DEAR DORIS

HOPE y

THIS BOO...

LOVE

KENNY

Great Novels of
THE BRONTË SISTERS

Great Novels of

THE BRONTË SISTERS

Charlotte Brontë
JANE EYRE

Emily Brontë
WUTHERING HEIGHTS

Anne Brontë
AGNES GREY

p

This is a Parragon Book
This edition published in 2000

Parragon
Queen Street House
4 Queen Street
Bath BA1 1HE, UK

Produced by Magpie Books, an imprint of
Constable & Robinson Ltd, London

Edition first published 1968

ISBN 0-75254-551-5 HARDBACK

ISBN 0-75254-617-1 PAPERBACK

Cover picture courtesy of
Ackermann and Johnson Ltd., London/Bridgeman Art Library
Cover design by John Dunne

A copy of the British Library Cataloguing-in-Publication Data
is available from the British Library

Printed and bound in the EC

Contents

INTRODUCTION

In 1846 a slim volume of poems was published in London, at the authors' expense, by Currer, Ellis and Acton Bell. Only two copies were sold but it attracted some critical attention. Next year, bookshops, libraries and fashionable London drawing-rooms were buzzing with excitement over a new novel by this same Currer Bell, entitled *Jane Eyre*, and published by the firm of Smith and Elder. It is to the credit of George Smith that he immediately recognised the merits of the book, which more than compensated for his previous rejection of Currer Bell's earlier novel, *The Professor*. Smith was so impressed with the new manuscript that he read it through in one day.

His decision to publish *Jane Eyre* was well justified by events. Though it received rough handling from some reviewers who found this passionate story of a governess's love for her employer too violent and crude, the book proved a tremendous popular success both in England and in America. It was followed a few months later by two more romantic novels, *Wuthering Heights* and *Agnes Grey*, published together in the popular three-volume form, and both bearing the surname Bell on the title page. Again the critics closed their ranks to attack these outspoken books; their harsh comments merely served to whet the reading public's interest.

Soon the most extraordinary rumours were circulating about the true identity of the authors. It was even suggested that all three books might have come from the same hand. The truth could no longer be concealed. The disguises were thrown off and to the astonishment of the literary world, and not least of their own publishers, it was revealed that the Bells were in reality three sisters, Charlotte, Emily and Anne Brontë, daughters of the rector of Haworth in Yorkshire.

Literary fame had never been the ambition of the Brontë sisters, but writing had from earliest childhood been as natural to them as breathing. The pages of their exercise books were filled with rhymes, poems, anecdotes, letters, stories, plays, incomplete novels—the irresistible outpouring of youthful hearts and minds, already distinguished by much mature observation and feeling, and by frequent flashes of fantasy and imagination.

Two younger sisters had died as children, shortly after their mother, and the family now consisted of the three girls, their brother Branwell, gifted but hopelessly undisciplined, the father Patrick Brontë—a stern, solitary man—an aunt and an elderly servant. All four children were devoted to one another, an exceptionally close bond of affection linking Charlotte with Branwell, Emily with Anne, and this sense of mutual dependence and responsibility lasted throughout their tragically brief lives.

The parsonage with its gloomy graveyard was an austere setting for the fantasies which they acted out and committed to paper; but beyond, stretching

for mile upon mile, were the wild, desolate moors which they loved with such intensity and returned to with such relief after temporary exile at school or in service. The absences at school were rare, for most of their formal education took place at home; but as time went by, to eke out Patrick Brontë's modest income, they all in turn took posts as governesses, a career for which they were singularly unsuited, for their health was never strong and they were physically and temperamentally unfitted to cope with recalcitrant children and indulgent parents. So again and again they returned to Haworth, storing up their experiences, prolonging their imaginary childhood games into adolescence, sitting up into the small hours reading to one another, feverishly writing and discussing their future. At one time they made plans for their own private school, even issuing a prospectus, but it was an unfulfilled dream. Nevertheless it was with this in mind, and particularly to improve their command of French, that Charlotte and Emily accepted teaching posts at M. Héger's school in Brussels, a decisive, liberating experience—at any rate for Charlotte.

For although illness at home cut short their stay Charlotte returned alone in 1843, the following year; and whether or not she fell in love with Constantin Héger (and her biographer Mrs. Gaskell discreetly ignores this possibility) the intellectual stimulation, the expanding social horizon—perhaps the emotional upheaval as well—were critical to Charlotte both as a person and as a writer. Those months away from home and family had a tremendous impact upon her. *Jane Eyre* perhaps might have been written had she never visited Brussels, but both *The Professor* and *Villette* were set in foreign boarding schools, with their chief characters largely modelled on the pupils and teachers encountered during this eventful year.

After Charlotte's return from Brussels the sisters put the finishing touches to their novels, working feverishly against time, and in the most arduous conditions, for Branwell was wasting away with drink and dissipation, Patrick Brontë was almost blind and both Emily and Anne were in poor health. It was Emily's strange, mystical poems which spurred Charlotte to take the plunge with the slim book of verse, using pseudonyms because, as she put it, 'we had a vague impression that authoresses are liable to be looked on with prejudice.'

The seven Brontë novels were published at intervals over the next ten years —*The Professor* not until 1857, after Charlotte's death. None achieved the popular success of *Jane Eyre* though as time passed *Wuthering Heights* came to be recognised as perhaps the finest of them all. But such was the fury of the critics' onslaught ('odiously and abominably pagan' said one reviewer) that Charlotte had to leap to the defence of Emily's book in her preface to the second edition; and even she failed to appreciate to the full the extraordinary power of Emily's talent. Certainly she underestimated the integrity and frequent beauties of Anne's simpler, less adorned prose style as it was revealed in *Agnes Grey*. And when Anne's more ambitious *Tenant of Wildfell Hall* appeared

in print, its central character owing much to the tragic figure of Branwell, now dead, even Charlotte admitted the theme was a mistake, virtually echoing the critics who, predictably, assailed the book for its 'coarseness' and 'brutality'.

So publication brought little financial reward and no relief from hardship for two of the shy, solitary Brontë sisters. Emily's haunting poems were never appreciated in her lifetime and her passionate tale of Cathy and Heathcliff, which in places attained tragic grandeur for all its faults of construction, was only acknowledged to be a masterpiece long after her death. To Charlotte's great grief and the world's loss both Emily and Anne died within a year of their books being published. Only Charlotte won some measure of peace and content—*Shirley*, a remarkable book set in the industrial north with the Luddite riots as a central feature, was followed by *Villette*, a penetrating study of social manners and behaviour in two countries, very moving in parts, and in many respects a more mature book than *Jane Eyre*. London society accepted her; she met a number of celebrities including Thackeray—and in 1853 she married Arthur Bell Nicholls, her father's curate. He was not of the Rochester mould—no man ever could be—nor did he possess Héger's qualities, but for a few brief months she seems to have enjoyed a quiet, uneventful married life. Then fate intervened again and after complications arising from childbirth she too died—the last of the five Brontë sisters.

All was not quite as stark as the bare outline of their lives would suggest. For if they knew loneliness, heartbreak and physical pain only too well, they also knew the joys of sisterly love and companionship, the release from drudgery which freely indulged fantasy can bring, and the fulfilment of literary creation in which all their innermost thoughts, feelings and longings found expression. Their contribution to the English novel, and incidentally to the cause of female emancipation, was vital and revolutionary; and though it would be foolish to claim for them a place among the greatest immortals of literature, no reader, who has derived pleasure and profit from their company, will deny them the admiration and gratitude which they scarcely knew in their lifetime.

JOHN GILBERT

AUTHOR'S PREFACE

A preface to the first edition of 'Jane Eyre' being unnecessary, I gave none: this second edition demands a few words both of acknowledgment and miscellaneous remark.

My thanks are due in three quarters.

To the Public, for the indulgent ear it has inclined to a plain tale with few pretensions.

To the Press, for the fair field its honest suffrage has opened to an obscure aspirant.

To my Publishers, for the aid their tact, their energy, their practical sense, and frank liberality have afforded an unknown and unrecommended Author.

The Press and the Public are but vague personifications for me, and I must thank them in vague terms; but my Publishers are definite: so are certain generous critics who have encouraged me as only large-hearted and high-minded men know how to encourage a struggling stranger; to them, *i.e.* to my Publishers and the select Reviewers, I say cordially, Gentlemen, I thank you from my heart.

Having thus acknowledged what I owe to those who have aided and approved me, I turn to another class; a small one, so far as I know, but not, therefore, to be overlooked. I mean the timorous or carping few who doubt the tendency of such books as 'Jane Eyre:' in whose eyes whatever is unusual is wrong; whose ears detect in each protest against bigotry—that parent of crime—an insult to piety, that regent of God on earth. I would suggest to such doubters certain obvious distinctions; I would remind them of certain simple truths.

Conventionality is not morality. Self-righteousness is not religion. To attack the first is not to assail the last. To pluck the mask from the face of the Pharisee, is not to lift an impious hand to the Crown of Thorns.

The things and deeds are diametrically opposed: they are as distinct as is vice from virtue. Men too often confound them; they should not be confounded: appearance should not be mistaken for truth; narrow human doctrines, that only tend to elate and magnify a few, should not be substituted for the world-redeeming creed of Christ. There is—I repeat it—a difference; and it is a good, and not a bad action to mark broadly and clearly the line of separation between them.

The world may not like to see these ideas dissevered, for it has been accustomed to blend them; finding it convenient to make external show pass for sterling worth—to let white-washed walls vouch for clean shrines. It may hate him who dares to scrutinise and expose—to rase the gilding, and show base metal under it—to penetrate the sepulchre, and reveal charnel relics: but, hate as it will, it is indebted to him.

Ahab did not like Micaiah, because he never prophesied good concerning him, but evil: probably he liked the sycophant son of Chenaanah better; yet might Ahab have escaped a bloody death, had he but stopped his ears to flattery, and opened them to faithful counsel.

There is a man in our own days whose words are not framed to tickle delicate ears: who, to my thinking, comes before the great ones of society, much as the son of Imlah came before the throned Kings of Judah and Israel; and who speaks truth as deep, with a power as prophetlike and as vital—a mien as dauntless and as daring. Is the satirist of 'Vanity Fair' admired in high places? I cannot tell; but I think if some of those amongst whom he hurls the Greek fire of his sarcasm, and over whom he flashes the levin-brand of his denunciation, were to take his warnings in time—they or their seed might yet escape a fatal Ramoth-Gilead.

Why have I alluded to this man? I have alluded to him, Reader, because I think I see in him an intellect profounder and more unique than his contemporaries have yet recognised; because I regard him as the first social regenerator of the day—as the very master of that working corps who would restore to rectitude the warped system of things; because I think no commentator on his writings has yet found the comparison that suits him, the terms which rightly characterise his talent. They say he is like Fielding: they talk of his wit, humour, comic powers. He resembles Fielding as an eagle does a vulture: Fielding could stoop on carrion, but Thackeray never does. His wit is bright, his humour attractive, but both bear the same relation to his serious genius, that the mere lambent sheet-lightning playing under the edge of the summer-cloud, does to the electric death-spark hid in its womb. Finally; I have alluded to Mr. Thackeray, because to him—if he will accept the tribute of a total stranger—I have dedicated this second edition of 'Jane Eyre.'

Dec. 21st, 1847. CURRER BELL

AUTHOR'S NOTE TO THE THIRD EDITION

I avail myself of the opportunity which a third edition of 'Jane Eyre' affords me, of again addressing a word to the Public, to explain that my claim to the title of novelist rests on this one work alone. If, therefore, the authorship of other works of fiction has been attributed to me, an honour is awarded where it is not merited; and consequently, denied where it is justly due.

This explanation will serve to rectify mistakes which may already have been made, and to prevent future errors.

April 13th, 1848. CURRER BELL

JANE EYRE

CHAPTER 1

There was no possibility of taking a walk that day. We had been wandering indeed, in the leafless shrubbery an hour in the morning; but since dinner (Mrs. Reed, when there was no company, dined early) the cold winter wind had brought with it clouds so sombre, and a rain so penetrating, that further out-door exercise was now out of the question.

I was glad of it: I never liked long walks, especially on chilly afternoons: dreadful to me was the coming home in the raw twilight, with nipped fingers and toes, and a heart saddened by the chidings of Bessie, the nurse, and humbled by the consciousness of my physical inferiority to Eliza, John, and Georgiana Reed.

The said Eliza, John, and Georgiana were now clustered round their mama in the drawing-room: she lay reclined on a sofa by the fireside, and with her darlings about her (for the time neither quarrelling nor crying) looked perfectly happy. Me, she had dispensed from joining the group; saying, 'She regretted to be under the necessity of keeping me at a distance; but that until she heard from Bessie, and could discover by her own observation that I was endeavour-ing in good earnest to acquire a more sociable and childlike disposition, a more attractive and sprightly manner,—something lighter, franker, more natural as it were—she really must exclude me from privileges intended only for contented, happy, little children.'

'What does Bessie say I have done?' I asked.

'Jane, I don't like cavillers or questioners: besides, there is something truly forbidding in a child taking up her elders in that manner. Be seated somewhere; and until you can speak pleasantly, remain silent.'

A small breakfast-room adjoined the drawing-room. I slipped in there. It contained a book-case: I soon possessed myself of a volume, taking care that it should be one stored with pictures. I mounted into the window-seat: gather-ing up my feet, I sat cross-legged, like a Turk; and, having drawn the red moreen curtain nearly close, I was shrined in double retirement.

Folds of scarlet drapery shut in my view to the right hand; to the left were the clear panes of glass, protecting, but not separating me from the drear November day. At intervals, while turning over the leaves of my book, I studied

the aspect of that winter afternoon. Afar, it offered a pale blank of mist and cloud; near, a scene of wet lawn and storm-beat shrub, with ceaseless rain sweeping away wildly before a long and lamentable blast.

I returned to my book—Bewick's History of British Birds: the letter-press thereof I cared little for, generally speaking; and yet there were certain introductory pages that, child as I was, I could not pass quite as a blank. They were those which treat of the haunts of sea-fowl; of 'the solitary rocks and promontories' by them only inhabited; of the coast of Norway, studded with isles from its southern extremity, the Lindeness, or Naze, to the North Cape—

> 'Where the Northern Ocean, in vast whirls,
> Boils round the naked, melancholy isles
> Of farthest Thule; and the Atlantic surge
> Pours in among the stormy Hebrides.'

Nor could I pass unnoticed the suggestion of the bleak shores of Lapland, Siberia, Spitzbergen, Nova Zembla, Iceland, Greenland, with 'the vast sweep of the Arctic Zone, and those forlorn regions of dreary space,—that reservoir of frost and snow, where firm fields of ice, the accumulation of centuries of winters, glazed in Alpine heights above heights, surround the pole, and concentre the multiplied rigors of extreme cold.' Of these death-white realms I formed an idea of my own: shadowy, like all the half-comprehended notions that float dim through children's brains, but strangely impressive. The words in these introductory pages connected themselves with the succeeding vignettes, and gave significance to the rock standing up alone in a sea of billow and spray; to the broken boat stranded on a desolate coast; to the cold and ghastly moon glancing through bars of cloud at a wreck just sinking.

I cannot tell what sentiment haunted the quiet solitary churchyard, with its inscribed headstone; its gate, its two trees, its low horizon, girdled by a broken wall, and its newly-risen crescent, attesting the hour of eventide.

The two ships becalmed on a torpid sea, I believed to be marine phantoms.

The fiend pinning down the thief's pack behind him, I passed over quickly: it was an object of terror.

So was the black, horned thing seated aloof on a rock, surveying a distant crowd surrounding a gallows.

Each picture told a story; mysterious often to my undeveloped understanding and imperfect feelings, yet ever profoundly interesting: as interesting as the tales Bessie sometimes narrated on winter evenings, when she chanced to be in good humour; and when, having brought her ironing-table to the nursery-hearth, she allowed us to sit about it, and while she got up Mrs. Reed's lace frills, and crimped her night-cap borders, fed our eager attention with passages of love and adventure taken from old fairy tales and older ballads; or (as at a later period I discovered) from the pages of Pamela, and Henry, Earl of Moreland.

With Bewick on my knee, I was then happy: happy at least in my way. I feared nothing but interruption, and that came too soon. The breakfast-room door opened.

'Boh! Madame Mope!' cried the voice of John Reed; then he paused: he found the room apparently empty.

'Where the dickens is she?' he continued. 'Lizzy! Georgy! (calling to his sisters) Joan is not here: tell mama she is run out into the rain—bad animal!''

'It is well I drew the curtain,' thought I; and I wished fervently he might not discover my hiding-place: nor would John Reed have found it out himself; he was not quick either of vision or conception; but Eliza just put her head in at the door, and said at once:—

'She is in the window-seat, to be sure, Jack.'

And I came out immediately, for I trembled at the idea of being dragged forth by the said Jack.

'What do you want?' I asked, with awkward diffidence.

'Say, "what do you want, Master Reed," ' was the answer. 'I want you to come here;' and seating himself in an armchair, he intimated by a gesture that I was to approach and stand before him.

John Reed was a schoolboy of fourteen years old; four years older than I, for I was but ten; large and stout for his age, with a dingy and unwholesome skin; thick lineaments in a spacious visage, heavy limbs and large extremities. He gorged himself habitually at table, which made him bilious, and gave him a dim and bleared eye and flabby cheeks. He ought now to have been at school; but his mama had taken him home for a month or two, 'on account of his delicate health.' Mr. Miles, the master, affirmed that he would do very well if he had fewer cakes and sweetmeats sent him from home; but the mother's heart turned from an opinion so harsh, and inclined rather to the more refined idea that John's sallowness was owing to over-application and, perhaps, to pining after home.

John had not much affection for his mother and sisters, and an antipathy to me. He bullied and punished me; not two or three times in the week, nor once or twice in the day, but continually: every nerve I had feared him, and every morsel of flesh on my bones shrank when he came near. There were moments when I was bewildered by the terror he inspired, because I had no appeal whatever against either his menaces or his inflictions; the servants did not like to offend their young master by taking my part against him, and Mrs. Reed was blind and deaf on the subject: she never saw him strike or heard him abuse me, though he did both now and then in her very presence; more frequently, however, behind her back.

Habitually obedient to John, I came up to his chair: he spent some three minutes in thrusting out his tongue at me as far as he could without damaging the roots: I knew he would soon strike, and while dreading the blow, I mused

on the disgusting and ugly appearance of him who would presently deal it. I wonder if he read that notion in my face; for, all at once, without speaking, he struck suddenly and strongly. I tottered, and on regaining my equilibrium retired back a step or two from his chair.

'That is for your impudence in answering mama awhile since,' said he, 'and for your sneaking way of getting behind curtains, and for the look you had in your eyes two minutes since, you rat!'

Accustomed to John Reed's abuse, I never had an idea of replying to it; my care was how to endure the blow which would certainly follow the insult.

'What were you doing behind the curtain?' he asked.

'I was reading.'

'Shew the book.'

I returned to the window and fetched it thence.

'You have no business to take our books; you are a dependant, mama says; you have no money; your father left you none; you ought to beg, and not to live here with gentlemen's children like us, and eat the same meals we do, and wear clothes at our mama's expense. Now, I'll teach you to rummage my book-shelves: for they *are* mine; all the house belongs to me, or will do in a few years. Go and stand by the door, out of the way of the mirror and the windows.'

I did so, not at first aware what was his intention; but when I saw him lift and poise the book and stand in act to hurl it, I instinctively started aside with a cry of alarm: not soon enough, however; the volume was flung, it hit me, and I fell, striking my head against the door and cutting it. The cut bled, the pain was sharp; my terror had passed its climax; other feelings succeeded.

'Wicked and cruel boy!' I said. 'You are like a murderer—you are like a slave-driver—you are like the Roman emperors!'

I had read Goldsmith's History of Rome, and had formed my opinion of Nero, Caligula, etc. Also I had drawn parallels in silence, which I never thought thus to have declared aloud.

'What! what!' he cried. 'Did you say that to me? Did you hear her, Eliza and Georgiana? Won't I tell mama? but first'—

He ran headlong at me: I felt him grasp my hair and my shoulder: he had closed with a desperate thing. I really saw in him a tyrant: a murderer. I felt a drop or two of blood from my head trickle down my neck, and was sensible of somewhat pungent sufferings: these sensations for the time predominated over fear, and I received him in frantic sort. I don't very well know what I did with my hands, but he called me 'Rat! rat!' and bellowed out aloud. Aid was near him: Eliza and Georgiana had run for Mrs. Reed, who was gone upstairs; she now came upon the scene, followed by Bessie and her maid Abbot. We were parted: I heard the words:—

'Dear! dear! What a fury to fly at Master John!'

14

'Did ever anybody see such a picture of passion!'

Then Mrs. Reed subjoined:—

'Take her away to the red-room, and lock her in there.' Four hands were immediately laid upon me, and I was borne upstairs.

CHAPTER 2

I resisted all the way: a new thing for me, and a circumstance which greatly strengthened the bad opinion Bessie and Miss Abbot were disposed to entertain of me. The fact is, I was a trifle beside myself; or rather *out* of myself, as the French would say: I was conscious that a moment's mutiny had already rendered me liable to strange penalties, and, like any other rebel slave, I felt resolved, in my desperation, to go all lengths.

'Hold her arms, Miss Abbot: she's like a mad cat.'

'For shame! for shame!' cried the lady's-maid. 'What shocking conduct, Miss Eyre, to strike a young gentleman, your benefactress's son! Your young master.'

'Master! How is he my master? Am I a servant?'

'No; you are less than a servant, for you do nothing for your keep. There, sit down, and think over your wickedness.'

They had got me by this time into the apartment indicated by Mrs. Reed, and had thrust me upon a stool: my impulse was to rise from it like a spring; their two pair of hands arrested me instantly.

'If you don't sit still, you must be tied down,' said Bessie. 'Miss Abbot, lend me your garters; she would break mine directly.'

Miss Abbot turned to divest a stout leg of the necessary ligature. This preparation for bonds, and the additional ignominy it inferred, took a little of the excitement out of me.

'Don't take them off,' I cried; 'I will not stir.'

In guarantee whereof, I attached myself to my seat by my hands.

'Mind you don't,' said Bessie; and when she had ascertained that I was really subsiding, she loosened her hold of me; then she and Miss Abbot stood with folded arms, looking darkly and doubtfully on my face, as incredulous of my sanity.

'She never did so before,' at last said Bessie, turning to the Abigail.

'But it was always in her,' was the reply. 'I've told Missis often my opinion about the child, and Missis agreed with me. She's an underhand little thing: I never saw a girl of her age with so much cover.'

Bessie answered not; but ere long, addressing me, she said,—

'You ought to be aware, Miss, that you are under obligations to Mrs. Reed: she keeps you: if she were to turn you off, you would have to go to the poorhouse.'

15

I had nothing to say to these words: they were not new to me: my very first recollections of existence included hints of the same kind. This reproach of my dependence had become a vague sing-song in my ear; very painful and crushing, but only half intelligible. Miss Abbot joined in:—

'And you ought not to think yourself on an equality with the Misses Reed and Master Reed, because Missis kindly allows you to be brought up with them. They will have a great deal of money, and you will have none: it is your place to be humble, and to try to make yourself agreeable to them.'

'What we tell you, is for your good,' added Bessie, in no harsh voice: 'you should try to be useful and pleasant, then, perhaps, you would have a home here; but if you become passionate and rude, Missis will send you away, I am sure.'

'Besides,' said Miss Abbot, 'God will punish her: he might strike her dead in the midst of her tantrums, and then where would she go? Come, Bessie, we will leave her: I wouldn't have her heart for anything. Say your prayers, Miss Eyre, when you are by yourself; for if you don't repent, something bad might be permitted to come down the chimney and fetch you away.'

They went, shutting the door, and locking it behind them.

The red-room was a spare chamber, very seldom slept in; I might say never, indeed, unless when a chance influx of visitors at Gateshead Hall rendered it necessary to turn to account all the accommodation it contained: yet it was one of the largest and stateliest chambers in the mansion. A bed supported on massive pillars of mahogany, hung with curtains of deep red damask, stood out like a tabernacle in the centre; the two large windows, with their blinds always drawn down, were half shrouded in festoons and falls of similar drapery; the carpet was red; the table at the foot of the bed was covered with a crimson cloth; the walls were a soft fawn colour, with a blush of pink in it; the wardrobe, the toilet-table, the chairs were of darkly polished old mahogany. Out of these deep surrounding shades rose high, and glared white, the piled-up mattresses and pillows of the bed, spread with a snowy Marseilles counterpane. Scarcely less prominent was an ample, cushioned easy-chair near the head of the bed, also white, with a footstool before it; and looking as I thought, like a pale throne.

This room was chill, because it seldom had a fire; it was silent, because remote from the nursery and kitchens; solemn, because it was known to be so seldom entered. The housemaid alone came here on Saturdays, to wipe from the mirrors and the furniture a week's quiet dust: and Mrs. Reed herself, at far intervals, visited it to review the contents of a certain secret drawer in the wardrobe, where were stored divers parchments, her jewel-casket, and a miniature of her deceased husband; and in those last words lies the secret of the bedroom—the spell which kept it so lonely in spite of its grandeur.

Mr. Reed had been dead nine years: it was in this chamber he breathed

his last; here he lay in state; hence his coffin was borne by the undertaker's men; and, since that day, a sense of dreary consecration had guarded it from frequent intrusion.

My seat, to which Bessie and the bitter Miss Abbot had left me riveted, was a low ottoman near the marble chimney-piece; the bed rose before me; to my right hand there was the high, dark wardrobe, with subdued, broken reflections varying the gloss of its panels; to my left were the muffled windows; a great looking-glass between them repeated the vacant majesty of the bed and room. I was not quite sure whether they had locked the door; and, when I dared move, I got up, and went to see. Alas! yes, no jail was ever more secure. Returning, I had to cross before the looking-glass; my fascinated glance involuntarily explored the depth it revealed. All looked colder and darker in that visionary hollow than in reality: and the strange little figure there gazing at me, with a white face and arms specking the gloom, and glittering eyes of fear moving where all else was still, had the effect of a real spirit: I thought it like one of the tiny phantoms, half fairy, half imp, Bessie's evening stories represented as coming up out of lone, ferny dells in moors, and appearing before the eyes of belated travellers. I returned to my stool.

Superstition was with me at that moment; but it was not yet her hour for complete victory: my blood was still warm; the mood of the revolted slave was still bracing me with its bitter vigour; I had to stem a rapid rush of retrospective thought before I quailed to the dismal present.

All John Reed's violent tyrannies, all his sisters' proud indifference, all his mother's aversion, all the servants' partiality, turned up in my disturbed mind like a dark deposit in a turbid well. Why was I always suffering, always brow-beaten, always accused, for ever condemned? Why could I never please? Why was it useless to try to win any one's favour? Eliza, who was headstrong and selfish, was respected. Georgiana, who had a spoiled temper, a very acrid spite, a captious and insolent carriage, was universally indulged. Her beauty, her pink cheeks and golden curls, seemed to give delight to all who looked at her, and to purchase indemnity for every fault. John, no one thwarted, much less punished; though he twisted the necks of the pigeons, killed the little pea-chicks, set the dogs at the sheep, stripped the hothouse vines of their fruit, and broke the buds off the choicest plants in the conservatory: he called his mother 'old girl,' too: sometimes reviled her for her dark skin, similar to his own; bluntly disregarded her wishes; not unfrequently tore and spoiled her silk attire; and he was still 'her own darling.' I dared commit no fault: I strove to fulfil every duty; and I was termed naughty and tiresome, sullen and sneaking, from morning to noon, and from noon to night.

My head still ached and bled with the blow and fall I had received: no one had reproved John for wantonly striking me; and because I had turned against him to avert farther irrational violence, I was loaded with general opprobrium.

'Unjust!—unjust!' said my reason, forced by the agonising stimulus into precocious though transitory power; and Resolve, equally wrought up, instigated some strange expedient to achieve escape from insupportable oppression—as running away, or, if that could not be effected, never eating or drinking more, and letting myself die.

What a consternation of soul was mine that dreary afternoon! How all my brain was in tumult, and all my heart in insurrection! Yet in what darkness, what dense ignorance, was the mental battle fought! I could not answer the ceaseless inward question—*why* I thus suffered; now, at the distance of—I will not say how many years, I see it clearly.

I was a discord in Gateshead Hall; I was like nobody there; I had nothing in harmony with Mrs. Reed or her children, or her chosen vassalage. If they did not love me in fact, as little did I love them. They were not bound to regard with affection a thing that could not sympathise with one amongst them; a heterogeneous thing; opposed to them in temperament, in capacity, in propensities; a useless thing, incapable of serving their interest, or adding to their pleasure; a noxious thing, cherishing the germs of indignation at their treatment, of contempt of their judgment. I know that had I been a sanguine, brilliant, careless, exacting, handsome, romping child—though equally dependent and friendless—Mrs. Reed would have endured my presence more complacently; her children would have entertained for me more of the cordiality of fellow-feeling; the servants would have been less prone to make me the scapegoat of the nursery.

Daylight began to forsake the red-room; it was past four o'clock, and the beclouded afternoon was tending to drear twilight. I heard the rain still beating continuously on the staircase window, and the wind howling in the grove behind the hall; I grew by degrees cold as a stone, and then my courage sank. My habitual mood of humiliation, self-doubt, forlorn depression, fell damp on the embers of my decaying ire. All said I was wicked, and perhaps I might be so; what thought had I been but just conceiving of starving myself to death? That certainly was a crime: and was I fit to die? Or was the vault under the chancel of Gateshead Church an inviting bourne? In such vault I had been told did Mr. Reed lie buried; and led by this thought to recall his idea, I dwelt on it with gathering dread. I could not remember him; but I knew that he was my own uncle—my mother's brother—that he had taken me when a parentless infant to his house; and that in his last moments he had required a promise of Mrs. Reed that she would rear and maintain me as one of her own children. Mrs. Reed probably considered she had kept this promise; and so she had, I dare say, as well as her nature would permit her; but how could she really like an interloper not of her race, and unconnected with her, after her husband's death, by any tie? It must have been most irksome to find herself bound by a hard-wrung pledge to stand in the stead of a parent to a strange child she

could not love, and to see an uncongenial alien permanently intruded on her own family group.

A singular notion dawned upon me. I doubted not—never doubted—that if Mr. Reed had been alive he would have treated me kindly; and now, as I sat looking at the white bed and overshadowed walls—occasionally also turning a fascinated eye towards the dimly gleaming mirror—I began to recall what I had heard of dead men, troubled in their graves by the violation of their last wishes, revisiting the earth to punish the perjured and avenge the oppressed; and I thought Mr. Reed's spirit, harassed by the wrongs of his sister's child, might quit its abode—whether in the church vault or in the unknown world of the departed—and rise before me in this chamber. I wiped my tears and hushed my sobs, fearful lest any sign of violent grief might waken a preternatural voice to comfort me, or elicit from the gloom some haloed face, bending over me with strange pity. This idea, consolatory in theory, I felt, would be terrible if realised: with all my might I endeavoured to stifle it—I endeavoured to be firm. Shaking my hair from my eyes, I lifted my head and tried to look boldly round the dark room: at this moment a light gleamed on the wall. Was it, I asked myself, a ray from the moon penetrating some aperture in the blind? No; moonlight was still, and this stirred; while I gazed, it glided up to the ceiling and quivered over my head. I can now conjecture readily that this streak of light was, in all likelihood, a gleam from a lantern, carried by some one across the lawn: but then, prepared as my mind was for horror, shaken as my nerves were by agitation, I thought the swift-darting beam was a herald of some coming vision from another world. My heart beat thick, my head grew hot; a sound filled my ears, which I deemed the rushing of wings: something seemed near me; I was oppressed, suffocated: endurance broke down; I rushed to the door and shook the lock in desperate effort. Steps came running along the outer passage; the key turned, Bessie and Abbot entered.

'Miss Eyre, are you ill?' said Bessie.

'What a dreadful noise! it went quite through me!' exclaimed Abbot.

'Take me out! Let me go into the nursery!' was my cry.

'What for! Are you hurt! Have you seen something?' again demanded Bessie.

'Oh! I saw a light, and I thought a ghost would come.' I had now got hold of Bessie's hand, and she did not snatch it from me.

'She has screamed out on purpose,' declared Abbot, in some disgust. 'And what a scream! If she had been in great pain one would have excused it, but she only wanted to bring us all here. I know her naughty tricks.'

'What is all this?' demanded another voice peremptorily; and Mrs. Reed came along the corridor, her cap flying wide, her gown rustling stormily. 'Abbot and Bessie, I believe I gave orders that Jane Eyre should be left in the red-room till I came to her myself.'

'Miss Jane screamed so loud, ma'am,' pleaded Bessie.

'Let her go,' was the only answer. 'Loose Bessie's hand, child: you cannot succeed in getting out by these means, be assured. I abhor artifice, particularly in children; it is my duty to show you that tricks will not answer: you will now stay here an hour longer, and it is only on condition of perfect submission and stillness that I shall liberate you then.'

'Oh aunt, have pity! Forgive me! I cannot endure it—let me be punished some other way! I shall be killed if'—

'Silence! This violence is all most repulsive:' and so, no doubt, she felt it. I was a precocious actress in her eyes: she sincerely looked on me as a compound of virulent passions, mean spirit, and dangerous duplicity.

Bessie and Abbot having retreated, Mrs. Reed, impatient of my now frantic anguish and wild sobs, abruptly thrust me back and locked me in, without farther parley. I heard her sweeping away; and soon after she was gone, I suppose I had a species of fit: unconsciousness closed the scene.

CHAPTER 3

The next thing I remember is, waking up with a feeling as if I had had a frightful night-mare, and seeing before me a terrible red glare, crossed with thick black bars. I heard voices, too, speaking with a hollow sound, and as if muffled by a rush of wind or water: agitation, uncertainty, and an all-predominating sense of terror confused my faculties. Ere long, I became aware that some one was handling me; lifting me up and supporting me in a sitting posture, and that more tenderly than I had ever been raised or upheld before. I rested my head against a pillow or an arm, and felt easy.

In five minutes more, the cloud of bewilderment dissolved: I knew quite well that I was in my own bed, and that the red glare was the nursery fire. It was night: a candle burnt on the table; Bessie stood at the bed-foot with a basin in her hand, and a gentleman sat in a chair near my pillow, leaning over me.

I felt an inexpressible relief, a soothing conviction of protection and security, when I knew that there was a stranger in the room, an individual not belonging to Gateshead, and not related to Mrs. Reed. Turning from Bessie (though her presence was far less obnoxious to me than that of Abbot, for instance, would have been), I scrutinised the face of the gentleman: I knew him; it was Mr. Lloyd, an apothecary, sometimes called in by Mrs. Reed when the servants were ailing: for herself and the children she employed a physician.

'Well, who am I?' he asked.

I pronounced his name, offering him at the same time my hand: he took it, smiling and saying, 'We shall do very well by-and-by.' Then he laid me down, and addressing Bessie, charged her to be very careful that I was not disturbed during the night. Having given some further directions, and intimated that

he should call again the next day, he departed; to my grief: I felt so sheltered and befriended while he sat in the chair near my pillow; and as he closed the door after him, all the room darkened and my heart again sank: inexpressible sadness weighed it down.

'Do you feel as if you should sleep, Miss?' asked Bessie, rather softly.

Scarcely dared I answer her; for I feared the next sentence might be rough. 'I will try.'

'Would you like to drink, or could you eat anything?'

'No, thank you, Bessie.'

'Then I think I shall go to bed, for it is past twelve o'clock; but you may call me if you want anything in the night.'

Wonderful civility this! It emboldened me to ask a question.

'Bessie, what is the matter with me? Am I ill?'

'You fell sick, I suppose, in the red-room with crying; you'll be better soon, no doubt.'

Bessie went into the housemaid's apartment which was near. I heard her say—

'Sarah, come and sleep with me in the nursery; I daren't for my life be alone with that poor child to-night; she might die; it's such a strange thing she should have that fit: I wonder if she saw anything. Missis was rather too hard.'

Sarah came back with her; they both went to bed; they were whispering together for half an hour before they fell asleep. I caught scraps of their conversation, from which I was able only too distinctly to infer the main subject discussed.

'Something passed her, all dressed in white, and vanished'—'A great black dog behind him'—'Three loud raps on the chamber door'—'A light in the churchyard just over his grave'—etc., etc.

At last both slept: the fire and the candle went out. For me, the watches of that long night passed in ghastly wakefulness; ear, eye, and mind were alike strained by dread: such dread as children only can feel.

No severe or prolonged bodily illness followed this incident of the red-room: it only gave my nerves a shock, of which I feel the reverberation to this day. Yes, Mrs. Reed, to you I owe some fearful pangs of mental suffering. But I ought to forgive you, for you knew not what you did: while rending my heart-strings, you thought you were only up-rooting my bad propensities.

Next day, by noon, I was up and dressed, and sat wrapped in a shawl by the nursery hearth. I felt physically weak and broken down: but my worse ailment was an unutterable wretchedness of mind: a wretchedness which kept drawing from me silent tears; no sooner had I wiped one salt drop from my cheek than another followed. Yet I thought, I ought to have been happy, for none of the Reeds were there; they were all gone out in the carriage with their

mama: Abbot, too, was sewing in another room, and Bessie, as she moved hither and thither, putting away toys and arranging drawers, addressed to me every now and then a word of unwonted kindness. This state of things should have been to me a paradise of peace, accustomed as I was to a life of ceaseless reprimand and thankless fagging; but, in fact, my racked nerves were now in such a state that no calm could soothe, and no pleasure excite them agreeably.

Bessie had been down into the kitchen, and she brought up with her a tart on a certain brightly painted china plate whose bird of paradise, nestling in a wreath of convolvuli and rosebuds, had been wont to stir in me a most enthusiastic sense of admiration; and which plate I had petitioned to be allowed to take in my hand in order to examine it more closely, but had always hitherto been deemed unworthy of such a privilege. This precious vessel was now placed on my knee, and I was cordially invited to eat the circlet of delicate pastry upon it. Vain favour! coming, like most other favours long deferred and often wished for, too late! I could not eat the tart: and the plumage of the bird, the tints of the flowers, seemed strangely faded: I put both plate and tart away. Bessie asked if I would have a book: the word *book* acted as a transient stimulus, and I begged her to fetch Gulliver's Travels from the library. This book I had again and again perused with delight. I considered it a narrative of facts, and discovered in it a vein of interest deeper than what I found in fairy tales: for as to the elves, having sought them in vain among foxglove leaves and bells, under mushrooms and beneath the ground-ivy mantling old wall-nooks, I had at length made up my mind to the sad truth, that they were all gone out of England to some savage country where the woods were wilder and thicker, and the population more scant; whereas, Lilliput and Brobdignag being, in my creed, solid parts of the earth's surface, I doubted not that I might one day, by taking a long voyage, see with my own eyes the little fields, houses, and trees, the diminutive people, the tiny cows, sheep, and birds of the one realm; and the corn-fields forest-high, the mighty mastiffs, the monster cats, the tower-like men and women, of the other. Yet, when this cherished volume was now placed in my hand—when I turned over its leaves, and sought in its marvellous pictures the charm I had, till now, never failed to find—all was eerie and dreary; the giants were gaunt goblins, the pigmies malevolent and fearful imps, Gulliver a most desolate wanderer in most dread and dangerous regions. I closed the book, which I dared no longer peruse, and put it on the table, beside the untasted tart.

Bessie had now finished dusting and tidying the room, and having washed her hands, she opened a certain little drawer, full of splendid shreds of silk and satin, and began making a new bonnet for Georgiana's doll. Meantime she sang: her song was—

'In the days when we went gipsying,
A long time ago.'

I had often heard the song before, and always with lively delight; for Bessie had a sweet voice,—at least, I thought so. But now, though her voice was still sweet, I found in its melody an indescribable sadness. Sometimes, pre-occupied with her work, she sang the refrain very low, very lingerly: 'A long time ago' came out like the saddest cadence of a funeral hymn. She passed into another ballad, this time a really doleful one.

'My feet they are sore, and my limbs they are weary;
 Long is the way, and the mountains are wild;
Soon will the twilight close moonless and dreary
 Over the path of the poor orphan child.

'Why did they send me so far and so lonely,
 Up where the moors spread and grey rocks are piled?
Men are hard-hearted, and kind angels only
 Watch'd o'er the steps of a poor orphan child.

'Yet distant and soft the night-breeze is blowing,
 Clouds there are none, and clear stars beam mild.
God, in His mercy, protection is showing,
 Comfort and hope to the poor orphan child.

'Ev'n should I fall o'er the broken bridge passing,
 Or stray in the marshes, by false lights beguiled,
Still will my Father, with promise and blessing,
 Take to His bosom the poor orphan child.

'There is a thought that for strength should avail me,
 Though both of shelter and kindred despoiled;
Heaven is a home, and a rest will not fail me;
 God is a friend to the poor orphan child.'

'Come, Miss Jane, don't cry,' said Bessie, as she finished. She might as well have said to the fire, 'don't burn!' but how could she divine the morbid suffering to which I was a prey? In the course of the morning, Mr. Lloyd came again.

'What, already up!' said he, as he entered the nursery. 'Well, nurse, how is she?'

Bessie answered that I was doing very well.

'Then she ought to look more cheerful. Come, here, Miss Jane: your name is Jane, is it not?'

'Yes, sir, Jane Eyre.'

'Well, you have been crying, Miss Jane Eyre, can you tell me what about? Have you any pain?'

'No, sir.'

'Oh! I daresay she is crying because she could not go out with Missis in the carriage,' interposed Bessie.

'Surely not! why, she is too old for such pettishness.'

I thought so too; and my self-esteem being wounded by the false charge, I answered promptly, 'I never cried for such a thing in my life: I hate going out in the carriage. I cry because I am miserable.'

'Oh fie, Miss!' said Bessie.

The good apothecary appeared a little puzzled. I was standing before him; he fixed his eyes on me very steadily: his eyes were small and grey; not very bright, but I daresay I should think them shrewd now: he had a hard-featured yet good-natured looking face. Having considered me at leisure, he said—

'What made you ill yesterday?'

'She had a fall,' said Bessie, again putting in her word.

'Fall! why that is like a baby again! Can't she manage to walk at her age? She must be eight or nine years old.'

'I was knocked down,' was the blunt explanation jerked out of me by another pang of mortified pride: 'but that did not make me ill,' I added; while Mr. Lloyd helped himself to a pinch of snuff.

As he was returning the box to his waistcoat pocket, a loud bell rang for the servants' dinner; he knew what it was. 'That's for you, nurse,' said he; 'you can go down; I'll give Miss Jane a lecture till you come back.'

Bessie would rather have stayed, but she was obliged to go, because punctuality at meals was rigidly enforced at Gateshead Hall.

'The fall did not make you ill; what did, then?' pursued Mr. Lloyd, when Bessie was gone.

'I was shut up in a room where there is a ghost, till after dark.'

I saw Mr. Lloyd smile and frown at the same time: 'Ghost! What, you are a baby after all! You are afraid of ghosts?'

'Of Mr. Reed's ghost I am: he died in that room, and was laid out there. Neither Bessie nor any one else will go into it at night, if they can help it; and it was cruel to shut me up alone without a candle,—so cruel that I think I shall never forget it.'

'Nonsense! And is it that makes you so miserable? Are you afraid now in daylight?'

'No: but night will come again before long: and besides,—I am unhappy,—very unhappy, for other things.'

'What other things? Can you tell me some of them?'

How much I wished to reply fully to this question! How difficult it was to frame any answer! Children can feel, but they cannot analyse their feelings; and if the analysis is partially effected in thought, they know not how to express the result of the process in words. Fearful, however, of losing this first and only opportunity of relieving my grief by imparting it, I, after a dis-

24

turbed pause, contrived to frame a meagre, though, as far as it went, true response.

'For one thing, I have no father or mother, brothers or sisters.'

'You have a kind aunt and cousins.'

Again I paused; then bunglingly enounced:

'But John Reed knocked me down, and my aunt shut me up in the red-room.' Mr. Lloyd a second time produced his snuff-box.

'Don't you think Gateshead Hall a very beautiful house?' asked he. 'Are you not very thankful to have such a fine place to live at?'

'It is not my house, sir; and Abbot says I have less right to be here than a servant.'

'Pooh! you can't be silly enough to wish to leave such a splendid place?'

'If I had anywhere else to go, I should be glad to leave it; but I can never get away from Gateshead till I am a woman.'

'Perhaps you may—who knows? Have you any relations besides Mrs. Reed?'

'I think not, sir.'

'None belonging to your father?'

'I don't know: I asked aunt Reed once, and she said possibly I might have some poor, low relations called Eyre, but she knew nothing about them.'

'If you had such, would you like to go to them?'

I reflected. Poverty looks grim to grown people; still more so to children: they have not much idea of industrious, working, respectable poverty; they think of the word only as connected with ragged clothes, scanty food, fireless grates, rude manners, and debasing vices: poverty for me was synonymous with the degradation.

'No; I should not like to belong to poor people,' was my reply.

'Not even if they were kind to you?'

I shook my head: I could not see how poor people had the means of being kind; and then to learn to speak like them, to adopt their manners, to be uneducated, to grow up like one of the poor women I saw sometimes nursing their children or washing their clothes at the cottage doors of the village of Gateshead: no, I was not heroic enough to purchase liberty at the price of caste.

'But are your relatives so very poor? Are they working people?'

'I cannot tell; aunt Reed says if I have any, they must be a beggarly set: I should not like to go a begging.'

'Would you like to go to school?'

Again I reflected: I scarcely knew what school was; Bessie sometimes spoke of it as a place where young ladies sat in the stocks, wore backboards, and were expected to be exceedingly genteel and precise: John Reed hated his school, and abused his master; but John Reed's tastes were no rule for mine, and if

Bessie's accounts of school-discipline (gathered from the young ladies of a family where she had lived before coming to Gateshead) were somewhat appalling, her details of certain accomplishments attained by these same young ladies were, I thought, equally attractive. She boasted of beautiful paintings of landscapes and flowers by them executed; of songs they could sing and pieces they could play, of purses they could net, of French books they could translate; till my spirit was moved to emulation as I listened. Besides, school would be a complete change: it implied a long journey, an entire separation from Gateshead, an entrance into a new life.

'I should indeed like to go to school,' was the audible conclusion of my musings.

'Well, well; who knows what may happen?' said Mr. Lloyd, as he got up: 'The child ought to have change of air and scene,' he added, speaking to himself; 'nerves not in a good state.'

Bessie now returned; at the same moment the carriage was heard rolling up the gravel-walk.

'Is that your mistress, nurse?' asked Mr. Lloyd. 'I should like to speak to her before I go.'

Bessie invited him to walk into the breakfast-room, and led the way out. In the interview which followed between him and Mrs. Reed, I presume, from after-occurrences, that the apothecary ventured to recommend my being sent to school; and the recommendation was no doubt readily enough adopted; for as Abbot said, in discussing the subject with Bessie when both sat sewing in the nursery one night, after I was in bed, and, as they thought, asleep, 'Missis was, she dared say, glad enough to get rid of such a tiresome, ill-conditioned child, who always looked as if she were watching everybody, and scheming plots underhand.' Abbot, I think, gave me credit for being a sort of infantine Guy Fawkes.

On that same occasion I learned, for the first time, from Miss Abbot's communications to Bessie, that my father had been a poor clergyman; that my mother had married him against the wishes of her friends, who considered the match beneath her; that my grandfather Reed was so irritated at her disobedience, he cut her off without a shilling; that after my mother and father had been married a year, the latter caught the typhus fever while visiting among the poor of a large manufacturing town where his curacy was situated, and where that disease was then prevalent; that my mother took the infection from him, and both died within a month of each other.

Bessie, when she heard this narrative, sighed and said, 'Poor Miss Jane is to be pitied, too, Abbot.'

'Yes,' responded Abbot; 'if she were a nice, pretty child, one might compassionate her forlornness; but one really cannot care for such a little toad as that.'

'Not a great deal to be sure,' agreed Bessie: 'at any rate, a beauty like Miss Georgiana would be more moving in the same condition.'

'Yes, I doat on Miss Georgiana!' cried the fervent Abbot. 'Little darling!—with her long curls and her blue eyes, and such a sweet colour as she has; just as if she were painted!—Bessie, I could fancy a Welsh rabbit for supper.'

'So could I—with a roast onion. Come, we'll go down.' They went.

CHAPTER 4

From my discourse with Mr. Lloyd, and from the above reported conference between Bessie and Abbot, I gathered enough of hope to suffice as a motive for wishing to get well: a change seemed near,—I desired and waited it in silence. It tarried, however: days and weeks passed: I had regained my normal state of health, but no new allusion was made to the subject over which I brooded. Mrs. Reed surveyed me at times with a severe eye, but seldom addressed me: since my illness, she had drawn a more marked line of separation than ever between me and her own children; appointing me a small closet to sleep in by myself, condemning me to take my meals alone, and pass all my time in the nursery, while my cousins were constantly in the drawing-room. Not a hint, however, did she drop about sending me to school: still I felt an instinctive certainty that she would not long endure me under the same roof with her: for her glance, now more than ever, when turned on me, expressed an insuperable and rooted aversion.

Eliza and Georgiana, evidently acting according to orders, spoke to me as little as possible: John thrust his tongue in his cheek whenever he saw me, and once attempted chastisement; but as I instantly turned against him, roused by the same sentiment of deep ire and desperate revolt which had stirred my corruption before, he thought it better to desist, and ran from me uttering execrations, and vowing I had burst his nose. I had indeed levelled at that prominent feature as hard a blow as my knuckles could inflict; and when I saw that either that or my look daunted him, I had the greatest inclination to follow up my advantage to purpose; but he was already with his mama. I heard him in a blubbering tone commence the tale of how 'that nasty Jane Eyre' had flown at him like a mad cat: he was stopped rather harshly—

'Don't talk to me about her, John: I told you not to go near her; she is not worthy of notice; I do not choose that either you or your sisters should associate with her.'

Here, leaning over the banister, I cried out suddenly, and without at all deliberating on my words,—

'They are not fit to associate with me.'

Mrs. Reed was rather a stout woman; but, on hearing this strange and audacious declaration, she ran nimbly up the stair, swept me like a whirlwind into the nursery, and crushing me down on the edge of my crib, dared me in an emphatic voice to rise from that place, or utter one syllable during the remainder of the day.

'What would uncle Reed say to you, if he were alive?' was my scarcely voluntary demand. I say scarcely voluntary, for it seemed as if my tongue pronounced words without my will consenting to their utterance: something spoke out of me over which I had no control.

'What?' said Mrs. Reed under her breath: her usually cold composed grey eye became troubled with a look like fear; she took her hand from my arm, and gazed at me as if she really did not know whether I were child or fiend. I was now in for it.

'My uncle Reed is in heaven, and can see all you do and think; and so can papa and mama: they know how you shut me up all day long, and how you wish me dead.'

Mrs. Reed soon rallied her spirits: she shook me most soundly, she boxed both my ears, and then left me without a word. Bessie supplied the hiatus by a homily of an hour's length, in which she proved beyond a doubt that I was the most wicked and abandoned child ever reared under a roof. I half believed her; for I felt indeed only bad feelings surging in my breast.

November, December, and half of January passed away. Christmas and the New Year had been celebrated at Gateshead with the usual festive cheer; presents had been interchanged, dinners and evening parties given. From every enjoyment I was, of course, excluded: my share of the gaiety consisted in witnessing the daily apparelling of Eliza and Georgiana, and seeing them descend to the drawing-room, dressed out in thin muslin frocks and scarlet sashes, with hair elaborately ringletted; and afterwards, in listening to the sound of the piano or the harp played below, to the passing to and fro of the butler and footman, to the jingling of glass and china as refreshments were handed, to the broken hum of conversation as the drawing-room doors opened and closed. When tired of this occupation, I would retire from the stairhead to the solitary and silent nursery: there, though somewhat sad, I was not miserable. To speak the truth, I had not the least wish to go into company, for in company I was very rarely noticed; and if Bessie had been kind and companionable, I should have deemed it a treat to spend the evenings quietly with her, instead of passing them under the formidable eye of Mrs. Reed, in a room full of ladies and gentlemen. But Bessie, as soon as she had dressed her young ladies, used to take herself off to the lively regions of the kitchen and housekeeper's room, generally bearing the candle along with her. I then sat with my doll on my knee, till the fire got low, glancing round occasionally to make sure that nothing worse than myself haunted the shadowy room; and

when the embers sank to a dull red, I undressed hastily, tugging at knot and strings as I best might, and sought shelter from cold and darkness in my crib. To this crib I always took my doll; human beings must love something, and in the dearth of worthier objects of affection, I contrived to find a pleasure in loving and cherishing a faded graven image, shabby as a miniature scarecrow. It puzzles me now to remember with what absurd sincerity I doated on this little toy, half fancying it alive and capable of sensation. I could not sleep unless it was folded in my night-gown; and when it lay there safe and warm, I was comparatively happy, believing it to be happy likewise.

Long did the hours seem while I waited the departure of the company, and listened for the sound of Bessie's step on the stairs: sometimes she would come up in the interval to seek her thimble or her scissors, or perhaps to bring me something by way of supper—a bun or a cheese-cake—then she would sit on the bed while I ate it, and when I had finished, she would tuck the clothes round me, and twice she kissed me, and said, 'Good-night, Miss Jane.' When thus gentle, Bessie seemed to me the best, prettiest, kindest being in the world; and I wished most intensely that she would always be so pleasant and amiable, and never push me about, or scold, or task me unreasonably, as she was too often wont to do. Bessie Lee must, I think, have been a girl of good natural capacity, for she was smart in all she did, and had a remarkable knack of narrative; so, at least, I judge from the impression made on me by her nursery tales. She was pretty, too, if my recollections of her face and person are correct. I remember her as a slim young woman, with black hair, dark eyes, very nice features, and good, clear complexion; but she had a capricious and hasty temper, and indifferent ideas of principle or justice: still, such as she was, I preferred her to any one else at Gateshead Hall.

It was the fifteenth of January, about nine o'clock in the morning: Bessie was gone down to breakfast; my cousins had not yet been summoned to their mama; Eliza was putting on her bonnet and warm garden-coat to go and feed her poultry, an occupation of which she was fond: and not less so of selling the eggs to the housekeeper and hoarding up the money she thus obtained. She had a turn for traffic, and a marked propensity for saving; shown not only in the vending of eggs and chickens, but also in driving hard bargains with the gardener about flower-roots, seeds, and slips of plants, that functionary having orders from Mrs. Reed to buy of his young lady all the products of her parterre she wished to sell: and Eliza would have sold the hair off her head if she could have made a handsome profit thereby. As to her money, she first secreted it in odd corners, wrapped in a rag or an old curl-paper; but some of these hoards having been discovered by the housemaid, Eliza, fearful of one day losing her valued treasure, consented to intrust it to her mother, at a usurious rate of interest—fifty or sixty per cent.; which interest she exacted every quarter, keeping her accounts in a little book with anxious accuracy.

Georgiana sat on a high stool, dressing her hair at the glass, and interweaving her curls with artificial flowers and faded feathers, of which she had found a store in a drawer in the attic. I was making my bed, having received strict orders from Bessie to get it arranged before she returned (for Bessie now frequently employed me as a sort of under-nurserymaid, to tidy the room, dust the chairs, etc.). Having spread the quilt and folded my night-dress, I went to the window-seat to put in order some picture-books and doll's house furniture scattered there; an abrupt command from Georgiana to let her playthings alone (for the tiny chairs and mirrors, the fairy plates and cups were her property) stopped my proceedings; and then, for lack of other occupation, I fell to breathing on the frost-flowers with which the window was fretted, and thus clearing a space in the glass through which I might look out on the grounds, where all was still and petrified under the influence of a hard frost.

From this window were visible the porter's lodge and the carriage-road, and just as I had dissolved so much of the silver-white foliage veiling the panes, as left room to look out, I saw the gates thrown open and a carriage roll through. I watched it ascending the drive with indifference: carriages often came to Gateshead, but none ever brought visitors in whom I was interested; it stopped in front of the house, the door-bell rang loudly, the new comer was admitted. All this being nothing to me, my vacant attention soon found livelier attraction in the spectacle of a little hungry robin, which came and chirruped on the twigs of the leafless cherry-tree nailed against the wall near the casement. The remains of my breakfast of bread and milk stood on the table, and having crumbled a morsel of roll, I was tugging at the sash to put out the crumbs on the window-sill, when Bessie came running upstairs into the nursery.

'Miss Jane, take off your pinafore: what are you doing there? Have you washed your hands and face this morning?' I gave another tug before I answered, for I wanted the bird to be secure of its bread: the sash yielded; I scattered the crumbs, some on the stone sill, some on the cherry-tree bough, then, closing the window, I replied:—

'No, Bessie; I have only just finished dusting.'

'Troublesome, careless child! and what are you doing now? You look quite red, as if you had been about some mischief: what were you opening the window for?'

I was spared the trouble of answering, for Bessie seemed in too great a hurry to listen to explanations; she hauled me to the wash-stand, inflicted a merciless, but happily brief scrub on my face and hands with soap, water, and a coarse towel; disciplined my head with a bristly brush, denuded me of my pinafore, and then hurrying me to the top of the stairs, bid me go down directly, as I was wanted in the breakfast-room.

I would have asked who wanted me: I would have demanded if Mrs. Reed was there; but Bessie was already gone, and had closed the nursery-door

upon me: I slowly descended. For nearly three months, I had never been called to Mrs. Reed's presence: restricted so long to the nursery, the breakfast, dining, and drawing-rooms were become for me awful regions, on which it dismayed me to intrude.

I now stood in the empty hall; before me was the breakfast-room door, and I stopped, intimidated and trembling. What a miserable little poltroon had fear, engendered of unjust punishment, made of me in those days! I feared to return to the nursery, and feared to go forward to the parlour; ten minutes I stood in agitated hesitation: the vehement ringing of the breakfast-room bell decided me; I *must* enter.

'Who could want me?' I asked inwardly, as with both hands I turned the stiff door-handle which, for a second or two, resisted my efforts. 'What should I see besides aunt Reed in the apartment?—a man or a woman?' The handle turned, the door unclosed, and passing through and curtseying low, I looked up at—a black pillar!—such, at least, appeared to me, at first sight, the straight, narrow, sable-clad shape standing erect on the rug: the grim face at the top was like a carved mask, placed above the shaft by way of capital.

Mrs. Reed occupied her usual seat by the fireside: she made a signal to me to approach: I did so, and she introduced me to the stony stranger with the words: 'This is the little girl respecting whom I applied to you.'

He, for it was a man, turned his head slowly towards where I stood, and having examined me with the two inquisitive-looking grey eyes which twinkled under a pair of bushy brows, said solemnly, and in a bass voice: 'Her size is small: what is her age?'

'Ten years.'

'So much?' was the doubtful answer; and he prolonged his scrutiny for some minutes. Presently he addressed me:— 'Your name, little girl?'

'Jane Eyre, sir.'

In uttering these words, I looked up: he seemed to me a tall gentleman; but then I was very little: his features were large, and they and all the lines of his frame were equally harsh and prim.

'Well, Jane Eyre, and are you a good child?'

Impossible to reply to this in the affirmative: my little world held a contrary opinion: I was silent. Mrs. Reed answered for me by an expressive shake of the head, adding soon, 'Perhaps the less said on that subject the better, Mr. Brocklehurst.'

'Sorry indeed to hear it! she and I must have some talk;' and bending from the perpendicular, he installed his person in the arm-chair, opposite Mrs. Reed's. 'Come here,' he said.

I stepped across the rug; he placed me square and straight before him. What a face he had, now that it was almost on a level with mine! what a great nose! and what a mouth! and what large prominent teeth!

'No sight so sad as that of a naughty child,' he began, 'especially a naughty little girl. Do you know where the wicked go after death?'

'They go to hell,' was my ready and orthodox answer.

'And what is hell? Can you tell me that?'

'A pit full of fire?'

'And should you like to fall into that pit, and to be burning there for ever?'

'No, sir.'

'What must you do to avoid it?'

I deliberated a moment; my answer, when it did come, was objectionable: 'I must keep in good health, and not die.'

'How can you keep in good health? Children younger than you die daily. I buried a little child of five years old only a day or two since,—a good little child whose soul is now in heaven. It is to be feared the same could not be said of you, were you to be called hence.'

Not being in a condition to remove his doubts I only cast my eyes down on the two large feet planted on the rug, and sighed, wishing myself far enough away.

'I hope that sigh is from the heart, and that you repent of ever having been the occasion of discomfort to your excellent benefactress.'

'Benefactress! benefactress!' said I, inwardly: 'they all call Mrs. Reed my benefactress; if so, a benefactress is a disagreeable thing.'

'Do you say your prayers night and morning?' continued my interrogator.

'Yes, sir.'

'Do you read your Bible?'

'Sometimes.'

'With pleasure? Are you fond of it?'

'I like Revelations, and the book of Daniel, and Genesis and Samuel, and a little bit of Exodus, and some parts of Kings and Chronicles, and Job and Jonah.'

'And the Psalms? I hope you like them?'

'No, sir.'

'No? oh, shocking! I have a little boy, younger than you, who knows six Psalms by heart: and when you ask him which he would rather have, a gingerbread nut to eat, or a verse of a Psalm to learn, he says: "Oh! the verse of a Psalm! angels sing Psalms;" says he, "I wish to be a little angel here below;" he then gets two nuts in recompense for his infant piety.'

'Psalms are not interesting,' I remarked.

'That proves you have a wicked heart; and you must pray to God to change it: to give you a new and clean one: to take away your heart of stone and give you a heart of flesh.'

I was about to propound a question, touching the manner in which that operation of changing my heart was to be performed, when Mrs. Reed inter-

posed, telling me to sit down; she then proceeded to carry on the conversation herself.

'Mr. Brocklehurst, I believe I intimated in the letter which I wrote to you three weeks ago, that this little girl has not quite the character and disposition I could wish: should you admit her into Lowood school, I should be glad if the superintendent and teachers were requested to keep a strict eye on her, and above all, to guard against her worst fault, a tendency to deceit. I mention this in your hearing, Jane, that you may not attempt to impose on Mr. Brocklehurst.'

Well might I dread, well might I dislike Mrs. Reed; for it was her nature to wound me cruelly: never was I happy in her presence: however carefully I obeyed, however strenuously I strove to please her, my efforts were still repulsed and repaid by such sentences as the above. Now, uttered before a stranger, the accusation cut me to the heart: I dimly perceived that she was already obliterating hope from the new phase of existence which she destined me to enter; I felt, though I could not have expressed the feeling, that she was sowing aversion and unkindness along my future path; I saw myself trans- formed under Mr. Brocklehurst's eye into an artful, noxious child, and what could I do to remedy the injury?

'Nothing, indeed!' thought I, as I struggled to repress a sob, and hastily wiped away some tears, the impotent evidences of my anguish.

'Deceit is, indeed, a sad fault in a child,' said Mr. Brocklehurst; 'it is akin to falsehood, and all liars will have their portion in the lake burning with fire and brimstone: she shall, however, be watched, Mrs. Reed; I will speak to Miss Temple and the teachers.'

'I should wish her to be brought up in a manner suiting her pros- pects,' continued my benefactress; 'to be made useful, to be kept humble: as for the vacations, she will, with your permission, spend them always at Lowood.'

'Your decisions are perfectly judicious, madam,' returned Mr. Brocklehurst. 'Humility is a Christian grace, and one peculiarly appropriate to the pupils of Lowood; I, therefore, direct that especial care shall be bestowed on its cultivation amongst them. I have studied how best to mortify in them the worldly sentiment of pride; and, only the other day, I had a pleasing proof of my success. My second daughter, Augusta, went with her mama to visit the school, and on her return she exclaimed: "Oh, dear papa, how quiet and plain all the girls at Lowood look; with their hair combed behind their ears, and their long pinafores, and those little holland pockets outside their frocks— they are almost like poor people's children! and," said she, "they looked at my dress and mama's, as if they had never seen a silk gown before." '

'This is the state of things I quite approve,' returned Mrs. Reed; 'had I sought all England over, I could scarcely have found a system more exactly

fitting a child like Jane Eyre. Consistency, my dear Mr. Brocklehurst; I advocate consistency in all things.'

'Consistency, madam, is the first of Christian duties; and it has been observed in every arrangement connected with the establishment of Lowood: plain fare, simple attire, unsophisticated accommodations, hardy and active habits; such is the order of the day in the house and its inhabitants.'

'Quite right, sir. I may then depend upon this child being received as a pupil at Lowood, and there being trained in conformity to her position and prospects?'

'Madam, you may: she shall be placed in that nursery of chosen plants—and I trust she will show herself grateful for the inestimable privilege of her election.'

'I will send her, then, as soon as possible, Mr. Brocklehurst; for, I assure you, I feel anxious to be relieved of a responsibility that was becoming too irksome.'

'No doubt, no doubt, madam, and now I wish you good morning. I shall return to Brocklehurst Hall in the course of a week or two: my good friend, the Archdeacon, will not permit me to leave him sooner. I shall send Miss Temple notice that she is to expect a new girl, so that there will be no difficulty about receiving her. Good bye.'

'Good bye, Mr. Brocklehurst; remember me to Mrs. and Miss Brocklehurst, and to Augusta and Theodore, and Master Broughton Brocklehurst.'

'I will, madam. Little girl, here is a book entitled the "Child's Guide"; read it with prayer, especially that part containing "an account of the awfully sudden death of Martha G——, a naughty child addicted to falsehood and deceit." '

With these words Mr. Brocklehurst put into my hand a thin pamphlet sewn in a cover, and having rung for his carriage, he departed.

Mrs. Reed and I were left alone: some minutes passed in silence; she was sewing, I was watching her. Mrs. Reed might be at that time some six or seven and thirty; she was a woman of robust frame, square-shouldered and strong-limbed, not tall, and, though stout, not obese: she had a somewhat large face, the under-jaw being much developed and very solid; her brow was low, her chin large and prominent, mouth and nose sufficiently regular; under her light eye-brows glimmered an eye devoid of ruth; her skin was dark and opaque, her hair nearly flaxen; her constitution was sound as a bell—illness never came near her; she was an exact, clever manager, her household and tenantry were thoroughly under her control; her children, only, at times defied her authority, and laughed it to scorn; she dressed well, and had a presence and port calculated to set off handsome attire.

Sitting on a low stool, a few yards from her arm-chair, I examined her figure; I perused her features. In my hand I held the tract, containing the sudden death of the Liar: to which narrative my attention had been pointed

as to an appropriate warning. What had just passed; what Mrs. Reed had said concerning me to Mr. Brocklehurst; the whole tenor of their conversation, was recent, raw, and stinging in my mind; I had felt every word as acutely as I had heard it plainly, and a passion of resentment fomented now within me.

Mrs. Reed looked up from her work; her eye settled on mine, her fingers at the same time suspended their nimble movements.

'Go out of the room; return to the nursery,' was her mandate. My look or something else must have struck her as offensive, for she spoke with extreme, though suppressed irritation. I got up, I went to the door; I came back again; I walked to the window, across the room, then close up to her.

Speak I must: I had been trodden on severely, and *must* turn: but how? What strength had I to dart retaliation at my antagonist? I gathered my energies and launched them in this blunt sentence:—

'I am not deceitful: if I were, I should say I loved *you*; but I declare I do not love you: I dislike you the worst of anybody in the world except John Reed; and this book about the liar, you may give to your girl, Georgiana, for it is she who tells lies, and not I.'

Mrs. Reed's hands still lay on her work inactive: her eye of ice continued to dwell freezingly on mine.

'What more have you to say?' she asked, rather in the tone in which a person might address an opponent of adult age than such as is ordinarily used to a child.

That eye of hers, that voice stirred every antipathy I had. Shaking from head to foot, thrilled with ungovernable excitement, I continued:—

'I am glad you are no relation of mine: I will never call you aunt again as long as I live. I will never come to see you when I am grown up; and if any one asks me how I liked you, and how you treated me, I will say the very thought of you makes me sick, and that you treated me with miserable cruelty.'

'How dare you affirm that, Jane Eyre?'

'How dare I, Mrs. Reed? How dare I? Because it is the *truth*. You think I have no feelings, and that I can do without one bit of love or kindness; but I cannot live so: and you have no pity. I shall remember how you thrust me back—roughly and violently thrust me back—into the red-room, and locked me up there, to my dying day; though I was in agony; though I cried out, while suffocating with distress, "Have mercy! Have mercy, aunt Reed!" And that punishment you made me suffer because your wicked boy struck me—knocked me down for nothing. I will tell anybody who asks me questions, this exact tale. People think you a good woman, but you are bad; hard-hearted. *You* are deceitful!'

Ere I had finished this reply, my soul began to expand, to exult, with the strangest sense of freedom, of triumph, I ever felt. It seemed as if an invisible bond had burst, and that I had struggled out into unhoped-for liberty. Not

without cause was this sentiment: Mrs. Reed looked frightened; her work had slipped from her knee; she was lifting up her hands, rocking herself to and fro, and even twisting her face as if she would cry.

'Jane, you are under a mistake: what is the matter with you? Why do you tremble so violently? Would you like to drink some water?'

'No, Mrs. Reed.'

'Is there anything else you wish for, Jane? I assure you, I desire to be your friend.'

'Not you. You told Mr. Brocklehurst I had a bad character, a deceitful disposition; and I'll let everybody at Lowood know what you are, and what you have done.'

'Jane, you don't understand these things: children must be corrected for their faults.'

'Deceit is not my fault!' I cried out in a savage, high voice.

'But you are passionate, Jane, that you must allow; and now return to the nursery—there's a dear—and lie down a little.'

'I am not your dear; I cannot lie down: send me to school soon, Mrs. Reed, for I hate to live here.'

'I will indeed send her to school soon,' murmured Mrs. Reed, *sotto voce*; and gathering up her work, she abruptly quitted the apartment.

I was left there alone—winner of the field. It was the hardest battle I had fought, and the first victory I had gained: I stood awhile on the rug, where Mr. Brocklehurst had stood, and I enjoyed my conqueror's solitude. First, I smiled to myself and felt elate; but this fierce pleasure subsided in me as fast as did the accelerated throb of my pulses. A child cannot quarrel with its elders, as I had done, cannot give its furious feelings uncontrolled play, as I had given mine, without experiencing afterwards the pang of remorse and the chill of reaction. A ridge of lighted heath, alive, glancing, devouring, would have been a meet emblem of my mind when I accused and menaced Mrs. Reed: the same ridge, black and blasted after the flames are dead, would have represented as meetly my subsequent condition, when half an hour's silence and reflection had shown me the madness of my conduct, and the dreariness of my hated and hating position.

Something of vengeance I had tasted for the first time; as aromatic wine it seemed, on swallowing, warm and racy: its after-flavour, metallic and corroding, gave me a sensation as if I had been poisoned. Willingly would I now have gone and asked Mrs. Reed's pardon; but I knew, partly from experience and partly from instinct, that was the way to make her repulse me with double scorn, thereby re-exciting every turbulent impulse of my nature.

I would fain exercise some better faculty than that of fierce speaking; fain find nourishment for some less fiendish feeling than that of sombre indignation. I took a book—some Arabian tales; I sat down and endeavoured to read.

I could make no sense of the subject; my own thoughts swam always between me and the page I had usually found fascinating. I opened the glass-door in the breakfast-room: the shrubbery was quite still: the black frost reigned, unbroken by sun or breeze, through the grounds. I covered my head and arms with the skirt of my frock, and went out to walk in a part of the plantation which was quite sequestered: but I found no pleasure in the silent trees, the falling fir-cones, the congealed relics of autumn, russet leaves, swept by past winds in heaps, and now stiffened together. I leaned against a gate, and looked into an empty field where no sheep were feeding, where the short grass was nipped and blanched. It was a very grey day; a most opaque sky, 'onding on snaw,' canopied all; thence flakes fell at intervals, which settled on the hard path and on the hoary lea without melting. I stood, a wretched child enough, whispering to myself over and over again, 'What shall I do?—what shall I do?'

All at once I heard a clear voice call, 'Miss Jane! where are you? Come to lunch!'

It was Bessie, I knew well enough; but I did not stir; her light step came tripping down the path.

'You naughty little thing!' she said. 'Why don't you come when you are called?'

Bessie's presence, compared with the thoughts over which I had been brooding, seemed cheerful; even though, as usual she was somewhat cross. The fact is, after my conflict with and victory over Mrs. Reed, I was not disposed to care much for the nursemaid's transitory anger; and I *was* disposed to bask in her youthful lightness of heart. I just put my two arms round her, and said, 'Come, Bessie! don't scold.'

The action was more frank and fearless than any I was habituated to indulge in: somehow it pleased her.

'You are a strange child, Miss Jane,' she said, as she looked down at me: 'a little roving, solitary thing: and you are going to school, I suppose?'

I nodded.

'And won't you be sorry to leave poor Bessie?'

'What does Bessie care for me? She is always scolding me.'

'Because you're such a queer, frightened, shy, little thing. You should be bolder.'

'What! to get more knocks?'

'Nonsense! But you are rather put upon, that's certain. My mother said, when she came to see me last week, that she would not like a little one of her own to be in your place. — Now, come in, and I've some good news for you.'

'I don't think you have, Bessie.'

'Child! what do you mean? What sorrowful eyes you fix on me! Well! but Missis and the young ladies and Master John are going out to tea this afternoon, and you shall have tea with me. I'll ask cook to bake you a little cake, and then

you shall help me to look over your drawers; for I am soon to pack your trunk. Missis intends you to leave Gateshead in a day or two, and you shall choose what toys you like to take with you.'

'Bessie, you must promise not to scold me any more till I go.'

'Well, I will: but mind you are a very good girl, and don't be afraid of me. Don't start when I chance to speak rather sharply: it's so provoking.'

'I don't think I shall ever be afraid of you again, Bessie, because I have got used to you: and I shall soon have another set of people to dread.'

'If you dread them, they'll dislike you.'

'As you do, Bessie?'

'I don't dislike you, Miss; I believe I am fonder of you than of all the others.'

'You don't show it.'

'You sharp little thing! you've got quite a new way of talking. What makes you so venturesome and hardy?'

'Why, I shall soon be away from you, and besides——' I was going to say something about what had passed between me and Mrs. Reed; but on second thoughts I considered it better to remain silent on that head.

'And so you're glad to leave me?'

'Not at all, Bessie; indeed, just now I am rather sorry.'

'Just now! and rather! How coolly my little lady says it! I daresay now if I were to ask you for a kiss you wouldn't give it to me: you'd say you'd *rather* not.'

'I'll kiss you and welcome: bend your head down.' Bessie stooped; we mutually embraced, and I followed her into the house quite comforted. That afternoon lapsed in peace and harmony; and in the evening Bessie told me some of her most enchanting stories, and sang me some of her sweetest songs. Even for me life had its gleams of sunshine.

CHAPTER 5

Five o'clock had hardly struck on the morning of the 19th of January, when Bessie brought a candle into my closet and found me already up and nearly dressed. I had risen half an hour before her entrance, and had washed my face, and put on my clothes by the light of a half-moon just setting, whose rays streamed through the narrow window near my crib. I was to leave Gateshead that day by a coach which passed the lodge gates at 6 A.M. Bessie was the only person yet risen; she had lit a fire in the nursery, where she now proceeded to make my breakfast. Few children can eat when excited with the thoughts of a journey; nor could I. Bessie, having pressed me in vain to take a few spoonfuls of the boiled milk and bread she had prepared for me, wrapped up some biscuits in a paper and put them into my bag; then she helped me on

with my pelisse and bonnet, and wrapping herself in a shawl, she and I left the nursery. As we passed Mrs. Reed's bedroom, she said, 'Will you go in and bid Missis good-bye?'

'No, Bessie: she came to my crib last night when you were gone down to supper, and said I need not disturb her in the morning, or my cousins either; and she told me to remember that she had always been my best friend, and to speak of her and be grateful to her accordingly.'

'What did you say, Miss!'

'Nothing: I covered my face with the bed-clothes, and turned from her to the wall.'

'That was wrong, Miss Jane.'

'It was quite right, Bessie: your Missis has not been my friend: she has been my foe.'

'Oh, Miss Jane! don't say so!'

'Good-bye to Gateshead!' cried I, as we passed through the hall and went out at the front door.

The moon was set, and it was very dark; Bessie carried a lantern, whose light glanced on wet steps and gravel road soddened by a recent thaw. Raw and chill was the winter morning: my teeth chattered as I hastened down the drive. There was a light in the porter's lodge: when we reached it, we found the porter's wife just kindling her fire: my trunk, which had been carried down the evening before, stood corded at the door. It wanted but a few minutes of six, and shortly after that hour had struck, the distant roll of wheels announced the coming coach; I went to the door and watched its lamps approach rapidly through the gloom.

'Is she going by herself?' asked the porter's wife.

'Yes.'

'And how far is it?'

'Fifty miles.'

'What a long way! I wonder Mrs. Reed is not afraid to trust her so far alone.'

The coach drew up; there it was at the gates with its four horses and its top laden with passengers: the guard and coachman loudly urged haste; my trunk was hoisted up; I was taken from Bessie's neck, to which I clung with kisses.

'Be sure and take good care of her,' cried she to the guard, as he lifted me into the inside.

'Ay, ay!' was the answer: the door was slapped to, a voice exclaimed, 'All right,' and on we drove. Thus was I severed from Bessie and Gateshead: thus whirled away to unknown, and, as I then deemed, remote and mysterious regions.

I remember but little of the journey: I only know that the day seemed to me of a preternatural length, and that we appeared to travel over hundreds of

miles of road. We passed through several towns, and in one, a very large one, the coach stopped; the horses were taken out, and the passengers alighted to dine. I was carried into an inn, where the guard wanted me to have some dinner; but, as I had no appetite, he left me in an immense room with a fire-place at each end, a chandelier pendent from the ceiling, and a little red gallery high up against the wall filled with musical instruments. Here I walked about for a long time, feeling very strange, and mortally apprehensive of some one coming in and kidnapping me; for I believed in kidnappers, their exploits having frequently figured in Bessie's fireside chronicles. At last the guard returned: once more I was stowed away in the coach, my protector mounted his own seat, sounded his hollow horn, and away we rattled over the 'stony street' of L——.

The afternoon came on wet and somewhat misty: as it waned into dusk, I began to feel that we were getting very far indeed from Gateshead: we ceased to pass through towns; the country changed; great grey hills heaved up round the horizon: as twilight deepened, we descended a valley, dark with wood, and long after night had overclouded the prospect, I heard a wild wind rushing amongst trees.

Lulled by the sound, I at last dropped asleep: I had not long slumbered when the sudden cessation of motion awoke me; the coach-door was open, and a person like a servant was standing at it: I saw her face and dress by the light of the lamps.

'Is there a little girl called Jane Eyre here?' she asked. I answered 'Yes,' and was then lifted out; my trunk was handed down, and the coach instantly drove away.

I was stiff with long sitting, and bewildered with the noise and motion of the coach: gathering my faculties, I looked about me. Rain, wind, and darkness filled the air; nevertheless, I dimly discerned a wall before me and a door open in it. Through this door I passed with my new guide: she shut and locked it behind her. There was now visible a house or houses—for the building spread far—with many windows, and lights burning in some; we went up a broad pebbly path, splashing wet, and were admitted at a door; then the servant led me through a passage into a room with a fire, where she left me alone.

I stood and warmed my numbed fingers over the blaze, then I looked round; there was no candle, but the uncertain light from the hearth showed, by inter-vals, papered walls, carpet, curtains, shining mahogany furniture: it was a parlour, not so spacious or splendid as the drawing-room at Gateshead, but comfortable enough. I was puzzling to make out the subject of a picture on the wall, when the door opened, and an individual carrying a light entered; another followed close behind.

The first was a tall lady with dark hair, dark eyes, and a pale and large

forehead; her figure was partly enveloped in a shawl, her countenance was grave, her bearing erect.

'The child is very young to be sent alone,' said she, putting her candle down on the table. She considered me attentively for a minute or two, then further added,—

'She had better be put to bed soon; she looks tired: are you tired?' she asked, placing her hand on my shoulder.

'A little, ma'am.'

'And hungry too, no doubt: let her have some supper before she goes to bed, Miss Miller. Is this the first time you have left your parents to come to school, my little girl?'

I explained to her that I had no parents. She inquired how long they had been dead; then how old I was, what was my name, whether I could read, write, and sew a little: then she touched my cheek gently with her forefinger, and saying, 'She hoped I should be a good child,' dismissed me along with Miss Miller.

The lady I had left might be about twenty-nine; the one who went with me appeared some years younger: the first impressed me by her voice, look, and air. Miss Miller was more ordinary; ruddy in complexion, though of a careworn countenance; hurried in gait and action, like one who had always a multiplicity of tasks on hand: she looked, indeed, what I afterwards found she really was, an under-teacher. Led by her, I passed from compartment to compartment, from passage to passage, of a large and irregular building; till, emerging from the total and somewhat dreary silence pervading that portion of the house we had traversed, we came upon the hum of many voices, and presently entered a wide, long room, with great deal tables, two at each end, on each of which burnt a pair of candles, and seated all round on benches, a congregation of girls of every age, from nine or ten to twenty. Seen by the dim light of the dips, their number to me appeared countless, though not in reality exceeding eighty; they were uniformly dressed in brown stuff frocks of quaint fashion, and long holland pinafores. It was the hour of study; they were engaged in conning over their to-morrow's task, and the hum I had heard was the combined result of their whispered repetitions.

Miss Miller signed to me to sit on a bench near the door, then walking up to the top of the long room, she cried out,—

'Monitors, collect the lesson-books and put them away!'

Four tall girls arose from different tables, and going round, gathered the books and removed them. Miss Miller again gave the word of command,—

'Monitors, fetch the supper-trays!'

The tall girls went out and returned presently, each bearing a tray, with portions of something, I knew not what, arranged thereon, and a pitcher of water and mug in the middle of each tray. The portions were handed round;

those who liked took a draught of the water, the mug being common to all. When it came to my turn, I drank, for I was thirsty, but did not touch the food, excitement and fatigue rendering me incapable of eating: I now saw, however, that it was a thin oaten cake, shared into fragments.

The meal over, prayers were read by Miss Miller, and the classes filed off, two and two, upstairs. Overpowered by this time with weariness, I scarcely noticed what sort of a place the bed-room was; except that, like the school-room, I saw it was very long. To-night I was to be Miss Miller's bed-fellow; she helped me to undress: when laid down I glanced at the long rows of beds, each of which was quickly filled with two occupants; in ten minutes the single light was extinguished; amid silence and complete darkness, I fell asleep.

The night passed rapidly: I was too tired even to dream; I only once awoke to hear the wind rave in furious gusts, and the rain fall in torrents, and to be sensible that Miss Miller had taken her place by my side. When I again unclosed my eyes, a loud bell was ringing: the girls were up and dressing; day had not yet begun to dawn, and a rushlight or two burnt in the room. I too rose reluctantly; it was bitter cold, and I dressed as well as I could for shivering, and washed when there was a basin at liberty, which did not occur soon, as there was but one basin to six girls, on the stands down the middle of the room. Again the bell rang: all formed in file, two and two, and in that order descended the stairs and entered the cold and dimly-lit school-room: here prayers were read by Miss Miller; afterwards she called out:—

'Form classes!'

A great tumult succeeded for some minutes, during which Miss Miller repeatedly exclaimed, 'Silence!' and 'Order!' When it subsided, I saw them all drawn up in four semi-circles, before four chairs, placed at the four tables; all held books in their hands, and a great book, like a Bible, lay on each table, before the vacant seat. A pause of some seconds succeeded, filled up by the low, vague hum of numbers; Miss Miller walked from class to class, hushing this indefinite sound.

A distant bell tinkled: immediately three ladies entered the room, each walked to a table and took her seat; Miss Miller assumed the fourth vacant chair, which was that nearest the door, and around which the smallest of the children were assembled: to this inferior class I was called, and placed at the bottom of it.

Business now began: the day's Collect was repeated, then certain texts of Scripture were said, and to these succeeded a protracted reading of chapters in the Bible, which lasted an hour. By the time that exercise was terminated, day had fully dawned. The indefatigable bell now sounded for the fourth time: the classes were marshalled and marched into another room to breakfast: how glad I was to behold a prospect of getting something to eat! I was now nearly sick from inanition, having taken so little the day before.

The refectory was a great, low-ceiled, gloomy room; on two long tables smoked basins of something hot, which, however, to my dismay, sent forth an odour far from inviting. I saw a universal manifestation of discontent when the fumes of the repast met the nostrils of those destined to swallow it; from the van of the procession, the tall girls of the first class, rose the whispered words:—

'Disgusting!' The porridge is burnt again!'

'Silence!' ejaculated a voice; not that of Miss Miller, but one of the upper teachers, a little and dark personage, smartly dressed, but of somewhat morose aspect, who installed herself at the top of one table, while a more buxom lady presided at the other. I looked in vain for her I had first seen the night before; she was not visible: Miss Miller occupied the foot of the table where I sat, and a strange, foreign looking, elderly lady, the French teacher, as I afterwards found, took the corresponding seat at the other board. A long grace was said and a hymn sung; then a servant brought in some tea for the teachers, and the meal began.

Ravenous, and now very faint, I devoured a spoonful or two of my portion without thinking of its taste; but the first edge of hunger blunted, I perceived I had got in hand a nauseous mess: burnt porridge is almost as bad as rotten potatoes; famine itself soon sickens over it. The spoons were moved slowly: I saw each girl taste her food and try to swallow it; but in most cases the effort was soon relinquished. Breakfast was over, and none had breakfasted. Thanks being returned for what we had not got, and a second hymn chanted, the refectory was evacuated for the school-room. I was one of the last to go out, and in passing the tables, I saw one teacher take a basin of the porridge and taste it; she looked at the others; all their countenances expressed displeasure, and one of them, the stout one, whispered:—

'Abominable stuff! How shameful!'

A quarter of an hour passed before lessons again began, during which the school-room was in a glorious tumult; for that space of time, it seemed to be permitted to talk loud and more freely, and they used their privilege. The whole conversation ran on the breakfast, which one and all abused roundly. Poor things! it was the sole consolation they had. Miss Miller was now the only teacher in the room: a group of great girls standing about her, spoke with serious and sullen gestures. I heard the name of Mr. Brocklehurst pronounced by some lips; at which Miss Miller shook her head disapprovingly; but she made no great effort to check the general wrath: doubtless she shared in it.

A clock in the school-room struck nine; Miss Miller left her circle, and standing in the middle of the room, cried:—

'Silence! To your seats!'

Discipline prevailed: in five minutes the confused throng was resolved into order, and comparative silence quelled the Babel clamour of tongues. The upper teachers now punctually resumed their posts: but still, all seemed to wait.

Ranged on benches down the sides of the room, the eighty girls sat motionless and erect: a quaint assemblage they appeared, all with plain locks combed from their faces, not a curl visible; in brown dresses, made high and surrounded by a narrow tucker about the throat, with little pockets of holland (shaped something like a Highlander's purse) tied in front of their frocks, and designed to serve the purpose of a work-bag: all too wearing woollen stockings and country-made shoes, fastened with brass buckles. Above twenty of those clad in this costume were full-grown girls, or rather young women: it suited them ill, and gave an air of oddity even to the prettiest.

I was still looking at them, and also at intervals examining the teachers—none of whom precisely pleased me; for the stout one was a little coarse, the dark one not a little fierce, the foreigner harsh and grotesque, and Miss Miller, poor thing! looked purple, weather-beaten, and over-worked—when, as my eye wandered from face to face, the whole school rose simultaneously, as if moved by a common spring.

What was the matter? I had heard no order given: I was puzzled. Ere I had gathered my wits, the classes were again seated: but as all eyes were now turned to one point, mine followed the general direction, and encountered the personage who had received me last night. She stood at the bottom of the long room, on the hearth; for there was a fire at each end: she surveyed the two rows of girls silently and gravely. Miss Miller approaching, seemed to ask her a question, and having received her answer, went back to her place, and said aloud,—

'Monitor of the first class, fetch the globes!'

While the direction was being executed, the lady consulted moved slowly up the room. I suppose I have a considerable organ of Veneration, for I retain yet the sense of admiring awe with which my eyes traced her steps. Seen now, in broad daylight, she looked tall, fair, and shapely; brown eyes, with a benignant light in their irids, and a fine pencilling of long lashes round, relieved the whiteness of her large front; on each of her temples her hair, of a very dark brown, was clustered in round curls, according to the fashion of those times, when neither smooth bands nor long ringlets were in vogue; her dress, also in the mode of the day, was of purple cloth, relieved by a sort of Spanish trimming of black velvet; a gold watch (watches were not so common then as now) shone at her girdle. Let the reader add, to complete the picture, refined features; a complexion, if pale, clear; and a stately air and carriage, and he will have, at least, as clearly as words can give it, a correct idea of the exterior of Miss Temple—Maria Temple, as I afterwards saw the name written in a prayer-book entrusted to me to carry to church.

The superintendent of Lowood (for such was this lady) having taken her seat before a pair of globes placed on one of the tables, summoned the first class round her, and commenced giving a lesson in geography; the lower

classes were called by the teachers: repetitions in history, grammar, etc., went on for an hour; writing and arithmetic succeeded, and music lessons were given by Miss Temple to some of the elder girls. The duration of each lesson was measured by the clock, which at last struck twelve. The superintendent rose:—

'I have a word to address to the pupils,' said she.

The tumult of cessation from lessons was already breaking forth, but it sank at her voice. She went on:—

'You had this morning a breakfast which you could not eat; you must be hungry:—I have ordered that a lunch of bread and cheese shall be served to all.'

The teachers looked at her with a sort of surprise.

'It is to be done on my responsibility,' she added, in an explanatory tone to them, and immediately afterwards left the room.

The bread and cheese was presently brought in and distributed, to the high delight and refreshment of the whole school. The order was now given 'To the garden!' Each put on a coarse straw bonnet, with strings of coloured calico, and a cloak of grey frieze. I was similarly equipped, and, following the stream, I made my way into the open air.

The garden was a wide enclosure, surrounded with walls so high as to exclude every glimpse of prospect; a covered verandah ran down one side, and broad walks bordered a middle space divided into scores of little beds: these beds were assigned as gardens for the pupils to cultivate, and each bed had an owner. When full of flowers they would doubtless look pretty; but now, at the latter end of January, all was wintry blight and brown decay. I shuddered as I stood and looked round me: it was an inclement day for out-door exercise; not positively rainy, but darkened by a drizzling yellow fog; all underfoot was still soaking wet with the floods of yesterday. The stronger among the girls ran about and engaged in active games, but sundry pale and thin ones herded together for shelter and warmth in the verandah; and amongst these, as the dense mist penetrated to their shivering frames, I heard frequently the sound of a hollow cough.

As yet I had spoken to no one, nor did anybody seem to take notice of me; I stood lonely enough: but to that feeling of isolation I was accustomed; it did not oppress me much. I leant against a pillar of the verandah, drew my grey mantle close about me, and, trying to forget the cold which nipped me without, and the unsatisfied hunger which gnawed me within, delivered myself up to the employment of watching and thinking. My reflections were too undefined and fragmentary to merit record: I hardly yet knew where I was; Gateshead and my past life seemed floated away to an immeasurable distance; the present was vague and strange, and of the future I could form no conjecture. I looked round the convent-like garden, and then up at the house; a large

building, half of which seemed grey and old, the other half quite new. The new part, containing the school-room and dormitory, was lit by mullioned and latticed windows, which gave it a church-like aspect; a stone tablet over the door, bore this inscription:—

'Lowood Institution.—This portion was rebuilt A.D.——, by Naomi Brocklehurst, of Brocklehurst Hall, in this county.' 'Let your light so shine before men that they may see your good works, and glorify your Father which is in heaven.' —St. Matt. v. 16.

I read these words over and over again: I felt that an explanation belonged to them, and was unable fully to penetrate their import. I was still pondering the signification of 'Institution,' and endeavouring to make out a connection between the first words and the verse of Scripture, when the sound of a cough close behind me, made me turn my head. I saw a girl sitting on a stone bench near; she had bent over a book, on the perusal of which she seemed intent: from where I stood I could see the title—it was 'Rasselas;' a name that struck me as strange, and consequently attractive. In turning a leaf she happened to look up, and I said to her directly:—

'Is your book interesting?' I had already formed the intention of asking her to lend it to me some day.

'I like it,' she answered, after a pause of a second or two, during which she examined me.

'What is it about?' I continued. I hardly know where I found the hardihood thus to open a conversation with a stranger; the step was contrary to my nature and habits: but I think her occupation touched a chord of sympathy somewhere; for I too liked reading, though of a frivolous and childish kind; I could not digest or comprehend the serious or substantial.

'You may look at it,' replied the girl, offering me the book.

I did so; a brief examination convinced me that the contents were less taking than the title: 'Rasselas' looked dull to my trifling taste; I saw nothing about fairies, nothing about genii: no bright variety seemed spread over the closely-printed pages. I returned it to her; she received it quietly, and without saying anything she was about to relapse into her former studious mood: again I ventured to disturb her:—

'Can you tell me what the writing on that stone over the door means? What is Lowood Institution?'

'This house where you are come to live.'

'And why do they call it Institution? Is it in any way different from other schools?'

'It is partly a charity-school: you and I, and all the rest of us, are charity-children. I suppose you are an orphan: are not either your father or your mother dead?'

'Both died before I can remember.'

'Well, all the girls here have lost either one or both parents, and this is called an institution for educating orphans.'

'Do we pay no money? Do they keep us for nothing?'

'We pay, or our friends pay, fifteen pounds a year for each.'

'Then why do they call us charity-children?'

'Because fifteen pounds is not enough for board and teaching, and the deficiency is supplied by subscription.'

'Who subscribes?'

'Different benevolent-minded ladies and gentlemen in this neighbourhood and in London.'

'Who was Naomi Brocklehurst?'

'The lady who built the new part of this house as that tablet records, and whose son overlooks and directs everything here.'

'Why?'

'Because he is treasurer and manager of the establishment.'

'Then this house does not belong to that tall lady who wears a watch, and who said we were to have some bread and cheese.'

'To Miss Temple? Oh, no! I wish it did: she has to answer to Mr. Brocklehurst for all she does. Mr. Brocklehurst buys all our food and all our clothes.'

'Does he live here?'

'No—two miles off, at a large hall.'

'Is he a good man?'

'He is a clergyman, and is said to do a great deal of good.'

'Did you say that tall lady was called Miss Temple?'

'Yes.'

'And what are the other teachers called?'

'The one with red cheeks is called Miss Smith; she attends to the work, and cuts out—for we make our own clothes, our frocks, and pelisses, and every thing; the little one with black hair is Miss Scatcherd; she teaches history and grammar, and hears the second class repetitions; and the one who wears a shawl, and has a pocket-handkerchief tied to her side with a yellow riband, is Madame Pierrot: she comes from Lisle, in France, and teaches French.'

'Do you like the teachers?'

'Well enough.'

'Do you like the little black one, and the Madame——?—I cannot pronounce her name as you do.'

'Miss Scatcherd is hasty—you must take care not to offend her; Madame Pierrot is not a bad sort of person.'

'But Miss Temple is the best—isn't she?'

'Miss Temple is very good, and very clever; she is above the rest, because she knows far more than they do.'

'Have you been long here?'

'Two years.'

'Are you an orphan?'

'My mother is dead.'

'Are you happy here?'

'You ask rather too many questions. I have given you answers enough for the present: now I want to read.'

But at that moment the summons sounded for dinner: all re-entered the house. The odour which now filled the refectory was scarcely more appetising than that which had regaled our nostrils at breakfast: the dinner was served in two huge tin-plated vessels, whence rose a strong steam redolent of rancid fat. I found the mess to consist of indifferent potatoes and strange shreds of rusty meat, mixed and cooked together. Of this preparation a tolerably abundant plateful was apportioned to each pupil. I ate what I could, and wondered within myself whether every day's fare would be like this.

After dinner, we immediately adjourned to the schoolroom: lessons recommenced, and were continued till five o'clock.

The only marked event of the afternoon was, that I saw the girl with whom I had conversed in the verandah, dismissed in disgrace, by Miss Scatcherd, from a history class, and sent to stand in the middle of the large school-room. The punishment seemed to me in a high degree ignominious, especially for so great a girl—she looked thirteen or upwards. I expected she would show signs of great distress and shame; but to my surprise she neither wept nor blushed: composed, though grave, she stood, the central mark of all eyes. 'How can she bear it so quietly—so firmly?' I asked of myself. 'Were I in her place, it seems to me I should wish the earth to open and swallow me up. She looks as if she were thinking of something beyond her punishment—beyond her situation: of something not round nor before her. I have heard of day-dreams—is she in a day-dream now? Her eyes are fixed on the floor, but I am sure they do not see it—her sight seems turned in, gone down into her heart: she is looking at what she can remember, I believe; not at what is really present. I wonder what sort of a girl she is—whether good or naughty.'

Soon after five P.M. we had another meal, consisting of a small mug of coffee, and half a slice of brown bread. I devoured my bread and drank my coffee with relish; but I should have been glad of as much more—I was still hungry. Half an hour's recreation succeeded, then study; then the glass of water and the piece of oat-cake, prayers, and bed. Such was my first day at Lowood.

CHAPTER 6

The next day commenced as before, getting up and dressing by rushlight: but this morning we were obliged to dispense with the ceremony of washing: the water in the pitchers was frozen. A change had taken place in the weather the preceding evening, and a keen north-east wind, whistling through the crevices of our bed-room windows all night long, had made us shiver in our beds, and turned the contents of the ewers to ice.

Before the long hour and a half of prayers and Bible reading was over, I felt ready to perish with cold. Breakfast-time came at last, and this morning the porridge was not burnt; the quality was eatable, the quantity small; how small my portion seemed! I wished it had been doubled.

In the course of the day I was enrolled a member of the fourth class, and regular tasks and occupations were assigned me: hitherto, I had only been a spectator of the proceedings at Lowood, I was now to become an actor therein. At first, being little accustomed to learn by heart, the lessons appeared to me both long and difficult: the frequent change from task to task, too, bewildered me; and I was glad, when, about three o'clock in the afternoon, Miss Smith put into my hands a border of muslin two yards long, together with needle, thimble, etc., and sent me to sit in a quiet corner of the school-room, with direction to hem the same. At that hour most of the others were sewing likewise; but one class still stood round Miss Scatcherd's chair reading, and as all was quiet, the subject of their lessons could be heard, together with the manner in which each girl acquitted herself, and the animadversions or commendations of Miss Scatcherd on the performance. It was English history: among the readers, I observed my acquaintance of the verandah: at the commencement of the lesson, her place had been at the top of the class, but for some error of pronunciation or some inattention to stops, she was suddenly sent to the very bottom. Even in that obscure position, Miss Scatcherd continued to make her an object of constant notice: she was continually addressing to her such phrases as the following:—

'Burns' (such it seems was her name: the girls here were all called by their surnames, as boys are elsewhere), 'Burns, you are standing on the side of your shoe, turn your toes out immediately.' 'Burns, you poke your chin most unpleasantly, draw it in.' 'Burns, I insist on your holding your head up; I will not have you before me in that attitude,' etc., etc.

A chapter having been read through twice, the books were closed and the girls examined. The lesson had comprised part of the reign of Charles I., and there were sundry questions about tonnage and poundage, and ship-money, which most of them appeared unable to answer; still, every little difficulty was solved instantly when it reached Burns: her memory seemed to have retained the substance of the whole lesson, and she was ready with answers

on every point. I kept expecting that Miss Scatcherd would praise her attention; but, instead of that, she suddenly cried out:—

'You dirty, disagreeable girl! you have never cleaned your nails this morning!'

Burns made no answer: I wondered at her silence.

'Why,' thought I, 'does she not explain that she could neither clean her nails nor wash her face, as the water was frozen?'

My attention was now called off by Miss Smith desiring me to hold a skein of thread: while she was winding it, she talked to me from time to time, asking whether I had ever been at school before, whether I could mark, stitch, knit, etc.; till she dismissed me, I could not pursue my observations on Miss Scatcherd's movements. When I returned to my seat, that lady was just delivering an order, of which I did not catch the import; but Burns immediately left the class, and, going into the small inner room where the books were kept, returned in half a minute, carrying in her hand a bundle of twigs tied together at one end. This ominous tool she presented to Miss Scatcherd with a respectful courtesy; then she quietly, and without being told, unloosed her pinafore, and the teacher instantly and sharply inflicted on her neck a dozen strokes with the bunch of twigs. Not a tear rose to Burns' eye; and, while I paused from my sewing, because my fingers quivered at this spectacle with a sentiment of unavailing and impotent anger, not a feature of her pensive face altered its ordinary expression.

'Hardened girl!' exclaimed Miss Scatcherd; 'nothing can correct you of your slatternly habits: carry the rod away.'

Burns obeyed; I looked at her narrowly as she emerged from the book-closet; she was just putting back her handkerchief into her pocket, and the trace of a tear glistened on her thin cheek.

The play-hour in the evening I thought the pleasantest fraction of the day at Lowood: the bit of bread, the draught of coffee swallowed at five o'clock had revived vitality, if it had not satisfied hunger; the long restraint of the day was slackened; the school-room felt warmer than in the morning—its fires being allowed to burn a little more brightly to supply, in some measure, the place of candles, not yet introduced: the ruddy gloaming, the licensed uproar, the confusion of many voices gave one a welcome sense of liberty.

On the evening of the day on which I had seen Miss Scatcherd flog her pupil, Burns, I wandered as usual among the forms and tables and laughing groups without a companion, yet not feeling lonely; when I passed the windows, I now and then lifted a blind and looked out; it snowed fast, a drift was already forming against the lower panes; putting my ear close to the window, I could distinguish from the gleeful tumult within, the disconsolate moan of the wind outside.

Probably, if I had lately left a good home and kind parents, this would have

been the hour when I should most keenly have regretted the separation: that wind would then have saddened my heart; this obscure chaos would have disturbed my peace: as it was, I derived from both a strange excitement, and reckless and feverish, I wished the wind to howl more wildly, the gloom to deepen to darkness, and the confusion to rise to clamour.

Jumping over forms, and creeping under tables, I made my way to one of the fire-places; there, kneeling by the high wire fender, I found Burns, absorbed, silent, abstracted from all round her by the companionship of a book, which she read by the dim glare of the embers.

'It is still Rasselas?' I asked, coming behind her.

'Yes,' she said, 'and I have just finished it.'

And in five minutes more she shut it up. I was glad of this.

'Now,' thought I, 'I can perhaps get her to talk.'

I sat down by her on the floor.

'What is your name besides Burns?'

'Helen.'

'Do you come a long way from here?'

'I come from a place further north; quite on the borders of Scotland.'

'Will you ever go back?'

'I hope so; but nobody can be sure of the future.'

'You must wish to leave Lowood?'

'No: why should I? I was sent to Lowood to get an education; and it would be of no use going away until I have attained that object.'

'But that teacher, Miss Scatcherd, is so cruel to you?'

'Cruel? No at all! She is severe: she dislikes my faults.'

'And if I were in your place I should dislike her; I should resist her; if she struck me with that rod, I should get it from her hand; I should break it under her nose.'

'Probably you would do nothing of the sort: but if you did, Mr. Brockle-hurst would expel you from the school; that would be a great grief to your relations. It is far better to endure patiently a smart which nobody feels but yourself, than to commit a hasty action whose evil consequences will extend to all connected with you; and, besides, the Bible bids us to return good for evil.'

'But then it seems disgraceful to be flogged, and to be sent to stand in the middle of a room full of people; and you are such a great girl: I am far younger than you, and I could not bear it.'

'Yet it would be your duty to bear it, if you could not avoid it: it is weak and silly to say you *cannot bear* what it is your fate to be required to bear.'

I heard her with wonder: I could not comprehend this doctrine of endurance; and still less could I understand or sympathise with the forbearance she expressed for her chastiser. Still I felt that Helen Burns considered things by a light

invisible to my eyes. I suspected she might be right and I wrong; but I would not ponder the matter deeply: like Felix, I put it off to a more convenient season.

'You say you have faults, Helen: what are they: To me you seem very good.'

'Then learn from me, not to judge by appearances: I am, as Miss Scatcherd said, slatternly; I seldom put, and never keep, things in order; I am careless; I forget rules; I read when I should learn my lessons; I have no method; and sometimes I say, like you, I cannot *bear* to be subjected to systematic arrangements. This is all very provoking to Miss Scatcherd, who is naturally neat, punctual, and particular.'

'And cross and cruel,' I added; but Helen Burns would not admit my addition; she kept silence.

'Is Miss Temple as severe to you as Miss Scatcherd?'

At the utterance of Miss Temple's name, a soft smile flitted over her grave face.

'Miss Temple is full of goodness: it pains her to be severe to any one, even the worst in the school: she sees my errors, and tells me of them gently; and, if I do anything worthy of praise, she gives me my meed liberally. One strong proof of my wretchedly defective nature is, that even her expostulations, so mild, so rational, have no influence to cure me of my faults; and even her praise, though I value it most highly, cannot stimulate me to continued care and foresight.'

'That is curious,' said I: 'it is so easy to be careful.'

'For *you* I have no doubt it is. I observed you in your class this morning, and saw you were closely attentive: your thoughts never seemed to wander while Miss Miller explained the lesson and questioned you. Now, mine continually rove away: when I should be listening to Miss Scatcherd, and collecting all she says with assiduity, often I lose the very sound of her voice; I fall into a sort of dream. Sometimes I think I am in Northumberland, and that the noises I hear round me are the bubbling of a little brook which runs through Deepden, near our house;—then, when it comes to my turn to reply, I have to be wakened; and, having heard nothing of what was read for listening to the visionary brook, I have no answer ready.'

'Yet how well you replied this afternoon.'

'It was mere chance: the subject on which we had been reading had interested me. This afternoon, instead of dreaming of Deepden, I was wondering how a man who wished to do right could act so unjustly and unwisely as Charles the First sometimes did; and I thought what a pity it was that, with his integrity and conscientiousness, he could see no farther than the prerogatives of the crown. If he had but been able to look to a distance, and see how what they call the spirit of the age was tending! Still, I like Charles—I respect him—I

pity him, poor murdered king! Yes, his enemies were the worst: they shed blood they had no right to shed. How dared they kill him!'

Helen was talking to herself now: she had forgotten I could not very well understand her—that I was ignorant, or nearly so, of the subject she discussed. I recalled her to my level.'

'And when Miss Temple teaches you, do your thoughts wander then?'

'No, certainly, not often; because Miss Temple has generally something to say which is newer than my own reflections: her language is singularly agreeable to me, and the information she communicates is often just what I wished to gain.'

'Well, then, with Miss Temple you are good?'

'Yes, in a passive way: I make no effort; I follow as inclination guides me. There is no merit in such goodness.'

'A great deal: you are good to those who are good to you. It is all I ever desire to be. If people were always kind and obedient to those who are cruel and unjust, the wicked people would have it all their own way: they would never feel afraid, and so they would never alter, but would grow worse and worse. When we are struck at without a reason, we should strike back again very hard; I am sure we should—so hard as to teach the person who struck us never to do it again.'

'You will change your mind, I hope, when you grow older: as yet you are but a little untaught girl.'

'But I feel this, Helen: I must dislike those who, whatever I do to please them, persist in disliking me; I must resist those who punish me unjustly. It is as natural as that I should love those who show me affection, or submit to punishment when I feel it is deserved.'

'Heathens and savage tribes hold that doctrine; but Christians and civilised nations disown it.'

'How? I don't understand.'

'It is not violence that best overcomes hate—nor vengeance that most certainly heals injury.'

'What then?'

'Read the New Testament, and observe what Christ says, and how he acts; make his word your rule, and his conduct your example.'

'What does he say?'

'Love your enemies; bless them that curse you; do good to them that hate you and despitefully use you.'

'Then I should love Mrs. Reed, which I cannot do; I should bless her son John, which is impossible.'

In her turn, Helen Burns asked me to explain; and I proceeded forthwith to pour out, in my own way, the tale of my sufferings and resentments. Bitter and truculent when excited, I spoke as I felt, without reserve or softening.

Helen heard me patiently to the end: I expected she would then make a remark, but she said nothing.

'Well,' I asked impatiently, 'is not Mrs. Reed a hard-hearted, bad woman?'

'She has been unkind to you, no doubt; because, you see, she dislikes your cast of character, as Miss Scatcherd does mine: but how minutely you remember all she has done and said to you! What a singularly deep impression her injustice seems to have made on your heart! No ill-usage so brands its record on my feelings. Would you not be happier if you tried to forget her severity, together with the passionate emotions it excited? Life appears to me too short to be spent in nursing animosity, or registering wrongs. We are, and must be, one and all, burdened with faults in this world: but the time will soon come when, I trust, we shall put them off in putting off our corruptible bodies; when debasement and sin will fall from us with this cumbrous frame of flesh, and only the spark of the spirit will remain,—the impalpable principle of life and thought, pure as when it left the Creator to inspire the creature: whence it came it will return; perhaps again to be communicated to some being higher than man—perhaps to pass through gradations of glory, from the pale human soul to brighten to the seraph! Surely it will never, on the contrary, be suffered to degenerate from man to fiend? No; I cannot believe that: I hold another creed; which no one ever taught me, and which I seldom mention; but in which I delight, and to which I cling: for it extends hope to all: it makes Eternity a rest—a mighty home, not a terror and an abyss. Besides, with this creed, I can so clearly distinguish between the criminal and his crime; I can so sincerely forgive the first while I abhor the last: with this creed revenge never worries my heart, degradation never too deeply disgusts me, injustice never crushes me too low: I live in calm, looking to the end.'

Helen's head, always drooping, sank a little lower as she finished this sentence I saw by her look she wished no longer to talk to me, but rather to converse with her own thoughts. She was not allowed much time for meditation: a monitor, a great rough girl, presently came up, exclaiming in a strong Cumberland accent,—

'Helen Burns, if you don't go and put your drawer in order, and fold up your work this minute, I'll tell Miss Scatcherd to come and look at it!'

Helen sighed as her reverie fled, and getting up, obeyed the monitor without reply as without delay.

CHAPTER 7

My first quarter at Lowood seemed an age; and not the golden age either: it comprised an irksome struggle with difficulties in habituating myself to new rules and unwonted tasks. The fear of failure in these points harassed me

worse than the physical hardships of my lot; though these were no trifles.

During January, February, and part of March, the deep snows, and, after their melting, the almost impassable roads, prevented our stirring beyond the garden walls, except to go to church; but within these limits we had to pass an hour every day in the open air. Our clothing was insufficient to protect us from the severe cold: we had no boots, the snow got into our shoes and melted there; our ungloved hands became numbed and covered with chilblains, as were our feet: I remember well the distracting irritation I endured from this cause every evening, when my feet inflamed; and the torture of thrusting the swelled, raw, and stiff toes into my shoes in the morning. Then the scanty supply of food was distressing: with the keen appetites of growing children, we had scarcely sufficient to keep alive a delicate invalid. From this deficiency of nourishment resulted an abuse, which pressed hardly on the younger pupils: whenever the famished great girls had an opportunity, they would coax or menace the little ones out of their portion. Many a time I have shared between two claimants the precious morsel of brown bread distributed at tea-time; and after relinquishing to a third, half the contents of my mug of coffee, I have swallowed the remainder with an accompaniment of secret tears, forced from me by the exigency of hunger.

Sundays were dreary days in that wintry season. We had to walk two miles to Brocklebridge Church, where our patron officiated. We set out cold, we arrived at church colder: during the morning service we became almost paralysed. It was too far to return to dinner, and an allowance of cold meat and bread, in the same penurious proportion observed in our ordinary meals, was served round between the services.

At the close of the afternoon service we returned by an exposed and hilly road, where the bitter winter wind, blowing over a range of snowy summits to the north, almost flayed the skin from our faces.

I can remember Miss Temple walking lightly and rapidly along our drooping line, her plaid cloak which the frosty wind fluttered, gathered close about her, and encouraging us, by precept, and example, to keep up our spirits, and march forward, as she said, 'like stalwart soldiers'. The other teachers, poor things, were generally themselves too much dejected to attempt the task of cheering others.

How we longed for the light and heat of a blazing fire when we got back! But, to the little ones at least, this was denied: each hearth in the school-room was immediately surrounded by a double row of great girls, and behind them the younger children crouched in groups, wrapping their starved arms in their pinafores.

A little solace came at tea-time, in the shape of a double ration of bread—a whole, instead of a half, slice—with the delicious addition of a thin scrape of butter: it was the hebdomadal treat to which we all looked forward from

Sabbath to Sabbath. I generally contrived to reserve a moiety of this bounteous repast for myself; but the remainder I was invariably obliged to part with.

The Sunday evening was spent in repeating, by heart, the Church Catechism, and the fifth, sixth, and seventh chapters of St. Matthew; and in listening to a long sermon, read by Miss Miller, whose irrepressible yawns attested her weariness. A frequent interlude of these performances was the enactment of the part of Eutychus by some half dozen of little girls; who, overpowered with sleep, would fall down, if not out of the third loft, yet off the fourth form, and be taken up half dead. The remedy was, to thrust them forward into the centre of the school-room, and oblige them to stand there till the sermon was finished. Sometimes, their feet failed them, and they sank together in a heap; they were then propped up with the monitors' high stools.

I have not yet alluded to the visits of Mr. Brocklehurst; and indeed that gentleman was from home during the greater part of the first month after my arrival; perhaps prolonging his stay with his friend the archdeacon: his absence was a relief to me. I need not say that I had my own reasons for dreading his coming: but come he did at last.

One afternoon (I had then been three weeks at Lowood), as I was sitting with a slate in my hand, puzzling over a sum in long division, my eyes, raised in abstraction to the window, caught sight of a figure just passing: I recognised almost instinctively that gaunt outline; and when, two minutes after, all the school, teachers included, rose *en masse*, it was not necessary for me to look up in order to ascertain whose entrance they thus greeted. A long stride measured the school-room, and presently beside Miss Temple, who herself had risen, stood the same black column which had frowned on me so ominously from the hearth-rug of Gateshead. I now glanced sideways at this piece of architecture. Yes, I was right: it was Mr. Brocklehurst, buttoned up in a surtout and looking longer, narrower, and more rigid than ever.

I had my own reasons for being dismayed at this apparition: too well I remembered the perfidious hints given by Mrs. Reed about my disposition, etc.; the promise pledged by Mr. Brocklehurst to apprise Miss Temple and the teachers of my vicious nature. All along I had been dreading the fulfilment of this promise,—I had been looking out daily for the 'Coming Man,' whose information respecting my past life and conversation was to brand me as a bad child for ever: now there he was. He stood at Miss Temple's side; he was speaking low in her ear: I did not doubt he was making disclosures of my villainy; and I watched her eye with painful anxiety, expecting every moment to see its dark orb turn on me a glance of repugnance and contempt. I listened too; and as I happened to be seated quite at the top of the room, I caught most of what he said: its import relieved me from immediate apprehension.

'I suppose, Miss Temple, the thread I bought at Lowton will do; it struck me that it would be just of the quality for the calico chemises, and I sorted

the needles to match. You may tell Miss Smith that I forgot to make a memo-randum of the darning needles, but she shall have some papers sent in next week; and she is not, on any account, to give out more than one at a time to each pupil: if they have more,.they are apt to be careless and lose.them. And, oh ma'am! I wish the woollen stockings were better looked to!—when I was here last, I went into the kitchen-garden and examined the clothes drying on the line; there was a quantity of black hose in a very bad state of repair: from the size of the holes in them I was sure they had not been well-mended from time to time.'

He paused.

'Your directions shall be attended to, sir,' said Miss Temple.

'And, ma'am,' he continued, 'the laundress tells me some of the girls have two clean tuckers in the week: it is too much; the rules limit them to one.'

'I think I can explain that circumstance, sir. Agnes and Catherine Johnstone were invited to take tea with some friends at Lowton last Thursday, and I gave them leave to put on clean tuckers for the occasion.'

Mr. Brocklehurst nodded.

'Well, for once it may pass; but please not to let the circumstance occur too often. And there is another thing which surprised me: I find, in settling accounts with the housekeeper, that a lunch consisting of bread and cheese, has twice been served out to the girls during the past fortnight. How is this? I look over the regulations, and I find no such meal as lunch mentioned. Who introduced this innovation! and by what authority?'

'I must be responsible for the circumstance, sir,' replied Miss Temple: 'the breakfast was so ill-prepared that the pupils could not possibly eat it; and I dared not allow them to remain fasting till dinner time.'

'Madam, allow me an instant.—You are aware that my plan in bringing up these girls is, not to accustom them to habits of luxury and indulgence, but to render them hardy, patient, self-denying. Should any little accidental disappointment of the appetite occur, such as the spoiling of a meal, the under or the over dressing of a dish, the incident ought not to be neutralised by replacing with something more delicate the comfort lost, thus pampering the body and obviating the aim of this institution; it ought to be improved to the spiritual edification of the pupils, by encouraging them to evince forti-tude under the temporary privation. A brief address on those occasions would not be mistimed, wherein a judicious instructor would take the opportunity of referring to the sufferings of the primitive Christians; to the torments of martyrs; to the exhortations of our blessed Lord himself, calling upon his disciples to take up their cross and follow him; to his warnings that man shall not live by bread alone, but by every word that proceedeth out of the mouth of God; to his divine consolations, "if ye suffer hunger or thirst for my sake, happy are ye." Oh, madam, when you put bread and cheese, instead of burnt

porridge, into these children's mouths, you may indeed feed their vile bodies, but you little think how you starve their immortal souls!'

Mr. Brocklehurst again paused—perhaps overcome by his feelings. Miss Temple had looked down when he first began to speak to her; but she now gazed straight before her, and her face, naturally pale as marble, appeared to be assuming also the coldness and fixity of that material; especially her mouth, closed as if it would have required a sculptor's chisel to open it, and her brow settled gradually into petrified severity.

Meantime, Mr. Brocklehurst, standing on the hearth with his hands behind his back, majestically surveyed the whole school. Suddenly his eye gave a blink, as if it had met something that either dazzled or shocked its pupil; turning, he said in more rapid accents than he had hitherto used:—

'Miss Temple, Miss Temple, what—*what* is that girl with curled hair? Red hair, ma'am, curled—curled all over?' And extending his cane he pointed to the awful object, his hand shaking as he did so.

'It is Julia Severn,' replied Miss Temple, very quietly.

'Julia Severn, ma'am! And why has she, or any other, curled hair? Why, in defiance of every precept and principle of this house, does she conform to the world so openly—here in an evangelical, charitable establishment—as to wear her hair one mass of curls?'

'Julia's hair curls naturally,' returned Miss Temple, still more quietly.

'Naturally! Yes, but we are not to conform to nature: I wish these girls to be the children of Grace: and why that abundance? I have again and again intimated that I desire the hair to be arranged closely, modestly, plainly. Miss Temple, that girl's hair must be cut off entirely; I will send a barber to-morrow: and I see others who have far too much of the excrescence—that tall girl, tell her to turn round. Tell all the first form to rise up and direct their faces to the wall.'

Miss Temple passed her handkerchief over her lips, as if to smooth away the involuntary smile that curled them; she gave the order, however, and when the first class could take in what was required of them, they obeyed. Leaning a little back on my bench, I could see the looks and grimaces with which they commented on this manœuvre: it was a pity Mr. Brocklehurst could not see them too; he would perhaps have felt that, whatever he might do with the outside of the cup and platter, the inside was further beyond his interference than he imagined.

He scrutinised the reverse of these living medals some five minutes, then pronounced sentence. These words fell like the knell of doom:—

'All these top-knots must be cut off.'

Miss Temple seemed to remonstrate.

'Madam,' he pursued, 'I have a Master to serve whose kingdom is not of this world: my mission is to mortify in these girls the lusts of the flesh; to teach them to clothe themselves with shame-facedness and sobriety, not with braided

hair and costly apparel; and each of the young persons before us has a string of hair twisted in plaits which vanity itself might have woven: these, I repeat, must be cut off; think of the time wasted, of——'

Mr. Brocklehurst was here interrupted: three other visitors, ladies, now entered the room. They ought to have come a little sooner to have heard his lecture on dress, for they were splendidly attired in velvet, silk, and furs. The two younger of the trio (fine girls of sixteen and seventeen) had grey beaver hats, then in fashion, shaded with ostrich plumes, and from under the brim of this graceful head-dress fell a profusion of light tresses, elaborately curled; the elderly lady was enveloped in a costly velvet shawl, trimmed with ermine, and she wore a false front of French curls.

These ladies were deferentially received by Miss Temple, as Mrs. and Misses Brocklehurst, and conducted to seats of honour at the top of the room. It seems they had come in the carriage with their reverend relative, and had been conducting a rummaging scrutiny of the rooms upstairs, while he transacted business with the housekeeper, questioned the laundress, and lectured the superintendent. They now proceeded to address divers remarks and reproofs to Miss Smith, who was charged with the care of the linen and the inspection of the dormitories: but I had no time to listen to what they said; other matters called off and enchained my attention.

Hitherto, while gathering up the discourse of Mr. Brocklehurst and Miss Temple, I had not, at the same time, neglected precautions to secure my personal safety; which I thought would be effected, if I could only elude observation. To this end, I had sat well back on the form, and while seeming to be busy with my sum, had held my slate in such a manner as to conceal my face: I might have escaped notice had not my treacherous slate somehow happened to slip from my hand, and falling with an obtrusive crash, directly drawn every eye upon me; I knew it was all over now, and, as I stooped to pick up the two fragments of slate, I rallied my forces for the worst. It came.

'A careless girl!' said Mr. Brocklehurst, and immediately after—'It is the new pupil, I perceive.' And before I could draw breath, 'I must not forget I have a word to say respecting her.' Then aloud: how loud it seemed to me! 'Let the child who broke her slate, come forward!'

Of my own accord, I could not have stirred; I was paralysed: but the two great girls who sat on each side of me, set me on my legs and pushed me towards the dread judge, and then Miss Temple gently assisted me to his very feet, and I caught her whispered counsel,—

'Don't be afraid, Jane, I saw it was an accident; you shall not be punished.'

The kind whisper went to my heart like a dagger.

'Another minute, and she will despise me for a hypocrite,' thought I; and an impulse of fury against Reed, Brocklehurst, and Co. bounded in my pulses at the conviction. I was no Helen Burns.

'Fetch that stool,' said Mr. Brocklehurst, pointing to a very high one from which a monitor had just risen: it was brought.

'Place the child upon it.'

And I was placed there, by whom I don't know: I was in no condition to note particulars; I was only aware that they had hoisted me up to the height of Mr. Brocklehurst's nose, that he was within a yard of me, and that a spread of shot orange and purple silk pelisses, and a cloud of silvery plumage extended and waved below me.

Mr. Brocklehurst hemmed.

'Ladies,' said he, turning to his family; 'Miss Temple, teachers, and children, you all see this girl?'

Of course they did; for I felt their eyes directed like burning-glasses against my scorched skin.

'You see she is yet young; you observe she possesses the ordinary form of childhood; God has graciously given her the shape that He has given to all of us; no signal deformity points her out as a marked character. Who would think that the Evil One had already found a servant and agent in her! Yet such, I grieve to say, is the case.'

A pause—in which I began to steady the palsy of my nerves, and to feel that the Rubicon was passed; and that the trial, no longer to be shirked, must be firmly sustained.

'My dear children,' pursued the black marble clergyman, with pathos, 'this is a sad, a melancholy occasion; for it becomes my duty to warn you, that this girl, who might be one of God's own lambs, is a little castaway: not a member of the true flock, but evidently an interloper and an alien. You must be on your guard against her; you must shun her example: if necessary, avoid her company, exclude her from your sports, and shut her out from your converse. Teachers, you must watch her: keep your eyes on her movements, weigh well her words, scrutinise her actions, punish her body to save her soul: if, indeed, such salvation be possible, for (my tongue falters while I tell it) this girl, this child, the native of a Christian land, worse than many a little heathen who says its prayers to Brahma and kneels before Juggernaut—this girl is—a liar!'

Now came a pause of ten minutes; during which I, by this time in perfect possession of my wits, observed all the female Brocklehursts produce their pocket-handkerchiefs and apply them to their optics, while the elderly lady swayed herself to and fro, and the two younger ones whispered, 'How shocking!'

Mr. Brocklehurst resumed.

'This I learned from her benefactress; from the pious and charitable lady who adopted her in her orphan state, reared her as her own daughter, and whose kindness, whose generosity the unhappy girl repaid by an ingratitude so bad, so dreadful, that at last her excellent patroness was obliged to separate

her from her own young ones, fearful lest her vicious example should contaminate their purity; she has sent her here to be healed, even as the Jews of old sent their diseased to the troubled pool of Bethesda; and, teachers, superintendent, I beg of you not to allow the waters to stagnate round her.'

With this sublime conclusion, Mr. Brocklehurst adjusted the top button of his surtout, muttered something to his family, who rose, bowed to Miss Temple, and then all the great people sailed in state from the room. Turning at the door, my judge said:—

'Let her stand half an hour longer on that stool, and let no one speak to her during the remainder of the day.'

There was I, then, mounted aloft; I, who had said I could not bear the shame of standing on my natural feet in the middle of the room, was now exposed to general view on a pedestal of infamy. What my sensations were, no language can describe; but just as they all rose, stifling my breath and constricting my throat, a girl came up and passed me: in passing, she lifted her eyes. What a strange light inspired them! What an extraordinary sensation that ray sent through me! How the new feeling bore me up! It was as if a martyr, a hero, had passed a slave or victim, and imparted strength in the transit. I mastered the rising hysteria, lifted up my head, and took a firm stand on the stool. Helen Burns asked some slight question about her work of Miss Smith, was chidden for the triviality of the inquiry, returned to her place, and smiled at me as she again went by. What a smile! I remember it now, and I know that it was the effluence of fine intellect, of true courage; it lit up her marked lineaments, her thin face, her sunken grey eye, like a reflection from the aspect of an angel. Yet at that moment Helen Burns wore on her arm 'the untidy badge'; scarcely an hour ago I had heard her condemned by Miss Scatcherd to a dinner of bread and water on the morrow, because she had blotted an exercise in copying it out. Such is the imperfect nature of man! such spots are there on the disc of the clearest planet; and eyes like Miss Scatcherd's can only see those minute defects, and are blind to the full brightness of the orb.

CHAPTER 8

Ere the half-hour ended, five o'clock struck; school was dismissed, and all were gone into the refectory to tea. I now ventured to descend: it was deep dusk; I retired into a corner and sat down on the floor. The spell by which I had been so far supported began to dissolve; reaction took place, and soon, so everwhelming was the grief that seized me, I sank prostrate with my face to the ground. Now I wept: Helen Burns was not here; nothing sustained me; left to myself I abandoned myself, and my tears watered the boards. I had

meant to be so good, and to do so much at Lowood: to make so many friends, to earn respect, and win affection. Already I had made visible progress: that very morning I had reached the head of my class; Miss Miller had praised me warmly; Miss Temple had smiled approbation; she had promised to teach me drawing, and to let me learn French, if I continued to make similar improvement two months longer: and then I was well-received by my fellow-pupils; treated as an equal by those of my own age, and not molested by any; now, here I lay again crushed and trodden on; and could I ever rise more?

'Never,' I thought; and ardently I wished to die. While sobbing out this wish in broken accents, some one approached: I started up—again Helen Burns was near me; the fading fires just showed her coming up the long, vacant room; she brought my coffee and bread.

'Come, eat something,' she said; but I put both away from me, feeling as if a drop or a crumb would have choked me in my present condition. Helen regarded me, probably with surprise: I could not now abate my agitation, though I tried hard; I continued to weep aloud. She sat down on the ground near me, embraced her knees with her arms, and rested her head upon them; in that attitude she remained silent as an Indian. I was the first who spoke:—

'Helen, why do you stay with a girl whom everybody believes to be a liar?'

'Everybody, Jane? Why, there are only eighty people who have heard you called so, and the world contains hundreds of millions.'

'But what have I to do with millions? The eighty I know despise me.'

'Jane, you are mistaken: probably not one in the school either despises or dislikes you: many, I am sure, pity you much.'

'How can they pity me after what Mr. Brocklehurst said?'

'Mr. Brocklehurst is not a god: nor is he even a great and admired man; he is little liked here; he never took steps to make himself liked. Had he treated you as an especial favourite, you would have found enemies, declared or covert, all around you; as it is, the greater number would offer you sympathy if they dared. Teachers and pupils may look coldly on you for a day or two, but friendly feelings are concealed in their hearts; and if you persevere in doing well, these feelings will ere long appear so much the more evidently for their temporary suppression. Besides, Jane,'——she paused.

'Well, Helen?' said I, putting my hand into hers: she chafed my fingers gently to warm them, and went on:—

'If all the world hated you, and believed you wicked, while your own conscience approved you, and absolved you from guilt, you would not be without friends.'

'No; I know I should think well of myself; but that is not enough: if others don't love me, I would rather die than live—I cannot bear to be solitary and hated, Helen. Look here; to gain some real affection from you, or Miss Temple, or any other whom I truly love, I would willingly submit to have the bone

of my arm broken, or to let a bull toss me, or to stand behind a kicking horse, and let it dash its hoof at my chest,'——

'Hush, Jane! you think too much of the love of human beings: you are too impulsive, too vehement: the sovereign hand that created your frame, and put life into it, has provided you with other resources than your feeble self, or than creatures feeble as you. Besides this earth, and besides the race of men, there is an invisible world and a kingdom of spirits: that world is round us, for it is everywhere; and those spirits watch us, for they are commissioned to guard us; and if we were dying in pain and shame, if scorn smote us on all sides, and hatred crushed us, angels see our tortures, recognise our innocence (if innocent we be: as I know you are of this charge which Mr. Brocklehurst has weakly and pompously repeated at second-hand from Mrs. Reed; for I read a sincere nature in your ardent eyes and on your clear front), and God waits only the separation of spirit from flesh to crown us with a full reward. Why, then, should we ever sink overwhelmed with distress, when life is so soon over, and death is so certain an entrance to happiness—to glory?'

I was silent: Helen had calmed me; but in the tranquillity she imparted there was an alloy of inexpressible sadness. I felt the impression of woe as she spoke, but I could not tell whence it came; and when, having done speaking, she breathed a little fast and coughed a short cough, I momentarily forgot my own sorrows to yield to a vague concern for her.

Resting my head on Helen's shoulder, I put my arms round her waist; she drew me to her, and we reposed in silence. We had not sat long thus, when another person came in. Some heavy clouds, swept from the sky by a rising wind, had left the moon bare; and her light, streaming in through a window near, shone full both on us and on the approaching figure, which we at once recognised as Miss Temple.

'I came on purpose to find you, Jane Eyre,' said she; 'I want you in my room; and as Helen Burns is with you, she may come too.'

We went; following the superintendent's guidance, we had to thread some intricate passages, and mount a staircase before we reached her apartment; it contained a good fire, and looked cheerful. Miss Temple told Helen Burns to be seated in a low arm-chair on one side of the hearth, and herself taking another, she called me to her side.

'Is it all over?' she asked, looking down at my face. 'Have you cried your grief away?'

'I am afraid I never shall do that.'

'Why?'

'Because I have been wrongly accused; and you, ma'am, and everybody else will now think me wicked.'

'We shall think you what you prove yourself to be, my child. Continue to act as a good girl, and you will satisfy me.'

'Shall I, Miss Temple?'

'You will,' said she, passing her arm round me. 'And now tell me who is the lady whom Mr. Brocklehurst called your benefactress?'

'Mrs. Reed, my uncle's wife. My uncle is dead, and he left me to her care.'

'Did she not, then, adopt you of her own accord?'

'No, ma'am; she was sorry to have to do it; but my uncle, as I have often heard the servants say, got her to promise before he died, that she would always keep me.'

'Well now, Jane, you know, or at least I will tell you, that when a criminal is accused, he is always allowed to speak in his own defence. You have been charged with falsehood; defend yourself to me as well as you can. Say whatever your memory suggests as true; but add nothing and exaggerate nothing.'

I resolved, in the depth of my heart, that I would be most moderate—most correct; and, having reflected a few minutes in order to arrange coherently what I had to say, I told her all the story of my sad childhood. Exhausted by emotion, my language was more subdued than it generally was when it developed that sad theme; and mindful of Helen's warnings against the indulgence of resentment, I infused into the narrative far less of gall and wormwood than ordinary. Thus restrained and simplified, it sounded more credible: I felt as I went on that Miss Temple fully believed me.

In the course of the tale I had mentioned Mr. Lloyd as having come to see me after the fit: for I never forgot the, to me, frightful episode of the red-room; in detailing which, my excitement was sure, in some degree, to break bounds; for nothing, could soften in my recollection the spasm of agony which clutched my heart when Mrs. Reed spurned my wild supplication for pardon, and locked me a second time in the dark and haunted chamber.

I had finished: Miss Temple regarded me a few minutes in silence; she then said—

'I know something of Mr. Lloyd; I shall write to him; if his reply agrees with your statement, you shall be publicly cleared from every imputation: to me, Jane, you are clear now.'

She kissed me, and still keeping me at her side (where I was well contented to stand, for I derived a child's pleasure from the contemplation of her face, her dress, her one or two ornaments, her white forehead, her clustered and shining curls, and beaming dark eyes), she proceeded to address Helen Burns.

'How are you to-night, Helen? Have you coughed much to-day?'

'Not quite so much I think, ma'am.'

'And the pain in your chest?'

'It is a little better.'

Miss Temple got up, took her hand and examined her pulse; then she returned to her own seat: as she resumed it, I heard her sigh low. She was pensive a few minutes, then rousing herself, she said cheerfully:—

'But you two are my visitors to-night; I must treat you as such.' She rang the bell.

'Barbara,' she said to the servant who answered it, 'I have not yet had tea; bring the tray, and place cups for these two young ladies.'

And a tray was soon brought. How pretty, to my eyes, did the china and bright teapot look, placed on the little round table near the fire! How fragrant was the steam of the beverage, and the scent of the toast! of which, however, I, to my dismay (for I was beginning to be hungry), discerned only a very small portion: Miss Temple discerned it too:—

'Barbara,' said she, 'can you not bring a little more bread and butter? There is not enough for three.'

Barbara went out: she returned soon:—

'Madam, Mrs. Harden says she has sent up the usual quantity.'

Mrs. Harden, be it observed, was the housekeeper: a woman after Mr. Brocklehurst's own heart, made up of equal parts of whalebone and iron.

'Oh, very well!' returned Miss Temple; 'we must make it do, Barbara, I suppose.' And as the girl withdrew, she added, smiling, 'Fortunately, I have it in my power to supply deficiencies for this once.'

Having invited Helen and me to approach the table, and placed before each of us a cup of tea with one delicious but thin morsel of toast, she got up, unlocked a drawer, and taking from it a parcel wrapped in paper, disclosed presently to our eyes a good-sized seed-cake.

'I meant to give each of you some of this to take with you,' said she; 'but as there is so little toast, you must have it now,' and she proceeded to cut slices with a generous hand.

We feasted that evening as on nectar and ambrosia; and not the least delight of the entertainment was the smile of gratification with which our hostess regarded us, as we satisfied our famished appetites on the delicate fare she liberally supplied. Tea over and the tray removed, she again summoned us to the fire; we sat one on each side of her, and now a conversation followed between her and Helen, which it was indeed a privilege to be admitted to hear.

Miss Temple had always something of serenity in her air, of state in her mien, of refined propriety in her language, which precluded deviation into the ardent, the excited, the eager: something which chastened the pleasure of those who looked on her and listened to her, by a controlling sense of awe; and such was my feeling now: but as to Helen Burns, I was struck with wonder.

The refreshing meal, the brilliant fire, the presence and kindness of her beloved instructress, or, perhaps, more than all these, something in her own unique mind, had roused her powers within her. They woke, they kindled: first, they glowed in the bright tint of her cheek, which till this hour I had never seen but pale and bloodless; then they shone in the liquid lustre of her eyes, which had suddenly acquired a beauty more singular than that of

Miss Temple's—a beauty neither of fine colour nor long eyelash, nor pencilled brow, but of meaning, of movement, of radiance. Then her soul sat on her lips, and language flowed, from what source I cannot tell: has a girl of fourteen a heart large enough, vigorous enough to hold the swelling spring of pure, full, fervid eloquence? Such was the characteristic of Helen's discourse on that, to me, memorable evening; her spirit seemed hastening to live within a very brief span as much as many live during a protracted existence.

They conversed of things I had never heard of; of nations and times past; of countries far away: of secrets of nature discovered or guessed at: they spoke of books: how many they had read! What stores of knowledge they possessed! Then they seemed so familiar with French names and French authors: but my amazement reached its climax when Miss Temple asked Helen if she sometimes snatched a moment to recall the Latin her father had taught her, and taking a book from a shelf, bade her read and construe a page of 'Virgil'; and Helen obeyed, my organ of Veneration expanding at every sounding line. She had scarcely finished ere the bell announced bedtime: no delay could be admitted; Miss Temple embraced us both, saying, as she drew us to her heart:—

'God bless you, my children!'

Helen she held a little longer than me: she let her go more reluctantly; it was Helen her eye followed to the door; it was for her she a second time breathed a sad sigh; for her she wiped a tear from her cheek.

On reaching the bed-room, we heard the voice of Miss Scatcherd: she was examining drawers; she had just pulled out Helen Burns's, and when we entered Helen was greeted with a sharp reprimand, and told that to-morrow she should have half a dozen of untidily folded articles pinned to her shoulder.

'My things were indeed in shameful disorder,' murmured Helen to me, in a low voice: 'I intended to have arranged them, but I forgot.'

Next morning, Miss Scatcherd wrote in conspicuous, characters on a piece of pasteboard the word 'Slattern,' and bound it like a phylactery round Helen's large, mild, intelligent, and benign-looking forehead. She wore it till evening, patient, unresentful, regarding it as a deserved punishment. The moment Miss Scatcherd withdrew after afternoon-school, I ran to Helen, tore it off, and thrust it into the fire: the fury of which she was incapable had been burning in my soul all day, and tears, hot and large, had continually been scalding my cheek; for the spectacle of her sad resignation gave me an intolerable pain at the heart.

About a week subsequently to the incidents above narrated, Miss Temple, who had written to Mr. Lloyd, received his answer: it appeared that what he said went to corroborate my account. Miss Temple, having assembled the whole school, announced that inquiry had been made into the charges alleged against Jane Eyre, and that she was most happy to be able to pronounce her completely cleared from every imputation. The teachers then shook hands

with me and kissed me, and a murmur of pleasure ran through the ranks of my companions.

Thus relieved of a grievous load, I from that hour set to work afresh, resolved to pioneer my way through every difficulty: I toiled hard, and my success was proportionate to my efforts; my memory, not naturally tenacious, improved with practice; exercise sharpened my wits; in a few weeks I was promoted to a higher class ; in less than two months I was allowed to commence French and drawing. I learned the first two tenses of the verb *Etre*, and sketched my first cottage (whose walls, by-the-by, outrivalled in slope those of the leaning tower of Pisa), on the same day. That night, on going to bed, I forgot to prepare in imagination the Barmecide supper of hot roast potatoes, or white bread and new milk, with which I was wont to amuse my inward cravings: I feasted instead on the spectacle of ideal drawings; which I saw in the dark; all the work of my own hands: freely pencilled houses and trees, picturesque rocks and ruins, Cuyp-like groups of cattle, sweet paintings of butterflies hovering over unblown roses, of birds picking at ripe cherries, of wrens' nests enclosing pearl-like eggs, wreathed about with young ivy sprays. I examined, too, in thought, the possibility of my ever being able to translate currently a certain little French story-book which Madame Pierrot had that day shown me; nor was that problem solved to my satisfaction ere I fell sweetly asleep.

Well has Solomon said—'Better is a dinner of herbs where love is, than a stalled ox and hatred therewith.'

I would not now have exchanged Lowood with all its privations, for Gateshead and its daily luxuries.

CHAPTER 9

But the privations, or rather the hardships, of Lowood lessened. Spring drew on, she was indeed already come; the frosts of winter had ceased; its snows were melted, its cutting winds ameliorated. My wretched feet, flayed and swollen to lameness by the sharp air of January, began to heal and subside under the gentler breathings of April; the nights and mornings no longer by their Canadian temperature froze the very blood in our veins; we could now endure the play-hour in the garden: sometimes on a sunny day it began even to be pleasant and genial, and a greenness grew over those brown beds, which, freshening daily, suggested the thought that Hope traversed them at night, and left each morning brighter traces of her steps. Flowers peeped out amongst the leaves; snow-drops, crocuses, purple auriculas, and golden-eyed pansies. On Thursday afternoons (half-holidays) we now took walks, and found still sweeter flowers opening by the wayside, under the hedges.

I discovered, too, that a great pleasure, an enjoyment which the horizon only bounded, lay all outside the high and spike-guarded walls of our garden: this pleasure consisted in prospect of noble summits girdling a great hill-hollow, rich in verdure and shadow: in a bright beck, full of dark stones and sparkling eddies. How different had this scene looked when I viewed it laid out beneath the iron sky of winter, stiffened in frost, shrouded with snow!—when mists as chill as death wandered to the impulse of east winds along those purple peaks, and rolled down 'ing' and holm till they blended with the frozen fog of the beck! That beck itself was then a torrent, turbid and curbless: it tore asunder the wood, and sent a raving sound through the air, often thickened with wild rain or whirling sleet; and for the forest on its banks, *that* showed only ranks of skeletons.

April advanced to May: a bright, serene May it was; days of blue sky, placid sunshine, and soft western or southern gales filled up its duration. And now vegetation matured with vigour; Lowood shook loose its tresses; it became all green, all flowery; its great elm, ash, and oak skeletons were restored to majestic life; woodland plants sprang up profusely in its recesses; unnumbered varieties of moss filled its hollows, and it made a strange ground-sunshine out of the wealth of its wild primrose plants: I have seen their pale gold gleam in overshadowed spots like scatterings of the sweetest lustre. All this I enjoyed often and fully, free, unwatched, and almost alone; for this unwonted liberty and pleasure there was a cause, to which it now becomes my task to advert.

Have I not described a pleasant site for a dwelling, when I speak of it as bosomed in hill and wood, and rising from the verge of a stream? Assuredly, pleasant enough: but whether healthy or not is another question.

That forest-dell, where Lowood lay, was the cradle of fog and fog-bred pestilence; which, quickening with the quickening spring, crept into the Orphan Asylum, breathed typhus through its crowded school-room and dormitory, and, ere May arrived, transformed the seminary into an hospital.

Semi-starvation and neglected colds had predisposed most of the pupils to receive infection: forty-five out of the eighty girls lay ill at one time. Classes were broken up, rules relaxed. The few who continued well were allowed almost unlimited licence; because the medical attendant insisted on the necessity of frequent exercise to keep them in health: and had it been otherwise, no one had leisure to watch or restrain them. Miss Temple's whole attention was absorbed by the patients: she lived in the sick-room, never quitting it except to snatch a few hours' rest at night. The teachers were fully occupied with packing up and making other necessary preparations for the departure of those girls who were fortunate enough to have friends and relations able and willing to remove them from the seat of contagion. Many, already smitten, went home only to die; some died at the school and were buried quietly and quickly, the nature of the malady forbidding delay.

While disease had thus become an inhabitant of Lowood, and death its frequent visitor; while there was gloom and fear within its walls; while its rooms and passages steamed with hospital smells, the drug and the pastille striving vainly to overcome the effluvia of mortality, that bright May shone unclouded over the bold hills and beautiful woodland out of doors. Its garden, too, glowed with flowers: hollyhocks had sprung up tall as trees, lilies had opened, tulips and roses were in bloom; the borders of the little beds were gay with pink thrift and crimson double-daisies; the sweet-briars gave out, morning and evening, their scent of spice and apples; and these fragrant treasures were all useless for most of the inmates of Lowood, except to furnish now and then a handful of herbs and blossoms to put in a coffin.

But I, and the rest who continued well, enjoyed fully the beauties of the scene and season: they let us ramble in the wood, like gipsies, from morning till night; we did what we liked, went where we liked: we lived better too. Mr. Brocklehurst and his family never came near Lowood now: household matters were not scrutinised into: the cross housekeeper was gone, driven away by the fear of infection; her successor, who had been matron at the Lowton Dispensary, unused to the ways of her new abode, provided with comparative liberality. Besides, there were fewer to feed: the sick could eat little; our breakfast-basins were better filled: when there was no time to prepare a regular dinner, which often happened, she would give us a large piece of cold pie, or a thick slice of bread and cheese, and this we carried away with us to the wood, where we each chose the spot we liked best, and dined sumptuously.

My favourite seat was a smooth and broad stone, rising white and dry from the very middle of the beck, and only to be got at by wading through the water; a feat I accomplished barefoot. The stone was just broad enough to accommodate, comfortably, another girl and me, at that time my chosen comrade—one Mary Ann Wilson; a shrewd observant personage, whose society I took pleasure in, partly because she was witty and original, and partly because she had a manner which set me at my ease. Some years older than I, she knew more of the world, and could tell me many things I liked to hear: with her my curiosity found gratification: to my faults also she gave ample indulgence, never imposing curb or rein on anything I said. She had a turn for narrative, I for analysis; she liked to inform, I to question; so we got on swimmingly together, deriving much entertainment, if not much improvement, from our mutual intercourse.

And where, meantime, was Helen Burns? Why did I not spend these sweet days of liberty with her? Had I forgotten her? or was I so worthless as to have grown tired of her pure society? Surely the Mary Ann Wilson I have mentioned was inferior to my first acquaintance: she could only tell me amusing stories, and reciprocate any racy and pungent gossip I chose to indulge in; while,

if I have spoken truth of Helen, she was qualified to give those who enjoyed the privilege of her converse, a taste of far higher things.

True, reader; and I knew and felt this: and though I am a defective being, with many faults and few redeeming points, yet I never tired of Helen Burns; nor ever ceased to cherish for her a sentiment of attachment, as strong, tender, and respectful as any that ever animated my heart. How could it be otherwise, when Helen, at all times and under all circumstances, evinced for me a quiet and faithful friendship, which ill-humour never soured, nor irritation ever troubled? But Helen was ill at present: for some weeks she had been removed from my sight to I knew not what room upstairs. She was not, I was told, in the hospital portion of the house with the fever patients; for her complaint was consumption, not typhus: and by consumption I, in my ignorance, understood something mild, which time and care would be sure to alleviate.

I was confirmed in this idea by the fact of her once or twice coming downstairs on very warm sunny afternoons, and being taken by Miss Temple into the garden: but, on these occasions, I was not allowed to go and speak to her; I only saw her from the schoolroom window, and then not distinctly; for she was much wrapped up, and sat at a distance under the verandah.

One evening, in the beginning of June, I had stayed out very late with Mary Ann in the wood; we had, as usual, separated ourselves from the others, and had wandered far: so far that we lost our way, and had to ask it at a lonely cottage, where a man and woman lived, who looked after a herd of half-wild swine that fed on the mast in the wood. When we got back, it was after moonrise: a pony, which we knew to be the surgeon's, was standing at the garden door. Mary Ann remarked that she supposed some one must be very ill, as Mr. Bates had been sent for at that time of the evening. She went into the house: I stayed behind a few minutes to plant in my garden a handful of roots I had dug up in the forest, and which I feared would wither if I left them till the morning. This done, I lingered yet a little longer: the flowers smelt so sweet as the dew fell; it was such a pleasant evening, so serene, so warm; the still glowing west promised so fairly another fine day on the morrow; the moon rose with such majesty in the grave east. I was noting these things and enjoying them as a child might, when it entered my mind as it had never done before:—

'How sad to be lying now on a sick bed, and to be in danger of dying! This world is pleasant—it would be dreary to be called from it, and to have to go who knows where?'

And then my mind made its first earnest effort to comprehend what had been infused into it concerning heaven and hell: and for the first time it recoiled, baffled; and for the first time glancing behind, on each side, and before it, it saw all round an unfathomed gulf: it felt the one point where it stood—the present; all the rest was formless cloud and vacant depth: and it

shuddered at the thought of tottering, and plunging amid that chaos. While pondering this new idea, I heard the front door open; Mr. Bates came out, and with him was a nurse. After she had seen him mount his horse and depart, she was about to close the door, but I ran up to her.

'How is Helen Burns?'

'Very poorly,' was the answer.

'Is it her Mr. Bates has been to see?'

'Yes.'

'And what does he say about her?'

'He says she'll not be here long.'

This phrase, uttered in my hearing yesterday, would have only conveyed the notion that she was about to be removed to Northumberland, to her own home. I should not have suspected that it meant she was dying; but I knew instantly now; it opened clear on my comprehension that Helen Burns was numbering her last days in this world, and that she was going to be taken to the region of spirits, if such region there were. I experienced a shock of horror, then a strong thrill of grief, then a desire—a necessity to see her; and I asked in what room she lay.

'She is in Miss Temple's room,' said the nurse.

'May I go up and speak to her?'

'Oh, no, child! It is not likely; and now it is time for you to come in; you'll catch the fever if you stop out when the dew is falling.'

The nurse closed the front door; I went in by the side entrance which led to the school-room: I was just in time; it was nine o'clock, and Miss Miller was calling the pupils to go to bed.

It might be two hours later, probably near eleven, when I—not having been able to fall asleep, and deeming, from the perfect silence of the dormitory, that my companions were all wrapt in profound repose—rose softly, put on my frock over my night-dress, and, without shoes, crept from the apartment, and set off in quest of Miss Temple's room. It was quite at the other end of the house; but I knew my way; and the light of the unclouded summer moon, entering here and there at passage windows, enabled me to find it without difficulty. An odour of camphor and burnt vinegar warned me when I came near the fever room: and I passed its door quickly, fearful lest the nurse who sat up all night should hear me. I dreaded being discovered and sent back; for I *must* see Helen,—I must embrace her before she died,—I must give her one last kiss, exchange with her one last word.

Having descended a staircase, traversed a portion of the house below, and succeeded in opening and shutting, without noise, two doors, I reached another flight of steps; these I mounted, and then just opposite to me was Miss Temple's room. A light shone through the key-hole, and from under the door; a profound stillness pervaded the vicinity. Coming near, I found the

door slightly ajar; probably to admit some fresh air into the close abode of sickness. Indisposed to hesitate, and full of impatient impulses—soul and senses quivering with keen throes—I put it back and looked in. My eye sought Helen, and feared to find death.

Close by Miss Temple's bed, and half covered, with its white curtains, there stood a little crib. I saw the outline of a form under the clothes, but the face was hid by the hangings: the nurse I had spoken to in the garden sat in an easy chair, asleep; an unsnuffed candle burnt dimly on the table. Miss Temple was not to be seen: I knew afterwards that she had been called to a delirious patient in the fever room. I advanced; then paused by the crib side: my hand was on the curtain, but I preferred speaking before I withdrew it. I still recoiled at the dread of seeing a corpse.

'Helen?' I whispered softly; 'are you awake?'

She stirred herself, put back the curtain, and I saw her face, pale, wasted, but quite composed: she looked so little changed that my fear was instantly dissipated.

'Can it be you, Jane?' she asked in her own gentle voice.

'Oh!' I thought, 'she is not going to die; they are mistaken: she could not speak and look so calmly if she were.'

I got on to her crib and kissed her; her forehead was cold, and her cheek both cold and thin, and so were her hand and wrist; but she smiled as of old.

'Why are you come here, Jane? It is past eleven o'clock: I heard it strike some minutes since.'

'I came to see you, Helen: I heard you were very ill, and I could not sleep till I had spoken to you.'

'You came to bid me good-bye, then: you are just in time probably.'

'Are you going somewhere, Helen? Are you going home?'

'Yes; to my long home—my last home.'

'No, no, Helen!' I stopped, distressed. While I tried to devour my tears, a fit of coughing seized Helen; it did not, however, wake the nurse; when it was over, she lay some minutes exhausted; then she whispered:—

'Jane, your little feet are bare; lie down and cover yourself with my quilt.'

I did so: she put her arm over me, and I nestled close to her. After a long silence, she resumed; still whispering,—

'I am very happy, Jane; and when you hear that I am dead, you must be sure and not grieve: there is nothing to grieve about. We all must die one day, and the illness which is removing me is not painful; it is gentle and gradual: my mind is at rest. I leave no one to regret me much: I have only a father; and he is lately married, and will not miss me. By dying young, I shall escape great sufferings. I had not qualities or talent to make my way very well in the world: I should have been continually at fault.'

'But where are you going to, Helen? Can you see? Do you know?'

'I believe; I have faith: I am going to God.'

'Where is God? What is God?'

'My Maker and yours, who will never destroy what he created. I rely implicitly on his power, and confide wholly in his goodness: I count the hours till that eventful one arrives which shall restore me to him, reveal him to me.'

'You are sure, then, Helen, that there is such a place as heaven; and that our souls can get to it when we die?'

'I am sure there is a future state; I believe God is good; I can resign my immortal part to him without any misgiving. God is my father; God is my friend: I love him; I believe he loves me.'

'And shall I see you again, Helen, when I die?'

'You will come to the same region of happiness: be received by the same mighty, universal Parent, no doubt, dear Jane.'

Again I questioned; but this time only in thought. 'Where is that region? Does it exist?' And I clasped my arms closer round Helen; she seemed dearer to me than ever; I felt as if I could not let her go; I lay with my face hidden on her neck. Presently she said in the sweetest tone,—

'How comfortable I am! That last fit of coughing has tired me a little; I feel as if I could sleep: but don't leave me, Jane; I like to have you near me.'

'I'll stay with you, *dear* Helen: no one shall take me away.'

'Are you warm, darling?'

'Yes.'

'Good-night, Jane.'

'Good-night, Helen.'

She kissed me, and I her; and we both soon slumbered.

When I awoke it was day; an unusual movement roused me; I looked up; I was in somebody's arms; the nurse held me; she was carrying me through the passage back to the dormitory. I was not reprimanded for leaving my bed; people had something else to think about: no explanation was afforded then to my many questions; but a day or two afterwards I learned that Miss Temple, on returning to her own room at dawn, had found me laid in a little crib; my face against Helen Burns's shoulder, my arms round her neck. I was asleep, and Helen was—dead.

Her grave is in Brocklebridge churchyard: for fifteen years after her death it was only covered by a grassy mound; but now a gray marble tablet marks the spot, inscribed with her name, and the word 'Resurgam.'

CHAPTER 10

Hitherto I have recorded in detail the events of my insignificant existence: to the first ten years of my life, I have given almost as many chapters. But this is not to be a regular autobiography: I am only bound to invoke memory

where I know her responses will possess some degree of interest; therefore I now pass a space of eight years almost in silence: a few lines only are necessary to keep up the links of connection.

When the typhus fever had fulfilled its mission of devastation at Lowood, it gradually disappeared from thence; but not till its virulence and the number of its victims had drawn public attention on the school. Inquiry was made into the origin of the scourge, and by degrees various facts came out which excited public indignation in a high degree. The unhealthy nature of the site; the quantity and quality of the children's food; the brackish, fetid water used in its preparation; the pupils' wretched clothing and accommodations: all these things were discovered; and the discovery produced a result mortifying to Mr. Brocklehurst, but beneficial to the institution.

Several wealthy and benevolent individuals in the county subscribed largely for the erection of a more convenient building in a better situation; new regulations were made; improvements in diet and clothing introduced; the funds of the school were entrusted to the management of a committee. Mr. Brocklehurst, who, from his wealth and family connections, could not be over-looked, still retained the post of treasurer; but he was aided in the discharge of his duties by gentlemen of rather more enlarged and sympathising minds: his office of inspector, too, was shared by those who knew how to combine reason with strictness, comfort with economy, compassion with uprightness. The school, thus improved, became in time a truly useful and noble institution. I remained an inmate of its walls, after its regeneration, for eight years: six as pupil, and two as teacher; and in both capacities I bear my testimony to its value and importance.

During these eight years my life was uniform: but not unhappy, because it was not inactive. I had the means of an excellent education placed within my reach; a fondness for some of my studies, and a desire to excel in all, together with a great delight in pleasing my teachers, especially such as I loved, urged me on: I availed myself fully of the advantages offered me. In time I rose to be the first girl of the first class; then I was invested with the office of teacher; which I discharged with zeal for two years: but at the end of that time I altered.

Miss Temple, through all changes, had thus far continued superintendent of the seminary: to her instruction I owed the best part of my acquirements; her friendship and society had been my continual solace; she had stood me in the stead of mother, governess, and latterly, companion. At this period she married, removed with her husband (a clergyman, an excellent man, almost worthy of such a wife) to a distant county, and consequently was lost to me.

From the day she left I was no longer the same: with her was gone every settled feeling, every association that had made Lowood in some degree a home to me. I had imbibed from her something of her nature and much of her habits: more harmonious thoughts: what seemed better regulated feelings

had become the inmates of my mind. I had given in allegiance to duty and order; I was quiet; I believed I was content: to the eyes of others, usually even to my own, I appeared a disciplined and subdued character.

But destiny, in the shape of the Rev. Mr. Nasmyth, came between me and Miss Temple: I saw her in her travelling dress step into a post-chaise, shortly after the marriage ceremony; I watched the chaise mount the hill and disappear beyond its brow; and then retired to my own room, and there spent in solitude the greatest part of the half-holiday granted in honour of the occasion.

I walked about the chamber most of the time. I imagined myself only to be regretting my loss, and thinking how to repair it; but when my reflections were concluded, and I looked up and found that the afternoon was gone, and evening far advanced, another discovery dawned on me, namely, that in the interval I had undergone a transforming process; that my mind had put off all it had borrowed of Miss Temple—or rather that she had taken with her the serene atmosphere I had been breathing in her vicinity—and that now I was left in my natural element, and beginning to feel the stirring of old emotions. It did not seem as if a prop were withdrawn, but rather as if a motive were gone: it was not the power to be tranquil which had failed me, but the reason for tranquillity was no more. My world had for some years been in Lowood: my experience had been of its rules and systems; now I remembered that the real world was wide, and that a varied field of hopes and fears, of sensations and excitements, awaited those who had courage to go forth into its expanse, to seek real knowledge, of life amidst its perils.

I went to my window, opened it, and looked out. There were the two wings of the building; there was the garden; there were the skirts of Lowood; there was the hilly horizon. My eye passed all other objects to rest on those most remote, the blue peaks: it was those I longed to surmount; all within their boundary of rock and heath seemed prison-ground, exile limit. I traced the white road winding round the base of one mountain, and vanishing in a gorge between two: how I longed to follow it further! I recalled the time when I had travelled that very road in a coach; I remembered descending that hill at twilight: an age seemed to have elapsed since the day which brought me first to Lowood, and I had never quitted it since. My vacations had all been spent at school: Mrs. Reed had never sent for me to Gateshead; neither she nor any of her family had ever been to visit me. I had had no communication by letter or message with the outer world: school-rules, school-duties, school-habits and notions, and voices, and faces, and phrases, and costumes, and preferences, and antipathies: such was what I knew of existence. And now I felt that it was not enough: I tired of the routine of eight years in one afternoon. I desired liberty; for liberty I gasped; for liberty I uttered a prayer; it seemed scattered on the wind then faintly blowing. I abandoned it and framed a humbler supplication; for change, stimulus: that petition, too,

seemed swept off into vague space: 'Then,' I cried, half desperate, 'grant me at least a new servitude!'

Here a bell, ringing the hour of supper, called me downstairs.

I was not free to resume the interrupted chain of my reflections till bedtime: even then a teacher who occupied the same room with me kept me from the subject to which I longed to recur, by a prolonged effusion of small talk. How I wished sleep would silence her! It seemed as if, could I but go back to the idea which had last entered my mind as I stood at the window, some inventive suggestion would rise for my relief.

Miss Gryce snored at last; she was a heavy Welshwoman, and till now her habitual nasal strains had never been regarded by me in any other light than as a nuisance; to-night I hailed the first deep notes with satisfaction; I was debarrassed of interruption; my half-effaced thought instantly revived.

'A new servitude! There is something in that,' I soliloquised (mentally, be it understood; I did not talk aloud). 'I know there is, because it does not sound too sweet; is it not like such words as Liberty, Excitement, Enjoyment: delightful sounds truly; but no more than sounds for me; and so hollow and fleeting that it is mere waste of time to listen to them. But Servitude! That must be matter of fact. Any one may serve: I have served here eight years; now all I want is to serve elsewhere. Can I not get so much of my own will? Is not the thing feasible? Yes—yes—the end is not so difficult; if I had only a brain active enough to ferret out the means of attaining it.'

I sat up in bed by way of arousing this said brain: it was a chilly night; I covered my shoulders with a shawl, and then I proceeded *to think* again with all my might.

'What do I want? A new place, in a new house, amongst new faces, under new circumstances: I want this because it is of no use wanting anything better. How do people do to get a new place? They apply to friends, I suppose: I have no friends. There are many others who have no friends, who must look about for themselves and be their own helpers: and what is their resource?'

I could not tell: nothing answered me; I then ordered my brain to find a response, and quickly. It worked and worked faster: I felt the pulses throb in my head and temples; but for nearly an hour it worked in chaos, and no result came of its efforts. Feverish with vain labour, I got up and took a turn in the room; undrew the curtain, and noted a star or two, shivered with cold, and again crept to bed.

A kind fairy, in my absence, had surely dropped the required suggestion on my pillow; for as I lay down it came quietly and naturally to my mind:—'Those who want situations advertise; you must advertise in the ——shire *Herald*.'

'How? I know nothing about advertising.'

Replies rose smooth and prompt now:—

'You must inclose the advertisement and the money to pay for it under a cover directed to the Editor of the *Herald*; you must put it, the first opportunity you have, into the post at Lowton; answers must be addressed to J. E. at the post-office there: you can go and inquire in about a week after you send your letter, if any are come, and act accordingly.'

This scheme I went over twice, thrice; it was then digested in my mind: I had it in a clear practical form; I felt satisfied, and fell asleep.

With earliest day, I was up: I had my advertisement written, enclosed, and directed before the bell rang to rouse the school; it ran thus:—

'A young lady accustomed to tuition' (had I not been a teacher two years?) 'is desirous of meeting with a situation in a private family where the children are under fourteen (I thought that as I was barely eighteen, it would not do to undertake the guidance of pupils nearer my own age). She is qualified to teach the usual branches of a good English education, together with French, Drawing, and Music' (in those days, reader, this now narrow catalogue of accomplishments, would have been held tolerably comprehensive). 'Address J. E., Post-office, Lowton, ——shire.'

This document remained locked in my drawer all day: after tea, I asked leave of the new superintendent to go to Lowton, in order to perform some small commissions for myself and one or two of my fellow-teachers; permission was readily granted; I went. It was a walk of two miles, and the evening was wet, but the days were still long; I visited a shop or two, slipped the letter into the post-office, and came back through heavy rain, with streaming garments, but with a relieved heart.

The succeeding week seemed long: it came to an end at last, however, like all sublunary things, and once more, towards the close of a pleasant autumn day, I found myself afoot on the road to Lowton. A picturesque track it was, by the way; lying along the side of the beck and through the sweetest curves of the dale: but that day I thought more of the letter, that might or might not be awaiting me at the little burgh whither I was bound, than of the charms of lea and water.

My ostensible errand on this occasion was to get measured for a pair of shoes; so I discharged that business first, and when it was done, I stepped across the clean and quiet little street from the shoemaker's to the post-office: it was kept by an old dame, who wore horn spectacles on her nose, and black mittens on her hands.

'Are there any letters for J. E.?' I asked.

She peered at me over her spectacles, and then she opened a drawer and fumbled among its contents for a long time, so long that my hopes began to falter. At last, having held a document before her glasses for nearly five minutes, she presented it across the counter, accompanying the act by another inquisitive and mistrustful glance—it was for J. E.

'Is there only one?' I demanded.

'There are no more,' said she; and I put it in my pocket and turned my face homeward: I could not open it then; rules obliged me to be back by eight, and it was already half-past seven.

Various duties awaited me on my arrival: I had to sit with the girls during their hour of study; then it was my turn to read prayers; to see them to bed: afterwards I supped with the other teachers. Even when we finally retired for the night, the inevitable Miss Gryce was still my companion: we had only a short end of a candle in our candlestick, and I dreaded lest she should talk till it was all burnt out; fortunately, however, the heavy supper she had eaten produced a soporific effect: she was already snoring, before I had finished undressing. There still remained an inch of candle: I now took out my letter; the seal was an initial F.; I broke it; the contents were brief.

'If J. E., who advertised in the ——shire *Herald* of last Thursday, possesses the acquirements mentioned; and if she is in a position to give satisfactory references as to character and competency; a situation can be offered her where there is but one pupil, a little girl, under ten years of age; and, where the salary is thirty pounds per annum. J. E. is requested to send references, name, address, and all particulars to the direction:—

'Mrs. Fairfax, Thornfield, near Millcote, ——shire.'

I examined the document long; the writing was old-fashioned and rather uncertain, like that of an elderly lady. This circumstance was satisfactory: a private fear had haunted me, that in thus acting for myself, and by my own guidance, I ran the risk of getting into some scrape; and, above all things, I wished the result of my endeavours to be respectable, proper, *en règle*. I now felt that an elderly lady was no bad ingredient in the business I had on hand. Mrs. Fairfax! I saw her in a black gown and widow's cap; frigid, perhaps, but not uncivil: a model of elderly English respectability. Thornfield! that, doubtless, was the name of her house: a neat, orderly spot, I was sure; though I failed in my efforts to conceive a correct plan of the premises. Millcote, ——shire; I brushed up my recollections of the map of England; yes, I saw it; both the shire and the town. ——shire was seventy miles nearer London than the remote county where I now resided: that was a recommendation to me. I longed to go where there was life and movement: Millcote was a large manufacturing town on the banks of the A——; a busy place enough, doubtless: so much the better; it would be a complete change at least. Not that my fancy was much captivated by the idea of long chimneys and clouds of smoke—'but,' I argued, 'Thornfield, will, probably, be a good way from the town.'

Here the socket of the candle dropped, and the wick went out.

Next day new steps were to be taken: my plans could no longer be confined to my own breast; I must impart them in order to achieve their success. Having sought and obtained an audience of the superintendent, during the noon-

tide recreation, I told her I had a prospect of getting a new situation where the salary would be double what I now received (for, at Lowood, I only got £15 per annum); and requested she would break the matter for me to Mr. Brocklehurst, or some of the committee, and ascertain whether they would permit me to mention them as references. She obligingly consented to act as mediatrix in the matter. The next day she laid the affair before Mr. Brockle-hurst, who said that Mrs. Reed must be written to, as she was my natural guardian. A note was accordingly addressed to that lady, who returned for answer, that 'I might do as I pleased: she had long relinquished all inter-ference in my affairs.' This note went the round of the committee, and at last, after what appeared to me most tedious delay, formal leave was given me to better my condition if I could; and an assurance added, that as I had always conducted myself well, both as teacher and pupil, at Lowood, a testi-monial of character and capacity, signed by the inspectors of that institution, should forthwith be furnished me.

This testimonial I accordingly received in about a month, forwarded a copy of it to Mrs. Fairfax, and got that lady's reply, stating that she was satisfied, and fixing that day fortnight as the period for my assuming the post of governess in her house.

I now busied myself in preparations: the fortnight passed rapidly. I had not a very large wardrobe, though it was adequate to my wants; and the last day sufficed to pack my trunk,—the same I had brought with me eight years ago from Gateshead.

The box was corded, the card nailed on. In half an hour the carrier was to call for it to take it to Lowton, whither I myself was to repair at an early hour the next morning to meet the coach. I had brushed my black stuff travelling dress, prepared my bonnet, gloves, and muff; sought in all my draw-ers to see that no article was left behind; and now, having nothing more to do, I sat down and tried to rest. I could not; though I had been on foot all day, I could not now repose an instant; I was too much excited. A phase of my life was closing to-night, a new one opening to-morrow: impossible to slumber in the interval; I must watch feverishly while the change was being accomplished.

'Miss,' said a servant who met me in the lobby, where I was wandering like a troubled spirit, 'a person below wishes to see you.'

'The carrier, no doubt,' I thought, and ran downstairs without enquiry. I was passing the back parlour, or teachers' sitting-room, the door of which was half open, to go to the kitchen, when some one ran out:—

'It's her, I am sure!—I could have told her anywhere!' cried the individual who stopped my progress and took my hand.

I looked: I saw a woman attired like a well-dressed servant, matronly, yet still young; very good-looking, with black hair and eyes, and lively com-plexion.

'Well, who is it?' she asked in a voice and with a smile I half recognised; 'you've not quite forgotten me, I think, Miss Jane?'

In another second I was embracing, and kissing her rapturously: 'Bessie! Bessie! Bessie!' that was all I said; whereat she half laughed, half cried, and we both went into the parlour. By the fire stood a little fellow of three years old, in plaid frock and trousers.

'That is my little boy,' said Bessie, directly.

'Then you are married, Bessie?'

'Yes: nearly five years since, to Robert Leaven, the coachman; and I've a little girl besides Bobby there, that I've christened Jane.'

'And you don't live at Gateshead?'

'I live at the lodge: the old porter has left.'

'Well, and how do they all get on? Tell me everything about them, Bessie: but sit down first; and, Bobby, come and sit on my knee, will you?' but Bobby preferred sidling over to his mother.

'You're not grown so very tall, Miss Jane, nor so very stout,' continued Mrs. Leaven. 'I dare say they've not kept you too well at school; Miss Reed is the head and shoulders taller than you are; and Miss Georgiana would make two of you in breadth.'

'Georgiana is handsome, I suppose, Bessie?'

'Very. She went up to London last winter with her mama, and there everybody admired her, and a young lord fell in love with her: but his relations were against the match; and—what do you think?—he and Miss Georgiana made it up to run away: but they were found out and stopped. It was Miss Reed that found them out: I believe she was envious; and now she and her sister lead a cat and dog life together; they are always quarrelling.'

'Well, and what of John Reed?'

'Oh, he is not doing so well as his mama could wish. He went to college, and he got—plucked, I think they call it: and then his uncles wanted him to be a barrister, and study the law: but he is such a dissipated young man, they will never make much of him, I think.'

'What does he look like?'

'He is very tall: some people call him a fine looking young man; but he has such thick lips.'

'And Mrs. Reed?'

'Missis looks stout and well enough in the face, but I think she's not quite easy in her mind: Mr. John's conduct does not please her—he spends a deal of money.'

'Did she send you here, Bessie?'

'No, indeed: but I have long wanted to see you, and when I heard that there had been a letter from you, and that you were going to another part of the country, I thought I'd just set off, and get a look at you before you were quite out of my reach.'

'I am afraid you are disappointed in me, Bessie.' I said this laughing:
I perceived that Bessie's glance, though it expressed regard, did in no shape
denote admiration.

'No, Miss Jane, not exactly: you are genteel enough; you look like a lady,
and it is as much as ever I expected of you: you were no beauty as a child.'

I smiled at Bessie's frank answer: I felt that it was correct, but I confess
I was not quite indifferent to its import: at eighteen most people wish to please,
and the conviction that they have not an exterior likely to second that desire
brings anything but gratification.

'I dare say you are clever, though,' continued Bessie, by way of solace.
'What can you do? Can you play on the piano?'

'A little.'

There was one in the room; Bessie went and opened it, and then asked me
to sit down and give her a tune: I played a waltz or two, and she was charmed.

'The Miss Reeds could not play as well!' said she exultingly, 'I always said
you would surpass them in learning: and can you draw?'

'That is one of my paintings over the chimney-piece.' It was a landscape
in water colours, of which I had made a present to the superintendent, in
acknowledgment of her obliging mediation with the committee on my behalf,
and which she had framed and glazed.

'Well, that is beautiful, Miss Jane! It is as fine a picture as any Miss Reed's
drawing-master could paint, let alone the young ladies themselves, who could
not come near it: and have you learnt French?'

'Yes, Bessie, I can both read it and speak it.'

'And you can work on muslin and canvass?'

'I can.'

'Oh, you are quite a lady, Miss Jane! I knew you would be: you will get
on whether your relations notice you or not. There was something I wanted
to ask you. Have you ever heard anything from your father's kinsfolk, the
Eyres?'

'Never in my life.'

'Well, you know Missis always said they were poor and quite despicable:
and they may be poor; but I believe they are as much gentry as the Reeds
are; for one day, nearly seven years ago, a Mr. Eyre came to Gateshead and
wanted to see you; Missis said you were at school fifty miles off; he seemed
so much disappointed, for he could not stay: he was going on a voyage to
a foreign country, and the ship was to sail from London in a day or two. He
looked quite a gentleman, and I believe he was your father's brother.'

'What foreign country was he going to, Bessie?'

'An island thousands of miles off, where they make wine—the butler did
tell me'——

'Madeira!' I suggested.

'Yes, that is it—that is the very word.'

'So he went?'

'Yes; he did not stay many minutes in the house: Missis was very high with him; she called him afterwards a "sneaking tradesman." My Robert believes he was a wine-merchant.'

'Very likely,' I returned; 'or perhaps clerk or agent to a wine-merchant.'

Bessie and I conversed about old times an hour longer, and then she was obliged to leave me: I saw her again for a few minutes the next morning at Lowton, while I was waiting for the coach. We parted finally at the door of the Brocklehurst Arms there: each went her separate way; she set off for the brow of Lowood Fell to meet the conveyance which was to take her back to Gateshead, I mounted the vehicle which was to bear me to new duties and a new life in the unknown environs of Millcote.

CHAPTER 11

A new chapter in a novel is something like a new scene in a play; and when I draw up the curtain this time, reader, you must fancy you see a room in the George Inn at Millcote, with such large figured papering on the walls as inn rooms have; such a carpet, such furniture, such ornaments on the mantel-piece, such prints; including a portrait of George the Third, and another of the Prince of Wales, and a representation of the death of Wolfe. All this is visible to you by the light of an oil lamp hanging from the ceiling, and by that of an excellent fire, near which I sit in my cloak and bonnet; my muff and umbrella lie on the table, and I am warming away the numbness and chill contracted by sixteen hours' exposure to the rawness of an October day: I left Lowton at four o'clock A.M., and the Millcote town clock is now just striking eight.

Reader, though I look comfortably accommodated, I am not very tranquil in my mind. I thought when the coach stopped here there would be some one to meet me; I looked anxiously round as I descended the wooden steps the 'boots' placed for my convenience, expecting to hear my name pronounced, and to see some description of carriage waiting to convey me to Thornfield. Nothing of the sort was visible: and when I asked a waiter if any one had been to inquire after a Miss Eyre, I was answered in the negative: so I had no resource but to request to be shown into a private room: and here I am waiting, while all sorts of doubts and fears are troubling my thoughts.

It is a very strange sensation to inexperienced youth to feel itself quite alone in the world, cut adrift from every connection, uncertain whether the port to which it is bound can be reached, and prevented by many impediments from returning to that it has quitted. The charm of adventure sweetens that sensation, the glow of pride warms it; but then the throb of fear disturbs it;

and fear with me became predominant, when half an hour elapsed and still I was alone. I bethought myself to ring the bell.

'Is there a place in this neighbourhood called Thornfield?' I asked of the waiter who answered the summons.

'Thornfield? I don't know, ma'am; I'll enquire at the bar.' He vanished, but reappeared instantly:—

'Is your name Eyre, Miss?'

'Yes.'

'Person here waiting for you.'

I jumped up, took my muff and umbrella, and hastened into the inn-passage: a man was standing by the open door, and in the lamp-lit street I dimly saw a one-horse conveyance.

'This will be your luggage, I suppose?' said the man rather abruptly when he saw me, pointing to my trunk in the passage.'

'Yes.' He hoisted it on to the vehicle, which was a sort of car, and then I got in: before he shut me up, I asked him how far it was to Thornfield.

'A matter of six miles.'

'How long shall we be before we get there?'

'Happen an hour and a half.'

He fastened the car door, climbed to his own seat outside, and we set off. Our progress was leisurely, and gave me ample time to reflect: I was content to be at length so near the end of my journey; and as I leaned back in the comfortable though not elegant conveyance, I meditated much at my ease.

'I suppose,' thought I, 'judging from the plainness of the servant and carriage, Mrs. Fairfax is not a very dashing person: so much the better; I never lived amongst fine people but once, and I was very miserable with them. I wonder if she lives alone except this little girl; if so, and if she is in any degree amiable, I shall surely be able to get on with her; I will do my best: it is a pity that doing one's best does not always answer. At Lowood, indeed, I took that resolution, kept it, and succeeded in pleasing; but with Mrs. Reed, I remember my best was always spurned with scorn. I pray God Mrs. Fairfax may not turn out a second Mrs. Reed; but if she does, I am not bound to stay with her: let the worst come to the worst, I can advertise again. How far are we on our road now, I wonder?'

I let down the window and looked out: Millcote was behind us; judging by the number of its lights, it seemed a place of considerable magnitude, much larger than Lowton. We were now, as far as I could see, on a sort of common; but there were houses scattered all over the district; I felt we were in a different region to Lowood, more populous, less picturesque; more stirring, less romantic.

The roads were heavy, the night misty; my conductor let his horse walk all the way, and the hour and a half extended, I verily believe, to two hours; at last he turned in his seat and said:—

'You're noan so far fro' Thornfield now.'

Again I looked out: we were passing a church: I saw its low broad tower against the sky, and its bell was tolling a quarter; I saw a narrow galaxy of lights too, on a hill-side, marking a village or hamlet. About ten minutes after, the driver got down and opened a pair of gates; we passed through, and they clashed to behind us. We now slowly ascended a drive, and came upon the long front of a house: candle-light gleamed from one curtained bow-window; all the rest were dark. The car stopped at the front door; it was opened by a maid-servant: I alighted and went in.

'Will you walk this way, ma'am,' said the girl: and I followed her across a square hall with high doors all round: she ushered me into a room whose double illumination of fire and candle at first dazzled me, contrasting as it did with the darkness to which my eyes had been for two hours inured; when I could see, however, a cozy and agreeable picture presented itself to my view.

A snug, small room; a round table by a cheerful fire; an arm-chair high-backed and old-fashioned, wherein sat the neatest imaginable little elderly lady, in widow's cap, black silk gown and snowy muslin apron; exactly like what I had fancied Mrs. Fairfax, only less stately and milder looking. She was occupied in knitting; a large cat sat demurely at her feet; nothing in short was wanting to complete the beau-ideal of domestic comfort. A more reassuring introduction for a new governess could scarcely be conceived: there was no grandeur to overwhelm, no stateliness to embarrass; and then, as I entered, the old lady got up, and promptly and kindly came forward to meet me.

'How do you do, my dear? I am afraid you have had a tedious ride; John drives so slowly: you must be cold, come to the fire.'

'Mrs. Fairfax, I suppose?' said I.

'Yes, you are right: do sit down.'

She conducted me to her own chair, and then began to remove my shawl and untie my bonnet-strings: I begged she would not give herself so much trouble.

'Oh, it is no trouble; I dare say your own hands are almost numbed with cold. Leah, make a little hot negus and cut a sandwich or two: here are the keys of the store-room.'

And she produced from her pocket a most housewifely bunch of keys, and delivered them to the servant.

'Now, then, draw nearer to the fire,' she continued. 'You've brought your luggage with you, haven't you, my dear?'

'Yes, ma'am.'

'I'll see it carried into your room,' she said, and bustled out.

'She treats me like a visitor,' thought I. 'I little expected such a reception; I anticipated only coldness and stiffness: this is not like what I have heard

of the treatment of governesses; but I must not exult too soon.'

She returned; with her own hands cleared her knitting apparatus and a book or two from the table, to make room for the tray which Leah now brought, and then herself handed me the refreshments. I felt rather confused at being the object of more attention than I had ever before received, and that, too, shown by my employer and superior; but as she did not herself seem to consider she was doing anything out of her place, I thought it better to take her civilities quietly.

'Shall I have the pleasure of seeing Miss Fairfax tonight?' I asked, when I had partaken of what she offered me.

'What did you say, my dear? I am a little deaf,' returned the good lady, approaching her ear to my mouth.

I repeated the question more distinctly.

'Miss Fairfax? Oh, you mean Miss Varens! Varens is the name of your future pupil.'

'Indeed! Then she is not your daughter?'

'No,—I have no family.'

I should have followed up my first inquiry, by asking in what way Miss Varens was connected with her; but I recollected it was not polite to ask too many questions: besides, I was sure to hear in time.

'I am so glad,' she continued, as she sat down opposite to me, and took the cat on her knee; 'I am so glad you are come; it will be quite pleasant living here now with a companion. To be sure it is pleasant at any time; for Thornfield is a fine old hall, rather neglected of late years perhaps, but still it is a respectable place; yet you know in winter time one feels dreary quite alone, in the best quarters. I say alone—Leah is a nice girl to be sure, and John and his wife are very decent people; but then you see they are only servants, and one can't converse with them on terms of equality: one must keep them at due distance, for fear of losing one's authority. I'm sure last winter (it was a very severe one, if you recollect, and when it did not snow, it rained and blew), not a creature but the butcher and postman came to the house, from November till February; and I really got quite melancholy with sitting night after night alone; I had Leah in to read to me sometimes; but I don't think the poor girl liked the task much: she felt it confining. In spring and summer one got on better: sunshine and long days make such a difference; and then, just at the commencement of this autumn, little Adela Varens came and her nurse: a child makes a house alive all at once; and now you are here I shall be quite gay.'

My heart really warmed to the worthy lady as I heard her talk; and I drew my chair a little nearer to her, and expressed my sincere wish that she might find my company as agreeable as she anticipated.

'But I'll not keep you sitting up late to-night,' said she; 'it is on the stroke

of twelve now, and you have been travelling all day: you must feel tired. If you have got your feet well warmed, I'll show you your bed-room. I've had the room next to mine prepared for you; it is only a small apartment, but I thought you would like it better than one of the large front chambers: to be sure they have finer furniture, but they are so dreary and solitary, I never sleep in them myself.'

I thanked her for her considerate choice, and as I really felt fatigued with my long journey, expressed my readiness to retire. She took her candle, and I followed her from the room. First she went to see if the hall-door was fastened; having taken the key from the lock, she led the way upstairs. The steps and banisters were of oak; the staircase window was high and latticed; both it and the long gallery into which the bed-room doors opened, looked as if they belonged to a church rather than a house. A very chill and vault-like air pervaded the stairs and gallery, suggesting cheerless ideas of space and solitude; and I was glad, when finally ushered into my chamber, to find it of small dimensions, and furnished in ordinary modern style.

When Mrs. Fairfax had bidden me a kind good-night, and I had fastened my door, gazed leisurely round, and in some measure effaced the eerie impression made by that wide hall, that dark and spacious staircase, and that long, cold gallery, by the livelier aspect of my little room, I remembered that after a day of bodily fatigue and mental anxiety, I was now at last in safe haven. The impulse of gratitude swelled my heart, and I knelt down at the bedside, and offered up thanks where thanks were due; not forgetting, ere I rose, to implore aid on my further path, and the power of meriting the kindness which seemed so frankly offered me before it was earned. My couch had no thorns in it that night; my solitary room no fears. At once weary and content, I slept soon and soundly; when I awoke it was broad day.

The chamber looked such a bright little place to me as the sun shone in between the gay blue chintz window curtains, showing papered walls and a carpeted floor, so unlike the bare planks and stained plaster of Lowood, that my spirits rose at the view. Externals have a great effect on the young: I thought that a fairer era of life was beginning for me, one that was to have its flowers and pleasures, as well as its thorns and toils. My faculties, roused by the change of scene, the new field offered to hope, seemed all astir. I cannot precisely define what they expected, but it was something pleasant: not perhaps that day or that month, but at an indefinite future period.

I rose; I dressed myself with care: obliged to be plain—for I had no article of attire that was not made with extreme simplicity—I was still by nature solicitous to be neat. It was not my habit to be disregardful of appearance, or careless of the impression I made: on the contrary, I ever wished to look as well as I could, and to please as much as my want of beauty would permit. I sometimes regretted that I was not handsomer: I sometimes wished to have

rosy cheeks, a straight nose, and small cherry mouth; I desired to be tall, stately, and finely developed in figure; I felt it a misfortune that I was so little, so pale, and had features so irregular and so marked. And why had I these aspirations and these regrets? It would be difficult to say: I could not then distinctly say it to myself; yet I had a reason, and a logical, natural reason too. However, when I had brushed my hair very smooth, and put on my black frock—which, Quakerlike as it was, at least had the merit of fitting to a nicety— and adjusted my clean white tucker, I thought I should do respectably enough to appear before Mrs. Fairfax; and that my new pupil would not at least recoil from me with antipathy. Having opened my chamber window, and seen that I left all things straight and neat on the toilet table, I ventured forth.

Traversing the long and matted gallery, I descended the slippery steps of oak; then I gained the hall: I halted there a minute; I looked at some pictures on the walls (one I remember represented a grim man in a cuirass, and one a lady with powdered hair and a pearl necklace), at a bronze lamp pendent from the ceiling, at a great clock whose case was of oak curiously carved, and ebon black with time and rubbing. Everything appeared very stately and imposing to me: but then I was so little accustomed to grandeur. The hall-door, which was half of glass, stood open; I stepped over the threshold. It was a fine autumn morning; the early sun shone serenely on embrowned groves and still green fields: advancing on to the lawn, I looked up and surveyed the front of the mansion. It was three stories high, of proportions not vast, though considerable: a gentleman's manorhouse, not a nobleman's seat: battlements round the top gave it a picturesque look. Its grey front stood out well from the background of a rookery, whose cawing tenants were now on the wing: they flew over the lawn and grounds to alight in a great meadow, from which these were separated by a sunk fence, and where an array of mighty old thorn trees, strong, knotty, and broad as oaks, at once explained the etymology of the mansion's designation. Farther off were hills: not so lofty as those round Lowood, nor so craggy, nor so like barriers of separation from the living world; but yet quiet and lonely hills enough, and seeming to embrace Thornfield with a seclusion I had not expected to find existent so near the stirring locality of Millcote. A little hamlet, whose roofs were blent with trees, straggled up the side of one of these hills; the church of the district stood nearer Thornfield: its old tower-top looked over a knoll between the house and gates.

I was yet enjoying the calm prospect and pleasant fresh air, yet listening with delight to the cawing of the rooks, yet surveying the wide, hoary front of the hall, and thinking what a great place it was for one lonely little dame like Mrs. Fairfax to inhabit, when that lady appeared at the door.

'What! out already?' said she. 'I see you are an early riser.' I went up to her and was received with an affable kiss and shake of the hand.

'How do you like Thornfield?' she asked. I told her I liked it very much.

'Yes,' she said, 'it is a pretty place; but I fear it will be getting out of order, unless Mr. Rochester should take it into his head to come and reside here permanently; or, at least, visit it rather oftener: great houses and fine grounds require the presence of the proprietor.'

'Mr. Rochester!' I exclaimed. 'Who is he?'

'The owner of Thornfield,' she responded quietly. 'Did you not know he was called Rochester?'

Of course I did not—I had never heard of him before; but the old lady seemed to regard his existence as a universally understood fact, with which everybody must be acquainted by instinct.

'I thought,' I continued, 'Thornfield belonged to you.'

'To me?' Bless you, child; what an idea! To me? I am only the housekeeper—the manager. To be sure I am distantly related to the Rochesters by the mother's side; or, at least, my husband was: he was a clergyman, incumbent of Hay—that little village yonder on the hill—and that church near the gates was his. The present Mr. Rochester's mother was a Fairfax, and second cousin to my husband; but I never presume on the connection—in fact it is nothing to me; I consider myself quite in the light of an ordinary housekeeper: my employer is always civil, and I expect nothing more.'

'And the little girl— my pupil?'

'She is Mr. Rochester's ward; he commissioned me to find a governess for her. He intends to have her brought up in——shire, I believe. Here she comes, with her "bonne," as she calls her nurse.' The enigma then was explained: this affable and kind little widow was no great dame, but a dependant like myself. I did not like her the worse for that; on the contrary, I felt better pleased than ever. The equality between her and me was real; not the mere result of condescension on her part: so much the better—my position was all the freer.

As I was meditating on this discovery, a little girl, followed by her attendant, came running up the lawn. I looked at my pupil, who did not at first appear to notice me: she was quite a child, perhaps, seven or eight years old, slightly built, with a pale, small-featured face, and a redundancy of hair falling in curls to her waist.

'Good morning, Miss Adela,' said Mrs. Fairfax. 'Come and speak to the lady who is to teach you, and to make you a clever woman some day.' She approached.

'C'est là ma gouvernante?' said she, pointing, to me and addressing her nurse; who answered:

'Mais oui, certainement.'

'Are they foreigners?' I inquired, amazed at hearing the French language.

'The nurse is a foreigner, and Adela was born on the Continent; and, I believe, never left it till within six months ago. When she first came here

she could speak no English; now she can make shift to talk it a little: I don't understand her, she mixes it so with French; but you will make out her meaning very well, I daresay.'

Fortunately I had had the advantage of being taught French by a French lady; and as I had always made a point of conversing with Madame Pierrot, as often as I could, and had, besides, during the last seven years, learnt a portion of French by heart daily—applying myself to take pains with my accent, and imitating as closely as possible the pronunciation of my teacher—I had acquired a certain degree of readiness and correctness in the language, and was not likely to be much at a loss with Mademoiselle Adela. She came and shook hands with me when she heard that I was her governess; and as I led her in to breakfast, I addressed some phrases to her in her own tongue: she replied briefly at first, but after we were seated at the table, and she had examined me some ten minutes with her large hazel eyes, she suddenly commenced chattering fluently.

'Ah,' cried she, in French, 'you speak my language as well as Mr. Rochester does: I can talk to you as I can to him, and so can Sophie. She will be glad: nobody here understands her: Madame Fairfax is all English. Sophie is my nurse; she came with me over the sea in a great ship with a chimney that smoked—how it did smoke!—and I was sick, and so was Sophie, and so was Mr. Rochester. Mr. Rochester lay down on a sofa in a pretty room called the salon, and Sophie and I had little beds in another place. I nearly fell out of mine; it was like a shelf. And, Mademoiselle——what is your name?'

'Eyre—Jane Eyre.'

'Aire? Bah! I cannot say it. Well: our ship stopped in the morning, before it was quite daylight, at a great city—a huge city, with very dark houses and all smoky; not at all like the pretty clean town I came from; and Mr. Rochester carried me in his arms over a plank to the land, and Sophie came after, and we all got into a coach, which took us to a beautiful large house, larger than this and finer, called an hotel. We stayed there nearly a week: I and Sophie used to walk every day in a great green place full of trees, called the Park; and there were many children there besides me, and a pond with beautiful birds in it, that I fed with crumbs.'

'Can you understand her when she runs on so fast?' asked Mrs. Fairfax.

I understood her very well, for I had been accustomed to the fluent tongue of Madame Pierrot.

'I wish,' continued the good lady, 'you would ask her a question or two about her parents: I wonder if she remembers them?'

'Adèle,' I inquired, 'with whom did you live when you were in that pretty clean town you spoke of?'

'I lived long ago with mama; but she is gone to the Holy Virgin. Mama used to teach me to dance and sing, and to say verses. A great many gentlemen

and ladies came to see mama, and I used to dance before them, or to sit on their knees and sing to them: I liked it. Shall I let you hear me sing now?'

She had finished her breakfast, so I permitted her to give a specimen of her accomplishments. Descending from her chair, she came and placed herself on my knee; then, folding her little hands demurely before her, shaking back her curls and lifting her eyes to the ceiling, she commenced singing a song from some opera. It was the strain of a forsaken lady, who, after bewailing the perfidy of her lover, calls pride to her aid; desires her attendant to deck her in her brightest jewels and richest robes, and resolves to meet the false one that night at a ball, and prove to him, by the gaiety of her demeanour, how little his desertion had affected her.

The subject seemed strangely chosen for an infant singer; but I suppose the point of the exhibition lay in hearing the notes of love and jealousy warbled with the lisp of childhood; and in very bad taste that point was, at least I thought so.

Adèle sang the canzonette tunefully enough, and with the naïveté of her age. This achieved, she jumped from my knee and said, 'Now, Mademoiselle, I will repeat you some poetry.'

Assuming an attitude, she began 'La Ligue des Rats, fable de la Fontaine.' She then declaimed the little piece with an attention to punctuation and emphasis, a flexibility of voice and an appropriateness of gesture, very unusual indeed at her age, and which proved she had been carefully trained.

'Was it your mama who taught you that piece?' I asked.

'Yes, and she just used to say it in this way: 'Qu'avez vous donc? lui dit un de ces rats; parlez!' She made me lift my hand—so—to remind me to raise my voice at the question. Now shall I dance for you?'

'No, that will do: but after your mama went to the Holy Virgin, as you say, with whom did you live then?'

'With Madame Frédéric and her husband: she took care of me, but she is nothing related to me. I think she is poor, for she had not so fine a house as mama. I was not long there. Mr. Rochester asked me if I would like to go and live with him in England, and I said yes; for I knew Mr. Rochester before I knew Madame Frédéric, and he was always kind to me and gave me pretty dresses and toys: but you see he has not kept his word, for he has brought me to England, and now he has gone back again himself, and I never see him.'

After breakfast, Adèle and I withdrew to the library; which room, it appears, Mr. Rochester had directed should be used as the school-room. Most of the books were locked up behind glass doors; but there was one bookcase left open containing everything that could be needed in the way of elementary works, and several volumes of light literature, poetry, biography, travels, a few romances, etc. I suppose he had considered that these were all the governess would require for her private perusal; and indeed, they contented me amply

for the present; compared with the scanty pickings I had now and then been able to glean at Lowood, they seemed to offer an abundant harvest of entertainment and information. In this room, too, there was a cabinet piano, quite new and of superior tone; also an easel for painting, and a pair of globes.

I found my pupil sufficiently docile, though disinclined to apply: she had not been used to regular occupation of any kind. I felt it would be injudicious to confine her too much at first; so, when I had talked to her a great deal, and got her to learn a little, and when the morning had advanced to noon, I allowed her to return to her nurse. I then proposed to occupy myself till dinner-time in drawing some little sketches for her use.

As I was going upstairs to fetch my portfolio and pencils, Mrs. Fairfax called to me: 'Your morning school-hours are over now, I suppose,' said she. She was in a room the folding-doors of which stood open: I went in when she addressed me. It was a large, stately apartment, with purple chairs and curtains, a Turkey carpet, walnut-panelled walls, one vast window rich in stained glass, and a lofty ceiling, nobly moulded. Mrs. Fairfax was dusting some vases of fine purple spar, which stood on a sideboard.

'What a beautiful room!' I exclaimed, as I looked round; for I had never before seen any half so imposing.

'Yes; this is the dining-room. I have just opened the window, to let in a little air and sunshine; for everything gets so damp in apartments that are seldom inhabited: the drawing-room yonder feels like a vault.'

She pointed to a wide arch corresponding to the window, and hung like it with a Tyrian-dyed curtain, now looped up. Mounting to it by two broad steps and looking though, I thought I caught a glimpse of a fairy place, so bright to my novice-eyes appeared the view beyond. Yet it was merely a very pretty drawing-room, and within it a boudoir, both spread with white carpets, on which seemed laid brilliant garlands of flowers; both ceiled with snowy mouldings of white grapes and vine-leaves, beneath which glowed in rich contrast crimson couches and ottomans; while the ornaments on the pale Parian mantel-piece were of sparkling Bohemian glass, ruby red; and between the windows large mirrors repeated the general blending of snow and fire.

'In what order you keep these rooms, Mrs. Fairfax!' said I. 'No dust, no canvass coverings: except that the air feels chilly, one would think they were inhabited daily.'

'Why, Miss Eyre, though Mr. Rochester's visits here are rare, they are always sudden and unexpected; and as I observed that it put him out to find everything swathed up, and to have a bustle of arrangement on his arrival, I thought it best to keep the rooms in readiness.'

'Is Mr. Rochester an exacting, fastidious sort of man?'

'Not particularly so; but he has a gentleman's tastes and habits, and he expects to have things managed in conformity to them.'

'Do you like him? Is he generally liked?'

'Oh, yes; the family have always been respected here. Almost all the land in this neighbourhood, as far as you can see, has belonged to the Rochesters time out of mind.'

'Well, but, leaving his land out of the question, do you like him? Is he liked for himself?'

'*I* have no cause to do otherwise than like him; and I believe he is considered a just and liberal landlord by his tenants: but he has never lived much amongst them.'

'But has he no peculiarities? What, in short, is his character?'

'Oh! his character is unimpeachable, I suppose. He is rather peculiar, perhaps: he has travelled a great deal, and seen a great deal of the world, I should think. I dare say he is clever: but I never had much conversation with him.'

'In what way is he peculiar?'

'I don't know—it is not easy to describe—nothing striking, but you feel it when he speaks to you: you cannot be always sure whether he is in jest or earnest, whether he is pleased or the contrary; you don't thoroughly understand him, in short—at least, I don't: but it is of no consequence, he is a very good master.'

This was all the account I got from Mrs. Fairfax, of her employer and mine. There are people who seem to have no notion of sketching a character, or observing and describing salient points, either in persons or things: the good lady evidently belonged to this class; my queries puzzled, but did not draw her out. Mr. Rochester was Mr. Rochester in her eyes; a gentleman, a landed proprietor—nothing more: she inquired and searched no further, and evidently wondered at my wish to gain a more definite notion of his identity.

When we left the dining-room, she proposed to show me over the rest of the house; and I followed her upstairs and downstairs, admiring as I went; for all was well-arranged and handsome. The large front chambers I thought especially grand; and some of the third story rooms, though dark and low, were interesting from their air of antiquity. The furniture once appropriated to the lower apartments had from time to time been removed here, as fashions changed: and the imperfect light entering by their narrow casements showed bedsteads of a hundred years old; chests in oak or walnut, looking, with their strange carvings of palm branches and cherubs' heads, like types of the Hebrew ark; rows of venerable chairs, high-backed and narrow; stools still more antiquated, on whose cushioned tops were yet apparent traces of half-effaced embroideries, wrought by fingers that for two generations had been coffin-dust. All these relics gave to the third story of Thornfield Hall the aspect of a home of the past: a shrine of memory. I liked the hush, the gloom, the quaintness of these retreats in the day; but I by no means coveted a night's repose on one

of those wide and heavy beds: shut in, some of them with doors of oak; shaded, others with wrought old English hangings crusted with thick work, portraying effigies of strange flowers, and stranger birds, and strangest, human beings,— all which would have looked strange, indeed, by the pallid gleam of moonlight.

'Do the servants sleep in these rooms?' I asked.

'No; they occupy a range of smaller apartments to the back; no one ever sleeps here: one would almost say that, if there were a ghost at Thornfield Hall, this would be its haunts.'

'So I think: you have no ghost, then?'

'None that I ever heard of,' returned Mrs. Fairfax, smiling.

'Nor any traditions of one? no legends or ghost stories?'

'I believe not. And yet it is said, the Rochesters have been rather a violent than a quiet race in their time: perhaps, though, that is the reason they rest tranquilly in their graves now.'

'Yes—"after life's fitful fever they sleep well," ' I muttered. 'Where are you going now, Mrs. Fairfax?' for she was moving away.

'On to the leads; will you come and see the view from thence?' I followed still, up a very narrow staircase to the attics, and thence by a ladder and through a trap-door to the roof of the hall. I was now on a level with the crow colony, and could see into their nests. Leaning over the battlements and looking far down, I surveyed the grounds laid out like a map: the bright and velvet lawn closely girding the grey base of the mansion; the field, wide as a park, dotted with its ancient timber; the wood, dun and sere, divided by a path visibly overgrown, greener with moss than the trees were with foliage; the church at the gates, the road, the tranquil hills, all reposing in the autumn day's sun; the horizon bounded by a propitious sky, azure, marbled with pearly white. No feature in the scene was extraordinary, but all was pleasing. When I turned from it and repassed the trap-door, I could scarcely see my way down the ladder; the attic seemed black as a vault compared with that arch of blue air to which I had been looking up, and to that sunlit scene of grove, pasture, and green hill of which the hall was the centre, and over which I had been gazing with delight.

Mrs. Fairfax stayed behind a moment to fasten the trap-door; I, by dint of groping, found the outlet from the attic, and proceeded to descend the narrow garret staircase. I lingered in the long passage to which this led, separating the front and back rooms of the third story: narrow, low, and dim, with only one little window at the far end, and looking, with its two rows of small black doors all shut, like a corridor in some Bluebeard's castle.

While I paced softly on, the last sound I expected to hear in so still a region, a laugh, struck my ear. It was a curious laugh; distinct, formal, mirthless. I stopped: the sound ceased, only for an instant; it began again, louder: for at first, though distinct, it was very low. It passed off in a clamorous peal that

seemed to wake an echo in every lonely chamber; though it originated but in one, and I could have pointed out the door whence the accents issued.

'Mrs. Fairfax!' I called out: for I now heard her descending the great stairs. 'Did you hear that loud laugh? Who is it?'

'Some of the servants, very likely,' she answered: 'perhaps Grace Poole.'

'Did you hear it?' I again inquired.

'Yes, plainly: I often hear her; she sews in one of these rooms. Sometimes Leah is with her: they are frequently noisy together.'

The laugh was repeated in its low, syllabic tone, and terminated in an odd murmur.

'Grace!' exclaimed Mrs. Fairfax.

I really did not expect any Grace to answer; for the laugh was as tragic, as preternatural, a laugh as any I ever heard; and, but that it was high noon, and that no circumstance of ghostliness accompanied the curious cachinnation, but that neither scene nor season favoured fear, I should have been superstitiously afraid. However, the event, showed me I was a fool for entertaining a sense even of surprise.

The door nearest me opened, and a servant came out,—a woman of between thirty and forty; a set, square-made figure, red-haired, and with a hard, plain face: any apparition less romantic or less ghostly could scarcely be conceived.

'Too much noise, Grace,' said Mrs. Fairfax. 'Remember directions!' Grace curtseyed silently and went in.

'She is a person we have to sew and assist Leah in her housemaid's work,' continued the widow; 'not altogether unobjectionable in some points, but she does well enough. By-the-bye, how have you got on with your new pupil this morning?'

The conversation, thus turned on Adèle, continued till we reached the light and cheerful region below. Adèle came running to meet us in the hall, exclaiming—

'Mesdames, vous êtes servies!' adding, 'J'ai bien faim, moi!'

We found dinner ready, and waiting for us in Mrs. Fairfax's room.

CHAPTER 12

The promise of a smooth career, which my first calm introduction to Thornfield Hall seemed to pledge, was not belied on a longer acquaintance with the place and its inmates. Mrs. Fairfax turned out to be what she appeared, a placid-tempered, kind-natured woman, of competent education and average intelligence. My pupil was a lively child, who had been spoilt and indulged, and therefore was sometimes wayward; but as she was committed entirely to

my care, and no injudicious interference from any quarter ever thwarted my plans for her improvement, she soon forgot her little freaks, and became obedient and teachable. She had no great talents, no marked traits of character, no peculiar development of feeling or taste which raised her one inch above the ordinary level of childhood; but neither had she any deficiency or vice which sunk her below it. She made reasonable progress, entertained for me a vivacious, though perhaps not very profound, affection; and by her simplicity, gay prattle, and efforts to please, inspired me, in return, with a degree of attachment sufficient to make us both content in each other's society.

This, *par parenthèse*, will be thought cool language by persons who entertain solemn doctrines about the angelic nature of children, and the duty of those charged with their education to conceive for them an idolatrous devotion: but I am not writing to flatter paternal egotism, to echo cant, or prop up humbug; I am merely telling the truth. I felt a conscientious solicitude for Adèle's welfare and progress, and a quiet liking to her little self; just as I cherished towards Mrs. Fairfax a thankfulness for her kindness, and a pleasure in her society proportionate to the tranquil regard she had for me, and the moderation of her mind and character.

Anybody may blame me who likes, when I add further, that, now and then, when I took a walk by myself in the grounds; when I went down to the gates and looked through them along the road; or when, while Adèle played with her nurse, and Mrs. Fairfax made jellies in the store-room, I climbed the three staircases, raised the trap-door of the attic, and having reached the leads, looked out afar over sequestered field and hill, and along dim sky-line—that then I longed for a power of vision which might overpass that limit; which might reach the busy world, towns, regions full of life I had heard of but never seen; that then I desired more of practical experience than I possessed; more of intercourse with my kind, of acquaintance with variety of character, than was here within my reach. I valued what was good in Mrs. Fairfax, and what was good in Adèle; but I believed in the existence of other and more vivid kinds of goodness, and what I believed in I wished to behold.

Who blames me? Many, no doubt; and I shall be called discontented. I could not help it: the restlessness was in my nature; it agitated me to pain sometimes. Then my sole relief was to walk along the corridor of the third story, backwards and forwards, safe in the silence and solitude of the spot, and allow my mind's eye to dwell on whatever bright visions rose before it— and, certainly, they were many and glowing; to let my heart be heaved by the exultant movement, which, while it swelled it in trouble, expanded it with life; and, best of all, to open my inward ear to a tale that was never ended—a tale my imagination created, and narrated continuously; quickened with all of incident, life, fire, feeling that I desired and had not in my actual existence.

It is in vain to say human beings ought to be satisfied with tranquillity:

they must have action; and they will make it if they cannot find it. Millions are condemned to a stiller doom than mine, and millions are in silent revolt against their lot. Nobody knows how many rebellions besides political rebellions ferment in the masses of life which people earth. Women are supposed to be very calm generally: but women feel just as men feel; they need exercise for their faculties, and a field for their efforts as much as their brothers do; they suffer from too rigid a constraint, too absolute a stagnation, precisely as men would suffer; and it is narrow-minded in their more privileged fellow-creatures to say that they ought to confine themselves to making puddings and knitting stockings, to playing on the piano and embroidering bags. It is thoughtless to condemn them or laugh at them, if they seek to do more or learn more than custom has pronounced necessary for their sex.

When thus alone, I not unfrequently heard Grace Poole's laugh: the same peal, the same low, slow ha! ha! which, when first heard, had thrilled me: I heard, too, her eccentric murmurs; stranger than her laugh. There were days when she was quite silent; but there were others when I could not account for the sounds she made. Sometimes I saw her: she would come out of her room with a basin, or a plate, or a tray in her hand, go down to the kitchen and shortly return, generally (oh, romantic reader, forgive me for telling the plain truth!) bearing a pot of porter. Her appearance always acted as a damper to the curiosity raised by her oral oddities: hard-featured and staid, she had no point to which interest could attach. I made some attempts to draw her into conversation, but she seemed a person of few words: a monosyllabic reply usually cut short every effort of that sort.

The other members of the household, viz., John and his wife, Leah the housemaid, and Sophie the French nurse, were decent people; but in no respect remarkable: with Sophie I used to talk French, and sometimes I asked her questions about her native country; but she was not of a descriptive or narrative turn, and generally gave such vapid and confused answers as were calculated rather to check than encourage inquiry.

October, November, December passed away. One afternoon in January, Mrs. Fairfax had begged a holiday for Adèle, because she had a cold; and, as Adèle seconded the request with an ardour that reminded me how precious occasional holidays had been to me in my own childhood, I accorded it, deeming that I did well in showing pliability on the point. It was a fine, calm day, though very cold; I was tired of sitting still in the library through a whole long morning: Mrs. Fairfax had just written a letter which was waiting to be posted, so I put on my bonnet and cloak and volunteered to carry it to Hay; the distance, two miles, would be a pleasant winter afternoon walk. Having seen Adèle comfortably seated in her little chair by Mrs. Fairfax's parlour fireside, and given her her best wax doll (which I usually kept enveloped in silver paper in a drawer) to play with, and a story-book for change of

amusement; and having replied to her 'Revenez bientôt, ma bonne amie, ma chère Mdlle. Jeannette,' with a kiss, I set out.

The ground was hard, the air was still, my road was lonely; I walked fast till I got warm, and then I walked slowly to enjoy and analyse the species of pleasure brooding for me in the hour and situation. It was three o'clock; the church bell tolled as I passed under the belfry; the charm of the hour lay in its approaching dimness, in the low-gliding and pale-beaming sun.

I was a mile from Thornfield, in a lane noted for wild roses in summer, for nuts and blackberries in autumn, and even now possessing a few coral treasures in hips and haws, but whose best winter delight lay in its utter solitude and leafless repose. If a breath of air stirred, it made no sound here; for there was not a holly, not an evergreen to rustle, and the stripped hawthorn and hazel bushes were as still as the white, worn stones which causewayed the middle of the path. Far and wide, on each side, there were only fields, where no cattle now browsed; and the little brown birds, which stirred occasionally in the hedge, looked like single russet leaves that had forgotten to drop.

This lane inclined up-hill all the way to Hay: having reached the middle, I sat down on a stile which led thence into a field. Gathering my mantle about me, and sheltering my hands in my muff, I did not feel the cold, though it froze keenly; as was attested by a sheet of ice covering the causeway, where a little brooklet, now congealed, had overflowed after a rapid thaw some days since. From my seat I could look down on Thornfield: the grey and battle-mented hall was the principal object in the vale below me; its woods and dark rookery rose against the west. I lingered till the sun went down amongst the trees, and sank crimson and clear behind them. I then turned eastward.

On the hill-top above me sat the rising moon; pale yet as a cloud, but brightening momently: she looked over Hay, which, half lost in trees, sent up a blue smoke from its few chimneys; it was yet a mile distant, but in the absolute hush I could hear plainly its thin murmurs of life. My ear too felt the flow of currents; in what dales and depths I could not tell: but there were many hills beyond Hay, and doubtless many becks threading their passes. That evening calm betrayed alike the tinkle of the nearest streams, the sough of the most remote.

A rude noise broke on these fine ripplings and whisperings, at once so far away and so clear: a positive tramp, tramp; a metallic clatter, which effaced the soft wave-wanderings; as, in a picture, the solid mass of a crag, or the rough boles of a great oak, drawn in dark and strong on the foreground, efface the aërial distance of azure hill, sunny horizon, and blended clouds, where tint melts into tint.

The din was on the causeway: a horse was coming; the windings of the lane yet hid it, but it approached. I was just leaving the stile; yet, as the path was narrow, I sat still to let it go by. In those days I was young, and all sorts of

fancies bright and dark tenanted my mind: the memories of nursery stories were there amongst other rubbish; and when they recurred, maturing youth added to them a vigour and vividness beyond what childhood could give. As this horse approached, and as I watched for it to appear through the dusk, I remembered certain of Bessie's tales, wherein figured a North-of-England spirit, called a 'Gytrash'; which, in the form of horse, mule, or large dog, haunted solitary ways, and sometimes came upon belated travellers, as this horse was now coming upon me.

It was very near, but not yet in sight; when, in addition to the tramp, tramp, I heard a rush under the hedge, and close down by the hazel stems glided a great dog, whose black and white colour made him a distinct object against the trees. It was exactly one mask of Bessie's Gytrash,—a lion-like creature with long hair and a huge head: it passed me, however, quietly enough; not staying to look up, with strange pretercanine eyes, in my face, as I half expected it would. The horse followed,—a tall steed and on its back a rider. The man, the human being, broke the spell at once. Nothing ever rode the Gytrash: it was always alone; and goblins, to my notions, though they might tenant the dumb carcasses of beasts, could scarce covet shelter in the commonplace human form. No Gytrash was this,—only a traveller taking the short cut to Millcote. He passed, and I went on; a few steps, and I turned: a sliding sound and an exclamation of 'What the deuce is to do now?' and a clattering tumble, arrested my attention. Man and horse were down; they had slipped on the sheet of ice which glazed the causeway. The dog came bounding back, and seeing his master in a predicament, and hearing the horse groan, barked till the evening hills echoed the sound, which was deep in proportion to his magnitude. He snuffed round the prostrate group, and then he ran up to me; it was all he could do,—there was no other help at hand to summon. I obeyed him, and walked down to the traveller, by this time struggling himself free of his steed. His efforts were so vigorous, I thought he could not be much hurt; but I asked him the question:—

'Are you injured, sir?'

I think he was swearing, but am not certain; however, he was pronouncing some formula which prevented him from replying to me directly.

'Can I do anything?' I asked again.

'You must stand on one side,' he answered as he rose, first to his knees, and then to his feet. I did; whereupon began a heaving, stamping, clattering process, accompanied by a barking and baying which removed me effectually some yards distance; but I would not be driven quite away till I saw the event. This was finally fortunate; the horse was re-established, and the dog was silenced with a 'Down, Pilot!' The traveller now, stooping, felt his foot and leg, as if trying whether they were sound; apparently something ailed them, for he halted to the stile whence I had just risen, and sat down.

I was in the mood for being useful, or at least officious, I think, for I now drew near him again.

'If you are hurt, and want help, sir, I can fetch some one either from Thornfield Hall or from Hay.'

'Thank you; I shall do: I have no broken bones,—only a sprain;' and again he stood up and tried his foot, but the result extorted an involuntary 'Ugh!'

Something of daylight still lingered, and the moon was waxing bright: I could see him plainly. His figure was enveloped in a riding cloak, fur collared, and steel clasped; its details were not apparent, but I traced the general points of middle height, and considerable breadth of chest. He had a dark face, with stern features and a heavy brow; his eyes and gathered eyebrows looked ireful and thwarted just now; he was past youth, but had not reached middle age; perhaps he might be thirty-five. I felt no fear of him, and but little shyness. Had he been a handsome, heroic-looking young gentleman, I should not have dared to stand thus questioning him against his will, and offering my services unasked. I had hardly ever seen a handsome youth; never in my life spoken to one. I had a theoretical reverence and homage for beauty, elegance, gallantry, fascination; but had I met those qualities incarnate in masculine shape, I should have known instinctively that they neither had nor could have sympathy with anything in me, and should have shunned them as one would fire, lightning, or anything else that is bright but antipathetic.

If even this stranger had smiled and been good-humoured to me when I addressed him; if he had put off my offer of assistance gaily and with thanks, I should have gone on my way and not felt any vocation to renew inquiries: but the frown, the roughness of the traveller set me at my ease: I retained my station when he waved to me to go, and announced:—

'I cannot think of leaving you, sir, at so late an hour, in this solitary lane, till I see you are fit to mount your horse.'

He looked at me when I said this: he had hardly turned his eyes in my direction before.

'I should think you ought to be at home yourself,' said he, 'if you have a home in this neighbourhood: were do you come from?'

'From just below; and I am not at all afraid of being out late when it is moonlight: I will run over to Hay for you with pleasure, if you wish it; indeed, I am going there to post a letter.'

'You live just below—do you mean at that house with the battlements?'— pointing to Thornfield Hall, on which the moon cast a hoary gleam, bringing it out distinct and pale from the woods, that, by contrast with the western sky, now seemed one mass of shadow.

'Yes, sir.'

'Whose house is it?'

'Mr. Rochester's.'

'Do you know Mr. Rochester?'

'No, I have never seen him.'

'He is not resident, then?'

'No.'

'Can you tell me where he is?'

'I cannot.'

'You are not a servant at the hall, of course. You are' —— He stopped, ran his eye over my dress, which, as usual, was quite simple: a black merino cloak, a black beaver bonnet; neither of them half fine enough for a lady's maid. He seemed puzzled to decide what I was: I helped him.

'I am the governess.'

'Ah, the governess!' he repeated; 'deuce take me, if I had not forgotten! The governess!' and again my raiment underwent scrutiny. In two minutes he rose from the stile: his face expressed pain when he tried to move.

'I cannot commission you to fetch help,' he said; 'but you may help me a little yourself, if you will be so kind.'

'Yes, sir.'

'You have not an umbrella that I can use as a stick?'

'No.'

'Try to get hold of my horse's bridle and lead him to me: you are not afraid?'

I should have been afraid to touch a horse when alone, but when told to do it, I was disposed to obey. I put down my muff on the stile, and went up to the tall steed; I endeavoured to catch the bridle, but it was a spirited thing, and would not let me come near its head; I made effort on effort, though in vain: meantime, I was mortally afraid of its trampling forefeet. The traveller waited and watched for some time, and at last he laughed.

'I see,' he said, 'the mountain will never be brought to Mahomet, so all you can do is to aid Mahomet to go to the mountain; I must beg of you to come here.'

I came. 'Excuse me,' he continued; 'necessity compels me to make you useful.' He laid a heavy hand on my shoulder, and leaning on me with some stress, limped to his horse. Having once caught the bridle, he mastered it directly, and sprang to his saddle; grimacing grimly as he made the effort, for it wrenched his sprain.

'Now,' said he, releasing his under lip from a hard bite, 'just hand me my whip; it lies there under the hedge.'

I sought it and found it.

'Thank you; now make haste with the letter to Hay, and return as fast as you can.'

A touch of a spurred heel made his horse first start and rear, and then bound away; the dog rushed in his traces: all three vanished,

'Like heath that, in the wilderness,
The wild wind whirls away.'

I took up my muff and walked on. The incident had occurred and was gone for me: it *was* an incident of no moment, no romance, no interest in a sense; yet it marked with change one single hour of a monotonous life. My help had been needed and claimed; I had given it: I was pleased to have done something; trivial, transitory though the deed was, it was yet an active thing, and I was weary of an existence all passive. The new face, too, was like a new picture introduced to the gallery of memory; and it was dissimilar to all the others hanging there: firstly, because it was masculine; and, secondly, because it was dark, strong, and stern. I had it still before me when I entered Hay, and slipped the letter into the post-office; I saw it as I walked fast down hill all the way home. When I came to the stile, I stopped a minute, looked round and listened, with an idea that a horse's hoofs might ring on the causeway again, and that a rider in a cloak, and a Gytrash-like Newfoundland dog, might be again apparent: I saw only the hedge and a pollard willow before me, rising up still and straight to meet the moonbeams; I heard only the faintest waft of wind roaming fitful among the trees round Thornfield, a mile distant; and when I glanced down in the direction of the murmur, my eye, traversing the hall-front, caught a light kindling in a window: it reminded me that I was late, and I hurried on.

I did not like re-entering Thornfield. To pass its threshold was to return to stagnation; to cross the silent hall, to ascend the darksome staircase, to seek my own lonely little room, and then to meet tranquil Mrs. Fairfax, and spend the long winter evening with her, and her only, was to quell wholly the faint excitement wakened by my walk,—to slip again over my faculties the viewless fetters of an uniform and too still existence; of an existence whose very privileges of security and ease I was becoming incapable of appreciating. What good it would have done me at that time to have been tossed in the storms of an uncertain struggling life, and to have been taught by rough and bitter experience to long for the calm amidst which I now repined! Yes, just as much good as it would do a man tired of sitting still in a 'too easy chair' to take a long walk: and just as natural was the wish to stir, under my circumstances, as it would be under his.

I lingered at the gates; I lingered on the lawn; I paced backwards and forwards on the pavement: the shutters of the glass door were closed; I could not see into the interior; and both my eyes and spirit seemed drawn from the gloomy house—from the grey hollow filled with rayless cells, as it appeared to me—to that sky expanded before me,—a blue sea absolved from taint of cloud; the moon ascending it in solemn march; her orb seeming to look up as she left the hill tops, from behind which she had come, far and farther below her, and aspired to the zenith, midnight-dark in its fathomless depth

and measureless distance: and for those trembling stars that followed her course; they made my heart tremble, my veins glow when I viewed them. Little things recall us to earth: the clock struck in the hall; that sufficed; I turned from moon and stars, opened a side-door, and went in.

The hall was not dark, nor yet was it lit, only by the high-hung bronze lamp: a warm glow suffused both it and the lower steps of the oak staircase. This ruddy shine issued from the great dining-room, whose two-leaved door stood open, and showed a genial fire in the grate, glancing on marble hearth and brass fire-irons, and revealing purple draperies and polished furniture, in the most pleasant radiance. It revealed, too, a group near the mantelpiece: I had scarcely caught it, and scarcely become aware of a cheerful mingling of voices, amongst which I seemed to distinguish the tones of Adèle, when the door closed.

I hastened to Mrs. Fairfax's room: there was a fire there too, but no candle, and no Mrs. Fairfax. Instead, all alone, sitting upright on the rug, and gazing with gravity at the blaze, I beheld a great black and white long-haired dog, just like the Gytrash of the lane. It was so like it that I went forward and said,—

'Pilot,' and the thing got up and came to me and snuffed me. I caressed him, and he wagged his great tail: but he looked an eerie creature to be alone with, and I could not tell whence he had come. I rang the bell, for I wanted a candle; and I wanted, too, to get an account of this visitant. Leah entered.

'What dog is this?'

'He came with master.'

'With whom?'

'With master—Mr. Rochester—he is just arrived.'

'Indeed! and is Mrs. Fairfax with him?'

'Yes, and Miss Adela; they are in the dining-room, and John is gone for a surgeon: for master has had an accident; his horse fell and his ankle is sprained.'

'Did the horse fall in Hay Lane?'

'Yes, coming down hill; it slipped on some ice.'

'Ah! Bring me a candle, will you, Leah?'

Leah brought it; she entered, followed by Mrs. Fairfax, who repeated the news; adding that Mr. Carter the surgeon was come, and was now with Mr. Rochester: then she hurried out to give orders about tea, and I went upstairs to take off my things.

CHAPTER 13

Mr. Rochester, it seems, by the surgeon's orders, went to bed early that night; nor did he rise soon next morning. When he did come down, it was to attend to business: his agent and some of his tenants were arrived, and waiting to speak with him.

Adèle and I had now to vacate the library: it would be in daily requisition as a reception-room for callers. A fire was lit in an apartment upstairs, and there I carried our books, and arranged it for the future school-room. I discerned in the course of the morning that Thornfield Hall was a changed place: no longer silent as a church, it echoed every hour or two to a knock at the door, or a clang of the bell; steps, too, often traversed the hall, and new voices spoke in different keys below; a rill from the outer world was flowing through it; it had a master: for my part, I liked it better.

Adèle was not easy to teach that day; she could not apply: she kept running to the door and looking over the banisters to see if she could get a glimpse of Mr. Rochester; then she coined pretexts to go downstairs, in order, as I shrewdly suspected, to visit the library, where I knew she was not wanted; then, when I got a little angry, and made her sit still, she continued to talk incessantly of her 'ami, Monsieur Edouard Fairfax *de* Rochester,' as she dubbed him (I had not before heard his prenomens), and to conjecture what presents he had brought her: for it appears he had intimated the night before, that when his luggage came from Millcote, there would be found amongst it a little box in whose contents she had an interest.

'Et cela doit signifier,' said she, 'qu'il y aura là dedans un cadeau pour moi, et peutêtre pour vous aussi, mademoiselle. Monsieur a parlé de vous: il m'a demandé le nom de ma gouvernante, et si elle n'était pas une petite personne, assez mince et un peu pâle. J'ai dit qu'oui: car c'est vrai, n'est-ce pas, mademoiselle?'

I and my pupil dined as usual in Mrs. Fairfax's parlour; the afternoon was wild and snowy, and we passed it in the school-room. At dark I allowed Adèle to put away books and work, and to run downstairs; for, from the comparative silence below, and from the cessation of appeals to the door-bell, I conjectured that Mr. Rochester was now at liberty. Left alone, I walked to the window; but nothing was to be seen thence: twilight and snow-flakes together thickened the air, and hid the very shrubs on the lawn. I let down the curtain and went back to the fireside.

In the clear embers I was tracing a view, not unlike a picture I remembered to have seen of the castle of Heidelberg, on the Rhine, when Mrs. Fairfax came in, breaking up by her entrance the fiery mosaic I had been piecing together, and scattering too some heavy unwelcome thoughts that were beginning to throng on my solitude.

meed teachers most covet; praise of their pupils' progress.'

'Humph!' said Mr. Rochester, and he took his tea in silence.

'Come to the fire,' said the master, when the tray was taken away, and Mrs. Fairfax had settled into a corner with her knitting; while Adèle was leading me by the hand round the room, showing me the beautiful books and ornaments on the consoles and chiffonnières. We obeyed, as in duty bound; Adèle wanted to take a seat on my knee, but she was ordered to amuse herself with Pilot.

'You have been resident in my house three months?'

'Yes, sir.'

'And you came from——?'

'From Lowood school, in ——shire.'

'Ah! a charitable concern.—How long were you there?'

'Eight years.'

'Eight years! you must be tenacious of life. I thought half the time in such a place would have done up any constitution! No wonder you have rather the look of another world. I marvelled where you had got that sort of face. When you came on me in Hay Lane last night, I thought unaccountably of fairy tales, and had half a mind to demand whether you had bewitched my horse: I am not sure yet. Who are your parents?'

'I have none.'

'Nor ever had, I suppose: do you remember them?'

'No.'

'I thought not. And so you were waiting for your people when you sat on that stile?'

'For whom, sir?'

'For the men in green: it was a proper moonlight evening for them. Did I break through one of your rings, that you spread that damned ice on the causeway?'

I shook my head. 'The men in green all forsook England a hundred years ago,' said I, speaking as seriously as he had done. 'And not even in Hay Lane, or the fields about it, could you find a trace of them. I don't think either summer or harvest, or winter moon, will ever shine on their revels more.'

Mrs. Fairfax had dropped her knitting, and, with raised eyebrows, seemed wondering what sort of talk this was.

'Well,' resumed Mr. Rochester, 'if you disown parents, you must have some sort of kinsfolk: uncles and aunts?'

'No; none that I ever saw.'

'And your home?'

'I have none.'

'Where do your brothers and sisters live?'

'I have no brothers or sisters.'

'Who recommended you to come here?'

'I advertised, and Mrs. Fairfax answered my advertisement.'

'Yes,' said the good lady, who now knew what ground we were upon, 'and I am daily thankful for the choice Providence led me to make. Miss Eyre has been an invaluable companion to me, and a kind and careful teacher to Adèle.'

'Don't trouble yourself to give her a character,' returned Mr. Rochester: 'eulogiums will not bias me; I shall judge for myself. She began by felling my horse.'

'Sir?' said Mrs. Fairfax.

'I have to thank her for this sprain.'

The widow looked bewildered.

'Miss Eyre, have you ever lived in a town?'

'No, sir.'

'Have you seen much society?'

'None but the pupils and teachers of Lowood; and now the inmates of Thornfield.'

'Have you read much?'

'Only such books as came in my way; and they have not been numerous, or very learned.'

'You have lived the life of a nun: no doubt you are well drilled in religious forms;—Brocklehurst, who I understand directs Lowood, is a parson, is he not?'

'Yes, sir.'

'And you girls probably worshipped him, as a convent full of religieuses would worship their director.'

'Oh, no.'

'You are very cool! No! What? a novice not worship her priest! That sounds blasphemous.'

'I disliked Mr. Brocklehurst; and I was not alone in the feeling. He is a harsh man; at once pompous and meddling: he cut off our hair; and for economy's sake bought us bad needles and thread, with which we could hardly sew.'

'That was very false economy,' remarked Mrs. Fairfax, who now again caught the drift of the dialogue.

'And was that the head and front of his offending?' demanded Mr. Rochester.

'He starved us when he had the sole superintendence of the provision department, before the committee was appointed; and he bored us with long lectures once a week, and with evening readings from books of his own inditing, about sudden deaths and judgments, which made us afraid to go to bed.'

'What age were you when you went to Lowood?'

'About ten.'

'And you stayed there eight years: and are now, then, eighteen?'

I assented.

'Arithmetic, you see, is useful: without its aid, I should hardly have been able to guess your age. It is a point difficult to fix where the features and countenance are so much at variance as in your case. And now what did you learn at Lowood? Can you play?'

'A little.'

'Of course: that is the established answer. Go into the library—I mean, if you please.—(Excuse my tone of command; I am used to say "Do this," and it is done: I cannot alter my customary habits for one new inmate.)—Go, then, into the library; take a candle with you; leave the door open; sit down to the piano, and play a tune.'

I departed, obeying his directions.

'Enough!' he called out in a few minutes. 'You play a *little*, I see; like any other English school-girl: perhaps rather better than some, but not well.'

I closed the piano, and returned. Mr. Rochester continued.

'Adèle showed me some sketches this morning, which she said were yours. I don't know whether they were entirely of your doing: probably a master aided you?'

'No, indeed!' I interjected.

'Ah! that pricks pride. Well, fetch me your portfolio, if you can vouch for its contents being original; but don't pass your word unless you are certain: I can recognise patchwork.'

'Then I will say nothing, and you shall judge for yourself, sir.'

I brought the portfolio from the library.

'Approach the table,' said he; and I wheeled it to his couch. Adèle and Mrs. Fairfax drew near to see the pictures.

'No crowding,' said Mr. Rochester: 'take the drawings from my hand as I finish with them; but don't push your faces up to mine.'

He deliberately scrutinised each sketch and painting. Three he laid aside; the others, when he had examined them, he swept from him.

'Take them off to the other table, Mrs. Fairfax,' said he, 'and look at them with Adèle;—you' (glancing at me) 'resume your seat, and answer my questions. I perceive these pictures were done by one hand: was that hand yours?'

'Yes.'

'And when did you find time to do them? They have taken much time, and some thought.'

'I did them in the last two vacations I spent at Lowood, when I had no other occupation.'

'Where did you get your copies?'

'Out of my head.'

'That head I see now on your shoulders?'

'Yes, sir.'

'Has it other furniture of the same kind within?'

'I should think it may have: I should hope—better.'

He spread the pictures before him, and again surveyed them alternately.

While he is so occupied, I will tell you, reader, what they are: and first, I must premise that they are nothing wonderful. The subjects had, indeed, risen vividly on my mind. As I saw them with the spiritual eye, before I attempted to embody them, they were striking; but my hand would not second my fancy, and in each case it had wrought out but a pale portrait of the thing I had conceived.

These pictures were in water colours. The first represented clouds low and livid, rolling over a swollen sea: all the distance was in eclipse; so, too, was the foreground; or, rather, the nearest billows, for there was no land. One gleam of light lifted into relief a half-submerged mast, on which sat a cormorant, dark and large, with wings flecked with foam; its beak held a gold bracelet, set with gems, that I had touched with as brilliant tints as my palette could yield, and as glittering distinctness as my pencil could impart. Sinking below the bird and mast, a drowned corpse glanced through the green water; a fair arm was the only limb clearly visible, whence the bracelet had been washed or torn.

The second picture contained for foreground only the dim peak of a hill, with grass and some leaves slanting as if by a breeze. Beyond and above spread an expanse of sky, dark blue as at twilight: rising into the sky was a woman's shape to the bust, portrayed in tints as dusk and soft as I could combine. The dim forehead was crowned with a star; the lineaments below were seen as through the suffusion of vapour; the eyes shone dark and wild; the hair streamed shadowy, like a beamless cloud torn by storm or by electric travail. On the neck lay a pale reflection like moonlight; the same faint lustre touched the train of thin clouds from which rose and bowed this vision of the Evening Star.

The third showed the pinnacle of an iceberg piercing a polar winter sky: a muster of northern lights reared their dim lances, close serried, along the horizon. Throwing these into distance, rose, in the foreground, a head,— a colossal head, inclined towards the iceberg, and resting against it. Two thin hands, joined under the forehead, and supporting it, drew up before the lower features a sable veil; a brow quite bloodless, white as bone, and an eye hollow and fixed, blank of meaning but for the glassiness of despair, alone were visible. Above the temples, amidst wreathed turban folds of black drapery, vague in its character and consistency as cloud, gleamed a ring of white flame, gemmed with sparkles of a more lurid tinge. This pale crescent was 'The likeness of a Kingly Crown'; what it diademed was 'the shape which shape had none.'

'Were you happy when you painted these pictures?' asked Mr. Rochester, presently.

'I was absorbed, sir: yes, and I was happy. To paint them, in short, was to enjoy one of the keenest pleasures I have ever known.'

'That is not saying much. Your pleasures, by your own account, have been few; but I daresay you did exist in a kind of artist's dreamland while you blent and arranged these strange tints. Did you sit at them long each day?'

'I had nothing else to do, because it was the vacation, and I sat at them from morning till noon, and from noon till night: the length of the midsummer days favoured my inclination to apply.'

'And you felt self-satisfied with the result of your ardent labours?'

'Far from it. I was tormented by the contrast between my ideas and my handiwork: in each case I had imagined something which I was quite powerless to realize.'

'Not quite: you have secured the shadow of your thought; but no more, probably. You had not enough of the artist's skill and science to give it full being: yet the drawings are, for a school girl, peculiar. As to the thoughts, they are elfish. These eyes in the Evening Star you must have seen in a dream. How could you make them look so clear, and yet not at all brilliant? for the planet above quells their rays. And what meaning is that in their solemn depth? And who taught you to paint wind? There is a high gale in that sky, and on this hill-top. Where did you see Latmos? For that is Latmos. There,— put the drawings away!'

I had scarce tied the strings of the portfolio, when, looking at his watch, he said abruptly—

'It is nine o'clock: what are you about, Miss Eyre, to let Adèle sit up so long? Take her to bed.'

Adèle went to kiss him before quitting the room: he endured the caress, but scarcely seemed to relish it more than Pilot would have done, nor so much.

'I wish you all good-night, now,' said he, making a movement of the hand towards the door, in token that he was tired of our company, and wished to dismiss us. Mrs. Fairfax folded up her knitting: I took my portfolio: we curt-seyed to him, received a frigid bow in return, and so withdrew.

'You said Mr. Rochester was not strikingly peculiar, Mrs. Fairfax, I observed, when I rejoined her in her room, after putting Adèle to bed.

'Well, is he?'

'I think so: he is very changeful and abrupt.'

'True: no doubt he may appear so to a stranger, but I am so accustomed to his manner, I never think of it; and then, if he has peculiarities of temper, allowance should be made.'

'Why?'

'Partly because it is his nature—and we can none of us help our nature; and, partly, he has painful thoughts, no doubt, to harass him, and make his spirits unequal.'

'What about?'

'Family troubles, for one thing.'

'But he has no family.'

'Not now, but he has had—or, at least, relatives. He lost his elder brother a few years since.'

'His *elder* brother?'

'Yes. The present Mr. Rochester has not been very long in possession of the property; only about nine years.'

'Nine years is a tolerable time. Was he so very fond of his brother as to be still inconsolable for his loss?'

'Why, no—perhaps not. I believe there were some misunderstandings between them. Mr. Rowland Rochester was not quite just to Mr. Edward; and, perhaps, he prejudiced his father against him. The old gentleman was fond of money, and anxious to keep the family estate together. He did not like to diminish the property by division, and yet he was anxious that Mr. Edward should have wealth, too, to keep up the consequence of the name; and, soon after he was of age, some steps were taken that were not quite fair, and made a great deal of mischief. Old Mr. Rochester and Mr. Rowland combined to bring Mr. Edward into what he considered a painful position, for the sake of making his fortune: what the precise nature of that position was I never clearly knew, but his spirit could not brook what he had to suffer in it. He is not very forgiving: he broke with his family, and now for many years he has led an unsettled kind of life. I don't think he has ever been resident at Thornfield for a fortnight together, since the death of his brother without a will left him master of the estate; and, indeed, no wonder he shuns the old place.'

'Why should he shun it?'

'Perhaps he thinks it gloomy.'

The answer was evasive—I should have liked something clearer; but Mrs. Fairfax either could not, or would not, give me more explicit information of the origin and nature of Mr. Rochester's trials. She averred they were a mystery to herself, and that what she knew was chiefly from conjecture. It was evident, indeed, that she wished me to drop the subject, which I did accordingly.

CHAPTER 14

For several subsequent days I saw little of Mr. Rochester. In the mornings he seemed much engaged with business, and, in the afternoon, gentlemen from Millcote or the neighbourhood called, and sometimes stayed to dine with him. When his sprain was well enough to admit of horse exercise, he rode out a good deal; probably to return these visits, as he generally did not come back till late at night.

During this interval, even Adèle was seldom sent for to his presence, and all my acquaintance with him was confined to an occasional rencontre in the hall, on the stairs, or in the gallery, when he would sometimes pass me haughtily and coldly, just acknowledging my presence by a distant nod or a cool glance, and sometimes bow and smile with gentleman-like affability. His changes of mood did not offend me, because I saw that I had nothing to do with their alternation; the ebb and flow depended on causes quite disconnected with me.

One day he had had company to dinner, and had sent for my portfolio; in order, doubtless, to exhibit its contents: the gentlemen went away early, to attend a public meeting at Millcote, as Mrs. Fairfax informed me; but the night being wet and inclement, Mr. Rochester did not accompany them. Soon after they were gone, he rang the bell: a message came that I and Adèle were to go downstairs. I brushed Adèle's hair and made her neat, and having ascertained that I was myself in my usual Quaker trim, where there was nothing to retouch—all being too close and plain, braided locks included, to admit of disarrangement—we descended, Adèle wondering whether the *petit coffre* was at length come; for, owing to some mistake, its arrival had hitherto been delayed. She was gratified: there it stood, a little carton, on the table when we entered the dining-room. She appeared to know it by instinct.

'Ma boite! ma boite!' exclaimed she, running towards it.

'Yes—there is your "boite" at last: take it into a corner, you genuine daughter of Paris, and amuse yourself with disembowelling it,' said the deep and rather sarcastic voice of Mr. Rochester, proceeding from the depths of an immense easy chair at the fireside. 'And mind,' he continued, 'don't bother me with any details of the anatomical process, or any notice of the condition of the entrails: let your operation be conducted in silence: tiens-toi tranquille, enfant; comprends-tu?'

Adèle seemed scarcely to need the warning; she had already retired to a sofa with her treasure, and was busy untying the cord which secured the lid. Having removed this impediment, and lifted certain silvery envelopes of tissue paper, she merely exclaimed:—

'Oh ciel! Que c'est beau!' and then remained absorbed in ecstatic contemplation.

'Is Miss Eyre there?' now demanded the master, half rising from his seat to look round to the door, near which I still stood.

'Ah! well; come forward: be seated here.' He drew a chair near his own. 'I am not fond of the prattle of children,' he continued; 'for, old bachelor as I am, I have no pleasant associations connected with their lisp. It would be intolerable to me to pass a whole evening *tête-à-tête* with a brat. Don't draw that chair further off, Miss Eyre; sit down exactly where I placed it—if you please, that is. Confound these civilities! I continually forget them. Nor do I particularly affect simple-minded old ladies. By-the-by, I must have mine in

mind; it won't do to neglect her; she is a Fairfax, or wed to one; and blood is said to be thicker than water.'

He rang and despatched an invitation to Mrs. Fairfax, who soon arrived, knitting-basket in hand.

'Good-evening, madam; I sent to you for a charitable purpose: I have forbidden Adèle to talk to me about her presents, and she is bursting with repletion; have the goodness to serve her as auditress and interlocutrice: it will be one of the most benevolent acts you ever performed.'

Adèle, indeed, no sooner saw Mrs. Fairfax, than she summoned her to her sofa and there quickly filled her lap with the porcelain, the ivory, the waxen contents of her 'boite'; pouring out, meantime, explanations and raptures in such broken English as she was mistress of.

'Now I have performed the part of a good host,' pursued Mr. Rochester, 'put my guests into the way of amusing each other, I ought to be at liberty to attend to my own pleasure. Miss Eyre, draw your chair still a little further forward: you are yet too far back; I cannot see you without disturbing my position in this comfortable chair, which I have no mind to do.'

I did as I was bid, though I would much rather have remained somewhat in the shade: but Mr. Rochester had such a direct way of giving orders, it seemed a matter of course to obey him promptly.

We were, as I have said, in the dining-room: the lustre, which had been lit for dinner, filled the room with a festal breadth of light; the large fire was all red and clear; the purple curtains hung rich and ample before the lofty window and loftier arch; everything was still, save the subdued chat of Adèle (she dared not speak loud), and, filling up each pause, the beating of winter rain against the panes.

Mr. Rochester, as he sat in his damask-covered chair, looked different to what I had seen him look before; not quite so stern—much less gloomy. There was a smile on his lips, and his eyes sparkled, whether with wine or not, I am not sure; but I think it very probable. He was, in short, in his after-dinner mood; more expanded and genial, and also more self-indulgent than the frigid and rigid temper of the morning: still he looked preciously grim, cushioning his massive head against the swelling back of his chair, and receiving the light of the fire on his granite-hewn features, and in his great, dark eyes; for he had great, dark eyes, and very fine eyes, too—not without a certain change in their depths sometimes, which, if it was not softness, reminded you, at least of that feeling.

He had been looking two minutes at the fire, and I had been looking the same length of time at him, when, turning suddenly, he caught my gaze fastened on his physiognomy.

'You examine me, Miss Eyre,' said he: 'do you think me handsome?'

I should, if I had deliberated, have replied to this question by something

conventionally vague and polite; but the answer somehow slipped from my tongue before I was aware:—'No, sir.'

'Ah! By my word! there is something singular about you,' said he: 'you have the air of a little nonnette; quaint, quiet, grave, and simple, as you sit with your hands before you, and your eyes generally bent on the carpet (except, by-the-by, when they are directed piercingly to my face; as just now, for instance); and when one asks you a question, or makes a remark to which you are obliged to reply, you rap out a round rejoinder, which, if not blunt, is at least brusque. What do you mean by it?'

'Sir, I was too plain: I beg your pardon. I ought to have replied that it was not easy to give an impromptu answer to a question about appearances; that tastes differ; that beauty is of little consequence, or something of that sort.'

'You ought to have replied no such thing. Beauty of little consequence, indeed! And so, under pretence of softening the previous outrage, of stroking and soothing me into placidity, you stick a sly penknife under my ear! Go on: what fault do you find with me, pray? I suppose I have all my limbs and all my features like any other man?'

'Mr. Rochester, allow me to disown my first answer: I intended no pointed repartee: it was only a blunder.'

'Just so: I think so: and you shall be answerable for it. Criticise me: does my forehead not please you?'

He lifted up the sable waves of hair which lay horizontally over his brow, and showed a solid enough mass of intellectual organs, but an abrupt deficiency where the suave sign of benevolence should have risen.

'Now, ma'am, am I a fool?'

'Far from it, sir. You would, perhaps, think me rude if I inquired in return whether you are a philanthropist?'

'There again! Another stick of the penknife, when she pretended to pat my head: and that is because I said I did not like the society of children and old women (low be it spoken!). No, young lady, I am not a general philanthropist; but I bear a conscience;' and he pointed to the prominences which are said to indicate that faculty, and which, fortunately for him, were sufficiently conspicuous; giving, indeed, a marked breadth to the upper part of his head: 'and, besides, I once had a kind of rude tenderness of heart. When I was as old as you, I was a feeling fellow enough; partial to the unfledged, unfostered, and unlucky; but fortune has knocked me about since: she has even kneaded me with her knuckles, and now I flatter myself I am hard and tough as an India-rubber ball; pervious, though, through a chink or two still, and with one sentient point in the middle of the lump. Yes: does that leave hope for me?'

'Hope of what, sir?'

'Of my final re-transformation from India-rubber back to flesh?'

114

'Decidedly he has had too much wine,' I thought; and I did not know what answer to make to his queer question: how could I tell whether he was capable of being re-transformed?

'You look very much puzzled, Miss Eyre; and though you are not pretty any more than I am handsome, yet a puzzled air becomes you; besides, it is convenient, for it keeps those searching eyes of yours away from my physiognomy, and busies them with the worsted flowers of the rug; so puzzle on. Young lady, I am disposed to be gregarious and communicative to-night.'

With this announcement he rose from his chair, and stood, leaning his arm on the marble mantelpiece: in that attitude his shape was seen plainly as well as his face; his unusual breadth of chest, disproportionate almost to his length of limb. I am sure most people would have thought him an ugly man; yet there was so much unconscious pride in his port: so much ease in his demeanour; such a look of complete indifference to his own external appearance; so haughty a reliance on the power of other qualities, intrinsic or adventitious, to atone for the lack of mere personal attractiveness, that, in looking at him, one inevitably shared the indifference, and, even in a blind, imperfect sense, put faith in the confidence.

'I am disposed to be gregarious and communicative to-night,' he repeated; 'and that is why I sent for you: the fire and the chandelier were not sufficient company for me; nor would Pilot have been, for none of these can talk. Adèle is a degree better, but still far below the mark; Mrs. Fairfax ditto; you, I am persuaded, can suit me if you will: you puzzled me the first evening I invited you down here. I have almost forgotten you since: other ideas have driven yours from my head; but to-night I am resolved to be at ease; to dismiss what importunes, and recall what pleases. It would please me now to draw you out—to learn more of you—therefore speak.'

Instead of speaking, I smiled; and not a very complacent or submissive smile either.

'Speak,' he urged.

'What about, sir?'

'Whatever you like. I leave both the choice of subject and the manner of treating it entirely to yourself.'

Accordingly I sat and said nothing: 'If he expects me to talk for the mere sake of talking and showing off, he will find he has addressed himself to the wrong person,' I thought.

'You are dumb, Miss Eyre.'

I was dumb still. He bent his head a little towards me, and with a single hasty glance seemed to dive into my eyes.

'Stubborn?' he said, 'and annoyed. Ah, it is consistent. I put my request in an absurd, almost insolent form. Miss Eyre, I beg your pardon. The fact is, once for all, I don't wish to treat you like an inferior: that is (correcting

himself), I claim only such superiority as must result from twenty years' difference in age and a century's advance in experience. This is legitimate, et j'y tiens, as Adèle would say; and it is by virtue of this superiority and this alone that I desire you to have the goodness to talk to me a little now, and divert my thoughts, which are galled with dwelling on one point—cankering as a rusty nail.'

He had deigned an explanation; almost an apology: I did not feel insensible to his condescension, and would not seem so.

'I am willing to amuse you if I can, sir: quite willing; but I cannot introduce a topic, because how do I know what will interest you? Ask me questions, and I will do my best to answer them.'

'Then, in the first place, do you agree with me that I have a right to be a little masterful, abrupt; perhaps exacting, sometimes, on the grounds I stated; namely, that I am old enough to be your father, and that I have battled through a varied experience with many men of many nations, and roamed over half the globe, while you have lived quietly with one set of people in one house?'

'Do as you please, sir.'

'That is no answer; or rather it is a very irritating, because a very evasive one; reply clearly.'

'I don't think, you have a right to command me, merely because you are older than I, or because you have seen more of the world than I have; your claim to superiority depends on the use you have made of your time and experience.'

'Humph! Promptly spoken. But I won't allow that, seeing that it would never suit my case; as I have made an indifferent, not to say a bad, use of both advantages. Leaving superiority out of the question then, you must still agree to receive my orders now and then, without being piqued or hurt by the tone of command—will you?'

I smiled: I thought to myself Mr. Rochester *is* peculiar—he seems to forget that he pays me £30 per annum for receiving his orders.

'The smile is very well,' said he, catching instantly the passing expression; 'but speak too.'

'I was thinking, sir, that very few masters would trouble themselves to inquire whether or not their paid subordinates were piqued and hurt by their orders.'

'Paid subordinates! What, you are my paid subordinate, are you? Oh yes, I had forgotten the salary! Well then, on that mercenary ground, will you agree to let me hector a little?'

'No, sir, not on that ground: but, on the ground that you did forget it, and that you care whether or not a dependent is comfortable in his dependency, I agree heartily.'

'And will you consent to dispense with a great many conventional forms and phrases, without thinking that the omission arises from insolence?'

'I am sure, sir, I should never mistake informality for insolence: one I rather like, the other nothing free-born would submit to, even for a salary.'

'Humbug! Most things free-born will submit to anything for a salary; therefore, keep to yourself, and don't venture on generalities of which you are intensely ignorant. However, I mentally shake hands with you for your answer, despite its inaccuracy; and as much for the manner in which it was said, as for the substance of the speech: the manner was frank and sincere; one does not often see such a manner: no, on the contrary, affectation, or coldness, or stupid, coarse-minded misapprehension of one's meaning are the usual rewards of candour. Not three in three thousand raw school-girl governesses would have answered me as you have just done. But I don't mean to flatter you: if you are cast in a different mould to the majority, it is no merit of yours: Nature did it. And then, after all, I go too fast in my conclusions: for what I yet know, you may be no better than the rest; you may have intolerable defects to counterbalance your few good points.'

'And so may you,' I thought. My eye met his as the idea crossed my mind: he seemed to read the glance, answering as if its import had been spoken as well as imagined:—

'Yes, yes, you are right,' said he; 'I have plenty of faults of my own: I know it, and I don't wish to palliate them, I assure you. God wot I need not be too severe about others; I have a past existence, a series of deeds, a colour of life to contemplate within my own breast, which might well call my sneers and censures from my neighbours to myself. I started, or rather (for, like other defaulters, I like to lay half the blame on ill fortune and adverse circumstances) was thrust on to a wrong tack at the age of one and twenty, and have never recovered the right course since: but I might have been very different; I might have been as good as you—wiser—almost as stainless. I envy you your peace of mind, your clean conscience, your unpolluted memory. Little girl, a memory without blot or contamination must be an exquisite treasure—an inexhaustible source of pure refreshment: is it not?'

'How was your memory when you were eighteen, sir?'

'All right then; limpid, salubrious: no gush of bilge water had turned it to fetid puddle. I was your equal at eighteen—quite your equal. Nature meant me to be, on the whole, a good man, Miss Eyre: one of the better end; and you see I am not so. You would say you don't see it: at least I flatter myself I read as much in your eye (beware, by-the-by, what you express with that organ, I am quick at interpreting its language). Then take my word for it,—I am not a villain: you are not to suppose that—not to attribute to me any such bad eminence; but, owing, I verily believe, rather to circumstances than to my natural bent, I am a trite common-place sinner, hackneyed in all the

poor petty dissipations with which the rich and worthless try to put on life. Do you wonder that I avow this to you? Know, that in the course of your future life you will often find yourself elected the involuntary confidant of your acquaintances' secrets: people will instinctively find out, as I have done, that it is not your forte to tell of yourself, but to listen while others talk of themselves; they will feel, too, that you listen with no malevolent scorn of their indiscretion, but with a kind of innate sympathy; not the less comforting and encouraging because it is very unobtrusive in its manifestations.'

'How do you know? — how can you guess all this, sir?'

'I know it well; therefore I proceed almost as freely as if I were writing my thoughts in a diary. You would say, I should have been superior to circumstances: so I should — so I should; but you see I was not. When fate wronged me, I had not the wisdom to remain cool: I turned desperate; then I degenerated. Now, when any vicious simpleton excites my disgust by his paltry ribaldry, I cannot flatter myself that I am better than he: I am forced to confess that he and I are on a level. I wish I had stood firm — God knows I do! Dread remorse when you are tempted to err, Miss Eyre: remorse is the poison of life.'

'Repentance is said to be its cure, sir.'

'It is not its cure. Reformation may be its cure; and I could reform — I have strength yet for that — if — but where is the use of thinking of it, hampered, burdened, cursed as I am? Besides, since happiness is irrevocably denied me, I have a right to get pleasure out of life: and I *will* get it, cost what it may.'

'Then you will degenerate still more, sir.'

'Possibly: yet why should I, if I can get sweet, fresh pleasure? And I may get it as sweet and fresh as the wild honey the bee gathers on the moor.'

'It will sting — it will taste bitter, sir.'

'How do you know? — you never tried it. How very serious — how very solemn you look; and you are as ignorant of the matter as this cameo head' (taking one from the mantelpiece). 'You have no right to preach to me, you neophyte, that have not passed the porch of life, and are absolutely unacquainted with its mysteries.'

'I only remind you of your own words, sir: you said error brought remorse, and you pronounced remorse the poison of existence.'

'And who talks of error now? I scarcely think the notion that flittered across my brain was an error. I believe it was an inspiration rather than a temptation: it was very genial, very soothing, — I know that. Here it comes again! It is no devil, I assure you; or if it be, it has put on the robes of an angel of light. I think I must admit so fair a guest when it asks entrance to my heart.'

'Distrust it, sir; it is not a true angel.'

'Once more, how do you know? By what instinct do you pretend to distinguish between a fallen seraph of the abyss and a messenger from the eternal

throne—between a guide and a seducer?'

'I judged by your countenance, sir; which was troubled: when you said the suggestion had returned upon you. I feel sure it will work you more misery if you listen to it.'

'Not at all—it bears the most gracious message in the world: for the rest, you are not my conscience-keeper, so don't make yourself uneasy. Here, come in, bonny wanderer!'

He said this as if he spoke to a vision, viewless to any eye but his own; then, folding his arms, which he had half extended, on his chest, he seemed to enclose in their embrace the invisible being.

'Now,' he continued, again addressing me, 'I have received the pilgrim— a disguised deity, as I verily believe. Already it has done me good: my heart was a sort of charnel; it will now be a shrine.'

'To speak truth, sir, I don't understand you at all: I cannot keep up the conversation, because it has got out of my depth. Only one thing I know: you said you were not as good as you should like to be, and that you regretted your own imperfection;—one thing I can comprehend: you intimated that to have a sullied memory was a perpetual bane. It seems to me, that if you tried hard, you would in time find it possible to become what you yourself would approve; and that if from this day you began with resolution to correct your thoughts and actions, you would in a few years have laid up a new and stainless store of recollections, to which you might revert with pleasure.'

'Justly thought; rightly said, Miss Eyre; and, at this moment, I am paving hell with energy.'

'Sir?'

'I am laying down good intentions, which I believe durable as flint. Certainly, my associates and pursuits shall be other than they have been.'

'And better?'

'And better—so much better as pure ore is than foul dross. You seem to doubt me; I don't doubt myself: I know what my aim is, and what my motives are; and at this moment I pass a law, unalterable as that of the Medes and Persians, that both are right.'

'They cannot be, sir, if they require a new statute to legalise them.'

'They are, Miss Eyre, though they absolutely require a new statute: unheard-of combinations of circumstances demand unheard-of rules.'

'That sounds a dangerous maxim, sir; because one can see at once that it is liable to abuse.'

'Sententious sage! so it is: but I swear by my household gods not to abuse it.'

'You are human and fallible.'

'I am: so are you—what then?'

'The human and fallible should not arrogate a power with which the divine and perfect alone can be safely entrusted.'

'What power?'

'That of saying of any strange, unsanctioned line of action,—"Let it be right." '

' "Let it be right"—the very words: you have pronounced them.'

'*May* it be right, then,' I said, as I rose, deeming it useless to continue a discourse which was all darkness to me; and, besides, sensible that the character of my interlocutor was beyond my penetration; at least, beyond its present reach; and feeling the uncertainty, the vague sense of insecurity, which accompanied a conviction of ignorance.

'Where are you going?'

'To put Adèle to bed: it is past her bedtime.'

'You are afraid of me, because I talk like a Sphynx.'

'Your language is enigmatical, sir: but though I am bewildered, I am certainly not afraid.'

'You *are* afraid—your self-love dreads a blunder.'

'In that sense I do feel apprehensive—I have no wish to talk nonsense.'

'If you did, it would be in such a grave, quiet manner, I should mistake it for sense. Do you never laugh, Miss Eyre? Don't trouble yourself to answer— I see, you laugh rarely; but you can laugh very merrily: believe me, you are not naturally austere, any more than I am naturally vicious. The Lowood constraint still clings to you somewhat; controlling your features, muffling your voice, and restricting your limbs; and you fear in the presence of a man and a brother—or father, or master, or what you will—to smile too gaily, speak too freely, or move too quickly: but, in time, I think you will learn to be natural with me, as I find it impossible to be conventional with you; and then your looks and movements will have more vivacity and variety than they dare offer now. I see at intervals the glance of a curious sort of bird through the close-set bars of a cage: a vivid, restless, resolute captive is there; were it but free, it would soar cloud-high. You are still bent on going?'

'It has struck nine, sir.'

'Never mind,—wait a minute: Adèle is not ready to go to bed yet. My position, Miss Eyre, with my back to the fire, and my face to the room, favours observation. While talking to you, I have also occasionally watched Adèle; (I have my own reasons for thinking her a curious study,—reasons that I may, nay that I shall, impart to you some day;) she pulled out of her box, about ten minutes ago, a little pink silk frock; rapture lit her face as she unfolded it; coquetry runs in her blood, blends with her brains, and seasons the marrow of her bones. "Il faut que je l'essaie!" cried she; "et à l'instant même!" and she rushed out of the room. She is now with Sophie, undergoing a robing process: in a few minutes she will re-enter; and I know what I shall see,—a miniature of Céline Varens, as she used to appear on the boards at the rising of——: but never mind that. However, my tenderest feelings are about

to receive a shock: such is my presentiment; stay now, to see whether it will be realised.'

Ere long, Adèle's little foot was heard tripping across the hall. She entered, transformed as her guardian had predicted. A dress of rose-coloured satin, very short, and as full in the skirt as it could be gathered, replaced the brown frock she had previously worn; a wreath of rosebuds circled her forehead; her feet were dressed in silk stockings and small white satin sandals.

'Est-ce que ma robe va bien?' cried she, bounding forwards; 'et mes souliers? et mes bas? Tenez, je crois que je vais danser!'

And spreading out her dress, she chasséed across the room; till, having reached Mr. Rochester, she wheeled lightly round before him on tip-toe, then dropped on one knee at his feet, exclaiming:—

'Monsieur, je vous remercie mille fois de votre bonté;' then rising, she added, 'C'est comme cela que maman faisait, n'est-ce pas, monsieur?'

'Pre-cise-ly!' was the answer; 'and, "comme cela," she charmed my English gold out of my British breeches' pocket. I have been green, too, Miss Eyre,—ay, grass green: not a more vernal tint freshens you now than once freshened me. My Spring is gone, however: but it has left me that French floweret on my hands: which, in some moods, I would fain be rid of. Not valuing now the root whence it sprang; having found that it was of a sort which nothing but gold dust could manure, I have but half a liking to the blossom: especially when it looks so artificial as just now. I keep it and rear it rather on the Roman Catholic principle of expiating numerous sins, great or small, by one good work. I'll explain all this some day. Good-night.'

CHAPTER 15

Mr. Rochester did, on a future occasion, explain it.

It was one afternoon, when he chanced to meet me and Adèle in the grounds; and while she played with Pilot and her shuttlecock, he asked me to walk up and down a long beech avenue within sight of her.

He then said that she was the daughter of a French opera-dancer, Céline Varens, towards whom he had once cherished what he called a 'grande passion.' This passion Céline had professed to return with even superior ardour. He thought himself her idol; ugly as he was: he believed, as he said, that she preferred his 'taille d'athlète' to the elegance of the Apollo Belvidere.

'And, Miss Eyre, so much was I flattered by this preference of the Gallic sylph for her British gnome, that I installed her in an hotel; gave her a complete establishment of servants, a carriage, cashmeres, diamonds, dentelles, etc. In short, I began the process of ruining myself in the received style, like any other spoony. I had not, it seems, the originality to chalk out a new road to

shame and destruction, but trode the old track with stupid exactness not to deviate an inch from the beaten centre. I had—as I deserved to have—the fate of all other spoonies. Happening to call one evening, when Céline did not expect me, I found her out; but it was a warm night, and I was tired with strolling through Paris, so I sat down in her boudoir; happy to breathe the air consecrated so lately by her presence. No,—I exaggerate; I never thought there was any consecrating virtue about her: it was rather a sort of pastille perfume she had left; a scent of musk and amber, than an odour of sanctity. I was just beginning to stifle with the fumes of conservatory flowers and sprinkled essences, when I bethought myself to open the window and step out on to the balcony. It was moonlight and gas-light besides, and very still and serene. The balcony was furnished with a chair or two; I sat down, took out a cigar.—I will take one now, if you will excuse me.'

Here ensued a pause, filled up by the producing and lighting of a cigar; having placed it to his lips and breathed a trail of Havannah incense on the freezing and sunless air, he went on:—

'I liked bonbons too, in those days, Miss Eyre, and I was *croquant*—(overlook the barbarism) *croquant* chocolate comfits, and smoking alternately, watching meantime the equipages that rolled along the fashionable streets towards the neighbouring opera-house, when in an elegant close carriage drawn by a beautiful pair of English horses, and distinctly seen in the brilliant city-night, I recognised the "voiture" I had given Céline. She was returning: of course my heart thumped with impatience against the iron rails I leant upon. The carriage stopped, as I had expected, at the hotel door; my flame (that is the very word for an opera inamorata) alighted: though muffled in a cloak—an unnecessary encumbrance, by-the-by, on so warm a June evening—I knew her instantly by her little foot, seen peeping from the skirt of her dress, as she skipped from the carriage-step. Bending over the balcony I was about to murmur, "Mon ange"—in a tone, of course, which should be audible to the ear of love alone—when a figure jumped from the carriage after her; cloaked also; but that was a spurred heel which had rung on the pavement, and that was a hatted head which now passed under the arched *porte cochère* of the hotel.

'You never felt jealousy, did you, Miss Eyre? Of course not: I need not ask you; because you never felt love. You have both sentiments yet to experience; your soul sleeps: the shock is yet to be given which shall waken it. You think all existence lapses in as quiet a flow as that in which your youth has hitherto slid away. Floating on with closed eyes and muffled ears, you neither see the rocks bristling not far off in the bed of the flood, nor hear the breakers boil at their base. But I tell you—and you may mark my words—you will come some day to a craggy pass of the channel, where the whole of life's stream will be broken up into whirl and tumult, foam and noise: either you will be dashed

to atoms on crag points, or lifted up and borne on by some master wave into a calmer current—as I am now.

'I like this day: I like that sky of steel; I like the sternness and stillness of the world under this frost. I like Thornfield; its antiquity; its retirement; its old crow-trees and thorn-trees; its grey façade, and lines of dark windows reflecting that metal welkin: and yet how long have I abhorred the very thought of it; shunned it like a great plague-house! How I do still abhor'——

He ground his teeth and was silent: he arrested his step and struck his boot against the hard ground. Some hated thought seemed to have him in its grip, and to hold him so tightly that he could not advance.

We were ascending the avenue when he thus paused; the hall was before us. Lifting his eye to its battlements, he cast over them a glare such as I never saw before or since. Pain, shame, ire—impatience, disgust, detestation—seemed momentarily to hold a quivering conflict in the large pupil dilating under his ebon eyebrow. Wild was the wrestle which should be paramount; but another feeling rose and triumphed: something hard and cynical; self-willed and resolute: it settled his passion and petrified his countenance: he went on:—

'During the moment I was silent, Miss Eyre, I was arranging a point with my destiny. She stood there, by that beech-trunk—a hag like one of those who appeared to Macbeth on the heath of Forres. "You like Thornfield?" she said, lifting her finger; and then she wrote in the air a memento, which ran in lurid hieroglyphics all along the house-front, between the upper and lower row of windows. "Like it if you can!" "Like it if you dare!"

' "I will like it," said I. "I dare like it;" and (he subjoined moodily) I will keep my word: I will break obstacles to happiness, to goodness—yes, goodness; I wish to be a better man than I have been; than I am—as Job's leviathan broke the spear, the dart and the habergeon, hinderances which others count as iron and brass, I will esteem but straw and rotten wood.'

Adèle here ran before him with her shuttlecock. 'Away!' he cried harshly; 'keep at a distance, child; or go in to Sophie!' Continuing then to pursue his walk in silence, I ventured to recall him to the point whence he had abruptly diverged:—

'Did you leave the balcony, sir,' I asked, 'when Mdlle. Varens entered?'

I almost expected a rebuff for this hardly well-timed question; but, on the contrary, waking out of his scowling abstraction, he turned his eyes towards me, and the shade seemed to clear off his brow. 'Oh, I had forgotten Céline! Well, to resume. When I saw my charmer thus come in accompanied by a cavalier, I seemed to hear a hiss, and the green snake of jealousy, rising on undulating coils from the moonlit balcony, glided within my waistcoat, and ate its way in two minutes to my heart's core. Strange!' he exclaimed, suddenly starting again from the point. 'Strange that I should choose you for the confidant of all this, young lady: passing strange that you should listen

to me quietly, as if it were the most usual thing in the world for a man like me to tell stories of his opera-mistresses to a quaint, inexperienced girl like you! But the last singularity explains the first, as I intimated once before: you, with your gravity, considerateness, and caution were made to be the recipient of secrets. Besides, I know what sort of a mind I have placed in communication with my own: I know it is not one liable to take infection: it is a peculiar mind; it is an unique one. Happily I do not mean to harm it: but, if I did, it would not take harm from me. The more you and I converse, the better; for while I cannot blight you, you may refresh me.' After this digression he proceeded:—

'I remained in the balcony. "They will come to her boudoir no doubt," thought I: "let me prepare an ambush." So putting my hand in through the open window, I drew the curtain over it, leaving only an opening through which I could take observations; then I closed the casement, all but a chink just wide enough to furnish an outlet to lovers' whispered vows: then I stole back to my chair; and as I resumed it the pair came in. My eye was quickly at the aperture. Céline's chamber-maid entered, lit a lamp, left it on the table and withdrew. The couple were thus revealed to me clearly: both removed their cloaks, and there was "the Varens" shining in satin and jewels,—my gifts of course,—and there was her companion in an officer's uniform; and I knew him for a young roué of a vicomte—a brainless and vicious youth whom I had sometimes met in society, and had never thought of hating because I despised him so absolutely. On recognising him, the fang of the snake, jealousy, was instantly broken; because at the same moment my love for Céline sank under an extinguisher. A woman who could betray me for such a rival was not worth contending for: she deserved only scorn; less, however, than I, who had been her dupe.

'They began to talk; their conversation eased me completely: frivolous, mercenary, heartless, and senseless, it was rather calculated to weary than enrage a listener. A card of mine lay on the table; this being perceived brought my name under discussion. Neither of them possessed energy or wit to belabour me soundly; but they insulted me as coarsely as they could in their little way: especially Céline; who even waxed rather brilliant on my personal defects—deformities she termed them. Now it had been her custom to launch out into fervent admiration of what she called my "beauté mâle": wherein she differed diametrically from you, who told me point blank, at the second interview, that you did not think me handsome. The contrast struck me at the time, and'—

Adèle here came running up again.

'Monsieur, John has just been to say that your agent has called and wishes to see you.'

'Ah! in that case I must abridge. Opening the window, I walked in upon

them; liberated Céline from my protection; gave her notice to vacate her hotel; offered her a purse for immediate exigencies; disregarded screams, hysterics, prayers, protestations, convulsions; made an appointment with the vicomte for a meeting at the Bois de Boulogne. Next morning I had the pleasure of encountering him; left a bullet in one of his poor, etiolated arms, feeble as the wing of a chicken in the pip, and then thought I had done with the whole crew. But unluckily the Varens, six months before, had given me this filette Adèle; who she affirmed was my daughter; and perhaps she may be, though I see no proofs of such grim paternity written in her countenance: Pilot is more like me than she. Some years after I had broken with the mother, she abandoned her child and ran away to Italy with a musician or singer. I acknowledged no natural claim on Adèle's part to be supported by me; nor do I now acknowledge any, for I am not her father; but hearing that she was quite destitute, I e'en took the poor thing out of the slime and mud of Paris, and transplanted it here, to grow up clean in the wholesome soil of an English country garden. Mrs. Fairfax found you to train it; but now you know that it is the illegitimate offspring of a French opera-girl, you will perhaps think differently of your post and protegée: you will be coming to me some day with notice that you have found another place—that you beg me to look out for a new governess, etc.—eh?'

'No: Adèle is not answerable for either her mother's faults or yours; I have a regard for her, and now that I know she is, in a sense, parentless— forsaken by her mother and disowned by you, sir—I shall cling closer to her than before. How could I possibly prefer the spoilt pet of a wealthy family, who would hate her governess as a nuisance, to a lonely little orphan, who leans towards her as a friend?'

'Oh, that is the light in which you view it! Well, I must go in now; and you too: it darkens.'

But I stayed out a few minutes longer with Adèle and Pilot—ran a race with her, and played a game of battledore and shuttlecock. When we went in and I had removed her bonnet and coat, I took her on my knee; kept her there an hour, allowing her to prattle as she liked: not rebuking even some little freedoms and trivialities into which she was apt to stray when much noticed: and which betrayed in her a superficiality of character, in- herited probably from her mother, hardly congenial to an English mind. Still she had her merits; and I was disposed to appreciate all that was good in her to the utmost. I sought in her countenance and features a likeness to Mr. Rochester, but found none: no trait, no turn of expression announced relation- ship. It was a pity: if she could but have been proved to resemble him, he would have thought more of her.

It was not till after I had withdrawn to my own chamber for the night, that I steadily reviewed the tale Mr. Rochester had told me. As he had

said, there was probably nothing at all extraordinary in the substance of the narrative itself: a wealthy Englishman's passion for a French dancer, and her treachery to him, were every-day matters enough, no doubt, in society; but there was something decidedly strange in the paroxysm of emotion which had suddenly seized him, when he was in the act of expressing the present contentment of his mood, and his newly revived pleasure in the old hall and its environs. I meditated wonderingly on this incident: but gradually quitting it, as I found it for the present inexplicable, I turned to the consideration of my master's manner to myself. The confidence he had thought fit to repose in me seemed a tribute to my discretion: I regarded and accepted it as such. His deportment had now for some weeks been more uniform towards me than at the first. I never seemed in his way; he did not take fits of chilling hauteur: when he met me unexpectedly, the encounter seemed welcome; he had always a word and sometimes a smile for me: when summoned by formal invitation to his presence, I was honoured by a cordiality of reception that made me feel I really possessed the power to amuse him, and that these evening conferences were sought as much for his pleasure as for my benefit.

I, indeed, talked comparatively little; but I heard him talk with relish. It was his nature to be communicative; he liked to open to a mind unacquainted with the world, glimpses of its scenes and ways (I do not mean its corrupt scenes and wicked ways, but such as derived their interest from the great scale on which they were acted, the strange novelty by which they were characterised); and I had a keen delight in receiving the new ideas he offered, in imagining the new pictures he portrayed, or followed him in thought through the new regions he disclosed, never startled or troubled by one noxious allusion.

The ease of his manner freed me from painful restraint: the friendly frankness, as correct as cordial, with which he treated me, drew me to him. I felt at times as if he were my relation, rather than my master: yet he was imperious sometimes still; but I did not mind that; I saw it was his way. So happy, so gratified did I become with this new interest added to life, that I ceased to pine after kindred: my thin crescent-destiny seemed to enlarge; the blanks of existence were filled up; my bodily health improved; I gathered flesh and strength.

And was Mr. Rochester now ugly in my eyes? No, reader: gratitude, and many associations, all pleasurable and genial, made his face the object I best liked to see; his presence in a room was more cheering than the brightest fire. Yet I had not forgotten his faults: indeed, I could not, for he brought them frequently before me. He was proud, sardonic, harsh to inferiority of every description: in my secret soul I knew that his great kindness to me was balanced by unjust severity to many others. He was moody, too; unac-

countably so: I more than once, when sent for to read to him, found him sitting in his library alone, with his head bent on his folded arms; and, when he looked up, a morose, almost a malignant scowl, blackened his features. But I believed that his moodiness, his harshness, and his former faults of morality (I say *former*, for now he seemed corrected of them) had their source in some cruel cross of fate. I believed he was naturally a man of better tendencies, higher principles, and purer tastes than such as circumstances had developed, education instilled, or destiny encouraged. I thought there were excellent materials in him; though for the present they hung together somewhat spoiled and tangled. I cannot deny that I grieved for his grief, whatever that was, and would have given much to assuage it.

Though I had now extinguished my candle and was laid down in bed, I could not sleep, for thinking of his look when he paused in the avenue, and told how his destiny had risen up before him, and dared him to be happy at Thornfield.

'Why not?' I asked myself. 'What alienates him from the house? Will he leave it again soon? Mrs. Fairfax said he seldom stayed here longer than a fortnight at a time; and he has now been resident eight weeks. If he does go, the change will be doleful. Suppose he should be absent, spring, summer, and autumn: how joyless sunshine and fine days will seem!'

I hardly knew whether I had slept or not after this musing; at any rate, I started wide awake on hearing a vague murmur, peculiar and lugubrious, which sounded, I thought, just above me. I wished I had kept my candle burning: the night was drearily dark; my spirits were depressed. I rose and sat up in bed, listening. The sound was hushed.

I tried again to sleep; but my heart beat anxiously: my inward tranquillity was broken. The clock, far down in the hall, struck two. Just then it seemed my chamber-door was touched; as if fingers had swept the panels in groping a way along the dark gallery outside. I said, 'Who is there?' Nothing answered. I was chilled with fear.

All at once I remembered that it might be Pilot: who, when the kitchen-door chanced to be left open, not unfrequently found his way up to the threshold of Mr. Rochester's chamber: I had seen him lying there myself, in the mornings. The idea calmed me somewhat: I lay down. Silence composes the nerves; and as an unbroken hush now reigned again through the whole house, I began to feel the return of slumber. But it was not fated that I should sleep that night. A dream had scarcely approached my ear, when it fled affrighted, scared by a marrow-freezing incident enough.

This was a demoniac laugh—low, suppressed, and deep—uttered, as it seemed, at the very key-hole of my chamber door. The head of my bed was near the door, and I thought at first the goblin-laughter stood at my bedside—or rather, crouched by my pillow: but I rose, looked round, and could see

nothing; while, as I still gazed, the unnatural sound was reiterated: and I knew it came from behind the panels. My first impulse was to rise and fasten the bolt; my next, again to cry out, 'Who is there?'

Something gurgled and moaned. Ere long, steps retreated up the gallery towards the third story staircase: a door had lately been made to shut in that staircase; I heard it open and close, and all was still.

'Was that Grace Poole? and is she possessed with a devil?' thought I. Impossible now to remain longer by myself: I must go to Mrs. Fairfax. I hurried on my frock and a shawl; I withdrew the bolt and opened the door with a trembling hand. There was a candle burning just outside, left on the matting in the gallery. I was surprised at this circumstance: but still more was I amazed to perceive the air quite dim, as if filled with smoke; and, while looking to the right hand and left, to find whence these blue wreaths issued, I became further aware of a strong smell of burning.

Something creaked: it was a door ajar, and that door was Mr. Rochester's, and the smoke rushed in a cloud from thence. I thought no more of Mrs. Fairfax; I thought no more of Grace Poole or the laugh: in an instant, I was within the chamber. Tongues of flame darted round the bed: the curtains were on fire. In the midst of blaze and vapour, Mr. Rochester lay stretched motionless, in deep sleep.

'Wake! wake!' I cried—I shook him, but he only murmured and turned: the smoke had stupified him. Not a moment could be lost: the very sheets were kindling. I rushed to his basin and ewer; fortunately, one was wide and the other deep, and both were filled with water. I heaved them up, deluged the bed and its occupant, flew back to my own room, brought my own water-jug, baptized the couch afresh, and, by God's aid, succeeded in extinguishing the flames which were devouring it.

The hiss of the quenched element, the breakage of a pitcher which I had flung from my hand when I had emptied it, and, above all, the splash of the shower-bath I had liberally bestowed, roused Mr. Rochester at last. Though it was now dark, I knew he was awake; because I heard him fulminating strange anathemas at finding himself lying in a pool of water.

'Is there a flood?' he cried.

'No, sir,' I answered; 'but there has been a fire: get up, do, you are quenched now; I will fetch you a candle.'

'In the name of all the elves in Christendom, is that Jane Eyre?' he demanded. 'What have you done with me, witch, sorceress? Who is in the room besides you? Have you plotted to drown me?'

'I will fetch you a candle, sir; and in Heaven's name, get up. Somebody has plotted something: you cannot too soon find out who and what it is.'

'There—I am up now; but at your peril you fetch a candle yet: wait two minutes till I get into some dry garments, if any dry there be—yes, here is

my dressing-gown. Now run!'

I did run; I brought the candle which still remained in the gallery. He took it from my hand, held it up, and surveyed the bed, all blackened and scorched, the sheets drenched, the carpet round swimming in water.

'What is it? and who did it?' he asked.

I briefly related to him what had transpired: the strange laugh I had heard in the gallery; the step ascending to the third story; the smoke,— the smell of fire which had conducted me to his room; in what state I had found matters there, and how I had deluged him with all the water I could lay hands on.

He listened very gravely; his face, as I went on, expressed more concern than astonishment; he did not immediately speak when I had concluded.

'Shall I call Mrs. Fairfax?' I asked.

'Mrs. Fairfax? No: what the deuce would you call her for? What can she do? Let her sleep unmolested.'

'Then I will fetch Leah, and wake John and his wife.'

'Not at all: just be still. You have a shawl on? if you are not warm enough, you may take my cloak yonder; wrap it about you, and sit down in the arm-chair: there,—I will put it on. Now place your feet on the stool, to keep them out of the wet. I am going to leave you a few minutes. I shall take the candle. Remain where you are till I return; be as still as a mouse. I must pay a visit to the second story. Don't move, remember, or call any one.'

He went: I watched the light withdraw. He passed up the gallery very softly, unclosed the staircase door with as little noise as possible, shut it after him, and the last ray vanished. I was left in total darkness. I listened for some noise, but heard nothing. A very long time elapsed. I grew weary: it was cold, in spite of the cloak; and then I did not see the use of staying, as I was not to rouse the house. I was on the point of risking Mr. Rochester's displeasure, by disobeying his orders, when the light once more gleamed dimly on the gallery-wall, and I heard his unshod feet tread the matting.

'I hope it is he,' thought I, 'and not something worse.'

He re-entered, pale and very gloomy. 'I have found it all out,' said he, setting his candle down on the washstand; 'it is as I thought.'

'How, sir?'

He made no reply, but stood with his arms folded, looking on the ground. At the end of a few minutes, he inquired in rather a peculiar tone:—

'I forget whether you said you saw anything when you opened your chamber door.'

'No, sir, only the candlestick on the ground.'

'But you heard an odd laugh? You have heard that laugh before, I should think, or something like it?'

'Yes, sir: there is a woman who sews here, called Grace Poole,—she laughs in that way. She is a singular person.'

'Just so. Grace Poole—you have guessed it. She is, as you say, singular,—very. Well, I shall reflect on the subject. Meantime, I am glad that you are the only person, besides myself, acquainted with the precise details of tonight's incident. You are no talking fool: say nothing about it. I will account for this state of affairs (pointing to the bed): and now return to your own room. I shall do very well on the sofa in the library for the rest of the night. It is near four:—in two hours the servants will be up.'

'Good-night, then, sir,' said I, departing.

He seemed surprised—very inconsistently so, as he had just told me to go.

'What!' he exclaimed,' are you quitting me already: and in that way?'

'You said I might go, sir,'

'But not without taking leave; not without a word or two of acknowledgment and good will: not, in short, in that brief, dry fashion. Why, you have saved my life!—snatched me from a horrible and excruciating death!—and you walk past me as if we were mutual strangers! At least shake hands.'

He held out his hand; I gave him mine: he took it first in one, then in both his own.

'You have saved my life: I have a pleasure in owing you so immense a debt. I cannot say more. Nothing else that has being would have been tolerable to me in the character of creditor for such an obligation: but you: it is different;—I feel your benefits no burden, Jane.'

He paused; gazed at me; words almost visible trembled on his lips,—but his voice was checked.

'Good-night again, sir. There is no debt, benefit, burden, obligation, in the case.'

'I knew,' he continued, 'you would do me good in some way, at some time;—I saw it in your eyes when I first beheld you: their expression and smile did not—(again he stopped)—did not (he proceeded hastily) strike delight to my very inmost heart so for nothing. People talk of natural sympathies; I have heard of·good genii:—there are grains of truth in the wildest fable. My cherished preserver, good-night!'

Strange energy was in his voice; strange fire in his look.

'I am glad I happened to be awake,' I said: and then I was going.

'What! you *will* go?'

'I am cold, sir.'

'Cold? Yes,—and standing in a pool! Go, then, Jane; go!' But he still retained my hand, and I could not free it. I bethought myself of an expedient.

'I think I hear Mrs. Fairfax move, sir,' said I.

'Well, leave me:' he relaxed his fingers, and I was gone.

I regained my couch, but never thought of sleep. Till morning dawned I was tossed on a buoyant but unquiet sea, where billows of trouble rolled under surges of joy. I thought sometimes I saw beyond its wild waters a shore,

sweet as the hills of Beulah; and now and then a freshening gale, wakened by hope, bore my spirit triumphantly towards the bourne: but I could not reach it, even in fancy,—a counteracting breeze blew off land, and continually drove me back. Sense would resist delirium: judgment would warn passion. Too feverish to rest, I rose as soon as day dawned.

CHAPTER 16

I both wished and feared to see Mr. Rochester on the day which followed this sleepless night: I wanted to hear his voice again, yet feared to meet his eye. During the early part of the morning, I momentarily expected his coming; he was not in the frequent habit of entering the school-room; but he did step in for a few minutes sometimes, and I had the impression that he was sure to visit it that day.

Bu t the morning passed just as usual: nothing happened to interrupt the quiet course of Adèle's studies; only, soon after breakfast, I heard some bustle in the neighbourhood of Mr. Rochester's chamber, Mrs. Fairfax's voice, and Leah's, and the cook's—that is, John's wife—and even John's own gruff tones. There were exclamations of 'What a mercy master was not burnt in his bed!' 'It is always dangerous to keep a candle lit at night.' 'How providential that he had presence of mind to think of the water-jug!' 'I wonder he waked nobody!' 'It is to be hoped he will not take cold with sleeping on the library sofa,' etc.

To much confabulation succeeded a sound of scrubbing and setting to rights; and when I passed the room, in going downstairs to dinner, I saw through the open door that all was again restored to complete order; only the bed was stripped of its hangings. Leah stood up in the windowseat, rubbing the panes of glass dimmed with smoke. I was about to address her, for I wished to know what account had been given of the affair: but, on advancing, I saw a second person in the chamber—a woman sitting on a chair by the bedside, and sewing rings to new curtains. That woman was no other than Grace Poole.

There she sat, staid and taciturn-looking, as usual, in her brown stuff gown, her check apron, white handkerchief, and cap. She was intent on her work, in which her whole thoughts seemed absorbed: on her hard forehead, and in her common-place features, was nothing either of the paleness or desperation one would have expected to see marking the countenance of a woman who had attempted murder; and whose intended victim had followed her last night to her lair, and (as I believed) charged her with the crime she wished to perpetrate. I was amazed—confounded. She looked up, while I still gazed at her: no start, no increase or failure of colour betrayed emotion, consciousness of guilt, or fear of detection. She said 'Good morning, Miss,' in her usual

phlegmatic and brief manner; and taking up another ring and more tape, went on with her sewing.

'I will put her to some test,' thought I: 'such absolute impenetrability is past comprehension.'

'Good morning, Grace,' I said. 'Has anything happened here? I thought I heard the servants all talking together a while ago.'

'Only master had been reading in his bed last night; he fell asleep with his candle lit, and the curtains got on fire; but, fortunately, he awoke before the bed-clothes or the wood-work caught, and contrived to quench the flame with the water in the ewer.'

'A strange affair!' I said, in a low voice: then, looking at her fixedly,—'Did Mr. Rochester wake nobody? Did no one hear him move?'

She again raised her eyes to me; and this time there was something of consciousness in their expression. She seemed to examine me warily; then she answered,—

'The servants sleep so far off, you know, Miss, they would not be likely to hear. Mrs. Fairfax's room and yours are the nearest to master's; but Mrs. Fairfax said she heard nothing: when people get elderly, they often sleep heavy.' She paused, and then added, with a sort of assumed indifference, but still in a marked and significant tone, 'But you are young, Miss; and I should say a light sleeper: perhaps you may have heard a noise?'

'I did,' said I, dropping my voice, so that Leah, who was still polishing the panes, could not hear me, 'and at first I thought it was Pilot: but Pilot cannot laugh; and I am certain I heard a laugh, and a strange one.'

She took a new needleful of thread, waxed it carefully, threaded her needle with a steady hand, and then observed, with perfect composure,—

'It is hardly likely master would laugh, I should think, Miss, when he was in such danger: you must have been dreaming.'

'I was not dreaming,' I said, with some warmth, for her brazen coolness provoked me. Again she looked at me; and with the same scrutinising and conscious eye.

'Have you told master that you heard a laugh?' she inquired.

'I have not had the opportunity of speaking to him this morning.'

'You did not think of opening your door and looking out into the gallery?' she further asked.

She appeared to be cross-questioning me; attempting to draw from me information unawares: the idea struck me that if she discovered I knew or suspected her guilt, she would be playing off some of her malignant pranks on me; I thought it advisable to be on my guard.

'On the contrary,' said I, 'I bolted my door.'

'Then you are not in the habit of bolting your door every night before you get into bed?'

'Fiend! she wants to know my habits, that she may lay her plans accordingly!' Indignation again prevailed over prudence; I replied sharply, 'Hitherto I have often omitted to fasten the bolt: I did not think it necessary. I was not aware any danger or annoyance was to be dreaded at Thornfield Hall: but in future' (and I laid marked stress on the words) 'I shall take good care to make all secure before I venture to lie down.'

'It will be wise so to do,' was her answer: 'this neighbourhood is as quiet as any I know, and I never heard of the hall being attempted by robbers since it was a house; though there are hundreds of pounds' worth of plate in the plate-closet, as is well known. And you see, for such a large house, there are very few servants, because master has never lived here much; and when he does come, being a bachelor, he needs little waiting on: but I always think it best to err on the safe side; a door is soon fastened, and it is as well to have a drawn bolt between one and any mischief that may be about. A deal of people, Miss, are for trusting all to Providence; but I say Providence will not dispense with the means, though he often blesses them when they are used discreetly.' And here she closed her harangue: a long one for her, and uttered with the demureness of a Quakeress.

I still stood absolutely dumbfoundered at what appeared to me her miraculous self-possession and most inscrutable hypocrisy, when the cook entered.

'Mrs. Poole,' said she, addressing Grace, 'the servants' dinner will soon be ready: will you come down?'

'No; just put my pint of porter and bit of pudding on a tray, and I'll carry it upstairs.'

'You'll have some meat?'

'Just a morsel, and a taste of cheese, that's all.'

'And the sago?'

'Never mind it, at present: I shall be coming down before tea-time: I'll make it myself.'

The cook here turned to me, saying that Mrs. Fairfax was waiting for me: so I departed.

I hardly heard Mrs. Fairfax's account of the curtain conflagration during dinner, so much was I occupied in puzzling my brains over the enigmatical character of Grace Poole; and still more in pondering the problem of her position at Thornfield: in questioning why she had not been given into custody that morning; or, at the very least, dismissed from her master's service. He had almost as much as declared his conviction of her criminality last night: what mysterious cause withheld him from accusing her? Why had he enjoined me, too, to secrecy? It was strange: a bold, vindictive, and haughty gentleman seemed somehow in the power of one of the meanest of his dependants; so much in her power, that even when she lifted her hand against his

life, he dared not openly charge her with the attempt, much less punish her for it.

Had Grace been young and handsome, I should have been tempted to think that tenderer feelings than prudence or fear influenced Mr. Rochester in her behalf; but, hard-favoured and matronly as she was, the idea could not be admitted. 'Yet,' I reflected, 'she has been young once; her youth would be contemporary with her master's: Mrs. Fairfax told me once, she had lived here many years. I don't think she can ever have been pretty; but, for aught I know, she may possess originality and strength of character to compensate for the want of personal advantages. Mr. Rochester is an amateur of the decided and eccentric: Grace is eccentric at least. What if a former caprice (a freak very possible to a nature so sudden and headstrong as his) has delivered him into her power, and she now exercises over his actions a secret influence, the result of his own indiscretion, which he cannot shake off, and dare not disregard?' But, having reached this point of conjecture, Mrs. Poole's square, flat figure, and uncomely, dry, even coarse face, recurred so distinctly to my mind's eye, that I thought, 'No; impossible! my supposition cannot be correct. Yet,' suggested the secret voice which talks to us in our hearts, '*you* are not beautiful either, and perhaps Mr. Rochester approves you: at any rate, you have often felt as if he did; and last night—remember his words; remember his look; remember his voice!'

I well remembered all: language, glance, and tone seemed at the moment vividly renewed. I was now in the school-room; Adéle was drawing; I bent over her and directed her pencil. She looked up with a sort of start.

'Qu'avez-vous, mademoiselle?' said she; 'Vos doigts tremblent comme la feuille, et vos joues sont rouges: mais, rouges comme des cerises!'

'I am hot, Adéle, with stooping!' She went on sketching, I went on thinking.

I hastened to drive from my mind the hateful notion I had been conceiving respecting Grace Poole: it disgusted me. I compared myself with her, and found we were different. Bessie Leaven had said I was quite a lady; and she spoke truth: I was a lady. And now I looked much better than I did when Bessie saw me: I had more colour and more flesh; more life, more vivacity; because I had brighter hopes and keener enjoyments.

'Evening approaches,' said I, as I looked towards the window. 'I have never heard Mr. Rochester's voice or step in the house to-day; but surely I shall see him before night: I feared the meeting in the morning: now I desire it, because expectation has been so long baffled that it is grown impatient.'

When dusk actually closed, and when Adéle left me to go and play in the nursery with Sophie, I did most keenly desire it. I listened for the bell to ring below; I listened for Leah coming up with a message; I fancied sometimes I heard Mr. Rochester's own tread, and I turned to the door, expecting it to open and admit him. The door remained shut: darkness only came in

through the window. Still it was not late: he often sent for me at seven and eight o'clock, and it was yet but six. Surely I should not be wholly disappointed to-night, when I had so many things to say to him! I wanted again to introduce the subject of Grace Poole, and to hear what he would answer; I wanted to ask him plainly if he really believed it was she who had made last night's hideous attempt; and if so, why he kept her wickedness a secret. It little mattered whether my curiosity irritated him; I knew the pleasure of vexing and soothing him by turns; it was one I chiefly delighted in, and a sure instinct always prevented me from going too far: beyond the verge of provocation I never ventured; on the extreme brink I liked well to try my skill. Retaining every minute form of respect, every propriety of my station, I could still meet him in argument without fear of uneasy restraint: this suited both him and me.

A tread creaked on the stairs at last; Leah made her appearance; but it was only to intimate that tea was ready in Mrs. Fairfax's room. Thither I repaired, glad at least to go downstairs; for that brought me, I imagined, nearer to Mr. Rochester's presence.

'You must want your tea,' said the good lady, as I joined her; 'you ate so little at dinner. I am afraid,' she continued, 'you are not well to-day: you look flushed and feverish.'

'Oh, quite well! I never felt better.'

'Then you must prove it by evincing a good appetite; will you fill the teapot while I knit off this needle?' Having completed her task, she rose to draw down the blind which she had hitherto kept up; by way, I suppose, of making the most of daylight: though dusk was now fast deepening into total obscurity.

'It is fair to-night,' said she, as she looked through the panes, 'though not starlight; Mr. Rochester has, on the whole, had a favourable day for his journey.'

'Journey!—Is Mr. Rochester gone anywhere? I did not know he was out.'

'Oh, he set off the moment he had breakfasted! He is gone to the Leas; Mr. Eshton's place, ten miles on the other side of Millcote; I believe there is quite a party assembled there; Lord Ingram, Sir George Lynn, Colonel Dent, and others.'

'Do you expect him back to-night?'

'No—nor to-morrow either; I should think he is very likely to stay a week or more: when these fine, fashionable people get together, they are so surrounded by elegance and gaiety; so well provided with all that can please and entertain, they are in no hurry to separate. Gentlemen, especially, are often in request on such occasions; and Mr. Rochester is so talented and so lively in society, that I believe he is a general favourite: the ladies are very fond of him; though you would not think his appearance calculated to re-

commend him particularly in their eyes: but I suppose his acquirements and abilities, perhaps his wealth and good blood, make amends for any little fault of look."

'Are there ladies at the Leas?'

'There are Mrs. Eshton and her three daughters—very elegant young ladies, indeed; and there are the Honourable Blanche and Mary Ingram; most beautiful women, I suppose: indeed I have seen Blanche, six or seven years since, when she was a girl of eighteen. She came here to a Christmas ball and party Mr. Rochester gave. You should have seen the dining-room that day—how richly it was decorated, how brilliantly lit up! I should think there were fifty ladies and gentlemen present—all of the first county-families; and Miss Ingram was considered the belle of the evening.'

'You saw her, you say, Mrs. Fairfax: what was she like?'

'Yes, I saw her. The dining-room doors were thrown open; and, as it was Christmas-time, the servants were allowed to assemble in the hall, to hear some of the ladies sing and play. Mr. Rochester would have me to come in, and I sat down in a quiet corner and watched them. I never saw a more splendid scene: the ladies were magnificently dressed; most of them—at least most of the younger ones—looked handsome; but Miss Ingram was certainly the queen.'

'And what was she like?'

'Tall, fine bust, sloping shoulders; long, graceful neck; olive complexion, dark and clear; noble features; eyes rather like Mr. Rochester's, large and black, and as brilliant as her jewels. And then she had such a fine head of hair; raven-black, and so becomingly arranged: a crown of thick plaits behind, and in front the longest, the glossiest curls I ever saw. She was dressed in pure white; an amber-coloured scarf was passed over her shoulder and across her breast, tied at the side, and descending in long, fringed ends below her knee. She wore an amber-coloured flower, too, in her hair: it contrasted well with the jetty mass of her curls.'

'She was greatly admired of course?'

'Yes, indeed: and not only for her beauty, but for her accomplishments. She was one of the ladies who sang: a gentleman accompanied her on the piano. She and Mr. Rochester sang a duet.'

'Mr. Rochester? I was not aware he could sing.'

'Oh! he has a fine bass voice, and an excellent taste for music.'

'And Miss Ingram: what sort of a voice had she?'

'A very rich and powerful one: she sang delightfully; it was a treat to listen to her;—and she played afterwards. I am no judge of music, but Mr. Rochester is; and I heard him say her execution was remarkably good.'

'And this beautiful and accomplished lady is not yet married?'

'It appears not: I fancy neither she nor her sister have very large fortunes.

Old Lord Ingram's estates were chiefly entailed, and the eldest son came in for everything almost.'

'But I wonder no wealthy nobleman or gentleman has taken a fancy to her: Mr. Rochester, for instance. He is rich, is he not?'

'Oh! yes. But you see there is a considerable difference in age: Mr. Rochester is near forty; she is but twenty-five.'

'What of that? More unequal matches are made every day.'

'True: yet I should scarcely fancy Mr. Rochester would entertain an idea of the sort. But you eat nothing: you have scarcely tasted since you began tea.'

'No: I am too thirsty to eat. Will you let me have another cup?'

I was about again to revert to the probability of a union between Mr. Rochester and the beautiful Blanche; but Adèle came in, and the conversation was turned into another channel.

When once more alone, I reviewed the information I had got; looked into my heart, examined its thoughts and feelings, and endeavoured to bring back with a strict hand such as had been straying through imagination's boundless and trackless waste, into the safe fold of common sense.

Arraigned at my own bar, Memory having given her evidence of the hopes, wishes, sentiments I had been cherishing since last night—of the general state of mind in which I had indulged for nearly a fortnight past; Reason having come forward and told in her own quiet way, a plain, unvarnished tale, showing how I had rejected the real, and rabidly devoured the ideal;—I pronounced judgment to this effect:—

That a greater fool than Jane Eyre had never breathed the breath of life: that a more fantastic idiot had never surfeited herself on sweet lies, and swallowed poison as if it were nectar.

'*You*,' I said, 'a favourite with Mr. Rochester? *You* gifted with the power of pleasing him? *You* of importance to him in any way? Go! your folly sickens me. And you have derived pleasure from occasional tokens of preference—equivocal tokens, shown by a gentleman of family, and a man of the world, to a dependant and a novice. How dared you? Poor stupid dupe!—Could not even self-interest make you wiser? You repeated to yourself this morning the brief scene of last night?—Cover your face and be ashamed! He said something in praise of your eyes, did he? Blind puppy! Open their bleared lids and look on your own accursed senselessness! It does good to no woman to be flattered by her superior, who cannot possibly intend to marry her; and it is madness in all women to let a secret love kindle within them, which, if unreturned and unknown, must devour the life that feeds it; and, if discovered and responded to, must lead, *ignis-fatuus*-like, into miry wilds whence there is no extrication.

'Listen, then, Jane Eyre, to your sentence: to-morrow, place the glass

before you, and draw in chalk your own picture, faithfully; without softening one defect: omit no harsh line, smooth away no displeasing irregularity; write under it, "Portrait of a Governess, disconnected, poor, and plain"

'Afterwards, take a piece of smooth ivory—you have one prepared in your drawing-box: take your pallette, mix your freshest, finest, clearest tints; choose your most delicate camel-hair pencils; delineate carefully the loveliest face you can imagine; paint it in your softest shades and sweetest hues, according to the description given by Mrs. Fairfax of Blanche Ingram: remember the raven ringlets, the oriental eye;—what! you revert to Mr. Rochester as a model! Order! No snivel!—no sentiment!—no regret! I will endure only sense and resolution. Recall the august yet harmonious lineaments, the Grecian neck and bust: let the round and dazzling arm be visible, and the delicate hand; omit neither diamond ring nor gold bracelet; portray faithfully the attire, aërial lace and glistening satin, graceful scarf and golden rose: call it "Blanche, an accomplished lady of rank."

'Whenever, in future, you should chance to fancy Mr. Rochester thinks well of you, take out these two pictures and compare them: say, "Mr. Rochester might probably win that noble lady's love, if he chose to strive for it; is it likely he would waste a serious thought on this indigent and insignificant plebeian?"'

'I'll do it,' I resolved; and having framed this determination, I grew calm, and fell asleep.

I kept my word. An hour or two sufficed to sketch my own portrait in crayons; and in less than a fortnight I had completed an ivory miniature of an imaginary Blanche Ingram. It looked a lovely face enough, and when compared with the real head in chalk, the contrast was as great as self-control could desire. I derived benefit from the task: it had kept my head and hands employed, and had given force and fixedness to the new impressions I wished to stamp indelibly on my heart.

Ere long, I had reason to congratulate myself on the course of wholesome discipline to which I had thus forced my feelings to submit: thanks to it, I was able to meet subsequent occurrences with a decent calm; which, had they found me unprepared, I should probably have been unequal to maintain, even externally.

CHAPTER 17

A week passed, and no news arrived of Mr. Rochester: ten days; and still he did not come. Mrs. Fairfax said she should not be surprised if he were to go straight from the Leas to London, and thence to the continent, and not show his face again at Thornfield for a year to come: he had not unfrequently

quitted it in a manner quite as abrupt and unexpected. When I heard this I was beginning to feel a strange chill and failing at the heart. I was actually permitting myself to experience a sickening sense of disappointment: but rallying my wits, and recollecting my principles, I at once called my sensations to order; and it was wonderful how I got over the temporary blunder—how I cleared up the mistake of supposing Mr. Rochester's movements a matter in which I had any cause to take a vital interest. Not that I humbled myself by a slavish notion of inferiority: on the contrary, I just said—

'You have nothing to do with the master of Thornfield, further than to receive the salary he gives you for teaching his protegée, and to be grateful for such respectful and kind treatment as, if you do your duty, you have a right to expect at his hands. Be sure that is the only tie he seriously acknowledges between you and him: so don't make him the object of your fine feelings, your raptures, agonies, and so forth. He is not of your order: keep to your caste; and be too self-respecting to lavish the love of the whole heart, soul, and strength, where such a gift is not wanted and would be despised.'

I went on with my day's business tranquilly; but ever and anon vague suggestions kept wandering across my brain of reasons why I should quit Thornfield; and I kept involuntarily framing advertisements and pondering conjectures about new situations: these thoughts I did not think it necessary to check; they might germinate and bear fruit if they could.

Mr. Rochester had been absent upwards of a fortnight, when the post brought Mrs. Fairfax a letter.

'It is from the master,' said she, as she looked at the direction. 'Now I suppose we shall know whether we are to expect his return or not.'

And while she broke the seal and perused the document, I went on taking my coffee (we were at breakfast): it was hot, and I attributed to that circumstance a fiery glow which suddenly rose to my face. Why my hand shook, and why I involuntarily spilt half the contents of my cup into my saucer, I did not choose to consider.

'Well—I sometimes think we are too quiet; but we run a chance of being busy enough now: for a little while at least,' said Mrs. Fairfax, still holding the note before her spectacles.

Ere I permitted myself to request an explanation, I tied the string of Adèle's pinafore, which happened to be loose: having helped her also to another bun and refilled her mug with milk, I said, nonchalantly:—

'Mr. Rochester is not likely to return soon, I suppose?'

'Indeed, he is—in three days, he says; that will be next Thursday; and not alone either. I don't know how many of the fine people at the Leas are coming with him: he sends directions for all the best bed-rooms to be prepared; and the library and drawing-rooms are to be cleaned out; and I am to get more kitchen hands from the George Inn, at Millcote, and from wherever else

I can; and the ladies will bring their maids and the gentlemen their valets: so we shall have a full house of it.' And Mrs. Fairfax swallowed her breakfast and hastened away to commence operations.

The three days were, as she had foretold, busy enough. I had thought all the rooms at Thornfield beautifully clean and well arranged: but it appears I was mistaken. Three women were got to help; and such scrubbing, such brushing, such washing of paint and beating of carpets, such taking down and putting up of pictures, such polishing of mirrors and lustres, such lighting of fires in bed-rooms, such airing of sheets and feather-beds on hearths, I never beheld, either before or since. Adèle ran quite wild in the midst of it: the preparations for company and the prospect of their arrival, seemed to throw her into ecstasies. She would have Sophie to look over all her 'toilettes,' as she called frocks; to furbish up any that were 'passées,' and to air and arrange the new. For herself, she did nothing but caper about in the front chambers, jump on and off the bedsteads, and lie on the mattresses and piled-up bolsters and pillows before the enormous fires roaring in the chimneys. From school duties she was exonerated: Mrs. Fairfax had pressed me into her service, and I was all day in the store-room, helping (or hindering) her and the cook; learning to make custards and cheesecakes and French pastry, to truss game and garnish dessert-dishes.

The party were expected to arrive on Thursday afternoon, in time for dinner at six. During the intervening period I had no time to nurse chimeras; and I believe I was as active and gay as anybody—Adèle excepted. Still, now and then, I received a damping check to my cheerfulness; and was, in spite of myself, thrown back on the region of doubts and portents, and dark conjectures. This was when I chanced to see the third story staircase door (which of late had always been kept locked) open slowly, and give passage to the form of Grace Poole, in prim cap, white apron, and handkerchief; when I watched her glide along the gallery, her quiet tread muffled in a list slipper; when I saw her look into the bustling, topsy-turvy bed-rooms,— just say a word, perhaps, to the charwoman about the proper way to polish a grate, or clean a marble mantel-piece, or take stains from papered walls, and then pass on. She would thus descend to the kitchen once a day, eat her dinner, smoke a moderate pipe on the hearth, and go back, carrying her pot of porter with her, for her private solace, in her own gloomy, upper haunt. Only one hour in the twenty-four did she pass with her fellow-servants below; all the rest of her time was spent in some low-ceiled, oaken chamber of the third story: there she sat and sewed—and probably laughed drearily to herself,—as companionless as a prisoner in his dungeon.

The strangest thing of all was, that not a soul in the house, except me, noticed her habits, or seemed to marvel at them; no one discussed her position or employment; no one pitied her solitude or isolation. I once, indeed, over-

heard part of a dialogue between Leah and one of the charwomen, of which Grace formed the subject. Leah had been saying something I had not caught, and the charwoman remarked:—

'She gets good wages, I guess?'

'Yes,' said Leah; 'I wish I had as good; not that mine are to complain of,—there's no stinginess at Thornfield; but they're not one-fifth of the sum Mrs. Poole receives. And she is laying by: she goes every quarter to the bank at Millcote. I should not wonder but she has saved enough to keep her independent if she liked to leave; but I suppose she's got used to the place; and then she's not forty yet, and strong and able for anything. It is too soon for her to give up business.'

'She is a good hand, I daresay,' said the charwoman.

'Ah!—she understands what she has to do,—nobody better,' rejoined Leah significantly; 'and it is not every one could fill her shoes; not for all the money she gets.'

"That it is not!' was the reply. 'I wonder whether master'—

The charwoman was going on; but here Leah turned and perceived me, and she instantly gave her companion a nudge.

'Doesn't she know?' I heard the woman whisper.

Leah shook her head, and the conversation was of course dropped. All I had gathered from it amounted to this,—that there was a mystery at Thornfield; and that from participation in that mystery, I was purposely excluded.

Thursday came: all work had been completed the previous evening; carpets were laid down, bed-hangings festooned, radiant white counterpanes spread, toilet tables arranged, furniture rubbed, flowers piled in vases: both chambers and saloons looked as fresh and bright as hands could make them. The hall, too, was scoured; and the great carved clock, as well as the steps and banisters of the staircase, were polished to the brightness of glass; in the dining-room, the side-board flashed resplendent with plate; in the drawing-room and boudoir, vases of exotics bloomed on all sides.

Afternoon arrived: Mrs. Fairfax assumed her best black satin gown, her gloves, and her gold watch; for it was her part to receive the company,—to conduct the ladies to their rooms, etc. Adèle, too, would be dressed: though I thought she had little chance of being introduced to the party that day at least. However, to please her, I allowed Sophie to apparel her in one of her short, full muslin frocks. For myself, I had no need to make any change; I should not be called upon to quit my sanctum of the school-room; for a sanctum it was now become to me,—'a very pleasant refuge in time of trouble.'

It had been a mild, serene spring day; one of those days which, towards the end of March or the beginning of April, rise shining over the earth as heralds of summer. It was drawing to an end now; but the evening was

even warm, and I sat at work in the school-room with the window open.

'It gets late,' said Mrs. Fairfax, entering in rustling state. 'I am glad I ordered dinner an hour after the time Mr. Rochester mentioned; for it is past six now. I have sent John down to the gates to see if there is anything on the road: one can see a long way from thence in the direction of Millcote.' She went to the window. 'Here he is!' said she. 'Well John' (leaning out) 'any news?'

'They're coming, ma'am,' was the answer. "They'll be here in ten minutes.'

Adèle flew to the window. I followed; taking care to stand on one side, so that, screened by the curtain, I could see without being seen.

The ten minutes John had given seemed very long, but at last wheels were heard; four equestrians galloped up the drive, and after them came two open carriages. Fluttering veils and waving plumes filled the vehicles; two of the cavaliers were young, dashing-looking gentlemen; the third was Mr. Rochester, on his black horse, Mesrour; Pilot bounding before him: at his side rode a lady, and he and she were the first of the party. Her purple riding-habit almost swept the ground, her veil streamed long on the breeze; mingling with its transparent folds, and gleaming through them shone rich raven ringlets.

'Miss Ingram!' exclaimed Mrs. Fairfax, and away she hurried to her post below.

The cavalcade, following the sweep of the drive, quickly turned the angle of the house, and I lost sight of it. Adèle now petitioned to go down; but I took her on my knee and gave her to understand that she must not on any account think of venturing in sight of the ladies, either now or at any other time, unless expressly sent for: that Mr. Rochester would be very angry, etc. 'Some natural tears she shed' on being told this; but as I began to look very grave, she consented at last to wipe them.

A joyous stir was now audible in the hall: gentlemen's deep tones, and ladies' silvery accents blent harmoniously together, and distinguishable above all, though not loud, was the sonorous, voice of the master of Thornfield Hall, welcoming his fair and gallant guests under its roof. Then light steps ascended the stairs; and there was a tripping through the gallery, and soft cheerful laughs, and opening and closing doors, and, for a time, a hush.

'Elles changent de toilettes,' said Adèle; who, listening attentively, had followed every movement; and she sighed.

'Chez maman,' said she, 'quand il y avait du monde, je le suivais partout, au salon et à leurs chambres; souvent je regardais les femmes de chambre coiffer et habiller les dames, et c'était si amusant: comme cela on apprend.'

'Don't you feel hungry, Adèle?'

'Mais oui, mademoiselle: voilà cinq ou six heures que nous n'avons pas mangé.'

'Well now, while the ladies are in their rooms, I will venture down and get you something to eat.'

And issuing from my asylum with precaution, I sought a back-stairs which conducted directly to the kitchen. All in that region was fire and commotion; the soup and fish were in the last stage of projection, and the cook hung over her crucibles in a frame of mind and body threatening spontaneous combustion. In the servants' hall two coachmen and three gentlemen's gentlemen stood or sat round the fire; the Abigails, I suppose, were upstairs with their mistresses: the new servants that had been hired from Millcote, were bustling about everywhere. Threading this chaos, I at last reached the larder; there I took possession of a cold chicken, a roll of bread, some tarts, a plate or two and a knife and fork: with this booty I made a hasty retreat. I had regained the gallery, and was just shutting the back-door behind me, when an accelerated hum warned me that the ladies were about to issue from their chambers. I could not proceed to the school-room without passing some of their doors, and running the risk of being surprised with my cargo of victualage; so I stood still at this end, which, being windowless, was dark: quite dark now, for the sun was set and twilight gathering.

Presently the chambers gave up their fair tenants one after another: each came out gaily and airily, with dress that gleamed lustrous through the dusk. For a moment they stood grouped together at the other extremity of the gallery, conversing in a key of sweet subdued vivacity; they then descended the staircase almost as noiselessly as a bright mist rolls down a hill. Their collective appearance had left on me an impression of high-born elegance, such as I had never before received.

I found Adèle peeping through the school-room door, which she held ajar. 'What beautiful ladies!' cried she in English. 'Oh, I wish I might go to them! Do you think Mr. Rochester will send for us by-and-by, after dinner?'

'No, indeed, I don't; Mr. Rochester has something else to think about. Never mind the ladies to-night; perhaps you will see them to-morrow: here is your dinner.'

She was really hungry, so the chicken and tarts served to divert her attention for a time. It was well I secured this forage; or both she, I and Sophie, to whom I conveyed a share of our repast, would have run a chance of getting no dinner at all: every one downstairs was too much engaged to think of us. The dessert was not carried out till after nine; and at ten, footmen were still running to and fro with trays and coffee-cups. I allowed Adèle to sit up much later than usual; for she declared she could not possibly go to sleep while the doors kept opening and shutting below, and people bustling about. Besides, she added, a message might possibly come from Mr. Rochester when she was undressed; 'et alors quel dommage!'

I told her stories as long as she would listen to them; and then for a change I took her out into the gallery. The hall lamp was now lit, and it amused her to look over the balustrade and watch the servants passing backwards

and forwards. When the evening was far advanced, a sound of music issued from the drawing-room, whither the piano had been removed; Adèle and I sat down on the top step of the stairs to listen. Presently a voice blent with the rich tones of the instrument; it was a lady who sang, and very sweet her notes were. The solo over, a duet followed, and then a glee: a joyous conversational murmur filled up the intervals. I listened long: suddenly I discovered that my ear was wholly intent on analysing the mingled sounds, and trying to discriminate amidst the confusion of accents those of Mr. Rochester; and when it caught them, which it soon did, it found a further task in framing the tones, rendered by distance inarticulate, into words.

The clock struck eleven. I looked at Adèle, whose head leant against my shoulder; her eyes were waxing heavy, so I took her up in my arms and carried her off to bed. It was near one before the gentlemen and ladies sought their chambers.

The next day was as fine as its predecessor; it was devoted by the party to an excursion to some site in the neighbourhood. They set out early in the forenoon, some on horseback, the rest in carriages; I witnessed both the departure and the return. Miss Ingram, as before, was the only lady equestrian; and, as before, Mr. Rochester galloped at her side; the two rode a little apart from the rest. I pointed out this circumstance to Mrs. Fairfax, who was standing at the window with me:—

'You said it was not likely they should think of being married,' said I, 'but you see Mr. Rochester evidently prefers her to any of the other ladies.'

'Yes; I daresay: no doubt he admires her.'

'And she him,' I added; 'look how she leans her head towards him as if she were conversing confidentially; I wish I could see her face; I have never had a glimpse of it yet.'

'You will see her this evening,' answered Mrs. Fairfax. 'I happened to remark to Mr. Rochester how much Adèle wished to be introduced to the ladies, and he said: 'Oh! let her come into the drawing-room after dinner; and request Miss Eyre to accompany her.''

'Yes—he said that from mere politeness: I need not go, I am sure,' I answered.

'Well—I observed to him that as you were unused to company, I did not think you would like appearing before so gay a party—all strangers; and he replied, in his quick way: "Nonsense! If she objects, tell her it is my particular wish; and if she resists, say I shall come and fetch her in case of contumacy."'

'I will not give him that trouble,' I answered. 'I will go, if no better may be: but I don't like it. Shall you be there, Mrs. Fairfax?'

'No; I pleaded off, and he admitted my plea. I'll tell you how to manage so as to avoid the embarrassment of making a formal entrance, which is the most disagreeable part of the business. You must go into the drawing-room

while it is empty, before the ladies leave the dinner-table; choose your seat in any quiet nook you like; you need not stay long after the gentlemen come in, unless you please: just let Mr. Rochester see you are there and then slip away—nobody will notice you.'

'Will these people remain long, do you think?'

'Perhaps two or three weeks; certainly not more. After the Easter recess, Sir George Lynn, who was lately elected member for Millcote, will have to go up to town and take his seat; I daresay Mr. Rochester will accompany him: it surprises me that he has already made so protracted a stay at Thornfield.'

It was with some trepidation that I perceived the hour approach when I was to repair with my charge to the drawing-room. Adèle had been in a state of ecstasy all day, after hearing she was to. be presented to the ladies in the evening; and it was not till Sophie commenced the operation of dressing her, that she sobered down. Then the importance of the process quickly steadied her; and by the time she had her curls arranged in well-smoothed, drooping clusters, her pink satin frock put on, her long sash tied, and her lace mittens adjusted, she looked as grave as any judge. No need to warn her not to disarrange her attire: when she was dressed, she sat demurely down in her little chair, taking care previously to lift up the satin skirt for fear she should crease it, and assured me she would not stir thence till I was ready. This I quickly was: my best dress (the silver-grey one, purchased for Miss Temple's wedding, and never worn since) was soon put on; my hair was soon smoothed; my sole ornament, the pearl brooch, soon assumed. We descended.

Fortunately there was another entrance to the drawing-room than that through the saloon where they were all seated at dinner. We found the apartment vacant; a large fire burning silently on the marble hearth, and wax candles shining in bright solitude, amid the exquisite flowers with which the tables were adorned. The crimson curtain hung before the arch: slight as was the separation this drapery formed from the party in the adjoining saloon, they spoke in so low a key that nothing of their conversation could be distinguished beyond a soothing murmur.

Adèle, who appeared to be still under the influence of a most solemnising impression, sat down, without a word, on the footstool I pointed out to her. I retired to a window-seat, and, taking a book from a table near, endeavoured to read. Adèle brought her stool to my feet; ere long she touched my knee.

'What is it, Adèle?'

'Est-ce que je ne puis pas prendre une seule de ces fleurs magnifiques, Mademoiselle? Seulement pour completer ma toilette.'

'You think too much of your "toilette," Adèle: but you may have a flower.'

And I took a rose from a vase and fastened it in her sash. She sighed a sigh of ineffable satisfaction, as if her cup of happiness were now full. I turned my face away to conceal a smile I could not suppress: there was something ludicrous as well as painful in the little Parisienne's earnest and innate devotion to matters of dress.

A soft sound of rising now became audible; the curtain was swept back from the arch; through it appeared the dining-room, with its lit lustre pouring down light on the silver and glass of a magnificent dessert-service covering a long table; a band of ladies stood in the opening; they entered, and the curtain fell behind them.

There were but eight; yet somehow as they flocked in, the gave the impression of a much larger number. Some of them were very tall, many were dressed in white, and all had a sweeping amplitude of array that seemed to magnify their persons as a mist magnifies the moon. I rose and curtseyed to them: one or two bent their heads in return; the others only stared at me.

They dispersed about the room; reminding me, by the lightness and buoyancy of their movements, of a flock of white plumy birds. Some of them threw themselves in half-reclining positions on the sofas and ottomans: some bent over the tables and examined the flowers and books: the rest gathered in a group round the fire: all talked in a low but clear tone which seemed habitual to them. I knew their names afterwards, and may as well mention them now.

First, there was Mrs. Eshton and two of her daughters. She had evidently been a handsome woman, and was well preserved still. Of her daughters, the eldest, Amy, was rather little; naive, and child-like in face and manner, and piquant in form: her white muslin dress and blue sash became her well. The second, Louisa, was taller and more elegant in figure; with a very pretty face, of that order the French term 'minois chiffonné': both sisters were fair as lilies.

Lady Lynn was a large and stout personage of about forty; very erect, very haughty-looking, richly dressed in a satin robe of changeful sheen: her dark hair shone glossily under the shade of an azure plume, and within the circlet of a band of gems.

Mrs. Colonel Dent was less showy; but, I thought, more lady-like. She had a slight figure, a pale, gentle face, and fair hair. Her black satin dress, her scarf of rich foreign lace, and her pearl ornaments, pleased me better than the rainbow radiance of the titled dame.

But the three most distinguished—partly, perhaps, because the tallest figures of the band—were the Dowager Lady Ingram and her daughters, Blanche and Mary. They were all three of the loftiest stature of woman. The dowager might be between forty and fifty: her shape was still fine; her hair (by candlelight at least) still black; her teeth, too, were still appar-

ently perfect. Most people would have termed her a splendid woman of her age: and so she was, no doubt, physically speaking; but then there was an expression of almost insupportable haughtiness in her bearing and countenance. She had Roman features and a double chin, disappearing into a throat like a pillar: these features appeared to me not only inflated and darkened, but even furrowed with pride; and the chin was sustained by the same principle, in a position of almost preternatural erectness. She had, likewise, a fierce and a hard eye: it reminded me of Mrs. Reed's; she mouthed her words in speaking; her voice was deep, its inflections very pompous, very dogmatical, —very intolerable, in short. A crimson velvet robe, and a shawl turban of some gold-wrought Indian fabric, invested her (I suppose she thought) with a truly imperial dignity.

Blanche and Mary were of equal stature,—straight and tall as poplars. Mary was too slim for her height; but Blanche was moulded like a Dian. I regarded her, of course, with special interest. First, I wished to see whether her appearance accorded with Mrs. Fairfax's description; secondly, whether it at all resembled the fancy miniature I had painted of her; and thirdly—it will out!—whether it were such as I should fancy likely to suit Mr. Rochester's taste.

As far as person went, she answered point for point, both to my picture and Mrs. Fairfax's description. The noble bust, the sloping shoulders, the graceful neck, the dark eyes and black ringlets were all there;—but her face? Her face was like her mother's; a youthful unfurrowed likeness: the same low brow, the same high features, the same pride. It was not, however, so saturnine a pride: she laughed continually; her laugh was satirical, and so was the habitual expression of her arched and haughty lip.

Genius is said to be self-conscious: I cannot tell whether Miss Ingram was a genius, but she was self-conscious—remarkably self-conscious indeed. She entered into a discourse on botany with the gentle Mrs. Dent. It seems Mrs. Dent had not studied that science: though, as she said, she liked flowers, 'especially wild ones;' Miss Ingram had, and she ran over its vocabulary with an air. I presently perceived she was (what is vernacularly termed) *trailing* Mrs. Dent; that is, playing on her ignorance: her *trail* might be clever, but it was decidedly not good-natured. She played: her execution was brilliant; she sang: her voice was fine; she talked French apart to her mama; and she talked it well, with fluency and with a good accent.

Mary had a milder and more open countenance than Blanche; softer features too, and a skin some shades fairer (Miss Ingram was dark as a Spaniard)—but Mary was deficient in life: her face lacked expression, her eye lustre; she had nothing to say, and having once taken her seat, remained fixed like a statue in its niche. The sisters were both attired in spotless white.

And did I now think Miss Ingram such a choice as Mr. Rochester would

be likely to make? I could not tell—I did not know his taste in female beauty. If he liked the majestic, she was the very type of majesty: then she was accomplished, sprightly. Most gentlemen would admire her, I thought; and that he *did* admire her, I already seemed to have obtained proof: to remove the last shade of doubt, it remained but to see them together.

You are not to suppose, reader, that Adèle has all this time been sitting motionless on the stool at my feet: no; when the ladies entered, she rose, advanced to meet them, made a stately reverence, and said, with gravity,—

'Bon jour, mesdames.'

And Miss Ingram had looked down at her with a mocking air, and exclaimed, 'Oh, what a little puppet!'

Lady Lynn had remarked, 'It is Mr. Rochester's ward, I suppose—the little French girl he was speaking of.'

Mrs. Dent had kindly taken her hand, and given her a kiss. Amy and Louisa Eshton had cried out simultaneously—

'What a love of a child!'

And then they had called her to a sofa, where she now sat, ensconced between them, chattering alternately in French and broken English; absorbing not only the young ladies' attention, but that of Mrs. Eshton and Lady Lynn, and getting spoilt to her heart's content.

At last coffee is brought in, and the gentlemen are summoned. I sit in the shade—if any shade there be in this brilliantly-lit apartment; the window-curtain half hides me. Again the arch yawns: they come. The collective appearance of the gentlemen, like that of the ladies, is very imposing: they are all costumed in black; most of them are tall, some young. Henry and Frederick Lynn are very dashing sparks, indeed; and Colonel Dent is a fine soldierly man. Mr. Eshton, the magistrate of the district, is gentleman-like: his hair is quite white, his eyebrows and whiskers still dark, which gives him something of the appearance of a 'père noble de théâtre.' Lord Ingram, like his sisters, is very tall; like them, also, he is handsome; but he shares Mary's apathetic and listless look: he seems to have more length of limb than vivacity of blood or vigour of brain.

And where is Mr. Rochester?

He comes in last: I am not looking at the arch, yet I see him enter. I try to concentrate my attention on those netting needles, on the meshes of the purse I am forming—I wish to think only of the work I have in my hands, to see only the silver beads and silk threads that lie in my lap; whereas, I distinctly behold his figure, and I inevitably recall the moment when I last saw it: just after I had rendered him, what he deemed, an essential service—and he, holding my hand, and looking down on my face, surveyed me with eyes that revealed a heart full and eager to overflow; in whose emotions I had a part. How near had I approached him at that moment! What had

occurred since, calculated to change his and my relative positions? Yet now, how distant, how far estranged we were! So far estranged, that I did not expect him to come and speak to me. I did not wonder, when, without looking at me, he took a seat at the other side of the room, and began conversing with some of the ladies.

No sooner did I see that his attention was riveted on them, and that I might gaze without being observed, than my eyes were drawn involuntarily to his face: I could not keep their lids under control: they would rise and the irids would fix on him. I looked, and had an acute pleasure in looking,—a precious, yet poignant pleasure; pure gold, with a steely point of agony: a pleasure like what the thirst-perishing man might feel who knows the well to which he has crept is poisoned, yet stoops and drinks divine draughts nevertheless.

Most true it is that 'beauty is in the eye of the gazer.' My master's colourless, olive face, square, massive brow, broad and jetty eyebrows, deep eyes, strong features, firm, grim mouth,—all energy, decision, will,—were not beautiful, according to rule; but they were more than beautiful to me: they were full of an interest, an influence that quite mastered me,—that took my feelings from my own power and fettered them in his. I had not intended to love him: the reader knows I had wrought hard to extirpate from my soul the germs of love there detected; and now, at the first renewed view of him, they spontaneously revived, green and strong! He made me love him without looking at me.

I compared him with his guests. What was the gallant grace of the Lynns, the languid elegance of Lord Ingram, — even the military distinction of Colonel Dent, contrasted with his look of native pith and genuine power? I had no sympathy in their appearance, their expression: yet I could imagine that most observers would call them attractive, handsome, imposing; while they would pronounce Mr. Rochester at once harsh-featured and melancholy-looking. I saw them smile, laugh—it was nothing: the light of the candles had as much soul in it as their smile; the tinkle of the bell as much significance as their laugh. I saw Mr. Rochester smile:—his stern features softened; his eye grew both brilliant and gentle, its ray both searching and sweet. He was talking, at the moment, to Louisa and Amy Eshton. I wondered to see them receive with calm that look which seemed to me so penetrating: I expected their eyes to fall, their colour to rise under it; yet I was glad when I found they were in no sense moved. 'He is not to them what he is to me,' I thought: 'he is not of their kind. I believe he is of mine;—I am sure he is, —I feel akin to him,—I understand the language of his countenance and movements: though rank and wealth sever us widely, I have something in my brain and heart, in my blood and nerves, that assimilates me mentally to him. Did I say, a few days since, that I had nothing to do with him but to receive my salary at his hands? Did I forbid myself to think of him in any

other light than as a paymaster? Blasphemy against nature! Every good, true, vigorous feeling I have, gathers impulsively round him. I know I must conceal my sentiments: I must smother hope; I must remember that he cannot care much for me. For when I say that I am of his kind, I do not mean that I have his force to influence, and his spell to attract: I mean only that I have certain tastes and feelings in common with him. I must, then, repeat continually that we are for ever sundered:—and yet, while I breathe and think I must love him.'

Coffee is handed. The ladies, since the gentlemen entered, have become lively as larks; conversation waxes brisk and merry. Colonel Dent and Mr. Eshton argue on politics; their wives listen. The two proud dowagers, Lady Lynn and Lady Ingram, confabulate together. Sir George—whom, by-the-by, I have forgotten to describe,—a very big, and very fresh-looking country gentleman, stands before their sofa, coffee-cup in hand, and occasionally puts in a word. Mr. Frederick Lynn had taken a seat beside Mary Ingram, and is showing her the engravings of a splendid volume: she looks, smiles now and then, but apparently says little. The tall and phlegmatic Lord Ingram leans with folded arms on the chair-back of the little and lively Amy Eshton; she glances up at him, and chatters like a wren: she likes him better than she does Mr. Rochester. Henry Lynn has taken possession of an ottoman at the feet of Louisa; Adèle shares it with him: he is trying to talk French with her, and Louisa laughs at his blunders. With whom will Blanche Ingram pair? She is standing alone at the table, bending gracefully over an album. She seems waiting to be sought; but she will not wait too long: she herself selects a mate.

Mr. Rochester, having quitted the Eshtons, stands on the hearth as solitary as she stands by the table: she confronts him, taking her station on the opposite side of the mantelpiece.

'Mr. Rochester, I thought you were not fond of children?'

'Nor am I.'

'Then, what induced you to take charge of such a little doll as that?' (pointing to Adèle). 'Where did you pick her up?'

'I did not pick her up, she was left on my hands.'

'You should have sent her to school.'

'I could not afford it: schools are so dear.'

'Why, I suppose you have a governess for her: I saw a person with her just now—is she gone? Oh, no! there she is still behind the window-curtain. You pay her, of course; I should think it quite as expensive,—more so; for you have them both to keep in addition.'

I feared—or should I say, hoped?—the allusion to me would make Mr. Rochester glance my way; and I involuntarily shrank further into the shade: but he never turned his eyes.

'I have not considered the subject,' said he indifferently, looking straight before him.

'No—you men never do consider economy and commonsense. You should hear mama on the chapter of governesses: Mary and I have had, I should think, a dozen at least in our day; half of them detestable and the rest ridiculous, and all incubi—were they not, mama?'

'Did you speak, my own?'

The young lady thus claimed as the dowager's special property, reiterated her question with an explanation.

'My dearest, don't mention governesses; the word makes me nervous. I have suffered a martyrdom from their incompetency and caprice; I thank Heaven I have now done with them!'

Mrs. Dent here bent over to the pious lady, and whispered something in her ear; I suppose from the answer elicited, I was a reminder that one of the anathematised race was present.

'Tant pis!' said her ladyship, 'I hope it may do her good!' Then, in a lower tone, but still loud enough for me to hear, 'I noticed her; I am a judge of physiognomy, and in hers I see all the faults of her class.'

'What are they, madam?' inquired Mr. Rochester aloud.

'I will tell you in your private ear,' replied she, wagging her turban three times with portentous significancy.

'But my curiosity will be past its appetite; it craves food now.'

'Ask Blanche; she is nearer you than I.'

'Oh, don't refer him to me, mama! I have just one word to say of the whole tribe; they are a nuisance. Not that I ever suffered much from them; I took care to turn the tables. What tricks Theodore and I used to play on our Miss Wilsons, and Mrs. Greys, and Madame Jouberts! Mary was always too sleepy to join in a plot with spirit. The best fun was with Madame Joubert: Miss Wilson was a poor sickly thing, lachrymose and low-spirited: not worth the trouble of vanquishing, in short; and Mrs. Grey was coarse and insensible: no blow took effect on her. But poor Madame Joubert! I see her yet in her raging passions, when we had driven her to extremities—spilt our tea, crumbled our bread and butter, tossed our books up to the ceiling, and played a charivari with the ruler and desk, the fender and fire-irons. Theodore, do you remember those merry days?'

'Yaas, to be sure I do,' drawled Lord Ingram; 'and the poor old stick used to cry out "Oh you villains childs!"—and then we sermonised her on the presumption of attempting to teach such clever blades as we were, when she was herself so ignorant.'

'We did; and Tedo, you know, I helped you in prosecuting (or persecuting) your tutor, whey-faced Mr. Vining—the parson in the pip, as we used to call him. He and Miss Wilson took the liberty of falling in love with each

other—at least Tedo and I thought so; we surprised sundry tender glances and sighs which we interpreted as tokens of 'la belle passion', and I promise you the public soon had the benefit of our discovery: we employed it as a sort of lever to hoist our deadweights from the house. Dear mama, there, as soon as she got an inkling of the business, found out that it was of an immoral tendency. Did you not, my lady-mother?'

'Certainly, my best. And I was quite right; depend on that: there are a thousand reasons why liaisons between governesses and tutors should never be tolerated a moment in any well-regulated house; firstly'—

'Oh gracious, mama! Spare us the enumeration! Au reste, we all know them: danger of bad example to innocence of childhood; distractions and consequent neglect of duty on the part of the attached—mutual alliance and reliance; confidence thence resulting—insolence accompanying—mutiny and general blow-up. Am I right, Baroness Ingram, of Ingram Park?'

'My lily-flower, you are right now, as always.'

'Then no more need be said: change the subject.'

Amy Eshton, not hearing or not heeding this dictum, joined in with her soft, infantine tone: 'Louisa and I used to quiz our governess too; but she was such a good creature, she would bear anything: nothing put her out. She was never cross with us; was she, Louisa?'

'No, never: we might do what we pleased; ransack her desk and her work-box, and turn her drawers inside out; and she was so good-natured, she would give us anything we asked for.'

'I suppose, now,' said Miss Ingram, curling her lip sarcastically, 'we shall have an abstract of the memoirs of all the governesses extant: in order to avert such a visitation, I again move the introduction of a new topic. Mr. Rochester, do you second my motion?'

'Madam, I support you on this point as on every other.'

'Then on me be the onus of bringing it forward. Signior Eduardo, are you in voice to-night?'

'Donna Bianca, if you command it, I will be.'

'Then, signior, I lay on you my sovereign behest to furbish up your lungs and other vocal organs, as they will be wanted on my royal service.'

'Who would not be the Rizzio of so divine a Mary?'

'A fig for Rizzio!' cried she, tossing her head with all its curls, as she moved to the piano. 'It is my opinion the fiddler David must have been an insipid sort of fellow: I like black Bothwell better: to my mind a man is nothing without a spice of the devil in him; and history may say what it will of James Hepburn, but I have a notion, he was just the sort of wild, fierce, bandit hero whom I could have consented to gift with my hand.'

'Gentlemen, you hear! Now which of you most resembles Bothwell?' cried Mr. Rochester.

'I should say the preference lies with you,' responded Colonel Dent.

'On my honour, I am much obliged to you,' was the reply.

Miss Ingram, who had now seated herself with proud grace at the piano, spreading out her snowy robes in queenly amplitude, commenced a brilliant prelude; talking meantime. She appeared to be on her high horse to-night; both her words and her air seemed intended to excite not only the admiration, but the amazement of her auditors: she was evidently bent on striking them as something very dashing and daring indeed.

'Oh, I am so sick of the young men of the present day!' exclaimed she, rattling away at the instrument. 'Poor, puny things not fit to stir a step beyond papa's park-gates: nor to go even so far without mama's permission and guardianship! Creatures so absorbed in care about their pretty faces and their white hands, and their small feet; as if a man had anything to do with beauty! As if loveliness were not the special prerogative of woman—her legitimate appanage and heritage! I grant an ugly *woman* is a blot on the fair face of creation; but as to the *gentlemen*, let them be solicitous to possess only strength and valour: let their motto be:—Hunt, shoot, and fight: the rest is not worth a fillip. Such should be my device, were I a man.'

'Whenever I marry,' she continued after a pause which none interrupted, 'I am resolved my husband shall not be a rival, but a foil to me. I will suffer no competitor near the throne; I shall exact an undivided homage: his devotions shall not be shared between me and the shape he sees in his mirror. Mr. Rochester, now sing, and I will play for you.'

'I am all obedience,' was the response.

'Here then is a Corsair-song. Know that I doat on Corsairs; and for that reason, sing it "con spirito."'

'Commands from Miss Ingram's lips would put spirit into a mug of milk and water.'

'Take care, then: if you don't please me, I will shame you by showing how such things *should* be done.'

'That is offering a premium on incapacity: I shall now endeavour to fail.'

'Gardez-vous en bien! If you err wilfully, I shall devise a proportionate punishment.'

'Miss Ingram ought to be clement, for she has it in her power to inflict a chastisement beyond mortal endurance.'

'Ha! explain!' commanded the lady.

'Pardon me, madam: no need of explanation; your own fine sense must inform you that one of your frowns would be a sufficient substitute for capital punishment.'

'Sing!' said she, and again touching the piano, she commenced an accompaniment in spirited style.

'Now is my time to slip away,' thought I: but the tones that then severed the air arrested me. Mrs. Fairfax had said Mr. Rochester possessed a fine voice: he did—a mellow, powerful bass, into which he threw his own feeling, his own force; finding a way through the ear to the heart, and there waking sensation strangely. I waited till the last deep and full vibration had expired —till the tide of talk, checked an instant, had resumed its flow; I then quitted my sheltered corner and made my exit by the side-door, which was fortunately near. Thence a narrow passage led into the hall: in crossing it, I perceived my sandal was loose; I stopped to tie it, kneeling down for that purpose on the mat at the foot of the staircase. I heard the dining-room door unclose; a gentleman came out; rising hastily, I stood face to face with him: it was Mr. Rochester.

'How do you do?' he asked.

'I am very well, sir.'

'Why did you not come and speak to me in the room?'

I thought I might have retorted the question on him who put it: but I would not take that freedom. I answered:—

'I did not wish to disturb you, as you seemed engaged, sir.'

'What have you been doing during my absence?'

'Nothing particular; teaching Adèle as usual.'

'And getting a good deal paler than you were—as I saw at first sight. What is the matter?'

'Nothing at all, sir.'

'Did you take any cold that night you half drowned me?'

'Not the least.'

'Return to the drawing-room: you are deserting too early.'

'I am tired, sir.'

He looked at me for a minute.

'And a little depressed,' he said. 'What about? Tell me.'

'Nothing—nothing, sir. I am not depressed.'

'But I affirm that you are: so much depressed that a few more words would bring tears to your eyes—indeed, they are there now, shining and swimming; and a bead has slipped from the lash and fallen on to the flag. If I had time, and was not in mortal dread of some prating prig of a servant passing, I would know what all this means. Well, to-night I excuse you; but understand that so long as my visitors stay, I expect you to appear in the drawing-room every evening; it is my wish; don't neglect it. Now go, and send Sophie for Adèle. Good-night, my'——He stopped, bit his lip, and abruptly left me.

CHAPTER 18

Merry days were those at Thornfield Hall; and busy days too: how different from the first three months of stillness, monotony, and solitude I had passed beneath its roof! All sad feelings seemed now driven from the house, all gloomy associations forgotten: there was life everywhere, movement all day long. You could not now traverse the gallery, once so hushed, nor enter the front chambers, once so tenantless, without encountering a smart lady's maid or a dandy valet.

The kitchen, the butler's pantry, the servants' hall, the entrance hall, were equally alive; and the saloons were only left void and still, when the blue sky and halcyon sunshine of the genial spring weather called their occupants out into the grounds. Even when that weather was broken, and continuous rain set in for some days, no damp seemed cast over enjoyment: in-door amusements only became more lively and varied, in consequence of the stop put to out-door gaiety.

I wondered what they were going to do the first evening a change of entertainment was proposed: they spoke of 'playing charades,' but in my ignorance I did not understand the term. The servants were called in, the dining-room tables wheeled away, the lights otherwise disposed, the chairs placed in a semi-circle opposite the arch. While Mr. Rochester and the other gentlemen directed these alterations, the ladies were running up and down stairs ringing for their maids. Mrs. Fairfax was summoned to give information respecting the resources of the house in shawls, dresses, draperies of any kind; and certain wardrobes of the third story were ransacked, and their contents, in the shape of brocaded and hooped petticoats, satin sacques, black modes, lace lappets, etc., were brought down in armfuls by the Abigails; then a selection was made, and such things as were chosen were carried to the boudoir within the drawing-room.

Meantime, Mr. Rochester had again summoned the ladies round him, and was selecting certain of their number to be of his party. 'Miss Ingram is mine, of course,' said he: afterwards he named the two Misses Eshton, and Mrs. Dent. He looked at me: I happened to be near him, as I had been fastening the clasp of Mrs. Dent's bracelet, which had got loose.

'Will you play?' he asked. I shook my head. He did not insist, which I rather feared he would have done: he allowed me to return quietly to my usual seat.

He and his aids now withdrew behind the curtain: the other party, which was headed by Colonel Dent, sat down on the crescent of chairs. One of the gentlemen, Mr. Eshton, observing me, seemed to propose that I should be asked to join them; but Lady Ingram instantly negatived the notion.

'No,' I heard her say: 'she looks too stupid for any game of the sort.'

Ere long, a bell tinkled, and the curtain drew up. Within the arch, the

bulky figure of Sir George Lynn, whom Mr. Rochester had likewise chosen, was seen enveloped in a white sheet: before him, on a table, lay open a large book; and at his side stood Amy Eshton, draped in Mr. Rochester's cloak, and holding a book in her hand. Somebody, unseen, rang the bell merrily; then Adèle (who had insisted on being one of her guardian's party), bounded forward, scattering round her the contents of a basket of flowers she carried on her arm. Then appeared the magnificent figure of Miss Ingram, clad in white, a long veil on her head, and a wreath of roses round her brow: by her side walked Mr. Rochester, and together they drew near the table. They knelt; while Mrs. Dent and Louisa Eshton, dressed also in white, took up their stations behind them. A ceremony followed, in dumb show, in which it was easy to recognise the pantomime of a marriage. At its termination, Colonel Dent and his party consulted in whispers for two minutes, then the colonel called out,—

'Bride!' Mr. Rochester bowed, and the curtain fell.

A considerable interval elapsed before it again rose. Its second rising displayed a more elaborately prepared scene than the last. The drawing-room, as I have before observed, was raised two steps above the dining-room, and on the top of the upper step, placed a yard or two back within the room, appeared a large marble basin, which I recognised as an ornament of the conservatory—where it usually stood, surrounded by exotics, and tenanted by gold-fish—and whence it must have been transported with some trouble, on account of its size and weight.

Seated on the carpet, by the side of this basin, was seen Mr. Rochester, costumed in shawls, with a turban on his head. His dark eyes and swarth skin and Paynim features suited the costume exactly: he looked the very model of an eastern emir; an agent or a victim of the bowstring. Presently advanced into view Miss Ingram. She, too, was attired in oriental fashion: a crimson scarf tied sash-like round the waist: an embroidered handkerchief knotted about her temples; her beautifully-moulded arms bare, one of them up-raised in the act of supporting a pitcher, poised gracefully on her head. Both her cast of form and feature, her complexion and her general air, suggested the idea of some Israelitish princess of the patriarchal days; and such was doubtless the character she intended to represent.

She approached the basin, and bent over it as if to fill her pitcher; she again lifted it to her head. The personage on the well-brink now seemed to accost her; to make some request:—'She hasted, let down her pitcher on her hand and gave him to drink.' From the bosom of his robe, he then produced a casket, opened it and showed magnificent bracelets and earrings: she acted astonishment and admiration; kneeling, he laid the treasure at her feet; incredulity and delight were expressed by her looks and gestures; the stranger fastened the bracelets on her arms, and the rings in her ears. It was Eliezer

and Rebecca: the camels only were wanting.

The divining party again laid their heads together: apparently they could not agree about the word or syllable this scene illustrated. Colonel Dent, their spokesman, demanded 'the tableau of the Whole'; whereupon the curtain again descended.

On its third rising only a portion of the drawing-room was disclosed; the rest being concealed by a screen, hung with some sort of dark and coarse drapery. The marble basin was removed; in its place stood a deal table and a kitchen chair: these objects were visible by a very dim light proceeding from a horn lantern, the wax candles being all extinguished.

Amidst this sordid scene, sat a man with his clenched hands resting on his knees, and his eyes bent on the ground. I knew Mr. Rochester; though the begrimed face, the disordered dress (his coat hanging loose from one arm, as if it had been almost torn from his back in a scuffle), the desperate and scowling countenance, the rough, bristling hair might well have disguised him. As he moved, a chain clanked; to his wrists were attached fetters.

'Bridewell!' exclaimed Colonel Dent, and the charade was solved.

A sufficient interval having elapsed for the performers to assume their ordinary costume, they re-entered the dining-room. Mr. Rochester led in Miss Ingram; she was complimenting him on his acting.

'Do you know,' said she, 'that, of the three characters, I liked you in the last best? Oh, had you but lived a few years earlier, what a gallant gentleman-highwayman you would have made!'

'Is all the soot washed from my face?' he asked, turning it towards her.

'Alas, yes; the more's the pity! Nothing could be more becoming to your complexion than that ruffian's rouge.'

'You would like a hero of the road then?'

'An English hero of the road would be the next best thing to an Italian bandit; and that could only be surpassed by a Levantine pirate.'

'Well, whatever I am, remember you are my wife; we were married an hour since, in the presence of all these witnesses.' She giggled, and her colour rose.

'Now, Dent,' continued Mr. Rochester, 'it is your turn.' And as the other party withdrew, he and his band took the vacated seats. Miss Ingram placed herself at her leader's right hand; the other diviners filled the chairs on each side of him and her. I did not now watch the actors; I no longer waited with interest for the curtain to rise; my attention was absorbed by the spectators; my eyes, erewhile fixed on the arch, were now irresistibly attracted to the semicircle of chairs. What charade Colonel Dent and his party played, what word they chose, how they acquitted themselves, I no longer remember! but I still see the consultation which followed each scene: I see Mr. Rochester turn to Miss Ingram, and Miss Ingram to him; I see her incline her head

towards him, till the jetty curls almost touch his shoulder and wave against his cheek; I hear their mutual whisperings; I recall their interchanged glances; and something even of the feeling roused by the spectacle returns in memory at this moment.

I have told you, reader, that I had learnt to love Mr. Rochester: I could not unlove him now, merely because I found that he had ceased to notice me—because I might pass hours in his presence, and he would never once turn his eyes in my direction—because I saw all his attentions appropriated by a great lady, who scorned to touch me with the hem of her robes as she passed; who, if ever her dark and imperious eye fell on me by chance, would withdraw it instantly as from an object too mean to merit observation. I could not unlove him, because I felt sure he would soon marry this very lady—because I read daily in her a proud security in his intentions respecting her—because I witnessed hourly in him a style of courtship which, if careless and choosing rather to be sought than to seek, was yet, in its very carelessness, captivating, and in its very pride, irresistible.

There was nothing to cool or banish love in these circumstances; though much to create despair. Much too, you will think, reader, to engender jealousy: if a woman, in my position, could presume to be jealous of a woman in Miss Ingram's. But I was not jealous: or very rarely;—the nature of the pain I suffered could not be explained by that word. Miss Ingram was a mark beneath jealousy: she was too inferior to excite that feeling. Pardon this seeming paradox: I mean what I say. She was very showy, but she was not genuine: she had a fine person, many brilliant attainments; but her mind was poor, her heart barren by nature: nothing bloomed spontaneously on that soil; no unforced natural fruit delighted by its freshness. She was not good; she was not original: she used to repeat sounding phrases from books: she never offered, nor had, an opinion of her own. She advocated a high tone of sentiment; but she did not know the sensations of sympathy and pity; tenderness and truth were not in her. Too often she betrayed this, by the undue vent she gave to a spiteful antipathy she had conceived against little Adèle: pushing her away with some contumelious epithet if she happened to approach her; sometimes ordering her from the room, and always treating her with coldness and acrimony. Other eyes besides mine watched these manifestations of character—watched them closely, keenly, shrewdly. Yes: the future bridegroom, Mr. Rochester himself, exercised over his intended a ceaseless surveillance: and it was from this sagacity—this guardedness of his—this perfect, clear consciousness of his fair one's defects—this obvious absence of passion in his sentiments towards her, that my ever-torturing pain arose.

I saw he was going to marry her, for family, perhaps political reasons; because her rank and connections suited him; I felt he had not given her his love, and that her qualifications were ill adapted to win from him that treasure.

This was the point—this was where the nerve was touched and teased—this was where the fever was sustained and fed: *she could not charm him.*

If she had managed the victory at once, and he had yielded and sincerely laid his heart at her feet, I should have covered my face, turned to the wall, and (figuratively) have died to them. If Miss Ingram had been a good and noble woman, endowed with force, fervour, kindness, sense, I should have had one vital struggle with two tigers—jealousy and despair: then, my heart torn out and devoured, I should have admired her—acknowledged her excellence, and been quiet for the rest of my days: and the more absolute her superiority, the deeper would have been my admiration—the more truly tranquil my quiescence. But as matters really stood, to watch Miss Ingram's efforts at fascinating Mr. Rochester; to witness their repeated failure, herself unconscious that they did fail; vainly fancying that each shaft launched, hit the mark, and infatuatedly pluming herself on success, when her pride and self-complacency repelled further and further what she wished to allure—to witness *this*, was to be at once under ceaseless excitation and ruthless restraint.

Because, when she failed, I saw how she might have succeeded. Arrows that continually glanced off from Mr. Rochester's breast and fell harmless at his feet, might, I knew, if shot by a surer hand, have quivered keen in his proud heart—have called love into his stern eye, and softness into his sardonic face: or, better still, without weapons a silent conquest might have been won.

'Why can she not influence him more, when she is privileged to draw so near to him?' I asked myself. 'Surely she cannot truly like him; or not like him with true affection! If she did, she need not coin her smiles so lavishly; flash her glances so unremittingly; manufacture airs so elaborate, graces so multitudinous. It seems to me, that she might, by merely sitting quietly at his side, saying little and looking less, get nigher his heart. I have seen in his face a far different expression from that which hardens it now while she is so vivaciously accosting him; but then it came of itself: it was not elicited by meretricious arts and calculated manoeuvres; and one had but to accept it—to answer what he asked without pretension, to address him when needful without grimace—and it increased and grew kinder and more genial, and warmed one like a fostering sunbeam. How will she manage to please him when they are married? I do not think she will manage it; and yet it might be managed; and his wife might, I verily believe, be the very happiest woman the sun shines on.'

I have not yet said anything condemnatory of Mr. Rochester's project of marrying for interest and connections. It surprised me when I first discovered that such was his intention: I had thought him a man unlikely to be influenced by motives so common-place in his choice of a wife; but the longer I considered the position, education, etc. of the parties, the less I felt justified in judging and blaming either him or Miss Ingram, for acting in conformity to ideas

and principles instilled into them, doubtless, from their childhood. All their class held these principles: I supposed, then, they had reasons for holding them such as I could not fathom. It seemed to me that, were I a gentleman like him, I would take to my bosom only such a wife as I could love; but the very obviousness of the advantages to the husband's own happiness, offered by this plan, convinced me that there must be arguments against its general adoption of which I was quite ignorant: otherwise I felt sure all the world would act as I wished to act.

But in other points, as well as this, I was growing very lenient to my master: I was forgetting all his faults, for which I had once kept a sharp look-out. It had formerly been my endeavour to study all sides of his character: to take the bad with the good; and from the just weighing of both, to form an equitable judgment. Now I saw no bad. The sarcasm that had repelled, the harshness that had startled me once, were only like keen condiments in a choice dish: their presence was pungent, but their absence would be felt as comparatively insipid. And as for the vague something—was it a sinister or a sorrowful, a designing or a desponding expression?—that opened upon a careful observer, now and then, in his eye, and closed again before one could fathom the strange depth partially disclosed; that something which used to make me fear and shrink, as if I had been wandering amongst volcanic-looking hills, and had suddenly felt the ground quiver, and seen it gape: that something, I, at intervals, beheld still; and with throbbing heart, but not with palsied nerves. Instead of wishing to shun, I longed only to dare—to divine it; and I thought Miss Ingram happy, because one day she might look into the abyss at her leisure, explore its secrets and analyse their nature.

Meantime, while I thought only of my master and his future bride—saw only them, heard only their discourse, and considered only their movements of importance—the rest of the party were occupied with their own separate interests and pleasures. The ladies Lynn and Ingram continued to consort in solemn conferences; where they nodded their two turbans at each other, and held up their four hands in confronting gestures of surprise, or mystery, or horror, according to the theme on which their gossip ran, like a pair of magnified puppets. Mild Mrs. Dent talked with good-natured Mrs. Eshton; and the two sometimes bestowed a courteous word or smile on me. Sir George Lynn, Colonel Dent, and Mr. Eshton discussed politics, or county affairs, or justice business. Lord Ingram flirted with Amy Eshton; Louisa played and sang to and with one of the Messrs. Lynn, and Mary Ingram listened languidly to the gallant speeches of the other. Sometimes all, as with one consent, suspended their by-play to observe and listen to the principal actors: for, after all, Mr. Rochester, and—because closely connected with him—Miss Ingram, were the life and soul of the party. If he were absent from the room an hour, a perceptible dulness seemed to steal over the spirits of his guests;

and his re-entrance was sure to give a fresh impulse to the vivacity of conversation.

The want of his animating influence appeared to be peculiarly felt one day that he had been summoned to Millcote on business, and was not likely to return till late. The afternoon was wet: a walk the party had proposed to take to see a gipsy camp, lately pitched on a common beyond Hay, was consequently deferred. Some of the gentlemen were gone to the stables: the younger ones, together with the younger ladies, were playing billiards in the billiard-room. The dowagers Ingram and Lynn sought solace in a quiet game at cards. Blanche Ingram, after having repelled, by supercilious taciturnity, some efforts of Mrs. Dent and Mrs. Eshton to draw her into conversation, had first murmured over some sentimental tunes and airs on the piano, and then, having fetched a novel from the library, had flung herself in haughty listlessness on a sofa, and prepared to beguile, by the spell of fiction, the tedious hours of absence. The room and the house were silent: only now and then the merriment of the billiard players was heard from above.

It was verging on dusk, and the clock had already given warning of the hour to dress for dinner, when little Adèle, who knelt by me in the drawing-room window-seat, exclaimed:—

'Voilà Monsieur Rochester, qui revient!'

I turned, and Miss Ingram darted forwards from her sofa: the others, too, looked up from their several occupations; for at the same time a crunching of wheels, and a splashing tramp of horse-hoofs became audible on the wet gravel. A post-chaise was approaching.

'What can possess him to come home in that style?' said Miss Ingram. 'He rode Mesrour (the black horse), did he not, when he went out? and Pilot was with him:— what has he done with the animals?'

As she said this, she approached her tall person and ample garments so near the window, that I was obliged to bend back almost to the breaking of my spine: in her eagerness she did not observe me at first, but when she did, she curled her lip and moved to another casement. The post-chaise stopped; the driver rang the door bell, and a gentleman alighted, attired in travelling garb; but it was not Mr. Rochester; it was a tall, fashionable-looking man, a stranger.

'Provoking!' exclaimed Miss Ingram: 'you tiresome monkey!' (apostrophising Adèle) 'who perched you up in the window to give false intelligence?' and she cast on me an angry glance, as if I were in fault.

Some parleying was audible in the hall, and soon the new comer entered. He bowed to Lady Ingram, as deeming her the eldest lady present.

'It appears I come at an inopportune time, madam,' said he; 'when my friend, Mr. Rochester, is from home; but I arrive from a very long journey, and I think I may presume so far on old and intimate acquaintance as to

instal myself here till he returns.'

His manner was polite; his accent, in speaking, struck me as being somewhat unusual,—not precisely foreign, but still not altogether English; his age might be about Mr. Rochester's,—between thirty and forty; his complexion was singularly sallow: otherwise he was a fine-looking man, at first sight especially. On closer examination, you detected something in his face that displeased; or rather, that failed to please. His features were regular, but too relaxed: his eye was large and well cut, but the life looking out of it was a tame, vacant life—at least so I thought.

The sound of the dressing-bell dispersed the party. It was not till after dinner that I saw him again: he then seemed quite at his ease. But I liked his physiognomy even less than before: it struck me as being, at the same time, unsettled, and inanimate. His eye wandered, and had no meaning in its wandering: this gave him an odd look, such as I never remembered to have seen. For a handsome and not an unamiable-looking man, he repelled me exceedingly: there was no power in that smooth-skinned face of a full oval shape; no firmness in that aquiline nose, and small, cherry mouth; there was no thought on the low, even forehead; no command in that blank, brown eye.

As I sat in my usual nook, and looked at him with the light of the girandoles on the mantel-piece beaming full over him—for he occupied an armchair, drawn close to the fire, and kept shrinking still nearer, as if he were cold—I compared him with Mr. Rochester. I think (with deference be it spoken) the contrast could not be much greater between a sleek gander and a fierce falcon: between a meek sheep and the rough-coated keen-eyed dog, its guardian.

He had spoken of Mr. Rochester as an old friend. A curious friendship theirs must have been: a pointed illustration indeed, of the old adage that 'extremes meet.'

Two or three of the gentlemen sat near him, and I caught at times scraps of their conversation across the room. At first I could not make much sense of what I heard; for the discourse of Louisa Eshton and Mary Ingram, who sat nearer to me, confused the fragmentary sentences that reached me at intervals. These last were discussing the stranger: they both called him 'a beautiful man.' Louisa said he was 'a love of a creature,' and she 'adored him': and Mary instanced his 'pretty little mouth, and nice nose,' as her ideal of the charming.

'And what a sweet-tempered forehead he has!' cried Louisa,—'so smooth—none of those frowning irregularities I dislike so much: and such a placid eye and smile!'

And then, to my great relief, Mr. Henry Lynn summoned them to the other side of the room, to settle some point about the deferred excursion to Hay Common.

I was now able to concentrate my attention on the group by the fire, and I presently gathered that the new comer was called Mr. Mason: then I learned that he was but just arrived in England, and that he came from some hot country: which was the reason, doubtless, his face was so sallow, and that he sat so near the hearth, and wore a surtout in the house. Presently the words Jamaica, Kingston, Spanish Town, indicated the West Indies as his residence; and it was with no little surprise I gathered, ere long, that he had there first seen and become acquainted with Mr. Rochester. He spoke of his friend's dislike of the burning heats, the hurricanes, and rainy seasons of that region. I knew Mr. Rochester had been a traveller: Mrs. Fairfax had said so; but I thought the continent of Europe had bounded his wanderings: till now I had never heard a hint given of visits to more distant shores.

I was pondering these things, when an incident, and a somewhat unexpected one, broke the thread of my musings. Mr. Mason, shivering as some one chanced to open the door, asked for more coal to be put on the fire, which had burnt out its flame, though its mass of cinder still shone hot and red. The footman who brought the coal, in going out, stopped near Mr. Eshton's chair, and said something to him in a low voice, of which I heard only the words, 'old woman,'—'quite troublesome.'

'Tell her she shall be put in the stocks if she does not take herself off,' replied the magistrate.

'No—stop!' interrupted Colonel Dent. 'Don't send her away, Eshton; we might turn the thing to account; better consult the ladies.' And speaking aloud, he continued, 'Ladies, you talked of going to Hay Common to visit the gipsy camp; Sam, here, says that one of the old Mother Bunches is in the servants' hall at this moment, and insists upon being brought in before "the quality," to tell them their fortunes. Would you like to see her?'

'Surely, colonel,' cried Lady Ingram, 'you would not encourage such a low impostor? Dismiss her, by all means, at once!'

'But I cannot persuade her to go away, my lady,' said the footman; 'nor can any of the servants: Mrs. Fairfax is with her just now, entreating her to be gone; but she has taken a chair in the chimney-corner, and says nothing shall stir her from it till she gets leave to come in here.'

'What does she want?' asked Mrs. Eshton.

' "To tell the gentry their fortunes," she says, ma'am; and she swears she must and will do it.'

'What is she like?' inquired the Misses Eshton in a breath.

'A shockingly ugly old creature, miss; almost as black as a crock.'

'Why, she's a real sorceress!' cried Frederick Lynn. 'Let us have her in, of course.'

'To be sure,' rejoined his brother; 'it would be a thousand pities to throw away such a chance of fun.'

'My dear boys, what are you thinking about?' exclaimed Mrs. Lynn.

'I cannot possibly countenance any such inconsistent proceeding,' chimed in the Dowager Ingram.

'Indeed, mamma, but you can—and will,' pronounced the haughty voice of Blanche, as she turned round on the piano-stool; where till now she had sat silent, apparently examining sundry sheets of music. 'I have a curiosity to hear my fortune told: therefore, Sam, order the beldame forwards.'

'My darling Blanche! recollect'——

'I do—I recollect all you can suggest; and I must have my will—quick, Sam!'

'Yes—yes—yes!' cried all the juveniles, both ladies and gentlemen. 'Let her come—it will be excellent sport!'

The footman still lingered. 'She looks such a rough one,' said he.

'Go!' ejaculated Miss Ingram, and the man went.

Excitement instantly seized the whole party: a running fire of raillery and jests was proceeding when Sam returned.

'She won't come now,' said he. 'She says it's not her mission to appear before the "vulgar herd" (them's her words). I must show her into a room by herself, and then those who wish to consult her must go to her one by one.'

'You see now, my queenly Blanche,' began Lady Ingram, 'she encroaches. Be advised, my angel girl—and'——

'Show her into the library, of course,' cut in the 'angel girl.' 'It is not my mission to listen to her before the vulgar herd either: I mean to have her all to myself. Is there a fire in the library?'

'Yes, ma'am—but she looks such a tinkler.'

'Cease that chatter, blockhead! and do my bidding.'

Again Sam vanished; and mystery, animation, expectation rose to full flow once more.

'She's ready now,' said the footman, as he reappeared. 'She wishes to know who will be her first visitor.'

'I think I had better just look in upon her before any of the ladies go,' said Colonel Dent.

'Tell her, Sam, a gentleman is coming.'

Sam went and returned.

'She says, sir, that she'll have no gentlemen; they need not trouble themselves to come near her: nor,' he added, with difficulty suppressing a titter, 'any ladies either, except the young and single.'

'By Jove, she has taste!' exclaimed Henry Lynn.

Miss Ingram rose solemnly: 'I go first,' she said, in a tone which might have befitted the leader of a forlorn hope, mounting a breach in the van of his men.

'Oh, my best! oh, my dearest! pause—reflect!' was her mama's cry; but she swept past her in stately silence, passed through the door which Colonel Dent held open, and we heard her enter the library.

A comparative silence ensued. Lady Ingram thought it 'le cas' to wring her hands: which she did accordingly. Miss Mary declared she felt, for her part, she never dared venture. Amy and Louisa Eshton tittered under their breath, and looked a little frightened.

The minutes passed very slowly: fifteen were counted before the library door again opened. Miss Ingram returned to us through the arch.

Would she laugh? Would she take it as a joke? All eyes met her with a glance of eager curiosity, and she met all eyes with one of rebuff and coldness: she looked neither flurried nor merry; she walked stiffly to her seat, and took it in silence.

'Well, Blanche?' said Lord Ingram.

'What did she say, sister?' asked Mary.

'What do you think? How do you feel? Is she a real fortune-teller?' demanded the Misses Eshton.

'Now, now, good people,' returned Miss Ingram, 'don't press upon me. Really your organs of wonder and credulity are easily excited: you seem by the importance you all—my good mama included—ascribe to this matter—absolutely to believe we have a genuine witch in the house, who is in close alliance with the old gentleman. I have seen a gipsy vagabond; she has practised in hackneyed fashion the science of palmistry, and told me what such people usually tell. My whim is gratified; and now I think Mr. Eshton will do well to put the hag in the stocks to-morrow morning, as he threatened.'

Miss Ingram took a book, leant back in her chair, and so declined further conversation. I watched her for nearly half an hour: during all that time she never turned a page, and her face grew momently darker, more dissatisfied, and more sourly expressive of disappointment. She had obviously not heard anything to her advantage: and it seemed to me, from her prolonged fit of gloom and taciturnity, that she herself, notwithstanding her professed indifference, attached undue importance to whatever revelations had been made her.

Meantime, Mary Ingram, Amy and Louisa Eshton, declared they dared not go alone; and yet they all wished to go. A negotiation was opened through the medium of the ambassador, Sam; and after much pacing to and fro, till, I think, the said Sam's calves must have ached with the exercise, permission was at last, with great difficulty, extorted from the rigorous Sybil, for the three to wait upon her in a body.

Their visit was not so still as Miss Ingram's had been: we heard hysterical giggling and little shrieks proceeding from the library; and at the end of about twenty minutes they burst the door open, and came running across the

hall, as if they were half-scared out of their wits.

'I'm sure she is something not right!' they cried, one and all. 'She told us such things! She knows all about us!' and they sank breathless into the various seats the gentlemen hastened to bring them.

Pressed for further explanation, they declared she had told them of things they had said and done when they were mere children; described books and ornaments they had in their boudoirs at home: keepsakes that different relations had presented to them. They affirmed that she had even divined their thoughts, and had whispered in the ear of each the name of the person she liked best in the world, and informed them of what they most wished for.

Here the gentlemen interposed with earnest petitions to be further enlightened on these two last-named points; but they got only blushes, ejaculations, tremors, and titters, in return for their importunity. The matrons, meantime, offered vinaigrettes and wielded fans; and again and again reiterated the expression of their concern that their warning had not been taken in time; and the elder gentlemen laughed, and the younger urged their services on the agitated fair ones.

In the midst of the tumult, and while my eyes and ears were fully engaged in the scene before me, I heard a hem close at my elbow: I turned, and saw Sam.

'If you please, Miss, the gipsy declares that there is another young single lady in the room who has not been to her yet, and she swears she will not go till she has seen all. I thought it must be you: there is no one else for it. What shall I tell her?'

'Oh, I will go by all means,' I answered; and I was glad of the unexpected opportunity to gratify my much excited curiosity. I slipped out of the room, unobserved by any eye—for the company were gathered in one mass about the trembling trio just returned—and I closed the door quietly behind me.

'If you like, miss,' said Sam, 'I'll wait in the hall for you; and if she frightens you, just call and I'll come in.'

'No, Sam, return to the kitchen: I am not in the least afraid.' Nor was I; but I was a good deal interested and excited.

CHAPTER 19

The library looked tranquil enough as I entered it, and the Sybil—if Sybil she were, was seated snugly enough in an easy chair at the chimney-corner. She had on a red cloak and a black bonnet; or rather, a broad-brimmed gipsy hat, tied down with a striped handkerchief under the chin. An extinguished candle stood on the table; she was bending over the fire, and seemed reading in a little black book, like a prayer-book, by the light of the blaze: she

muttered the words to herself, as most old women do, while she read; she did not desist immediately on my entrance: it appeared she wished to finish a paragraph.

I stood on the rug and warmed my hands, which were rather cold with sitting at a distance from the drawing-room fire. I felt now as composed as ever I did in my life: there was nothing indeed in the gipsy's appearance to trouble one's calm. She shut her book and slowly looked up; her hat-brim partially shaded her face, yet I could see, as she raised it, that it was a strange one. It looked all brown and black: elf-locks bristled out from beneath a white band which passed under her chin, and came half over her cheeks, or rather jaws; her eye confronted me at once, with a bold and direct gaze.

'Well, and you want your fortune told?' she said in a voice as decided as her glance, as harsh as her features.

'I don't care about it, mother; you may please yourself: but I ought to warn you, I have no faith.'

'It's like your impudence to say so: I expected it of you; I heard it in your step as you crossed the threshold.'

'Did you? You've a quick ear.'

'I have; and a quick eye, and a quick brain.'

'You need them all in your trade.'

'I do; especially when I've customers like you to deal with. Why don't you tremble?'

'I'm not cold.'

'Why don't you turn pale?'

'I am not sick.'

'Why don't you consult my art?'

'I'm not silly.'

The old crone 'nichered' a laugh under her bonnet and bandage: she then drew out a short black pipe, and lighting it began to smoke. Having indulged a while in this sedative, she raised her bent body, took the pipe from her lips, and while gazing steadily at the fire, said very deliberately:—

'You are cold; you are sick; and you are silly.'

'Prove it,' I rejoined.

'I will; in few words. You are cold, because you are alone: no contact strikes the fire from you that is in you. You are sick: because the best of feelings, the highest and the sweetest given to man, keeps far away from you. You are silly, because, suffer as you may, you will not beckon it to approach; nor will you stir one step to meet it where it waits you.'

She again put her short, black pipe to her lips, and renewed her smoking with vigour.

'You might say all that to almost any one who, you knew, lived as a solitary dependant in a great house.'

'I might say it to almost any one; but would it be true of almost any one?'

'In my circumstances.'

'Yes; just so, in *your* circumstances: but find me another precisely placed as you are.'

'It would be easy to find you thousands.'

'You could scarcely find me one. If you knew it, you are peculiarly situated: very near happiness; yes; within reach of it. The materials are all prepared; there only wants a movement to combine them. Chance laid them somewhat apart; let them be once approached and bliss results.'

'I don't understand enigmas. I never could guess a riddle in my life.'

'If you wish me to speak more plainly, show me your palm.'

'And I must cross it with silver, I suppose?'

'To be sure.'

I gave her a shilling: she put it into an old stocking-foot which she took out of her pocket, and having tied it round and returned it, she told me to hold out my hand. I did. She approached her face to the palm, and pored over it without touching it.

'It is too fine,' said she. 'I can make nothing of such a hand as that; almost without lines; besides, what is in a palm? Destiny is not written there.'

'I believe you,' said I.

'No,' she continued, 'it is in the face: on the forehead, about the eyes, in the eyes themselves, in the lines of the mouth. Kneel, and lift up your head.'

'Ah! now you are coming to reality,' I said as I obeyed her. 'I shall begin to put some faith in you presently.'

I knelt within half a yard of her. She stirred the fire, so that a ripple of light broke from the disturbed coal: the glare, however, as she sat, only threw her face into deeper shadow: mine, it illumined.

'I wonder with what feelings you came to me to-night,' she said, when she had examined me a while. 'I wonder what thoughts are busy in your heart during all the hours you sit in yonder room with the fine people flitting before you like shapes in a magic lantern: just as little sympathetic communion passing between you and them, as if they were really mere shadows of human forms, and not the actual substance.'

'I feel tired often, sleepy sometimes; but seldom sad.'

'Then you have some secret hope to buoy you up and please you with whispers of the future?'

'Not I. The utmost I hope is, to save money enough out of my earnings to set up a school some day in a little house rented by myself.'

'A mean nutriment for the spirit to exist on: and sitting in that window-seat (you see I know your habits)'——

'You have learned them from the servants.'

'Ah! you think yourself sharp. Well—perhaps I have: to speak truth, I have an acquaintance with one of them—Mrs. Poole'——

I started to my feet when I heard the name.

'You have—have you?' thought I; 'there is diablerie in the business after all, then!'

'Don't be alarmed,' continued the strange being; 'she's a safe hand, is Mrs. Poole: close and quiet: any one may repose confidence in her. But, as I was saying: sitting in that window-seat, do you think of nothing but your future school? Have you no present interest in any of the company who occupy the sofas and chairs before you? Is there not one face you study? One figure whose movements you follow with, at least, curiosity?'

'I like to observe all the faces, and all the figures.'

'But do you never single one from the rest—or it may be, two?'

'I do, frequently; when the gestures or looks of a pair seem telling a tale: it amuses me to watch them.'

'What tale do you like best to hear?'

'Oh, I have not much choice! They generally run on the same theme—courtship; and promise to end in the same catastrophe—marriage.'

'And do you like that monotonous theme?'

'Positively, I don't care about it: it is nothing to me.'

'Nothing to you? When a lady, young and full of life and health, charming with beauty and endowed with the gifts of rank and fortune, sits and smiles in the eyes of a gentleman you'——

'I what?'

'You know—and, perhaps, think well of.'

'I don't know the gentlemen here. I have scarcely interchanged a syllable with one of them; and as to thinking well of them, I consider some respectable and stately, and middle-aged, and others young, dashing, handsome and lively; but certainly they are all at liberty to be the recipients of whose smiles they please, without my feeling disposed to consider the transaction of any moment to me.'

'You don't know the gentlemen here? You have not exchanged a syllable with one of them? Will you say that of the master of the house?'

'He is not at home.'

'A profound remark! A most ingenious quibble! He went to Millcote this morning, and will be back here tonight, or to-morrow: does that circumstance exclude him from the list of your acquaintance—blot him, as it were, out of existence?'

'No; but I can scarcely see what Mr. Rochester has to do with the theme you had introduced.'

'I was talking of ladies smiling in the eyes of gentlemen; and of late so many smiles have been shed into Mr. Rochester's eyes that they overflow like two

cups filled above the brim: have you never remarked that?'

'Mr. Rochester has a right to enjoy the society of his guests.'

'No question about his right: but have you never observed that, of all the tales told here about matrimony, Mr. Rochester has been favoured with the most lively and the most continuous?'

'The eagerness of a listener quickens the tongue of a narrator.' I said this rather to myself than to the gipsy; whose strange talk, voice, manner, had by this time wrapped me in a kind of dream. One unexpected sentence came from her lips after another, till I got involved in a web of mystification; and wondered what unseen spirit had been sitting for weeks by my heart watching its workings, and taking record of every pulse.

'Eagerness of a listener;' repeated she: 'yes; Mr. Rochester has sat by the hour, his ear inclined to the fascinating lips that took such delight in their task of communicating; and Mr. Rochester was so willing to receive and looked so grateful for the pastime given him: you have noticed this?'

'Grateful! I cannot remember detecting gratitude in his face.'

'Detecting! You have analysed, then. And what did you detect, if not gratitude?'

I said nothing.

'You have seen love: have you not?—and, looking forward, you have seen him married, and beheld his bride happy?'

'Humph! Not exactly. Your witch's skill is rather at fault sometimes.'

'What the devil have you seen, then?'

'Never mind: I came here to inquire, not to confess. Is it known that Mr. Rochester is to be married?'

'Yes; and to the beautiful Miss Ingram.'

'Shortly?'

'Appearances would warrant that conclusion; and, no doubt (though, with an audacity that wants chastising out of you, you seem to question it), they will be a superlatively happy pair. He must love such a handsome, noble, witty, accomplished lady; and probably she loves him: or, if not his person, at least his purse. I know she considers the Rochester estate eligible to the last degree; though (God pardon me!) I told her something on that point about an hour ago, which made her look wondrous grave: the corners of her mouth fell half an inch. I would advise her black-aviced suitor to look out: if another comes, with a longer or clearer rent-roll,—he's dished'——

'But, mother, I did not come to hear Mr. Rochester's fortune: I came to hear my own; and you have told me nothing of it.'

'Your fortune is yet doubtful: when I examined your face, one trait contradicted another. Chance has meted you a measure of happiness: that I know. I knew it before I came here this evening. She has laid it carefully on one side for you. I saw her do it. It depends on yourself to stretch out your hand,

and take it up: but whether you will do so, is the problem I study. Kneel again on the rug.'

'Don't keep me long; the fire scorches me.'

I knelt. She did not stoop towards me, but only gazed, leaning back in her chair. She began muttering,—

'The flame flickers in the eye; the eye shines like dew; it looks soft and full of feeling; it smiles at my jargon: it is susceptible; impression follows impression through its clear sphere; where it ceases to smile, it is sad; an unconscious lassitude weighs on the lid: that signifies melancholy resulting from loneliness. It turns from me; it will not suffer farther scrutiny; it seems to deny, by a mocking glance, the truth of the discoveries I have already made,—to disown the charge both of sensibility and chagrin: its pride and reserve only confirm me in my opinion. The eye is favourable.

'As to the mouth, it delights at times in laughter; it is disposed to impart all that the brain conceives; though I daresay it would be silent on much the heart experiences. Mobile and flexible, it was never intended to be compressed in the eternal silence of solitude: it is a mouth which should speak much and smile often, and have human affection for its interlocutor. That feature too is propitious.

'I see no enemy to a fortunate issue but in the brow; and that brow professes to say,—"I can live alone, if self-respect and circumstances require me so to do. I need not sell my soul to buy bliss. I have an inward treasure, born with me, which can keep me alive if all extraneous delights should be withheld. or offered only at a price I cannot afford to give." The forehead declares, "Reason sits firm and holds the reins, and she will not let the feelings burst away and hurry her to wild chasms. The passions may rage furiously, like true heathens, as they are; and the desires may imagine all sorts of vain things: but judgment shall still have the last word in every argument, and the casting vote in every decision. Strong wind, earthquake-shock, and fire may pass by: but I shall follow the guiding of that still small voice which interprets the dictates of conscience."

'Well said, forehead; your declaration shall be respected. I have formed my plans—right plans I deem them—and in them I have attended to the claims of conscience, the counsels of reason. I know how soon youth would fade and bloom perish, if, in the cup of bliss offered, but one dreg of shame, or one flavour of remorse were detected; and I do not want sacrifice, sorrow, dissolution—such is not my taste. I wish to foster, not to blight—to earn gratitude, not to wring tears of blood—no, nor of brine: my harvest must be in smiles, in endearments, in sweet—That will do. I think I rave in a kind of exquisite delirium. I should wish now to protract this moment *ad infinitum*; but I dare not. So far I have governed myself thoroughly. I have acted as I inwardly swore I would act; but farther might try me beyond my strength.

Rise, Miss Eyre: leave me; "the play is played out." '

Where was I? Did I wake or sleep? Had I been dreaming? Did I dream still? The old woman's voice had changed: her accent, her gesture, and all were familiar to me as my own face in a glass—as the speech of my own tongue. I got up, but did not go. I looked; I stirred the fire, and I looked again: but she drew her bonnet and her bandage closer about her face, and again beckoned me to depart. The flame illuminated her hand stretched out; roused now, and on the alert for discoveries, I at once noticed that hand. It was no more the withered limb of eld than my own; it was a rounded supple member, with smooth fingers, symmetrically turned; a broad ring flashed on the little finger, and stooping forward, I looked at it, and saw a gem I had seen a hundred times before. Again I looked at the face; which was no longer turned from me—on the contrary, the bonnet was doffed, the bandage displaced, the head advanced.

'Well, Jane, do you know me?' asked the familiar voice.

'Only take off the red cloak, sir, and then'——

'But the string is in a knot—help me.'

'Break it, sir.'

'There, then—"Off, ye lendings!" ' And Mr. Rochester stepped out of his disguise.

'Now, sir, what a strange idea!'

'But well carried out, eh? Don't you think so?'

'With the ladies you must have managed well.'

'But not with you?'

'You did not act the character of a gipsy with me.'

'What character did I act? My own?'

'No; some unaccountable one. In short, I believe you have been trying to draw me out—or in; you have been talking nonsense to make me talk nonsense. It is scarcely fair, sir.'

'Do you forgive me, Jane?'

'I cannot tell till I have thought it all over. If, on reflection, I find I have fallen into no great absurdity, I shall try to forgive you; but it was not right.'

'Oh! you have been very correct—very careful, very sensible.'

I reflected, and thought, on the whole, I had. It was a comfort; but, indeed, I had been on my guard almost from the beginning of the interview. Something of masquerade I suspected. I knew gipsies and fortune-tellers did not express themselves as this seeming old woman had expressed herself; besides, I had noted her feigned voice, her anxiety to conceal her features. But my mind had been running on Grace Poole—that living enigma, that mystery of mysteries, as I considered her. I had never thought of Mr. Rochester.

'Well,' said he, 'what are you musing about? What does that grave smile signify?'

'Wonder and self-congratulation, sir. I have your permission to retire now, I suppose?'

'No; stay a moment; and tell me what the people in the drawing-room yonder are doing.'

'Discussing the gipsy, I daresay.'

'Sit down!—Let me hear what they said about me.'

. 'I had better not stay long, sir; it must be near eleven o'clock. Oh! are you aware, Mr. Rochester, that a stranger has arrived here since you left this morning?'

'A stranger!—no; who can it be? I expected no one; is he gone?'

'No; he said he had known you long, and that he could take the liberty of installing himself here till you returned.'

'The devil he did! Did he give his name?'

'His name is Mason, sir; and he comes from the West Indies; from Spanish Town, in Jamaica, I think.'

Mr. Rochester was standing near me; he had taken my hand, as if to lead me to a chair. As I spoke, he gave my wrist a convulsive grip; the smile on his lips froze: apparently a spasm caught his breath.

'Mason!—the West Indies!' he said, in the tone one might fancy a speaking automaton to enounce its single words; 'Mason!—the West Indies!' he re-iterated; and he went over the syllables three times, growing, in the intervals of speaking, whiter than ashes: he hardly seemed to know what he was doing.

'Do you feel ill, sir?' I inquired.

'Jane, I've got a blow;—I've got a blow, Jane!' He staggered.

'Oh!—lean on me, sir.'

'Jane, you offered me your shoulder once before; let me have it now.'

'Yes, sir, yes; and my arm.'

He sat down, and made me sit beside him. Holding my hand in both his own, he chafed it; gazing on me, at the same time, with the most troubled and dreary look.

'My little friend!' said he, 'I wish I were in a quiet island with only you; and trouble, and danger, and hideous recollections removed from me.'

'Can I help you, sir?—I'd give my life to serve you.'

'Jane, if aid is wanted, I'll seek it at your hands; I promise you that.'

'Thank you, sir; tell me what to do,—I'll try, at least, to do it.'

'Fetch me now, Jane, a glass of wine from the dining-room; they will be at supper there; and tell me if Mason is with them, and what he is doing.'

I went. I found all the party in the dining-room at supper, as Mr. Rochester had said; they were not seated at table,—the supper was arranged on the side-board; each had taken what he chose, and they stood about here and there in groups, their plates and glasses in their hands. Every one seemed

with a candle: he had just descended from the upper story. One of the ladies ran to him directly; she seized his arm: it was Miss Ingram.

'What awful event has taken place?' said she. 'Speak! let us know the worst at once!'

'But don't pull me down or strangle me,' he replied: for the misses Eshton were clinging about him now; and the two dowagers, in vast white wrappers, were bearing down on him like ships in full sail.

'All's right!—all's right!' he cried. 'It's a mere rehearsal of Much Ado About Nothing. Ladies, keep off; or I shall wax dangerous.'

And dangerous he looked: his black eyes darted sparks. Calming himself by an effort, he added:—

'A servant has had the nightmare; that is all. She's an excitable, nervous person: she construed her dream into an apparition, or something of that sort, no doubt; and has taken a fit with fright. Now then, I must see you all back into your rooms; for, till the house is settled, she cannot be looked after. Gentlemen, have the goodness to set the ladies the example. Miss Ingram, I am sure you will not fail in evincing superiority to idle terrors. Amy and Louisa, return to your nests like a pair of doves, as you are. Mesdames' (to the dowagers), 'you will take cold to a dead certainty, if you stay in this chill gallery any longer.'

And so, by dint of alternate coaxing and commanding, he contrived to get them all once more enclosed in their separate dormitories. I did not wait to be ordered back to mine; but retreated unnoticed: as unnoticed as I had left it.

Not, however, to go to bed: on the contrary, I began and dressed myself carefully. The sounds I had heard after the scream, and the words that had been uttered, had probably been heard only by me; for they had proceeded from the room above mine: but they assured me that it was not a servant's dream which had thus struck horror through the house; and that the explanation Mr. Rochester had given was merely an invention framed to pacify his guests. I dressed, then, to be ready for emergencies. When dressed, I sat a long time by the window, looking out over the silent grounds and silvered fields, and waiting for I knew not what. It seemed to me that some event must follow the strange cry, struggle, and call.

No: stillness returned: each murmur and movement ceased gradually, and in about an hour Thornfield Hall was again as hushed as a desert. It seemed that sleep and night had resumed their empire. Meantime the moon declined: she was about to set. Not liking to sit in the cold and darkness, I thought I would lie down on my bed, dressed as I was. I left the window, and moved with little noise across the carpet; as I stooped to take off my shoes, a cautious hand tapped low at the door.

'Am I wanted?' I asked.

with a candle: he had just descended from the upper story. One of the ladies ran to him directly; she seized his arm: it was Miss Ingram.

'What awful event has taken place?' said she. 'Speak! let us know the worst at once!'

'But don't pull me down or strangle me,' he replied: for the misses Eshton were clinging about him now; and the two dowagers, in vast white wrappers, were bearing down on him like ships in full sail.

'All's right!—all's right!' he cried. 'It's a mere rehearsal of Much Ado About Nothing. Ladies, keep off; or I shall wax dangerous.'

And dangerous he looked: his black eyes darted sparks. Calming himself by an effort, he added:—

'A servant has had the nightmare; that is all. She's an excitable, nervous person: she construed her dream into an apparition, or something of that sort, no doubt; and has taken a fit with fright. Now then, I must see you all back into your rooms; for, till the house is settled, she cannot be looked after. Gentlemen, have the goodness to set the ladies the example. Miss Ingram, I am sure you will not fail in evincing superiority to idle terrors. Amy and Louisa, return to your nests like a pair of doves, as you are. Mesdames' (to the dowagers), 'you will take cold to a dead certainty, if you stay in this chill gallery any longer.'

And so, by dint of alternate coaxing and commanding, he contrived to get them all once more enclosed in their separate dormitories. I did not wait to be ordered back to mine; but retreated unnoticed: as unnoticed as I had left it.

Not, however, to go to bed: on the contrary, I began and dressed myself carefully. The sounds I had heard after the scream, and the words that had been uttered, had probably been heard only by me; for they had proceeded from the room above mine: but they assured me that it was not a servant's dream which had thus struck horror through the house; and that the explanation Mr. Rochester had given was merely an invention framed to pacify his guests. I dressed, then, to be ready for emergencies. When dressed, I sat a long time by the window, looking out over the silent grounds and silvered fields, and waiting for I knew not what. It seemed to me that some event must follow the strange cry, struggle, and call.

No: stillness returned: each murmur and movement ceased gradually, and in about an hour Thornfield Hall was again as hushed as a desert. It seemed that sleep and night had resumed their empire. Meantime the moon declined: she was about to set. Not liking to sit in the cold and darkness, I thought I would lie down on my bed, dressed as I was. I left the window, and moved with little noise across the carpet; as I stooped to take off my shoes, a cautious hand tapped low at the door.

'Am I wanted?' I asked.

CHAPTER 20

I had forgotten to draw my curtain, which I usually did; and also to let down my window-blind. The consequence was, that when the moon, which was full and bright (for the night was fine), came in her course to that space in the sky opposite my casement, and looked in at me through the unveiled panes, her glorious gaze roused me. Awaking in the dead of night, I opened my eyes on her disk—silver-white and crystal-clear. It was beautiful, but too solemn: I half rose, and stretched my arm to draw the curtain.

Good God! What a cry!

The night—its silence—its rest, was rent in twain by a savage, a sharp, a shrilly sound that ran from end to end of Thornfield Hall.

My pulse stopped: my heart stood still; my stretched arm was paralysed. The cry died, and was not renewed. Indeed, whatever being uttered that fearful shriek could not soon repeat it: not the widest-winged condor on the Andes could, twice in succession, send out such a yell from the cloud shrouding his eyrie. The thing delivering such utterance must rest ere it could repeat the effort.

It came out of the third story; for it passed overhead. And overhead—yes, in the room just above my chamber-ceiling—I now heard a struggle: a deadly one it seemed from the noise; and a half-smothered voice shouted—

'Help! help! help!' three times rapidly.

'Will no one come?' it cried; and then, while the staggering and stamping went on wildly, I distinguished through plank and plaster:—

'Rochester! Rochester! for God's sake, come!'

A chamber-door opened: some one ran, or rushed, along the gallery. Another step stamped on the flooring above and something fell; and there was silence.

I put on some clothes, though horror shook all my limbs: I issued from my apartment. The sleepers were all aroused: ejaculations, terrified murmurs sounded in every room; door after door unclosed; one looked out and another looked out; the gallery filled. Gentlemen and ladies alike had quitted their beds; and 'Oh! what is it?'—'Who is hurt?'—'What has happened?'—'Fetch a light!'—'Is it fire?'—'Are there robbers?'—'Where shall we run?' was demanded confusedly on all hands. But for the moonlight they would have been in complete darkness. They ran to and fro; they crowded together: some sobbed, some stumbled: the confusion was inextricable.

'Where the devil is Rochester?' cried Colonel Dent. 'I cannot find him in his bed.'

'Here! here!' was shouted in return. 'Be composed, all of you: I'm coming.'

And the door at the end of the gallery opened, and Mr. Rochester advanced

in high glee; laughter and conversation were general and animated. Mr. Mason stood near the fire, talking to Colonel and Mrs. Dent, and appeared as merry as any of them. I filled a wine-glass (I saw Miss Ingram watch me frowningly as I did so: she thought I was taking a liberty, I daresay), and I returned to the library.

Mr. Rochester's extreme pallor had disappeared, and he looked once more firm and stern. He took the glass from my hand.

'Here is to your health, ministrant spirit!' he said: he swallowed the contents and returned it to me. 'What are they doing, Jane?'

'Laughing and talking, sir.'

'They don't look grave and mysterious, as if they had heard something strange?'

'Not at all:—they are full of jests and gaiety.'

'And Mason?'

'He was laughing too.'

'If all these people came in a body and spat at me, what would you do, Jane?'

'Turn them out of the room, sir, if I could.'

He half smiled. 'But if I were to go to them, and they only looked at me coldly, and whispered sneeringly amongst each other, and then dropt off and left me one by one, what then? Would you go with them?'

'I rather think not, sir: I should have more pleasure in staying with you.'

'To comfort me?'

'Yes, sir, to comfort you as well as I could.'

'And if they laid you under a ban for adhering to me?'

'I, probably, should know nothing about their ban; and if I did, I should care nothing about it.'

'Then, you could dare censure for my sake?'

'I could dare it for the sake of any friend who deserved my adherence; as you, I am sure, do.'

'Go back now into the room; step quietly up to Mason, and whisper in his ear that Mr. Rochester is come and wishes to see him: show him in here and then leave me.'

'Yes, sir.'

I did his behest. The company all stared at me as I passed straight among them. I sought Mr. Mason, delivered the message, and preceded him from the room: I ushered him into the library, and then I went upstairs.

At a late hour, after I had been in bed some time, I heard the visitors repair to their chambers: I distinguished Mr. Rochester's voice, and heard him say 'This way, Mason; this is your room.'

He spoke cheerfully: the gay tones set my heart at ease. I was soon asleep.

'Wonder and self-congratulation, sir. I have your permission to retire now, I suppose?'

'No; stay a moment; and tell me what the people in the drawing-room yonder are doing.'

'Discussing the gipsy, I daresay.'

'Sit down!—Let me hear what they said about me.'

'I had better not stay long, sir; it must be near eleven o'clock. Oh! are you aware, Mr. Rochester, that a stranger has arrived here since you left this morning?'

'A stranger!—no; who can it be? I expected no one; is he gone?'

'No; he said he had known you long, and that he could take the liberty of installing himself here till you returned.'

'The devil he did! Did he give his name?'

'His name is Mason, sir; and he comes from the West Indies; from Spanish Town, in Jamaica, I think.'

Mr. Rochester was standing near me; he had taken my hand, as if to lead me to a chair. As I spoke, he gave my wrist a convulsive grip; the smile on his lips froze: apparently a spasm caught his breath.

'Mason!—the West Indies!' he said, in the tone one might fancy a speaking automaton to enounce its single words; 'Mason!—the West Indies!' he re-iterated; and he went over the syllables three times, growing, in the intervals of speaking, whiter than ashes: he hardly seemed to know what he was doing.

'Do you feel ill, sir?' I inquired.

'Jane, I've got a blow;—I've got a blow, Jane!' He staggered.

'Oh!—lean on me, sir.'

'Jane, you offered me your shoulder once before; let me have it now.'

'Yes, sir, yes; and my arm.'

He sat down, and made me sit beside him. Holding my hand in both his own, he chafed it; gazing on me, at the same time, with the most troubled and dreary look.

'My little friend!' said he, 'I wish I were in a quiet island with only you; and trouble, and danger, and hideous recollections removed from me.'

'Can I help you, sir?—I'd give my life to serve you.'

'Jane, if aid is wanted, I'll seek it at your hands; I promise you that.'

'Thank you, sir; tell me what to do,—I'll try, at least, to do it.'

'Fetch me now, Jane, a glass of wine from the dining-room; they will be at supper there; and tell me if Mason is with them, and what he is doing.'

I went. I found all the party in the dining-room at supper, as Mr. Rochester had said; they were not seated at table,—the supper was arranged on the side-board; each had taken what he chose, and they stood about here and there in groups, their plates and glasses in their hands. Every one seemed

'Are you up?' asked the voice I expected to hear, viz., my master's.

'Yes, sir.'

'And dressed?'

'Yes.'

'Come out, then, quietly.'

I obeyed. Mr. Rochester stood in the gallery, holding a light.

'I want you,' he said: 'come this way: take your time, and make no noise.'

My slippers were thin: I could walk the matted floor as softly as a cat. Ie glided up the gallery and up the stairs, and stopped in the dark, low orridor of the fateful third story: I had followed and stood at his side.

'Have you a sponge in your room?' he asked in a whisper.

'Yes, sir.'

'Have you any salts—volatile salts?'

'Yes.'

'Go back and fetch both.'

I returned, sought the sponge on the wash-stand, the salts in my drawer, nd once more retraced my steps. He still waited; he held a key in his hand: pproaching one of the small, black doors, he put it in the lock; he paused nd addressed me again.

'You don't turn sick at the sight of blood?'

'I think I shall not: I have never been tried yet.'

I felt a thrill while I answered him; but no coldness, and no faintness. 'Just give me your hand,' he said; 'it will not do to risk a fainting t.'

I put my fingers into his. 'Warm and steady,' was his remark: he turned the ey and opened the door.

I saw a room I remembered to have seen before; the day Mrs. Fairfax howed me over the house: it was hung with tapestry; but the tapestry was ow looped up in one part, and there was a door apparent, which had then een concealed. This door was open; a light shone out of the room within: heard thence a snarling, snatching sound, almost like a dog quarrelling. Ir. Rochester, putting down his candle, said to me, 'What a minute,' and e went forward to the inner apartment. A shout of laughter greeted his ntrance; noisy at first, and terminating in Grace Poole's own goblin ha! ha! he then was there. He made some sort of arrangement, without speaking: hough I heard a low voice address him: he came out and closed the door ehind him.

'Here, Jane!' he said; and I walked round to the other side of a large ed, which with its drawn curtains concealed a considerable portion of the hamber. An easy-chair was near the bed-head: a man sat in it, dressed ith the exception of his coat; he was still; his head leant back; his eyes were losed. Mr. Rochester held the candle over him; I recognised in his pale and

seemingly lifeless face—the stranger, Mason: I saw too that his linen on one side, and one arm, was almost soaked in blood.

'Hold the candle,' said Mr. Rochester, and I took it; he fetched a basin of water from the wash-stand: 'Hold that,' said he. I obeyed. He took the sponge, dipped it in and moistened the corpse-like face: he asked for my smelling-bottle, and applied it to the nostrils. Mr. Mason shortly unclosed his eyes; he groaned. Mr. Rochester opened the shirt of the wounded man whose arm and shoulder were bandaged: he sponged away blood, trickling fast down.

'Is there immediate danger?' murmured Mr. Mason.

'Pooh! No—a mere scratch. Don't be so overcome, man: bear up! I'll fetch a surgeon for you now, myself: you'll be able to be removed by morning I hope. Jane,' he continued.

'Sir?'

'I shall have to leave you in this room with this gentleman, for an hour or perhaps two hours; you will sponge the blood as I do when it returns: if he feels faint, you will put the glass of water on that stand to his lips, and your salts to his nose. You will not speak to him on any pretext —and—Richard— will be at the peril of your life if you speak to her: open your lips—agitate yourself—and I'll not answer for the consequences.'

Again the poor man groaned: he looked as if he dared not move: fear either of death or of something else, appeared almost to paralyse him. Mr. Rochester put the now bloody sponge into my hand, and I proceeded to use it as he had done. He watched me a second, then saying, 'Remember!—No conversation,' he left the room. I experienced a strange feeling as the key grated in the lock, and the sound of his retreating step ceased to be heard.

Here then I was in the third story, fastened into one of its mystic cells; night around me; a pale and bloody spectacle under my eyes and hands; a murderess hardly separated from me by a single door: yes—that was appalling—the rest I could bear; but I shuddered at the thought of Grace Poole bursting out upon me.

I must keep to my post, however. I must watch this ghastly countenance— these blue, still lips forbidden to unclose—these eyes now shut, now opening, now wandering through the room, now fixing on me, and ever glazed with the dulness of horror. I must dip my hand again and again in the basin of blood and water, and wipe away the trickling gore. I must see the light of the unsnuffed candle wane on my employment; the shadow darken on the wrought antique tapestry round me, and grow black under the hangings of the vast old bed, and quiver strangely over the doors of a great cabinet opposite— whose front, divided into twelve panels, bore, in grim design, the heads of the twelve apostles, each inclosed in its separate panel as in a frame; while above them at the top rose an ebon crucifix and a dying Christ.

According as the shifting obscurity and flickering gleam hovered here or glanced there, it was now the bearded physician, Luke, that bent his brow; St. John's long hair that waved; and anon the devilish face of Judas, that grew out of the panel, and seemed gathering life and threatening a revelation of the arch-traitor—of Satan himself—in his subordinate's form.

Amidst all this, I had to listen as well as watch: to listen for the movements of the wild beast or the fiend in yonder side den. But since Mr. Rochester's visit it seemed spellbound: all the night I heard but three sounds at three long intervals,—a step creak, a momentary renewal of the snarling, canine noise, and a deep human groan.

Then my own thoughts worried me. What crime was this, that lived incarnate in this sequestered mansion, and could neither be expelled nor subdued by the owner?— What mystery, that broke out, now in fire and now in blood, at the deadest hours of night? What creature was it, that, masked in an ordinary woman's face and shape, uttered the voice, now of a mocking demon, and anon of a carrion-seeking bird of prey?

And this man I bent over—this common-place, quiet stranger—how had he become involved in the web of horror? and why had the Fury flown at him? What made him seek this quarter of the house at an untimely season, when he should have been asleep in bed? I had heard Mr. Rochester assign him an apartment below—what brought him here? And why, now, was he so tame under the violence or treachery done him? Why did he so quietly submit to the concealment Mr. Rochester enforced? Why *did* Mr. Rochester enforce this concealment? His guest had been outraged, his own life on a former occasion had been hideously plotted against; and both attempts he smothered in secrecy and sank in oblivion! Lastly, I saw Mr. Mason was submissive to Mr. Rochester; that the impetuous will of the latter held complete sway over the inertness of the former: the few words which had passed between them assured me of this. It was evident that in their former intercourse, the passive disposition of the one had been habitually influenced by the active energy of the other: whence then had arisen Mr. Rochester's dismay when he heard of Mr. Mason's arrival? Why had the mere name of this unresisting individual—whom his word now sufficed to control like a child— fallen on him, a few hours since, as a thunderbolt might fall on an oak?

Oh! I could not forget his look and his paleness when he whispered: 'Jane, I have got a blow—I have got a blow, Jane.' I could not forget how the arm had trembled which he rested on my shoulder: and it was no light matter which could thus bow the resolute spirit and thrill the vigorous frame of Fairfax Rochester.

'When will he come? When will he come?' I cried inwardly, as the night lingered and lingered—as my bleeding patient drooped, moaned, sickened: and neither day nor aid arrived. I had, again and again, held the water to

Mason's white lips; again and again offered him the stimulating salts: my efforts seemed ineffectual: either bodily or mental suffering, or loss of blood, or all three combined, were fast prostrating his strength. He moaned so, and looked so weak, wild, and lost, I feared he was dying; and I might not even speak to him!

The candle, wasted at last, went out; as it expired, I perceived streaks o grey light edging the window curtains; dawn was approaching. Presently I heard Pilot bark far below, out of his distant kennel in the court-yard hope revived. Nor was it unwarranted: in five minutes more the grating key the yielding lock, warned me my watch was relieved. It could not have lasted more than two hours: many a week has seemed shorter.

Mr. Rochester entered, and with him the surgeon he had been to fetch.

'Now, Carter, be on the alert,' he said to this last: 'I give you but half an hour for dressing the wound, fastening the bandages, getting the patien downstairs and all.'

'But is he fit to move, sir?'

'No doubt of it; it is nothing serious: he is nervous, his spirits must be kept up. Come, set to work.'

Mr. Rochester drew back the thick curtain, drew up the holland blind, let in all the daylight he could; and I was surprised and cheered to see how far dawn was advanced: what rosy streaks were beginning to brighten the east Then he approached Mason, whom the surgeon was already handling.

'Now, my good fellow, how are you?' he asked.

"She's done for me, I fear,' was the faint reply.

'Not a whit!—courage! This day fortnight you'll hardly be a pin the wors of it: you've lost a little blood; that's all. Carter, assure him there's no danger

'I can do that conscientiously,' said Carter, who had now undone the ban dages; 'only I wish I could have got here sooner: he would not have bled s much—but how is this? The flesh on the shoulder is torn as well as cut. Th wound was not done with a knife: there have been teeth here!'

'She bit me,' he murmured. 'She worried me like a tigress, when Rocheste got the knife from her.'

'You should not have yielded: you should have grappled with her at once said Mr. Rochester.

'But under such circumstances what could one do?' returned Maso 'Oh, it was frightful!' he added, shuddering. 'And I did not expect it: sh looked so quiet at first.'

'I warned you,' was his friend's answer; 'I said—be on your guard whe you go near her. Besides, you might have waited till to-morrow, and had m with you: it was mere folly to attempt the interview to-night, and alone

'I thought I could have done some good.'

'You thought! you thought! Yes; it makes me impatient to hear you

180

but, however, you have suffered, and are likely to suffer enough for not taking my advice; so I'll say no more. Carter—hurry!—hurry! The sun will soon rise, and I must have him off.'

'Directly, sir; the shoulder is just bandaged. I must look to this other wound in the arm: she has had her teeth here too, I think.'

'She sucked the blood: she said she'd drain my heart,' said Mason.

I saw Mr. Rochester shudder: a singularly marked expression of disgust, horror, hatred, warped his countenance almost to distortion; but he only said:—

'Come, be silent, Richard, and never mind her gibberish: don't repeat it.'

'I wish I could forget it,' was the answer.

'You will when you are out of the country: when you get back to Spanish Town, you may think of her as dead and buried—or rather, you need not think of her at all.'

'Impossible to forget this night!'

'It is not impossible: have some energy, man. You thought you were as dead as a herring two hours since, and you are all alive and talking now. There!—Carter has done with you or nearly so; I'll make you decent in a trice. Jane' (he turned to me for the first time since his re-entrance) 'take this key: go down into my bedroom, and walk straight forward into my dressing-room; open the top drawer of the wardrobe and take out a clean shirt and neck-handkerchief: bring them here; and be nimble.'

I went; sought the repository he had mentioned, found the articles named, and returned with them.

'Now,' said he, 'go to the other side of the bed while I order his toilet; but don't leave the room: you may be wanted again.'

I retired as directed.

'Was anybody stirring below when you went down, Jane?' inquired Mr. Rochester, presently.

'No, sir; all was very still.'

'We shall get you off cannily, Dick: and it will be bettter, both for your sake, and for that of the poor creature in yonder. I have striven long to avoid exposure, and I should not like it to come at last. Here, Carter, help him on with his waistcoat. Where did you leave your furred cloak? You can't travel a mile without that, I know, in this damned cold climate. In your room?—Jane, run down to Mr. Mason's room,—the one next mine,—and fetch a cloak you will see there.'

Again I ran, and again returned, bearing an immense mantle lined and edged with fur.

'Now, I've another errand for you,' said my untiring master; 'you must away to my room again. What a mercy you are shod with velvet, Jane!—a clod-hopping messenger would never do at this juncture. You must open

the middle drawer of my toilet-table and take out a little phial and a little glass you will find there,—quick!' I flew thither and back, bringing the desired vessels.

'That's well! Now, doctor, I shall take the liberty of administering a dose myself; on my own responsibility. I got this cordial at Rome, of an Italian charlatan—a fellow you would have kicked, Carter. It is not a thing to be used indiscriminately, but it is good upon occasion: as now, for instance Jane, a little water.'

He held out the tiny glass, and I half filled it from the water bottle on the wash-stand.

'That will do:—now wet the lip of the phial.'

I did so: he measured twelve drops of a crimson liquid, and presented it to Mason.

'Drink, Richard: it will give you the heart you lack, for an hour or so.'

'But will it hurt me?—is it inflammatory?'

'Drink! drink! drink!'

Mr. Mason obeyed, because it was evidently useless to resist. He was dressed now: he still looked pale, but he was no longer gory and sullied. Mr. Rochester let him sit three minutes after he had swallowed the liquid; he then took his arm:—

'Now I am sure you can get on your feet,' he said:—'try.'

The patient rose.

'Carter, take him under the other shoulder. Be of good cheer, Richard step out:—that's it!'

'I do feel better,' remarked Mr. Mason.

'I am sure you do. Now, Jane, trip on before us away to the back-stairs unbolt the side-passage door, and tell the driver of the post-chaise you will see in the yard—or just outside, for I told him not to drive his rattling wheel over the pavement—to be ready; we are coming: and, Jane, if any one is about, come to the foot of the stairs and hem.'

It was by this time half-past five, and the sun was on the point of rising but I found the kitchen still dark and silent. The side-passage door was fastened; I opened it with as little noise as possible: all the yard was quiet but the gates stood wide open, and there was a post-chaise, with horses ready harnessed, and driver seated on the box, stationed outside. I approached him, and said the gentlemen were coming; he nodded: and then I looked carefully round and listened. The stillness of early morning slumbered everywhere; the curtains were yet drawn over the servants' chamber windows; little birds were just twittering in the blossom-blanched orchard trees whose boughs drooped like white garlands over the wall enclosing one side of the yard; the carriage horses stamped from time to time in their close stables: all else was still.

The gentlemen now appeared. Mason, supported by Mr. Rochester and he surgeon, seemed to walk with tolerable ease; they assisted him into the chaise; Carter followed.

'Take care of him,' said Mr. Rochester to the latter, 'and keep him at your house till he is quite well: I shall ride over in a day or two to see how he gets on. Richard, how is it with you?'

'The fresh air revives me, Fairfax.'

'Leave the window open on his side, Carter; there is no wind—good-bye, Dick.'

'Fairfax'——

'Well, what is it?'

'Let her be taken care of; let her be treated as tenderly as may be: let her'——he stopped and burst into tears.

'I do my best; and have done it, and will do it,' was the answer: he shut up the chaise door, and the vehicle drove away.

'Yet would to God there was an end of all this!' added Mr. Rochester, as he closed and barred the heavy yard-gates. This done, he moved with slow step and abstracted air towards a door in the wall bordering the orchard. , supposing he had done with me, prepared to return to the house; again, however, I heard him call 'Jane!' He had opened the portal and stood at it, waiting for me.

'Come where there is some freshness, for a few moments,' he said; 'that house is a mere dungeon: don't you feel it so?'

'It seems to me a splendid mansion, sir.'

'The glamour of inexperience is over your eyes,' he answered; 'and you see it through a charmed medium: you cannot discern that the gilding is slime and the silk draperies cobwebs; that the marble is sordid slate, and the polished woods mere refuse chips and scaly bark. Now *here* (he pointed to the leafy enclosure we had entered? all is real, sweet, and pure.'

He strayed down a walk edged with box; with apple trees, pear trees, and cherry trees on one side, and a border on the other, full of all sorts of old-fashioned flowers, stocks, sweet-williams, primroses, pansies, mingled with southern-wood, sweet-briar, and various fragrant herbs. They were fresh now as a succession of April showers and gleams, followed by a lovely spring morning, could make them: the sun was just entering the dappled east, and his light illumined the wreathed and dewy orchard trees and shone down the quiet walks under them.

'Jane, will you have a flower?'

He gathered a half-blown rose, the first on the bush, and offered it to me.

'Thank you, sir.'

'Do you like this sunrise, Jane? That sky with its high and light clouds

which are sure to melt away as the day waxes warm—this placid and balmy atmosphere?'

'I do, very much.'

'You have passed a strange night, Jane?'

'Yes, sir.'

'And it has made you look pale—were you afraid when I left you alone with Mason?'

'I was afraid of some one coming out of the inner room.'

'But I had fastened the door—I had the key in my pocket: I should have been a careless shepherd if I had left a lamb—my pet lamb—so near a wolf's den unguarded: you were safe.'

'Will Grace Poole live here still, sir?'

'Oh, yes! don't trouble your head about her—put the thing out of your thoughts.'

'Yet it seems to me your life is hardly secure while she stays.'

'Never fear—I will take care of myself.'

'Is the danger you apprehended last night gone by now, sir?'

'I cannot vouch for that till Mason is out of England: nor even then. To live, for me, Jane, is to stand on a crater-crust which may crack and spue fire any day.'

'But Mr. Mason seems a man easily led. Your influence, sir, is evidently potent with him: he will never set you at defiance, or wilfully injure you.'

'Oh, no! Mason will not defy me; nor, knowing it, will he hurt me—but, unintentionally, he might in a moment, by one careless word, deprive me if not of life, yet for ever of happiness.'

'Tell him to be cautious, sir: let him know what you fear, and show him how to avert the danger.'

He laughed sardonically, hastily took my hand, and as hastily threw it from him.

'If I could do that, simpleton, where would the danger be? Annihilated in a moment. Ever since I have known Mason, I have only had to say to him "Do that," and the thing has been done. But I cannot give him orders in this case: I cannot say "Beware of harming me, Richard;" for it is imperative that I should keep him ignorant that harm to me is possible. Now you look puzzled; and I will puzzle you farther. You are my little friend, are you not?'

'I like to serve you, sir, and to obey you in all that is right.'

'Precisely: I see you do. I see genuine contentment in your gait, and mien, your eye and face, when you are helping me and pleasing me—working for me, and with me, in, as you characteristically say, "*all that is right:*" for if I bid you do what you thought wrong, there would be no light-footed running, no neat-handed alacrity, no lively glance and animated complexion. My

iend would then turn to me, quiet and pale, and would say, "No, sir; that impossible: I cannot do it, because it is wrong;" and would become immutable as a fixed star. Well, you too have power over me, and may injure e: yet I dare not show you where I am vulnerable, lest, faithful and friendly you are, you should transfix me at once.'

'If you have no more to fear from Mr. Mason than you have from me, sir, u are very safe.'

'God grant it may be so! Here, Jane, is an arbour; sit down.'

The arbour was an arch in the wall, lined with ivy; it contained a rustic at. Mr. Rochester took it, leaving room, however, for me: but I stood fore him.

'Sit,' he said; 'the bench is long enough for two. You don't hesitate to take place at my side, do you? Is that wrong, Jane?'

I answered him by assuming it: to refuse would, I felt have been unwise.

'Now, my little friend, while the sun drinks the dew—while all the flowers in is old garden awake and expand, and the birds fetch their young ones' eakfast out of the Thornfield, and the early bees do their first spell of work I'll put a case to you; which you must endeavour to suppose your own: but st, look at me, and tell me you are at ease, and not fearing that I err in taining you, or that you err in staying.'

'No, sir; I am content.'

'Well, then, Jane, call to aid your fancy:—suppose you were no longer girl well reared and disciplined, but a wild boy indulged from childhood wards; imagine yourself in a remote foreign land; conceive that you there mmit a capital error, no matter of what nature or from what motives, but e whose consequences must follow you through life and taint all your exisnce. Mind, I don't say a *crime*; I am not speaking of shedding of blood or y other guilty act, which might make the perpetrator amenable to the w: my word is *error*. The results of what you have done become in time to u utterly insupportable; you take measures to obtain relief: unusual meases, but neither unlawful nor culpable. Still you are miserable; for hope as quitted you on the very confines of life: your sun at noon darkens in an lipse, which you feel will not leave it till the time of setting. Bitter and base sociations have become the sole food of your memory: you wander here d there, seeking rest in exile: happiness in pleasure—I mean in heartless, nsual pleasure—such as dulls intellect and blights feeling. Heart-weary d soul-withered, you come home after years of voluntary banishment; u make a new acquaintance—how or where no matter: you find in this ranger much of the good and bright qualities which you have sought for venty years, and never before encountered; and they are all fresh, healthy, ithout soil and without taint. Such society revives, regenerates: you feel etter days come back—higher wishes, purer feelings; you desire to recom-

mence your life, and to spend what remains to you of days in a way mo
worthy of an immortal being. To attain this end, are you justified in ove
leaping an obstacle of custom—a mere conventional impediment, whic
neither your conscience sanctifies nor your judgment approves?'

He paused for an answer: and what was I to say? Oh, for some good spir
to suggest a judicious and satisfactory response! Vain aspiration! The we
wind whispered in the ivy round me; but no gentle Ariel borrowed its brea
as a medium of speech: the birds sang in the tree-tops; but their song, howev
sweet, was inarticulate.

Again Mr. Rochester propounded his query:

'Is the wandering and sinful, but now rest-seeking and repentant, m
justified in daring the world's opinion, in order to attach to him for ever th
gentle, gracious, genial stranger; thereby securing his own peace of mir
and regeneration of life?'

'Sir,' I answered, 'a wanderer's repose or a sinner's reformation shou
never depend on a fellow-creature. Men and women die; philosophers falt
in wisdom, and Christians in goodness: if any one you know has suffere
and erred, let him look higher than his equals for strength to amend, ar
solace to heal.'

'But the instrument—the instrument! God, who does the work, ordair
the instrument. I have myself—I tell it you without parable—been a worldl
dissipated, restless man; and I believe I have found the instrument for n
cure, in'——

He paused: the birds went on carolling, the leaves lightly rustling. I almc
wondered they did not check their songs and whispers to catch the suspende
revelation: but they would have had to wait many minutes—so long was th
silence protracted. At last I looked up at the tardy speaker: he was lookir
eagerly at me.

'Little friend,' said he, in quite a changed tone—while his face changed to
losing all its softness and gravity, and becoming harsh and sarcastic—'yc
have noticed my tender penchant for Miss Ingram: don't you think if
married her she would regenerate me with a vengeance?'

He got up instantly, went quite to the other end of the walk, and when
came back he was humming a tune.

'Jane, Jane,' said he, stopping before me, 'you are quite pale with yo
vigils: don't you curse me for disturbing your rest?'

'Curse you? No, sir.'

'Shake hands in confirmation of the word. What cold fingers! They we
warmer last night when I touched them at the door of the mysterious chambe
Jane, when will you watch with me again?'

'Whenever I can be useful, sir.'

'For instance, the night before I am married! I am sure I shall not be at

ɔ sleep. Will you promise to sit up with me to bear me company? To you can talk of my lovely one: for now you have seen her and know her.'

'Yes, sir.'

'She's a rare one, is she not, Jane?'

'Yes, sir.'

'A strapper—a real strapper, Jane: big, brown, and buxom; with hair ɪst such as the ladies of Carthage must have had. Bless me! there's Dent and ·ynn in the stables! Go in by the shrubbery, through that wicket.'

As I went one way, he went another, and I heard him in the yard, saying heeringly:—

'Mason got the start of you all this morning; he was gone before sunrise: rose at four to see him off.'

CHAPTER 21

resentiments are strange things! and so are sympathies; and so are signs ⁻ nd the three combined make one mystery to which humanity has not yet ·und the key. I never laughed at presentiments in my life; because I have ad strange ones of my own. Sympathies, I believe, exist: (for instance, between ɪr-distant, long-absent, wholly estranged relatives; asserting, notwithstanding ɪeir alienation, the unity of the source to which each traces his origin) ·hose workings baffle mortal comprehension. And signs, for aught we know, ɪay be but the sympathies of Nature with man.

When I was a little girl, only six years old, I, one night, heard Bessie eaven say to Martha Abbott that she had been dreaming about a little ɪild; and that to dream of children was a sure sign of trouble, either to ɪe's self or one's kin. The saying might have worn out of my memory, ad not a circumstance immediately followed which served indelibly to fix there. The next day Bessie was sent for home to the deathbed of her little sister.

Of late I had often recalled this saying and this incident; for during the ast week scarcely a night had gone over my couch that had not brought ·ith it a dream of an infant: which I sometimes hushed in my arms, sometimes andled on my knee, sometimes watched playing with daisies on a lawn; ɪ again, dabbling its hands in running water. It was a wailing child this ɪght, and a laughing one the next: now it nestled close to me, and now it ɪn from me; but whatever mood the apparition evinced, whatever aspect wore, it failed not for seven successive nights to meet me the moment I entered ɪe land of slumber.

I did not like this iteration of one idea—this strange recurrence of one ɪnage; and I grew nervous as bedtime approached and the hour of the vision ɪew near. It was from companionship with this baby-phantom I had been

roused on that moonlight night when I heard the cry; and it was on the after
noon of the day following I was summoned downstairs by a message tha
some one wanted me in Mrs. Fairfax's room. On repairing thither, I foun
a man waiting for me, having the appearance of a gentleman's servant: h
was dressed in deep mourning, and the hat he held in his hand was surrounde
with a crape band.

'I daresay you hardly remember me, miss,' he said, rising as I entered
'but my name is Leaven; I lived coachman with Mrs. Reed when you wer
at Gateshead eight or nine years since, and I live there still.'

'Oh, Robert! how do you do? I remember you very well: you used to giv
me a ride sometimes on Miss Georgiana's bay pony. And how is Bessie
You are married to Bessie?'

'Yes, miss: my wife is very hearty, thank you; she brought me anothe
little one about two months since—we have three now—and both mother an
child are thriving.'

'And are the family well at the house, Robert?'

'I am sorry I can't give you better news of them, miss: they are very bad
at present—in great trouble.'

'I hope no one is dead,' I said, glancing at his black dress. He too looke
down at the crape round his hat and replied,—

'Mr. John died yesterday was a week, at his chambers in London.'

'Mr. John?'

'Yes.'

'And how does his mother bear it?'

'Why you see, Miss Eyre, it is not a common mishap: his life has bee
very wild: these last three years he gave himself up to strange ways; and h
death was shocking.'

'I heard from Bessie he was not doing well.'

'Doing well! He could not do worse: he ruined his health and his estat
amongst the worst men and the worst women. He got into debt and int
jail: his mother helped him out twice, but as soon as he was free he returne
to his old companions and habits. His head was not strong: the knaves h
lived amongst fooled him beyond anything I ever heard. He came down t
Gateshead about three weeks ago and wanted missis to give up all to hin
Missis refused: her means have long been much reduced by his extravaganc
so he went back again, and the next news was that he was dead. How h
died, God knows!—they say he killed himself.'

I was silent: the tidings were frightful. Robert Leaven resumed:—

'Missis had been out of health herself for some time: she had got very stou
but was not strong with it; and the loss of money and fear of poverty wer
quite breaking her down. The information about Mr. John's death an
the manner of it came too suddenly: it brought on a stroke. She was thre

lays without speaking; but last Tuesday she seemed rather better: she appeared as if she wanted to say something, and kept making signs to my wife and mumbling. It was only yesterday morning, however, that Bessie understood she was pronouncing your name; and at last she made out the words, 'Bring Jane—fetch Jane Eyre: I want to speak to her." Bessie is not sure whether she is in her right mind, or means anything by the words; but she old Miss Reed and Miss Georgiana, and advised them to send for you. The young ladies put it off at first: but their mother grew so restless, and said, Jane, Jane," so many times, that at last they consented. I left Gateshead esterday; and if you can get ready, Miss, I should like to take you back with me early to-morrow morning.'

'Yes, Robert, I shall be ready: it seems to me that I ought to go.'

'I think so too, Miss. Bessie said she was sure you would not refuse: but suppose you will have to ask leave before you can get off?'

'Yes; and I will do it now;' and having directed him to the servants' all, and recommended him to the care of John's wife, and the attentions f John himself, I went in search of Mr. Rochester.

He was not in any of the lower rooms; he was not in the yard, the stables, r the grounds. I asked Mrs. Fairfax if she had seen him;—yes: she believed e was playing billiards with Miss Ingram. To the billiard-room I hastened: he click of balls and the hum of voices resounded thence; Mr. Rochester, Miss Ingram, the two Misses Eshton, and their admirers, were all busied the game. It required some courage to disturb so interesting a party; ay errand, however, was one I could not defer, so I approached the master where he stood at Miss Ingram's side. She turned as I drew near, and looked t me haughtily: her eyes seemed to demand, 'What can the creeping creature want now?' and when I said, in a low voice, 'Mr. Rochester,' she made movement as if tempted to order me away. I remember her appearance t the moment,—it was very graceful and very striking: she wore a morning obe of sky-blue crape; a gauzy azure scarf was twisted in her hair. She ad been all animation with the game, and irritated pride did not lower he expression of her haughty lineaments.

'Does that person want you?' she inquired of Mr. Rochester; and Mr. ochester turned to see who the 'person' was. He made a curious grimace, —one of his strange and equivocal demonstrations—threw down his cue and llowed me from the room.

'Well, Jane?' he said, as he rested his back against the school-room door, hich he had shut.

'If you please, sir, I want leave of absence for a week or two.'

'What to do?—Where to go?'

'To see a sick lady who has sent for me.'

'What sick lady?—Where does she live?'

'At Gateshead, in——shire.'

'——shire? That is a hundred miles off! Who may she be that sends for people to see her that distance?'

'Her name is Reed, sir,—Mrs. Reed.'

'Reed of Gateshead? There was a Reed of Gateshead, a magistrate.'

'It is his widow, sir.'

'And what have you to do with her? How do you know her?'

'Mr. Reed was my uncle,—my mother's brother.'

'The deuce he was! You never told me that before: you always said you had no relations.'

'None that would own me, sir. Mr. Reed is dead, and his wife cast me off.'

'Why?'

'Because I was poor, and burdensome, and she disliked me.'

'But Reed left children?—you must have cousins? Sir George Lynn was talking of a Reed of Gateshead, yesterday—who, he said, was one of the veriest rascals on town; and Ingram was mentioning a Georgiana Reed of the same place, who was much admired for her beauty, a season or two ago in London.'

'John Reed is dead, too, sir: he ruined himself and half-ruined his family, and is supposed to have committed suicide. The news so shocked his mother that it brought on an apoplectic attack.'

'And what good can you do her? Nonsense, Jane! I would never think of running a hundred miles to see an old lady who will, perhaps, be dead before you reach her: besides, you say she cast you off.'

'Yes, sir, but that is long ago; and when her circumstances were very different: I could not be easy to neglect her wishes now.'

'How long will you stay?'

'As short a time as possible, sir.'

'Promise me only to stay a week'——

'I had better not pass my word: I might be obliged to break it.'

'At all events you *will* come back: you will not be induced under any pretext to take up a permanent residence with her?'

'Oh no! I shall certainly return if all be well.'

'And who goes with you? You don't travel a hundred miles alone.'

'No, sir, she has sent her coachman.'

'A person to be trusted?'

'Yes, sir, he has lived ten years in the family.'

Mr. Rochester meditated. 'When do you wish to go?'

'Early to-morrow morning, sir.'

'Well, you must have some money; you can't travel without money, and I daresay you have not much: I have given you no salary yet. How much have you in the world, Jane?' he asked, smiling.

I drew out my purse; a meagre thing it was. 'Five shillings, sir.' He took the
purse, poured the hoard into his palm and chuckled over it as if its scantiness
pleased him. Soon he produced his pocket-book: 'Here,' said he, offering
me a note: it was fifty pounds, and he owed me but fifteen. I told him I had
no change.

'I don't want change: you know that. Take your wages.'

I declined accepting more than was my due. He scowled at first; then,
as if recollecting something, he said:—

'Right, right! Better not give you all now: you would, perhaps, stay away
three months if you had fifty pounds. There are ten: is it not plenty?'

'Yes, sir, but now you owe five.'

'Come back for it then: I am your banker for forty pounds.'

'Mr. Rochester, I may as well mention another matter of business to you
while I have the opportunity.'

'Matter of business? I'm curious to hear it.'

'You have as good as informed me, sir, that you are going shortly to be
married?'

'Yes: what then?'

'In that case, sir, Adèle ought to go to school: I am sure you will perceive
the necessity of it.'

'To get her out of my bride's way; who might otherwise walk over her
rather too emphatically. There's sense in the suggestion; not a doubt of it:
Adèle, as you say, must go to school; and you, of course, must march straight
to—the devil?'

'I hope not, sir: but I must seek another situation somewhere.'

'In course!' he exclaimed, with a twang of voice and a distortion of features
equally fantastic and ludicrous. He looked at me some minutes.

'And old Madam Reed, or the Misses, her daughters, will be solicited by
you to seek a place, I suppose?'

'No, sir; I am not on such terms with my relatives as would justify me in
asking favours of them—but I shall advertise.'

'You shall walk up the pyramids of Egypt!' he growled. 'At your peril
you advertise! I wish I had only offered you a sovereign instead of ten pounds.
Give me back nine pounds, Jane; I've a use for it.'

'And so have I, sir,' I returned, putting my hands and my purse behind
me. 'I could not spare the money on any account.'

'Little niggard!' said he, 'refusing me a pecuniary request! Give me five
pounds, Jane.'

'Not five shillings, sir; nor five pence.'

'Just let me look at the cash.'

'No, sir; you are not to be trusted.'

'Jane!'

'Sir?'

'Promise me one thing.'

'I'll promise you anything, sir, that I think I am likely to perform.'

'Not to advertise: and to trust this quest of a situation to me. I'll find you one in time.'

'I shall be glad so to do, sir, if you, in your turn, will promise that I and Adèle shall be both safe out of the house before your bride enters it.'

'Very well! very well! I'll pledge my word on it. You go to-morrow, then.'

'Yes, sir; early.'

'Shall you come down to the drawing-room after dinner?'

'No, sir, I must prepare for the journey.'

'Then you and I must bid good-bye for a little while?'

'I suppose so, sir.'

'And how do people perform that ceremony of parting, Jane? Teach me; I'm not quite up to it.'

'They say, Farewell; or any other form they prefer.'

'Then say it.'

'Farewell, Mr. Rochester, for the present.'

'What must I say?'

'The same, if you like, sir.'

'Farewell, Miss Eyre, for the present: is that all?'

'Yes.'

'It seems stingy, to my notions, and dry, and unfriendly. I should like something else: a little addition to the rite. If one shook hands, for instance; but no,—that would not content me either. So you'll do no more than say Farewell, Jane?'

'It is enough, sir: as much good-will may be conveyed in one hearty word as in many.'

'Very likely; but it is blank and cool—"farewell." '

'How long is he going to stand with his back against that door?' I asked myself; 'I want to commence my packing.' The dinner-bell rang, and suddenly away he bolted, without another syllable: I saw him no more during the day, and was off before he had risen in the morning.

I reached the lodge at Gateshead about five o'clock in the afternoon of the first of May: I stepped in there before going up to the hall. It was very clean and neat: the ornamental windows were hung with little white curtains; the floor was spotless; the grate and fire-irons were burnished bright, and the fire burnt clear. Bessie sat on the hearth, nursing her last-born, and Robert and his sister played quietly in a corner.

'Bless you!—I knew you would come!' exclaimed Mrs. Leaven, as I entered.

'Yes, Bessie,' said I, after I had kissed her; 'and I trust I am not too late. How is Mrs. Reed?—Alive still, I hope.'

'Yes, she is alive; and more sensible and collected than she was. The doctor ays she may linger a week or two yet; but he hardly thinks she will finally ecover.'

'Has she mentioned me lately?'

'She was talking of you only this morning, and wishing you would come: ut she is sleeping now; or was ten minutes ago, when I was up at the house. he generally lies in a kind of lethargy all the afternoon, and wakes up about ix or seven. Will you rest yourself here an hour, miss, and then I will go up ith you?'

Robert here entered, and Bessie laid her sleeping child in the cradle and ent to welcome him: afterwards she insisted on my taking off my bonnet nd having some tea; for she said I looked pale and tired. I was glad to accept er hospitality; and I submitted to be relieved of my travelling garb just as assively as I used to let her undress me when a child.

Old times crowded fast back on me as I watched her bustling about—setting ut the tea-tray with her best china, cutting bread and butter, toasting a tea-ake, and, between whiles, giving little Robert or Jane an occasional tap or ush, just as she used to give me in former days. Bessie had retained her uick temper as well as her light foot and good looks.

Tea ready, I was going to approach the table; but she desired me to sit ill, quite in her old, peremptory tones. I must be served at the fireside, she aid; and she placed before me a little round stand with my cup and a plate f toast, absolutely as she used to accommodate me with some privately pur-ined dainty on a nursery chair: and I smiled and obeyed her as in bygone ays.

She wanted to know if I was happy at Thornfield Hall, and what sort of person the mistress was; and when I told her there was only a master, hether he was a nice gentleman, and if I liked him. I told her he was rather n ugly man, but quite a gentleman; and that he treated me kindly, and I was ontent. Then I went on to describe to her the gay company that had lately een staying at the house; and to these details Bessie listened with interest: hey were precisely of the kind she relished.

In such conversation an hour was soon gone: Bessie restored to me my onnet, etc., and, accompanied by her, I quitted the lodge for the hall. t was also accompanied by her that I had, nearly nine years ago, walked own the path I was now ascending. On a dark, misty, raw morning in anuary, I had left a hostile roof with a desperate and embittered heart—a ense of outlawry and almost of reprobation—to seek the chilly harbourage f Lowood: that bourne so far away and unexplored. The same hostile roof ow again rose before me: my prospects were doubtful yet; and I had yet an ching heart. I still felt as a wanderer on the face of the earth; but I experien-ed firmer trust in myself and my own powers, and less withering dread of

oppression. The gaping wound of my wrongs, too, was now quite healed and the flame of resentment extinguished.

'You shall go into the breakfast-room first,' said Bessie, as she preceded me through the hall; 'the young ladies will be there.'

In another moment I was within that apartment. There was every article of furniture looking just as it did on the morning I was first introduced to Mr Brocklehurst: the very rug he had stood upon still covered the hearth. Glancing at the book-case, I thought I could distinguish the two volumes of Bewick's British Birds occupying their old place on the third shelf, and Gulliver's Travels and the Arabian Nights ranged just above. The inanimate objects were not changed: but the living things had altered past recognition.

Two young ladies appeared before me; one very tall, almost as tall as Miss Ingram,—very thin too, with a sallow face and severe mien. There was something ascetic in her look, which was augmented by the extreme plainness of a straight-skirted, black, stuff dress, a starched linen collar, hair combed away from the temples, and the nun-like ornament of a string of ebony beads and a crucifix. This I felt sure was Eliza, though I could trace little resemblance to her former self in that elongated and colourless visage.

The other was as certainly Georgiana: but not the Georgiana I remembered—the slim and fairy-like girl of eleven. This was a full-blown, very plump damsel, fair as waxwork; with handsome and regular features, languishing blue eyes, and ringleted yellow hair. The hue of her dress was black too: but its fashion was so different from her sister's—so much more flowing and becoming—it looked as stylish as the other's looked puritanical.

In each of the sisters there was one trait of the mother—and only one: the thin and pallid elder daughter had her parent's Cairngorm eye: the blooming and luxuriant younger girl had her contour of jaw and chin,—perhaps a little softened, but still imparting an indescribable hardness to the countenance, otherwise so voluptuous and buxom.

Both ladies, as I advanced, rose to welcome me, and both addressed me by the name of 'Miss Eyre.' Eliza's greeting was delivered in a short, abrupt voice, without a smile; and then she sat down again, fixed her eyes on the fire, and seemed to forget me. Georgiana added to her 'How d'ye do?' several commonplaces about my journey, the weather and so on, uttered in rather a drawling tone: and accompanied by sundry side-glances that measured me from head to foot—now traversing the folds of my drab merino pelisse, and now lingering on the plain trimming of my cottage bonnet. Young ladies have a remarkable way of letting you know that they think you a 'quiz' without actually saying the words. A certain superciliousness of look, coolness of manner, nonchalance of tone, express fully their sentiments on the point without committing them by any positive rudeness in word or deed.

A sneer, however, whether covert or open, had now no longer that power

over me it once possessed: as I sat between my cousins, I was surprised to find how easy I felt under the total neglect of the one and the semi-sarcastic attentions of the other—Eliza did not mortify, nor Georgiana ruffle me. The fact was, I had other things to think about; within the last few months feelings had been stirred in me so much more potent than any they could raise—pains and pleasures so much more acute and exquisite had been excited, than any it was in their power to inflict or bestow—that their airs gave me no concern either for good or bad.

'How is Mrs. Reed?' I asked soon, looking calmly at Georgiana; who thought fit to bridle at the direct address, as if it were an unexpected liberty.

'Mrs. Reed? Ah! mama you mean; she is extremely poorly: I doubt if you can see her to-night.'

'If,' said I, 'you would just step upstairs and tell her I am come, I should be much obliged to you.'

Georgiana almost started, and she opened her blue eyes wild and wide. I know she had a particular wish to see me,' I added, 'and I would not defer attending to her desire longer than is absolutely necessary.'

'Mama dislikes being disturbed in an evening,' remarked Eliza. I soon rose, quietly took off my bonnet and gloves, uninvited, and said I would just step out to Bessie—who was, I dared say, in the kitchen—and ask her to ascertain whether Mrs. Reed was disposed to receive me or not to-night. I went, and having found Bessie and despatched her on my errand, I proceeded to take further measures. It had heretofore been my habit always to shrink from arrogance: received as I had been to-day, I should, a year ago, have resolved to quit Gateshead the very next morning; now, it was disclosed to me all at once, that that would be a foolish plan. I had taken a journey of a hundred miles to see my aunt, and I must stay with her till she was better—or dead: as to her daughters' pride and folly, I must put it on one side; make myself independent of it. So I addressed the housekeeper; asked her to show me a room, told her I should probably be a visitor for a week or two, had my trunk conveyed to my chamber, and followed it thither myself: met Bessie on the landing.

'Missis is awake,' said she; 'I have told her you are here: come and let us see if she will know you.'

I did not need to be guided to the well-known room: to which I had so often been summoned for chastisement or reprimand in former days. I hastened before Bessie, I softly opened the door: a shaded light stood on the table, for it was now getting dark. There was the great four-post bed with amber hangings as of old; there the toilet-table, the arm-chair, and the foot-stool: at which I had a hundred times been sentenced to kneel, to ask pardon for offences, by me, uncommitted. I looked into a certain corner near, half-expecting to see the slim outline of a once-dreaded switch; which used to

lurk there, waiting to leap out imp-like and lace my quivering palm or shrink ing neck. I approached the bed; I opened the curtains and leant over the high-piled pillows.

Well did I remember Mrs. Reed's face, and I eagerly sought the familiar image. It is a happy thing that time quells the longings of vengeance, and hushes the promptings of rage and aversion: I had left this woman in bitterness and hate, and I came back to her now with no other emotion than a sort of ruth for her great sufferings, and a strong yearning to forget and forgive all injuries—to be reconciled and clasp hands in amity.

The well-known face was there: stern, relentless as ever—there was that peculiar eye which nothing could melt; and the somewhat raised, imperious, despotic eyebrow. How often had it lowered on me menace and hate! and how the recollection of childhood's terrors and sorrows revived as I traced its harsh line now! And yet I stooped down and kissed her: she looked at me.

'Is this Jane Eyre?' she said.

'Yes, aunt Reed. How are you, dear aunt?'

I had once vowed that I would never call her aunt again: I thought it no sin to forget and break that vow now. My fingers had fastened on her hand which lay outside the sheet: had she pressed mine kindly, I should at that moment have experienced true pleasure. But unimpressionable natures are not so soon softened, nor are natural antipathies so readily eradicated: Mrs. Reed took her hand away, and, turning her face rather from me, she remarked that the night was warm. Again she regarded me, so icily, I felt at once that her opinion of me—her feeling towards me—was unchanged, and unchangeable. I knew by her stony eye—opaque to tenderness, indissoluble to tears— that she was resolved to consider me bad to the last; because to believe me good, would give her no generous pleasure: only a sense of mortification.

I felt pain, and then I felt ire; and then I felt a determination to subdue her—to be her mistress in spite both of her nature and her will. My tears had risen, just as in childhood: I ordered them back to their source. I brought a chair to the bed-head: I sat down and leaned over the pillow.

'You sent for me,' I said, 'and I am here; and it is my intention to stay till I see how you get on.'

'Oh, of course! You have seen my daughters?'

'Yes.'

'Well, you may tell them I wish you to stay till I can talk some things over with you I have on my mind: to-night it is too late, and I have a difficulty in recalling them. But there was something I wished to say—let me see'——

The wandering look and changed utterance told what wreck had taken place in her once-vigorous frame. Turning restlessly, she drew the bed-clothes round her; my elbow, resting on a corner of the quilt, fixed it down: she was at once irritated.

'Sit up!' said she; 'don't annoy me with holding the clothes fast—are you Jane Eyre?'

'I am Jane Eyre.'

'I have had more trouble with that child than any one would believe. Such a burden to be left on my hands—and so much annoyance as she caused me, daily and hourly, with her incomprehensible disposition, and her sudden starts of temper, and her continual, unnatural watchings of one's movements! I declare she talked to me once like something mad, or like a fiend—no child ever spoke or looked as she did; I was glad to get her away from the house. What did they do with her at Lowood? The fever broke out there, and many of the pupils died. She, however, did not die: but I said she did—I wish she had died!'

'A strange wish, Mrs. Reed: why do you hate her so?'

'I had a dislike to her mother always; for she was my husband's only sister, and a great favourite with him: he opposed the family's disowning her when she made her low marriage; and when news came of her death, he wept like a simpleton. He would send for the baby; though I entreated him rather to put it out to nurse and pay for its maintenance. I hated it the first time I set my eyes on it—a sickly, whining, pining thing! It would wail in its cradle all night long—not screaming heartily like any other child, but whimpering and moaning. Reed pitied it; and he used to nurse it and notice it as if it had been his own: more, indeed, than he ever noticed his own at that age. He would try to make my children friendly to the little beggar: the darlings could not bear it, and he was angry with them when they showed their dislike. In his last illness, he had it brought continually to his bedside; and but an hour before he died, he bound me by vow to keep the creature. I would as soon have been charged with a pauper brat out of a workhouse: but he was weak, naturally weak. John does not at all resemble his father, and I'm glad of it: John is like me and like my brothers—he is quite a Gibson. Oh, I wish he would cease tormenting me with letters for money! I have no more money to give him: we are getting poor. I must send away half the servants and shut up part of the house; or let it off. I can never submit to do that—yet how are we to get on? Two-thirds of my income goes in paying the interest of mortgages. John gambles dreadfully, and always loses—poor boy! He is beset by sharpers: John is sunk and degraded—his look is frightful—I feel ashamed for him when I see him.'

She was getting much excited. 'I think I had better leave her now,' said I to Bessie, who stood on the other side of the bed.

'Perhaps you had, Miss: but she often talks in this way towards night—in the morning she is calmer.'

I rose. 'Stop!' exclaimed Mrs. Reed. 'There is another thing I wished to say. He threatens me—he continually threatens me with his own death,

or mine: and I dream sometimes that I see him laid out with a great wound in his throat, or with a swollen and blackened face. I am come to a strange pass: I have heavy troubles. What is to be done? How is the money to be had?'

Bessie now endeavoured to persuade her to take a sedative draught: she succeeded with difficulty. Soon after, Mrs. Reed grew more composed, and sank into a dozing state. I then left her.

More than ten days elapsed before I had again any conversation with her. She continued either delirious or lethargic; and the doctor forbade everything which could painfully excite her. Meantime, I got on as well as I could with Georgiana and Eliza. They were very cold, indeed, at first. Eliza would sit half the day sewing, reading, or writing, and scarcely utter a word either to me or her sister. Georgiana would chatter nonsense to her canary bird by the hour, and take no notice of me. But I was determined not to seem at a loss for occupation or amusement: I had brought my drawing materials with me, and they served me for both.

Provided with a case of pencils, and some sheets of paper, I used to take a seat apart from them, near the window, and busy myself in sketching fancy vignettes, representing any scene that happened momentarily to shape itself in the ever-shifting kaleidoscope of imagination: a glimpse of sea between two rocks; the rising moon, and a ship crossing its disk; a group of reeds and water-flags, and a naiad's head, crowned with lotus-flowers, rising out of them; an elf sitting in a hedge-sparrow's nest, under a wreath of hawthorn-bloom.

One morning I fell to sketching a face: what sort of a face it was to be I did not care or know. I took a soft black pencil, gave it a broad point, and worked away. Soon I had traced on the paper a broad and prominent forehead and a square lower outline of visage: that contour gave me pleasure; my fingers proceeded actively to fill it with features. Strongly-marked horizontal eyebrows must be traced under that brow; then followed, naturally, a well defined nose, with a straight ridge and full nostrils; then a flexible-looking mouth, by no means narrow; then a firm chin, with a decided cleft down the middle of it: of course, some black whiskers were wanted, and some jetty hair, tufted on the temples, and waved above the forehead. Now for the eyes: I had left them to the last, because they required the most careful working. I drew them large; I shaped them well: the eyelashes I traced long and sombre; the irids lustrous and large. 'Good! but not quite the thing,' I thought as I surveyed the effect: 'They want more force and spirit;' and I wrought the shades blacker, that the lights might flash more brilliantly—a happy touch or two secured success. There, I had a friend's face under my gaze; and what did it signify that those young ladies turned their backs on me? I looked at it; I smiled at the speaking likeness: I was absorbed and content.

'Is that a portrait of some one you know?' asked Eliza, who had approached

ne unnoticed. I responded that it was merely a fancy head, and hurried it
beneath the other sheets. Of course, I lied: it was, in fact, a very faithful
representation of Mr. Rochester. But what was that to her, or to any one
but myself? Georgiana also advanced to look. The other drawings pleased
her much, but she called that 'an ugly man.' They both seemed surprised
at my skill. I offered to sketch their portraits; and each, in turn, sat for a pencil
outline. Then Georgiana produced her album. I promised to contribute
a water-colour drawing: this put her at once into good humour. She proposed
a walk in the grounds. Before we had been out two hours, we were deep in
confidential conversation: she had favoured me with a description of the
brilliant winter she had spent in London two seasons ago—of the admiration
she had there excited—the attention she had received; and I even got hints
of the titled conquest she had made. In the course of the afternoon and
evening these hints were enlarged on: various soft conversations were reported,
and sentimental scenes represented; and, in short, a volume of a novel of
fashionable life was that day improvised by her for my benefit. The com-
munications were renewed from day to day: they always ran on the same
theme—herself, her loves, and woes. It was strange she never once adverted
either to her mother's illness, or her brother's death, or the present gloomy
state of the family prospects. Her mind seemed wholly taken up with remi-
niscences of past gaiety, and aspirations after dissipations to come. She
passed about five minutes each day in her mother's sick-room and no more.

Eliza still spoke little: she had evidently no time to talk. I never saw a busier
person than she seemed to be; yet it was difficult to say what she did: or
rather, to discover any result of her diligence. She had an alarum to call her
up early. I know not how she occupied herself before breakfast, but after
that meal she divided her time into regular portions; and each hour had
its allotted task. Three times a day she studied a little book, which I found,
on inspection, was a Common Prayer Book. I asked her once what was the
great attraction of that volume, and she said 'the Rubric.' Three hours she
gave to stitching, with gold thread, the border of a square crimson cloth,
almost large enough for a carpet. In answer to my inquiries after the use
of this article, she informed me it was a covering for the altar of a new church
lately erected near Gateshead. Two hours she devoted to her diary; two to
working by herself in the kitchen-garden; and one to the regulation of her
accounts. She seemed to want no company; no conversation. I believe she
was happy in her way: this routine sufficed to her; and nothing annoyed her
so much as the occurrence of any incident which forced her to vary its
clock-work regularity.

She told me one evening, when more disposed to be communicative than
usual, that John's conduct, and the threatened ruin of the family, had been
a source of profound affliction to her: but she had now, she said, settled her

mind, and formed her resolution. Her own fortune she had taken care to secure; and when her mother died,—and it was wholly improbable, she tranquilly remarked, that she should either recover or linger long,—she would execute a long-cherished project: seek a retirement where punctual habits would be permanently secured from disturbance, and place safe barriers between herself and a frivolous world. I asked if Georgiana would accompany her

'Of course not. Georgiana and she had nothing in common: they never had had. She would not be burdened with her society for any consideration Georgiana should take her own course; and she, Eliza, would take hers.

Georgiana, when not unburdening her heart to me, spent most of her time in lying on the sofa, fretting about the dulness of the house, and wishing over and over again that her aunt Gibson would send her an invitation up to town. 'It would be so much better,' she said, 'if she could only get out of the way for a month or two, till all was over.' I did not ask her what she meant by 'all being over,' but I suppose she referred to the expected decease of her mother and the gloomy sequel of funeral rites. Eliza generally took no more notice of her sister's indolence and complaints than if no such murmuring, lounging object had been before her. One day, however, as she put away her account-book, and unfolded her embroidery, she suddenly took her up thus:—

'Georgiana, a more vain and absurd animal than you, was certainly never allowed to cumber the earth. You had no right to be born; for you make no use of life. Instead of living for, in, and with yourself, as a reasonable being ought, you seek only to fasten your feebleness on some other person's strength: if no one can be found willing to burden her or himself with such a fat, weak, puffy, useless thing, you cry out that you are ill-treated, neglected, miserable. Then, too, existence for you must be a scene of continual change and excitement, or else the world is a dungeon: you must be admired, you must be courted, you must be flattered—you must have music, dancing, and society—or you languish, you die away. Have you no sense to devise a system which will make you independent of all efforts, and all wills, but your own? Take one day; share it into sections; to each section apportion its task: leave no stray unemployed quarters of an hour, ten minutes, five minutes, include all; do each piece of business in its turn with method, with rigid regularity. The day will close almost before you are aware it has begun; and you are indebted to no one for helping you to get rid of one vacant moment: you have had to seek no one's company, conversation, sympathy, forbearance; you have lived, in short, as an independent being ought to do. Take this advice: the first and last I shall offer you; then you will not want me or any one else, happen what may. Neglect it—go on as heretofore, craving, whining, and idling—and suffer the results of your idiocy, however bad and insufferable they may be. I tell you this plainly; and listen: for though

I shall no more repeat what I am now about to say, I shall steadily act on it. After my mother's death, I wash my hands of you: from the day her coffin is carried to the vault in Gateshead Church, you and I will be as separate as if we had never known each other. You need not think that because we chanced to be born of the same parents, I shall suffer you to fasten me down by even the feeblest claim: I can tell you this—if the whole human race, ourselves excepted, were swept away, and we two stood alone on the earth, I would leave you in the old world, and betake myself to the new.'

She closed her lips.

'You might have spared yourself the trouble of delivering that tirade,' answered Georgiana. 'Everybody knows you are the most selfish heartless creature in existence: and I know your spiteful hatred towards me: I have had a specimen of it before in the trick you played me about Lord Edwin Vere: you could not bear me to be raised above you, to have a title, to be received into circles where you dare not show your face, and so you acted the spy and informer, and ruined my prospects for ever.' Georgiana took out her handkerchief and blew her nose for an hour afterwards; Eliza sat cold, impassable, and assiduously industrious.

True, generous feeling is made small account of by some; but here were two natures rendered, the one intolerably acrid, the other despicably savourless for the want of it. Feeling without judgment is a washy draught indeed; but judgment untempered by feeling is too bitter and husky a morsel for human deglutition.

It was a wet and windy afternoon: Georgiana had fallen asleep on the sofa over the perusal of a novel; Eliza was gone to attend a saint's-day service at the new church—for in matters of religion she was a rigid formalist: no weather ever prevented the punctual discharge of what she considered her devotional duties; fair or foul, she went to church thrice every Sunday, and as often on week-days as there were prayers.

I bethought myself to go upstairs and see how the dying woman sped, who lay there almost unheeded: the very servants paid her but a remittent attention: the hired nurse, being little looked after, would slip out of the room whenever she could. Bessie was faithful; but she had her own family to mind, and could only come occasionally to the hall. I found the sick-room unwatched, as I had expected: no nurse was there; the patient lay still, and seemingly lethargic; her livid face sunk in the pillows: the fire was dying in the grate. I renewed the fuel, re-arranged the bed-clothes, gazed awhile on her who could not now gaze on me, and then I moved away to the window.

The rain beat strongly against the panes, the wind blew tempestuously: 'One lies there,' I thought, 'who will soon be beyond the war of earthly elements. Whither will that spirit—now struggling to quit its material tenement—flit when at length released?'

In pondering the great mystery, I thought of Helen Burns: recalled her dying words—her faith—her doctrine of the equality of disembodied souls. I was still listening in thought to her well-remembered tones—still picturing her pale and spiritual aspect, her wasted face and sublime gaze, as she lay on her placid deathbed, and whispered her longing to be restored to her divine Father's bosom—when a feeble voice murmured from the couch behind: 'Who is that?'

I knew Mrs. Reed had not spoken for days: was she reviving? I went up to her.

'It is I, aunt Reed.'

'Who—I?' was her answer. 'Who are you?' looking at me with surprise and a sort of alarm, but still not wildly.

'You are quite a stranger to me—where is Bessie?'

'She is at the lodge, aunt.'

'Aunt,' she repeated. 'Who calls me Aunt? You are not one of the Gibsons; and yet I know you—that face, and the eyes and forehead are quite familiar to me: you are like—why, you are like Jane Eyre!'

I said nothing: I was afraid of occasioning some shock by declaring my identity.

'Yet,' said she, 'I am afraid it is a mistake: my thoughts deceive me. I wished to see Jane Eyre, and I fancy a likeness where none exists: besides, in eight years she must be so changed.' I now gently assured her that I was the person she supposed and desired me to be: and seeing that I was understood, and that her senses were quite collected, I explained how Bessie had sent her husband to fetch me from Thornfield.

'I am very ill, I know,' she said ere long. 'I was trying to turn myself a few minutes since, and find I cannot move a limb. It is as well I should ease my mind before I die: what we think little of in health, burdens us at such an hour as the present is to me. Is the nurse here? or is there no one in the room but you?'

I assured her we were alone.

'Well, I have twice done you a wrong which I regret now. One was in breaking the promise which I gave my husband to bring you up as my own child; the other'—she stopped. 'After all, it is of no great importance, perhaps,' she murmured to herself: 'and then I may get better; and to humble myself so to her is painful.'

She made an effort to alter her position, but failed: her face changed; she seemed to experience some inward sensation—the precursor, perhaps, of the last pang.

'Well: I must get it over. Eternity is before me: I had better tell her.—Go to my dressing-case, open it, and take out a letter you will see there.'

I obeyed her directions. 'Read the letter,' she said. It was short, and thus conceived:—

'MADAM,

'Will you have the goodness to send me the address of my niece, Jane Eyre, and to tell me how she is: it is my intention to write shortly and desire her to come to me at Madeira. Providence has blessed my endeavours to secure a competency; and as I am unmarried and childless, I wish to adopt her during my life, and bequeath her at my death whatever I may have to leave.

'I am, Madam, etc., etc.
'JOHN EYRE, Madeira.'

It was dated three years back.

'Why did I never hear of this?' I asked.

'Because I disliked you too fixedly and thoroughly ever to lend a hand in lifting you to prosperity. I could not forget your conduct to me, Jane—the fury with which you once turned on me; the tone in which you declared you abhorred me the worst of anybody in the world; the unchildlike look and voice with which you affirmed that the very thought of me made you sick, and asserted that I had treated you with miserable cruelty. I could not forget my own sensations when you thus started up and poured out the venom of your mind: I felt fear, as if an animal that I had struck or pushed had looked up at me with human eyes and cursed me in a man's voice.—Bring me some water! Oh! make haste!'

'Dear Mrs. Reed,' said I, as I offered her the draught she required, 'think no more of all this, let it pass away from your mind. Forgive me for my passionate language: I was a child then; eight, nine years have passed since that day.'

She heeded nothing of what I said; but when she had tasted the water and drawn breath, she went on thus:—

'I tell you I could not forget it; and I took my revenge: for you to be adopted by your uncle, and placed in a state of ease and comfort, was what I could not endure. I wrote to him; I said I was sorry for his disappointment, but Jane Eyre was dead: she had died of typhus fever at Lowood. Now act as you please: write and contradict my assertion—expose my falsehood as soon as you like. You were born, I think, to be my torment: my last hour is racked by the recollection of a deed, which, but for you, I should never have been tempted to commit.'

'If you could but be persuaded to think no more of it, aunt, and to regard me with kindness and forgiveness'—

'You have a very bad disposition,' said she, 'and one to this day I feel it impossible to understand: how for nine years you could be patient and quiescent under any treatment, and in the tenth break out all fire and violence, I can never comprehend.'

'My disposition is not so bad as you think: I am passionate, but not vin-

dictive. Many a time, as a little child, I should have been glad to love you if you would have let me; and I long earnestly to be reconciled to you now: kiss me, aunt.'

I approached my cheek to her lips: she would not touch it. She said I oppressed her by leaning over the bed; and again demanded water. As I laid her down—for I raised her and supported her on my arm while she drank—I covered her ice-cold and clammy hand with mine: the feeble fingers shrank from my touch—the glazing eyes shunned my gaze.

'Love me, then, or hate me, as you will,' I said at last, 'you have my full and free forgiveness: ask now for God's; and be at peace.'

Poor, suffering woman! it was too late for her to make now the effort to change her habitual frame of mind: living, she had ever hated me—dying she must hate me still.

The nurse now entered, and Bessie followed. I yet lingered half an hour longer, hoping to see some sign of amity: but she gave none. She was fast relapsing into stupor; nor did her mind again rally: at twelve o'clock that night she died. I was not present to close her eyes; nor were either of her daughters. They came to tell us the next morning that all was over. She was by that time laid out. Eliza and I went to look at her: Georgiana, who had burst out into loud weeping, said she dared not go. There was stretched Sarah Reed's once robust and active frame, rigid and still: her eye of flint was covered with its cold lid; her brow and strong traits wore yet the impress of her inexorable soul. A strange and solemn object was that corpse to me. I gazed on it with gloom and pain: nothing soft, nothing sweet, nothing pitying or hopeful, or subduing, did it inspire; only a grating anguish for *her* woes—not *my* loss—and a sombre tearless dismay at the fearfulness of death in such a form.

Eliza surveyed her parent calmly. After a silence of some minutes she observed,—

'With her constitution she should have lived to a good old age: her life was shortened by trouble.' And then a spasm constricted her mouth for an instant: as it passed away she turned and left the room, and did I. Neither of us had dropt a tear.

CHAPTER 22

Mr. Rochester had given me but one week's leave of absence: yet a month elapsed before I quitted Gateshead. I wished to leave immediately after the funeral; but Georgiana entreated me to stay till she could get off to London: whither she was now at last invited by her uncle, Mr. Gibson, who had come down to direct his sister's interment, and settle the family affairs. Georgiana said she dreaded being left alone with Eliza; from her she got

either sympathy in her dejection, support in her fears, nor aid in her preparations; so I bore with her feeble-minded quailings, and selfish lamentations, as well as I could, and did my best in sewing for her and packing her dresses. It is true, that while I worked, she would idle; and I thought to myself, If you and I were destined to live always together, cousin, we would commence matters on a different footing. I should not settle tamely down into being the forbearing party; I should assign you your share of labour, and compel you to accomplish it, or else it should be left undone: I should insist, also, on your keeping some of those drawling, half-insincere complaints hushed in your own breast. It is only because our connection happens to be very transitory, and comes at a peculiarly mournful season, that I consent thus to render it so patient and compliant on my part.'

At last I saw Georgiana off; but now it was Eliza's turn to request me to stay another week. Her plans required all her time and attention, she said: she was about to depart for some unknown bourne; and all day long she stayed in her own room, her door bolted within, filling trunks, emptying drawers, burning papers, and holding no communication with any one. She wished me to look after the house, to see callers, and answer notes of condolence.

One morning, she told me I was at liberty. 'And,' she added, 'I am obliged to you for your valuable services and discreet conduct! There is some difference between living with such a one as you, and with Georgiana: you perform your own part in life, and burden no one. Tomorrow,' she continued, 'I set out for the Continent. I shall take up my abode in a religious house, near Lisle—a nunnery you would call it: there I shall be quiet and unmolested. I shall devote myself for a time to the examination of the Roman Catholic dogmas, and to a careful study of the workings of their system; if I find it to be, as I half suspect it is, the one best calculated to ensure the doing of all things decently and in order, I shall embrace the tenets of Rome and probably take the veil.'

I neither expressed surprise at this resolution nor attempted to dissuade her from it. 'The vocation will fit you to a hair,' I thought: 'much good may do you!'

'When we parted, she said: 'Good-bye, cousin Jane Eyre; I wish you well: you have some sense.'

I then returned: 'You are not without sense, cousin Eliza; but what you have, I suppose in another year will be walled up alive in a French convent. However, it is not my business, and so it suits you—I don't much care.'

'You are in the right,' said she: and with these words we each went our separate way. As I shall not have occasion to refer either to her or her sister again, I may as well mention here, that Georgiana made an advantageous match with a wealthy worn-out man of fashion; and that Eliza actually took

the veil, and is at this day superior of the convent where she passed the period of her novitiate: and which she endowed with her fortune.

How people feel when they are returning home from an absence, long or short, I did not know: I had never experienced the sensation. I had known what it was to come back to Gateshead when a child, after a long walk—to be scolded for looking cold or gloomy; and later, what it was to come back from church to Lowood—to long for a plenteous meal and a good fire, and to be unable to get either. Neither of these returnings were very pleasant or desirable: no magnet drew me to a given point, increasing in its strength of attraction the nearer I came. The return to Thornfield was yet to be tried.

My journey seemed tedious—very tedious: fifty miles one day, a night spent at an inn; fifty miles the next day. During the first twelve hours I thought of Mrs. Reed in her last moments: I saw her disfigured and discoloured face, and heard her strangely altered voice. I mused on the funeral day, the coffin, the hearse, the black train of tenants and servants—few was the number of relatives—the gaping vault, the silent church, the solemn service. Then I thought of Eliza and Georgiana: I beheld one the cynosure of a ball-room, the other the inmate of a convent cell: and I dwelt on and analysed their separate peculiarities of person and character. The evening arrival at the great town of——scattered these thoughts; night gave them quite another turn: laid down on my traveller's bed, I left reminiscence for anticipation.

I was going back to Thornfield: but how long was I to stay there? Not long; of that I was sure. I had heard from Mrs. Fairfax in the interim of my absence: the party at the hall was dispersed; Mr. Rochester had left for London three weeks ago, but he was then expected to return in a fortnight. Mrs. Fairfax surmised that he was gone to make arrangements for his wedding, as he had talked of purchasing a new carriage: she said the idea of his marrying Miss Ingram still seemed strange to her; but from what everybody said, and from what she had herself seen, she could no longer doubt that the event would shortly take place. 'You would be strangely incredulous if you did doubt it,' was my mental comment. 'I don't doubt it.'

The question followed, 'Where was I to go?' I dreamt of Miss Ingram all the night: in a vivid morning dream I saw her closing the gates of Thornfield against me and pointing me out another road; and Mr. Rochester looked on with his arms folded—smiling sardonically, as it seemed, at both her and me.

I had not notified to Mrs. Fairfax the exact day of my return; for I did not wish either car or carriage to meet me at Millcote. I proposed to walk the distance quietly by myself; and very quietly, after leaving my box in the ostler's care, did I slip away from the George Inn, about six o'clock of a June evening, and take the old road to Thornfield: a road which lay chiefly through fields, and was now little frequented.

It was not a bright or splendid summer evening, though fair and soft: the

haymakers were at work all along the road; and the sky, though far from cloudless, was such as promised well for the future: its blue—where blue was visible—was mild and settled, and its cloud strata high and thin. The west, too, was warm: no watery gleam chilled it—it seemed as if there was a fire lit, an altar burning behind its screen of marbled vapour, and out of apertures shone a golden redness.

I felt glad as the road shortened before me: so glad that I stopped once to ask myself what that joy meant: and to remind reason that it was not to my home I was going, or to a permanent resting-place, or to a place where fond friends looked out for me and waited my arrival. 'Mrs. Fairfax will smile you a calm welcome, to be sure,' said I; 'and little Adèle will clap her hands and jump to see you: but you know very well you are thinking of another than they; and that he is not thinking of you.'

But what is so headstrong as youth? What so blind as inexperience? These affirmed that it was pleasure enough to have the privilege of again looking on Mr. Rochester, whether he looked on me or not; and they added—'Hasten! be with him while you may: but a few more days or weeks at most, and you are parted with him for ever!' And then I strangled a new-born agony—a deformed thing which I could not persuade myself to own and rear—and ran on.

They are making hay, too, in Thornfield meadows; or rather, the labourers are just quitting their work, and returning home with their rakes on their shoulders: now, at the hour I arrive. I have but a field or two to traverse, and then I shall cross the road and reach the gates. How full the hedges are of roses! But I have no time to gather any; I want to be at the house. I passed a tall briar, shooting leafy and flowery branches across the path; I see the narrow stile with stone steps; and I see—Mr. Rochester sitting there, a book and a pencil in his hand: he is writing.

Well, he is not a ghost; yet every nerve I have is unstrung: for a moment I am beyond my own mastery. What does it mean? I did not think I should tremble in this way when I saw him—or lose my voice or the power of motion in his presence. I will go back as soon as I can stir: I need not make an absolute fool of myself. I know another way to the house. It does not signify if I knew twenty ways; for he has seen me.

'Hillo!' he cries; and he puts up his book and his pencil. 'There you are! Come on, if you please.'

I suppose I do come on; though in what fashion I know not: being scarcely cognisant of my movements, and solicitous only to appear calm; and, above all, to control the working muscles of my face—which I feel rebel insolently against my will, and struggle to express what I had resolved to conceal. But I have a veil—it is down: I make shift yet to behave with decent composure.

'And this is Jane Eyre? Are you coming from Millcote, and on foot? Yes—

just one of your tricks: not to send for a carriage, and come clattering ove street and road like a common mortal, but to steal into the vicinage of you home along with twilight, just as if you were a dream or a shade. What th deuce have you done with yourself this last month?'

'I have been with my aunt, sir, who is dead.'

'A true Janian reply! Good angels be my guard! She comes from the othe world—from the abode of people who are dead; and tells me so when sh meets me alone here in the gloaming! If I dared I'd touch you to see if you ar substance or shadow, you elf!—but I'd as soon offer to take hold of a blu *ignis fatuus* light in a march. Truant! truant!' he added, when he had pause an instant. 'Absent from me a whole month: and forgetting me quite, I' be sworn!'

I knew there would be pleasure in meeting my master again; even though broken by the fear that he was so soon to cease to be my master, and by th knowledge that I was nothing to him: but there was ever in Mr. Rochester (s at least I thought) such a wealth of the power of communicating happiness that to taste but of the crumbs he scattered to stray and stranger birds lik me, was to feast genially. His last words were balm: they seemed to impl that it imported something to him whether I forgot him or not. And he ha spoken of Thornfield as my home—would that it were my home!

He did not leave the stile, and I hardly liked to ask to go by. I inquire soon if he had not been to London.

'Yes: I suppose you found that out by second-sight?'

'Mrs. Fairfax told me in a letter.'

'And did she inform you what I went to do?'

'Oh, yes, sir! Everybody knew your errand.'

'You must see the carriage, Jane, and tell me if you don't think it will su Mrs. Rochester exactly; and whether she won't look like Queen Boadice leaning back against those purple cushions. I wish, Jane, I were a trifl better adapted to match with her externally. Tell me, now, fairy as you are,— can't you give me a charm, or a philter, or something of that sort, to mak me a handsome man?'

'It would be past the power of magic, sir;' and, in thought, I added, 'a lovin eye is all the charm needed: to such you are handsome enough; or rathe your sternness has a power beyond beauty.'

Mr. Rochester had sometimes read my unspoken thoughts with an acume to me incomprehensible: in the present instance he took no notice of m abrupt vocal response; but he smiled at me with a certain smile he had of h own, and which he used but on rare occasions. He seemed to think it too goo for common purposes: it was the real sunshine of feeling—he shed it ove me now.

'Pass, Janet,' said he, making room for me to cross the stile: 'go up home

and stay your weary little wandering feet at a friend's threshold.'

All I had now to do was to obey him in silence: no need for me to colloquise further. I got over the stile without a word, and meant to leave him calmly. An impulse held me fast,—a force turned me round. I said—or something in me said for me, and in spite of me:—

'Thank you, Mr. Rochester, for your great kindness. I am strangely glad to get back again to you; and wherever you are is my home—my only home.'

I walked on so fast that even he could hardly have overtaken me had he tried. Little Adèle was half wild with delight when she saw me. Mrs. Fairfax received me with her usual plain friendliness. Leah smiled; and even Sophie bid me 'bon soir' with glee. This was very pleasant: there is no happiness like that of being loved by your fellow-creatures, and feeling that your presence is an addition to their comfort.

I, that evening, shut my eyes resolutely against the future: I stopped my ears against the voice that kept warning me of near separation and coming grief. When tea was over and Mrs. Fairfax had taken her knitting, and I had assumed a low seat near her, and Adèle, kneeling on the carpet, had nestled close up to me, and a sense of mutual affection seemed to surround us with a ring of golden peace, I uttered a silent prayer that we might not be parted far or soon; but when, as we thus sat, Mr. Rochester entered, unannounced, and looking at us, seemed to take pleasure in the spectacle of a group so amicable—when he said he supposed the old lady was all right now that he had got her adopted daughter back again, and added that he saw Adèle was 'prête à croquer sa petite maman Anglaise'—I half ventured to hope that he would, even after his marriage, keep us together somewhere under the shelter of his protection, and not quite exiled from the sunshine of his presence.

A fortnight of dubious calm succeeded my return to Thornfield Hall. Nothing was said of the master's marriage, and I saw no preparation going on for such an event. Almost every day I asked Mrs. Fairfax if she had yet heard anything decided: her answer was always in the negative. Once, she said, she had actually put the question to Mr. Rochester as to when he was going to bring his bride home; but he had answered her only by a joke, and one of his queer looks, and she could not tell what to make of him.

One thing specially surprised me, and that was, there were no journeyings backward and forward, no visits to Ingram Park: to be sure it was twenty miles off, on the borders of another county; but what was that distance to an ardent lover? To so practised and indefatigable a horseman as Mr. Rochester, it would be but a morning's ride. I began to cherish hopes I had no right to conceive: that the match was broken off; that rumour had been mistaken; that one or both parties had changed their minds. I used to look at my master's face to see if it were sad or fierce; but I could not remember the time when it had been so uniformly clear of clouds or evil feelings. If, in the moments

I and my pupil spent with him, I lacked spirits and sank into inevitable dejection, he became even gay. Never had he called me more frequently to his presence; never been kinder to me when there—and, alas! never had I loved him so well.

CHAPTER 23

A splendid Midsummer shone over England: skies so pure, suns so radiant as were then seen in long succession, seldom favour, even singly, our wave-girt land. It was as if a band of Italian days had come from the South, like a flock of glorious passenger birds, and lighted to rest them on the cliffs of Albion. The hay was all got in; the fields round Thornfield were green and shorn; the roads white and baked; the trees were in their dark prime; hedge and wood, full-leaved and deeply tinted, contrasted well with the sunny hue of the clear meadows between.

On Midsummer-eve, Adèle, weary with gathering wild strawberries in Hay Lane half the day, had gone to bed with the sun. I watched her drop asleep, and when I left her I sought the garden.

It was now the sweetest hour of the twenty-four:—'Day its fervid fires had wasted,' and dew fell cool on panting plain and scorched summit. Where the sun had gone down in simple state—pure of the pomp of clouds—spread a solemn purple, burning with the light of red jewel and furnace flame at one point, on one hill-peak, and extending high and wide, soft and still softer over half heaven. The east had its own charm of fine, deep blue, and its own modest gem, a rising and solitary star: soon it would boast the moon; but she was yet beneath the horizon.

I walked a while on the pavement; but a subtle, well-known scent—that of a cigar—stole from some window; I saw the library casement open a hand breadth; I knew I might be watched thence; so I went apart into the orchard. No nook in the grounds more sheltered and more Eden-like; it was full of trees, it bloomed with flowers: a very high wall shut it out from the court, on one side; on the other, a beech avenue screened it from the lawn. At the bottom was a sunk fence; its sole separation from lonely fields: a winding walk bordered with laurels and terminating in a giant horse-chesnut, circled at the base by a seat, led down to the fence. Here one could wander unseen. While such honey-dew fell, such silence reigned, such gloaming gathered, I felt as if I could haunt such shade for ever: but in threading the flower and fruit parterres at the upper part of the inclosure, enticed there by the light the now risen moon casts on this more open quarter, my step is stayed—not by sound not by sight, but once more by a warning fragrance.

Sweet briar and southernwood, jasmine, pink, and rose, have long been

yielding their evening sacrifice of incense: this new scent is neither of shrub nor flower; it is—I know it well—it is Mr. Rochester's cigar. I look round and I listen. I see trees laden with ripening fruit. I hear a nightingale warbling in a wood half a mile off; no moving form is visible, no coming step audible; but that perfume increases: I must flee. I make for the wicket leading to the shrubbery, and I see Mr. Rochester entering. I step aside into the ivy recess, he will not stay long: he will soon return whence he came, and if I sit still he will never see me.

But no—eventide is as pleasant to him as to me, and this antique garden as attractive; and he strolls on, now lifting the gooseberry-tree branches to look at the fruit, large as plums, with which they are laden; now taking a ripe cherry from the wall; now stooping towards a knot of flowers, either to inhale their fragrance or to admire the dew-beads on their petals. A great moth goes humming by me: it alights on a plant at Mr. Rochester's foot: he sees it, and bends to examine it.

'Now, he has his back towards me,' thought I, 'and he is occupied too; perhaps, if I walk softly, I can slip away unnoticed.'

I trode on an edging of turf that the crackle of the pebbly gravel might not betray me: he was standing among the beds at a yard or two distant from where I had to pass; the moth apparently engaged him. 'I shall get by very well,' I meditated. As I crossed his shadow, thrown long over the garden by the moon, not yet risen high, he said quietly without turning:—

'Jane, come and look at this fellow.'

I had made no noise: he had not eyes behind—could his shadow feel? I started at first, and then I approached him.

'Look at his wings,' said he, 'he reminds me rather of a West Indian insect; one does not often see so large and gay a night-rover in England: there! he is flown.'

The moth roamed away. I was sheepishly retreating also; but Mr. Rochester followed me, and when we reached the wicket, he said:—

'Turn back: on so lovely a night it is a shame to sit in the house; and surely no one can wish to go to bed while sunset is thus at meeting with moonrise.'

It is one of my faults, that though my tongue is sometimes prompt enough at an answer, there are times when it sadly fails me in framing an excuse; and always the lapse occurs at some crisis, when a facile word or plausible pretext is specially wanted to get me out of painful embarrassment. I did not like to walk at this hour alone with Mr. Rochester in the shadowy orchard; but I could not find a reason to allege for leaving him. I followed with lagging step, and thoughts busily bent on discovering a means of extrication; but he himself looked so composed and so grave also, I became ashamed of feeling any confusion: the evil—if evil existent or prospective there was—seemed to be with me only; his mind was unconscious and quiet.

'Jane,' he recommenced, as we entered the laurel walk, and slowly strayed down in the direction of the sunk fence and the horse-chesnut, 'Thornfield is a pleasant place in summer, is it not?'

'Yes, sir.'

'You must have become in some degree attached to the house,—you, who have an eye for natural beauties, and a good deal of the organ of Adhesiveness?'

'I am attached to it, indeed.'

'And though I don't comprehend how it is, I perceive you have acquired a degree of regard for that foolish little child Adèle, too; and even for simple dame Fairfax?'

'Yes, sir; in different ways, I have an affection for both.'

'And would be sorry to part with them?'

'Yes.'

'Pity!' he said, and sighed and paused. 'It is always the way of events in this life,' he continued presently: 'no sooner have you got settled in a pleasant resting-place, than a voice calls out to you to rise and move on, for the hour of repose is expired.'

'Must I move on, sir?' I asked. 'Must I leave Thornfield?'

'I believe you must, Jane. I am sorry, Janet, but I believe indeed you must.'

This was a blow: but I did not let it prostrate me.

'Well, sir, I shall be ready when the order to march comes.'

'It is come now—I must give it to-night.'

'Then you are going to be married, sir?'

'Ex-act-ly—pre-cise-ly: with your usual acuteness, you have hit the nail straight on the head.'

'Soon, sir?'

'Very soon, my——that is, Miss Eyre: and you'll remember, Jane, the first time I, or Rumour, plainly intimated to you that it was my intention to put my old bachelor's neck into the sacred noose, to enter into the holy estate of matrimony—to take Miss Ingram to my bosom, in short (she's an extensive armful: but that's not to the point—one can't have too much of such a very excellent thing as my beautiful Blanche): well, as I was saying—listen to me, Jane! You're not turning your head to look after more moths, are you? That was only a lady-clock, child, "flying away home." I wish to remind you that it was you who first said to me, with that discretion I respect in you—with that foresight, prudence and humility which befit your responsible and dependent position—that in case I married Miss Ingram—both you and little Adèle had better trot forthwith. I pass over the sort of slur conveyed in this suggestion on the character of my beloved; indeed, when you are far away, Janet, I'll try to forget it: I shall notice only its wisdom; which is such that I have made it my law of action. Adèle must go to school; and you, Miss Eyre, must get a new situation.'

'Yes, sir, I will advertise immediately: and meantime, I suppose'——I was going to say, 'I suppose I may stay here, till I find another shelter to betake myself to:' but I stopped, feeling it would not do to risk a long sentence, for my voice was not quite under command.

'In about a month I hope to be a bridegroom,' continued Mr. Rochester; 'and in the interim I shall myself look out for employment and an asylum for you.'

'Thank you, sir; I am sorry to give'——

'Oh, no need to apologise! I consider that when a dependent does her duty as well as you have done yours, she has a sort of claim upon her employer for any little assistance he can conveniently render her; indeed I have already, through my future mother-in-law, heard of a place that I think will suit: it is to undertake the education of the five daughters of Mrs. Dionysius O'Gall of Bitternutt Lodge, Connaught, Ireland. You'll like Ireland, I think: they're such warm-hearted people there, they say.'

'It is a long way off, sir.'

'No matter—a girl of your sense will not object to the voyage or the distance.'

'Not the voyage, but the distance: and then the sea is a barrier'——

'From what, Jane?'

'From England and from Thornfield: and'——

'Well?'

'From *you*, sir.'

I said this almost involuntarily; and, with as little sanction of free will, my ears gushed out. I did not cry so as to be heard, however; I avoided sobbing. The thought of Mrs. O'Gall and Bitternutt Lodge struck cold to my heart; and colder the thought of all the brine and foam, destined, as it seemed, to rush between me and the master at whose side I now walked; and coldest the remembrance of the wider ocean—wealth, caste, custom intervened between me and what I naturally and inevitably loved.

'It is a long way,' I again said.

'It is, to be sure; and when you get to Bitternutt Lodge, Connaught, Ireland, I shall never see you again, Jane: that's morally certain. I never go over to Ireland, not having myself much of a fancy for the country. We have been good friends, Jane; have we not?'

'Yes, sir.'

'And when friends are on the eve of separation, they like to spend the little time that remains to them close to each other. Come—we'll talk over the voyage and the parting quietly, half an hour or so, while the stars enter into their shining life up in heaven yonder: here is the chestnut tree: here is the bench at its old roots. Come, we will sit there in peace to-night, though we should never more be destined to sit there together.' He seated me and himself.

'It is a long way to Ireland, Janet, and I am sorry to send my little friend

on such weary travels: but if I can't do better, how is it to be helped? Are you anything akin to me, do you think, Jane?'

I could risk no sort of answer by this time: my heart was full.

'Because,' he said, 'I sometimes have a queer feeling with regard to you—especially when you are near me, as now: it is as if I had a string somewhere under my left ribs, tightly and inextricably knotted to a similar string situated in the corresponding quarter of your little frame. And if that boisterous channel, and two hundred miles or so of land come broad between us, I am afraid that cord of communion will be snapt; and then I've a nervous notion I should take to bleeding inwardly. As for you,—you'd forget me.'

'That I *never* should, sir: you know'——impossible to proceed.

'Jane, do you hear that nightingale singing in the wood? Listen!'

In listening, I sobbed convulsively; for I could repress what I endured no longer; I was obliged to yield, and I was shaken from head to foot with acute distress. When I did speak, it was only to express an impetuous wish that I had never been born, or never come to Thornfield.

'Because you are sorry to leave it?'

The vehemence of emotion, stirred by grief and love within me, was claiming mastery, and struggling for full sway; and asserting a right to predominate: to overcome, to live, rise, and reign at last; yes,—and to speak.

'I grieve to leave Thornfield: I love Thornfield:—I love it, because I have lived in it a full and delightful life,—momentarily at least. I have not been trampled on. I have not been petrified. I have not been buried with inferior minds, and excluded from every glimpse of communion with what is bright and energetic, and high. I have talked, face to face, with what I reverence; with what I delight in,—with an original, a vigorous, an expanded mind. I have known you, Mr. Rochester; and it strikes me with terror and anguish to feel I absolutely must be torn from you for ever. I see the necessity of departure and it is like looking on the necessity of death.'

'Where do you see the necessity?' he asked, suddenly.

'Where? You sir, have placed it before me.'

'In what shape?'

'In the shape of Miss Ingram; a noble and beautiful woman,—your bride.'

'My bride! What bride? I have no bride!'

'But you will have.'

'Yes:—I will!—I will!' He set his teeth.

'Then I must go:—you have said it yourself.'

'No: you must stay! I swear it—and the oath shall be kept.'

'I tell you I must go!' I retorted, roused to something like passion. 'Do you think I can stay to become nothing to you? Do you think I am an automaton—a machine without feelings? and can bear to have my morsel of bread snatched from my lips, and my drop of living water dashed from my cup? D

you think, because I am poor, obscure, plain, and little, I am soulless and heartless? You think wrong!—I have as much soul as you,—and full as much heart! And if God had gifted me with some beauty, and much wealth, I should have made it as hard for you to leave me, as it is now for me to leave you. I am not talking to you now through the medium of custom, conventionalities, or even of mortal flesh:—it is my spirit that addresses your spirit; just as if both had passed through the grave, and we stood at God's feet, equal,—as we are!'

'As we are!' repeated Mr. Rochester—'so,' he added, enclosing me in his arms, gathering me to his breast, pressing his lips on my lips: 'so, Jane!'

'Yes, so, sir,' I rejoined: 'and yet not so; for you are a married man—or as good as a married man, and wed to one inferior to you—to one with whom you have no sympathy—whom I do not believe you truly love; for I have seen and heard you sneer at her. I would scorn such a union: therefore I am better than you—let me go!'

'Where, Jane? To Ireland?'

'Yes—to Ireland. I have spoken my mind, and can go anywhere now.'

'Jane, be still; don't struggle so, like a wild, frantic bird that is rending its own plumage in its desperation.'

'I am no bird; and no net ensnares me; I am a free human being with an independent will; which I now exert to leave you.'

Another effort set me at liberty, and I stood erect before him.

'And your will shall decide your destiny,' he said: 'I offer you my hand, my heart, and a share of all my possessions.'

'You play a farce, which I merely laugh at.'

'I ask you to pass through life at my side—to be my second self and best earthly companion.'

'For that fate you have already made your choice, and must abide by it.'

'Jane, be still a few moments: you are over-excited: I will be still too.'

A waft of wind came sweeping down the laurel-walk, and trembled through the boughs of the chesnut: it wandered away—away—to an indefinite distance —it died. The nightingale's song was then the only voice of the hour: in listening to it, I again wept. Mr. Rochester sat quiet, looking at me gently and seriously. Some time passed before he spoke: he at last said:—

'Come to my side, Jane, and let us explain and understand one another.'

'I will never again come to your side: I am torn away now, and cannot return.'

'But, Jane, I summon you as my wife: it is you only I intend to marry.'

I was silent: I thought he mocked me.

'Come, Jane—come hither.'

'Your bride stands between us.'

He rose, and with a stride reached me.

'My bride is here,' he said, again drawing me to him, 'because my equal is here, and my likeness. Jane, will you marry me?'

Still I did not answer, and still I writhed myself from his grasp: for I was still incredulous.

'Do you doubt me, Jane?'

'Entirely.'

'You have no faith in me?'

'Not a whit.'

'Am I a liar in your eyes?' he asked passionately. 'Little sceptic, you *shall* be convinced. What love have I for Miss Ingram? None: and that you know. What love has she for me? None: as I have taken pains to prove: I caused a rumour to reach her that my fortune was not a third of what was supposed, and after that I presented myself to see the result; it was coldness both from her and her mother. I would not—I could not—marry Miss Ingram. You— you strange—you almost unearthly thing!—I love as my own flesh. You—poor and obscure, and small and plain as you are—I entreat to accept me as a husband.'

'What, me!' I ejaculated: beginning in his earnestness—and especially in his incivility—to credit his sincerity: 'me who have not a friend in the world but you—if you are my friend: not a shilling but what you have given me?'

'You, Jane. I must have you for my own—entirely my own. Will you be mine? Say yes, quickly.'

'Mr. Rochester, let me look at your face: turn to the moonlight.'

'Why?'

'Because I want to read your countenance; turn!'

'There: you will find it scarcely more legible than a crumpled, scratched page. Read on: only make haste, for I suffer.'

His face was very much agitated and very much flushed, and there were strong workings in the features, and strange gleams in the eyes.

'Oh, Jane, you torture me!' he exclaimed. 'With that searching and yet faithful and generous look, you torture me!'

'How can I do that? If you are true and your offer real, my only feelings to you must be gratitude and devotion—they cannot torture.'

'Gratitude!' he ejaculated; and added wildly—'Jane, accept me quickly. Say Edward—give me my name—Edward—I will marry you.'

'Are you in earnest?—Do you truly love me?—Do you sincerely wish me to be your wife?'

'I do; and if an oath is necessary to satisfy you, I swear it.'

'Then, sir, I will marry you.'

'Edward—my little wife!'

'Dear Edward!'

'Come to me—come to me entirely now,' said he: and added, in his deepest

tone, speaking in my ear as his cheek was laid on mine, 'Make my happiness—
I will make yours.'

'God pardon me!' he subjoined ere long, 'and man meddle not with me:
I have her, and will hold her.'

'There is no one to meddle, sir. I have no kindred to interfere.'

'No—that is the best of it,' he said. And if I had loved him less I should
have thought his accent and look of exultation savage: but sitting by him,
roused from the nightmare of parting—called to the paradise of union—
I thought only of the bliss given me to drink in so abundant a flow. Again and
again he said, 'Are you happy, Jane?' and again and again I answered, 'Yes.'
After which he murmured, 'It will atone—it will atone. Have I not found her
friendless, and cold, and comfortless? Will I not guard, and cherish, and
solace her? Is there not love in my heart, and constancy in my resolves? It
will expiate at God's tribunal. I know my Maker sanctions what I do.
For the world's judgment—I wash my hands thereof. For man's opinion—I
defy it.'

But what had befallen the night? The moon was not yet set, and we were
all in shadow: I could scarcely see my master's face, near as I was. And what
ailed the chesnut tree? it writhed and groaned; while wind roared in the laurel
walk, and came sweeping over us.

'We must go in,' said Mr. Rochester: 'the weather changes. I could have
sat with thee till morning, Jane.'

'And so,' thought I, 'could I with you.' I should have said so, perhaps, but
a livid, vivid spark leapt out of a cloud at which I was looking, and there was
a crack, a crash, and a close rattling peal; and I thought only of hiding my
dazzled eyes against Mr. Rochester's shoulder.

The rain rushed down. He hurried me up the walk, through the grounds,
and into the house; but we were quite wet before we could pass the threshold.
He was taking off my shawl in the hall, and shaking the water out of my
loosened hair, when Mrs. Fairfax emerged from her room. I did not observe
her at first, nor did Mr. Rochester. The lamp was lit. The clock was on the
stroke of twelve.

'Hasten to take off your wet things,' said he: 'and before you go, good-
night—good-night, my darling!'

He kissed me repeatedly. When I looked up, on leaving his arms, there stood
the widow, pale, grave, and amazed. I only smiled at her, and ran upstairs.
'Explanation will do for another time,' thought I. Still, when I reached my
chamber, I felt a pang at the idea she should even temporarily misconstrue
what she had seen. But joy soon effaced every other feeling; and loud as the
wind blew, near and deep as the thunder crashed, fierce and frequent as the
lightning gleamed, cataract-like as the rain fell during a storm of two hours'
duration, I experienced no fear, and little awe. Mr. Rochester came thrice

to my door in the course of it, to ask if I was safe and tranquil: and that was comfort, that was strength for anything.

Before I left my bed in the morning, little Adèle came running in to tell me that the great horse-chesnut at the bottom of the orchard had been struck by lightning in the night, and half of it split away.

CHAPTER 24

As I rose and dressed, I thought over what had happened, and wondered if it were a dream. I could not be certain of the reality till I had seen Mr. Rochester again, and heard him renew his words of love and promise.

While arranging my hair, I looked at my face in the glass, and felt it was no longer plain: there was hope in its aspect, and life in its colour: and my eyes seemed as if they had beheld the fount of fruition, and borrowed beams from the lustrous ripple. I had often been unwilling to look at my master, because I feared he could not be pleased at my look; but I was sure I might lift my face to his now, and not cool his affection by its expression. I took a plain but clean and light summer dress from my drawer and put it on: it seemed no attire had ever so well become me; because none had I ever worn in so blissful a mood.

I was not surprised, when I ran down into the hall, to see that a brilliant June morning had succeeded to the tempest of the night; and to feel, through the open glass door, the breathing of a fresh and fragrant breeze. Nature must be gladsome when I was so happy. A beggar-woman and her little boy—pale, ragged objects both—were coming up the walk, and I ran down and gave them all the money I happened to have in my purse—some three or four shillings: good or bad, they must partake of my jubilee. The rooks cawed, and blither birds sang; but nothing was so merry or so musical as my own rejoicing heart.

Mrs. Fairfax surprised me by looking out of the window with a sad countenance, and saying gravely:—'Miss Eyre, will you come to breakfast?' During the meal she was quiet and cool: but I could not undeceive her then. I must wait for my master to give explanations; and so must she. I ate what I could and then I hastened upstairs. I met Adèle leaving the school-room.

'Where are you going? It is time for lessons.'

'Mr. Rochester has sent me away to the nursery.'

'Where is he?'

'In there,' pointing to the apartment she had left; and I went in, and there he stood.

'Come and bid me good-morning,' said he. I gladly advanced; and it was not merely a cold word now, or even a shake of the hand that I received, but

an embrace and a kiss. It seemed natural: it seemed genial to be so well-loved, so caressed by him.

'Jane, you look blooming, and smiling, and pretty,' said he: 'truly pretty this morning. Is this my pale little elf? Is this my mustard-seed? This little sunny-faced girl with the dimpled cheek and rosy lips; the satin-smooth hazel hair, and the radiant hazel eyes?' (I had green eyes, reader; but you must excuse the mistake: for him they were new-dyed, I suppose.)

'It is Jane Eyre, sir.'

'Soon to be Jane Rochester,' he added: 'in four weeks, Janet; not a day more. Do you hear that?'

I did, and I could not quite comprehend it: it made me giddy. The feeling, the annoucement sent through me, was something stronger than was consistent with joy—something that smote and stunned: it was, I think, almost fear.

'You blushed, and now you are white, Jane: what is that for?'

'Because you gave me a new name—Jane Rochester; and it seems so strange.'

'Yes; Mrs. Rochester,' said he; 'young Mrs. Rochester—Fairfax Rochester's girl-bride.'

'It can never be, sir; it does not sound likely. Human beings never enjoy complete happiness in this world. I was not born for a different destiny to the rest of my species; to imagine such a lot befalling me is a fairy tale—a day-dream.'

'Which I can and will realise. I shall begin to-day. This morning I wrote to my banker in London to send me certain jewels he has in his keeping,—heirlooms for the ladies of Thornfield. In a day or two I hope to pour them into your lap: for every privilege, every attention shall be yours, that I would accord a peer's daughter if about to marry her.'

'Oh, sir!—never mind jewels! I don't like to hear them spoken of. Jewels for Jane Eyre sounds unnatural and strange: I would rather not have them.'

'I will myself put the diamond chain round your neck, and the circlet on your forehead,—which it will become: for nature, at least, has stamped her patent of nobility on this brow, Jane; and I will clasp the bracelets on these fine wrists, and load these fairy-like fingers with rings.'

'No, no, sir! think of other subjects, and speak of other things, and in another strain. Don't address me as if I were a beauty; I am your plain, Quakerish governess.'

'You are a beauty, in my eyes; and a beauty just after the desire of my heart,—delicate and aërial.'

'Puny and insignificant, you mean. You are dreaming, sir,—or you are neering. For God's sake, don't be ironical!'

'I will make the world acknowledge you a beauty, too,' he went on, while ͺ really became uneasy at the strain he had adopted; because I felt he was ither deluding himself, or trying to delude me. 'I will attire my Jane in

satin and lace, and she shall have roses in her hair; and I will cover the head I love best with a priceless veil.'

'And then you won't know me, sir; and I shall not be your Jane Eyre any longer, but an ape in a harlequin's jacket,—a jay in borrowed plumes. I would as soon see you, Mr. Rochester, tricked out in stage-trappings, as myself clad in a court-lady's robe; and I don't call you handsome, sir, though I love you most dearly; far too dearly to flatter you. Don't flatter me.'

He pursued his theme, however, without noticing my deprecation. 'This very day I shall take you in the carriage to Millcote, and you must choose some dresses for yourself. I told you we shall be married in four weeks. The wedding is to take place quietly, in the church down below yonder; and then I shall waft you away at once to town. After a brief stay there, I shall bear my treasure to regions nearer the sun: to French vineyards and Italian plains; and she shall see whatever is famous in old story and in modern record: she shall taste, too, of the life of cities; and she shall learn to value herself by just comparison with others.'

'Shall I travel?—and with you, sir?'

'You shall sojourn at Paris, Rome, and Naples: at Florence, Venice, and Vienna: all the ground I have wandered over shall be re-trodden by you: wherever I stamped my hoof, your sylph's foot shall step also. Ten years since, I flew through Europe half mad; with disgust, hate, and rage, as my companions: now I shall revisit it healed and cleansed, with a very angel as my comforter.'

I laughed at him as he said this. 'I am not an angel,' I asserted; 'and I will not be one till I die: I will be myself, Mr. Rochester, you must neither expect nor exact anything celestial of me—for you will not get it, any more than I shall get it of you: which I do not at all anticipate.'

'What do you anticipate of me?'

'For a little while you will perhaps be as you are now,—a very little while; and then you will turn cool; and then you will be capricious; and then you will be stern, and I shall have much ado to please you: but when you get well used to me, you will perhaps like me again,—*like* me, I say, not *love* me. I suppose your love will effervesce in six months, or less. I have observed in books written by men, that period assigned as the farthest to which a husband's ardour extends. Yet, after all, as a friend and companion, I hope never to become quite distasteful to my dear master.'

'Distasteful! and like you again! I think I shall like you again and yet again; and I will make you confess I do not only *like*, but *love* you—with truth, fervour, constancy.'

'Yet are you not capricious, sir?'

'To women who please me only by their faces, I am the very devil when I find out they have neither souls nor hearts—when they open to me a perspec-

ive of flatness, triviality, and perhaps imbecility, coarseness, and ill-temper: but to the clear eye and eloquent tongue, to the soul made of fire, and the character that bends but does not break—at once supple and stable, tractable and consistent—I am ever tender and true.'

'Had you ever experience of such a character, sir? Did you ever love such an one?'

'I love it now.'

'But before me: if I, indeed, in any respect come up to your difficult standard?'

'I never met your likeness, Jane: you please me, and you master me—you seem to submit, and I like the sense of pliancy you impart; and while I am twining the soft, silken skein round my finger, it sends a thrill up my arm to my heart. I am influenced—conquered; and the influence is sweeter than I can express; and the conquest I undergo has a witchery beyond any triumph I can win. Why do you smile, Jane? What does that inexplicable, that uncanny turn of countenance mean?'

'I was thinking, sir (you will excuse the idea; it was involuntary), I was thinking of Hercules and Samson with their charmers'——

'You were, you little elfish'——

'Hush, sir! You don't talk very wisely just now; any more than those gentlemen acted very wisely. However, had they been married, they would no doubt by their severity as husbands have made up for their softness as suitors; and so will you, I fear. I wonder how you will answer me a year hence, should I ask a favour it does not suit your convenience or pleasure to grant.'

'Ask me something now, Janet—the least thing: I desire to be entreated'——

'Indeed, I will, sir; I have my petition all ready.'

'Speak! But if you look up and smile with that countenance, I shall swear concession before I know to what, and that will make a fool of me.'

'Not at all, sir; I ask only this: don't send for the jewels, and don't crown me with roses: you might as well put a border of gold lace round that plain pocket handkerchief you have there.'

'I might as well "gild refined gold." I know it: your request is granted then—for the time. I will remand the order I despatched to my banker. But you have not yet asked for anything: you have prayed a gift to be withdrawn: try again.'

'Well, then, sir, have the goodness to gratify my curiosity, which is much piqued on one point.'

He looked disturbed. 'What? what?' he said hastily. 'Curiosity is a dangerous petition: it is well I have not taken a vow to accord every request'——

'But there can be no danger in complying with this, sir.'

'Utter it, Jane: but I wish that instead of a mere inquiry into, perhaps, a secret, it was a wish for half my estate.'

'Now, king Ahasuerus! What do I want with half your estate? Do you think I am a Jew-usurer, seeking good investment in land? I would much rather have all your confidence. You will not exclude me from your confidence, if you admit me to your heart?'

'You are welcome to all my confidence that is worth having, Jane: but for God's sake, don't desire a useless burden! Don't long for poison—don't turn out a downright Eve on my hands!'

'Why not, sir? You have just been telling me how much you liked to be conquered, and how pleasant over-persuasion is to you. Don't you think I had better take advantage of the confession, and begin and coax and entreat—even cry and be sulky if necessary—for the sake of a mere essay of my power?'

'I dare you to any such experiment. Encroach, presume, and the game is up.

'Is it, sir? You soon give in. How stern you look now! Your eyebrows have become as thick as my finger, and your forehead resembles, what, in some very astonishing poetry, I once saw styled, "a blue-piled thunderloft." That will be your married look, sir, I suppose?'

'If that will be *your* married look, I, as a Christian, will soon give up the notion of consorting with a mere sprite or salamander. But what had you to ask, thing?—out with it!'

'There, you are less than civil now; and I like rudeness a great deal better than flattery. I had rather be a *thing* than an angel. This is what I have to ask,—Why did you take such pains to make me believe you wished to marry Miss Ingram?'

'Is that all! Thank God, it is no worse!' And now he unknit his black brows looked down, smiling at me, and stroked my hair, as if well pleased at seeing a danger averted. 'I think I may confess,' he continued, 'even although I should make you a little indignant, Jane—and I have seen what a fire-spirit you can be when you are indignant. You glowed in the cool moonlight last night, when you mutinied against fate, and claimed your rank as my equal. Janet, by-the-by, it was you who made me the offer.'

'Of course, I did. But to the point if you please, sir—Miss Ingram?'

'Well, I feigned courtship of Miss Ingram, because I wished to render you as madly in love with me as I was with you; and I knew jealousy would be the best ally I could call in for the furtherance of that end.'

'Excellent!—Now you are small—not one whit bigger than the end of my little finger. It was a burning shame, and a scandalous disgrace to act in that way. Did you think nothing of Miss Ingram's feelings, sir!'

'Her feelings are concentrated in one—pride; and that needs humbling. Were you jealous, Jane?'

'Never mind, Mr. Rochester: it is in no way interesting to you to know that. Answer me truly once more. Do you think Miss Ingram will not suffer from your dishonest coquetry? Won't she feel forsaken and deserted?'

'Impossible!—when I told you how she, on the contrary, deserted me: the idea of my insolvency cooled, or rather extinguished, her flame in a moment.'

'You have a curious, designing mind, Mr. Rochester. I am afraid your principles on some points are eccentric.'

'My principles were never trained, Jane: they may have grown a little awry for want of attention.'

'Once again, seriously; may I enjoy the great good that has been vouchsafed to me, without fearing that any one else is suffering the bitter pain I myself felt a while ago?'

'That you may, my good little girl: there is not another being in the world has the same pure love for me as yourself—for I lay that pleasant unction to my soul, Jane, a belief in your affection.'

I turned my lips to the hand that lay on my shoulder. I loved him very much —more than I could trust myself to say—more than words had power to express.

'Ask something more,' he said presently; 'it is my delight to be entreated, and to yield.'

I was again ready with my request. 'Communicate your intentions to Mrs. Fairfax, sir: she saw me with you last night in the hall, and she was shocked. Give her some explanation before I see her again. It pains me to be misjudged by so good a woman.'

'Go to your room, and put on your bonnet,' he replied. 'I mean you to accompany me to Millcote this morning; and while you prepare for the drive, I will enlighten the old lady's understanding. Did she think, Janet, you had given the world for love, and considered it well lost?'

'I believe she thought I had forgotten my station, and yours, sir.'

'Station! station!—your station is in my heart, and on the necks of those who would insult you, now or hereafter.—Go.'

I was soon dressed; and when I heard Mr. Rochester quit Mrs. Fairfax's parlour, I hurried down to it. The old lady had been reading her morning portion of Scripture—the lesson for the day; her Bible lay open before her, and her spectacles were upon it. Her occupation, suspended by Mr. Rochester's announcement, seemed now forgotten: her eyes, fixed on the blank wall opposite, expressed the surprise of a quiet mind, stirred by unwonted tidings. Seeing me, she roused herself: she made a sort of effort to smile, and framed a few words of congratulation: but the smile expired, and the sentence was abandoned unfinished. She put up her spectacles, shut the Bible, and pushed her chair back from the table.

'I feel so astonished,' she began, 'I hardly know what to say to you, Miss Eyre. I have surely not been dreaming, have I? Sometimes I half fall asleep when I am sitting alone, and fancy things that have never happened. It has seemed to me more than once when I have been in a doze, that my dear

husband, who died fifteen years since, has come in and sat down beside me; and that I have even heard him call me by my name, Alice, as he used to do. Now, can you tell me whether it is actually true that Mr. Rochester has asked you to marry him? Don't laugh at me. But I really thought he came in here five minutes ago, and said, that in a month you would be his wife.'

'He has said the same thing to me,' I replied.

'He has! Do you believe him? Have you accepted him?'

'Yes.' She looked at me bewildered.

'I could never have thought it. He is a proud man: all the Rochesters were proud: and his father, at least, liked money. He, too, has always been careful. He means to marry you?'

'He tells me so.'

She surveyed my whole person: in her eyes I read that they had there found no charm powerful enough to solve the enigma.

'It passes me!' she continued: 'but no doubt it is true since you say so. How it will answer, I cannot tell: I really don't know. Equality of position and fortune is often advisable in such cases; and there are twenty years of difference in your ages. He might almost be your father.'

'No, indeed, Mrs. Fairfax!' exclaimed I, nettled: 'he is nothing like my father! No one, who saw us together, would suppose it for an instant. Mr. Rochester looks as young, and is as young as some men at five-and-twenty.'

'Is it really for love he is going to marry you?' she asked.

I was so hurt by her coldness and scepticism, that the tears rose to my eyes.

'I am sorry to grieve you,' pursued the widow; 'but you are so young, and so little acquainted with men, I wished to put you on your guard. It is an old saying that "all is not gold that glitters"; and in this case I do fear there will be something found to be different to what either you or I expect.'

'Why!—am I a monster?' I said: 'is it impossible that Mr. Rochester should have a sincere affection for me?'

'No: you are very well; and much improved of late; and Mr. Rochester, I daresay, is fond of you. I have always noticed that you were a sort of pet of his. There are times when, for your sake, I have been a little uneasy at his marked preference, and have wished to put you on your guard: but I did not like to suggest even the possibility of wrong. I knew such an idea would shock, perhaps offend you; and you were so discreet, and so thoroughly modest and sensible, I hoped you might be trusted to protect yourself. Last night I cannot tell you what I suffered when I sought all over the house, and could find you nowhere, nor the master either; and then, at twelve o'clock, saw you come in with him.'

'Well, never mind that now,' I interrupted impatiently: 'it is enough that all was right.'

'I hope all will be right in the end,' she said: 'but, believe me, you canno

be too careful. Try and keep Mr. Rochester at a distance: distrust yourself as well as him. Gentlemen in his station are not accustomed to marry their governesses.'

I was growing truly irritated: happily, Adèle ran in.

'Let me go,—let me go to Millcote too!' she cried. 'Mr. Rochester won't; though there is so much room in the new carriage. Beg him to let me go, mademoiselle.'

'That I will, Adèle;' and I hastened away with her, glad to quit my gloomy monitress. The carriage was ready; they were bringing it round to the front, and my master was pacing the pavement, Pilot following him backwards and forwards.

'Adèle may accompany us, may she not, sir?'

'I told her no. I'll have no brats!—I'll have only you.'

'Do let her go, Mr. Rochester, if you please: it would be better.'

'Not it: she will be a restraint.'

He was quite peremptory, both in look and voice. The chill of Mrs. Fairfax's warnings, and the damp of her doubts were upon me: something of unsubstantiality and uncertainty had beset my hopes. I half lost the sense of power over him. I was about mechanically to obey him, without further remonstrance: but as he helped me into the carriage, he looked at my face.

'What is the matter?' he asked; 'all the sunshine is gone. Do you really wish the bairn to go? Will it annoy you if she is left behind?'

'I would far rather she went, sir.'

'Then off for your bonnet, and back, like a flash of lightning!' cried he to Adèle. She obeyed him with what speed she might.

'After all, a single morning's interruption will not matter much,' said he, 'when I mean shortly to claim you—your thoughts, conversation, and company —for life.'

Adèle, when lifted in, commenced kissing me, by way of expressing her gratitude for my intercession; she was instantly stowed away into a corner on the other side of him. She then peeped round to where I sat; so stern a neighbour was too restrictive: to him, in his present fractious mood, she dared whisper no observations, nor ask of him any information.

'Let her come to me,' I entreated: 'she will, perhaps, trouble you, sir: there is plenty of room on this side.'

He handed her over as if she had been a lap-dog: 'I'll send her to school yet,' he said, but now he was smiling.

Adèle heard him, and asked if she was to go to school 'sans mademoiselle?'

'Yes,' he replied, 'absolutely sans mademoiselle; for I am to take mademoiselle to the moon, and there I shall seek a cave in one of the white valleys among the volcano-tops, and mademoiselle shall live with me there and only me.'

'She will have nothing to eat: you will starve her,' observed Adèle.

'I shall gather manna for her morning and night: the plains and hill-sides in the moon are bleached with manna, Adèle.'

'She will want to warm herself: what will she do for a fire?'

'Fire rises out of the lunar mountains: when she is cold, I'll carry her up to a peak and lay her down on the edge of a crater.'

'Oh, qu'elle y sera mal—peu comfortable! And her clothes, they will wear out: how can she get new ones?'

Mr. Rochester professed to be puzzled. 'Hem!' said he. 'What would you do, Adèle? Cudgel your brains for an expedient. How would a white or a pink cloud answer for a gown, do you think? And one could cut a pretty enough scarf out of a rainbow.'

'She is far better as she is,' concluded Adèle, after musing some time: 'besides, she would get tired of living with only you in the moon. If I were mademoiselle, I would never consent to go with you.'

'She has consented: she has pledged her word.'

'But you can't get her there: there is no road to the moon: it is all air; and neither you nor she can fly.'

'Adèle, look at that field.' We were now outside Thornfield gates, and bowling lightly along the smooth road to Millcote, where the dust was well laid by the thunder-storm, and where the low hedges and lofty timber trees on each side glistened green, and rain-refreshed.

'In that field, Adèle, I was walking late one evening about a fortnight since—the evening of the day you helped me to make hay in the orchard meadows; and as I was tired with raking swaths, I sat down to rest me on a stile; and there I took out a little book and a pencil, and began to write about a misfortune that befell me long ago, and a wish I had for happy days to come: I was writing away very fast, though daylight was fading from the leaf, when something came up the path and stopped two yards off me. I looked at it. It was a little thing with a veil of gossamer on its head. I beckoned it to come near me: it stood soon at my knee. I never spoke to it, and it never spoke to me in words: but I read its eyes, and it read mine; and our speechless colloquy was to this effect:—

'It was a fairy, and come from Elf-land, it said; and its errand was to make me happy: I must go with it out of the common world to a lonely place—such as the moon, for instance—and it nodded its head towards her horn, rising over Hay-hill: it told me of the alabaster cave and silver vale where we might live. I said I should like to go: but reminded it, as you did me, that I had no wings to fly.'

' "Oh," returned the fairy, "that does not signify! Here is a talisman will remove all difficulties;" and she held out a pretty gold ring. "Put it," she said "on the fourth finger of my left hand, and I am yours, and you are mine; and

we shall leave earth, and make our own heaven yonder." She nodded again at the moon. The ring, Adèle, is in my breeches-pocket, under the disguise of a sovereign: but I mean soon to change it to a ring again.'

'But what has mademoiselle to do with it? I don't care for the fairy: you said it was mademoiselle you would take to the moon?'——

'Mademoiselle is a fairy,' he said, whispering mysteriously. Whereupon I told her not to mind his badinage; and she, on her part, evinced a fund of genuine French scepticism: denominating Mr. Rochester 'un vrai menteur,' and assuring him that she made no account whatever of his 'Contes de fée,' and that 'du reste, il n'y avait pas de fées, et quand même il y en avait:' she was sure they would never appear to him, nor ever give him rings, or offer to live with him in the moon.

The hour spent at Millcote was a somewhat harassing one to me. Mr. Rochester obliged me to go to a certain silk warehouse: there I was ordered to choose half a dozen dresses. I hated the business, I begged leave to defer it: no—it should be gone through with now. By dint of entreaties expressed in energetic whispers, I reduced the half-dozen to two: these, however, he vowed he would select himself. With anxiety I watched his eye rove over the gay stores: he fixed on a rich silk of the most brilliant amethyst dye, and a superb pink satin. I told him in a new series of whispers, that he might as well buy me a gold gown and a silver bonnet at once: I should certainly never venture to wear his choice. With infinite difficulty, for he was stubborn as a stone, I persuaded him to make an exchange in favour of a sober black satin and pearl-grey silk. 'It might pass for the present,' he said; 'but he would yet see me glittering like a parterre.'

Glad was I to get him out of the silk warehouse, and then out of a jeweller's shop: the more he bought me, the more my cheek burned with a sense of annoyance and degradation. As we re-entered the carriage, and I sat back feverish and fagged, I remembered what in the hurry of events, dark and bright, I had wholly forgotten—the letter of my uncle, John Eyre, to Mrs. Reed: his intention to adopt me and make me his legatee. 'It would, indeed, be a relief,' I thought, 'if I had ever so small an independency; I never can bear being dressed like a doll by Mr. Rochester, or sitting like a second Danae with the golden shower falling daily round me. I will write to Madeira the moment I get home, and tell my uncle John I am going to be married, and to whom: if I had but a prospect of one day bringing Mr. Rochester an accession of fortune, I could better endure to be kept by him now.' And somewhat relieved by this idea (which I failed not to execute that day), I ventured once more to meet my master's and lover's eye; which most pertinaciously sought mine, though I averted both face and gaze. He smiled; and I thought his smile was such as a sultan might, in a blissful and fond moment, bestow on a slave his gold and gems had enriched: I crushed his hand, which was ever hunting

mine, vigorously, and thrust it back to him red with the passionate pressure—

'You need not look in that way,' I said: 'if you do, I'll wear nothing but my old Lowood frocks to the end of the chapter. I'll be married in this lilac gingham—you may make a dressing-gown for yourself out of the pearl grey silk, and an infinite series of waitcoats out of the black satin.'

He chuckled; he rubbed his hands: 'Oh, it is rich to see and hear her!' he exclaimed. 'Is she original? Is she piquant? I would not exchange this one little English girl for the grand Turk's whole seraglio; gazelle-eyes, houri forms and all!'

The eastern allusion bit me again: 'I'll not stand you an inch in the stead of a seraglio,' I said: 'so don't consider me an equivalent for one; if you have a fancy for anything in that line, away with you, sir, to the bazars of Stamboul without delay; and lay out in extensive slave-purchases some of that spare cash you seem at a loss to spend satisfactorily here.'

'And what will you do, Janet, while I am bargaining for so many tons of flesh and such an assortment of black eyes?'

'I'll be preparing myself to go out as a missionary to preach liberty to them that are enslaved—your harem inmates amongst the rest. I'll get admitted there, and I'll stir up mutiny; and you, three-tailed bashaw as you are, sir, shall in a trice find yourself fettered amongst our hands: nor will I, for one, consent to cut your bonds till you have signed a charter, the most liberal that despot ever yet conferred.'

'I would consent to be at your mercy, Jane.'

'I would have no mercy, Mr. Rochester, if you supplicated for it with an eye like that. While you looked so, I should be certain that whatever charter you might grant under coercion, your first act, when released, would be to violate its conditions.'

'Why, Jane, what would you have? I fear you will compel me to go through a private marriage ceremony, besides that performed at the altar. You will stipulate, I see, for peculiar terms—what will they be?'

'I only want an easy mind, sir; not crushed by crowded obligations. Do you remember what you said of Céline Varens?—of the diamonds, the cashmeres you gave her? I will not be your English Céline Varens. I shall continue to act as Adèle's governess; by that I shall earn my board and lodging, and thirty pounds a year besides. I'll furnish my own wardrobe out of that money, and you shall give me nothing but'——

'Well, but what?'

'Your regard: and if I give you mine in return, that debt will be quit.'

'Well, for cool native impudence, and pure innate pride, you haven't your equal,' said he. We were now approaching Thornfield. 'Will it please you to dine with me to-day?' he asked, as we re-entered the gates.

'No, thank you, sir.'

'And what for "no, thank you"? if one may inquire.'

'I never have dined with you, sir: and I see no reason why I should now: till'——

'Till what? You delight in half-phrases.'

'Till I can't help it.'

'Do you suppose I eat like an ogre, or a ghoul, that you dread being the companion of my repast?'

'I have formed no supposition on the subject, sir; but I want to go on as usual for another month.'

'You will give up your governessing slavery at once.'

'Indeed! begging your pardon, sir, I shall not. I shall just go on with it as usual. I shall keep out of your way all day, as I have been accustomed to do: you may send for me in the evening, when you feel disposed to see me, and I'll come then, but at no other time.'

'I want a smoke, Jane, or a pinch of snuff, to comfort me under all this "pour me donner une contenance," as Adèle would say; and unfortunately I have neither my cigar-case, nor my snuff-box. But listen—whisper—it is your time now, little tyrant, but it will be mine presently: and when once I have fairly seized you, to have and to hold, I'll just—figuratively speaking— attach you to a chain like this' (touching his watch-guard). 'Yes, bonny wee thing, I'll wear you in my bosom, lest my jewel I should tyne.'

He said this as he helped me to alight from the carriage: and while he afterwards lifted out Adèle, I entered the house, and made good my retreat upstairs.

He duly summoned me to his presence in the evening. I had prepared an occupation for him; for I was determined not to spend the whole time in a *tête-à-tête* conversation. I remembered his fine voice: I knew he liked to sing—good singers generally do. I was no vocalist myself, and, in his fastidious judgment, no musician, either; but I delighted in listening when the performance was good. No sooner had twilight, that hour of romance, began to lower her blue and starry banner over the lattice, than I rose, opened the piano, and entreated him, for the love of heaven, to give me a song. He said I was a capricious witch, and that he would rather sing another time; but I averred that no time was like the present.

'Did I like his voice?' he asked.

'Very much.' I was not fond of pampering that susceptible vanity of his; but for once, and from motives of expediency, I would e'en soothe and stimulate it.

'Then, Jane, you must play the accompaniment.'

'Very well, sir, I will try.'

I did try, but was presently swept off the stool and denominated, 'a little bungler.' Being pushed unceremoniously to one side—which was precisely what I wished—he usurped my place, and proceeded to accompany himself:

for he could play as well as sing. I hied me to the window-recess; and while I sat there and looked out on the still trees and dim lawn, to a sweet air was sung in mellow tones the following strain:—

> The truest love that ever heart
> Felt at its kindled core
> Did through each vein, in quickened start,
> The tide of being pour.
>
> Her coming was my hope each day,
> Her parting was my pain;
> The chance that did her steps delay
> Was ice in every vein.
>
> I dreamed it would be nameless bliss,
> As I loved, loved to be;
> And to this object did I press
> As blind as eagerly.
>
> But wide as pathless was the space
> That lay, our lives, between,
> And dangerous as the foamy race
> Of ocean-surges green.
>
> And haunted as a robber path
> Through wilderness or wood;
> For Might and Right, and Woe and Wrath,
> Between our spirits stood.
>
> I dangers dared; I hind'rance scorned;
> I omens did defy;
> Whatever menaced, harassed, warned,
> I passed impetuous by.
>
> On sped my rainbow, fast as light;
> I flew as in a dream;
> For glorious rose upon my sight
> That child of Shower and Gleam.
>
> Still bright on clouds of suffering dim
> Shines that soft, solemn joy;
> Nor care I now, how dense and grim
> Disasters gather nigh.
>
> I care not in this moment sweet,
> Though all I have rushed o'er
> Should come on pinion, strong and fleet,
> Proclaiming vengeance sore:
>
> Though haughty Hate should strike me down,
> Right, bar approach to me,
> And grinding Might, with furious frown,
> Swear endless enmity.

My love has placed her little hand
　　With noble faith in mine,
And vowed that wedlock's sacred band
　　Our nature shall entwine.

My love has sworn, with sealing kiss,
　　With me to live—to die;
I have at last my nameless bliss:
　　As I love.—loved am I!

He rose and came towards me, and I saw his face all kindled, and his full falcon-eye flashing, and tenderness and passion in every lineament. I quailed momentarily—then I rallied. Soft scene, daring demonstration, I would not have; and I stood in peril of both: a weapon of defence must be prepared—I whetted my tongue; as he reached me, I asked with asperity, 'whom he was going to marry now?'

'That was a strange question to be put by his darling Jane.'

'Indeed! I considered it a very natural and necessary one: he had talked of his future wife dying with him. What did he mean by such a pagan idea? I had no intention of dying with him—he might depend on that.'

'Oh, all he longed, all he prayed for, was that I might live with him! Death was not for such as I.'

'Indeed it was: I had as good a right to die when my time came as he had: but I should bide that time, and not be hurried away in a suttee.'

'Would I forgive him for the selfish idea, and prove my pardon by a reconciling kiss?'

'No: I would rather be excused.'

Here I heard myself apostrophised as a 'hard little thing'; and it was added, 'any other woman would have been melted to marrow at hearing such stanzas crooned in her praise.'

I assured him I was naturally hard—very flinty, and that he would often find me so; and that, moreover, I was determined to show him divers rugged points in my character before the ensuing four weeks elapsed: he should know fully what sort of a bargain he had made, while there was yet time to rescind it.

'Would I be quiet, and talk rationally?'

'I would be quiet if he liked; and as to talking rationally, I flattered myself I was doing that now.'

He fretted, pished, and pshawed. 'Very good,' I thought; 'you may fume and fidget as you please: but this is the best plan to pursue with you, I am certain. I like you more than I can say; but I'll not sink into a bathos of sentiment; and with this needle of repartee I'll keep you from the edge of the gulph too; and, moreover, maintain by its pungent aid that distance between you and myself most conducive to our real mutual advantage.'

From less to more, I worked him up to considerable irritation; then, after he had retired, in dudgeon, quite to the other end of the room, and I got up, saying, 'I wish you good-night, sir,' in my natural and wonted respectful manner, I slipped out by the side-door and got away.

The system thus entered on, I pursued during the whole season of probation; and with the best success. He was kept, to be sure, rather cross and crusty: but on the whole I could see he was excellently entertained; and that a lamb-like submission and turtle-dove sensibility, while fostering his despotism more, would have pleased his judgment, satisfied his common-sense, and even suited his taste, less.

In other people's presence I was, as formerly, deferential and quiet; any other line of conduct being uncalled for: it was only in the evening conferences I thus thwarted and afflicted him. He continued to send for me punctually the moment the clock struck seven; though when I appeared before him now, he had no such honeyed terms as 'love' and 'darling' on his lips: the best words at my service were 'provoking puppet', 'malicious elf', 'sprite', 'change-ling,' etc. For caresses, too, I now got grimaces; for a pressure of the hand, a pinch on the arm; for a kiss on the cheek, a severe tweak of the ear. It was all right: at present I decidedly preferred these fierce favours to anything more tender. Mrs. Fairfax, I saw, approved me: her anxiety on my account vanished; therefore I was certain I did well. Meantime, Mr. Rochester affirmed I was wearing him to skin and bone, and threatened awful vengeance for my present conduct at some period fast coming. I laughed in my sleeve at his menaces: 'I can keep you in reasonable check now,' I reflected; 'and I don't doubt to be able to do it hereafter: if one expedient loses its virtue another must be devised.'

Yet after all my task was not an easy one; often I would rather have pleased than teased him. My future husband was becoming to me my whole world; and more than the world: almost my hope of heaven. He stood between me and every thought of religion, as an eclipse intervenes between man and the broad sun. I could not, in those days, see God for his creature: of whom I had made an idol.

CHAPTER 25

The month of courtship had wasted: its very last hours were being numbered There was no putting off the day that advanced—the bridal day; and al preparations for its arrival were complete. I, at least, had nothing more to do there were my trunks, packed, locked, corded, ranged in a row along th wall of my little chamber; to-morrow, at this time, they would be far o their road to London: and so should I (D.V.),—or rather, not I, but on

ane Rochester, a person whom as yet I knew not. The cards of address lone remained to nail on: they lay, four little squares on the drawer. Mr. Rochester had himself written the direction, 'Mrs. Rochester, Hotel London,' on each: I could not persuade myself to affix them, or to have them affixed. Mrs. Rochester! She did not exist: she would not be born till to-morrow, some time after eight o'clock A.M.: and I would wait to be assured he had come into the world alive, before I assigned to her all that property. t was enough that in yonder closet, opposite my dressing-table, garments said to be hers had already displaced my black stuff Lowood frock and straw bonnet: for not to me appertained that suit of wedding raiment; the pearl-coloured robe, the vapoury veil, pendent from the usurped portmanteau. shut the closet, to conceal the strange, wraithlike apparel it contained; which, at this evening hour—nine o'clock—gave out certainly a most ghostly shimmer through the shadow of my apartment. 'I will leave you by yourself, white dream,' I said. 'I am feverish: I heard the wind blowing: I will go out f doors and feel it.'

It was not only the hurry of preparation that made me feverish; not only he anticipation of the great change—the new life which was to commence to-morrow; both these circumstances had their share, doubtless, in producing that restless, excited mood which hurried me forth at this late hour into the darkening grounds: but a third cause influenced my mind more than hey.

I had at heart a strange and anxious thought. Something had happened which I could not comprehend; no one knew of or had seen the event but myself: it had taken place the preceding night. Mr. Rochester that night was absent from home; nor was he yet returned: business had called him to a small estate of two or three farms he possessed thirty miles off—business it was requisite he should settle in person, previously to his meditated depar-ure from England. I waited now his return; eager to disburthen my mind, and to seek of him the solution of the enigma that perplexed me. Stay till he comes, reader; and, when I disclose my secret to him, you shall share the confidence.

I sought the orchard: driven to its shelter by the wind, which all day had blown strong and full from the south; without, however, bringing a speck of rain. Instead of subsiding as night drew on, it seemed to augment its rush and deepen its roar: the trees blew stedfastly one way, never writhing round, and scarcely tossing back their boughs once in an hour; so continuous was the strain bending their branchy heads northward—the clouds drifted from pole to pole, fast following, mass on mass: no glimpse of blue sky had been visible that July day.

It was not without a certain wild pleasure I ran before the wind delivering my trouble of mind to the measureless air-torrent thundering through space.

Descending the laurel walk, I faced the wreck of the chesnut-tree; it stood up, black and riven: the trunk, split down the centre, gasped ghastly. The cloven halves were not broken from each other, for the firm base and strong roots kept them unsundered below; though community of vitality was destroyed—the sap could flow no more: their great boughs on each side were dead, and next winter's tempests would be sure to fell one or both to earth as yet, however, they might be said to form one tree—a ruin, but an entire ruin.

'You did right to hold fast to each other,' I said: as if the monster-splinter were living things, and could hear me. 'I think, scathed as you look, and char red and scorched, there must be a little sense of life in you yet: rising out o that adhesion at the faithful, honest roots: you will never have green leave more—never more see birds making nests and singing idylls in your boughs the time of pleasure and love is over with you: but you are not desolate each of you has a comrade to sympathise with him in his decay.' As I looked up at them, the moon appeared momentarily in that part of the sky which filled their fissure; her disk was blood-red, and half overcast; she seemed to throw on me one bewildered, dreary glance, and buried herself again instantly in the deep drift of cloud. The wind fell, for a second, round Thornfield but far away over wood and water, poured a wild, melancholy wail: it wa sad to listen to, and I ran off again.

Here and there I strayed through the orchard, gathered up the apple with which the grass round the tree roots was thickly strewn: then I employee myself in dividing the ripe from the unripe; I carried them into the hous and put them away in the store-room. Then I repaired to the library t ascertain whether the fire was lit; for, though summer, I knew on such a gloom evening, Mr. Rochester would like to see a cheerful hearth when he came in yes, the fire had been kindled some time, and burnt well. I placed his arm chair by the chimney-corner: I wheeled the table near it: I let down th curtain, and had the candles brought in ready for lighting. More restles than ever, when I had completed these arrangements I could not sit still nor even remain in the house: a little time-piece in the room and the ol clock in the hall simultaneously struck ten.

'How late it grows!' I said: 'I will run down to the gates: it is moonligh at intervals: I can see a good way on the road. He may be coming now, an to meet him will save some minutes of suspense.'

The wind roared high in the great trees which embowered the gates; bu the road as far as I could see, to the right hand and the left, was all still an solitary: save for the shadows of clouds crossing it at intervals, as the moo looked out, it was but a long pale line, unvaried by one moving speck.

A puerile tear dimmed my eye while I looked—a tear of disappointmer and impatience: ashamed of it, I wiped it away. I lingered; the moon shu

herself wholly within her chamber, and drew close her curtain of dense cloud: the night grew dark; rain came driving fast on the gale.

'I wish he would come! I wish he would come!' I exclaimed, seized with hypochondriac foreboding. I had expected his arrival before tea; now it was dark: what could keep him? Had an accident happened? The event of last night again recurred to me. I interpreted it as a warning of disaster. I feared my hopes were too bright to be realised; and I had enjoyed so much bliss lately that I imagined my fortune had passed its meridian, and must now decline.

'Well, I cannot return to the house,' I thought; 'I cannot sit by the fireside, while he is abroad in inclement weather: better tire my limbs than strain my heart; I will go forward and meet him.'

I set out; I walked fast, but not far: ere I had measured a quarter of a mile, I heard the tramp of hoofs; a horseman came on, full gallop; a dog ran by his side. Away with evil presentiment! It was he: here he was, mounted on Mesrour, followed by Pilot. He saw me; for the moon had opened a blue field in the sky, and rode in it watery bright: he took his hat off, and waved it round his head. I now ran to meet him.

'There!' he exclaimed, as he stretched out his hand and bent from the saddle: 'You can't do without me, that is evident. Step on my boot-toe; give me both hands: mount!'

I obeyed; joy made me agile: I sprang up before him. A hearty kissing I got for a welcome; and some boastful triumph, which I swallowed as well as I could. He checked himself in his exultation to demand, 'But is there anything the matter, Janet, that you come to meet me at such an hour: Is there anything wrong?'

'No; but I thought you would never come. I could not bear to wait in the house for you, especially with this rain and wind.'

'Rain and wind, indeed! Yes, you are dripping like a mermaid; pull my cloak round you: but I think you are feverish, Jane: both your cheek and hand are burning hot. I ask again, is there anything the matter?'

'Nothing, now: I am neither afraid nor unhappy.'

'Then you have been both?'

'Rather: but I'll tell you all about it by-and-by, sir; and I daresay you will only laugh at me for my pains.'

'I'll laugh at you heartily when to-morrow is past; till then I dare not: my prize is not certain. This is you; who have been as slippery as an eel this last month, and as thorny as a briar-rose? I could not lay a finger anywhere but I was pricked; and now I seem to have gathered up a stray lamb in my arms: you wandered out of the fold to seek your shepherd, did you, Jane?'

'I wanted you, but don't boast. Here we are at Thornfield: now let me get down.'

He landed me on the pavement. As John took his horse, and he followed me into the hall, he told me to make haste and put something dry on, and then return to him in the library; and he stopped me, as I made for the staircase, to extort a promise that I would not be long: nor was I long; in five minutes I rejoined him. I found him at supper.

'Take a seat and bear me company, Jane: please God, it is the last meal but one you will eat at Thornfield Hall for a long time.'

I sat down near him; but told him I could not eat.

'Is it because you have the prospect of a journey before you, Jane? Is it the thoughts of going to London that takes away your appetite?'

'I cannot see my prospects clearly to-night, sir: and I hardly know what thoughts I have in my head. Everything in life seems unreal.'

'Except me: I am substantial enough:—touch me.'

'You, sir, are the most phantom-like of all: you are a mere dream.'

He held out his hand, laughing: 'Is that a dream?' said he, placing it close to my eyes. He had a rounded, muscular, and vigorous hand, as well as a long, strong arm.

'Yes; though I touch it, it is a dream,' said I, as I put it down from before my face. 'Sir, have you finished supper?'

'Yes, Jane.'

I rang the bell, and ordered away the tray. When we were again alone, I stirred the fire, and then took a low seat at my master's knee.

'It is near midnight,' I said.

'Yes: but remember, Jane, you promised to wake with me the night before my wedding.'

'I did; and I will keep my promise, for an hour or two at least; I have no wish to go to bed.'

'Are all your arrangements complete?'

'All, sir.'

'And on my part, likewise,' he returned, 'I have settled everything; and we leave Thornfield to-morrow, within half an hour after our return from church.'

'Very well, sir.'

'With what an extraordinary smile you uttered that word—"very well," Jane! What a bright spot of colour you have on each cheek! and how strangely your eyes glitter! Are you well?'

'I believe I am.'

'Believe! What is the matter?—Tell me what you feel.'

'I could not, sir: no words could tell you what I feel. I wish this present hour would never end: who knows with what fate the next may come charged?'

'This is hypochondria, Jane. You have been over-excited or over-fatigued.'

'Do you, sir, feel calm and happy?'

'Calm?—no: but happy—to the heart's core.'

I looked up at him to read the signs of bliss in his face: it was ardent and flushed.

'Give me your confidence, Jane,' he said: 'relieve your mind of any weight that oppresses it, by imparting it to me. What do you fear?—that I shall not prove a good husband?'

'It is the idea farthest from my thoughts.'

'Are you apprehensive of the new sphere you are about to enter?—of the new life into which you are passing?'

'No.'

'You puzzle me, Jane: your look and tone of sorrowful audacity perplex and pain me. I want an explanation.'

'Then, sir,—listen. You were from home last night?'

'I was:—I know that; and you hinted a while ago at something which had happened in my absence:—nothing, probably, of consequence; but, in short, it has disturbed you. Let me hear it. Mrs. Fairfax has said something, perhaps? or you have overheard the servants talk?—your sensitive self-respect has been wounded?'

'No, sir.' It struck twelve—I waited till the time-piece had concluded its silver chime, and the clock its hoarse, vibrating stroke, and then I proceeded.

'All day, yesterday, I was very busy, and very happy in my ceaseless bustle: for I am not, as you seem to think, troubled by any haunting fears about the new sphere, et cetera: I think it a glorious thing to have the hope of living with you, because I love you. No, sir, don't caress me now—let me talk undisturbed. Yesterday I trusted well in Providence, and believed that events were working together for your good and mine: it was a fine day, if you recollect—the calmness of the air and sky forbade apprehensions regarding your safety or comfort on your journey. I walked a little while on the pavement after tea, thinking of you; and I beheld you in imagination so near me, I scarcely missed your actual presence. I thought of the life that lay before me—*your* life, sir—an existence more expansive and stirring than my own: as much more so as the depths of the sea to which the brook runs, are than the shallows of its own strait channel. I wondered why moralists call this world a dreary wilderness: for me it blossomed like a rose. Just at sunset, the air turned cold and the sky cloudy: I went in. Sophie called me upstairs to look at my wedding-dress, which they had just brought; and under it in the box I found your present—the veil which, in your princely extravagance, you sent for from London: resolved, I suppose, since I would not have jewels, to cheat me into accepting something as costly. I smiled as I unfolded it, and devised how I would tease you about your aristocratic tastes, and your efforts to masque your plebeian bride in the attributes of a peeress. I thought how I would carry down to you the square of unembroidered blond I had myself prepared as a covering for my low-born head, and ask if that was not good enough

for a woman who could bring her husband neither fortune, beauty, nor connections. I saw plainly how you would look; and heard your impetuous republican answers, and your haughty disavowal of any necessity on your part to augment your wealth, or elevate your standing, by marrying either a purse or a coronet.'

'How well you read me, you witch!' interposed Mr. Rochester: 'but what did you find in the veil besides its embroidery? Did you find poison or a dagger that you look so mournful now?'

'No, no, sir; besides the delicacy and richness of the fabric, I found nothing save Fairfax Rochester's pride; and that did not scare me, because I am used to the sight of the demon. But, sir, as it grew dark, the wind rose: it blew yesterday evening, not as it blows now—wild and high—but "with a sullen moaning sound" far more eerie. I wished you were at home. I came into this room, and the sight of the empty chair and fireless hearth chilled me. For some time after I went to bed, I could not sleep—a sense of anxious excitement distressed me. The gale still rising, seemed to my ear to muffle a mournful under-sound; whether in the house or abroad I could not at first tell, but it recurred, doubtful yet doleful at every lull: at last I made out it must be some dog howling at a distance. I was glad when it ceased. On sleeping, I continued in dreams the idea of a dark and gusty night. I continued also the wish to be with you, and experienced a strange, regretful consciousness, of some barrier dividing us. During all my first sleep, I was following the winding of an unknown road; total obscurity environed me; rain pelted me; I was burdened with the charge of a little child: a very small creature, too young and feeble to walk, and which shivered in my cold arms, and wailed piteously in my ear. I thought, sir, that you were on the road a long way before me; and I strained every nerve to overtake you, and made effort on effort to utter your name and entreat you to stop—but my movements were fettered; and my voice still died away inarticulate; while you, I felt, withdrew farther and farther every moment.'

'And these dreams weigh on your spirits now, Jane, when I am close to you? Little nervous subject! Forget visionary woe, and think only of real happiness! You say you love me, Janet: yes—I will not forget that; and you cannot deny it. *Those* words did not die inarticulate on your lips. I heard them clear and soft: a thought too solemn perhaps, but sweet as music—"I think it is a glorious thing to have the hope of living with you, Edward, because I love you."—Do you love me, Jane? repeat it.'

'I do, sir.—I do, with my whole heart.'

'Well,' he said, after some minutes' silence, 'it is strange; but that sentence has penetrated my breast painfully. Why? I think because you said it with such an earnest, religious energy; and because your upward gaze at me now is the very sublime of faith, truth, and devotion: it is too much as

some spirit were near me. Look wicked, Jane; as you know well how to look: coin one of your wild, shy, provoking smiles; tell me you hate me—tease me, vex me: do anything but move me: I would rather be incensed than saddened.'

'I will tease you and vex you to your heart's content, when I have finished my tale: but hear me to the end.'

'I thought, Jane, you had told me all. I thought I had found the source of your melancholy in a dream!'

I shook my head. 'What! is there more? But I will not believe it to be anything important. I warn you of incredulity beforehand. Go on.'

The disquietude of his air, and somewhat apprehensive impatience of his manner, surprised me: but I proceeded.

'I dreamt another dream, sir: that Thornfield Hall was a dreary ruin, the retreat of bats and owls. I thought that of all the stately front nothing remained but a shell-like wall, very high, and very fragile-looking. I wandered, on a moonlight night, through the grass-grown enclosure within: here I stumbled over a marble hearth, and there over a fallen fragment of cornice. Wrapped up in a shawl, I still carried the unknown little child: I might not lay it down anywhere, however tired were my arms—however much its weight impeded my progress, I must retain it. I heard a gallop of a horse at a distance on the road: I was sure it was you; and you were departing for many years, and for a distant country. I climbed the thin wall with frantic perilous haste, eager to catch one glimpse of you from the top: the stones rolled from under my feet, the ivy branches I grasped gave way, the child clung round my neck in terror, and almost strangled me: at last I gained the summit. I saw you like a speck on a white track, lessening every moment. The blast blew so strong I could not stand. I sat down on the narrow ledge; I hushed the scared infant in my lap: you turned an angle in the road; I bent forward to take a last look; the wall crumbled; I was shaken; the child rolled from my knee, I lost my balance, fell, and woke.'

'Now, Jane, that is all.'

'All the preface, sir; the tale is yet to come. On waking, a gleam dazzled my eyes: I thought—oh, it is daylight! But I was mistaken: it was only candle-light. Sophie, I supposed, had come in. There was a light on the dressing table, and the door of the closet, where, before going to bed, I had hung my wedding dress and veil, stood open: I heard a rustling there. I asked, "Sophie, what are you doing?" No one answered; but a form emerged from the closet: it took the light, held it aloft and surveyed the garments pendent from the portmanteau. "Sophie! Sophie!" I again cried: and still it was silent. I had risen up in bed, I bent forward: first, surprise, then bewilderment, came over me; and then my blood crept cold through my veins. Mr. Rochester, this was not Sophie, it was not Leah, it was not Mrs. Fairfax: it was not—

no, I was sure of it, and am still—it was not even that strange woman, Grace Poole.'

'It must have been one of them,' interrupted my master.

'No, sir, I solemnly assure you to the contrary. The shape standing before me had never crossed my eyes within the precincts of Thornfield Hall before; the height, the contour were new to me.'

'Describe it, Jane.'

'It seemed, sir, a woman, tall and large, with thick and dark hair hanging long down her back. I know not what dress she had on: it was white and straight; but whether gown, sheet, or shroud, I cannot tell.'

'Did you see her face?'

'Not at first. But presently she took my veil from its place; she held it up; gazed at it long, and then she threw it over her own head, and turned to the mirror. At that moment I saw the reflection of the visage and features quite distinctly in the dark oblong glass.'

'And how were they?'

'Fearful and ghastly to me—oh, sir, I never saw a face like it! It was a discoloured face—it was a savage face. I wish I could forget the roll of the red eyes and the fearful blackened inflation of the lineaments!'

'Ghosts are usually pale, Jane.'

'This, sir, was purple: the lips were swelled and dark; the brow furrowed; the back eyebrows widely raised over the blood-shot eyes. Shall I tell you of what it reminded me?'

'You may.'

'Of the foul German specter—the Vampyre.'

'Ah!—what did it do?'

'Sir, it removed my veil from its gaunt head, rent it in two parts, and flinging both on the floor, trampled on them.'

'Afterwards?'

'It drew aside the window-curtain and looked out: perhaps it saw dawn approaching, for, taking the candle, it retreated to the door. Just at my bedside the figure stopped: the fiery eye glared upon me—she thrust up her candle close to my face, and extinguished it under my eyes. I was aware her lurid visage flamed over mine, and I lost consciousness: for the second time in my life—only the second time—I became insensible from terror.'

'Who was with you when you revived?'

'No one, sir; but the broad day. I rose, bathed my head and face in water; drank a long draught; felt that though enfeebled I was not ill, and determined that to none but you would I impart this vision. Now, sir, tell me who and what that woman was?'

'The creature of an over-stimulated brain; that is certain. I must be careful of you, my treasure: nerves like yours were not made for rough handling.'

'Sir, depend upon it, my nerves were not in fault; the thing was real: the transaction actu ally took place.'

'And your previous dreams: were they real too? Is Thornfield Hall a ruin? Am I severed from you by insuperable obstacles? Am I leaving you without a tear—without a kiss—without a word?'

'Not yet.'

'Am I about to do it?—Why, the day is already commenced which is to bind us indissolubly; and when we are once united, there shall be no recurrence of these mental terrors: I guarantee that.'

'Mental terrors, sir! I wish I could believe them to be only such: I wish it more than ever; since even you cannot explain to me the mystery of that awful visitant.'

'And since I cannot do it, Jane, it must have been unreal.'

'But, sir, when I said so to myself on rising this morning, and when I looked round the room to gather courage and comfort from the cheerful aspect of each familiar object in full daylight, there—on the carpet—I saw what gave the distinct lie to my hypothesis,—the veil, torn from top to bottom in two halves!'

I felt Mr. Rochester start and shudder; he hastily flung his arms round me: 'Thank God!' he exclaimed, 'that if anything malignant did come near you last night, it was only the veil that was harmed.—Oh, to think what might have happened!'

He drew his breath short, and strained me so close to him, I could scarcely pant. After some minutes' silence, he continued, cheerily:—

'Now, Janet, I'll explain to you all about it. It was half dream, half reality: a woman did, I doubt not, enter your room: and that woman was—must have been—Grace Poole. You call her a strange being yourself: from all you know, you have reason so to call her—what did she do to me? what to Mason? In a state between sleeping and waking, you noticed her entrance and her actions; but feverish, almost delirious as you were, you ascribed to her a goblin appearance different from her own: the long dishevelled hair, the swelled black face, the exaggerated stature, were figments of imagination; results of nightmare: the spiteful tearing of the veil was real: and it is like her. I see you would ask why I keep such a woman in my house: when we have been married a year and a day, I will tell you: but not now. Are you satisfied, Jane? Do you accept my solution of the mystery?'

I reflected, and in truth it appeared to me the only possible one: satisfied I was not, but to please him I endeavoured to appear so—relieved, I certainly did feel; so I answered him with a contented smile. And now, as it was long past one, I prepared to leave him.

'Does not Sophie sleep with Adèle in the nursery?' he asked, as I lit my candle.

'Yes, sir.'

'And there is room enough in Adèle's little bed for you. You must share it with her to-night, Jane: it is no wonder that the incident you have related should make you nervous, and I would rather you did not sleep alone: promise me to go to the nursery.'

'I shall be very glad to do so, sir.'

'And fasten the door securely on the inside. Wake Sophie when you go upstairs, under pretence of requesting her to rouse you in good time to-morrow for you must be dressed and have finished breakfast before eight. And now no more sombre thoughts: chase dull care away, Janet. Don't you hear to what soft whispers the wind has fallen? and there is no more beating of rain against the window-panes: look here' (he lifted up the curtain) — 'it is a lovely night!'

It was. Half heaven was pure and stainless: the clouds, now trooping before the wind, which had shifted to the west, were filing off eastward, in long, silvered columns. The moon shone peacefully.

'Well,' said Mr. Rochester, gazing inquiringly into my eyes, 'how is my Janet now?'

'The night is serene, sir; and so am I.'

'And you will not dream of separation and sorrow to-night; but of happy love and blissful union.'

This prediction was but half fulfilled: I did not indeed dream of sorrow but as little did I dream of joy; for I never slept at all. With little Adèle in my arms, I watched the slumber of childhood—so tranquil, so passionless so innocent—and waited for the coming day: all my life was awake and astir in my frame: and as soon as the sun rose I rose too. I remember Adèle clung to me as I left her: I remember I kissed her as I loosened her little hand from my neck; and I cried over her with strange emotion, and quitted her because I feared my sobs would break her still sound repose. She seemed the emblem of my past life; and he, I was now to array myself to meet, the dread, but adored, type of my unknown future day.

CHAPTER 26

Sophie came at seven to dress me; she was very long indeed in accomplishing her task; so long that Mr. Rochester, grown, I suppose, impatient of my delay, sent up to ask why I did not come. She was just fastening my veil (the plain square of blond after all) to my hair with a brooch; I hurried from under her hands as soon as I could.

'Stop!' she cried in French. 'Look at yourself in the mirror: you have not taken one peep.'

So I turned at the door: I saw a robed and veiled figure, so unlike my usual self that it seemed almost the image of a stranger. 'Jane!' called a voice, and I hastened down. I was received at the foot of the stairs by Mr. Rochester.

'Lingerer,' he said, 'my brain is on fire with impatience; and you tarry so long!'

He took me into the dining-room, surveyed me keenly all over, pronounced me 'fair as a lily, and not only the pride of his life, but the desire of his eyes,' and then telling me he would give me but ten minutes to eat some breakfast, he rang the bell. One of his lately hired servants, a footman, answered it. 'Is John getting the carriage ready?'

'Yes, sir.'

'Is the luggage brought down?'

'They are bringing it down, sir.'

'Go you to the church: see if Mr. Wood (the clergyman) and the clerk are there: return and tell me.'

The church, as the reader knows, was but just beyond the gates; the footman soon returned.

'Mr. Wood is in the vestry, sir, putting on his surplice.'

'And the carriage?'

'The horses are harnessing.'

'We shall not want it to go to church; but it must be ready the moment we return: all the boxes and luggage arranged and strapped on, and the coachman in his seat.'

'Yes, sir.'

'Jane, are you ready?'

I rose. There were no groomsmen, no bridesmaids, no relatives to wait for or marshal: none but Mr. Rochester and I. Mrs. Fairfax stood in the hall as we passed. I would fain have spoken to her, but my hand was held by a grasp of iron: I was hurried along by a stride I could hardly follow; and to look at Mr. Rochester's face was to feel that not a second of delay would be tolerated for any purpose. I wonder what other bridegroom ever looked as he did—so bent up to a purpose, so grimly resolute: or who, under such stedfast brows, ever revealed such flaming and flashing eyes.

I know not whether the day was fair or foul; in descending the drive, I gazed neither on sky nor earth: my heart was with my eyes; and both seemed migrated into Mr. Rochester's frame. I wanted to see the invisible thing on which, as we went along, he appeared to fasten a glance fierce and fell. I wanted to feel the thoughts whose force he seemed breasting and resisting.

At the churchyard wicket he stopped: he discovered I was quite out of breath. 'Am I cruel in my love?' he said. 'Delay an instant: lean on me, Jane.'

And now I can recall the picture of the grey old house of God rising calm before me, of a rook wheeling round the steeple, of a ruddy morning sky

beyond. I remember something, too, of the green grave-mounds; and I have not forgotten, either, two figures of strangers, straying amongst the low hillocks, and reading the mementoes graven on the few mossy head-stones. I noticed them, because, as they saw us, they passed round to the back of the church; and I doubted not they were going to enter by the side-aisle door, and witness the ceremony. By Mr. Rochester they were not observed; he was earnestly looking at my face, from which the blood had, I daresay, momentarily fled: for I felt my forehead dewy, and my cheeks and lips cold. When I rallied, which I soon did, he walked gently with me up the path to the porch.

We entered the quiet and humble temple; the priest waited in his white surplice at the lowly altar, the clerk beside him. All was still: two shadows only moved in a remote corner. My conjecture had been correct: the strangers had slipped in before us, and they now stood by the vault of the Rochesters, their backs towards us, viewing through the rails the old time-stained marble tomb, where a kneeling angel guarded the remains of Damer de Rochester, slain at Marston Moor in the time of the civil wars; and of Elizabeth, his wife.

Our place was taken at the communion rails. Hearing a cautious step behind me, I glanced over my shoulder: one of the strangers—a gentleman evidently—was advancing up the chancel. The service began. The explanation of the intent of matrimony was gone through; and then the clergyman came a step further forward, and, bending slightly towards Mr. Rochester, went on

'I require and charge you both (as ye will answer at the dreadful day of judgment, when the secrets of all hearts shall be disclosed), that if either of you know any impediment why ye may not lawfully be joined together in matrimony, ye do now confess it; for be ye well assured that so many as are coupled together otherwise than God's word doth allow, are not joined together by God, neither is their matrimony lawful.'

He paused, as the custom is. When is the pause after that sentence ever broken by reply? Not, perhaps, once in a hundred years. And the clergyman who had not lifted his eyes from his book, and had held his breath but for a moment, was proceeding: his hand was already stretched towards Mr. Rochester, as his lips unclosed to ask, 'Wilt thou have this woman for thy wedded wife?'—when a distinct and near voice said:—

'The marriage cannot go on: I declare the existence of an impediment.'

The clergyman looked up at the speaker, and stood mute; the clerk did the same; Mr. Rochester moved slightly, as if an earthquake had rolled under his feet: taking a firmer footing, and not turning his head or eyes, he said 'Proceed'.

Profound silence fell when he had uttered that word, with deep but low intonation. Presently Mr. Wood said:—

'I cannot proceed without some investigation into what has been asserted, and evidence of its truth or falsehood.'

'The ceremony is quite broken off,' subjoined the voice behind us. 'I am in a condition to prove my allegation: an insuperable impediment to this marriage exists.'

Mr. Rochester heard, but heeded not: he stood stubborn and rigid: making no movement, but to possess himself of my hand. What a hot and strong grasp he had!—and how like quarried marble was his pale, firm, massive front at this moment! How his eye shone, still, watchful, and yet wild beneath!

Mr. Wood seemed at a loss. 'What is the nature of the impediment?' he asked. 'Perhaps it may be got over—explained away?'

'Hardly,' was the answer: 'I have called it insuperable, and I speak advisedly.'

The speaker came forwards, and leaned on the rails. He continued, uttering each word distinctly, calmly, steadily, but not loudly.

'It simply consists in the existence of a previous marriage. Mr. Rochester has a wife now living.'

My nerves vibrated to those low-spoken words as they had never vibrated to thunder—my blood felt their subtle violence as it had never felt frost or fire: but I was collected, and in no danger of swooning. I looked at Mr. Rochester: I made him look at me. His whole face was colourless rock: his eye was both spark and flint. He disavowed nothing; he seemed as if he would defy all things. Without speaking; without smiling; without seeming to recognise in me a human being, he only twined my waist with his arm, and riveted me to his side.

'Who are you?' he asked of the intruder.

'My name is Briggs—a solicitor of —— Street, London.'

'And you would thrust on me a wife?'

'I would remind you of your lady's existence, sir; which the law recognises, if you do not.'

'Favour me with an account of her—with her name, her parentage, her place of abode.'

'Certainly.' Mr. Briggs calmly took a paper from his pocket, and read out in a sort of official, nasal voice:—

' "I affirm and can prove that on the 20th of October, A.D., ——, (a date of fifteen years back) Edward Fairfax Rochester, of Thornfield Hall, in the county of ——, and of Ferndean Manor, in ——shire, England, was married to my sister, Bertha Antoinetta Mason, daughter of Jonas Mason, merchant, and of Antoinetta his wife, a Creole—at —— church, Spanish Town, Jamaica. The record of the marriage will be found in the register of that church—a copy of it is now in my possession. Signed, Richard Mason." '

'That—if a genuine document—may prove I have been married, but it

does not prove that the woman mentioned therein as my wife is still living.'

'She was living three months ago,' returned the lawyer.

'How do you know?'

'I have a witness to the fact; whose testimony even you, sir, will scarcely controvert.'

'Produce him—or go to hell.'

'I will produce him first—he is on the spot: Mr. Mason, have the goodness to step forward.'

Mr. Rochester, on hearing the name, set his teeth; he experienced, too, a sort of strong convulsive quiver; near to him as I was, I felt the spasmodic movement of fury or despair run through his frame. The second stranger, who had hitherto lingered in the background, now drew near; a pale face looked over the solicitor's shoulder—yes, it was Mason himself. Mr. Rochester turned and glared at him. His eye, as I have often said, was a black eye: it had now a tawny, nay a bloody light in its gloom; and his face flushed— olive cheek, and hueless forehead received a glow, as from spreading, ascending heart-fire: and he stirred, lifted his strong arm—he could have struck Mason—dashed him on the church floor—shocked by ruthless blow the breath from his body—but Mason shrank away, and cried faintly, 'Good God!' Contempt fell cool on Mr. Rochester—his passion died as if a blight had shrivelled it up: he only asked, 'What have *you* to say?'

An inaudible reply escaped Mason's white lips.

'The devil is in it if you cannot answer distinctly. I again demand, what have *you* to say?'

'Sir—sir'—interrupted the clergyman, 'do not forget you are in a sacred place.' Then addressing Mason, he inquired gently, 'Are you aware, sir, whether or not this gentleman's wife is still living?'

'Courage,' urged the lawyer,—'speak out.'

'She is now living at Thornfield Hall;' said Mason, in more articulate tones: 'I saw her there last April. I am her brother.'

'At Thornfield Hall!' ejaculated the clergyman. 'Impossible! I am an old resident in this neighbourhood, sir, and I never heard of a Mrs. Rochester at Thornfield Hall.'

I saw a grim smile contort Mr. Rochester's lip, and he muttered:—

'No—by God! I took care that none should hear of it—or of her under that name.' He mused—for ten minutes he held counsel with himself: he formed his resolve, and announced it:—

'Enough—all shall bolt out at once, like the bullet from the barrel.—Wood close your book, and take off your surplice; John Green (to the clerk), leave the church: there will be no wedding to-day:' the man obeyed.

Mr. Rochester continued, hardily and recklessly: 'Bigamy is an ugly word —I meant, however, to be a bigamist: but fate has out-manœuvred me

246

or Providence has checked me, perhaps the last. I am little better than a devil at this moment; and, as my pastor there would tell me, deserve no doubt the sternest judgments of God,—even to the quenchless fire and deathless worm. Gentlemen, my plan is broken up!—what this lawyer and his client say is true: I have been married: and the woman to whom I was married lives! You say you never heard of a Mrs. Rochester at the house up yonder, Wood: but I daresay you have many a time inclined your ear to gossip about the mysterious lunatic kept there under watch and ward. Some have whispered to you that she is my bastard half-sister: some, my cast-off mistress; I now inform you that she is my wife, whom I married fifteen years ago,—Bertha Mason by name; sister of this resolute personage, who is now, with his quivering limbs and white cheeks, showing you what a stout heart men may bear. Cheer up, Dick!—never fear me!—I'd almost as soon strike a woman as you. Bertha Mason is mad; and she came of a mad family;—idiots and maniacs through three generations! Her mother, the Creole, was both a mad woman and a drunkard!—as I found out after I had wed the daughter: for they were silent on family secrets before. Bertha, like a dutiful child, copied her parent in both points. I had a charming partner—pure, wise, modest: you can fancy I was a happy man.—I went through rich scenes! Oh! my experience has been heavenly, if you only knew it! But I owe you no further explanation. Briggs, Wood, Mason,—I invite you all to come up to the house and visit Mrs. Poole's patient, and *my wife*!—You shall see what sort of a being I was cheated into espousing, and judge whether or not I had a right to break the compact, and seek sympathy with something at least human. This girl,' he continued, looking at me, 'knew no more than you, Wood, of the disgusting secret: she thought all was fair and legal; and never dreamt she was going to be entrapped into a feigned union with a defrauded wretch, already bound to a bad, mad, and embruted partner! Come all of you, follow!'

Still holding me fast, he left the church: the three gentlemen came after. At the front door of the hall we found the carriage.

'Take it back to the coach-house, John,' said Mr. Rochester, coolly; 'it will not be wanted to-day.'

At our entrance, Mrs. Fairfax, Adèle, Sophie, Leah, advanced to meet and greet us.

'To the right about—every soul!' cried the master: 'away with your congratulations! Who wants them?—Not I!—they are fifteen years too late!'

He passed on and ascended the stairs, still holding my hand, and still beckoning the gentlemen to follow him; which they did. We mounted the first staircase, passed up the gallery, proceeded to the third story: the low, black door, opened by Mr. Rochester's master key, admitted us to the tapestried room, with its great bed, and its pictorial cabinet.

'You know this place, Mason,' said our guide; 'she bit and stabbed you here.'

He lifted the hangings from the wall, uncovering the second door: this, too, he opened. In a room without a window, there burnt a fire, guarded by a high and strong fender, and a lamp suspended from the ceiling by a chain. Grace Poole bent over the fire, apparently cooking something in a saucepan. In the deep shade, at the further end of the room, a figure ran backwards and forwards. What it was, whether beast or human being, one could not, at first sight, tell: it grovelled, seemingly, on all fours; it snatched and growled like some strange wild animal: but it was covered with clothing; and a quantity of dark, grizzled hair, wild as a mane, hid its head and face.

'Good-morrow, Mrs. Poole!' said Mr. Rochester. 'How are you? and how is your charge to-day?'

'We're tolerable, sir, I thank you,' replied Grace, lifting the boiling mess carefully on to the hob: 'rather snappish, but not 'rageous.'

A fierce cry seemed to give the lie to her favourable report: the clothed hyena rose up, and stood tall on its hind feet.

'Ah, sir, she sees you!' exclaimed Grace: 'you'd better not stay.'

'Only a few moments, Grace: you must allow me a few moments.'

'Take care then, sir!—for God's sake, take care!'

The maniac bellowed: she parted her shaggy locks from her visage, and gazed wildly at her visitors. I recognised well that purple face,—those bloated features. Mrs. Poole advanced.

'Keep out of the way,' said Mr. Rochester, thrusting her aside: 'she has no knife, now, I suppose? and I'm on my guard.'

'One never knows what she has, sir: she is so cunning: it is not in mortal discretion to fathom her craft.'

'We had better leave her,' whispered Mason.

'Go to the devil!' was his brother-in-law's recommendation.

'Ware!' cried Grace. The three gentlemen retreated simultaneously. Mr Rochester flung me behind him: the lunatic sprang and grappled his throat viciously, and laid her teeth to his cheek: they struggled. She was a big woman in stature almost equalling her husband, and corpulent besides: she showed virile force in the contest—more than once she almost throttled him, athletic as he was. He could have settled her with a well-planted blow; but he would not strike: he would only wrestle. At last he mastered her arms; Grace Poole gave him a cord, and he pinioned them behind her: with more rope, which was at hand, he bound her to a chair. The operation was performed amidst the fiercest yells, and the most convulsive plunges. Mr. Rochester then turned to the spectators: he looked at them with a smile both acrid and desolate.

'That is *my wife*,' said he. 'Such is the sole conjugal embrace I am ever to know—such are the endearments which are to solace my leisure hours! And *this* is what I wished to have' (laying his hand on my shoulder): 'this young girl, who stands so grave and quiet at the mouth of hell, looking collectedly

t the gambols of a demon. I wanted her just as a change after that fierce ragout. Wood and Briggs, look at the difference! Compare these clear eyes with the red balls yonder—this face with that mask—this form with that bulk; then judge me, priest of the gospel and man of the law, and remember, with what judgment ye judge ye shall be judged! Off with you now. I must shut up my prize.'

We all withdrew. Mr. Rochester stayed a moment behind us, to give some further order to Grace Poole. The solicitor addressed me as he descended the stair.

'You, madam,' said he, 'are cleared from all blame: your uncle will be glad to hear it—if, indeed, he should be still living—when Mr. Mason returns to Madeira.'

'My uncle! What of him? Do you know him?'

'Mr. Mason does: Mr. Eyre has been the Funchal correspondent of his house for some years. When your uncle received your letter intimating the contemplated union between yourself and Mr. Rochester, Mr. Mason, who was staying at Madeira to recruit his health, on his way back to Jamaica, happened to be with him. Mr. Eyre mentioned the intelligence; for he knew that my client here was acquainted with a gentleman of the name of Rochester. Mr. Mason, astonished and distressed as you may suppose, revealed the real state of matters. Your uncle, I am sorry to say, is now on a sick bed; from which, considering the nature of his disease—decline—and the stage it has reached, it is unlikely he will ever rise. He could not then hasten to England himself, to extricate you from the snare into which you had fallen, but he implored Mr. Mason to lose no time in taking steps to prevent the false marriage. He referred him to me for assistance. I used all despatch, and am thankful I was not too late: as you, doubtless, must be also. Were I not morally certain that your uncle will be dead ere you reach Madeira, I would advise you to accompany Mr. Mason back: but as it is, I think you had better remain in England till you can hear further, either from or of Mr. Eyre. Have we anything else to stay for?' he inquired of Mr. Mason.

'No, no—let us be gone,' was the anxious reply; and without waiting to take leave of Mr. Rochester, they made their exit at the hall door. The clergyman stayed to exchange a few sentences, either of admonition or reproof, with his haughty parishioner; this duty done, he too departed.

I heard him go as I stood at the half open door of my own room, to which I had now withdrawn. The house cleared, I shut myself in, fastened the bolt that none might intrude, and proceeded—not to weep, not to mourn, I was yet too calm for that, but—mechanically to take off the wedding dress, and replace it by the stuff gown I had worn yesterday, as I thought for the last time. I then sat down: I felt weak and tired. I leaned my arms on a table, and my head dropped on them. And now I thought: till now I had only

heard, seen, moved—followed up and down where I was led or dragged—watched event rush on event, disclosure open beyond disclosure: but *now*, *I thought.*

The morning had been a quiet morning enough—all except the brief scene with the lunatic: the transaction in the church had not been noisy; there there was no explosion of passion, no loud altercation, no dispute, no defiance or challenge, no tears, no sobs: a few words had been spoken, a calmly pronounced objection to the marriage made; some stern short questions put by Mr. Rochester; answers, explanations given, evidence adduced; an open admission of the truth had been uttered by my master; then the living proof had been seen: the intruders were gone, and all was over.

I was in my own room as usual—just myself, without obvious change nothing had smitten me, or scathed me, or maimed me. And yet where was the Jane Eyre of yesterday?—where was her life?—where were her prospects?

Jane Eyre, who had been an ardent, expectant woman—almost a bride—was a cold, solitary girl again: her life was pale, her prospects were desolate. A Christmas frost had come at midsummer; a white December storm had whirled over June; ice glazed the ripe apples, drifts crushed the blowing roses on hay-field and corn-field lay a frozen shroud: lanes which last night blushed full of flowers, to-day were pathless with untrodden snow; and the wood which twelve hours since waved leafy and fragrant as groves between the tropics, now spread, waste, wild and white as pine-forests in wintry Norway. My hopes were all dead—struck with a subtle doom, such as, in one night, fell on all the first-born in the land of Egypt. I looked on my cherished wishes yesterday so blooming and glowing; they lay stark, chill, livid corpses, that could never revive. I looked at my love: that feeling which was my master's —which he had created; it shivered in my heart, like a suffering child in a cold cradle; sickness and anguish had seized it; it could not seek Mr. Rochester's arms—it could not derive warmth from his breast. Oh, never more could it turn to him; for faith was blighted—confidence destroyed! Mr. Rochester was not to me what he had been; for he was not what I had thought him. I would not ascribe vice to him; I would not say he had betrayed me: but the attribute of stainless truth was gone from his idea; and from his presence I must go: *that* I perceived well. When--how—whither, I could not yet discern: but he himself, I doubted not, would hurry me from Thornfield. Real affection, it seemed, he could not have for me; it had been only fitful passion, that was balked; he would want me no more. I should fear even to cross his path now: my view must be hateful to him. Oh, how blind had been my eyes! How weak my conduct!

My eyes were covered and closed: eddying darkness seemed to swim round me, and reflection came in as black and confused a flow. Self-abandoned relaxed, and effortless, I seemed to have laid me down in the dried-up bed

of a great river; I heard a flood loosened in remote mountains, and felt the torrent come: to rise I had no will, to flee I had no strength. I lay faint; longing to be dead. One idea only still throbbed life-like within me—a remembrance of God: it begot an unuttered prayer: these words went wandering up and down in my rayless mind, as something that should be whispered; but no energy was found to express them:—

'Be not far from me, for trouble is near: there is none to help.'

It was near: and as I had lifted no petition to Heaven to avert it—as I had neither joined my hands, nor bent my knees, nor moved my lips—it came: in full, heavy swing the torrent poured over me. The whole consciousness of my life lorn, my love lost, my hope quenched, my faith death-struck, swayed full and mighty above me in one sullen mass. That bitter hour cannot be described: in truth, 'the waters came into my soul; I sank in deep mire: I felt no standing; I came into deep waters; the floods overflowed me.'

CHAPTER 27

Some time in the afternoon I raised my head, and looking round and seeing the western sun gilding the sign of its decline on the wall, I asked, 'What am I to do?'

But the answer my mind gave—'Leave Thornfield at once'—was so prompt, so dread, that I stopped my ears: I said, I could not bear such words now. 'That I am not Edward Rochester's bride is the least part of my woe,' I alleged: 'that I have wakened out of most glorious dreams, and found them all void and vain, is a horror I could bear and master; but that I must leave him decidedly, instantly, entirely, is intolerable. I cannot do it.'

But, then, a voice within me averred that I could do it; and foretold that I should do it. I wrestled with my own resolution: I wanted to be weak that I might avoid the awful passage of further suffering I saw laid out for me; and conscience, turned tyrant, held passion by the throat, told her tauntingly, she had yet but dipped her dainty foot in the slough, and swore that with that arm of iron, he would thrust her down to unsounded depths of agony.

'Let me be torn away, then!' I cried. 'Let another help me!'

'No; you shall tear yourself away, none shall help you: you shall, yourself, pluck out your right eye: yourself cut off your right hand: your heart shall be the victim; and you, the priest, to transfix it.'

I rose up suddenly, terror-struck at the solitude which so ruthless a judge haunted,—at the silence which so awful a voice filled. My head swam as I stood erect: I perceived that I was sickening from excitement and inanition; neither meat nor drink had passed my lips that day, for I had taken no breakfast. And, with a strange pang, I now reflected that, long as I had been shut

up here, no message had been sent to ask how I was, or to invite me to come down: not even little Adèle had tapped at the door; not even Mrs. Fairfax had sought me. 'Friends always forget those whom fortune forsakes,' I murmured, as I undrew the bolt and passed out. I stumbled over an obstacle: my head was still dizzy, my sight was dim, and my limbs were feeble. I could not soon recover myself. I fell, but not on to the ground: an out-stretched arm caught me; I looked up—I was supported by Mr. Rochester, who sat in a chair across my chamber threshold.

'You have come out at last,' he said. 'Well, I have been waiting for you long, and listening: yet not one movement have I heard, nor one sob: five minutes more of that death-like hush, and I should have forced the lock like a burglar. So, you shun me?—you shut yourself up and grieve alone! I would rather you had come and upbraided me with vehemence. You are passionate: I expected a scene of some kind. I was prepared for the hot rain of tears; only I wanted them to be shed on my breast: now a senseless floor has received them, or your drenched handkerchief. But I err: you have not wept at all! I see a white cheek and a faded eye, but no trace of tears. I suppose, then, your heart has been weeping blood?

'Well, Jane; not a word of reproach? Nothing bitter—nothing poignant? Nothing to cut a feeling or sting a passion? You sit quietly where I have placed you, and regard me with a weary, passive look.

'Jane, I never meant to wound you thus. If the man who had but one little ewe lamb that was dear to him as a daughter, that ate of his bread and drank of his cup, and lay in his bosom, had by some mistake slaughtered it at the shambles, he would not have rued his bloody blunder more than I now rue mine. Will you ever forgive me?'

Reader!—I forgave him at the moment, and on the spot. There was such deep remorse in his eye, such true pity in his tone, such manly energy in his manner; and, besides, there was such unchanged love in his whole look and mien—I forgave him all: yet not in words, not outwardly; only at my heart's core.

'You know I am a scoundrel, Jane?' ere long he inquired wistfully—wondering, I suppose, at my continued silence and tameness: the result rather of weakness than of will.

'Yes, sir.'

'Then tell me so roundly and sharply—don't spare me.'

'I cannot: I am tired and sick. I want some water.' He heaved a sort of shuddering sigh, and taking me in his arms, carried me downstairs. At first I did not know to what room he had borne me; all was cloudy to my glazed sight: presently I felt the reviving warmth of a fire; for, summer as it was, I had become icy cold in my chamber. He put wine to my lips; I tasted it and revived; then I ate something he offered me, and was soon myself. I was

in the library—sitting in his chair—he was quite near. 'If I could go out of life, now, without too sharp a pang, it would be well for me,' I thought; then I should not have to make the effort of cracking my heart-strings in rending them from among Mr. Rochester's. I must leave him, it appears. I do not want to leave him—I cannot leave him.'

'How are you now, Jane?'

'Much better, sir: I shall be well soon.'

'Taste the wine again, Jane.'

I obeyed him; then he put the glass on the table, stood before me, and looked at me attentively. Suddenly he turned away, with an inarticulate exclamation, full of passionate emotion of some kind; he walked fast through the room and came back: he stooped towards me as if to kiss me; but I remembered caresses were now forbidden. I turned my face away, and put his aside.

'What!—how is this?' he exclaimed hastily. 'Oh, I know! you won't kiss the husband of Bertha Mason? You consider my arms filled, and my embraces appropriated?'

'At any rate, there is neither room nor claim for me, sir.'

'Why, Jane? I will spare you the trouble of much talking: I will answer for you—because I have a wife already, you would reply.—I guess rightly?'

'Yes.'

'If you think so, you must have a strange opinion of me; you must regard me as a plotting profligate—a base and low rake who has been simulating disinterested love in order to draw you into a snare deliberately laid, and strip you of honour, and rob you of self-respect. What do you say to that? I see you can say nothing: in the first place, you are faint, still, and have enough to do to draw your breath; in the second place, you cannot yet accustom yourself to accuse and revile me; and, besides, the flood-gates of tears are opened, and they would rush out if you spoke much; and you have no desire to expostulate, to upbraid, to make a scene: you are thinking how *to act*—*talking*, you consider, is of no use. I know you—I am on my guard.'

'Sir, I do not wish to act against you,' I said; and my unsteady voice warned me to curtail my sentence.

'Not in *your* sense of the word but in *mine*, you are scheming to destroy me. You have as good as said that I am a married man—as a married man you will shun me, keep out of my way: just now you have refused to kiss me. You intend to make yourself a complete stranger to me; to live under this roof only as Adèle's governess; if ever I say a friendly word to you; if ever a friendly feeling inclines you again to me, you will say,—"That man had nearly made me his mistress: I must be ice and rock to him;" and ice and rock you will accordingly become.'

I cleared and steadied my voice to reply: 'All is changed about me, sir; I must change too—there is no doubt of that: and to avoid fluctuations of

253

feeling, and continual combats with recollections and associations, there is only one way—Adèle must have a new governess, sir.'

'Oh, Adèle will go to school—I have settled that already; nor do I mean to torment you with the hideous associations and recollections of Thornfield Hall—this accursed place—this tent of Achan—this insolent vault, offering the ghastliness of living death to the light of the open sky—this narrow stone hell, with its one real fiend, worse than a legion of such as we imagine.— Jane, you shall not stay here, nor will I. I was wrong ever to bring you to Thornfield Hall, knowing as I did how it was haunted. I charged them to conceal from you, before I ever saw you, all knowledge of the curse of the place; merely because I feared Adèle never would have a governess to stay if she knew with what inmate she was housed, and my plans would not permit me to remove the maniac elsewhere—though I possess an old house, Ferndean Manor, even more retired and hidden than this, where I could have lodged her safely enough, had not a scruple about the unhealthiness of the situation in the heart of a wood, made my conscience recoil from the arrangement. Probably those damp walls would soon have eased me of her charge: but to each villain his own vice; and mine is not a tendency to indirect assassination, even of what I most hate.

'Concealing the mad-woman's neighbourhood, from you, however, was something like covering a child with a cloak, and laying it down near a upas tree: that demon's vicinage is poisoned, and always was. But I'll shut up Thornfield Hall: I'll nail up the front door, and board the lower windows: I'll give Mrs. Poole two hundred a year to live here with *my wife*, as you term that fearful hag: Grace will do much for money, and she shall have her son, the keeper at Grimsby Retreat, to bear her company and be a hand to give her aid, in the paroxysms, when *my wife* is prompted by her familiar to burn people in their beds at night, to stab them, to bite their flesh from their bones, and so on'—

'Sir,' I interrupted him, 'you are inexorable for that unfortunate lady: you speak of her with hate—with vindictive antipathy. It is cruel—she cannot help being mad.'

'Jane, my little darling (so I will call you, for so you are), you don't know what you are talking about; you misjudge me again: it is not because she is mad I hate her. If you were mad, do you think I should hate you?'

'I do indeed, sir.'

'Then you are mistaken, and you know nothing about me, and nothing about the sort of love of which I am capable. Every atom of your flesh is as dear to me as my own: in pain and sickness it would still be dear. Your mind is my treasure, and if it were broken, it would be my treasure still: if you raved, my arms should confine you, and not a strait waistcoat—your grasp, even in fury, would have a charm for me: if you flew at me as wildly as that

woman did this morning, I should receive you in an embrace, at least as fond as it would be restrictive. I should not shrink from you with disgust as I did from her: in your quiet moments you should have no watcher and no nurse but me; and I could hang over you with untiring tenderness, though you gave me no smile in return; and never weary of gazing into your eyes, though they had no longer a ray of recognition for me.—But why do I follow that train of ideas? I was talking of removing you from Thornfield. All, you know, is prepared for prompt departure: to-morrow you shall go. I only ask you to endure one more night under this roof, Jane: and then, farewell to its miseries and terrors for ever! I have a place to repair to, which will be a secure sanctuary from hateful reminiscences, from unwelcome intrusion—even from falsehood and slander.'

'And take Adèle with you, sir,' I interrupted; 'she will be a companion for you.'

'What do you mean, Jane? I told you I would send Adèle to school: and what do I want with a child for a companion? and not my own child,—a French dancer's bastard. Why do you importune me about her? I say, why do you assign Adèle to me for a companion?'

'You spoke of a retirement, sir; and retirement and solitude are dull: too dull for you.'

'Solitude! solitude!' he reiterated, with irritation. 'I see I must come to an explanation. I don't know what sphynx-like expression is forming in your countenance. *You* are to share my solitude. Do you understand?'

I shook my head: it required a degree of courage, excited as he was becoming, even to risk that mute sign of dissent. He had been walking fast about the room, and he stopped, as if suddenly rooted to one spot. He looked at me long and hard: I turned my eyes from him, fixed them on the fire, and tried to assume and maintain a quiet, collected aspect.

'Now for the hitch in Jane's character,' he said at last, speaking more calmly than from his look I had expected him to speak. 'The reel of silk has run smoothly enough so far; but I always knew there would come a knot and a puzzle: here it is. Now for vexation, and exasperation, and endless trouble! By God! I long to exert a fraction of Samson's strength, and break the entanglement like tow!'

He recommenced his walk: but soon again stopped, and this time just before me.

'Jane! will you hear reason?' (he stooped and approached his lips to my ear) 'because, if you won't, I'll try violence.' His voice was hoarse; his look that of a man who is just about to burst an insufferable bond and plunge headlong into wild licence. I saw that in another moment, and with one impetus of frenzy more, I should be able to do nothing with him. The present—the passing second of time—was all I had in which to control and

restrain him: a movement of repulsion, flight, fear, would have sealed m doom,—and his. But I was not afraid: not in the least. I felt an inward power a sense of influence, which supported me. The crisis was perilous; but no without its charm: such as the Indian, perhaps, feels when he slips over th rapid in his canoe. I took hold of his clenched hand; loosened the contorte fingers; and said to him, soothingly,—

'Sit down; I'll talk to you as long as you like, and hear all you have t say, whether reasonable or unreasonable.'

He sat down: but he did not get leave to speak directly. I had been strugglin with tears for some time: I had taken great pains to repress them, becaus I knew he would not like to see me weep. Now, however, I considered it wel to let them flow as freely and as long as they liked. If the flood annoye him, so much the better. So I gave way and cried heartily.

Soon I heard him earnestly entreating me to be composed. I said I coul not while he was in such a passion.

'But I am not angry, Jane: I only love you too well; and you had steele your little pale face with such a resolute, frozen look, I could not endure it Hush, now, and wipe your eyes.'

His softened voice announced that he was subdued; so I, in my turn became calm. Now he made an effort to rest his head on my shoulder: but would not permit it. Then he would draw me to him: no.

'Jane! Jane!' he said—in such an accent of bitter sadness it thrilled alon every nerve I had; 'you don't love me, then? It was only my station, and th rank of my wife, that you valued? Now that you think me disqualified t become your husband, you recoil from my touch as if I were some toad or ape.

These words cut me: yet what could I do or say? I ought probably to hav done or said nothing: but I was so tortured by a sense of remorse at thu hurting his feelings, I could not control the wish to drop balm where I ha wounded.

'I *do* love you,' I said, 'more than ever: but I must not show or indulg the feeling: and this is the last time I must express it.'

'The last time, Jane! What! do you think you can live with me, and se me daily, and yet, if you still love me, be always cold and distant?'

'No, sir; that I am certain I could not; and therefore I see there is but on way: but you will be furious if I mention it.'

'Oh, mention it! If I storm, you have the art of weeping.'

'Mr. Rochester, I must leave you.'

'For how long, Jane? For a few minutes, while you smooth your hair—whic is somewhat dishevelled; and bathe your face—which looks feverish?'

'I must leave Adèle and Thornfield. I must part with you for my whole life I must begin a new existence amongst strange faces and strange scenes.'

'Of course: I told you you should. I pass over the madness about partin

from me. You mean you must become a part of me. As to the new existence, it is all right: you shall yet be my wife: I am not married. You shall be Mrs. Rochester—both virtually and nominally. I shall keep only to you so long as you and I live. You shall go to a place I have in the south of France: a white-washed villa on the shores of the Mediterranean. There you shall live a happy, and guarded, and most innocent life. Never fear that I wish to lure you into error—to make you my mistress. Why do you shake your head? Jane, you must be reasonable; or in truth I shall again become frantic.'

His voice and hand quivered: his large nostrils dilated: his eye blazed: still dared to speak:—

'Sir, your wife is living: that is a fact acknowledged this morning by your-self. If I lived with you as you desire, I should then be your mistress: to say otherwise is sophistical—is false.'

'Jane, I am not a gentle-tempered man—you forget that: I am not long-enduring; I am not cool and dispassionate. Out of pity to me and yourself, put your finger on my pulse, feel how it throbs, and—beware!'

He bared his wrist, and offered it to me: the blood was forsaking his cheek and lips, they were growing livid; I was distressed on all hands. To agitate him thus deeply, by a resistance he so abhorred, was cruel: to yield was out of the question. I did what human beings do instinctively when they are driven to utter extremity—looked for aid to one higher than man: the words 'God help me!' burst involuntarily from my lips.

'I am a fool!' cried Mr. Rochester, suddenly. 'I keep telling her I am not married, and do not explain to her why. I forget she knows nothing of the character of that woman, or of the circumstances attending my infernal union with her. Oh, I am certain Jane will agree with me in opinion, when she knows all that I know! Just put your hand in mine, Janet—that I may have the evidence of touch as well as sight, to prove you are near me—and I will in a few words show you the real state of the case. Can you listen to me?'

'Yes, sir; for hours if you will.'

'I ask only minutes. Jane, did you ever hear, or know that I was not the eldest son of my house: that I had once a brother older than I?'

'I remember Mrs. Fairfax told me so once.'

'And did you ever hear that my father was an avaricious, grasping man?'

'I have understood something to that effect.'

'Well, Jane, being so, it was his resolution to keep the property together; he could not bear the idea of dividing his estate and leaving me a fair portion: all, he resolved, should go to my brother, Rowland. Yet as little could he endure that a son of his should be a poor man. I must be provided for by a wealthy marriage. He sought me a partner betimes. Mr. Mason, a West India planter and merchant, was his old acquaintance. He was certain his possessions were real and vast: he made inquiries. Mr. Mason, he found, had

a son and daughter; and he learned from him that he could and would give the latter a fortune of thirty thousand pounds: that sufficed. When I left college, I was sent out to Jamaica, to espouse a bride already courted for me. My father said nothing about her money; but he told me Miss Mason was the boast of Spanish Town for her beauty: and this was no lie. I found her a fine woman, in the style of Blanche Ingram; tall, dark, majestic. Her family wished to secure me because I was of a good race; and so did she. They showed her to me in parties, splendidly dressed. I seldom saw her alone, and had very little private conversation with her. She flattered me, and lavishly displayed for my pleasure her charms and accomplishments. All the men in her circle seemed to admire her and envy me. I was dazzled, stimulated: my senses were excited; and being ignorant, raw, and inexperienced, I thought I loved her. There is no folly so besotted that the idiotic rivalries of society, the prurience, the rashness, the blindness of youth, will not hurry a man to its commission. Her relatives encouraged me; competitors piqued me; she allured me: a marriage was achieved almost before I knew where I was. Oh, I have no respect for myself when I think of that act!—an agony of inward contempt masters me. I never loved, I never esteemed, I did not even know her. I was not sure of the existence of one virtue in her nature: I had marked neither modesty, nor benevolence, nor candour, nor refinement in her mind or manners—and, I married her:—gross, grovelling, mole-eyed blockhead that I was! With less sin I might have—but let me remember to whom I am speaking.

'My bride's mother I had never seen: I understood she was dead. The honey-moon over, I learned my mistake; she was only mad, and shut up in a lunatic asylum. There was a younger brother, too; a complete dumb idiot. The elder one, whom you have seen (and whom I cannot hate, whilst I abhor all his kindred, because he has some grains of affection in his feeble mind, shown in the continued interest he takes in his wretched sister and also in a dog-like attachment he once bore me), will probably be in the same state one day. My father and my brother Rowland, knew all this; but they thought only of the thirty thousand pounds, and joined in the plot against me.

'These were vile discoveries; but, except for the treachery of concealment, I should have made them no subject of reproach to my wife: even when I found her nature wholly alien to mine; her tastes obnoxious to me; her cast of mind common, low, narrow, and singularly incapable of being led to anything higher, expanded to anything larger—when I found that I could not pass a single evening nor a single hour of the day with her in comfort; that kindly conversation could not be sustained between us, because whatever topic I started, immediately received from her a turn at once coarse and trite, perverse and imbecile—when I perceived that I should never have a quiet or settled household, because no servant would bear the continued outbreak

of her violent and unreasonable temper, or the vexations of her absurd, contradictory, exacting orders—even then I restrained myself: I eschewed upbraiding, I curtailed remonstrance; I tried to devour my repentance and disgust in secret; I repressed the deep antipathy I felt.

'Jane, I will not trouble you with abominable details: some strong words shall express what I have to say. I lived with that woman upstairs four years, and before that time she had tried me indeed: her character ripened and developed with frightful rapidity; her vices sprang up fast and rank: they were so strong, only cruelty could check them; and I would not use cruelty. What a pigmy intellect she had—and what giant propensities! How fearful were the curses those propensities entailed on me! Bertha Mason,—the true daughter of an infamous mother,—dragged me through all the hideous and degrading agonies which must attend a man bound to a wife at once intemperate and unchaste.

'My brother in the interval was dead; and at the end of the four years my father died too. I was rich enough now—yet poor to hideous indigence: a nature the most gross, impure, depraved I ever saw, was associated with mine, and called by the law and by society a part of me. And I could not rid myself of it by any legal proceedings: for the doctors now discovered that *my wife* was mad—her excesses had prematurely developed the germs of insanity: Jane, you don't like my narrative; you look almost sick—shall I defer the rest to another day?'

'No, sir, finish it now: I pity you—I do earnestly pity you.'

'Pity, Jane, from some people is a noxious and insulting sort of tribute, which one is justified in hurling back in the teeth of those who offer it; but that is a sort of pity native to callous, selfish hearts: it is a hybrid, egotistical pain at hearing of woes, crossed with ignorant contempt for those who have endured them. But that is not your pity, Jane: it is not the feeling of which your whole face is full at this moment—with which your eyes are now almost overflowing—with which your heart is heaving—with which your hand is trembling in mine. Your pity, my darling, is the suffering mother of love: its anguish is the very natal pang of the divine passion. I accept it, Jane; let the daughter have free advent—my arms wait to receive her.'

'Now, sir, proceed: what did you do when you found she was mad?'

'Jane—I approached the verge of despair: a remnant of self-respect was all that intervened between me and the gulf. In the eyes of the world, I was doubtless covered with grimy dishonour: but I resolved to be clean in my own sight—and to the last I repudiated the contamination of her crimes, and wrenched myself from connection with her mental defects. Still, society associated my name and person with hers; I yet saw her and heard her daily: something of her breath (faugh!) mixed with the air I breathed; and, besides, I remembered I had once been her husband—that recollection was then, and

is now, inexpressibly odious to me; moreover, I knew that while she lived I could never be the husband of another and better wife; and, though five years my senior (her family and her father had lied to me even in the particular of her age), she was likely to live as long as I, being as robust in frame as she was infirm in mind. Thus, at the age of twenty-six, I was hopeless.

'One night I had been awakened by her yells—(since the medical men had pronounced her mad, she had of course been shut up)—it was a fiery West Indian night; one of the description that frequently precedes the hurricanes of those climates; being unable to sleep in bed, I got up and opened the window. The air was like sulphur-steams—I could find no refreshment anywhere. Mosquitoes came buzzing in and hummed sullenly round the room; the sea, which I could hear from thence, rumbled dull like an earthquake—black clouds were casting up over it; the moon was setting in the waves, broad and red, like a hot cannon-ball—she threw her last bloody glance over a world quivering with the ferment of tempest. I was physically influenced by the atmosphere and scene, and my ears were filled with the curses the maniac still shrieked out; wherein she momentarily mingled my name with such a tone of demon-hate, with such language!—no professed harlot ever had a fouler vocabulary than she: though two rooms off, I heard every word—the thin partitions of the West India house opposing but slight obstruction to her wolfish cries.

' "This life," said I at last, "is hell! this is the air—those are the sounds of the bottomless pit! I have a right to deliver myself from it if I can. The sufferings of this mortal state will leave me with the heavy flesh that now cumbers my soul. Of the fanatic's burning eternity I have no fear: there is not a future state worse than this present one—let me break away and go home to God!"

'I said this whilst I knelt down at, and unlocked a trunk which contained a brace of loaded pistols: I meant to shoot myself. I only entertained the intention for a moment; for, not being insane, the crisis of exquisite and unalloyed despair which had originated the wish and design of self-destruction was past in a second.

'A wind fresh from Europe blew over the ocean and rushed through the open casement: the storm broke, streamed, thundered, blazed, and the air grew pure. I then framed and fixed a resolution. While I walked under the dripping orange-trees of my wet garden, and amongst its drenched pomegranates and pine-apples, and while the refulgent dawn of the tropics kindled round me—I reasoned thus, Jane:—and now listen; for it was true Wisdom that consoled me in that hour, and showed me the right path to follow.

'The sweet wind from Europe was still whispering in the refreshed leaves, and the Atlantic was thundering in glorious liberty; my heart, dried up and scorched for a long time, swelled to the tone, and filled with living blood—my being longed for renewal—my soul thirsted for a pure draught. I saw Hope

revive—and felt Regeneration possible. From a flowery arch at the bottom of my garden I gazed over the sea—bluer than the sky; the old world was beyond; clear prospects opened thus:—

' "Go," said Hope, "and live again in Europe: there it is not known what a sullied name you bear, nor what a filthy burden is bound to you. You may take the maniac with you to England; confine her with due attendance and precautions at Thornfield: then travel yourself to what clime you will, and form what new tie you like. That woman, who has so abused your long-suffering—so sullied your name; so outraged your honour; so blighted your youth—is not your wife; nor are you her husband. See that she is cared for as her condition demands, and you have done all that God and Humanity require of you. Let her identity, her connection with yourself, be buried in oblivion: you are bound to impart them to no living being. Place her in safety and comfort: shelter her degradation with secrecy, and leave her."

'I acted precisely on this suggestion. My father and brother had not made my marriage known to their acquaintance; because, in the very first letter I wrote to apprise them of the union—having already begun to experience extreme disgust of its consequences; and from the family character and consti-tution, seeing a hideous future opening to me—I added an urgent charge to keep it secret: and very soon, the infamous conduct of the wife my father had elected for me, was such as to make him blush to own her as his daughter-in-law. Far from desiring to publish the connection, he became as anxious to conceal it as myself.

'To England, then, I conveyed her; a fearful voyage I had with such a monster in the vessel. Glad was I when I at last got her to Thornfield, and saw her safely lodged in that third story room, of whose secret inner cabinet she has now for ten years made a wild beast's den—a goblin's cell. I had some trouble in finding an attendant for her: as it was necessary to select one on whose fidelity dependence could be placed; for her ravings would inevitably betray my secret: besides, she had lucid intervals of days—sometimes weeks—which she filled up with abuse of me. At last I hired Grace Poole, from the Grimsby Retreat. She and the surgeon, Carter (who dressed Mason's wounds that night he was stabbed and worried), are the only two I have ever admitted to my confidence. Mrs. Fairfax may indeed have suspected something; but she could have gained no precise knowledge as to facts. Grace has, on the whole, proved a good keeper; though, owing partly to a fault of her own, of which it appears nothing can cure her, and which is incident to her harassing profession, her vigilance has been more than once lulled and baffled. The lunatic is both cunning and malignant; she has never failed to take advantage of her guardian's temporary lapses; once to secrete the knife with which she stabbed her brother, and twice to possess herself of the key of her cell, and issue therefrom in the night-time. On the first of these occasions, she perpetrated

the attempt to burn me in my bed; on the second she paid that ghastly visit to you. I thank Providence, who watched over you, that she then spent her fury on your wedding apparel; which perhaps brought back vague reminiscences of her own bridal days: but on what might have happened, I cannot endure to reflect. When I think of the thing which flew at my throat this morning, hanging its black and scarlet visage over the nest of my dove, my blood curdles'——

'And what, sir,' I asked, while he paused, 'did you do when you had settled her here? Where did you go?'

'What did I do, Jane? I transformed myself into a Will-o'-the-wisp. Where did I go? I pursued wanderings as wild as those of the March-spirit. I sought the Continent, and went devious through all its lands. My fixed desire was to seek and find a good and intelligent woman, whom I could love: a contrast to the fury I left at Thornfield'——

'But you could not marry, sir.'

'I had determined, and was convinced that I could and ought. It was not my original intention to deceive, as I have deceived you. I meant to tell my tale plainly, and make my proposals openly: and it appeared to me so absolutely rational that I should be considered free to love and be loved, I never doubted some woman might be found willing and able to understand my case and accept me, in spite of the curse with which I was burdened.'

'Well, sir?'

'When you are inquisitive, Jane, you always make me smile. You open your eyes like an eager bird, and make every now and then a restless movement, as if answers in speech did not flow fast enough for you, and you wanted to read the tablet of one's heart. But before I go on, tell me what you mean by your "Well, sir?" It is a small phrase very frequent with you; and which many a time has drawn me on and on through interminable talk: I don't very well know why.'

'I mean,—What next? How did you proceed? What came of such an event?'

'Precisely: and what do you wish to know now?'

'Whether you found any one you liked: whether you asked her to marry you; and what she said.'

'I can tell you whether I found any one I liked, and whether I asked her to marry me: but what she said is yet to be recorded in the book of Fate. For ten long years I roved about, living first in one capital, then another: sometimes in St. Petersburgh; oftener in Paris; occasionally in Rome, Naples, and Florence. Provided with plenty of money, and the passport of an old name, I could choose my own society: no circles were closed against me. I sought my ideal of a woman amongst English ladies, French countesses, Italian signoras, and German gräfinnen. I could not find her. Sometimes, for a fleeting moment, I thought I caught a glance, heard a tone, beheld a form,

which announced the realisation of my dream: but I was presently undeceived. You are not to suppose that I desired perfection, either of mind or person. I longed only for what suited me—for the antipodes of the Creole: and I longed vainly. Amongst them all I found not one, whom, had I been ever so free, —warned as I was of the risks, the horrors, the loathings of incongruous unions—would have asked to marry me. Disappointment made me reckless. I tried dissipation—never debauchery: that I hated, and hate. That was my Indian Messalina's attribute: rooted disgust at it and her restrained me much, even in pleasure. Any enjoyment that bordered on riot seemed to approach me to her and her vices, and I eschewed it.

'Yet I could not live alone; so I tried the companionship of mistresses. The first I chose was Céline Varens—another of those steps which make a man spurn himself when he recalls them. You already know what she was, and how my liaison with her terminated. She had two successors: an Italian, Giacinta, and a German, Clara; both considered singularly handsome. What was their beauty to me in a few weeks? Giacinta was unprincipled and violent: I tired of her in three months. Clara was honest and quiet; but heavy, mindless, unimpressible: not one whit to my taste. I was glad to give her a sufficient sum to set her up in a good line of business, and so get decently rid of her. But, Jane, I see by your face you are not forming a very favourable opinion of me just now. You think me an unfeeling, loose-principled rake: don't you?'

'I don't like you so well as I have done sometimes, indeed, sir. Did it not seem to you in the least wrong to live in that way: first with one mistress and then another? You talk of it as a mere matter of course.'

'It was with me; and I did not like it. It was a grovelling fashion of existence: I should never like to return to it. Hiring a mistress is the next worse thing to buying a slave: both are often by nature, and always by position, inferior: and to live familiarly with inferiors is degrading. I now hate the recollection of the time I passed with Céline, Giacinta, and Clara.'

I felt the truth of these words; and I drew from them the certain inference, that if I were so far to forget myself and all the teaching that had ever been instilled into me, as—under any pretext—with any justification—through any temptation—to become the successor of these poor girls, he would one day regard me with the same feeling which now in his mind desecrated their memory. I did not give utterance to this conviction: it was enough to feel it. I impressed it on my heart, that it might remain there to serve me as aid in the time of trial.

'Now, Jane, why don't you say "Well, sir?" I have not done. You are looking grave. You disapprove of me still, I see. But let me come to the point. Last January, rid of all mistresses—in a harsh, bitter, frame of mind, the result of a useless, roving, lonely life—corroded with disappointment, sourly disposed

against all men, and especially against all *woman*kind (for I began to regard the notion of an intellectual, faithful, loving woman as a mere dream), recalled by business, I came back to England.

'On a frosty winter afternoon, I rode in sight of Thornfield Hall. Abhorred spot! I expected no peace—no pleasure there. On a stile in Hay Lane I saw a quiet little figure sitting by itself. I passed it as negligently as I did the pollard willow opposite to it: I had no presentiment of what it would be to me; no inward warning that the arbitress of my life—my genius for good or evil—waited there in humble guise. I did not know it, even when, on the occasion of Mesrour's accident, it came up and gravely offered me help. Childish and slender creature! It seemed as if a linnet had hopped to my foot and proposed to bear me on its tiny wing. I was surly; but the thing would not go: it stood by me with strange perseverance, and looked and spoke with a sort of authority. I must be aided, and by that hand: and aided I was.

'When once I had pressed the frail shoulder, something new—a fresh sap and sense—stole into my frame. It was well I had learnt that this elf must return to me—that it belonged to my house down below—or I could not have felt it pass away from under my hand, and seen it vanish behind the dim hedge, without singular regret. I heard you come home that night, Jane, though probably you were not aware that I thought of you, or watched for you. The next day I observed you—myself unseen—for half an hour, while you played with Adèle in the gallery. It was a snowy day, I recollect, and you could not go out of doors. I was in my room; the door was ajar: I could both listen and watch. Adèle claimed your outward attention for a while; yet I fancied your thoughts were elsewhere: but you were very patient with her, my little Jane; you talked to her and amused her a long time. When at last she left you, you lapsed at once into deep reverie: you betook yourself slowly to pace the gallery. Now and then, in passing a casement, you glanced out at the thick-falling snow; you listened to the sobbing wind, and again you paced gently on and dreamed. I think those day visions were not dark: there was a pleasurable illumination in your eye occasionally, a soft excitement in your aspect, which told of no bitter, bilious, hypochondriac brooding: your look revealed rather the sweet musings of youth, when its spirit follows on willing wings the flight of Hope, up and on to an ideal heaven. The voice of Mrs. Fairfax, speaking to a servant in the hall, wakened you: and how curiously you smiled to and at yourself, Jane! There was much sense in your smile. It was very shrewd, and seemed to make light of your own abstraction. I seemed to say—' My fine visions are all very well, but I must not forget they are absolutely unreal. I have a rosy sky, and a green flowery Eden in my brain; but without, I am perfectly aware, lies at my feet a rough tract to travel, and around me gather black tempests to encounter." You ran downstairs and demanded of Mrs. Fairfax some occupation: the weekly house accounts to

make up, or something of that sort, I think it was. I was vexed with you for getting out of my sight.

'Impatiently I waited for evening, when I might summon you to my presence. An unusual—to me—a perfectly new character I suspected was yours: I desired to search it deeper, and know it better. You entered the room with a look and air at once shy and independent: you were quaintly dressed—much as you are now. I made you talk: ere long I found you full of strange contrasts. Your garb and manner were restricted by rule; your air was often diffident, and altogether that of one refined by nature, but absolutely unused to society, and a good deal afraid of making herself disadvantageously conspicuous by some solecism or blunder; yet when addressed, you lifted a keen, a daring and a glowing eye to your interlocutor's face: there was penetration and power in each glance you gave; when plied by close questions, you found ready and round answers. Very soon, you seemed to get used to me: I believe you felt the existence of sympathy between you and your grim and cross master, Jane; for it was astonishing to see how quickly a certain pleasant ease tranquil-lised your manner: snarl as I would, you showed no surprise, fear, annoyance, or displeasure at my moroseness; you watched me, and now and then smiled at me with a simple yet sagacious grace I cannot describe. I was at once content and stimulated with what I saw: I liked what I had seen, and wished to see more. Yet, for a long time, I treated you distantly, and sought your company rarely. I was an intellectual epicure, and wished to prolong the gratification of making this novel and piquant acquaintance: besides, I was for a while troubled with a haunting fear that if I handled the flower freely its bloom would fade—the sweet charm of freshness would leave it. I did not then know that it was no transitory blossom; but rather the radiant resemblance of one, cut in an indestructible gem. Moreover, I wished to see whether you would seek me if I shunned you—but you did not; you kept in the school-room as still as your own desk and easel; if by chance I met you, you passed me as soon, and with as little token of recognition, as was consistent with respect. Your habitual expression in those days, Jane, was a thoughtful look; not despondent, for you were not sickly; but not buoyant, for you had little hope, and no actual pleasure. I wondered what you thought of me—or if you ever thought of me; to find this out, I resumed my notice of you. There was some-thing glad in your glance, and genial in your manner, when you conversed: I saw you had a social heart; it was the silent school-room—it was the tedium of your life—that made you mournful. I permitted myself the delight of being kind to you; kindness stirred emotion soon: your face became soft in expression, your tones gentle: I liked my name pronounced by your lips in a grateful happy accent. I used to enjoy a chance meeting with you, Jane, at this time: there was a curious hesitation in your manner: you glanced at me with a slight trouble—a hovering doubt: you did not know what my caprice might be—

whether I was going to play the master and be stern, or the friend and be benignant. I was now too fond of you often to simulate the first whim; and, when I stretched my hand out cordially, such bloom and light and bliss rose to your young, wistful features, I had much ado often to avoid straining you then and there to my heart.'

'Don't talk any more of those days, sir,' I interrupted, furtively dashing away some tears from my eyes; his language was torture to me; for I knew what I must do—and do soon—and all these reminiscences, and these revelations of his feelings only made my work more difficult.

'No, Jane,' he returned: 'what necessity is there to dwell on the Past, when the Present is so much surer—the Future so much brighter?'

I shuddered to hear the infatuated assertion.

'You see now how the case stands—do you not?' he continued. 'After a youth and manhood passed half in unutterable misery and half in dreary solitude, I have for the first time found what I can truly love—I have found *you*. You are my sympathy—my better self—my good angel—and I am bound to you with a strong attachment. I think you good, gifted, lovely: a fervent a solemn passion is conceived in my heart; it leans to you, draws you to my centre and spring of life, wraps my existence about you—and, kindling in pure powerful flame, fuses you and me in one.

'It was because I felt and knew this, that I resolved to marry you. To tell me that I had already a wife is empty mockery: you know now that I had but a hideous demon. I was wrong to attempt to deceive you; but I feared a stubbornness that exists in your character. I feared early instilled prejudice I wanted to have you safe before hazarding confidences. This was cowardly I should have appealed to your nobleness and magnanimity at first, as I do now—opened to you plainly my life of agony—described to you my hunger and thirst after a higher and worthier existence—shown to you, not my *resolution* (that word is weak), but my resistless *bent* to love faithfully and well, where I am faithfully and well loved in return. Then I should have asked you to accept my pledge of fidelity, and to give me yours: Jane—give it me now.'

A pause.

'Why are you silent, Jane?'

I was experiencing an ordeal: a hand of fiery iron grasped my vitals. Terrible moment: full of struggle, blackness, burning! Not a human being that ever lived could wish to be loved better than I was loved; and him who thus loved me I absolutely worshipped: and I must renounce love and idol. One dread word comprised my intolerable duty—'Depart!'

'Jane, you understand what I want of you? Just this promise—"I will be yours, Mr. Rochester."'

'Mr. Rochester, I will *not* be yours.'

Another long silence.

'Jane!' recommenced he, with a gentleness that broke me down with grief, and turned me stone-cold with ominous terror—for this still voice was the pant of a lion rising—'Jane, do you mean to go one way in the world, and to let me go another?'

'I do.'

'Jane' (bending towards and embracing me), 'do you mean it now?'

'I do.'

'And now?' softly kissing my forehead and cheek.

'I do'—extricating myself from restraint rapidly and completely.

'Oh, Jane, this is bitter! This—this is wicked. It would not be wicked to love me.'

'It would to obey you.'

A wild look raised his brows—crossed his features: he rose; but he forbore yet. I laid my hand on the back of a chair for support: I shook, I feared—but I resolved.

'One instant, Jane. Give one glance to my horrible life when you are gone. All happiness will be torn away with you. What then is left? For a wife I have but the maniac upstairs: as well might you refer me to some corpse in yonder churchyard. What shall I do, Jane? Where turn for a companion, and for some hope?'

'Do as I do: trust in God and yourself. Believe in heaven. Hope to meet again there.'

'Then you will not yield?'

'No.'

'Then you condemn me to live wretched, and to die accursed?' His voice rose.

'I advise you to live sinless: and I wish you to die tranquil.'

'Then you snatch love and innocence from me? You fling me back on lust for a passion—vice for an occupation?'

'Mr. Rochester, I no more assign this fate to you than I grasp at it for myself. We were born to strive and endure—you as well as I: do so. You will forget me before I forget you.'

'You make me a liar by such language: you sully my honour. I declared I could not change: you tell me to my face I shall change soon. And what a distortion in your judgment, what a perversity in your ideas, is proved by your conduct! Is it better to drive a fellow-creature to despair than to transgress a mere human law—no man being injured by the breach? for you have neither relatives nor acquaintances whom you need fear to offend by living with me.'

This was true: and while he spoke my very conscience and reason turned traitors against me, and charged me with crime in resisting him. They spoke almost as loud as Feeling: and that clamoured wildly. 'Oh, comply!' it said. Think of his misery; think of his danger—look at his state when left alone; remember his headlong nature; consider the recklessness following on despair—

soothe him; save him; love him; tell him you love him and will be his. Who in the world cares for *you*? or who will be injured by what you do?'

Still indomitable was the reply—'*I* care for myself. The more solitary, the more friendless, the more unsustained I am, the more I will respect myself. I will keep the law given by God; sanctioned by man. I will hold to the principles received by me when I was sane, and not mad—as I am now. Laws and principles are not for the times when there is no temptation: they are for such moments as this, when body and soul rise in mutiny against their rigour; stringent are they; inviolate they shall be. If at my individual convenience I might break them, what would be their worth? They have a worth—so I have always believed; and if I cannot believe it now, it is because I am insane—quite insane: with my veins running fire, and my heart beating faster than I can count its throbs. Preconceived opinions, foregone determinations, are all I have at this hour to stand by: there I plant my foot.'

I did. Mr. Rochester, reading my countenance, saw I had done so. His fury was wrought to the highest: he must yield to it for a moment, whatever followed; he crossed the floor and seized my arm, and grasped my waist. He seemed to devour me with his flaming glance: physically, I felt, at the moment, powerless as stubble exposed to the draught and glow of a furnace—mentally, I still possessed my soul, and with it the certainty of ultimate safety. The soul, fortunately, has an interpreter—often an unconscious, but still a truthful interpreter—in the eye. My eye rose to his; and while I looked in his fierce face, I gave an involuntary sigh: his gripe was painful, and my over-tasked strength almost exhausted.

'Never,' said he, as he ground his teeth, 'never was anything at once so frail and so indomitable. A mere reed she feels in my hand!' (And he shook me with the force of his hold.) 'I could bend her with my finger and thumb: and what good would it do if I bent, if I uptore, if I crushed her? Consider that eye: consider the resolute, wild, free thing looking out of it, defying me with more than courage—with a stern triumph. Whatever I do with its cage, I cannot get at it—the savage, beautiful creature! If I tear, if I rend the slight prison, my outrage will only let the captive loose. Conqueror I might be of the house; but the inmate would escape to heaven before I could call myself possessor of its clay dwelling-place. And it is you, spirit—with will and energy and virtue and purity—that I want: not alone your brittle frame. Of yourself you could come with soft flight and nestle against my heart, if you would: seized against your will you will elude the grasp like an essence—you will vanish ere I inhale your fragrance. Oh! come, Jane, come!'

As he said this, he released me from his clutch, and only looked at me. The look was far worse to resist than the frantic strain: only an idiot, however, would have succumbed now. I had dared and baffled his fury; I must elude his sorrow: I retired to the door.

'You are going, Jane?'

'I am going, sir.'

'You are leaving me?'

'Yes.'

'You will not come?—You will not be my comforter, my rescuer?—My deep love, my wild woe, my frantic prayer, are all nothing to you?'

What unutterable pathos was in his voice! How hard it was to reiterate firmly, 'I am going.'

'Jane!'

'Mr. Rochester!'

'Withdraw, then,—I consent—but remember, you leave me here in anguish. Go up to your own room; think over all I have said, Jane, cast a glance on my sufferings—think of me.'

He turned away; he threw himself on his face on the sofa. 'Oh, Jane! my hope—my love—my life!' broke in anguish from his lips. Then came a deep, strong sob.

I had already gained the door: but, reader, I walked back—walked back as determinedly as I had retreated. I knelt down by him; I turned his face from the cushion to me; I kissed his cheek; I smoothed his hair with my hand. 'God bless you, my dear master!' I said. 'God keep you from harm and wrong—direct you, solace you—reward you well for your past kindness to me.'

'Little Jane's love would have been my best reward,' he answered: 'without it, my heart is broken. But Jane will give me her love: yes—nobly, generously.'

Up the blood rushed to his face; forth flashed the fire from his eyes; erect he sprang; he held his arms out; but I evaded the embrace, and at once quitted the room.

'Farewell!' was the cry of my heart as I left him. Despair added, 'Farewell, for ever!'

*　　*　　*　　*　　*　　*　　*

That night I never thought to sleep; but a slumber fell on me as soon as I lay down in bed. I was transported in thought to the scenes of childhood: I dreamt I lay in the red-room at Gateshead; that the night was dark, and my mind impressed with strange fears. The light that long ago had struck me into syncope, recalled in this vision, seemed glidingly to mount the wall, and tremblingly to pause in the centre of the obscured ceiling. I lifted up my head to look: the roof resolved to clouds, high and dim; the gleam was such as the moon imparts to vapours she is about to sever. I watched her come—watched with the strangest anticipation; as though some word of doom were to be written on her disk. She broke forth as never moon yet burst from cloud: a hand first penetrated the sable folds and waved them away; then, not the moon, but a white human form shone in the azure, inclining a glorious brow

earthward. It gazed and gazed on me. It spoke to my spirit: immeasurably distant was the tone, yet so near, it whispered in my heart—

'My daughter, flee temptation!'

'Mother, I will.'

So I answered after I had waked from the trance-like dream. It was yet night, but July nights are short: soon after midnight, dawn comes. 'It cannot be too early to commence the task I have to fulfil,' thought I. I rose: I was dressed; for I had taken off nothing but my shoes. I knew where to find in my drawers some linen, a locket, a ring. In seeking these articles, I encountered the beads of a pearl necklace Mr. Rochester had forced me to accept a few days ago. I left that; it was not mine: it was the visionary bride's, who had melted in air. The other articles I made up in a parcel; my purse, containing twenty shillings (it was all I had), I put in my pocket: I tied on my straw bonnet, pinned my shawl, took the parcel and my slippers, which I would not put on yet, and stole from my room.

'Farewell, kind Mrs. Fairfax!' I whispered, as I glided past her door. 'Farewell, my darling Adèle!' I said as I glanced towards the nursery. No thought could be admitted of entering to embrace her. I had to deceive a fine ear: for aught I knew, it might now be listening.

I would have got past Mr. Rochester's chamber without a pause; but my heart momentarily stopping its beat at that threshold, my foot was forced to stop also. No sleep was there: the inmate was walking restlessly from wall to wall; and again and again he sighed while I listened. There was a heaven—a temporary heaven—in this room for me, if I chose: I had but to go in and to say—

'Mr. Rochester, I will love you and live with you through life till death,' and a fount of rapture would spring to my lips. I thought of this.

That kind master, who could not sleep now, was waiting with impatience for day. He would send for me in the morning; I should be gone. He would have me sought for: vainly. He would feel himself forsaken; his love rejected: he would suffer; perhaps grow desperate. I thought of this too. My hand moved towards the lock: I caught it back, and glided on.

Drearily I wound my way downstairs: I knew what I had to do, and I did it mechanically. I sought the key of the side-door in the kitchen; I sought, too, a phial of oil and a feather; I oiled the key and the lock. I got some water, I got some bread: for perhaps I should have to walk far; and my strength, sorely shaken of late, must not break down. All this I did without one sound. I opened the door, passed out, shut it softly. Dim dawn glimmered in the yard. The great gates were closed and locked; but a wicket in one of them was only latched. Through that I departed: it, too, I shut; and now I was out of Thornfield.

A mile off, beyond the fields, lay a road which stretched in the contrary

direction to Millcote; a road I had never travelled, but often noticed, and wondered where it led: thither I bent my steps. No reflection was to be allowed now: not one glance was to be cast back; not even one forward. Not one thought was to be given either to the past or the future. The first was a page so heavenly sweet—so deadly sad—that to read one line of it would dissolve my courage and break down my energy. The last was an awful blank: something like the world when the deluge was gone by.

I skirted fields, and hedges, and lanes, till after sunrise. I believe it was a lovely summer morning: I knew my shoes, which I had put on when I left the house, were soon wet with dew. But I looked neither to rising sun, nor smiling sky, nor wakening nature. He who is taken out to pass through a fair scene to the scaffold, thinks not of the flowers that smile on his road, but of the block and axe-edge; of the disseverment of bone and vein; of the grave gaping at the end: and I thought of drear flight and homeless wandering—and oh! with agony I thought of what I left. I could not help it. I thought of him now—in his room—watching the sunrise; hoping I should soon come to say I would stay with him, and be his. I longed to be his; I panted to return: it was not too late; I could yet spare him the bitter pang of bereavement. As yet my flight, I was sure, was undiscovered. I could go back and be his comforter—his pride; his redeemer from misery; perhaps from ruin. Oh, that fear of his self-abandonment—far worse than my abandonment—how it goaded me! It was a barbed arrow-head in my breast; it tore me when I tried to extract it; it sickened me when remembrance thrust it further in. Birds began singing in brake and copse: birds were faithful to their mates; birds were emblems of love. What was I? In the midst of my pain of heart, and frantic effort of principle, I abhorred myself. I had no solace from self-approbation: none even from self-respect. I had injured—wounded—left my master. I was hateful in my own eyes. Still I could not turn, nor retrace one step. God must have led me on. As to my own will or conscience, impassioned grief had trampled one and stifled the other. I was weeping wildly as I walked along my solitary way: fast, fast I went like one delirious. A weakness, beginning inwardly, extending to the limbs, seized me, and I fell: I lay on the ground some minutes, pressing my face to the wet turf. I had some fear—or hope—that here I should die: but I was soon up; crawling forward on my hands and knees, and then again raised to my feet—as eager and as determined as ever to reach the road.

When I got there I was forced to sit to rest me under the hedge; and while I sat, I heard wheels, and saw a coach come on. I stood up and lifted my hand; it stopped. I asked where it was going: the driver named a place a long way off, and where I was sure Mr. Rochester had no connections. I asked for what sum he would take me there; he said thirty shillings; I answered I had but twenty; well, he would try to make it do. He further gave me leave to get

into the inside, as the vehicle was empty: I entered, was shut in, and it rolled
on its way.

Gentle reader, may you never feel what I then felt! May your eyes never
shed such stormy, scalding, heart-wrung tears as poured from mine. May you
never appeal to Heaven in prayers so hopeless and so agonised as in that hour
left my lips: for never may you, like me, dread to be the instrument of evil to
what you wholly love.

CHAPTER 28

Two days are passed. It is a summer evening; the coachman has set me down
at a place called Whitcross; he could take me no farther for the sum I had
given, and I was not possessed of another shilling in the world. The coach is
a mile off by this time; I am alone. At this moment I discover that I forgot
to take my parcel out of the pocket of the coach, where I had placed it for
safety; there it remains, there it must remain; and now, I am absolutely
destitute.

Whitcross is no town, nor even a hamlet; it is but a stone pillar set up where
four roads meet: white-washed, I suppose to be more obvious at a distance
and in darkness. Four arms spring from its summit: the nearest town to
which these point is, according to the inscription, distant ten miles; the farthest
above twenty. From the well known names of these towns I learn in what
county I have lighted; a north-midland shire, dusk with moorland, ridged
with mountain: this I see. There are great moors behind and on each hand of
me; there are waves of mountains far beyond that deep valley at my feet.
The population here must be thin, and I see no passengers on these roads:
they stretch out east, west, north, and south—white, broad, lonely; they are
all cut in the moor, and the heather grows deep and wild to their very verge.
Yet a chance traveller might pass by; and I wish no eye to see me now:
strangers would wonder what I am doing, lingering here at the signpost,
evidently objectless and lost. I might be questioned: I could give no answer
but what would sound incredible, and excite suspicion. Not a tie holds me to
human society at this moment—not a charm or hope calls me where my
fellow-creatures are—none that saw me would have a kind thought or good
wish for me. I have no relative but the universal mother, Nature: I will seek
her breast and ask repose.

I struck straight into the heath; I held on to a hollow I saw deeply furrowing
the brown moorside; I waded knee-deep in its dark growth; I turned with its
turnings, and finding a moss-blackened granite crag in a hidden angle, I sat
down under it. High banks of moor were about me; the crag protected my
head: the sky was over that.

Some time passed before I felt tranquil even here: I had a vague dread that wild cattle might be near, or that some sportsman or poacher might discover me. If a gust of wind swept the waste, I looked up, fearing it was the rush of a bull; if a plover whistled, I imagined it a man. Finding my apprehensions unfounded, however, and calmed by the deep silence that reigned as evening declined at nightfall, I took confidence. As yet I had not thought; I had only listened, watched, dreaded; now I regained the faculty of reflection.

What was I to do? Where to go? Oh, intolerable questions, when I could do nothing and go nowhere!—when a long way must yet be measured by my weary, trembling limbs, before I could reach human habitation—when cold charity must be entreated before I could get a lodging: reluctant sympathy importuned: almost certain repulse incurred: before my tale could be listened to, or one of my wants relieved!

I touched the heath: it was dry, and yet warm with the heat of the summer-day. I looked at the sky; it was pure: a kindly star twinkled just above the chasm ridge. The dew fell, but with propitious softness; no breeze whispered. Nature seemed to me benign and good; I thought she loved me, outcast as I was; and I, who from man could anticipate only mistrust, rejection, insult, clung to her with filial fondness. To-night, at least, I would be her guest—as I was her child: my mother would lodge me without money and without price. I had one morsel of bread yet: the remnant of a roll I had bought in a town we passed through at noon with a stray penny—my last coin. I saw ripe bilberries gleaming here and there, like jet beads in the heath: I gathered a handful and ate them with the bread. My hunger, sharp before, was, if not satisfied, appeased by this hermit's meal. I said my evening prayers at its conclusion, and then chose my couch.

Beside the crag, the heath was very deep: when I lay down my feet were buried in it; rising high on each side, it left only a narrow space for the night-air to invade. I folded my shawl double, and spread it over me for a coverlet; a low, mossy swell was my pillow. Thus lodged, I was not, at least at the commencement of the night, cold.

My rest might have been blissful enough, only a sad heart broke it. It plained of its gaping wounds, its inward bleeding, its riven chords. It trembled for Mr. Rochester and his doom: it bemoaned him with bitter pity; it demanded him with ceaseless longing: and, impotent as a bird with both wings broken, it still quivered its shattered pinions in vain attempts to seek him.

Worn out with this torture of thought, I rose to my knees. Night was come, and her planets were risen: a safe, still night; too serene for the companionship of fear. We know that God is everywhere; but certainly we feel His presence most when His works are on the grandest scale spread before us: and it is in the unclouded night-sky, where His worlds wheel their silent course, that we read clearest His infinitude, His omnipotence, His omnipresence. I had risen

to my knees to pray for Mr. Rochester. Looking up, I, with tear-dimmed eyes, saw the mighty Milky-way. Remembering what it was—what countless systems swept space like a soft trace of light—I felt the might and strength of God. Sure was I of His efficiency to save what He had made: convinced I grew that neither earth should perish, nor one of the souls it treasured. I turned my prayer to thanks-giving: the Source of Life was also the Saviour of spirits. Mr. Rochester was safe: he was God's and by God would he be guarded. I again nestled to the breast of the hill; and ere long, in sleep, forgot sorrow.

But next day, Want came to me, pale and bare. Long after the little birds had left their nests; long after bees had come in the sweet prime of day to gather the heath honey before the dew was dried—when the long morning shadows were curtailed, and the sun filled earth and sky—I got up, and I looked round me.

What a still, hot, perfect day! What a golden desert this spreading moor! Everywhere sunshine. I wished I could live in it and on it. I saw a lizard run over the crag; I saw a bee busy among the sweet bilberries. I would fain at the moment have become bee or lizard, that I might have found fitting nutriment, permanent shelter here. But I was a human being, and had a human being's wants: I must not linger where there was nothing to supply them. I rose, I looked back at the bed I had left. Hopeless of the future, I wished but this—that my Maker had that night thought good to require my soul of me while I slept; and that this weary frame, absolved by death from further conflict with fate, had now but to decay quietly, and mingle in peace with the soil of this wilderness. Life, however, was yet in my possession: with all its requirements and pains, and responsibilities. The burden must be carried; the want provided for; the suffering endured; the responsibility fulfilled. I set out.

Whitcross regained, I followed a road which led from the sun, now fervent and high. By no other circumstance had I will to decide my choice. I walked a long time, and when I thought I had nearly done enough, and might conscientiously yield to the fatigue that almost overpowered me—might relax this forced action, and, sitting down on a stone I saw near, submit restlessly to the apathy that clogged heart and limb—I heard a bell chime—a church bell.

I turned in the direction of the sound, and there, amongst the romantic hills, whose changes and aspect I had ceased to note an hour ago, I saw a hamlet and a spire. All the valley at my right hand was full of pasture-fields and cornfields, and wood; and a glittering stream ran zig-zag through the varied shades of green, the mellowing grain, the sombre wood-land, the clear and sunny lea. Recalled by the rumbling of wheels to the road before me, I saw a heavily-laden waggon labouring up the hill; and not far beyond were two cows and their drover. Human life and human labour were near. I must struggle on: strive to live and bend to toil like the rest.

About two o'clock, P.M., I entered the village. At the bottom of its one street

there was a little shop with some cakes of bread in the window. I coveted a cake of bread. With that refreshment I could perhaps regain a degree of energy; without it, it would be difficult to proceed. The wish to have some strength and some vigour returned to me as soon as I was amongst my fellow-beings. I felt it would be degrading to faint with hunger on the causeway of a hamlet. Had I nothing about me I could offer in exchange for one of these rolls? I considered. I had a small silk handkerchief tied round my throat; I had my gloves. I could hardly tell how men and women in extremities of destitution proceeded. I did not know whether either of these articles would be accepted: probably they would not; but I must try.

I entered the shop: a woman was there. Seeing a respectably-dressed person, a lady as she supposed, she came forward with civility. How could she serve me? I was seized with shame: my tongue would not utter the request I had prepared. I dared not offer her the half-worn gloves, the creased handkerchief: besides, I felt it would be absurd. I only begged permission to sit down a moment, as I was tired. Disappointed in the expectation of a customer, she coolly acceded to my request. She pointed to a seat; I sank into it. I felt sorely urged to weep; but conscious how unseasonable such a manifestation would be, I restrained it. Soon I asked her, 'if there were any dressmaker or plain-work-woman in the village?'

'Yes; two or three. Quite as many as there was employment for.'

I reflected. I was driven to the point now. I was brought face to face with Necessity. I stood in the position of one without a resource: without a friend; without a coin. I must do something. What? I must apply somewhere. Where?

'Did she know of any place in the neighbourhood where a servant was wanted?'

'Nay; she couldn't say.'

'What was the chief trade in this place? What did most of the people do?'

'Some were farm labourers; a good deal worked at Mr. Oliver's needle-factory, and at the foundry.'

'Did Mr. Oliver employ women?'

'Nay; it was men's work.'

'And what do the women do?'

'I knawn't,' was the answer. 'Some does one thing, and some another. Poor folk mun get on as they can.'

She seemed to be tired of my questions: and, indeed, what claim had I to importune her? A neighbour or two came in; my chair was evidently wanted. I took leave.

I passed up the street, looking as I went at all the houses to the right hand and to the left: but I could discover no pretext, nor see an inducement, to enter any. I rambled round the hamlet, going sometimes to a little distance and returning again, for an hour or more. Much exhausted, and suffering greatly

now for want of food, I turned aside into a lane and sat down under the hedge. Ere many minutes had elapsed, I was again on my feet, however, and again searching something—a resource, or at least an informant. A pretty little house stood at the top of the lane, with a garden before it; exquisitely neat, and brilliantly blooming. I stopped at it. What business had I to approach the white door, or touch the glittering knocker? In what way could it possibly be the interest of the inhabitants of that dwelling to serve me? Yet I drew near and knocked. A mild-looking, cleanly-attired young woman opened the door. In such a voice as might be expected from a hopeless heart and fainting frame—a voice wretchedly low and faltering—I asked if a servant was wanted here?

'No,' said she; 'we do not keep a servant.'

'Can you tell me where I could get employment of any kind?' I continued. 'I am a stranger, without acquaintance, in this place. I want some work: no matter what.'

But it was not her business to think for me, or to seek a place for me: besides, in her eyes, how doubtful must have appeared my character, position, tale. She shook her head, she 'was sorry she could give me no information,' and the white door closed, quite gently and civilly: but it shut me out. If she had held it open a little longer, I believe I should have begged a piece of bread; for I was now brought low.

I could not bear to return to the sordid village; where, besides, no prospect of aid was visible. I should have longed rather to deviate to a wood I saw not far off, which appeared in its thick shade to offer inviting shelter; but I was so sick, so weak, so gnawed with nature's cravings, instinct kept me roaming round abodes where there was a chance of food. Solitude would be no solitude—rest no rest—while the vulture, hunger, thus sank beak and talons in my side.

I drew near houses; I left them, and came back again, and again I wandered away: always repelled by the consciousness of having no claim to ask—no right to expect interest in my isolated lot. Meantime, the afternoon advanced, while I thus wandered about like a lost and starving dog. In crossing a field I saw the church spire before me: I hastened towards it. Near the churchyard, and in the middle of a garden, stood a well-built though small house, which I had no doubt was the parsonage. I remembered that strangers who arrive at a place where they have no friends, and who want employment, sometimes apply to the clergyman for introduction and aid. It is the clergyman's function to help—at least with advice—those who wished to help themselves. I seemed to have something like a right to seek counsel here. Renewing then, my courage and gathering my feeble remains of strength, I pushed on. I reached the house and knocked at the kitchen-door. An old woman opened: I asked was this the parsonage?

'Yes.'

'Was the clergyman in?'

'No.'

'Would he be in soon?'

'No, he was gone from home.'

'To a distance?'

'Not so far—happen three mile. He had been called away by the sudden death of his father: he was at Marsh End now, and would very likely stay there a fortnight longer.'

'Was there any lady of the house?'

'Nay, there was naught but her, and she was housekeeper;' and of her, reader, I could not bear to ask the relief for want of which I was sinking; I could not yet beg; and again I crawled away.

Once more I took off my handkerchief—once more I thought of the cakes of bread in the little shop. Oh, for but a crust! for but one mouthful to allay the pang of famine! Instinctively I turned my face again to the village; I found the shop again, and I went in; and though others were there besides the woman, I ventured the request: 'Would she give me a roll for this hand-kerchief?'

She looked at me with evident suspicion: 'Nay, she never sold stuff i' that way.'

Almost desperate, I asked for half a cake; she again refused. 'How could she tell where I had got the handkerchief,' she said.

'Would she take my gloves?'

'No! what could she do with them?'

Reader, it is not pleasant to dwell on these details. Some say there is enjoy-ment in looking back to painful experience past; but at this day I can scarcely bear to review the times to which I allude: the moral degradation, blent with the physical suffering, form too distressing a recollection ever to be willingly dwelt on. I blamed none of those who repulsed me. I felt it was what was to be expected, and what could not be helped: an ordinary beggar is frequently an object of suspicion; a well-dressed beggar inevitably so. To be sure what I begged was employment: but whose business was it to provide me with employment? Not, certainly, that of persons who saw me then for the first time, and who knew nothing about my character. And as to the woman who would not take my handkerchief in exchange for her bread, why, she was right; if the offer appeared to her sinister, or the exchange unprofitable. Let me condense now. I am sick of the subject.

A little before dark I passed a farm-house, at the open door of which the farmer was sitting, eating his supper of bread and cheese; I stopped, and said:—

'Will you give me a piece of bread? for I am very hungry.' He cast on me a glance of surprise; but without answering, he cut a thick slice from his loaf, and gave it to me. I imagine he did not think I was a beggar, but only an

eccentric sort of lady, who had taken a fancy to his brown loaf. As soon as I was out of sight of his house, I sat down and ate it.

I could not hope to get a lodging under a roof, and sought it in the wood I have before alluded to. But my night was wretched, my rest broken: the ground was damp, the air cold: besides, intruders passed near me more than once, and I had again and again to change my quarters: no sense of safety or tranquillity befriended me. Towards morning it rained; the whole of the following day was wet. Do not ask me, reader, to give a minute account of that day; as before, I sought work; as before, I was repulsed; as before, I starved; but once did food pass my lips. At the door of a cottage I saw a little girl about to throw a mess of cold porridge into a pig trough. 'Will you give me that?' I asked.

She stared at me. 'Mother!' she exclaimed; 'there is a woman wants me to give her these porridge.'

'Well, lass,' replied a voice within, 'give it her if she's a beggar. T' pig doesn't want it.'

The girl emptied the stiffened mould into my hand, and I devoured it ravenously.

As the wet twilight deepened, I stopped in a solitary bridle path, which I had been pursuing an hour or more.

'My strength is quite failing me,' I said, in soliloquy. 'I feel I cannot go much further. Shall I be an outcast again this night? While the rain descends so, must I lay my head on the cold, drenched ground! I fear I cannot do otherwise: for who will receive me? But it will be very dreadful: with this feeling of hunger, faintness, chill, and this sense of desolation—this total prostration of hope. In all likelihood, though, I should die before morning. And why cannot I reconcile myself to the prospect of death? Why do I struggle to retain a valueless life? Because I know, or believe, Mr. Rochester is still living: and then, to die of want and cold, is a fate to which nature cannot submit passively. Oh, Providence! sustain me a little longer! Aid—direct me!'

My glazed eye wandered over the dim and misty landscape. I saw I had strayed far from the village: it was quite out of sight. The very cultivation surrounding it had disappeared. I had, by cross-ways and by-paths, once more drawn near the tract of moorland; and now, only a few fields, almost as wild and unproductive as the heath from which they were scarcely reclaimed, lay between me and the dusky hill.

'Well, I would rather die yonder than in a street, or on a frequented road,' I reflected. 'And far better that crows and ravens—if any ravens there be in these regions—should pick my flesh from my bones, than that they should be prisoned in a workhouse coffin and moulder in a pauper's grave.'

To the hill, then, I turned. I reached it. It remained now only to find a hollow where I could lie down, and feel at least hidden, if not secure: but

all the surface of the waste looked level. It showed no variation but of tint: green, where rush and moss overgrew the marshes; black, where the dry soil bore only heath. Dark as it was getting, I could still see these changes: though but as mere alterations of light and shade: for colour had faded with the daylight.

My eye still roved over the sullen swell, and along the moor-edge, vanishing amidst the wildest scenery; when at one dim point, far among the marshes and the ridges, a light sprang up. 'That is an *ignis fatuus*,' was my first thought; and I expected it would soon vanish. It burnt on, however, quite steadily; neither receding nor advancing. 'Is it, then, a bonfire just kindled?' I questioned. I watched to see whether it would spread: but no, as it did not diminish, so it did not enlarge. 'It may be a candle in a house,' I then conjectured: 'but if so, I can never reach it. It is much too far away: and were it within a yard of me, what would it avail? I should but knock at the door to have it shut in my face.'

And I sank down where I stood, and hid my face against the ground. I lay still a while: the night-wind swept over the hill and over me, and died moaning in the distance; the rain fell fast, wetting me afresh to the skin. Could I but have stiffened to the still frost—the friendly numbness of death—it might have pelted on: I should not have felt it; but my yet living flesh shuddered to its chilling influence. I rose ere long.

The light was yet there: shining dim, but constant, through the rain. I tried to walk again: I dragged my exhausted limbs slowly towards it. It led me aslant over the hill, through a wide bog; which would have been impassable in winter, and was splashy and shaking even now, in the height of summer. Here I fell twice; but as often I rose and rallied my faculties. This light was my forlorn hope: I must gain it.

Having crossed the marsh, I saw a trace of white over the moor. I approached it; it was a road or a track: it led straight up to the light, which now beamed from a sort of knoll, amidst a clump of trees—firs, apparently, from what I could distinguish of the character of their forms and foliage through the gloom. My star vanished as I drew near: some obstacle had intervened between me and it. I put out my hand to feel the dark mass before me; I discriminated the rough stones of a low wall—above it, something like palisades, and within, a high and prickly hedge. I groped on. Again a whitish object gleamed before me: it was a gate—a wicket; it moved on its hinges as I touched it. On each side stood a sable bush—holly or yew.

Entering the gate and passing the shrubs, the silhouette of a house rose to view; black, low, and rather long; but the guiding light shone nowhere. All was obscurity. Were the inmates retired to rest? I feared it must be so. In seeking the door, I turned an angle: there shot out the friendly gleam again, from the lozenged panes of a very small latticed window, within a foot of the

ground; made still smaller by the growth of ivy or some other creeping plant, whose leaves clustered thick over the portion of the house wall in which it was set. The aperture was so screened and narrow, that curtain or shutter had been deemed unnecessary; and when I stooped down and put aside the spray of foliage shooting over it, I could see all within. I could see clearly a room with a sanded floor, clean scoured; a dresser of walnut, with pewter plates ranged in rows, reflecting the redness and radiance of a glowing peat-fire. I could see a clock, a white deal table, some chairs. The candle, whose ray had been my beacon, burnt on the table; and by its light an elderly woman, somewhat rough-looking, but scrupulously clean, like all about her, was knitting a stocking.

I noted these objects cursorily only—in them there was nothing extraordinary. A group of more interest appeared near the hearth, sitting still amidst the rosy peace and warmth suffusing it. Two young, graceful women—ladies in every point—sat, one on a low rocking-chair, the other on a lower stool; both wore deep mourning of crape and bombazeen, which sombre garb singularly set off very fair necks and faces: a large old pointer dog rested its massive head on the knee of one girl—in the lap of the other was cushioned a black cat.

A strange place was this humble kitchen for such occupants! Who were they? They could not be the daughters of the elderly person at the table; for she looked like a rustic, and they were all delicacy and cultivation. I had nowhere seen such faces as theirs: and yet, as I gazed on them, I seemed intimate with every lineament. I cannot call them handsome—they were too pale and grave for the word: as they each bent over a book, they looked thoughtful almost to severity. A stand between them supported a second candle and two great volumes, to which they frequently referred; comparing them seemingly with the smaller books they held in their hands, like people consulting a dictionary to aid them in the task of translation. This scene was as silent as if all the figures had been shadows, and the fire-lit apartment a picture: so hushed was it, I could hear the cinders fall from the grate, the clock tick in its obscure corner; and I even fancied I could distinguish the click-click of the woman's knitting-needles. When, therefore, a voice broke the strange stillness at last, it was audible enough to me.

'Listen, Diana,' said one of the absorbed students: 'Franz and old Daniel are together in the night-time, and Franz is telling a dream from which he has awakened in terror—listen!' And in a low voice she read something, of which not one word was intelligible to me; for it was in an unknown tongue—neither French nor Latin. Whether it were Greek or German I could not tell.

'That is strong,' she said, when she had finished: 'I relish it.' The other girl who had lifted her head to listen to her sister, repeated, while she gazed at the fire, a line of what had been read. At a later day, I knew the language

and the book; therefore I will here quote the line: though when I first heard it, it was only like a stroke on sounding brass to me—conveying no meaning:—
' "Da trat hervor Einer, anzusehen wie die Sternen Nacht." Good! good!' she exclaimed, while her dark and deep eye sparkled. 'There you have a dim and mighty archangel, fitly set before you! The line is worth a hundred pages of fustian. "Ich wäge die Gedanken in der Schale meines Zornes und die Werke mit dem Gewichte meines Grimms." I like it!'

Both were again silent.

'Is there ony country where they talk i' that way?' asked the old woman, looking up from her knitting.

'Yes, Hannah—a far larger country than England; where they talk in no other way.'

'Well, for sure case, I knawn't how they can understand t' one t' other: and if either o' ye went there, ye could tell what they said, I guess?'

'We could probably tell something of what they said, but not all—for we are not as clever as you think us, Hannah. We don't speak German, and we cannot read it without a dictionary to help us.'

'And what good does it do you?'

'We mean to teach it some time—or at least the elements, as they say; and then we shall get more money than we do now.'

'Varry like: but give ower studying: ye've done enough for to-night.'

'I think we have: at least I'm tired. Mary, are you?'

'Mortally: after all, it's tough work fagging away at a language with no master but a lexicon.'

'It is: especially such a language as this crabbed but glorious Deutsch. wonder when St. John will come home.'

'Surely he will not be long now: it is just ten' (looking at a little gold watch he drew from her girdle). 'It rains fast. Hannah, will you have the goodness o look at the fire in the parlour?'

The woman rose: she opened a door, through which I dimly saw a passage: oon I heard her stir a fire in an inner room; she presently came back.

'Ah, childer!' said she, 'it fair troubles me to go into yond' room now; it ooks so lonesome wi' the chair empty and set back in a corner.'

She wiped her eyes with her apron: the two girls, grave before, looked ad now.

'But he is in a better place,' continued Hannah: 'we shouldn't wish him ere again. And then, nobody need to have a quieter death nor he had.'

'You say he never mentioned us?' inquired one of the ladies.

'He hadn't time, bairn: he was gone in a minute—was your father. He had een a bit ailing like the day before, but naught to signify; and when Mr.
t. John asked if he would like either o' ye to be sent for, he fair laughed at him.
e began again with a bit of a heaviness in his head the next day—that is,

a fortnight sin'—and he went to sleep and niver wakened; he wor a'most stark when your brother went into t' chamber and fand him. Ah, childer! that's t' last o' t' old stock—for ye and Mr. St. John is like of a different soart to them 'at's gone; for all your mother wor mich i' your way; and a'most as book-learned. She wor the pictur' o' ye, Mary: Diana is more like your father.'

I thought them so similar I could not tell where the old servant (for such I now concluded her to be) saw the difference. Both were fair complexioned and slenderly made; both possessed faces full of distinction and intelligence. One, to be sure, had hair a shade darker than the other, and there was a differ-ence in their style of wearing it: Mary's pale brown locks were parted and braided smooth; Diana's duskier tresses covered her neck with thick curls. The clock struck ten.

'You'll want your supper, I am sure,' observed Hannah; 'and so will Mr. St. John when he comes in.'

And she proceeded to prepare the meal. The ladies rose; they seemed about to withdraw to the parlour. Till this moment, I had been so intent on watching them, their appearance and conversation had excited in me so keen an interest I had half-forgotten my own wretched position: now it recurred to me. More desolate, more desperate than ever, it seemed from contrast. And how impos-sible did it appear to touch the inmates of this house with concern on my behalf; to make them believe in the truth of my wants and woes—to induce them to vouchsafe a rest for my wanderings! As I groped out the door, and knocked at it hesitatingly, I felt that last idea to be a mere chimera. Hannah opened.

'What do you want?' she inquired, in a voice of surprise, as she surveyed me by the light of the candle she held.

'May I speak to your mistresses?' I said.

'You had better tell me what you have to say to them. Where do you come from?'

'I am a stranger.'

'What is your business here at this hour?'

'I want a night's shelter in an out-house or anywhere, and a morsel of bread to eat.'

Distrust, the very feeling I dreaded, appeared in Hannah's face. 'I'll give you a piece of bread,' she said, after a pause; 'but we can't take in a vagrant to lodge. It isn't likely.'

'Do let me speak to your mistresses.'

'No; not I. What can they do for you? You should not be roving about now it looks very ill.'

'But where shall I go if you drive me away? What shall I do?'

'Oh, I'll warrant you know where to go, and what to do. Mind you don do wrong, that's all. Here is a penny; now go'——

'A penny cannot feed me, and I have no strength to go farther. Don't shut the door:—oh, don't, for God's sake!'

'I must; the rain is driving in'——

'Tell the young ladies.—Let me see them'——

'Indeed, I will not. You are not what you ought to be, or you wouldn't make such a noise. Move off.'

'But I must die if I am turned away.'

'Not you. I'm fear'd you have some ill plans agate, that bring you about folk's houses at this time o' night. If you've any followers—housebreakers or such like—anywhere near, you may tell them we are not by ourselves in the house; we have a gentleman, and dogs, and guns.' Here the honest but inflexible servant clapped the door to and bolted it within.

This was the climax. A pang of exquisite suffering—a throe of true despair—rent and heaved my heart. Worn out, indeed, I was; not another step could I stir. I sank on the wet door-step: I groaned—I wrung my hands—I wept in utter anguish. Oh, this spectre of death! Oh, this last hour, approaching in such horror! Alas, this isolation—this banishment from my kind! Not only the anchor of home, but the footing of fortitude was gone—at least for a moment: but the last I soon endeavoured to regain.

'I can but die,' I said, 'and I believe in God. Let me try to wait His will in silence.'

These words I not only thought, but uttered; and thrusting back all my misery into my heart, I made an effort to compel it to remain there—dumb and still.

'All men must die,' said a voice quite close at hand; 'but all are not condemned to meet a lingering and premature doom, such as yours would be if you perished here of want.'

'Who or what speaks?' I asked, terrified at the unexpected sound, and incapable now of deriving from any occurrence a hope of aid. A form was near—what form, the pitch-dark night and my enfeebled vision prevented me from distinguishing. With a loud long knock, the new comer appealed to the door.

'Is it you, Mr. St. John?' cried Hannah.

'Yes—yes; open quickly.'

'Well, how wet and cold you must be, such a wild night as it is! Come in—our sisters are quite uneasy about you, and I believe there are bad folks about. There has been a beggar-woman—I declare she is not gone yet!—laid down here. Get up! for shame! Move off, I say!'

'Hush, Hannah! I have a word to say to the woman. You have done your duty in excluding, now let me do mine in admitting her. I was near, and listened to both you and her. I think this is a peculiar case—I must at least examine into it. Young woman, rise, and pass before me into the house.'

With difficulty I obeyed him. Presently I stood within that clean, bright kitchen—on the very hearth—trembling, sickening; conscious of an aspect in the last degree ghastly, wild, and weather-beaten. The two ladies, their brother, Mr. St. John, the old servant, were all gazing at me.

'St. John, who is it?' I heard one ask.

'I cannot tell: I found her at the door,' was the reply.

'She does look white,' said Hannah.

'As white as clay or death,' was responded. 'She will fall: let her sit.'

And indeed my head swam: I dropped; but a chair received. I still possessed my senses; though just now I could not speak.

'Perhaps a little water would restore her. Hannah, fetch some. But she is worn to nothing. How very thin, and how very bloodless!'

'A mere spectre!'

'Is she ill, or only famished?'

'Famished, I think. Hannah, is that milk? Give it me, and a piece of bread.'

Diana (I knew her by the long curls which I saw drooping between me and the fire as she bent over me) broke some bread, dipped it in milk, and put it to my lips. Her face was near mine: I saw there was pity in it, and I felt sympathy in her hurried breathing. In her simple words, too, the same balm-like emotion spoke: 'Try to eat.'

'Yes—try,' repeated Mary gently; and Mary's hand removed my sodden bonnet and lifted my head. I tasted what they offered me: feebly at first, eagerly soon.

'Not too much at first—restrain her,' said the brother; 'she has had enough.' And he withdrew the cup of milk and the plate of bread.

'A little more, St. John—look at the avidity in her eyes.'

'No more at present, sister. Try if she can speak now—ask her her name.

I felt I could speak, and I answered—'My name is Jane Elliott.' Anxious as ever to avoid discovery, I had before resolved to assume an *alias*.

'And where do you live? Where are your friends?'

I was silent.

'Can we send for any one you know?'

I shook my head.

'What account can you give of yourself?'

Somehow, now that I had once crossed the threshold of this house, and once was brought face to face with its owners, I felt no longer outcast, vagrant, and disowned by the wide world. I dared to put off the mendicant—to resume my natural manner and character. I began once more to know myself; and when Mr. St. John demanded an account—which at present I was far too weak to render—I said after a brief pause,—

'Sir, I can give you no details to-night.'

'But what, then,' said he, 'do you expect me to do for you?'

'Nothing,' I replied. My strength sufficed for but short answers. Diana took he word:—

'Do you mean,' she asked, 'that we have now given you what aid you require? and that we may dismiss you to the moor and the rainy night?'

I looked at her. She had, I thought, a remarkable countenance; instinct both with power and goodness. I took sudden courage. Answering her compassionate gaze with a smile, I said: 'I will trust you. If I were a masterless and stray dog, I know that you would not turn me from your hearth to-night: as it is, I really have no fear. Do with me and for me as you like; but excuse me from much discourse—my breath is short—I feel a spasm when I speak.'

All three surveyed me, and all three were silent.

'Hannah,' said Mr. St. John, at last, 'let her sit there at present, and ask her no questions; in ten minutes more, give her the remainder of that milk and bread. Mary and Diana, let us go into the parlour and talk the matter over.'

They withdrew. Very soon one of the ladies returned—I could not tell which. A kind of pleasant stupor was stealing over me as I sat by the genial fire. In an under tone she gave some directions to Hannah. Ere long, with the servant's aid, I contrived to mount a staircase; my dripping clothes were removed; soon, a warm, dry bed received me. I thanked God—experienced amidst unutterable exhaustion a glow of grateful joy—and slept.

CHAPTER 29

The recollection of about three days and nights succeeding this is very dim in my mind. I can recall some sensations felt in the interval; but few thoughts framed, and no actions performed. I knew I was in a small room, and in a narrow bed. To that bed I seemed to have grown; I lay on it motionless as a stone; and to have torn me from it would have been almost to kill me. I took no note of the lapse of time—of the change from morning to noon, from noon to evening. I observed when any one entered or left the apartment; I could even tell who they were; I could understand what was said when the speaker stood near to me; but I could not answer; to open my lips or move my limbs was equally impossible. Hannah, the servant, was my most frequent visitor. Her coming disturbed me. I had a feeling that she wished me away: that she did not understand me or my circumstances: that she was prejudiced against me. Diana and Mary appeared in the chamber once or twice a day. They would whisper sentences of this sort at my bedside:—

'It is very well we took her in.'

'Yes; she would certainly have been found dead at the door in the morning, had she been left out all night. I wonder what she has gone through?'

'Strange hardships, I imagine—poor, emaciated, pallid wanderer!'

'She is not an uneducated person, I should think, by her manner of speaking; her accent was quite pure; and the clothes she took off, though splashed and wet, were little worn and fine.'

'She has a peculiar face; fleshless and haggard as it is, I rather like it; and when in good health and animated, I can fancy her physiognomy would be agreeable.'

Never once in their dialogues did I hear a syllable of regret at the hospitality they had extended to me; or of suspicion of, or aversion to, myself. I was comforted.

Mr. St. John came but once: he looked at me, and said my state of lethargy was the result of reaction from excessive and protracted fatigue. He pronounced it needless to send for a doctor: nature, he was sure, would manage best, left to herself. He said every nerve had been overstrained in some way, and the whole system must sleep torpid a while. There was no disease. He imagined my recovery would be rapid enough when once commenced. These opinions he delivered in a few words, in a quiet, low voice; and added, after a pause, in the tone of a man little accustomed to expansive comment, 'rather an unusual physiognomy; certainly, not indicative of vulgarity or degradation.'

'Far otherwise,' responded Diana. 'To speak truth, St. John, my heart rather warms to the poor little soul. I wish we may be able to benefit her permanently.'

'That is hardly likely,' was the reply. 'You will find she is some young lady who has had a misunderstanding with her friends and has probably injudiciously left them. We may, perhaps, succeed in restoring her to them, if she is not obstinate: but I trace lines of force in her face which make me sceptical of her tractability.' He stood considering me some minutes; then added, 'She looks sensible, but not at all handsome.'

'She is so ill, St. John.'

'Ill or well, she would always be plain. The grace and harmony of beauty are quite wanting in those features.'

On the third day, I was better; on the fourth, I could speak, move, rise in bed, and turn. Hannah had brought me some gruel and dry toast, about, as I supposed, the dinner hour. I had eaten with relish: the food was good—void of the feverish flavour which had hitherto poisoned what I had swallowed. When she left me, I felt comparatively strong and revived: ere long satiety of repose, and desire for action stirred me. I wished to rise; but what could I put on? Only my damp and bemired apparel; in which I had slept on the ground and fallen in the marsh. I felt ashamed to appear before my benefactors so clad. I was spared the humiliation.

On a chair by the bedside were all my own things, clean and dry. My black silk frock hung against the wall. The traces of the bog were removed from it

the creases left by the wet smoothed out: it was quite decent. My very shoes and stockings were purified and rendered presentable. There were the means of washing in the room, and a comb and brush to smooth my hair. After a weary process, and resting every five minutes, I succeeded in dressing myself. My clothes hung loose on me; for I was much wasted, but I covered deficiencies with a shawl, and once more, clean and respectable-looking—no speck of the dirt, no trace of the disorder I so hated, and which seemed so to degrade me, left—I crept down a stone staircase with the aid of the banisters, to a narrow low passage, and found my way presently to the kitchen.

It was full of the fragrance of new bread, and the warmth of a generous fire. Hannah was baking. Prejudices, it is well known, are most difficult to eradicate from the heart whose soil has never been loosened or fertilised by education: they grow there, firm as weeds among stones. Hannah had been cold and stiff, indeed, at the first: latterly she had begun to relent a little; and when she saw me come in tidy and well-dressed, she even smiled.

'What, you have got up?' she said. 'You are better, then. You may sit you down in my chair on the hearthstone, if you will.'

She pointed to the rocking chair: I took it. She bustled about, examining me every now and then with the corner of her eye. Turning to me, as she took some loaves from the oven, she asked, bluntly—

'Did you ever go a-begging afore you came here?'

I was indignant for a moment; but remembering that anger was out of the question, and that I had indeed appeared as a beggar to her, I answered quietly; but still not without a certain marked firmness—

'You are mistaken in supposing me a beggar. I am no beggar; any more than yourself or your young ladies.'

After a pause, she said, 'I dunnut understand that: you've no house, nor no brass, I guess?'

'The want of house or brass (by which I suppose you mean money) does not make a beggar in your sense of the word.'

'Are you book-learned?' she inquired, presently.

'Yes, very.'

'But you've never been to a boarding-school!'

'I was at a boarding-school eight years.'

She opened her eyes wide. 'Whatever cannot ye keep yourself for, then?'

'I have kept myself; and, I trust, shall keep myself again. What are you going to do with these gooseberries?' I inquired, as she brought out a basket of the fruit.

'Mak'em into pies.'

'Give them to me and I'll pick them.'

'Nay; I dunnut want ye to do nought.'

'But I must do something. Let me have them.'

She consented; and she even brought me a clean towel to spread over my dress, 'lest,' as she said, 'I should mucky it.'

'Ye've not been used to sarvant's wark, I see by your hands,' she remarked. 'Happen ye've been a dressmaker.'

'No, you are wrong. And, now, never mind what I have been: don't trouble your head further about me; but tell me the name of the house where we are.'

'Some calls it Marsh End, and some calls it Moor House.'

'And the gentleman who lives here is called Mr. St. John?'

'Nay; he doesn't live here: he is only staying a while. When he is at home, he is in his own parish at Morton.'

'That village a few miles off?'

'Aye.'

'And what is he?'

'He is a parson.'

I remembered the answer of the old housekeeper at the parsonage, when I had asked to see the clergyman. 'This, then, was his father's residence?'

'Aye; old Mr. Rivers lived here, and his father, and grandfather, and gurt (great) grandfather afore him.'

'The name, then, of that gentleman, is Mr. St. John Rivers?'

'Aye; St. John is like his kirstened name.'

'And his sisters are called Diana and Mary Rivers?'

'Yes.'

'Their father is dead?'

'Dead three weeks sin' of a stroke.'

'They have no mother?'

'The mistress has been dead this mony a year.'

'Have you lived with the family long?'

'I've lived here thirty year. I nursed them all three.'

'That proves you must have been an honest and faithful servant. I will say so much for you, though you have had the incivility to call me a beggar.'

She again regarded me with a surprised stare. 'I believe,' she said, 'I was quite mista'en in my thoughts of you: but there is so mony cheats goes about you mun forgie me.'

'And though,' I continued, rather severely, 'you wished to turn me from the door, on a night when you should not have shut out a dog.'

'Well, it was hard: but what can a body do? I thought more o' the childer nor of mysel: poor things! They've like nobody to tak' care on 'em but me. I'm like to look sharpish.'

I maintained a grave silence for some minutes.

'You munnut think too hardly of me,' she again remarked.

'But I do think hardly of you,' I said; 'and I'll tell you why—not so much because you refused to give me shelter, or regarded me as an impostor, a

because you just now made it a species of reproach that I had no "brass," and no house. Some of the best people that ever lived have been as destitute as I am; and if you are a Christian, you ought not to consider poverty a crime.'

'No more I ought,' said she: 'Mr. St. John tells me so too; and I see I wor wrang—but I've clear a different notion on you now to what I had. You look a raight down dacent little crater.'

'That will do—I forgive you now. Shake hands.'

She put her floury and horny hand into mine; another and heartier smile illumined her rough face; and from that moment we were friends.

Hannah was evidently fond of talking. While I picked the fruit, and she made the paste for the pies, she proceeded to give me sundry details about her deceased master and mistress, and 'the childer, 'as she called the young people.

Old Mr. Rivers, she said, was a plain man enough; but a gentleman, and of as ancient a family as could be found. Marsh End had belonged to the Rivers' ever since it was a house: and it was, she affirmed, 'aboon two hundred year old—for all it looked but a small, humble place, naught to compare wi' Mr. Oliver's grand hall down i' Morton Vale. But she could remember Bill Oliver's father a journeyman needle-maker; and th' Rivers wor gentry i' th' owd days o' th' Henrys, as onybody might see by looking into th' registers ' Morton Church vestry.' Still, she allowed, 'the owd maister was like other 'olk—naught mich out o' t' common way: stark mad o' shooting, and farming, and sich like.' The mistress was different. She was a great reader, and studied a deal; and the 'bairns' had taken after her. There was nothing like them in these parts, nor ever had been; they had liked learning, all three, almost from the time they could speak; and they had always been 'of a mak' of their own.' Mr. St. John, when he grew up, would go to college and be a parson; and the girls, as soon as they left school, would seek places as governesses: for they had told her their father had some years ago lost a great deal of money, by a man he had trusted turning bankrupt; and as he was now not rich enough to give them fortunes, they must provide for themselves. They had lived very little at home for a long while, and were only come now to stay a few weeks on account of their father's death: but they did so like Marsh End and Morton, and all these moors and hills about. They had been in London, and many other grand towns; but they always said there was no place like home; and then they were so agreeable with each other—never fell out nor 'threaped.' She did not know where there was such a family for being united.

Having finished my task of gooseberry picking, I asked where the two ladies and their brother were now.

'Gone over to Morton for a walk; but they would be back in half an hour o tea.'

They returned within the time Hannah had allotted them: they entered by the kitchen door. Mr. St. John, when he saw me, merely bowed and passed

through; the two ladies stopped: Mary, in a few words, kindly and calmly expressed the pleasure she felt in seeing me well enough to be able to come down; Diana took my hand: she shook her head at me.

'You should have waited for my leave to descend,' she said. 'You still look very pale—and so thin! Poor child!—poor girl!'

Diana had a voice toned, to my ear, like the cooing of a dove. She possessed eyes whose gaze I delighted to encounter. Her whole face seemed to me full of charm. Mary's countenance was equally intelligent—her features equally pretty: but her expression was more reserved; and her manners, though gentle, more distant. Diana looked and spoke with a certain authority: she had a will, evidently. It was my nature to feel pleasure in yielding to authority supported like hers; and to bend, where my conscience and self-respect permitted, to an active will.

'And what business have you here?' she continued. 'It is not your place. Mary and I sit in the kitchen sometimes, because at home we like to be free, even to licence—but you are a visitor, and must go into the parlour.'

'I am very well here.'

'Not at all—with Hannah bustling about and covering you with flour.'

'Besides, the fire is too hot for you,' interposed Mary.

'To be sure,' added her sister. 'Come, you must be obedient.' And still holding my hand she made me rise, and led me into the inner room.

'Sit there,' she said, placing me on the sofa, 'while we take our things off and get the tea ready; it is another privilege we exercise in our little moorland home—to prepare our own meals when we are so inclined; or when Hannah is baking, brewing, washing, or ironing.'

She closed the door, leaving me solus with Mr. St. John, who sat opposite; a book or newspaper in his hand. I examined, first, the parlour, and then its occupant.

The parlour was rather a small room, very plainly furnished; yet comfortable, because clean and neat. The old-fashioned chairs were very bright, and the walnut-wood table was like a looking-glass. A few strange, antique portraits of the men and women of other days decorated the stained walls; a cupboard with glass doors contained some books and an ancient set of china. There was no superfluous ornament in the room—not one modern piece of furniture, save a brace of work-boxes and a lady's desk in rosewood, which stood on a side-table: everything—including the carpet and curtains—looked at once well worn and well saved.

Mr. St. John—sitting as still as one of the dusky pictures on the walls, keeping his eyes fixed on the page he perused and his lips mutely sealed—was easy enough to examine. Had he been a statue instead of a man, he could not have been easier. He was young—perhaps from twenty-eight to thirty—tall, slender; his face riveted the eye; it was like a Greek face, very pure in outline

quite a straight, classic nose; quite an Athenian mouth and chin. It is seldom, indeed, an English face comes so near the antique models as did his. He might well be a little shocked at the irregularity of my lineaments, his own being so harmonious. His eyes were large and blue, with brown lashes; his high forehead, colourless as ivory, was partially streaked over by careless locks of fair hair.

This is a gentle delineation, is it not, reader? Yet he whom it describes scarcely impressed one with the idea of a gentle, a yielding, an impressible, or even of a placid nature. Quiescent as he now sat, there was something about his nostril, his mouth, his brow, which, to my perceptions, indicated elements within either restless, or hard, or eager. He did not speak to me one word nor even direct to me one glance, till his sisters returned. Diana, as she passed in and out, in the course of preparing tea, brought me a little cake, baked on the top of the oven.

'Eat that now,' she said: 'you must be hungry. Hannah says you have had nothing but some gruel since breakfast.'

I did not refuse it, for my appetite was awakened and keen. Mr. Rivers now closed his book, approached the table, and, as he took a seat, fixed his blue pictorial-looking eyes full on me. There was an unceremonious directness, a searching, decided steadfastness in his gaze now, which told that intention, and not diffidence, had hitherto kept it averted from the stranger.

'You are very hungry,' he said.

'I am, sir.' It is my way—it always was my way, by instinct—ever to meet the brief with brevity, the direct with plainness.

'It is well for you that a low fever has forced you to abstain for the last three days: there would have been danger in yielding to the cravings of your appetite at first. Now you may eat; though still not immoderately.'

'I trust I shall not eat long at your expense, sir,' was my very clumsily-contrived, unpolished answer.

'No,' he said, coolly: 'when you have indicated to us the residence of your friends, we can write to them, and you may be restored to home.'

'That, I must plainly tell you, is out of my power to do; being absolutely without home and friends.'

The three looked at me; but not distrustfully; I felt there was no suspicion in their glances: there was more of curiosity. I speak particularly of the young ladies. St. John's eyes, though clear enough in a literal sense, in a figurative one were difficult to fathom. He seemed to use them rather as instruments to search other people's thoughts, than as agents to reveal his own: the which combination of keenness and reserve was considerably more calculated to embarrass than to encourage.

'Do you mean to say,' he asked, 'that you are completely isolated from every connection?'

'I do. Not a tie links me to any living thing: not a claim do I possess to admittance under any roof in England.'

'A most singular position at your age!'

Here I saw his glance directed to my hands, which were folded on the table before me. I wondered what he sought there: his words soon explained the quest.

'You have never been married? You are a spinster?'

Diana laughed. 'Why, she can't be above seventeen or eighteen years old, St. John,' she said.

'I am near nineteen; but I am not married. No.'

I felt a burning glow mount to my face; for bitter and agitating recollections were awakened by the allusion to marriage. They all saw the embarrassment, and the emotion. Diana and Mary relieved me by turning their eyes elsewhere than to my crimsoned visage; but the colder and sterner brother continued to gaze, till the trouble he had excited forced out tears as well as colour.

'Where did you last reside?' he now asked.

'You are too inquisitive, St. John,' murmured Mary, in a low voice; but he leaned over the table and required an answer, by a second firm and piercing look.

'The name of the place where, and of the person with whom I lived, is my secret,' I replied, concisely.

'Which, if you like, you have, in my opinion, a right to keep, both from St. John and every other questioner,' remarked Diana.

'Yet if I know nothing about you or your history, I cannot help you,' he said. 'And you need help: do you not?'

'I need it, and I seek it; so far, sir, that some true philanthropist will put me in the way of getting work which I can do, and the remuneration for which will keep me: if but in the barest necessaries of life.'

'I know not whether I am a true philanthropist; yet I am willing to aid you to the utmost of my power, in a purpose so honest. First, then, tell me what you have been accustomed to do, and what you *can* do.'

I had now swallowed my tea. I was mightily refreshed by the beverage; a much so as a giant with wine: it gave new tone to my unstrung nerves, and enabled me to address this penetrating young judge steadily.

'Mr. Rivers,' I said, turning to him, and looking at him, as he looked at me openly and without diffidence, 'you and your sisters have done me a grea service—the greatest man can do his fellow-being; you have rescued me, by your noble hospitality, from death. This benefit conferred gives you an unlimited claim on my gratitude; and a claim to a certain extent, on my confidence. I will tell you as much of the history of the wanderer you have harboured, as I can tell without compromising my own peace of mind—my own security, moral and physical, and that of others.

'I am an orphan; the daughter of a clergyman. My parents died before I could know them. I was brought up a dependant; educated in a charitable institution. I will even tell you the name of the establishment, where I passed six years as a pupil, and two as a teacher—Lowood Orphan Asylum, ——shire: you will have heard of it, Mr. Rivers?—the Rev. Robert Brocklehurst is the treasurer.'

'I have heard of Mr. Brocklehurst, and I have seen the school.'

'I left Lowood nearly a year since to become a private governess. I obtained a good situation, and was happy. This place I was obliged to leave four days before I came here. The reason of my departure I cannot and ought not to explain: it would be useless—dangerous; and would sound incredible. No blame attached to me: I am as free from culpability as any one of you three. Miserable I am, and must be for a time; for the catastrophe which drove me from the house I had found a paradise was of a strange and direful nature. I observed but two points in planning my departure—speed, secrecy: to secure these, I had to leave behind me everything I possessed except a small parcel; which, in my hurry and trouble of mind, I forgot to take out of the coach that brought me to Whitcross. To this neighbourhood, then, I came, quite destitute. I slept two nights in the open air, and wandered about two days without crossing a threshold: but twice in that space of time did I taste food; and it was when brought by hunger, exhaustion, and despair, almost to the last gasp, that you, Mr. Rivers, forbade me to perish of want at your door, and took me under the shelter of your roof. I know all your sisters have done for me since—for I have not been insensible during my seeming torpor—and I owe to their spontaneous, genuine, genial compassion, as large a debt as to your evangelical charity.'

'Don't make her talk any more now, St. John,' said Diana, as I paused; she is evidently not yet fit for excitement. Come to the sofa, and sit down now, Miss Elliott.'

I gave an involuntary half-start at hearing the *alias*: I had forgotten my new name. Mr. Rivers, whom nothing seemed to escape, noticed it at once.

'You said your name was Jane Elliott?' he observed.

'I did say so; and it is the name by which I think it expedient to be called at present: but it is not my real name, and when I hear it, it sounds strange to me.'

'Your real name you will not give?'

'No: I fear discovery above all things; and whatever disclosure would lead to it, I avoid.'

'You are quite right, I am sure,' said Diana. 'Now do, brother, let her be at peace awhile.'

But when St. John had mused a few moments, he recommenced, as imperturbably, and with as much acumen as ever.

293

'You would not like to be long dependent on our hospitality—you would wish, I see, to dispense as soon as may be with my sisters' compassion; and, above all, with my *charity* (I am quite sensible of the distinction drawn, nor do I resent it—it is just): you desire to be independent of us?'

'I do: I have already said so. Show me how to work, or how to seek work: that is all I now ask; then let me go, if it be but to the meanest cottage—but *till then*, allow me to stay here: I dread another essay of the horrors of homeless destitution.'

'Indeed, you *shall* stay here,' said Diana, putting her white hand on my head. 'You *shall*,' repeated Mary, in the tone of undemonstrative sincerity, which seemed natural to her.

'My sisters, you see, have a pleasure in keeping you,' said Mr. St. John, 'as they would have a pleasure in keeping and cherishing a half-frozen bird, some wintry wind might have driven through their casement. *I* feel more inclination to put you in the way of keeping yourself: and shall endeavour to do so: but observe, my sphere is narrow. I am but the incumbent of a poor country parish: my aid must be of the humblest sort. And if you are inclined to despise the day of small things, seek some more efficient succour than such as I can offer.'

'She has already said that she is willing to do anything honest she *can* do,' answered Diana, for me; 'and you know, St. John, she has no choice of helpers: she is forced to put up with such crusty people as you.'

'I will be a dressmaker: I will be a plain work-woman; I will be a servant, a nurse-girl, if I can be no better,' I answered.

'Right,' said Mr. St. John, quite coolly. 'If such is your spirit, I promise to aid you; in my own time and way.'

He now resumed the book with which he had been occupied before tea. I soon withdrew; for I had talked as much, and sat up as long, as my present strength would permit.

CHAPTER 30

The more I knew of the inmates of Moor House, the better I liked them. In a few days I had so far recovered my health that I could sit up all day, and walk out sometimes. I could join with Diana and Mary in all their occupations, converse with them as much as they wished, and aid them when and where they would allow me. There was a reviving pleasure in this intercourse, of a kind now tasted by me for the first time—the pleasure arising from perfect congeniality of tastes, sentiments, and principles.

I liked to read what they liked to read: what they enjoyed, delighted me; what they approved, I reverenced. They loved their sequestered home. I, too, in the grey, small, antique structure, with its low roof, its latticed casement,

its mouldering walls, its avenue of aged firs—all grown aslant under the stress of mountain winds; its garden, dark with yew and holly—and where no flowers but of the hardiest species would bloom—found a charm both potent and permanent. They clung to the purple moors behind and around their dwelling—to the hollow vale into which the pebbly bridle-path leading from their gate descended; and which wound between fern-banks first, and then amongst a few of the wildest little pasture-fields that ever bordered a wilderness of heath, or gave sustenance to a flock of grey moorland sheep, with their little mossy-faced lambs:—they clung to this scene, I say, with a perfect enthusiasm of attachment. I could comprehend the feeling, and share both its strength and truth. I saw the fascination of the locality. I felt the consecration of its loneliness: my eye feasted on the outline of swell and sweep—on the wild colouring communicated to ridge and dell, by moss, by heath-bell, by flower-sprinkled turf, by brilliant bracken, and mellow granite crag. These details were just to me what they were to them—so many pure and sweet sources of pleasure. The strong blast and the soft breeze; the rough and the halcyon day; the hours of sunrise and sunset; the moonlight and the clouded night, developed for me, in these regions, the same attraction as for them—wound round my faculties the same spell that entranced theirs.

In-doors we agreed equally well. They were both more accomplished and better read than I was: but with eagerness I followed in the path of knowledge they had trodden before me. I devoured the books they lent me: then it was full satisfaction to discuss with them in the evening what I had perused during the day. Thought fitted thought; opinion met opinion: we coincided, in short, perfectly.

If in our trio there was a superior and a leader, it was Diana. Physically, she far excelled me: she was handsome; she was vigorous. In her animal spirits, there was an affluence of life, and certainty of flow, such as excited my wonder, while it baffled my comprehension. I could talk a while when the evening commenced: but the first gush of vivacity and fluency gone, I was fain to sit on a stool at Diana's feet, to rest my head on her knee, and listen alternately to her and Mary; while they sounded thoroughly the topic on which I had but touched. Diana offered to teach me German. I liked to learn of her; I saw the part of instructress pleased and suited her; that of scholar pleased and suited me no less. Our natures dovetailed: mutual affection—of the strongest kind—was the result. They discovered I could draw: their pencils and colour-boxes were immediately at my service. My skill, greater in this one point than theirs, surprised and charmed them. Mary would sit and watch me by the hour together: then she would take lessons; and a docile, intelligent, assiduous pupil, she made. Thus occupied, and mutually entertained, days passed like hours, and weeks like days.

As to Mr. St. John, the intimacy which had arisen so naturally and rapidly

between me and his sisters, did not extend to him. One reason of the distance yet observed between us was, that he was comparatively seldom at home: a large proportion of his time appeared devoted to visiting the sick and poor among the scattered population of his parish.

No weather seemed to hinder him in these pastoral excursions: rain or fair, he would, when his hours of morning study were over, take his hat, and followed by his father's old pointer, Carlo, go out on his mission of love or duty—I scarcely know in which light he regarded it. Sometimes, when the day was very unfavourable, his sisters would expostulate. He would then say, with a peculiar smile, more solemn than cheerful,—

'And if I let a gust of wind or a sprinkling of rain turn me aside from these easy tasks, what preparation would such sloth be for the future I propose to myself?'

Diana and Mary's general answer to this question was a sigh, and some minutes of apparently mournful meditation.

But besides his frequent absences, there was another barrier to friendship with him: he seemed of a reserved, an abstracted, and even of a brooding nature. Zealous in his ministerial labours, blameless in his life and habits, he yet did not appear to enjoy that mental serenity, that inward content, which should be the reward of every sincere Christian and practical philanthropist. Often, of an evening, when he sat at the window, his desk and papers before him, he would cease reading or writing, rest his chin on his hand, and deliver himself up to I know not what course of thought: but that it was perturbed and exciting might be seen in the frequent flash and changeful dilation of his eye.

I think, moreover, that Nature was not to him that treasury of delight it was to his sisters. He expressed once, and but once in my hearing, a strong sense of the rugged charm of the hills, and an inborn affection for the dark roof and hoary walls he called his home: but there was more of gloom than pleasure in the tone and words in which the sentiment was manifested; and never did he seem to roam the moors for the sake of their soothing silence—never seek out or dwell upon the thousand peaceful delights they could yield.

Incommunicative as he was, some time elapsed before I had an opportunity of gauging his mind. I first got an idea of its calibre when I heard him preach in his own church at Morton. I wish I could describe that sermon but it is past my power. I cannot even render faithfully the effect it produced on me.

It began calm—and indeed, as far as delivery and pitch of voice went, i was calm to the end: an earnestly felt, yet strictly restrained zeal breathed soon in the distinct accents, and prompted the nervous language. This grew to force—compressed, condensed, controlled. The heart was thrilled, the mind astonished, by the power of the preacher: neither were softened. Throughout

there was a strange bitterness; an absence of consolatory gentleness; stern allusions to Calvinistic doctrines—election, predestination, reprobation—were frequent; and each reference to these points sounded like a sentence pronounced for doom. When he had done, instead of feeling better, calmer, more enlightened by his discourse, I experienced an inexpressible sadness; for it seemed to me—I know not whether equally so to others—that the eloquence to which I had been listening had sprung from a depth where lay turbid dregs of disappointment—where moved troubling impulses of insatiate yearnings and disquieting aspirations. I was sure St. John Rivers—pure-lived, conscientious, zealous as he was—had not yet found that peace of God which passeth all understanding: he had no more found it, I thought, than had I; with my concealed and racking regrets for my broken idol and lost elysium—regrets to which I have latterly avoided referring; but which possessed me and tyrannised over me ruthlessly.

Meantime a month was gone. Diana and Mary were soon to leave Moor House, and return to the far different life and scene which awaited them, as governesses in a large, fashionable, south-of-England city; where each held a situation in families, by whose wealthy and haughty members they were regarded only as humble dependants, and who neither knew nor sought one of their innate excellences, and appreciated only their acquired accomplishments as they appreciated the skill of their cook, or the taste of their waiting-woman. Mr. St. John had said nothing to me yet about the employment he had promised to obtain for me; yet it became urgent that I should have a vocation of some kind. One morning, being left alone with him a few minutes in the parlour, I ventured to approach the window-recess—which his table, chair, and desk consecrated as a kind of study—and I was going to speak; though not very well knowing in what words to frame my inquiry—for it is at all times difficult to break the ice of reserve glassing over such natures as his—when he saved me the trouble, by being the first to commence a dialogue.

Looking up as I drew near—'You have a question to ask of me?' he said.

'Yes; I wish to know whether you have heard of any service I can offer myself to undertake.'

'I found or devised something for you three weeks ago; but as you seemed both useful and happy here—as my sisters had evidently become attached to you, and your society gave them unusual pleasure—I deemed it inexpedient to break in on your mutual comfort, till their approaching departure from Marsh End should render yours necessary.'

'And they will go in three days now?' I said.

'Yes; and when they go, I shall return to the parsonage at Morton: Hannah will accompany me; and this old house will be shut up.'

I waited a few moments, expecting he would go on with the subject first broached: but he seemed to have entered another train of reflection: his look

denoted abstraction from me and my business. I was obliged to recall him to a theme which was of necessity one of close and anxious interest to me.

'What is the employment you had in view, Mr. Rivers? I hope this delay will not have increased the difficulty of securing it.'

'Oh, no; since it is an employment which depends only on me to give, and you to accept.'

He again paused: there seemed a reluctance to continue. I grew impatient: a restless movement or two, and an eager and exacting glance fastened on his face, conveyed the feeling to him as effectually as words could have done, and with less trouble.

'You need be in no hurry to hear,' he said: 'let me frankly tell you, I have nothing eligible or profitable to suggest. Before I explain, recall, if you please, my notice, clearly given, that if I helped you, it must be as the blind man would help the lame. I am poor; for I find that, when I have paid my father's debts, all the patrimony remaining to me will be this crumbling grange, the row of scathed firs behind, and the patch of moorish soil, with the yew-trees and holly-bushes in front. I am obscure: Rivers is an old name; but of the three sole descendants of the race, two earn the dependant's crust among strangers, and the third considers himself an alien from his native country—not only for life, but in death. Yes, and deems, and is bound to deem, himself honoured by the lot, and aspires but after the day when the cross of separation from fleshly ties shall be laid on his shoulders, and when the Head of that church-militant of whose humblest members he is one, shall give the word, "Rise, follow me!" '

St. John said these words as he pronounced his sermons, with a quiet, deep voice; with an unflushed cheek, and a coruscating radiance of glance. He resumed:—

'And since I am myself poor and obscure. I can offer you but a service of poverty and obscurity. *You* may even think it degrading—for I see now your habits have been what the world calls refined: your tastes lean to the ideal and your society has at least been amongst the educated—but *I* consider that no service degrades which can better our race. I hold that the more arid and unreclaimed the soil where the Christian labourer's task of tillage is appointed him—the scantier the meed his toil brings—the higher the honour. His, under such circumstances, is the destiny of the pioneer; and the first pioneers of the Gospel were the Apostles—their captain was Jesus, the Redeemer himself.'

'Well?' I said, as he again paused—'proceed.'

He looked at me before he proceeded: indeed, he seemed leisurely to read my face, as if its features and lines were characters on a page. The conclusions drawn from this scrutiny he partially expressed in his succeeding observations.

'I believe you will accept the post I offer you,' said he; 'and hold it for a while: not permanently, though: any more than I could permanently keep

the narrow and narrowing—the tranquil, hidden office of English country incumbent: for in your nature is an alloy as detrimental to repose as that in mine; though of a different kind.'

'Do explain,' I urged, when he halted once more.

'I will; and you shall hear how poor the proposal is,—how trivial—how cramping. I shall not stay long at Morton, now that my father is dead, and that I am my own master. I shall leave the place probably in the course of a twelvemonth: but while I do stay, I will exert myself to the utmost for its improvement. Morton, when I came to it two years ago, had no school: the children of the poor were excluded from every hope of progress. I established one for boys: I mean now to open a second school for girls. I have hired a building for the purpose, with a cottage of two rooms attached to it for the mistress's house. Her salary will be thirty pounds a year: her house is already furnished, very simply, but sufficiently, by the kindness of a lady, Miss Oliver; the only daughter of the sole rich man in my parish—Mr. Oliver, the proprietor of a needle-factory and iron-foundry in the valley. The same lady pays for the education and clothing of an orphan from the workhouse; on condition that she shall aid the mistress in such menial offices connected with her own house and the school, as her occupation of teaching will prevent her having time to discharge in person. Will you be this mistress?'

He put the question rather hurriedly; he seemed half to expect an indignant, or at least a disdainful rejection of the offer: not knowing all my thoughts and feelings, though guessing some, he could not tell in what light the lot would appear to me. In truth it was humble—but then it was sheltered, and I wanted a safe asylum: it was plodding—but then, compared with that of a governess in a rich house, it was independent; and the fear of servitude with strangers entered my soul like iron: it was not ignoble—not unworthy—not mentally degrading. I made my decision.

'I thank you for the proposal, Mr. Rivers; and I accept it with all my heart.'

'But you comprehend me?' he said. 'It is a village school: your scholars will be only poor girls—cottagers' children—at the best, farmers' daughters. Knitting, sewing, reading, writing, cyphering, will be all you will have to teach. What will you do with your accomplishments? What, with the largest portion of your mind—sentiments—tastes?'

'Save them till they are wanted. They will keep.'

'You know what you undertake, then?'

'I do.'

He now smiled: not a bitter or a sad smile; but one well pleased and deeply gratified.

'And when will you commence the exercise of your function?'

'I will go to my house to-morrow; and open the school, if you like, next week.'

'Very well: so be it.'

He rose and walked through the room. Standing still, he again looked at me. He shook his head.

'What do you disapprove of, Mr. Rivers?' I asked.

'You will not stay at Morton long: no, no!'

'Why! What is your reason for saying so?'

'I read it in your eye; it is not of that description which promises the maintenance of an even tenor on life.'

'I am not ambitious.'

He started at the word 'ambitious.' He repeated, 'No. What made you think of ambition? Who is ambitious? I know I am: but how did you find it out?'

'I was speaking of myself.'

'Well, if you are not ambitious, you are'—— He paused.

'What?'

'I was going to say, impassioned: but perhaps you would have misunderstood the word, and been displeased. I mean that human affections and sympathies have a most powerful hold on you. I am sure you cannot long be content to pass your leisure in solitude, and to devote your working hours to a monotonous labour wholly void of stimulus; any more than I can be content,' he added, with emphasis, 'to live here buried in morass, pent in with mountain—my nature, that God gave me, contravened; my faculties, heaven-bestowed, paralysed—made useless. You hear now how I contradict myself. I, who preached contentment with a humble lot, and justified the vocation even of hewers of wood, and drawers of water, in God's service—I, his ordained minister, almost rave in my restlessness. Well, propensities and principles must be reconciled by some means.'

He left the room. In this brief hour I had learnt more of him than in the whole previous month: yet still he puzzled me.

Diana and Mary Rivers became more sad and silent as the day approached for leaving their brother, and their home. They both tried to appear as usual; but the sorrow they had to struggle against was one that could not be entirely conquered or concealed. Diana intimated that this would be a different parting from any they had ever yet known. It would probably, as far as St. John was concerned, be a parting for years: it might be a parting for life.

'He will sacrifice all to his long-framed resolves,' she said: 'natural affection and feelings more potent still. St. John looks quiet, Jane; but he hides a fever in his vitals. You would think him gentle, yet in some things he is inexorable as death; and the worst of it is, my conscience will hardly permit me to dissuade him from his severe decision: certainly, I cannot for a moment blame him for it. It is right, noble, Christian: yet it breaks my heart.' And the tears gushed to her fine eyes. Mary bent her head low over her work.

'We are now without father: we shall soon be without home and brother,' she murmured.

At that moment a little accident supervened, which seemed decreed by fate, purposely to prove the truth of the adage, that 'misfortunes never come singly:' and to add to their distresses the vexing one of the slip between the cup and the lip. St. John passed the window reading a letter. He entered.

'Our uncle John is dead,' said he.

Both the sisters seemed struck: not shocked or appalled; the tidings appeared in their eyes rather momentous than afflicting.

'Dead?' repeated Diana.

'Yes.'

She riveted a searching gaze on her brother's face. 'And what then?' she demanded, in a low voice.

'What then, Die?' he replied, maintaining a marble immobility of feature. 'What then? Why—nothing. Read.'

He threw the letter into her lap. She glanced over it, and handed it to Mary. Mary perused it in silence, and returned it to her brother. All three looked at each other, and all three smiled—a dreary, pensive smile enough.

'Amen! We can yet live,' said Diana, at last.

'At any rate, it makes us no worse off than we were before,' remarked Mary.

'Only it forces rather strongly on the mind the picture of what *might have been*,' said Mr. Rivers; 'and contrasts it somewhat too vividly with what *is*.'

He folded the letter, and locked it in his desk, and again went out.

For some minutes no one spoke. Diana then turned to me.

'Jane, you will wonder at us and our mysteries,' she said; 'and think us hard-hearted beings not to be more moved at the death of so near a relation as an uncle; but we have never seen him or known him. He was my mother's brother. My father and he quarrelled long ago. It was by his advice that my father risked most of his property in the speculation that ruined him. Mutual recrimination passed between them: they parted in anger, and were never reconciled. My uncle engaged afterwards in more prosperous undertakings: it appears he realised a fortune of twenty thousand pounds. He was never married and had no near kindred but ourselves, and one other person, not more closely related than we. My father always cherished the idea that he would atone for his error, by leaving his possessions to us; that letter informs us that he has bequeathed every penny to the other relation; with the exception of thirty guineas, to be divided between St. John, Diana, and Mary Rivers, for the purchase of three mourning rings. He had a right, of course, to do as he pleased: and yet a momentary damp is on the spirits by the receipt of such news. Mary and I would have esteemed ourselves rich with a thousand pounds each; and to St. John such a sum would have been valuable, for the good it would have enabled him to do.'

This explanation given, the subject was dropped, and no further reference made to it, by either Mr. Rivers or his sisters. The next day, I left Marsh End for Morton. The day after, Diana and Mary quitted it for distant B——. In a week, Mr. Rivers and Hannah repaired to the parsonage: and so the old grange was abandoned.

CHAPTER 31

My home, then,—when I at last find a home,—is a cottage: a little room with white-washed walls, and a sanded floor; containing four painted chairs and a table, a clock, a cupboard, with two or three plates and dishes, and a set of tea-things in delf. Above, a chamber of the same dimensions as the kitchen, with a deal bedstead, and chest of drawers; small, yet too large to be filled with my scanty wardrobe: though the kindness of my gentle and generous friends has increased that, by a modest stock of such things as are necessary.

It is evening. I have dismissed, with the fee of an orange, the little orphan who serves me as a handmaid. I am sitting alone on the hearth. This morning, the village school opened. I had twenty scholars. But three of the number can read: none write or cypher. Several knit, and a few sew a little. They speak with the broadest accent of the district. At present, they and I have a difficulty in understanding each other's language. Some of them are unmannered, rough, intractable, as well as ignorant; but others are docile, have a wish to learn, and evince a disposition that pleases me. I must not forget that these coarsely-clad little peasants are of flesh and blood as good as the scions of gentlest genealogy; and that the germs of native excellence, refinement, intelligence, kind feeling, are as likely to exist in their hearts as in those of the best-born. My duty will be to develop these germs: surely I shall find some happiness in discharging that office. Much enjoyment I do not expect in the life opening before me: yet it will, doubtless, if I regulate my mind, and exert my powers as I ought, yield me enough to live on from day to day.

Was I very gleeful, settled, content, during the hours I passed in yonder bare, humble school-room this morning and afternoon? Not to deceive myself, I must reply—No: I felt desolate to a degree. I felt—yes, idiot that I am—I felt degraded. I doubted I had taken a step which sank instead of raising me in the scale of social existence. I was weakly dismayed at the ignorance, the poverty, the coarseness of all I heard and saw round me. But let me not hate and despise myself too much for these feelings: I know them to be wrong—that is a great step gained; I shall strive to overcome them. To-morrow, I trust I shall get the better of them partially; and in a few weeks, perhaps, they will be quite subdued. In a few months, it is possible, the happiness of seeing progress

and a change for the better in my scholars, may substitute gratification for disgust.

Meantime, let me ask myself one question—Which is better?—To have surrendered to temptation; listened to passion; made no painful effort—no struggle;—but to have sunk down in the silken snare; fallen asleep on the flowers covering it; wakened in a southern clime, amongst the luxuries of a pleasure villa: to have been now living in France, Mr. Rochester's mistress; delirious with his love half my time—for he would—oh, yes, he would have loved me well for a while. He *did* love me—no one will ever love me so again. I shall never more know the sweet homage given to beauty, youth, and grace—for never to any one else shall I seem to possess these charms. He was fond and proud of me—it is what no man besides will ever be.—But where am I wandering, and what am I saying; and, above all, feeling? Whether is it better, I ask, to be a slave in a fool's paradise at Marseilles—fevered with delusive bliss one hour—suffocating with the bitterest tears of remorse and shame the next—or to be a village-schoolmistress, free and honest, in a breezy mountain nook in the healthy heart of England?

Yes; I feel now that I was right when I adhered to principle and law, and scorned and crushed the insane promptings of a frenzied moment. God directed me to a correct choice: I thank His providence for the guidance!

Having brought my eventide musings to this point, I rose, went to my door, and looked at the sunset of the harvest-day, and at the quiet fields before my cottage; which, with the school, was distant half a mile from the village. The birds were singing their last strains—

'The air was mild; the dew was balm.'

While I looked, I thought myself happy, and was surprised to find myself ere long weeping—and why? For the doom which had reft me from adhesion to my master: for him I was no more to see; for the desperate grief and fatal fury—consequences of my departure—which might now, perhaps, be dragging him from the path of right, too far to leave hope of ultimate restoration thither. At this thought, I turned my face aside from the lovely sky of eve and lonely vale of Morton—I say *lonely*, for in that bed of it visible to me, there was no building apparent save the church and the parsonage, half-hid in trees; and, quite at the extremity, the roof of Vale Hall, where the rich Mr. Oliver and his daughter lived. I hid my eyes, and leant my head against the stone frame of my door; but soon a slight noise near the wicket which shut in my tiny garden from the meadow beyond it, made me look up. A dog—old Carlo, Mr. Rivers' pointer, as I saw in a moment—was pushing the gate with his nose, and St. John himself leant upon it with folded arms; his brow knit, his gaze, grave almost to displeasure, fixed on me. I asked him to come in.

'No, I cannot stay; I have only brought you a little parcel my sisters left for you. I think it contains a colour-box, pencils, and paper.'

I approached to take it: a welcome gift it was. He examined my face, I thought, with austerity, as I came near: the traces of tears were doubtless very visible upon it.

'Have you found your first day's work harder than you expected?' he asked.

'Oh, no! On the contrary, I think in time I shall get on with my scholars very well.'

'But perhaps your accommodations—your cottage—your furniture—have disappointed your expectations? They are, in truth, scanty enough; but'——I interrupted:

'My cottage is clean and weather-proof; my furniture sufficient and commodious. All I see has made me thankful, not despondent. I am not absolutely such a fool and sensualist as to regret the absence of a carpet, a sofa, and silver plate: besides, five weeks ago I had nothing—I was an outcast, a beggar, a vagrant; now I have acquaintance, a home, a business. I wonder at the goodness of God; the generosity of my friends; the bounty of my lot. I do not repine.'

'But you feel solitude an oppression? The little house there behind you is dark and empty.'

'I have hardly had time yet to enjoy a sense of tranquillity, much less to grow impatient under one of loneliness.'

'Very well; I hope you feel the content you express: at any rate, your good sense will tell you that it is too soon yet to yield to the vacillating fears of Lot's wife. What you had left before I saw you, of course I do not know; but I counsel you to resist, firmly, every temptation which would incline you to look back: pursue your present career steadily, for some months at least.'

'It is what I mean to do,' I answered. St. John continued:—

'It is hard work to control the workings of inclination, and turn the bent of nature: but that it may be done, I know from experience. God has given us, in a measure, the power to make our own fate; and when our energies seem to demand a sustenance they cannot get—when our will strains after a path we may not follow—we need neither starve from inanition, nor stand still in despair: we have but to seek another nourishment for the mind, as strong as the forbidden food it longed to taste—and perhaps purer; and to hew out for the adventurous foot a road as direct and broad as the one Fortune has blocked up against us, if rougher than it.

'A year ago, I was myself intensely miserable, because I thought I had made a mistake in entering the ministry: its uniform duties wearied me to death. I burnt for the more active life of the world—for the more exciting toils of a literary career—for the destiny of an artist, author, orator; anything rather than that of a priest: yes, the heart of a politician, of a soldier, of a votary of

lory, a lover of renown, a luster after power, beat under my curate's surplice. considered; my life was so wretched, it must be changed, or I must die. After season of darkness and struggling, light broke and relief fell: my cramped xistence all at once spread out to a plain without bounds—my powers heard call from heaven to rise, gather their full strength, spread their wings, and mount beyond ken. God had an errand for me; to bear which afar, to deliver t well, skill and strength, courage and eloquence, the best qualifications of oldier, statesman, and orator, were all needed: for these all centre in the good nissionary.

'A missionary I resolved to be. From that moment my state of mind changed; he fetters dissolved and dropped from every faculty, leaving nothing of ondage but its galling soreness—which time only can heal. My father, indeed, pposed the determination, but since his death, I have not a legitimate obstacle o contend with, some affairs settled, a successor for Morton provided, an ntanglement or two of the feelings broken through or cut asunder—a last onflict with human weakness, in which I know I shall overcome, because have vowed that I *will* overcome—and I leave Europe for the East.'

He said this, in his peculiar, subdued, yet emphatic voice; looking, when he ad ceased speaking, not at me, but at the setting sun, at which I looked too. oth he and I had our backs towards the path leading up the field to the ricket. We had heard no step on that grass-grown track; the water running 1 the vale was the one lulling sound of the hour and scene; we might well hen start, when a gay voice, sweet as a silver bell, exclaimed:—

'Good evening, Mr. Rivers. And good evening, old Carlo. Your dog is uicker to recognise his friends than you are, sir; he pricked his ears and ragged his tail when I was at the bottom of the field, and you have your back owards me now.'

It was true. Though Mr. Rivers had started at the first of those musical ccents, as if a thunderbolt had split a cloud over his head, he stood yet, at the lose of the sentence, in the same attitude in which the speaker had surprised im—his arm resting on the gate, his face directed towards the west. He turned t last, with measured deliberation. A vision, as it seemed to me, had risen at is side. There appeared, within three feet of him, a form clad in pure white— youthful, graceful form: full, yet fine in contour; and when, after bending caress Carlo, it lifted up its head, and threw back a long veil, there bloomed nder his glance a face of perfect beauty. Perfect beauty is a strong expression; ut I do not retrace or qualify it: as sweet features as ever the temperate clime f Albion moulded; as pure hues of rose and lily as ever her humid gales and apoury skies generated and screened, justified, in this instance, the term. o charm was wanting, no defect was perceptible; the young girl had regular nd delicate lineaments; eyes shaped and coloured as we see them in lovely ictures, large, and dark, and full; the long and shadowy eyelash which

encircles a fine eye with so soft a fascination; the pencilled brow which give
such clearness; the white, smooth forehead, which adds such repose to th
livelier beauties of tint and ray; the cheek, oval, fresh and smooth; the lips
fresh too, ruddy, healthy, sweetly formed; the even and gleaming teeth withou
flaw; the small dimpled chin; the ornament of rich, plenteous tresses—al
advantages, in short, which, combined, realise the ideal of beauty, were full
hers. I wondered, as I looked at this fair creature: I admired her with my whol
heart. Nature had surely formed her in a partial mood; and, forgetting he
usual stinted step-mother dole of gifts, had endowed this, her darling, wit
a granddame's bounty.

What did St. John Rivers think of this earthly angel? I naturally aske
myself that question as I saw him turn to her and look at her; and, as naturally
I sought the answer to the inquiry in his countenance. He had already with
drawn his eye from the Peri, and was looking at a humble tuft of daisies whicl
grew by the wicket.

'A lovely evening, but late for you to be out alone,' he said, as he crushe
the snowy heads of the closed flowers with his foot.

'Oh, I only came home from S——' (she mentioned the name of a larg
town some twenty miles distant) 'this afternoon. Papa told me you had opene
your school, and that the new mistress was come; and so I put on my bonne
after tea, and ran up the valley to see her: this is she?' pointing to me.

'It is,' said St. John.

'Do you think you shall like Morton?' she asked of me, with a direct an
naïve simplicity of tone and manner, pleasing, if child-like.

'I hope I shall. I have many inducements to do so.'

'Did you find your scholars as attentive as you expected?'

'Quite.'

'Do you like your house?'

'Very much.'

'Have I furnished it nicely?'

'Very nicely, indeed.'

'And made a good choice of an attendant for you in Alice Wood?'

'You have, indeed. She is teachable and handy.' (This, then, I thought,
Miss Oliver, the heiress; favoured, it seems, in the gifts of fortune, as well as i
those of nature! What happy combination of the planets presided over he
birth, I wonder?)

'I shall come up and help you to teach sometimes,' she added. 'It will b
a change for me to visit you now and then; and I like a change. Mr. River
I have been *so* gay during my stay at S——. Last night, or rather this mornin
I was dancing till two o'clock. The——th regiment are stationed there since th
riots; and the officers are the most agreeable men in the world: they put all ou
young knife-grinders and scissor merchants to shame.'

It seemed to me that Mr. St. John's under lip protruded, and his upper lip curled a moment. His mouth certainly looked a good deal compressed, and the lower part of his face unusually stern and square, as the laughing girl gave him this information. He lifted his gaze, too, from the daisies, and turned it on her. An unsmiling, a searching, a meaning gaze it was. She answered it with a second laugh, and laughter well became her youth, her roses, her dimples, her bright eyes.

As he stood, mute and grave, she again fell to caressing Carlo. 'Poor Carlo loves me,' said she. '*He* is not stern and distant to his friends; and if he could speak, he would not be silent.'

As she patted the dog's head, bending with native grace before his young and austere master, I saw a glow rise to that master's face. I saw his solemn eye melt with sudden fire, and flicker with resistless emotion. Flushed and kindled thus, he looked nearly as beautiful for a man as she for a woman. His chest heaved once, as if his large heart, weary of despotic constriction, had expanded, despite the will, and made a vigorous bound for the attainment of liberty. But he curbed it, I think, as a resolute rider would curb a rearing steed. He responded neither by word nor movement to the gentle advances made him.

'Papa says you never come to see us now,' continued Miss Oliver, looking up. 'You are quite a stranger at Vale Hall. He is alone this evening, and not very well: will you return with me and visit him?'

'It is not a seasonable hour to intrude on Mr. Oliver,' answered St. John.

'Not a seasonable hour! But, I declare, it is. It is just the hour when papa most wants company: when the works are closed, and he has no business to occupy him. Now, Mr. Rivers, *do* come. Why are you so very shy, and so very sombre?' She filled up the hiatus his silence left by a reply of her own.

'I forgot!' she exclaimed, shaking her beautiful curled head, as if shocked at herself. 'I am so giddy and thoughtless! *Do* excuse me. It had slipped my memory that you have good reasons to be indisposed for joining in my chatter. Diana and Mary have left you, and Moor House is shut up, and you are so lonely. I am sure I pity you. Do come and see papa.'

'Not to-night, Miss Rosamond, not to-night.'

Mr. St. John spoke almost like an automaton: himself only knew the effect it cost him thus to refuse.

'Well, if you are so obstinate, I will leave you; for I dare not stay any longer: the dew begins to fall. Good evening!'

She held out her hand. He just touched it. 'Good evening!' he repeated, in a voice low and hollow as an echo. She turned; but in a moment returned.

'Are you well?' she asked. Well might she put the question: his face was blanched as her gown.

'Quite well,' he enunciated; and, with a bow, she left the gate. She went one

way; he another. She turned twice to gaze after him, as she tripped fairy-like down the field; he, as he strode firmly across, never turned at all.

This spectacle of another's suffering and sacrifice, rapt my thoughts from exclusive meditation on my own. Diana Rivers had designated her brother 'inexorable as death.' She had not exaggerated.

CHAPTER 32

I continued the labours of the village-school as actively and faithfully as I could. It was truly hard work at first. Some time elapsed before, with all my efforts, I could comprehend my scholars and their nature. Wholly untaught, with faculties quite torpid, they seemed to me hopelessly dull; and, at first sight, all dull alike: but I soon found I was mistaken. There was a difference amongst them as amongst the educated; and when I got to know them, and they me, this difference rapidly developed itself. Their amazement at me, my language, my rules, and ways, once subsided, I found some of these heavy looking, gaping rustics wake up into sharp-witted girls enough. Many showed themselves obliging, and amiable too; and I discovered amongst them no a few examples of natural politeness, and innate self-respect, as well as of excellent capacity, that won my goodwill and my admiration. These soon took a pleasure in doing their work well; in keeping their persons neat; in learning their tasks regularly; in acquiring quiet and orderly manners. The rapidity of their progress, in some instances, was even surprising; and an honest and happy pride I took in it: besides, I began personally to like some of the best girls; and they liked me. I had amongst my scholars several farmers' daughters young women grown, almost. These could already read, write, and sew; and to them I taught the elements of grammar, geography, history, and the finer kinds of needlework. I found estimable characters amongst them—characters desirous of information, and disposed for improvement—with whom I passed many a pleasant evening hour in their own homes. Their parents then (the farmer and his wife) loaded me with attentions. There was an enjoyment in accepting their simple kindness, and in repaying it by a consideration—a scrupulous regard to their feelings—to which they were not, perhaps, at all times accustomed, and which both charmed and benefited them; because while it elevated them in their own eyes, it made them emulous to merit the deferential treatment they received.

I felt I became a favourite in the neighbourhood. Whenever I went out I heard on all sides cordial salutations, and was welcomed with friendly smiles. To live amidst general regard, though it be but the regard of working-people, like 'sitting in sunshine, calm and sweet:' serene inward feelings bud and bloom

under the ray. At this period of my life, my heart far oftener swelled with thankfulness than sank with dejection: and yet, reader, to tell you all, in the midst of this calm, this useful existence—after a day passed in honourable exertion amongst my scholars, an evening spent in drawing or reading contentedly alone—I used to rush into strange dreams at night: dreams many-coloured, agitated, full of the ideal, the stirring, the stormy—dreams where, amidst unusual scenes, charged with adventure, with agitating risk and romantic chance, I still again and again met Mr. Rochester, always at some exciting crisis; and then the sense of being in his arms, hearing his voice, meeting his eye, touching his hand and cheek, loving him, being loved by him—the hope of passing a lifetime at his side, would be renewed, with all its first force and fire. Then I awoke. Then I recalled where I was, and how situated. Then I rose up on my curtainless bed, trembling and quivering; and then the still, dark night witnessed the convulsion of despair, and heard the burst of passion. By nine o'clock the next morning I was punctually opening the school; tranquil, settled, prepared for the steady duties of the day.

Rosamond Oliver kept her word in coming to visit me. Her call at the school was generally made in the course of her morning ride. She would canter up to the door on her pony, followed by a mounted livery servant. Anything more exquisite than her appearance, in her purple habit, with her Amazon's cap of black velvet placed gracefully above the long curls that kissed her cheek and floated to her shoulders, can scarcely be imagined: and it was thus she would enter the rustic building, and glide through the dazzled ranks of the village children. She generally came at the hour when Mr. Rivers was engaged in giving his daily catechising lesson. Keenly, I fear, did the eye of the visitress pierce the young pastor's heart. A sort of instinct seemed to warn him of her entrance, even when he did not see it; and when he was looking quite away from the door, if she appeared at it, his cheek would glow, and his marble-seeming features, though they refused to relax, changed indescribably; and in their very quiescence became expressive of a repressed fervour, stronger than working muscle or darting glance could indicate.

Of course, she knew her power: indeed, he did not, because he could not, conceal it from her. In spite of his Christian stoicism, when she went up and addressed him, and smiled gaily, encouragingly, even fondly in his face, his hand would tremble, and his eye burn. He seemed to say, with his sad and resolute look, if he did not say it with his lips, 'I love you, and I know you prefer me. It is not despair of success that keeps me dumb. If I offered my heart, I believe you would accept it. But that heart is already laid on a sacred altar: the fire is arranged round it. It will soon be no more than a sacrifice consumed.'

And then she would pout like a disappointed child; a pensive cloud would soften her radiant vivacity; she would withdraw her hand hastily from his,

and turn in transient petulance from his aspect at once so heroic and so martyr-like. St. John, no doubt, would have given the world to follow, recall, retain her, when she thus left him; but he would not give one chance of Heaven; nor relinquish, for the elysium of her love, one hope of the true, eternal Paradise. Besides, he could not bound all that he had in his nature—the rover, the aspirant, the poet, the priest—in the limits of a single passion. He could not—he would not—renounce his wild field of mission warfare for the parlours and the peace of Vale Hall. I learnt so much from himself, in an inroad I once, despite his reserve, had the daring to make on his confidence.

Miss Oliver already honoured me with frequent visits to my cottage. I had learnt her whole character; which was without mystery or disguise: she was coquettish, but not heartless; exacting, but not worthlessly selfish. She had been indulged from her birth, but was not absolutely spoilt. She was hasty, but good-humoured; vain (she could not help it, when every glance in the glass showed her such a flush of loveliness), but not affected; liberal-handed; innocent of the pride of wealth; ingenuous; sufficiently intelligent; gay, lively, and unthinking: she was very charming, in short, even to a cool observer of her own sex like me; but she was not profoundly interesting or thoroughly impressive. A very different sort of mind was hers from that, for instance, of the sisters of St. John. Still, I liked her almost as I liked my pupil Adèle; except that, for a child whom we have watched over and taught, a closer affection is engendered than we can give an equally attractive adult acquaintance.

She had taken an amiable caprice to me. She said I was like Mr. Rivers (only, certainly, she allowed, 'not one-tenth so handsome, though I was a nice neat little soul enough, but he was an angel'). I was, however, good, clever, composed, and firm, like him. I was a *lusus naturae*, she affirmed, as a village schoolmistress: she was sure my previous history, if known, would make a delightful romance.

One evening, while, with her usual child-like activity, and thoughtless yet not offensive inquisitiveness, she was rummaging the cupboard and the table drawer of my little kitchen, she discovered first two French books, a volume of Schiller, a German grammar and dictionary; and then my drawing materials and some sketches, including a pencil-head of a pretty, little cherub like girl, one of my scholars, and sundry views from nature, taken in the Vale of Morton and on the surrounding moors. She was first transfixed with surprise and then electrified with delight.

'Had I done these pictures? Did I know French and German? What a love—what a miracle I was! I drew better than her master in the first school in S—— Would I sketch a portrait of her, to show to papa?'

'With pleasure,' I replied; and I felt a thrill of artist-delight at the idea of copying from so perfect and radiant a model. She had then on a dark-blue silk dress; her arms and her neck were bare; her only ornament was he

hestnut tresses, which waved over her shoulders with all the wild grace of natural curls. I took a sheet of fine card-board, and drew a careful outline. promised myself the pleasure of colouring it; and, as it was getting late then, told her she must come and sit another day.

She made such a report of me to her father, that Mr. Oliver himself accompanied her next evening—a tall, massive-featured, middle-aged, and grey-headed man, at whose side his lovely daughter looked like a bright flower near a hoary turret. He appeared a taciturn, and perhaps a proud personage; but he was very kind to me. The sketch of Rosamond's portrait pleased him highly he said I must make a finished picture of it. He insisted, too, on my coming the next day to spend the evening at Vale Hall.

I went. I found it a large, handsome residence, showing abundant evidences of wealth in the proprietor. Rosamond was full of glee and pleasure all the time I stayed. Her father was affable; and when he entered into conversation with me after tea, he expressed in strong terms his approbation of what had done in Morton school; and said he only feared, from what he saw and heard, I was too good for the place, and would soon quit it for one more suitable.

'Indeed!' cried Rosamond, 'she is clever enough to be a governess in a high family, papa.'

I thought—I would far rather be where I am than in any high family in the land. Mr. Oliver spoke of Mr. Rivers—of the Rivers family—with great respect. He said it was a very old name in that neighbourhood; that the ancestors of the house were wealthy; that all Morton had once belonged to them; that even now he considered the representative of that house might, if he liked, make an alliance with the best. He accounted it a pity that so fine and talented a young man should have formed the design of going out as a missionary; it was quite throwing a valuable life away. It appeared, then, that her father would throw no obstacle in the way of Rosamond's union with St. John. Mr. Oliver evidently regarded the young clergyman's good birth, old name, and sacred profession, as sufficient compensation for the want of fortune.

It was the 5th of November, and a holiday. My little servant, after helping me to clean my house, was gone, well satisfied with the fee of a penny for her aid. All about me was spotless and bright—scoured floor, polished grate, and well rubbed chairs. I had also made myself neat, and had now the afternoon before me to spend as I would.

The translation of a few pages of German occupied an hour; then I got my palette and pencils, and fell to the more soothing, because easier occupation, of completing Rosamond Oliver's miniature. The head was finished already; there was but the background to tint, and the drapery to shade off; a touch of carmine, too, to add to the ripe lips—a soft curl here and there to the tresses

—a deeper tinge to the shadow of the lash under the azure eyelid. I was absorbed in the execution of these nice details, when, after one rapid tap, my door unclosed, admitting St. John Rivers.

'I am come to see how you are spending your holiday,' he said. 'Not, I hope. in thought? No, that is well: while you draw you will not feel lonely. You see I mistrust you still: though you have borne up wonderfully so far. I have brought you a book for evening solace,' and he laid on the table a new publica-tion—a poem: one of those genuine productions so often vouchsafed to the fortunate public of those days—the golden age of modern literature. Alas! the readers of our era are less favoured. But, courage! I will not pause either to accuse or repine. I know poetry is not dead, nor genius lost; nor has Mammon gained power over either, to bind or slay: they will both assert their existence, their presence, their liberty and strength again one day. Powerful angels, safe in heaven! they smile when sordid souls triumph, and feeble ones weep over their destruction. Poetry destroyed? Genius banished? No! Mediocrity, no do not let envy prompt you to the thought. No; they not only live, but reign and redeem: and without their divine influence spread everywhere, you would be in hell—the hell of your own meanness.

While I was eagerly glancing at the bright pages of Marmion (for Marmion it was), St. John stooped to examine my drawing. His tall figure sprang erect again with a start: he said nothing. I looked up at him: he shunned my eye I knew his thoughts well, and could read his heart plainly; at the moment I felt calmer and cooler than he: I had then temporarily the advantage of him and I conceived an inclination to do him some good, if I could.

'With all his firmness and self-control,' thought I, 'he tasks himself too far locks every feeling and pang within—expresses, confesses, imparts nothing I am sure it would benefit him to talk a little about this sweet Rosamond whom he thinks he ought to marry: I will make him talk.'

I said first: 'Take a chair, Mr. Rivers.' But he answered, as he always did that he could not stay. 'Very well,' I responded mentally, 'stand if you like but you shall not go just yet, I am determined: solitude is at least as bad for you as it is for me. I'll try if I cannot discover the secret spring of your confidence, and find an aperture in that marble breast through which I can shed one drop of the balm of sympathy.'

'Is this portrait like?' I asked bluntly.

'Like! Like whom! I did not observe it closely.'

'You did, Mr. Rivers.'

He almost started at my sudden and strange abruptness: he looked at me astonished. 'Oh, that is nothing yet,' I muttered within. 'I don't mean to be baffled by a little stiffness on your part; I'm prepared to go to considerable lengths.' I continued, 'You observed it closely and distinctly: but I have no objection to your looking at it again,' and I rose and placed it in his hand

'A well-executed picture,' he said; 'very, soft, clear colouring; very graceful and correct drawing.'

'Yes, yes; I know all that. But what of the resemblance? Who is it like?'

Mastering some hesitation, he answered, 'Miss Oliver, I presume.'

'Of course. And now, sir, to reward you for the accurate guess, I will promise to paint you a careful and faithful duplicate of this very picture, provided you admit that the gift would be acceptable to you. I don't wish to throw away my time and trouble on an offering you would deem worthless.'

He continued to gaze at the picture: the longer he looked, the firmer he held it, the more he seemed to covet it. 'It is like!' he murmured; 'the eye is well managed: the colour, light, expression, are perfect. It smiles!'

'Would it comfort, or would it wound you to have a similar painting? Tell me that. When you are at Madagascar, or at the Cape, or in India, would it be a consolation to have that memento in your possession? or would the sight of it bring recollections calculated to enervate and distress?'

He now furtively raised his eyes: he glanced at me, irresolute, disturbed: he again surveyed the picture.

'That I should like to have it, is certain: whether it would be judicious or wise is another question.'

Since I had ascertained that Rosamond really preferred him, and that her father was not likely to oppose the match, I—less exalted in my views than St. John—had been strongly disposed in my own heart to advocate their union. It seemed to me that, should he become the possessor of Mr. Oliver's large fortune, he might do as much good with it as if he went and laid his genius out to wither, and his strength to waste, under a tropical sun. With this persuasion I now answered:—

'As far as I can see, it would be wiser and more judicious if you were to take to yourself the original at once.'

By this time he had sat down: he had laid the picture on the table before him, and with his brow supported on both hands, hung fondly over it. I discerned he was now neither angry nor shocked at my audacity. I saw even that to be thus frankly addressed on a subject he had deemed unapproachable—to hear it thus freely handled—was beginning to be felt by him as a new pleasure—an unhoped-for relief. Reserved people often really need the frank discussion of their sentiments and griefs more than the expansive. The sternest-seeming stoic is human after all; and to 'burst' with boldness and good will into 'the silent sea' of their souls, is often to confer on them the first of obligations.

'She likes you, I am sure,' said I, as I stood behind his chair, 'and her father respects you. Moreover, she is a sweet girl—rather thoughtless; but you would have sufficient thought for both yourself and her. You ought to marry her.'

'*Does* she like me?' he asked.

'Certainly; better than she likes any one else. She talks of you continually there is no subject she enjoys so much, or touches upon so often.'

'It is very pleasant to hear this,' he said—'very: go on for another quarter of an hour.' And he actually took out his watch and laid it upon the table to measure the time.

'But where is the use of going on,' I asked, 'when you are probably preparing some iron blow of contradiction, or forging a fresh chain to fetter your heart?'

'Don't imagine such hard things. Fancy me yielding and melting, as I am doing: human love rising like a freshly opened fountain in my mind and over flowing with sweet inundation all the field I have so carefully, and with such labour prepared—so assiduously sown with the seeds of good intentions, o self-denying plans. And now it is deluged with a nectarous flood—the young germs swamped—delicious poison cankering them: now I see myself stretched on an ottoman in the drawing-room at Vale Hall, at my bride Rosamond Oliver's feet: she is talking to me with her sweet voice—gazing down on me with those eyes your skilful hand has copied so well—smiling at me with these cora lips. She is mine—I am hers—this present life and passing world suffice to me Hush! say nothing—my heart is full of delight—my senses are entranced—le the time I marked pass in peace.'

I humoured him: the watch ticked on: he breathed fast and low: I stood silent. Amidst this hush the quarter sped; he replaced the watch, laid the picture down, rose, and stood on the hearth.

'Now,' said he, 'that little space was given to delirium and delusion. I rested my temples on the breast of temptation, and put my neck voluntarily under her yoke of flowers; I tasted her cup. The pillow was burning: there is an asp in the garland: the wine has a bitter taste: her promises are hollow—her offer false: I see and know all this.'

I gazed at him in wonder.

'It is strange,' pursued he, 'that while I love Rosamond Oliver so wildly—with all the intensity, indeed, of a first passion, the object of which is exquisitel beautiful, graceful, and fascinating—I experience at the same time a calm unwarped consciousness, that she would not make me a good wife; that she is not the partner suited to me; that I should discover this within a year after marriage; and that to twelve months' rapture would succeed a lifetime of regret. This I know.'

'Strange, indeed!' I could not help ejaculating.

'While something in me,' he went on, 'is acutely sensible to her charms something else is as deeply impressed with her defects: they are such that she could sympathise in nothing I aspired to—co-operate in nothing I undertook Rosamond a sufferer, a labourer, a female apostle? Rosamond a missionary wife? No!'

'But you need not be a missionary. You might relinquish that scheme.'

'Relinquish! What! my vocation? My great work? My foundation laid on earth for a mansion in heaven? My hopes of being numbered in the band who have merged all ambitions in the glorious one of bettering their race—of carrying knowledge into the realms of ignorance—of substituting peace for war—freedom for bondage—religion for superstition—the hope of heaven for the fear of hell? Must I relinquish that? It is dearer than the blood in my veins. It is what I have to look forward to, and to live for.'

After a considerable pause, I said,—'And Miss Oliver? Are her disappointment and sorrow of no interest to you?'

'Miss Oliver is ever surrounded by suitors and flatterers: in less than a month, my image will be effaced from her heart. She will forget me; and will marry, probably, some one who will make her far happier than I should do.'

'You speak coolly enough; but you suffer in the conflict. You are wasting away.'

'No. If I get a little thin, it is with anxiety about my prospects, yet unsettled— my departure, continually procrastinated. Only this morning, I received intelligence that the successor, whose arrival I have been so long expecting, cannot be ready to replace me for three months to come yet; and perhaps the three months may extend to six.'

'You tremble and become flushed whenever Miss Oliver enters the school-room.'

Again the surprised expression crossed his face. He had not imagined that a woman would dare to speak so to a man. For me, I felt at home in this sort of discourse. I could never rest in communication with strong, discreet, and refined minds, whether male or female, till I had passed the outworks of conventional reserve, and crossed the threshold of confidence, and won a place by their heart's very hearthstone.

'You *are* original,' said he, 'and not timid. There is something brave in your spirit, as well as penetrating in your eye: but allow me to assure you that you partially misinterpret emotions. You think them more profound and potent than they are. You give me a larger allowance of sympathy than I have a just claim to. When I colour, and when I shake before Miss Oliver, I do not pity myself. I scorn the weakness. I know it is ignoble; a mere fever of the flesh: not, I declare, the convulsion of the soul. *That* is just as fixed as a rock, firm set in the depths of a restless sea. Know me to be what I am—a cold hard man.'

I smiled incredulously.

'You have taken my confidence by storm,' he continued: 'and now it is much at your service. I am simply, in my original state—stripped of that blood-bleached robe with which Christianity covers human deformity—a cold, hard, ambitious man. Natural affection only, of all the sentiments, has permanent power over me. Reason, and not Feeling, is my guide; my ambition is unlimited; my desire to rise higher, to do more than others insatiable. I honour endurance, perseverance, industry, talent; because these are the means by

315

which men achieve great ends, and mount to lofty eminence. I watch your career with interest, because I consider you a specimen of a diligent, orderly, energetic woman: not because I deeply compassionate what you have gone through, or what you still suffer.'

'You would describe yourself as a mere pagan philosopher,' I said.

'No. There is this difference between me and deistic philosophers: I believe, and I believe the Gospel. You missed your epithet. I am not a pagan, but a Christian philosopher—a follower of the sect of Jesus. As his disciple I adopt his pure, his merciful, his benignant doctrines. I advocate them: I am sworn to spread them. Won in youth to religion, she has cultivated my original qualities thus:—From the minute germ, natural affection, she has developed the over-shadowing tree, philanthropy. From the wild, stringy root of human uprightness, she has reared a due sense of the Divine justice. Of the ambition to win power and renown for my wretched self, she has formed the ambition to spread my Master's kingdom; to achieve victories for the standard of the cross. So much has religion done for me; turning the original materials to the best account; pruning and training nature. But she could not eradicate nature nor will it be eradicated "till this mortal shall put on immortality." '

Having said this, he took his hat, which lay on the table beside my palette Once more he looked at the portrait.

'She *is* lovely,' he murmured. 'She is well named the Rose of the World indeed!'

'And may I not paint one like it for you?'

'*Cui bono?* No.'

He drew over the picture the sheet of thin paper on which I was accustomed to rest my hand in painting, to prevent the card-board from being sullied What he suddenly saw on this blank paper, it was impossible for me to tell but something had caught his eye. He took it up with a snatch; he looked at the edge; then shot a glance at me, inexpressibly peculiar, and quite incomprehensible: a glance that seemed to take and make note of every point in my shape, face, and dress; for it traversed all, quick, keen as lightning. His lips parted, as if to speak: but he checked the coming sentence, whatever it was

'What is the matter?' I asked.

'Nothing in the world,' was the reply: and, replacing the paper, I saw him dexterously tear a narrow slip from the margin. It disappeared in his glove and, with one hasty nod and 'good-afternoon,' he vanished.

'Well!' I exclaimed, using an expression of the district; 'that caps the globe however!'

I, in my turn, scrutinised the paper; but saw nothing on it save a few dingy stains of paint where I had tried the tint in my pencil. I pondered the mystery a minute or two; but finding it insolvable, and being certain it could not be of much moment, I dismissed, and soon forgot it.

CHAPTER 33

When Mr. St. John went, it was beginning to snow; the whirling storm continued all night. The next day a keen wind brought fresh and blinding falls; by twilight the valley was drifted up and almost impassable. I had closed my shutter, laid a mat to the door to prevent the snow from blowing in under it, trimmed my fire, and after sitting nearly an hour on the hearth listening to the muffled fury of the tempest, I lit a candle, took down Marmion, and beginning—

> 'Day set on Norham's castled steep,
> And Tweed's fair river broad and deep,
> And Cheviot's mountains lone;
> The massive towers, the donjon keep,
> The flanking walls that round them sweep,
> In yellow lustre shone.'

soon forgot storm in music.

I heard a noise: the wind, I thought, shook the door. No; it was St. John Rivers, who, lifting the latch, came in out of the frozen hurricane—the howling darkness—and stood before me: the cloak that covered his tall figure all white as a glacier. I was almost in consternation; so little had I expected any guest from the blocked-up vale that night.

'Any ill news?' I demanded. 'Has anything happened?'

'No. How very easily alarmed you are!' he answered, removing his cloak and hanging it up against the door, towards which he again coolly pushed the mat which his entrance had deranged. He stamped the snow from his boots.

'I shall sully the purity of your floor,' said he, 'but you must excuse me for once.' Then he approached the fire: 'I have had hard work to get here, I assure you,' he observed, as he warmed his hands over the flame. 'One drift took me up to the waist; happily the snow is quite soft yet.'

'But why are you come?' I could not forbear saying.

'Rather an inhospitable question to put to a visitor; but since you ask it, I answer simply to have a little talk with you; I got tired of my mute books and empty rooms. Besides, since yesterday, I have experienced the excitement of a person to whom a tale has been half-told, and who is impatient to hear the sequel.'

He sat down. I recalled his singular conduct of yesterday, and really I began to fear his wits were touched. If he were insane, however, his was a very cool and collected insanity: I had never seen that handsome-featured face of his look more like chiselled marble than it did just now, as he put aside his snow-wet hair from his forehead and let the firelight shine free on his pale brow and cheek as pale, where it grieved me to discover the hollow trace of care or

317

sorrow now so plainly graved. I waited, expecting he would say somethin
I could at least comprehend; but his hand was now at his chin, his finger o
his lip: he was thinking. It struck me that his hand looked wasted like his fac
A perhaps uncalled-for gush of pity came over my heart: I was moved to say:–

'I wish Diana or Mary would come and live with you: it is too bad that yo
should be quite alone; and you are recklessly rash about your own health

'Not at all,' said he: 'I care for myself when necessary. I am well now. Wha
do you see amiss in me?'

This was said with a careless, abstracted indifference, which showed tha
my solicitude was, at least in his opinion, wholly superfluous. I was silencec

He still slowly moved his finger over his upper lip, and still his eye dwe
dreamily on the glowing grate; thinking it urgent to say something, I aske
him presently if he felt any cold draught from the door, which was behind hin

'No, no;' he responded, shortly and somewhat testily.

'Well,' I reflected, 'if you won't talk, you may be still; I'll let you alone nov
and return to my book.'

So I snuffed the candle, and resumed the perusal of Marmion. He soo
stirred; my eye was instantly drawn to his movements; he only took ov
a morocco pocket-book, thence produced a letter, which he read in silence
folded it, put it back, relapsed into meditation. It was vain to try to read wit
such an inscrutable fixture before me; nor could I, in my impatience, conser
to be dumb; he might rebuff me if he liked, but talk I would.

'Have you heard from Diana and Mary lately?'

'Not since the letter I showed you a week ago.'

'There has not been any change made about your own arrangements? Yo
will not be summoned to leave England sooner than you expected?'

'I fear not, indeed: such chance is too good to befall me.' Baffled so fa
I changed my ground—I bethought myself to talk about the school and m
scholars.

'Mary Garrett's mother is better, and Mary came back to the school th
morning, and I shall have four new girls next week from the Foundry Close-
they would have come to-day but for the snow.'

'Indeed!'

'Mr. Oliver pays for two.'

'Does he?'

'He means to give the whole school a treat at Christmas.'

'I know.'

'Was it your suggestion?'

'No.'

'Whose then?'

'His daughter's, I think.'

'It is like her: she is so good-natured.'

318

'Yes.'

Again came the blank of a pause: the clock struck eight strokes. It aroused him; he uncrossed his legs, sat erect, turned to me.

'Leave your book a moment, and come a little nearer the fire,' he said.

Wondering, and of my wonder finding no end, I complied.

'Half an hour ago,' he pursued, 'I spoke of my impatience to hear the sequel of a tale: on reflection, I find the matter will be better managed by my assuming the narrator's part, and converting you into a listener. Before commencing, it is but fair to warn you that the story will sound somewhat hackneyed in your ears: but stale details often regain a degree of freshness when they pass through new lips. For the rest, whether trite or novel, it is short.

'Twenty years ago, a poor curate—never mind his name at this moment—fell in love with a rich man's daughter; she fell in love with him, and married him, against the advice of all her friends; who consequently disowned her immediately after the wedding. Before two years passed, the rash pair were both dead, and laid quietly side by side under one slab. (I have seen their grave; it formed part of the pavement of a huge churchyard surrounding the grim, soot-black old cathedral of an overgrown manufacturing town in ——shire.) They left a daughter, which, at its very birth, Charity received in her lap—cold as that of the snow-drift I almost stuck fast in to-night. Charity carried the friendless thing to the house of its rich, maternal relations; it was reared by an aunt-in-law, called (I come to names now) Mrs. Reed of Gateshead—you start—did you hear a noise? I daresay it is only a rat scrambling along the rafters of the adjoining schoolroom: it was a barn before I had it repaired and altered, and barns are generally haunted by rats.—To proceed. Mrs. Reed kept the orphan ten years: whether it was happy or not with her, I cannot say, never having been told; but at the end of that time she transferred it to a place you know—being no other than Lowood School, where you so long resided yourself. It seems her career there was very honourable: from a pupil, she became a teacher, like yourself—really it strikes me there are parallel points in her history and yours—she left it to be a governess: there, again, your fates were analogous: she undertook the education of the ward of a certain Mr. Rochester.'

'Mr. Rivers!' I interrupted.

'I can guess your feelings,' he said, 'but restrain them for a while: I have nearly finished; hear me to the end. Of Mr. Rochester's character I know nothing, but the one fact that he professed to offer honourable marriage to this young girl, and that at the very altar she discovered he had a wife yet alive, though a lunatic. What his subsequent conduct and proposals were is a matter of pure conjecture; but when an event transpired which rendered inquiry after the governess necessary, it was discovered she was gone—no one could tell when, where, or how. She had left Thornfield Hall in the night; every

research after her course had been vain: the country had been scoured far and wide; no vestige of information could be gathered respecting her. Yet that she should be found is become a matter of serious urgency: advertisements have been put in all the papers; I myself have received a letter from one Mr. Briggs, a solicitor, communicating the details I have just imparted. Is it not an odd tale?'

'Just tell me this,' said I, 'and since you know so much, you surely *can* tell it me—what of Mr. Rochester? How and where is he? What is he doing? Is he well?'

'I am ignorant of all concerning Mr. Rochester: the letter never mentions him but to narrate the fraudulent and illegal attempt I have adverted to. You should rather ask the name of the governess—the nature of the event which requires her appearance.'

'Did no one go to Thornfield Hall then? Did no one see Mr. Rochester?'

'I suppose not.'

'But they wrote to him?'

'Of course.'

'And what did he say? Who has his letters?'

'Mr. Briggs intimates that the answer to his application was not from Mr. Rochester, but from a lady: it is signed "Alice Fairfax." '

I felt cold and dismayed: my worst fears then were probably true: he had in all probability left England and rushed in reckless desperation to some former haunt on the Continent. And what opiate for his severe sufferings—what object for his strong passions—had he sought there? I dared not answer the question. Oh, my poor master—once almost my husband—whom I had often called 'my dear Edward!'

'He must have been a bad man,' observed Mr. Rivers.

'You don't know him—don't pronounce an opinion upon him,' I said, with warmth.

'Very well,' he answered, quietly: 'and indeed my head is otherwise occupied than with him: I have my tale to finish. Since you won't ask the governess' name, I must tell it of my own accord—stay—I have it here—it is always more satisfactory to see important points written down, fairly committed to black and white.'

And the pocket-book was again deliberately produced, opened, sought through; from one of its compartments was extracted a shabby slip of paper hastily torn off: I recognised in its texture and its stains of ultra-marine, and lake, and vermilion, the ravished margin of the portrait-cover. He got up, held it close to my eyes: and I read, traced in Indian ink, in my own hand-writing the words 'JANE EYRE'—the work doubtless of some moment of abstraction.

'Briggs wrote to me of a Jane Eyre:' he said, 'the advertisements demanded a Jane Eyre: I knew a Jane Elliott.—I confess I had my suspicions, but it was

nly yesterday afternoon they were at once resolved into certainty. You own he name and renounce the *alias*?'

'Yes—yes—but where is Mr. Briggs? He perhaps knows more of Mr. Rochster than you do.'

'Briggs is in London; I should doubt his knowing anything at all about Mr. Rochester; it is not in Mr. Rochester he is interested. Meantime, you orget essential points in pursuing trifles: you do not inquire why Mr. Briggs ought after you—what he wanted with you.'

'Well, what did he want?'

'Merely to tell you that your uncle, Mr. Eyre of Madeira, is dead; that he as left you all his property, and that you are now rich—merely that—nothing nore.'

'I! rich?'

'Yes, you, rich—quite an heiress.'

Silence succeeded.

'You must prove your identity of course,' resumed St. John, presently: a step which will offer no difficulties; you can then enter on immediate ossession. Your fortune is vested in the English funds; Briggs has the will and ne necessary documents.'

Here was a new card turned up! It is a fine thing, reader, to be lifted in moment from indigence to wealth—a very fine thing: but not a matter one an comprehend, or consequently enjoy, all at once. And then there are other hances in life far more thrilling and rapture-giving: *this* is solid, an affair of ne actual world, nothing ideal about it: all its associations are solid and sober, nd its manifestations are the same. One does not jump, and spring, and shout urrah! at hearing one has got a fortune, one begins to consider responsibilities, nd to ponder business; on a base of steady satisfaction rise certain grave ares—and we contain ourselves, and brood over our bliss with a solemn brow.

Besides, the words Legacy, Bequest, go side by side with the words Death, uneral. My uncle I had heard was dead—my only relative; ever since being nade aware of his existence, I had cherished the hope of one day seeing him: ow, I never should. And then this money came only to me: not to me and rejoicing family, but to my isolated self. It was a grand boon doubtless; and ndependence would be glorious—yes, I felt that—*that* thought swelled my eart.

'You unbend your forehead at last,' said Mr. Rivers: 'I thought Medusa had ooked at you, and that you were turning to stone—perhaps now you will ask ow much you are worth?'

'How much am I worth?'

'Oh, a trifle! Nothing of course to speak of—twenty thousand pounds, think they say—but what is that?'

'Twenty thousand pounds?'

Here was a new stunner—I had been calculating on four or five thousand. This news actually took my breath for a moment: Mr. St. John, whom I had never heard laugh before, laughed now.

'Well,' said he, 'if you had committed a murder, and I had told you your crime was discovered, you could scarcely look more aghast.'

'It is a large sum—don't you think there is a mistake?'

'No mistake at all.'

'Perhaps you have read the figures wrong—it may be 2,000!'

'It is written in letters, not figures,—twenty thousand.'

I again felt rather like an individual of but average gastronomical powers sitting down to feast alone at a table spread with provisions for a hundred. Mr. Rivers rose now and put his cloak on.

'If it were not such a very wild night,' he said, 'I would send Hannah down to keep you company: you look too desperately miserable to be left alone. But Hannah, poor woman! could not stride the drifts so well as I: her legs are not quite so long: so I must e'en leave you to your sorrows. Good-night.'

He was lifting the latch: a sudden thought occurred to me.

'Stop one minute!' I cried.

'Well?'

'It puzzles me to know why Mr. Briggs wrote to you about me; or how he knew you, or could fancy that you, living in such an out-of-the-way place, had the power to aid in my discovery.'

'Oh! I am a clergyman,' he said; 'and the clergy are often appealed to about odd matters.' Again the latch rattled.

'No: that does not satisfy me!' I exclaimed: and, indeed, there was something in the hasty and unexplanatory reply, which, instead of allaying, piqued my curiosity more than ever.

'It is a very strange piece of business,' I added. 'I must know more about it.'

'Another time.'

'No: to-night!—to-night!' and as he turned from the door, I placed myself between it and him. He looked rather embarrassed.

'You certainly shall not go till you have told me all!' I said.

'I would rather not, just now.'

'You shall!—you must!'

'I would rather Diana or Mary informed you.'

Of course these objections wrought my eagerness to a climax: gratified it must be, and that without delay; and I told him so.

'But I apprised you that I was a hard man,' said he; 'difficult to persuade.'

'And I am a hard woman,—impossible to put off.'

'And then,' he pursued, 'I am cold: no fervour infects me.'

'Whereas I am hot, and fire dissolves ice. The blaze there has thawed all the snow from your cloak; by the same token, it has streamed on to my floor,

and made it like a trampled street. As you hope ever to be forgiven, Mr. Rivers, the high crime and misdemeanour of spoiling a sanded kitchen, tell me what I wish to know.'

'Well, then,' he said, 'I yield; if not to your earnestness, to your perseverance: as stone is worn by continual dropping. Besides, you must know some day,—as well now as later. Your name is Jane Eyre?'

'Of course: that was all settled before.'

'You are not, perhaps, aware that I am your namesake?—that I was christened St. John Eyre Rivers?'

'No, indeed! I remember now seeing the letter E. comprised in your initials written in books you have at different times lent me; but I never asked for what name it stood. But what then? Surely'——

I stopped: I could not trust myself to entertain, much less to express, the thought that rushed upon me—that embodied itself,—that, in a second, stood out a strong, solid probability. Circumstances knit themselves, fitted themselves, shot into order: the chain that had been lying hitherto a formless lump of links, was drawn out straight,—every ring was perfect, the connection complete. I knew, by instinct, how the matter stood, before St. John had said another word: but I cannot expect the reader to have the same intuitive perception, so I must repeat his explanation.

'My mother's name was Eyre; she had two brothers; one a clergyman, who married Miss Jane Reed, of Gateshead; the other, John Eyre, Esq., merchant, late of Funchal, Madeira. Mr. Briggs, being Mr. Eyre's solicitor, wrote to us last August to inform us of our uncle's death; and to say that he had left his property to his brother the clergyman's orphan daughter; overlooking us, in consequence of a quarrel, never forgiven, between him and my father. He wrote again a few weeks since, to intimate that the heiress was lost; and asking if we knew anything of her. A name casually written on a slip of paper has enabled me to find her out. You know the rest.' Again he was going, but I set my back against the door.

'Do let me speak,' I said; 'let me have one moment to draw breath and reflect.' I paused—he stood before me, hat in hand, looking composed enough. I resumed:—

'Your mother was my father's sister.'

'Yes.'

'My aunt, consequently?'

He bowed.

'My uncle John was your uncle John? You, Diana and Mary, are his sister's children; as I am his brother's child?'

'Undeniably.'

'You three, then, are my cousins; half our blood on each side flows from the same source?'

'We are cousins; yes.'

I surveyed him. It seemed I had found a brother: one I could be proud of,—one I could love; and two sisters, whose qualities were such, that, when I knew them but as mere strangers, they had inspired me with genuine affection and admiration. The two girls, on whom, kneeling down on the wet ground, and looking through the low, latticed window of Moor House kitchen I had gazed with so bitter a mixture of interest and despair, were my dear kinswomen; and the young and stately gentleman who had found me almost dying at his threshold, was my blood relation. Glorious discovery to a lonely wretch! This was wealth indeed!—wealth to the heart!—a mine of pure genial affections. This was a blessing, bright, vivid, and exhilarating;—not like the ponderous gift of gold: rich and welcome enough in its way, but sobering from its weight. I now clapped my hands in sudden joy—my pulse bounded, my veins thrilled.

'Oh, I am glad!—I am glad!' I exclaimed.

St. John smiled. 'Did I not say you neglected essential points to pursue trifles?' he asked. 'You were serious when I told you you had got a fortune and now, for a matter of no moment, you are excited.'

'What *can* you mean? It may be of no moment to you; you have sisters, and don't care for a cousin; but I had nobody; and now three relations,—or two if you don't choose to be counted,—are born into my world full grown. I say again, I am glad!'

I walked fast through the room: I stopped, half suffocated with the thoughts that rose faster than I could receive, comprehend, settle them:—thoughts of what might, could, would, and should be, and that ere long. I looked at the blank wall: it seemed a sky, thick with ascending stars,—every one lit me to a purpose or delight. Those who had saved my life, whom, till this hour, I had loved barrenly, I could now benefit. They were under a yoke: I could free them: they were scattered,—I could reunite them—the independence, the affluence which was mine, might be theirs too. Were we not four? Twenty thousand pounds shared equally, would be five thousand each,—enough and to spare: justice would be done,—mutual happiness secured. Now the wealth did not weigh on me: now it was not a mere bequest of coin,—it was a legacy of life, hope, enjoyment.

How I looked while these ideas were taking my spirit by storm, I cannot tell; but I perceived soon that Mr. Rivers had placed a chair behind me, and was gently attempting to make me sit down on it. He also advised me to be composed: I scorned the insinuation of helplessness and distraction, shook off his hand, and began to walk about again.

'Write to Diana and Mary to-morrow,' I said, 'and tell them to come home directly; Diana said they would both consider themselves rich with a thousand pounds, so with five thousand, they will do very well.'

'Tell me where I can get a glass of water,' said St. John; 'you must really make an effort to tranquillise your feelings.'

'Nonsense! and what sort of an effect will the bequest have on you? Will it keep you in England, induce you to marry Miss Oliver, and settle down like an ordinary mortal?'

'You wander: your head becomes confused, I have been too abrupt in communicating the news; it has excited you beyond your strength.'

'Mr. Rivers! you quite put me out of patience; I am rational enough; it is you who misunderstand; or rather who affect to misunderstand.'

'Perhaps if you explained yourself a little more fully, I should comprehend better.'

'Explain! What is there to explain? You cannot fail to see that twenty thousand pounds, the sum in question, divided equally between the nephew and three nieces of our uncle, will give five thousand to each? What I want is, that you should write to your sisters and tell them of the fortune that has accrued to them.'

'To you, you mean.'

'I have intimated my view of the case: I am incapable of taking any other. I am not brutally selfish, blindly unjust, or fiendishly ungrateful. Besides, I am resolved I will have a home and connections. I like Moor House, and I will live at Moor House; I like Diana and Mary, and I will attach myself for life to Diana and Mary. It would please and benefit me to have five thousand pounds; it would torment and oppress me to have twenty thousand; which, moreover, could never be mine in justice, though it might in law. I abandon to you, then, what is absolutely superfluous to me. Let there be no opposition, and no discussion about it; let us agree amongst each other, and decide the point at once.'

'This is acting on first impulses; you must take days to consider such a matter, ere your word can be regarded as valid.'

'Oh! if all you doubt is my sincerity, I am easy: you see the justice of the case?'

'I *do* see a certain justice; but it is contrary to all custom. Besides, the entire fortune is your right: my uncle gained it by his own efforts; he was free to leave it to whom he would: he left it to you. After all, justice permits you to keep it: you may, with a clear conscience, consider it absolutely your own.'

'With me,' said I, 'it is fully as much a matter of feeling as of conscience: I must indulge my feelings; I so seldom have had an opportunity of doing so. Were you to argue, object, and annoy me for a year, I could not forego the delicious pleasure of which I have caught a glimpse—that of repaying, in part, a mighty obligation, and winning to myself life-long friends.'

'You think so now,' rejoined St. John; 'because you do not know what it is to possess, nor consequently to enjoy wealth: you cannot form a notion of the

importance twenty thousand pounds would give you; of the place it would enable you to take in society; of the prospects it would open to you: you cannot'——

'And you,' I interrupted, 'cannot at all imagine the craving I have for fraternal and sisterly love. I never had a home, I never had brother or sisters; I must and will have them now: you are not reluctant to admit me and own me, are you?'

'Jane: I will be your brother—my sisters will be your sisters—without stipulating for this sacrifice of your just rights.'

'Brother? Yes; at the distance of a thousand leagues! Sisters? Yes; slaving amongst strangers! I, wealthy—gorged with gold I never earned and do not merit! You, penniless! Famous equality and fraternisation! Close union! Intimate attachment!'

'But, Jane, your aspirations after family ties and domestic happiness may be realised otherwise than by the means you contemplate: you may marry.'

'Nonsense, again! Marry! I don't want to marry, and never shall marry.'

'That is saying too much: such hazardous affirmations are a proof of the excitement under which you labour.'

'It is not saying too much: I know what I feel, and how averse are my inclinations to the bare thought of marriage. No one would take me for love; and I will not be regarded in the light of a mere money-speculation. And I do not want a stranger—unsympathising alien, different from me; I want my kindred: those with whom I have full fellow-feeling. Say again you will be my brother: when you uttered the words I was satisfied, happy; repeat them, if you can, repeat them sincerely.'

'I think I can. I know I have always loved my own sisters; and I know on what my affection for them is grounded,—respect for their worth, and admiration of their talents. You too have principle and mind: your tastes and habits resemble Diana's and Mary's; your presence is always agreeable to me; in your conversation I have already for some time found a salutary solace. I feel I can easily and naturally make room in my heart for you, as my third and youngest sister.'

'Thank you: that contents me for to-night. Now you had better go; for if you stay longer, you will perhaps irritate me afresh by some mistrustful scruple.'

'And the school, Miss Eyre? It must now be shut up, I suppose?'

'No. I will retain my post of mistress till you get a substitute.'

He smiled approbation: we shook hands, and he took leave.

I need not narrate in detail the further struggles I had, and arguments I used to get matters regarding the legacy settled as I wished. My task was a very hard one: but, as I was absolutely resolved—as my cousins saw at length that my mind was really and immutably fixed on making a just division of the

property—as they must in their own hearts have felt the equity of the intention; and must, besides, have been innately conscious that in my place they would have done precisely what I wished to do—they yielded at length so far as to consent to put the affair to arbitration. The judges chosen were Mr. Oliver and an able lawyer: both coincided in my opinion: I carried my point. The instruments of transfer were drawn out: St. John, Diana, Mary, and I, each became possessed of a competency.

CHAPTER 34

It was near Christmas by the time all was settled: the season of general holiday approached. I now closed Morton school; taking care that the parting should not be barren on my side. Good fortune opens the hand as well as the heart wonderfully; and to give somewhat when we have largely received, is but to afford a vent to the unusual ebullition of the sensations. I had long felt with pleasure that many of my rustic scholars liked me, and when we parted, that consciousness was confirmed: they manifested their affection plainly and strongly. Deep was my gratification to find I had really a place in their unsophisticated hearts: I promised them that never a week should pass in future that I did not visit them, and give them an hour's teaching in their school.

Mr. Rivers came up, as—having seen the classes, now numbering sixty girls, file out before me, and locked the door—I stood with the key in my hand, exchanging a few words of special farewell with some half-dozen of my best scholars: as decent, respectable, modest, and well-informed young women as could be found in the ranks of the British peasantry. And that is saying a great deal; for after all, the British peasantry are the best taught, best mannered, most self-respecting of any in Europe: since those days I have seen paysannes and Bäuerinnen; and the best of them seemed to me ignorant, coarse, and besotted, compared with my Morton girls.

'Do you consider you have got your reward for a season of exertion?' asked Mr. Rivers, when they were gone. 'Does not the consciousness of having done some real good in your day and generation give pleasure?'

'Doubtless.'

'And you have only toiled a few months! Would not a life devoted to the task of regenerating your race be well spent?'

'Yes,' I said; 'but I could not go on for ever so: I want to enjoy my own faculties as well as to cultivate those of other people. I must enjoy them now; don't recall either my mind or body to the school; I am out of it and disposed for full holiday.'

He looked grave. 'What now? What sudden eagerness is this you evince? What are you going to do?'

'To be active: as active as I can. And first I must beg you to set Hannah at liberty, and get somebody else to wait on you.'

'Do you want her?'

'Yes, to go with me to Moor House: Diana and Mary will be at home in a week, and I want to have everything in order against their arrival.'

'I understand: I thought you were for flying off on some excursion. It is better so: Hannah shall go with you.'

'Tell her to be ready by to-morrow then; and here is the schoolroom key: I will give you the key of my cottage in the morning.'

He took it. 'You give it up very gleefully,' said he: 'I don't quite understand your light-heartedness; because I cannot tell what employment you propose to yourself as a substitute for the one you are relinquishing. What aim, what purpose, what ambition in life have you now?'

'My first aim will be to *clean down* (do you comprehend the full force of the expression?)—to *clean down* Moor House from chamber to cellar; my next to rub it up with bees-wax, oil, and an indefinite number of cloths, till it glitters again; my third, to arrange every chair, table, bed, carpet, with mathematical precision; afterwards I shall go near to ruin you in coals and peat to keep up good fires in every room; and lastly, the two days preceding that on which your sisters are expected, will be devoted by Hannah and me to such a beating of eggs, sorting of currants, grating of spices, compounding of Christmas cakes, chopping up of materials for mince-pies, and solemnising of other culinary rites, as words can convey but an inadequate notion of to the uninitiated like you. My purpose, in short, is to have all things in an absolutely perfect state of readiness for Diana and Mary, before next Thursday; and my ambition is to give them a beau-ideal of a welcome when they come.'

St. John smiled slightly: still he was dissatisfied.

'It is all very well for the present,' said he: 'but seriously, I trust that when the first flush of vivacity is over, you will look a little higher than domestic endearments and household joys.'

'The best things the world has!' I interrupted.

'No, Jane, no: this world is not the scene of fruition; do not attempt to make it so: nor of rest; do not turn slothful.'

'I mean, on the contrary, to be busy.'

'Jane, I excuse you for the present: two months' grace I allow you for the full enjoyment of your new position, and for pleasing yourself with this late found charm of relationship; but *then*, I hope you will begin to look beyond Moor House and Morton, and sisterly society, and the selfish calm and sensual comfort of civilised affluence. I hope your energies will then once more trouble you with their strength.'

I looked at him with surprise. 'St. John,' I said, 'I think you are almost wicked to talk so. I am disposed to be as content as a queen, and you try to

tir me up to restlessness! To what end?'

'To the end of turning to profit the talents which God has committed to your keeping; and of which he will surely one day demand a strict account. Jane, I shall watch you closely and anxiously—I warn you of that. And try to restrain disproportionate fervour with which you throw yourself into common-place home pleasures. Don't cling so tenaciously to ties of the flesh; save your constancy and ardour for an adequate cause; forbear to waste them on trite transient objects. Do you hear, Jane?'

'Yes; just as if you were speaking Greek. I feel I have adequate cause to be happy, and I *will* be happy. Good-bye!'

Happy at Moor House I was, and hard I worked; and so did Hannah: she was charmed to see how jovial I could be amidst the bustle of a house turned topsy-turvy—how I could dust, and brush, and clean, and cook. And really after a day or two of confusion worse confounded, it was delightful, by degrees, to invoke order from the chaos ourselves had made. I had previously taken a journey to S——, to purchase some new furniture: my cousins having given me carte blanche to effect what alterations I pleased, and a sum having been set aside for that purpose. The ordinary sitting-rooms and bedrooms I left much as they were: for I knew Diana and Mary would derive more pleasure from seeing again the old homely tables, and chairs, and beds, than from the spectacle of the smartest innovations. Still some novelty was necessary, to give to their return the piquancy with which I wished it to be invested. Dark handsome new carpets and curtains, an arrangement of some carefully selected antique ornaments in porcelain and bronze, new coverings, and mirrors, and dressing-cases for the toilet tables, answered the end: they looked fresh without being glaring. A spare parlour and bedroom I refurnished entirely, with old mahogany and crimson upholstery: I laid canvas on the passage, and carpets on the stairs. When all was finished, I thought Moor House as complete a model of bright modest snugness within, as it was, at this season, a specimen of wintry waste and desert dreariness without.

The eventful Thursday at length came. They were expected about dark, and ere dusk, fires were lit upstairs and below; the kitchen was in perfect trim; Hannah and I were dressed and all was in readiness.

St. John arrived first. I had entreated him to keep quite clear of the house till everything was arranged: and, indeed, the bare idea of the commotion, at once sordid and trivial, going on within its walls sufficed to scare him to estrangement. He found me in the kitchen, watching the progress of certain cakes for tea, then baking. Approaching the hearth, he asked, 'If I was at last satisfied with housemaid's work?' I answered by inviting him to accompany me on a general inspection of the result of my labours. With some difficulty, I got him to make the tour of the house. He just looked in at the doors I opened: and when he had wandered upstairs and downstairs, he said I must

have gone through a great deal of fatigue and trouble to have effected such considerable changes in so short a time: but not a syllable did he utter indicating pleasure in the improved aspect of his abode.

This silence damped me. I thought perhaps the alterations had disturbed some old associations he valued. I inquired whether this was the case: no doubt in a somewhat crest-fallen tone.

'Not at all; he had, on the contrary, remarked that I had scrupulously respected every association: he feared, indeed, I must have bestowed more thought on the matter than it was worth. How many minutes, for instance, had I devoted to studying the arrangement of this very room?—By-the-by, could I tell him where such a book was?'

I showed him the volume on the shelf: he took it down, and withdrawing to his accustomed window recess, he began to read it.

Now, I did not like this, reader. St. John was a good man; but I began to feel he had spoken truth of himself, when he said he was hard and cold. The humanities and amenities of life had no attraction for him—its peaceful enjoyments no charm. Literally, he lived only to aspire—after what was good and great, certainly: but still would never rest; nor approve of others resting round him. As I looked at his lofty forehead, still and pale as a white stone—at his fine lineaments fixed in study—I comprehended all at once that he would hardly make a good husband: that it would be a trying thing to be his wife. I understood, as by inspiration, the nature of his love for Miss Oliver; I agreed with him that it was but a love of the senses. I comprehended how he should despise himself for the feverish influence it exercised over him; how he should wish to stifle and destroy it; how he should mistrust its ever conducing permanently to his happiness, or hers. I saw he was of the material from which nature hews her heroes—Christian and Pagan—her lawgivers, her statesmen, her conquerors: a steadfast bulwark for great interests to rest upon; but, at the fireside, too often a cold cumbrous column, gloomy and out of place.

'This parlour is not his sphere,' I reflected: 'the Himalayan ridge, or Caffre bush, even the plague-cursed Guinea Coast swamp, would suit him better. Well may he eschew the calm of domestic life; it is not his element: there his faculties stagnate—they cannot develop or appear to advantage. It is in scenes of strife and danger—where courage is proved, and energy exercised, and fortitude tasked—that he will speak and move, the leader and superior. A merry child would have the advantage of him on this hearth. He is right to choose a missionary's career—I see it now.'

'They are coming! they are coming!' cried Hannah, throwing open the parlour door. At the same moment old Carlo barked joyfully. Out I ran. It was now dark; but a rumbling of wheels was audible. Hannah soon had a lantern lit. The vehicle had stopped at the wicket: the driver opened the door: first one well-known form, then another, stepped out. In a minute I had

my face under their bonnets, in contact first with Mary's soft cheek, then with Diana's flowing curls. They laughed—kissed me—then Hannah: patted Carlo, who was half wild with delight, asked eagerly if all was well; and being assured in the affirmative, hastened into the house.

They were stiff with their long and jolting drive from Whitcross, and chilled with the frosty night air; but their pleasant countenances expanded to the cheerful firelight. While the driver and Hannah brought in the boxes, they demanded St. John. At this moment he advanced from the parlour. They both threw their arms round his neck at once. He gave each one quiet kiss, said in a low tone a few words of welcome, stood a while to be talked to, and then, intimating that he supposed they would soon rejoin him in the parlour, withdrew there as to a place of refuge.

I had lit their candles to go upstairs, but Diana had first to give hospitable orders respecting the driver; this done, both followed me. They were delighted with the renovation and decoration of their rooms; with the new drapery, and fresh carpets, and rich tinted china vases: they expressed their gratification ungrudgingly. I had the pleasure of feeling that my arrangements met their wishes exactly; and that what I had done added a vivid charm to their joyous return home.

Sweet was that evening. My cousins, full of exhilaration, were so eloquent in narrative and comment, that their fluency covered St. John's taciturnity: he was sincerely glad to see his sisters; but in their glow of fervour and flow of joy he could not sympathise. The event of the day—that is, the return of Diana and Mary—pleased him; but the accompaniments of that event, the glad tumult, the garrulous glee of reception, irked him: I saw he wished the quieter morrow was come. In the very meridian of the night's enjoyment, about an hour after tea, a rap was heard at the door. Hannah entered with the intimation that 'a poor lad was come, at that unlikely time, to fetch Mr. Rivers to see his mother, who was drawing away.'

'Where does she live, Hannah?'

'Clear up at Whitcross Brow, almost four miles off; and moor and moss all the way.'

'Tell him I will go.'

'I'm sure, sir, you had better not. It's the worst road to travel after dark that can be: there's no track at all over the bog. And then it is such a bitter night—the keenest wind you ever felt. You had better send word, sir, that you will be there in the morning.'

But he was already in the passage, putting on his cloak; and without one objection, one murmur, he departed. It was then nine o'clock: he did not return till midnight. Starved and tired enough he was: but he looked happier than when he set out. He had performed an act of duty; made an exertion; felt his own strength to do and deny, and was on better terms with himself.

I am afraid the whole of the ensuing week tried his patience. It was Christmas week: we took to no settled employment, but spent it in a sort of merry domestic dissipation. The air of the moors, the freedom of home, the dawn of prosperity, acted on Diana and Mary's spirits like some life-giving elixir: they were gay from morning till noon, and from noon till night. They could always talk; and their discourse, witty, pithy, original, had such charms for me, that I preferred listening to, and sharing in it, to doing anything else. St. John did not rebuke our vivacity; but he escaped from it: he was seldom in the house, his parish was large, the population scattered, and he found daily business in visiting the sick and poor in its different districts.

One morning, at breakfast, Diana, after looking a little pensive for some minutes, asked him, 'If his plans were yet unchanged?'

'Unchanged and unchangeable,' was the reply. And he proceeded to inform us that his departure from England was now definitely fixed for the ensuing year.

'And Rosamond Oliver?' suggested Mary: the words seeming to escape her lips involuntarily: for no sooner had she uttered them, than she made a gesture as if wishing to recall them. St. John had a book in his hand—it was his unsocial custom to read at meals—he closed it, and looked up.

'Rosamond Oliver,' said he, 'is about to be married to Mr. Granby; one of the best connected and most estimable residents in S——, grandson and heir to Sir Frederic Granby: I had the intelligence from her father yesterday.'

His sisters looked at each other, and at me; we all three looked at him: he was serene as glass.

'The match must have been got up hastily,' said Diana: 'they cannot have known each other long.'

'But two months: they met in October at the county ball at S——. But where there are no obstacles to a union, as in the present case, where the connection is in every point desirable, delays are unnecessary: they will be married as soon as S—— Place, which Sir Frederic gives up to them, can be refitted for their reception.'

The first time I found St. John alone after this communication, I felt tempted to inquire if the event distressed him: but he seemed so little to need sympathy, that, so far from venturing to offer him more, I experienced some shame at the recollection of what I had already hazarded. Besides, I was out of practice in talking to him: his reserve was again frozen over, and my frankness was congealed beneath it. He had not kept his promise of treating me like his sisters; he continually made little, chilling differences between us, which did not at all tend to the development of cordiality: in short, now that I was acknowledged his kinswoman, and lived under the same roof with him, I felt the distance between us to be far greater than when he had known me only as the village schoolmistress. When I remembered how far I had once been

admitted to his confidence, I could hardly comprehend his present frigidity.

Such being the case, I felt not a little surprised when he raised his head suddenly from the desk over which he was stooping, and said:—

'You see, Jane, the battle is fought and the victory won.'

Startled at being thus addressed, I did not immediately reply: after a moment's hesitation I answered:—

'But are you sure, you are not in the position of those conquerors whose triumphs have cost them too dear? Would not such another ruin you?'

'I think not; and if I were, it does not much signify; I shall never be called upon to contend for such another. The event of the conflict is decisive: my way is now clear; I thank God for it!' So saying, he returned to his papers and his silence.

As our mutual happiness (i.e. Diana's, Mary's, and mine) settled into a quieter character, and we resumed our usual habits and regular studies, St. John stayed more at home: he sat with us in the same room, sometimes for hours together. While Mary drew, Diana pursued a course of encyclopedic reading she had (to my awe and amazement) undertaken, and I fagged away at German, he pondered a mystic lore of his own: that of some Eastern tongue, the acquisition of which he thought necessary to his plans.

Thus engaged, he appeared, sitting in his own recess, quiet and absorbed enough; but that blue eye of his had a habit of leaving the outlandish-looking grammar, and wandering over, and sometimes fixing upon us, his fellow-students, with a curious intensity of observation: if caught, it would be instantly withdrawn; yet ever and anon, it returned searchingly to our table. I wondered what it meant: I wondered, too, at the punctual satisfaction he never failed to exhibit on an occasion that seemed to me of small moment, namely,—my weekly visit to Morton School; and still more was I puzzled when, if the day was unfavourable, if there was snow, or rain, or high wind, and his sisters urged me not to go, he would invariably make light of their solicitude, and encourage me to accomplish the task without regard to the elements.

'Jane is not such a weakling as you would make her,' he would say: 'she can bear a mountain blast, or a shower, or a few flakes of snow, as well as any of us. Her constitution is both sound and elastic:—better calculated to endure variations of climate than many more robust.'

And when I returned, sometimes a good deal tired, and not a little weather-beaten, I never dared complain, because I saw that to murmur would be to vex him: on all occasions fortitude pleased him: the reverse was a special annoyance.

One afternoon, however, I got leave to stay at home, because I really had a cold. His sisters were gone to Morton in my stead: I sat reading Schiller; he, deciphering his crabbed Oriental scrolls. As I exchanged a translation for an exercise, I happened to look his way: there I found myself under the

influence of the ever-watchful blue eye. How long it had been searching me through and through, and over and over, I cannot tell: so keen was it, and yet so cold, I felt for the moment superstitious—as if I were sitting in the room with something uncanny.

'Jane, what are you doing?'

'Learning German.'

'I want you to give up German, and learn Hindostanee.'

'You are not in earnest?'

'In such earnest that I must have it so: and I will tell you why.'

He then went on to explain that Hindostanee was the language he himself was at present studying: that, as he advanced, he was apt to forget the commencement: that it would assist him greatly to have a pupil with whom he might again and again go over the elements, and so fix them thoroughly in his mind; that his choice had hovered for some time between me and his sisters, but that he had fixed on me, because he saw I could sit at a task the longest of the three. Would I do him this favour? I should not, perhaps, have to make the sacrifice long; as it wanted now barely three months to his departure.

St. John was not a man to be lightly refused: you felt that every impression made on him, either for pain or pleasure, was deep-graved and permanent. I consented. When Diana and Mary returned, the former found her scholar transferred from her to her brother: she laughed; and both she and Mary agreed that St. John should never have persuaded them to such a step. He answered, quietly:—

'I know it.'

I found him a very patient, very forbearing, and yet an exacting master: he expected me to do a great deal; and when I fulfilled his expectations, he, in his own way, fully testified his approbation. By degree, he acquired a certain influence over me that took away my liberty of mind: his praise and notice were more restraining than his indifference. I could no longer talk or laugh freely when he was by; because a tiresomely importunate instinct reminded me that vivacity (at least in me) was distasteful to him. I was so fully aware that only serious moods and occupations were acceptable, that in his presence every effort to sustain or follow any other became vain: I fell under a freezing spell. When he said 'go,' I went: 'come,' I came; 'do this,' I did it. But I did not love my servitude: I wished, many a time, he had continued to neglect me.

One evening, when, at bedtime, his sisters and I stood round him, bidding him good-night, he kissed each of them, as was his custom; and, as was equally his custom, he gave me his hand. Diana, who chanced to be in a frolicsome humour (*she* was not painfully controlled by his will; for hers, in another way, was as strong), exclaimed:—

'St. John! you used to call Jane your third sister, but you don't treat her as such: you should kiss her too.'

She pushed me towards him. I thought Diana very provoking, and felt uncomfortably confused; and while I was thus thinking and feeling, St. John bent his head; his Greek face was brought to a level with mine, his eyes questioned my eyes piercingly—he kissed me. There are no such things as marble kisses, or ice kisses, or I should say, my ecclesiastical cousin's salute belonged to one of these classes; but there may be experiment kisses, and his was an experiment kiss. When given, he viewed me to learn the esrult; it was not striking: I am sure I did not blush: perhaps I might have turned a little pale, for I felt as if the kiss were a seal affixed to my fetters. He never omitted the ceremony afterwards, and the gravity and quiescence with which I underwent it, seemed to invest it for him with a certain charm.

As for me, I daily wished more to please him: but to do so, I felt daily more and more that I must disown half my nature, stifle half my faculties, wrest my tastes from their original bent, force myself to the adoption of pursuits for which I had no natural vocation. He wanted to train me to an elevation I could never reach; it racked me hourly to aspire to the standard he uplifted. The thing was as impossible as to mould my irregular features to his correct and classic pattern, to give to my changeable green eyes the sea-blue tint and solemn lustre of his own.

Not his ascendancy, alone, however, held me in thrall at present. Of late it had been easy enough for me to look sad: a cankering evil sat at my heart and drained my happiness at its source—the evil of suspense.

Perhaps you think I had forgotten Mr. Rochester, reader, amidst these changes of place and fortune. Not for a moment. His idea was still with me; because it was not a vapour sunshine could disperse; nor a sand-traced effigy storms could wash away: it was a name graven on a tablet, fated to last as long as the marble it inscribed. The craving to know what had become of him followed me everywhere; when I was at Morton, I re-entered my cottage every evening to think of that; and now at Moor House, I sought my bedroom each night to brood over it.

In the course of my necessary correspondence with Mr. Briggs about the will, I had inquired if he knew anything of Mr. Rochester's present residence and state of health; but, as St. John had conjectured, he was quite ignorant of all concerning him. I then wrote to Mrs. Fairfax, entreating information on the subject. I had calculated with certainty on this step answering my end: I felt sure it would elicit an early answer. I was astonished when a fortnight passed without reply; but when two months wore away, and day after day the post arrived and brought nothing for me, I fell a prey to the keenest anxiety.

I wrote again: there was a chance of my first letter having missed. Renewed hope followed renewed effort: it shone like the former for some weeks, then, like it, faded, flickered: not a line, not a word reached me. When half a year wasted in vain expectancy my hope died out: and then I felt dark indeed.

A fine spring shone round me, which I could not enjoy. Summer approached: Diana tried to cheer me: she said I looked ill, and wished to accompany me to the sea-side. This St. John opposed; he said I did not want dissipation, I wanted employment; my present life was too purposeless, I required an aim: and, I suppose, by way of supplying deficiencies, he prolonged still further my lessons in Hindostanee, and grew more urgent in requiring their accomplishment: and I, like a fool, never thought of resisting him—I could not resist him.

One day I had come to my studies in lower spirits than usual; the ebb was occasioned by a poignantly felt disappointment: Hannah had told me in the morning there was a letter for me, and when I went down to take it, almost certain that the long looked-for tidings were vouchsafed me at last, I found only an unimportant note from Mr. Briggs on business. The bitter check had wrung from me some tears; and now as I sat poring over the crabbed characters and flourishing tropes of an Indian scribe, my eyes filled again.

St. John called me to his side to read; in attempting to do this my voice failed me: words were lost in sobs. He and I were the only occupants of the parlour: Diana was practising her music in the drawing-room, Mary was gardening—it was a very fine May-day, clear, sunny, and breezy. My companion expressed no surprise at this emotion, nor did he question me as to its cause; he only said:—

'We will wait a few minutes, Jane, till you are more composed.' And while I smothered the paroxysm with all haste, he sat calm and patient, leaning on his desk and looking like a physician watching with the eye of science an expected and fully-understood crisis in a patient's malady. Having stifled my sobs, wiped my eyes, and muttered something about not being very well that morning, I resumed my task, and succeeded in completing it. St. John put away my books and his, locked his desk, and said:—

'Now, Jane, you shall take a walk; and with me.'

'I will call Diana and Mary.'

'No. I want only one companion this morning, and that must be you: put on your things; go out by the kitchen door: take the road towards the head of Marsh Glen: I will join you in a moment.'

I know no medium: I never in my life have known any medium in my dealings with positive, hard characters, antagonistic to my own, between absolute submission and determined revolt. I have always faithfully observed the one, up to the very moment of bursting, sometimes with volcanic vehemence, into the other; and as neither present circumstances warranted nor my present mood inclined me to mutiny, I observed careful obedience to St. John's directions; and in ten minutes I was treading the wild track of the glen, side by side with him.

The breeze was from the west: it came over the hills, sweet with scents of

heath and rush; the sky was of stainless blue; the stream descending the ravine, swelled with past spring rains, poured along plentiful and clear, catching golden gleams from the sun, and sapphire tints from the firmament. As we advanced and left the track, we trod a soft turf, mossy fine and emerald green, minutely enamelled with a tiny white flower, and spangled with a star-like yellow blossom: the hills, meantime, shut us quite in; for the glen, towards its head, wound to their very core.

'Let us rest here,' said St. John, as we reached the first stragglers of a battalion of rocks, guarding a sort of pass, beyond which the beck rushed down a water-fall; and where, still a little further, the mountain shook off turf and flower, had only heath for raiment, and crag for gem—where it exaggerated the wild to the savage, and exchanged the fresh for the frowning—where it guarded the forlorn hope of solitude, and a last refuge for silence.

I took a seat: St. John stood near me. He looked up the pass and down the hollow; his glance wandered away with the stream, and returned to traverse the unclouded heaven which coloured it: he removed his hat, let the breeze stir his hair and kiss his brow. He seemed in communion with the genius of the haunt: with his eye he bade farewell to something.

'And I shall see it again,' he said aloud, 'in dreams, when I sleep by the Ganges: and again, in a more remote hour—when another slumber overcomes me—on the shore of a darker stream.'

Strange words of a strange love! An austere patriot's passion for his father-land! He sat down; for half an hour we never spoke; neither he to me nor I to him: that interval passed, he recommenced:—

'Jane, I go in six weeks: I have taken my berth in an East Indiaman which sails on the twentieth of June.'

'God will protect you; for you have undertaken His work,' I answered.

'Yes,' said he, 'there is my glory and joy. I am the servant of an infallible master. I am not going out under human guidance, subject to the defective laws and erring control of my feeble fellow-worms: my king, my lawgiver, my captain, is the All-perfect. It seems strange to me that all round me do not burn to enlist under the same banner,—to join in the same enter-prise.'

'All have not your powers: and it would be folly for the feeble to wish to march with the strong.'

'I do not speak to the feeble, or think of them: I address only such as are worthy of the work, and competent to accomplish it.'

'Those are few in number, and difficult to discover.'

'You say truly: but when found, it is right to stir them up—to urge and exhort them to the effort—to show them what their gifts are, and why they were given—to speak Heaven's message in their ear,—to offer them, direct from God, a place in the ranks of His chosen.'

'If they are really qualified for the task, will not their own hearts be the first to inform them of it?'

I felt as if an awful charm was framing round and gathering over me: I trembled to hear some fatal word spoken which would at once declare and rivet the spell.

'And what does *your* heart say?' demanded St. John.

'My heart is mute,—my heart is mute,' I answered, struck and thrilled.

'Then I must speak for it,' continued the deep, relentless voice. 'Jane, come with me to India: come as my helpmeet and fellow-labourer.'

The glen and sky spun round: the hills heaved! It was as if I had heard a summons from Heaven—as if a visionary messenger, like him of Macedonia, had enounced, 'Come over and help us!' But I was no apostle,—I could not behold the herald,—I could not receive his call.

'Oh, St. John!' I cried, 'have some mercy!'

I appealed to one who, in the discharge of what he believed his duty, knew neither mercy nor remorse. He continued:—

'God and nature intended you for a missionary's wife. It is not personal but mental endowments they have given you: you are formed for labour, not for love. A missionary's wife you must—shall be. You shall be mine: I claim you—not for my pleasure, but for my Sovereign's service.'

'I am not fit for it: I have no vocation,' I said.

He had calculated on these first objections: he was not irritated by them. Indeed, as he leaned back against the crag behind him, folded his arms on his chest, and fixed his countenance, I saw he was prepared for a long and trying opposition, and had taken in a stock of patience to last him to its close—resolved, however, that that close should be conquest for him.

'Humility, Jane,' said he, 'is the groundwork of Christian virtues: you say right that you are not fit for the work. Who is fit for it? Or who, that ever was truly called, believed himself worthy of the summons? I, for instance, am but dust and ashes. With St. Paul, I acknowledge myself the chiefest of sinners; but I do not suffer this sense of my personal vileness to daunt me. I know my Leader: that He is just as well as mighty; and while He has chosen a feeble instrument to perform a great task, He will, from the boundless stores of His providence, supply the inadequacy of the means to the end. Think like me, Jane—trust like me. It is the Rock of Ages I ask you to lean on: do not doubt but it will bear the weight of your human weakness.'

'I do not understand a missionary life: I have never studied missionary labours.'

'There, I, humble as I am, can give you the aid you want: I can set your task from hour to hour; stand by you always; help you from moment to moment. This I could do in the beginning: soon (for I know your powers) you would be as strong and apt as myself, and would not require my help.'

'But my powers—where are they for this undertaking? I do not feel them. Nothing speaks or stirs in me while you talk. I am sensible of no light kindling—no life quickening—no voice counselling or cheering. Oh, I wish I could make you see how much my mind is at this moment like a rayless dungeon, with one shrinking fear fettered in its depths—the fear of being persuaded by you to attempt what I cannot accomplish!'

'I have an answer for you—hear it. I have watched you ever since we first met: I have made you my study for ten months. I have proved you in that time by sundry tests: and what have I seen and elicited? In the village school I found you could perform well, punctually, uprightly, labour uncongenial to your habits and inclinations; I saw you could perform it with capacity and tact: you could win while you controlled. In the calm with which you learnt you had become suddenly rich, I read a mind clear of the vice of Demas:—lucre had no undue power over you. In the resolute readiness with which you cut your wealth into four shares, keeping but one to yourself, and relinquishing the three others to the claim of abstract justice, I recognised a soul that revelled in the flame and excitement of sacrifice. In the tractability with which, at my wish, you forsook a study in which you were interested, and adopted another because it interested me; in the untiring assiduity with which you have since persevered in it—in the unflagging energy and unshaken temper with which you have met its difficulties—I acknowledge the complement of the qualities I seek. Jane, you are docile, diligent, disinterested, faithful, constant, and courageous; very gentle, and very heroic: cease to mistrust yourself—I can trust you unreservedly. As a conductress of Indian schools, and a helper amongst Indian women, your assistance will be to me invaluable.'

My iron shroud contracted round me; persuasion advanced with slow sure step. Shut my eyes as I would, these last words of his succeeded in making the way, which had seemed blocked up, comparatively clear. My work, which had appeared so vague, so hopelessly diffuse, condensed itself as he proceeded, and assumed a definite form under his shaping hand. He waited for an answer. I demanded a quarter of an hour to think, before I again hazarded a reply.

'Very willingly,' he rejoined: and rising, he strode a little distance up the pass, threw himself down on a swell of heath, and there lay still.

'I *can* do what he wants me to do: I am forced to see and acknowledge that,' I meditated—'That is, if life be spared me. But I feel mine is not the existence to be long protracted under an Indian sun.—What then? He does not care for that: when my time came to die he would resign me, in all serenity and sanctity, to the God who gave me. The case is very plain before me. In leaving England, I should leave a loved but empty land—Mr. Rochester is not there: and if he were, what is, what can that ever be to me? My business is to live without him now: nothing so absurd, so weak as to drag on from day to day, as if I were waiting some impossible change in circumstances, which might reunite me

to him. Of course (as St. John once said) I must seek another interest in life to replace the one lost: is not the occupation he now offers me truly the most glorious man can adopt or God assign? Is it not, by its noble cares and sublime results, the one best calculated to fill the void left by uptorn affections and demolished hopes? I believe I must say, Yes—and yet I shudder. Alas! If I join St. John, I abandon half myself: if I go to India, I go to premature death. And how will the interval between leaving England for India, and India for the grave, be filled? Oh, I know well! That, too, is very clear to my vision. By straining to satisfy St. John till my sinews ache, I *shall* satisfy him—to the finest central point and farthest outward circle of his expectations. If I *do* go with him—if I *do* make the sacrifice he urges, I will make it absolutely: I will throw all on the altar—heart, vitals, the entire victim. He will never love me; but he shall approve me; I will show him energies he has not seen, resources he has never suspected. Yes: I can work as hard as he can; and with as little grudging.

'Consent, then, to his demand is possible: but for one item—one dreadful item. It is—that he asks me to be his wife, and has no more of a husband's heart for me than that frowning giant of a rock, down which the stream is foaming in yonder gorge. He prizes me as a soldier would a good weapon; and that is all. Unmarried to him, this would never grieve me; but can I let him complete his calculations—coolly put into practice his plans—go through the wedding ceremony? Can I receive from him the bridal ring, endure all the forms of love (which I doubt not he would scrupulously observe) and know that the spirit was quite absent? Can I bear the consciousness that every endearment he bestows is a sacrifice made on principle? No: such a martyrdom would be monstrous. I will never undergo it. As his sister, I might accompany him—not as his wife: I will tell him so.'

I looked towards the knoll: there he lay, still as a prostrate column; his face turned to me: his eye beaming watchful, and keen. He started to his feet, and approached me.

'I am ready to go to India, if I may go free.'

'Your answer requires a commentary,' he said; 'it is not clear.'

'You have hitherto been my adopted brother: I, your adopted sister; let us continue as such: you and I had better not marry.'

He shook his head. 'Adopted fraternity will not do in this case. If you were my real sister it would be different: I should take you, and seek no wife. But as it is, either our union must be consecrated and sealed by marriage or it cannot exist: practical obstacles oppose themselves to any other plan. Do you not see it, Jane? Consider a moment—your strong sense will guide you.'

I did consider: and still my sense, such as it was, directed me only to the fact that we did not love each other as man and wife should; and therefore

it inferred we ought not to marry. I said so. 'St. John,' I returned, 'I regard you as a brother—you, me as a sister: so let us continue.'

'We cannot—we cannot,' he answered, with short, sharp determination: 'it would not do. You have said you will go with me to India: remember—you have said that.'

'Conditionally.'

'Well—well. To the main point—the departure with me from England, the co-operation with me in my future labours—you do not object. You have already as good as put your hand to the plough: you are too consistent to withdraw it. You have but one end to keep in view—how the work you have undertaken can best be done. Simplify your complicated interests, feelings, thoughts, wishes, aims; merge all considerations in one purpose: that of fulfilling with effect—with power—the mission of your great Master. To do so, you must have a coadjutor—not a brother; that is a loose tie; but a husband. I, too, do not want a sister; a sister might any day be taken from me. I want a wife: the sole helpmeet I can influence efficiently in life, and retain absolutely till death.'

I shuddered as he spoke: I felt his influence in my marrow—his hold on my limbs.

'Seek one elsewhere than in me, St. John: seek one fitted to you.'

'One fitted to my purpose, you mean—fitted to my vocation. Again I tell you it is not the insignificant private individual—the mere man, with the man's selfish senses—I wish to mate: it is a missionary.'

'And I will give the missionary my energies—it is all he wants—but not myself: that would be only adding the husk and shell to the kernel. For them he has no use: I retain them.'

'You cannot—you ought not. Do you think God will be satisfied with half an oblation? Will he accept a mutilated sacrifice? It is the cause of God I advocate: it is under his standard I enlist you. I cannot accept on His behalf a divided allegiance: it must be entire.'

'Oh! I will give my heart to God,' I said. '*You* do not want it.'

I will not swear, reader, that there was not something of repressed sarcasm both in the tone in which I uttered this sentence, and in the feeling that accompanied it. I had silently feared St. John till now, because I had not understood him. He had held me in awe, because he had held me in doubt. How much of him was saint, how much mortal, I could not heretofore tell: but revelations were being made in this conference: the analysis of his nature was proceeding before my eyes. I saw his fallibilities: I comprehended them. I understood that, sitting there where I did, on the bank of heath, and with that handsome form before me, I sat at the feet of a man, erring as I. The veil fell from his hardness and despotism. Having felt in him the presence of these qualities, I felt his imperfection, and took courage. I was with an equal—one

with whom I might argue—one whom, if I saw good, I might resist.

He was silent after I had uttered the last sentence, and I presently risked an upward glance at his countenance. His eye, bent on me, expressed at once stern surprise and keen inquiry. 'Is she sarcastic, and sarcastic to *me*!' it seemed to say.

'What does this signify?'

'Do not let us forget that this is a solemn matter,' he said ere long; 'one of which we may neither think nor talk lightly without sin. I trust, Jane, you are in earnest when you say you will give your heart to God: it is all I want. Once wrench your heart from man, and fix it on your Maker, the advancement of that Maker's spiritual kingdom on earth will be your chief delight and endeavour; you will be ready to do at once whatever furthers that end. You will see what impetus would be given to your efforts and mine by our physical and mental union in marriage: the only union that gives a character of permanent conformity to the destinies and designs of human beings: and passing over all minor caprices—all trivial difficulties and delicacies of feeling— all scruple about the degree, kind, strength, or tenderness of mere personal inclination—you will hasten to enter into that union at once.'

'Shall I?' I said, briefly; and I looked at his features, beautiful in their harmony, but strangely formidable in their still severity; at his brow, commanding but not open; at his eyes, bright and deep, and searching, but never soft; at his tall, imposing figure; and fancied myself in idea *his wife*. Oh! it would never do! As his curate, his comrade, all would be right: I would cross oceans with him in that capacity; toil under eastern suns, in Asian deserts with him in that office; admire and emulate his courage, and devotion, and vigour; accommodate quietly to his masterhood; smile undisturbed at his ineradicable ambition; discriminate the Christian from the man; profoundly esteem the one, and freely forgive the other. I should suffer often, no doubt, attached to him only in this capacity: my body would be under rather a stringent yoke, but my heart and mind would be free. I should still have my unblighted self to turn to: my natural unenslaved feelings with which to communicate in moments of loneliness. There would be recesses in my mind which would be only mine, to which he never came; and sentiments growing there fresh and sheltered, which his austerity could never blight, nor his measured warrior-march trample down: but as his wife—at his side always, and always restrained, and always checked—forced to keep the fire of my nature continually low, to compel it to burn inwardly and never utter a cry, though the imprisoned flame consumed vital after vital—*this* would be unendurable.

'St. John!' I exclaimed, when I had got so far in my meditation.

'Well?' he answered, icily.

'I repeat: I freely consent to go with you as your fellow-missionary; but not as your wife; I cannot marry you and become part of you.'

342

'A part of me you must become,' he answered steadily; 'otherwise the whole bargain is void. How can I, a man not yet thirty, take out with me to India a girl of nineteen, unless she be married to me? How can we be for ever together—sometimes in solitudes, sometimes amidst savage tribes—and unwed?'

'Very well,' I said shortly; 'under the circumstances, quite as well as if I were either your real sister, or a man and a clergyman like yourself.'

'It is known that you are not my sister; I cannot introduce you as such: to attempt it would be to fasten injurious suspicions on us both. And for the rest, though you have a man's vigorous brain, you have a woman's heart, and—it would not do.'

'It would do,' I affirmed with some disdain, 'perfectly well. I have a woman's heart; but not where you are concerned; for you I have only a comrade's constancy; a fellow-soldier's frankness, fidelity, fraternity, if you like; a neophyte's respect and submission to his hierophant: nothing more—don't fear.'

'It is what I want,' he said, speaking to himself; 'it is just what I want. And there are obstacles in the way: they must be hewn down. Jane, you would not repent marrying me; be certain of that; we *must* be married. I repeat it: there is no other way; and undoubtedly enough of love would follow upon marriage to render the union right even in your eyes.'

'I scorn your idea of love,' I could not help saying; as I rose up and stood before him, leaning my back against the rock. 'I scorn the counterfeit sentiment you offer: yes, St. John, and I scorn you when you offer it.'

He looked at me fixedly: compressing his well-cut lips while he did so. Whether he was incensed or surprised, or what, it was not easy to tell: he could command his countenance thoroughly.

'I scarcely expected to hear that expression from you,' he said: 'I think I have done and uttered nothing to deserve scorn.'

I was touched by his gentle tone, and overawed by his high, calm mien.

'Forgive me the words, St. John: but it is your own fault that I have been roused to speak so unguardedly. You have introduced a topic on which our natures are at variance—a topic we should never discuss: the very name of love is an apple of discord between us—if the reality were required what should we do? How should we feel? My dear cousin, abandon your scheme of marriage —forget it.'

'No,' said he; 'it is a long-cherished scheme, and the only one which can secure my great end: but I shall urge you no further at present. To-morrow, I leave home for Cambridge: I have many friends there to whom I should wish to say farewell. I shall be absent a fortnight—take that space of time to consider my offer: and do not forget that if you reject it, it is not me you deny, but God. Through my means, He opens to you a noble career; as my wife only can you enter upon it. Refuse to be my wife, and you limit yourself for

ever to a track of selfish ease and barren obscurity. Tremble lest in that case you should be numbered with those who have denied the faith, and are worse than infidels!'

He had done. Turning from me, he once more—

'Looked to river, looked to hill:'

But this time his feelings were all pent in his heart: I was not worthy to hear them uttered. As I walked by his side homeward, I read well in his iron silence all he felt towards me: the disappointment of an austere and despotic nature, which has met resistance where it expected submission—the disapprobation of a cool, inflexible judgment, which has detected in another feelings and views in which it has no power to sympathise: in short, as a man, he would have wished to coerce me into obedience: it was only as a sincere Christian he bore so patiently with my perversity, and allowed so long a space for reflection and repentance.

That night, after he had kissed his sisters, he thought proper to forget even to shake hands with me; but left the room in silence. I—who, though I had no love, had much friendship for him—was hurt by the marked omission: so much hurt that tears started to my eyes.

'I see you and St. John have been quarrelling, Jane,' said Diana, 'during your walk on the moor. But go after him; he is now lingering in the passage expecting you—he will make it up.'

I have not much pride under such circumstances: I would always rather be happy than dignified; and I ran after him—he stood at the foot of the stairs.

'Good-night, St. John,' said I.

'Good-night, Jane,' he replied calmly.

'Then shake hands,' I added.

What a cold, loose touch he impressed on my fingers! He was deeply displeased by what had occurred that day: cordiality would not warm, nor tears move him. No happy reconciliation was to be had with him—no cheering smile or generous word: but still the Christian was patient and placid; and when I asked him if he forgave me, he answered that he was not in the habit of cherishing the remembrance of vexation; that he had nothing to forgive: not having been offended.

And with that answer he left me. I would much rather he had knocked me down.

CHAPTER 35

He did not leave for Cambridge the next day, as he had said he would. He deferred his departure a whole week; and during that time he made me feel what severe punishment, a good, yet stern, a conscientious, yet implacable man can inflict on one who has offended him. Without one overt act of hostility, one upbraiding word, he contrived to impress me momently with the conviction that I was put beyond the pale of his favour.

Not that St. John harboured a spirit of unchristian vindictiveness—not that he would have injured a hair of my head, if it had been fully in his power to do so. Both by nature and principle, he was superior to the mean gratification of vengeance: he had forgiven me for saying I scorned him and his love, but he had not forgotten the words; and as long as he and I lived he never would forget them. I saw by his look, when he turned to me, that they were always written on the air between me and him; whenever I spoke, they sounded in my voice to his ear; and their echo toned every answer he gave me.

He did not abstain from conversing with me: he even called me as usual each morning to join him at his desk; and I fear the corrupt man within him had a pleasure unimparted to, and unshared by, the pure Christian, in evincing with what skill he could, while acting and speaking apparently just as usual, extract from every deed and every phrase the spirit of interest and approval which had formerly communicated a certain austere charm to his language and manner. To me, he was in reality become no longer flesh, but marble; his eye was a cold, bright, blue gem; his tongue, a speaking instrument—nothing more.

All this was torture to me—refined, lingering torture. It kept up a slow fire of indignation, and a trembling trouble of grief, which harassed and crushed me altogether. I felt how—if I were his wife, this good man, pure as the deep unless source, could soon kill me: without drawing from my veins a single drop of blood, or receiving on his own crystal conscience the faintest stain of crime. Especially I felt this, when I made any attempt to propitiate him. No ruth met my ruth. *He* experienced no suffering from estrangement—no yearning after reconciliation; and though, more than once, my fast falling tears blistered the page over which we both bent, they produced no more effect on him than if his heart had been really a matter of stone or metal. To his sisters, meantime, he was somewhat kinder than usual: as if afraid that mere coldness would not sufficiently convince me how completely I was banished and banned, he added the force of contrast: and this I am sure he did, not by malice, but on principle.

The night before he left home, happening to see him walking in the garden about sunset, and remembering, as I looked at him, that this man, alienated as he now was, had once saved my life, and that we were near relations, I was

moved to make a last attempt to regain his friendship. I went out and approached him, as he stood leaning over the little gate: I spoke to the point at once.

'St. John, I am unhappy, because you are still angry with me. Let us be friends.'

'I hope we are friends,' was the unmoved reply; while he still watched the rising of the moon, which he had been contemplating as I approached.

'No, St. John, we are not friends as we were. You know that.'

'Are we not? That is wrong. For my part, I wish you no ill and all good.'

'I believe you, St. John; for I am sure you are incapable of wishing any one ill; but, as I am your kinswoman, I should desire somewhat more of affection than that sort of general philanthropy you extend to mere strangers.'

'Of course,' he said. 'Your wish is reasonable; and I am far from regarding you as a stranger.'

This, spoken in a cool, tranquil tone, was mortifying and baffling enough. Had I attended to the suggestions of pride and ire, I should immediately have left him: but something worked within me more strongly than those feelings could. I deeply venerated my cousin's talent and principle. His friendship was of value to me: to lose it tried me severely. I would not so soon relinquish the attempt to reconquer it.

'Must we part in this way, St. John? And when you go to India, will you leave me so, without a kinder word than you have yet spoken?'

He now turned quite from the moon, and faced me.

'When I go to India, Jane, will I leave you? What! do you not go to India?'

'You said I could not, unless I married you.'

'And you will not marry me? You adhere to that resolution?'

Reader, do you know, as I do, what terror those cold people can put into the ice of their questions? How much of the fall of the avalanche is in their anger? of the breaking up of the frozen sea in their displeasure?

'No, St. John, I will not marry you. I adhere to my resolution.'

The avalanche had shaken and slid a little forward; but it did not yet crash down.

'Once more, why this refusal?' he asked.

'Formerly,' I answered, 'because you did not love me; now, I reply, because you almost hate me. If I were to marry you, you would kill me. You are killing me now.'

His lips and cheeks turned white—quite white.

'*I should kill you—I am killing you?* Your words are such as ought not to be used: violent, unfeminine, and untrue. They betray an unfortunate state of mind: they merit severe reproof: they would seem inexcusable; but that it is the duty of man to forgive his fellow, even until seventy-and-seven times.'

I had finished the business now. While earnestly wishing to erase from his

mind the trace of my former offence, I had stamped on that tenacious surface, another and far deeper impression: I had burnt it in.

'Now, you will indeed hate me,' I said. 'It is useless to attempt to conciliate you: I see I have made an eternal enemy of you.'

A fresh wrong did these words inflict: the worse, because they touched on the truth. That bloodless lip quivered to a temporary spasm. I knew the steely ire I had whetted. I was heart-wrung.

'You utterly misinterpret my words,' I said, at once seizing his hand: 'I have no intention to grieve or pain you—indeed, I have not.'

Most bitterly he smiled—most decidedly he withdrew his hand from mine. 'And now you recall your promise, and will not go to India at all, I presume?' said he, after a considerable pause.

'Yes I will, as your assistant,' I answered.

A very long silence succeeded. What struggle there was in him between Nature and Grace in this interval, I cannot tell: only singular gleams scintillated in his eyes, and strange shadows passed over his face. He spoke at last.

'I before proved to you the absurdity of a single woman of your age proposing to accompany abroad a single man of mine. I proved it to you in such terms as, I should have thought, would have prevented your ever again alluding to the plan. That you have done so, I regret—for your sake.'

I interrupted him. Anything like a tangible reproach gave me courage at once. 'Keep to common sense, St. John: you are verging on nonsense. You pretend to be shocked by what I have said. You are not really shocked; for, with your superior mind, you cannot be either so dull or so conceited as to misunderstand my meaning. I say again, I will be your curate, if you like, but never your wife.'

Again he turned lividly pale; but, as before, controlled his passion perfectly. He answered emphatically, but calmly:—

'A female curate, who is not my wife, would never suit me. With me, then, it seems, you cannot go: but if you are sincere in your offer, I will, while in own, speak to a married missionary, whose wife needs a coadjutor. Your own fortune will make you independent of the Society's aid; and thus you may still be spared the dishonour of breaking your promise, and deserting the band you engaged to join.'

Now I never had, as the reader knows, either given any formal promise, or entered into any engagement; and this language was much too hard, and much too despotic for the occasion. I replied:—

'There is no dishonour; no breach of promise; no desertion in the case. I am not under the slightest obligation to go to India: especially with strangers. With you I would have ventured much; because I admire, confide in, and, as a sister, I love you: but I am convinced that, go when and with whom

I would, I should not live long in that climate.'

'Ah! you are afraid of yourself,' he said, curling his lip.

'I am. God did not give me my life to throw away; and to do as you wish me would, I begin to think, be almost equivalent to committing suicide. Moreover, before I definitely resolve on quitting England, I will know for certain, whether I cannot be of greater use by remaining in it than by leaving it.'

'What do you mean?'

'It would be fruitless to attempt to explain: but there is a point on which I have long endured painful doubt; and I can go nowhere till by some means that doubt is removed.'

'I know where your heart turns, and to what it clings. The interest you cherish is lawless and unconsecrated. Long since you ought to have crushed it: now you should blush to allude to it. You think of Mr. Rochester?'

It was true. I confessed it by silence.

'Are you going to seek Mr. Rochester?'

'I must find out what has become of him.'

'It remains for me, then,' he said, 'to remember you in my prayers; and to entreat God for you, in all earnestness, that you may not indeed become a castaway. I had thought I recognised in you one of the chosen. But God sees not as man sees: *His* will be done.'

He opened the gate, passed through it, and strayed away down the glen. He was soon out of sight.

On re-entering the parlour, I found Diana standing at the window, looking very thoughtful. Diana was a great deal taller than I: she put her hand on my shoulder, and, stooping, examined my face.

'Jane,' she said, 'you are always agitated and pale now. I am sure there is something the matter. Tell me what business St. John and you have on hands. I have watched you this half hour from the window: you must forgive my being such a spy, but for a long time I have fancied I hardly know what. St. John is a strange being'——

She paused—I did not speak: soon she resumed:—

'That brother of mine cherishes peculiar views of some sort respecting you, I am sure: he has long distinguished you by a notice and interest he never showed to anyone else—to what end? I wish he loved you—does he, Jane?'

I put her cool hand to my hot forehead: 'No, Die, not one whit.'

'Then why does he follow you so with his eyes—and get you so frequently alone with him, and keep you so continually at his side? Mary and I had both concluded he wished you to marry him.'

'He does—he has asked me to be his wife.'

Diana clapped her hands. 'That is just what we hoped and thought! And you will marry him, Jane, won't you? And then he will stay in England.'

'Far from that, Diana; his sole idea in proposing to me is to procure a fitting

fellow-labourer in his Indian toils.'

'What! He wishes you to go to India?'

'Yes.'

'Madness!' she exclaimed. 'You would not live three months there, I am certain. You never shall go: you have not consented—have you, Jane?'

'I have refused to marry him——'

'And have consequently displeased him?' she suggested.

'Deeply: he will never forgive me, I fear: yet I offered to accompany him as his sister.'

'It was frantic folly to do so, Jane. Think of the task you undertook—one of incessant fatigue: where fatigue kills even the strong; and you are weak. St. John—you know him—would urge you to impossibilities—with him there would be no permission to rest during the hot hours; and unfortunately, I have noticed, whatever he exacts, you force yourself to perform. I am astonished you found courage to refuse his hand. You do not love him then, Jane?'

'Not as a husband.'

'Yet he is a handsome fellow.'

'And I am so plain you see, Die. We should never suit.'

'Plain! You? Not at all. You are much too pretty, as well as too good, to be grilled alive in Calcutta.' And again she earnestly conjured me to give up all thoughts of going out with her brother.

'I must, indeed,' I said: 'for when just now I repeated the offer of serving him for a deacon, he expressed himself shocked at my want of decency. He seemed to think I had committed an impropriety in proposing to accompany him unmarried: as if I had not from the first hoped to find in him a brother; and habitually regarded him as such.'

'What makes you say he does not love you, Jane?'

'You should hear himself on the subject. He has again and again explained that it is not himself, but his office he wishes to mate. He has told me I am formed for labour—not for love: which is true, no doubt. But, in my opinion, if I am not formed for love, it follows that I am not formed for marriage. Would it not be strange, Die, to be chained for life to a man who regarded one but as a useful tool?'

'Insupportable—unnatural—out of the question!'

'And then,' I continued, 'though I have only sisterly affection for him now, yet, if forced to be his wife, I can imagine the possibility of conceiving an inevitable, strange, torturing kind of love for him: because he is so talented; and there is often a certain heroic grandeur in his look, manner, and conversation. In that case, my lot would become unspeakably wretched. He would not want me to love him; and if I showed the feeling, he would make me sensible that it was a superfluity unrequired by him, unbecoming in me. I know he would.'

'And yet, St. John is a good man,' said Diana.

'He is a good and a great man: but he forgets, pitilessly, the feelings and claims of little people, in pursuing his own large views. It is better, therefore, for the insignificant to keep out of his way; lest, in his progress, he should trample them down. Here he comes! I will leave you, Diana.' And I hastened upstairs, as I saw him entering the garden.

But I was forced to meet him again at supper. During that meal he appeared just as composed as usual. I had thought he would hardly speak to me, and I was certain he had given up the pursuit of his matrimonial scheme: the sequel showed I was mistaken on both points. He addressed me precisely in his ordinary manner; or what had, of late, been his ordinary manner; one scrupulously polite. No doubt he had invoked the help of the Holy Spirit to subdue the anger I had roused in him, and now believed he had forgiven me once more.

For the evening reading before prayers, he selected the twenty-first chapter of Revelation. It was at all times pleasant to listen, while from his lips fell the words of the Bible: never did his fine voice sound at once so sweet and full— never did his manner become so impressive in its noble simplicity, as when he delivered the oracles of God: and to-night that voice took a more solemn tone—that manner a more thrilling meaning—as he sat in the midst of his household circle (the May moon shining in through the uncurtained window and rendering almost unnecessary the light of the candle on the table): as he sat there, bending over the great old Bible, and described from its page the vision of the new heaven and the new earth—told how God would come to dwell with men, how he would wipe away all tears from their eyes, and promised that there should be no more death, neither sorrow nor crying, nor any more pain, because the former things were passed away.

The succeeding words thrilled me strangely as he spoke them: especially as I felt, by the slight, indescribable alteration in sound, that in uttering them his eye had turned on me.

'He that overcometh shall inherit all things; and I will be his God, and he shall be my son. But,' was slowly, distinctly read, 'the fearful, the unbelieving etc., shall have their part in the lake which burneth with fire and brimstone which is the second death.'

Henceforward, I knew what fate St. John feared for me.

A calm, subdued triumph, blent with a longing earnestness, marked his enunciation of the last glorious verses of that chapter. The reader believed his name was already written in the Lamb's book of life, and he yearned after the hour which should admit him to the city to which the kings of the earth bring their glory and honour; which has no need of sun or moon to shine in it, because the glory of God lightens it, and the Lamb is the light thereof.

In the prayer following the chapter, all his energy gathered—all his stern

zeal woke: he was in deep earnest, wrestling with God, and resolved on a conquest. He supplicated strength for the weak-hearted; guidance for wanderers from the fold: a return, even at the eleventh hour, for those whom the temptations of the world and the flesh were luring from the narrow path. He asked, he urged, he claimed the boon of a brand snatched from the burning. Earnestness is ever deeply solemn: first, as I listened to that prayer, I wondered at his; then, when it continued and rose, I was touched by it, and at last awed. He felt the greatness and goodness of his purpose so sincerely: others who heard him plead for it, could not but feel it too.

The prayer over, we took leave of him: he was to go at a very early hour in the morning. Diana and Mary having kissed him, left the room—in compliance, I think, with a whispered hint from him: I tendered my hand, and wished him a pleasant journey.

'Thank you, Jane. As I said, I shall return from Cambridge in a fortnight: that space, then, is yet left you for reflection. If I listened to human pride, I should say no more to you of marriage with me; but I listen to my duty, and keep steadily in view my first aim—to do all things to the glory of God. My Master was long-suffering: so will I be. I cannot give you up to perdition as a vessel of wrath: repent—resolve; while there is yet time. Remember, we are bid to work while it is day—warned that "the night cometh when no man shall work." Remember the fate of Dives, who had his good things in this life. God give you strength to choose that better part which shall not be taken from you!'

He laid his hand on my head as he uttered the last words. He had spoken earnestly, mildly: his look was not, indeed, that of a lover beholding his mistress; but it was that of a pastor recalling his wandering sheep—or better, of a guardian angel watching the soul for which he is responsible. All men of talent, whether they be men of feeling or not; whether they be zealots, or aspirants, or despots—provided only they be sincere—have their sublime moments: when they subdue and rule. I felt veneration for St. John—veneration so strong that its impetus thrust me at once to the point I had so long shunned. I was tempted to cease struggling with him—to rush down the torrent of his will into the gulf of his existence, and there lose my own. I was almost as hard beset by him now as I had been once before, in a different way, by another. I was a fool both times. To have yielded then would have been an error of principle; to have yielded now would have been an error of judgment. So I think at this hour, when I look back to the crisis through the ' quiet medium of time: I was unconscious of folly at the instant.

I stood motionless under my hierophant's touch. My refusals were forgotten —my fears overcome—my wrestlings paralysed. The Impossible—*i.e.* my marriage with St. John—was fast becoming the Possible. All was changing utterly, with a sudden sweep. Religion called—Angels beckoned—God

commanded—life rolled together like a scroll—death's gates opening, showed eternity beyond: it seemed, that for safety and bliss there, all here might be sacrificed in a second. The dim room was full of visions.

'Could you decide now?' asked the missionary. The inquiry was put in gentle tones: he drew me to him gently. Oh, that gentleness! how far more potent is it than force! I could resist St. John's wrath: I grew pliant as a reed under his kindness. Yet I knew all the time, if I yielded now, I should not the less be made to repent, some day, of my former rebellion. His nature was not changed by one hour of solemn prayer: it was only elevated.

'I could decide if I were but certain,' I answered: 'were I but convinced that it is God's will I should marry you, I could vow to marry you here and now—come afterwards what would!'

'My prayers are heard!' ejaculated St. John. He pressed his hand firmer on my head, as if he claimed me: he surrounded me with his arm, *almost* as if he loved me (I say *almost*—I knew the difference—for I had felt what it was to be loved; but, like him, I had now put love out of the question, and thought only of duty): I contended with my inward dimness of vision, before which clouds yet rolled. I sincerely, deeply, fervently longed to do what was right; and only that. 'Show me, show me the path!' I entreated of Heaven. I was excited more than I had ever been; and whether what followed was the effect of excitement, the reader shall judge.

All the house was still; for I believe all, except St. John and myself, were now retired to rest. The one candle was dying out: the room was full of moonlight. My heart beat fast and thick: I heard its throb. Suddenly it stood still to an inexpressible feeling that thrilled it through, and passed at once to my head and extremities. The feeling was not like an electric shock; but it was quite as sharp, as strange, as startling: it acted on my senses as if their utmost activity hitherto had been but torpor; from which they were now summoned and forced to wake. They rose expectant: eye and ear waited, while the flesh quivered on my bones.

'What have you heard? What do you see?' asked St. John. I saw nothing but I heard a voice somewhere cry—

'Jane! Jane! Jane!' nothing more.

'Oh God! what is it?' I gasped.

I might have said, 'Where is it?' for it did not seem in the room—nor in the house—nor in the garden: it did not come out of the air—nor from under the earth—nor from overhead. I had heard it—where, or whence, for ever impossible to know! And it was the voice of a human being—a known, loved, well-remembered voice—that of Edward Fairfax Rochester; and it spoke in pain and woe wildly, eerily, urgently.

'I am coming!' I cried. 'Wait for me! Oh, I will come!' I flew to the door and looked into the passage: it was dark. I ran out into the garden: it was void

'Where are you?' I exclaimed.

The hills beyond Marsh Glen sent the answer faintly back—'Where are you?' I listened. The wind sighed low in the firs: all was moorland loneliness and midnight hush.

'Down superstition!' I commented, as that spectre rose up black by the black yew at the gate. 'This is not thy deception, not thy witchcraft: it is the work of nature. She was roused, and did—no miracle—but her best.'

I broke from St. John; who had followed, and would have detained me. It was *my* time to assume ascendancy. *My* powers were in play, and in force. I told him to forbear question or remark; I desired him to leave me: I must, and would be alone. He obeyed at once. Where there is energy to command well enough, obedience never fails. I mounted to my chamber; locked myself in; fell on my knees; and prayed in my way—a different way to St. John's, but effective in its own fashion. I seemed to penetrate very near a Mighty Spirit; and my soul rushed out in gratitude at His feet. I rose from the thanksgiving—took a resolve—and lay down, unscared, enlightened—eager but for the daylight.

CHAPTER 36

The daylight came. I rose at dawn. I busied myself for an hour or two with arranging my things in my chamber, drawers and wardrobe, in the order wherein I should wish to leave them during a brief absence. Meantime, I heard St. John quit his room. He stopped at my door: I feared he would knock—no, but a slip of paper was passed under the door. I took it up. It bore these words—

'You left me too suddenly last night. Had you stayed but a little longer, you would have laid your hand on the Christian's cross and the angel's crown. shall expect your clear decision when I return this day fortnight. Meantime, watch and pray that you enter not into temptation: the spirit, I trust, is willing, but the flesh, I see, is weak. I shall pray for you hourly,—Yours, St. John.'

'My spirit,' I answered, mentally, 'is willing to do what is right; and my flesh, I hope, is strong enough to accomplish the will of Heaven, when once that will is distinctly known to me. At any rate, it shall be strong enough to search—inquire—to grope an outlet from this crowd of doubt, and find the open day of certainty.'

It was the first of June; yet the morning was overcast and chilly: rain beat fast on my casement. I heard the front-door open, and St. John pass out. Looking through the window, I saw him traverse the garden. He took the way over the misty moors in the direction of Whitcross—there he would meet the coach.

'In a few more hours I shall succeed you in that track, cousin,' thought I: 'I too have a coach to meet at Whitcross. I too have some to see and ask after in England, before I depart for ever.'

It wanted yet two hours of breakfast-time. I filled the interval in walking softly about my room, and pondering the visitation which had given my plans their present bent. I recalled that inward sensation I had experienced: for I could recall it, with all its unspeakable strangeness. I recalled the voice I had heard; again I questioned whence it came, as vainly as before: it seemed in *me*—not in the external world. I asked, was it a mere nervous impression—a delusion? I could not conceive or believe: it was more like an inspiration. The wondrous shock of feeling had come like the earthquake which shook the foundations of Paul and Silas's prison; it had opened the doors of the soul's cell, and loosed its bands—it had wakened it out of its sleep, whence it sprang trembling, listening, aghast; then vibrated thrice a cry on my startled ear, and in my quaking heart, and through my spirit; which neither feared nor shook, but exulted as if in joy over the success of one effort it had been privileged to make, independent of the cumbrous body.

'Ere many days,' I said, as I terminated my musings, 'I will know something of him whose voice seemed last night to summon me. Letters have proved of no avail—personal inquiry shall replace them.'

At breakfast I announced to Diana and Mary that I was going a journey and should be absent at least four days.

'Alone, Jane?' they asked.

'Yes; it was to see, or hear news of, a friend about whom I had for some time been uneasy.'

They might have said, as I have no doubt they thought, that they had believed me to be without any friends save them: for, indeed, I had often said so; but with their true natural delicacy, they abstained from comment except that Diana asked me if I was sure I was well enough to travel. I looked very pale, she observed. I replied, that nothing ailed me save anxiety of mind which I hoped soon to alleviate.

It was easy to make my further arrangements; for I was troubled with no inquiries—no surmises. Having once explained to them that I could not now be explicit about my plans, they kindly and wisely acquiesced in the silence with which I pursued them; according to me the privilege of free action I should, under similar circumstances, have accorded them.

I left Moor House at three o'clock P.M., and soon after four, I stood at the foot of the sign-post of Whitcross, waiting the arrival of the coach which was to take me to distant Thornfield. Amidst the silence of those solitary roads and desert hills, I heard it approach from a great distance. It was the same vehicle whence, a year ago, I had alighted one summer evening on this very spot—how desolate, and hopeless, and objectless! It stopped as I beckoned. I entered-

not now obliged to part with my whole fortune as the price of its accommodation. Once more on the road to Thornfield, I felt like the messenger-pigeon flying home.

It was a journey of six-and-thirty hours. I had set out from Whitcross on a Tuesday afternoon, and early on the succeeding Thursday morning the coach stopped to water the horses at a wayside inn, situated in the midst of scenery whose green hedges and large fields, and low pastoral hills (how mild of feature and verdant of hue compared with the stern north-midland moors of Morton!) met my eye like the lineaments of a once familiar face. Yes, I knew the character of this landscape: I was sure we were near my bourne.

'How far is Thornfield Hall from here?' I asked of the ostler.

'Just two miles, ma'am, across the fields.'

'My journey is closed,' I thought to myself. I got out of the coach, gave a box I had into the ostler's charge, to be kept till I called for it; paid my fare; satisfied the coachman, and was going: the brightening day gleamed on the sign of the inn, and I read in gilt letters, 'The Rochester Arms.' My heart leapt up: I was already on my master's very lands. It fell again: the thought struck it:—

'Your master himself may be beyond the British Channel, for aught you know: and then, if he is at Thornfield Hall, towards which you hasten, who besides him is there? His lunatic wife: and you have nothing to do with him: you dare not speak to him or seek his presence. You have lost your labour—you had better go no farther,' urged the monitor. 'Ask information of the people at the inn; they can give you all you seek: they can solve your doubts at once. Go up to that man, and inquire if Mr. Rochester be at home.'

The suggestion was sensible; and yet I could not force myself to act on it. So dreaded a reply that would crush me with despair. To prolong doubt was to prolong hope. I might yet once more see the Hall under the ray of her star. There was the stile before me—the very fields through which I had hurried, blind, deaf, distracted, with a revengeful fury tracking and scourging me, on the morning I fled from Thornfield: ere I well knew what course I had resolved to take, I was in the midst of them. How fast I walked! How I ran sometimes! How I looked forward to catch the first view of the well-known woods! With what feelings I welcomed single trees I knew, and familiar glimpses of meadow and hill between them!

At last the woods rose; the rookery clustered dark; a loud cawing broke the morning stillness. Strange delight inspired me: on I hastened. Another field crossed—a lane threaded—and there were the courtyard walls—the back offices: the house itself, the rookery still hid. 'My first view of it shall be in front,' I determined, 'where its bold battlements will strike the eye nobly at once, and where I can single out my master's very window: perhaps he will be standing at it—he rises early: perhaps he is now walking in the orchard, or

on the pavement in front. Could I but see him!—but a moment! Surely, in that case, I should not be so mad as to run to him? I cannot tell—I am not certain. And if I did—what then? God bless him! What then? Who would be hurt by my once more tasting the life his glance can give me—I rave: perhaps at this moment he is watching the sun rise over the Pyrenees, or on the tideless sea of the south.'

I had coasted along the lower wall of the orchard—turned its angle: there was a gate just there, opening into the meadow, between two stone pillars, crowned by stone balls. From behind one pillar, I could peep round quietly at the full front of the mansion. I advanced my head with precaution, desirous to ascertain if any bedroom window-blinds were yet drawn up: battlements, windows, long front—all from this sheltered station were at my command.

The crows sailing overhead perhaps watched me while I took this survey. I wonder what they thought: they must have considered I was very careful and timid at first, and that gradually I grew very bold and reckless. A peep, and then a long stare; and then a departure from my niche and a straying out into the meadow; and a sudden stop full in front of the great mansion, and a protracted, hardy gaze towards it. 'What affectation of diffidence was this at first?' they might have demanded, 'What stupid regardlessness now?'

Hear an illustration, reader.

A lover finds his mistress asleep on a mossy bank; he wishes to catch a glimpse of her fair face without waking her. He steals softly over the grass, careful to make no sound; he pauses—fancying she has stirred: he withdraws; not for worlds would he be seen. All is still: he again advances: he bends over her; a light veil rests on her features: he lifts it, bends lower; now his eyes anticipate the vision of beauty—warm, and blooming, and lovely, in rest. How hurried was their first glance! But how they fix! How he starts! How he suddenly and vehemently clasps in both arms the form he dared not, a moment since, touch with his finger! How he calls aloud a name, and drops his burden, and gazes on it wildly! He thus grasps and cries, and gazes, because he no longer fears to waken by any sound he can utter—by any movement he can make. He thought his love slept sweetly: he finds she is stone-dead.

I looked with timorous joy towards a stately house: I saw a blackened ruin.

No need to cower behind a gate-post, indeed!—to peep up at chamber lattices, fearing life was astir behind them! No need to listen for doors opening —to fancy steps on the pavement or the gravel-walk! The lawn, the grounds were trodden and waste: the portal yawned void. The front was, as I had once seen it in a dream, but a shell-like wall, very high and very fragile looking, perforated with paneless windows: no roof, no battlements, no chimneys—all had crashed in.

And there was the silence of death about it: the solitude of a lonesome wild. No wonder that letters addressed to people here had never received an answer:

as well despatch epistles to a vault in a church aisle. The grim blackness of the stones told by what fate the Hall had fallen—by conflagration: but how kindled? What story belonged to this disaster? What loss, besides mortar and marble, and woodwork, had followed upon it? Had life been wrecked, as well as property? If so, whose? Dreadful question: there was no one here to answer it—not even dumb sign, mute token.

In wandering round the shattered walls and through the devastated interior, I gathered evidence that the calamity was not of late occurrence. Winter snows, I thought, had drifted through that void arch; winter rains beaten in at those hollow casements; for, amidst the drenched piles of rubbish, spring had cherished vegetation: grass and weed grew here and there between the stones and fallen rafters. And oh! where, meantime, was the hapless owner of this wreck? In what land? Under what auspices? My eye involuntarily wandered to the grey church tower near the gates, and I asked, 'Is he with Damer de Rochester, sharing the shelter of his narrow marble house?'

Some answer must be had to these questions. I could find it nowhere but at the inn, and thither, ere long, I returned. The host himself brought my breakfast into the parlour. I requested him to shut the door and sit down: I had some questions to ask him. But when he complied, I scarcely knew how to begin; such horror had I of the possible answers. And yet the spectacle of desolation I had just left, prepared me in a measure for a tale of misery. The host was a respectable-looking, middle-aged man.

'You know Thornfield Hall, of course?' I managed to say at last.

'Yes, ma'am; I lived there once.'

'Did you?' Not in my time, I thought; you are a stranger to me.

'I was the late Mr. Rochester's butler,' he added.

The late! I seemed to have received with full force, the blow I had been trying to evade.

'The late!' I gasped. 'Is he dead?'

'I mean the present gentleman, Mr. Edward's father,' he explained. I breathed again: my blood resumed its flow. Fully assured by these words that Mr. Edward—_my_ Mr. Rochester (God bless him, wherever he was!) was at least alive: was, in short, 'the present gentleman.' Gladdening words! It seemed I could hear all that was to come—whatever the disclosures might be—with comparative tranquillity. Since he was not in the grave, I could bear, I thought, to learn that he was at the Antipodes.

'Is Mr. Rochester living at Thornfield now?' I asked, knowing, of course, what the answer would be, but yet desirous of deferring the direct question as to where he really was.

'No, ma'am—oh, no! No one is living there. I suppose you are a stranger in these parts, or you would have heard what happened last autumn,—Thornfield Hall is quite a ruin: it was burnt down just about harvest time. A dreadful

calamity! such an immense quantity of valuable property destroyed: hardly any of the furniture could be saved. The fire broke out at dead of night, and before the engines arrived from Millcote, the building was one mass of flame. It was a terrible spectacle: I witnessed it myself.'

'At dead of night!' I muttered. Yes, that was ever the hour of fatality at Thornfield. 'Was it known how it originated?' I demanded.

'They guessed, ma'am: they guessed. Indeed, I should say it was ascertained beyond a doubt. You are not perhaps aware,' he continued, edging his chair a little nearer the table, and speaking low, 'that there was a lady,—a—a lunatic, kept in the house?'

'I have heard something of it.'

'She was kept in very close confinement, ma'am; people even for years was not absolutely certain of her existence. No one saw her: they only knew by rumour that such a person was at the Hall; and who or what she was it was difficult to conjecture. They said Mr. Edward had brought her from abroad; and some believed she had been his mistress. But a queer thing happened a year since—a very queer thing.'

I feared now to hear my own story. I endeavoured to recall him to the main fact.

'And this lady?'

'This lady, ma'am,' he answered, 'turned out to be Mr. Rochester's wife! The discovery was brought about in the strangest way. There was a young lady, a governess at the Hall, that Mr. Rochester fell in'——

'But the fire,' I suggested.

'I'm coming to that, ma'am—that Mr. Edward fell in love with. The servants say they never saw anybody so much in love as he was: he was after her continually. They used to watch him—servants will, you know, ma'am—and he set store on her past everything: for all, nobody but him thought her so very handsome. She was a little small thing, they say, almost like a child. I never saw her myself; but I've heard Leah, the housemaid, tell of her. Leah liked her well enough. Mr. Rochester was about forty, and this governess not twenty; and you see, when gentlemen of his age fall in love with girls, they are often like as if they were bewitched: well, he would marry her.'

'You shall tell me this part of the story another time,' I said; 'but now I have a particular reason for wishing to hear all about the fire. Was it suspected that this lunatic, Mrs. Rochester, had any hand in it?'

'You've hit it, ma'am: it's quite certain that it was her and nobody but her that set it going. She had a woman to take care of her called Mrs. Poole—an able woman in her line, and very trustworthy, but for one fault—a fault common to a deal of them nurses and matrons—*she kept a private bottle of gin by her*, and now and then took a drop over much. It is excusable, for she had a hard life of it: but still it was dangerous; for when Mrs. Poole was fast asleep

after the gin and water, the mad lady, who was as cunning as a witch, would take the keys out of her pocket, let herself out of her chamber, and go roaming about the house, doing any wild mischief that came into her head. They say she had nearly burnt her husband in his bed once: but I don't know about that. However, on this night, she set fire first to the hangings of the room next to her own; and then she got down to a lower story, and made her way to the chamber that had been the governess's—(she was like as if she knew somehow matters had gone on, and had a spite at her)—and she kindled the bed there; but there was nobody sleeping in it fortunately. The governess had run away two months before; and for all Mr. Rochester sought her as if she had been the most precious thing he had in the world, he never could hear a word of her; and he grew savage—quite savage on his disappointment: he never was a wild man, but he got dangerous after he lost her. He would be alone, too. He sent Mrs. Fairfax, the housekeeper, away to her friends at a distance; but he did it handsomely, for he settled an annuity on her for life: and she deserved it—she was a very good woman. Miss Adèle, a ward he had, was put to school. He broke off acquaintance with all the gentry, and shut himself up, like a hermit, at the Hall.'

'What! did he not leave England?'

'Leave England? Bless you, no! He would not cross the door-stones of the house; except at night, when he walked just like a ghost about the grounds and in the orchard as if he had lost his senses—which it is my opinion he had; for a more spirited, bolder, keener gentleman than he was before that midge of a governess crossed him, you never saw, ma'am. He was not a man given to wine, or cards, or racing, as some are, and he was not so very handsome; but he had a courage and a will of his own, if ever man had. I knew him from a boy, you see: and for my part I have often wished that Miss Eyre had been sunk in the sea before she came to Thornfield Hall.'

'Then Mr. Rochester was at home when the fire broke out?'

'Yes, indeed was he; and he went up to the attics when all was burning above and below, and got the servants out of their beds and helped them down himself—and went back to get his mad wife out of her cell. And then they called out to him that she was on the roof; where she was standing, waving her arms, above the battlements, and shouting out till they could hear her a mile off: I saw her and heard her with my own eyes. She was a big woman, and had long, black hair: we could see it streaming against the flames as she stood. I witnessed, and several more witnessed Mr. Rochester ascend through the skylight on to the roof: we heard him call "Bertha!" We saw him approach her; and then, ma'am, she yelled, and gave a spring, and the next minute she lay smashed on the pavement.'

'Dead?'

'Dead? Ay, dead as the stones on which her brains and blood were scattered.'

'Good God!'

'You may well say so, ma'am: it was frightful!'

He shuddered.

'And afterwards?' I urged.

'Well, ma'am, afterwards the house was burnt to the ground: there are only some bits of walls standing now.'

'Were any other lives lost?'

'No—perhaps it would have been better if there had.'

'What do you mean?'

'Poor Mr. Edward!' he ejaculated, 'I little thought ever to have seen it! Some say it was a just judgment on him for keeping his first marriage secret, and wanting to take another wife while he had one living: but I pity him, for my part.'

'You said he was alive?' I exclaimed.

'Yes, yes: he is alive; but many think he had better be dead.'

'Why? How?' My blood was again running cold.

'Where is he?' I demanded. 'Is he in England?'

'Ay—ay—he's in England; he can't get out of England, I fancy—he's a fixture now.'

What agony was this! And the man seemed resolved to protract it.

'He is stone-blind,' he said at last. 'Yes—he is stone-blind—is Mr. Edward.'

I had dreaded worse. I had dreaded he was mad. I summoned strength to ask what had caused this calamity.

'It was all his own courage, and a body may say, his kindness, in a way, ma'am: he wouldn't leave the house till every one else was out before him. As he came down the great staircase at last, after Mrs. Rochester had flung herself from the battlements, there was a great crash—all fell. He was taken out from under the ruins, alive, but sadly hurt: a beam had fallen in such a way as to protect him partly; but one eye was knocked out, and one hand so crushed that Mr. Carter, the surgeon, had to amputate it directly. The other eye inflamed: he lost the sight of that also. He is now helpless, indeed—blind and a cripple.'

'Where is he? Where does he now live?'

'At Ferndean, a manor-house on a farm he has, about thirty miles off quite a desolate spot.'

'Who is with him?'

'Old John and his wife: he would have none else. He is quite broken down they say.'

'Have you any sort of conveyance?'

'We have a chaise, ma'am, a very handsome chaise.'

'Let it be got ready instantly; and if your post-boy can drive me to Ferndean before dark this day, I'll pay both you and him twice the hire you usually demand.

CHAPTER 37

The manor-house of Ferndean was a building of considerable antiquity, moderate size, and no architectural pretensions, deep buried in a wood. I had heard of it before. Mr. Rochester often spoke of it, and sometimes went there. His father had purchased the estate for the sake of the game covers. He would have let the house: but could find no tenant, in consequence of its ineligible and insalubrious site. Ferndean then remained uninhabited and unfurnished; with the exception of some two or three rooms fitted up for the accommodation of the squire when he went there in the season to shoot.

To this house I came, just ere dark, on an evening marked by the characteristics of sad sky, cold gale, and continued small, penetrating rain. The last mile I performed on foot, having dismissed the chaise and driver with the double remuneration I had promised. Even when within a very short distance of the manor-house, you could see nothing of it; so thick and dark grew the timber of the gloomy wood about it. Iron gates between granite pillars showed me where to enter, and passing through them, I found myself at once in the twilight of close-ranked trees. There was a grass-grown track descending the forest aisle, between hoar and knotty shafts and under branched arches. I followed it, expecting soon to reach the dwelling; but it stretched on and on, it wound far and farther: no sign of habitation or grounds was visible.

I thought I had taken a wrong direction and lost my way. The darkness of natural as well as of sylvan dusk gathered over me. I looked round in search of another road. There was none: all was interwoven stem, columnar trunk, dense, summer foliage—no opening anywhere.

I proceeded: at last my way opened, the trees thinned a little; presently I beheld a railing, then the house—scarce, by this dim light, distinguishable from the trees; so dank and green were its decaying walls. Entering a portal, fastened only by a latch, I stood amidst a space of enclosed ground, from which the wood swept away in a semicircle. There were no flowers, no garden-beds; only a broad gravel-walk girdling a grass-plat, and this set in the heavy frame of the forest. The house presented two pointed gables in its front: the windows were latticed and narrow: the front-door was narrow too, one step led up to it. The whole looked, as the host of the Rochester Arms had said, 'quite a desolate spot.' It was as still as a church on a week-day: the pattering rain on the forest leaves was the only sound audible in its vicinage.

'Can there be life here?' I asked.

Yes: life of some kind there was; for I heard a movement—that narrow front-door was unclosing, and some shape was about to issue from the grange.

It opened slowly; a figure came out into the twilight and stood on the step; a man without a hat: he stretched forth his hand as if to feel whether it rained. Dusk as it was, I had recognised him—it was my master, Edward Fairfax

Rochester, and no other.

I stayed my step, almost my breath, and stood to watch him—to examine him, myself unseen, and alas! to him invisible. It was a sudden meeting, and one in which rapture was kept well in check by pain. I had no difficulty in restraining my voice from exclamation, my step from hasty advance.

His form was of the same strong and stalwart contour as ever: his port was still erect, his hair was still raven-black; nor were his features altered or sunk: not in one year's space, by any sorrow, could his athletic strength be quelled, or his vigorous prime blighted. But in his countenance, I saw a change: that looked desperate and brooding—that reminded me of some wronged and fettered wild beast or bird, dangerous to approach in his sullen woe. The caged eagle, whose gold-ringed eyes cruelty has extinguished, might look as looked that sightless Samson.

And, reader, do you think I feared him in his blind ferocity?—if you do, you little know me. A soft hope blent with my sorrow that soon I should dare to drop a kiss on that brow of rock, and on those lips so sternly sealed beneath it: but not yet. I would not accost him yet.

He descended the one step, and advanced slowly and gropingly towards the grass-plat. Where was his daring stride now? Then he paused, as if he knew not which way to turn. He lifted his hand and opened his eyelids; gazed blank, and with a straining effort, on the sky, and towards the amphitheatre of trees: one saw that all to him was void darkness. He stretched his right hand (the left arm, the mutilated one, he kept hidden in his bosom); he seemed to wish by touch to gain an idea of what lay around him: he met but vacancy still; for the trees were some yards off where he stood. He relinquished the endeavour, folded his arms, and stood quiet and mute in the rain, now falling fast on his uncovered head. At this moment John approached him from some quarter.

'Will you take my arm, sir?' he said; 'there is a heavy shower coming on; had you not better go in?'

'Let me alone,' was the answer.

John withdrew, without having observed me. Mr. Rochester now tried to walk about: vainly,—all was too uncertain. He groped his way back to the house, and, re-entering it, closed the door.

I now drew near and knocked: John's wife opened for me. 'Mary,' I said 'how are you?'

She started as if she had seen a ghost: I calmed her. To her hurried 'Is it really you, miss, come at this late hour to this 'only place?' I answered by taking her hand; and then I followed her into the kitchen, where John now sat by a good fire. I explained to them, in a few words, that I had heard all which had happened since I left Thornfield, and that I was come to see Mr. Rochester. I asked John to go down to the turnpike-house, where I had dismissed the chaise, and bring my trunk, which I had left there: and then

while I removed my bonnet and shawl, I questioned Mary as to whether I could be accommodated at the Manor House for the night; and finding that arrangements to that effect, though difficult, would not be impossible, I informed her I should stay. Just at this moment the parlour-bell rang.

'When you go in,' said I, 'tell your master that a person wishes to speak to him, but do not give my name.'

'I don't think he will see you,' she answered; 'he refuses every body.'

When she returned, I inquired what he had said.

'You are to send in your name and your business,' she replied. She then proceeded to fill a glass with water, and place it on a tray, together with candles.

'Is that what he rang for?' I asked.

'Yes: he always has candles brought in at dark, though he is blind.'

'Give the tray to me, I will carry it in.'

I took it from her hand: she pointed me out the parlour door. The tray shook as I held it; the water spilt from the glass; my heart struck my ribs loud and fast. Mary opened the door for me, and shut it behind me.

This parlour looked gloomy: a neglected handful of fire burnt low in the grate; and, leaning over it, with his head supported against the high, old-fashioned mantel-piece, appeared the blind tenant of the room. His old dog, Pilot, lay on one side, removed out of the way, and coiled up as if afraid of being inadvertently trodden upon. Pilot pricked up his ears when I came in: then he jumped up with a yelp and a whine, and bounded towards me: he almost knocked the tray from my hands. I set it on the table; then patted him, and said softly, 'Lie down!' Mr. Rochester turned mechanically to *see* what the commotion was: but as he *saw* nothing, he returned and sighed.

'Give me the water, Mary,' he said.

I approached him with the now only half-filled glass. Pilot followed me, still excited.

'What is the matter?' he inquired.

'Down, Pilot!' I again said. He checked the water on its way to his lips, and seemed to listen: he drank, and put the glass down. 'This is you, Mary, is it not?'

'Mary is in the kitchen,' I answered.

He put out his hand with a quick gesture, but not seeing where I stood, he did not touch me. 'Who is this? Who is this?' he demanded, trying, as it seemed, to *see* with those sightless eyes—unavailing and distressing attempt! Answer me—speak again!' he ordered, imperiously and aloud.

'Will you have a little more water, sir? I spilt half of what was in the glass,' said.

'*Who* is it? *What* is it? Who speaks?'

'Pilot knows me, and John and Mary know I am here. I came only this

evening,' I answered.

'Great God!—what delusion has come over me? What sweet madness has seized me?'

'No delusion—no madness: your mind, sir, is too strong for delusion, your health too sound for frenzy.'

'And where is the speaker? Is it only a voice? Oh! I *cannot* see, but I must feel, or my heart will stop and my brain burst. Whatever—whoever you are—be perceptible to the touch or I cannot live!'

He groped; I arrested his wandering hand, and prisoned it in both mine.

'Her very fingers!' he cried; 'her small, slight fingers! If so, there must be more of her.'

The muscular hand broke from my custody; my arm was seized, my shoulder —neck—waist—I was entwined and gathered to him.

'Is it Jane? *What* is it? This is her shape—this is her size'——

'And this her voice,' I added. 'She is all here: her heart, too. God bless you sir! I am glad to be so near you again.'

'Jane Eyre!—Jane Eyre,' was all he said.

'My dear master,' I answered, 'I am Jane Eyre: I have found you out—I am come back to you.'

'In truth?—in the flesh? My living Jane?'

'You touch me, sir,—you hold me, and fast enough: I am not like a corpse nor vacant like air, am I?'

'My living darling! These are certainly her limbs, and these her features but I cannot be so blest, after all my misery. It is a dream; such dreams a I have had at night when I have clasped her once more to my heart, as I do now; and kissed her, as thus—and felt that she loved me, and trusted that she would not leave me.'

'Which I never will, sir, from this day.'

'Never will, says the vision? But I always woke and found it an empty mockery; and I was desolate and abandoned—my life dark, lonely, hopeless— my soul athirst and forbidden to drink—my heart famished and never to be fed Gentle, soft dream, nestling in my arms now, you will fly, too, as your sister have all fled before you: but kiss me before you go—embrace me, Jane.'

'There, sir—and there!'

I pressed my lips to his once brilliant and now rayless eyes—I swept his hair from his brow, and kissed that too. He suddenly seemed to arouse himself: the conviction of the reality of all this seized him.

'It is you—is it, Jane? You are come back to me, then?'

'I am.'

'And you do not lie dead in some ditch under some stream? And you are not a pining outcast amongst strangers?'

'No, sir; I am an independent woman now.'

'Independent! What do you mean, Jane?'

'My uncle in Madeira is dead, and he left me five thousand pounds.'

'Ah, this is practical—this is real!' he cried: 'I should never dream that. Besides, there is that peculiar voice of hers, so animating and piquant, as well as soft: it cheers my withered heart; it puts life into it.—What, Janet! Are you an independent woman? A rich woman?'

'Quite rich, sir. If you won't let me live with you, I can build a house of my own close up to your door, and you may come and sit in my parlour when you want company of an evening.'

'But as you are rich, Jane, you have now, no doubt, friends who will look after you, and not suffer you to devote yourself to a blind lameter like me?'

'I told you I am independent, sir, as well as rich: I am my own mistress.'

'And you will stay with me?'

'Certainly—unless you object. I will be your neighbour, your nurse, your housekeeper. I find you lonely: I will be your companion—to read to you, to walk with you, to sit with you, to wait on you, to be eyes and hands to you. Cease to look so melancholy, my dear master; you shall not be left desolate, so long as I live.'

He replied not: he seemed serious—abstracted; he sighed; he half-opened his lips as if to speak: he closed them again. I felt a little embarrassed. Perhaps I had too rashly overleaped conventionalities; and he, like St. John, saw impropriety in my inconsiderateness. I had indeed made my proposal from the idea that he wished and would ask me to be his wife: an expectation, not the less certain because unexpressed, had buoyed me up, that he would claim me at once as his own. But no hint to that effect escaping him and his countenance becoming more overcast, I suddenly remembered that I might have been all wrong, and was perhaps playing the fool unwittingly; and I began gently to withdraw myself from his arms—but he eagerly snatched me closer.

'No—no—Jane; you must not go. No—I have touched you, heard you, felt the comfort of your presence—the sweetness of your consolation: I cannot give up these joys. I have little left in myself—I must have you. The world may laugh—may call me absurd, selfish—but it does not signify. My very soul demands you: it will be satisfied: or it will take deadly vengeance on its frame.'

'Well, sir, I will stay with you: I have said so.'

'Yes—but you understand one thing by staying with me: and I understand another. You, perhaps, could make up your mind to be about my hand and chair—to wait on me as a kind little nurse (for you have an affectionate heart and a generous spirit, which prompt you to make sacrifices for those you pity), and that ought to suffice for me no doubt. I suppose I should now entertain none but fatherly feelings for you; do you think so? Come—tell me.'

'I will think what you like, sir: I am content to be only your nurse, if you think it better.'

'But you cannot always be my nurse, Janet: you are young—you must marry one day.'

'I don't care about being married.'

'You should care, Janet: if I were what I once was, I would try to make you care—but—a sightless block!'

He relapsed again into gloom. I, on the contrary, became more cheerful and took fresh courage: these last words gave me an insight as to where the difficulty lay; and as it was no difficulty with me, I felt quite relieved from my previous embarrassment. I resumed a livelier vein of conversation.

'It is time some one undertook to rehumanise you,' said I, parting his thick and long uncut locks; 'for I see you are being metamorphosed into a lion, or something of that sort. You have a "faux air" of Nebuchadnezzar in the field about you, that is certain: your hair reminds me of eagles' feathers; whether your nails are grown like birds' claws or not, I have not yet noticed.'

'On this arm, I have neither hand nor nails,' he said, drawing the mutilated limb from his breast, and showing it to me. 'It is a mere stump—a ghastly sight! Don't you think so, Jane?'

'It is a pity to see it; and a pity to see your eyes—and the scar of fire on your forehead: and the worst of it is, one is in danger of loving you too well for all this; and making too much of you.'

'I thought you would be revolted, Jane, when you saw my arm, and my cicatrised visage.'

'Did you? Don't tell me so—lest I should say something disparaging to your judgment. Now, let me leave you an instant, to make a better fire, and have the hearth swept up. Can you tell when there is a good fire?'

'Yes; with the right eye I see a glow—a ruddy haze.'

'And you see the candles?'

'Very dimly—each is a luminous cloud.'

'Can you see me?'

'No, my fairy: but I am only too thankful to hear and feel you.'

'When do you take supper?'

'I never take supper.'

'But you shall have some to-night. I am hungry: so are you, I daresay, only you forget.'

Summoning Mary, I soon had the room in more cheerful order: I prepared him, likewise, a comfortable repast. My spirits were excited, and with pleasure and ease I talked to him during supper, and for a long time after. There was no harassing restraint, no repressing of glee and vivacity with him; for with him I was at perfect ease, because I knew I suited him: all I said or did seemed either to console or revive him. Delightful consciousness! It brought to life and light my whole nature: in his presence I thoroughly lived; and he lived in mine. Blind as he was, smiles played over his face, joy dawned on his fore

head: his lineaments softened and warmed.

After supper, he began to ask me many questions, of where I had been, what I had been doing, how I had found him out; but I gave him only very partial replies: it was too late to enter into particulars that night. Besides, I wished to touch no deep-thrilling chord—to open no fresh well of emotion in his heart: my sole present aim was to cheer him. Cheered, as I have said, he was: and yet but by fits. If a moment's silence broke the conversation, he would turn restless, touch me, then say, 'Jane.'

'You are altogether a human being, Jane? You are certain of that?'

'I conscientiously believe so, Mr. Rochester.'

'Yet how, on this dark and doleful evening, could you so suddenly rise on my lone hearth? I stretched my hand to take a glass of water from a hireling, and it was given me by you: I asked a question, expecting John's wife to answer me, and your voice spoke at my ear.'

'Because I had come in, in Mary's stead, with the tray.'

'And there is enchantment in the very hour I am now spending with you. Who can tell what a dark, dreary, hopeless life I have dragged on for months past? Doing nothing, expecting nothing; merging night in day; feeling but the sensation of cold when I let the fire go out, of hunger when I forgot to eat: and then a ceaseless sorrow, and, at times, a very delirium of desire to behold my Jane again. Yes: for her restoration I longed, far more than for that of my lost sight. How can it be that Jane is with me, and says she loves me? Will she not depart as suddenly as she came? To-morrow, I fear I shall find her no more.'

A common-place, practical reply, out of the train of his own disturbed ideas, was, I was sure, the best and most reassuring for him in this frame of mind. I passed my finger over his eyebrows, and remarked that they were scorched, and that I would apply something which should make them grow as broad and black as ever.

'What is the use of doing me good in any way, beneficent spirit, when, at some fatal moment, you will again desert me—passing like a shadow, whither and how to me unknown; and for me, remaining afterwards undiscoverable?'

'Have you a pocket-comb about you, sir?'

'What for, Jane?'

'Just to comb out this shaggy black mane. I find you rather alarming, when I examine you close at hand: you talk of my being a fairy; but I am sure, you are more like a brownie.'

'Am I hideous, Jane?'

'Very, sir: you always were, you know.'

'Humph! The wickedness has not been taken out of you, wherever you have sojourned.'

'Yet I have been with good people; far better than you: a hundred times

better people; possessed of ideas and views you never entertained in your life: quite more refined and exalted.'

'Who the deuce have you been with?'

'If you twist in that way you will make me pull the hair out of your head; and then I think you will cease to entertain doubts of my substantiality.'

'Who have you been with, Jane?'

'You shall not get it out of me to-night, sir; you must wait till to-morrow; to leave my tale half-told, will, you know, be a sort of security that I shall appear at your breakfast-table to finish it. By-the-by, I must mind not to rise on your hearth with only a glass of water, then: I must bring an egg at the least, to say nothing of fried ham.'

'You mocking changeling—fairy-born and human-bred! You make me feel as I have not felt these twelve months. If Saul could have had you for his David, the evil spirit would have been exorcised without the aid of the harp.'

'There, sir, you are redd up and made decent. Now I'll leave you: I have been travelling these last three days, and I believe I am tired. Good-night.'

'Just one word, Jane: were there only ladies in the house where you have been?'

I laughed and made my escape, still laughing as I ran upstairs. 'A good idea!' I thought, with glee. 'I see I have the means of fretting him out of his melancholy for some time to come.'

Very early the next morning, I heard him up and astir, wandering from one room to another. As soon as Mary came down I heard the question: 'Is Miss Eyre here?' Then: 'Which room did you put her into? Was it dry? Is she up? Go and ask if she wants anything: and when she will come down.'

I came down as soon as I thought there was a prospect of breakfast. Entering the room very softly, I had a view of him before he discovered my presence. It was mournful, indeed, to witness the subjugation of that vigorous spirit to a corporeal infirmity. He sat in his chair,—still, but not at rest: expectant evidently; the lines of now habitual sadness marking his strong features. His countenance reminded one of a lamp quenched, waiting to be relit—and alas! it was not himself that could now kindle the lustre of animated expression: he was dependent on another for that office! I had meant to be gay and careless, but the powerlessness of the strong man touched my heart to the quick: still I accosted him with what vivacity I could:—

'It is a bright, sunny morning, sir,' I said. 'The rain is over and gone, and there is a tender shining after it: you shall have a walk soon.'

I had wakened the glow: his features beamed.

'Oh, you are indeed there, my skylark! Come to me. You are not gone: not vanished? I heard one of your kind an hour ago, singing high over the wood: but its song had no music for me, any more than the rising sun had rays. All the melody on earth is concentrated in my Jane's tongue to my ear (I am

glad it is not naturally a silent one): all the sunshine I can feel is in her presence.'

The water stood in my eyes to hear this avowal of his dependence: just as if a royal eagle, chained to a perch, should be forced to entreat a sparrow to become its purveyor. But I would not be lachrymose: I dashed off the salt drops, and busied myself with preparing breakfast.

Most of the morning was spent in the open air. I led him out of the wet and wild wood into some cheerful fields: I described to him how brilliantly green they were; how the flowers and hedges looked refreshed; how sparklingly blue was the sky. I sought a seat for him in a hidden and lovely spot: a dry stump of a tree; nor did I refuse to let him, when seated, place me on his knee: why should I, when both he and I were happier near than apart? Pilot lay beside us: all was quiet. He broke out suddenly while clasping me in his arms:—

'Cruel, cruel deserter! Oh, Jane, what did I feel when I discovered you had fled from Thornfield, and when I could nowhere find you; and, after examining your apartment, ascertained that you had taken no money, nor anything which could serve as an equivalent! A pearl necklace I had given you lay untouched in its little casket; your trunks were left corded and locked as they had been prepared for the bridal tour. What could my darling do, I asked, left destitute and penniless? And what did she do? Let me hear now.'

Thus urged, I began the narrative of my experience for the last year. I softened considerably what related to the three days of wandering and starvation, because to have told him all would have been to inflict unnecessary pain: the little I did say lacerated his faithful heart deeper than I wished.

I should not have left him thus, he said, without any means of making my way: I should have told him my intention. I should have confided in him: he would never have forced me to be his mistress. Violent as he had seemed in his despair, he, in truth, loved me far too well and too tenderly to constitute himself my tyrant: he would have given me half his fortune, without demanding so much as a kiss in return, rather than I should have flung myself friendless on the wide world. I had endured, he was certain, more than I had confessed to him.

'Well, whatever my sufferings had been, they were very short,' I answered: and then I proceeded to tell him how I had been received at Moor House; how I had obtained the office of schoolmistress, etc. The accession of fortune, the discovery of my relations, followed in due order. Of course, St. John Rivers' name came in frequently in the progress of my tale. When I had done, that name was immediately taken up.

'This St. John, then, is your cousin?'

'Yes.'

'You have spoken of him often: did you like him?'

'He was a very good man, sir; I could not help liking him.'

'A good man? Does that mean a respectable, well-conducted man of fifty? Or what does it mean?'

'St. John was only twenty-nine, sir.'

' "*Jeune encore*," as the French say. Is he a person of low stature, phlegmatic and plain? A person whose goodness consists rather in his guiltlessness of vice than in his prowess in virtue?'

'He is untiringly active. Great and exalted deeds are what he lives to perform.'

'But his brain? That is probably rather soft? He means well: but you shrug your shoulders to hear him talk?'

'He talks little, sir: what he does say is ever to the point. His brain is first rate, I should think not impressible, but vigorous.'

'Is he an able man, then?'

'Truly able.'

'A thoroughly educated man?'

'St. John is an accomplished and profound scholar.'

'His manners, I think, you said are not to your taste?—priggish and parsonic?'

'I never mentioned his manners; but, unless I had a very bad taste, they must suit it; they are polished, calm, and gentlemanlike.'

'His appearance,—I forget what description you gave of his appearance;— a sort of raw curate, half strangled with his white neckcloth, and stilted up on his thick-soled high-lows, eh?'

'St. John dresses well. He is a handsome man: tall, fair with blue eyes, and a Grecian profile.'

(*Aside.*) 'Damn him!'—(*To me.*) 'Did you like him, Jane?'

'Yes, Mr. Rochester, I liked him: but you asked me that before.'

I perceived, of course, the drift of my interlocutor. Jealousy had got hold of him: she stung him; but the sting was salutary: it gave him respite from the gnawing fang of melancholy. I would not, therefore, immediately charm the snake.

'Perhaps you would rather not sit any longer on my knee, Miss Eyre?' was the next somewhat unexpected observation.

'Why not, Mr. Rochester?'

'The picture you have just drawn is suggestive of a rather too overwhelming contrast. Your words have delineated very prettily a graceful Apollo: he is present to your imagination,—tall, fair, blue-eyed, and with a Grecian profile. Your eyes dwell on a Vulcan,—a real blacksmith, brown, broad-shouldered and blind and lame into the bargain.'

'I never thought of it before; but you certainly are rather like Vulcan, sir.'

'Well,—you can leave me, ma'am: but before you go' (and he retained me by a firmer grasp than ever), 'you will be pleased just to answer me a question or two.' He paused.

'What questions, Mr. Rochester?'

Then followed this cross-examination.

'St. John made you schoolmistress of Morton before he knew you were his cousin?'

'Yes.'

'You would often see him? He would visit the school sometimes?'

'Daily.'

'He would approve of your plans, Jane? I know they would be clever, for you are a talented creature.'

'He approved of them—yes.'

'He would discover many things in you he could not have expected to find? Some of your accomplishments are not ordinary.'

'I don't know about that.'

'You had a little cottage near the school, you say: did he ever come there to see you?'

'Now and then.'

'Of an evening?'

'Once or twice.'

A pause.

'How long did you reside with him and his sisters after the cousinship was discovered?'

'Five months.'

'Did Rivers spend much time with the ladies of his family?'

'Yes; the back parlour was both his study and ours: he sat near the window, and we by the table.'

'Did he study much?'

'A good deal.'

'What?'

'Hindostanee.'

'And what did you do meantime?'

'I learnt German, at first.'

'Did he teach you?'

'He did not understand German.'

'Did he teach you nothing?'

'A little Hindostanee.'

'Rivers taught you Hindostanee?'

'Yes, sir.'

'And his sisters also?'

'No.'

'Only you?'

'Only me.'

'Did you ask to learn?'

'No.'

'He wished to teach you?'

'Yes.'

A second pause.

'Why did he wish it? Of what use could Hindostanee be to you?'

'He intended me to go with him to India.'

'Ah! here I reach the root of the matter. He wanted you to marry him?'

'He asked me to marry him.'

'That is a fiction—an impudent invention to vex me.'

'I beg your pardon, it is the literal truth: he asked me more than once, and was as stiff about urging his point as ever you could be.'

'Miss Eyre, I repeat it, you can leave me. How often am I to say the same thing? Why do you remain pertinaciously perched on my knee, when I have given you notice to quit?'

'Because I am comfortable there.'

'No, Jane, you are not comfortable there, because your heart is not with me it is with this cousin—this St. John. Oh, till this moment, I thought my little Jane was all mine! I had a belief she loved me even when she left me: that was an atom of sweet in much bitter. Long as we have been parted, hot tears as I have wept over our separation, I never thought that while I was mourning her, she was loving another! But it is useless grieving. Jane, leave me: go and marry Rivers.'

'Shake me off, then, sir,—push me away, for I'll not leave you of my own accord.'

'Jane, I ever like your tone of voice: it still renews hope, it sounds so truthful When I hear it, it carries me back a year. I forget that you have formed a new tie. But I am not a fool—go'——

'Where must I go, sir?'

'Your own way—with the husband you have chosen.'

'Who is that?'

'You know—this St. John Rivers.'

'He is not my husband, nor ever will be. He does not love me: I do not love him. He loves (as he *can* love, and that is not as you love) a beautiful young lady called Rosamond. He wanted to marry me only because he thought I should make a suitable missionary's wife, which she would not have done He is good and great, but severe; and, for me, cold as an iceberg. He is not like you, sir: I am not happy at his side, nor near him, nor with him. He has no indulgence for me—no fondness. He sees nothing attractive in me; not even youth—only a few useful mental points.—Then I must leave you, sir, to go to him?'

I shuddered involuntarily, and clung instinctively closer to my blind but beloved master. He smiled.

'What Jane! Is this true? Is such really the state of matters between you and Rivers?'

'Absolutely, sir. Oh, you need not be jealous! I wanted to tease you a little to make you less sad: I thought anger would be better than grief. But if you wish me to love you, could you but see how much I *do* love you, you would be proud and content. All my heart is yours, sir: it belongs to you; and with you it would remain, were fate to exile the rest of me from your presence for ever.'

Again, as he kissed me, painful thoughts darkened his aspect.

'My seared vision! My crippled strength!' he murmured regretfully.

I caressed, in order to soothe him. I knew of what he was thinking, and wanted to speak for him; but dared not. As he turned aside his face a minute, I saw a tear slide from under the sealed eyelid, and trickle down the manly cheek. My heart swelled.

'I am no better than the old lightning-struck chesnut-tree in Thornfield orchard,' he remarked, ere long. 'And what right would that ruin have to bid a budding woodbine cover its decay with freshness?'

'You are no ruin, sir—no lightning-struck tree: you are green and vigorous. Plants will grow about your roots, whether you ask them or not, because they take delight in your bountiful shadow; and as they grow they will lean towards you, and wind round you, because your strength offers them so safe a prop.'

Again he smiled: I gave him comfort.

'You speak of friends, Jane?' he asked.

'Yes; of friends,' I answered, rather hesitatingly: for I knew I meant more than friends, but could not tell what other word to employ. He helped me!

'Ah! Jane. But I want a wife.'

'Do you, sir?'

'Yes: is it news to you?'

'Of course: you said nothing about it before.'

'Is it unwelcome news?'

'That depends on circumstances, sir—on your choice.'

'Which you shall make for me, Jane. I will abide by your decision.'

'Choose then, sir—*her who loves you best.*'

'I will at least choose—*her I love best.* Jane, will you marry me?'

'Yes, sir.'

'A poor blind man, whom you will have to lead about by the hand?'

'Yes, sir.'

'A crippled man, twenty years older than you, whom you will have to wait on?'

'Yes, sir.'

'Truly, Jane?'

'Most truly, sir.'

'Oh! my darling! God bless you and reward you!'

'Mr. Rochester, if ever I did a good deed in my life—if ever I thought a good thought—if ever I prayed a sincere and blameless prayer—if ever I wished a righteous wish,—I am rewarded now. To be your wife is, for me, to be as happy as I can be on earth.'

'Because you delight in sacrifice.'

'Sacrifice! What do I sacrifice? Famine for food, expectation for content. To be privileged to put my arms round what I value—to press my lips to what I love—to repose on what I trust: is that to make a sacrifice? If so, then certainly I delight in sacrifice.'

'And to bear with my infirmities, Jane: to overlook my deficiencies.'

'Which are none, sir, to me. I love you better now, when I can really be useful to you, than I did in your state of proud independence, when you disdained every part but that of the giver and protector.'

'Hitherto I have hated to be helped—to be led: henceforth, I feel, I shall hate it no more. I did not like to put my hand into a hireling's, but it is pleasant to feel it circled by Jane's little fingers. I preferred utter loneliness to the constant attendance of servants; but Jane's soft ministry will be a perpetual joy. Jane suits me: do I suit her?'

'To the finest fibre of my nature, sir.'

'The case being so, we have nothing in the world to wait for: we must be married instantly.'

He looked and spoke with eagerness: his old impetuosity was rising.

'We must become one flesh without any delay, Jane: there is but the licence to get—then we marry.'

'Mr. Rochester, I have just discovered the sun is far declined from its meridian, and Pilot is actually gone home to his dinner. Let me look at your watch.'

'Fasten it into your girdle, Janet, and keep it henceforward: I have no use for it.'

'It is nearly four o'clock in the afternoon, sir. Don't you feel hungry?'

'The third day from this must be our wedding-day, Jane. Never mind fine clothes and jewels, now: all that is not worth a fillip.'

'The sun has dried up all the rain-drops, sir. The breeze is still: it is quite hot.'

'Do you know, Jane, I have your little pearl necklace at this moment fastened round my bronze scrag under my cravat? I have worn it since the day I lost my only treasure: as a memento of her.'

'We will go home through the wood: that will be the shadiest way.'

He pursued his own thoughts without heeding me.

'Jane! you think me, I daresay, an irreligious dog: but my heart swells with gratitude to the beneficent God of this earth just now. He sees not as man sees, but far clearer: judges not as man judges, but far more wisely. I did wrong: I would have sullied my innocent flower—breathed guilt on its purity:

the Omnipotent snatched it from me. I, in my stiff-necked rebellion, almost cursed the dispensation: instead of bending to the decree, I defied it. Divine justice pursued its course; disasters came thick on me: I was forced to pass through the valley of the shadow of death. *His* chastisements are mighty; and one smote me which has humbled me for ever. You know I was proud of my strength: but what is it now, when I must give it over to foreign guidance, as a child does its weakness? Of late, Jane—only—only—of late—I began to see and acknowledge the hand of God in my doom. I began to experience remorse, repentance; the wish for reconcilement to my Maker. I began sometimes to pray: very brief prayers they were, but very sincere.

'Some days since: nay, I can number them—four; it was last Monday night, a singular mood came over me: one in which grief replaced frenzy—sorrow, sullenness. I had long had the impression that since I could nowhere find you, you must be dead. Late that night—perhaps it might be between eleven and twelve o'clock—ere I retired to my dreary rest, I supplicated God, that, if it seemed good to Him, I might soon be taken from this life, and admitted to that world to come, where there was still hope of rejoining Jane.

'I was in my own room, and sitting by the window, which was open: it soothed me to feel the balmy night-air; though I could see no stars, and only by a vague, luminous haze, knew the presence of a moon. I longed for thee, Janet! Oh, I longed for thee both with soul and flesh! I asked of God, at once in anguish and humility, if I had not been long enough desolate, afflicted, tormented; and might not soon taste bliss and peace once more. That I merited all I endured, I acknowledged—that I could scarcely endure more, I pleaded; and the alpha and omega of my heart's wishes broke involuntarily from my lips in the words—"Jane! Jane! Jane!" '

'Did you speak these words aloud?'

'I did, Jane. If any listener had heard me, he would have thought me mad: I pronounced them with such frantic energy.'

'And it was last Monday night: somewhere near midnight?'

'Yes; but the time is of no consequence: what followed is the strange point. You will think me superstitious,—some superstition I have in my blood, and always had: nevertheless, this is true—true at least it is that I heard what I now relate.

'As I exclaimed "Jane! Jane! Jane!" a voice—I cannot tell whence the voice came, but I know whose voice it was—replied, "I am coming: wait for me;" and a moment after, went whispering on the wind, the words—"Where are you?"

'I'll tell you, if I can, the idea, the picture these words opened to my mind: yet it is difficult to express what I want to express. Ferndean is buried, as you see, in a heavy wood, where sound falls dull, and dies unreverberating. "Where are you?" seemed spoken amongst mountains; for I heard a hill-sent

echo repeat the words. Cooler and fresher at the moment the gale seemed to visit my brow: I could have deemed that in some wild, lone scene, I and Jane were meeting. In spirit, I believe we must have met. You no doubt were, at that hour, in unconscious sleep, Jane: perhaps your soul wandered from its cell to comfort mine; for those were your accents—as certain as I live—they were yours!'

Reader, it was on Monday night—near midnight—that I too had received the mysterious summons: those were the very words by which I replied to it I listened to Mr. Rochester's narrative; but made no disclosure in return. The coincidence struck me as too awful and inexplicable to be communicated or discussed. If I told anything, my tale would be such as must necessarily make a profound impression on the mind of my hearer: and that mind, yet from its sufferings too prone to gloom, needed not the deeper shade of the supernatural I kept these things then, and pondered them in my heart.

'You cannot now wonder,' continued my master, 'that when you rose upon me so unexpectedly last night, I had difficulty in believing you any other than a mere voice and vision: something that would melt to silence and annihilation as the midnight whisper and mountain echo had melted before. Now, I thank God! I knew it to be otherwise. Yes, I thank God!'

He put me off his knee, rose, and reverently lifting his hat from his brow, and bending his sightless eyes to the earth, he stood in mute devotion. Only the last words of the worship were audible.

'I thank my Maker, that in the midst of judgment he has remembered mercy. I humbly entreat my Redeemer to give me strength to lead henceforth a purer life than I have done hitherto!'

Then he stretched his hand out to be led. I took that dear hand, held it a moment to my lips, then let it pass round my shoulder: being so much lower of stature than he, I served both for his prop and guide. We entered the wood, and wended homeward.

CHAPTER 38

CONCLUSION

Reader, I married him. A quiet wedding we had: he and I, the parson and clerk, were alone present. When we got back from church, I went into the kitchen of the manor-house, where Mary was cooking the dinner, and John cleaning the knives, and I said:—

'Mary, I have been married to Mr. Rochester this morning.' The house keeper and her husband were both of that decent phlegmatic order of people to whom one may at any time safely communicate a remarkable piece of news without incurring the danger of having one's ears pierced by some shrill ejaculation, and subsequently stunned by a torrent of wordy wonderment

Mary did look up, and she did stare at me: the ladle with which she was basting a pair of chickens roasting at the fire, did for some three minutes hang suspended in the air; and for the same space of time John's knives also had rest from the polishing process: but Mary, bending again over the roast, said only—

'Have you, Miss? Well, for sure!'

A short time after she pursued: 'I seed you go out with the master, but didn't know you were gone to church to be wed;' and she basted away. John, when I turned to him, was grinning from ear to ear.

'I telled Mary how it would be,' he said: 'I knew what Mr. Edward' (John was an old servant, and had known his master when he was the cadet of the house, therefore, he often gave him his Christian name)—'I knew what Mr. Edward would do; and I was certain he would not wait long neither: and he's done right, for aught I know. I wish you joy, Miss!' and he politely pulled his forelock.

'Thank you, John. Mr. Rochester told me to give you and Mary this.' I put into his hand a five-pound note. Without waiting to hear more, I left the kitchen. In passing the door of that sanctum some time after, I caught the words,—

'She'll happen do better for him nor ony o' t' grand ladies.' And again, 'f she ben't one o' th' handsomest, she's noan faâl and varry good-natured; and i' his een she's fair beautiful, onybody may see that.'

I wrote to Moor House and to Cambridge immediately, to say what I had done: fully explaining also why I had thus acted. Diana and Mary approved the step unreservedly. Diana announced that she would just give me time to get over the honey-moon, and then she would come and see me.

'She had better not wait till then, Jane,' said Mr. Rochester, when I read her letter to him; 'if she does, she will be too late, for our honey-moon will shine our life-long: its beams will only fade over your grave or mine.'

How St. John received the news, I don't know; he never answered the letter in which I communicated it: yet six months after he wrote to me; without, however, mentioning Mr. Rochester's name, or alluding to my marriage. His letter was then calm; and, though very serious, kind. He has maintained a regular, though not frequent correspondence ever since: he hopes I am happy, and trusts I am not of those who live without God in the world, and only mind earthly things.

You have not quite forgotten little Adèle, have you, reader? I had not; I soon asked and obtained leave of Mr. Rochester, to go and see her at the school where he had placed her. Her frantic joy at beholding me again moved me much. She looked pale and thin: she said she was not happy. I found the rules of the establishment were too strict, its course of study too severe, for a child of her age: I took her home with me. I meant to become her governess

once more; but I soon found this impracticable; my time and cares were now required by another—my husband needed them all. So I sought out a school conducted on a more indulgent system; and near enough to permit of my visiting her often, and bringing her home sometimes. I took care she should never want for anything that could contribute to her comfort: she soon settled in her new abode, became very happy there, and made fair progress in her studies. As she grew up, a sound English education corrected in a great measure her French defects; and when she left school, I found in her a pleasing and obliging companion: docile, good-tempered, and well-principled. By her grateful attention to me and mine, she has long since well repaid any little kindness I ever had it in my power to offer her.

My tale draws to its close: one word respecting my experience of married life, and one brief glance at the fortunes of those whose names have most frequently recurred in this narrative, and I have done.

I have now been married ten years. I know what it is to live entirely for and with what I love best on earth. I hold myself supremely blest—blest beyond what language can express; because I am my husband's life as fully as he is mine. No woman was ever nearer to her mate than I am: ever more absolutely bone of his bone, and flesh of his flesh. I know no weariness of my Edward's society: he knows none of mine, any more than we each do of the pulsation of the heart that beats in our separate bosoms; consequently, we are ever together. To be together is for us to be at once, as free as in solitude, as gay as in company. We talk, I believe, all day long: to talk to each other is but a more animated and an audible thinking. All my confidence is bestowed on him, all his confidence is devoted to me; we are precisely suited in character—perfect concord is the result.

Mr. Rochester continued blind the first two years of our union: perhaps it was that circumstance that drew us so very near—that knit us so very close; for I was then his vision, as I am still his right hand. Literally, I was (what he often called me) the apple of his eye. He saw nature—he saw books through me; and never did I weary of gazing for his behalf, and of putting into words the effect of field, tree, town, river, cloud, sunbeam—of the landscape before us; of the weather round us—and impressing by sound on his ear what light could no longer stamp on his eye. Never did I weary of reading to him; never did I weary of conducting him where he wished to go: of doing for him what he wished to be done. And there was a pleasure in my services, most full, most exquisite, even though sad—because he claimed these services without painful shame or damping humiliation. He loved me so truly, that he knew no reluctance in profiting by my attendance: he felt that I loved him so fondly, that to yield that attendance was to indulge my sweetest wishes.

One morning at the end of the two years, as I was writing a letter to his dictation, he came and bent over me, and said—

378

'Jane, have you a glittering ornament round your neck?'

I had a gold watch-chain: I answered 'Yes.'

'And have you a pale blue dress on?'

I had. He informed me then, that for some time he had fancied the obscurity clouding one eye was becoming less dense; and that now he was sure of it.

He and I went up to London. He had the advice of an eminent oculist; and he eventually recovered the sight of that one eye. He cannot now see very distinctly: he cannot read or write much; but he can find his way without being led by the hand: the sky is no longer a blank to him—the earth no longer a void. When his first-born was put into his arms, he could see that the boy had inherited his own eyes, as they once were—large, brilliant, and black. On that occasion, he again, with a full heart, acknowledged that God had tempered judgment with mercy.

My Edward and I, then, are happy: and the more so, because those we most love are happy likewise. Diana and Mary Rivers are both married: alternately, once every year, they come to see us, and we go to see them. Diana's husband is a captain in the navy; a gallant officer, and a good man. Mary's is a clergyman; a college friend of her brother's; and, from his attainments and principles, worthy of the connection. Both Captain Fitzjames and Mr. Wharton love their wives, and are loved by them.

As to St. John Rivers, he left England: he went to India. He entered on the path he had marked for himself; he pursues it still. A more resolute, indefatigable pioneer never wrought amidst rocks and dangers. Firm, faithful, and devoted; full of energy, and zeal, and truth, he labours for his race: he clears their painful way to improvement: he hews down like a giant the prejudices of creed and caste that encumber it. He may be stern; he may be exacting; he may be ambitious yet; but his is the sternness of the warrior Great-heart, who guards his pilgrim convoy from the onslaught of Apollyon. His is the exaction of the apostle, who speaks but for Christ, when he says—'Whosoever will come after me, let him deny himself, and take up his cross and follow me.' His is the ambition of the high master-spirit, which aims to fill a place in the first rank of those who are redeemed from the earth—who stand without fault before the throne of God; who share the last mighty victories of the Lamb; who are called, and chosen, and faithful.

St. John is unmarried: he never will marry now. Himself has hitherto sufficed to the toil; and the toil draws near its close: his glorious sun hastens to its setting. The last letter I received from him drew from my eyes human tears, and yet filled my heart with Divine joy: he anticipated his sure reward, his incorruptible crown. I know that a stranger's hand will write to me next, to say that the good and faithful servant has been called at length into the joy of his Lord. And why weep for this? No fear of death will darken St. John's last hour: his mind will be unclouded; his heart will be undaunted; his hope

will be sure; his faith steadfast. His own words are a pledge of this:—

'My Master,' he says, 'has forewarned me. Daily he announces more distinctly,—"Surely I come quickly!" and hourly I more eagerly respond,— "Amen; even so come, Lord Jesus!" '

BIOGRAPHICAL NOTICE OF
ELLIS AND ACTON BELL

t has been thought that all the works published under the names of Currer, Ellis, and Acton Bell, were, in reality, the production of one person. This mistake I endeavoured to rectify by a few words of disclaimer prefixed to the third edition of 'Jane Eyre.' These, too, it appears, failed to gain general credence, and now, on the occasion of a reprint of 'Wuthering Heights' and 'Agnes Grey,' I am advised distinctly to state how the case really stands.

Indeed, I feel myself that it is time the obscurity attending those two names—Ellis and Acton—was done away. The little mystery, which formerly yielded some harmless pleasure, has lost its interest; circumstances are changed. It becomes, then, my duty to explain briefly the origin and authorship of the books written by Currer, Ellis, and Acton Bell.

About five years ago, my two sisters and myself, after a somewhat prolonged period of separation, found ourselves reunited, and at home. Resident in a remote district, where education had made little progress, and where, consequently, there was no inducement to seek social intercourse beyond our own domestic circle, we were wholly dependent on ourselves and each other, on books and study, for the enjoyments and occupations of life. The highest stimulus, as well as the liveliest pleasure we had known from childhood upwards, lay in attempts at literary composition; formerly we used to show each other what we wrote, but of late years this habit of communication and consultation had been discontinued; hence it ensued, that we were mutually ignorant of the progress we might respectively have made.

One day, in the autumn of 1845, I accidentally lighted on a MS. volume of verse in my sister Emily's handwriting. Of course, I was not surprised, knowing that she could and did write verse: I looked it over, and something more than surprise seized me,—a deep conviction that these were not common effusions, nor at all like the poetry women generally write. I thought them condensed and terse, vigorous and genuine. To my ear, they had also a peculiar music—wild, melancholy, and elevating.

My sister Emily was not a person of demonstrative character, nor one on the recesses of whose mind and feelings, even those nearest and dearest to her could, with impunity, intrude unlicensed; it took hours to reconcile her to the discovery I had made, and days to persuade her that such poems merited publication. I knew, however, that a mind like hers could not be without some latent spark of honourable ambition, and refused to be discouraged in my attempts to fan that spark to flame.

Meantime, my younger sister quietly produced some of her own compositions, intimating that, since Emily's had given me pleasure, I might like to look

at hers. I could not but be a partial judge, yet I thought that these verses, too, had a sweet sincere pathos of their own.

We had very early cherished the dream of one day becoming authors. This dream, never relinquished even when distance divided and absorbing tasks occupied us, now suddenly acquired strength and consistency: it took the character of a resolve. We agreed to arrange a small selection of our poems, and, if possible, get them printed. Averse to personal publicity, we veiled our own names under those of Currer, Ellis, and Acton Bell; the ambiguous choice being dictated by a sort of conscientious scruple at assuming Christian names positively masculine, while we did not like to declare ourselves women, because—without at that time suspecting that our mode of writing and thinking was not what is called 'feminine'—we had a vague impression that authoresses are liable to be looked on with prejudice; we had noticed how critics sometimes use for their chastisement the weapon of personality, and for their reward, a flattery which is not true praise.

The bringing out of our little book was hard work. As was to be expected, neither we nor our poems were at all wanted; but for this we had been prepared at the outset; though inexperienced ourselves, we had read the experience of others. The great puzzle lay in the difficulty of getting answers of any kind from the publishers to whom we applied. Being greatly harassed by this obstacle, I ventured to apply to the Messrs. Chambers, of Edinburgh, for a word of advice; *they* may have forgotten the circumstance, but *I* have not, for from them I received a brief and business-like, but civil and sensible reply, on which we acted, and at last made a way.

The book was printed: it is scarcely known, and all of it that merits to be known are the poems of Ellis Bell. The fixed conviction I held, and hold, of the worth of these poems has not indeed received the confirmation of much favourable criticism; but I must retain it notwithstanding.

Ill-success failed to crush us: the mere effort to succeed had given a wonderful zest to existence; it must be pursued. We each set to work on a prose tale: Ellis Bell produced 'Wuthering Heights,' Acton Bell 'Agnes Grey,' and Currer Bell also wrote a narrative in one volume. These MSS. were perseveringly obtruded upon various publishers for the space of a year and a half; usually their fate was an ignominious and abrupt dismissal.

At last 'Wuthering Heights' and 'Agnes Grey' were accepted on terms somewhat impoverishing to the two authors; Currer Bell's book found acceptance nowhere, nor any acknowledgment of merit, so that something like the chill of despair began to invade his heart. As a forlorn hope, he tried one publishing house more—Messrs. Smith, Elder and Co. Ere long, in a much shorter space than that on which experience had taught him to calculate—there came a letter, which he opened in the dreary expectation of finding two hard hopeless lines, intimating that Messrs. Smith, Elder and Co. 'were

not disposed to publish the MS.,' and, instead, he took out of the envelope a letter of two pages. He read it trembling. It declined, indeed, to publish that tale, for business reasons, but it discussed its merits and demerits so courteously, so considerately, in a spirit so rational, with a discrimination so enlightened, that this very refusal cheered the author better than a vulgarly-expressed acceptance would have done. It was added, that a work in three volumes would meet with careful attention.

I was just then completing 'Jane Eyre,' at which I had been working while the one-volume tale was plodding its weary round in London: in three weeks I sent it off; friendly and skilful hands took it in. This was in the commencement of September 1847; it came out before the close of October following, while 'Wuthering Heights' and 'Agnes Grey,' my sisters' works, which had already been in the press for months, still lingered under a different management.

They appeared at last. Critics failed to do them justice. The immature but very real powers revealed in 'Wuthering Heights' were scarcely recognised; its import and nature were misunderstood; the identity of its author was misrepresented; it was said that this was an earlier and ruder attempt of the same pen which had produced 'Jane Eyre.' Unjust and grievous error! We laughed at it at first, but I deeply lament it now. Hence, I fear, arose a prejudice against the book. That writer who could attempt to palm off an inferior and immature production under cover of one successful effort, must indeed be unduly eager after the secondary and sordid result of authorship, and pitiably indifferent to its true and honourable meed. If reviewers and the public truly believed this, no wonder that they looked darkly on the cheat.

Yet I must not be understood to make these things subject for reproach or complaint; I dare not do so; respect for my sister's memory forbids me. By her any such querulous manifestation would have been regarded as an unworthy and offensive weakness.

It is my duty, as well as my pleasure, to acknowledge one exception to the general rule of criticism. One writer,[1] endowed with the keen vision and fine sympathies of genius, has discerned the real nature of 'Wuthering Heights,' and has, with equal accuracy, noted its beauties and touched on its faults. Too often do reviewers remind us of the mob of Astrologers, Chaldeans, and Soothsayers gathered before the 'writing on the wall,' and unable to read the characters or make known the interpretation. We have a right to rejoice when a true seer comes at last, some man in whom is an excellent spirit, to whom have been given light, wisdom, and understanding; who can accurately read the 'Mene, Mene, Tekel, Upharsin' of an original mind (however unripe, however inefficiently cultured and partially expanded that mind may be); and who can say with confidence, 'This is the interpretation thereof.'

See the *Palladium* for September 1850.

Yet even the writer to whom I allude shares the mistake about the author ship, and does me the injustice to suppose that there was equivoque in m former rejection of this honour (as an honour I regard it). May I assure hin that I would scorn in this and in every other case to deal in equivoque I believe language to have been given us to make our meaning clear, an(not to wrap it in dishonest doubt.

'The Tenant of Wildfell Hall,' by Acton Bell, had likewise an unfavourabl reception. At this I cannot wonder. The choice of subject was an entir mistake. Nothing less congruous with the writer's nature could be conceived The motives which dictated this choice were pure, but, I think, slightly morbid She had, in the course of her life, been called on to contemplate, near a hand, and for a long time, the terrible effects of talents misused and facultie abused; hers was naturally a sensitive, reserved, and dejected nature; wha she saw sank very deeply into her mind; it did her harm. She brooded ove it till she believed it to be a duty to reproduce every detail (of course witl fictitious characters, incidents, and situations), as a warning to others. Sh hated her work, but would pursue it. When reasoned with on the subject she regarded such reasonings as a temptation to self-indulgence. She mus be honest: she must not varnish, soften, or conceal. This well-meant resolutio brought on her misconstruction, and some abuse, which she bore, as it wa her custom to bear whatever was unpleasant, with mild, steady patience She was a very sincere and practical Christian, but the tinge of religiou melancholy communicated a sad shape to her brief, blameless life.

Neither Ellis nor Acton allowed herself for one moment to sink unde want of encouragement; energy nerved the one, and endurance upheld th other. They were both prepared to try again; I would fain think that hop and the sense of power was yet strong within them. But a great change ap proached: affliction came in that shape which to anticipate is dread: to loo back on, grief. In the very heat and burden of the day, the labourers faile over their work.

My sister Emily first declined. The details of her illness are deep-brande in my memory, but to dwell on them, either in thought or narrative, is no in my power. Never in all her life had she lingered over any task that la before her, and she did not linger now. She sank rapidly. She made hast to leave us. Yet, while physically she perished, mentally she grew stronge than we had yet known her. Day by day, when I saw with what a front sh met suffering, I looked on her with an anguish of wonder and love. I hav seen nothing like it; but, indeed, I have never seen her parallel in anything Stronger than a man, simpler than a child, her nature stood alone. Th awful point was, that while full of ruth for others, on herself she had no pity the spirit was inexorable to the flesh; from the trembling hand, the unnerve limbs, the faded eyes, the same service was exacted as they had rendere

n health. To stand by and witness this, and not dare to remonstrate, was a pain no words can render.

Two cruel months of hope and fear passed painfully by, and the day came at last when the terrors and pains of death were to be undergone by this treasure, which had grown dearer and dearer to our hearts as it wasted before our eyes. Towards the decline of that day, we had nothing of Emily but her mortal remains as consumption left them. She died December 19, 848.

We thought this enough: but we were utterly and presumptuously wrong. She was not buried ere Anne fell ill. She had not been committed to the grave a fortnight, before we received distinct intimation that it was necessary to prepare our minds to see the younger sister go after the elder. Accordingly, he followed in the same path with slower step, and with a patience that qualled the other's fortitude. I have said that she was religious, and it was by leaning on those Christian doctrines in which she firmly believed, that he found support through her most painful journey. I witnessed their efficacy n her latest hour and greatest trial, and must bear my testimony to the calm triumph with which they brought her through. She died May 28, 1849.

What more shall I say about them? I cannot and need not say much more. n externals, they were two unobtrusive women; a perfectly secluded life gave them retiring manners and habits. In Emily's nature the extremes of igour and simplicity seemed to meet. Under an unsophisticated culture, nartificial tastes, and an unpretending outside, lay a secret power and fire hat might have informed the brain and kindled the veins of a hero; but he had no wordly wisdom; her powers were unadapted to the practical business f life: she would fail to defend her most manifest rights, to consult her most egitimate advantage. An interpreter ought always to have stood between her and the world. Her will was not very flexible, and it generally opposed her interest. Her temper was magnanimous, but warm and sudden; her pirit altogether unbending.

Anne's character was milder and more subdued; she wanted the power, he fire, the originality of her sister, but was well endowed with quiet virtues f her own. Long-suffering, self-denying, reflective, and intelligent, a consti- utional reserve and taciturnity placed and kept her in the shade, and covered er mind, and especially her feelings, with a sort of nun-like veil, which was arely lifted. Neither Emily nor Anne was learned; they had no thought of lling their pitchers at the well-spring of other minds; they always wrote from he impulse of nature, the dictates of intuition, and from such stores of observa- ion as their limited experience had enabled them to amass. I may sum p all by saying, that for strangers they were nothing, for superficial observers ess than nothing; but for those who had known them all their lives in the ntimacy of close relationship, they were genuinely good and truly great.

This notice has been written, because I felt it a sacred duty to wipe the dust off their gravestones, and leave their dear names free from soil.

CURRER BELL

September 19, 1850.

CHARLOTTE BRONTË'S PREFACE
TO THE SECOND EDITION

I have just read over 'Wuthering Heights,' and, for the first time, have obtained a clear glimpse of what are termed (and, perhaps, really are) its faults; have gained a definite notion of how it appears to other people—to strangers who knew nothing of the author; who are unacquainted with the locality where the scenes of the story are laid; to whom the inhabitants, the customs, the natural characteristics of the outlying hills and hamlets in the West Riding of Yorkshire are things alien and unfamiliar.

To all such 'Wuthering Heights' must appear a rude and strange production. The wild moors of the north of England can for them have no interest; the language, the manners, the very dwellings and household customs of the scattered inhabitants of those districts, must be to such readers in a great measure unintelligible, and—where intelligible—repulsive. Men and women who, perhaps naturally very calm, and with feelings moderate in degree, and little marked in kind, have been trained from their cradle to observe the utmost evenness of manner and guardedness of language, will hardly know what to make of the rough, strong utterance, the harshly manifested passions, the unbridled aversions, and headlong partialities of unlettered moorland hinds and rugged moorland squires, who have grown up untaught and unchecked, except by mentors as harsh as themselves. A large class of readers, likewise, will suffer greatly from the introduction into the pages of this work of words printed with all their letters, which it has become the custom to represent by the initial and final letter only—a blank line filling the interval. I may as well say at once that, for this circumstance, it is out of my power to apologise; deeming it, myself, a rational plan to write words at full length. The practice of hinting by single letters those expletives with which profane and violent persons are wont to garnish their discourse, strikes me as a proceeding which, however well meant, is weak and futile, I cannot tell what good it does—what feeling it spares—what horror it conceals.

With regard to the rusticity of 'Wuthering Heights,' I admit the charge, for I feel the quality. It is rustic all through. It is moorish, and wild, and knotty as a root of heath. Nor was it natural that it should be otherwise; the author being herself a native and nursling of the moors. Doubtless, had her lot been cast in a town, her writings, if she had written at all, would have possessed another character. Even had chance or taste led her to choose a similar subject

she would have treated it otherwise. Had Ellis Bell been a lady or gentleman accustomed to what is called 'the world,' her view of a remote and unreclaimed region, as well as of the dwellers therein, would have differed greatly from that actually taken by the homebred country girl. Doubtless it would have been wider—more comprehensive: whether it would have been more original or more truthful is not so certain. As far as the scenery and locality are concerned, it could scarcely have been so sympathetic: Ellis Bell did not describe as one whose eye and taste alone found pleasure in the prospect; her native hills were far more to her than a spectacle; they were what she lived in, and by, as much as the wild birds, their tenants, or as the heather, their produce. Her descriptions, then, of natural scenery, are what they should be, and all they should be.

Where delineation of human character is concerned, the case is different. I am bound to avow that she had scarcely more practical knowledge of the peasantry amongst whom she lived, than a nun has of the country people who sometimes pass her convent gates. My sister's disposition was not naturally gregarious; circumstances favoured and fostered her tendency to seclusion; except to go to church or take a walk on the hills, she rarely crossed the threshold of home. Though her feeling for the people round was benevolent, intercourse with them she never sought; nor, with very few exceptions, ever experienced. And yet she knew them: knew their ways, their language, their family histories; she could hear of them with interest, and talk of them with detail, minute, graphic, and accurate; but *with* them, she rarely exchanged a word. Hence it ensued that what her mind had gathered of the real concerning them, was too exclusively confined to those tragic and terrible traits of which, in listening to the secret annals of every rude vicinage, the memory is sometimes compelled to receive the impress. Her imagination, which was a spirit more sombre than sunny, more powerful than sportive, found in such traits material whence it wrought creations like Heathcliff, like Earnshaw, like Catherine. Having formed these beings she did not know what she had done. If the auditor of her work when read in manuscript, shuddered under the grinding influence of natures so relentless and implacable, of spirits so lost and fallen; if it was complained that the mere hearing of certain vivid and fearful scenes banished sleep by night, and disturbed mental peace by day, Ellis Bell would wonder what was meant, and suspect the complainant of affectation. Had she but lived, her mind would of itself have grown like a strong tree, loftier, straighter, wider-spreading, and its matured fruits would have attained a mellower ripeness and sunnier bloom; but on that mind time and experience alone could work: to the influence of other intellects, it was not amenable.

Having avowed that over much of 'Wuthering Heights' there broods 'a horror of great darkness'; that, in its storm-heated and electrical atmosphere,

we seem at times to breathe lightning, let me point to those spots where clouded daylight and the eclipsed sun still attest their existence. For a speci men of true benevolence and homely fidelity, look at the character of Nelly Dean; for an example of constancy and tenderness, remark that of Edgar Linton. (Some people will think these qualities do not shine so well incarnate in a man as they would do in a woman, but Ellis Bell could never be brough to comprehend this notion: nothing moved her more than any insinuation that the faithfulness and clemency, the long-suffering and loving-kindness which are esteemed virtues in the daughters of Eve, become foibles in the sons of Adam. She held that mercy and forgiveness are the divinest attribute of the Great Being who made both man and woman, and that what clothes the Godhead in glory, can disgrace no form of feeble humanity.) There is a dry saturnine humour in the delineation of old Joseph, and some glimpses of grace and gaiety animate the younger Catherine. Nor is even the first heroine of the name destitute of a certain strange beauty in her fierceness, or of honesty in the midst of perverted passion and passionate perversity.

Heathcliff, indeed, stands unredeemed; never once swerving in his arrow straight course to perdition, from the time when 'the little black-haired swarthy thing, as dark as if it came from the Devil,' was first unrolled out of the bundle and set on its feet in the farmhouse kitchen, to the hour when Nelly Dean found the grim, stalwart corpse laid on its back in the panel-enclosed bed with wide-gazing eyes that seemed 'to sneer at her attempt to close them, and parted lips and sharp white teeth that sneered too.'

Heathcliff betrays one solitary human feeling, and that is *not* his love for Catherine; which is a sentiment fierce and inhuman; a passion such as might boil and glow in the bad essence of some evil genius; a fire that might from the tormented centre—the ever-suffering soul of a magnate of the infernal world: and by its quenchless and ceaseless ravage effect the execution of the decree which dooms him to carry Hell with him wherever he wanders. No the single link that connects Heathcliff with humanity is his rudely-confessed regard for Hareton Earnshaw—the young man whom he has ruined; and then his half-implied esteem for Nelly Dean. These solitary traits omitted, we should say he was child neither of Lascar nor gipsy, but a man's shape animated by demon life—a Ghoul—an Afreet.

Whether it is right or advisable to create beings like Heathcliff, I do no know: I scarcely think it is. But this I know: the writer who possesses the creative gift owns something of which he is not always master—something that, at times, strangely wills and works for itself. He may lay down rules and devise principles, and to rules and principles it will perhaps for years lie in subjection; and then, haply without any warning of revolt, there come a time when it will no longer consent to 'harrow the valleys, or be bound with a band in the furrow'—when it 'laughs at the multitude of the city, and regard

ot the crying of the driver'—when, refusing absolutely to make ropes out of sea-sand any longer, it sets to work on statue-hewing, and you have a Pluto or a Jove, a Tisiphone or a Psyche, a Mermaid or a Madonna, as Fate or inspiration direct. Be the work grim or glorious, dread or divine, you have little choice left but quiescent adoption. As for you—the nominal artist—your share in it has been to work passively under dictates you neither delivered nor could question—that would not be uttered at your prayer, nor suppressed nor changed at your caprice. If the result be attractive, the World will praise you, who little deserve praise; if it be repulsive, the same World will blame you, who almost as little deserve blame.

'Wuthering Heights' was hewn in a wild workshop, with simple tools out of homely materials. The statuary found a granite block on a solitary moor; gazing thereon, he saw how from the crag might be elicited a head, savage, swart, sinister; a form moulded with at least one element of grandeur—power. He wrought with a rude chisel, and from no model but the vision of his meditations. With time and labour, the crag took human shape; and there it stands colossal, dark, and frowning, half statue, half rock: in the former sense, terrible and goblin-like; in the latter, almost beautiful, for its colouring is of mellow grey, and moorland moss clothes it; and heath, with its blooming bells and balmy fragrance, grows faithfully close to the giant's foot.

CURRER BELL

WUTHERING HEIGHTS

CHAPTER 1

1801.—

I have just returned from a visit to my landlord—the solitary neighbour that I shall be troubled with. This is certainly a beautiful country! In all England, I do not believe that I could have fixed on a situation so completely removed from the stir of society. A perfect misanthropist's heaven: and Mr. Heathcliff and I are such a suitable pair to divide the desolation between us. A capital fellow! He little imagined how my heart warmed towards him when I beheld his black eyes withdraw so suspiciously under their brows, as I rode up, and when his fingers sheltered themselves, with a jealous resolution, still further in his waistcoat, as I announced my name.

'Mr. Heathcliff!' I said.

A nod was the answer.

'Mr. Lockwood, your new tenant, sir. I do myself the honour of calling as soon as possible after my arrival, to express the hope that I have not inconvenienced you by my perseverance in soliciting the occupation of Thrushcross Grange: I heard yesterday you had had some thoughts'——

'Thrushcross Grange is my own, sir,' he interrupted, wincing. 'I should not allow any one to inconvenience me, if I could hinder it—walk in!'

The 'walk in' was uttered with closed teeth, and expressed the sentiment 'Go to the deuce': even the gate over which he leant manifested no sympathising movement to the words; and I think that circumstance determined me to accept the invitation: I felt interested in a man who seemed more exaggeratedly reserved than myself.

When he saw my horse's breast fairly pushing the barrier, he did put out his hand to unchain it, and then sullenly preceded me up the causeway, calling, as we entered the court—' Joseph, take Mr. Lockwood's horse and bring up some wine.'

'Here we have the whole establishment of domestics, I suppose,' was the reflection suggested by this compound order. No wonder the grass grows up between the flags, and cattle are the only hedge-cutters.'

Joseph was an elderly, nay, an old man: very old, perhaps, though hale and sinewy. 'The Lord help us!' he soliloquised in an undertone of peevish displeasure, while relieving me of my horse: looking, meantime, in my face so sourly that I charitably conjectured he must have need of divine aid to digest his dinner, and his pious ejaculation had no reference to my unexpected advent.

Wuthering Heights is the name of Mr. Heathcliff's dwelling. 'Wuthering' being a significant provincial adjective, descriptive of the atmospheric tumult to which its station is exposed in stormy weather. Pure, bracing ventilation they must have up there at all times, indeed; one may guess the power of the north wind blowing over the edge, by the excessive slant of a few stunted firs at the end of the house; and by a range of gaunt thorns all stretching their limbs one way, as if craving alms of the sun. Happily, the architect had foresight to build it strong: the narrow windows are deeply set in the wall, and the corners defended with large jutting stones.

Before passing the threshold, I paused to admire a quantity of grotesque carving lavished over the front, and especially about the principal door; above which, among a wilderness of crumbling griffins and shameless little boys, I detected the date '1500,' and the name 'Hareton Earnshaw.' I would have made a few comments, and requested a short history of the place from the surly owner; but his attitude at the door appeared to demand my speedy entrance, or complete departure, and I had no desire to aggravate his impatience previous to inspecting the penetralium.

One step brought us into the family sitting-room, without any introductory lobby or passage: they call it here 'the house' pre-eminently. It includes kitchen and parlour, generally; but I believe at Wuthering Heights the kitchen is forced to retreat altogether into another quarter: at least I distinguished a chatter of tongues, and a clatter of culinary utensils, deep within; and I observed no signs of roasting, boiling, or baking, about the huge fire-place; nor any glitter of copper saucepans and tin cullenders on the walls. One end indeed, reflected splendidly both light and heat from ranks of immense pewter dishes, interspersed with silver jugs and tankards, towering row after row, on a vast oak dresser, to the very roof. The latter had never been underdrawn: its entire anatomy lay bare to an inquiring eye, except where a frame of wood laden with oatcakes and clusters of legs of beef, mutton, and ham, concealed it. Above the chimney were sundry villainous old guns, and a couple of horse-pistols: and, by way of ornament, three gaudily-painted canisters disposed along its ledge. The floor was of smooth, white stone; the chairs, high-backed, primitive structures, painted green: one or two heavy black ones lurking in the shade. In an arch under the dresser, reposed a huge, liver-coloured bitch pointer, surrounded by a swarm of squealing puppies; and other dogs haunted other recesses.

The apartment and furniture would have been nothing extraordinary as belonging to a homely, northern farmer, with a stubborn countenance, and stalwart limbs set out to advantage in knee-breeches and gaiters. Such an individual seated in his arm-chair, his mug of ale frothing on the round table before him, is to be seen in any circuit of five or six miles among these hills, if you go at the right time after dinner. But Mr. Heathcliff forms a singular

contrast to his abode and style of living. He is a dark-skinned gipsy in aspect in dress and manners a gentleman: that is, as much a gentleman as many a country squire: rather slovenly, perhaps, yet not looking amiss with his negligence, because he has an erect and handsome figure; and rather morose Possibly, some people might suspect him of a degree of under-bred pride I have a sympathetic chord within that tells me it is nothing of the sort I know, by instinct, his reserve springs from an aversion to showy display of feeling—to manifestations of mutual kindliness. He'll love and hate equally under cover, and esteem it a species of impertinence to be loved or hated again. No, I'm running on too fast: I bestow my own attributes over liberally on him. Mr. Heathcliff may have entirely dissimilar reasons for keeping his hand out of the way when he meets a would-be acquaintance, to those which actuate me. Let me hope my constitution is almost peculiar: my dear mother used to say I should never have a comfortable home; and only last summer I proved myself perfectly unworthy of one.

While enjoying a month of fine weather at the sea-coast, I was thrown into the company of a most fascinating creature: a real goddess in my eyes as long as she took no notice of me. I 'never told my love' vocally; still, if looks have language, the merest idiot might have guessed I was over head and ears: she understood me at last, and looked a return—the sweetest of all imaginable looks. And what did I do? I confess it with shame—shrunk icily into myself, like a snail; at every glance retired colder and farther; till finally the poor innocent was led to doubt her own senses, and, overwhelmed with confusion at her supposed mistake, persuaded her mamma to decamp. By this curious turn of disposition I have gained the reputation of deliberate heartlessness; how undeserved, I alone can appreciate.

I took a seat at the end of the hearthstone opposite that towards which my landlord advanced, and filled up an interval of silence by attempting to caress the canine mother, who had left her nursery, and was sneaking wolfishly to the back of my legs, her lip curled up, and her white teeth watering for a snatch. My caress provoked a long, guttural gnarl.

'You'd better let the dog alone,' growled Mr. Heathcliff in unison, checking fiercer demonstrations with a punch of his foot. 'She's not accustomed to be spoiled—not kept for a pet.' Then, striding to a side door, he shouted again 'Joseph!'

Joseph mumbled indistinctly in the depths of the cellar, but gave no intimation of ascending; so his master dived down to him, leaving me *vis-à-vis* the ruffianly bitch and a pair of grim shaggy sheep-dogs, who shared with her a jealous guardianship over all my movements. Not anxious to come in contact with their fangs, I sat still; but, imagining they would scarcely understand tacit insults, I unfortunately indulged in winking and making faces at the trio, and some turn of my physiognomy so irritated madam, that

she suddenly broke into a fury and leapt on my knees. I flung her back, and hastened to interpose the table between us. This proceeding roused the whole hive: half-a-dozen four-footed fiends, of various sizes and ages, issued from hidden dens to the common centre. I felt my heels and coat-laps peculiar subjects of assault; and parrying off the larger combatants as effectually as I could with the poker, I was constrained to demand, aloud, assistance from some of the household in re-establishing peace.

Mr. Heathcliff and his man climbed the cellar steps with vexatious phlegm: I don't think they moved one second faster than usual, though the hearth was an absolute tempest of worrying and yelping. Happily, an inhabitant of the kitchen made more despatch: a lusty dame, with tucked-up gown, bare arms, and fire-flushed cheeks, rushed into the midst of us flourishing a frying-pan: and used that weapon, and her tongue, to such purpose, that the storm subsided magically, and she only remained, heaving like a sea after a high wind, when her master entered on the scene.

'What the devil is the matter?' he asked, eyeing me in a manner that I could ill endure after this inhospitable treatment.

'What the devil, indeed!' I muttered. 'The herd of possessed swine could have had no worse spirits in them than those animals of yours, sir. You might as well leave a stranger with a brood of tigers!'

'They won't meddle with persons who touch nothing.' he remarked. putting the bottle before me, and restoring the displaced table. 'The dogs do right to be vigilant. Take a glass of wine?'

'No, thank you.'

'Not bitten, are you?'

'If I had been, I would have set my signet on the biter.'

Heathcliff's countenance relaxed into a grin.

'Come, come,' he said, 'you are flurried, Mr. Lockwood. Here, take a little wine. Guests are so exceedingly rare in this house that I and my dogs, I am willing to own, hardly know how to receive them. Your health, sir!'

I bowed and returned the pledge; beginning to perceive that it would be foolish to sit sulking for the misbehaviour of a pack of curs: besides, I felt loath to yield the fellow further amusement at my expense; since the humour took that turn. He—probably swayed by prudential consideration of the folly of offending a good tenant—relaxed a little in the laconic style of chipping off his pronouns and auxiliary verbs, and introduced what he supposed would be a subject of interest to me,—a discourse on the advantages and disadvantages of my present place of retirement. I found him very intelligent on the topics we touched; and before I went home, I was encouraged so far as to volunteer another visit to-morrow. He evidently wished no repetition of my intrusion. I shall go, notwithstanding. It is astonishing how sociable I feel myself compared with him.

CHAPTER 2

Yesterday afternoon set in misty and cold. I had half a mind to spend it by my study fire, instead of wading through heath and mud to Wuthering Heights. On coming up from dinner however (N.B.—I dine between twelve and one o'clock; the housekeeper, a matronly lady, taken as a fixture along with the house, could not, or would not, comprehend my request that I might be served at five), on mounting the stairs with this lazy intention, and stepping into the room, I saw a servant-girl on her knees surrounded by brushes and coal-scuttles, and raising an infernal dust as she extinguished the flames with heaps of cinders. This spectacle drove me back immediately; I took my hat, and, after a four miles' walk, arrived at Heathcliff's garden gate just in time to escape the first feathery flakes of a snow-shower.

On that bleak hill-top the earth was hard with a black frost, and the air made me shiver through every limb. Being unable to remove the chain, I jumped over, and, running up the flagged causeway bordered with straggling gooseberry bushes, knocked vainly for admittance, till my knuckles tingled and the dogs howled.

'Wretched inmates!' I ejaculated mentally, 'you deserve perpetual isolation from your species for your churlish inhospitality. At least, I would not keep my doors barred in the day-time. I don't care—I will get in!' So resolved, I grasped the latch and shook it vehemently. Vinegar-faced Joseph projected his head from a round window of the barn.

'Whet are ye for?' he shouted. 'T' maister's dahn i' t' fowld. Go rahnd by th' end ut' laith, if yah went tuh spake tull him.'

'Is there nobody inside to open the door?' I hallooed, responsively.

'They's nobbut t' missis; and shoo'll nut oppen't an ye mak yer flaysome dins till neegt.'

'Why? Cannot you tell her who I am, eh, Joseph?'

'Nor-ne me! Aw'll hae noa hend wi't,' muttered the head, vanishing.

The snow began to drive thickly. I seized the handle to essay another trial; when a young man without coat, and shouldering a pitchfork, appeared in the yard behind. He hailed me to follow him, and, after marching through a washhouse, and a paved area containing a coal-shed, pump, and pigeon-cot, we at length arrived in the huge, warm cheerful apartment, where I was formerly received. It glowed delightfully in the radiance of an immense fire, compounded of coal, peat, and wood; and near the table, laid for a plentiful evening meal, I was pleased to observe the 'missis', an individual whose existence I had never previously suspected. I bowed and waited, thinking she would bid me take a seat. She looked at me, leaning back in her chair, and remained motionless and mute.

'Rough weather!' I remarked. 'I'm afraid, Mrs. Heathcliff, the door must

bear the consequence of your servants' leisure attendance: I had hard work to make them hear me.'

She never opened her mouth. I stared—she stared also: at any rate, she kept her eyes on me in a cool, regardless manner, exceedingly embarrassing and disagreeable.

'Sit down,' said the young man gruffly. 'He'll be in soon.'

I obeyed; and hemmed, and called the villain Juno, who deigned, at this second interview, to move the extreme tip of her tail, in token of owning my acquaintance.

'A beautiful animal!' I commenced again. 'Do you intend parting with the little ones, madam?'

'They are not mine,' said the amiable hostess, more repellingly than Heathcliff himself could have replied.

'Ah, your favourites are among these?' I continued, turning to an obscure cushion full of something like cats.

'A strange choice of favourites!' she observed scornfully.

Unluckily, it was a heap of dead rabbits. I hemmed once more, and drew closer to the hearth, repeating my comment on the wildness of the evening.

'You should not have come out,' she said, rising and reaching from the chimney-piece two of the painted canisters.

Her position before was sheltered from the light; now, I had a distinct view of her whole figure and countenance. She was slender, and apparently scarcely past girlhood: an admirable form, and the most exquisite little face that I have ever had the pleasure of beholding; small features, very fair; flaxen ringlets, or rather golden, hanging loose on her delicate neck; and eyes, had they been agreeable in expression, they would have been irresistible: fortunately for my susceptible heart, the only sentiment they evinced hovered between scorn, and a kind of desperation, singularly unnatural to be detected there. The canisters were almost out of her reach; I made a motion to aid her; she turned upon me as a miser might turn if anyone attempted to assist him in counting his gold.

'I don't want your help,' she snapped; 'I can get them for myself.'

'I beg your pardon!' I hastened to reply.

'Were you asked to tea?' she demanded, tying an apron over her neat black frock, and standing with a spoonful of the leaf poised over the pot.

'I shall be glad to have a cup,' I answered.

'Were you asked?' she repeated.

'No,' I said, half smiling. 'You are the proper person to ask me.'

She flung the tea back, spoon and all, and resumed her chair in a pet; her forehead corrugated, and her red under-lip pushed out, like a child's ready to cry.

Meanwhile, the young man had slung on to his person a decidedly shabby

upper garment, and, erecting himself before the blaze, looked down on me from the corner of his eyes, for all the world as if there were some mortal feud unavenged between us. I began to doubt whether he were a servant or not: his dress and speech were both rude, entirely devoid of the superiority observable in Mr. and Mrs. Heathcliff; his thick, brown curls were rough and uncultivated, his whiskers encroached bearishly over his cheeks, and his hands were embrowned like those of a common labourer: still his bearing was free, almost haughty, and he showed none of a domestic's assiduity in attending on the lady of the house. In the absence of clear proofs of his condition, I deemed it best to abstain from noticing his curious conduct; and, five minutes afterwards, the entrance of Heathcliff relieved me, in some measure, from my uncomfortable state.

'You see, sir, I am come, according to promise!' I exclaimed, assuming the cheerful 'and I fear I shall be weather-bound for half an hour, if you can afford me shelter during that space.'

'Half-an-hour?' he said, shaking the white flakes from his clothes; 'I wonder you should select the thick of a snowstorm to ramble about in. Do you know that you run a risk of being lost in the marshes? People familiar with these moors often miss their road on such evenings; and I can tell you there is no chance of a change at present.'

'Perhaps I can get a guide among your lads, and he might stay at the Grange till morning—could you spare me one?'

'No, I could not.'

'Oh, indeed! Well, then, I must trust to my own sagacity.'

'Umph!'

'Are you going to mak th' tea?' demanded he of the shabby coat, shifting his ferocious gaze from me to the young lady.

'Is *he* to have any?' she asked, appealing to Heathcliff.

'Get it ready, will you?' was the answer, uttered so savagely that I started. The tone in which the words were said revealed a genuine bad nature. I no longer felt inclined to call Heathcliff a capital fellow. When the preparations were finished, he invited me with—'Now, sir, bring forward your chair.' And we all, including the rustic youth, drew round the table: an austere silence prevailing while we discussed our meal.

I thought, if I had caused the cloud, it was my duty to make an effort to dispel it. They could not every day sit so grim and taciturn; and it was impossible, however ill-tempered they might be, that the universal scowl they wore was their every-day countenance.

'It is strange,' I began, in the interval of swallowing one cup of tea and receiving another—' it is strange how custom can mould our tastes and ideas: many could not imagine the existence of happiness in a life of such complete exile from the world as you spend, Mr. Heathcliff; yet I'll venture to say,

that, surrounded by your family, and with your amiable lady as the presiding genius over your home and heart'——

'My amiable lady!' he interrupted, with an almost diabolical sneer on his face. 'Where is she—my amiable lady?'

'Mrs. Heathcliff, your wife, I mean.'

'Well, yes—Oh, you would intimate that her spirit has taken the post of ministering angel, and guards the fortunes of Wuthering Heights even when her body is gone. Is that it?'

Perceiving myself in a blunder, I attempted to correct it. I might have seen there was too great a disparity between the ages of the parties to make it likely that they were man and wife. One was about forty: a period of mental vigour at which men seldom cherish the delusion of being married for love by girls: that dream is reserved for the solace of our declining years. The other did not look seventeen.

Then it flashed upon me—'The clown at my elbow, who is drinking his tea out of a basin and eating his bread with unwashed hands, may be her husband: Heathcliff, junior, of course. Here is the consequence of being buried alive: she has thrown herself away upon that boor from sheer ignorance that better individuals existed! A sad pity—I must beware how I cause her to regret her choice.' The last reflection may seem conceited; it was not. My neighbour struck me as bordering on repulsive; I knew, through experience, that I was tolerably attractive.

'Mrs. Heathcliff is my daughter-in-law,' said Heathcliff, corroborating my surmise. He turned, as he spoke, a peculiar look in her direction: a look of hatred; unless he has a most perverse set of facial muscles that will not, like those of other people, interpret the language of his soul.

'Ah, certainly—I see now: you are the favoured possessor of the beneficent fairy,' I remarked, turning to my neighbour.

This was worse than before: the youth grew crimson, and clenched his fist, with every appearance of a meditated assault. But he seemed to recollect himself presently, and smothered the storm in a brutal curse, muttered on my behalf: which, however, I took care not to notice.

'Unhappy in your conjectures, sir,' observed my host; 'we neither of us have the privilege of owning your good fairy; her mate is dead. I said she was my daughter-in-law, therefore, she must have married my son.'

'And this young man is'——

'Not my son, assuredly.'

Heathcliff smiled again, as if it were rather too bold a jest to attribute the paternity of that bear to him.

'My name is Hareton Earnshaw,' growled the other; 'and I'd counsel you to respect it!'

'I've shown no disrespect,' was my reply, laughing internally at the dignity

with which he announced himself.

He fixed his eye on me longer than I cared to return the stare, for fear I might be tempted either to box his ears or render my hilarity audible. I began to feel unmistakably out of place in that pleasant family circle. The dismal spiritual atmosphere overcame, and more than neutralised, the glowing physical comforts round me; and I resolved to be cautious how I ventured under those rafters a third time.

The business of eating being concluded, and no one uttering a word of sociable conversation, I approached a window to examine the weather. A sorrowful sight I saw: dark night coming down prematurely, and sky and hills mingled in one bitter whirl of wind and suffocating snow.

'I don't think it possible for me to get home now without a guide,' I could not help exclaiming. 'The roads will be buried already; and, if they were bare, I could scarcely distinguish a foot in advance.'

'Hareton, drive those dozen sheep into the barn porch. They'll be covered if left in the fold all night: and put a plank before them,' said Heathcliff.

'How must I do?' I continued, with rising irritation.

There was no reply to my question; and on looking round I saw only Joseph bringing in a pail of porridge for the dogs, and Mrs. Heathcliff leaning over the fire, diverting herself with burning a bundle of matches which had fallen from the chimney-piece as she restored the tea canister to its place. The former, when he had deposited his burden, took a critical survey of the room, and in cracked tones, grated out:

'Aw woonder hagh yah can faishion tuh stand thear i' idleness un war, when all on 'em's goan aght! Bud yah're a nowt, and it's noa use talking— yah'll niver mend uh yer ill ways, bud goa raight tuh t' divil, like yer mother afore ye!'

I imagined, for a moment, that this piece of eloquence was addressed to me; and, sufficiently enraged, stepped towards the aged rascal with an intention of kicking him out of the door. Mrs. Heathcliff, however, checked me by her answer.

'You scandalous old hypocrite!' she replied. 'Are you not afraid of being carried away bodily, whenever you mention the devil's name? I warn you to refrain from provoking me, or I'll ask your abduction as a special favour! Stop! look here, Joseph,' she continued, taking a long, dark book from a shelf; 'I'll show you how far I've progressed in the Black Art: I shall soon be competent to make a clear house of it. The red cow didn't die by chance and your rheumatism can hardly be reckoned among providential visitations!'

'Oh, wicked, wicked!' gasped the elder; 'may the Lord deliver us from evil!'

'No, reprobate! you are a castaway—be off, or I'll hurt you seriously! I'll have you all modelled in wax and clay; and the first who passes the limit

I fix, shall—I'll not say what he shall be done to—but, you'll see! Go, I'm looking at you!'

The little witch put a mock malignity into her beautiful eyes, and Joseph, trembling with sincere horror, hurried out praying and ejaculating 'wicked' as he went. I thought her conduct must be prompted by a species of dreary fun; and, now that we were alone, I endeavoured to interest her in my distress.

'Mrs. Heathcliff,' I said earnestly, 'you must excuse me for troubling you. I presume, because, with that face, I'm sure you cannot help being good-hearted. Do point out some landmarks by which I may know my way home: I have no more idea how to get there than you would have how to get to London!'

'Take the road you came,' she answered, ensconcing herself in a chair, with a candle, and the long book open before her. 'It is brief advice, but as sound as I can give.'

'Then, if you hear of me being discovered dead in a bog or a pit full of snow, your conscience won't whisper that it is partly your fault?'

'How so? I cannot escort you. They wouldn't let me go to the end of the garden-wall.'

'*You*! I should be sorry to ask you to cross the threshold, for my convenience, on such a night,' I cried. 'I want you to *tell* me my way, not to *show* it; or else to persuade Mr. Heathcliff to give me a guide.'

'Who? There is himself, Earnshaw, Zillah, Joseph, and I. Which would you have?'

'Are there no boys at the farm?'

'No, those are all.'

'Then, it follows that I am compelled to stay.'

'That you may settle with your host. I have nothing to do with it.'

'I hope it will be a lesson to you to make no more rash journeys on these hills,' cried Heathcliff's stern voice from the kitchen entrance. 'As to staying here, I don't keep accommodations for visitors: you must share a bed with Hareton or Joseph, if you do.'

'I can sleep on a chair in this room,' I replied.

'No, no! A stranger is a stranger, be he rich or poor: it will not suit me to permit any one the range of the place while I am off guard!' said the unmannerly wretch.

With this insult, my patience was at an end. I uttered an expression of disgust, and pushed past him into the yard, running against Earnshaw in my haste. It was so dark that I could not see the means of exit; and, as I wandered round, I heard another specimen of their civil behaviour amongst each other. At first the young man appeared about to befriend me.

'I'll go with him as far as the park,' he said.

'You'll go with him to hell!' exclaimed his master, or whatever relation

he bore. 'And who is to look after the horses, eh?'

'A man's life is of more consequence than one evening's neglect of the horses somebody must go,' murmured Mrs. Heathcliff, more kindly than I expected

'Not at your command!' retorted Hareton. 'If you set store on him, you'd better be quiet.'

'Then I hope his ghost will haunt you; and I hope Mr. Heathcliff will never get another tenant till the Grange is a ruin!' she answered sharply.

'Hearken, hearken, shoo's cursing on 'em!' muttered Joseph, toward whom I had been steering.

He sat within earshot, milking the cows by the light of a lantern, which I seized unceremoniously, and, calling out that I would send it back on the morrow, rushed to the nearest postern.

'Maister, maister, he's staling t' lantern!' shouted the ancient, pursuing my retreat. 'Hey, Gnasher! Hey, dog! Hey, Wolf, holld him, holld him!'

On opening the little door, two hairy monsters flew at my throat, bearing me down and extinguishing the light; while a mingled guffaw from Heathcliff and Hareton, put the copestone on my rage and humiliation. Fortunately the beasts seemed more bent on stretching their paws and yawning and flourishing their tails, than devouring me alive; but they would suffer no resurrection, and I was forced to lie till their malignant masters pleased to deliver me: then, hatless and trembling with wrath, I ordered the miscreants to let me out—on their peril to keep me one minute longer—with several incoherent threats of retaliation that, in their indefinite depth of virulency, smacked of King Lear.

The vehemence of my agitation brought on a copious bleeding at the nose and still Heathcliff laughed, and still I scolded. I don't know what would have concluded the scene, had there not been one person at hand rather more rational than myself, and more benevolent than my entertainer. This was Zillah, the stout housewife; who at length issued forth to inquire into the nature of the uproar. She thought that some of them had been laying violent hands on me; and, not daring to attack her master, she turned her vocal artillery against the younger scoundrel.

'Well, Mr. Earnshaw,' she cried, 'I wonder what you'll have agait next Are we going to murder folk on our very doorstones? I see this house will never do for me—look at t' poor lad, he's fair choking! Wisht, wisht! you mun'n't go on so. Come in, and I'll cure that: there now, hold ye still.'

With these words she suddenly splashed a pint of icy water down my neck and pulled me into the kitchen. Mr. Heathcliff followed, his accidental merriment expiring quickly in his habitual moroseness.

I was sick exceedingly, and dizzy and faint; and thus compelled perforce to accept lodgings under his roof. He told Zillah to give me a glass of brandy and then passed on to the inner room; while she condoled with me on my sorry

predicament, and having obeyed his orders, whereby I was somewhat revived,
ushered me to bed.

CHAPTER 3

While leading the way upstairs, she recommended that I should hide the
candle, and not make a noise; for her master had an odd notion about the
chamber she would put me in, and never let anybody lodge there willingly.
I asked the reason. She did not know, she answered: she had only lived there
a year or two; and they had so many queer goings on, she could not begin to
be curious.

Too stupified to be curious myself, I fastened my door and glanced round
for the bed. The whole furniture consisted of a chair, a clothes-press, and
a large oak case, with squares cut out near the top resembling coach windows.
Having approached this structure I looked inside, and perceived it to be
a singular sort of old-fashioned couch, very conveniently designed to obviate
the necessity for every member of the family having a room to himself. In
fact, it formed a little closet, and the ledge of a window, which it enclosed,
served as a table. I slid back the panelled sides, got in with my light, pulled
them together again, and felt secure against the vigilance of Heathcliff,
and every one else.

The ledge, where I placed my candle, had a few mildewed books piled up
in one corner; and it was covered with writing scratched on the paint. This
writing, however, was nothing but a name repeated in all kinds of characters,
large and small—*Catherine Earnshaw*, here and there varied to *Catherine Heath-
cliff*, and then again to *Catherine Linton*.

In vapid listlessness I leant my head against the window, and continued
spelling over Catherine Earnshaw—Heathcliff—Linton, till my eyes closed;
but they had not rested five minutes when a glare of white letters started from
the dark as vivid as specters—the air swarmed with Catherines; and rousing
myself to dispel the obtrusive name, I discovered my candle wick reclining
on one of the antique volumes, and perfuming the place with an odour of
roasted calf-skin. I snuffed it off, and, very ill at ease under the influence of
cold and lingering nausea, sat up and spread open the injured tome on my
knee. It was a Testament, in lean type, and smelling dreadfully musty:
a fly-leaf bore the inscription—'Catherine Earnshaw, her book,' and a date
some quarter of a century back. I shut it, and took up another, and another,
till I had examined all. Catherine's library was select, and its state of dilapi-
dation proved it to have been well used; though not altogether for a legitimate
purpose: scarcely one chapter had escaped a pen-and-ink commentary—at
least, the appearance of one—covering every morsel of blank that the printer

had left. Some were detached sentences; other parts took the form of a regular diary, scrawled in an unformed childish hand. At the top of an extra page (quite a treasure, probably, when first lighted on) I was greatly amused to behold an excellent caricature of my friend Joseph,—rudely, yet powerfully sketched. An immediate interest kindled within me for the unknown Catherine, and I began forthwith to decipher her faded hieroglyphics.

'An awful Sunday!' commenced the paragraph beneath. 'I wish my father were back again. Hindley is a detestable substitute—his conduct to Heathcliff is atrocious—H. and I are going to rebel—we took our initiatory step this evening.

'All day had been flooding with rain; we could not go to church, so Joseph must needs get up a congregation in the garret; and, while Hindley and his wife basked downstairs before a comfortable fire—doing anything but reading their Bibles, I'll answer for it—Heathcliff, myself, and the unhappy plough-boy, were commanded to take our Prayer-books, and mount: we were ranged in a row, on a sack of corn, groaning and shivering, and hoping that Joseph would shiver too, so that he might give us a short homily for his own sake. A vain idea! The service lasted precisely three hours; and yet my brother had the face to exclaim, when he saw us descending, "What, done already?" On Sunday evenings we used to be permitted to play, if we did not make much noise; now a mere titter is sufficient to send us into corners!

' "You forget you have a master here," says the tyrant. "I'll demolish the first who puts me out of temper! I insist on perfect sobriety and silence. Oh, boy! was that you? Frances, darling, pull his hair as you go by: I heard him snap his fingers." Frances pulled his hair heartily, and then went and seated herself on her husband's knee; and there they were, like two babies, kissing and talking nonsense by the hour—foolish palaver that we should be ashamed of. We made ourselves as snug as our means allowed in the arch of the dresser. I had just fastened our pinafores together, and hung them up for a curtain, when in comes Joseph on an errand from the stables. He tears down my handiwork, boxes my ears, and croaks—

' "T' maister nobbut just buried, and Sabbath nut o'ered, und t' sahnd uh t' gospel still i' yer lugs, and yah darr be laiking! Shame on ye! sit ye dahn, ill childer! they's good books eneugh if ye'll read 'em! sit ye dahn, and think uh yer sowls!"

'Saying this, he compelled us so to square our positions that we might receive from the far-off fire a dull ray to show us the text of the lumber thrust upon us. I could not bear the employment. I took my dingy volume by the scroop, and hurled it into the dog-kennel, vowing I hated a good book. Heathcliff kicked his to the same place. Then there was a hubbub!

' "Maister Hindley!" shouted our chaplain. "Maister, coom hither Miss Cathy's riven th' back off 'Th' Helmet uh Salvation,' un' Heathcliff'

pawsed his fit intuh t'first part uh 'T' Brooad Way to Destruction!' It's fair flaysome ut yah let 'em goa on this gait. Ech! th' owd man ud uh laced 'em properly—but he's goan!''

'Hindley hurried up from his paradise on the hearth, and seizing one of us by the collar, and the other by the arm, hurled both into the back kitchen; where, Joseph asseverated, "owd Nick" would fetch us as sure as we were living: and, so comforted, we each sought a separate nook to await his advent. I reached this book, and a pot of ink from a shelf, and pushed the house-door ajar to give me light, and I have got the time on with writing for twenty minutes; but my companion is impatient, and proposes that we should appropriate the dairywoman's cloak, and have a scamper on the moors, under its shelter. A pleasant suggestion—and then, if the surly old man come in, he may believe his prophecy verified—we cannot be damper, or colder, in the rain than we are here.'

* * * * * *

I suppose Catherine fulfilled her project, for the next sentence took up another subject: she waxed lachrymose.

'How little did I dream that Hindley would ever make me cry so!' she wrote. My head aches, till I cannot keep it on the pillow; and still I can't give over. Poor Heathcliff! Hindley calls him a vagabond, and won't let him sit with us, nor eat with us any more; and he says, he and I must not play together, and threatens to turn him out of the house if we break his orders. He has been blaming our father (how dared he?) for treating H. too liberally; and swears he will reduce him to his right place'—

* * * * * *

I began to nod drowsily over the dim page: my eye wandered from manu-script to print. I saw a red ornamented title—'Seventy Times Seven, and the First of the Seventy-First. A Pious Discourse delivered by the Reverend Jabes Branderham, in the Chapel, of Gimmerden Sough.' And while I was, half consciously, worrying my brain to guess what Jabes Branderham would make of his subject, I sank back in bed, and fell asleep. Alas, for the effects of bad tea and bad temper! what else could it be that made me pass such a terrible night? I don't remember another that I can at all compare with it since I was capable of suffering.

I began to dream, almost before I ceased to be sensible of my locality. I thought it was morning; and I had set out on my way home, with Joseph for a guide. The snow lay yards deep in our road; and, as we floundered on, my companion wearied me with constant reproaches that I had not brought a pilgrim's staff: telling me that I could never get into the house without one, and boastfully flourishing a heavy-headed cudgel, which I understood

to be so denominated. For a moment I considered it absurd that I should need such a weapon to gain admittance into my own residence. Then a new idea flashed across me. I was not going there: we were journeying to hear the famous Jabes Branderham preach from the text—'Seventy Times Seven'; and either Joseph, the preacher, or I had committed the 'First of the Seventy-First,' and were to be publicly exposed and excommunicated.

We came to the chapel. I have passed it really in my walks, twice or thrice; it lies in a hollow, between two hills: an elevated hollow, near a swamp, whose peaty moisture is said to answer all the purposes of embalming on the few corpses deposited there. The roof has been kept whole hitherto; but as the clergyman's stipend is only twenty pounds per annum, and a house with two rooms, threatening speedily to determine into one, no clergyman will undertake the duties of pastor: especially as it is currently reported that his flock would rather let him starve than increase the living by one penny from their own pockets. However, in my dream, Jabes had a full and attentive congregation; and he preached—good God! what a sermon; divided into *four hundred and ninety* parts, each fully equal to an ordinary address from the pulpit, and each discussing a separate sin! Where he searched for them, I cannot tell. He had his private manner of interpreting the phrase, and it seemed necessary the brother should sin different sins on every occasion. They were of the most curious character: odd transgressions that I never imagined previously.

Oh, how weary I grew. How I writhed, and yawned, and nodded, and revived! How I pinched and pricked myself, and rubbed my eyes, and stood up, and sat down again, and nudged Joseph to inform me if he would *ever* have done. I was condemned to hear all out: finally, he reached the '*First of the Seventy-First.*' At that crisis, a sudden inspiration descended on me; I was moved to rise and denounce Jabes Branderham as the sinner of the sin that no Christian need pardon.

'Sir,' I exlaimed, 'sitting here within these four walls, at one stretch, I have endured and forgiven the four hundred and ninety heads of your discourse. Seventy times seven times have I plucked up my hat and been about to depart—Seventy times seven times have you preposterously forced me to resume my seat. The four hundred and ninety-first is too much. Fellow-martyrs, have at him! Drag him down, and crush him to atoms, that the place which knows him may know him no more!'

'*Thou art the Man!*' cried Jabes, after a solemn pause, leaning over his cushion. 'Seventy times seven times didst thou gapingly contort thy visage—seventy times seven did I take counsel with my soul—Lo, this is human weakness: this also may be absolved! The First of the Seventy-First is come. Brethren, execute upon him the judgment written. Such honour have all His saints!'

With that concluding word, the whole assembly, exalting their pilgrim

staves, rushed round me in a body; and I, having no weapon to raise in self-defence, commenced grappling with Joseph, my nearest and most ferocious assailant, for his. In the confluence of the multitude, several clubs crossed; blows, aimed at me, fell on other sconces. Presently the whole chapel resounded with rappings and counter-rappings: every man's hand was against his neighbour; and Branderham, unwilling to remain idle, poured forth his zeal in a shower of loud taps on the boards of the pulpit, which responded so smartly that, at last, to my unspeakable relief, they woke me. And what was it that had suggested the tremendous tumult? What had played Jabes's part in the row? Merely, the branch of a fir-tree that touched my lattice, as the blast wailed by, and rattled its dry cones against the panes! I listened doubtingly an instant; detected the disturber, then turned and dozed, and dreamt again: if possible, still more disagreeably than before.

This time, I remembered I was lying in the oak closet, and I heard distinctly the gusty wind, and the driving of the snow; I heard, also, the fir-bough repeat its teasing sound, and ascribed it to the right cause: but it annoyed me so much, that I resolved to silence it, if possible; and, I thought, I rose and endeavoured to unhasp the casement. The hook was soldered into the staple: a circumstance observed by me when awake, but forgotten. 'I must stop it, nevertheless!' I muttered, knocking my knuckles through the glass, and stretching an arm out to seize the importunate branch; instead of which, my fingers closed on the fingers of a little, ice-cold hand! The intense horror of nightmare came over me: I tried to draw back my arm, but the hand clung to it, and a most melancholy voice sobbed, 'Let me in—let me in!' 'Who are you?' I asked, struggling, meanwhile, to disengage myself. 'Catherine Linton,' it replied, shiveringly (why did I think of *Linton*? I had read *Earnshaw* twenty times for Linton); 'I'm come home: I'd lost my way on the moor!' As it spoke, I discerned, obscurely, a child's face looking through the window. Terror made me cruel; and, finding it useless to attempt shaking the creature off, I pulled its wrist on to the broken pane, and rubbed it to and fro till the blood ran down and soaked the bedclothes: still it wailed, 'Let me in!' and maintained its tenacious gripe, almost maddening me with fear. 'How can I?' I said at length. 'Let *me* go, if you want me to let you in!' The fingers relaxed, I snatched mine through the hole, hurriedly piled the books up in a pyramid against it, and stopped my ears to exclude the lamentable prayer. I seemed to keep them closed above a quarter of an hour; yet, the instant I listened again, there was the doleful cry moaning on! 'Begone!' I shouted, 'I'll never let you in, not if you beg for twenty years.' 'It is twenty years,' mourned the voice: 'twenty years. I've been a waif for twenty years!' Thereat began a feeble scratching outside, and the pile of books moved as if thrust forward. I tried to jump up; but could not stir a limb; and so yelled aloud, in a frenzy of fright. To my confusion, I discovered the yell was not ideal:

hasty footsteps approached my chamber door; somebody pushed it open, with a vigorous hand, and a light glimmered through the squares at the top of the bed. I sat shuddering yet, and wiping the perspiration from my forehead: the intruder appeared to hesitate, and muttered to himself. At last, he said in a half-whisper, plainly not expecting an answer, 'Is any one here?' I considered it best to confess my presence; for I knew Heathcliff's accents, and feared he might search further, if I kept quiet. With this intention, I turned and opened the panels. I shall not soon forget the effect my action produced.

Heathcliff stood near the entrance, in his shirt and trousers: with a candle dripping over his fingers, and his face as white as the wall behind him. The first creak of the oak startled him like an electric shock! the light leaped from his hold to a distance, of some feet, and his agitation was so extreme, that he could hardly pick it up.

'It is only your guest, sir,' I called out, desirous to spare him the humiliation of exposing his cowardice further. 'I had the misfortune to scream in my sleep, owing to a frightful night-mare. I'm sorry I disturbed you.'

'Oh, God confound you, Mr. Lockwood! I wish you were at the——' commenced my host, setting the candle on a chair, because he found it impossible to hold it steady. 'And who showed you up into this room?' he continued, crushing his nails into his palms, and grinding his teeth to subdue the maxillary convulsions. 'Who was it? I've a good mind to turn them out of the house this moment!'

'It was your servant, Zillah,' I replied, flinging myself on to the floor, and rapidly resuming my garments. 'I should not care if you did, Mr. Heathcliff; she richly deserves it. I suppose that she wanted to get another proof that the place was haunted, at my expense. Well, it is —swarming with ghosts and goblins! You have reason in shutting it up, I assure you. No one will thank you for a doze in such a den!'

'What do you mean?' asked Heathcliff, 'and what are you doing? Lie down and finish out the night, since you *are* here; but, for Heaven's sake! don't repeat that horrid noise; nothing could excuse it, unless you were having your throat cut!'

'If the little fiend had got in at the window, she probably would have strangled me!' I returned. 'I'm not going to endure the persecutions of your hospitable ancestors again. Was not the Reverend Jabes Branderham akin to you on the mother's side? And that minx, Catherine Linton, or Earnshaw, or however she was called—she must have been a changeling—wicked little soul! She told me she had been walking the earth those twenty years: a just punishment for her mortal transgressions, I've no doubt!'

Scarcely were these words uttered, when I recollected the association of Heathcliff's with Catherine's name in the book, which had completely slipped

rom my memory, till thus awakened. I blushed at my inconsideration; but, without showing further consciousness of the offence, I hastened to add— The truth is, sir, I passed the first part of the night in'—Here I stopped afresh —I was about to say 'perusing those old volumes,' then it would have revealed my knowledge of their written, as well as their printed, contents: so, correcting myself, I went on, 'in spelling over the name scratched on that window-edge. A monotonous occupation, calculated to set me asleep, like counting, or'—

'What *can* you mean by talking in this way to *me*?' thundered Heathcliff with savage vehemence. 'How—how *dare* you, under my roof? — God! he's mad to speak so! And he struck his forehead with rage.

I did not know whether to resent this language or pursue my explanation; but he seemed so powerfully affected that I took pity and proceeded with my dreams; affirming I had never heard the appellation of 'Catherine Linton' before, but reading it often over produced an impression which personified itself when I had no longer my imagination under control. Heathcliff gradually fell back into the shelter of the bed, as I spoke; finally sitting down almost concealed behind it. I guessed, however, by his irregular and intercepted breathing, that he struggled to vanquish an excess of violent emotion. Not liking to show him that I had heard the conflict, I continued my toilette rather noisily, looked at my watch, and soliloquised on the length of the night: 'Not three o'clock yet! I could have taken oath it had been six. Time stagnates here: we must surely have retired to rest at eight!'

'Always at nine in winter, and always rise at four,' said my host, suppressing a groan: and, as I fancied, by the motion of his shadow's arm, dashing a tear from his eyes. 'Mr. Lockwood,' he added, 'you may go into my room: you'll only be in the way, coming downstairs so early; and your childish outcry has sent sleep to the devil for me.'

'And for me, too,' I replied. 'I'll walk in the yard till daylight, and then I'll be off; and you need not dread a repetition of my intrusion. I'm now quite cured of seeking pleasure in society, be it country or town. A sensible man ought to find sufficient company in himself.'

'Delightful company!' muttered Heathcliff. 'Take the candle, and go where you please. I shall join you directly. Keep out of the yard, though, the dogs are unchained; and the house—Juno mounts sentinel there, and—nay, you can only ramble about the steps and passages. But, away with you! I'll come in two minutes!'

I obeyed, so far as to quit the chamber; when, ignorant where the narrow lobbies led, I stood still, and was witness, involuntarily, to a piece of superstition on the part of my landlord, which belied, oddly his apparent sense. He got on to the bed, and wrenched open the lattice, bursting, as he pulled at it, into an uncontrollable passion of tears. 'Come in! come in!' he sobbed.

'Cathy, do come. Oh do—*once* more! Oh! my heart's darling! hear me *this* time, Catherine, at last!' The spectre showed a spectre's ordinary caprice: it gave no sign of being; but the snow and wind whirled wildly through, even reaching my station, and blowing out the light.

There was such anguish in the gush of grief that accompanied this raving, that my compassion made me overlook its folly, and I drew off, half angry to have listened at all, and vexed at having related my ridiculous nightmare, since it produced that agony; though *why*, was beyond my comprehension. I descended cautiously to the lower regions, and landed in the back-kitchen, where a gleam of fire, raked compactly together, enabled me to rekindle my candle. Nothing was stirring except a brindled, grey cat, which crept from the ashes, and saluted me with a querulous mew.

Two benches, shaped in sections of a circle, nearly enclosed the hearth; on one of these I stretched myself, and Grimalkin mounted the other. We were both of us nodding, ere any one invaded our retreat, and then it was Joseph, shuffling down a wooden ladder that vanished in the roof, through a trap: the ascent to his garret, I suppose. He cast a sinister look at the little flame which I had enticed to play between the ribs, swept the cat from its elevation, and bestowing himself in the vacancy, commenced the operation of stuffing a three-inch pipe with tobacco. My presence in his sanctum was evidently esteemed a piece of impudence too shameful for remark: he silently applied the tube to his lips, folded his arms, and puffed away. I let him enjoy the luxury unannoyed; and after sucking out his last wreath, and heaving a profound sigh, he got up, and departed as solemnly as he came.

A more elastic footstep entered next; and now I opened my mouth for a 'good morning,' but closed it again, the salutation unachieved; for Hareton Earnshaw was performing his orisons *sotto voce*, in a series of curses directed against every object he touched, while he rummaged a corner for a spade or shovel to dig through the drifts. He glanced over the back of the bench dilating his nostrils and thought as little of exchanging civilities with me as with my companion the cat. I guessed, by his preparations, that egress was allowed, and, leaving my hard couch, made a movement to follow him. He noticed this, and thrust at an inner door with the end of his spade, intimating by an inarticulate sound that there was the place where I must go, if I changed my locality.

It opened into the house, where the females were already astir. Zillah urging flakes of flame up the chimney with a colossal bellows; and Mrs. Heathcliff kneeling on the hearth, reading a book by the aid of the blaze. She held her hand interposed between the furnace-heat and her eyes, and seemed absorbed in her occupation; desisting from it only to chide the servant for covering her with sparks, or to push away a dog, now and then, that snoozled its nose over-forwardly into her face. I was surprised to see Heathcliff there also. He

stood by the fire, his back towards me, just finishing a stormy scene to poor Zillah; who ever and anon interrupted her labour to pluck up the corner of her apron, and heave an indignant groan.

'And you, you worthless'—he broke out as I entered, turning to his daughter-in-law, and employing an epithet as harmless as duck, or sheep, but generally represented by a dash——. 'There you are, at your idle tricks again! The rest of them do earn their bread—you live on my charity! Put your trash away, and find something to do. You shall pay me for the plague of having you eternally in my sight—do you hear, damnable jade?'

'I'll put my trash away, because you can make me, if I refuse,' answered the young lady, closing her book, and throwing it on a chair. 'But I'll not do anything, though you should swear your tongue out, except what I please!'

Heathcliff lifted his hand, and the speaker sprang to a safer distance obviously acquainted with its weight. Having no desire to be entertained by a cat-and-dog combat, I stepped forward briskly, as if eager to partake the warmth of the hearth, and innocent of any knowledge of the interrupted dispute. Each had enough decorum to suspend further hostilities: Heathcliff placed his fists, out of temptation, in his pockets; Mrs. Heathcliff curled her lip, and walked to a seat far off, where she kept her word by playing the part of a statue during the remainder of my stay. That was not long. I declined joining their breakfast, and, at the first gleam of dawn, took an opportunity of escaping into the free air, now clear, and still, and cold as impalpable ice.

My landlord hallooed for me to stop, ere I reached the bottom of the garden, and offered to accompany me across the moor. It was well he did, for the whole hill-back was one billowy, white ocean; the swells and falls not indicating corresponding rises and depressions in the ground: many pits, at least, were filled to a level; and entire ranges of mounds, the refuse of the quarries, blotted from the chart which my yesterday's walk left pictured in my mind. I had remarked on one side of the road, at intervals of six or seven yards, a line of upright stones, continued through the whole length of the barren: these were erected, and daubed with lime on purpose to serve as guides in the dark; and also when a fall, like the present, confounded the deep swamps on either hand with the firmer path: but, excepting a dirty dot pointing up here and there, all traces of their existence had vanished: and my companion found it necessary to warn me frequently to steer to the right or left, when I imagined I was following, correctly, the windings of the road. We exchanged little conversation, and he halted at the entrance of Thrushcross Park, saying, I could make no error there. Our adieux were limited to a hasty bow, and then I pushed forward, trusting to my own resources; for the porter's lodge is untenanted as yet. The distance from the gate to the Grange is two miles: I believe I managed to make it four; what with losing myself among the trees, and sinking up to the neck in snow: a predicament which only those who

have experienced it can appreciate. At any rate, whatever were my wanderings, the clock chimed twelve as I entered the house; and that gave exactly an hour for every mile of the usual way from Wuthering Heights.

My human fixture and her satellites rushed to welcome me; exclaiming, tumultuously, they had completely given me up; everybody conjectured that I perished last night; and they were wondering how they must set about the search for my remains. I bid them be quiet, now that they saw me returned, and, benumbed to my very heart, I dragged upstairs; whence, after putting on dry clothes, and pacing to and fro thirty or forty minutes, to restore the animal heat, I am adjourned to my study, feeble as a kitten: almost too much so to enjoy the cheerful fire and smoking coffee which the servant has prepared for my refreshment.

CHAPTER 4

What vain weather-cocks we are! I, who had determined to hold myself independent of all social intercourse, and thanked my stars that, at length, I had lighted on a spot where it was next to impracticable—I, weak wretch, after maintaining till dusk a struggle with low spirits and solitude, was finally compelled to strike my colours; and, under pretence of gaining information concerning the necessities of my establishment, I desired Mrs. Dean, when she brought in supper, to sit down while I ate it; hoping sincerely she would prove a regular gossip, and either rouse me to animation or lull me to sleep by her talk.

'You have lived here a considerable time,' I commenced; 'did you not say sixteen years?'

'Eighteen, sir. I came, when the mistress was married, to wait on her; after she died, the master retained me for his housekeeper.'

'Indeed.'

There ensued a pause. She was not a gossip, I feared; unless about her own affairs, and those could hardly interest me. However, having studied for an interval, with a fist on either knee, and a cloud of meditation over her ruddy countenance, she ejaculated:

'Ah, times are greatly changed since then!'

'Yes,' I remarked, 'You've seen a good many alterations, I suppose?'

'I have: and troubles too,' she said.

'Oh, I'll turn the talk on my landlord's family!' I thought to myself. 'A good subject to start—and that pretty girl-widow, I should like to know her history: whether she be a native of the country, or, as is more probable, an exotic that the surly *indigenæ* will not recognise for kin.' With this intention I asked Mrs. Dean why Heathcliff let Thrushcross Grange, and preferred

410

living in a situation and residence so much inferior. 'Is he not rich enough to keep the estate in good order?' I inquired.

'Rich, sir!' she returned. 'He has, nobody knows what money, and every year it increases. Yes, yes, he's rich enough to live in a finer house than this: but he's very near—close-handed; and, if he had meant to flit to Thrushcross Grange, as soon as he heard of a good tenant he could not have borne to miss the chance of getting a few hundreds more. It is strange people should be so greedy, when they are alone in the world!'

'He had a son, it seems?'

'Yes, he had one—he is dead.'

'And that young lady, Mrs. Heathcliff, is his widow?'

'Yes.'

'Where did she come from originally?'

'Why, sir, she is my late master's daughter: Catherine Linton was her maiden name. I nursed her, poor thing! I did wish Mr. Heathcliff would remove here, and then we might have been together again.'

'What! Catherine Linton?' I exclaimed, astonished. But a minute's reflection convinced me it was not my ghostly Catherine. 'Then,' I continued, 'my predecessor's name was Linton?'

'It was.'

'And who is that Earnshaw, Hareton Earnshaw, who lives with Mr. Heathcliff? are they relations?'

'No; he is the late Mrs. Linton's nephew.'

'The young lady's cousin, then?'

'Yes; and her husband was her cousin also: one on the mother's, the other on the father's side: Heathcliff married Mr. Linton's sister.'

'I see the house at Wuthering Heights has "Earnshaw" carved over the front door. Are they an old family?'

'Very old, sir; and Hareton is the last of them, as our Miss Cathy is of us—I mean of the Lintons. Have you been to Wuthering Heights? I beg pardon for asking; but I should like to hear how she is!'

'Mrs. Heathcliff? She looked very well, and very handsome; yet, I think, not very happy.'

'O dear, I don't wonder! And how did you like the master?'

'A rough fellow, rather, Mrs. Dean. Is not that his character?'

'Rough as a saw-edge, and hard as whinstone! The less you meddle with him the better.'

'He must have had some ups and downs in life to make him such a churl. Do you know anything of his history?'

'It's a cuckoo's, sir—I know all about it: except where he was born, and who were his parents, and how he got his money, at first. And Hareton has been cast out like an unfledged dunnock! The unfortunate lad is the only

one in all this parish that does not guess how he has been cheated.'

'Well, Mrs. Dean, it will be a charitable deed to tell me something of my neighbours: I feel I shall not rest, if I go to bed; so be good enough to sit and chat an hour.'

'Oh, certainly, sir! I'll just fetch a little sewing, and then I'll sit as long as you please. But you've caught cold: I saw you shivering, and you must have some gruel to drive it out.'

The worthy woman bustled off, and I crouched nearer the fire; my head felt hot, and the rest of me chill: moreover, I was excited, almost to a pitch of foolishness, through my nerves and brain. This caused me to feel, not uncomfortable, but rather fearful (as I am still) of serious effects from the incidents of to-day and yesterday. She returned presently, bringing a smoking basin and a basket of work; and, having placed the former on the hob, drew in her seat, evidently pleased to find me so companionable.

Before I came to live here, she commenced—waiting no further invitation to her story—I was almost always at Wuthering Heights; because my mother had nursed Mr. Hindley Earnshaw, that was Hareton's father, and I got used to playing with the children: I ran errands too, and helped to make hay, and hung about the farm ready for anything that anybody would set me to. One fine summer morning—it was the beginning of harvest, I remember—Mr. Earnshaw, the old master, came downstairs, dressed for a journey; and after he had told Joseph what was to be done during the day, he turned to Hindley, and Cathy, and me—for I sat eating my porridge with them—and he said, speaking to his son, 'Now my bonny man, I'm going to Liverpool to-day, what shall I bring you? You may choose what you like: only let it be little, for I shall walk there and back: sixty miles each way, that is a long spell!' Hindley named a fiddle, and then he asked Miss Cathy; she was hardly six years old, but she could ride any horse in the stable, and she chose a whip. He did not forget me; for he had a kind heart, though he was rather severe sometimes. He promised to bring me a pocketful of apples and pears, and then he kissed his children good-bye and set off.

It seemed a long while to us all—the three days of his absence—and often did little Cathy ask when he would be home. Mrs. Earnshaw expected him by supper-time on the third evening, and she put the meal off hour after hour; there were no signs of his coming, however, and at last the children got tired of running down to the gate to look. Then it grew dark; she would have had them to bed, but they begged sadly to be allowed to stay up; and just about eleven o'clock, the door-latch was raised quietly and in stepped the master. He threw himself into a chair, laughing and groaning, and bid them all stand off, for he was nearly killed—he would not have such another walk for the three kingdoms.

412

'And at the end of it, to be flighted to death!' he said, opening his great-coat, which he held bundled up in his arms. 'See here, wife! I was never so beaten with anything in my life: but you must e'en take it as a gift of God; though it's as dark almost as if it came from the devil.'

We crowded round, and over Miss Cathy's head, I had a peep at a dirty, ragged, black-haired child; big enough both to walk and talk: indeed, its face looked older than Catherine's; yet, when it was set on its feet, it only stared round, and repeated over and over again some gibberish, that nobody could understand. I was frightened, and Mrs. Earnshaw was ready to fling it out of doors: she did fly up, asking how he could fashion to bring that gipsy brat into the house, when they had their own bairns to feed and fend for? What he meant to do with it, and whether he were mad? The master tried to explain the matter; but he was really half-dead with fatigue, and all that I could make out, amongst her scolding, was a tale of his seeing it starving, and houseless, and as good as dumb, in the streets of Liverpool; where he picked it up and inquired for its owner. Not a soul knew to whom it belonged, he said; and his money and time being both limited, he thought it better to take it home with him at once, than run into vain expenses there: because he was determined he would not leave it as he found it. Well, the conclusion was that my mistress grumbled herself calm; and Mr. Earnshaw told me to wash it, and give it clean things, and let it sleep with the children.

Hindley and Cathy contented themselves with looking and listening till peace was restored: then, both began searching their father's pockets for the presents he had promised them. The former was a boy of fourteen, but when he drew out what had been a fiddle crushed to morsels in the great-coat, he blubbered aloud; and Cathy, when she learned the master had lost her whip in attending on the stranger, showed her humour by grinning and spitting at the stupid little thing; earning for her pains a sound blow from her father to teach her cleaner manners. They entirely refused to have it in bed with them, or even in their room; and I had no more sense, so I put it on the landing of the stairs, hoping it might be gone on the morrow. By chance, or else attracted by hearing his voice, it crept to Mr. Earnshaw's door, and there he found it on quitting his chamber. Inquiries were made as to how it got there; I was obliged to confess, and in recompense for my cowardice and inhumanity was sent out of the house.

This was Heathcliff's first introduction to the family. On coming back a few days afterwards (for I did not consider my banishment perpetual) I found they had christened him 'Heathcliff': it was the name of a son who died in childhood, and it has served him ever since, both for Christian and surname. Miss Cathy and he were now very thick; but Hindley hated him! and to say the truth I did the same; and we plagued and went on with him shamefully: for I wasn't reasonable enough to feel my injustice, and the mistress never

put in a word on his behalf when she saw him wronged.

He seemed a sullen, patient child; hardened, perhaps to ill-treatment: he would stand Hindley's blows without winking or shedding a tear, and my pinches moved him only to draw in a breath and open his eyes, as if he had hurt himself by accident and nobody was to blame. This endurance made old Earnshaw furious, when he discovered his son persecuting the poor, fatherless child, as he called him. He took to Heathcliff strangely, believing all he said (for that matter, he said precious little, and generally the truth), and petting him up far above Cathy, who was too mischievous and wayward for a favourite.

So, from the very beginning, he bred bad feeling in the house; and at Mrs. Earnshaw's death, which happened in less than two years after, the young master had learned to regard his father as an oppressor rather than a friend, and Heathcliff as a usurper of his parent's affections and his privileges; and he grew bitter with brooding over these injuries. I sympathised awhile; but when the children fell ill of the measles, and I had to tend them, and take on me the cares of a woman at once, I changed my ideas. Heathcliff was dangerously sick: and while he lay at the worst he would have me constantly by his pillow: I suppose he felt I did a good deal for him, and he hadn't wit to guess that I was compelled to do it. However, I will say this, he was the quietest child that ever nurse watched over. The difference between him and the others forced me to be less partial. Cathy and her brother harassed me terribly: *he* was as un-complaining as a lamb; though hardness, not gentleness, made him give little trouble.

He got through, and the doctor affirmed it was in a great measure owing to me, and praised me for my care. I was vain of his commendations, and softened towards the being by whose means I earned them, and thus Hindley lost his last ally: still I couldn't dote on Heathcliff, and I wondered often what my master saw to admire so much in the sullen boy, who never, to my recollection repaid his indulgence by any sign of gratitude. He was not insolent to his bene-factor, he was simply insensible; though knowing perfectly the hold he had on his heart, and conscious he had only to speak and all the house would be obliged to bend to his wishes. As an instance, I remember Mr. Earnshaw once bought a couple of colts at the parish fair, and gave the lads each one. Heath-cliff took the handsomest, but it soon fell lame, and when he discovered it, he said to Hindley—

'You must exchange horses with me: I don't like mine; and if you won't I shall tell your father of the three thrashings you've given me this week, and show him my arm, which is black to the shoulder.' Hindley put out his tongue and cuffed him over the ears. 'You'd better do it at once,' he persisted, escaping to the porch (they were in the stable): 'you will have to; and if I speak of these blows, you'll get them again with interest.' 'Off, dog!' cried Hindley, threaten-ing him with an iron weight used for weighing potatoes and hay. 'Throw it

he replied, standing still, 'and then I'll tell how you boasted that you would turn me out of doors as soon as he died, and see whether he will not turn you out directly.' Hindley threw it, hitting him on the breast, and down he fell, but staggered up immediately, breathless and white; and, had not I prevented it, he would have gone just so to the master, and got full revenge by letting his condition plead for him, intimating who had caused it. 'Take my colt, gipsy, then!' said young Earnshaw. 'And I pray that he may break your neck: take him, and be damned, you beggarly interloper! and wheedle my father out of all he has: only afterwards show him what you are, imp of Satan—And take that, I hope he'll kick out your brains!'

Heathcliff had gone to loose the beast, and shift it to his own stall; he was passing behind it, when Hindley finished his speech by knocking him under its feet, and without stopping to examine whether his hopes were fulfilled, ran away as fast as he could. I was surprised to witness how coolly the child gathered himself up, and went on with his intention; exchanging saddles and all, and then sitting down on a bundle of hay to overcome the qualm which the violent blow occasioned, before he entered the house. I persuaded him easily to let me lay the blame of his bruises on the horse: he minded little what tale was told since he had what he wanted. He complained so seldom, indeed, of such stirs as these, that I really thought him not vindictive: I was deceived completely, as you will hear.

CHAPTER 5

In the course of time, Mr. Earnshaw began to fail. He had been active and healthy, yet his strength left him suddenly; and when he was confined to the chimney-corner he grew grievously irritable. A nothing vexed him; and suspected slights of his authority nearly threw him into fits. This was especially to be remarked if any one attempted to impose upon, or domineer over, his favourite: he was painfully jealous lest a word should be spoken amiss to him; seeming to have got into his head the notion that, because he liked Heathcliff, all hated, and longed to do him an ill turn. It was a disadvantage to the lad; for the kinder among us did not wish to fret the master, so we humoured his partiality; and that humouring was rich nourishment to the child's pride and black tempers. Still it became in a manner necessary; twice, or thrice, Hindley's manifestation of scorn, while his father was near, roused the old man to a fury: he seized his stick to strike him, and shook with rage that he could not do it.

At last, our curate (we had a curate then who made the living answer by teaching the little Lintons and Earnshaws, and farming his bit of land himself), he advised that the young man should be sent to college; and Mr. Earnshaw agreed, though with a heavy spirit, for he said—'Hindley was nought, and

would never thrive as where he wandered.'

I hoped heartily we should have peace now. It hurt me to think the master should be made uncomfortable by his own good deed. I fancied the discontent of age and disease arose from his family disagreements: as he would have it that it did: really, you know, sir, it was in his sinking frame. We might have got on tolerably, notwithstanding, but for two people, Miss Cathy and Joseph, the servant: you saw him, I daresay, up yonder. He was, and is yet most likely, the wearisomest self-righteous Pharisee that ever ransacked a Bible to rake the promises to himself and fling the curses on his neighbours. By his knack of sermonising and pious discoursing, he contrived to make a great impression on Mr. Earnshaw; and the more feeble the master became, the more influence he gained. He was relentless in worrying him about his soul's concerns, and about ruling his children rigidly. He encouraged him to regard Hindley as a reprobate; and, night after night, he regularly grumbled out a long string of tales against Heathcliff and Catherine: always minding to flatter Earnshaw's weakness by heaping the heaviest blame on the last.

Certainly, she had ways with her such as I never saw a child take up before; and she put all of us past our patience fifty times and oftener in a day: from the hour she came downstairs till the hour she went to bed, we had not a minute's security that she wouldn't be in mischief. Her spirits were always at high-water mark, her tongue always going—singing, laughing, and plaguing everybody who would not do the same. A wild, wicked slip she was—but she had the bonniest eye, the sweetest smile, and lightest foot in the parish and, after all, I believe she meant no harm; for when once she made you cry in good earnest, it seldom happened that she would not keep you company and oblige you to be quiet that you might comfort her. She was much too fond of Heathcliff. The greatest punishment we could invent for her was to keep her separate from him: yet she got chided more than any of us on his account. In play, she liked exceedingly to act the little mistress; using her hands freely, and commanding her companions: she did so to me, but I would not bear shopping and ordering; and so I let her know.

Now, Mr. Earnshaw did not understand jokes from his children: he had always been strict and grave with them; and Catherine, on her part, had no idea why her father should be crosser and less patient in his ailing condition than he was in his prime. His peevish reproofs wakened in her a naughty delight to provoke him: she was never so happy as when we were all scolding her at once, and she defying us with her bold, saucy look, and her ready words; turning Joseph's religious curses into ridicule, baiting me, and doing just what her father hated most—showing how her pretended insolence which he thought real, had more power over Heathcliff than his kindness how the boy would do *her* bidding in anything, and *his* only when it suited his own inclination. After behaving as badly as possible all day, she sometimes

came fondling to make it up at night. 'Nay, Cathy,' the old man would say, 'I cannot love thee; thou'rt worse than thy brother. Go, say thy prayers, child, and ask God's pardon. I doubt thy mother and I must rue that we ever reared thee!' That made her cry, at first: and then being repulsed continually hardened her, and she laughed if I told her to say she was sorry for her faults, and beg to be forgiven.

But the hour came, at last, that ended Mr. Earnshaw's troubles on earth. He died quietly in his chair one October evening, seated by the fireside. A high wind blustered round the house, and roared in the chimney: it sounded wild and stormy, yet it was not cold, and we were all together—I, a little removed from the hearth, busy at my knitting, and Joseph reading his Bible near the table (for the servants generally sat in the house then, after their work was done). Miss Cathy had been sick, and that made her still; she leant against her father's knee, and Heathcliff was lying on the floor with his head in her lap. I remember the master, before he fell into a doze, stroking her bonny hair—it pleased him rarely to see her gentle—and saying—'Why canst thou not always be a good lass, Cathy?' And she turned her face up to his, and laughed, and answered, 'Why cannot you always be a good man, father?' But as soon as she saw him vexed again, she kissed his hand, and said she would sing him to sleep. She began singing very low, till his fingers dropped from hers, and his head sank on his breast. Then I told her to hush, and not stir, for fear she should wake him. We all kept as mute as mice a full half-hour, and should have done longer, only Joseph, having finished his chapter, got up and said that he must rouse the master for prayers and bed. He stepped forward, and called him by name, and touched his shoulder; but he would not move, so he took the candle and looked at him. I thought there was something wrong as he set down the light; and seizing the children each by an arm, whispered them to 'frame upstairs, and make little din—they might pray alone that evening—he had summut to do.'

'I shall bid father good-night first,' said Catherine, putting her arms round his neck, before we could hinder her. The poor thing discovered her loss directly—she screamed out—'Oh, he's dead, Heathcliff! he's dead!' And they both set up a heart-breaking cry.

I joined my wail to theirs, loud and bitter; but Joseph asked what we could be thinking of to roar in that way over a saint in heaven. He told me to put on my cloak and run to Gimmerton for the doctor and the parson. I could not guess the use that either would be of, then. However, I went, through wind and rain, and brought one, the doctor, back with me; the other said he would come in the morning. Leaving Joseph to explain matters; I ran to the children's room: their door was ajar, I saw they had never laid down, though it was past midnight; but they were calmer, and did not need me to console them. The little souls were comforting each other with better

thoughts than I could have hit on: no parson in the world ever pictured heaven so beautifully as they did, in their innocent talk: and, while I sobbed and listened, I could not help wishing we were all there safe together.

CHAPTER 6

Mr. Hindley came home to the funeral; and—a thing that amazed us, and set the neighbours gossiping right and left—he brought a wife with him. What she was, and where she was born, he never informed us: probably she had neither money nor name to recommend her, or he would scarcely have kept the union from his father.

She was not one that would have disturbed the house much on her own account. Every object she saw, the moment she crossed the threshold, appeared to delight her; and every circumstance that took place about her: except the preparing for the burial, and the presence of the mourners. I thought she was half silly, from her behaviour while that went on: she ran into her chamber, and made me come with her, though I should have been dressing the children; and there she sat shivering and clasping her hands, and asking repeatedly: 'Are they gone yet?' Then she began describing with hysterical emotion the effect it produced on her to see black; and started, and trembled, and, at last, fell a-weeping—and when I asked what was the matter? answered, she didn't know; but she felt so afraid of dying! I imagined her as little likely to die as myself. She was rather thin, but young, and fresh-complexioned, and her eyes sparkled as bright as diamonds. I did remark, to be sure, that mounting the stairs made her breathe very quick: that the least sudden noise set her all in a quiver, and that she coughed troublesomely sometimes: but I knew nothing of what these symptoms portended, and had no impulse to sympathise with her. We don't in general take to foreigners here, Mr Lockwood, unless they take to us first.

Young Earnshaw was altered considerably in the three years of his absence. He had grown sparer, and lost his colour, and spoke and dressed quite differently; and, on the very day of his return, he told Joseph and me we must thenceforth quarter ourselves in the back-kitchen, and leave the house for him. Indeed, he would have carpeted and papered a small spare room for a parlour; but his wife expressed such pleasure at the white floor and huge glowing fire-place, at the pewter dishes and delf-case, and dog-kennel, and the wide space there was to move about in where they usually sat, that he thought it unnecessary to her comfort, and so dropped the intention.

She expressed pleasure, too, at finding a sister among her new acquaintance; and she prattled to Catherine, and kissed her, and ran about with her, and gave her quantities of presents, at the beginning. Her affection tired ver

soon, however, and when she grew peevish, Hindley became tyrannical. A few words from her, evincing a dislike to Heathcliff, were enough to rouse in him all his old hatred of the boy. He drove him from their company to the servants, deprived him of the instructions of the curate, and insisted that he should labour out of doors instead; compelling him to do so as hard as any other lad on the farm.

Heathcliff bore his degradation pretty well at first, because Cathy taught him what she learnt, and worked or played with him in the fields. They both promised fair to grow up as rude as savages; the young master being entirely negligent how they behaved, and what they did, so they kept clear of him. He would not even have seen after their going to church on Sundays, only Joseph and the curate reprimanded his carelessness when they absented themselves; and that reminded him to order Heathcliff a flogging, and Catherine a fast from dinner or supper. But it was one of their chief amusements to run away to the moors in the morning and remain there all day, and the after punishment grew a mere thing to laugh at. The curate might set as many chapters as he pleased for Catherine to get by heart, and Joseph might thrash Heathcliff till his arm ached; they forgot everything the minute they were together again: at least the minute they had contrived some naughty plan of revenge; and many a time I've cried to myself to watch them growing more reckless daily, and I not daring to speak a syllable, for fear of losing the small power I still retained over the unfriended creatures. One Sunday evening, it chanced that they were banished from the sitting-room, for making a noise, or a light offence of the kind; and when I went to call them to supper, I could discover them nowhere. We searched the house, above and below, and the yard and stables; they were invisible: and at last, Hindley in a passion told us to bolt the doors, and swore nobody should let them in that night. The household went to bed; and I, too anxious to lie down, opened my lattice and put my head out to hearken, though it rained: determined to admit them in spite of the prohibition, should they return. In a while, I distinguished steps coming up the road, and the light of a lantern glimmered through the gate. I threw a shawl over my head and ran to prevent them from waking Mr. Earnshaw by knocking. There was Heathcliff, by himself: it gave me a start to see him alone.

'Where is Miss Catherine?' I cried hurriedly. 'No accident, I hope?' 'At Thrushcross Grange,' he answered; 'and I would have been there too, but they had not the manners to ask me to stay.' 'Well, you will catch it!' I said: 'you'll never be content till you're sent about your business. What in the world led you wandering to Thrushcross Grange?' 'Let me get off my wet clothes, and I'll tell you all about it, Nelly,' he replied. I bid him beware of rousing the master, and while he undressed and I waited to put out the candle, he continued—'Cathy and I escaped from the wash-house to have

a ramble at liberty, and getting a glimpse of the Grange lights, we thought we would just go and see whether the Lintons passed their Sunday evenings standing shivering in corners, while their father and mother sat eating and drinking, and singing and laughing, and burning their eyes out before the fire. Do you think they do? Or reading sermons, and being catechised by their man-servant, and set to learn a column of Scripture names, if they don't answer properly?' 'Probably not,' I responded. 'They are good children, no doubt, and don't deserve the treatment you receive, for your bad conduct.' 'Don't you cant, Nelly,' he said: 'nonsense! We ran from the top of the Heights to the park, without stopping—Catherine completely beaten in the race, because she was barefoot. You'll have to seek for her shoes in the bog to-morrow. We crept through a broken hedge, groped our way up the path, and planted ourselves on a flower-plot under the drawing-room window. The light came from thence; they had not put up the shutters, and the curtains were only half closed. Both of us were able to look in by standing on the basement, and clinging to the ledge, and we saw—ah! it was beautiful—a splendid place carpeted with crimson, and crimson-covered chairs and tables, and a pure white ceiling bordered by gold, a shower of glass-drops hanging in silver chains from the centre, and shimmering with little soft tapers. Old Mr. and Mrs. Linton were not there; Edgar and his sister had it entirely to themselves. Shouldn't they have been happy? We should have thought ourselves in heaven! And now, guess what your good children were doing? Isabella—I believe she is eleven, a year younger than Cathy—lay screaming at the farther end of the room, shrieking as if witches were running red-hot needles into her. Edgar stood on the hearth weeping silently, and in the middle of the table sat a little dog, shaking its paw and yelping; which, from their mutual accusations, we understood they had nearly pulled in two between them. The idiots! That was their pleasure! to quarrel who should hold a heap of warm hair, and each begin to cry because both, after struggling to get it, refused to take it. We laughed outright at the petted things; we did despise them! When would you catch me wishing to have what Catherine wanted? or find us by ourselves, seeking entertainment in yelling, and sobbing, and rolling on the ground, divided by the whole room? I'd not exchange, for a thousand lives, my condition here, for Edgar Linton's at Thrushcross Grange —not if I might have the privilege of flinging Joseph off the highest gable and painting the house-front with Hindley's blood!'

'Hush, hush!' I interrupted. 'Still you have not told me, Heathcliff, how Catherine is left behind?'

'I told you we laughed,' he answered. 'The Lintons heard us, and with one accord, they shot like arrows to the door; there was silence, and then a cry, "Oh, mamma, mamma! Oh, papa! Oh, mamma, come here. Oh, papa, oh!" They really did howl out something in that way. We made frightful

noises to terrify them still more, and then we dropped off the ledge, because somebody was drawing the bars, and we felt we had better flee. I had Cathy by the hand, and was urging her on, when all at once she fell down. "Run, Heathcliff, run!" she whispered. "They have let the bull-dog loose, and he holds me!" The devil had seized her ankle, Nelly: I heard his abominable snorting. She did not yell out—no! she would have scorned to do it, if she had been spitted on the horns of a mad cow. I did, though! I vociferated curses enough to annihilate any fiend in Christendom; and I got a stone and thrust it between his jaws, and tried with all my might to cram it down his throat. A beast of a servant came up with a lantern, at last, shouting— "Keep fast, Skulker, keep fast!" He changed his note, however, when he saw Skulker's game. The dog was throttled off; his huge, purple tongue hanging half a foot out of his mouth, and his pendent lips streaming with bloody slaver. The man took Cathy up: she was sick: not from fear, I'm certain, but from pain. He carried her in; I followed, grumbling execrations and vengeance. "What prey, Robert!" hallooed Linton from the entrance. "Skulker has caught a little girl, sir," he replied; "and there's a lad here," he added, making a clutch at me, "who looks an out-and-outer! Very like, the robbers were for putting them through the window to open the doors to the gang after all were asleep, that they might murder us at their ease. Hold your tongue, you foul-mouthed thief, you! you shall go to the gallows for this. Mr. Linton, sir, don't lay by your gun." "No, no, Robert," said the old fool. "The rascals knew that yesterday was my rent day: they thought to have me cleverly. Come in; I'll furnish them a reception. There, John, fasten the chain. Give Skulker some water, Jenny. To beard a magistrate in his stronghold, and on the Sabbath, too! Where will their insolence stop? Oh, my dear Mary, look here! Don't be afraid, it is but a boy—yet the villain scowls so plainly in his face; would it not be a kindness to the country to hang him at once, before he shows his nature in acts as well as features?" He pulled me under the chandelier, and Mrs. Linton placed her spectacles on her nose and raised her hands in horror. The cowardly children crept nearer also, Isabella lisping—"Frightful thing! Put him in the cellar, papa. He's exactly like the son of the fortune-teller that stole my tame pheasant. Isn't he, Edgar?"

'While they examined me, Cathy came round; she heard the last speech, and laughed. Edgar Linton, after an inquisitive stare, collected sufficient wit to recognise her. They see us at church, you know, though we seldom meet them elsewhere. "That's Miss Earnshaw!" he whispered to his mother, "and look how Skulker has bitten her—how her foot bleeds!"

' "Miss Earnshaw? Nonsense!" cried the dame; "Miss Earnshaw scouring the country with a gipsy! And yet, my dear, the child is in mourning—surely it is—and she may be lamed for life!"

' "What culpable carelessness in her brother!" exclaimed Mr. Linton,

turning from me to Catherine. "I've understood from Shielders" (that was the curate, sir) "that he lets her grow up in absolute heathenism. But who is this? Where did she pick up this companion? Oho! I declare he is that strange acquisition my late neighbour made, in his journey to Liverpool—a little Lascar, or an American or Spanish castaway."

' "A wicked boy, at all events," remarked the old lady, "and quite unfit for a decent house! Did you notice his language, Linton? I'm shocked that my children should have heard it."

'I recommenced cursing—don't be angry, Nelly—and so Robert was ordered to take me off. I refused to go without Cathy; he dragged me into the garden, pushed the lantern into my hand, assured me that Mr. Earnshaw should be informed of my behaviour, and, bidding me march directly, secured the door again. The curtains were still looped up at one corner, and I resumed my station as spy; because, if Catherine had wished to return, I intended shattering their great glass panes to a million of fragments, unless they let her out. She sat on the sofa quietly. Mrs. Linton took off the grey cloak of the dairymaid which we had borrowed for our excursion, shaking her head and expostulating with her, I suppose: she was a young lady, and they made a distinction between her treatment and mine. Then the woman-servant brought a basin of warm water, and washed her feet; and Mr. Linton mixed a tumbler of negus, and Isabella emptied a plateful of cakes into her lap, and Edgar stood gaping at a distance. Afterwards, they dried and combed her beautiful hair, and gave her a pair of enormous slippers, and wheeled her to the fire; and I left her, as merry as she could be, dividing her food between the little dog and Skulker, whose nose she pinched as he ate; and kindling a spark of spirit in the vacant blue eyes of the Lintons—a dim reflection from her own enchanting face. I saw they were full of stupid admiration; she is so immeasurably superior to them—to everybody on earth, is she not, Nelly?'

'There will more come of this business than you reckon on,' I answered, covering him up and extinguishing the light. 'You are incurable, Heathcliff; and Mr. Hindley will have to proceed to extremities, see if he won't.' My words came truer than I desired. The luckless adventure made Earnshaw furious. And then Mr. Linton, to mend matters, paid us a visit himself on the morrow; and read the young master such a lecture on the road he guided his family, that he was stirred to look about him, in earnest. Heathcliff received no flogging, but he was told that the first word he spoke to Miss Catherine should ensure a dismissal; and Mrs. Earnshaw undertook to keep her sister-in-law in due restraint when she returned home; employing art, not force: with force she would have found it impossible.

CHAPTER 7

Cathy stayed at Thrushcross Grange five weeks: till Christmas. By that time her ankle was thoroughly cured, and her manners much improved. The mistress visited her often in the interval, and commenced her plan of reform by trying to raise her self-respect with fine clothes and flattery, which she took readily; so that, instead of a wild, hatless little savage jumping into the house, and rushing to squeeze us all breathless, there lighted from a handsome black pony a very dignified person, with brown ringlets falling from the cover of a feathered beaver, and a long cloth habit, which she was obliged to hold up with both hands that she might sail in. Hindley lifted her from her horse, exclaiming delightedly, 'Why, Cathy, you are quite a beauty! I should scarcely have known you: you look like a lady now. Isabella Linton is not to be compared with her, is she, Frances?' 'Isabella has not her natural advantages,' replied his wife: 'but she must mind and not grow wild again here. Ellen, help Miss Catherine off with her things—stay, dear, you will disarrange your curls—let me untie your hat.'

I removed the habit, and there shone forth, beneath a grand plaid silk frock, white trousers, and burnished shoes; and, while her eyes sparkled joyfully when the dogs came bounding up to welcome her, she dare hardly touch them lest they should fawn upon her splendid garments. She kissed me gently: I was all flour making the Christmas cake, and it would not have done to give me a hug; and, then, she looked round for Heathcliff. Mr. and Mrs. Earnshaw watched anxiously their meeting; thinking it would enable them to judge, in some measure, what grounds they had for hoping to succeed in separating the two friends.

Heathcliff was hard to discover, at first. If he were careless, and uncared for, before Catherine's absence, he had been ten times more so, since. Nobody but I even did him the kindness to call him a dirty boy, and bid him wash himself, once a week; and children of his age seldom have a natural pleasure in soap and water. Therefore, not to mention his clothes, which had seen three months' service in mire and dust, and his thick uncombed hair, the surface of his face and hands was dismally beclouded. He might well skulk behind the settle, on beholding such a bright, graceful damsel enter the house, instead of a rough-headed counterpart of himself, as he expected. 'Is Heathcliff not here?' she demanded, pulling off her gloves, and displaying fingers wonderfully whitened with doing nothing and staying indoors.

'Heathcliff, you may come forward,' cried Mr. Hindley, enjoying his discomfiture, and gratified to see what a forbidding young blackguard he would be compelled to present himself. 'You may come and wish Miss Catherine welcome, like the other servants.'

Cathy, catching a glimpse of her friend in his concealment, flew to embrace him; she bestowed seven or eight kisses on his cheek within the second, and then stopped, and drawing back, burst into a laugh, exclaiming, 'Why, how very black and cross you look! and how—how funny and grim! But that's because I'm used to Edgar and Isabella Linton. Well, Heathcliff, have you forgotten me?'

She had some reason to put the question, for shame and pride threw double gloom over his countenance, and kept him immovable.

'Shake hands, Heathcliff,' said Mr. Earnshaw, condescendingly; 'once in a way, that is permitted.'

'I shall not,' replied the boy, finding his tongue at last; 'I shall not stand to be laughed at. I shall not bear it!'

And he would have broken from the circle, but Miss Cathy seized him again.

'I did not mean to laugh at you,' she said; 'I could not hinder myself: Heathcliff, shake hands at least! What are you sulky for? It was only that you looked odd. If you wash your face and brush your hair, it will be all right: but you are so dirty!'

She gazed concernedly at the dusky fingers she held in her own, and also at her dress; which she feared had gained no embellishment from its contact with his.

'You needn't have touched me!' he answered, following her eye and snatching away his hand. 'I shall be as dirty as I please: and I like to be dirty, and I will be dirty.'

With that he dashed head foremost out of the room, amid the merriment of the master and mistress, and to the serious disturbance of Catherine, who could not comprehend how her remarks should have produced such an exhibition of bad temper.

After playing lady's-maid to the new-comer, and putting my cakes in the oven, and making the house and kitchen cheerful with great fires, befitting Christmas eve, I prepared to sit down and amuse myself by singing carols all alone; regardless of Joseph's affirmations that he considered the merry tunes I chose as next door to songs. He had retired to private prayer in his chamber, and Mr. and Mrs. Earnshaw were engaging Missy's attention by sundry gay trifles bought for her to present to the little Lintons, as an acknowledgment of their kindness. They had invited them to spend the morrow at Wuthering Heights, and the invitation had been accepted, on one condition Mrs. Linton begged that her darlings might be kept carefully apart from that 'naughty swearing boy.'

Under these circumstances I remained solitary. I smelt the rich scent of the heating spices; and admired the shining kitchen utensils, the polished clock, decked in holly, the silver mugs ranged on a tray ready to be filled with

mulled ale for supper; and above all, the speckless purity of my particular care—the scoured and well-swept floor. I gave due inward applause to every object, and then I remembered how old Earnshaw used to come in when all was tidied, and call me a cant lass, and slip a shilling into my hand as a Christmas-box; and from that I went on to think of his fondness for Heathcliff, and his dread lest he should suffer neglect after death had removed him; and that naturally led me to consider the poor lad's situation now, and from singing I changed my mind to crying. It struck me soon, however, there would be more sense in endeavouring to repair some of his wrongs than shedding tears over them: I got up and walked into the court to seek him. He was not far; I found him smoothing the glossy coat of the new pony in the stable, and feeding the other beasts, according to custom.

'Make haste, Heathcliff!' I said, 'the kitchen is so comfortable; and Joseph is upstairs: make haste, and let me dress you smart before Miss Cathy comes out, and then you can sit together, with the whole hearth to yourselves, and have a long chatter till bedtime.'

He proceeded with his task and never turned his head towards me.

'Come—are you coming?' I continued. 'There's a little cake for each of you, nearly enough; and you'll need half an hour's donning.'

I waited five minutes, but getting no answer, left him. Catherine supped with her brother and sister-in-law: Joseph and I joined in an unsociable meal, seasoned with reproofs on one side and sauciness on the other. His cake and cheese remained on the table all night for the fairies. He managed to continue work till nine o'clock, and then marched dumb and dour to his chamber. Cathy sat up late, having a world of things to order for the reception of her new friends: she came into the kitchen once to speak to her old one; but he was gone, and she only stayed to ask what was the matter with him, and then went back. In the morning he rose early; and as it was a holiday carried his ill-humour on to the moors; not re-appearing till the family were departed for church. Fasting and reflection seemed to have brought him to a better spirit. He hung about me for a while, and having screwed up his courage, exclaimed abruptly:

'Nelly, make me decent, I'm going to be good.'

'High time, Heathcliff,' I said; 'you *have* grieved Catherine: she's sorry she ever came home, I dare say! It looks as if you envied her, because she is more thought of than you.'

The notion of *envying* Catherine was incomprehensible to him, but the notion of grieving her he understood clearly enough.

'Did she say she was grieved?' he inquired, looking very serious.

'She cried when I told her you were off again this morning.'

'Well, *I* cried last night,' he returned, 'and I had more reason to cry than she.'

425

'Yes: you had the reason of going to bed with a proud heart and an empty stomach,' said I. 'Proud people breed sad sorrows for themselves. But, if you be ashamed of your touchiness, you must ask pardon, mind, when she comes in. You must go up and offer to kiss her, and say—you know best what to say; only do it heartily, and not as if you thought her converted into a stranger by her grand dress. And now, though I have dinner to get ready. I'll steal time to arrange you so that Edgar Linton shall look quite a doll beside you: and that he does. You are younger, and yet, I'll be bound, you are taller and twice as broad across the shoulders: you could knock him down in a twinkling? don't you feel that you could?'

Heathcliff's face brightened a moment; then it was overcast afresh, and he sighed.

'But, Nelly, if I knocked him down twenty times, that wouldn't make him less handsome or me more so. I wish I had light hair and a fair skin, and was dressed and behaved as well, and had a chance of being as rich as he will be!'

'And cried for mamma at every turn,' I added, 'and trembled if a country lad heaved his fist against you, and sat at home all day for a shower of rain. Oh, Heathcliff, you are showing a poor spirit! Come to the glass, and I'll let you see what you should wish. Do you mark those two lines between your eyes; and those thick brows, that instead of rising arched, sink in the middle; and that couple of black fiends, so deeply buried, who never open their windows boldly, but lurk glinting under them, like devil's spies? Wish and learn to smooth away the surly wrinkles, to raise your lids frankly, and change the fiends to confident, innocent angels, suspecting and doubting nothing, and always seeing friends where they are not sure of foes. Don't get the expression of a vicious cur that appears to know the kicks it gets are its desert, and yet hates all the world as well as the kicker, for what it suffers.'

'In other words, I must wish for Edgar Linton's great blue eyes and even forehead,' he replied. 'I do—and that won't help me to them.'

'A good heart will help you to a bonny face, my lad.' I continued, 'if you were a regular black; and a bad one will turn the bonniest into something worse than ugly. And now that we've done washing, and combing, and sulking—tell me whether you don't think yourself rather handsome? I'll tell you, I do. You're fit for a prince in disguise. Who knows but your father was Emperor of China, and your mother an Indian queen, each of them able to buy up, with one week's income, Wuthering Heights and Thrushcross Grange together? And you were kidnapped by wicked sailors and brought to England. Were I in your place, I would frame high notions of my birth; and the thought of what I was should give me courage and dignity to support the oppression of a little farmer!'

So I chattered on; and Heathcliff gradually lost his frown and began to look quite pleasant, when all at once our conversation was interrupted by a rumbling sound moving up the road and entering the court. He ran to the window and I to the door, just in time to behold the two Lintons descend from the family carriage, smothered in cloaks and furs, and the Earnshaws dismount from their horses: they often rode to church in winter. Catherine took a hand of each of the children, and brought them into the house and set them before the fire, which quickly put colour into their white faces.

I urged my companion to hasten now and show his amiable humour, and he willingly obeyed; but ill luck would have it that, as he opened the door leading from the kitchen on one side, Hindley opened it on the other. They met, and the master, irritated at seeing him clean and cheerful; or, perhaps, eager to keep his promise to Mrs. Linton, shoved him back with a sudden thrust, and angrily bade Joseph 'keep the fellow out of the room—send him into the garret till dinner is over. He'll be cramming his fingers in the tarts and stealing the fruit, if left alone with them a minute.'

'Nay, sir,' I could not avoid answering, 'he'll touch nothing, not he: and I suppose he must have his share of the dainties as well as we.'

'He shall have his share of my hand, if I catch him downstairs again till dark,' cried Hindley. 'Begone, you vagabond! What! you are attempting the coxcomb, are you? Wait till I get hold of those elegant locks—see if I won't pull them a bit longer.'

'They are long enough, already,' observed Master Linton, peeping from the doorway; 'I wonder they don't make his head ache. It's like a colt's mane over his eyes!'

He ventured his remark without any intention to insult; but Heathcliff's violent nature was not prepared to endure the appearance of impertinence from one whom he seemed to hate, even then, as a rival. He seized a tureen of hot apple sauce (the first thing that come under his gripe) and dashed it all against the speaker's face and neck; who instantly commenced a lament that brought Isabella and Catherine hurrying to the place. Mr. Earnshaw snatched up the culprit directly and conveyed him to his chamber; where, doubtless, he administered a rough remedy to cool the fit of passion, for he reappeared red and breathless. I got the dish-cloth, and rather spitefully scrubbed Edgar's nose and mouth, affirming it served him right for meddling. His sister began weeping to go home, and Cathy stood by confounded, blushing for all.

'You should not have spoken to him!' she expostulated with Master Linton. 'He was in a bad temper, and now you've spoilt your visit; and he'll be flogged: I hate him to be flogged! I can't eat my dinner. Why did you speak to him, Edgar?'

'I didn't,' sobbed the youth, escaping from my hands, and finishing the

remainder of the purification with his cambric pocket-handkerchief. 'I promised mamma that I wouldn't say one word to him, and I didn't.'

'Well, don't cry,' replied Catherine, contemptuously, 'you're not killed. Don't make more mischief; my brother is coming: be quiet! Give over, Isabella! Has anybody hurt *you*?'

'There, there, children—to your seats!' cried Hindley, bustling in. 'That brute of a lad has warmed me nicely. Next time, Master Edgar, take the law into your own fists—it will give you an appetite!'

The little party recovered its equanimity at sight of the fragrant feast. They were hungry after their ride, and easily consoled, since no real harm had befallen them. Mr. Earnshaw carved bountiful platefuls, and the mistress made them merry with lively talk. I waited behind her chair, and was pained to behold Catherine, with dry eyes and an indifferent air, commence cutting up the wing of a goose before her. 'An unfeeling child,' I thought to myself; 'how lightly she dismisses her old playmate's troubles. I could not have imagined her to be so selfish.' She lifted a mouthful to her lips; then she set it down again: her cheeks flushed, and the tears gushed over them. She slipped her fork to the floor, and hastily dived under the cloth to conceal her emotion. I did not call her unfeeling long; for I perceived she was in purgatory throughout the day, and wearying to find an opportunity of getting by herself or paying a visit to Heathcliff, who had been locked up by the master: as I discovered, on endeavouring to introduce to him a private mess of victuals.

In the evening we had a dance. Cathy begged that he might be liberated then, as Isabella Linton had no partner; her entreaties were vain, and I was appointed to supply the deficiency. We got rid of all gloom in the excitement of the exercise, and our pleasure was increased by the arrival of the Gimmerton band, mustering fifteen strong: a trumpet, a trombone, clarionets, bassoons, French horns, and a bass viol, besides singers. They go the rounds of all the respectable houses, and receive contributions every Christmas, and we esteemed it a first-rate treat to hear them. After the usual carols had been sung, we set them to songs and glees. Mrs. Earnshaw loved the music, and so they gave us plenty.

Catherine loved it too; but she said it sounded sweetest at the top of the steps, and she went up in the dark; I followed. They shut the house door below, never noting our absence, it was so full of people. She made no stay at the stair's head, but mounted farther, to the garret where Heathcliff was confined, and called him. He stubbornly declined answering for a while; she persevered, and finally persuaded him to hold communion with her through the boards. I let the poor things converse unmolested, till I supposed the songs were going to cease, and the singers to get some refreshment; then I clambered up the ladder to warn her. Instead of finding her outside, I heard her voice within. The little monkey had crept by the skylight of one garret

along the roof, into the skylight of the other, and it was with the utmost difficulty I could coax her out again. When she did come Heathcliff came with her, and she insisted that I should take him into the kitchen, as my fellow-servant had gone to a neighbour's to be removed from the sound of our 'devil's psalmody,' as it pleased him to call it. I told them I intended by no means to encourage their tricks; but as the prisoner had never broken his fast since yesterday's dinner, I would wink at his cheating Mr. Hindley that once. He went down; I set him a stool by the fire, and offered him a quantity of good things; but he was sick and could eat little, and my attempts to entertain him were thrown away. He leant his two elbows on his knees, and his chin on his hands, and remained wrapt in dumb meditation. On my inquiring the subject of his thoughts, he answered gravely:

'I'm trying to settle how I shall pay Hindley back. I don't care how long I wait, if I can only do it at last. I hope he will not die before I do!'

'For shame, Heathcliff!' said I. 'It is for God to punish wicked people; we should learn to forgive.'

'No, God won't have the satisfaction that I shall,' he returned. 'I only wish I knew the best way! Let me alone, and I'll plan it out: while I'm thinking of that I don't feel pain.'

But, Mr. Lockwood, I forget these tales cannot divert you. I'm annoyed how I should dream of chattering on at such a rate; and your gruel cold, and you nodding for bed! I could have told Heathcliff's history, all that you need hear, in half-a-dozen words.

Thus interrupting herself, the housekeeper rose, and proceeded to lay aside her sewing; but I felt incapable of moving from the hearth, and I was very far from nodding. 'Sit still, Mrs. Dean,' I cried, 'do sit still, another half-hour! You've done just right to tell the story leisurely. That is the method I like; and you must finish it in the same style. I am interested in every charac-ter you have mentioned, more or less.'

'The clock is on the stroke of eleven, sir.'

'No matter—I'm not accustomed to go to bed in the long hours. One or two is early enough for a person who lies till ten.'

'You shouldn't lie till ten. There's the very prime of the morning gone long before that time. A person who has not done one half his day's work by ten o'clock, runs a chance of leaving the other half undone.'

'Nevertheless, Mrs. Dean, resume your chair; because to-morrow I intend lengthening the night till afternoon. I prognosticate for myself an obstinate cold, at least.'

'I hope not, sir. Well, you must allow me to leap over some three years; during that space Mrs. Earnshaw'—

'No, no, I'll allow nothing of the sort! Are you acquainted with the mood of mind in which, if you were seated alone, and the cat licking its kitten on the rug before you, you would watch the operation so intently that puss's neglect of one ear would put you seriously out of temper?'

'A terribly lazy mood, I should say.'

'On the contrary, a tiresomely active one. It is mine, at present; and, therefore, continue minutely. I perceive that people in these regions acquire over people in towns the value that the spider in a dungeon does over a spider in a cottage, to their various occupants; and yet the deepened attraction is not entirely owing to the situation of the looker-on. They *do* live more in earnest more in themselves, and less in surface-change, and frivolous external things I could fancy a love for life here almost possible; and I was a fixed unbeliever in any love of a year's standing. One state resembles setting a hungry man down to a single dish, on which he may concentrate his entire appetite and do it justice; the other, introducing him to a table laid out by French cooks he can perhaps extract as much enjoyment from the whole; but each part is a mere atom in his regard and remembrance.'

'Oh, here we are the same as anywhere else, when you get to know us,' observed Mrs. Dean, somewhat puzzled at my speech.

'Excuse me,' I responded; 'you, my good friend, are a striking evidence against that assertion. Excepting a few provincialisms of slight consequence you have no marks of the manners which I am habituated to consider as peculiar to your class. I am sure you have thought a great deal more than the generality of servants think. You have been compelled to cultivate your reflective faculties for want of occasions for frittering your life away in silly trifles.'

Mrs. Dean laughed.

'I certainly esteem myself a steady, reasonable kind of body,' she said 'not exactly from living among the hills and seeing one set of faces, and one series of actions, from year's end to year's end; but I have undergone sharp discipline, which has taught me wisdom; and then, I have read more than you would fancy, Mr. Lockwood. You could not open a book in this library that I have not looked into, and got something out of also: unless it be that range of Greek and Latin, and that of French; and those I know one from another: it is as much as you can expect of a poor man's daughter. However if I am to follow my story in true gossip's fashion, I had better go on; and instead of leaping three years, I will be content to pass to the next summer—the summer of 1778, that is, nearly twenty-three years ago.'

CHAPTER 8

On the morning of a fine June day, my first bonny little nursling, and the last of the ancient Earnshaw stock, was born. We were busy with the hay in a far away field, when the girl that usually brought our breakfasts, came running an hour too soon, across the meadow and up the lane, calling me as she ran.

'Oh, such a grand bairn!' she panted out. 'The finest lad that ever breathed! But the doctor says missis must go: he says she's been in a consumption these many months. I heard him tell Mr. Hindley: and now she has nothing to keep her, and she'll be dead before winter. You must come home directly. You're to nurse it, Nelly: to feed it with sugar and milk, and take care of it day and night. I wish I were you, because it will be all yours when there is no missis!'

'But is she very ill?' I asked, flinging down my rake, and tying my bonnet.

'I guess she is; yet she looks bravely,' replied the girl, 'and she talks as if she thought of living to see it grow a man. She's out of her head for joy, it's such a beauty! If I were her, I'm certain I should not die: I should get better at the bare sight of it, in spite of Kenneth. I was fairly mad at him. Dame Archer brought the cherub down to master, in the house, and his face just began to light up, then the old croaker steps forward, and says he: "Earnshaw, it's a blessing your wife has been spared to leave you this son. When she came, I felt convinced we shouldn't keep her long; and now, I must tell you, the winter will probably finish her. Don't take on, and fret about it too much! It can't be helped. And besides, you should have known better than to choose such a rush of a lass!" '

'And what did the master answer?' I inquired.

'I think he swore: but I didn't mind him, I was straining to see the bairn,' and she began again to describe it rapturously. I, as zealous as herself, hurried eagerly home to admire, on my part; though I was very sad for Hindley's sake. He had room in his heart only for two idols—his wife and himself: he doted on both, and adored one, and I couldn't conceive how he would bear the loss.

When we got to Wuthering Heights, there he stood at the front door; and, as I passed in, I asked, 'How was the baby?'

'Nearly ready to run about, Nell;' he replied, putting on a cheerful smile.

'And the mistress?' I ventured to inquire; 'the doctor says she's'——

'Damn the doctor!' he interrupted, reddening. 'Frances is quite right; she'll be perfectly well by this time next week. Are you going upstairs? will you tell her that I'll come, if she'll promise not to talk. I left her because she would not hold her tongue; and she must—tell her Mr. Kenneth says she must be quiet.'

I delivered this message to Mrs. Earnshaw; she seemed in flighty spirits and replied merrily:

'I hardly spoke a word, Ellen, and there he has gone out twice, crying Well, say I promise I won't speak: but that does not bind me not to laugh at him!'

Poor soul! Till within a week of her death that gay heart never failed her and her husband persisted doggedly, nay, furiously, in affirming her health improved every day. When Kenneth warned him that his medicines were useless at that stage of the malady, and he needn't put him to further expense by attending her, he retorted:

'I know you need not—she's well—she does not want any more attendance from you! She never was in a consumption. It was a fever; and it is gone her pulse is as slow as mine now, and her cheek as cool.'

He told his wife the same story, and she seemed to believe him; but one night, while leaning on his shoulder, in the act of saying she thought she should be able to get up to-morrow, a fit of coughing took her—a very slight one—he raised her in his arms; she put her two hands about his neck, her face changed and she was dead.

As the girl had anticipated, the child Hareton fell wholly into my hands Mr. Earnshaw, provided he saw him healthy and never heard him cry, was contented, as far as regarded him. For himself, he grew desperate: his sorrow was of that kind that will not lament. He neither wept nor prayed: he cursed and defied: execrated God and man, and gave himself up to reckless dissipation The servants could not bear his tyrannical and evil conduct long: Joseph and I were the only two that would stay. I had not the heart to leave my charge; and besides, you know I had been his foster-sister, and excused his behaviour more readily than a stranger would. Joseph remained to hector over tenants and labourers; and because it was his vocation to be where he had plenty of wickedness to reprove.

The master's bad ways and bad companions formed a pretty example for Catherine and Heathcliff. His treatment of the latter was enough to make a fiend of a saint. And, truly, it appeared as if the lad *were* possessed of something diabolical at that period. He delighted to witness Hindley degrading himself past redemption; and became daily more notable for savage sullenness and ferocity. I could not half tell what an infernal house we had. The curate dropped calling, and nobody decent came near us, at last; unless Edgar Linton' visits to Miss Cathy might be an exception. At fifteen she was the queen of the country side; she had no peer; and she did turn out a haughty, head strong creature! I own I did not like her, after her infancy was past; and I vexed her frequently by trying to bring down her arrogance: she never took an aversion to me, though. She had a wondrous constancy to old attach ments: even Heathcliff kept his hold on her affections unalterably; and young

Linton, with all his superiority, found it difficult to make an equally deep impression. He was my late master: that is his portrait over the fireplace. It used to hang on one side, and his wife's on the other; but hers has been removed, or else you might see something of what she was. Can you make that out?

Mrs. Dean raised the candle, and I discerned a soft-featured face, exceedingly resembling the young lady at the Heights, but more pensive and amiable in expression. It formed a sweet picture. The long light hair curled slightly on the temples; the eyes were large and serious; the figure almost too graceful. I did not marvel how Catherine Earnshaw could forget her first friend for such an individual. I marvelled much how he, with a mind to correspond with his person, could fancy my idea of Catherine Earnshaw.

'A very agreeable portrait,' I observed to the housekeeper. 'Is it like?'

'Yes,' she answered; 'but he looked better when he was animated; that is his everyday countenance: he wanted spirit in general.'

Catherine had kept up her acquaintance with the Lintons since her five weeks' residence among them; and as she had no temptation to show her rough side in their company, and had the sense to be ashamed of being rude where she experienced such invariable courtesy, she imposed unwittingly on the old lady and gentleman, by her ingenious cordiality; gained the admiration of Isabella, and the heart and soul of her brother: acquisitions that flattered her from the first, for she was full of ambition, and led her to adopt a double character without exactly intending to deceive any one. In the place where she heard Heathcliff termed a 'vulgar young ruffian,' and 'worse than a brute,' she took care not to act like him; but at home she had small inclination to practise politeness that would only be laughed at, and restrain an unruly nature when it would bring her neither credit nor praise.

Mr. Edgar seldom mustered courage to visit Wuthering Heights openly. He had a terror of Earnshaw's reputation, and shrunk from encountering him; and yet he was always received with our best attempts at civility: the master himself avoided offending him, knowing why he came; and if he could not be gracious, kept out of the way. I rather think his appearance there was distasteful to Catherine: she was not artful, never played the coquette, and had evidently an objection to her two friends meeting at all; for when Heathcliff expressed contempt of Linton in his presence, she could not half coincide, as she did in his absence; and when Linton evinced disgust and antipathy to Heathcliff, she dared not treat his sentiments with indifference, as if depreciation of her playmate were of scarcely any consequence to her. I've had many a laugh at her perplexities and untold troubles, which she vainly strove to hide from my mockery. That sounds ill-natured: but she was so proud, it became really impossible to pity her distresses, till she should be chastened into more humility. She did bring herself, finally, to confess, and

confide in me: there was not a soul else that she might fashion into an adviser.

Mr. Hindley had gone from home one afternoon, and Heathcliff presumed to give himself a holiday on the strength of it. He had reached the age of sixteen then, I think, and without having bad features, or being deficient in intellect, he contrived to convey an impression of inward and outward repulsiveness that his present aspect retains no traces of. In the first place, he had by that time lost the benefit of his early education: continual hard work, begun soon and concluded late, had extinguished any curiosity he once possessed in pursuit of knowledge, and any love for books or learning. His childhood's sense of superiority, instilled into him by the favours of old Mr. Earnshaw, was faded away. He struggled long to keep up an equality with Catherine in her studies, and yielded with poignant though silent regret: but he yielded completely; and there was no prevailing on him to take a step in the way of moving upward, when he found he must, necessarily, sink beneath his former level. Then personal appearance sympathised with mental deterioration: he acquired a slouching gait, and ignoble look; his naturally reserved disposition was exaggerated into an almost idiotic excess of unsociable moroseness; and he took a grim pleasure, apparently, in exciting the aversion rather than the esteem of his few acquaintance.

Catherine and he were constant companions still at his seasons of respite from labour; but he had ceased to express his fondness for her in words, and recoiled with angry suspicion from her girlish caresses, as if conscious there could be no gratification in lavishing such marks of affection on him. On the before-named occasion he came into the house to announce his intention of doing nothing, while I was assisting Miss Cathy to arrange her dress: she had not reckoned on his taking it into his head to be idle; and imagining she would have the whole place to herself, she managed, by some means, to inform Mr. Edgar of her brother's absence, and was then preparing to receive him.

'Cathy, are you busy, this afternoon?' asked Heathcliff. 'Are you going anywhere?'

'No, it is raining,' she answered.

'Why have you that silk frock on, then?' he said. 'Nobody coming here I hope?'

'Not that I know of,' stammered Miss: 'but you should be in the field now, Heathcliff. It is an hour past dinner time: I thought you were gone.'

'Hindley does not often free us from his accursed presence,' observed the boy. 'I'll not work any more to-day: I'll stay with you.'

'Oh, but Joseph will tell,' she suggested; 'you'd better go!'

'Joseph is loading lime on the further side of Pennistow Crag; it will take him till dark, and he'll never know.'

So saying, he lounged to the fire, and sat down. Catherine reflected an instant, with knitted brows—she found it needful to smooth the way for an

ntrusion. 'Isabella and Edgar Linton talked of calling this afternoon,' she said, at the conclusion of a minute's silence. 'As it rains, I hardly expect them; but they may come, and if they do, you run the risk of being scolded for no good.'

'Order Ellen to say you are engaged, Cathy,' he persisted; 'don't turn me out for those pitiful, silly friends of yours! I'm on the point, sometimes, of complaining that they—but I'll not'——

'That they what?' cried Catherine, gazing at him with a troubled countenance. 'Oh, Nelly!' she added petulantly; jerking her head away from my hands, 'you've combed my hair quite out of curl! That's enough; let me alone. What are you on the point of complaining about, Heathcliff?'

'Nothing—only look at the almanac on that wall;' he pointed to a framed sheet hanging near the window, and continued—'The crosses are for the evenings you have spent with the Lintons, the dots for those spent with me. Do you see? I've marked every day.'

'Yes—very foolish: as if I took notice!' replied Catherine in a peevish tone. 'And where is the sense of that?'

'To show that I *do* take notice,' said Heathcliff.

'And should I always be sitting with you?' she demanded, growing more irritated. 'What good do I get? What do you talk about? You might be dumb, or a baby, for anything you say to amuse me, or for anything you do, either!'

'You never told me before that I talked too little, or that you disliked my company, Cathy!' exclaimed Heathcliff, in much agitation.

'It's no company at all, when people know nothing and say nothing,' she muttered.

Her companion rose up, but he hadn't time to express his feelings further, for a horse's feet were heard on the flags, and having knocked gently, young Linton entered, his face brilliant with delight at the unexpected summons he had received. Doubtless Catherine marked the difference between her friends, as one came in and the other went out. The contrast resembled what you see in exchanging a bleak, hilly, coal country for a beautiful fertile valley; and his voice and greeting were as opposite as his aspect. He had a sweet, low manner of speaking, and pronounced his words as you do: that's less gruff than we talk here, and softer.

'I'm not come too soon, am I?' he said, casting a look at me: I had begun to wipe the plate, and tidy some drawers at the far end in the dresser.

'No,' answered Catherine. 'What are you doing there, Nelly?'

'My work, miss,' I replied. (Mr. Hindley had given me directions to make a third party in any private visits Linton chose to pay.)

She stepped behind me and whispered crossly, 'Take yourself and your dusters off; when company are in the house, servants don't commence scouring and cleaning in the room where they are!'

'It's a good opportunity, now that the master is away,' I answered aloud:

'he hates me to be fidgeting over these things in his presence. I'm sure Mr. Edgar will excuse me.'

'I hate you to be fidgeting in *my* presence,' exclaimed the young lady imperiously, not allowing her guest time to speak: she had failed to recover her equanimity since the little dispute with Heathcliff.

'I'm sorry for it, Miss Catherine,' was my response; and I proceeded assiduously with my occupation.

She, supposing Edgar could not see her, snatched the cloth from my hand, and pinched me, with a prolonged wrench, very spitefully on the arm. I've said I did not love her, and rather relished mortifying her vanity now and then besides, she hurt me extremely; so I started up from my knees, and screamed out, 'Oh, miss, that's a nasty trick! You have no right to nip me, and I'm not going to bear it.'

'I didn't touch you, you lying creature!' cried she, her fingers tingling to repeat the act, and her ears red with rage. She never had power to conceal her passion, it always set her whole complexion in a blaze.

'What's that, then?' I retorted, showing a decided purple witness to refute her.

She stamped her foot, wavered a moment, and then irresistibly impelled by the naughty spirit within her, slapped me on the cheek a stinging blow that filled both eyes with water.

'Catherine, love! Catherine!' interposed Linton, greatly shocked at the double fault of falsehood and violence which his idol had committed.

'Leave the room, Ellen!' she repeated, trembling all over.

Little Hareton, who followed me everywhere, and was sitting near me on the floor, at seeing my tears commenced crying himself, and sobbed out complaints against 'wicked aunt Cathy,' which drew her fury on to his unlucky head: she seized his shoulders, and shook him till the poor child waxed livid and Edgar thoughtlessly laid hold of her hands to deliver him. In an instant one was wrung free, and the astonished young man felt it applied over his own ear in a way that could not be mistaken for jest. He drew back in consternation I lifted Hareton in my arms, and walked off to the kitchen with him, leaving the door of communication open, for I was curious to watch how they would settle their disagreement. The insulted visitor moved to the spot where he had laid his hat, pale and with a quivering lip.

'That's right!' I said to myself. 'Take warning and begone! It's a kindness to let you have a glimpse of her genuine disposition.'

'Where are you going?' demanded Catherine, advancing to the door.

He swerved aside, and attempted to pass.

'You must not go!' she exclaimed energetically.

'I must and shall!' he replied in a subdued voice.

'No,' she persisted, grasping the handle; 'not yet, Edgar Linton: sit down

you shall not leave me in that temper. I should be miserable all night, and I won't be miserable for you!'

'Can I stay after you have struck me?' asked Linton.

Catherine was mute.

'You've made me afraid and ashamed of you,' he continued; 'I'll not come here again!'

Her eyes began to glisten, and her lids to twinkle.

'And you told a deliberate untruth!' he said.

'I didn't!' she cried, recovering her speech; 'I did nothing deliberately. Well, go, if you please—get away! And now I'll cry—I'll cry myself sick!'

She dropped down on her knees by a chair, and set to weeping in serious earnest. Edgar persevered in his resolution as far as the court; there he lingered. I resolved to encourage him.

'Miss is dreadfully wayward, sir,' I called out. 'As bad as any marred child: you'd better be riding home, or else she will be sick only to grieve us.'

The soft thing looked askance through the window: he possessed the power to depart, as much as a cat possesses the power to leave a mouse half killed, or a bird half eaten. Ah, I thought, there will be no saving him: he's doomed, and flies to his fate! And so it was: he turned abruptly, hastened into the house again, shut the door behind him; and when I went in a while after to inform them that Earnshaw had come home rabid drunk, ready to pull the whole place about our ears (his ordinary frame of mind in that condition), I saw the quarrel had merely effected a closer intimacy—had broken the outworks of youthful timidity, and enabled them to forsake the disguise of friendship, and confess themselves lovers.

Intelligence of Mr. Hindley's arrival drove Linton speedily to his horse, and Catherine to her chamber. I went to hide little Hareton, and to take the shot out of the master's fowling-piece, which he was fond of playing with in his insane excitement, to the hazard of the lives of any who provoked, or even attracted his notice too much; and I had hit upon the plan of removing it, that he might do less mischief if he did go the length of firing the gun.

CHAPTER 9

He entered, vociferating oaths dreadful to hear; and caught me in the act of stowing his son away in the kitchen cupboard. Hareton was impressed with a wholesome terror of encountering either his wild beast's fondness or his madman's rage; for in one he ran a chance of being squeezed and kissed to death, and in the other of being flung into the fire, or dashed against the wall; and the poor thing remained perfectly quiet wherever I chose to put him.

'There, I've found it out at last!' cried Hindley, pulling me back by the skin of my neck, like a dog. 'By heaven and hell, you've sworn between you to murder that child! I know how it is, now, that he is always out of my way. But, with the help of Satan, I shall make you swallow the carving-knife, Nelly! You needn't laugh; for I've just crammed Kenneth, head-downmost, in the Blackhorse marsh; and two is the same as one—and I want to kill some of you: I shall have no rest till I do!'

'But I don't like the carving-knife, Mr. Hindley,' I answered: 'it has been cutting red herrings. I'd rather be shot, if you please.'

'You'd rather be damned!' he said; 'and so you shall. No law in England can hinder a man from keeping his house decent, and mine's abominable! open your mouth.'

He held the knife in his hand, and pushed its point between my teeth: but for my part, I was never much afraid of his vagaries. I spat out, and affirmed it tasted detestably—I would not take it on any account.

'Oh!' said he, releasing me, 'I see that hideous little villain is not Hareton I beg your pardon, Nell. If it be, he deserves flaying alive for not running to welcome me, and for screaming as if I were a goblin. Unnatural cub, come hither! I'll teach thee to impose on a good-hearted, deluded father. Now don't you think the lad would be handsomer cropped? It makes a dog fiercer and I love something fierce—get me a scissors—something fierce and trim Besides, it's infernal affectation—devilish conceit it is, to cherish our ears— we're asses enough without them. Hush, child, hush! Well then, it is my darling! wisht, dry thy eyes—there's a joy; kiss me. What! it won't? Kiss me Hareton! Damn thee, kiss me! By God, as if I would rear such a monster! A sure as I'm living, I'll break the brat's neck.'

Poor Hareton was squalling and kicking in his father's arms with all his might, and redoubled his yells when he carried him upstairs and lifted him over the banister. I cried out that he would frighten the child into fits, and ran to rescue him. As I reached them, Hindley leant forward on the rails to listen to a noise below; almost forgetting what he had in his hands. 'Who is that? he asked, hearing some one approaching the stair's foot. I leant forward also for the purpose of signing to Heathcliff, whose step I recognised, not to come further; and, at the instant when my eye quitted Hareton, he gave a sudden spring, delivered himself from the careless grasp that held him, and fell.

There was scarcely time to experience a thrill of horror before we saw that the little wretch was safe. Heathcliff arrived underneath just at the critical moment; by a natural impulse, he arrested his descent, and setting him on his feet, looked up to discover the author of the accident. A miser who has parted with a lucky lottery ticket for five shillings, and finds next day he has lost in the bargain five thousand pounds, could not show a blanker countenance than did he on beholding the figure of Mr. Earnshaw above. It expressed

plainer than words could do, the intense anguish at having made himself the instrument of thwarting his own revenge. Had it been dark, I dare say, he would have tried to remedy the mistake by smashing Hareton's skull on the steps; but we witnessed his salvation; and I was presently below with my precious charge pressed to my heart. Hindley descended more leisurely, sobered and abashed.

'It is your fault, Ellen,' he said; 'you should have kept him out of sight: you should have taken him from me! Is he injured anywhere?'

'Injured!' I cried angrily; 'if he's not killed, he'll be an idiot! Oh! I wonder his mother does not rise from her grave to see how you use him. You're worse than a heathen—treating your own flesh and blood in that manner!'

He attempted to touch the child, who, on finding himself with me, sobbed off his terror directly. At the first finger his father laid on him, however, he shrieked again louder than before, and struggled as if he would go into convulsions.

'You shall not meddle with him!' I continued. 'He hates you—they all hate you—that's the truth! A happy family you have: and a pretty state you're come to!'

'I shall come to a prettier, yet, Nelly,' laughed the misguided man, recovering his hardness. 'At present, convey yourself and him away. And, hark you, Heathcliff! clear you too, quite from my reach and hearing. I wouldn't murder you to-night; unless, perhaps, I set the house on fire: but that's as my fancy goes.'

While saying this he took a pint bottle of brandy from the dresser, and poured some into a tumbler.

'Nay, don't!' I entreated. 'Mr. Hindley, do take warning. Have mercy on this unfortunate boy, if you care nothing for yourself!'

'Any one will do better for him than I shall,' he answered.

'Have mercy on your own soul!' I said, endeavouring to snatch the glass from his hand.

'Not I! On the contrary, I shall have great pleasure in sending it to perdition to punish its Maker,' exclaimed the blasphemer. 'Here's to its hearty damnation!'

He drank the spirits and impatiently bade us go; terminating his command with a sequel of horrid imprecations, too bad to repeat or remember.

'It's a pity he cannot kill himself with drink,' observed Heathcliff, muttering an echo of curses back when the door was shut. 'He's doing his very utmost; but his constitution defies him. Mr. Kenneth says he would wager his mare, that he'll outlive any man on this side Gimmerton, and go to the grave a hoary sinner, unless some happy chance out of the common course befall him.'

I went into the kitchen, and sat down to lull my little lamb to sleep. Heathcliff, as I thought, walked through to the barn. It turned out afterwards that

he only got as far as the other side the settle, when he flung himself on a bench by the wall, removed from the fire, and remained silent.

I was rocking Hareton on my knee, and humming a song that began:

> It was far in the night, and the bairnies grat,
> The mither beneath the mools heard that—

when Miss Cathy, who had listened to the hubbub from her room, put her head in, and whispered:

'Are you alone, Nelly?'

'Yes, miss,' I replied.

She entered and approached the hearth. I, supposing she was going to say something, looked up. The expression of her face seemed disturbed and anxious. Her lips were half asunder, as if she meant to speak, and she drew a breath but it escaped in a sigh instead of a sentence. I resumed my song; not having forgotten her recent behaviour.

'Where's Heathcliff?' she said, interrupting me.

'About his work in the stable,' was my answer.

He did not contradict me; perhaps he had fallen into a doze. There followed another long pause, during which I perceived a drop or two trickle from Catherine's cheek to the flags. Is she sorry for her shameful conduct? I asked myself. That will be a novelty: but she may come to the point as she will— I shan't help her! No, she felt small trouble regarding any subject, save her own concerns.

'Oh, dear!' she cried at last. 'I'm very unhappy!'

'A pity,' observed I. 'You're hard to please: so many friends and so few cares, and can't make yourself content!'

'Nelly, will you keep a secret for me?' she pursued, kneeling down by me and lifting her winsome eyes to my face with that sort of look which turns off bad temper, even when one has all the right in the world to indulge it.

'Is it worth keeping?' I inquired, less sulkily.

'Yes, and it worries me, and I must let it out! I want to know what I should do. To-day, Edgar Linton has asked me to marry him, and I've given him an answer. Now, before I tell you whether it was a consent or denial, you tell me which it ought to have been.'

'Really, Miss Catherine, how can I know?' I replied. 'To be sure, considering the exhibition you performed in his presence this afternoon, I might say it would be wise to refuse him: since he asked you after that, he must either be hopelessly stupid or a venturesome fool.'

'If you talk so, I won't tell you any more,' she returned peevishly, rising to her feet. 'I accepted him, Nelly. Be quick, and say whether I was wrong!'

'You accepted him! then what good is it discussing the matter? You have pledged your word, and cannot retract.'

'But, say whether I should have done so—do!' she exclaimed in an irritated tone; chafing her hands together, and frowning.

'There are many things to be considered before that question can be answered properly,' I said sententiously. 'First and foremost, do you love Mr. Edgar?'

'Who can help it? Of course I do,' she answered.

Then I put her through the following catechism: for a girl of twenty-two it was not injudicious.

'Why do you love him, Miss Cathy?'

'Nonsense, I do—that's sufficient.'

'By no means; you must say why?'

'Well, because he is handsome, and pleasant to be with.'

'Bad!' was my commentary.

'And because he is young and cheerful.'

'Bad, still.'

'And because he loves me.'

'Indifferent, coming there.'

'And he will be rich, and I shall like to be the greatest woman of the neighbourhood, and I shall be proud of having such a husband.'

'Worst of all. And now, say how you love him?'

'As everybody loves—You're silly, Nelly.'

'Not at all—Answer.'

'I love the ground under his feet, and the air over his head, and everything he touches, and every word he says. I love all his looks, and all his actions, and him entirely and altogether. There now!'

'And why?'

'Nay; you are making a jest of it; it is exceedingly ill-natured! It's no jest to me!' said the young lady, scowling, and turning her face to the fire.

'I'm very far from jesting, Miss Catherine,' I replied. 'You love Mr. Edgar because he is handsome, and young, and cheerful, and rich, and loves you. The last, however, goes for nothing: you would love him without that, probably; and with it you wouldn't, unless he possessed the four former attractions.'

'No, to be sure not: I should only pity him—hate him, perhaps, if he were ugly, and a clown.'

'But there are several other handsome, rich young men in the world: handsomer, possibly, and richer than he is. What should hinder you from loving them?'

'If there be any, they are out of my way! I've seen none like Edgar.'

'You may see some; and he won't always be handsome, and young, and may not always be rich.'

'He is now; and I have only to do with the present. I wish you would speak rationally.'

'Well, that settles it: if you have only to do with the present, marry Mr Linton.'

'I don't want your permission for that—I *shall* marry him: and yet you have not told me whether I'm right.'

'Perfectly right; if people be right to marry only for the present. And now let us hear what you are unhappy about. Your brother will be pleased; the old lady and gentleman will not object, I think; you will escape from a disorderly comfortless home into a wealthy, respectable one; and you love Edgar, and Edgar loves you. All seems smooth and easy: where is the obstacle?'

'*Here!* and *here!*' replied Catherine, striking one hand on her forehead, and the other on her breast: 'in whichever place the soul lives. In my soul and in my heart, I'm convinced I'm wrong!'

'That's very strange! I cannot make it out.'

'It's my secret. But if you will not mock at me, I'll explain it: I can't do it distinctly: but I'll give you a feeling of how I feel.'

She seated herself by me again: her countenance grew sadder and graver, and her clasped hands trembled.

'Nelly, do you never dream queer dreams?' she said, suddenly, after some minutes' reflection.

'Yes, now and then,' I answered.

'And so do I. I've dreamt in my life dreams that have stayed with me ever after, and changed my ideas: they've gone through and through me, like wine through water, and altered the colour of my mind. And this is one; I'm going to tell it—but take care not to smile at any part of it.'

'Oh! don't, Miss Catherine!' I cried. 'We're dismal enough without conjuring up ghosts and visions to perplex us. Come, come, be merry and like yourself! Look at little Hareton! *he's* dreaming nothing dreary. How sweetly he smiles in his sleep!'

'Yes; and how sweetly his father curses in his solitude! You remember him, I daresay, when he was just such another as that chubby thing: nearly as young and innocent. However, Nelly, I shall oblige you to listen: it's not long; and I've no power to be merry to-night.'

'I won't hear it, I won't hear it!' I repeated hastily.

I was superstitious about dreams then, and am still; and Catherine had an unusual gloom in her aspect, that made me dread something from which I might shape a prophecy, and foresee a fearful catastrophe. She was vexed, but she did not proceed. Apparently taking up another subject, she recommenced in a short time.

'If I were in heaven, Nelly, I should be extremely miserable.'

'Because you are not fit to go there,' I answered. 'All sinners would be miserable in heaven.'

'But it is not for that. I dreamt once that I was there.'

442

'I tell you I won't hearken to your dreams, Miss Catherine! I'll go to bed,' I interrupted again.

She laughed, and held me down; for I made a motion to leave my chair. 'This is nothing,' cried she: 'I was only going to say that heaven did not seem to be my home; and I broke my heart with weeping to come back to earth; and the angels were so angry that they flung me out into the middle of the heath on the top of Wuthering Heights; where I woke sobbing for joy. That will do to explain my secret, as well as the other. I've no more business to marry Edgar Linton than I have to be in heaven; and if the wicked man in there had not brought Heathcliff so low, I shouldn't have thought of it. It would degrade me to marry Heathcliff now; so he shall never know how I love him: and that, not because he's handsome, Nelly, but because he's more myself than I am. Whatever our souls are made of, his and mine are the same; and Linton's is as different as a moonbeam from lightning, or frost from fire.'

Ere this speech ended, I became sensible of Heathcliff's presence. Having noticed a slight movement, I turned my head, and saw him rise from the bench, and steal out noiselessly. He had listened till he heard Catherine say it would degrade her to marry him, and then he stayed to hear no further. My companion, sitting on the ground, was prevented by the back of the settle from remarking his presence or departure; but I started, and bade her hush!

'Why?' she asked, gazing nervously round.

'Joseph is here,' I answered, catching opportunely the roll of his cart-wheels up the road; 'and Heathcliff will come in with him. I'm not sure whether he were not at the door this moment.'

'Oh, he couldn't overhear me at the door!' said she. 'Give me Hareton, while you get the supper, and when it is ready ask me to sup with you. I want to cheat my uncomfortable conscience, and be convinced that Heathcliff has no notion of these things. He has not, has he? He does not know what being in love is?'

'I see no reason that he should not know, as well as you,' I returned; 'and if *you* are his choice, he will be the most unfortunate creature that ever was born! As soon as you become Mrs. Linton, he loses friend, and love, and all! Have you considered how you'll bear the separation, and how he'll bear to be quite deserted in the world? Because, Miss Catherine'——

'He quite deserted! we separated!' she exclaimed, with an accent of indignation. 'Who is to separate us, pray? They'll meet the fate of Milo! Not as long as I live, Ellen: for no mortal creature. Every Linton on the face of the earth might melt into nothing, before I could consent to forsake Heathcliff. Oh, that's not what I intend—that's not what I mean! I shouldn't be Mrs. Linton were such a price demanded! He'll be as much to me as he has been all his lifetime. Edgar must shake off his antipathy, and tolerate him, at least. He will, when he learns my true feelings towards him. Nelly, I see now, you

443

think me a selfish wretch; but did it never strike you that if Heathcliff and I married, we should be beggars? whereas, if I marry Linton, I can aid Heathcliff to rise, and place him out of my brother's power.'

'With your husband's money, Miss Catherine?' I asked. 'You'll find him no so pliable as you calculate upon: and, though I'm hardly a judge, I think that' the worst motive you've given yet for being the wife of young Linton.'

'It is not,' retorted she; 'it is the best! The others were the satisfaction of m whims: and for Edgar's sake, too, to satisfy him. This is for the sake of one wh comprehends in his person my feelings to Edgar and myself. I cannot express it; but surely you and everybody have a notion that there is or should be a existence of yours beyond you. What were the use of my creation, if I wer entirely contained here? My great miseries in this world have been Heathcliff' miseries, and I watched and felt each from the beginning: my great thought i living is himself. If all else perished, and *he* remained, *I* should still continu to be; and if all else remained, and he were annihilated, the universe woul turn to a mighty stranger: I should not seem a part of it. My love for Linto is like the foliage in the woods: time will change it, I'm well aware, as winte changes the trees. My love for Heathcliff resembles the eternal rocks beneath a source of little visible delight, but necessary. Nelly, I *am* Heathcliff! He always, always in my mind: not as a pleasure, any more than I am alway a pleasure to myself, but as my own being. So don't talk of our separation again it is impracticable; and'——

She paused, and hid her face in the folds of my gown; but I jerked it forcibl away. I was out of patience with her folly!

'If I can make any sense of your nonsense, miss,' I said, 'it only goes t convince me that you are ignorant of the duties you undertake in marrying or else that you are a wicked, unprincipled girl. But trouble me with no mor secrets: I'll not promise to keep them.'

'You'll keep that?' she asked eagerly.

'No, I'll not promise,' I repeated.

She was about to insist, when the entrance of Joseph finished our conversa tion; and Catherine removed her seat to a corner, and nursed Hareton, whil I made the supper. After it was cooked, my fellow-servant and I began t quarrel who should carry some to Mr. Hindley; and we didn't settle it till a was nearly cold. Then we came to the agreement that we would let him ask if he wanted any; for we feared particularly to go into his presence when h had been some time alone.

'Und hah isn't that nowt comed in frough th' field, be this time? What is h abaht? girt eedle seeght!' demanded the old man, looking round for Heathcliff

'I'll call him,' I replied. 'He's in the barn, I've no doubt.'

I went and called, but got no answer. On returning, I whispered to Catherin that he had heard a good part of what she said, I was sure; and told ho

I saw him quit the kitchen just as she complained of her brother's conduct regarding him. She jumped up in a fine fright, flung Hareton on to the settle, and ran to seek for her friend herself; not taking leisure to consider why she was so flurried, or how her talk would have affected him. She was absent such a while that Joseph proposed we should wait no longer. He cunningly conjectured they were staying away in order to avoid hearing his protracted blessing. They were 'ill enough for ony fahl manners,' he affirmed. And on their behalf he added that night a special prayer to the usual quarter of an hour's supplication before meat, and would have tacked another to the end of the grace, had not his young mistress broken in upon him with a hurried command that he must run down the road, and wherever Heathcliff had rambled, find and make him re-enter directly!

'I want to speak to him, and I *must*, before I go upstairs,' she said. 'And the gate is open: he is somewhere out of hearing; for he would not reply, though I shouted at the top of the fold as loud as I could.'

Joseph objected at first; she was too much in earnest, however, to suffer contradiction; and at last he placed his hat on his head, and walked grumbling forth. Meantime, Catherine paced up and down the floor, exclaiming:

'I wonder where he is—I wonder where he *can* be? What did I say, Nelly? I've forgotten. Was he vexed at my bad humour this afternoon? Dear! tell me what I've said to grieve him? I do wish he'd come. I do wish he would!'

'What a noise for nothing!' I cried, though rather uneasy myself. 'What a trifle scares you! It's surely no great cause of alarm that Heathcliff should take a moonlight saunter on the moors, or even lie too sulky to speak to us in the hay-loft. I'll engage he's lurking there. See if I don't ferret him out!'

I departed to renew my search; its result was disappointment, and Joseph's quest ended in the same.

'Yon lads gets war un war!' observed he on re-entering. 'He's left th' yate at t' full swing, and Miss's pony has trodden dahn two rigs uh corn, un plottered through, raight o'er intuh t' meadow! Hahsomdiver, t' maister 'ull play t' devil to-morn, and he'll do weel. He's patience itsseln wi' sich careless, offald craters—patience itsseln he is! Bud he'll nut be soa allus—yah's see, all on ye! Zah mum'nt drive him aht uf his heead for nowt!'

'Have you found Heathcliff, you ass?' interrupted Catherine. 'Have you been looking for him, as I ordered?'

'Aw sud more likker look for th' horse,' he replied. 'It 'ud be tuh more sense. Bud, Aw can look for norther horse nur man uf a neeght loike this—as black as t' chimbley! und Hathecliff's noan t' chap to coom at *maw* whistle—happen he'll be less hard uh hearing wi' *ye*!'

It *was* a very dark evening for summer: the clouds appeared inclined to thunder, and I said we had better all sit down; the approaching rain would be certain to bring him home without further trouble. However, Catherine

would not be persuaded into tranquillity. She kept wandering to and fro, from the gate to the door, in a state of agitation which permitted no repose; and at length took up a permanent situation on one side of the wall, near the road; where, heedless of my expostulations and the growling thunder, and the great drops that began to plash around her, she remained, calling at intervals, and then listening, and then crying outright. She beat Hareton, or any child, at a good passionate fit of crying.

About midnight, while we still sat up, the storm came rattling over the Heights in full fury. There was a violent wind, as well as thunder, and either one or the other split a tree off at the corner of the building: a huge bough fell across the roof, and knocked down a portion of the east chimney-stack, sending a clatter of stones and soot into the kitchen fire. We thought a bolt had fallen in the middle of us; and Joseph swung on to his knees beseeching the Lord to remember the patriarchs Noah and Lot, and, as in former times, spare the righteous, though He smote the ungodly. I felt some sentiment that it must be a judgment on us also. The Jonah, in my mind, was Mr. Earnshaw; and I shook the handle of his den that I might ascertain if he were yet living. He replied audibly enough, in a fashion which made my companion vociferate, more clamorously than before, that a wide distinction might be drawn between saints like himself and sinners like his master. But the uproar passed away in twenty minutes, leaving us all unharmed; excepting Cathy, who got thoroughly drenched for her obstinacy in refusing to take shelter, and standing bonnetless and shawl-less to catch as much water as she could with her hair and clothes. She came in and lay down on the settle, all soaked as she was, turning her face to the back, and putting her hands before it.

'Well, miss!' I exclaimed, touching her shoulder; 'you are not bent on getting your death, are you? Do you know what o'clock it is? Half-past twelve. Come, come to bed! there's no use waiting longer on that foolish boy: he'll be gone to Gimmerton, and he'll stay there now. He guesses we shouldn't wait for him till this late hour: at least, he guesses that only Mr. Hindley would be up; and he'd rather avoid having the door opened by the master.'

'Nay, nay, he's noan at Gimmerton,' said Joseph. 'Aw's niver wonder, but he's at t' bothom uf a bog-hoile. This visitation worn't for nowt, and I wod hev ye to look out, miss—yah muh be t' next. Thank Hiven for all! All wark togither for gooid to them as is chozzen, and piked out fro' th' rubbidge! Ya knaw whet t' Scripture ses.' And he began quoting several texts, referring us to the chapters and verses where we might find them.

I, having vainly begged the wilful girl to rise and remove her wet things, left him preaching and her shivering, and betook myself to bed with little Hareton, who slept as fast as if every one had been sleeping round him. I heard Joseph read on a while afterwards; then I distinguished his slow step on the ladder, and then I dropped asleep.

Coming down somewhat later than usual, I saw, by the sunbeams piercing the chinks of the shutters, Miss Catherine still seated near the fire-place. The house door was ajar, too; light entered from its unclosed windows; Hindley had come out, and stood on the kitchen hearth, haggard and drowsy.

'What ails you, Cathy?' he was saying when I entered: 'you look as dismal as a drowned whelp. Why are you so damp and pale, child?'

'I've been wet,' she answered reluctantly, 'and I'm cold, that's all.'

'Oh, she is naughty!' I cried, perceiving the master to be tolerably sober. 'She got steeped in the shower of yesterday evening, and there she has sat the night through, and I couldn't prevail on her to stir.'

Mr. Earnshaw stared at us in surprise. 'The night through,' he repeated. 'What kept her up? not fear of the thunder, surely? That was over hours since.'

Neither of us wished to mention Heathcliff's absence, as long as we could conceal it; so I replied, I didn't know how she took it into her head to sit up; and she said nothing. The morning was fresh and cool; I threw back the lattice, and presently the room filled with sweet scents from the garden; but Catherine called peevishly to me, 'Ellen, shut the window. I'm starving!' And her teeth chattered as she shrunk closer to the almost extinguished embers.

'She's ill,' said Hindley, taking her wrist; 'I suppose that's the reason she would not go to bed. Damn it! I don't want to be troubled with more sickness here. What took you into the rain!'

'Running after t' lads, as usuald!' croaked Joseph, catching an opportunity, from our hesitation, to thrust in his evil tongue. 'If I war yah, maister, I'd just slam t' boards i' their faces all on 'em, gentle and simple! Never a day ut yah're off, but yon cat o' Linton comes sneaking hither; and Miss Nelly, hoo's a fine lass! shoo sits watching for ye i' t' kitchen; and as yah're in at ne door, he's out at t'other; and, then, wer grand lady goes a coorting of er side! It's bonny behaviour, lurking amang t' fields, after twelve o' t' night, wi' that fahl, flaysome divil of a gipsy, Heathcliff! They think I'm blind; but 'm noan: nowt ut t' soart!—I seed young Linton boath coming and going, nd I seed yah' (directing his discourse to me), 'yah gooid fur nowt, slattenly ritch! nip up and bolt into th' house, t' minute yah heard t' maister's horse fit latter up t' road.'

'Silence, eavesdropper!' cried Catherine; 'none of your insolence before me! Edgar Linton came yesterday by chance, Hindley; and it was I who told him to be off: because I knew you would not like to have met him as you were.'

'You lie, Cathy, no doubt,' answered her brother, 'and you are a confounded simpleton! But never mind Linton at present: tell me, were you not with Heathcliff last night? Speak the truth, now, You need not be afraid of harming him: though I hate him as much as ever, he did me a good turn a short time since, that will make my conscience tender of breaking his neck. To prevent it, I shall send him about his business, this very morning; and after he's gone, I'd advise

you all to look sharp: I shall only have the more humour for you.'

'I never saw Heathcliff last night,' answered Catherine, beginning to sob bitterly: 'and if you do turn him out of doors, I'll go with him. But, perhaps you'll never have an opportunity: perhaps he's gone.' Here she burst into uncontrollable grief, and the remainder of her words were inarticulate.

Hindley lavished on her a torrent of scornful abuse, and bade her get to her room immediately, or she shouldn't cry for nothing! I obliged her to obey; and I shall never forget what a scene she acted when we reached her chamber: it terrified me. I thought she was going mad, and I begged Joseph to run for the doctor. It proved the commencement of delirium: Mr. Kenneth, as soon as he saw her, pronounced her dangerously ill; she had a fever. He bled her, and he told me to let her live on whey and water-gruel, and take care she did not throw herself downstairs or out of the window; and then he left: for he had enough to do in the parish, where two or three miles was the ordinary distance between cottage and cottage.

Though I cannot say I made a gentle nurse, and Joseph and the master were no better; and though our patient was as wearisome and headstrong as a patient could be, she weathered it through. Old Mrs. Linton paid us several visits, to be sure, and set things to rights, and scolded and ordered us all; and when Catherine was convalescent, she insisted on conveying her to Thrushcross Grange: for which deliverance we were very grateful. But the poor dame had reason to repent of her kindness: she and her husband both took the fever, and died within a few days of each other.

Our young lady returned to us, saucier and more passionate, and haughtier than ever. Heathcliff had never been heard of since the evening of the thunder storm; and one day I had the misfortune, when she had provoked me exceedingly, to lay the blame of his disappearance on her: where indeed it belonged, as she well knew. From that period, for several months, she ceased to hold any communication with me, save in the relation of a mere servant. Joseph fell under a ban also: he *would* speak his mind, and lecture her all the same as if she were a little girl; and she esteemed herself a woman, and our mistress, and thought that her recent illness gave her a claim to be treated with consideration. Then the doctor had said that she would not bear crossing much; she ought to have her own way; and it was nothing less than murder in her eyes for any one to presume to stand up and contradict her. From Mr. Earnshaw and his companions she kept aloof; and tutored by Kenneth, and serious threats of a fit that often attended her rages, her brother allowed her whatever she pleased to demand, and generally avoided aggravating her fiery temper. He was rather *too* indulgent in humouring her caprices; not from affection, but from pride: he wished earnestly to see her bring honour to the family by an alliance with the Lintons, and as long as she let him alone she might trample us like slaves, for aught he cared! Edgar Linton, as multitudes have been before

and will be after him, was infatuated; and believed himself the happiest man alive on the day he led her to Gimmerton Chapel, three years subsequent to his father's death.

Much against my inclination, I was persuaded to leave Wuthering Heights and accompany her here. Little Hareton was nearly five years old, and I had just begun to teach him his letters. We made a sad parting; but Catherine's tears were more powerful than ours. When I refused to go, and when she found her entreaties did not move me, she went lamenting to her husband and brother. The former offered me munificent wages; the latter ordered me to pack up: he wanted no women in the house, he said, now that there was no mistress; and as to Hareton, the curate should take him in hand, by-and-by. And so I had but one choice left: to do as I was ordered. I told the master he got rid of all decent people only to run to ruin a little faster; I kissed Hareton good-bye; and since then he has been a stranger: and it's very queer to think it, but I've no doubt he has completely forgotten all about Ellen Dean, and that he was ever more than all the world to her, and she to him!

At this point of the housekeeper's story, she chanced to glance towards the timepiece over the chimney; and was in amazement on seeing the minute-hand measure half-past one. She would not hear of staying a second longer: in truth, I felt rather disposed to defer the sequel of her narrative, myself. And now that she is vanished to her rest, and I have meditated for another hour or two, I shall summon courage to go, also, in spite of aching laziness of head and limbs.

CHAPTER 10

A charming introduction to a hermit's life! Four weeks' torture, tossing, and sickness! Oh! these bleak winds and bitter northern skies, and impassable roads, and dilatory country surgeons! And, oh, this dearth of the human physiognomy! and, worse than all, the terrible intimation of Kenneth that I need not expect to be out of doors till spring!

Mr. Heathcliff has just honoured me with a call. About seven days ago he sent me a brace of grouse—the last of the season. Scoundrel! He is not altogether guiltless in this illness of mine; and that I had a great mind to tell him. But, alas! how could I offend a man who was charitable enough to sit at my bedside a good hour, and talk on some other subject than pills and draughts, blisters and leeches? This is quite an easy interval. I am too weak to read; yet I feel as if I could enjoy something interesting. Why not have up Mrs. Dean to finish her tale? I can recollect its chief incidents as far as she had gone. Yes: I remember her hero had run off, and never been heard of for three years; and

the heroine was married. I'll ring: she'll be delighted to find me capable o
talking cheerfully. Mrs. Dean came.

'It wants twenty minutes, sir, to taking the medicine,' she commenced.

'Away, away with it!' I replied; 'I desire to have'——

'The doctor says you must drop the powders.'

'With all my heart! Don't interrupt me. Come and take your seat here
Keep your fingers from that bitter phalanx of vials. Draw your knitting out o
your pocket—that will do—now continue the history of Mr. Heathcliff, from
where you left off, to the present day. Did he finish his education on the Conti
nent, and come back a gentleman? or did he get a sizar's place at college, o
escape to America, and earn honours by drawing blood from his foster-country
or make a fortune more promptly on the English highways?'

'He may have done a little in all these vocations, Mr. Lockwood; bu
I couldn't give my word for any. I stated before that I didn't know how h
gained his money; neither am I aware of the means he took to raise his min
from the savage ignorance into which it was sunk: but, with your leave, I'
proceed in my own fashion, if you think it will amuse and not weary you
Are you feeling better this morning?'

'Much.'

'That's good news. I got Miss Catherine and myself to Thrushcross Grange
and, to my agreeable disappointment, she behaved infinitely better tha
I dared to expect. She seemed almost over-fond of Mr. Linton; and even to hi
sister she showed plenty of affection. They were both very attentive to he
comfort, certainly. It was not the thorn bending to the honeysuckles, but th
honeysuckles embracing the thorn. There were no mutual concessions; on
stood erect, and the others yielded: and who *can* be ill-natured and bad
tempered when they encounter neither opposition nor indifference? I observe
that Mr. Edgar had a deep-rooted fear of ruffling her humour. He concealed i
from her; but if ever he heard me answer sharply, or saw any other servan
grow cloudy at some imperious order of hers, he would show his trouble b
a frown of displeasure that never darkened on his own account. He man
a time spoke sternly to me about my pertness; and averred that the stab
a knife could not inflict a worse pang than he suffered at seeing his lady vexe
Not to grieve a kind master, I learned to be less touchy; and, for the space
half a year, the gunpowder lay as harmless as sand, because no fire came nea
to explode it. Catherine had seasons of gloom and silence now and then: the
were respected with sympathising silence by her husband, who ascribed the
to an alteration in her constitution, produced by her perilous illness; as sh
was never subject to depression of spirits before. The return of sunshine wa
welcomed by answering sunshine from him. I believe I may assert that the
were really in possession of deep and growing happiness.

It ended. Well, we *must* be for ourselves in the long run; the mild and gene

450

ous are only more justly selfish than the domineering; and it ended when circumstances caused each to feel that the one's interest was not the chief consideration in the other's thoughts. On a mellow evening in September, I was coming from the garden with a heavy basket of apples which I had been gathering. It had got dusk, and the moon looked over the high wall of the court, causing undefined shadows to lurk in the corners of the numerous projecting portions of the building. I set my burden on the house steps by the kitchen door, and lingered to rest, and drew in a few more breaths of the soft, sweet air; my eyes were on the moon, and my back to the entrance, when I heard a voice behind me say—

'Nelly, is that you?'

It was a deep voice, and foreign in tone; yet there was something in the manner of pronouncing my name which made it sound familiar. I turned about to discover who spoke, fearfully; for the doors were shut, and I had seen nobody on approaching the steps. Something stirred in the porch; and, moving nearer, I distinguished a tall man dressed in dark clothes, with dark face and hair. He leant against the side, and held his fingers on the latch as if intending to open for himself. 'Who can it be?' I thought. 'Mr. Earnshaw? Oh, no! The voice has no resemblance to his.'

'I have waited here an hour,' he resumed, while I continued staring; 'and the whole of that time all round has been as still as death. I dared not enter. You do not know me? Look, I'm not a stranger!'

A ray fell on his features; the cheeks were sallow, and half covered with black whiskers; the brows lowering, the eyes deep set and singular. I remembered the eyes.

'What!' I cried, uncertain whether to regard him as a worldly visitor, and I raised my hands in amazement. 'What! you come back? Is it really you? Is it?'

'Yes, Heathcliff,' he replied, glancing from me up to the windows, which reflected a score of glittering moons, but showed no lights from within. 'Are they at home? where is she? Nelly, you are not glad! you needn't be so disturbed. Is she here? Speak! I want to have one word with her—your mistress. Go, and say some person from Gimmerton desires to see her.'

'How will she take it?' I exclaimed. 'What will she do? The surprise bewilders me—it will put her out of her head! And you *are* Heathcliff! But altered! Nay, there's no comprehending it. Have you been for a soldier?'

'Go and carry my message,' he interrupted impatiently. 'I'm in hell till you do!'

He lifted the latch, and I entered; but when I got to the parlour where Mr. and Mrs. Linton were, I could not persuade myself to proceed. At length, I resolved on making an excuse to ask if they would have the candles lighted, and I opened the door.

They sat together in a window whose lattice lay back against the wall, and displayed, beyond the garden trees and the wild green park, the valley of Gimmerton, with a long line of mist winding nearly to its top (for very soon after you pass the chapel, as you may have noticed, the sough that runs from the marshes joins a beck which follows the bend of the glen). Wuthering Heights rose above this silvery vapour; but our old house was invisible; it rather dips down on the other side. Both the room and its occupants, and the scene they gazed on, looked wondrously peaceful. I shrank reluctantly from performing my errand; and was actually going away leaving it unsaid, after having put my question about the candles, when a sense of my folly compelled me to return, and mutter—'A person from Gimmerton wishes to see you, ma'am.'

'What does he want?' asked Mrs. Linton.

'I did not question him,' I answered.

'Well, close the curtains, Nelly,' she said; 'and bring up tea. I'll be back again directly.'

She quitted the apartment; Mr. Edgar inquired, carelessly, who it was.

'Some one mistress does not expect,' I replied. 'That Heathcliff—you recollect him, sir,—who used to live at Mr. Earnshaw's.'

'What! the gipsy—the ploughboy?' he cried. 'Why did you not say so to Catherine?'

'Hush! you must not call him by those names, master,' I said. 'She'd be sadly grieved to hear you. She was nearly heartbroken when he ran off. I guess his return will make a jubilee to her.'

Mr. Linton walked to a window on the other side of the room that overlooked the court. He unfastened it and leant out. I suppose they were below, for he exclaimed quickly—'Don't stand there, love! Bring the person in, if it be any one particular.' Ere long I heard the click of the latch, and Catherine flew upstairs, breathless and wild; too excited to show gladness: indeed, by her face, you would rather have surmised an awful calamity.

'Oh, Edgar, Edgar!' she panted, flinging her arms round his neck. 'Oh Edgar, darling! Heathcliff's come back—he is!' And she tightened her embrace to a squeeze.

'Well, well,' cried her husband crossly, 'don't strangle me for that! He never struck me as such a marvellous treasure. There is no need to be frantic!'

'I know you didn't like him,' she answered, repressing a little the intensity of her delight. 'Yet, for my sake, you must be friends now. Shall I tell him to come up?'

'Here?' he said, 'into the parlour?'

'Where else?' she asked.

He looked vexed, and suggested the kitchen as a more suitable place for him

Mrs. Linton eyed him with a droll expression—half angry, half laughing at his fastidiousness.

'No,' she added after a while; 'I cannot sit in the kitchen. Set two tables here, Ellen: one for your master and Miss Isabella, being gentry; the other for Heathcliff and myself, being of the lower orders. Will that please you, dear? Or must I have a fire lighted elsewhere? If so, give directions. I'll run down and secure my guest. I'm afraid the joy is too great to be real!'

She was about to dart off again; but Edgar arrested her.

'*You* bid him step up,' he said, addressing me; 'and, Catherine, try to be glad, without being absurd! the whole household need not witness the sight of your welcoming a runaway servant as a brother.'

I descended and found Heathcliff waiting under the porch, evidently anticipating an invitation to enter. He followed my guidance without waste of words, and I ushered him into the presence of the master and mistress, whose flushed cheeks betrayed signs of warm talking. But the lady's glowed with another feeling when her friend appeared at the door: she sprang forward took both his hands, and led him to Linton; and then she seized Linton's reluctant fingers and crushed them into his. Now fully revealed by the fire and candlelight, I was amazed, more than ever, to behold the transformation of Heathcliff. He had grown a tall, athletic, well-formed man; beside whom, my master seemed quite slender and youth-like. His upright carriage suggested the idea of his having been in the army. His countenance was much older in expression and decision of feature than Mr. Linton's; it looked intelligent, and retained no marks of former degradation. A half-civilised ferocity lurked yet in the depressed brows and eyes full of black fire, but it was subdued; and his manner was even dignified: quite divested of roughness, though too stern for grace. My master's surprise equalled or exceeded mine: he remained for a minute at a loss how to address the ploughboy, as he had called him. Heathcliff dropped his slight hand, and stood looking at him coolly till he chose to speak.

'Sit down, sir,' he said, at length. 'Mrs. Linton, recalling old times, would have me give you a cordial reception; and, of course, I am gratified when anything occurs to please her.'

'And I also,' answered Heathcliff, 'especially if it be anything in which I have a part. I shall stay an hour or two willingly.'

He took a seat opposite Catherine, who kept her gaze fixed on him as if she feared he would vanish were she to remove it. He did not raise his to her often: a quick glance now and then sufficed; but it flashed back, each time more confidently, the undisguised delight he drank from hers. They were too much absorbed in their mutual joy to suffer embarrassment. Not so Mr. Edgar: he grew pale with pure annoyance: a feeling that reached its climax when his lady rose, and stepping across the rug, seized Heathcliff's hands again, and

laughed like one beside herself.

'I shall think it a dream to-morrow!' she cried. 'I shall not be able to believe that I have seen, and touched, and spoken to you once more. And yet, cruel Heathcliff! you don't deserve this welcome. To be absent and silent for three years, and never to think of me!'

'A little more than you have thought of me,' he murmured. 'I heard of your marriage, Cathy, not long since, and, while waiting in the yard below, I meditated this plan:—just to have one glimpse of your face, a stare of surprise perhaps, and pretended pleasure; afterwards settle my score with Hindley and then prevent the law by doing execution on myself. Your welcome has put these ideas out of my mind; but beware of meeting me with another aspect next time! Nay, you'll not drive me off again. You were really sorry for me, were you? Well, there was cause. I've fought through a bitter life since I last heard your voice; and you must forgive me, for I struggled only for you!'

'Catherine, unless we are to have cold tea, please to come to the table,' interrupted Linton, striving to preserve his ordinary tone, and a due measure of politeness. 'Mr. Heathcliff will have a long walk, wherever he may lodge to-night; and I'm thirsty.'

She took her post before the urn; and Miss Isabella came, summoned by the bell; then, having handed their chairs forward, I left the room. The meal hardly endured ten minutes. Catherine's cup was never filled: she could neither eat nor drink. Edgar had made a slop in his saucer, and scarcely swallowed a mouthful. Their guest did not protract his stay that evening above an hour longer. I asked, as he departed, if he went to Gimmerton?

'No, to Wuthering Heights,' he answered: 'Mr. Earnshaw invited me, when I called this morning.'

Mr. Earnshaw invited *him*! and *he* called on Mr. Earnshaw! I pondered this sentence painfully, after he was gone. Is he turning out a bit of a hypocrite, and coming into the country to work mischief under a cloak? I mused: I had a presentiment in the bottom of my heart that he had better have remained away.

About the middle of the night, I was wakened from my first nap by Mrs. Linton gliding into my chamber, taking a seat on my bedside, and pulling me by the hair to rouse me.

'I cannot rest, Ellen,' she said, by way of apology. 'And I want some living creature to keep me company in my happiness! Edgar is sulky, because I'm glad of a thing that does not interest him: he refuses to open his mouth except to utter pettish, silly speeches; and he affirmed I was cruel and selfish for wishing to talk when he was so sick and sleepy. He always contrives to be sick at the least cross! I gave a few sentences of commendation to Heathcliff, and he, either for a headache or a pang of envy, began to cry: so I got up and left him.'

'What use is it praising Heathcliff to him?' I answered. 'As lads they had

an aversion to each other, and Heathcliff would hate just as much to hear him praised: it's human nature. Let Mr. Linton alone about him, unless you would like an open quarrel between them.'

'But does it not show great weakness?' pursued she. 'I'm not envious: I never feel hurt at the brightness of Isabella's yellow hair and the whiteness of her skin, at her dainty elegance, and the fondness all the family exhibit for her. Even you, Nelly, if we have a dispute sometimes, you back Isabella at once; and I yield like a foolish mother: I call her a darling, and flatter her into a good temper. It pleases her brother to see us cordial, and that pleases me. But they are very much alike: they are spoiled children, and fancy the world was made for their accommodation; and though I humour both, I think a smart chastisement might improve them, all the same.'

'You're mistaken, Mrs. Linton,' said I. 'They humour you: I know what there would be to do if they did not. You can well afford to indulge their passing whims as long as their business is to anticipate all your desires. You may, however, fall out, at last, over something of equal consequence to both sides; and then those you term weak are very capable of being as obstinate as you.'

'And then we shall fight to the death, shan't we, Nelly?' she returned, laughing. 'No! I tell you, I have such faith in Linton's love, that I believe I might kill him, and he wouldn't wish to retaliate.'

I advised her to value him the more for his affection.

'I do:' she answered, 'but he needn't resort to whining for trifles. It is childish; and, instead of melting into tears because I said that Heathcliff was now worthy of any one's regard, and it would honour the first gentleman in the country to be his friend, he ought to have said it for me, and been delighted from sympathy. He must get accustomed to him, and he may as well like him: considering how Heathcliff has reason to object to him, I'm sure he behaved excellently!'

'What do you think of his going to Wuthering Heights?' I inquired. 'He is reformed in every respect, apparently: quite a Christian: offering the right hand of fellowship to his enemies all around!'

'He explained it,' she replied. 'I wondered as much as you. He said he called to gather information concerning me from you, supposing you resided here still; and Joseph told Hindley, who came out and fell to questioning him of what he had been doing, and how he had been living; and finally, desired him to walk in. There were some persons sitting at cards; Heathcliff joined them; my brother lost some money to him, and, finding him plentifully supplied, he requested that he would come again in the evening: to which he consented. Hindley is too reckless to select his acquaintance prudently: he doesn't trouble himself to reflect on the causes he might have for mistrusting one whom he has basely injured. But Heathcliff affirms his principal reason

for resuming a connection with his ancient persecutor is a wish to instal himself in quarters at walking distance from the Grange, and an attachment to the house where we lived together; and likewise a hope that I shall have more opportunities of seeing him there than I could have if he settled in Gimmerton. He means to offer liberal payment for permission to lodge at the Heights; and doubtless my brother's covetousness will prompt him to accept the terms: he was always greedy; though what he grasps with one hand he flings away with the other.'

'It's a nice place for a young man to fix his dwelling in!' said I. 'Have you no fear of the consequences, Mrs. Linton?'

'None for my friend,' she replied: 'his strong head will keep him from danger; a little for Hindley: but he can't be made morally worse than he is and I stand between him and bodily harm. The event of this evening has reconciled me to God and humanity! I had risen in angry rebellion against Providence. Oh, I've endured very, very bitter misery, Nelly! If that creature knew how bitter, he'd be ashamed to cloud its removal with idle petulance It was kindness for him which induced me to bear it alone: had I expressed the agony I frequently felt, he would have been taught to long for its alleviation as ardently as I. However, it's over, and I'll take no revenge on his folly; I can afford to suffer anything hereafter! Should the meanest thing alive slap me on the cheek, I'd not only turn the other, but, I'd ask pardon for provoking it; and, as a proof, I'll go make my peace with Edgar instantly Good-night! I'm an angel!'

In this self-complacent conviction she departed; and the success of her fulfilled resolution was obvious on the morrow: Mr. Linton had not only abjured his peevishness (though his spirits seemed still subdued by Catherine's exuberance of vivacity), but he ventured no objection to her taking Isabella with her to Wuthering Heights in the afternoon; and she rewarded him with such a summer of sweetness and affection in return, as made the house a paradise for several days; both master and servants profiting from the perpetual sunshine.

Heathcliff—Mr. Heathcliff I should say in future—used the liberty of visiting at Thrushcross Grange cautiously, at first: he seemed estimating how far its owner would bear his intrusion. Catherine, also, deemed it judicious to moderate her expressions of pleasure in receiving him; and he gradually established his right to be expected. He retained a great deal of the reserve for which his boyhood was remarkable; and that served to repress all startling demonstrations of feeling. My master's uneasiness experienced a lull, and further circumstances diverted it into another channel for a space.

His new source of trouble sprang from the not-anticipated misfortune of Isabella Linton evincing a sudden and irresistible attraction towards the tolerated guest. She was at that time a charming young lady of eighteen

infantile in manners, though possessed of keen wit, keen feelings, and a keen temper, too, if irritated. Her brother, who loved her tenderly, was appalled at this fantastic preference. Leaving aside the degradation of an alliance with a nameless man, and the possible fact that his property, in default of heirs male, might pass into such a one's power, he had sense to comprehend Heathcliff's disposition: to know that, though his exterior was altered, his mind was unchangeable and unchanged. And he dreaded that mind: it revolted him: he shrank forebodingly from the idea of committing Isabella to his keeping. He would have recoiled still more had he been aware that her attachment rose unsolicited, and was bestowed where it awakened no reciprocation of sentiment; for the minute he discovered its existence, he laid the blame on Heathcliff's deliberate designing.

We had all remarked, during some time, that Miss Linton fretted and pined over something. She grew cross and wearisome; snapping at and teasing Catherine continually, at the imminent risk of exhausting her limited patience. We excused her, to a certain extent, on the plea of ill-health: she was dwindling and fading before our eyes. But one day, when she had been peculiarly wayward, rejecting her breakfast, complaining that the servants did not do what she told them; that the mistress would allow her to be nothing in the house, and Edgar neglected her; that she had caught a cold with the doors being left open, and we let the parlour fire go out on purpose to vex her, with a hundred yet more frivolous accusations, Mrs. Linton peremptorily insisted that she should get to bed; and, having scolded her heartily, threatened to send for the doctor. Mention of Kenneth caused her to exclaim, instantly, that her health was perfect, and it was only Catherine's harshness which made her unhappy.

'How can you say I am harsh, you naughty fondling?' cried the mistress, amazed at the unreasonable assertion. 'You are surely losing your reason. When have I been harsh, tell me?'

'Yesterday,' sobbed Isabella, 'and now!'

'Yesterday!' said her sister-in-law. 'On what occasion?'

'In our walk along the moor: you told me to ramble where I pleased, while you sauntered on with Mr. Heathcliff!'

'And that's your notion of harshness?' said Catherine, laughing. 'It was no hint that your company was superfluous: we didn't care whether you kept with us or not; I merely thought Heathcliff's talk would have nothing entertaining for your ears.'

'Oh no,' wept the young lady: 'you wished me away, because you knew I liked to be there!'

'Is she sane?' asked Mrs. Linton, appealing to me. 'I'll repeat our conversation, word for word, Isabella; and you point out any charm it could have had for you.'

'I don't mind the conversation,' she answered: 'I wanted to be with'——

'Well!' said Catherine, perceiving her hesitate to complete the sentence

'With him: and I won't be always sent off!' she continued, kindling up

'You are a dog in the manger, Cathy, and desire no one to be loved but yourself!'

'You are an impertinent little monkey!' exclaimed Mrs. Linton, in surprise 'But I'll not believe this idiocy! It is impossible that you can covet the admiration of Heathcliff—that you consider him an agreeable person! I hope I have misunderstood you, Isabella?'

'No, you have not,' said the infatuated girl. 'I love him more than ever you loved Edgar; and he might love me, if you would let him!'

'I wouldn't be you for a kingdom, then!' Catherine declared emphatically and she seemed to speak sincerely. 'Nelly, help me to convince her of her madness. Tell her what Heathcliff is: an unreclaimed creature, without refinement, without cultivation: an arid wilderness of furze and whinstone I'd as soon put that little canary into the park on a winter's day, as recommend you to bestow your heart on him! It is deplorable ignorance of his character, child, and nothing else, which makes that dream enter your head. Pray, don't imagine that he conceals depths of benevolence and affection beneath a stern exterior! He's not a rough diamond—a pearl-containing oyster of a rustic: he's a fierce, pitiless, wolfish man. I never say to him, "Let this or that enemy alone, because it would be ungenerous or cruel to harm them;" I say, "Let them alone, because I should hate them to be wronged:" and he'd crush you like a sparrow's egg, Isabella, if he found you a troublesome charge. I know he couldn't love a Linton; and yet he'd be quite capable of marrying your fortune and expectations! avarice is growing with him a besetting sin. There's my picture: and I'm his friend—so much so, that had he thought seriously to catch you, I should, perhaps, have held my tongue, and let you fall into his trap.'

Miss Linton regarded her sister-in-law with indignation.

'For shame! for shame!' she repeated angrily, 'you are worse then twenty foes, you poisonous friend!'

'Ah! you won't believe me, then!' said Catherine. 'You think I speak from wicked selfishness?'

'I'm certain you do,' retorted Isabella; 'and I shudder at you!'

'Good!' cried the other. 'Try for yourself, if that be your spirit: I have done and yield the argument to your saucy insolence.'

'And I must suffer for her egotism!' she sobbed, as Mrs. Linton left the room. 'All, all is against me; she has blighted my single consolation. But she uttered falsehoods, didn't she? Mr. Heathcliff is not a fiend: he has an honourable soul, and a true one, or how could he remember her?'

'Banish him from your thoughts, miss,' I said. 'He's a bird of bad omen

no mate for you. Mrs. Linton spoke strongly, and yet I can't contradict her. She is better acquainted with his heart than I, or any one besides; and she would never represent him as worse than he is. Honest people don't hide their deeds. How has he been living? how has he got rich? why is he staying at Wuthering Heights, the house of a man whom he abhors? They say Mr. Earnshaw is worse and worse since he came. They sit up all night together continually, and Hindley has been borrowing money on his land, and does nothing but play and drink: I heard only a week ago—it was Joseph who told me—I met him at Gimmerton: "Nelly," he said, "we's hae a crahnr's 'quest enah, at ahr folks. One on 'em's a'most getten his finger cut off wi' hauding t'other froo' sticking hisseln loike a cawlf. That's maister, yah knaw, 'ut's soa up uh going tuh t' grand 'sizes. He's noan feard uh t' bench uh judges, norther Paul, nur Peter, nur John, nur Matthew, nor noan on 'em, nut he! He fair likes—he langs to set his brazened face agean 'em! And yon bonny lad Heathcliff, yah mind, he's a rare 'un! He can girn a laugh as weel's onybody at a raight divil's jest. Does he niver say nowt of his fine living amang us, when he goas tuh t' Grange? This is t' way on't:—up at sundahn; dice, brandy, cloised shutters, und can'le-lught till next day at nooin: then, t' fooil gangs banning un raving to his cham'er, makking dacent fowks dig thur fingers i' thur lugs fur varry shaume; un' the knave, wah he carn cahnt his brass, un' ate, un' sleep, un' off to his neighbour's tuh gossip wi' t' wife. I' course, he tells Dame Catherine hah hor father's goold runs intuh his pocket, and her father's son gallops dahn t' Broad road, while he flees afore to oppen t' pikes?" Now, Miss Linton, Joseph is an old rascal, but no liar; and, if his account of Heathcliff's conduct be true, you would never think of desiring such a husband, would you?'

'You are leagued with the rest, Ellen!' she replied. 'I'll not listen to your slanders. What malevolence you must have to wish to convince me that there is no happiness in the world!'

Whether she would have got over this fancy if left to herself, or persevered in nursing it perpetually, I cannot say: she had little time to reflect. The day after, there was a justice-meeting at the next town; my master was obliged to attend; and Mr. Heathcliff, aware of his absence, called rather earlier than usual. Catherine and Isabella were sitting in the library, on hostile terms, but silent. The latter alarmed at her recent indiscretion, and the disclosure she had made of her secret feelings in a transient fit of passion; the former, on mature consideration, really offended with her companion; and, if she laughed again at her pertness, inclined to make it no laughing matter to *her*. She did laugh as she saw Heathcliff pass the window. I was sweeping the hearth, and I noticed a mischievous smile on her lips. Isabella, absorbed in her meditations, or a book, remained till the door opened; and it was too late to attempt an escape, which she would gladly have done

had it been practicable.

'Come in, that's right!' exclaimed the mistress gaily, pulling a chair to the fire. 'Here are two people sadly in need of a third to thaw the ice between them; and you are the very one we should both of us choose. Heathcliff, I'm proud to show you, at last, somebody that dotes on you more than myself. I expect you to feel flattered. Nay, it's not Nelly; don't look at her! My poor little sister-in-law is breaking her heart by mere contemplation of your physical and moral beauty. It lies in your own power to be Edgar's brother! No, no, Isabella, you shan't run off,' she continued, arresting, with feigned playfulness, the confounded girl, who had risen indignantly. 'We were quarrelling like cats about you, Heathcliff; and I was fairly beaten in protestations of devotion and admiration: and, moreover, I was informed that if I would but have the manners to stand aside, my rival, as she will have herself to be, would shoot a shaft into your soul that would fix you for ever, and send my image into eternal oblivion!'

'Catherine!' said Isabella, calling up her dignity, and disdaining to struggle from the tight grasp that held her. 'I'd thank you to adhere to the truth and not slander me, even in joke! Mr. Heathcliff, be kind enough to bid this friend of yours release me: she forgets that you and I are not intimate acquaintances; and what amuses her is painful to me beyond expression.'

As the guest answered nothing, but took his seat, and looked thoroughly indifferent what sentiments she cherished concerning him, she turned and whispered an earnest appeal for liberty to her tormentor.

'By no means!' cried Mrs. Linton in answer. 'I won't be named a dog in the manger again. You *shall* stay: now then! Heathcliff, why don't you evince satisfaction at my pleasant news? Isabella swears that the love Edgar has for me is nothing to that she entertains for you. I'm sure she made some speech of the kind; did she not, Ellen? And she has fasted ever since the day before yesterday's walk, from sorrow and rage that I despatched her out of your society under the idea of its being unacceptable.'

'I think you belie her,' said Heathcliff, twisting his chair to face them. 'She wishes to be out of my society now, at any rate!'

And he stared hard at the object of discourse, as one might do at a strange repulsive animal: a centipede from the Indies, for instance, which curiosity leads one to examine in spite of the aversion it raises. The poor thing couldn't bear that: she grew white and red in rapid succession, and, while tears beaded her lashes, bent the strength of her small fingers to loosen the firm clutch of Catherine; and perceiving that as fast as she raised one finger off her arm another closed down, and she could not remove the whole together, she began to make use of her nails; and their sharpness presently ornamented the detainer's with crescents of red.

'There's a tigress!' exclaimed Mrs. Linton, setting her free, and shaking

her hand with pain. 'Begone, for God's sake, and hide your vixen face! How foolish to reveal those talons to *him*. Can't you fancy the conclusions he'll draw? Look, Heathcliff! they are instruments that will do execution—you must beware of your eyes'.

'I'd wrench them off her fingers, if they ever menaced me,' he answered brutally, when the door had closed after her. 'But what did you mean by teasing the creature in that manner, Cathy? You were not speaking the truth, were you?'

'I assure you I was,' she returned. 'She has been pining for your sake several weeks; and raving about you this morning, and pouring forth a deluge of abuse, because I represented your failings in a plain light, for the purpose of mitigating her adoration. But don't notice it further: I wished to punish her sauciness, that's all. I like her too well, my dear Heathcliff, to let you absolutely seize and devour her up.'

'And I like her too ill to attempt it,' said he, 'except in a very ghoulish fashion. You'd hear of odd things if I lived alone with that mawkish, waxen face: the most ordinary would be painting on its white the colours of the rainbow, and turning the blue eyes, black, every day or two: they detestably resemble Linton's.'

'Delectably!' observed Catherine. 'They are dove's eyes—angel's!'

'She's her brother's heir, is she not?' he asked, after a brief silence.

'I should be sorry to think so,' returned his companion. 'Half-a-dozen nephews shall erase her title, please Heaven! Abstract your mind from the subject at present: you are too prone to covet your neighbour's goods; remember *this* neighbour's goods are mine.'

'If they were *mine*, they would be none the less that,' said Heathcliff; 'but though Isabella Linton may be silly, she is scarcely mad; and, in short, we'll dismiss the matter, as you advise.'

From their tongues they did dismiss it; and Catherine, probably, from her thoughts. The other, I felt certain, recalled it often in the course of the evening. I saw him smile to himself—grin rather—and lapse into ominous musing whenever Mrs. Linton had occasion to be absent from the apartment.

I determined to watch his movements. My heart invariably cleaved to the master's, in preference to Catherine's side: with reason I imagined, for he was kind, and trustful, and honourable; and she—she could not be called the *opposite*, yet she seemed to allow herself such wide latitude, that I had little faith in her principles, and still less sympathy for her feelings. I wanted something to happen which might have the effect of freeing both Wuthering Heights and the Grange of Mr. Heathcliff, quietly; leaving us as we had been prior to his advent. His visits were a continual nightmare to me; and, I suspected, to my master also. His abode at the Heights was an oppression past explaining. I felt that God had forsaken the stray sheep there to its own

461

wicked wanderings, and an evil beast prowled between it and the fold, waiting his time to spring and destroy.

CHAPTER 11

Sometimes, while meditating on these things in solitude, I've got up in a sudden terror, and put on my bonnet to go see how all was at the farm. I've persuaded my conscience that it was a duty to warn him how people talked regarding his ways; and then I've recollected his confirmed bad habits and, hopeless of benefiting him, have flinched from re-entering the dismal house, doubting if I could bear to be taken at my word.

One time I passed the old gate, going out of my way, on a journey to Gimmerton. It was about the period that my narrative has reached: a bright frosty afternoon; the ground bare, and the road hard and dry. I came to a stone where the highway branches off on to the moor at your left hand; a rough sand-pillar, with the letters W.H. cut on its north side, on the east G., and on the south-west T.G. It serves as guide-post to the Grange, the Heights, and village. The sun shone yellow on its grey head, reminding me of summer; and I cannot say why, but all at once, a gush of child's sensation flowed into my heart. Hindley and I held it a favourite spot twenty years before. I gazed long at the weather-worn block, and, stooping down, perceived a hole near the bottom still full of snail-shells and pebbles, which we were fond of storing there with more perishable things; and, as fresh as reality, it appeared that I beheld my early playmate seated on the withered turf, his dark, square head bent forward, and his little hand scooping out the earth with a piece of slate. 'Poor Hindley!' I exclaimed involuntarily. I started; my bodily eye cheated into a momentary belief that the child lifted its face and stared straight into mine! It vanished in a twinkling; but immediately I felt an irresistible yearning to be at the Heights. Superstition urged me to comply with this impulse: supposing he should be dead! I thought—or should die soon!—supposing it were a sign of death! The nearer I got to the house the more agitated I grew; and on catching sight of it I trembled in every limb. The apparition had outstripped me: it stood looking through the gate. That was my first idea on observing an elf-locked, brown-eyed boy setting his ruddy countenance against the bars. Further reflection suggested this must be Hareton, *my* Hareton, not altered greatly since I left him, ten months since.

'God bless thee, darling!' I cried, forgetting instantaneously my foolish fears. 'Hareton, it's Nelly! Nelly, thy nurse.'

He retreated out of arm's length, and picked up a large flint.

'I am come to see thy father, Hareton,' I added, guessing from the action

that Nelly, if she lived in his memory at all, was not recognised as one with me.

He raised his missile to hurl it; I commenced a soothing speech, but could not stay his hand: the stone struck my bonnet; and then ensued, from the stammering lips of the little fellow, a string of curses, which, whether he comprehended them or not, were delivered with practised emphasis, and distorted his baby features into a shocking expression of malignity. You may be certain this grieved more than angered me. Fit to cry, I took an orange from my pocket, and offered it to propitiate him. He hesitated, and then snatched it from my hold; as if he fancied I only intended to tempt and disappoint him. I showed another, keeping it out of his reach.

'Who has taught you those fine words, my bairn?' I inquired. 'The curate?'

'Damn the curate, and thee! Gie me that,' he replied.

'Tell us where you got your lessons, and you shall have it,' said I. 'Who's your master?'

'Devil daddy,' was his answer.

'And what do you learn from daddy?' I continued.

He jumped at the fruit; I raised it higher. 'What does he teach you?' I asked.

'Naught,' said he, 'but to keep out of his gait. Daddy cannot bide me, because I swear at him.'

'Ah! and the devil teaches you to swear at daddy?' I observed.

'Ah—nay,' he drawled.

'Who then?'

'Heathcliff.'

I asked if he liked Mr. Heathcliff.

'Ay!' he answered again.

Desiring to have his reasons for liking him, I could only gather the sentences—'I known't: he pays dad back what he gies to me—he curses daddy for cursing me. He says I mun do as I will.'

'And the curate does not teach you to read and write then?' I pursued.

'No, I was told the curate should have his—— teeth dashed down his—— throat, if he stepped over the threshold—Heathcliff had promised that!'

I put the orange in his hand, and bade him tell his father that a woman called Nelly Dean was waiting to speak with him, by the garden gate. He went up the walk, and entered the house; but, instead of Hindley, Heathcliff appeared on the door stones; and I turned directly and ran down the road as hard as ever I could race, making no halt till I gained the guide-post, and feeling as scared as if I had raised a goblin. This is not much connected with Miss Isabella's affair: except that it urged me to resolve further on mounting vigilant guard, and doing my utmost to check the spread of such bad influence at the Grange: even though I should wake a domestic storm, by thwarting Mrs. Linton's pleasure.

The next time Heathcliff came, my young lady chanced to be feeding some pigeons in the court. She had never spoken a word to her sister-in-law for three days; but she had likewise dropped her fretful complaining, and we found it a great comfort. Heathcliff had not the habit of bestowing a single unnecessary civility on Miss Linton, I knew. Now, as soon as he beheld her, his first precaution was to take a sweeping survey of the house-front. I was standing by the kitchen window, but I drew out of sight. He then stepped across the pavement to her, and said something: she seemed embarrassed, and desirous of getting away; to prevent it, he laid his hand on her arm. She averted her face: he apparently put some question which she had no mind to answer. There was another rapid glance at the house, and supposing himself unseen, the scoundrel had the impudence to embrace her.

'Judas! traitor!' I ejaculated. 'You are a hypocrite, too, are you? A deliberate deceiver.'

'Who is, Nelly?' said Catherine's voice at my elbow: I had been over intent on watching the pair outside to mark her entrance.

'Your worthless friend!' I answered warmly: 'the sneaking rascal yonder. Ah, he has caught a glimpse of us—he is coming in! I wonder will he have the art to find a plausible excuse for making love to Miss, when he told you he hated her?'

Mrs. Linton saw Isabella tear herself free, and run into the garden; and a minute after, Heathcliff opened the door. I couldn't withhold giving some loose to my indignation; but Catherine angrily insisted on silence, and threatened to order me out of the kitchen, if I dared to be so presumptuous as to put in my insolent tongue.

'To hear you, people might think you were the mistress!' she cried. 'You want setting down in your right place! Heathcliff, what are you about, raising this stir? I said you must let Isabella alone!—I beg you will, unless you are tired of being received here, and wish Linton to draw the bolts against you!'

'God forbid that he should try!' answered the black villain. I detested him just then. 'God keep him meek and patient! Every day I grow madder after sending him to heaven!'

'Hush!' said Catherine, shutting the inner door. 'Don't vex me. Why have you disregarded my request? Did she come across you on purpose?'

'What is it to you?' he growled. 'I have a right to kiss her, if she chooses and you have no right to object. I'm not *your* husband: *you* needn't be jealou of me!'

'I'm not jealous *of* you,' replied the mistress, 'I'm jealous *for* you. Clea your face: you shan't scowl at me! If you like Isabella, you shall marry her But do you like her? Tell the truth, Heathcliff! There, you won't answer I'm certain you don't!'

'And would Mr. Linton approve of his sister marrying that man?' I inquired

'Mr. Linton should approve,' returned my lady, decisively.

'He might spare himself the trouble,' said Heathcliff: 'I could do as well without his approbation. And as to you, Catherine, I have a mind to speak a few words now, while we are at it. I want you to be aware that I *know* you have treated me infernally—infernally! Do you hear? And if you flatter yourself that I don't perceive it, you are a fool; and if you think I can be consoled by sweet words, you are an idiot; and if you fancy I'll suffer unrevenged, I'll convince you of the contrary, in a very little while! Meantime, thank you for telling me your sister-in-law's secret: I swear I'll make the most of it. And stand you aside!'

'What new phase of his character is this?' exclaimed Mrs. Linton, in amazement. 'I've treated you infernally—and you'll take your revenge! How will you take it, ungrateful brute? How have I treated you infernally?'

'I seek no revenge on you,' replied Heathcliff less vehemently. 'That's not the plan. The tyrant grinds down his slaves and they don't turn against him; they crush those beneath them. You are welcome to torture me to death for your amusement, only allow me to amuse myself a little in the same style, and refrain from insult as much as you are able. Having levelled my palace, don't erect a hovel and complacently admire your own charity in giving me that for a home. If I imagined you really wished me to marry Isabella, I'd cut my throat!'

'Oh, the evil is that I am *not* jealous, is it?' cried Catherine. 'Well, I won't repeat my offer of a wife: it is as bad as offering Satan a lost soul. Your bliss lies, like his, in inflicting misery. You prove it. Edgar is restored from the ill-temper he gave way to at your coming; I begin to be secure and tranquil; and you, restless to know us at peace, appear resolved on exciting a quarrel. Quarrel with Edgar, if you please, Heathcliff, and deceive his sister: you'll hit on exactly the most efficient method of revenging yourself on me.'

The conversation ceased. Mrs. Linton sat down by the fire, flushed and gloomy. The spirit which served her was growing intractable: she could neither lay nor control it. He stood on the hearth with folded arms, brooding on his evil thoughts; and in this position I left them to seek the master, who was wondering what kept Catherine below so long.

'Ellen,' said he, when I entered, 'have you seen your mistress?'

'Yes; she's in the kitchen, sir,' I answered. 'She's sadly put out by Mr. Heathcliff's behaviour: and, indeed, I do think it's time to arrange his visits on another footing. There's harm in being too soft, and now it's come to this'—— And I related the scene in the court, and, as near as I dared, the whole subsequent dispute. I fancied it could not be very prejudicial to Mrs. Linton; unless she made it so afterwards, by assuming the defensive for her guest. Edgar Linton had difficulty in hearing me to the close. His first words revealed that he did not clear his wife of blame.

'This is insufferable!' he exclaimed. 'It is disgraceful that she should own him for a friend, and force his company on me! Call me two men out of the hall, Ellen. Catherine shall linger no longer to argue with the low ruffian—I have humoured her enough.'

He descended, and bidding the servants wait in the passage, went, followed by me, to the kitchen. Its occupants had recommenced their angry discussion: Mrs. Linton, at least, was scolding with renewed vigour; Heathcliff had moved to the window, and hung his head, somewhat cowed by her violent rating apparently. He saw the master first, and made a hasty motion that she should be silent; which she obeyed, abruptly, on discovering the reason of his intimation.

'How is this?' said Linton, addressing her; 'what notion of propriety must you have to remain here, after the language which has been held to you by that blackguard? I suppose, because it is his ordinary talk, you think nothing of it; you are habituated to his baseness, and, perhaps, imagine I can get used to it too!'

'Have you been listening at the door, Edgar?' asked the mistress, in a tone particularly calculated to provoke her husband, implying both carelessness and contempt of his irritation. Heathcliff, who had raised his eyes at the former speech, gave a sneering laugh at the latter; on purpose, it seemed, to draw Mr. Linton's attention to him. He succeeded; but Edgar did not mean to entertain him with any high flights of passion.

'I have been so far forbearing with you, sir,' he said quietly; 'not that I was ignorant of your miserable, degraded character, but I felt you were only partly responsible for that; and Catherine wishing to keep up your acquaintance, I acquiesced — foolishly. Your presence is a moral poison that would contaminate the most virtuous: for that cause, and to prevent worse consequences, I shall deny you hereafter admission into this house, and give notice now that I require your instant departure. Three minutes' delay will render it involuntary and ignominious.'

Heathcliff measured the height and breadth of the speaker with an eye full of derision.

'Cathy, this lamb of yours threatens like a bull!' he said. 'It is in danger of splitting its skull against my knuckles. By God! Mr. Linton, I'm mortally sorry that you are not worth knocking down!'

My master glanced towards the passage, and signed me to fetch the men. he had no intention of hazarding a personal encounter. I obeyed the hint, but Mrs. Linton, suspecting something, followed; and when I attempted to call them, she pulled me back, slammed the door to, and locked it.

'Fair means!' she said, in answer to her husband's look of angry surprise 'If you have not courage to attack him, make an apology, or allow yourself to be beaten. It will correct you of feigning more valour than you possess. No

I'll swallow the key before you shall get it! I'm delightfully rewarded for my kindness to each! After constant indulgence of one's weak nature, and the other's bad one, I earn for thanks two samples of blind ingratitude, stupid to absurdity! Edgar, I was defending you and yours; and I wish Heathcliff may flog you sick, for daring to think an evil thought of me!'

It did not need the medium of a flogging to produce that effect on the master. He tried to wrest the key from Catherine's grasp, and for safety she flung it into the hottest part of the fire; whereupon Mr. Edgar was taken with a nervous trembling, and his countenance grew deadly pale. For his life he could not avert that access of emotion; mingled anguish and humiliation overcame him completely. He leant on the back of a chair, and covered his face.

'Oh, heavens! In old days, this would win you knighthood!' exclaimed Mrs. Linton. 'We are vanquished! we are vanquished! Heathcliff would as soon lift a finger at you as a king would march his army against a colony of mice. Cheer up! you shan't be hurt! Your type is not a lamb, it's a sucking leveret.'

'I wish you joy of the milk-blooded coward, Cathy!' said her friend. 'I compliment you on your taste. And that is the slavering, shivering thing you preferred to me! I would not strike him with my fist, but I'd kick him with my foot, and experience considerable satisfaction. Is he weeping, or is he going to faint for fear?'

The fellow approached and gave the chair on which Linton rested a push. He'd better have kept his distance; my master quickly sprang erect, and struck him full on the throat a blow that would have levelled a slighter man. It took his breath for a minute; and while he choked, Mr. Linton walked out by the back door into the yard, and from thence to the front entrance.

'There! you've done with coming here,' cried Catherine. 'Get away, now; he'll return with a brace of pistols, and half-a-dozen assistants. If he did overhear us, of course he'd never forgive you. You've played him an ill turn, Heathcliff! But go—make haste! I'd rather see Edgar at bay than you.'

'Do you suppose I'm going with that blow burning in my gullet?' he thundered. 'By hell, no! I'll crush his ribs in like a rotten hazel-nut before I cross the threshold! If I don't floor him now, I shall murder him some time; so, as you value his existence, let me get at him!'

'He's not coming,' I interposed, framing a bit of a lie. 'There's the coachman and the two gardeners; you'll surely not wait to be thrust into the road by them! Each has a bludgeon; and master will, very likely, be watching from the parlour windows, to see that they fulfil his orders.'

The gardeners and coachman *were* there; but Linton was with them. They had already entered the court. Heathcliff, on second thoughts, resolved to avoid a struggle against the three underlings; he seized the poker, smashed the lock from the inner door, and made his escape as they tramped in.

Mrs. Linton, who was very much excited, bade me accompany her upstairs. She did not know my share in contributing to the disturbance, and I was anxious to keep her in ignorance.

'I'm nearly distracted, Nelly!' she exclaimed, throwing herself on the sofa. 'A thousand smiths' hammers are beating in my head! Tell Isabella to shun me; this uproar is owing to her; and should she or any one else aggravate my anger at present, I shall get wild. And, Nelly, say to Edgar, if you see him again to-night, that I'm in danger of being seriously ill. I wish it may prove true. He has startled and distressed me shockingly! I want to frighten him. Besides, he might come and begin a string of abuse or complainings; I'm certain I should recriminate, and God knows where we should end! Will you do so, my good Nelly? You are aware that I am in no way blamable in this matter. What possessed him to turn listener? Heathcliff's talk was outrageous, after you left us; but I could soon have diverted him from Isabella, and the rest meant nothing. Now all is dashed wrong by the fool's-craving to hear evil of self, that haunts some people like a demon! Had Edgar never gathered our conversation, he would never have been the worse for it. Really, when he opened on me in that unreasonable tone of displeasure after I had scolded Heathcliff till I was hoarse for *him*, I did not care, hardly, what they did to each other; especially as I felt that, however the scene closed, we should all be driven asunder for nobody knows how long! Well, if I cannot keep Heathcliff for my friend—if Edgar will be mean and jealous, I'll try to break their hearts by breaking my own. That will be a prompt way of finishing all, when I am pushed to extremity! But it's a deed to be reserved for a forlorn hope; I'd not take Linton by surprise with it. To this point he has been discreet in dreading to provoke me; you must represent the peril of quitting that policy, and remind him of my passionate temper, verging, when kindled, on frenzy. I wish you could dismiss that apathy out of your countenance, and look rather more anxious about me.'

The stolidity with which I received these instructions was, no doubt, rather exasperating: for they were delivered in perfect sincerity; but I believed a person who could plan the turning of her fits of passion to account, beforehand, might, by exerting her will, manage to control herself tolerably, even while under their influence; and I did not wish to 'frighten' her husband, as she said, and multiply his annoyances for the purpose of serving her selfishness. Therefore I said nothing when I met the master coming towards the parlour; but I took the liberty of turning back to listen whether they would resume their quarrel together. He began to speak first.

'Remain where you are, Catherine,' he said; without any anger in his voice, but with much sorrowful despondency. 'I shall not stay. I am neither come to wrangle nor be reconciled; but I wish just to learn whether, after this evening's events, you intend to continue your intimacy with'——

'Oh, for mercy's sake,' interrupted the mistress, stamping her foot, 'for mercy's sake, let us hear no more of it now! Your cold blood cannot be worked into a fever: your veins are full of ice-water; but mine are boiling, and the sight of such chillness makes them dance.'

'To get rid of me, answer my question,' persevered Mr. Linton. 'You *must* anwer it; and that violence does not alarm me. I have found that you can be as stoical as any one, when you please. Will you give up Heathcliff hereafter, or will you give up me? It is impossible for you to be *my* friend and *his* at the same time; and I absolutely *require* to know which you choose.'

'I require to be let alone!' exclaimed Catherine furiously. 'I demand it! Don't you see I can scarcely stand? Edgar, you—you leave me!'

She rang the bell till it broke with a twang; I entered leisurely. It was enough to try the temper of a saint, such senseless, wicked rages! There she lay dashing her head against the arm of the sofa, and grinding her teeth, so that you might fancy she would crash them to splinters! Mr. Linton stood looking at her in sudden compunction and fear. He told me to fetch some water. She had no breath for speaking. I brought a glass full; and as she would not drink, I sprinkled it on her face. In a few seconds she stretched herself out stiff, and turned up her eyes, while her cheeks, at once blanched and livid, assumed the aspect of death. Linton looked terrified.

'There is nothing in the world the matter,' I whispered. I did not want him to yield, though I could not help being afraid in my heart.

'She has blood on her lips!' he said, shuddering.

'Never mind!' I answered tartly. And I told him how she had resolved, previous to his coming, on exhibiting a fit of frenzy. I incautiously gave the account aloud, and she heard me; for she started up—her hair flying over her shoulders, her eyes flashing, the muscles of her neck and arms standing out preternaturally. I made up my mind for broken bones, at least; but she only glared about her for an instant, and then rushed from the room. The master directed me to follow; I did, to her chamber door: she hindered me from going further by securing it against me.

As she never offered to descend to breakfast next morning, I went to ask whether she would have some carried up. 'No!' she replied peremptorily. The same question was repeated at dinner and tea; and again on the morrow after, and received the same answer. Mr. Linton, on his part, spent his time in the library, and did not inquire concerning his wife's occupations. Isabella and he had had an hour's interview, during which he tried to elicit from her some sentiment of proper horror for Heathcliff's advances: but he could make nothing of her evasive replies, and was obliged to close the examination unsatisfactorily; adding, however, a solemn warning, that if she were so insane as to encourage that worthless suitor, it would dissolve all bonds of relationship between herself and him.

CHAPTER 12

While Miss Linton moped about the park and garden, always silent, and almost always in tears; and her brother shut himself up among books that he never opened—wearying, I guessed, with a continual vague expectation that Catherine, repenting her conduct, would come of her own accord to ask pardon, and seek a reconciliation—and *she* fasted pertinaciously, under the idea, probably, that at every meal, Edgar was ready to choke for her absence, and pride alone held him from running to cast himself at her feet: I went about my household duties, convinced that the Grange had but one sensible soul in its walls, and that lodged in my body. I wasted no condolences on Miss, nor any expostulations on my mistress; nor did I pay much attention to the sighs of my master, who yearned to hear his lady's name, since he might not hear her voice. I determined they should come about as they pleased for me; and though it was a tiresomely slow process, I began to rejoice at length in a faint dawn of its progress: as I thought at first.

Mrs. Linton, on the third day, unbarred her door, and having finished the water in her pitcher and decanter, desired a renewed supply, and a basin of gruel, for she believed she was dying. That I set down as a speech meant for Edgar's ears; I believed no such thing, so I kept it to myself and brought her some tea and dry toast. She ate and drank eagerly; and sank back on her pillow again clenching her hands and groaning. 'Oh, I will die,' she exclaimed 'since no one cares anything about me. I wish I had not taken that.' Then a good while after I heard her murmur, 'No, I'll not die—he'd be glad—he does not love me at all—he would never miss me!'

'Did you want anything, ma'am?' I inquired, still preserving my external composure, in spite of her ghastly countenance, and strange exaggerated manner.

'What is that apathetic being doing?' she demanded, pushing her thick entangled locks from her wasted face. 'Has he fallen into a lethargy, or is he dead?'

'Neither,' replied I; 'if you mean Mr. Linton. He's tolerably well, I think though his studies occupy him rather more than they ought: he is continually among his books, since he has no other society.'

I should not have spoken so, if I had known her true condition, but I could not get rid of the notion that she acted a part of her disorder.

'Among his books!' she cried, confounded. 'And I dying! I on the brink of the grave! My God! does he know how I'm altered?' continued she, staring at her reflection in a mirror hanging against the opposite wall. 'Is that Catherine Linton! He imagines me in a pet—in play, perhaps. Cannot you inform him that it is frightful earnest? Nelly, if it be not too late, as soon as I learn how he feels, I'll choose between these two; either to starve at once—that

would be no punishment unless he had a heart—or to recover, and leave the country. Are you speaking the truth about him now? Take care. Is he actually so utterly indifferent for my life?'

'Why, ma'am,' I answered, 'the master has no idea of your being deranged; and of course he does not fear that you will let yourself die of hunger.'

'You think not? Cannot you tell him I will?' she returned. 'Persuade him! speak of your own mind: say you are certain I will!'

'No, you forget, Mrs. Linton,' I suggested, 'that you have eaten some food with a relish this evening, and tomorrow you will perceive its good effects.'

'If I were only sure it would kill him,' she interrupted, 'I'd kill myself directly! These three awful nights, I've never closed my lids—and oh, I've been tormented! I've been haunted, Nelly! But I begin to fancy you don't like me. How strange! I thought, though everybody hated and despised each other, they could not avoid loving me. And they have all turned to enemies in a few hours: *they* have, I'm positive; the people *here*. How dreary to meet death, surrounded by their cold faces! Isabella terrified and repelled, afraid to enter the room, it would be so dreadful to watch Catherine go. And Edgar standing solemnly by to see it over; then offering prayers of thanks to God for restoring peace to his house, and going back to his *books*! What in the name of all that feels has he to do with *books*, when I am dying?'

She could not bear the notion which I had put into her head of Mr. Linton's philosophical resignation. Tossing about, she increased her feverish bewilderment to madness, and tore the pillow with her teeth; then raising herself up all burning, desired that I would open the window. We were in the middle of winter, the wind blew strong from the north-east, and I objected. Both the expressions flitting over her face, and the changes of her moods, began to alarm me terribly; and brought to my recollection her former illness, and the doctor's injunction that she should not be crossed. A minute previously she was violent; now, supported on one arm, and not noticing my refusal to obey her, she seemed to find childish diversion in pulling the feathers from the rents she had just made, and ranging them on the sheet according to their different species: her mind had strayed to other associations.

'That's a turkey's, she murmured to herself; 'and this is a wild duck's; and this is a pigeon's. Ah, they put pigeons' feathers in the pillows—no wonder I couldn't die! Let me take care to throw it on the floor when I lie down. And here is a moor-cock's; and this—I should know it among a thousand—it's a lapwing's. Bonny bird; wheeling over our heads in the middle of the moor. It wanted to get to its nest, for the clouds had touched the swells, and it felt rain coming. This feather was picked up from the heath, the bird was not shot: we saw its nest in the winter, full of little skeletons. Heathcliff set a trap over it, and the old ones dare not come. I made him promise he'd never shoot a lapwing after that, and he didn't. Yes, here are more! Did he

shoot my lapwings, Nelly? Are they red, any of them! Let me look.'

'Give over with that baby-work!' I interrupted, dragging the pillow away, and turning the holes towards the mattress, for she was removing its contents by handfuls. 'Lie down and shut your eyes: you're wandering. There's a mess! The down is flying about like snow.'

I went here and there collecting it.

'I see in you, Nelly,' she continued dreamily, 'an aged woman: you have grey hair and bent shoulders. This bed is the fairy cave under Peniston Crag, and you are gathering elf-bolts to hurt our heifers; pretending, while I am near, that they are only locks of wool. That's what you'll come to fifty years hence: I know you are not so now. I'm not wandering: you're mistaken, or else I should believe you really *were* that withered hag, and I should think I *was* under Peniston Crag; and I'm conscious it's night, and there are two candles on the table making the black press shine like jet.'

'The black press? where is that?' I asked. 'You are talking in your sleep!'

'It's against the wall, as it always is,' she replied. 'It *does* appear odd—I see a face in it!'

'There's no press in the room, and never was,' said I, resuming my seat, and looping up the curtain that I might watch her.

'Don't *you* see that face?' she inquired, gazing earnestly at the mirror.

And say what I could, I was incapable of making her comprehend it to be her own; so I rose and covered it with a shawl.

'It's behind there still!' she pursued anxiously. 'And it stirred. Who is it? I hope it will not come out when you are gone! Oh! Nelly, the room is haunted! I'm afraid of being alone!'

I took her hand in mine, and bid her be composed: for a succession of shudders convulsed her frame, and she *would* keep straining her gaze towards the glass.

'There's nobody here!' I insisted. 'It was *yourself*, Mrs. Linton: you knew it a while since.'

'Myself!' she gasped, 'and the clock is striking twelve! It's true, then! that's dreadful!'

Her fingers clutched the clothes, and gathered them over her eyes. I attempted to steal to the door with an intention of calling her husband; but I was summoned back by a piercing shriek—the shawl had dropped from the frame.

'Why, what *is* the matter?' cried I. 'Who is coward now? Wake up! That is the glass—the mirror, Mrs. Linton; and you see yourself in it, and there am I too, by your side.'

Trembling and bewildered, she held me fast, but the horror gradually passed from her countenance; its paleness gave place to a glow of shame.

'Oh, dear! I thought I was at home,' she sighed. 'I thought I was lying in my chamber at Wuthering Heights. Because I'm weak, my brain got confused

and I screamed unconsciously. Don't say anything; but stay with me. I dread sleeping: my dreams appal me.'

'A sound sleep would do you good, ma'am,' I answered; 'and I hope this suffering will prevent your trying starving again.'

'Oh, if I were but in my own bed in the old house!' she went on bitterly, wringing her hands, 'And that wind sounding in the firs by the lattice. Do let me feel it—it comes straight down the moor—do let me have one breath!'

To pacify her, I held the casement ajar a few seconds. A cold blast rushed through; I closed it, and returned to my post. She lay still now, her face bathed in tears. Exhaustion of body had entirely subdued her spirit: our fiery Catherine was no better than a wailing child.

'How long is it since I shut myself in here?' she asked, suddenly reviving.

'It was Monday evening,' I replied, 'and this is Thursday night, or rather Friday morning, at present.'

'What! of the same week?' she exclaimed. 'Only that brief time?'

'Long enough to live on nothing but cold water and ill-temper,' observed I.

'Well, it seems a weary number of hours,' she muttered doubtfully: 'it must be more. I remember being in the parlour after they had quarrelled, and Edgar being cruelly provoking, and me running into this room desperate. As soon as ever I had barred the door, utter blackness overwhelmed me, and I fell on the floor. I couldn't explain to Edgar how certain I felt of having a fit, or going raging mad, if he persisted in teasing me! I had no command of tongue, or brain, and he did not guess my agony, perhaps: it barely left me sense to try to escape from him and his voice. Before I recovered sufficiently to see and hear, it began to be dawn, and, Nelly, I'll tell you what I thought, and what has kept recurring and recurring till I feared for my reason. I thought as I lay there, with my head against that table leg, and my eyes dimly discerning the grey square of the window, that I was enclosed in the oak-panelled bed at home; and my heart ached with some great grief which, just waking, I could not recollect. I pondered, and worried myself to discover what it could be, and, most strangely, the whole last seven years of my life grew a blank! I did not recall that they had been at all. I was a child; my father was just buried, and my misery arose from the separation that Hindley had ordered between me and Heathcliff. I was laid alone, for the first time; and, rousing from a dismal doze after a night of weeping, I lifted my hand to push the panels aside: it struck the table-top! I swept it along the carpet, and then memory burst in: my late anguish was swallowed in a paroxysm of despair. I cannot say why I felt so wildly wretched: it must have been temporary derangement, for there is scarcely cause. But, supposing at twelve years old I had been wrenched from the Heights, and every early association, and my all in all, as Heathcliff was at that time, and been converted at a stroke into Mrs. Linton, the lady of Thrushcross Grange, and the wife of a stranger:

an exile, and outcast, thenceforth, from what had been my world. You may fancy a glimpse of the abyss where I grovelled! Shake your head as you will, Nelly, *you* have helped to unsettle me! You should have spoken to Edgar, indeed you should, and compelled him to leave me quiet! Oh, I'm burning! I wish I were out of doors! I wish I were a girl again, half savage and hardy, and free; and laughing at injuries, not maddening under them! Why am I so changed? Why does my blood rush into a hell of tumult at a few words? I'm sure I should be myself were I once among the heather on those hills. Open the window again wide: fasten it open! Quick, why don't you move?'

'Because I won't give you your death of cold,' I answered.

'You won't give me a chance of life, you mean,' she said sullenly. 'However, I'm not helpless, yet: I'll open it myself.'

And sliding from the bed before I could hinder her, she crossed the room, walking very uncertainly, threw it back, and bent out, careless of the frosty air that cut about her shoulders as keen as a knife. I entreated, and finally attempted to force her to retire. But I soon found her delirious strength much surpassed mine (she *was* delirious, I became convinced by her subsequent actions and ravings). There was no moon, and everything beneath lay in misty darkness: not a light gleamed from any house, far or near— all had been extinguished long ago; and those at Wuthering Heights were never visible—still she asserted she caught their shining.

'Look!' she cried eagerly, 'that's my room with the candle in it, and the trees swaying before it: and the other candle is in Joseph's garret. Joseph sits up late, doesn't he? He's waiting till I come home that he may lock the gate. Well, he'll wait a while yet. It's a rough journey, and a sad heart to travel it; and we must pass by Gimmerton Kirk, to go that journey! We've braved its ghosts often together, and dared each other to stand among the graves and ask them to come. But, Heathcliff, if I dare you now, will you venture? If you do, I'll keep you. I'll not lie there by myself: they may bury me twelve feet deep, and throw the church down over me, but I won't rest till you are with me. I never will!'

She paused, and resumed with a strange smile. 'He's considering—he'd rather I'd come to him! Find a way, then! not through that kirkyard. You are slow! Be content, you always followed me!'

Perceiving it vain to argue against her insanity, I was planning how I could reach something to wrap about her, without quitting my hold of herself (for I could not trust her alone by the gaping lattice), when, to my consternation, I heard the rattle of the door-handle, and Mr. Linton entered. He had only then come from the library; and, in passing through the lobby, had noticed our talking and been attracted by curiosity, or fear, to examine what it signified at that late hour.

'Oh, sir!' I cried, checking the exclamation risen to his lips at the sight

which met him, and the bleak atmosphere of the chamber. 'My poor mistress is ill, and she quite masters me: I cannot manage her at all; pray, come and persuade her to go to bed. Forget your anger, for she's hard to guide any way but her own.'

'Catherine ill?' he said, hastening to us. 'Shut the window, Ellen! Catherine! why'——

He was silent. The haggardness of Mrs. Linton's appearance smote him speechless, and he could only glance from her to me in horrified astonishment.

'She's been fretting here,' I continued, 'and eating scarcely anything, and never complaining; she would admit none of us till this evening, and so we couldn't inform you of her state as we were not aware of it ourselves; but it is nothing.'

I felt I uttered my explanations awkwardly; the master frowned. 'It is nothing, is it, Ellen Dean?' he said sternly. 'You shall account more clearly for keeping me ignorant of this!' And he took his wife in his arms, and looked at her with anguish.

At first she gave him no glance of recognition; he was invisible to her abstracted gaze. The delirium was not fixed, however; having weaned her eyes from contemplating the outer darkness, by degrees she centred her attention on him, and discovered who it was that held her.

'Ah! you are come, are you, Edgar Linton?' she said, with angry animation. 'You are one of those things that are ever found when least wanted, and when you are wanted, never! I suppose we shall have plenty of lamentations now—I see we shall—but they can't keep me from my narrow home out yonder: my resting-place, where I'm bound before spring is over! There it is: not among the Lintons, mind, under the chapel-roof, but in the open air, with a head-stone; and you may please yourself, whether you go to them or come to me!'

'Catherine, what have you done?' commenced the master. 'Am I nothing to you any more? Do you love that wretch Heath——'

'Hush!' cried Mrs. Linton. 'Hush, this moment! You mention that name and I end the matter instantly, by a spring from the window! What you touch at present you may have; but my soul will be on that hill-top before you lay hands on me again. I don't want you, Edgar: I'm past wanting you. Return to your books. I'm glad you possess a consolation, for all you had in me is gone.'

'Her mind wanders, sir,' I interposed. 'She has been talking nonsense the whole evening; but let her have quiet, and proper attendance, and she'll rally. Hereafter, we must be cautious how we vex her.'

'I desire no further advice from you,' answered Mr. Linton. 'You know your mistress's nature, and you encouraged me to harass her. And not to give me one hint of how she has been these three days! It was heartless!

Months of sickness could not cause such a change!'

I began to defend myself, thinking it too bad to be blamed for another's wicked waywardness. 'I knew Mrs. Linton's nature to be headstrong and domineering,' cried I; 'but I didn't know that you wished to foster her fierce temper! I didn't know that, to humour her, I should wink at Mr. Heathcliff. I performed the duty of a faithful servant in telling you, and I have got a faithful servant's wages! Well, it will teach me to be careful next time. Next time you may gather intelligence for yourself!'

'The next time you bring a tale to me, you shall quit my service, Ellen Dean,' he replied.

'You'd rather hear nothing about it, I suppose, then, Mr. Linton?' said I. 'Heathcliff has your permission to come a courting to miss, and to drop in at every opportunity your absence offers, on purpose to poison the mistress against you?'

Confused as Catherine was, her wits were alert applying our conversation.

'Ah! Nelly has played traitor,' she exclaimed passionately. 'Nelly is my hidden enemy. You witch! So you do seek elf-bolts to hurt us! Let me go, I'll make her rue! I'll make her howl a recantation!'

A maniac's fury kindled under her brows; she struggled desperately to disengage herself from Linton's arms. I felt no inclination to tarry the event; and, resolving to seek medical aid on my own responsibility, I quitted the chamber.

In passing the garden to reach the road, at a place where a bridle hook is driven into the wall, I saw something white moved irregularly, evidently by another agent than the wind. Notwithstanding my hurry, I stayed to examine it, lest ever after I should have the conviction impressed on my imagination that it was a creature of the other world. My surprise and perplexity were great to discover, by touch more than vision, Miss Isabella's springer, Fanny, suspended by a handkerchief, and nearly at its last gasp. I quickly released the animal, and lifted it into the garden. I had seen it follow its mistress upstairs when she went to bed; and wondered much how it could have got out there, and what mischievous person had treated it so. While untying the knot round the hook, it seemed to me that I repeatedly caught the beat of horses' feet galloping at some distance; but there were such a number of things to occupy my reflections that I hardly gave the circumstance a thought: though it was a strange sound, in that place, at two o'clock in the morning.

Mr. Kenneth was fortunately just issuing from his house to see a patient in the village as I came up the street; and my account of Catherine Linton's malady induced him to accompany me back immediately. He was a plain rough man; and he made no scruple to speak his doubts of her surviving this second attack; unless she were more submissive to his directions than she

had shown hersell before.

'Nelly Dean,' said he, 'I can't help fancying there's an extra cause for this. What has there been to do at the Grange? We've odd reports up here. A stout, hearty lass like Catherine, does not fall ill for a trifle; and that sort of people should not either. It's hard work bringing them through fevers, and such things. How did it begin?'

'The master will inform you,' I answered; 'but you are acquainted with the Earnshaws' violent dispositions, and Mrs. Linton caps them all. I may say this: it commenced in a quarrel. She was struck during a tempest of passion with a kind of fit. That's her account, at least; for she flew off in the height of it, and locked herself up. Afterwards, she refused to eat, and now she alternately raves and remains in a half dream; knowing those about her, but having her mind filled with all sorts of strange ideas and illusions.'

'Mr. Linton will be sorry?' observed Kenneth, interrogatively.

'Sorry? he'll break his heart should anything happen!' I replied. 'Don't alarm him more than necessary.'

'Well, I told him to beware,' said my companion; 'and he must bide the consequences of neglecting my warning! Hasn't he been thick with Mr. Heathcliff, lately?'

'Heathcliff frequently visits at the Grange,' answered I, 'though more on the strength of the mistress having known him when a boy, than because the master likes his company. At present, he's discharged from the trouble of calling; owing to some presumptuous aspirations after Miss Linton which he manifested. I hardly think he'll be taken in again.'

'And does Miss Linton turn a cold shoulder on him?' was the doctor's next question.

'I'm not in her confidence,' returned I, reluctant to continue the subject.

'No, she's a sly one,' he remarked, shaking his head. 'She keeps her own counsel! But she's a real little fool. I have it from good authority, that, last night (and a pretty night it was!) she and Heathcliff were walking in the plantation at the back of your house, above two hours; and he pressed her not to go in again, but just mount his horse and away with him! My informant said she could only put him off by pledging her word of honour to be prepared on their first meeting after that: when it was to be, he didn't hear; but you urge Mr. Linton to look sharp!'

This news filled me with fresh fears; I outstripped Kenneth, and ran most of the way back. The little dog was yelping in the garden yet. I spared a minute to open the gate for it, but instead of going to the house door, it coursed up and down snuffing the grass, and would have escaped to the road, had I not seized and conveyed it in with me. On ascending to Isabella's room, my suspicions were confirmed: it was empty. Had I been a few hours sooner, Mrs. Linton's illness might have arrested her rash step. But what

could be done now? There was a bare possibility of overtaking them if pursued instantly. *I* could not pursue them, however; and I dare not rouse the family, and fill the place with confusion; still less unfold the business to my master, absorbed as he was in his present calamity, and having no heart to spare for a second grief! I saw nothing for it but to hold my tongue, and suffer matters to take their course; and Kenneth being arrived, I went with a badly composed countenance to announce him. Catherine lay in a troubled sleep: her husband had succeeded in soothing the access of frenzy: he now hung over her pillow, watching every shade, and every change of her painfully expressive features.

The doctor, on examining the case for himself, spoke hopefully to him of its having a favourable termination, if we could only preserve around her perfect and constant tranquillity. To me, he signified the threatening danger was not so much death, as permanent alienation of intellect.

I did not close my eyes that night, nor did Mr. Linton: indeed, we never went to bed; and the servants were all up long before the usual hour, moving through the house with stealthy tread, and exchanging whispers as they encountered each other in their vocations. Every one was active, but Miss Isabella; and they began to remark how sound she slept: her brother, too, asked if she had risen, and seemed impatient for her presence, and hurt that she showed so little anxiety for her sister-in-law. I trembled lest he should send me to call her; but I was spared the pain of being the first proclaimant of her flight. One of the maids, a thoughtless girl, who had been on an early errand to Gimmerton, came panting upstairs, open mouthed, and dashed into the chamber, crying:

'Oh, dear, dear! What mun we have next? Master, master, our young lady'—

'Hold your noise!' cried I hastily, enraged at her clamorous manner.

'Speak lower, Mary—What is the matter?' said Mr. Linton. 'What ails your young lady?'

'She's gone, she's gone! Yon' Heathcliff's run off wi' her!' gasped the girl

'That is not true!' exclaimed Linton, rising in agitation. 'It cannot be how has the idea entered your head? Ellen Dean, go and seek her. It is incredible: it cannot be.'

As he spoke he took the servant to the door, and then repeated his demand to know her reasons for such an assertion.

'Why, I met on the road a lad that fetches milk here,' she stammered 'and he asked whether we weren't in trouble at the Grange. I thought he meant for missis's sickness, so I answered, yes. Then says he, "They's somebody gone after 'em, I guess?" I stared. He saw I knew nought about it, and he told how a gentleman and lady had stopped to have a horse's shoe fastened a a blacksmith's shop, two miles out of Gimmerton, not very long after midnight and how the blacksmith's lass had got up to spy who they were: she knew them

both directly. And she noticed the man—Heathcliff it was, she felt certain: nob'dy could mistake him, besides—put a sovereign in her father's hand for payment. The lady had a cloak about her face; but having desired a sup of water, while she drank, it fell back, and she saw her very plain. Heathcliff held both bridles as they rode on, and they set their faces from the village, and went as fast as the rough roads would let them. The lass said nothing to her father, but she told it all over Gimmerton this morning.'

I ran and peeped, for form's sake, into Isabella's room; confirming, when I returned, the servant's statement. Mr. Linton had resumed his seat by the bed; on my re-entrance, he raised his eyes, read the meaning of my blank aspect, and dropped them without giving an order, or uttering a word.

'Are we to try any measures for overtaking and bringing her back?' I inquired. 'How should we do?'

'She went of her own accord,' answered the master; 'she had a right to go if she pleased. Trouble me no more about her. Hereafter she is only my sister in name: not because I disown her, but because she has disowned me.'

And that was all he said on the subject: he did not make a single inquiry further, or mention her in any way, except directing me to send what property she had in the house to her fresh home, wherever it was, when I knew it.

CHAPTER 13

For two months the fugitives remained absent; in those two months, Mrs. Linton encountered and conquered the worst shock of what was denominated a brain fever. No mother could have nursed an only child more devotedly than Edgar tended her. Day and night he was watching, and patiently enduring all the annoyances that irritable nerves and a shaken reason could inflict: and, though Kenneth remarked that what he saved from the grave would only recompense his care by forming the source of constant future anxiety—in fact, that his health and strength were being sacrificed to preserve a mere ruin of humanity—he knew no limits in gratitude and joy when Catherine's life was declared out of danger; and hour after hour he would sit beside her, tracing the gradual return to bodily health, and flattering his too sanguine hopes with the illusion that her mind would settle back to its right balance also, and she would soon be entirely her former self.

The first time she left her chamber was at the commencement of the following March. Mr. Linton had put on her pillow, in the morning, a handful of golden crocuses; her eye, long stranger to any gleam of pleasure, caught them in waking, and shone delighted as she gathered them eagerly together.

'These are the earliest flowers at the Heights,' she exclaimed. 'They remind me of soft thaw winds, and warm sunshine, and nearly melted snow. Edgar,

is there not a south wind, and is not the snow almost gone?'

'The snow is quite gone down here, darling,' replied her husband; 'and I only see two white spots on the whole range of moors: the sky is blue, and the larks are singing, and the becks and brooks are all brim full. Catherine, last spring at this time, I was longing to have you under this roof, now, I wish you were a mile or two up those hills: the air blows so sweetly, I feel that it would cure you.'

'I shall never be there but once more,' said the invalid; 'and then you'll leave me; and I shall remain for ever. Next spring you'll long again to have me under this roof, and you'll look back and think you were happy to-day.'

Linton lavished on her the kindest caresses, and tried to cheer her by the fondest words; but, vaguely regarding the flowers, she let the tears collect on her lashes and stream down her cheeks unheeding. We knew she was really better, and, therefore, decided that long confinement to a single place produced much of this despondency, and it might be partially removed by a change of scene. The master told me to light a fire in the many-weeks-deserted parlour, and to set an easy-chair in the sunshine by the window; and then he brought her down, and she sat a long while enjoying the genial heat, and, as we expected, revived by the objects round her: which, though familiar, were free from the dreary associations investing her hated sick chamber. By evening, she seemed greatly exhausted; yet no arguments could persuade her to return to that apartment, and I had to arrange the parlour sofa for her bed, till another room could be prepared. To obviate the fatigue of mounting and descending the stairs, we fitted up this, where you lie at present: on the same floor with the parlour; and she was soon strong enough to move from one to the other, leaning on Edgar's arm. Ah, I thought myself she might recover, so waited on as she was. And there was double cause to desire it, for on her existence depended that of another: we cherished the hope that in a little while, Mr. Linton's heart would be gladdened, and his lands secured from a stranger's gripe, by the birth of an heir.

I should mention that Isabella sent to her brother, some six weeks from her departure, a short note, announcing her marriage with Heathcliff. It appeared dry and cold; but at the bottom was dotted in with pencil an obscure apology, and an entreaty for kind remembrance and reconciliation if her proceeding had offended him: asserting that she could not help it then and being done, she had now no power to repeal it. Linton did not reply to this, I believe; and, in a fortnight more, I got a long letter which I considered odd, coming from the pen of a bride just out of the honeymoon. I'll read it for I keep it yet. Any relic of the dead is precious, if they were valued living

DEAR ELLEN, it begins:—

I came last night to Wuthering Heights, and heard, for the first time that Catherine has been, and is yet, very ill. I must not write to her, I sup

pose, and my brother is either too angry or too distressed to answer what I sent him. Still, I must write to somebody, and the only choice left me is you.

Inform Edgar that I'd give the world to see his face again—that my heart returned to Thrushcross Grange in twenty-four hours after I left it, and is there at this moment, full of warm feelings for him, and Catherine! *I can't follow it, though*—(those words are underlined) they need not expect me, and they may draw what conclusions they please; taking care, however, to lay nothing at the door of my weak will or deficient affection.

The remainder of the letter is for yourself alone. I want to ask you two questions: the first is—How did you contrive to preserve the common sympathies of human nature when you resided here? I cannot recognise any sentiment which those around share with me.

The second question, I have great interest in; it is this—Is Mr. Heathcliff a man? If so, is he mad? And if not, is he a devil? I shan't tell my reasons for making this inquiry; but, I beseech you to explain, if you can, what I have married: that is, when you call to see me; and you must call, Ellen, very soon. Don't write, but come, and bring me something from Edgar.

Now, you shall hear how I have been received in my new home, as I am led to imagine the Heights will be. It is to amuse myself that I dwell on such subjects as the lack of external comforts: they never occupy my thoughts, except at the moment when I miss them. I should laugh and dance for joy, if I found their absence was the total of my miseries, and the rest was an unnatural dream!

The sun set behind the Grange, as we turned on to the moors; by that, I judged it to be six o'clock; and my companion halted half-an-hour, to inspect the park, and the gardens, and, probably, the place itself, as well as he could; so it was dark when we dismounted in the paved yard of the farm-house, and your old fellow-servant, Joseph, issued out to receive us by the light of a dip candle. He did it with a courtesy that redounded to his credit. His first act was to elevate his torch to a level with my face, squint malignantly, project his under lip, and turn away. Then he took the two horses, and led them into the stables; reappearing for the purpose of locking the outer gate, as if we lived in an ancient castle.

Heathcliff stayed to speak to him, and I entered the kitchen—a dingy, untidy hole; I daresay you would not know it, it is so changed since it was in your charge. By the fire stood a ruffianly child, strong in limb and dirty in garb, with a look of Catherine in his eyes and about his mouth.

'This is Edgar's legal nephew,' I reflected—'mine in a manner; I must shake hands, and—yes—I must kiss him. It is right to establish a good understanding at the beginning.'

I approached, and, attempting to take his chubby fist, said:

'How do you do, my dear?'

He replied in a jargon I did not comprehend.

'Shall you and I be friends, Hareton?' was my next essay at conversation.

An oath, and a threat to set Throttler on me if I did not 'frame off,' rewarded my perseverance.

'Hey, Throttler, lad!' whispered the little wretch, rousing a half-bred bull-dog from its lair in a corner. 'Now, wilt tuh be ganging?' he asked authoritatively.

Love for my life urged a compliance; I stepped over the threshold to wait till the others should enter. Mr. Heathcliff was nowhere visible; and Joseph, whom I followed to the stables, and requested to accompany me in, after staring and muttering to himself, screwed up his nose, and replied:

'Mim! mim! mim! Did iver Christian body hear aught like it? Minching un' munching! How can Aw tell whet ye say?'

'I say, I wish you to come with me into the house!' I cried, thinking him deaf, yet highly disgusted at his rudeness.

'Nor nuh me! I getten summat else to do,' he answered, and continued his work; moving his lantern jaws meanwhile, and surveying my dress and countenance (the former a great deal too fine, but the latter, I'm sure, as sad as he could desire) with sovereign contempt.

I walked round the yard, and through a wicket to another door, at which I took the liberty of knocking, in hopes some more civil servant might show himself. After a short suspense, it was opened by a tall, gaunt man, without neckerchief, and otherwise extremely slovenly; his features were lost in masses of shaggy hair that hung on his shoulders; and *his* eyes, too, were like a ghostly Catherine's with all their beauty annihilated.

'What's your business here?' he demanded grimly. 'Who are you?'

'My name *was* Isabella Linton,' I replied. 'You've seen me before, sir. I'm lately married to Mr. Heathcliff, and he has brought me here—I suppose by your permission.'

'Is he come back, then?' asked the hermit, glaring like a hungry wolf.

'Yes—we came just now,' I said; 'but he left me by the kitchen door; and when I would have gone in, your little boy played sentinel over the place, and frightened me off by the help of a bull-dog.'

'It's well the hellish villain has kept his word!' growled my future host, searching the darkness beyond me in expectation of discovering Heathcliff; and then he indulged in a soliloquy of execrations, and threats of what he would have done had the 'fiend' deceived him.

I repented having tried this second entrance, and was almost inclined to slip away before he finished cursing, but ere I could execute that intention, he ordered me in, and shut and re-fastened the door. There was a great fire, and that was all the light in the huge apartment, whose floor had grown a uniform grey; and the once brilliant pewter dishes, which used to attract

my gaze when I was a girl, partook of a similar obscurity, created by tarnish and dust. I inquired whether I might call the maid, and be conducted to a bed-room? Mr. Earnshaw vouchsafed no answer. He walked up and down, with his hands in his pockets, apparently quite forgetting my presence; and his abstraction was evidently so deep, and his whole aspect so misanthropical, that I shrank from disturbing him again.

You'll not be surprised, Ellen, at my feeling particularly cheerless, seated in worse than solitude on that inhospitable hearth, and remembering that four miles distant lay my delightful home, containing the only people I loved on earth; and there might as well be the Atlantic to part us, instead of those four miles: I could not overpass them! I questioned with myself—where must I turn for comfort? and—mind you don't tell Edgar, or Catherine— above every sorrow beside, this rose pre-eminent: despair at finding nobody who could or would be my ally against Heathcliff! I had sought shelter at Wuthering Heights, almost gladly, because I was secured by that arrange- ment from living alone with him; but he knew the people we were coming amongst, and he did not fear their intermeddling.

I sat and thought a doleful time: the clock struck eight, and nine, and still my companion paced to and fro, his head bent on his breast, and perfectly silent, unless a groan or a bitter ejaculation forced itself out at intervals. I listened to detect a woman's voice in the house, and filled the interim with wild regrets and dismal anticipations, which, at last, spoke audibly in irrepressible sighing and weeping. I was not aware how openly I grieved, till Earnshaw halted opposite, in his measured walk, and gave me a stare of newly-awakened surprise. Taking advantage of his recovered attention, I exclaimed:

'I'm tired with my journey, and I want to go to bed! Where is the maid- servant? Direct me to her, as she won't come to me!'

'We have none,' he answered; 'you must wait on yourself!'

'Where must I sleep, then?' I sobbed: I was beyond regarding self-respect, weighed down by fatigue and wretchedness.

'Joseph will show you Heathcliff's chamber,' said he; 'open that door—he's in there.'

I was going to obey, but he suddenly arrested me, and added in the strangest tone:

'Be so good as to turn your lock, and draw your bolt—don't omit it!'

'Well!' I said. 'But why, Mr. Earnshaw?' I did not relish the notion of deliberately fastening myself in with Heathcliff.

'Look here!' he replied, pulling from his waist-coat a curiously constructed pistol, having a double-edged spring knife attached to the barrel. 'That's a great tempter to a desperate man, is it not? I cannot resist going up with this every night, and trying his door. If once I find it open he's done for! I do it

invariably, even though the minute before I have been recalling a hundred reasons that should make me refrain: it is some devil that urges me to thwart my own schemes by killing him. You fight against that devil for love as long as you may; when the time comes, not all the angels in heaven shall save him!'

I surveyed the weapon inquisitively. A hideous notion struck me: how powerful I should be possessing such an instrument! I took it from his hand, and touched the blade. He looked astonished at the expression my face assumed during a brief second: it was not horror, it was covetousness. He snatched the pistol back, jealously; shut the knife, and returned it to its concealment.

'I don't care if you tell him,' said he. 'Put him on his guard, and watch for him. You know the terms we are on, I see: his danger does not shock you.'

'What has Heathcliff done to you?' I asked. 'In what has he wronged you, to warrant this appalling hatred? Wouldn't it be wiser to bid him quit the house?'

'No!' thundered Earnshaw, 'should he offer to leave me, he's a dead man: persuade him to attempt it, and you are a murderess! Am I to lose *all*, without a chance of retrieval? Is Hareton to be a beggar? Oh, damnation! I *will* have it back; and I'll have *his* gold too; and then his blood; and hell shall have his soul! It will be ten times blacker with that guest than ever it was before!'

You've acquainted me, Ellen, with your old master's habits, He is clearly on the verge of madness: he was so last night at least. I shuddered to be near him, and thought on the servant's ill-bred moroseness as comparatively agreeable. He now recommenced his moody walk, and I raised the latch, and escaped into the kitchen. Joseph was bending over the fire, peering into a large pan that swung above it; and a wooden bowl of oatmeal stood on the settle close by. The contents of the pan began to boil, and he turned to plunge his hand into the bowl; I conjectured that this preparation was probably for our supper, and, being hungry, I resolved it should be eatable; so, crying out sharply, '*I'll* make the porridge!' I removed the vessel out of his reach, and proceeded to take off my hat and riding habit. 'Mr. Earnshaw,' I continued, 'directs me to wait on myself: I will. I'm not going to act the lady among you, for fear I should starve.'

'Gooid Lord!' he muttered, sitting down, and stroking his ribbed stockings from the knee to the ankle. 'If they's tuh be fresh ortherings—just when Aw getten used tuh two maisters, if Aw mun hev a *mistress* set o'er my heead, it's loike time tuh be flitting. Aw niver *did* think tuh say t' day ut Aw mud lave th' owld place—but Aw daht it's nigh at hend!'

This lamentation drew no notice from me: I went briskly to work, sighing to remember a period when it would have been all merry fun; but compelled speedily to drive off the remembrance. It racked me to recall past happiness, and the greater peril there was of conjuring up its apparition, the quicker

the thible ran round, and the faster the handfuls of meal fell into the water. Joseph beheld my style of cookery with growing indignation.

'Thear!' he ejaculated, 'Hareton, thah willut sup thy porridge tuh neight; they'll be nowt bud lumpsas big as maw nàve. Thear, agean! Aw'd fling in bowl un all, if Aw wer yah! There, pale t' guilp off, un' then yah'll hae done wi't. Bang, bang. It's marcy t' bothom isn't deàved aht!'

It *was* rather a rough mess, I own, when poured into the basins; four had been provided, and a gallon pitcher of new milk was brought from the dairy, which Hareton seized and commenced drinking and spilling from the expansive lip. I expostulated, and desired that he should have his in a mug; affirming that I could not taste the liquid treated so dirtily. The old cynic chose to be vastly offended at this nicety; assuring me, repeatedly, that 'the barn was every bit as good' as I, 'and every bit as wollsome,' and wondering how I could fashion to be so conceited. Meanwhile, the infant ruffian continued sucking; and glowered at me defyingly, as he slavered into the jug.

'I shall have my supper in another room,' I said. 'Have you no place you call a parlour?'

'*Parlour!*' he echoed sneeringly, '*parlour!* Nay, we've noa *parlours.* If yah dunnut loike wer company, there's maister's; un' if yah dunnut loike maister, there's us.'

'Then I shall go upstairs!' I answered; 'show me a chamber.'

I put my basin on a tray, and went myself to fetch some more milk. With great grumblings, the fellow rose, and preceded me in my ascent: we mounted to the garrets; he opening a door, now and then, to look into the apartments we passed.

'Here's a rahm,' he said, at last, flinging back a cranky board on hinges. 'It's weel eneugh tuh ate a few porridge in. They's a pack o' corn i' t' corner, thear, meeterly clane; if yah're feared uh muckying yer grand silk cloes, spread yer hankerchir o' t' top on't.'

The 'rahm' was a kind of lumber-hole smelling strong of malt and grain; various sacks of which articles were piled around, leaving a wide, bare space in the middle.

'Why, man!' I exclaimed, facing him angrily, 'this is not a place to sleep in. I wish to see my bedroom.'

'*Bed-rume!*' he repeated, in a tone of mockery. 'Yah's see all t' *bed-rumes* hear is—yon's mine.'

He pointed into the second garret, only differing from the first in being more naked about the walls, and having a large low, curtainless bed, with an indigo-coloured quilt at one end.

'What do I want with yours?' I retorted. 'I suppose Mr. Heathcliff does not lodge at the top of the house, does he?'

'Oh! it's Maister *Hathecliff's* yah're wenting!' cried he, as if making a new

discovery. 'Couldn't ye uh said soa, at onst? un then, Aw mud uh telled ye, baht all this wark, ut that's just one yah cannut sea—he allas keeps it locked, un nob'dy iver mells on't but hisseln.'

'You've a nice house, Joseph,' I could not refrain from observing, 'and pleasant inmates; and I think the concentrated essence of all the madness in the world took up its abode in my brain the day I linked my fate with theirs! However, that is not to the present purpose—there are other rooms. For heaven's sake be quick, and let me settle somewhere!'

He made no reply to this adjuration; only plodding doggedly down the wooden steps, and halting before an apartment which, from that halt and the superior quality of its furniture, I conjectured to be the best one. There was a carpet: a good one, but the pattern was obliterated by dust; a fireplace hung with cut paper, dropping to pieces; a handsome oak bedstead with ample crimson curtains of rather expensive material and modern make; but they had evidently experienced rough usage: the valances hung in festoons, wrenched from their rings, and the iron rod supporting them was bent in an arc on one side, causing the drapery to trail upon the floor. The chairs were also damaged, many of them severely; and deep indentations deformed the panels of the walls. I was endeavouring to gather resolution for entering and taking possession, when my fool of a guide announced, 'This here is t' maister's.' My supper by this time was cold, my appetite gone, and my patience exhausted. I insisted on being provided instantly with a place of refuge, and means of repose.

'Whear the divil?' began the religious elder. 'The Lord bless us! The Lord forgie us! Whear the *hell* wold ye gang? ye marred, wearisome nowt! Yah seen all bud Hareton's bit uf a cham'er. They's not another hoile tuh lig dahn in i' th' hahse!'

I was so vexed, I flung my tray and its contents on the ground; and then seated myself at the stairs-head, hid my face in my hands, and cried.

'Ech! ech!' exclaimed Joseph. 'Weel done, Miss Cathy! weel done, Miss Cathy! Hahsiver, t' maister sall just tum'le o'er them brocken pots; un then we's hear summut; we's hear hah it's tuh be. Gooid-for-nowt madling yah desarve pining froo this to Churstmas, flinging t' precious gifts uh God under fooit i' yer flaysome rages! Bud Aw'm mista'en if yah shew yer sperrit lang. Will Hathecliff bide sich bonny ways, think ye? Aw nobbut wish he much cotch ye i' that plisky. Aw nobbut wish he may.'

And so he went on scolding to his den beneath, taking the candle with him and I remained in the dark. The period of reflection succeeding this silly action compelled me to admit the necessity of smothering my pride and choking my wrath, and bestirring myself to remove its effects. An unexpected aid presently appeared in the shape of Throttler, whom I now recognised as a son of our old Skulker: it had spent its whelphood at the Grange, and was

given by my father to Mr. Hindley. I fancy it knew me: it pushed its nose against mine by way of salute, and then hastened to devour the porridge; while I groped from step to step, collecting the shattered earthenware, and drying the spatters of milk from the banister with my pocket-handkerchief. Our labours were scarcely over when I heard Earnshaw's tread in the passage; my assistant tucked in his tail, and pressed to the wall; I stole into the nearest doorway. The dog's endeavour to avoid him was unsuccessful; as I guessed by a scutter downstairs, and a prolonged, piteous yelping. I had better luck! he passed on, entered his chamber, and shut the door. Directly after Joseph came up with Hareton, to put him to bed. I had found shelter in Hareton's room, and the old man, on seeing me, said:

'They's rahm for boath ye un yer pride, now, I sud think, i' the hahse. It's empty; ye may hev it all to yerseln, un Him as allas maks a third, i' such ill company!'

Gladly did I take advantage of this intimation; and the minute I flung myself into a chair, by the fire, I nodded, and slept. My slumber was deep and sweet, though over far too soon. Mr. Heathcliff awoke me; he had just come in, and demanded, in his loving manner, what I was doing there? I told him the cause of my staying up so late—that he had the key of our room in his pocket. The adjective *our* gave mortal offence. He swore it was not, nor ever should be, mine; and he'd—But I'll not repeat his language, nor describe his habitual conduct: he is ingenious and unresting in seeking to gain my abhorrence! I sometimes wonder at him with an intensity that deadens my fear: yet, I assure you, a tiger or a venomous serpent could not rouse terror in me equal to that which he wakens. He told me of Catherine's illness, and accused my brother of causing it; promising that I should be Edgar's proxy in suffering, till he could get hold of him.

I do hate him—I am wretched—I have been a fool! Beware of uttering one breath of this to any one at the Grange. I shall expect you every day—don't disappoint me!

<div align="right">Isabella.</div>

CHAPTER 14

As soon as I had perused this epistle, I went to the master, and informed him that his sister had arrived at the Heights, and sent me a letter expressing her sorrow for Mrs. Linton's situation, and her ardent desire to see him; with a wish that he would transmit to her, as early as possible, some token of forgiveness by me.

'Forgiveness!' said Linton. 'I have nothing to forgive her, Ellen. You may call at Wuthering Heights this afternoon, if you like, and say that I am not

angry, but I'm *sorry* to have lost her; especially as I can never think she'll be happy. It is out of the question my going to see her, however: we are eternally divided; and should she really wish to oblige me, let her persuade the villain she has married to leave the country.'

'And you won't write her a little note, sir?' I asked imploringly.

'No,' he answered. 'It is needless. My communication with Heathcliff's family shall be as sparing as his with mine. It shall not exist!'

Mr. Edgar's coldness depressed me exceedingly; and all the way from the Grange I puzzled my brains how to put more heart into what he said, when I repeated it; and how to soften his refusal of even a few lines to console Isabella. I dare say she had been on the watch for me since morning: I saw her looking through the lattice, as I came up the garden causeway, and I nodded to her; but she drew back, as if afraid of being observed. I entered without knocking. There never was such a dreary, dismal scene as the formerly cheerful house presented! I must confess, that if I had been in the young lady's place, I would, at least, have swept the hearth, and wiped the tables with a duster. But she already partook of the pervading spirit of neglect which encompassed her. Her pretty face was wan and listless; her hair uncurled: some locks hanging lankly down, and some carelessly twisted round her head. Probably she had not touched her dress since yester evening. Hindley was not there. Mr. Heathcliff sat at a table, turning over some papers in his pocket-book; but he rose when I appeared, asked me how I did, quite friendly, and offered me a chair. He was the only thing there that seemed decent: and I thought he never looked better. So much had circumstances altered their positions, that he would certainly have struck a stranger as a born and bred gentleman; and his wife as a thorough little slattern! She came forward eagerly to greet me; and held out one hand to take the expected letter. I shook my head. She wouldn't understand the hint, but followed me to a sideboard, where I went to lay my bonnet, and importuned me in a whisper to give her directly what I had brought. Heathcliff guessed the meaning of her manoeuvres, and said:

'If you have got anything for Isabella (as no doubt you have, Nelly), give it to her. You needn't make a secret of it! we have no secrets between us.'

'Oh, I have nothing,' I replied, thinking it best to speak the truth at once. 'My master bid me tell his sister that she must not expect either a letter or a visit from him at present. He sends his love, ma'am, and his wishes for your happiness, and his pardon for the grief you have occasioned; but he thinks that after this time, his household and the household here should drop intercommunication, as nothing good could come of keeping it up.'

Mrs. Heathcliff's lip quivered slightly, and she returned to her seat in the window. Her husband took his stand on the hearthstone, near me, and began to put questions concerning Catherine. I told him as much as I thought

proper of her illness, and he extorted from me, by cross-examination, most of the facts connected with its origin. I blamed her, as she deserved, for bringing it all on herself; and ended by hoping that he would follow Mr. Linton's example and avoid future interference with his family, for good or evil.

'Mrs. Linton is now just recovering,' I said; 'she'll never be like she was, but her life is spared; and if you really have a regard for her, you'll shun crossing her way again: nay, you'll move out of this country entirely; and that you may not regret it, I'll inform you Catherine Linton is as different now from your old friend Catherine Earnshaw, as that young lady is different from me. Her appearance is changed greatly, her character much more so; and the person who is compelled, of necessity, to be her companion, will only sustain his affection hereafter by the remembrance of what she once was, by common humanity, and a sense of duty!'

'That is quite possible,' remarked Heathcliff, forcing himself to seem calm: 'quite possible that your master should have nothing but common humanity and a sense of duty to fall back upon. But do you imagine that I shall leave Catherine to his *duty* and *humanity*? and can you compare my feelings respecting Catherine to his? Before you leave this house, I must exact a promise from you, that you'll get me an interview with her: consent or refuse, I *will* see her! What do you say?'

'I say, Mr. Heathcliff,' I replied, 'you must not: you never shall, through my means. Another encounter between you and the master would kill her altogether.'

'With your aid, that may be avoided,' he continued; 'and should there be danger of such an event—should he be the cause of adding a single trouble more to her existence—why, I think I shall be justified in going to extremes! I wish you had sincerity enough to tell me whether Catherine would suffer greatly from his loss: the fear that she would restrains me. And there you see the distinctions between our feelings: had he been in my place, and I in his, though I hated him with a hatred that turned my life to gall, I never would have raised a hand against him. You may look incredulous, if you please! I never would have banished him from her society as long as she desired his. The moment her regard ceased, I would have torn his heart out, and drunk his blood! But, till then—if you don't believe me, you don't know me—till then, I would have died by inches before I touched a single hair of his head!'

'And yet,' I interrupted, 'you have no scruples in completely ruining all hopes of her perfect restoration, by thrusting yourself into her remembrance now, when she has nearly forgotten you, and involving her in a new tumult of discord and distress.'

'You suppose she has nearly forgotten me?' he said. 'Oh, Nelly! you know she has not! You know as well as I do, that for every thought she spends on Linton, she spends a thousand on me! At a most miserable period of my

life, I had a notion of the kind: it haunted me on my return to the neighbour-hood last summer; but only her own assurance could make me admit the horrible idea again. And then, Linton would be nothing, nor Hindley, nor all the dreams that ever I dreamt. Two words would comprehend my future—*death* and *hell*: existence, after losing her, would be hell. Yet I was a fool to fancy for a moment that she valued Edgar Linton's attachment more than mine. If he loved with all the powers of his puny being, he couldn't love as much in eighty years as I could in a day. And Catherine has a heart as deep as I have: the sea could be as readily contained in that horse-trough, as her whole affection be monopolised by him! Tush! He is scarcely a degree dearer to her than her dog, or her horse. It is not in him to be loved like me: how can she love in him what he has not?'

'Catherine and Edgar are as fond of each other as any two people can be,' cried Isabella, with sudden vivacity. 'No one has a right to talk in that manner, and I won't hear my brother depreciated in silence!'

'Your brother is wondrous fond of you too, isn't he?' observed Heathcliff scornfully. 'He turns you adrift on the world with surprising alacrity.'

'He is not aware of what I suffer,' she replied. 'I didn't tell him that.'

'You have been telling him something, then: you have written, have you?'

'To say that I was married, I did write—you saw the note.'

'And nothing since?'

'No.'

'My young lady is looking sadly the worse for her change of condition,' I remarked. 'Somebody's love comes short in her case, obviously: whose, I may guess; but, perhaps, I shouldn't say.'

'I should guess it was her own,' said Heathcliff. 'She degenerates into a mere slut! She is tired of trying to please me uncommonly early. You'd hardly credit it, but the very morrow of our wedding, she was weeping to go home. However, she'll suit this house so much the better for not being over nice, and I'll take care she does not disgrace me by rambling abroad.'

'Well, sir,' returned I, 'I hope you'll consider that Mrs. Heathcliff is accustomed to be looked after and waited on; and that she has been brought up like an only daughter, whom every one was ready to serve. You must let her have a maid to keep things tidy about her, and you must treat her kindly. Whatever be your notion of Mr. Edgar, you cannot doubt that she has a capacity for strong attachments, or she wouldn't have abandoned the elegances, and comforts, and friends of her former home, to fix contentedly, in such a wilderness as this, with you.'

'She abandoned them under a delusion,' he answered; 'picturing in me a hero of romance, and expecting unlimited indulgences from my chivalrous devotion. I can hardly regard her in the light of a rational creature, so obstinately has she persisted in forming a fabulous notion of my character and acting

on the false impressions she cherished. But, at last, I think she begins to know me: I don't perceive the silly smiles and grimaces that provoked me at first; and the senseless incapability of discerning that I was in earnest when I gave her my opinion of her infatuation and herself. It was a marvellous effort of perspicacity to discover that I did not love her. I believed, at one time, no lessons could teach her that! And yet it is poorly learnt; for this morning she announced, as a piece of appalling intelligence, that I had actually succeeded in making her hate me! A positive labour of Hercules, I assure you! If it be achieved, I have cause to return thanks. Can I trust your assertion, Isabella? Are you sure you hate me? If I let you alone for half a day, won't you come sighing and wheedling to me again? I dare say she would rather I had seemed all tenderness before you: it wounds her vanity to have the truth exposed. But I don't care who knows that the passion was wholly on one side; and I never told her a lie about it. She cannot accuse me of showing a bit of deceitful softness. The first thing she saw me do, on coming out of the Grange, was to hang up her little dog; and when she pleaded for it, the first words I uttered were a wish that I had the hanging of every being belonging to her, except one: possibly she took that exception for herself. But no brutality disgusted her: I suppose she has an innate admiration of it, if only her precious person were secure from injury! Now, was it not the depth of absurdity—of genuine idiocy, for that pitiful, slavish, mean-minded brach to dream that I could love her? Tell your master, Nelly, that I never, in all my life, met with such an abject thing as she is. She even disgraces the name of Linton; and I've sometimes relented, from pure lack of invention, in my experiments on what she could endure, and still creep shamefully cringing back! But tell him, also, to set his fraternal and magisterial heart at ease: that I keep strictly within the limits of the law. I have avoided, up to this period, giving her the slightest right to claim a separation; and, what's more, she'd thank nobody for dividing us. If she desired to go, she might: the nuisance of her presence outweighs the gratification to be derived from tormenting her!'

'Mr. Heathcliff,' said I, 'this is the talk of a madman, and your wife, most likely, is convinced you are mad; and, for that reason, she has borne with you hitherto: but now that you say she may go, she'll doubtless avail herself of the permission. You are not so bewitched, ma'am, are you, as to remain with him of your own accord?'

'Take care, Ellen!' answered Isabella, her eyes sparkling irefully; there was no misdoubting by their expression the full success of her partner's endeavours to make himself detested. 'Don't put faith in a single word he speaks. He's a lying fiend! a monster, and not a human being! I've been told I might leave him before; and I've made the attempt, but I dare not repeat it! Only, Ellen, promise you'll not mention a syllable of his infamous conversation to my brother or Catherine. Whatever he may pretend, he wishes to provoke

Edgar to desperation: he says he has married me on purpose to obtain power over him; and he shan't obtain it—I'll die first! I just hope, I pray, that he may forget his diabolical prudence and kill me! The single pleasure I can imagine is to die or see him dead!'

'There—that will do for the present!' said Heathcliff. 'If you are called upon in a court of law, you'll remember her language, Nelly! And take a good look at that countenance: she's near the point which would suit me. No; you're not fit to be your own guardian, Isabella, now; and I, being your legal protector, must detain you in my custody, however distasteful the obligation may be. Go upstairs; I have something to say to Ellen Dean in private. That's not the way: upstairs, I tell you! Why, this is the road upstairs, child!'

He seized, and thrust her from the room: and returned muttering:

'I have no pity! I have no pity! The more the worms writhe, the more I yearn to crush out their entrails! It is a moral teething; and I grind with greater energy, in proportion to the increase of pain.'

'Do you understand what the word pity means?' I said, hastening to resume my bonnet. 'Did you ever feel a touch of it in your life?'

'Put that down!' he interrupted, perceiving my intention to depart. 'You are not going yet. Come here now, Nelly: I must either persuade or compel you to aid me in fulfilling my determination to see Catherine, and that without delay. I swear that I meditate no harm: I don't desire to cause any disturbance, or to exasperate or insult Mr. Linton; I only wish to hear from herself how she is, and why she has been ill; and to ask if anything that I could do would be of use to her. Last night, I was in the Grange garden six hours, and I'll return there to-night; and every night I'll haunt the place, and every day, till I find an opportunity of entering. If Edgar Linton meets me, I shall not hesitate to knock him down, and give him enough to insure his quiescence while I stay. If his servants oppose me, I shall threaten them off with these pistols. But wouldn't it be better to prevent my coming in contact with them, or their master? And you could do it so easily. I'd warn you when I came, and then you might let me in unobserved, as soon as she was alone, and watch till I departed, your conscience quite calm: you would be hindering mischief.'

I protested against playing that treacherous part in my employer's house: and, besides, I urged the cruelty and selfishness of his destroying Mrs. Linton's tranquillity for his satisfaction. 'The commonest occurrence startles her painfully,' I said. 'She's all nerves, and she couldn't bear the surprise I'm positive. Don't persist, sir! or else, I shall be obliged to inform my master of your designs; and he'll take measures to secure his house and its inmates from any such unwarrantable intrusions!'

'In that case, I'll take measures to secure you, woman!' exclaimed Heath

cliff; 'you shall not leave Wuthering Heights till to-morrow morning. It is a foolish story to assert that Catherine could not bear to see me; and as to surprising her, I don't desire it: you must prepare her—ask her if I may come. You say she never mentions my name, and that I am never mentioned to her. To whom should she mention me if I am a forbidden topic in the house? She thinks you are all spies for her husband. Oh, I've no doubt she's in hell among you! I guess by her silence, as much as anything, what she feels. You say she is often restless, and anxious-looking; is that a proof of tranquillity? You talk of her mind being unsettled. How the devil could it be otherwise in her frightful isolation? And that insipid, paltry creature attending her from *duty* and *humanity*! From *pity* and *charity*! He might as well plant an oak in a flower-pot, and expect it to thrive, as imagine he can restore her to vigour in the soil of his shallow cares! Let us settle it at once: will you stay here, and am I to fight my way to Catherine over Linton and his footmen? Or will you be my friend, as you have been hitherto, and do what I request? Decide! because there is no reason for my lingering another minute, if you persist in your stubborn ill-nature!'

Well, Mr. Lockwood, I argued and complained, and flatly refused him fifty·times; but in the long run he forced me to an agreement. I engaged to carry a letter from him. to my mistress; and should she consent, I promised to let him have intelligence of Linton's next absence from home, when he might come, and get in as he was able: I wouldn't be there, and my fellow-servants should be equally out of the way. Was it right or wrong? I fear it was wrong, though expedient. I thought I prevented another explosion by my compliance; and I thought, too, it might create a favourable crisis in Catherine's mental illness: and then I remembered Mr. Edgar's stern rebuke of my carrying tales; and I tried to smooth away all disquietude on the subject, by affirming, with frequent iteration, that that betrayal of trust, if it merited so harsh an appellation, should be the last. Notwithstanding, my journey homeward was sadder than my journey thither; and many misgivings I had, ere I could prevail on myself to put the missive into Mrs. Linton's hand.

But here is Kenneth; I'll go down, and tell him how much better you are. My history is *dree*, as we say, and will serve to while away another morning.

Dree, and dreary! I reflected as the good woman descended to receive the doctor; and not exactly of the kind which I should have chosen to amuse me. But never mind! I'll extract wholesome medicines from Mrs. Dean's bitter herbs; and firstly, let me beware the fascination that lurks in Catherine Heathcliff's brilliant eyes. I should be in a curious taking if I surrendered my heart to that young person, and the daughter turned out a second edition of the mother!

CHAPTER 15

Another week over—and I am so many days nearer health, and spring! I have now heard all my neighbour's history, at different sittings, as the housekeeper could spare time from more important occupations. I'll continue it in her own words, only a little condensed. She is, on the whole, a very fair narrator, and I don't think I could improve her style.

In the evening, she said, the evening of my visit to the Heights, I knew, as well as if I saw him, that Mr. Heathcliff was about the place; and I shunned going out, because I still carried his letter in my pocket, and didn't want to be threatened or teased any more. I had made up my mind not to give it till my master went somewhere, as I could not guess how its receipt would affect Catherine. The consequence was, that it did not reach her before the lapse of three days. The fourth was Sunday, and I brought it into her room after the family were gone to church. There was a man-servant left to keep the house with me, and we generally made a practice of locking the doors during the hours of service; but on that occasion the weather was so warm and pleasant that I set them wide open, and, to fulfil my engagement, as I knew who would be coming, I told my companion that the mistress wished very much for some oranges, and he must run over to the village and get a few, to be paid for on the morrow. He departed, and I went upstairs.

Mrs. Linton sat in a loose, white dress, with a light shawl over her shoulders, in the recess of the open window, as usual. Her thick, long hair had been partly removed at the beginning of her illness, and now she wore it simply combed in its natural tresses over her temples and neck. Her appearance was altered, as I had told Heathcliff; but when she was calm, there seemed unearthly beauty in the change. The flash of her eyes had been succeeded by a dreamy and melancholy softness; they no longer gave the impression of looking at the objects around her: they appeared always to gaze beyond and far beyond—you would have said out of this world. Then the paleness of her face—its haggard aspect having vanished as she recovered flesh—and the peculiar expression arising from her mental state, though painfully suggestive of their causes, added to the touching interest which she awakened and—invariably to me, I know, and to any person who saw her, I should think—refuted more tangible proofs of convalescence, and stamped her as one doomed to decay.

A book lay spread on the sill before her, and the scarcely perceptible wind fluttered its leaves at intervals. I believe Linton had laid it there: for she never endeavoured to divert herself with reading, or occupation of any kind, and he would spend many an hour in trying to entice her attention to some subject which had formerly been her amusement. She was conscious of his aim, and in her better moods endured his efforts placidly, only showing their

uselessness by now and then suppressing a wearied sigh, and checking him at last with the saddest of smiles and kisses. At other times, she would turn petulantly away, and hide her face in her hands, or even push him off angrily; and then he took care to let her alone, for he was certain of doing no good.

Gimmerton chapel bells were still ringing; and the full, mellow flow of the beck in the valley came soothingly on the ear. It was a sweet substitute for the yet absent murmur of the summer foliage, which drowned that music about the Grange when the trees were in leaf. At Wuthering Heights it always sounded on quiet days following a great thaw or a season of steady rain. And of Wuthering Heights Catherine was thinking as she listened: that is, if she thought or listened at all; but she had the vague, distant look I mentioned before, which expressed no recognition of material things either by ear or eye.

'There's a letter for you, Mrs. Linton,' I said, gently inserting it in one hand that rested on her knee. 'You must read it immediately, because it wants an answer. Shall I break the seal?' 'Yes,' she answered, without altering the direction of her eyes. I opened it—it was very short. 'Now,' I continued, 'read it.' She drew away her hand, and let it fall. I replaced it in her lap, and stood waiting till it should please her to glance down; but that movement was so long delayed that at last I resumed:

'Must I read it, ma'am? It is from Mr. Heathcliff.'

There was a start and a troubled gleam of recollection, and a struggle to arrange her ideas. She lifted the letter, and seemed to peruse it; and when she came to the signature she sighed: yet still I found she had not gathered its import, for, upon my desiring to hear her reply, she merely pointed to the name, and gazed at me with mournful and questioning eagerness.

'Well, he wishes to see you,' said I, guessing her need of an interpreter. 'He's in the garden by this time, and impatient to know what answer I shall bring.'

As I spoke, I observed a large dog lying on the sunny grass beneath raise its ears as if about to bark, and then smoothing them back, announce, by a wag of the tail, that some one approached whom it did not consider a stranger. Mrs. Linton bent forward, and listened breathlessly. The minute after a step traversed the hall; the open house was too tempting for Heathcliff to resist walking in: most likely he supposed that I was inclined to shirk my promise, and so resolved to trust to his own audacity. With straining eagerness Catherine gazed towards the entrance of her chamber. He did not hit the right room directly, she motioned me to admit him, but he found it out ere I could reach the door, and in a stride or two was at her side, and had her grasped in his arms.

He neither spoke nor loosed his hold for some five minutes, during which period he bestowed more kisses than ever he gave in his life before, I dare say:

but then my mistress had kissed him first, and I plainly saw that he could hardly bear, for downright agony, to look into her face! The same conviction had stricken him as me, from the instant he beheld her, that there was no prospect of ultimate recovery there—she was fated, sure to die.

'Oh, Cathy! Oh, my life! how can I bear it?' was the first sentence he uttered, in a tone that did not seek to disguise his despair. And now he stared at her so earnestly that I thought the very intensity of his gaze would bring tears into his eyes; but they burned with anguish: they did not melt.

'What now?' said Catherine, leaning back, and returning his look with a suddenly clouded brow: her humour was a mere vane for constantly varying caprices. 'You and Edgar have broken my heart, Heathcliff! And you both came to bewail the deed to me, as if you were the people to be pitied! I shall not pity you, not I. You have killed me—and thriven on it, I think. How strong you are! How many years do you mean to live after I am gone?'

Heathcliff had knelt on one knee to embrace her; he attempted to rise, but she seized his hair, and kept him down.

'I wish I could hold you,' she continued bitterly, 'till we were both dead! I shouldn't care what you suffered. I care nothing for your sufferings. Why shouldn't you suffer? I do! Will you forget me? Will you be happy when I am in the earth? Will you say twenty years hence, "That's the grave of Catherine Earnshaw. I loved her long ago, and was wretched to lose her; but it is past. I've loved many others since: my children are dearer to me than she was; and at death, I shall not rejoice that I going to her: I shall be sorry that I must leave them!" Will you say so, Heathcliff?'

'Don't torture me till I am as mad as yourself,' cried he, wrenching his head free, and grinding his teeth.

The two, to a cool spectator, made a strange, and fearful picture. Well might Catherine deem that heaven would be a land of exile to her, unless with her mortal body she cast away her moral character also. Her present countenance had a wild vindictiveness in its white cheek, and a bloodless lip and scintillating eye; and she retained in her closed fingers a portion of the locks she had been grasping. As to her companion, while raising himself with one hand, he had taken her arm with the other; and so inadequate was his stock of gentleness to the requirements of her condition, that on his letting go I saw four distinct impressions left blue in the colourless skin

'Are you possessed with a devil,' he pursued savagely, 'to talk in that manner to me when you are dying? Do you reflect that all those words will be branded on my memory, and eating deeper eternally after you have left me? You know you lie to say I have killed you: and, Catherine, you know that I could as soon forget you as my existence! Is it not sufficient for your infernal selfishness that while you are at peace I shall writhe in the torments of hell?'

'I shall not be at peace,' moaned Catherine, recalled to a sense of physica

weakness by the violent, unequal throbbing of her heart, which beat visibly and audibly under this excess of agitation. She said nothing further till the paroxysm was over; then she continued, more kindly—

'I'm not wishing you greater torment than I have, Heathcliff. I only wish us never to be parted: and should a word of mine distress you hereafter, think I feel the same distress underground, and for my own sake, forgive me! Come here and kneel down again! You never harmed me in your life. Nay, if you nurse anger, that will be worse to remember than my harsh words! Won't you come here again? Do!'

Heathcliff went to the back of her chair, and leant over, but not so far as to let her see his face, which was livid with emotion. She bent round to look at him; he would not permit it: turning abruptly, he walked to the fireplace, where he stood, silent, with his back towards us. Mrs. Linton's glance followed him suspiciously: every movement woke a new sentiment in her. After a pause and a prolonged gaze, she resumed; addressing me in accents of indignant disappointment—

'Oh, you see, Nelly, he would not relent a moment to keep me out of the grave. *That* is how I'm loved! Well never mind. That is not *my* Heathcliff. I shall love mine yet; and take him with me: he's in my soul. And,' added she, musingly,' the thing that irks me most in this shattered prison, after all. I'm tired, tired of being enclosed here. I'm wearying to escape into that glorious world, and to be always there: not seeing it dimly through tears, and yearning for it through the walls of an aching heart; but really with it, and in it. Nelly, you think you are better and more fortunate than I; in full health and strength: you are sorry for me—very soon that will be altered. I shall be sorry for *you*. I shall be incomparably beyond and above you all. I *wonder* he won't be near me!' She went on to herself. 'I thought he wished it. Heathcliff, dear! you should not be sullen now. Do come to me, Heathcliff.'

In her eagerness she rose and supported herself on the arm of the chair. At that earnest appeal he turned to her, looking absolutely desperate. His eyes, wide and wet, at last flashed fiercely on her; his breast heaved convulsively. An instant they held asunder, and then how they met I hardly saw, but Catherine made a spring, and he caught her, and they were locked in an embrace from which I thought my mistress would never be released alive: in fact, to my eyes, she seemed directly insensible. He flung himself into the nearest seat, and on my approaching hurriedly to ascertain if she had fainted, he gnashed at me, and foamed like a mad dog, and gathered her to him with greedy jealousy. I did not feel as if I were in the company of a creature of my own species: it appeared that he would not understand, though I spoke to him; so I stood off, and held my tongue, in great perplexity.

A movement of Catherine's relieved me a little presently: she put up her hand to clasp his neck, and bring her cheek to his as he held her; while he,

in return, covering her with frantic caresses, said wildly—

'You teach me now how cruel you've been—cruel and false. *Why* did you despise me? *Why* did you betray your own heart, Cathy? I have not one word of comfort. You deserve this. You have killed yourself. Yes, you may kiss me, and cry; and ring out my kisses and tears: they'll blight you—they'll damn you. You loved me—then what *right* had you to leave me? What right—answer me—for the poor fancy you felt for Linton? Because misery and degradation, and death, and nothing that God or Satan could inflict would have parted us, *you*, of your own will, did it. I have not broken your heart—*you* have broken it; and in breaking it, you have broken mine. So much the worse for me, that I am strong. Do I want to live? What kind of living will it be when you—oh, God! would *you* like to live with your soul in the grave?'

'Let me alone. Let me alone,' sobbed Catherine. 'If I have done wrong I'm dying for it. It is enough! You left me too: but I won't upbraid you! I forgive you. Forgive me!'

'It is hard to forgive, and to look at those eyes, and feel those wasted hands,' he answered. 'Kiss me again; and don't let me see your eyes! I forgive what you have done to me. I love *my* murderer—but *yours*! How can I?'

They were silent—their faces hid against each other, and washed by each other's tears. At least, I suppose the weeping was on both sides; as it seemed Heathcliff *could* weep on a great occasion like this.

I grew very uncomfortable, meanwhile; for the afternoon wore fast away, the man whom I had sent off returned from his errand, and I could distinguish, by the shine of the westering sun up the valley, a concourse thickening outside Gimmerton chapel porch.

'Service is over,' I announced. 'My master will be here in half-an-hour.'

Heathcliff groaned a curse, and strained Catherine closer: she never moved.

Ere long I perceived a group of the servants passing up the road toward the kitchen wing. Mr. Linton was not far behind; he opened the gate himself and sauntered slowly up, probably enjoying the lovely afternoon that breathed as soft as summer.

'Now he is here,' I exclaimed. 'For Heaven's sake, hurry down! You'll not meet any one on the front stairs. Do be quick; and stay among the trees till he is fairly in.'

'I must go, Cathy,' said Heathcliff, seeking to extricate himself from his companion's arms. 'But if I live, I'll see you again before you are asleep. I won't stray five yards from your window.'

'You must not go!' she answered, holding him as firmly as her strength allowed. 'You shall not, I tell you.'

'For one hour,' he pleaded earnestly.

'Not for one minute,' she replied.

'I *must*—Linton will be up immediately,' persisted the alarmed intruder. He would have risen, and unfixed her fingers by the act—she clung fast, gasping: there was mad resolution in her face.

'No!' she shrieked. 'Oh, don't, don't go. It is the last time! Edgar will not hurt us. Heathcliff, I shall die! I shall die!'

'Damn the fool! There he is,' cried Heathcliff, sinking back into his seat. 'Hush, my darling! Hush, hush, Catherine! I'll stay. If he shot me so, I'd expire with a blessing on my lips.'

And there they were fast again. I heard my master mounting the stairs—the cold sweat ran from my forehead: I was horrified.

'Are you going to listen to her ravings?' I said passionately. 'She does not know what she says. Will you ruin her, because she has not wit to help herself? Get up! You could be free instantly. That is the most diabolical deed that ever you did. We are all done for—master, mistress, and servant.'

I wrung my hands, and cried out; and Mr. Linton hastened his step at the noise. In the midst of my agitation, I was sincerely glad to observe that Catherine's arms had fallen relaxed, and her head hung down.

'She's fainted or dead,' I thought: 'so much the better. Far better that she should be dead, than lingering a burden and a misery-maker to all about her.'

Edgar sprang to his unbidden guest, blanched with astonishment and rage. What he meant to do, I cannot tell; however, the other stopped all demonstrations, at once, by placing the lifeless-looking form in his arms.

'Look there!' he said; 'unless you be a fiend, help her first—then you shall speak to me!'

He walked into the parlour, and sat down. Mr. Linton summoned me, and with great difficulty, and after resorting to many means, we managed to restore her to sensation; but she was all bewildered; she sighed, and moaned, and knew nobody. Edgar, in his anxiety for her, forgot her hated friend. I did not. I went, at the earliest opportunity, and besought him to depart; affirming that Catherine was better, and he should hear from me in the morning how she passed the night.

'I shall not refuse to go out of doors,' he answered; 'but I shall stay in the garden: and, Nelly, mind you keep your word to-morrow. I shall be under those larch trees. Mind! or I pay another visit, whether Linton be in or not.'

He sent a rapid glance through the half-open door of the chamber, and, ascertaining that what I stated was apparently true, delivered the house of his luckless presence.

CHAPTER 16

About twelve o'clock that night, was born the Catherine you saw at Wuthering Heights: a puny, seven months' child; and two hours after the mother died, having never recovered sufficient consciousness to miss Heathcliff, or know Edgar. The latter's distraction at his bereavement is a subject too painful to be dwelt on; its after effects showed how deep the sorrow sunk. A great addition, in my eyes, was his being left without an heir. I bemoaned that, as I gazed on the feeble orphan; and I mentally abused old Linton for (what was only natural partiality) the securing his estate to his own daughter, instead of his son's. An unwelcomed infant it was, poor thing! It might have wailed out of life, and nobody cared a morsel, during those first hours of existence. We redeemed the neglect afterwards; but its beginning was as friendless as its end is likely to be.

Next morning—bright and cheerful out of doors—stole softened in through the blinds of the silent room, and suffused the couch and its occupant with a mellow, tender glow. Edgar Linton had his head laid on the pillow, and his eyes shut. His young and fair features were almost as deathlike as those of the form beside him, and almost as fixed: but *his* was the hush of exhausted anguish, and *hers* of perfect peace. Her brow smooth, her lids closed, her lips wearing the expression of a smile; no angel in heaven could be more beautiful than she appeared. And I partook of the infinite calm in which she lay: my mind was never in a holier frame than while I gazed on that untroubled image of Divine rest. I instinctively echoed the words she had uttered a few hours before: 'Incomparably beyond and above us all! Whether still on earth or now in heaven, her spirit is at home with God!'

I don't know if it be a peculiarity in me, but I am seldom otherwise than happy, while watching in the chamber of death, should no frenzied or despairing mourner share the duty with me. I see a repose that neither earth nor hell can break, and I feel an assurance of the endless and shadowless hereafter—the Eternity they have entered—where life is boundless in its duration, and love in its sympathy, and joy in its fulness. I noticed on that occasion how much selfishness there is even in a love like Mr. Linton's, when he so regretted Catherine's blessed release! To be sure, one might have doubted, after the wayward and impatient existence she had led, whether she merited a haven of peace at last. One might doubt in seasons of cold reflection; but not then in the presence of her corpse. It asserted its own tranquillity, which seemed a pledge of equal quiet to its former inhabitant.

Do you believe such people *are* happy in the other world sir? I'd give a great deal to know.

I declined answering Mrs. Dean's question, which struck me as something heterodox. She proceeded—

Retracing the course of Catherine Linton, I fear we have no right to think she is; but we'll leave her with her Maker.

The master looked asleep, and I ventured soon after sunrise to quit the room and steal out to the pure refreshing air. The servants thought me gone to shake off the drowsiness of my protracted watch; in reality, my chief motive was seeing Mr. Heathcliff. If he had remained among the larches all night, he would have heard nothing of the stir at the Grange; unless, perhaps, he might catch the gallop of the messenger going to Gimmerton. If he had come nearer, he would probably be aware, from the lights flitting to and fro, and the opening and shutting of the outer doors, that all was not right within. I wished, yet feared, to find him. I felt the terrible news must be told, and I longed to get it over; but *how* to do it, I did not know. He was there—at least a few yards further in the park; leant against an old ash tree, his hat off, and his hair soaked with the dew that had gathered on the budded branches, and fell pattering round him. He had been standing a long time in that position, for I saw a pair of ousels passing and repassing scarcely three feet from him, busy in building their nest, and regarding his proximity no more than that of a piece of timber. They flew off at my approach, and he raised his eyes and spoke—

'She's dead!' he said; 'I've not waited for you to learn that. Put your handkerchief away—don't snivel before me. Damn you all! she wants none of *your* tears!'

I was weeping as much for him as her; we do sometimes pity creatures that have none of the feeling either for themselves or others; and when I first looked into his face, I perceived that he had got intelligence of the catastrophe; and a foolish notion struck me that his heart was quelled and he prayed, because his lips moved and his gaze was bent on the ground.

'Yes, she's dead!' I answered, checking my sobs and drying my cheeks. 'Gone to heaven, I hope; where we may, every one, join her, if we take due warning and leave our evil ways to follow good!'

'Did *she* take due warning, then?' asked Heathcliff, attempting a sneer. 'Did she die like a saint? Come, give me a true history of the event. How did'—

He endeavoured to pronounce the name, but could not manage it; and compressing his mouth he held a silent combat with his inward agony, defying, meanwhile, my sympathy with an unflinching ferocious stare. 'How did she die?' he resumed at last—fain, notwithstanding his hardihood, to have a support behind him; for, after the struggle, he trembled, in spite of himself, to his very finger-ends.

'Poor wretch!' I thought; 'you have a heart and nerves the same as your brother men! Why should you be anxious to conceal them? Your pride cannot blind God! You tempt Him to wring them, till He forces a cry of humiliation.'

'Quietly as a lamb!' I answered aloud. 'She drew a sigh, and stretched

herself, like a child reviving, and sinking again to sleep; and five minutes after I felt one little pulse at her heart, and nothing more!'

'And—did she ever mention me?' he asked, hesitating, as if he dreaded the answer to his question would introduce details that he could not bear to hear.

'Her senses never returned; she recognised nobody from the time you left her,' I said. 'She lies with a sweet smile on her face; and her latest ideas wandered back to pleasant early days. Her life closed in a gentle dream—may she wake as kindly in the other world!'

'May she wake in torment!' he cried, with frightful vehemence, stamping his foot, and groaning in a sudden paroxysm of ungovernable passion. 'Why, she's a liar to the end! Where is she? Not *there*—not in heaven—not perished—where? Oh! you said you cared nothing for my sufferings! And I pray one prayer—I repeat it till my tongue stiffens—Catherine Earnshaw, may you not rest as long as I am living! You said I killed you—haunt me, then! The murdered *do* haunt their murderers, I believe. I know that ghosts *have* wandered on earth. Be with me always—take any form—drive me mad! only *do* not leave me in this abyss, where I cannot find you! Oh, God! it is unutterable! I *cannot* live without my life! I *cannot* live without my soul!'

He dashed his head against the knotted trunk; and, lifting up his eyes, howled, not like a man, but like a savage beast getting goaded to death with knives and spears. I observed several splashes of blood about the bark of the tree, and his hand and forehead were both stained; probably the scene I witnessed was a repetition of others acted during the night. It hardly moved my compassion—it appalled me: still, I felt reluctant to quit him so. But the moment he recollected himself enough to notice me watching, he thundered a command for me to go, and I obeyed. He was beyond my skill to quiet or console!

Mrs. Linton's funeral was appointed to take place on the Friday following her decease; and till then her coffin remained uncovered, and strewn with flowers and scented leaves, in the great drawing-room. Linton spent his day and nights there, a sleepless guardian; and—a circumstance concealed from all but me—Heathcliff spent his nights, at least, outside, equally a stranger to repose. I held no communication with him; still, I was conscious of his design to enter, if he could; and on the Tuesday, a little after dark, when my master, from sheer fatigue, had been compelled to retire a couple of hours, I went and opened one of the windows; moved by his perseverance to give him a chance of bestowing on the faded image of his idol one final adieu. He did not omit to avail himself of the opportunity, cautiously and briefly: too cautiously to betray his presence by the slightest noise. Indeed I shouldn't have discovered that he had been there, except for the disarrangement of the drapery about the corpse's face, and for observing on the floor

a curl of light hair, fastened with a silver thread; which, on examination, I ascertained to have been taken from a locket hung round Catherine's neck. Heathcliff had opened the trinket and cast out its contents, replacing them by a black lock of his own. I twisted the two, and enclosed them together.

Mr. Earnshaw was, of course, invited to attend the remains of his sister to the grave; and he sent no excuse, but he never came; so that, besides her husband, the mourners were wholly composed of tenants and servants. Isabella was not asked.

The place of Catherine's interment, to the surprise of the villagers, was neither in the chapel under the carved monument of the Lintons, nor yet by the tombs of her own relations, outside. It was dug on a green slope in a corner of the kirkyard, where the wall is so low that heath and bilberry plants have climbed over it from the moor; and peat mould almost buries it. Her husband lies in the same spot now; and they have each a simple headstone above, and a plain grey block at their feet, to mark the graves.

CHAPTER 17

That Friday made the last of our fine days for a month. In the evening, the weather broke: the wind shifted from south to north-east, and brought rain first, and then sleet and snow. On the morrow one could hardly imagine that there had been three weeks of summer: the primroses and crocuses were hidden under wintry drifts; the larks were silent, the young leaves of the early trees smitten and blackened. And dreary, and chill, and dismal, that morrow did creep over! My master kept his room; I took possession of the lonely parlour, converting it into a nursery: and there I was, sitting with the moaning doll of a child laid on my knee; rocking it to and fro, and watching, meanwhile, the still driving flakes build up the uncurtained window, when the door opened, and some person entered, out of breath and laughing! My anger was greater than my astonishment for a minute. I supposed it one of the maids, and I cried—

'Have done! How dare you show your giddiness here? What would Mr. Linton say if he heard you?'

'Excuse me!' answered a familiar voice; 'but I know Edgar is in bed, and I cannot stop myself.'

With that the speaker came forward to the fire, panting and holding her hand to her side.

'I have run the whole way from Wuthering Heights!' she continued, after a pause; 'except where I've flown. I couldn't count the number of falls I've had. Oh, I'm aching all over! Don't be alarmed! There shall be an explanation as soon as I can give it; only just have the goodness to step out and order

the carriage to take me on to Gimmerton, and tell a servant to seek up a few clothes in my wardrobe.'

The intruder was Mrs. Heathcliff. She certainly seemed in no laughing predicament: her hair streamed on her shoulders, dripping with snow and water; she was dressed in the girlish dress she commonly wore, befitting her age more than her position: a low frock with short sleeves, and nothing on either head or neck. The frock was of light silk, and clung to her with wet, and her feet were protected merely by thin slippers; add to this a deep cut under one ear, which only the cold prevented from bleeding profusely, a white face scratched and bruised, and a frame hardly able to support itself, through fatigue; and you may fancy my first fright was not much allayed when I had had leisure to examine her.

'My dear young lady,' I exclaimed, 'I'll stir nowhere, and hear nothing till you have removed every article of your clothes, and put on dry things and certainly you shall not go to Gimmerton to-night, so it is needless to order the carriage.'

'Certainly, I shall,' she said; 'walking or riding: yet I've no objection to dress myself decently. And—ah, see how it flows down my neck now! The fire does make it smart.'

She insisted on my fulfilling her directions, before she would let me touch her and not till after the coachman had been instructed to get ready, and a maid set to pack up some necessary attire, did I obtain her consent for binding the wound and helping to change her garments.

'Now, Ellen,' she said, when my task was finished and she was seated in an easy chair on the hearth, with a cup of tea before her, 'you sit down opposite me, and put poor Catherine's baby away: I don't like to see it! You mustn't think I care little for Catherine, because I behaved so foolishly on entering: I've cried, too, bitterly—yes, more than any one else has reason to cry. We parted unreconciled, you remember, and I shan't forgive myself. But, for all that I was not going to sympathise with him—the brute beast! Oh, give me the poker! This is the last thing of his I have about me:' she slipped the gold ring from her third finger, and threw it on the floor. 'I'll smash it!' she continued, striking it with childish spite, 'and then I'll burn it!' and she took and dropped the misused article among the coals. 'There! he shall buy another if he gets me back again. He'd be capable of coming to seek me, to tease Edgar. I dare not stay, lest that notion should possess his wicked head! And besides, Edgar has not been kind, has he? And I won't come suing for his assistance; nor will I bring him into more trouble. Necessity compelled me to seek shelter here; though, if I had not learned he was out of the way, I'd have halted at the kitchen, washed my face, warmed myself, got you to bring what I wanted, and departed again to anywhere out of the reach of my accursed—of that incarnate goblin! Ah! he was in such a fury! If he had caught me! It's

pity Earnshaw is not his match in strength: I wouldn't have run till I'd seen him all but demolished, had Hindley been able to do it!'

'Well, don't talk so fast, miss!' I interrupted; 'you'll disorder the handkerchief I have tied round your face, and make the cut bleed again. Drink your tea, and take breath, and give over laughing: laughter is sadly out of place under this roof, and in your condition!'

'An undeniable truth,' she replied. 'Listen to that child! It maintains a constant wail—send it out of my hearing for an hour; I shan't stay any longer.'

I rang the bell, and committed it to a servant's care; and then I inquired what had urged her to escape from Wuthering Heights in such an unlikely plight, and where she meant to go, as she refused remaining with us.

'I ought, and I wish to remain,' answered she, 'to cheer Edgar and take care of the baby, for two things, and because the Grange is my right home. But I tell you he wouldn't let me! Do you think he could bear to see me grow fat and merry; and could bear to think that we were tranquil, and not resolve on poisoning our comfort? Now, I have the satisfaction of being sure that he detests me, to the point of its annoying him seriously to have me within earshot or eyesight: I notice, when I enter his presence, the muscles of his countenance are involuntarily distorted into an expression of hatred; partly arising from his knowledge of the good causes I have to feel that sentiment for him, and partly from original aversion. It is strong enough to make me feel pretty certain that he would not chase me over England, supposing I contrived a clear escape; and therefore I must get quite away. I've recovered from my first desire to be killed by him: I'd rather he'd kill himself! He has extinguished my love effectually, and so I'm at my ease. I can recollect yet how I loved him; and can dimly imagine that I could still be loving him, if—no, no! Even if he had doted on me, the devilish nature would have revealed its existence somehow. Catherine had an awfully perverted taste to esteem him so dearly, knowing him so well. Monster! would that he could be blotted out of creation, and out of my memory!'

'Hush, hush! He's a human being,' I said. 'Be more charitable: there are worse men than he is yet!'

'He's not a human being,' she retorted; 'and he has no claim on my charity. I gave him my heart, and he took and pinched it to death, and flung it back to me. People feel with their hearts, Ellen: and since he has destroyed mine, I have not power to feel for him: and I would not, though he groaned from this to his dying day, and wept tears of blood for Catherine! No, indeed, indeed, I wouldn't!' And here Isabella began to cry; but, immediately lashing the water from her lashes, she recommenced. 'You asked, what has driven me to flight at last? I was compelled to attempt it, because I had succeeded in rousing his rage a pitch above his malignity. Pulling out the nerves with redhot pincers requires more coolness than knocking on the head. He

was worked up to forget the fiendish prudence he boasted of, and proceeded to murderous violence. I experienced pleasure in being able to exasperate him; the sense of pleasure woke my instinct of self-preservation, so I fairly broke free; and if ever I come into his hands again he is welcome to a signal revenge.

'Yesterday, you know, Mr. Earnshaw should have been at the funeral. He kept himself sober for the purpose—tolerably sober: not going to bed mad at six o'clock and getting up drunk at twelve. Consequently he rose, in suicidal low spirits, as fit for the church as for a dance; and instead, he sat down by the fire and swallowed gin or brandy by tumblerfuls.

'Heathcliff—I shudder to name him! has been a stranger in the house from last Sunday till to-day. Whether the angels have fed him, or his kin beneath I cannot tell; but he has not eaten a meal with us for nearly a week. He has just come home at dawn, and gone upstairs to his chamber; locking himself in—as if anybody dreamt of coveting his company! There he has continued praying like a Methodist: only the deity he implored in senseless dust and ashes; and God, when addressed was curiously confounded with his own black father! After concluding these precious orisons—and they lasted generally till he grew hoarse and his voice was strangled in his throat—he would be off again; always straight down to the Grange! I wonder Edgar did not send for a constable, and give him into custody! For me, grieved as I was about Catherine, it was impossible to avoid regarding this season of deliverance from degrading oppression as a holiday.

'I recovered spirits sufficient to hear Joseph's eternal lectures without weeping, and to move up and down the house less with the foot of a frightened thief than formerly. You wouldn't think that I should cry at anything Joseph could say; but he and Hareton are detestable companions. I'd rather sit with Hindley, and hear his awful talk, than with "t' little maister" and his staunch supporter, that odious old man! When Heathcliff is in, I'm often obliged to seek the kitchen and their society, or starve among the damp uninhabited chambers; when he is not, as was the case this week, I establish a table and chair at one corner of the house fire, and never mind how Mr Earnshaw may occupy himself; and he does not interfere with my arrangements. He is quieter now than he used to be, if no one provokes him: more sullen and depressed, and less furious. Joseph affirms he's sure he's an altered man: that the Lord has touched his heart, and he is saved "so as by fire." I'm puzzled to detect signs of the favourable change: but it is not my business.

'Yester-evening I sat in my nook reading some old books till late on toward twelve. It seemed so dismal to go upstairs, with the wild snow blowing outside, and my thoughts continually reverting to the kirkyard and the new-made grave! I dared hardly lift my eyes from the page before me, that melancholy scene so instantly usurped its place. Hindley sat opposite, his head leant on

his hand; perhaps meditating on the same subject. He had ceased drinking at a point below irrationality, and had neither stirred nor spoken during two or three hours. There was no sound through the house but the moaning wind, which shook the windows every now and then, the faint crackling of the coals, and the click of my snuffers as I removed at intervals the long wick of the candle. Hareton and Joseph were probably fast asleep in bed. It was very, very sad: and while I read I sighed, for it seemed as if all joy had vanished from the world, never to be restored.

'The doleful silence was broken at length by the sound of the kitchen latch: Heathcliff had returned from his watch earlier than usual; owing, I suppose, to the sudden storm. That entrance was fastened, and we heard him coming round to get in by the other. I rose with an irrepressible expression of what I felt on my lips, which induced my companion, who had been staring towards the door, to turn and look at me.

' "I'll keep him out five minutes." he exclaimed. "You won't object?"

' "No, you may keep him out the whole night for me," I answered. "Do! put the key in the lock, and draw the bolts."

'Earnshaw accomplished this ere his guest reached the front; he then came and brought his chair to the other side of my table, leaning over it, and searching in my eyes, a sympathy with the burning hate that gleamed from his: as he both looked and felt like an assassin, he couldn't exactly find that; but he discovered enough to encourage him to speak.

' "You and I," he said, "have each a great debt to settle with the man out yonder! If we were neither of us cowards, we might combine to discharge it. Are you as soft as your brother? Are you willing to endure to the last, and not once attempt a repayment?"

' "I'm weary of enduring now," I replied; "and I'd be glad of a retaliation that wouldn't recoil on myself; but treachery and violence are spears pointed at both ends: they wound those who resort to them worse than their enemies."

' "Treachery and violence are a just return for treachery and violence!" cried Hindley. "Mrs. Heathcliff, I'll ask you to do nothing; but sit still and be dumb. Tell me now, can you? I'm sure you would have as much pleasure as I in witnessing the conclusion of the fiend's existence; he'll be *your* death unless you overreach him; and he'll be *my* ruin. Damn the hellish villain! He knocks at the door as if he were master here already! Promise to hold your tongue, and before that clock strikes—it wants three minutes of one—you're a free woman!"

'He took the implements which I described to you in my letter from his breast, and would have turned down the candle. I snatched it away, however, and seized his arm.

' "I'll not hold my tongue!" I said; "you mustn't touch him. Let the door remain shut, and be quiet!"

' "No! I've formed my resolution, and by God I'll execute it!" cried the desperate being. "I'll do you a kindness in spite of yourself, and Hareton justice! And you needn't trouble your head to screen me; Catherine is gone. Nobody alive would regret me, or be ashamed, though I cut my throat this minute—and it's time to make an end!"

'I might as well have struggled with a bear, or reasoned with a lunatic. The only resource left me was to run to a lattice and warn his intended victim of the fate which awaited him.

' "You'd better seek shelter somewhere else to-night!" I exclaimed in a rather triumphant tone. "Mr. Earnshaw has a mind to shoot you, if you persist in endeavouring to enter."

' "You'd better open the door, you——' he answered, addressing me by some elegant term that I don't care to repeat.

' "I shall not meddle in the matter," I retorted again. "Come in and get shot, if you please! I've done my duty.

'With that I shut the window and returned to my place by the fire; having too small a stock of hypocrisy at my command to pretend any anxiety for the danger that menaced him. Earnshaw swore passionately at me: affirming that I loved the villain yet; and calling me all sorts of names for the base spirit I evinced. And I, in my secret heart (and conscience never reproached me), thought what a blessing it would be for *him* should Heathcliff put him out of misery; and what a blessing for *me* should he send Heathcliff to his right abode! As I sat nursing these reflections, the casement behind me was banged on to the floor by a blow from the latter individual, and his black countenance looked blightingly through. The stanchions stood too close to suffer his shoulders to follow, and I smiled, exulting in my fancied security. His hair and clothes were whitened with snow, and his sharp cannibal teeth, revealed by cold and wrath, gleamed through the dark.

' "Isabella, let me in, or I'll make you repent!" he 'girned,' as Joseph calls it.

' "I cannot commit murder," I replied. "Mr. Hindley stands sentinel with a knife and loaded pistol."

' "Let me in by the kitchen door," he said.

' "Hindley will be there before you," I answered: "and that's a poor love of yours that cannot bear a shower of snow! We were left at peace on our beds as long as the summer moon shone, but the moment a blast of winter returns, you must run for shelter! Heathcliff, if I were you, I'd go stretch myself over her grave and die like a faithful dog. The world is surely not worth living in now, is it? You had distinctly impressed on me the idea that Catherine was the whole joy of your life: I can't imagine how you think of surviving her loss.'

' "He's there, is he!" exclaimed my companion, rushing to the gap. "If I can get my arm out I can hit him!"

'I'm afraid, Ellen, you'll set me down as really wicked; but you don't know all, so don't judge. I wouldn't have aided or abetted an attempt on even *his* life for anything. Wish that he were dead, I must; and therefore I was fearfully disappointed, and unnerved by terror for the consequences of my taunting speech, when he flung himself on Earnshaw's weapon and wrenched it from his grasp.

'The charge exploded, and the knife, in springing back, closed into its owner's wrist. Heathcliff pulled it away by main force, slitting up the flesh as it passed on, and thrust it dripping into his pocket. He then took a stone, struck down the division between two windows, and sprang in. His adversary had fallen senseless with excessive pain and the flow of blood, that gushed from an artery or a large vein. The ruffian kicked and trampled on him, and dashed his head repeatedly aaginst the flags, holding me with one hand, meantime, to prevent me summoning Joseph. He exerted preterhuman self-denial in abstaining from finishing him completely; but getting out of breath he finally desisted, and dragged the apparently inanimate body on to the settle. There he tore off the sleeve of Earnshaw's coat, and bound up the wound with brutal roughness; spitting and cursing during the operation as energetically as he had kicked before. Being at liberty, I lost no time in seeking the old servant; who, having gathered by degrees the purport of my hasty tale, hurried below, gasping, as he descended the steps two at once.

'"What is ther to do, now? what is ther to do, now?"

'"There's this to do," thundered Heathcliff, "that your master's mad; and should he last another month, I'll have him to an asylum. And how the devil did you come to fasten me out, you toothless hound? Don't stand muttering and mumbling there. Come, I'm not going to nurse him. Wash that stuff away; and mind the sparks of your candle—it is more than half brandy!"

'"And so, ye've been murthering on him?" exclaimed Joseph, lifting his hands and eyes in horror. "If iver I seed a seeght loike this! May the Lord"—

'Heathcliff gave him a push on to his knees in the midddle of the blood, and flung a towel to him; but instead of proceeding to dry it up, he joined his hands and began a prayer, which excited my laughter from its odd phraseo-ogy. I was in the condition of mind to be shocked at nothing: in fact, I was as reckless as some malefactors show themselves at the foot of the gallows.

'"Oh, I forgot you," said the tyrant. "You shall do that. Down with you. And you conspire with him against me, do you, viper? There, that is work fit for you!"

'He shook me till my teeth rattled, and pitched me beside Joseph, who steadily concluded his supplications and then rose, vowing he would set off for the Grange directly. Mr. Linton was a magistrate, and though he had fifty wives dead, he should inquire into this. He was so obstinate in his resolu-ion, that Heathcliff deemed it expedient to compel from my lips a recapitu-

lation of what had taken place; standing over me, heaving with malevolence as I reluctantly delivered the account in answer to his questions. It required a great deal of labour to satisfy the old man that Heathcliff was not the aggressor; especially with my hardly-wrung replies. However, Mr. Earnshaw soon convinced him that he was alive still; Joseph hastened to administer a dose of spirits, and by their succour his master presently regained motion and consciousness. Heathcliff, aware that his opponent was ignorant of the treatment received while insensible, called him deliriously intoxicated; and said he should not notice his atrocious conduct further, but advised him to get to bed. To my joy, he left us, after giving this judicious counsel, and Hindley stretched himself on the hearthstone. I departed to my own room marvelling that I had escaped so easily.

'This morning, when I came down, about half-an-hour before noon, Mr Earnshaw was sitting by the fire, deadly sick; his evil genius, almost as gaunt and ghastly, leant against the chimney. Neither appeared inclined to dine and, having waited till all was cold on the table, I commenced alone. Nothing hindered me from eating heartily, and I experienced a certain sense of satisfaction and superiority, as, at intervals, I cast a look towards my silent companions, and felt the comfort of a quiet conscience within me. After I had done, I ventured on the unusual liberty of drawing near the fire, going round Earnshaw's seat, and kneeling in the corner beside him.

'Heathcliff did not glance my way, and I gazed up, and contemplated his features almost as confidently as if they had been turned to stone. His forehead, that I once thought so manly, and that I now think so diabolical, was shaded with a heavy cloud; his basilisk eyes were nearly quenched by sleeplessness, and weeping, perhaps, for the lashes were wet then; his lips devoid of their ferocious sneer, and sealed in an expression of unspeakable sadness. Had it been another, I would have covered my face in the presence of such grief. In *his* case, I was gratified; and, ignoble as it seems to insult a fallen enemy, I couldn't miss this chance of sticking in a dart: his weakness was the only time when I could taste the delight of paying wrong for wrong.'

'Fie, fie, miss!' I interrupted. 'One might suppose you had never opened a Bible in your life. If God afflict your enemies, surely that ought to suffice you. It is both mean and presumptuous to add your torture to His!'

'In general I'll allow that it would be, Ellen,' she continued; 'but what misery laid on Heathcliff could content me, unless I have a hand in it? I'd rather he suffered *less*, if I might cause his sufferings and he might *know* that was the cause. O, I owe him so much. On only one condition can I hope to forgive him. It is, if I may take an eye for an eye, a tooth for a tooth; for every wrench of agony return a wrench: reduce him to my level. As he was the first to injure, make him the first to implore pardon; and then—why then, Ellen, I might show you some generosity. But it is utterly impossible I can ever

be revenged, and therefore I cannot forgive him. Hindley wanted some water, and I handed him a glass, and asked him how he was.

' "Not as ill as I wish," he replied. "But leaving out my arm, every inch of me is as sore as if I had been fighting with a legion of imps!"

' "Yes, no wonder," was my next remark. "Catherine used to boast that she stood between you and bodily harm: she meant that certain persons would not hurt you for fear of offending her. It's well people don't *really* rise from their grave, or, last night, she might have witnessed a repulsive scene! Are not you bruised and cut over your chest and shoulders?"

' "I can't say," he answered: "but what do you mean? Did he dare to strike me when I was down?"

' "He trampled on and kicked you, and dashed you on the ground," I whispered. "And his mouth watered to tear you with his teeth; because he's only half a man—not so much."

'Mr. Earnshaw looked up, like me, to the countenance of our mutual foe; who, absorbed in his anguish, seemed insensible to anything around him: the longer he stood, the plainer his reflections revealed their blackness through his features.

' "Oh, if God would but give me strength to strangle him in my last agony, I'd go to hell with joy," groaned the impatient man, writhing to rise, and sinking back in despair, convinced of his inadequacy for the struggle.

' "Nay, it's enough that he has murdered one of you," I observed aloud. "At the Grange, every one knows your sister would have been living now, had it not been for Mr. Heathcliff. After all, it is preferable to be hated than loved by him. When I recollect how happy we were—how happy Catherine was before he came—I'm fit to curse the day."

'Most likely, Heathcliff noticed more the truth of what was said, than the spirit of the person who said it. His attention was roused, I saw, for his eyes rained down tears among the ashes, and he drew his breath in suffocating sighs. I stared full at him, and laughed scornfully. The clouded windows of hell flashed a moment towards me; the fiend which usually looked out, however, was so dimmed and drowned that I did not fear to hazard another sound of derision.

' "Get up, and begone out of my sight," said the mourner.

'I guessed he uttered those words, at least, though his voice was hardly intelligible.

' "I beg your pardon," I replied. "But I loved Catherine too; and her brother requires attendance, which, for her sake, I shall supply. Now that she's dead, I see her in Hindley: Hindley has exactly her eyes, if you had not tried to gouge them out, and made them black and red; and her'——

' "Get up, wretched idiot, before I stamp you to death!" he cried, making a movement that caused me to make one also.

511

' "But then," I continued, holding myself ready to flee; "if poor Catherine had trusted you, and assumed the ridiculous, contemptible, degrading title of Mrs. Heathcliff, she would soon have presented a similar picture! *She* wouldn't have borne your abominable behaviour quietly: her detestation and disgust must have found voice."

'The back of the settle and Earnshaw's person interposed between me and him: so instead of endeavouring to reach me, he snatched a dinner knife from the table and flung it at my head. It struck beneath my ear, and stopped the sentence I was uttering; but, pulling it out, I sprang to the door and delivered another; which I hope went a little deeper than his missile. The last glimpse I caught of him was a furious rush on his part, checked by the embrace of his host; and both fell locked together on the hearth. In my flight through the kitchen I bid Joseph speed to his master; I knocked over Hareton, who was hanging a litter of puppies from a chair-back in the doorway; and blest as a soul escaped from purgatory, I bounded, leaped, and flew down the steep road; then, quitting its windings, shot direct across the moor, rolling over banks, and wading through marshes: precipitating myself, in fact, toward the beacon light of the Grange. And far rather would I be condemned to a perpetual dwelling in the infernal regions, than, even for one night, abide beneath the roof of Wuthering Heights again.'

Isabella ceased speaking, and took a drink of tea; then she rose, and bidding me put on her bonnet, and a great shawl I had brought, and turning a deaf ear to my entreaties for her to remain another hour, she stepped on to a chair, kissed Edgar's and Catherine's portraits, bestowed a similar salute on me, and descended to the carriage, accompanied by Fanny, who yelped wild with joy at recovering her mistress. She was driven away, never to revisit this neighbourhood: but a regular correspondence was established between her and my master when things were more settled. I believe her new abode was in the south, near London; there she had a son born, a few months subsequent to her escape. He was christened Linton, and, from the first, she reported him to be an ailing, peevish creature.

Mr. Heathcliff, meeting me one day in the village, inquired where she lived. I refused to tell. He remarked that it was not of any moment, only she must beware of coming to her brother: she should not be with him, if he had to keep her himself. Though I would give no information, he discovered through some of the other servants, both her place of residence and the existence of the child. Still he didn't molest her: for which forbearance she might thank his aversion, I suppose. He often asked about the infant, when he saw me; and on hearing its name, smiled grimly, and observed:

'They wish me to hate it too, do they?'

'I don't think they wish you to know anything about it,' I answered.

'But I'll have it,' he said, 'when I want it. They may reckon on that!'

Fortunately, its mother died before the time arrived; some thirteen years after the decease of Catherine, when Linton was twelve, or a little more.

On the day succeeding Isabella's unexpected visit, I had no opportunity of speaking to my master: he shunned conversation, and was fit for discussing nothing. When I could get him to listen, I saw it pleased him that his sister had left her husband; whom he abhorred with an intensity which the mildness of his nature would scarcely seem to allow. So deep and sensitive was his aversion, that he refrained from going anywhere where he was likely to see or hear of Heathcliff. Grief, and that together, transformed him into a complete hermit: he threw up his office of magistrate, ceased even to attend church, avoided the village on all occasions, and spent a life of entire seclusion within the limits of his park and grounds; only varied by solitary rambles on the moors, and visits to the grave of his wife, mostly at evening, or early morning before other wanderers were abroad. But he was too good to be thoroughly unhappy long. *He* didn't pray for Catherine's soul to haunt him. Time brought resignation, and a melancholy sweeter than common joy. He recalled her memory with ardent, tender love, and hopeful aspiring to the better world; where he doubted not she was gone.

And he had earthly consolation and affections also. For a few days, I said, he seemed regardless of the puny succesor to the departed: the coldness melted as fast as snow in April, and ere the tiny thing could stammer a word or totter a step, it wielded a despot's sceptre in his heart. It was named Catherine; but he never called it the name in full, as he had never called the first Catherine short; probably because Heathcliff had a habit of doing so. The little one was always Cathy; it formed to him a distinction from the mother, and yet a connection with her; and his attachment sprang from its relation to her far more than from its being his own.

I used to draw a comparison between him and Hindley Earnshaw, and perplex myself to explain satisfactorily why their conduct was so opposite in similar circumstances. They had both been fond husbands, and were both attached to their children; and I could not see how they shouldn't both have taken the same road, for good or evil. But, I thought in my mind, Hindley, with apparently the stronger head, has shown himself sadly the worse and the weaker man. When his ship struck, the captain abandoned his post; and the crew, instead of trying to save her, rushed into riot and confusion, leaving no hope for their luckless vessel. Linton, on the contrary, displayed the true courage of a loyal and faithful soul: he trusted God; and God comforted him. One hoped, and the other despaired: they chose their own lots, and were righteously doomed to endure them. But you'll not want to hear my moralising, Mr. Lockwood: you'll judge as well as I can, all these things: at least, you'll think you will, and that's the same. The end of Earnshaw was what might have been expected; it followed fast on his sister's: there was

scarcely six months between them. We, at the Grange, never got a very succinc
account of his state preceding it; all that I did learn, was on occasion of going
to aid in the preparations for the funeral. Mr. Kenneth came to announc
the event to my master.

'Well, Nelly,' said he, riding into the yard one morning, too early not t
alarm me with an instant presentiment of bad news, 'it's yours and my turn t
go into mourning at present. Who's given us the slip now, do you think?'

'Who?' I asked in a flurry.

'Why, guess!' he returned, dismounting, and slinging his bridle on a hoo
by the door. 'And nip up the corner of your apron: I'm certain you'll need it

'Not Mr. Heathcliff, surely?' I exlaimed.

'What! would you have tears for him?' said the doctor. 'No, Heathcliff
a tough young fellow: he looks blooming to-day. I've just seen him. He
rapidly regaining flesh since he lost his better half.'

'Who is it then, Mr. Kenneth?' I repeated impatiently.

'Hindley Earnshaw! Your old friend Hindley,' he replied, 'and my wicke
gossip: though he's been too wild for me this long while. There! I said w
should draw water. But cheer up. He died true to his character: drunk a
a lord. Poor lad! I'm sorry, too. One can't help missing an old companion
though he had the worst tricks with him that ever man imagined, and ha
done me many a rascally turn. He's barely twenty-seven, it seems; that
your own age: who would have thought you were born in one year?'

I confess this blow was greater to me than the shock of Mrs. Linton's death
ancient associations lingered round my heart; I sat down in the porch an
wept as for a blood relation, desiring Kenneth to get another servant to intr
duce him to the master. I could not hinder myself from pondering on th
question—'Had he had fair play?' Whatever I did, that idea would bother me
it was so tiresomely pertinacious that I resolved on requesting leave to g
to Wuthering Heights, and assist in the last duties to the dead. Mr. Linto
was extremely reluctant to consent, but I pleaded eloquently for the friendle
condition in which he lay; and I said my old master and foster-brother ha
a claim on my services as strong as his own. Besides, I reminded him that th
child Hareton was his wife's nephew, and, in the absence of nearer kin, h
ought to act as its guardian; and he ought to and must inquire how the pr
perty was left, and look over the concerns of his brother-in-law. He was unf
for attending to such matters then, but he bid me speak to his lawyer; an
at length permitted me to go. His lawyer had been Earnshaw's also: I calle
at the village, and asked him to accompany me. He shook his head, an
advised that Heathcliff should be let alone; affirming, if the truth wer
known, Hareton would be found little else than a beggar.

'His father died in debt,' he said; 'the whole property is mortgaged, an
the sole chance for the natural heir is to allow him an opportunity of creatin

ome interest in the creditor's heart, that he may be inclined to deal leniently owards him.'

When I reached the Heights, I explained that I had come to see everything arried on decently; and Joseph, who appeared in sufficient distress, expressed atisfaction at my presence. Mr. Heathcliff said he did not perceive that I was vanted; but I might stay and order the arrangements for the funeral, if chose.

'Correctly,' he remarked, 'that fool's body should be buried at the crossoads, without ceremony of any kind. I happened to leave him ten minutes esterday afternoon, and in that interval he fastened the two doors of the rouse against me, and he has spent the night in drinking himself to death leliberately! We broke in this morning, for we heard him snorting like a horse; nd there he was, laid over the settle; flaying and scalping would not have vakened him. I sent for Kenneth, and he came; but not till the beast had hanged into carrion: he was both dead and cold, and stark; and so you'll llow it was useless making more stir about him!'

The old servant confirmed this statement, but muttered:

'Aw'd rayther he'd goan hisseln fur t' doctor! Aw sud uh taen tent uh t' naister better nur him—un he warn't deead when Aw left, nowt uh t' soart!'

I insisted on the funeral being respectable. Mr. Heathcliff said I might have ny own way there too; only, he desired me to remember that the money for he whole affair came out of his pocket. He maintained a hard, careless deportnent, indicative of neither joy nor sorrow; if anything, it expressed a flinty ratification at a piece of difficult work successfully executed. I observed once, ndeed, something like exultation in his aspect: it was just when the people vere bearing the coffin from the house. He had the hypocrisy to represent . mourner: and previous to following with Hareton, he lifted the unfortunate :hild on to the table and muttered, with peculiar gusto, 'Now, my bonny lad, ou are *mine*! And we'll see if one tree won't grow as crooked as another, with he same wind to twist it!' The unsuspecting thing was pleased at this speech: ie played with Heathcliff's whiskers, and stroked his cheek; but I divined :s meaning, and observed tartly, 'That boy must go back with me to Thrushross Grange, sir. There is nothing in the world less yours than he is!'

'Does Linton say so?' he demanded.

'Of course—he has ordered me to take him,' I replied.

'Well,' said the scoundrel, 'we'll not argue the subject now: but I have fancy to try my hand at rearing a young one; so intimate to your master hat I must supply the place of this with my own, if he attempt to remove it. don't engage to let Hareton go undisputed; but I'll be pretty sure to make he other come! Remember to tell him.'

This hint was enough to bind our hands. I repeated its substance on my eturn; and Edgar Linton, little interested at the commencement, spoke no

more of interfering. I'm not aware that he could have done it to any purpose, had he been ever so willing.

The guest was now the master of Wuthering Heights: he held firm possession, and proved to the attorney—who, in his turn, proved it to Mr. Linton—that Earnshaw had mortgaged every yard of land he owned, for cash to supply his mania for gaming; and he, Heathcliff, was the mortgagee. In that manner Hareton, who should now be the first gentleman in the neighbourhood, was reduced to a state of complete dependence on his father's inveterate enemy, and lives in his own house as a servant, deprived of the advantage of wages, and quite unable to right himself, because of his friendlessness, and his ignorance that he has been wronged.

CHAPTER 18

The twelve years, continued Mrs. Dean, following that dismal period, were the happiest of my life: my greatest troubles in their passage rose from our little lady's trifling illnesses, which she had to experience in common with all children, rich and poor. For the rest, after the first six months, she grew like a larch, and could walk and talk too, in her own way, before the heath blossomed a second time over Mrs. Linton's dust. She was the most winning thing that ever brought sunshine into a desolate house: a real beauty in face, with the Earnshaws' handsome dark eyes, but the Lintons' fair skin and small features, and yellow curling hair. Her spirit was high, though not rough, and qualified by a heart sensitive and lively to excess in its affections. That capacity for intense attachments reminded me of her mother: still she did not resemble her; for she could be soft and mild as a dove, and she had a gentle voice and pensive expression: her anger was never furious; her love never fierce: it was deep and tender. However, it must be acknowledged, she had faults to foil her gifts. A propensity to be saucy was one; and a perverse will, that indulged children invariably acquire, whether they be good-tempered or cross. If a servant chanced to vex her, it was always—'I shall tell papa!' And if he reproved her, even by a look, you would have thought it a heart-breaking business: I don't believe he ever did speak a harsh word to her. He took her education entirely on himself, and made it an amusement. Fortunately curiosity and a quick intellect urged her into an apt scholar: she learned rapidly and eagerly, and did honour to his teaching.

Till she reached the age of thirteen, she had not once been beyond the range of the park by herself. Mr. Linton would take her with him a mile or so outside on rare occasions; but he trusted her to no one else. Gimmerton was an unsubstantial name in her ears; the chapel, the only building she had approached or entered, except her own home. Wuthering Heights and Mr. Heathcliff

did not exist for her: she was a perfect recluse; and, apparently, perfectly contented. Sometimes, indeed, while surveying the country from her nursery window, she would observe:

'Ellen, how long will it be before I can walk to the top of those hills? I wonder what lies on the other side—is it the sea?'

'No, Miss Cathy,' I would answer; 'it is hills again, just like these.'

'And what are those golden rocks like when you stand under them?' she once asked.

The abrupt descent of Penistone Crags particularly attracted her notice; especially when the setting sun shone on it and the topmost heights, and the whole extent of landscape besides lay in shadow. I explained that they were bare masses of stone, with hardly enough earth in their clefts to nourish a stunted tree.

'And why are they bright so long after it is evening here?' she pursued.

'Because they are a great deal higher up than we are,' replied I; 'you could not climb them, they are too high and steep. In winter the frost is always there before it comes to us; and deep into summer I have found snow under that black hollow on the north-east side!'

'Oh, you have been on them!' she cried gleefully. 'Then I can go, too, when I am a woman. Has papa been, Ellen?'

'Papa would tell you, miss,' I answered hastily, 'that they are not worth the trouble of visiting. The moors, where you ramble with him, are much nicer; and Thrushcross Park is the finest place in the world.'

'But I know the park, and I don't know those,' she murmured to herself. And I should delight to look round me from the brow of that tallest point: my little pony Minny shall take me some time.'

One of the maids mentioning the Fairy Cave, quite turned her head with a desire to fulfil this project: she teased Mr. Linton about it; and he promised she should have the journey when she got older. But Miss Catherine measured her age by months, and, 'Now, am I old enough to go to Penistone Crags?' was the constant question in her mouth. The road thither wound close by Wuthering Heights. Edgar had not the heart to pass it; so she received as constantly the answer, 'Not yet, love: not yet.'

I said Mrs. Heathcliff lived above a dozen years after quitting her husband. Her family were of a delicate constitution: she and Edgar both lacked the ruddy health that you will generally meet in these parts. What her last illness was, I am not certain: I conjecture, they died of the same thing, a kind of fever, slow at its commencement, but incurable, and rapidly consuming life towards the close. She wrote to inform her brother of the probable conclusion of a four months' indisposition under which she had suffered, and entreated him to come to her, if possible; for she had much to settle, and she wished to bid him adieu, and deliver Linton safely into his hands. Her hope was, that

Linton might be left with him, as he had been with her: his father, she would fain convince herself, had no desire to assume the burden of his maintenance or education. My master hesitated not a moment in complying with her request: reluctant as he was to leave home at ordinary calls, he flew to answer this; commending Catherine to my peculiar vigilance, in his absence, with reiterated orders that she must not wander out of the park, even under my escort: he did not calculate on her going unaccompanied.

He was away three weeks. The first day or two, my charge sat in a corner of the library, too sad for either reading or playing: in that quiet state she caused me little trouble; but it was succeeded by an interval of impatient fretful weariness; and being too busy, and too old then, to run up and down amusing her, I hit on a method by which she might entertain herself. I used to send her on her travels round the grounds—now on foot, and now on a pony; indulging her with a patient audience of all her real and imaginary adventures when she returned.

The summer shone in full prime; and she took such a taste for this solitary rambling that she often contrived to remain out from breakfast till tea; and then the evenings were spent in recounting her fanciful tales. I did not fear her breaking bounds; because the gates were generally locked, and I thought she would scarcely venture forth alone, if they had stood wide open. Unluckily, my confidence proved misplaced. Catherine came to me, one morning, at eight o'clock, and said she was that day an Arabian merchant, going to cross the Desert with his caravan; and I must give her plenty of provision for herself and beasts: a horse, and three camels, personated by a large hound and a couple of pointers. I got together good store of dainties, and slung them in a basket on one side of the saddle; and she sprang up as gay as a fairy, sheltered by her wide-brimmed hat and gauze veil from the July sun, and trotted off with a merry laugh, mocking my cautious counsel to avoid galloping, and come back early. The naughty thing never made her appearance at tea. One traveller, the hound, being an old dog and fond of its ease, returned; but neither Cathy, nor the pony, nor the two pointers were visible in any direction: I despatched emissaries down this path, and that path, and at last went wandering in search of her myself. There was a labourer working at a fence round a plantation, on the borders of the grounds. I inquired of him if he had seen our young lady.

'I saw her at morn,' he replied; 'she would have me to cut her a hazel switch, and then she leapt her Galloway over the hedge yonder, where it is lowest, and galloped out of sight.'

You may guess how I felt at hearing this news. It struck me directly she must have started for Penistone Crags. 'What will become of her?' I ejaculated, pushing through a gap which the man was repairing, and making straight to the highroad. I walked as if for a wager, mile after mile, till a turn brought

ne in view of the Heights; but no Catherine could I detect far or near. The
Crags lie about a mile and a half beyond Mr. Heathcliff's place, and that is
our from the Grange, so I began to fear night would fall ere I could reach
hem. 'And what if she should have slipped in clambering among them?'
reflected, 'and been killed, or broken some of her bones?' My suspense
was truly painful; and, at first, it gave me delightful relief to observe, in
urrying by the farmhouse, Charlie, the fiercest of the pointers, lying under
, window, with swelled head and bleeding ear. I opened the wicket and ran to
he door, knocking vehemently for admittance. A woman whom I knew, and
who formerly lived at Gimmerton, answered: she had been servant there since
he death of Mr. Earnshaw.

'Ah', said she, 'you are come a seeking your little mistress! don't be frightened.
he's here safe: but I'm glad it isn't the master.'

'He is not at home then, is he?' I panted, quite breathless with quick
walking and alarm.

'No, no,' she replied: 'both he and Joseph are off, and I think they won't
return this hour or more. Step in and rest you a bit.'

I entered, and beheld my stray lamb seated on the hearth, rocking herself
n a little chair that had been her mother's when a child. Her hat was hung
gainst the wall, and she seemed perfectly at home, laughing and chattering,
n the best spirits imaginable, to Hareton—now a great, strong lad of eighteen—
who stared at her with considerable curiosity and astonishment: comprehend-
ng precious little of the fluent succession of remarks and questions which her
ongue never ceased pouring forth.

'Very well, miss!' I exclaimed, concealing my joy under an angry counte-
ance. 'This is your last ride, till papa comes back. I'll not trust you over
he threshold again, you naughty, naughty girl!'

'Aha, Ellen!' she cried gaily, jumping up and running to my side. 'I shall
ave a pretty story to tell to-night: and so you've found me out. Have you
ver been here in your life before?'

'Put that hat on, and home at once,' said I. 'I'm dreadfully grieved at you,
Miss Cathy: you've done extremely wrong. It's no use pouting and crying:
hat won't repay the trouble I've had, scouring the country after you. To think
ow Mr. Linton charged me to keep you in; and you stealing off so! it shows
ou are a cunning little fox, and nobody will put faith in you any more.'

'What have I done?' sobbed she, instantly checked. 'Papa charged me
othing: he'll not scold me, Ellen—he's never cross, like you!'

'Come, come!' I repeated. 'I'll tie the riband. Now, let us have no petulance.
Oh, for shame! You thirteen years old, and such a baby!'

This exclamation was caused by her pushing the hat from her head, and
etreating to the chimney out of my reach.

'Nay,' said the servant, 'don't be hard on the bonny lass, Mrs. Dean. We

made her stop: she'd fain have ridden forwards, afeard you should be uneasy
But Hareton offered to go with her, and I thought he should: it's a wild
road over the hills.'

Hareton, during the discussion, stood with his hands in his pockets, too
awkward to speak; though he looked as if he did not relish my intrusion

'How long am I to wait?' I continued, disregarding the woman's inter
ference. 'It will be dark in ten minutes. Where is the pony, Miss Cathy? And
where is Phoenix? I shall leave you, unless you be quick; so please yourself.

'The pony is in the yard,' she replied, 'and Phoenix is shut in there. He'
bitten—and so is Charlie. I was going to tell you all about it; but you are in
a bad temper, and don't deserve to hear.'

I picked up her hat, and approached to reinstate it; but perceiving that the
people of the house took her part, she commenced capering round the room
and on my giving chase, ran like a mouse over and under and behind the
furniture, rendering it ridiculous for me to pursue. Hareton and the woman
laughed, and she joined them, and waxed more impertinent still; till I cried
in great irritation:

'Well, Miss Cathy, if you were aware whose house this is, you'd be glad
enough to get out.'

'It's *your* father's, isn't it?' said she, turning to Hareton.

'Nay,' he replied, looking down, and blushing bashfully.

He could not stand a steady gaze from her eyes, though they were just his
own.

'Whose then—your master's?' she asked.

He coloured deeper, with a different feeling, muttered an oath, and turned
away.

'Who is his master?' continued the tiresome girl, appealing to me. 'He
talked about "our house," and "our folk." I thought he had been the owner's
son. And he never said, Miss; he should have done, shouldn't he, if he's a ser
vant?'

Hareton grew black as a thunder-cloud, at this childish speech. I silently
shook my questioner, and at last succeeded in equipping her for departure

'Now, get my horse,' she said, addressing her unknown kinsman as she
would one of the stable-boys at the Grange. 'And you may come with me
I want to see where the goblin-hunter rises in the marsh, and to hear about
the *fairishes*, as you call them: but make haste! What's the matter? Get my
horse, I say.'

'I'll see thee damned before I be *thy* servant!' growled the lad.

'You'll see me *what*?' asked Catherine in surprise.

'Damned—thou saucy witch!' he replied.

'There, Miss Cathy! you see you have got into pretty company,' I inter
posed. 'Nice words to be used to a young lady! Pray don't begin to disput

with him. Come, let us seek for Minny ourselves, and begone.'

'But, Ellen,' cried she, staring, fixed in astonishment, 'how dare he speak to to me? Mustn't he be made to do as I ask him? You wicked creature, I shall tell papa what you said.—Now, then!'

Hareton did not appear to feel this threat; so the tears sprang into her eyes with indignation. 'You bring the pony,' she exclaimed, turning to the woman, 'and let my dog free this moment!'

'Softly, miss,' answered the addressed: 'you'll lose nothing by being civil. Though Mr. Hareton, there, be not the master's son, he's your cousin; and I was never hired to serve you.'

'*He* my cousin!' cried Cathy, with a scornful laugh.

'Yes, indeed,' responded her reprover.

'Oh, Ellen! don't let them say such things,' she pursued, in great trouble. 'Papa is gone to fetch my cousin from London: my cousin is a gentleman's son. That my'—she stopped, and wept outright; upset at the bare notion of relationship with such a clown.

'Hush, hush!' I whispered, 'people can have many cousins, and of all sorts, Miss Cathy, without being any the worse for it; only they needn't keep their company, if they be disagreeable and bad.'

'He's not—he's not my cousin, Ellen!' she went on, gathering fresh grief from reflection, and flinging herself into my arms for refuge from the idea.

I was much vexed at her and the servant for their mutual revelations; having no doubt of Linton's approaching arrival, communicated by the former, being reported to Mr. Heathcliff; and feeling as confident that Catherine's first thought on her father's return, would be to seek an explanation of the latter's assertion concerning her rude-bred kindred. Hareton, recovering from his disgust at being taken for a servant, seemed moved by her distress; and, having fetched the pony round to the door, he took, to propitiate her, a fine crooked-legged terrier-whelp from the kennel, and putting it into her hand bid her wisht! for he meant nought. Pausing in her lamentations, she surveyed him with a glance of awe and horror, then burst forth anew.

I could scarcely refrain from smiling at this antipathy to the poor fellow; who was a well-made, athletic youth, good-looking in features, and stout and healthy, but attired in garments befitting his daily occupations of working on the farm, and lounging among the moors after rabbits and game. Still, I thought I could detect in his physiognomy a mind owning better qualities than his father ever possessed. Good things lost amid a wilderness of weeds, to be sure, whose rankness far overtopped their neglected growth; yet, notwithstanding, evidence of a wealthy soil, that might yield luxuriant crops under other and favourable circumstances. Mr. Heathcliff, I believe, had not treated him physically ill; thanks to his fearless nature, which offered no temptation to that course of oppression: it had none of the timid susceptibility that would

have given zest to ill-treatment, in Heathcliff's judgment. He appeared to have bent his malevolence on making him a brute: he was never taught to read or write; never rebuked for any bad habit which did not annoy his keeper; never led a single step towards virtue, or guarded by a single precept against vice. And from what I heard, Joseph contributed much to his deterioration, by a narrow-minded partiality which prompted him to flatter and pet him, as a boy, because he was the head of the old family. And as he had been in the habit of accusing Catherine Earnshaw and Heathcliff, when children, of putting the master past his patience, and compelling him to seek solace in drink by what he termed their 'offalld ways,' so at present he laid the whole burden of Hareton's faults on the shoulders of the usurper of his property. If the lad swore, he wouldn't correct him: nor however culpably he behaved. It gave Joseph satisfaction, apparently, to watch him go the worst lengths: he allowed that he was ruined: that his soul was abandoned to perdition; but then, he reflected that Heathcliff must answer for it. Hareton's blood would be required at his hands; and there lay immense consolation in that thought. Joseph had instilled into him a pride of name, and of his lineage; he would, had he dared, have fostered hate between him and the present owner of the Heights: but his dread of that owner amounted to superstition; and he confined his feelings regarding him to muttered innuendoes and private comminations. I don't pretend to be intimately acquainted with the mode of living customary in those days at Wuthering Heights: I only speak from hearsay; for I saw little. The villagers affirmed Mr. Heathcliff was *near*, and a cruel hard landlord to his tenants; but the house, inside, had regained its ancient aspect of comfort under female management, and the scenes of riot common in Hindley's time were not now enacted within its walls. The master was too gloomy to seek companionship with any people good or bad; and he is yet.

This, however, is not making progress with my story. Miss Cathy rejected the peace-offering of the terrier, and demanded her own dogs, Charlie and Phoenix. They came limping, and hanging their heads; and we set out for home, sadly out of sorts, every one of us. I could not wring from my little lady how she had spent the day; except that, as I supposed, the goal of her pilgrimage was Penistone Crags; and she arrived without adventure to the gate of the farmhouse, when Hareton happened to issue forth, attended by some canine followers, who attacked her train. They had a smart battle before their owners could separate them: that formed an introduction. Catherine told Hareton who she was, and where she was going; and asked him to show her the way: finally, beguiling him to accompany her. He opened the mysteries of the Fairy Cave, and twenty other queer places. But, being in disgrace, I was not favoured with a description of the interesting objects she saw. I could gather, however, that her guide had been a favourite ti

she hurt his feelings by addressing him as a servant; and Heathcliff's house-keeper hurt hers by calling her her cousin. Then the language he had held to her rankled in her heart; she who was always 'love,' and 'darling,' and 'queen,' and 'angel,' with everybody at the Grange, to be insulted so shockingly by a stranger! She did not comprehend it; and hard work I had to obtain a promise that she would not lay the grievance before her father. I explained how he objected to the whole household at the Heights, and how sorry he would be to find she had been there; but I insisted most on the fact, that if she revealed my negligence of his orders, he would perhaps be so angry, that I should have to leave; and Cathy couldn't bear that prospect: she pledged her word, and kept it, for my sake. After all, she was a sweet little girl.

CHAPTER 19

A letter, edged with black, announced the day of my master's return. Isabella was dead; and he wrote to bid me get mourning for his daughter, and arrange a room, and other accommodations, for his youthful nephew. Catherine ran wild with joy at the idea of welcoming her father back; and indulged most sanguine anticipations of the innumerable excellences of her 'real' cousin. The evening of their expected arrival came. Since early morning, she had been busy ordering her own small affairs; and now, attired in her new black frock—poor thing! her aunt's death impressed her with no definite sorrow—she obliged me, by constant worrying, to walk with her down through the grounds to meet them.

'Linton is just six months younger than I am,' she chattered, as we strolled leisurely over the swells and hollows of mossy turf, under shadow of the trees. 'How delightful it will be to have him for a play-fellow! Aunt Isabella sent papa a beautiful lock of his hair; it was lighter than mine—more flaxen, and quite as fine. I have it carefully preserved in a little glass box: and I've often thought what pleasure it would be to see its owner. Oh! I am happy—and papa, dear, dear papa! Come, Ellen, let us run! come, run.'

She ran, and returned and ran again, many times before my sober footsteps reached the gate, and then she seated herself on the grassy bank beside the path, and tried to wait patiently; but that was impossible: she couldn't be still a minute.

'How long they are!' she exclaimed. 'Ah, I see some dust on the road—they're coming? No! When will they be here? May we not go a little way—half a mile, Ellen: only just half a mile? Do say yes: to that clump of birches at the turn!'

I refused staunchly. At length her suspense was ended: the travelling

carriage rolled in sight. Miss Cathy shrieked and stretched out her arms, as soon as she caught her father's face looking from the window. He descended nearly as eager as herself: and a considerable interval elapsed ere they had a thought to spare for any but themselves. While they exchanged caresses I took a peep in to see after Linton. He was asleep in a corner, wrapped in a warm, fur-lined cloak, as if it had been winter. A pale, delicate, effeminate boy, who might have been taken for my master's younger brother, so strong was the resemblance: but there was a sickly peevishness in his aspect, that Edgar Linton never had. The latter saw me looking; and having shaken hands, advised me to close the door, and leave him undisturbed; for the journey had fatigued him. Cathy would fain have taken one glance, but her father told her to come on, and they walked together up the park, while I hastened before to prepare the servants.

'Now, darling,' said Mr. Linton, addressing his daughter, as they halted at the bottom of the front steps; 'your cousin is not so strong or so merry as you are, and he has lost his mother, remember, a very short time since therefore, don't except him to play and run about with you directly. And don't harass him much by talking: let him be quiet this evening, at least will you?'

'Yes, yes, papa,' answered Catherine: 'but I do want to see him; and he hasn't once looked out.'

The carriage stopped; and the sleeper being roused, was lifted to the ground by his uncle.

'This is your cousin Cathy, Linton,' he said, putting their little hands together. 'She's fond of you already; and mind you don't grieve her by crying to-night. Try to be cheerful now; the travelling is at an end, and you have nothing to do but rest and amuse yourself as you please.'

'Let me go to bed, then,' answered the boy, shrinking from Catherine' salute; and he put his fingers to his eyes to remove incipient tears.

'Come, come, there's a good child,' I whispered, leading him in. 'You'l make her weep too—see how sorry she is for you!'

I do not know whether it were sorrow for him, but his cousin put on as sad a countenance as himself, and returned to her father. All three entered and mounted to the library, where tea was laid ready. I proceeded to remove Linton's cap and mantle, and placed him on a chair by the table; but he was no sooner seated than he began to cry afresh. My master inquired what was the matter.

'I can't sit on a chair,' sobbed the boy.

'Go to the sofa, then, and Ellen shall bring you some tea,' answered his uncle patiently.

He had been greatly tried during the journey, I felt convinced, by his fretful ailing charge. Linton slowly trailed himself off, and lay down. Cath

arried a footstool and her cup to his side. At first she sat silent; but that ould not last: she had resolved to make a pet of her little cousin, as she would have him to be; and she commenced stroking his curls, and kissing his cheek, and offering him tea in her saucer, like a baby. This pleased him, or he was not much better: he dried his eyes, and lightened into a faint smile.

'Oh, he'll do very well,' said the master to me, after watching them a minute. Very well, if we can keep him, Ellen. The company of a child of his own age will instil new spirit into him soon, and by wishing for strength he'll gain it.'

'Ay, if we can keep him!' I mused to myself; and sore misgivings came over me that there was slight hope of that. And then, I thought, however will that weakling live at Wuthering Heights, between his father and Hareton, what playmates and instructors they'll be. Our doubts were presently decided— even earlier than I expected. I had just taken the children upstairs, after tea was finished, and seen Linton asleep—he would not suffer me to leave him till that was the case—I had come down, and was standing by the table in the hall, lighting a bedroom candle for Mr. Edgar, when a maid stepped out of the kitchen and informed me that Mr. Heathcliff's servant Joseph was at the door, and wished to speak with the master.

'I shall ask him what he wants first,' I said, in considerable trepidation. 'A very unlikely hour to be troubling people, and the instant they have returned from a long journey. I don't think the master can see him.'

Joseph had advanced through the kitchen as I uttered these words, and now presented himself in the hall. He was donned in his Sunday garments, with his most sanctimonious and sourest face, and, holding his hat in one hand and his stick in the other, he proceeded to clean his shoes on the mat.

'Good evening, Joseph,' I said coldly. 'What business brings you here to-night?'

'It's Maister Linton Aw mun spake tull,' he answered, waving me disdainfully aside.

'Mr. Linton is going to bed; unless you have something particular to say, I'm sure he won't hear it now,' I continued. 'You had better sit down in here, and entrust your message to me.'

'Which is his rahm?' pursued the fellow, surveying the range of closed doors.

I perceived he was bent on refusing my mediation, so very reluctantly I went up to the library, and announced the unseasonable visitor, advising that he should be dismissed till next day. Mr. Linton had no time to empower me to do so, for Joseph mounted close at my heels, and, pushing into the apartment, planted himself at the far side of the table, with his two fists clapped on the head of his stick, and began in an elevated tone, as if anticipating opposition:

'Hathecliff has send me for his lad, and Aw munn't goa back 'bout him.

Edgar Linton was silent a minute; an expression of exceeding sorrow over cast his features: he would have pitied the child on his own account; but recalling Isabella's hopes and fears, and anxious wishes for her son, and he commendations of him to his care, he grieved bitterly at the prospect o yielding him up, and searched in his heart how it might be avoided. No plan offered itself: the very exhibition of any desire to keep him would have ren dered the claimant more peremptory: there was nothing left but to resign him. However, he was not going to rouse him from his sleep.

'Tell Mr. Heathcliff,' he answered calmly, 'that his son shall come to Wuthering Heights to-morrow. He is in bed, and too tired to go the distance now. You may also tell him that the mother of Linton desired him to remain under my guardianship; and, at present, his health is very precarious.'

'Noa!' said Joseph, giving a thud with his prop on the floor, and assuming an authoritative air; 'noa! that manes nowt. Hathecliff maks noa 'cahn uh t' mother, nur yah norther; bud he'll hev his lad; und Aw mun tak him— soa nah yah knaw!'

'You shall not to-night!' answered Linton decisively. 'Walk downstair at once, and repeat to your master what I have said. Ellen, show him down Go'—

And, aiding the indignant elder with a lift by the arm, he rid the room of him, and closed the door.

'Varrah weell!' shouted Joseph, as he slowly drew off. 'Tuh-morn, he' come hisseln, un thrust *him* aht, if yah darr!'

CHAPTER 20

To obviate the danger of this threat being fulfilled, Mr. Linton commissioned me to take the boy home early, on Catherine's pony; and, said he: 'As we shall now have no influence over his destiny, good or bad, you must say nothing of where he is gone, to my daughter: she cannot associate with him hereafter, and it is better for her to remain in ignorance of his proximity; lest she should be restless, and anxious to visit the Heights. Merely tell her his father sent for him suddenly, and he has been obliged to leave us.'

Linton was very reluctant to be roused from his bed at five o'clock, and astonished to be informed that he must prepare for further travelling; but I softened off the matter by stating that he was going to spend some time with his father, Mr. Heathcliff, who wished to see him so much, he did not like to defer the pleasure till he should recover from his late journey.

'My father!' he cried, in strange perplexity. 'Mamma never told me I had a father. Where does he live? I'd rather stay with uncle.'

'He lives a little distance from the Grange,' I replied; 'just beyond those hills: not so far, but you may walk over here when you get hearty. And you should be glad to go home, and to see him. You must try to love him, as you did your mother, and then he will love you.'

'But why have I not heard of him before?' asked Linton, 'Why didn't mamma and he live together, as other people do?'

'He had business to keep him in the north,' I answered, 'and your mother's health required her to reside in the south.'

'And why didn't mamma speak to me about him?' persevered the child. 'She often talked of uncle, and I learnt to love him long ago. How am I to love papa? I don't know him.'

'Oh, all children love their parents,' I said. 'Your mother, perhaps, thought you would want to be with him if she mentioned him often to you. Let us make haste. An early ride on such a beautiful morning is much preferable to an hour's more sleep.'

'Is *she* to go with us,' he demanded: 'the little girl I saw yesterday?'

'Not now,' replied I.

'Is uncle?' he continued.

'No, I shall be your companion there,' I said.

Linton sank back on his pillow and fell into a brown study.

'I won't go without uncle,' he cried at length: 'I can't tell where you mean to take me.'

I attempted to persuade him of the naughtiness of showing reluctance to meet his father; still he obstinately resisted any progress towards dressing, and I had to call for my master's assistance in coaxing him out of bed. The

poor thing was finally got off, with several delusive assurances that his absence should be short; that Mr. Edgar and Cathy would visit him, and other promises, equally ill-founded, which I invented and reiterated at intervals throughout the way. The pure heather-scented air, and the bright sunshine, and the gentle canter of Minny, relieved his despondency after a while. He began to put questions concerning his new home, and its inhabitants, with greater interest and liveliness.

'Is Wuthering Heights as pleasant a place as Thrushcross Grange?' he inquired, turning to take a last glance into the valley, whence a light mist mounted and formed a fleecy cloud on the skirts of the blue.

'It is not so buried in trees,' I replied, 'and it is not quite so large, but you can see the country beautifully all round; and the air is healthier for you—fresher and dryer. You will, perhaps, think the building old and dark at first; though it is a respectable house: the next best in the neighbourhood. And you will have such nice rambles on the moors. Hareton Earnshaw—that is Miss Cathy's other cousin, and so yours in a manner—will show you all the sweetest spots; and you can bring a book in fine weather, and make a green hollow your study; and, now and then, your uncle may join you in a walk: he does, frequently, walk out on the hills.'

'And what is my father like?' he asked. 'Is he as young and handsome as uncle?'

'He's as young,' said I; 'but he has black hair and eyes, and looks sterner; and he is taller and bigger altogether. He'll not seem to you so gentle and kind at first, perhaps, because it is not his way: still, mind you, be frank and cordial with him; and naturally he'll be fonder of you than any uncle, for you are his own.'

'Black hair and eyes!' mused Linton. 'I can't fancy him. Then I am not like him, am I?'

'Not much,' I answered: not a morsel, I thought, surveying with regret the white complexion and slim frame of my companion, and his large languid eyes—his mother's eyes, save that, unless a morbid touchiness kindled them a moment, they had not a vestige of her sparkling spirit.

'How strange that he should never come to see mamma and me!' he murmured. 'Has he ever seen me? If he have, I must have been a baby. I remember not a single thing about him!'

'Why, Master Linton,' said I, 'three hundred miles is a great distance; and ten years seem very different in length to a grown-up person compared with what they do to you. It is probable Mr. Heathcliff proposed going from summer to summer, but never found a convenient opportunity; and now it is too late. Don't trouble him with questions on the subject: it will disturb him, for no good.'

The boy was fully occupied with his own cogitations for the remainder of

the ride, till we halted before the farmhouse garden gate. I watched to catch his impressions in his countenance. He surveyed the carved front and low-browed lattices, the straggling gooseberry bushes and crooked firs, with solemn intentness, and then shook his head: his private feelings entirely disapproved of the exterior of his new abode. But he had sense to postpone complaining: there might be compensation within. Before he dismounted, I went and opened the door. It was half-past six; the family had just finished breakfast; the servant was clearing and wiping down the table. Joseph stood by his master's chair telling some tale concerning a lame horse; and Hareton was preparing for the hay field.

'Hallo, Nelly!' cried Mr. Heathcliff, when he saw me. 'I feared I should have to come down and fetch my property myself. You've brought it, have you? Let us see what we can make of it.'

He got up and strode to the door. Hareton and Joseph followed in gaping curiosity. Poor Linton ran a frightened eye over the faces of the three.

'Sure-ly,' said Joseph, after a grave inspection, 'he's swopped wi' ye, maister, an' yon's his lass!'

Heathcliff, having stared his son into an ague of confusion, uttered a scornful laugh.

'God! what a beauty! what a lovely, charming thing!' he exclaimed. 'Haven't they reared it on snails and sour milk, Nelly? Oh, damn my soul! but that's worse than I expected—and the devil knows I was not sanguine!'

I bid the trembling and bewildered child get down, and enter. He did not thoroughly comprehend the meaning of his father's speech, or whether it were intended for him: indeed, he was not yet certain that the grim, sneering stranger was his father. But he clung to me with growing trepidation; and on Mr. Heathcliff's taking a seat and bidding him 'come hither,' he hid his face on my shoulder and wept.

'Tut, tut!' said Heathcliff, stretching out a hand and dragging him roughly between his knees, and then holding up his head by the chin. 'None of that nonsense! We're not going to hurt thee, Linton—isn't that thy name? Thou art thy mother's child, entirely! Where is *my* share in thee, puling chicken?'

He took off the boy's cap and pushed back his thick flaxen curls, felt his slender arms and his small fingers; during which examination, Linton ceased crying, and lifted his great blue eyes to inspect the inspector.

'Do you know me?' asked Heathcliff, having satisfied himself that the limbs were all equally frail and feeble.

'No,' said Linton, with a gaze of vacant fear.

'You've heard of me, I dare say?'

'No,' he replied again.

'No? What a shame of your mother, never to waken your filial regard for me! You are my son, then, I'll tell you; and your mother was a wicked slut

to leave you in ignorance of the sort of father you possessed. Now, don't wince, and colour up! Though it *is* something to see you have not white blood. Be a good lad; and I'll do for you. Nelly, if you be tired you may sit down; if not, get home again. I guess you'll report what you hear and see to the cipher at the Grange; and this thing won't be settled while you linger about it.'

'Well,' replied I, 'I hope you'll be kind to the boy, Mr. Heathcliff, or you'll not keep him long; and he's all you have akin in the wide world, that you will ever know—remember.'

'I'll be *very* kind to him, you needn't fear,' he said, laughing. 'Only nobody else must be kind to him: I'm jealous of monopolising his affection. And, to begin my kindness, Joseph, bring the lad some breakfast. Hareton, you infernal calf, begone to your work. Yes, Nell,' he added, when they had departed, 'my son is prospective owner of your place, and I should not wish him to die till I was certain of being his successor. Besides, he's *mine*, and I want the triumph of seeing *my* descendant fairly lord of their estates: my child hiring their children to till their father's lands for wages. That is the sole consideration which can make me endure the whelp: I despise him for himself, and hate him for the memories he revives! But that consideration is sufficient: he's as safe with me, and shall be tended as carefully as your master tends his own. I have a room upstairs, furnished for him in handsome style: I've engaged a tutor, also, to come three times a week, from twenty miles distance, to teach him what he pleases to learn. I've ordered Hareton to obey him; and in fact I've arranged everything with a view to preserve the superior and the gentleman in him, above his associates. I do regret, however, that he so little deserves the trouble; if I wished any blessing in the world, it was to find him a worthy object of pride; and I'm bitterly disappointed with the whey-faced whining wretch!'

While he was speaking, Joseph returned bearing a basin of milk-porridge and placed it before Linton. He stirred round the homely mess with a look of aversion, and affirmed he could not eat it. I saw the old man-servant shared largely in his master's scorn of the child; though he was compelled to retain the sentiment in his heart, because Heathcliff plainly meant his underlings to hold him in honour.

'Cannot ate it?' repeated he, peering in Linton's face, and subduing his voice to a whisper, for fear of being overheard. 'But Maister Hareton nivir ate naught else, when he wer a little un; and what were gooid eneugh for him' gooid eneugh for ye, Aw's rayther think!'

'I *shant* eat it!' answered Linton snappishly. 'Take it away.'

Joseph snatched up the food indignantly, and brought it to us.

'Is there aught ails th' victuals?' he asked thrusting the tray under Heathcliff's nose.

'What should ail them?' he said.

'Wah!' answered Joseph, 'yon dainty chap says he cannut ate 'em. But Aw guess it's raight! His mother wer just soa—we wer a'most too mucky to sow t' corn for makking her breead.'

'Don't mention his mother to me,' said the master angrily. 'Get him some-thing that he can eat, that's all. What is his food, Nelly?'

I suggested boiled milk or tea; and the housekeeper received instructions to prepare some. Come, I reflected, his father's selfishness may contribute to his comfort. He perceives his delicate constitution, and the necessity of treating him tolerably. I'll console Mr. Edgar by acquainting him with the turn Heathcliff's humour has taken. Having no excuse for lingering longer I slipped out, while Linton was engaged in timidly rebuilding the advances of a friendly sheep-dog. But he was too much on the alert to be cheated: as I closed the door, I heard a cry, and a frantic repetition of the words:

'Don't leave me! I'll not stay here! I'll not stay here!'

Then the latch was raised and fell: they did not suffer him to come forth. I mounted Minny, and urged her to a trot; and so my brief guardianship ended.

CHAPTER 21

We had sad work with little Cathy that day; she rose in high glee, eager to join her cousin, and such passionate tears and lamentations followed the news of his departure, that Edgar himself was obliged to soothe her, by affirming he should come back soon: he added, however, 'if I can get him;' and there were no hopes of that. This promise poorly pacified her: but time was more potent; and though still at intervals she inquired of her father when Linton would return, before she did see him again his features had waxed so dim in her memory that she did not recognise him.

When I chanced to encounter the housekeeper of Wuthering Heights in paying business-visits to Gimmerton, I used to ask how the young master got on; for he lived almost as secluded as Catherine herself, and was never to be seen. I could gather from her that he continued in weak health, and was a tiresome inmate. She said Mr. Heathcliff seemed to dislike him ever longer and worse, though he took some trouble to conceal it: he had an antipathy to the sound of his voice, and could not do at all with his sitting in the same room with him many minutes together. There seldom passed much talk between them: Linton learnt his lessons and spent his evenings in a small apartment they called the parlour: or else lay in bed all day: for he was constantly getting coughs, and colds, and aches, and pains of some sort.

'And I never knew such a faint-hearted creature,' added the woman; 'nor one so careful of hisseln. He *will* go on, if I leave the window open a bit late in the evening. Oh! it's killing! a breath of night air! And he must have a fire

in the middle of summer; and Joseph's bacca pipe is poison; and he must always have sweets and dainties, and always milk, milk for ever—heeding naught how the rest of us are pinched in winter; and there he'll sit, wrapped in his furred cloak in his chair by the fire, some toast and water or other slop on the hob to sip at; and if Hareton, for pity, comes to amuse him— Hareton is not bad-natured, though he's rough—they're sure to part, one swearing and the other crying. I believe the master would relish Earnshaw's thrashing him to a mummy, if he were not his son; and I'm certain he would be fit to turn him out of doors, if he knew half the nursing he gives hisseln But then, he won't go into danger of temptation: he never enters the parlour and should Linton show those ways in the house where he is, he sends him upstairs directly.'

I divined, from this account, that utter lack of sympathy had rendered young Heathcliff selfish and disagreeable, if he were not so originally; and my interest in him, consequently, decayed: though still I was moved with a sense of grief at his lot, and a wish that he had been left with us. Mr. Edgar encouraged me to gain information: he thought a great deal about him, I fancy and would have run some risk to see him; and he told me once to ask the housekeeper whether he ever came into the village? She said he had only been twice, on horseback, accompanying his father, and both times he pretended to be quite knocked up for three or four days afterwards. The housekeeper left, if I recollect rightly, two years after he came; and another, whom I did not know, was her successor: she lives there still.

Time wore on at the Grange in its former pleasant way, till Miss Cathy reached sixteen. On the anniversary of her birth we never manifested any signs of rejoicing, because it was also the anniversary of my late mistress' death. Her father invariably spent that day alone in the library; and walked at dusk, as far as Gimmerton kirkyard, where he would frequently prolong his stay beyond midnight. Therefore Catherine was thrown on her own resources for amusement. This 20th of March was a beautiful spring day, and when her father had retired, my young lady came down dressed for going out and said she had asked to have a ramble on the edge of the moors with me and Mr. Linton had given her leave, if we went only a short distance and were back within the hour.

'So make haste, Ellen!' she cried. 'I know where I wish to go; where a colony of moor game are settled: I want to see whether they have made their nest yet.'

'That must be a good distance up,' I answered; 'they don't breed on the edge of the moor.'

'No, it's not,' she said. 'I've gone very near with papa.'

I put on my bonnet and sallied out, thinking nothing more of the matter She bounded before me, and returned to my side, and was off again like

young grey-hound; and, at first, I found plenty of entertainment in listening to the larks singing far and near, and enjoying the sweet, warm sunshine; and watching her, my pet, and my delight, with her golden ringlets flying loose behind, and her bright cheek, as soft and pure in its bloom as a wild rose, and her eyes radiant with cloudless pleasure. She was a happy creature, and an angel, in those days. It's a pity she could not be content.

'Well,' said I, 'where are your moor-game, Miss Cathy? We should be at them: the Grange park-fence is a great way off now.'

'Oh, a little further—only a little further, Ellen,' was her answer continually. 'Climb to that hillock, pass that bank, and by the time you reach the other side I shall have raised the birds.'

But there were so many hillocks and banks to climb and pass, that, at length, I began to be weary, and told her we must halt, and retrace our steps. I shouted to her, as she had outstripped me a long way; she either did not hear or did not regard, for she still sprang on, and I was compelled to follow. Finally, she dived into a hollow; and before I came in sight of her again, she was two miles nearer Wuthering Heights than her own home; and I beheld a couple of persons arrest her, one of whom I felt convinced was Mr. Heathcliff himself.

Cathy had been caught in the fact of plundering, or, at least, hunting out the nests of the grouse. The Heights were Heathcliff's land, and he was reproving the poacher.

'I've neither taken any nor found any,' she said, as I toiled to them, expanding her hands in corroboration of the statement. 'I didn't mean to take them; but papa told me there were quantities up here, and I wished to see the eggs.'

Heathcliff glanced at me with an ill-meaning smile, expressing his acquaintance with the party, and, consequently, his malevolence towards it, and demanded who 'papa' was?

'Mr. Linton of Thrushcross Grange,' she replied. 'I thought you did not know me, or you wouldn't have spoken in that way.'

'You suppose papa is highly esteemed and respected then?' he said sarcastically.

'And what are you?' inquired Catherine, gazing curiously on the speaker. 'That man I've seen before. Is he your son?'

She pointed to Hareton, the other individual, who had gained nothing but increased bulk and strength by the addition of two years to his age: he seemed as awkward and rough as ever.

'Miss Cathy,' I interrupted, 'it will be three hours instead of one that we're out, presently. We really must go back.'

'No, that man is not my son,' answered Heathcliff, pushing me aside. 'But I have one, and you have seen him before too; and, though your nurse is in a hurry, I think both you and she would be the better for a little rest.

Will you just turn this nab of heath, and walk into my house? You'll get home earlier for the ease; and you shall receive a kind welcome.'

I whispered Catherine that she mustn't, on any account, accede to the proposal: it was entirely out of the question.

'Why?' she asked, aloud. 'I'm tired of running, and the ground is dewy I can't sit here. Let us go, Ellen. Besides, he says I have seen his son. He's mistaken, I think; but I guess where he lives: at the farm-house I visited in coming from Penistone Crags. Don't you?'

'I do. Come, Nelly, hold your tongue—it will be a treat for her to look in on us. Hareton, get forwards with the lass. You shall walk with me, Nelly.

'No, she's not going to any such place,' I cried, struggling to release my arm, which he had seized: but she was almost at the door-stones already scampering round the brow at full speed. Her appointed companion did not pretend to escort her: he shied off by the road-side, and vanished.

'Mr. Heathcliff, it's very wrong,' I continued: 'you know you mean no good. And there she'll see Linton, and all will be told as soon as ever we return; and I shall have the blame.'

'I want her to see Linton,' he answered; 'he's looking better these few days it's not often he's fit to be seen. And we'll soon persuade her to keep the visit secret: where is the harm of it?'

'The harm of it is, that her father would hate me if he found I suffered her to enter your house; and I am convinced you have a bad design in encouraging her to do so,' I replied.

'My design is as honest as possible. I'll inform you of its whole scope,' he said. 'That the two cousins may fall in love, and get married. I'm acting generously to your master: his young chit has no expectations, and should she second my wishes, she'll be provided for at once as joint successor with Linton.'

'If Linton died,' I answered, 'and his life is quite uncertain, Catherine would be the heir.'

'No, she would not,' he said. 'There is no clause in the will to secure it so his property would go to me; but, to prevent disputes, I desire their union and am resolved to bring it about.'

'And I'm resolved she shall never approach your house with me again I returned, as we reached the gate, where Miss Cathy waited our coming.

Heathcliff bid me be quiet; and, preceding us up the path, hastened to open the door. My young lady gave him several looks, as if she could not exactly make up her mind what to think of him; but now he smiled when he met her eye, and softened his voice in addressing her; and I was foolish enough to imagine the memory of her mother might disarm him from desiring her injury. Linton stood on the hearth. He had been out walking in the fields for his cap was on, and he was calling to Joseph to bring him dry shoes. H

ad grown tall of his age, still wanting some months of sixteen. His features were pretty yet, and his eye and complexion brighter than I remembered them, though with merely temporary lustre borrowed from the salubrious air and genial sun.

'Now, who is that?' asked Mr. Heathcliff, turning to Cathy. 'Can you tell?'

'Your son?' she said, having doubtfully surveyed, first one and then the other.

'Yes, yes,' answered he: 'but is this the only time you have beheld him? Think! Ah! you have a short memory. Linton, don't you recall your cousin, that you used to tease us so with wishing to see?'

'What, Linton!' cried Cathy, kindling into joyful surprise at the name. 'Is that little Linton? He's taller than I am! Are you Linton?'

The youth stepped forward, and acknowledged himself: she kissed him fervently, and they gazed with wonder at the change time had wrought in the appearance of each. Catherine had reached her full height; her figure was both plump and slender, elastic as steel, and her whole aspect sparkling with health and spirits. Linton's looks and movements were very languid, and his form extremely slight; but there was a grace in his manner that mitigated these defects, and rendered him not unpleasing. After exchanging numerous marks of fondness with him his cousin went to Mr. Heathcliff, who lingered by the door, dividing his attention between the objects inside and those that lay without: pretending, that is, to observe the latter, and really noting the former alone.

'And you are my uncle, then!' she cried, reaching up to salute him. 'I thought I liked you, though you were cross at first. Why don't you visit at the Grange with Linton? To live all these years such close neighbours, and never see us, is odd: what have you done so for?'

'I visited it once or twice too often before you were born,' he answered. 'There—damn it! If you have any kisses to spare, give them to Linton: they are thrown away on me.'

'Naughty Ellen!' exclaimed Catherine, flying to attack me next with her lavish caresses. 'Wicked Ellen! to try to hinder me from entering. But I'll take this walk every morning in future: may I, uncle? and sometimes bring papa. Won't you be glad to see us?'

'Of course!' replied the uncle, with a hardly suppressed grimace, resulting from his deep aversion to both the proposed visitors. 'But stay,' he continued, turning towards the young lady. 'Now I think of it, I'd better tell you. Mr. Linton has a prejudice against me: we quarrelled at one time of our lives, with unchristian ferocity; and, if you mention coming here to him, he'll put a veto on your visits altogether. Therefore, you must not mention it, unless you be careless of seeing your cousin hereafter: you may come, if you will, but you must not mention it.'

'Why did you quarrel?' asked Catherine, considerably crestfallen.

'He thought me too poor to wed his sister,' answered Heathcliff, 'and was grieved that I got her: his pride was hurt, and he'll never forgive it.'

'That's wrong!' said the young lady: 'some time, I'll tell him so. But Linton and I have no share in your quarrel. I'll not come here, then; he shall come to the Grange.'

'It will be too far for me,' murmured her cousin: 'to walk four miles would kill me. No, come here, Miss Catherine, now and then: not every morning but once or twice a week.'

The father launched towards his son a glance of bitter contempt.

'I am afraid, Nelly, I shall lose my labour,' he muttered to me. 'Miss Catherine, as the ninny calls her, will discover his value, and send him to the devil. Now, if it had been Hareton!—Do you know that, twenty times a day, I covet Hareton, with all his degradation? I'd have loved the lad had he been some one else. But I think he's safe from *her* love. I'll pit him against that paltry creature, unless it bestir itself briskly. We calculate it will scarcely last till it is eighteen. Oh, confound the vapid thing! He's absorbed in drying his feet, and never looks at her.—Linton!'

'Yes, father,' answered the boy.

'Have you nothing to show your cousin anywhere about? not even a rabbit or a weasel's nest? Take her into the garden, before you change your shoes and into the stable to see your horse.'

'Wouldn't you rather sit here?' asked Linton, addressing Cathy in a tone which expressed reluctance to move again.

'I don't know,' she replied, casting a longing look to the door, and evidently eager to be active.

He kept his seat, and shrank closer to the fire. Heathcliff rose and went into the kitchen, and from thence to the yard, calling out for Hareton. Hareton responded, and presently the two re-entered. The young man had been washing himself, as was visible by the glow on his cheeks and his wetted hair.

'Oh, I'll ask *you*, uncle,' cried Miss Cathy, recollecting the housekeeper's assertion. 'That is not my cousin, is he?'

'Yes,' he replied, 'your mother's nephew. Don't you like him?'

Catherine looked queer.

'Is he not a handsome lad?' he continued.

The uncivil little thing stood on tiptoe, and whispered a sentence in Heathcliff's ear. He laughed; Hareton darkened: I perceived he was very sensitive to suspected slights, and had obviously a dim notion of his inferiority. But his master or guardian chased the frown by exclaiming:

'You'll be the favourite among us, Hareton! She says you are a—What was it? Well, something very flattering. Here! you go with her round the farm. And behave like a gentleman, mind! Don't use any bad words; and

don't stare when the young lady is not looking at you, and be ready to hide your face when she is; and, when you speak, say your words slowly, and keep your hands out of your pockets. Be off, and entertain her as nicely as you can.'

He watched the couple walking past the window. Earnshaw had his countenance completely averted from his companion. He seemed studying the familiar landscape with a stranger's and an artist's interest. Catherine took a sly look at him, expressing small admiration. She then turned her attention to seeking out objects of amusement for herself, and tripped merrily on, lilting a tune to supply the lack of conversation.

'I've tied his tongue,' observed Heathcliff. 'He'll not venture a single syllable, all the time! Nelly, you recollect me at his age—nay, some years younger. Did I ever look so stupid: so "gaumless," as Joseph calls it?'

'Worse,' I replied, 'because more sullen with it.'

'I've a pleasure in him' he continued, reflecting aloud. 'He has satisfied my expectations. If he were a born fool I should not enjoy it half so much. But he's no fool; and I can sympathise with all his feelings, having felt them myself I know what he suffers now, for instance, exactly: it is merely a beginning of what he shall suffer, though. And he'll never be able to emerge from his bathos of coarseness and ignorance. I've got him faster than his scoundrel of a father secured me, and lower; for he takes a pride in his brutishness. I've taught him to scorn everything extra-animal as silly and weak. Don't you think Hindley would be proud of his son, if he could see him? almost as proud as I am of mine. But there's this difference; one is gold put to the use of paving-stones, and the other is tin polished to ape a service of silver. *Mine* has nothing valuable about it; yet I shall have the merit of making it go as far as such poor stuff can go. *His* had first-rate qualities, and they are lost: rendered worse than unavailing. I have nothing to regret; he would have more than any but I are aware of. And the best of it is, Hareton is damnably fond of me! You'll own that I've out-matched Hindley there. If the dead villain could rise from his grave to abuse me for his offsprings's wrongs, I should have the fun of seeing the said offspring fight him back again, indignant that he should dare to rail at the one friend he has in the world!'

Heathcliff chuckled a fiendish laugh at the idea. I made no reply, because I saw that he expected none. Meantime, our young companion, who sat too removed from us to hear what was said, began to evince symptoms of uneasiness, probably repenting that he had denied himself the treat of Catherine's society for fear of a little fatigue. His father remarked the restless glances wandering to the window, and the hand irresolutely extended towards his cap.

'Get up, you idle boy!' he exclaimed, with assumed heartiness. 'Away after them! they are just at the corner, by the stand of hives.'

Linton gathered his energies, and left the hearth. The lattice was open,

and, as he stepped out, I heard Cathy inquiring of her unsociable attendant, what was that inscription over the door? Hareton stared up, and scratched his head like a true clown.

'It's some damnable writing,' he answered. 'I cannot read it.'

'Can't read it?' cried Catherine; 'I can read it: it's English. But I want to know why it is there.'

Linton giggled: the first appearance of mirth he had exhibited.

'He does not know his letters,' he said to his cousin. 'Could you believe in the existence of such a colossal dunce?'

'Is he all as he should be?' asked Miss Cathy seriously; 'or is he simple: not right? I've questioned him twice now, and each time he looked so stupid I think he does not understand me. I can hardly understand *him*, I'm sure!'

Linton repeated his laugh, and glanced at Hareton tauntingly; who certainly did not seem quite clear of comprehension at that moment.

'There's nothing the matter but laziness; is there, Earnshaw?' he said. 'My cousin fancies you are an idiot. There you experience the consequence of scorning "booklarning," as you would say. Have you noticed, Catherine, his frightful Yorkshire pronunciation?'

'Why, where the devil is the use on't?' growled Hareton, more ready in answering his daily companion. He was about to enlarge further, but the two youngsters broke into a noisy fit of merriment; my giddy miss being delighted to discover that she might turn his strange talk to matter of amusement.

'Where is the use of the devil in that sentence?' tittered Linton. 'Papa told you not to say any bad words, and you can't open your mouth without one Do try to behave like a gentleman, now do!'

'If thou weren't more a lass than a lad, I'd fell thee this minute, I would pitiful lath of a crater!' retorted the angry boor, retreating, while his face burnt with mingled rage and mortification; for he was conscious of being insulted, and embarrassed how to resent it.

Mr. Heathcliff having overheard the conversation, as well as I, smiled when he saw him go; but immediately afterwards cast a look of singular aversion on the flippant pair, who remained chattering in the doorway: the boy finding animation enough while discussing Hareton's faults and deficiencies and relating anecdotes of his goings-on; and the girl relishing his pert and spiteful sayings, without considering the ill-nature they evinced: but I began to dislike, more than to compassionate Linton, and to excuse his father, in some measure, for holding him cheap.

We stayed till afternoon: I could not tear Miss Cathy away, before; but happily my master had not quitted his apartment, and remained ignorant of our prolonged absence. As we walked home, I would fain have enlightened my charge on the characters of the people we had quitted; but she got it into her head that I was prejudiced against them.

'Aha!' she cried, 'you take papa's side, Ellen: you are partial, I know; or else you wouldn't have cheated me so many years into the notion that Linton lived a long way from here. I'm really extremely angry; only I'm so pleased I can't show it! But you must hold your tongue about my uncle: he's *my* uncle, remember; and I'll scold papa for quarrelling with him.'

And so she ran on, till I dropped endeavouring to convince her of her mistake. She did not mention the visit that night, because she did not see Mr. Linton. Next day it all came out, sadly to my chagrin; and still I was not altogether sorry: I thought the burden of directing and warning would be more efficiently borne by him than me. But he was too timid in giving satisfactory reasons for his wish that she should shun connection with the household of the Heights, and Catherine liked good reasons for every restraint that harassed her petted will.

'Papa!' she exclaimed, after the morning's salutations, 'guess whom I saw yesterday, in my walk on the moors. Ah, papa, you started! you've not done right, have you, now? I saw—But listen, and you shall hear how I found you out; and Ellen, who is in league with you, and yet pretended to pity me so, when I kept hoping, and was always disappointed about Linton's coming back!'

She gave a faithful account of her excursion and its consequences; and my master, though he cast more than one reproachful look at me, said nothing till she had concluded. Then he drew her to him, and asked if she knew why he had concealed Linton's near neighbourhood from her. Could she think it was to deny her a pleasure that she might harmlessly enjoy?

'It was because you disliked Mr. Heathcliff,' she answered.

'Then you believe I care more for my own feelings than yours, Cathy?' he said. 'No, it was not because I disliked Mr. Heathcliff, but because Mr. Heathcliff dislikes me; and is a most diabolical man, delighting to wrong and ruin those he hates, if they give him the slightest opportunity. I knew that you could not keep up an acquaintance with your cousin, without being brought into contact with him; and I knew he would detest you on my account; so for your own good, and nothing else, I took precautions that you should not see Linton again. I meant to explain this some time as you grew older, and I'm sorry I delayed it.'

'But Mr. Heathcliff was quite cordial, papa,' observed Catherine, not at all convinced; 'and *he* didn't object to our seeing each other: he said I might come to his house when I pleased; only I must not tell you, because you had quarrelled with him, and would not forgive him for marrying aunt Isabella. And you won't. *You* are the one to be blamed: he is willing to let *us* be friends, at least; Linton and I; and you are not.'

My master, perceiving that she would not take his word for her uncle-in-law's evil disposition, gave a hasty sketch of his conduct to Isabella, and the

manner in which Wuthering Heights became his property. He could not bear to discourse long upon the topic; for though he spoke little of it, he still felt the same horror and detestation of his ancient enemy that had occupied his heart ever since Mrs. Linton's death. 'She might have been living yet, if it had not been for him!' was his constant bitter reflection; and, in his eyes, Heathcliff seemed a murderer. Miss Cathy—conversant with no bad deeds except her own slight acts of disobedience, injustice, and passion, rising from hot temper and thoughtlessness, and repented of on the day they were committed—was amazed at the blackness of spirit that could brood on and cover revenge for years, and deliberately prosecute its plans without a visitation of remorse. She appeared so deeply impressed and shocked at this new view of human nature—excluded from all her studies and all her ideas till now—that Mr. Edgar deemed it unnecessary to pursue the subject. He merely added:

'You will know hereafter, darling, why I wish you to avoid his house and family; now return to your old employments and amusements, and think no more about them.'

Catherine kissed her father and sat down quietly to her lessons for a couple of hours, according to custom; then she accompanied him into the grounds, and the whole day passed as usual: but in the evening, when she had retired to her room, and I went to help her to undress, I found her crying, on her knees by the bedside.

'Oh, fie, silly child!' I exclaimed. 'If you had any real griefs, you'd be ashamed to waste a tear on this little contrariety. You never had one shadow of substantial sorrow, Miss Catherine. Suppose, for a minute, that master and I were dead, and you were by yourself in the world: how would you feel then? Compare the present occasion with such an affliction as that, and be thankful for the friends you have, instead of coveting more.'

'I'm not crying for myself, Ellen,' she answered, 'it's for him. He expected to see me again to-morrow, and there he'll be so disappointed: and he'll wait for me, and I shan't come!'

'Nonsense,' said I, 'do you imagine he has thought as much of you as you have of him? Hasn't he Hareton for a companion? Not one in a hundred would weep at losing a relation they had just seen twice, for two afternoons. Linton will conjecture how it is, and trouble himself no further about you.'

'But may I not write a note to tell him why I cannot come?' she asked, rising to her feet. 'And just send those books I promised to lend him? His books are not as nice as mine, and he wanted to have them extremely, when I told him how interesting they were. May I not, Ellen?'

'No, indeed! no, indeed!' replied I, with decision. 'Then he would write to you, and there'd never be an end of it. No, Miss Catherine, the acquaintance must be dropped entirely: so papa expects, and I shall see that it is done.'

'But how can one little note'——she recommenced, putting on an imploring countenance.

'Silence!' I interrupted. 'We'll not begin with your little notes. Get into bed.'

She threw at me a very naughty look, so naughty that I would not kiss her good-night at first: I covered her up, and shut her door, in great displeasure; but, repenting halfway, I returned softly, and lo! there was miss standing at the table with a bit of blank paper before her and a pencil in her hand, which she guiltily slipped out of sight, on my entrance.

'You'll get nobody to take that, Catherine,' I said, 'if you write it; and at present I shall put out your candle.'

I set the extinguisher on the flame, receiving as I did so a slap on my hand, and a petulant 'Cross thing!' I then quitted her again, and she drew the bolt in one of her worst, most peevish humours. The letter was finished and forwarded to its destination by a milk-fetcher who came from the village: but that I didn't learn till some time afterwards. Weeks passed on, and Cathy recovered her temper; though she grew wondrous fond of stealing off to corners by herself; and often, if I came near her suddenly while reading, she would start and bend over the book, evidently desirous to hide it; and I detected edges of loose paper sticking out beyond the leaves. She also got a trick of coming down early in the morning and lingering about the kitchen, as if she were expecting the arrival of something: and she had a small drawer in a cabinet in the library, which she would trifle over for hours, and whose key she took special care to remove when she left it.

One day, as she inspected this drawer, I observed that the playthings, and trinkets which recently formed its contents, were transmuted into bits of folded paper. My curiosity and suspicions were aroused; I determined to take a peep at her mysterious treasures; so, at night, as soon as she and my master were safe upstairs, I searched and readily found among my house-keys one that would fit the lock. Having opened, I emptied the whole contents into my apron, and took them with me to examine at leisure in my own chamber. Though I could not but suspect, I was still surprised to discover that they were a mass of correspondence—daily almost, it must have been—from Linton Heathcliff: answers to documents forwarded by her. The earlier dated were embarrassed and short; gradually, however, they expanded into copious love letters, foolish, as the age of the writer rendered natural, yet with touches here and there which I thought were borrowed from a more experienced source. Some of them struck me as singularly odd compounds of ardour and flatness; commencing in strong feeling, and concluding in the affected, wordy way that a schoolboy might use to a fancied, incorporeal sweetheart. Whether they satisfied Cathy, I don't know; but they appeared, very worthless trash to me. After turning over as many as I thought proper

I tied them in a handkerchief and set them aside, re-locking the vacant drawer.

Following her habit, my young lady descended early, and visited the kitchen: I watched her go to the door, on the arrival of a certain little boy; and, while the dairy-maid filled his can, she tucked something into his jacket pocket and plucked something out. I went round by the garden, and laid wait for the messenger; who fought valorously to defend his trust, and we spilt the milk between us; but I succeeded in abstracting the epistle; and, threatening serious consequences if he did not look sharp home, I remained under the wall and perused Miss Cathy's affectionate composition. It was more simple and more eloquent than her cousin's; very pretty and very silly. I shook my head, and went meditating into the house. The day being wet, she could not divert herself with rambling about the park; so at the conclusion of her morning studies, she resorted to the solace of the drawer. Her father sat reading at the table; and I, on purpose, had sought a bit of work in some unripped fringes of the window curtain, keeping my eye steadily fixed on her proceedings. Never did any bird flying back to a plundered nest which it had left brimful of chirping young ones, express more complete despair in its anguished cries and flutterings, than she by her single 'Oh!' and the change that transfigured her late happy countenance. Mr. Linton looked up.

'What is the matter, love? Have you hurt yourself?' he said.

His tone and look assured her *he* had not been the discoverer of the hoard.

'No, papa!' she gasped. 'Ellen! Ellen! come upstairs—I'm sick!'

I obeyed her summons, and accompanied her out.

'Oh, Ellen! you have got them,' she commenced immediately, dropping on her knees, when we were enclosed alone. 'Oh, give them to me, and I'll never, never do so again! Don't tell papa. You have not told papa, Ellen, say you have not? I've been exceedingly naughty, but I won't do it any more!'

With a grave severity in my manner, I bid her stand up.

'So,' I exclaimed, 'Miss Catherine, you are tolerably far on, it seems: you may well be ashamed of them! A fine bundle of trash you study in your leisure hours, to be sure: why, it's good enough to be printed! And what do you suppose the master will think, when I display it before him? I haven't shown it yet, but you needn't imagine I shall keep your ridiculous secret. For shame! and you must have led the way in writing such absurdities: he would not have thought of beginning, I'm certain.'

'I didn't! I didn't!' sobbed Cathy, fit to break her heart. 'I didn't once think of loving him till'——

'*Loving!*' cried I, as scornfully as I could utter the word. '*Loving!* Did anybody ever hear the like! I might just as well talk of loving the miller who comes once a year to buy our corn. Pretty loving, indeed! and both times together you have seen Linton hardly four hours in your life! Now here is the babyish

trash. I'm going with it to the library; and we'll see what your father says to such *loving*.'

She sprang at her precious epistles, but I held them above my head; and then she poured out further frantic entreaties that I would burn them—do anything rather than show them. And being really fully as inclined to laugh as scold—for I esteemed it all girlish vanity—I at length relented in a measure, and asked:

If I consent to burn them, will you promise faithfully neither to send nor receive a letter again, nor a book (for I perceive you have sent him books), nor locks of hair, nor rings, nor playthings?'

'We don't send playthings!' cried Catherine, her pride overcoming her shame.

'Nor anything at all, then, my lady,' I said. 'Unless you will, here I go.'
'I promise, Ellen!' she cried, catching my dress. 'Oh, put them in the fire, do, do!'

But when I proceeded to open a place with the poker, the sacrifice was too painful to be borne. She earnestly supplicated that I would spare her one or two.

'One or two, Ellen, to keep for Linton's sake!'

I unknotted the handkerchief, and commenced dropping them in from an angle, and the flame curled up the chimney.

'I will have one, you cruel wretch!' she screamed, darting her hand into the fire, and drawing forth some half consumed fragments, at the expense of her fingers.

'Very well—and I will have some to exhibit to papa!' I answered, shaking back the rest into the bundle, and turning anew to the door.

She emptied her blackened pieces into the flames, and motioned me to finish the immolation. It was done; I stirred up the ashes, and interred them under a shovelful of coals; and she mutely, and with a sense of intense injury, retired to her private apartment. I descended to tell my master that the young lady's qualm of sickness was almost gone, but I judged it best for her to lie down a while. She wouldn't dine; but she reappeared at tea, pale, and red about the eyes, and marvellously subdued in outward aspect. Next morning, I answered the letter by a slip of paper, inscribed, 'Master Heathcliff requested to send no more notes to Miss Linton, as she will not receive them.' And, thenceforth, the little boy came with vacant pockets.

CHAPTER 22

Summer drew to an end, and early autumn: it was past Michaelmas, but the harvest was late that year, and a few of our fields were still uncleared. Mr. Linton and his daughter would frequently walk out among the reapers; at the carrying of the last sheaves, they stayed till dusk, and the evening happening to be chill and damp, my master caught a bad cold, that settling obstinately on his lungs, confined him indoors throughout the whole of the winter, nearly without intermission.

Poor Cathy, frightened from her little romance, had been considerably sadder and duller since its abandonment; and her father insisted on her reading less, and taking more exercise. She had his companionship no longer; I esteemed it a duty to supply its lack, as much as possible, with mine: an inefficient substitute; for I could only spare two or three hours, from my numerous diurnal occupations, to follow her footsteps, and then my society was obviously less desirable than his.

On an afternoon in October, or the beginning of November—a fresh watery afternoon, when the turf and paths were rustling with moist, withered leaves, and the cold, blue sky was half hidden by clouds—dark grey streamers rapidly mounting from the west, and boding abundant rain—I requested my young lady to forego her ramble, because I was certain of showers. She refused; and I unwillingly donned a cloak, and took my umbrella to accompany her on a stroll to the bottom of the park: a formal walk which she generally affected if low-spirited—and that she invariably was when Mr. Edgar had been worse than ordinary, a thing never known from his confession, but guessed both by her and me, from his increased silence and the melancholy of his countenance. She went sadly on: there was no running or bounding now, though the chill wind might well have tempted her to a race. And often, from the side of my eye, I could detect her raising a hand, and brushing something off her cheek. I gazed round for a means of diverting her thoughts. On one side of the road rose a high, rough bank, where hazels and stunted oaks, with their roots half-exposed, held uncertain tenure: the soil was too loose for the latter; and strong winds had blown some nearly horizontal. In summer Miss Catherine delighted to climb along these trunks, and sit in the branches swinging twenty feet above the ground; and I, pleased with her agility and her light, childish heart, still considered it proper to scold every time I caught her at such an elevation, but so that she knew there was no necessity for descending. From dinner to tea she would lie in her breeze-rocked cradle, doing nothing except singing old songs—my nursery lore—to herself, or watching the birds, joint tenants, feed and entice their young ones to fly: or nestling with closed lids, half thinking, half dreaming, happier than words can express.

'Look, miss!' I exclaimed, pointing to a nook under the roots of one twisted tree. 'Winter is not here yet. There's a little flower up yonder, the last bud from the multitude of bluebells that clouded those turf steps in July with a lilac mist. Will you clamber up, and pluck it to show to papa?'

Cathy stared a long time at the lonely blossom trembling in its earthy shelter, and replied, at length:

'No, I'll not touch it: but it looks melancholy, does it not, Ellen?'

'Yes,' I observed, 'about as starved and sackless as you: your cheeks are bloodless; let us take hold of hands and run. You're so low, I dare say I shall keep up with you.'

'No,' she repeated, and continued sauntering on, pausing, at intervals, to muse over a bit of moss, or a tuft of blanched grass, or a fungus spreading its bright orange among the heaps of brown foliage; and, ever and anon, her hand was lifted to her averted face.

'Catherine, why are you crying, love?' I asked, approaching and putting my arm over her shoulder. 'You mustn't cry because papa has a cold; be thankful it is nothing worse.'

She now put no further restraint on her tears; her breath was stifled by sobs.

'Oh, it *will* be something worse,' she said. 'And what shall I do when papa and you leave me, and I am by myself? I can't forget your words, Ellen; they are always in my ear. How life will be changed, how dreary the world will be, when papa and you are dead.'

'None can tell, whether you won't die before us,' I replied. 'It's wrong to anticipate evil. We'll hope there are years and years to come before any of us go: master is young, and I am strong, and hardly forty-five. My mother lived till eighty, a canty dame to the last. And suppose Mr. Linton were spared till he saw sixty, that would be more years than you have counted, miss. And would it not be foolish to mourn a calamity above twenty years beforehand?'

'But Aunt Isabella was younger than papa,' she remarked, gazing up with timid hope to seek further consolation.

'Aunt Isabella had not you and me to nurse her,' I replied. 'She wasn't as happy as master: she hadn't as much to live for. All you need do, is to wait well on your father, and cheer him by letting him see you cheerful; and avoid giving him anxiety on any subject: mind that, Cathy! I'll not disguise but you might kill him, if you were wild and reckless, and cherished a foolish, fanciful affection for the son of a person who would be glad to have him in his grave; and allowed him to discover that you fretted over the separation he has judged it expedient to make.'

'I fret about nothing on earth except papa's illness,' answered my companion. 'I care for nothing in comparison with papa. And I'll never—never—oh,

never, while I have my senses, do an act or say a word to vex him. I love him better than myself, Ellen; and I know it by this: I pray every night that I may live after him; because I would rather be miserable than that he should be: that proves I love him better than myself.'

'Good words,' I replied. 'But deeds must prove it also; and after he is well, remember you don't forget resolutions formed in the hour of fear.'

As we talked, we neared a door that opened on the road; and my young lady, lightening into sunshine again, climbed up and seated herself on the top of the wall, reaching over to gather some hips that bloomed scarlet on the summit branches of the wild rose trees, shadowing the highway side: the lower fruit had disappeared, but only birds could touch the upper, except from Cathy's present station. In stretching to pull them, her hat fell off; and as the door was locked, she proposed scrambling down to recover it. I bid her be cautious lest she got a fall, and she nimbly disappeared. But the return was no such easy matter: the stones were smooth and neatly cemented, and the rosebushes and blackberry stragglers could yield no assistance in re-ascending. I, like a fool, didn't recollect that, till I heard her laughing and exclaiming:

'Ellen, you'll have to fetch the key, or else I must run round to the porter's lodge. I can't scale the ramparts on this side!'

'Stay where you are,' I answered, 'I have my bundle of keys in my pocket; perhaps I may manage to open it; if not I'll go.'

Catherine amused herself with dancing to and fro before the door, while I tried all the large keys in succession. I had applied the last, and found that none would do; so, repeating my desire that she would remain there, I was about to hurry home as fast as I could, when an approaching sound arrested me. It was the trot of a horse; Cathy's dance stopped, and in a minute the horse stopped also.

'Who is that?' I whispered.

'Ellen, I wish you could open the door,' whispered back my companion anxiously.

'Ho, Miss Linton!' cried a deep voice (the rider's), 'I'm glad to meet you. Don't be in haste to enter, for I have an explanation to ask and obtain.'

'I shan't speak to you, Mr. Heathcliff,' answered Catherine. 'Papa says you are a wicked man, and you hate both him and me; and Ellen says the same.'

'That is nothing to the purpose,' said Heathcliff. (He it was.) 'I don't hate my son, I suppose; and it is concerning him that I demand your attention. Yes; you have cause to blush. Two or three months since, were you not in the habit of writing to Linton? making love in play, eh? You deserved, both of you, flogging for that! You especially, the elder; and less sensitive, as it turns out. I've got your letters, and if you give me any pertness I'll send

them to your father. I presume you grew weary of the amusement and dropped it, didn't you? Well, you dropped Linton with it into a Slough of Despond. He was in earnest: in love, really. As true as I live, he's dying for you; breaking his heart at your fickleness: not figuratively, but actually. Though Hareton has made him a standing jest for six weeks, and I have used more serious measures, and attempted to frighten him out of his idiotcy, he gets worse daily; and he'll be under the sod before summer, unless you restore him!'

'How can you lie so glaringly to the poor child?' I called from the inside. 'Pray ride on! How can you deliberately get up such paltry falsehoods? Miss Cathy, I'll knock the lock off with a stone: you won't believe that vile nonsense. You can feel in yourself, it is impossible that a person should die for love of a stranger.'

'I was not aware there were eavesdroppers,' muttered the detected villain. 'Worthy Mrs. Dean, I like you, but I don't like your double-dealing,' he added aloud. 'How could *you* lie so glaringly, as to affirm I hated the "poor child"? and invent bugbear stories to terrify her from my door-stones? Cathe-ine Linton (the very name warms me), my bonnie lass, I shall be from home all this week; go and see if I have not spoken truth: do, there's a darling! Just imagine your father in my place, and Linton in yours; then think how you would value your careless lover if he refused to stir a step to comfort you, when your father himself entreated him; and don't, from pure stupidity, fall into the same error. I swear, on my salvation, he's going to his grave, and none but you can save him!'

The lock gave way and I issued out.

'I swear Linton is dying,' repeated Heathcliff, looking hard at me. 'And grief and disappointment are hastening his death. Nelly, if you won't let her go, you can walk over yourself. But I shall not return till this time next week; and I think your master himself would scarcely object to her visiting her cousin!'

'Come in,' said I, taking Cathy by the arm and half-forcing her to re-enter; for she lingered, viewing with troubled eyes the features of the speaker, too stern to express his inward deceit.

He pushed his horse close, and, bending down, observed:

'Miss Catherine, I'll own to you that I have little patience with Linton; and Hareton and Joseph have less. I'll own that he's with a harsh set. He pines for kindness, as well as love; and a kind word from you would be his best medicine. Don't mind Mrs. Dean's cruel cautions; but be generous, and contrive to see him. He dreams of you day and night, and cannot be persuaded that you don't hate him, since you neither write nor call.'

I closed the door, and rolled a stone to assist the loosened lock in holding it; and spreading my umbrella, I drew my charge underneath: for the rain began to drive through the moaning branches of the trees, and warned us to

avoid delay. Our hurry prevented any comment on the encounter with Heathcliff, as we stretched towards home; but I divined instinctively that Catherine's heart was clouded now in double darkness. Her features were so sad, they did not seem hers: she evidently regarded what she had heard as every syllable true.

The master had retired to rest before we came in. Cathy stole to his room to inquire how he was; he had fallen asleep. She returned, and asked me to sit with her in the library. We took our tea together; and afterwards she lay down on the rug, and told me not to talk, for she was weary. I got a book and pretended to read. As soon as she supposed me absorbed in my occupation she recommenced her silent weeping: it appeared, at present, her favourite diversion. I suffered her to enjoy it a while; then I expostulated: deriding and ridiculing all Mr. Heathcliff's assertions about his son, as if I were certain she would coincide. Alas! I hadn't skill to counteract the effect his account had produced: it was just what he intended.

'You may be right, Ellen,' she answered; 'but I shall never feel at ease till I know. And I must tell Linton it is not my fault that I don't write, and convince him that I shall not change.'

What use were anger and protestations against her silly credulity? We parted that night—hostile; but next day beheld me on the road to Wuthering Heights, by the side of my wilful young mistress's pony. I couldn't bear to witness her sorrow: to see her pale dejected countenance, and heavy eyes: and I yielded, in the faint hope that Linton himself might prove, by his reception of us, how little of the tale was founded on fact.

CHAPTER 23

The rainy night had ushered in a misty morning—half-frost, half-drizzle—and temporary brooks crossed our path—gurgling from the uplands. My feet were thoroughly wetted; I was cross and low; exactly the humour suited for making the most of these disagreeable things. We entered the farmhouse by the kitchen way, to ascertain whether Mr. Heathcliff were really absent; because I put slight faith in his own affirmation.

Joseph seemed sitting in a sort of elysium alone, beside a roaring fire: a quart of ale on the table near him, bristling with large pieces of toasted oat-cake; and his black, short pipe in his mouth. Catherine ran to the hearth to warm herself. I asked if the master was in? My question remained so long unanswered, that I thought the old man had grown deaf, and repeated it louder.

'Na—ay!' he snarled, or rather screamed through his nose. 'Na—ay! ya

muh goa back whear yah coom frough.'

'Joseph!' cried a peevish voice, simultaneously with me, from the inner room. 'How often am I to call you? There are only a few red ashes now. Joseph! come this moment.'

Vigorous puffs, and a resolute stare into the grate declared he had no ear for this appeal. The housekeeper and Hareton were invisible; one gone on an errand, and the other at his work, probably. We knew Linton's tones, and entered.

'Oh, I hope you'll die in a garret! starved to death,' said the boy, mistaking our approach for that of his negligent attendant.

He stopped, on observing his error; his cousin flew to him.

'Is that you, Miss Linton?' he said, raising his head from the arm of the great chair, in which he reclined. 'No—don't kiss me: it takes my breath. Dear me! Papa said you would call,' continued he, after recovering a little from Catherine's embrace; while she stood by looking very contrite. 'Will you shut the door, if you please? you left it open; and those—those *detestable* creatures won't bring coals to the fire. It's so cold!'

I stirred up the cinders, and fetched a scuttleful myself. The invalid complained of being covered with ashes; but he had a tiresome cough, and looked feverish and ill, so I did not rebuke his temper.

'Well, Linton,' murmured Catherine, when his corrugated brow relaxed. 'Are you glad to see me? Can I do you any good?'

'Why didn't you come before?' he asked. 'You should have come, instead of writing. It tired me dreadfully, writing those long letters. I'd far rather have talked to you. Now, I can neither bear to talk, nor anything else. I wonder where Zillah is! Will you (looking at me) step into the kitchen and see?'

I had received no thanks for my other service; and being unwilling to run to and fro at his behest, I replied:

'Nobody is out there but Joseph.'

'I want to drink,' he exclaimed fretfully, turning away. 'Zillah is constantly gadding off to Gimmerton since papa went: it's miserable! And I'm obliged to come down here—they resolved never to hear me upstairs.'

'Is your father attentive to you, Master Heathcliff?' I asked, perceiving Catherine to be checked in her friendly advances.

'Attentive? He makes *them* a little more attentive at least,' he cried. 'The wretches! Do you know, Miss Linton, that brute Hareton laughs at me! I hate him! indeed, I hate them all: they are odious beings.'

Cathy began searching for some water; she lighted on a pitcher in the dresser, filled a tumbler, and brought it. He bid her add a spoonful of wine from a bottle on the table; and having swallowed a small portion, appeared more tranquil, and said she was very kind.

'And are you glad to see me?' asked she, reiterating her former question,

and pleased to detect the faint dawn of a smile.

'Yes, I am. It's something new to hear a voice like yours!' he replied. 'But I *have* been vexed, because you wouldn't come. And papa swore it was owing to me: he called me a pitiful, shuffling, worthless thing; and said you despised me; and if he had been in my place, he would be more the master of the Grange than your father, by this time. But you don't despise me, do you, Miss'——

'I wish you would say Catherine, or Cathy,' interrupted my young lady. 'Despise you? No! Next to papa and Ellen, I love you better than anybody living. I don't love Mr. Heathcliff, though; and I dare not come when he returns; will he stay away many days?'

'Not many,' answered Linton; 'but he goes on to the moors frequently since the shooting season commenced; and you might spend an hour or two with me in his absence. Do say you will. I think I should not be peevish with you: you'd not provoke me, and you'd always be ready to help me wouldn't you?'

'Yes,' said Catherine, stroking his long soft hair; 'if I could only get papa's consent, I'd spend half my time with you. Pretty Linton! I wish you were my brother.'

'And then you would like me as well as your father?' observed he, more cheerfully. 'But papa says you would love me better than him and all the world if you were my wife; so I'd rather you were that.'

'No, I should never love anybody better than papa,' she returned gravely. And people hate their wives, sometimes; but not their sisters and brothers; and if you were the latter you would live with us, and papa would be as fond of you as he is of me.'

Linton denied that people ever hated their wives; but Cathy affirmed they did, and, in her wisdom, instanced his own father's aversion to her aunt. I endeavoured to stop her thoughtless tongue. I couldn't succeed till everything she knew was out. Master Heathcliff, much irritated, asserted her relation was false.

'Papa told me; and papa does not tell falsehoods,' she answered pertly.

'*My* papa scorns yours!' cried Linton. 'He calls him a sneaking fool!'

'Yours is a wicked man,' retorted Catherine, 'and you are very naughty to dare to repeat what he says. He must be wicked to have made Aunt Isabella leave him as she did!'

'She didn't leave him,' said the boy; 'you shan't contradict me!'

'She did!' cried my young lady.

'Well, I'll tell *you* something!' said Linton. 'Your mother hated your father, now then.'

'Oh!' exclaimed Catherine, too enraged to continue.

'And she loved mine!' added he.

'You little liar! I hate you now,' she panted, and her face grew red with passion.

'She did! she did!' sang Linton, sinking into the recess of his chair, and leaning back his head to enjoy the agitation of the other disputant, who stood behind.

'Hush, Master Heathcliff!' I said; 'that's your father's tale, too, I suppose.'

'It isn't: you hold your tongue!' he answered. 'She did, she did, Catherine! she did, she did!'

Cathy, beside herself, gave the chair a violent push, and caused him to fall against one arm. He was immediately seized by a suffocating cough that soon ended his triumph. It lasted so long that it frightened even me. As to his cousin, she wept, with all her might; aghast at the mischief she had done: though she said nothing. I held him till the fit exhausted itself. Then he thrust me away, and leant his head down silently. Catherine quelled her lamentations also, took a seat opposite, and looked solemnly into the fire.

'How do you feel now, Master Heathcliff?' I inquired, after waiting ten minutes.

'I wish *she* felt as I do,' he replied: 'spiteful, cruel thing! Hareton never touches me: he never struck me in his life. And I was better to-day: and there' ——his voice died in a whimper.

'*I* didn't strike you!' muttered Cathy, chewing her lip to prevent another burst of emotion.

He sighed and moaned like one under great suffering, and kept it up for a quarter of an hour; on purpose to distress his cousin apparently, for whenever he caught a stifled sob from her he put renewed pain and pathos into the inflections of his voice.

'I'm sorry I hurt you, Linton,' she said at length, racked beyond endurance. 'But *I* couldn't have been hurt by that little push, and I had no idea that you could, either: you're not much, are you, Linton? Don't let me go home thinking I've done you harm. Answer! speak to me.'

'I can't speak to you,' he murmured; 'you've hurt me so, that I shall lie awake all night choking with this cough. If you had it you'd know what it was; but *you'll* be comfortably asleep while I'm in agony, and nobody near me. I wonder how you would like to pass those fearful nights!' And he began to wail aloud, for very pity of himself.

'Since you are in the habit of passing dreadful nights,' I said, 'it won't be miss who spoils your ease: you'd be the same had she never come. However, she shall not disturb you again; and perhaps you'll get quieter when we leave you.'

'Must I go?' asked Catherine dolefully, bending over him. 'Do you want me to go, Linton?'

'You can't alter what you've done,' he replied pettishly, shrinking from

her, 'unless you alter it for the worse by teasing me into a fever.'

'Well, then, I must go?' she repeated.

'Let me alone, at least,' said he; 'I can't bear your talking.'

She lingered, and resisted my persuasions to departure a tiresome while but as he neither looked up nor spoke, she finally made a movement to the door and I followed. We were recalled by a scream. Linton had slid from his seat on to the hearthstone, and lay writhing in the mere perverseness of an indulged plague of a child, determined to be as grievous and harassing as he can. I thoroughly gauged his disposition from his behaviour, and saw at once it would be folly to attempt humouring him. Not so my companion: she ran back in terror, knelt down, and cried, and soothed, and entreated, till he grew quiet from lack of breath: by no means from compunction at distressing her.

'I shall lift him on the settle,' I said, 'and he may roll about as he pleases we can't stop to watch him. I hope you are satisfied, Miss Cathy, that you are not the person to benefit him; and that his condition of health is no occasioned by attachment to you. Now, then, there he is! Come away: as soon as he knows there is nobody by to care for his nonsense, he'll be glad to lie still.'

She placed a cushion under his head, and offered him some water; he rejected the latter, and tossed uneasily on the former, as if it were a stone or a block of wood. She tried to put it more comfortably.

'I can't do with that,' he said; 'it's not high enough.'

Catherine brought another to lay above it.

'That's *too* high,' murmured the provoking thing.

'How must I arrange it, then?' she asked despairingly.

He twined himself up to her, as she half knelt by the settle, and converted her shoulder into a support.

'No, that won't do,' I said. 'You'll be content with the cushion, Master Heathcliff. Miss has wasted too much time on you already: we cannot remain five minutes longer.'

'Yes, yes, we can!' replied Cathy. 'He's good and patient now. He's beginning to think I shall have far greater misery than he will to-night, if I believe he is the worse for my visit; and then I dare not come again. Tell the truth about it, Linton; for I mustn't come, if I have hurt you.'

'You must come, to cure me,' he answered. 'You ought to come, because you have hurt me: you know you have extremely! I was not as ill when you entered as I am at present—was I?'

'But you've made yourself ill by crying and being in a passion.'

'I didn't do it at all,' said his cousin. 'However, we'll be friends now. And you want me: you would wish to see me sometimes, really?'

'I told you I did,' he replied impatiently. 'Sit on the settle and let me lean

n your knee. That's as mamma used to do, whole afternoons together. Sit quite still and don't talk: but you may sing a song, if you can sing; or you may say a nice long interesting ballad—one of those you promised to teach me: or a story. I'd rather have a ballad, though: begin.'

Catherine repeated the longest she could remember. The employment pleased both mightily. Linton would have another; and after that another, notwithstanding my strenuous objections; and so they went on until the clock struck twelve, and we heard Hareton in the court, returning for his dinner.

'And to-morrow, Catherine, will you be here to-morrow?' asked young Heathcliff, holding her frock as she rose reluctantly.

'No,' I answered, 'nor next day neither.' She, however, gave a different response evidently, for his forehead cleared as she stooped and whispered in his ear.

'You won't go to-morrow, recollect, miss!' I commenced, when we were out of the house. 'You are not dreaming of it, are you?'

She smiled.

'Oh, I'll take good care,' I continued: 'I'll have that lock mended, and you can escape by no way else.'

'I can get over the wall,' she said, laughing. 'The Grange is not a prison, Ellen, and you are not my gaoler. And besides, I'm almost seventeen: I'm a woman. And I'm certain Linton would recover quickly if he had me to look after him. I'm older than he is, you know, and wiser: less childish, am I not? And he'll soon do as I direct him, with some slight coaxing. He's a pretty little darling when he's good. I'd make such a pet of him, if he were mine. We should never quarrel, should we, after we were used to each other? Don't you like him, Ellen?'

'Like him?' I exclaimed. 'The worst-tempered bit of a sickly slip that ever struggled into its teens. Happily, as Mr. Heathcliff conjectured, he'll not win twenty. I doubt whether he'll see spring, indeed. And small loss to his family whenever he drops off. And lucky it is for us that his father took him: the kinder he was treated, the more tedious and selfish he'd be. I'm glad you have no chance of having him for a husband, Miss Catherine.'

My companion waxed serious at hearing this speech. To speak of his death so regardlessly, wounded her feelings.

'He's younger than I,' she answered, after a protracted pause of meditation, 'and he ought to live the longest: he will—he must live as long as I do. He's as strong now as when he first came into the north; I'm positive of that. It's only a cold that ails him, the same as papa has. You say papa will get better, and why shouldn't he?'

'Well, well,' I cried, 'after all, we needn't trouble ourselves; for listen, miss, and mind, I'll keep my word,—if you attempt going to Wuthering Heights

again, with or without me, I shall inform Mr. Linton, and, unless he allow it, the intimacy with your cousin must not be revived.'

'It has been revived,' muttered Cathy sulkily.

'Must not be continued, then,' I said.

'We'll see,' was her reply, and she set off at a gallop, leaving me to toil in the rear.

We both reached home before our dinner-time; my master supposed we had been wandering through the park, and therefore he demanded no explanation of our absence. As soon as I entered, I hastened to change my soaked shoes and stockings; but sitting such a while at the Heights had done the mischief. On the succeeding morning I was laid up, and during three weeks I remained incapacitated for attending to my duties: a calamity never experienced prior to that period, and never, I am thankful to say, since.

My little mistress behaved like an angel, in coming to wait on me, and cheer my solitude: the confinement brought me exceedingly low. It is wearisome, to a stirring active body: but few have slighter reasons for complaint than I had. The moment Catherine left Mr. Linton's room, she appeared at my bedside. Her day was divided between us; no amusement usurped a minute she neglected her meals, her studies, and her play; and she was the fondest nurse that ever watched. She must have had a warm heart, when she loved her father so, to give so much to me. I said her days were divided between us; but the master retired early, and I generally needed nothing after six o'clock thus the evening was her own. Poor thing! I never considered what she did with herself after tea. And though frequently, when she looked in to bid me good-night, I remarked a fresh colour in her cheeks and a pinkness over her slender fingers; instead of fancying the hue borrowed from a cold ride across the moors, I laid it to the charge of a hot fire in the library.

CHAPTER 24

AT the close of three weeks, I was able to quit my chamber, and move about the house. And on the first occasion of my sitting up in the evening, I asked Catherine to read to me, because my eyes were weak. We were in the library the master having gone to bed: she consented, rather unwillingly, I fancied and imagining my sort of books did not suit her, I bid her place herself in the choice of what she perused. She selected one of her own favourites, and got forward steadily about an hour; then came frequent questions.

'Ellen, are not you tired? Hadn't you better lie down now? You'll be sick keeping up so long, Ellen.'

'No, no, dear, I'm not tired,' I returned continually.

Perceiving me immovable, she essayed another method of showing her

disrelish for her occupation. It changed to yawning, and stretching, and: 'Ellen, I'm tired.'

'Give over then and talk,' I answered.

That was worse: she fretted and sighed, and looked at her watch till eight, and finally went to her room, completely over-done with sleep; judging by her peevish, heavy look, and the constant rubbing she inflicted on her eyes. The following night she seemed more impatient still; and on the third from recovering my company, she complained of a headache, and left me. I thought her conduct odd; and having remained alone a long while, I resolved on going and inquiring whether she were better, and asking her to come and lie on the sofa, instead of upstairs in the dark. No Catherine could I discover upstairs, and none below. The servants affirmed they had not seen her. I listened at Mr. Edgar's door; all was silence. I returned to her apartment, extinguished my candle, and seated myself in the window.

The moon shone bright; a sprinkling of snow covered the ground, and reflected that she might, possibly, have taken it into her head to walk about the garden, for refreshment. I did detect a figure creeping along the inner fence of the park; but it was not my young mistress: on its merging into the light, I recognised one of the grooms. He stood a considerable period, viewing the carriage-road through the grounds; then started off at a brisk pace, as if he had detected something, and reappeared presently, leading miss's pony; and there she was, just dismounted, and walking by its side. The man took his charge stealthily across the grass towards the stable. Cathy entered by the casement-window of the drawing-room, and glided noiselessly up to where I awaited her. She put the door gently to, slipped off her snowy shoes, untied her hat, and was proceeding, unconscious of my espionage, to lay aside her mantle, when I suddenly rose and revealed myself. The surprise petrified her an instant: she uttered an inarticulate exclamation, and stood fixed.

'My dear Miss Catherine,' I began, too vividly impressed by her recent kindness to break into a scold, 'where have you been riding out at this hour? And why should you try to deceive me, by telling a tale? Where have you been? Speak.'

'To the bottom of the park,' she stammered. 'I didn't tell a tale.'

'And nowhere else?' I demanded.

'No,' was the muttered reply.

'Oh, Catherine!' I cried sorrowfully. 'You know you have been doing wrong, or you wouldn't be driven to uttering an untruth to me. That does grieve me. I'd rather be three months ill, than hear you frame a deliberate lie.'

She sprang forward, and bursting into tears, threw her arms round my neck. 'Well, Ellen, I'm so afraid of you being angry,' she said. 'Promise not to be angry, and you shall know the very truth: I hate to hide it.'

We sat down in the window-seat; I assured her I would not scold, whatever her secret might be, and I guessed it of course; so she commenced:

'I've been to Wuthering Heights, Ellen, and I've never missed going a day since you fell ill; except thrice before, and twice after you left your room. I gave Michael books and pictures to prepare Minny every evening, and to put her back in the stable: you mustn't scold *him* either, mind. I was at the Heights by half-past six, and generally stayed till half-past eight, and then galloped home. It was not to amuse myself that I went: I was often wretched all the time. Now and then I was happy; once in a week perhaps. At first, I expected there would be sad work persuading you to let me keep my word to Linton: for I had engaged to call again next day, when we quitted him; but, as you stayed upstairs on the morrow, I escaped that trouble; and while Michael was refastening the lock of the park door in the afternoon, I got possession of the key, and told him how my cousin wished me to visit him, because he was sick, and couldn't come to the Grange; and how papa would object to my going: and then I negotiated with him about the pony. He is fond of reading, and he thinks of leaving soon to get married so he offered, if I would lend him books out of the library, to do what I wished but I preferred giving him my own, and that satisfied him better.

'On my second visit, Linton seemed in lively spirits; and Zillah (that is their housekeeper) made us a clean room and a good fire, and told us that as Joseph was out at a prayer-meeting and Hareton Earnshaw was off with his dogs—robbing our woods of pheasants, as I heard afterwards—we might do what we liked. She brought me some warm wine and gingerbread, and appeared exceedingly good-natured; and Linton sat in the arm chair and I in the little rocking-chair on the hearth-stone, and we laughed and talked so merrily, and found so much to say: we planned where we would go, and what we would do in summer. I needn't repeat that, because you would call it silly.

'One time, however, we were near quarrelling. He said the pleasantest manner of spending a hot July day was lying from morning till evening on a bank of heath in the middle of the moors, with the bees humming dreamily about among the bloom, and the larks singing high up overhead, and the blue sky and bright sun shining steadily and cloudlessly. That was his most perfect idea of heaven's happiness: mine was rocking in a rustling green tree with a west wind blowing, and bright white clouds flitting rapidly above and not only larks, but throstles, and blackbirds, and linnets, and cuckoo pouring out music on every side, and the moors seen at a distance, broken into cool dusky dells; but close by great swells of long grass undulating in waves to the breeze; and woods and sounding water, and the whole world awake and wild with joy. He wanted all to lie in an ecstasy of peace; I wanted all to sparkle and dance in a glorious jubilee. I said his heaven would be only

alf alive; and he said mine would be drunk: I said I should fall asleep in
is; and he said he could not breathe in mine, and began to grow very snappish.
t last, we agreed to try both, as soon as the right weather came; and then we
issed each other and were friends.

'After sitting still an hour, I looked at the great room with its smooth un-
arpeted floor, and thought how nice it would be to play in, if we removed
ie table; and I asked Linton to call Zillah in to help us, and we'd have
game at blind-man's buff; she should try to catch us: you used to, you know,
llen. He wouldn't: there was no pleasure in it, he said; but he consented to
lay at ball with me. We found two in a cupboard, among a heap of old toys,
ips, and hoops, and battledores, and shuttlecocks. One was marked C.,
nd the other H.; I wished to have the C., because that stood for Catherine,
nd the H. might be for Heathcliff, his name; but the bran came out of H.,
nd Linton didn't like it. I beat him constantly, and he got cross again,
nd coughed, and returned to his chair. That night, though, he easily reco-
ered his good humour: he was charmed with two or three pretty songs—*your*
ings, Ellen; and when I was obliged to go, he begged and entreated me
i come the following evening; and I promised. Minny and I went flying
ome as light as air; and I dreamt of Wuthering Heights and my sweet, darling
ousin, till morning.

'On the morrow I was sad; partly because you were poorly, and partly that
wished my father knew, and approved of my excursions: but it was beautiful
ioonlight after tea; and, as I rode on, the gloom cleared. I shall have another
appy evening, I thought to myself; and what delights me more, my pretty
inton will. I trotted up their garden, and was turning round to the back,
hen that fellow Earnshaw met me, took my bridle, and bid me go in by
ie front entrance. He patted Minny's neck, and said she was a bonny beast,
nd appeared as if he wanted me to speak to him. I only told him to leave
iy horse alone, or else it would kick him. He answered in his vulgar
ccent, "It wouldn't do mitch hurt if it did"; and surveyed its legs with a smile.
was half inclined to make it try; however, he moved off to open the door,
nd, as he raised the latch, he looked up to the inscription above, and
iid, with a stupid mixture of awkwardness and elation:

' "Miss Catherine! I can read yon, nah."

' "Wonderful," I exclaimed. "Pray let us hear you—you *are* grown clever!"

'He spelt, and drawled over by syllables, the name—"Hareton Earnshaw."

' "And the figures?" I cried encouragingly, perceiving that he came to
dead halt.

' "I cannot tell them yet," he answered.

' "Oh, you dunce!" I said, laughing heartily at his failure.

'The fool stared, with a grin hovering about his lips, and a scowl gathering
ver his eyes, as if uncertain whether he might not join in my mirth: whether

it were not pleasant familiarity, or what it really was, contempt. I settled hi
doubts, by suddenly retrieving my gravity and desiring him to walk away
for I came to see Linton, not him. He reddened—I saw that by the moonligh
—dropped his hand from the latch, and skulked off, a picture of mortifie
vanity. He imagined himself to be as accomplished as Linton, I suppose
because he could spell his own name; and was marvellously discomfited tha
I didn't think the same.'

'Stop, Miss Catherine, dear!' I interrupted. 'I shall not scold, but I don
like your conduct there. If you had remembered that Hareton was you
cousin as much as Master Heathcliff, you would have felt how improper
it was to behave in that way. At least, it was praiseworthy ambition for hir
to desire to be as accomplished as Linton; and probably he did not learn merel
to show off: you had made him ashamed of his ignorance before, I have n
doubt; and he wished to remedy it and please you. To sneer at his imperfec
attempt was very bad breeding. Had *you* been brought up in his circumstance
would you be less rude? He was as quick and as intelligent a child as ever yo
were; and I'm hurt that he should be despised now, because that base Heat
cliff has treated him so unjustly.'

'Well, Ellen, you won't cry about it, will you?' she exclaimed, surprised a
my earnestness. 'But wait, and you shall hear if he conned his A B C to pleas
me; and if it were worth while being civil to the brute. I entered; Linto
was lying on the settle, and half got up to welcome me.

' "I'm ill to-night, Catherine, love," he said; "and you must have all th
talk, and let me listen. Come, and sit by me. I was sure you wouldn't brea
your word, and I'll make you promise again, before you go."

'I knew now that I mustn't tease him, as he was ill; and I spoke softly an
put no questions, and avoided irritating him in any way. I had brought son
of my nicest books for him; he asked me to read a little of one, and I wa
about to comply, when Earnshaw burst the door open: having gathere
venom with reflection. He advanced direct to us, seized Linton by the arn
and swung him off the seat.

' "Get to thy own room!" he said, in a voice almost inarticulate with passio
and his face looked swelled and furious. "Take her there if she comes to se
thee: thou shalln't keep me out of this. Begone wi' ye both!"

'He swore at us, and left Linton no time to answer, nearly throwing hi
into the kitchen; and he clenched his fist as I followed, seemingly longir
to knock me down. I was afraid for a moment, and I let one volume fal
he kicked it after me, and shut us out. I heard a malignant, crackly laug
by the fire, and turning, beheld that odious Joseph standing rubbing his bo
hands, and quivering.

' "Aw wer sure he'd sarve ye eht! He's a grand lad! He's getten t' raig
sperrit in him! *He* knaws—Aye, he knaws, as weel as Aw do, who sud l

'maister yonder—Ech, ech, ech! He mad ye skift properly! Ech, ech, ech!"

' "Where must we go?" I said to my cousin, disregarding the old wretch's mockery.

'Linton was white and trembling. He was not pretty then, Ellen: oh no! he looked frightful; for his thin face and large eyes were wrought into an xpression of frantic, powerless fury. He grasped the handle of the door, and shook it: it was fastened inside.

' "If you don't let me in I'll kill you!—If you don't let me in, I'll kill you!" he rather shrieked than said. "Devil! devil!—I'll kill you—I'll kill you!"

'Joseph uttered his croaking laugh again.

' "Thear, that's t' father!" he cried. "That's father! We've allas summut h orther side in us. Niver heed Hareton, lad—dunnut be 'feard—he cannot et at thee!"

'I took hold of Linton's hands, and tried to pull him away; but he shrieked o shockingly that I dared not proceed. At last his cries were choked by a dreadful fit of coughing; blood gushed from his mouth, and he fell on the round. I ran into the yard, sick with terror; and called for Zillah, as loud s I could. She soon heard me: she was milking the cows in a shed behind the barn, and hurrying from her work, she inquired what there was to do? I hadn't reath to explain; dragging her in, I looked about for Linton. Earnshaw ad come out to examine the mischief he had caused, and he was then con-eying the poor thing upstairs. Zillah and I ascended after him; but he topped me at the top of the steps, and said I shouldn't go in: I must go ome. I exclaimed that he had killed Linton, and I *would* enter. Joseph ocked the door, and declared I should do "no sich stuff," and asked me whether I were "bahn to be as mad as him." I stood crying, till the housekeeper eappeared. She affirmed he would be better in a bit, but he couldn't do with hat shrieking and din; and she took me, and nearly carried me into the ouse.

'Ellen, I was ready to tear my hair off my head! I sobbed and wept so hat my eyes were almost blind; and the ruffian you have such sympathy vith stood opposite: presuming every now and then to bid me "wisht," nd denying that it was his fault; and, finally, frightened by my assertions hat I would tell papa, and that he should be put in prison and hanged, he ommenced blubbering himself, and hurried out to hide his cowardly agitation. till, I was not rid of him: when at length they compelled me to depart, nd I had got some hundred yards off the premises, he suddenly issued from he shadow of the roadside, and checked Minny and took hold of me.

' "Miss Catherine, I'm ill grieved," he began, "but it's rayther too bad"——

'I gave him a cut with my whip, thinking perhaps he would murder me. He let go, thundering one of his horrid curses, and I galloped home more han half out of my senses.

'I didn't bid you good night that evening, and I didn't go to Wuthering Heights the next: I wished to, exceedingly; but I was strangely excited, and dreaded to hear that Linton was dead, sometimes; and sometimes shuddered at the thought of encountering Hareton. On the third day I took courage at least, I couldn't bear longer suspense, and stole off once more. I went at five o'clock, and walked; fancying I might manage to creep into the house and up to Linton's room, unobserved. However, the dogs gave notice of my approach. Zillah received me, and saying, "the lad was mending nicely," showed me into a small, tidy, carpeted apartment, where, to my inexpressible joy, I beheld Linton laid on a little sofa, reading one of my books. But he would neither speak to me nor look at me, through a whole hour, Ellen: he has such an unhappy temper. And what quite confounded me, when he did open his mouth, it was to utter the falsehood that I had occasioned the uproar and Hareton was not to blame! Unable to reply, except passionately, I got up and walked from the room. He sent after me a faint "Catherine!" He did not reckon on being answered so: but I wouldn't turn back; and the morrow was the second day on which I stayed at home, nearly determined to visit him no more. But it was so miserable going to bed and getting up, and never hearing anything about him, that my resolution melted into air before it was properly formed. It *had* appeared wrong to take the journey once; now it seemed wrong to refrain. Michael came to ask if he must saddle Minny; I said "Yes," and considered myself doing a duty as she bore me over the hills. I was forced to pass the front windows to get to the court: it was no use trying to conceal my presence.

' "Young master is in the house," said Zillah, as she saw me making for the parlour. I went in; Earnshaw was there also, but he quitted the room directly. Linton sat in the great arm-chair half asleep; walking up to the fire, I began in a serious tone, partly meaning it to be true:

' "As you don't like me, Linton, and as you think I come on purpose to hurt you, and pretend that I do so every time, this is our last meeting: let us say good-bye; and tell Mr. Heathcliff that you have no wish to see me, and that he mustn't invent any more falsehoods on the subject.'

' "Sit down and take your hat off, Catherine," he answered. "You are so much happier than I am, you ought to be better. Papa talks enough of my defects, and shows enough scorn of me, to make it natural I should doubt myself. I doubt whether I am not altogether as worthless as he calls me frequently; and then I feel so cross and bitter, I hate everybody! I *am* worthless, and bad in temper, and bad in spirit, almost always; and, if you choose, you may say good-bye: you'll get rid of an annoyance. Only, Catherine, do me this justice: believe that if I might be as sweet, and as kind, and as good as you are, I would be; as willingly, and more so, than as happy and as healthy. And believe that your kindness has made me love you deeper than if I deserved

your love: and though I couldn't, and cannot help showing my nature to you, I regret it and repent it; and shall regret and repent it till I die!"

'I felt he spoke the truth; and I felt I must forgive him: and, though he should quarrel the next moment, I must forgive him again. We were reconciled; but we cried, both of us, the whole time I stayed: not entirely for sorrow; yet I *was* sorry Linton had that distorted nature. He'll never let his friends be at ease, and he'll never be at ease himself! I have always gone to his little parlour, since that night; because his father returned the day after.

'About three times, I think, we have been merry and hopeful, as we were the first evening; the rest of my visits were dreary and troubled: now with his selfishness and spite, and now with his sufferings: but I've learned to endure the former with nearly as little resentment as the latter. Mr. Heathcliff purposely avoids me: I have hardly seen him at all. Last Sunday, indeed, coming earlier than usual, I heard him abusing poor Linton, cruelly, for his conduct of the night before. I can't tell how he knew of it, unless he listened. Linton had certainly behaved provokingly: however, it was the business of nobody but me, and I interrupted Mr. Heathcliff's lecture by entering and telling him so. He burst into a laugh, and went away, saying he was glad I took that view of the matter. Since then, I've told Linton he must whisper his bitter things. Now Ellen, you have heard all; and I can't be prevented from going to Wuthering Heights except by inflicting misery on two people; whereas, if you'll only not tell papa, my going need disturb the tranquillity of none. You'll not tell, will you? It will be very heartless if you do.'

'I'll make up my mind on that point by to-morrow, Miss Catherine,' I replied. 'It requires some study; and so I'll leave you to your rest, and go think it over.'

I thought it over aloud, in my master's presence; walking straight from her room to his, and relating the whole story: with the exception of her conversations with her cousin, and any mention of Hareton. Mr. Linton was alarmed and distressed, more than he would acknowledge to me. In the morning, Catherine learnt my betrayal of her confidence, and she learnt also that her secret visits were to end. In vain she wept and writhed against the interdict, and implored her father to have pity on Linton: all she got to comfort her was a promise that he would write and give him leave to come to the Grange when he pleased; but explaining that he must no longer expect to see Catherine at Wuthering Heights. Perhaps, had he been aware of his nephew's disposition and state of health, he would have seen fit to withhold, even that slight consolation.

CHAPTER 25

'These things happened last winter, sir,' said Mrs. Dean; 'hardly more than a year ago. Last winter, I did not think, at another twelve months' end I should be amusing a stranger to the family with relating them! Yet, who knows how long you'll be a stranger? You're too young to rest always contented, living by yourself; and I some way fancy no one could see Catherine Linton and not love her. You smile; but why do you look so lively and interested when I talk about her? and why have you asked me to hang her picture over your fireplace? and why'——

'Stop, my good friend!' I cried. 'It may be very possible that *I* should love her; but would she love me? I doubt it too much to venture my tranquillity by running into temptation: and then my home is not here. I'm of the busy world, and to its arms I must return. Go on. Was Catherine obedient to her father's commands?'

'She was,' continued the housekeeper. 'Her affection for him was still the chief sentiment in her heart; and he spoke without anger: he spoke in the deep tenderness of one about to leave his treasure amid perils and foes, where his remembered words would be the only aid that he could bequeath to guide her. He said to me, a few days afterwards:

' "I wish my nephew would write, Ellen, or call. Tell me, sincerely, what you think of him: is he changed for the better, or is there a prospect of improvement, as he grows a man?"

' "He's very delicate, sir," I replied; "and scarcely likely to reach manhood; but this I can say, he does not resemble his father; and if Miss Catherine had the misfortune to marry him, he would not be beyond her control: unless she were extremely and foolishly indulgent. However, master, you'll have plenty of time to get acquainted with him, and see whether he would suit her: it wants four years and more to his being of age." '

Edgar sighed; and walking to the window, looked out towards Gimmerton Kirk. It was a misty afternoon, but the February sun shone dimly, and we could just distinguish the two fir-trees in the yard, and the sparely scattered grave-stones.

'I've prayed often,' he half soliloquised, 'for the approach of what is coming; and now I begin to shrink, and fear it. I thought the memory of the hour I came down that glen a bridegroom would be less sweet than the anticipation that I was soon, in a few months, or, possibly, weeks, to be carried up, and laid in its lonely hollow! Ellen, I've been very happy with my little Cathy: through winter nights and summer days she was a living hope at my side. But I've been as happy musing by myself among those stones, under that old church: lying, through the long June evenings, on the green mound of her mother's grave and wishing—yearning for the time when I might lie be-

eath it. What can I do for Cathy? How must I quit her? I'd not care one moment for Linton being Heathcliff's son; nor for his taking her from me, f he could console her for my loss. I'd not care that Heathcliff gained his nds, and triumphed in robbing me of my last blessing! But should Linton e unworthy—only a feeble tool to his father—I cannot abandon her to im! And, hard though it be to crush her buoyant spirit, I must persevere n making her sad while I live, and leaving her solitary when I die. Darling! 'd rather resign her to God, and lay her in the earth before me.'

'Resign her to God, as it is, sir,' I answered, 'and if we should lose you— vhich may He forbid—under His providence, I'll stand her friend and coun-ellor to the last. Miss Catherine is a good girl: I don't fear that she will o wilfully wrong; and people who do their duty are always finally rewarded.'

Spring advanced; yet my master gathered no real strength, though he resu-ned his walks in the grounds with his daughter. To her inexperienced notions, his itself was a sign of convalescence; and then his cheek was often flushed, nd his eyes were bright: she felt sure of his recovering. On her seventeenth irthday, he did not visit the churchyard: it was raining, and I observed:

'You'll surely not go out to-night, sir?'

He answered:

'No, I'll defer it this year a little longer.'

He wrote again to Linton, expressing his great desire to see him; and, had he invalid been presentable, I've no doubt his father would have permitted im to come. As it was, being instructed, he returned an answer, intimating hat Mr. Heathcliff objected to his calling at the Grange; but his uncle's ind remembrance delighted him, and he hoped to meet him, sometimes, a his rambles, and personally to petition that his cousin and he might not emain long so utterly divided.

That part of his letter was simple, and probably his own. Heathcliff, knew e could plead eloquently enough for Catherine's company, then.

'I do not ask,' he said, 'that she may visit here; but, am I never to see her, ecause my father forbids me to go to her home, and you forbid her to come o mine? Do now and then, ride with her towards the Heights; and let us xchange a few words, in your presence! We have done nothing to deserve is separation; and you are not angry with me; you have no reason to dislike e, you allow, yourself. Dear uncle! send me a kind note to-morrow, and ave to join you anywhere you please, except at Thrushcross Grange. I believe n interview would convince you that my father's character is not mine: e affirms I am more your nephew than his son; and though I have faults vhich render me unworthy of Catherine, she has excused them, and for er sake, you should also. You inquire after my health—it is better; but while remain cut off from all hope, and doomed to solitude, or the society of those ho never did and never will like me, how can I be cheerful and well?'

Edgar, though he felt for the boy, could not consent to grant this request because he could not accompany Catherine. He said, in summer, perhaps they might meet: meantime, he wished him to continue writing at intervals, and engaged to give him what advice and comfort he was able by letter; being well aware of his hard position in his family. Linton complied; and had he been unrestrained, would probably have spoiled all by filling his epistle with complaints and lamentations: but his father kept a sharp watch over him, and, of course, insisted on every line that my master sent being shown; so instead of penning his peculiar personal sufferings and distresses, the theme constantly uppermost in his thoughts, he harped on the cruel obligation of being held asunder from his friend and love; and gently intimated that Mr. Linton must allow an interview soon, or he should fear he was purposely deceiving him with empty promises.

Cathy was a powerful ally at home; and, between them, they at length persuaded my master to acquiesce in their having a ride or a walk together about once a week, under my guardianship, and on the moors nearest the Grange: for June found him still declining; and though he had set aside yearly a portion of his income for my young lady's fortune, he had a natural desire that she might retain—or at least return in a short time to—the house of her ancestors; and he considered her only prospect of doing that was by a union with his heir; he had no idea that the latter was failing almost as fast as himself; nor had any one, I believe: no doctor visited the Heights, and no one saw Master Heathcliff to make report of his condition among us. I, for my part, began to fancy my forebodings were false, and that he must be actually rallying, when he mentioned riding and walking on the moors, and seemed so earnest in pursuing his object. I could not picture a father treating a dying child as tyrannically and wickedly as I afterwards learned Heathcliff had treated him, to compel this apparent eagerness: his efforts redoubling the more imminently his avaricious and unfeeling plans were threatened with defeat by death.

CHAPTER 26

Summer was already past its prime, when Edgar reluctantly yielded his assent to their entreaties, and Catherine and I set out on our first ride to join her cousin. It was a close, sultry day: devoid of sunshine, but with a sky too dappled and hazy to threaten rain; and our place of meeting had been fixed at the guide-stone, by the cross-roads. On arriving there, however, a little herd-boy, despatched as a messenger, told us that:

'Maister Linton wer just ut this side th' Heights: and he'd be mitch obleeged to us to gang on a bit further.'

'Then Master Linton has forgot the first injunction of his uncle,' I observed: he bid us keep on the Grange land, and here we are off at once.'

'Well, we'll turn our horses' heads round, when we reach him,' answered my companion, 'our excursion shall lie towards home.'

But when we reached him, and that was scarcely a quarter of a mile from his own door, we found he had no horse; and we were forced to dismount, and leave ours to graze. He lay on the heath, awaiting our approach, and did not rise till we came within a few yards. Then he walked so feebly, and looked so pale, that I immediately exclaimed:

'Why, Master Heathcliff, you are not fit for enjoying a ramble, this morning. How ill you do look!'

Catherine surveyed him with grief and astonishment; and changed the ejaculation of joy on her lips, to one of alarm; and the congratulation on their long-postponed meeting, to an anxious inquiry, whether he were worse than usual?

'No—better—better!' he panted, trembling, and retaining her hand as if he needed its support, while his large blue eyes wandered timidly over her; the hollowness round them transforming to haggard wildness the languid expression they once possessed.

'But you have been worse,' persisted his cousin; 'worse than when I saw you last; you are thinner, and'——

'I'm tired,' he interrupted hurriedly. 'It is too hot for walking, let us rest here. And, in the morning, I often feel sick—papa says I grow so fast.'

Badly satisfied, Cathy sat down, and he reclined beside her.

'This is something like your paradise,' said she, making an effort at cheerfulness. 'You recollect the two days we agreed to spend in the place and way each thought pleasantest? This is surely yours, only there are clouds: but then they are so soft and mellow: it is nicer than sunshine. Next week, if you can, we'll ride down to the Grange Park, and try mine.'

Linton did not appear to remember what she talked of; and he had evidently great difficulty in sustaining any kind of conversation. His lack of interest in the subjects she started, and his equal incapacity to contribute to her entertainment, were so obvious that she could not conceal her disappointment. An indefinite alteration had come over his whole person and manner. The pettishness that might be caressed into fondness, had yielded to a listless apathy; there was less of the peevish temper of a child which frets and teases on purpose to be soothed, and more of the self-absorbed moroseness of a confirmed invalid, repelling consolation, and ready to regard the good-humoured mirth of others as an insult. Catherine perceived, as well as I did, that he held it rather a punishment, than a gratification, to endure our company; and she made no scruple of proposing, presently, to depart. That proposal, unexpectedly, roused Linton from his lethargy, and threw him into a strange

state of agitation. He glanced fearfully towards the Heights, begging she would remain another half-hour at least.

'But I think,' said Cathy, 'you'd be more comfortable at home than sitting here; and I cannot amuse you to-day, I see, by my tales, and songs, and chatter; you have grown wiser than I, in these six months; you have little taste for my diversions now: or else, if I could amuse you, I'd willingly stay.'

'Stay to rest yourself,' he replied. 'And Catherine, don't think, or say that I'm *very* unwell: it is the heavy weather and heat that make me dull; and I walked about, before you came, a great deal for me. Tell uncle I'm in tolerable health, will you?'

'I'll tell him that *you* say so, Linton. I couldn't affirm that you are,' observed my young lady, wondering at his pertinacious assertion of what was evidently an untruth.

'And be here again next Thursday,' continued he, shunning her puzzled gaze. 'And give him my thanks for permitting you to come—my best thanks, Catherine. And—and, if you *did* meet my father, and he asked you about me, don't lead him to suppose that I've been extremely silent and stupid; don't look sad and downcast, as you *are* doing—he'll be angry.'

'I care nothing for his anger,' exclaimed Cathy, imagining she would be its object.

'But I do,' said her cousin, shuddering. '*Don't* provoke him against me, Catherine, for he is very hard.'

'Is he severe to you, Master Heathcliff?' I inquired. 'Has he grown weary of indulgence, and passed from passive to active hatred?'

Linton looked at me, but did not answer; and, after keeping her seat by his side another ten minutes, during which his head fell drowsily on his breast, and he uttered nothing except suppressed moans of exhaustion or pain, Cathy, began to seek solace in looking for bilberries, and sharing the produce of her researches with me: she did not offer them to him, for she saw further notice would only weary and annoy.

'Is it half-an-hour now, Ellen?' she whispered in my ear, at last. 'I can't tell why we should stay. He's asleep, and papa will be wanting us back.'

'Well, we must not leave him asleep,' I answered; 'wait till he wakes, and be patient. You were mighty eager to set off, but your longing to see poor Linton has soon evaporated!'

'Why did *he* wish to see me?' returned Catherine. 'In his crossest humours formerly, I liked him better than I do in his present curious mood. It's just as if it were a task he was compelled to perform—this interview—for fear his father should scold him. But I'm hardly going to come to give Mr. Heathcliff pleasure; whatever reason he may have for ordering Linton to undergo this penance. And, though I'm glad he's better in health, I'm sorry he's so much less pleasant, and so much less affectionate to me.'

'You think *he is* better in health then?' I said.

'Yes,' she answered; 'because he always made such a great deal of his sufferings, you know. He is not tolerably well, as he told me to tell papa; but he's better, very likely.'

'There you differ with me, Miss Cathy,' I remarked; 'I should conjecture him to be far worse.'

Linton here started from his slumber in bewildered terror, and asked if any one had called his name.

'No,' said Catherine; 'unless in dreams. I cannot conceive how you manage to doze out of doors, in the morning.'

'I thought I heard my father,' he gasped, glancing up to the frowning nab above us. 'You are sure nobody spoke?'

'Quite sure,' replied his cousin. 'Only Ellen and I were disputing concerning your health. Are you truly stronger, Linton, than when we separated a winter? If you be I'm certain one thing is not stronger—your regard for me: speak,—are you?'

The tears gushed from Linton's eyes as he answered, 'Yes, yes, I am!' And, still under the spell of the imaginary voice, his gaze wandered up and down to detect its owner. Cathy rose. 'For to-day we must part,' she said. 'And I won't conceal that I have been sadly disappointed with our meeting; though I'll mention it to nobody but you: not that I stand in awe of Mr. Heathcliff.'

'Hush,' murmured Linton: 'for God's sake, hush! He's coming.' And he clung to Catherine's arm, striving to detain her; but at that announcement she hastily disengaged herself, and whistled to Minny, who obeyed her like a dog.

'I'll be here next Thursday,' she cried, springing to the saddle. 'Good-bye. Quick, Ellen!'

And so we left him, scarcely conscious of our departure, so absorbed was he in anticipating his father's approach.

Before we reached home, Catherine's displeasure softened into a perplexed sensation of pity and regret, largely blended with vague, uneasy doubts about Linton's actual circumstances, physical and social; in which I partook, though I counselled her not to say much; for a second journey would make us better judges. My master requested an account of our ongoings. His nephew's offering of thanks was duly delivered, Miss Cathy gently touching on the rest: I also threw little light on his inquiries, for I hardly knew what to hide, and what to reveal.

CHAPTER 27

Seven days glided away, every one marking its course by the henceforth rapid alteration of Edgar Linton's state. The havoc that months had previously wrought was now emulated by the inroads of hours. Catherine, we would fain have deluded yet: but her own quick spirit refused to delude her: it divined in secret, and brooded on the dreadful probability, gradually ripening into certainty. She had not the heart to mention her ride, when Thursday came round; I mentioned it for her, and obtained permission to order her out of doors: for the library, where her father stopped a short time daily—the brief period he could bear to sit up—and his chamber, had become her whole world. She grudged each moment that did not find her bending over his pillow, or seated by his side. Her countenance grew wan with watching and sorrow, and my master gladly dismissed her to what he flattered himself would be a happy change of scene and society; drawing comfort from the hope that she would not now be left entirely alone after his death.

He had a fixed idea, I guessed by several observations he let fall, that, as his nephew resembled him in person, he would resemble him in mind; for Linton's letters bore few or no indications of his defective character. And I, through pardonable weakness, refrained from correcting the error; asking myself what good there would be in disturbing his last moments with information that he had neither power nor opportunity to turn to account.

We deferred our excursion till the afternoon; a golden afternoon of August every breath from the hills so full of life, that it seemed whoever respired it, though dying, might revive. Catherine's face was just like the landscape—shadows and sunshine flitting over it in rapid succession; but the shadows rested longer, and the sunshine was more transient; and her poor little heart reproached itself for even that passing forgetfulness of its cares.

We discerned Linton watching at the same spot he had selected before. My young mistress alighted, and told me that, as she was resolved to stay a very little while, I had better hold the pony and remain on horseback; but I dissented: I wouldn't risk losing sight of the charge committed to me a minute; so we climbed the slope of heath together. Master Heathcliff received us with greater animation on this occasion: not the animation of high spirits though, nor yet of joy; it looked more like fear.

'It is late!' he said, speaking short and with difficulty. 'Is not your father very ill? I thought you wouldn't come.'

'*Why* won't you be candid?' cried Catherine, swallowing her greeting. 'Why cannot you say at once you don't want me? It is strange, Linton, that for the second time you have brought me here on purpose, apparently, to distress us both, and for no reason besides!'

Linton shivered, and glanced at her, half supplicating, half ashamed; ut his cousin's patience was not sufficient to endure this enigmatical behaviour. 'My father *is* very ill,' she said; 'and why am I called from his bedside? Thy didn't you send to absolve me from my promise, when you wished I wouldn't keep it? Come! I desire an explanation: playing and trifling are ompletely banished out of my mind; and I can't dance attendance on your ffectations now!'

'My affections!' he murmured; 'what are they? For Heaven's sake, atherine, don't look so angry! Despise me as much as you please; I am worthless, cowardly wretch: I can't be scorned enough; but I'm too mean r your anger. Hate my father, and spare me for contempt.'

'Nonsense!' cried Catherine, in a passion. 'Foolish, silly boy! And there! e trembles, as if I were really going to touch him! You needn't bespeak ontempt, Linton: anybody will have it spontaneously at your service. et off! I shall return home: it is folly dragging you from the hearthstone, nd pretending—what do we pretend? Let go my frock! If I pitied you r crying and looking so very frightened, you should spurn such pity. Ellen, ll him how disgraceful this conduct is. Rise, and don't degrade yourself to an abject reptile—*don't*!'

With streaming face and an expression of agony, Linton had thrown his erveless frame along the ground: he seemed convulsed with exquisite terror. 'Oh!' he sobbed, 'I cannot bear it! Catherine, Catherine, I'm a traitor, o, and I dare not tell you! But leave me, and I shall be killed! *Dear* Cathene, my life is in your hands: and you have said you loved me, and if you d, it wouldn't harm you. You'll not go, then? kind, sweet, good Catherine! nd perhaps you *will* consent—and he'll let me die with you!'

My young lady, on witnessing his intense anguish, stooped to raise him. he old feeling of indulgent tenderness overcame her vexation, and she grew oroughly moved and alarmed.

'Consent to what?' she asked. 'To stay? Tell me the meaning of this strange lk, and I will. You contradict your own words, and distract me! Be calm d frank, and confess at once all that weighs on your heart. You wouldn't jure me, Linton, would you?' You wouldn't let any enemy hurt me, if u could prevent it? I'll believe you are a coward for yourself, but not cowardly betrayer of your best friend.'

'But my father threatened me,' gasped the boy, clasping his attenuated gers, 'and I dread him—I dread him! I *dare* not tell!'

'Oh, well!' said Catherine, with scornful compassion, 'keep your secret: m no coward. Save yourself: I'm not afraid!'

Her magnanimity provoked his tears: he wept wildly, kissing her supporting nds, and yet could not summon courage to speak out. I was cogitating hat the mystery might be, and determined Catherine should never suffer,

to benefit him or any one else, by my good will; when hearing a rustle among the ling, I looked up and saw Mr. Heathcliff almost close upon us, descending the Heights. He didn't cast a glance towards my companions, though they were sufficiently near for Linton's sobs to be audible; but hailing me in the almost hearty tone he assumed to none besides, and the sincerity of which I couldn't avoid doubting, he said:

'It is something to see you so near to my house, Nelly. How are you at the Grange? Let us hear. The rumour goes,' he added in a lower tone, 'that Edgar Linton is on his deathbed: perhaps they exaggerate his illness!'

'No; my master is dying,' I replied: 'it is true enough. A sad thing it will be for us all, but a blessing for him!'

'How long will he last, do you think?' he asked.

'I don't know,' I said.

'Because,' he continued, looking at the two young people, who were fixed under his eye—Linton appeared as if he could not venture to stir or raise his head, and Catherine could not move, on his account—'because that lad yonder seems determined to beat me; and I'd thank his uncle to be quick, and go before him. Hallo! has the whelp been playing that game long? I *did* give him some lessons about snivelling. Is he pretty lively with Miss Linton generally?'

'Lively? no—he has shown the greatest distress,' I answered. 'To see him I should say, that instead of rambling with his sweetheart on the hills, he ought to be in bed, under the hands of a doctor.'

'He shall be in a day or two,' muttered Heathcliff. 'But first—get up, Linton! Get up!' he shouted. 'Don't grovel on the ground there: up, the moment!'

Linton had sunk prostrate again in another paroxysm of helpless fear, caused by his father's glance towards him, I suppose: there was nothing else to produce such humiliation. He made several efforts to obey, but his little strength was annihilated for the time, and he fell back again with a moan. Mr. Heathcliff advanced, and lifted him to lean against a ridge of turf.

'Now,' said he, with curbed ferocity, 'I'm getting angry; and if you don't command that paltry spirit of yours—*Damn* you! get up directly!'

'I will, father,' he panted. 'Only, let me alone, or I shall faint. I've done as you wished, I'm sure. Catherine will tell you that I—that I—have been cheerful. Ah! keep by me, Catherine: give me your hand.'

'Take mine,' said his father; 'stand on your feet. There now—she'll lend you her arm: that's right, look at *her*. You would imagine I was the devil himself, Miss Linton, to excite such horror. Be so kind as to walk home with him, will you? He shudders if I touch him.'

'Linton, dear!' whispered Catherine, 'I can't go to Wuthering Heights: papa has forbidden me. He'll not harm you: why are you so afraid?'

'I can never re-enter that house,' he answered. 'I'm *not* to re-enter it without ou!'

'Stop!' cried his father. 'We'll respect Catherine's filial scruples. Nelly, ake him in, and I'll follow your advice concerning the doctor, without delay.'

'You'll do well,' replied I. 'But I must remain with my mistress: to mind our son is not my business.'

'You are very stiff,' said Heathcliff, 'I know that: but you'll force me to inch the baby and make it scream before it moves your charity. Come, then, ny hero. Are you willing to return, escorted by me?'

He approached once more, and made as if he would seize the fragile being; ut, shrinking back, Linton clung to his cousin, and implored her to accompany im, with a frantic importunity that admitted no denial. However I disapproved, I couldn't hinder her: indeed, how could she have refused him erself? What was filling him with dread we had no means of discerning: ut there he was, powerless under its grip, and any addition seemed capable f shocking him into idiotcy. We reached the threshold: Catherine walked a, and I stood waiting till she had conducted the invalid to a chair, expecting er out immediately; when Mr. Heathcliff, pushing me forward, exclaimed:

'My house is not stricken with the plague, Nelly; and I have a mind to e hospitable to-day: sit down, and allow me to shut the door.'

He shut and locked it also. I started.

'You shall have tea before you go home,' he added. 'I am by myself. Hareton s gone with some cattle to the Lees, and Zillah and Joseph are off on a journey f pleasure; and, though I'm used to being alone, I'd rather have some nteresting company, if I can get it. Miss Linton, take your seat by *him*. I give ou what I have: the present is hardly worth accepting; but I have nothing lse to offer. It is Linton, I mean. How she does stare! It's odd what a savage eeling I have to anything that seems afraid of me! Had I been born where aws are less strict and tastes less dainty, I should treat myself to a slow vivisction of those two, as an evening's amusement.'

He drew in his breath, struck the table, and swore to himself, 'By hell! hate them.'

'I'm not afraid of you!' exclaimed Catherine, who could not hear the atter part of his speech. She stepped close up; her black eyes flashing with assion and resolution. 'Give me that key: I will have it!' she said. 'I wouldn't at or drink here, if I were starving.'

Heathcliff had the key in his hand that remained on the table. He looked p, seized with a sort of surprise at her boldness; or, possibly, reminded by er voice and glance, of the person from whom she inherited it. She snatched t the instrument, and half-succeeded in getting it out of his loosened fingers: ut her action recalled him to the present; he recovered it speedily.

'Now, Catherine Linton,' he said, 'stand off, or I shall knock you down;

and that will make Mrs. Dean mad.'

Regardless of this warning, she captured his closed hand and its content again. 'We *will* go!' she repeated, exerting her utmost efforts to cause th iron muscles to relax; and finding that her nails made no impression, sh applied her teeth pretty sharply. Heathcliff glanced at me a glance that kep me from interfering a moment. Catherine was too intent on his fingers t notice his face. He opened them suddenly, and resigned the object of dispute but, ere she had well secured it, he seized her with the liberated hand, and pulling her on his knee, administered with the other a shower of terrific slap on the side of the head, each sufficient to have fulfilled his threat, had sh been able to fall.

At this diabolical violence I rushed on him furiously. 'You villain!' I bega to cry, 'you villain!' A touch on the chest silenced me: I am stout, and soo put out of breath; and, what with that and the rage, I staggered dizzil back, and felt ready to suffocate, or to burst a blood-vessel. The scene wa over in two minutes; Catherine, released, put her two hands to her temple and looked just as if she were not sure whether her ears were off or on. Sh trembled like a reed, poor thing, and leant against the table perfectly bewil dered.

'I know how to chastise children, you see,' said the scoundrel grimly, as h stooped to repossess himself of the key, which had dropped to the floo 'Go to Linton now, as I told you; and cry at your ease! I shall be your fathe to-morrow—all the father you'll have in a few days—and you shall hav plenty of that. You can bear plenty; you're no weakling: you shall hav a daily taste, if I catch such a devil of a temper in your eyes again!'

Cathy ran to me instead of Linton, and knelt down and put her burnin cheek on my lap, weeping aloud. Her cousin had shrunk into a corner the settle, as quiet as a mouse, congratulating himself, I dare say, that th correction had lighted on another than him. Mr. Heathcliff, perceiving all confounded, rose, and expeditiously made the tea himself. The cups an saucers were laid ready. He poured it out, and handed me a cup.

'Wash away your spleen,' he said. 'And help your own naughty pet an mine. It is not poisoned, though I prepared it. I'm going out to seek you horses.'

Our first thought, on his departure, was to force an exit somewhere. W tried the kitchen door, but that was fastened outside: we looked at the window —they were too narrow for even Cathy's little figure.

'Master Linton,' I cried, seeing we were regularly imprisoned: 'yo know what your diabolical father is after, and you shall tell us, or I'll bo your ears, as he has done your cousin's.'

'Yes, Linton, you must tell,' said Catherine. 'It was for your sake I cam and it will be wickedly ungrateful if you refuse.'

'Give me some tea, I'm thirsty, and then I'll tell you,' he answered. 'Mrs. ean, go away. I don't like you standing over me. Now, Catherine, you are tting your tears fall into my cup. I won't drink that. Give me another.'

Catherine pushed another to him, and wiped her face. I felt disgusted t the little wretch's composure, since he was no longer in terror for himself. he anguish he had exhibited on the moor subsided as soon as ever he entered 'uthering Heights; so I guessed he had been menaced with an awful visita- on of wrath if he failed in decoying us there; and, that accomplished, he ad no further immediate fears.

'Papa wants us to be married,' he continued, after sipping some of the quid. 'And he knows your papa wouldn't let us marry now; and he's afraid f my dying, if we wait; so we are to be married in the morning, and you are stay here all night; and if you do as he wishes, you shall return home xt day, and take me with you.'

'Take you with her, pitiful changeling?' I exclaimed. '*You* marry? Why, e man is mad; or he thinks us fools, every one. And do you imagine that eautiful young lady, that healthy, hearty girl, will tie herself to a little erishing monkey like you! Are you cherishing the notion that *anybody*, let one Miss Catherine Linton, would have you for a husband? You want hipping for bringing us in here at all, with your dastardly puling tricks; d—don't look so silly, now! I've a very good mind to shake you severely, r your contemptible treachery, and your imbecile conceit.'

I did give him a slight shaking; but it brought on the cough, and he took his ordinary resource of moaning and weeping, and Catherine rebuked e.

'Stay all night? No,' she said, looking slowly round. 'Ellen, I'll burn that oor down, but I'll get out.'

And she would have commenced the execution of her threat directly, ut Linton was up in alarm for his dear self again. He clasped her in his two eble arms, sobbing:

'Won't you have me, and save me? not let me come to the Grange? Oh! arling Catherine! you mustn't go and leave me, after all. You *must* obey y father—you *must*!'

'I must obey my own,' she replied, 'and relieve him from this cruel suspense. he whole night! What would he think? he'll be distressed already. I'll ther break or burn a way out of the house. Be quiet! You're in no danger; ut if you hinder me—Linton, I love papa better than you!'

The mortal terror he felt of Mr. Heathcliff's anger, restored to the boy his ward's eloquence. Catherine was near distraught: still, she persisted that e must go home, and tried entreaty in her turn, persuading him to subdue s selfish agony. While they were thus occupied, our gaoler re-entered.

'Your beasts have trotted off,' he said, 'and—now, Linton! snivelling

again? What has she been doing to you? Come, come—have done, and g
to bed. In a month or two, my lad, you'll be able to pay her back her preser
tyrannies with a vigorous hand. You're pining for pure love, are you not
nothing else in the world: and she shall have you! There, to bed! Zillah won
be here to-night; you must undress yourself. Hush! hold your noise! Onc
in your own room, I'll not come near you: you needn't fear. By chance you'v
managed tolerably. I'll look to the rest.'

He spoke these words, holding the door open for his son to pass; and th
latter achieved his exit exactly as a spaniel might, which suspected the perso
who attended on it of designing a spiteful squeeze. The lock was re-securec
Heathcliff approached the fire, where my mistress and I stood silent. Catherir
looked up, and instinctively raised her hand to her cheek: his neighbourhoo
revived a painful sensation. Anybody else would have been incapable
regarding the childish act with sternness, but he scowled on her, and mutterec

'Oh! you are not afraid of me? Your courage is well disguised: you *see*
damnably afraid!'

'I *am* afraid now,' she replied, 'because, if I stay, papa will be miserabl
and how can I endure making him miserable:—when he—when he—M
Heathcliff, *let* me go home! I promise to marry Linton: papa would like m
to, and I love him—why should you wish to force me to do what I'll willing
do of myself?'

'Let him dare to force you!' I cried. 'There's law in the land, thank Gc
there is; though we *be* in an out-of-the-way place. I'd inform if he were m
own son: and it's felony without benefit of clergy!'

'Silence!' said the ruffian. 'To the devil with your clamour! I don't wa
you to speak. Miss Linton, I shall enjoy myself remarkably in thinking yo
father will be miserable: I shall not sleep for satisfaction. You could ha
hit on no surer way of fixing your residence under my roof for the ne
twenty-four hours, than informing me that such an event would follow.
to your promise to marry Linton, I'll take care you shall keep it; for you sha
not quit this place till it is fulfilled.'

'Send Ellen, then, to let papa know I'm safe!' exclaimed Catherine, weepir
bitterly. 'Or marry me now. Poor papa! Ellen, he'll think we're lost. Wh
shall we do?'

'Not he! He'll think you are tired of waiting on him, and run off for a litt
amusement,' answered Heathcliff. 'You cannot deny that you entered m
house of your own accord, in contempt of his injunctions to the contrary. An
it is quite natural that you should desire amusement at your age; and th
you would weary of nursing a sick man, and that man *only* your father. Cath
rine, his happiest days were over when your days began. He cursed yo
I dare say, for coming into the world (I did, at least); and it would just
if he cursed you as *he* went out of it. I'd join him. I don't love you! How shou

Weep away. As far as I can see, it will be your chief diversion hereafter; unless Linton make amends for other losses: and your provident parent appears to fancy he may. His letters of advice and consolation entertained me vastly. In his last he recommended my jewel to be careful of his; and kind to her when he got her. Careful and kind—that's paternal. But Linton requires his whole stock of care and kindness for himself. Linton can play the little tyrant well. He'll undertake to torture any number of cats, if their teeth be drawn and their claws pared. You'll be able to tell his uncle fine tales of his *kindness*, when you get home again, I assure you.'

'You're right there!' I said; 'explain your son's character. Show his resemblance to yourself; and then, I hope, Miss Cathy will think twice before she takes the cockatrice!'

'I don't much mind speaking of his amiable qualities now,' he answered; 'because she must either accept him or remain a prisoner, and you along with her, till your master dies. I can detain you both, quite concealed, here. If you doubt, encourage her to retract her word, and you'll have an opportunity of judging!'

'I'll not retract my word,' said Catherine. 'I'll marry him within this hour, if I may go to Thrushcross Grange afterwards. Mr. Heathcliff, you're a cruel man, but you're not a fiend; and you won't, from *mere* malice, destroy irrevocably all my happiness. If papa thought I had left him on purpose, and if he died before I returned, could I bear to live? I've given over crying: but I'm going to kneel here, at your knee; and I'll not get up, and I'll not take my eyes from your face till you look back at me! No, don't turn away! *do* look! You'll see nothing to provoke you. I don't hate you. I'm not angry that you struck me. Have you never loved *anybody* in all your life, uncle? *never*? Ah! you must look once. I'm so wretched, you can't help being sorry and pitying me.'

'Keep your eft's fingers off; and move, or I'll kick you!' cried Heathcliff, brutally repulsing her. 'I'd rather be hugged by a snake. How the devil can you dream of fawning on me? I *detest* you!'

He shrugged his shoulders: shook himself, indeed, as if his flesh crept with aversion; and thrust back his chair; while I got up, and opened my mouth, to commence a downright torrent of abuse. But I was rendered dumb in the middle of the first sentence, by a threat that I should be shown into a room by myself the very next syllable I uttered. It was growing dark—we heard a sound of voices at the garden gate. Our host hurried out instantly: *he* had his wits about him; *we* had not. There was a talk of two or three minutes, and he returned alone.

'I thought it had been your cousin Hareton,' I observed to Catherine. 'I wish he would arrive! Who knows but he might take our part?'

'It was three servants sent to seek you from the Grange,' said Heathcliff, overhearing me. 'You should have opened a lattice and called out: but I could

swear that chit is glad you didn't. She's glad to be obliged to stay, I'm certain

At learning the chance we had missed, we both gave vent to our grief without control; and he allowed us to wail on till nine o'clock. Then he bade us go upstairs, through the kitchen, to Zillah's chamber; and I whispered my companion to obey: perhaps we might contrive to get through the window there, or into a garret, and out by its skylight. The window, however, was narrow, like those below, and the garret trap was safe from our attempts, for we were fastened in as before. We neither of us lay down: Catherine took her station by the lattice, and watched anxiously for morning; a deep sigh being the only answer I could obtain to my frequent entreaties that she would try to rest. I seated myself in a chair, and rocked to and fro, passing harsh judgment on my many derelictions of duty; from which, it struck me then, all the misfortunes of all my employers sprang. It was not the case in reality, I am aware; but it was, in my imagination, that dismal night and I thought Heathcliff himself less guilty than I.

At seven o'clock he came, and inquired if Miss Linton had risen. She ran to the door immediately, and answered, 'Yes.' 'Here, then,' he said, opening it, and pulling her out. I rose to follow, but he turned the lock again. I demanded my release.

'Be patient,' he replied; 'I'll send up your breakfast in a while.'

I thumped on the panels, and rattled the latch angrily; and Catherine asked why I was still shut up? He answered, I must try to endure it another hour, and they went away. I endured it two or three hours; at length, I heard a footstep: not Heathcliff's.

'I've brought you something to eat,' said a voice; 'oppen t' door!'

Complying eagerly, I beheld Hareton, laden with food enough to last me a day.

'Tak it,' he added, thrusting the tray into my hand.

'Stay one minute,' I began.

'Nay,' cried he, and retired, regardless of any prayers I could pour forth to detain him.

And there I remained enclosed the whole day, and the whole of the next night; and another, and another. Five nights and four days I remained altogether, seeing nobody but Hareton, once every morning; and he was a model of a gaoler: surly, and dumb, and deaf to every attempt at moving his sense of justice or compassion.

CHAPTER 28

On the fifth morning, or rather afternoon, a different step approached—
lighter and shorter; and, this time, the person entered the room. It was
Zillah; donned in her scarlet shawl, with a black silk bonnet on her head,
and a willow basket swung to her arm.

'Eh, dear! Mrs. Dean!' she exclaimed. 'Well! there is a talk about you at
Gimmerton. I never thought but you were sunk in the Blackhorse marsh,
and missy with you, till master told me you'd been found, and he'd lodged
you here! What! and you must have got on an island, sure? And how long
were you in the hole? Did master save you, Mrs. Dean? But you're not so
thin—you've not been so poorly, have you?'

'Your master is a true scoundrel!' I replied. 'But he shall answer for it.
He needn't have raised that tale: it shall all be laid bare!'

'What do you mean?' asked Zillah. 'It's not his tale: they tell that in the
village—about your being lost in the marsh: and I calls to Earnshaw, when
I come in—"Eh, they's queer things, Mr. Hareton, happened since I went
off. It's a sad pity of that likely young lass, and cant Nelly Dean." He stared.
I thought he had not heard aught, so I told him the rumour. The master
listened, and he just smiled to himself, and said, "If they have been in the
marsh, they are out now, Zillah. Nelly Dean is lodged, at this minute, in
your room. You can tell her to flit, when you go up; here is the key. The bog-
water got into her head, and she would have run home quite flighty; but
I fixed her till she came round to her senses. You can bid her go to the Grange
at once, if she be able, and carry a message from me, that her young lady
will follow in time to attend the squire's funeral."'

'Mr. Edgar is not dead?' I gasped. 'Oh! Zillah, Zillah!'

'No, no; sit you down, my good mistress,' she replied, 'you're right sickly
yet. He's not dead; Doctor Kenneth thinks he may last another day. I met
him on the road and asked.'

Instead of sitting down, I snatched my outdoor things, and hastened below,
for the way was free. On entering the house, I looked about for some one to
give information of Catherine. The place was filled with sunshine, and the
door stood wide open; but nobody seemed at hand. As I hesitated whether
to go off at once, or return and seek my mistress, a slight cough drew my
attention to the hearth. Linton lay on the settle, sole tenant, sucking a stick
of sugar-candy, and pursuing my movements with apathetic eyes. 'Where
is Miss Catherine?' I demanded sternly, supposing I could frighten him into
giving intelligence, by catching him thus, alone. He sucked on like an innocent.

'Is she gone?' I said.

'No,' he replied; 'she's upstairs: she's not to go; we won't let her.'

'You won't let her, little idiot!' I exclaimed. 'Direct me to her room

577

immediately, or I'll make you sing out sharply.'

'Papa would make you sing out, if you attempted to get there,' he answered
'He says I'm not to be soft with Catherine: she's my wife, and it's shameful
that she should wish to leave me. He says, she hates me and wants me to
die, that she may have my money; but she shan't have it: and she shan't
go home! She never shall!—she may cry, and be sick as much as she pleases

He resumed his former occupation, closing his lids, as if he meant to drop
asleep.

'Master Heathcliff,' I resumed, 'have you forgotten all Catherine's kindness
to you last winter, when you affirmed you loved her, and when she brought
you books and sung you songs, and came many a time through wind and
snow to see you? She wept to miss one evening, because you would be disap-
pointed; and you felt then that she was a hundred times too good to you
and now you believe the lies your father tells, though you know he detests
you both. And you join him against her. That's fine gratitude, is it not?'

The corner of Linton's mouth fell, and he took the sugar-candy from his
lips.

'Did she come to Wuthering Heights, because she hated you?' I continued
'Think for yourself! As to your money, she does not even know that you will
have any. And you say she's sick; and yet, you leave her alone, up there in
a strange house! *You* who have felt what it is to be so neglected! You could
pity your own sufferings; and she pitied them too; but you won't pity hers!
I shed tears, Master Heathcliff, you see—an elderly woman, and a servant
merely—and you, after pretending such affection, and having reason to worship
her almost, store every tear you have for yourself, and lie there quite at ease
Ah! you're a heartless, selfish boy!'

'I can't stay with her,' he answered crossly. 'I'll not stay by myself. She
cries so I can't bear it. And she won't give over, though I say I'll call my
father. I did call him once, and he threatened to strangle her, if she was
not quiet; but she began again the instant he left the room, moaning and
grieving all night long, though I screamed for vexation that I couldn't sleep

'Is Mr. Heathcliff out?' I inquired, perceiving that the wretched creature
had no power to sympathise with his cousin's mental tortures.

'He's in the court,' he replied, 'talking to Dr. Kenneth; who says uncle
dying, truly, at last. I'm glad, for I shall be master of the Grange after him—
and Catherine always spoke of it as *her* house. It isn't hers! It's mine: papa
says everything she has is mine. All her nice books are mine; she offered to
give me them, and her pretty birds, and her pony Minny, if I would get the
key, of our room, and let her out; but I told her she had nothing to give
they were all, all mine. And then she cried, and took a little picture from
her neck, and said I should have that; two pictures in a gold case, on one
side her mother, and on the other, uncle, when they were young. That was

esterday—I said *they* were mine, too; and tried to get them from her. The piteful thing wouldn't let me: she pushed me off, and hurt me. I shrieked out—that frightens her—she heard papa coming, and she broke the hinges nd divided the case, and gave me her mother's portrait; the other she attempted to hide: but papa asked what was the matter, and I explained it. He took he one I had away, and ordered her to resign hers to me; she refused, and e—he struck her down, and wrenched it off the chain, and crushed it with is foot.'

'And were you pleased to see her struck?' I asked: having my designs in ncouraging his talk.

'I winked,' he answered: 'I wink to see my father strike a dog or a horse, e does it so hard. Yet I was glad at first—she deserved punishing for pushing ne: but when papa was gone, she made me come to the window and showed ne her cheek cut on the inside, against her teeth, and her mouth filling with lood; and then she gathered up the bits of the picture, and went and sat lown with her face to the wall, and she has never spoken to me since: and sometimes think she can't speak for pain. I don't like to think so; but she's naughty thing for crying continually; and she looks so pale and wild, I'm fraid of her.'

'And you can get the key if you choose?' I said.

'Yes, when I'm upstairs,' he answered; 'but I can't walk upstairs now.'

'In what apartment is it?' I asked.

'Oh,' he cried, 'I shan't tell *you* where it is! It is our secret. Nobody, neither Hareton nor Zillah, is to know. There! you've tired me—go away, go away!' And he turned his face on to his arm, and shut his eyes again.

I considered it best to depart without seeing Mr. Heathcliff, and bring rescue for my young lady from the Grange. On reaching it, the astonishment f my fellow-servants to see me, and their joy also, was intense; and when hey heard that their little mistress was safe, two or three were about to urry up and shout the news at Mr. Edgar's door: but I bespoke the announcement of it, myself. How changed I found him, even in those few days! He ay an image of sadness and resignation waiting his death. Very young he ooked; though his actual age was thirty-nine, one would have called him en years younger, at least. He thought of Catherine; for he murmured her ame. I touched his hand, and spoke.

'Catherine is coming, dear master!' I whispered; 'she is alive and well; nd will be here, I hope, to-night.'

I trembled at the first effects of this intelligence: he half rose up, looked agerly round the apartment, and then sank back in a swoon. As soon as e recovered, I related our compulsory visit, and detention at the Heights. said Heathcliff forced me to go in: which was not quite true. I uttered as ttle as possible against Linton; nor did I describe all his father's brutal

conduct—my intentions being to add no bitterness, if I could help it, t
his already overflowing cup.

He divined that one of his enemy's purposes was to secure the person:
property, as well as the estate, to his son: or rather himself; yet why he di
not wait till his decease was a puzzle to my master, because ignorant ho
nearly he and his nephew would quit the world together. However, he fe
that his will had better be altered: instead of leaving Catherine's fortune
her own disposal, he determined to put it in the hands of trustees for her us
during life, and for her children, if she had any, after her. By that mean
it could not fall to Mr. Heathcliff should Linton die.

Having received his orders, I despatched a man to fetch the attorney
and four more, provided with serviceable weapons, to demand my youn
lady of her gaoler. Both parties were delayed very late. The single servar
returned first. He said Mr. Green, the lawyer, was out when he arrived
his house, and he had to wait two hours for his re-entrance; and then M
Green told him he had a little business in the village that must be done
but he would be at Thrushcross Grange before morning. The four me
came back unaccompanied also. They brought word that Catherine wa
ill: too ill to quit her room; and Heathcliff would not suffer them to see he
I scolded the stupid fellows well for listening to that tale, which I woul
not carry to my master; resolving to take a whole bevy up to the Height
at daylight, and storm it literally, unless the prisoner were quietly surrendere
to us. Her father *shall* see her, I vowed, and vowed again, if that devil be kille
on his own doorstones in trying to prevent it!

Happily, I was spared the journey and the trouble. I had gone downstai
at three o'clock to fetch a jug of water; and was passing through the ha
with it in my hand, when a sharp knock at the front door made me jum
'Oh! it is Green,' I said, recollecting myself—'only Green,' and I went or
intending to send somebody else to open it; but the knock was repeated
not loud, and still importunately. I put the jug on the banister and hastene
to admit him myself. The harvest moon shone clear outside. It was not th
attorney. My own sweet little mistress sprang on my neck, sobbing:

'Ellen! Ellen! is papa alive?'

'Yes,' I cried: 'yes, my angel, he is. God be thanked, you are safe with u
again!'

She wanted to run, breathless as she was, upstairs to Mr. Linton's room
but I compelled her to sit down on a chair, and made her drink, and washe
her pale face, chafing it into a faint colour with my apron. Then I said I mus
go first, and tell of her arrival; imploring her to say, she should be happ
with young Heathcliff. She stared, but soon comprehending why I counselle
her to utter the falsehood, she assured me she would not complain.

I couldn't abide to be present at their meeting. I stood outside the chambe

or a quarter of an hour, and hardly ventured near the bed, then. All was composed, however: Catherine's despair was as silent as her father's joy. he supported him calmly, in appearance; and he fixed on her features his raised eyes, that seemed dilating with ecstasy.

He died blissfully, Mr. Lockwood: he died so. Kissing her cheek, he murmured:

'I am going to her; and you, darling child, shall come to us!' and never stirred or spoke again; but continued that rapt, radiant gaze, till his pulse imperceptibly stopped and his soul departed. None could have noticed the exact minute of his death, it was so entirely without a struggle.

Whether Catherine had spent her tears, or whether the grief were too weighty to let them flow, she sat there dry-eyed till the sun rose: she sat till noon, and would still have remained brooding over that deathbed, but I insisted on her coming away and taking some repose. It was well I succeeded . removing her; for at dinner-time appeared the lawyer, having called at Wuthering Heights to get his instructions how to behave. He had sold himself to Mr. Heathcliff, and that was the cause of his delay in obeying my master's summons. Fortunately, no thought of worldly affairs crossed the latter's mind, to disturb him, after his daughter's arrival.

Mr. Green took upon himself to order everything and everybody about the place. He gave all the servants, but me, notice to quit. He would have carried his delegated authority to the point of insisting that Edgar Linton should not be buried beside his wife, but in the chapel, with his family. There was the will, however, to hinder that, and my loud protestations against any infringement of its directions. The funeral was hurried over; Catherine, Mrs. Linton Heathcliff now, was suffered to stay at the Grange till her father's corpse had quitted it.

She told me that her anguish had at last spurred Linton to incur the risk of liberating her. She heard the men I sent disputing at the door, and she gathered the sense of Heathcliff's answer. It drove her desperate. Linton, who had been conveyed up to the little parlour soon after I left, was terrified into fetching the key before his father re-ascended. He had the cunning to unlock and re-lock the door, without shutting it; and when he should have gone to bed, he begged to sleep with Hareton, and his petition was granted for once. Catherine stole out before break of day. She dare not try the doors, lest the dogs should raise an alarm; she visited the empty chambers and examined their windows; and, luckily, lighting on her mother's, she got easily out of its lattice, and on to the ground, by means of the fir-tree close by. Her accomplice suffered for his share in the escape, notwithstanding his timid contrivances.

CHAPTER 29

The evening after the funeral, my young lady and I were seated in the library, now musing mournfully—one of us despairingly—on our loss, now venturing conjectures as to the gloomy future.

We had just agreed the best destiny which could await Catherine, would be a permission to continue resident at the Grange; at least, during Linton's life: he being allowed to join her there, and I to remain as housekeeper. That seemed rather too favourable an arrangement to be hoped for: and yet I did hope, and began to cheer up under the prospect of retaining my home and my employment, and, above all, my beloved young mistress; when a servant—one of the discarded ones, not yet departed—rushed hastily in, and said 'that devil Heathcliff' was coming through the court: should I fasten the door in his face?

If we had been mad enough to order that proceeding, we had not time. He made no ceremony of knocking or announcing his name: he was master, and availed himself of the master's privilege to walk straight in, without saying a word. The sound of our informant's voice directed him to the library: he entered, and motioning him out, shut the door.

It was the same room into which he had been ushered, as a guest, eighteen years before: the same moon shone through the window; and the same autumn landscape lay outside. We had not yet lighted a candle, but all the apartment was visible, even to the portraits on the wall: the splendid head of Mrs Linton, and the graceful one of her husband. Heathcliff advanced to the hearth. Time had little altered his person either. There was the same man: his dark face rather sallower and more composed, his frame a stone or two heavier, perhaps, and no other difference. Catherine had risen, with an impulse to dash out, when she saw him.

'Stop!' he said, arresting her by the arm. 'No, more runnings away! Where would you go? I'm come to fetch you home; and I hope you'll be a dutiful daughter, and not encourage my son to further disobedience. I was embarrassed how to punish him when I discovered his part in the business: he's such a cobweb, a pinch would annihilate him; but you'll see by his look that he has received his due! I brought him down one evening, the day before yesterday, and just set him in a chair, and never touched him afterwards. I sent Hareton out, and we had the room to ourselves. In two hours, I called Joseph to carry him up again; and since then my presence is as potent on his nerves as a ghost; and I fancy he sees me often, though I am not near. Hareton says he wakes and shrieks in the night by the hour together, and calls you to protect him from me; and, whether you like your precious mate or not, you must come: he's your concern now; I yield all my interest in him to you.

'Why not let Catherine continue here?' I pleaded, 'and send Master Linton
her. As you hate them both, you'd not miss them: they *can* only be a daily
ague to your unnatural heart.'

'I'm seeking a tenant for the Grange,' he answered; 'and I want my children
out me, to be sure. Besides, that lass owes me her services for her bread.
m not going to nurture her in luxury and idleness after Linton has gone.
ake haste and get ready, now; and don't oblige me to compel you.'

'I shall,' said Catherine. 'Linton is all I have to love in the world, and though
u have done what you could to make him hateful to me, and me to him,
u *cannot* make us hate each other. And I defy you to hurt him when I am
, and I defy you to frighten me!'

'You are a boastful champion,' replied Heathcliff; 'but I don't like you
ell enough to hurt him: you shall get the full benefit of the torment, as
ng as it lasts. It is not I who will make him hateful to you—it is his own
eet spirit. He's as bitter as gall at your desertion and its consequences: don't
pect thanks for this noble devotion. I heard him draw a pleasant picture
Zillah of what he would do if he were as strong as I: the inclination is
ere, and his very weakness will sharpen his wits to find a substitute for
ength.'

'I know he has a bad nature,' said Catherine: 'he's your son. But I'm glad
e a better, to forgive it; and I know he loves me, and for that reason I love
m. Mr. Heathcliff, *you* have *nobody* to love you; and, however miserable
u make us, we shall still have the revenge of thinking that your cruelty
ises from your greater misery. You *are* miserable, are you not? Lonely,
e the devil, and envious like him? *Nobody* loves you—*nobody* will cry for
u when you die! I wouldn't be you!'

Catherine spoke with a kind of dreary triumph: she seemed to have made
her mind to enter into the spirit of her future family, and draw pleasure
om the griefs of her enemies.

'You shall be sorry to be yourself presently,' said her father-in-law, 'if
u stand there another minute. Begone, witch, and get your things!'

She scornfully withdrew. In her absence, I began to beg for Zillah's place
the Heights, offering to resign mine to her; but he would suffer it on no
count. He bid me be silent; and then, for the first time, allowed himself
glance round the room and a look at the pictures. Having studied Mrs.
nton, he said:

'I shall have that home. Not because I need it, but'——He turned abruptly
the fire, and continued, with what, for lack of a better word, I must call
smile—'I'll tell you what I did yesterday! I got the sexton, who was digging
nton's grave, to remove the earth off her coffin-lid, and I opened it. I thought,
ce, I would have stayed there: when I saw her face again—it is hers yet!—
had hard work to stir me; but he said it would change if the air blew on

it, and so I struck one side of the coffin loose, and covered it up: not Linton's
side, damn him! I wish he'd been soldered in lead. And I bribed the sexton
to pull it away when I'm laid there, and slide mine out too; I'll have it made
so: and then, by the time Linton gets to us he'll not know which is which!'

'You were very wicked, Mr. Heathcliff!' I exclaimed, 'were you not ashamed
to disturb the dead?'

'I disturbed nobody, Nelly,' he replied; 'and I gave some ease to myself.
I shall be a great deal more comfortable now; and you'll have a better chance
of keeping me underground, when I get there. Disturbed her? No! she has
disturbed me, night and day, through eighteen years—incessantly—remorselessly—till yesternight; and yesternight I was tranquil. I dreamt I was
sleeping the last sleep by that sleeper, with my heart stopped and my cheek
frozen against hers.'

'And if she had been dissolved into earth, or worse, what would you have
dreamt of then?' I said.

'Of dissolving with her, and being more happy still!' he answered. 'Do
you suppose I dread any change of that sort? I expected such a transformation
on raising the lid: but I'm better pleased that it should not commence till
I share it. Besides, unless I had received a distinct impression of her passionless
features, that strange feeling would hardly have been removed. It began
oddly. You know I was wild after she died; and eternally, from dawn to dawn,
praying her to return to me her spirit! I have a strong faith in ghosts: I have
a conviction that they can, and do, exist among us! The day she was buried
there came a fall of snow. In the evening I went to the churchyard. It blew
bleak as winter—all round was solitary. I didn't fear that her fool of a husband
would wander up the den so late; and no one else had business to bring them
there. Being alone, and conscious two yards of loose earth was the sole barrier
between us, I said to myself—"I'll have her in my arms again! If she be cold,
I'll think it is this north wind that chills me; and if she be motionless, it is
sleep." I got a spade from the tool-house, and began to delve with all my
might—it scraped the coffin; I fell to work with my hands; the wood commenced cracking about the screws; I was on the point of attaining my object,
when it seemed that I heard a sigh from some one above, close at the edge
of the grave, and bending down. "If I can only get this off," I muttered, "I
wish they may shovel in the earth over us both!" and I wrenched at it more
desperately still. There was another sigh, close at my ear. I appeared to feel
the warm breath of it displacing the sleet-laden wind. I knew no living thing
in flesh and blood was by; but, as certainly as you perceive the approach of
some substantial body in the dark, though it cannot be discerned, so certainly
I felt that Cathy was there: not under me, but on the earth. A sudden sense
of relief flowed from my heart through every limb. I relinquished my labour
of agony, and turned consoled at once: unspeakably consoled. Her presence

was with me: it remained while I refilled the grave, and led me home. You may laugh, if you will; but I was sure I should see her there. I was sure she was with me, and I could not help talking to her. Having reached the Heights, I rushed eagerly to the door. It was fastened; and, I remember, that accursed Earnshaw and my wife opposed my entrance. I remember stopping to kick the breath out of him, and then hurrying upstairs, to my room and hers. I looked round impatiently—I felt her by me—I could *almost* see her, and yet I *could not*! I ought to have sweat blood then, from the anguish of my yearning — from the fervour of my supplications to have but one glimpse! I had not one. She showed herself, as she often was in life, a devil to me! And, since then, sometimes more and sometimes less, I've been the sport of that intolerable torture! Infernal! keeping my nerves at such a stretch, that, if they had not resembled catgut, they would long ago have relaxed to the feebleness of Linton's. When I sat in the house with Hareton, it seemed that on going out, I should meet her; when I walked on the moors I should meet her coming in. When I went from home, I hastened to return: she *must* be somewhere at the Heights, I was certain! And when I slept in her chamber—I was beaten out of that. I couldn't lie there; for the moment I closed my eyes, she was either outside the window, or sliding back the panels, or entering the room, or even resting her darling head on the same pillow as she did when a child; and I must open my lids to see. And so I opened and closed them a hundred times a night—to be always disappointed! It racked me! I've often groaned aloud, till that old rascal Joseph no doubt believed that my conscience was playing the fiend inside of me. Now, since I've seen her, I'm pacified—a little. It was a strange way of killing! not by inches, but by fractions and hairbreadths, to beguile me with the spectre of a hope, through eighteen years!'

Mr. Heathcliff paused and wiped his forehead; his hair clung to it, wet with perspiration; his eyes were fixed on the red embers of the fire, the brows not contracted, but raised next the temples; diminishing the grim aspect of his countenance, but imparting a peculiar look of trouble, and a painful appearance of mental tension towards one absorbing subject. He only half addressed me, and I maintained silence. I didn't like to hear him talk! After a short period he resumed his meditation on the picture, took it down and leant it against the sofa to contemplate it at better advantage; and while so occupied Catherine entered, announcing that she was ready, when her pony should be saddled.

'Send that over to-morrow,' said Heathcliff to me; then turning to her, he added—'You may do without your pony: it is a fine evening, and you'll need no ponies at Wuthering Heights; for what journeys you take, your own feet will serve you. Come along.'

'Good-bye, Ellen!' whispered my dear little mistress. As she kissed me,

her lips felt like ice. 'Come and see me, Ellen; don't forget.'

'Take care you do no such thing, Mrs. Dean!' said her new father. 'Whe I wish to speak to you I'll come here. I want none of your prying at m house!'

He signed her to precede him; and casting back a look that cut my hear she obeyed. I watched them from the window, walk down the garden. Heathcli fixed Catherine's arm under his: though she disputed the act at first evidently and with rapid strides he hurried her into the alley, whose trees conceale them.

CHAPTER 30

I have paid a visit to the Heights, but I have not seen her since she left Joseph held the door in his hand when I called to ask after her, and wouldn let me pass. He said Mrs. Linton was 'thrang,' and the master was not ir Zillah has told me something of the way they go on, otherwise I should hardl know who was dead and who living. She thinks Catherine haughty, an does not like her, I can guess by her talk. My young lady asked some ai of her when she first came; but Mr. Heathcliff told her to follow her ow business, and let his daughter-in-law look after herself; and Zillah willingl acquiesced, being a narrow-minded, selfish woman. Catherine evinced a child annoyance at this neglect; repaid it with contempt, and thus enlisted m informant among her enemies, as securely as if she had done her some grea wrong. I had a long talk with Zillah about six weeks ago, a little before yo came, one day when we foregathered on the moor; and this is what she told me

'The first thing Mrs. Linton did,' she said, 'on her arrival at the Height was to run upstairs, without even wishing good evening to me and Josepl she shut herself into Linton's room, and remained till morning. Then, whi the master and Earnshaw were at breakfast, she entered the house, an asked all in a quiver if the doctor might be sent for? her cousin was very il

' "We know that!" answered Heathcliff; "but his life is not worth a farthing and I won't spend a farthing on him."

' "But I cannot tell how to do," she said; "and if nobody will help me, he die!"

' "Walk out of the room," cried the master, "and let me never hear a wor more about him! None here care what becomes of him; if you do, act th nurse; if you do not, lock him up and leave him."

'Then she began to bother me, and I said I'd had enough plague with th tiresome thing; we each had our tasks, and hers was to wait on Linton, M Heathcliff bid me leave that labour to her.

'How they managed together, I can't tell. I fancy he fretted a great dea and moaned hisseln night and day; and she had precious little rest: one coul

uess by her white face and heavy eyes. She sometimes came into the kitchen
ll wildered like, and looked as if she would fain beg assistance; but I was
ot going to disobey the master: I never dare disobey him, Mrs. Dean; and,
hough I thought it wrong that Kenneth should not be sent for, it was no
oncern of mine either to advise or complain, and I always refused to meddle.
Once or twice, after we had gone to bed, I've happened to open my door
gain and seen her sitting crying on the stairs' top; and then I've shut myself
a quick, for fear of being moved to interfere. I did pity her then, I'm sure:
till I didn't wish to lose my place, you know.

'At last, one night she came boldly into my chamber, and frightened me
ut of my wits, by saying:

' "Tell Mr. Heathcliff that his son is dying—I'm sure he is, this time. Get up,
nstantly, and tell him."

'Having uttered this speech, she vanished again. I lay a quarter of an hour
stening and trembling. Nothing stirred—the house was quiet.

'She's mistaken, I said to myself. He's got over it. I needn't disturb them;
nd I began to doze. But my sleep was marred a second time by a sharp
inging of the bell—the only bell we have, put up on purpose for Linton;
nd the master called to me to see what was the matter, and inform them that
e wouldn't have that noise repeated.

'I delivered Catherine's message. He cursed to himself, and in a few minutes
ame out with a lighted candle, and proceeded to their room. I followed. Mrs.
Heathcliff was seated by the bedside, with her hands folded on her knees.
Her father-in-law went up, held the light to Linton's face, looked at him,
nd touched him; afterwards he turned to her.

' "Now—Catherine," he said, "how do you feel?"

'She was dumb.

' "How do you feel, Catherine?" he repeated.

' "He's safe, and I'm free," she answered: "I should feel well—but," she
ontinued, with a bitterness she couldn't conceal, "you have left me so long
o struggle against death alone, that I feel and see only death! I feel like death!"

'And she looked like it, too! I gave her a little wine. Hareton and Joseph,
ho had been wakened by the ringing and the sound of feet, and heard
ur talk from outside, now entered. Joseph was fain, I believe, of the lad's
emoval; Hareton seemed a thought bothered: though he was more taken
p with staring at Catherine than thinking of Linton. But the master bid him
et off to bed again: we didn't want his help. He afterwards made Joseph
emove the body to his chamber, and told me to return to mine, and Mrs.
Heathcliff remained by herself.

'In the morning, he sent me to tell her she must come down to breakfast:
ae had undressed, and appeared going to sleep, and said she was ill; at which
hardly wondered. I informed Mr. Heathcliff, and he replied:

' "Well, let her be till after the funeral; and go up now and then to get he what is needful; and, as soon as she seems better, tell me." '

Cathy stayed upstairs a fortnight, according to Zillah; who visited he twice a day, and would have been rather more friendly, but her attempts a increasing kindness were proudly and promptly repelled.

Heathcliff went up once, to show her Linton's will. He had bequeathed th whole of his, and what had been her, movable property to his father: th poor creature was threatened, or coaxed, into that act during her week' absence, when his uncle died. The lands, being a minor, he could not medd with. However, Mr. Heathcliff has claimed and kept them in his wife's righ and his also: I suppose legally: at any rate, Catherine, destitute of cash an friends, cannot disturb his possession.

'Nobody,' said Zillah, 'ever approached her door, except that once, but I and nobody asked anything about her. The first occasion of her comin down into the house was on a Sunday afternoon. She had cried out, when carried up her dinner, that she couldn't bear any longer being in the cold: an I told her the master was going to Thrushcross Grange, and Earnshaw an I needn't hinder her from descending; so, as soon as she heard Heathcliff horse trot off, she made her appearance donned in black, and her yellov curls combed back behind her ears as plain as a Quaker: she couldn't com them out.

'Joseph and I generally go to chapel on Sundays;' the kirk, you know, ha no minister now, explained Mrs. Dean; and they call the Methodists' o Baptists' place (I can't say which it is), at Gimmerton, a chapel. 'Joseph ha gone,' she continued, 'but I thought proper to bide at home. Young folk are always the better for an elder's over-looking; and Hareton, with all h bashfulness, isn't a model of nice behaviour. I let him know that his cousin woul very likely sit with us, and she had been always used to see the Sabbath respec ted; so he had as good leave his guns and bits of indoor work alone, whil she stayed. He coloured up at the news, and cast his eyes over his hands an clothes. The train-oil and gunpowder were shoved out of sight in a minut I saw he meant to give her his company; and I guessed, by his way, he wante to be presentable; so, laughing, as I durst not laugh when the master is by I offered to help him, if he would, and joked at his confusion. He grew sulle and began to swear.

'Now, Mrs. Dean,' Zillah went on, seeing me not pleased by her manne 'you happen think your young lady too fine for Mr. Hareton; and happe you're right: but I own I should love well to bring her pride a peg lowe And what will all her learning and her daintiness do for her, now? She as poor as you or I: poorer I'll be bound: you're saving, and I'm doing m little all that road.'

Hareton allowed Zillah to give him her aid; and she flattered him int

good humour: so, when Catherine came, half forgetting her former insults,
e tried to make himself agreeable, by the housekeeper's account.

'Missis walked in,' she said, 'as chill as an icicle, and as high as a princess.
 got up and offered her my seat in the arm-chair. No, she turned up her
ose at my civility. Earnshaw rose, too, and bid her come to the settle, and
t close by the fire: he was sure she was starved.

' "I've been starved a month and more," she answered, resting on the
ord as scornful as she could.

'And she got a chair for herself, and placed it at a distance from both of us.
aving sat till she was warm, she began, to look round, and discovered
 number of books in the dresser; she was instantly upon her feet again,
retching to reach them: but they were too high up. Her cousin, after watch-
g her endeavours a while, at last summoned courage to help her; she held
er frock, and he filled it with the first that came to hand.

'That was a great advance for the lad. She didn't thank him; still, he felt
 atified that she had accepted his assistance, and ventured to stand behind
 she examined them, and even to stoop and point out what struck his fancy in
 rtain old pictures which they contained; nor was he daunted by the saucy
yle in which she jerked the page from his finger: he contented himself with
 ing a bit farther back, and looking at her instead of the book. She continued
 ading, or seeking for something to read. His attention became, by degrees,
 ite centred in the study of her thick, silky curls: her face he couldn't see,
 d she couldn't see him. And, perhaps, not quite awake to what he did,
 ut attracted like a child to a candle, at last he proceeded from staring to
 uching; he put out his hand and stroked one curl, as gently as if it were
 bird. He might have stuck a knife into her neck, she started round in such
 taking.

' "Get away, this moment! How dare you touch me? Why are you stopping
 ere?" she cried, in a tone of disgust. "I can't endure you! I'll go upstairs
 ain, if you come near me."

'Mr. Hareton recoiled, looking as foolish as he could do: he sat down in
 e settle very quiet, and she continued turning over her volumes another
 alf-hour; finally, Earnshaw crossed over, and whispered to me:

' "Will you ask her to read to us, Zillah? I'm stalled of doing naught; and
 do like—I could like to hear her! Dunnot say I wanted it, but ask of yourseln."

' "Mr. Hareton wishes you would read to us, ma'am," I said immediately.
 He'd take it very kind—he'd be much obliged."

'She frowned; and looking up, answered:

' "Mr. Hareton, and the whole set of you, will be good enough to under-
 and that I reject any pretence at kindness you have the hypocrisy to offer!
 despise you, and will have nothing to say to any of you! When I would
 ave given my life for one kind word, even to see one of your faces, you all

kept off. But I won't complain to you! I'm driven down here by the cold not either to amuse you or enjoy your society."

' "What could I ha' done?" began Earnshaw. "How was I to blame?"

' "Oh! you are an exception," answered Mrs. Heathcliff. "I never misse such a concern as you."

' "But I offered more than once, and asked," he said, kindling up at h pertness, "I asked Mr. Heathcliff to let me wake for you"——

' "Be silent! I'll go out of doors, or anywhere, rather than have your di agreeable voice in my ear!" said my lady.

'Hareton muttered she might go to hell, for him! and unslinging his gu restrained himself from his Sunday occupations no longer. He talked nov freely enough; and she presently saw fit to retreat to her solitude: but th frost had set in, and, in spite of her pride, she was forced to condescend our company, more and more. However, I took care there should be n further scorning at my good-nature: ever since, I've been as stiff as herse and she has no lover or liker among us: and she does not deserve one; for, l them say the least word to her, and she'll curl back without respect of ar one! She'll snap at the master himself, and as good as dares him to thra her; and the more hurt she gets, the more venomous she grows.'

At first, on hearing this account from Zillah, I determined to leave n situation, take a cottage, and get Catherine to come and live with me: b Mr. Heathcliff would as soon permit that as he would set up Hareton in a independent house; and I can see no remedy, at present, unless she cou marry again: and that scheme it does not come within my province to arrang

Thus ended Mrs. Dean's story. Notwithstanding the doctor's prophec I am rapidly recovering strength; and though it be only the second we in January, I propose getting out on horseback in a day or two, and ridi over to Wuthering Heights, to inform my landlord that I shall spend th next six months in London; and, if he likes, he may look out for anoth tenant to take the place after October. I would not pass another winter he for much.

CHAPTER 31

esterday was bright, calm, and frosty. I went to the Heights as I proposed;
y housekeeper entreated me to bear a little note from her to her young lady,
nd I did not refuse, for the worthy woman was not conscious of anything
dd in her request. The front door stood open, but the jealous gate was fastened,
at my last visit; I knocked, and invoked Earnshaw from among the garden
eds; he unchained it, and I entered. The fellow is as handsome a rustic
need be seen. I took particular notice of him this time; but then he does
is best, apparently, to make the least of his advantages.

I asked if Mr. Heathcliff were at home? He answered, No; but he would be
at dinner-time. It was eleven o'clock, and I announced my intention of going
and waiting for him, at which he immediately flung down his tools and
ccompanied me, in the office of watchdog, not as a substitute for the host.

We entered together; Catherine was there, making herself useful in prepar-
g some vegetables for the approaching meal; she looked more sulky and less
irited than when I had seen her first. She hardly raised her eyes to notice
e, and continued her employment with the same disregard to common forms
politeness as before; never returning my bow and good-morning by the slight-
t acknowledgment.

'She does not seem so amiable,' I thought, 'as Mrs. Dean would persuade me
believe. She's a beauty, it is true; but not an angel.'

Earnshaw surlily bid her remove her things to the kitchen. 'Remove them
urself,' she said, pushing them from her as soon as she had done; and retiring
a stool by the window, where she began to carve figures of birds and beasts
t of the turnip parings in her lap. I approached her, pretending to desire
view of the garden; and, as I fancied, adroitly dropped Mrs. Dean's note
to her knee, unnoticed by Hareton—but she asked aloud, 'What is that?'
d chucked it off.

'A letter from your old acquaintance, the housekeeper at the Grange,'
answered; annoyed at her exposing my kind deed, and fearful lest it should
imagined a missive of my own. She would gladly have gathered it up at
is information, but Hareton beat her; he seized and put it in his waistcoat,
ying Mr. Heathcliff should look at it first. Thereat, Catherine silently turned
r face from us, and, very stealthily, drew out her pocket-handkerchief and
plied it to her eyes; and her cousin, after struggling a while to keep down
s softer feelings, pulled out the letter and flung it on the floor beside her,
ungraciously as he could. Catherine caught and perused it eagerly; then
e put a few questions to me concerning the inmates, rational and irrational,
her former home; and gazing towards the hills, murmured in soliloquy:
'I should like to be riding Minny down there! I should like to be climbing
there! Oh! I'm tired—I'm *stalled*, Hareton!' And she leant her pretty head

back against the sill, with half a yawn and half a sigh, and lapsed into an aspect of abstracted sadness: neither caring nor knowing whether we remarked her.

'Mrs. Heathcliff,' I said, after sitting some time mute, 'you are not aware that I am an acquaintance of yours? so intimate that I think it strange you won't come and speak to me. My housekeeper never wearies of talking about and praising you; and she'll be greatly disappointed if I return with no news of or from you, except that you received her letter and said nothing!'

She appeared to wonder at this speech, and asked:

'Does Ellen like you?'

'Yes, very well,' I replied unhesitatingly.

'You must tell her,' she continued, 'that I would answer her letter, but I have no materials for writing: not even a book from which I might tear a leaf.'

'No books!' I exclaimed. 'How do you contrive to live here without them, if I may take the liberty to inquire. Though provided with a large library, I'm frequently very dull at the Grange; take my books away, and I should be desperate!'

'I was always reading, when I had them,' said Catherine; 'and Mr. Heath cliff never reads; so he took it into his head to destroy my books. I have not had a glimpse of one for weeks. Only once, I searched through Joseph's store of theology, to his great irritation; and once, Hareton, I came upon a secret stock in your room—some Latin and Greek, and some tales and poetry all old friends. I brought the last here—and you gathered them, as a magpie gathers silver spoons, for the mere love of stealing! They are of no use to you or else you concealed them in the bad spirit that as you cannot enjoy them nobody else shall. Perhaps *your* envy counselled Mr. Heathcliff to rob me my treasures? But I've most of them written on my brain and printed my heart, and you cannot deprive me of those!'

Earnshaw blushed crimson when his cousin made this revelation of his private literary accumulations, and stammered an indignant denial of her accusation.

'Mr. Hareton is desirous of increasing his amount of knowledge,' I said coming to his rescue. 'He is not *envious* but *emulous* of your attainments. He'll be a clever scholar in a few years.'

'And he wants *me* to sink into a dunce, meantime,' answered Catherine. 'Yes, I hear him trying to spell and read to himself, and pretty blunders he makes! I wish you would repeat Chevy Chase as you did yesterday: it was extremely funny. I heard you; and I heard you turning over the dictionary to seek out the hard words, and then cursing because you couldn't read the explanations!'

The young man evidently thought it too bad that he should be laughed at for his ignorance, and then laughed at for trying to remove it. I had a similar

otion; and, remembering Mrs. Dean's anecdote of his first attempt at en-
ghtening the darkness in which he had been reared, I observed:

'But, Mrs. Heathcliff, we have each had a commencement, and each
tumbled and tottered on the threshold; had our teachers scorned instead
f aiding us, we should stumble and totter yet.'

'Oh!' she replied, 'I don't wish to limit his acquirements: still, he has no
ight to appropriate what is mine, and make it ridiculous to me with his
ile mistakes and mispronunciations! Those books, both prose and verse,
vere consecrated to me by other associations; and I hate to have them debased
nd profaned in his mouth! Besides, of all, he has selected my favourite pieces
hat I love the most to repeat, as if out of deliberate malice.'

Hareton's chest heaved in silence a minute: he laboured under a severe
nse of mortification and wrath, which it was no easy task to suppress. I rose,
nd, from a gentlemanly idea of relieving his embarrassment, took up my
ation in the doorway, surveying the external prospect as I stood. He followed
y example, and left the room; but presently reappeared, bearing half-a-dozen
olumes in his hands, which he threw into Catherine's lap, exclaiming:

'Take them! I never want to hear, or read, or think of them again!'

'I won't have them now,' she answered. 'I shall connect them with you, and
ate them.'

She opened one that had obviously been often turned over, and read a por-
on in the drawling tone of a beginner; then laughed, and threw it from her.
And listen,' she continued provokingly, commencing a verse of an old
allad in the same fashion.

But his self-love would endure no further torment: I heard, and not alto-
ether disapprovingly, a manual check given to her saucy tongue. The
ttle wretch had done her utmost to hurt her cousin's sensitive though un-
ultivated feelings, and a physical argument was the only mode he had of
alancing the account, and repaying its effects on the inflicter. He afterwards
athered the books and hurled them on the fire. I read in his countenance
hat anguish it was to offer that sacrifice to spleen. I fancied that as they
onsumed, he recalled the pleasure they had already imparted, and the
iumph and ever-increasing pleasure he had anticipated from them; and
fancied I guessed the incitement to his secret studies also. He had been
ontent with daily labour and rough animal enjoyments, till Catherine
ossed his path. Shame at her scorn, and hope of her approval, were his
rst prompters to higher pursuits; and, instead of guarding him from one
nd winning him to the other, his endeavours to rise himself had produced
ist the contrary result.

'Yes; that's all the good that such a brute as you can get from them!' cried
atherine, sucking her damaged lip, and watching the conflagration with
idignant eyes.

'You'd *better* hold your tongue, now,' he answered fiercely.

And his agitation precluding further speech, he advanced hastily to th
entrance, where I made way for him to pass. But ere he had crossed the door
stones, Mr. Heathcliff, coming up the causeway, encountered him, and layin
hold of his shoulder, asked:

'What's to do now, my lad?'

'Naught, naught,' he said, and broke away to enjoy his grief and anger i
solitude.

Heathcliff gazed after him, and sighed.

'It will be odd if I thwart myself,' he muttered, unconscious that I wa
behind him. 'But when I look for his father in his face, I find *her* every da
more. How the devil is he so like? I can hardly bear to see him.'

He bent his eyes to the ground, and walked moodily in. There was a restles
anxious expression in his countenance I had never remarked there before
and he looked sparer in person. His daughter-in-law, on perceiving hir
through the window, immediately escaped to the kitchen, so that I remaine
alone.

'I'm glad to see you out of doors again, Mr. Lockwood,' he said, in rep
to my greeting; 'from selfish motives partly: I don't think I could readi
supply your loss in this desolation. I've wondered more than once wh
brought you here.'

'An idle whim, I fear, sir,' was my answer; 'or else an idle whim is goir
to spirit me away. I shall set out for London, next week; and I must give yc
warning that I feel no disposition to retain Thrushcross Grange beyond th
twelve months I agreed to rent it. I believe I shall not live there any more

'Oh, indeed; you're tired of being banished from the world, are you?' he sai
'But if you be coming to plead off paying for a place you won't occupy, yo
journey is useless: I never relent in exacting my due from any one.'

'I'm coming to plead off nothing about it,' I exclaimed, considerably irrit
ted. 'Should you wish it, I'll settle with you now,' and I drew my note-boc
from my pocket.

'No, no,' he replied coolly; 'you'll leave sufficient behind to cover yo
debts, if you fail to return: I'm not in such a hurry. Sit down and take yo
dinner with us; a guest that is safe from repeating his visit can generally
made welcome. Catherine, bring the things in: where are you?'

Catherine reappeared, bearing a tray of knives and forks.

'You may get your dinner with Joseph,' muttered Heathcliff aside, 'ar
remain in the kitchen till he is gone.'

She obeyed his directions very punctually: perhaps she had no temptati
to transgress. Living among clowns and misanthropists, she probably cann
appreciate a better class of people when she meets them.

With Mr. Heathcliff, grim and saturnine, on the one hand, and Haretc

bsolutely dumb, on the other, I made a somewhat cheerless meal, and bid dieu early. I would have departed by the back way, to get a last glimpse f Catherine and annoy old Joseph; but Hareton received orders to lead p my horse, and my host himself escorted me to the door, so I could not fulfil y wish.

'How dreary life gets over in that house!' I reflected, while riding down the ad. 'What a realisation of something more romantic than a fairy tale it ould have been for Mrs. Linton Heathcliff, had she and I struck up an ttachment, as her good nurse desired, and migrated together into the stirring tmosphere of the town!'

CHAPTER 32

1802.—

his September I was invited to devastate the moors of a friend in the north, nd on my journey to his abode, I unexpectedly came within fifteen miles f Gimmerton. The ostler at a roadside public-house was holding a pail of ater to refresh my horses, when a cart of very green oats, newly reaped, assed by, and he remarked:

'Yon's frough Gimmerton, nah! They're allas three wick after other folk i' ther harvest.'

'Gimmerton?' I repeated—my residence in that locality had already grown im and dreamy. 'Ah! I know. How far is it from this?'

'Happen fourteen mile o'er th' hills; and a rough road,' he answered.

A sudden impulse seized me to visit Thrushcross Grange. It was scarcely oon, and I conceived that I might as well pass the night under my own roof s in an inn. Besides, I could spare a day easily to arrange matters with my andlord, and thus save myself the trouble of invading the neighbourhood gain. Having rested a while, I directed my servant to inquire the way to the illage; and, with great fatigue to our beasts, we managed the distance in me three hours.

I left him there, and proceeded down the valley alone. The grey church oked greyer, and the lonely churchyard lonelier. I distinguished a moor eep cropping the short turf on the graves. It was sweet, warm weather—too arm for travelling; but the heat did not hinder me from enjoying the delightful enery above and below: had I seen it nearer August, I'm sure it would ave tempted me to waste a month among its solitudes. In winter nothing ore dreary, in summer nothing more divine, than those glens shut in by ills, and those bluff, bold swells of heath.

I reached the Grange before sunset, and knocked for admittance; but the mily had retreated into the back premises, I judged, by one thin, blue

595

wreath curling from the kitchen chimney, and they did not hear. I rod
into the court. Under the porch, a girl of nine or ten sat knitting, and a
old woman reclined on the house-steps, smoking a meditative pipe.

'Is Mrs. Dean within?' I demanded of the dame.

'Mistress Dean? Nay!' she answered, 'shoo doesn't bide here: shoo's u
at th' Heights.'

'Are you the housekeeper, then?' I continued.

'Ea, Aw keep th' house,' she replied.

'Well, I'm Mr. Lockwood, the master. Are there any rooms to lodge m
in, I wonder? I wish to stay here all night.'

'T' maister!' she cried in astonishment. 'Whet, whoiver knew yah wu
coming? Yah sud ha' send word. They's nowt norther dry nor mensful abal
t' place: nowt there isn't!'

She threw down her pipe and bustled in, the girl followed, and I entere
too; soon perceiving that her report was true, and, moreover, that I ha
almost upset her wits by my unwelcome apparition, I bid her be composec
I would go out for a walk; and, meantime, she must try to prepare a corne
of a sitting-room for me to sup in, and a bedroom to sleep in. No sweepin
and dusting, only good fire and dry sheets were necessary. She seemed willir
to do her best; though she thrust the hearth-brush into the grates in mistak
for the poker, and mal-appropriated several other articles of her craft: bι
I retired, confiding in her energy for a resting-place against my return. Wuthe
ing Heights was the goal of my proposed excursion. An after-thought brougl
me back, when I had quitted the court.

'All well at the Heights?' I inquired of the woman.

'Eea, f'r owt Ee knaw,' she answered, skurrying away with a pan of hι
cinders.

I would have asked why Mrs. Dean had deserted the Grange, but it wa
impossible to delay her at such a crisis, so I turned away and made my exι
rambling leisurely along with the glow of a sinking sun behind, and th
mild glory of a rising moon in front—one fading, and the other brightening—ι
I quitted the park, and climbed the stony by-road branching off to M
Heathcliff's dwelling. Before I arrived in sight of it, all that remained
day was a beamless amber light along the west: but I could see every pebb
on the path, and every blade of grass, by that splendid moon. I had neith
to climb the gate nor to knock—it yielded to my hand. That is an improvemen
I thought. And I noticed another, by the aid of my nostrils; a fragrance
stocks and wallflowers wafted on the air from amongst the homely fruit-tree

Both doors and lattices were open; and yet, as is usually the case in a co
district, a fine, red fire illumined the chimney: the comfort which the eι
derives from it renders the extra heat endurable. But the house of Wutheriι
Heights is so large, that the inmates have plenty of space for withdrawing o

f its influence; and accordingly, what inmates there were had stationed
hemselves not far from one of the windows. I could both see them and hear
hem talk before I entered, and looked and listened in consequence; being
noved thereto by a mingled sense of curiosity and envy, that grew as I lin-
ered.

'Con-*trary*!' said a voice as sweet as a silver bell—'That for the third time,
ou dunce! I'm not going to tell you again. Recollect, or I'll pull your hair!'

'Contrary, then,' answered another, in deep but softened tones. 'And
ow, kiss me, for minding so well.'

'No, read it over first correctly, without a single mistake.'

The male speaker began to read: he was a young man, respectably dressed
nd seated at a table, having a book before him. His handsome features
lowed with pleasure, and his eyes kept impatiently wandering from the
age to a small white hand over his shoulder, which recalled him by a smart
ap on the cheek, whenever its owner detected such signs of inattention. Its
wner stood behind; her light, shining ringlets blending, at intervals, with
is brown locks, as she bent to superintend his studies; and her face—it
as lucky he could not see her face, or he would never have been so steady.
could; and I bit my lip in spite, at having thrown away the chance I might
ave had of doing something besides staring at its smiling beauty.

The task was done, not free from further blunders; but the pupil claimed
reward, and received at least five kisses: which, however, he generously
turned. Then they came to the door, and from their conversation I judged
ey were about to issue out and have a walk on the moors. I supposed I should
e condemned in Hareton Earnshaw's heart, if not by his mouth, to the lowest
it in the infernal regions, if I showed my unfortunate person in his neigh-
ourhood then; and feeling very mean and malignant, I skulked round to
ek refuge in the kitchen. There was unobstructed admittance on that side
so, and at the door sat my old friend Nelly Dean, sewing and singing a song;
hich was often interrupted from within by harsh words of scorn and intol-
ance, uttered in far from musical accents.

'Aw'd rayther, by th' haulf, hev 'em swearing i' my lugs frough morn to
eeght, nur hearken yah, hahsiver!' said the tenant of the kitchen, in answer
an unheard speech of Nelly's. 'It's a blazing shaime, ut Aw cannut oppen
blessed Book, bud yah set up them glories tuh Sattan, un' all t' flaysome
ickednesses ut iver wer born intuh t' warld! Oh! yah'er a raight nowt;
' shoo's another; un' that poor lad'll be lost atween ye. Poor lad!' he added,
ith a groan; 'he's witched: Aw'm sartin on't! O Lord, judge 'em, fur they's
rther law nur justice amang wer rullers!'

'No! or we should be sitting in flaming fagots, I suppose,' retorted the
ager. 'But wisht, old man, and read your Bible like a Christian, and never
ind me. This is "Fairy Annie's Wedding"—a bonny tune—it goes to a dance.'

Mrs. Dean was about to recommence, when I advanced; and recognising me directly, she jumped to her feet, crying:

'Why, bless you, Mr. Lockwood! How could you think of returning in this way? All's shut up at Thrushcross Grange. You should have given us notice!'

'I've arranged to be accommodated there, for as long as I shall stay,' I answered. 'I depart again to-morrow. And how are you transplanted here Mrs. Dean? tell me that.'

'Zillah left, and Mr. Heathcliff wished me to come, soon after you went to London, and stay till you returned. But, step in, pray! Have you walked from Gimmerton this evening?'

'From the Grange,' I replied; 'and while they make me lodging room there I want to finish my business with your master; because I don't think of having another opportunity in a hurry.'

'What business, sir?' said Nelly, conducting me into the house. 'He's gone out at present, and won't return soon.'

'About the rent,' I answered.

'Oh! then it is with Mrs. Heathcliff you must settle,' she observed; 'or rather with me. She has not learnt to manage her affairs yet, and I act for her: there's nobody else.'

I looked surprised.

'Ah! you have not heard of Heathcliff's death, I see,' she continued.

'Heathcliff dead!' I exclaimed, astonished. 'How long ago?'

'Three months since: but sit down and let me take your hat, and I'll tell you all about it. Stop, you have had nothing to eat, have you?'

'I want nothing: I have ordered supper at home. You sit down too. I never dreamt of his dying! Let me hear how it came to pass. You say you don't expect them back for some time—the young people?'

'No—I have to scold them every evening for their late rambles: but they don't care for me. At least have a drink of our old ale; it will do you good you seem weary.'

She hastened to fetch it before I could refuse, and I heard Joseph asking whether 'it warn't a crying scandal that she should have fellies at her time of life? And then, to get them jocks out uh' t' maister's cellar! He fair shaamed to 'bide still and see it.'

She did not stay to retaliate, but re-entered in a minute, bearing a reaming silver pint, whose contents I lauded with becoming earnestness. And afterwards she furnished me with the sequel of Heathcliff's history. He had a 'queer' end, as she expressed it.

I was summoned to Wuthering Heights, within a fortnight of your leaving us, she said; and I obeyed joyfully, for Catherine's sake. My first interview with her grieved and shocked me: she had altered so much since our separa

ion. Mr. Heathcliff did not explain his reasons for taking a new mind about my coming here; he only told me he wanted me, and he was tired of seeing Catherine: I must make the little parlour my sitting-room, and keep her with me. It was enough if he were obliged to see her once or twice a day. She seemed pleased at this arrangement; and, by degrees, I smuggled over a great number of books, and other articles, that had formed her amusement at the Grange; and flattered myself we should get on in tolerable comfort. The delusion did not last long. Catherine, contented at first, in a brief space grew irritable and restless. For one thing, she was forbidden to move out of the garden, and it fretted her sadly to be confined to its narrow bounds as spring drew on; for another, in following the house, I was forced to quit her frequently, and she complained of loneliness: she preferred quarrelling with Joseph in the kitchen to sitting at peace in her solitude. I did not mind their skirmishes: but Hareton was often obliged to seek the kitchen also, when the master wanted to have the house to himself; and though in the beginning she either left it at his approach, or quietly joined in my occupations, and shunned remarking or addressing him—and though he was always as sullen and silent as possible—after a while she changed her behaviour, and became incapable of letting him alone: talking at him; commenting on his stupidity and idleness; expressing her wonder how he could endure the life he lived—how he could sit a whole evening staring into the fire and dozing.

'He's just like a dog, is he not, Ellen?' she once observed, 'or a cart-horse? He does his work, eats his food, and sleeps eternally! What a blank, dreary mind he must have! Do you ever dream, Hareton? And, if you do, what is it about? But you can't speak to me!'

Then she looked at him; but he would neither open his mouth nor look again.

'He's, perhaps, dreaming now,' she continued. 'He twitched his shoulder as Juno twitches hers. Ask him, Ellen.'

'Mr. Hareton will ask the master to send you upstairs, if you don't behave!' I said. He had not only twitched his shoulder but clenched his fist, as if tempted to use it.

'I know why Hareton never speaks, when I am in the kitchen.' she exclaimed, on another occasion. 'He is afraid I shall laugh at him. Ellen, what do you think? He began to teach himself to read once; and because I laughed, he burned his books, and dropped it: was he not a fool?'

'Were not you naughty?' I said; 'answer me that.'

'Perhaps I was,' she went on; 'but I did not expect him to be so silly. Hareton, if I gave you a book, would you take it now? I'll try!'

She placed one she had been perusing on his hand; he flung it off, and muttered, if she did not give over, he would break her neck.

'Well, I shall put it here,' she said, 'in the table drawer; and I'm going to bed.'

Then she whispered me to watch whether he touched it, and departed.
But he would not come near it; and so I informed her in the morning, to her
great disappointment. I saw she was sorry for his persevering sulkiness and
indolence: her conscience reproved her for frightening him off improving
himself: she had done it effectually. But her ingenuity was at work to remedy
the injury: while I ironed, or pursued other stationary employments I could
not well do in the parlour, she would bring some pleasant volume and read
it aloud to me. When Hareton was there, she generally paused in an interesting
part, and left the book lying about: that she did repeatedly; but he was as
obstinate as a mule, and, instead of snatching at her bait, in wet weather he
took to smoking with Joseph; and they sat like automatons, one on each side
of the fire, the elder happily too deaf to understand her wicked nonsense,
as he would have called it, the younger doing his best to seem to disregard it.
On fine evenings the latter followed his shooting expeditions, and Catherine
yawned and sighed, and teased me to talk to her, and ran off into the court
or garden, the moment I began; and, as a last resource, cried, and said she
was tired of living: her life was useless.

Mr. Heathcliff, who grew more and more disinclined to society, had almost
banished Earnshaw out of his apartment. Owing to an accident at the com-
mencement of March, he became for some days a fixture in the kitchen.
His gun burst while out on the hills by himself; a splinter cut his arm, and
he lost a good deal of blood before he could reach home. The consequence
was that, perforce, he was condemned to the fireside and tranquillity, till he
made it up again. It suited Catherine to have him there: at any rate, it made
her hate her room upstairs more than ever: and she would compel me to
find out business below, that she might accompany me.

On Easter Monday, Joseph went to Gimmerton fair with some cattle;
and, in the afternoon, I was busy getting up linen in the kitchen. Earnshaw
sat, morose as usual, at the chimney-corner, and my little mistress was be-
guiling an idle hour with drawing pictures on the window panes; varying
her amusement by smothered bursts of songs, and whispered ejaculations, and
quick glances of annoyance and impatience in the direction of her cousin,
who steadfastly smoked, and looked into the grate. At a notice that I could
do with her no longer intercepting my light, she removed to the hearth-
stone. I bestowed little attention on her proceedings, but, presently, I heard
her begin:

'I've found out, Hareton, that I want—that I'm glad—that I should like
you to be my cousin now, if you had not grown so cross to me, and so
rough.'

Hareton returned no answer.

'Hareton, Hareton, Hareton! do you hear?' she continued.

'Get off wi' ye!' he growled, with uncompromising gruffness.

'Let me take that pipe,' she said, cautiously advancing her hand and abstracting it from his mouth.

Before he could attempt to recover it, it was broken, and behind the fire. He swore at her and seized another.

'Stop,' she cried, 'you must listen to me first; and I can't speak while those clouds are floating in my face.'

'Will you go to the devil!' he exclaimed ferociously, 'and let me be!'

'No,' she persisted, 'I won't: I can't tell what to do to make you talk to me; and you are determined not to understand. When I call you stupid, I don't mean anything: I don't mean that I despise you. Come, you shall take notice of me, Hareton! you are my cousin, and you shall own me.'

'I shall have naught to do wi' you and your mucky pride, and your damned mocking tricks!' he answered. 'I'll go to hell, body and soul, before I look sideways after you again. Side out o' t' gait, now; this minute!'

Catherine frowned, and retreated to the window-seat chewing her lip, and endeavouring, by humming an eccentric tune, to conceal a growing tendency to sob.

'You should be friends with your cousin, Mr. Hareton,' I interrupted, 'since she repents of her sauciness. It would do you a great deal of good: it would make you another man to have her for a companion.'

'A companion?' he cried; 'when she hates me, and does not think me fit to wipe her shoon! Nay! if it made me a king, I'd not be scorned for seeking her good-will any more.'

'It is not I who hate you, it is you who hate me!' wept Cathy, no longer disguising her trouble. 'You hate me as much as Mr. Heathcliff does, and more.'

'You're a damned liar,' began Earnshaw: 'why have I made him angry, by taking your part, then, a hundred times? and that when you sneered at and despised me, and—Go on plaguing me, and I'll step in yonder, and say you worried me out of the kitchen!'

'I didn't know you took my part,' she answered, drying her eyes; 'and I was miserable and bitter at everybody; but now I thank you, and beg you to forgive me: what can I do besides?'

She returned to the hearth, and frankly extended her hand. He blackened and scowled like a thunder-cloud, and kept his fists resolutely clenched, and his gaze fixed on the ground. Catherine, by instinct, must have divined it was obdurate perversity, and not dislike, that prompted this dogged conduct; for, after remaining an instant undecided, she stooped and impressed on his cheek a gentle kiss. The little rogue thought I had not seen her, and, drawing back, she took her former station by the window, quite demurely. I shook my head reprovingly, and then she blushed and whispered:

'Well! what should I have done, Ellen? He wouldn't shake hands, and he

wouldn't look: I must show him some way that I like him—that I want to be friends.'

Whether the kiss convinced Hareton, I cannot tell: he was very careful, for some minutes, that his face should not be seen, and when he did raise it, he was sadly puzzled where to turn his eyes.

Catherine employed herself in wrapping a handsome book neatly in white paper, and having tied it with a bit of ribband, and addressed it to 'Mr. Hareton Earnshaw,' she desired me to be her ambassadress, and convey the present to its destined recipient.

'And tell him, if he'll take it I'll come and teach him to read it right,' she said; 'and, if he refuse it, I'll go upstairs, and never tease him again.'

I carried it, and repeated the message; anxiously watched by my employer. Hareton would not open his fingers, so I laid it on his knee. He did not strike off, either. I returned to my work. Catherine leaned her head and arms on the table, till she heard the slight rustle of the covering being removed; then she stole away, and quietly seated herself beside her cousin. He trembled, and his face glowed: all his rudeness and all his surly harshness had deserted him: he could not summon courage, at first, to utter a syllable in reply to her questioning look, and her murmured petition.

'Say you forgive me, Hareton, do? You can make me so happy by speaking that little word.'

He muttered something inaudible.

'And you'll be my friend?' added Catherine interrogatively.

'Nay, you'll be ashamed of me every day of your life,' he answered; 'and the more, the more you know me; and I cannot bide it.'

'So you won't be my friend?' she said, smiling as sweet as honey, and creeping close up.

I overheard no further distinguishable talk, but, on looking round again, I perceived two such radiant countenances bent over the page of the accepted book, that I did not doubt the treaty had been ratified on both sides; and the enemies were, thenceforth, sworn allies.

The work they studied was full of costly pictures; and those and their position had charm enough to keep them unmoved till Joseph came home. He, poor man, was perfectly aghast at the spectacle of Catherine seated on the same bench with Hareton Earnshaw, leaning her hand on his shoulder; and confounded at his favourite's endurance of her proximity: it affected him too deeply to allow an observation on the subject that night. His emotion was only revealed by the immense sighs he drew, as he solemnly spread his large Bible on the table, and overlaid it with dirty bank-notes from his pocket-book, the produce of the day's transactions. At length, he summoned Hareton from his seat.

'Tak' these in tuh t' maister, lad,' he said, 'un' bide thar. Aw's gang up tu

my awn rahm. This hoile's norther mensful nor seemly fur us: we mun side aht and seearch another.'

'Come, Catherine,' I said, 'we must "side out" too; I've done my ironing, are you ready to go?'

'It is not eight o'clock!' she answered, rising unwillingly. 'Hareton, I'll leave this book upon the chimney-piece, and I'll bring some more to-morrow.'

'Ony books ut yah leave, Aw suall tak' intuh th' hahse,' said Joseph, 'un it'll be mitch if yah find em agean; soa, yah muh plase yourseln!'

Cathy threatened that his library should pay for hers; and smiling as she passed Hareton, went singing upstairs: lighter of heart, I venture to say, than ever she had been under that roof before; except, perhaps, during her earliest visits to Linton.

The intimacy thus commenced, grew rapidly; though it encountered temporary interruptions. Earnshaw was not to be civilised with a wish, and my young lady was no philosopher, and no paragon of patience; but both their minds tending to the same point—one loving and desiring to esteem, and the other loving and desiring to be esteemed—they contrived in the end to reach it.

You see, Mr. Lockwood, it was easy enough to win Mrs. Heathcliff's heart. But now, I'm glad you did not try. The crown of all my wishes will be the union of those two. I shall envy no one on their wedding-day: there won't be a happier woman than myself in England!

CHAPTER 33

On the morrow of that Monday, Earnshaw being still unable to follow his ordinary employments, and therefore remaining about the house, I speedily found it would be impracticable to retain my charge beside me, as heretofore. She got downstairs before me, and out into the garden, where she had seen her cousin performing some easy work; and when I went to bid them come to breakfast, I saw she had persuaded him to clear a large space of ground from currant and gooseberry bushes, and they were busy planning together an importation of plants from the Grange.

I was terrified at the devastation which had been accomplished in a brief half-hour; the black currant trees were the apple of Joseph's eye, and she had just fixed her choice of a flower-bed in the midst of them.

'There! That will be all shown to the master,' I exclaimed, 'the minute it is discovered. And what excuse have you to offer for taking such liberties with the garden? We shall have a fine explosion on the head of it: see if we don't! Mr. Hareton, I wonder you should have no more wit, than to go and make that mess at her bidding!'

'I'd forgotten they were Joseph's,' answered Earnshaw, rather puzzled; 'but I'll tell him I did it.'

We always ate our meals with Mr. Heathcliff. I held the mistress's post in making tea and carving; so I was indispensable at table. Catherine usually sat by me, but to-day she stole nearer to Hareton; and I presently saw she would have no more discretion in her friendship than she had in her hostility.

'Now, mind you don't talk with and notice your cousin too much,' were my whispered instructions as we entered the room. 'It will certainly annoy Mr. Heathcliff, and he'll be mad at you both.'

'I'm not going to,' she answered.

The minute after, she had sidled to him, and was sticking primroses in his plate of porridge.

He dared not speak to her there: he dared hardly look; and yet she went on teasing, till he was twice on the point of being provoked to laugh; and I frowned, and then she glanced towards the master: whose mind was occupied on other subjects than his company, as his countenance evinced; and she grew serious for an instant, scrutinising him with deep gravity. Afterwards she turned, and recommenced her nonsense; at last, Hareton uttered a smothered laugh. Mr. Heathcliff started; his eye rapidly surveyed our faces. Catherine met it with her accustomed look of nervousness and yet defiance, which he abhorred.

'It is well you are out of my reach,' he exclaimed. 'What fiend possesses you to stare back at me, continually, with those infernal eyes? Down with them! and don't remind me of your existence again. I thought I had cured you of laughing.'

'It was me,' muttered Hareton.

'What do you say?' demanded the master.

Hareton looked at his plate, and did not repeat the confession. Mr. Heathcliff looked at him a bit, and then silently resumed his breakfast and his interrupted musing. We had nearly finished, and the two young people prudently shifted wider asunder, so I anticipated no further disturbance during that sitting: when Joseph appeared at the door, revealing by his quivering lip and furious eyes, that the outrage committed on his precious shrubs was detected. He must have seen Cathy and her cousin about the spot before he examined it, for while his jaws worked like those of a cow chewing its cud, and rendered his speech difficult to understand, he began:

'Aw mun hev my wage, and Aw mun goa! Aw *hed* aimed tuh dee, wheare Aw'd sarved fur sixty year; 'un Aw thowt Aw'd lug my books up intuh t' garret, un' all my bits uh stuff, un' they sud hev t' kitchen tuh theirseln; fur t' sake uh quietness. It wur hard tuh gie up my awn hearthstun, bud Aw thowt Aw *could* do that! Bud, nah, shoo's taan my garden frough me, un, by th' heart, maister, Aw cannot stand it! Yah muh bend tuh th' yoak, an ye

vill—*Aw* noan used to 't, and an ow'd man dosen't sooin get used tuh new
arthens. Aw'd rayther arn my bite an' my sup wi' a hammer in th' road!'

'Now, now, idiot!' interrupted Heathcliff, 'cut it short! What's your griev-
nce? I'll interfere in no quarrels between you and Nelly. She may thrust
ou into the coal-hole for anything I care.'

'It's noan Nelly!' answered Joseph. 'Aw sudn't shift fur Nellie—nasty ill
owt as shoo is. Thank God! *shoo* cannot stale t' sowl o' nob'dy! Shoo wer
iver soa handsome, bud whet a body mud look at her 'baht winking. It's
on flaysome, graceless quean, ut's witched ahr lad, wi' her bold een un'
er forrard ways—till—Nay! it fair brusts my heart! He's forgetten all Ee
one for him, un' made on him, un' goan un' riven up a hole row ut t' grandest
urrant trees, i' t' garden!' And here he lamented outright; unmanned by
sense of his bitter injuries, and Earnshaw's ingratitude and dangerous
ondition.

'Is the fool drunk?' asked Mr. Heathcliff. 'Hareton, is it you he's finding
ult with?'

'I've pulled up two or three bushes,' replied the young man; 'but I'm
oing to set 'em again.'

'And why have you pulled them up?' said the master.

Catherine unwisely put in her tongue.

'We wanted to plant some flowers there,' she cried. 'I'm the only person
blame, for I wished him to do it.'

'And who the devil gave *you* leave to touch a stick about the place?' de-
anded her father-in-law, much surprised. 'And who ordered *you* to obey
er?' he added, turning to Hareton.

The latter was speechless; his cousin replied:

'You shouldn't grudge a few yards of earth for me to ornament, when you
ave taken all my land!'

'Your land, insolent slut! You never had any,' said Heathcliff.

'And my money,' she continued; returning his angry glare, and meantime
ting a piece of crust, the remnant of her breakfast.

'Silence!' he exclaimed. 'Get done, and begone!'

'And Hareton's land, and his money,' pursued the reckless thing. 'Hareton
d I are friends now; and I shall tell him all about you!'

The master seemed confounded a moment: he grew pale, and rose up,
eing her all the while, with an expression of mortal hate.

'If you strike me, Hareton will strike you,' she said; 'so you may as well sit
wn.'

'If Hareton does not turn you out of the room, I'll strike him to hell,'

thundered Heathcliff. 'Damnable witch! dare you pretend to rouse him against me? Off with her! Do you hear? Fling her into the kitchen! I'll kill her, Ellen Deane, if you let her come into my sight again!'

Hareton tried, under his breath, to persuade her to go.

'Drag her away!' he cried savagely. 'Are you staying to talk?' And he approached to execute his own command.

'He'll not obey you, wicked man, any more,' said Catherine; 'and he'll soon detest you as much as I do.'

'Wisht! wisht!' muttered the young man reproachfully. 'I will not hear you speak so to him. Have done.'

'But you won't let him strike me?' she cried.

'Come, then,' he whispered earnestly.

It was too late: Heathcliff had caught hold of her.

'Now you go!' he said to Earnshaw. 'Accursed witch! this time she has provoked me when I could not bear it; and I'll make her repent it for ever!'

He had his hand in her hair; Hareton attempted to release the locks, entreating him not to hurt her that once. Heathcliff's black eyes flashed he seemed ready to tear Catherine in pieces, and I was just worked up to risk coming to the rescue, when of a sudden his fingers relaxed; he shifted his grasp from her head to her arm, and gazed intently in her face. Then he drew his hand over his eyes, stood a moment to collect himself apparently, and turning anew to Catherine, said with assumed calmness: 'You must learn to avoid putting me in a passion, or I shall really murder you some time! Go with Mrs. Dean, and keep with her; and confine your insolence to her ears. As to Hareton Earnshaw, if I see him listen to you, I'll send him seeking his bread where he can get it! Your love will make him an outcast and a beggar. Nelly, take her; and leave me, all of you! Leave me!'

I led my young lady out; she was too glad of her escape to resist; the other followed, and Mr. Heathcliff had the room to himself till dinner. I had counselled Catherine to get hers upstairs; but, as soon as he perceived her vacant seat, he sent me to call her. He spoke to none of us, ate very little, and went out directly afterwards, intimating that he should not return before evening.

The two new friends established themselves in the house during his absence when I heard Hareton sternly check his cousin, on her offering a revelation of her father-in-law's conduct to his father. He said he wouldn't suffer a word to be uttered to him, in his disparagement: if he were the devil, it didn't signify: he would stand by him; and he'd rather she would abuse himself as she used to, than begin on Mr. Heathcliff. Catherine was waxing cross at this; but he found means to make her hold her tongue, by asking how she would like him to speak ill of her father? and then she comprehended that Earnshaw took the master's reputation home to himself; and was attached by ties stronger than reason could break—chains, forged by habit, which

would be cruel to attempt to loosen. She showed a good heart, thenceforth, in avoiding both complaints and expressions of antipathy concerning Heathcliff; and confessed to me her sorrow that she had endeavoured to raise a bad spirit between him and Hareton: indeed, I don't believe she has ever breathed a syllable, in the latter's hearing, against her oppressor since.

When this slight disagreement was over, they were thick again, and as busy as possible in their several occupations of pupil and teacher. I came in to sit with them, after I had done my work; and I felt so soothed and comforted to watch them, that I did not notice how time got on. You know, they both appeared in a measure my children: I had long been proud of one; and now, I was sure, the other would be a source of equal satisfaction. His honest, warm, and intelligent nature shook off rapidly the clouds of ignorance and degradation in which it had been bred; and Catherine's sincere commendations acted as a spur to his industry. His brightening mind brightened his features, and added spirit and nobility to their aspect: I could hardly fancy it the same individual I had beheld on the day I discovered my little lady at Wuthering Heights, after her expedition to the Crags. While I admired and they laboured, dusk grew on, and with it returned the master. He came upon us quite unexpectedly, entering by the front way, and had full view of the whole three, ere we could raise our heads to glance at him. Well, I reflected, there was never a pleasanter, or more harmless sight; and will be a burning shame to scold them. The red firelight glowed on their two bonny heads, and revealed their faces animated with the eager interest of children; for, though he was twenty-three and she eighteen, each had so much of novelty to feel and learn, that neither experienced nor evinced the sentiments of sober disenchanted maturity.

They lifted their eyes together, to encounter Mr. Heathcliff: perhaps you have never remarked that their eyes are precisely similar, and they are those of Catherine Earnshaw. The present Catherine has no other likeness to her, except a breadth of forehead, and a certain arch of the nostril that makes her appear rather haughty, whether she will or not. With Hareton the resemblance is carried farther: it is singular at all times, then it was particularly striking; because his senses were alert, and his mental faculties wakened to unwonted activity. I suppose this resemblance disarmed Mr. Heathcliff: he walked to the hearth in evident agitation; but it quickly subsided as he looked at the young man: or, I should say, altered its character; for it was there yet. He took the book from his hand, and glanced at the open page, then returned it without any observation; merely signing Catherine away: her companion lingered very little behind her, and I was about to depart also, but he bid me sit still.

'It is a poor conclusion, is it not?' he observed, having brooded a while on the scene he had just witnessed: 'an absurd termination to my violent exertions?

I get levers and mattocks to demolish the two houses, and train myself to be capable of working like Hercules, and when everything is ready and in my power, I find the will to lift a slate off either roof has vanished! My old enemies have not beaten me; now would be the precise time to revenge myself on their representatives: I could do it; and none could hinder me. But where is the use? I don't care for striking; I can't take the trouble to raise my hand. That sounds as if I had been labouring the whole time only to exhibit a fine trait of magnanimity. It is far from being the case: I have lost the faculty of enjoying their destruction, and I am too idle to destroy for nothing.

'Nelly, there is a strange change approaching: I'm in its shadow at present. I take so little interest in my daily life, that I hardly remember to eat and drink. Those two who have left the room are the only objects which retain a distinct material appearance to me; and that appearance causes me pain amounting to agony. About *her* I won't speak; and I don't desire to think, but I earnestly wish she were invisible: her presence invokes only maddening sensations. *He* moves me differently: and yet if I could do it without seeming insane, I'd never see him again. You'll perhaps think me rather inclined to become so,' he added, making an effort to smile, 'if I try to describe the thousand forms of past associations and ideas he awakens or embodies. But you'll not talk of what I tell you; and my mind is so eternally secluded in itself, it is tempting at last to turn it out to another.

'Five minutes ago, Hareton seemed a personification of my youth, not a human being: I felt to him in such a variety of ways, that it would have been impossible to have accosted him rationally. In the first place, his startling likeness to Catherine connected him fearfully with her. That, however, which you may suppose the most potent to arrest my imagination, is actually the least: for what is not connected with her to me? and what does not recall her? I cannot look down to this floor, but her features are shaped in the flags! In every cloud, in every tree—filling the air at night, and caught by glimpses in every object by day—I am surrounded with her image! The most ordinary faces of men and women—my own features—mock me with a resemblance. The entire world is a dreadful collection of memoranda that she did exist, and that I have lost her! Well, Hareton's aspect was the ghost of my immortal love; of my wild endeavours to hold my right; my degradation, my pride, my happiness, and my anguish:

'But it is frenzy to repeat these thoughts to you: only it will let you know why, with a reluctance to be always alone, his society is no benefit; rather an aggravation of the constant torment I suffer; and it partly contributes to render me regardless how he and his cousin go on together. I can give them no attention, any more.'

'But what do you mean by a *change*, Mr. Heathcliff?' I said, alarmed his manner: though he was neither in danger of losing his senses, nor dying

according to my judgment; he was quite strong and healthy: and, as to his reason, from childhood he had a delight in dwelling on dark things, and entertaining odd fancies. He might have had a monomania on the subject of his departed idol; but on every other point his wits were as sound as mine.

'I shall not know that till it comes,' he said, 'I'm only half conscious of it now.'

'You have no feelings of illness, have you?' I asked.

'No, Nelly, I have not,' he answered.

'Then you are not afraid of death?' I pursued.

'Afraid? No!' he replied. 'I have neither a fear, nor a presentiment, nor a hope of death. Why should I? With my hard constitution and temperate mode of living, and unperilous occupations, I ought to, and probably *shall*, remain above ground till there is scarcely a black hair on my head. And yet I cannot continue in this condition! I have to remind myself to breathe— almost to remind my heart to beat! And it is like bending back a stiff spring: it is by compulsion that I do the slightest act not prompted by one thought; and by compulsion that I notice anything alive or dead, which is not associated with one universal idea. I have a single wish, and my whole being and faculties are yearning to attain it. They have yearned towards it so long, and so unwaveringly, that I'm convinced it *will* be reached—and *soon*— because it has devoured my existence: I am swallowed up in the anticipation of its fulfilment. My confessions have not relieved me; but they may account for some otherwise unaccountable phases of humour which I show. O God! It is a long fight, I wish it were over!'

He began to pace the room, muttering terrible things to himself, till I was inclined to believe, as he said Joseph did, that conscience had turned his heart to an earthly hell. I wondered greatly how it would end. Though he seldom before had revealed this state of mind, even by looks, it was his habitual mood, I had no doubt: he asserted it himself; but not a soul, from his general bearing, would have conjectured the fact. You did not when you saw him, Mr. Lockwood: and at the period of which I speak he was just the same as then; only fonder of continued solitude, and perhaps still more laconic in company.

CHAPTER 34

For some days after that evening, Mr. Heathcliff shunned meeting us at meals; yet he would not consent formally to exclude Hareton and Cathy. He had an aversion to yielding so completely to his feelings, choosing rather to absent himself; and eating once in twenty-four hours seemed sufficient sustenance for him.

One night, after the family were in bed, I heard him go down-stairs, and out at the front door. I did not hear him re-enter, and in the morning I found he was still away. We were in April then: the weather was sweet and warm, the grass as green as showers and sun could make it, and the two dwarf apple-trees near the southern wall in full bloom. After breakfast, Catherine insisted on my bringing a chair and sitting with my work under the fir-trees at the end of the house; and she beguiled Hareton, who had perfectly recovered from his accident, to dig and arrange her little garden, which was shifted to that corner by the influence of Joseph's complaints. I was comfortably revelling in the spring fragrance around, and the beautiful soft blue overhead, when my young lady, who had run down near the gate to procure some primrose roots for a border, returned only half laden, and informed us that Mr. Heathcliff was coming in. 'And he spoke to me,' she added, with a perplexed countenance.

'What did he say?' asked Hareton.

'He told me to begone as fast as I could,' she answered. 'But he looked so different from his usual look that I stopped a moment to stare at him.'

'How?' he inquired.

'Why, almost bright and cheerful. No, *almost* nothing—*very much* excited and wild and glad!' she replied.

'Night-walking amuses him, then,' I remarked, affecting a careless manner in reality as surprised as she was, and anxious to ascertain the truth of her statement; for to see the master looking glad would not be an every-day spectacle. I framed an excuse to go in. Heathcliff stood at the open door, he was pale, and he trembled: yet, certainly, he had a strange, joyful glitter in his eyes, that altered the aspect of his whole face.

'Will you have some breakfast?' I said. 'You must be hungry, rambling about all night!' I wanted to discover where he had been, but I did not like to ask directly.

'No, I'm not hungry,' he answered, averting his head, and speaking rather contemptuously, as if he guessed I was trying to divine the occasion of his good-humour.

I felt perplexed: I didn't know whether it were not a proper opportunity to offer a bit of admonition.

'I don't think it right to wander out of doors,' I observed, 'instead of being

610

in bed: it is not wise, at any rate, this moist season. I dare say you'll catch a bad cold, or a fever: you have something the matter with you now!'

'Nothing but what I can bear,' he replied; 'and with the greatest pleasure, provided you'll leave me alone; get in, and don't annoy me.'

I obeyed: and, in passing, I noticed he breathed as fast as a cat.

'Yes!' I reflected to myself, 'we shall have a fit of illness. I cannot conceive what he has been doing.'

That noon he sat down to dinner with us, and received a heaped-up plate from my hands, as if he intended to make amends for previous fasting.

'I've neither cold nor fever, Nelly,' he remarked, in allusion to my morning's speech; 'and I'm ready to do justice to the food you give me.'

He took his knife and fork, and was going to commence eating, when the inclination appeared to become suddenly extinct. He laid them on the table, looked eagerly towards the window, then rose and went out. We saw him walking to and fro in the garden while we concluded our meal, and Earnshaw said he'd go and ask why he would not dine: he thought we had grieved him some way.

'Well, is he coming?' cried Catherine, when her cousin returned.

'Nay,' he answered; 'but he's not angry: he seemed rare and pleased indeed; only I made him impatient by speaking to him twice; and then he bid me be off to you: he wondered how I could want the company of anybody else.'

I set his plate to keep warm on the fender; and after an hour or two he re-entered, when the room was clear, in no degree calmer: the same unnatural –it was unnatural–appearance of joy under his black brows; the same blood-less hue, and his teeth visible, now and then, in a kind of smile; his frame shivering, not as one shivers with chill or weakness, but as a tight-stretched cord vibrates—a strong thrilling, rather than trembling.

I will ask what is the matter, I thought; or who should? And I exclaimed: 'Have you heard any good news, Mr. Heathcliff? You look uncommonly animated.'

'Where should good news come from to me?' he said. 'I'm animated with hunger; and, seemingly, I must not eat.'

'Your dinner is here,' I returned; 'why won't you get it?'

'I don't want it now,' he muttered hastily; 'I'll wait till supper. And, Nelly, once for all, let me beg you to warn Hareton and the other away from me. I wish to be troubled by nobody: I wish to have this place to myself.'

'Is there some new reason for this banishment?' I inquired. 'Tell me why you are so queer, Mr. Heathcliff? Where were you last night? I'm not putting the question through idle curiosity, but'——

'You are putting the question through very idle curiosity,' he interrupted, with a laugh. 'Yet I'll answer it. Last night I was on the threshold of hell. To-day, I am within sight of my heaven. I have my eyes on it: hardly three

feet to sever me! And now you'd better go! You'll neither see nor hear anything to frighten you, if you refrain from prying.'

Having swept the hearth and wiped the table, I departed; more perplexed then ever.

He did not quit the house again that afternoon, and no one intruded on his solitude; till, at eight o'clock, I deemed it proper, though unsummoned, to carry a candle and his supper to him. He was leaning against the ledge of an open lattice, but not looking out: his face was turned to the interior gloom. The fire had smouldered to ashes; the room was filled with the damp, mild air of the cloudy evening; and so still, that not only the murmur of the beck down Gimmerton was distinguishable, but its ripples and its gurgling over the pebbles, or through the large stones which it could not cover. I uttered an ejaculation of discontent at seeing the dismal grate, and commenced shutting the casements, one after another, till I came to his.

'Must I close this?' I asked, in order to rouse him; for he would not stir.

The light flashed on his features as I spoke. Oh, Mr. Lockwood, I cannot express what a terrible start I got by the momentary view! Those deep black eyes! That smile, and ghastly paleness! It appeared to me, not Mr. Heathcliff, but a goblin; and, in my terror, I let the candle bend towards the wall and it left me in darkness.

'Yes, close it,' he replied, in his familiar voice. 'There, that is pure awkwardness! Why did you hold the candle horizontally? Be quick, and bring another.'

I hurried out in a foolish state of dread, and said to Joseph:

'The master wishes you to take him a light and rekindle the fire.' For I dare not go in myself again just then.

Joseph rattled some fire into the shovel, and went; but he brought it back immediately, with the supper-tray in his other hand, explaining that Mr Heathcliff was going to bed, and he wanted nothing to eat till morning. We heard him mount the stairs directly; he did not proceed to his ordinary chamber, but turned into that with the panelled bed: its window, as I mentioned before, is wide enough for anybody to get through; and it struck me that he plotted another midnight excursion, of which he had rather we had no suspicion.

'Is he a ghoul or a vampire?' I mused. I had read of such hideous incarnate demons. And then I set myself to reflect how I had tended him in infancy and watched him grow to youth, and followed him almost through his whole course; and what absurd nonsense it was to yield to that sense of horror. 'But where did he come from, the little dark thing, harboured by a good man to his bane?' muttered Superstition, as I dozed into unconsciousness. And I began, half dreaming, to weary myself with imagining some fit parentage for him; and, repeating my waking meditations, I tracked his existence over again, with grim variations; at last, picturing his death and funeral: of which

all I can remember is, being exceedingly vexed at having the task of dictating an inscription for his monument, and consulting the sexton about it; and, as he had no surname, and we could not tell his age, we were obliged to content ourselves with the single word, 'Heathcliff.' That came true: we were. If you enter the kirkyard, you'll read on his headstone, only that, and the date of his death.

Dawn restored me to common sense. I rose, and went into the garden, as soon as I could see, to ascertain if there were any footmarks under his window. There were none. 'He has stayed at home,' I thought, 'and he'll be all right to-day.' I prepared breakfast for the household, as was my usual custom, but told Hareton and Catherine to get theirs ere the master came down, for he lay late. They preferred taking it out of doors, under the trees, and I set a little table to accommodate them.

On my re-entrance, I found Mr. Heathcliff below. He and Joseph were conversing about some farming business; he gave clear, minute directions concerning the matter discussed, but he spoke rapidly, and turned his head continually aside, and had the same excited expression, even more exaggerated. When Joseph quitted the room he took his seat in the place he generally chose, and I put a basin of coffee before him. He drew it nearer, and then rested his arms on the table, and looked at the opposite wall, as I supposed, surveying one particular portion, up and down, with glittering, restless eyes, and with such eager interest that he stopped breathing during half a minute together.

'Come now,' I exclaimed, pushing some bread against his hand, 'eat and drink that, while it is hot: it has been waiting near an hour.'

He didn't notice me, and yet he smiled. I'd rather have seen him gnash his teeth than smile so.

'Mr. Heathcliff! master!' I cried, 'don't, for God's sake, stare as if you saw an unearthly vision.'

'Don't, for God's sake, shout so loud,' he replied. 'Turn round, and tell me, are we by ourselves?'

'Of course,' was my answer; 'of course we are.'

Still I involuntarily obeyed him, as if I were not quite sure. With a sweep of his hand he cleared a vacant space in front among the breakfast things, and leant forward to gaze more at his ease.

Now, I perceived he was not looking at the wall; for when I regarded him alone, it seemed exactly that he gazed at something within two yards' distance. And whatever it was, it communicated, apparently, both pleasure and pain in exquisite extremes: at least the anguished, yet raptured, expression of his countenance suggested that idea. The fancied object was not fixed: either his eyes pursued it with unwearied diligence, and, even in speaking to me, were never weaned away. I vainly reminded him of his protracted abstinence from food: if he stirred to touch anything in compliance with my entrea-

ties, if he stretched his hand out to get a piece of bread, his fingers clenched before they reached it, and remained on the table, forgetful of their aim.

I sat, a model of patience, trying to attract his absorbed attention from its engrossing speculation; till he grew irritable, and got up, asking why I would not allow him to have his own time in taking his meals? and saying that on the next occasion, I needn't wait: I might set the things down and go. Having uttered these words he left the house, slowly sauntered down the garden path, and disappeared through the gate.

The hours crept anxiously by: another evening came. I did not retire to rest till late, and when I did, I could not sleep. He returned after midnight, and instead of going to bed, shut himself into the room beneath. I listened and tossed about, and, finally, dressed and descended. It was too irksome to lie up there, harassing my brain with a hundred idle misgivings.

I distinguished Mr. Heathcliff's step, restlessly measuring the floor, and he frequently broke the silence by a deep inspiration, resembling a groan. He muttered detached words also; the only one I could catch was the name of Catherine, coupled with some wild term of endearment or suffering; and spoken as one would speak to a person present: low and earnest, and wrung from the depth of his soul. I had not courage to walk straight into the apartment; but I desired to divert him from his reverie, and therefore fell foul of the kitchen fire, stirred it, and began to scrape the cinders. It drew him forth sooner than I expected. He opened the door immediately, and said

'Nelly, come here—is it morning? Come in with your light.'

'It is striking four,' I answered. 'You want a candle to take upstairs: you might have lit one at this fire.'

'No, I don't wish to go upstairs,' he said. 'Come in, and kindle *me* a fire, and do anything there is to do about the room.'

'I must blow the coals red first, before I can carry any,' I replied, getting a chair and the bellows.

He roamed to and fro, meantime, in a state approaching distraction; his heavy sighs succeeding each other so thick as to leave no space for common breathing between.

'When day breaks I'll send for Green,' he said; 'I wish to make some legal inquiries of him while I can bestow a thought on those matters, and while I can act calmly. I have not written my will yet; and how to leave my property I cannot determine. I wish I could annihilate it from the face of the earth.'

'I would not talk so, Mr. Heathcliff,' I interposed. 'Let your will be a while; you'll be spared to repent of your many injustices yet. I never expected that your nerves would be disordered: they are, at present, marvellously so, however; and almost entirely through your own fault. The way you've passed these three last days might knock up a Titan. Do take some food, and some repose. You need only look at yourself in a glass to see how you require both.

Your cheeks are hollow, and your eyes bloodshot, like a person starving with hunger and going blind with loss of sleep.'

'It is not my fault that I cannot eat or rest,' he replied. 'I assure you it is through no settled designs. I'll do both as soon as I possibly can. But you might as well bid a man struggling in the water rest within arm's length of the shore! I must reach it first, and then I'll rest. Well, never mind Mr. Green: as to repenting of my injustices, I've done no injustice, and I repent of nothing. I'm too happy; and yet I'm not happy enough. My soul's bliss kills my body, but does not satisfy itself.'

'Happy, master?' I cried. 'Strange happiness! If you would hear me without being angry, I might offer some advice that would make you happier.'

'What is that?' he asked. 'Give it.'

'You are aware, Mr. Heathcliff,' I said, 'that from the time you were thirteen years old, you have lived a selfish, unchristian life; and probably hardly had a Bible in your hands during all that period. You must have forgotten the contents of the book, and you may not have space to search it now. Could it be hurtful to send for some one—some minister of any denomination, it does not matter which—to explain it, and show you how very far you have erred from its precepts; and how unfit you will be for its heaven, unless a change takes place before you die?'

'I'm rather obliged than angry, Nelly,' he said, 'for you remind me of the manner that I desire to be buried in. It is to be carried to the churchyard in the evening. You and Hareton may, if you please, accompany me: and mind, particularly, to notice that the sexton obeys my directions concerning the two coffins! No minister need come; nor need anything be said over me.—I tell you I have nearly attained *my* heaven; and that of others is altogether unvalued and uncoveted by me.'

'And supposing you persevered in your obstinate fast, and died by that means, and they refused to bury you in the precincts of the Kirk?' I said, shocked at his godless indifference. 'How would you like it?'

'They won't do that,' he replied: 'if they did, you must have me removed secretly: and if you neglect it you shall prove, practically, that the dead are not annihilated!'

As soon as he heard the other members of the family stirring he retired to his den, and I breathed freer. But in the afternoon, while Joseph and Hareton were at their work, he came into the kitchen again, and, with a wild look, bid me come and sit in the house: he wanted somebody with him. I declined: telling him plainly that his strange talk and manner frightened me, and I had neither the nerve nor the will to be his companion alone.

'I believe you think me a fiend,' he said, with his dismal laugh: 'something too horrible to live under a decent roof.' Then turning to Catherine, who was there, and who drew behind me at his approach, he added, half-sneeringly

—'Will *you* come, chuck? I'll not hurt you. No! to you I've made myself worse than the devil. Well, there is *one* who won't shrink from my company! By God! she's relentless. Oh, damn it! It's unutterably too much for flesh and blood to bear—even mine.'

He solicited the society of no one more. At dusk, he went into his chamber. Through the whole night, and far into the morning, we heard him groaning and murmuring to himself. Hareton was anxious to enter; but I bade him fetch Mr. Kenneth, and he should go in and see him. When he came, and I requested admittance and tried to open the door, I found it locked; and Heathcliff bid us be damned. He was better, and would be left alone; so the doctor went away.

The following evening was very wet: indeed it poured down till day-dawn; and, as I took my morning walk round the house, I observed the master's window swinging open, and the rain driving straight in. He cannot be in bed, I thought: those showers would drench him through. He must either be up or out. But I'll make no more ado, I'll go boldly and look.

Having succeeded in obtaining entrance with another key, I ran to unclose the panels, for the chamber was vacant; quickly pushing them aside, I peeped in. Mr. Heathcliff was there—laid on his back. His eyes met mine so keen and fierce, I started; and then he seemed to smile. I could not think him dead but his face and throat were washed with rain; the bedclothes dripped, and he was perfectly still. The lattice, flapping to and fro, had grazed one hand that rested on the sill; no blood trickled from the broken skin, and when I put my fingers to it, I could doubt no more: he was dead and stark!

I hasped the window; I combed his black long hair from his forehead I tried to close his eyes: to extinguish, if possible, that frightful, life-like gaze of exultation before any one else beheld it. They would not shut: they seemed to sneer at my attempts: and his parted lips and sharp white teeth sneered too! Taken with another fit of cowardice, I cried out for Joseph. Joseph shuffled up and made a noise; but resolutely refused to meddle with him.

'Th' divil's harried off his soul,' he cried, 'and he muh hev his carcas intuh t' bargain, for ow't Aw care! Ech! what a wicked un he looks girnin at death!' and the old sinner grinned in mockery. I thought he intended t cut a caper round the bed; but, suddenly composing himself, he fell on hi knees, and raised his hands, and returned thanks that the lawful master an the ancient stock were restored to their rights.

I felt stunned by the awful event; and my memory unavoidably recurre to former times with a sort of oppressive sadness. But poor Hareton, the mo wronged, was the only one that really suffered much. He sat by the corpse a night, weeping in bitter earnest. He pressed its hand, and kissed the sarcast savage face that every one else shrank from contemplating; and bemoane him with that strong grief which springs naturally from a generous hear

though it be tough as tempered steel.

Mr. Kenneth was perplexed to pronounce of what disorder the master died. I concealed the fact of his having swallowed nothing for four days, fearing it might lead to trouble, and then, I am persuaded, he did not abstain on purpose: it was the consequence of his strange illness, not the cause.

We buried him, to the scandal of the whole neighbourhood, as he wished. Earnshaw and I, the sexton, and six men to carry the coffin, comprehended the whole attendance. The six men departed when they had let it down into the grave: we stayed to see it covered. Hareton, with a streaming face, dug green sods, and laid them over the brown mould himself: at present it is as smooth and verdant as its companion mounds—and I hope its tenant sleeps as soundly. But the country folk, if you ask them, would swear on the Bible that he *walks*: there are those who speak to having met him near the church, and on the moor, and even in this house. Idle tales, you'll say, and so say I. Yet that old man by the kitchen fire affirms he has seen two on 'em, looking out of his chamber window, on every rainy night since his death: and an odd thing happened to me about a month ago. I was going to the Grange one evening—a dark evening, threatening thunder—and, just at the turn of the Heights, I encountered a little boy with a sheep and two lambs before him; he was crying terribly; and I supposed the lambs were skittish, and would not be guided.

'What's the matter, my little man?' I asked.

'There's Heathcliff and a woman, yonder, under t' nab,' he blubbered, 'an' I darnut pass 'em.'

I saw nothing; but neither the sheep nor he would go on; so I bid him take the road lower down. He probably raised the phantoms from thinking, as he traversed the moors alone, on the nonsense he had heard his parents and companions repeat. Yet, still, I don't like being out in the dark now; and I don't like being left by myself in this grim house: I cannot help it; I shall be glad when they leave it, and shift to the Grange.

'They are going to the Grange, then,' I said.

'Yes,' answered Mrs. Dean, 'as soon as they are married, and that will be on New Years' day.'

'And who will live here, then?'

'Why, Joseph will take care of the house, and, perhaps, a lad to keep him company. They will live in the kitchen, and the rest will be shut up.'

'For the use of such ghosts as choose to inhabit it,' I observed.

'No, Mr. Lockwood,' said Nelly, shaking her head. 'I believe the dead are at peace: but it is not right to speak of them with levity.'

At that moment the garden gate swung to; the ramblers were returning.

'*They* are afraid of nothing.' I grumbled, watching their approach through the window. 'Together they would brave Satan and all his legions.'

As they stepped on to the door-stones, and halted to take a last look at th
moon—or, more correctly, at each other by her light—I felt irresistibl
impelled to escape them again; and, pressing a remembrance into the han
of Mrs. Dean, and disregarding her expostulations at my rudeness, I vanishe
through the kitchen as they opened the house-door; and so should have con
firmed Joseph in his opinion of his fellow-servant's gay indiscretions, had h
not fortunately recognised me for a respectable character by the sweet rin
of a sovereign at his feet.

My walk home was lengthened by a diversion in the direction of the kirl
When beneath its walls, I perceived decay had made progress, even in seve
months: many a window showed black gaps deprived of glass; and slates jutte
off, here and there, beyond the right line of the roof, to be gradually worke
off in coming autumn storms.

I sought, and soon discovered, the three head-stones on the slope next th
moor: the middle one grey, and half buried in heath: Edgar Linton's onl
harmonised by the turf and moss creeping up its foot: Heathcliff's still bar

I lingered round them, under that benign sky; watched the moths flutterin
among the heath and harebells, listened to the soft wind breathing through th
grass, and wondered how any one could ever imagine unquiet slumbers fc
the sleepers in that quiet earth.

AGNES GREY

CHAPTER 1

THE PARSONAGE

All true histories contain instruction; though, in some, the treasure may be hard to find, and when found, so trivial in quantity, that the dry, shrivelled kernel scarcely compensates for the trouble of cracking the nut. Whether this be the case with my history or not, I am hardly competent to judge. I sometimes think it might prove useful to some, and entertaining to others; but the world may judge for itself. Shielded by my own obscurity, and by the lapse of years, and a few fictitious names, I do not fear to venture; and will candidly lay before the public what I would not disclose to the most intimate friend.

My father was a clergyman of the north of England, who was deservedly respected by all who knew him; and, in his younger days, lived pretty comfortably on the joint income of a small incumbency and a snug little property of his own. My mother, who married him against the wishes of her friends, was a squire's daughter, and a woman of spirit. In vain it was represented to her, that if she became the poor parson's wife, she must relinquish her carriage and her lady's-maid, and all the luxuries and elegancies of affluence; which to her were little less than the necessaries of life. A carriage and a lady's-maid were great conveniences; but, thank Heaven, she had feet to carry her, and hands to minister to her own necessities. An elegant house and spacious grounds were not to be despised; but she would rather live in a cottage with Richard Grey than in a palace with any other man in the world.

Finding arguments of no avail, her father, at length, told the lovers they might marry if they pleased; but, in so doing, his daughter would forfeit every fraction of her fortune. He expected this would cool the ardour of both; but he was mistaken. My father knew too well my mother's superior worth not to be sensible that she was a valuable fortune in herself: and if she would but consent to embellish his humble hearth, he should be happy to take her on any terms; while she, on her part, would rather labour with her own hands than be divided from the man she loved, whose happiness it would be her joy to make, and who was already one with her in heart and soul. So her fortune went to swell the purse of a wiser sister, who had married a rich nabob; and she, to the wonder and compassionate regret of all who knew her, went to bury herself in the homely village parsonage among the hills of—. And yet, in spite of all

this, and in spite of my mother's high spirit and my father's whims, I believ
you might search all England through, and fail to find a happier couple.

Of six children, my sister Mary and myself were the only two that survive
the perils of infancy and early childhood. I, being the younger by five or si
years, was always regarded as the *child*, and the pet of the family: fathe
mother, and sister, all combined to spoil me—not by foolish indulgence, t
render me fractious and ungovernable, but by ceaseless kindness, to make m
too helpless and dependent—too unfit for buffeting with the cares and tui
moils of life.

Mary and I were brought up in the strictest seclusion. My mother, being a
once highly accomplished, well-informed, and fond of employment, took th
whole charge of our education on herself, with the exception of Latin—whic
my father undertook to teach us—so that we never even went to school; and
as there was no society in the neighbourhood, our only intercourse with th
world consisted in a stately tea-party, now and then, with the principal farme
and trades-people of the vicinity (just to avoid being stigmatized as too prou
to consort with our neighbours), and an annual visit to our paternal granc
father's; where himself, our kind grandmamma, a maiden aunt, and two c
three elderly ladies and gentlemen, were the only persons we ever saw. Som
times our mother would amuse us with stories and anecdotes of her younge
days, which, while they entertained us amazingly, frequently awoke—in m
at least—a secret wish to see a little more of the world.

I thought she must have been very happy: but she never seemed to regre
past times. My father, however, whose temper was neither tranquil nor cheerf
by nature, often unduly vexed himself with thinking of the sacrifices his de
wife had made for him; and troubled his head with revolving endless scheme
for the augmentation of his little fortune, for her sake and ours. In vain m
mother assured him she was quite satisfied; and if he would but lay by a littl
for the children, we should all have plenty, both for time present and to come
but saving was not my father's forte. He would not run in debt (at least, m
mother took good care he should not), but while he had money he must spen
it: he liked to see his house comfortable, and his wife and daughters we
clothed, and well attended; and besides, he was charitably disposed, and like
to give to the poor, according to his means: or, as some might think, beyon
them.

At length, however, a kind friend suggested to him a means of doubling h
private property at one stroke; and further increasing it, hereafter, to an untol
amount. This friend was a merchant, a man of enterprising spirit and u
doubted talent, who was somewhat straitened in his mercantile pursuits fc
want of capital; but generously proposed to give my father a fair share of h
profits, if he would only entrust him with what he could spare; and he thoug
he might safely promise that whatever sum the latter chose to put into h

nds, it should bring him in cent per cent. The small patrimony was speedily
ld, and the whole of its price was deposited in the hands of the friendly
erchant; who as promptly proceeded to ship his cargo, and prepare for his
oyage.

My father was delighted, so were we all, with our brightening prospects. For
e present, it is true, we were reduced to the narrow income of the curacy;
t my father seemed to think there was no necessity for scrupulously restricting
r expenditure to that; so, with a standing bill at Mr. Jackson's, another at
mith's, and a third at Hobson's, we got along even more comfortably than
fore: though my mother affirmed we had better keep within bounds, for our
ospects of wealth were but precarious, after all; and if my father would only
ust everything to her management, he should never feel himself stinted: but
, for once, was incorrigible.

What happy hours Mary and I have passed, while sitting at our work by
e fire, or wandering on the heath-clad hills, or idling under the weeping birch
he only considerable tree in the garden), talking of future happiness to
urselves and our parents, of what we would do, and see, and possess; with no
mer foundation for our goodly superstructure, than the riches that were
pected to flow in upon us from the success of the worthy merchant's specula-
ons. Our father was nearly as bad as ourselves; only, that he affected not
be so much in earnest: expressing his bright hopes and sanguine expectations,
jests and playful sallies, that always struck me as being exceedingly witty and
easant. Our mother laughed with delight to see him so hopeful and happy:
t still she feared he was setting his heart too much upon the matter; and
ce I heard her whisper as she left the room, 'God grant he be not disap-
inted! I know not how he would bear it.'

Disappointed he was; and bitterly, too. It came like a thunder-clap on us
, that the vessel which contained our fortune had been wrecked, and gone to
e bottom with all its stores, together with several of the crew, and the un-
rtunate merchant himself. I was grieved for him; I was grieved for the
erthrow of all our air-built castles: but, with the elasticity of youth, I soon
covered the shock.

Though riches had charms, poverty had no terrors for an inexperienced girl
e me. Indeed, to say the truth, there was something exhilarating in the idea
being driven to straits, and thrown upon our own resources. I only wished
pa, mamma, and Mary, were all of the same mind as myself; and then,
stead of lamenting past calamities, we might all cheerfully set to work to
medy them; and the greater the difficulties, the harder our present privations,
e greater should be our cheerfulness to endure the latter, and our vigour to
ntend against the former.

Mary did not lament, but she brooded continually over the misfortune, and
nk into a state of dejection from which no effort of mine could rouse her.

621

I could not possibly bring her to regard the matter on its bright side as I did
and indeed I was so fearful of being charged with childish frivolity, or stupi
insensibility, that I carefully kept most of my bright ideas and cheering notior
to myself; well knowing they could not be appreciated.

My mother thought only of consoling my father, and paying our debts an
retrenching our expenditure by every available means; but my father wa
completely overwhelmed by the calamity: health, strength, and spirits san
beneath the blow; and he never wholly recovered them. In vain my mothe
strove to cheer him, by appealing to his piety, to his courage, to his affectio
for herself and us. That very affection was his greatest torment: it was for ou
sakes he had so ardently longed to increase his fortune—it was our interest tha
had lent such brightness to his hopes, and that imparted such bitterness to h
present distress. He now tormented himself with remorse at having neglecte
my mother's advice; which would at least have saved him from the additiona
burden of debt—he vainly reproached himself for having brought her from th
dignity, the ease, the luxury of her former station to toil with him through th
cares and toils of poverty. It was gall and wormwood to his soul to see tha
splendid, highly accomplished woman, once so courted and admired, tran
formed into an active managing housewife, with hands and head continual
occupied with household labours and household economy. The very willingne
with which she performed these duties, the cheerfulness with which she bo
her reverses, and the kindness which withheld her from imputing the smalle
blame to him, were all perverted by this ingenious self-tormentor, into furthe
aggravations of his sufferings. And thus the mind preyed upon the body, an
disordered the system of the nerves, and they in turn increased the troubles
the mind, till by action and reaction his health was seriously impaired; an
not one of us could convince him that the aspect of our affairs was not half
gloomy, so utterly hopeless, as his morbid imagination represented it to be.

The useful pony phaeton was sold, together with the stout well-fed pony—th
old favourite that we had fully determined should end its days in peace, an
never pass from our hands; the little coach-house and stable were let; th
servant boy, and the more efficient (being the more expensive) of the two mai
servants were dismissed. Our clothes were mended, turned, and darned to th
utmost verge of decency; our food, always plain, was now simplified to an u
precedented degree—except my father's favourite dishes; our coals and candl
were painfully economized—the pair of candles reduced to one, and that mo
sparingly used; the coals carefully husbanded in the half-empty grate: esp
cially when my father was out on his parish duties, or confined to bed throug
illness—then we sat with our feet on the fender, scraping the perishing embe
together from time to time, and occasionally adding a slight scattering
the dust and fragments of coal, just to keep them alive. As for our carpets, th
in time were worn threadbare, and patched and darned even to a great

xtent than our garments. To save the expense of a gardener, Mary and I under-
ook to keep the garden in order; and all the cooking and household work that
ould not easily be managed by one servant girl, was done by my mother and
ister, with a little occasional help from me: only a little, because, though
 woman in my own estimation, I was still a child in theirs; and my mother,
ke most active, managing women, was not gifted with very active daughters:
or this reason—that being so clever and diligent herself, she was never tempted
o trust her affairs to a deputy, but on the contrary, was willing to act and
hink for others as well as for number one; and whatever was the business in
and, she was apt to think that no one could do it so well as herself: so that
whenever I offered to assist her, I received such an answer as—'No, love, you
annot indeed—there's nothing here you can do. Go and help your sister, or
et her to take a walk with you—tell her she must not sit so much, and stay so
onstantly in the house as she does—she may well look thin and dejected.'

'Mary, mamma says I'm to help you; or get you to take a walk with me: she
ays you may well look thin and dejected, if you sit so constantly in the house.'

'Help me you cannot, Agnes; and I cannot go out with _you_—I have far too
much to do.'

'Then let me help you.'

'You cannot, indeed, dear child. Go and practise your music, or play with
he kitten.'

There was always plenty of sewing on hand; but I had not been taught to
ut out a single garment, and except plain hemming and seaming, there was
ittle I could do, even in that line; for they both asserted that it was far easier
o do the work themselves than to prepare it for me: and, besides, they liked
etter to see me prosecuting my studies, or amusing myself—it was time
nough for me to sit bending over my work, like a grave matron, when my
avourite little pussy was become a steady old cat. Under such circumstances,
lthough I was not many degrees more useful than the kitten, my idleness was
ot entirely without excuse.

Through all our troubles, I never but once heard my mother complain of
ur want of money. As summer was coming on, she observed to Mary and me,
What a desirable thing it would be for your papa to spend a few weeks at
 watering-place. I am convinced the sea-air and the change of scene would be
f incalculable service to him. But then, you see, there's no money,' she added,
vith a sigh. We both wished exceedingly that the thing might be done, and
mented greatly that it could not. 'Well, well!' said she, 'it's no use com-
laining. Possibly something might be done to further the project after all.
Iary, you are a beautiful drawer. What do you say to doing a few more
ictures in your best style, and getting them framed, with the water-coloured
rawings you have already done, and trying to dispose of them to some liberal
icture-dealer, who has the sense to discern their merits?'

'Mamma, I should be delighted if you think they *could* be sold; and fo
anything worth while.'

'It's worth while trying, however, my dear: do you procure the drawing
and I'll endeavour to find a purchaser.'

'I wish *I* could do something,' said I.

'You Agnes! well, who knows? You draw pretty well, too: if you choos
some simple piece for your subject, I dare say you will be able to produce some
thing we shall all be proud to exhibit.'

'But I have another scheme in my head, mamma, and have had long, onl
I did not like to mention it.'

'Indeed! pray tell us what it is.'

'I should like to be a governess.'

My mother uttered an exclamation of surprise, and laughed. My siste
dropped her work in astonishment, exclaiming, '*You* a governess, Agnes! Wha
can you be dreaming of?'

'Well! I don't see anything so *very* extraordinary in it. I do not pretend t
be able to instruct great girls; but surely, I could teach little ones: and I shoul
like it *so* much: I am so fond of children. Do let me, mamma!'

'But, my love, you have not learned to take care of *yourself* yet: and youn
children require more judgement and experience to manage than elde ones

'But, mamma, I am above eighteen, and quite able to take care of mysel
and others too. You do not know half the wisdom and prudence I posses
because I have never been tried.'

'Only think,' said Mary, 'what would you do in a house full of stranger
without me or mamma to speak and act for you—with a parcel of childre
besides yourself, to attend to; and no one to look to for advice? You would n
even know what clothes to put on.'

'You think, because I always do as you bid me, I have no judgement of m
own: but only try me—that is all I ask—and you shall see what I can do.'

At that moment my father entered, and the subject of our discussion wa
explained to him.

'What, my little Agnes, a governess!' cried he, and, in spite of his dejectio
he laughed at the idea.

'Yes, papa, don't *you* say anything against it: I should like it *so* much; an
I am sure I could manage delightfully.'

'But, my darling, we could not spare you.' And a tear glistened in his ey
as he added—'No, no! afflicted as we are, surely we are not brought to tha
pass yet.'

'Oh, no!' said my mother. 'There is no necessity whatever for such a step
it is merely a whim of her own. So you must hold your tongue, you naught
girl; for, though you are so ready to leave *us*, you know very well we cann
part with *you*.'

I was silenced for that day, and for many succeeding ones; but still I did not wholly relinquish my darling scheme. Mary got her drawing materials, and readily set to work. I got mine too; but while I drew, I thought of other things. How delightful it would be to be a governess! To go out into the world; to enter upon a new life; to act for myself; to exercise my unused faculties; to try my unknown powers; to earn my own maintenance, and something to comfort and help my father, mother, and sister, besides exonerating them from the provision of my food and clothing; to show papa what his little Agnes could do; to convince mamma and Mary that I was not quite the helpless, thoughtless being they supposed. And then, how charming to be entrusted with the care and education of children! Whatever others said, I felt I was fully competent to the task: the clear remembrance of my own thoughts in early childhood would be a surer guide than the instructions of the most mature adviser. I had but to turn from my little pupils to myself at their age, and I should know, at once, how to win their confidence and affections: how to waken the contrition of the erring; how to embolden the timid, and console the afflicted; how to make Virtue practicable, Instruction desirable, and Religion lovely and comprehensible.

—Delightful task!
To teach the young idea how to shoot!

To train the tender plants, and watch their buds unfolding day by day!

Influenced by so many inducements, I determined still to persevere; though the fear of displeasing my mother, or distressing my father's feelings, prevented me from resuming the subject for several days. At length, again, I mentioned it to my mother in private; and, with some difficulty, got her to promise to assist me with her endeavours. My father's reluctant consent was next obtained, and then, though Mary still sighed her disapproval, my dear, kind mother began to look out for a situation for me. She wrote to my father's relations, and consulted the newspaper advertisements—her own relations she had long dropped all communication with: a formal interchange of occasional letters was all she had ever had since her marriage, and she would not at any time have applied to them in a case of this nature. But so long and so entire had been my parents' seclusion from the world, that many weeks elapsed before a suitable situation could be procured. At last, to my great joy, it was decreed that I should take charge of the young family of a certain Mrs. Bloomfield; whom my kind, prim aunt Grey had known in her youth, and asserted to be a very nice woman. Her husband was a retired tradesman, who had realized a very comfortable fortune; but could not be prevailed upon to give a greater salary than twenty-five pounds to the instructress of his children. I, however, was glad to accept this, rather than refuse the situation—which my parents were inclined to think the better plan.

But some weeks more were yet to be devoted to preparation. How long, how tedious those weeks appeared to me! Yet they were happy ones in the main—full of bright hopes and ardent expectations. With what peculiar pleasure I assisted at the making of my new clothes, and, subsequently, the packing of my trunks! But there was a feeling of bitterness mingling with the latter occupation too; and when it was done—when all was ready for my departure on the morrow, and the last night at home approached—a sudden anguish seemed to swell my heart. My dear friends looked so sad, and spoke so very kindly, that I could scarcely keep my eyes from overflowing: but I still affected to be gay. I had taken my last ramble with Mary on the moors, my last walk in the garden, and round the house; I had fed, with her, our pet pigeons for the last time—the pretty creatures that we had tamed to peck their food from our hands: I had given a farewell stroke to all their silky backs as they crowded in my lap. I had tenderly kissed my own peculiar favourites, the pair of snow white fantails; I had played my last tune on the old familiar piano, and sung my last song to papa: not the last, I hoped, but the last for, what appeared to me, a very long time. And, perhaps, when I did these things again, it would be with different feelings: circumstances might be changed, and this house might never be my settled home again. My dear little friend, the kitten, would certainly be changed: she was already growing a fine cat; and when I returned even for a hasty visit at Christmas, would, most likely, have forgotten both her playmate and her merry pranks. I had romped with her for the last time; and when I stroked her soft bright fur, while she lay purring herself to sleep in my lap, it was with a feeling of sadness I could not easily disguise. Then, at bed time, when I retired with Mary to our quiet little chamber, where already my drawers were cleared out and my share of the bookcase was empty—and where hereafter, she would have to sleep alone, in dreary solitude, as she expressed it—my heart sank more than ever: I felt as if I had been selfish and wrong to persist in leaving her; and when I knelt once more beside our little bed, I prayed for a blessing on her and on my parents more fervently than ever I had done before. To conceal my emotion, I buried my face in my hands, and they were presently bathed in tears. I perceived, on rising, that she had been crying too: but neither of us spoke; and in silence we betook ourselves to our repose, creeping more closely together from the consciousness that we were to part so soon.

But the morning brought a renewal of hope and spirits. I was to depart early, that the conveyance which took me (a gig, hired from Mr. Smith, the draper, grocer, and tea-dealer of the village) might return the same day. I rose, washed, dressed, swallowed a hasty breakfast, received the fond embraces of my father, mother, and sister, kissed the cat—to the great scandal of Sally, the maid—shook hands with her, mounted the gig, drew my veil over my face, and then, but not till then, burst into a flood of tears. The gig rolled on; I looked

ack; my dear mother and sister were still standing at the door, looking after
ᴇe, and waving their adieux. I returned their salute, and prayed God to
ᴌess them from my heart: we descended the hill, and I could see them no more.

'It's a coldish mornin' for you, Miss Agnes,' observed Smith; 'and a dark-
ᴗme un too; but we's happen get to yon' spot afore there come much rain
ᴑ signify.'

'Yes, I hope so,' replied I, as calmly as I could.

'It's comed a good sup last night too.'

'Yes.'

'But this cold wind will happen keep it off.'

'Perhaps it will.'

Here ended our colloquy. We crossed the valley, and began to ascend the
ᴑpposite hill. As we were toiling up, I looked back again: there was the village
ᴗire, and the old grey parsonage beyond it, basking in a slanting beam of
ᴗnshine—it was but a sickly ray, but the village and surrounding hills were
ᴌl in sombre shade, and I hailed the wandering beam as a propitious omen
ᴑ my home. With clasped hands, I fervently implored a blessing on its in-
ᴌbitants, and hastily turned away; for I saw the sunshine was departing; and
carefully avoided another glance, lest I should see it in gloomy shadow, like
ᴌe rest of the landscape.

CHAPTER 2

FIRST LESSONS IN THE ART OF INSTRUCTION

ᴌs we drove along, my spirits revived again, and I turned, with pleasure, to
ᴌe contemplation of the new life upon which I was entering. But though it was
ᴑt far past the middle of September, the heavy clouds and strong north-
ᴌsterly wind combined to render the day extremely cold and dreary; and the
ᴗurney seemed a very long one, for, as Smith observed, the roads were 'very
ᴇavy'; and certainly, his horse was very heavy too: it crawled up the hills, and
ᴇept down them, and only condescended to shake its sides in a trot where the
ᴑad was at a dead level or a very gentle slope, which was rarely the case in
ᴌose rugged regions; so that it was nearly one o'clock before we reached the
ᴌace of our destination. Yet, after all, when we entered the lofty iron gateway,
ᴌhen we drove softly up the smooth, well-rolled carriage road, with the green
ᴌwn on each side, studded with young trees, and approached the new but
ᴌately mansion of Wellwood, rising above its mushroom poplar-groves, my
ᴇart failed me, and I wished it were a mile or two farther off. For the first
ᴇme in my life, I must stand alone: there was no retreating now. I must
ᴌter that house, and introduce myself among its strange inhabitants. But

how was it to be done? True, I was near nineteen; but, thanks to my retire
life and the protecting care of my mother and sister, I well knew that man
a girl of fifteen, or under, was gifted with a more womanly address, and greate
ease and self-possession, than I was. Yet, if Mrs. Bloomfield were a kind
motherly woman, I might do very well, after all; and the children, of course
I should soon be at ease with them—and Mr. Bloomfield, I hoped, I shoul
have but little to do with.

'Be calm, be calm, whatever happens,' I said within myself; and trul
I kept this resolution so well, and was so fully occupied in steadying my nerve
and stilling the rebellious flutter of my heart, that when I was admitted in
the hall, and ushered into the presence of Mrs. Bloomfield, I almost forgot t
answer her polite salutation; and it afterwards struck me, that the little I di
say was spoken in the tone of one half-dead or half-asleep. The lady, too, wa
somewhat chilly in her manner, as I discovered when I had time to reflec
She was a tall, spare, stately woman, with thick black hair, cold grey eyes, an
extremely sallow complexion.

With due politeness, however, she showed me my bedroom, and left m
there to take a little refreshment. I was somewhat dismayed at my appearanc
on looking in the glass: the cold wind had swelled and reddened my hand
uncurled and entangled my hair, and dyed my face of a pale purple; add t
this my collar was horribly crumpled, my frock splashed with mud, my fee
clad in stout new boots, and as the trunks were not brought up, there was n
remedy; so having smoothed my hair as well as I could, and repeatedl
twitched my obdurate collar, I proceeded to clomp down the two flights
stairs, philosophizing as I went; and with some difficulty found my way in
the room where Mrs. Bloomfield awaited me.

She led me into the dining-room, where the family luncheon had been lai
out. Some beefsteaks and half-cold potatoes were set before me; and whil
I dined upon these, she sat opposite, watching me (as I thought) and endeav
ouring to sustain something like a conversation—consisting chiefly of a succe
sion of commonplace remarks, expressed with frigid formality: but this migl
be more my fault than hers, for I really *could* not converse. In fact, my attentio
was almost wholly absorbed in my dinner: not from ravenous appetite, b
from distress at the toughness of the beefsteaks, and the numbness of my hand
almost palsied by their five hours' exposure to the bitter wind. I would gladl
have eaten the potatoes and let the meat alone, but having got a large pie
of the latter on to my place, I could not be so impolite as to leave it; so, aft
many awkward and unsuccessful attempts to cut it with the knife, or tear it wit
the fork, or pull it asunder between them, sensible that the awful lady wa
a spectator to the whole transaction, I at last desperately grasped the kni
and fork in my fists, like a child of two years old, and fell to work with all th
little strength I possessed. But this needed some apology—with a feeble attemp

628

a laugh, I said, 'My hands are so benumbed with the cold that I can scarcely handle my knife and fork.'

'I dare say you would find it cold,' replied she with a cool, immutable gravity that did not serve to reassure me.

When the ceremony was concluded, she led me into the sitting-room again, where she rang and sent for the children.

'You will find them not very far advanced in their attainments,' said she, 'for I have had so little time to attend to their education myself, and we have thought them too young for a governess till now; but I think they are clever children, and very apt to learn, especially the little boy: he is, I think, the flower of the flock—a generous, noble-spirited boy, one to be led, but not driven, and remarkable for always speaking the truth. He seems to scorn deception' (this was good news). 'His sister Mary Ann will require watching,' continued she, 'but she is a very good girl upon the whole: though I wish her to be kept out of the nursery as much as possible, as she is now almost six years old, and might acquire bad habits from the nurses. I have ordered her crib to be placed in your room, and if you will be so kind as to overlook her washing and dressing, and take charge of her clothes, she need have nothing further to do with the nursery maid.'

I replied I was quite willing to do so; and at that moment my young pupils entered the apartment, with their two younger sisters. Master Tom Bloomfield was a well-grown boy of seven, with a somewhat wiry frame, flaxen hair, blue eyes, small turned-up nose, and fair complexion. Mary Ann was a tall girl too, somewhat dark like her mother, but with a round face and a high colour in her cheeks. The second sister was Fanny, a very pretty little girl; Mrs. Bloomfield assured me she was a remarkably gentle child, and required encouragement: she had not learned anything yet; but in a few days, she would be four years old, and then she might take her first lesson in the alphabet, and be promoted to the schoolroom. The remaining one was Harriet, a little broad, fat, merry, playful thing of scarcely two, that I coveted more than all the rest—but with her I had nothing to do.

I talked to my little pupils as well as I could, and tried to render myself agreeable; but with little success I fear, for their mother's presence kept me under an unpleasant restraint. They, however, were remarkably free from shyness. They seemed bold, lively children, and I hoped I should soon be on friendly terms with them—the little boy especially, of whom I had heard such a favourable character from his mamma. In Mary Ann there was a certain affected simper, and a craving for notice, that I was sorry to observe. But her brother claimed all my attention to himself; he stood bolt upright between me and the fire, with his hands behind his back, talking away like an orator, occasionally interrupting his discourse with a sharp reproof to his sisters when they made too much noise.

'O Tom, what a darling you are!' exclaimed his mother. 'Come and ki[s]
dear mamma; and then won't you show Miss Grey your schoolroom, and yo[u]
nice new books?'

'I won't kiss *you*, mamma; but I *will* show Miss Grey my schoolroom, an[d]
my new books.'

'And *my* schoolroom, and *my* new books, Tom,' said Mary Ann. 'They'[re]
mine too.'

'They're *mine*,' replied he decisively. 'Come along, Miss Grey—I'll escort you[.]'

When the room and books had been shown, with some bickerings betwee[n]
the brother and sister that I did my utmost to appease or mitigate, Mary An[n]
brought me her doll, and began to be very loquacious on the subject of its fi[ne]
clothes, its bed, its chest of drawers, and other appurtenances; but Tom told h[er]
to hold her clamour, that Miss Grey might see his rocking-horse, which, wi[th]
a most important bustle, he dragged forth from its corner into the middle [of]
the room, loudly calling on me to attend to it. Then, ordering his sister to ho[ld]
the reins, he mounted, and made me stand for ten minutes, watching how ma[n]
fully he used his whip and spurs. Meantime, however, I admired Mary Ann['s]
pretty doll, and all its possessions; and then told Master Tom he was a capit[al]
rider, but I hoped he would not use his whip and spurs so much when he ro[de]
a real pony.

'Oh, yes, I will!' said he, laying on with redoubled ardour. 'I'll cut into hi[m]
like smoke! Eeh! my word! but he shall sweat for it.'

This was very shocking: but I hoped in time to be able to work a reformatio[n.]

'Now you must put on your bonnet and shawl,' said the little hero, 'and I[']
show you my garden.'

'And *mine*,' said Mary Ann.

Tom lifted his fist with a menacing gesture; she uttered a loud, shrill screa[m,]
ran to the other side of me, and made a face at him.

'Surely, Tom, you would not strike your sister! I hope I shall *never* see y[ou]
do that.'

'You will sometimes: I'm obliged to do it now and then to keep her in orde[r.]'

'But it is not your business to keep her in order, you know—that is for—[-]'

'Well, now go and put on your bonnet.'

'I don't know—it is so very cloudy and cold, it seems likely to rain;—a[nd]
you know I have had a long drive.'

'No matter—you *must* come; I shall allow of no excuses,' replied the co[n]
sequential little gentleman. And as it was the first day of our acquaintan[ce]
I thought I might as well indulge him. It was too cold for Mary Ann to ventu[re]
so she stayed with her mamma; to the great relief of her brother, who lik[ed]
to have me all to himself.

The garden was a large one, and tastefully laid out; besides several splend[id]
dahlias, there were some other fine flowers still in bloom: but my compani[on]

ould not give me time to examine them: I must go with him, across the wet grass, to a remote sequestered corner, the most important place in the grounds, because it contained *his* garden. There were two round beds, stocked with variety of plants. In one there was a pretty little rose tree. I paused to admire its lovely blossoms.

'Oh, never mind that!' said he contemptuously. 'That's only *Mary Ann's* garden; look, THIS is mine.'

After I had observed every flower, and listened to a disquisition on every plant, I was permitted to depart; but first, with great pomp, he plucked a polyanthus and presented it to me, as one conferring a prodigious favour. I observed, on the grass about his garden, certain apparatus of sticks and cord, and asked what they were.

'Traps for birds.'

'Why do you catch them?'

'Papa says they do harm.'

'And what do you do with them when you catch them?'

'Different things. Sometimes I give them to the cat; sometimes I cut them in pieces with my penknife; but the next, I mean to roast alive.'

'And why do you mean to do such a horrible thing?'

'For two reasons; first, to see how long it will live—and then, to see what it will taste like.'

'But don't you know it is extremely wicked to do such things. Remember, the birds can feel as well as you; and think, how would you like it yourself.'

'Oh, that's nothing! I'm not a bird, and I can't feel what I do to them.'

'But you will have to feel it some time, Tom: you have heard where wicked people go to when they die; and if you don't leave off torturing innocent birds, remember, you will have to go there, and suffer just what you have made them suffer.'

'Oh, pooh! I shan't. Papa knows how I treat them, and he never blames me for it: he says it is just what *he* used to do when *he* was a boy. Last summer, he gave me a nest full of young sparrows, and he saw me pulling off their legs and wings, and heads, and never said anything; except that they were nasty things, and I must not let them soil my trousers: and Uncle Robson was there too, and he laughed, and said I was a fine boy.'

'But what would your mamma say?'

'Oh, she doesn't care! she says it's a pity to kill the pretty singing birds, but the naughty sparrows, and mice and rats, I may do what I like with. So now, Miss Grey, you see it is *not* wicked.'

'I still think it is, Tom; and perhaps your papa and mamma would think so too, if they thought much about it. However,' I internally added, 'they may say what they please, but I am determined you shall do nothing of the kind, as long as I have power to prevent it.'

He next took me across the lawn to see his mole-traps, and then into the stack-yard to see his weasel-traps: one of which, to his great joy, contained a dead weasel; and then into the stable to see, not the fine carriage horses, but a little rough colt, which he informed me had been bred on purpose for him, and he was to ride it as soon as it was properly trained. I tried to amuse the little fellow, and listened to all his chatter as complacently as I could; for I thought if he had any affections at all, I would endeavour to win them, and then, in time, I might be able to show him the error of his ways: but I looked in vain for that generous, noble spirit, his mother talked of; though I could see he was not without a certain degree of quickness and penetration when he chose to exert it.

When we re-entered the house it was nearly tea-time. Master Tom told me that, as papa was from home, he and I and Mary Ann were to have tea with mamma, for a treat; for, on such occasions, she always dined at luncheon time with them, instead of at six o'clock. Soon after tea, Mary Ann went to bed, but Tom favoured us with his company and conversation till eight. After he was gone, Mrs. Bloomfield further enlightened me on the subject of her children's dispositions and acquirements, and on what they were to learn, and how they were to be managed, and cautioned me to mention their defects to no one but herself. My mother had warned me before to mention them as little as possible to *her*, for people did not like to be told of their children's faults, and so I concluded I was to keep silence on them altogether. About half-past nine, Mrs. Bloomfield invited me to partake of a frugal supper of cold meat and bread. I was glad when that was over, and she took her bedroom candlestick and retired to rest; for though I wished to be pleased with her, her company was extremely irksome to me; and I could not help feeling that she was cold, grave, and forbidding—the very opposite of the kind, warm-hearted matron my hopes had depicted her to be.

CHAPTER 3

A FEW MORE LESSONS

I rose next morning with a feeling of hopeful exhilaration, in spite of the disappointments already experienced; but I found the dressing of Mary Ann was no light matter, as her abundant hair was to be smeared with pomade, plaited in three long tails, and tied with bows of ribbon: a task my unaccustomed fingers found great difficulty in performing. She told me her nurse could do it in half the time, and, by keeping up a constant fidget of impatience, contrived to render me still longer. When all was done, we went into the schoolroom, where I met my other pupil, and chatted with the two till it was

me to go down to breakfast. That meal being concluded, and a few civil words
aving been exchanged with Mrs. Bloomfield, we repaired to the schoolroom
gain, and commenced the business of the day. I found my pupils very back-
ard, indeed; but Tom, though averse to every species of mental exertion, was
ot without abilities. Mary Ann could scarcely read a word, and was so careless
nd inattentive that I could hardly get on with her at all. However, by dint of
reat labour and patience, I managed to get something done in the course of
ae morning, and then accompanied my young charges out into the garden
nd adjacent grounds, for a little recreation before dinner. There we got along
olerably together, except that I found they had no notion of going with *me*:
must go with *them* wherever they chose to lead me. I must run, walk, or stand,
xactly as it suited their fancy. This, I thought, was reversing the order of
aings; and I found it doubly disagreeable, as on this as well as subsequent
ccasions, they seemed to prefer the dirtiest places and the most dismal
ccupations. But there was no remedy; either I must follow them, or keep
ntirely apart from them, and thus appear neglectful of my charge. To-day,
aey manifested a particular attachment to a well at the bottom of the lawn,
here they persisted in dabbling with sticks and pebbles for above half an hour.
was in constant fear that their mother would see them from the window, and
lame me for allowing them thus to draggle their clothes and wet their feet and
ands, instead of taking exercise; but no arguments, commands, or entreaties
ould draw them away. If *she* did not see them, some one else did—a gentleman
n horseback had entered the gate and was proceeding up the road; at the
istance of a few paces from us he paused, and calling to the children in
waspish penetrating tone, bade them 'Keep out of that water.' 'Miss Grey,'
aid he, '(I suppose it *is* Miss Grey) I am surprised that you should allow them
o dirty their clothes in that manner! Don't you see how Miss Bloomfield has
oiled her frock? and that Master Bloomfield's socks are quite wet? and both
f them without gloves? Dear, dear! Let me *request* that in future you will
eep them *decent* at least!' so saying, he turned away, and continued his ride up
o the house. This was Mr. Bloomfield. I was surprised that he should nominate
is children Master and Miss Bloomfield; and still more so, that he should
peak so uncivilly to me, their governess, and a perfect stranger to himself.
resently the bell rang to summon us in. I dined with the children at one,
hile he and his lady took their luncheon at the same table. His conduct there
id not greatly raise him in my estimation. He was a man of ordinary stature—
ather below than above—and rather thin than stout, apparently between
airty and forty years of age: he had a large mouth, pale, dingy complexion
ailky blue eyes, and hair the colour of a hempen cord. There was a roast leg of
autton before him: he helped Mrs. Bloomfield, the children, and me, desiring
ae to cut up the children's meat; then, after twisting about the mutton in
arious directions, and eyeing it from different points, he pronounced it not

fit to be eaten, and called for the cold beef.

'What is the matter with the mutton, my dear?' asked his mate.

'It is quite overdone. Don't you taste, Mrs. Bloomfield, that all the goodne is roasted out of it? And can't you see that all that nice, red gravy is complete dried away?'

'Well, I think the *beef* will suit you.'

The beef was set before him, and he began to carve, but with the mo rueful expressions of discontent.

'What is the matter with the *beef*, Mr. Bloomfield? I'm sure I thought it w very nice.'

'And so it *was* very nice. A nicer joint could not be; but it is *quite* spoiled replied he, dolefully.

'How so?'

'How so! Why, don't you see how it is cut? Dear—dear! it is quite shocking

'They must have cut it wrong in the kitchen, then, for I'm sure I carved quite properly here, yesterday.'

'No *doubt* they cut it wrong in the kitchen—the savages! Dear—dear! Di ever anyone see such a fine piece of beef so completely ruined? But rememb(that, in future, when a decent dish leaves this table, they shall not *touch* it i the kitchen. Remember *that*, Mrs. Bloomfield!'

Notwithstanding the ruinous state of the beef, the gentleman managed to ct himself some delicate slices, part of which he ate in silence. When he next spok(it was, in a less querulous tone, to ask what there was for dinner.'

'Turkey and grouse,' was the concise reply.

'And what besides?'

'Fish.'

'What kind of fish?'

'I don't know.'

'*You don't know?*' cried he, looking solemnly up from his plate, and suspendin(his knife and fork in astonishment.

'No. I told the cook to get some fish—I did not particularize what.'

'Well, that beats everything! A lady professes to keep house, and doesn't eve know what fish is for dinner! professes to order fish, and doesn't specify what

'Perhaps, Mr. Bloomfield, you will order dinner yourself in future.'

Nothing more was said; and I was very glad to get out of the room with m pupils; for I never felt so ashamed and uncomfortable in my life for anythin(that was not my own fault.

In the afternoon we applied to lessons again: then went out again; then ha tea in the schoolroom; then I dressed Mary Ann for dessert; and when sh and her brother had gone down to the dining-room, I took the opportunity (beginning a letter to my dear friends at home: but the children came up befo(I had half completed it. At seven I had to put Mary Ann to bed; then I playe

ith Tom till eight, when he, too, went; and I finished my letter and unpacked my clothes, which I had hitherto found no opportunity for doing, and, finally, ent to bed myself.

But this is a very favourable specimen of a day's proceedings.

My task of instruction and surveillance, instead of becoming easier as my harges and I got better accustomed to each other, became more arduous as heir characters unfolded. The name of governess, I soon found, was a mere mockery as applied to me: my pupils had no more notion of obedience than wild, unbroken colt. The habitual fear of their father's peevish temper, and he dread of the punishments he was wont to inflict when irritated, kept them enerally within bounds in his immediate presence. The girls, too, had some ar of their mother's anger; and the boy might occasionally be bribed to do as he bid him by the hope of reward: but I had no rewards to offer; and as for unishments, I was given to understand, the parents reserved that privilege to hemselves; and yet they expected me to keep my pupils in order. Other hildren might be guided by the fear of anger and the desire of approbation; ut neither the one nor the other had any effect upon these.

Master Tom, not content with refusing to be ruled, must needs set up as ruler, and manifested a determination to keep, not only his sisters, but his overness in order, by violent manual and pedal applications; and, as he was tall, strong boy of his years, this occasioned no trifling inconvenience. A few und boxes in the ear, on such occasions, might have settled the matter easily nough: but as, in that case, he might make up some story to his mother, which he would be sure to believe, as she had such unshaken faith in his veracity— hough I had already discovered it to be by no means unimpeachable—I etermined to refrain from striking him, even in self-defence; and, in his most iolent moods, my only resource was to throw him on his back, and hold his ands and feet till the frenzy was somewhat abated. To the difficulty of reventing him from doing what he ought not, was added that of forcing him o do what he ought. Often he would positively refuse to learn, or to repeat his ssons, or even to look at his book. Here, again, a good birch rod might have een serviceable; but, as my powers were so limited, I must make the best se of what I had.

As there were no settled hours for study and play, I resolved to give my pupils certain task, which, with moderate attention, they could perform in a short me; and till this was done, however weary I was, or however perverse they ight be, nothing short of parental interference should induce me to suffer hem to leave the schoolroom; even if I should sit with my chair against the oor to keep them in. Patience, Firmness, and Perseverance, were my only eapons; and these I resolved to use to the utmost. I determined always strictly fulfil the threats and promises I made; and, to that end, I must be cautious threaten and promise nothing that I could not perform. Then, I would

carefully refrain from all useless irritability and indulgence of my own il temper: when they behaved tolerably, I would be as kind and obliging as was in my power to be, in order to make the widest possible distinction betwee good and bad conduct; I would reason with them, too, in the simplest and mo effective manner. When I reproved them, or refused to gratify their wishe after a glaring fault, it should be more in sorrow than in anger: their litt hymns and prayers I would make plain and clear to their understanding; whe they said their prayers at night, and asked pardon for their offences, I woul remind them of the sins of the past day, solemnly, but in perfect kindness, avoid raising a spirit of opposition; penitential hymns should be said by th naughty; cheerful ones by the comparatively good; and every kind of instruc tion I would convey to them, as much as possible, by entertaining discourse- apparently with no other object than their present amusement in view.

By these means I hoped, in time, both to benefit the children and to gain th approbation of their parents; and also to convince my friends at home tha I was not so wanting in skill and prudence as they supposed. I knew the diff culties I had to contend with were great; but I knew (at least I believec unremitting patience and perseverance could overcome them; and night an morning I implored Divine assistance to this end. But either the children wei so incorrigible, the parents so unreasonable, or myself so mistaken in my view or so unable to carry them out, that my best intentions and most strenuou efforts seemed productive of no better result than sport to the children, di satisfaction to their parents, and torment to myself.

The task of instruction was as arduous for the body as the mind. I had to ru after my pupils to catch them, to carry or drag them to the table, and ofte forcibly to hold them there till the lesson was done. Tom I frequently put int a corner, seating myself before him in a chair, with a book which contained th little task that must be said or read, before he was released, in my hand. He wa not strong enough to push both me and the chair away, so he would stan twisting his body and face into the most grotesque and singular contortions- laughable, no doubt, to an unconcerned spectator, but not to me—and utterin loud yells and doleful outcries, intended to represent weeping, but wholl without the accompaniment of tears. I knew this was done solely for the purpos of annoying me; and, therefore, however I might inwardly tremble wit impatience and irritation, I manfully strove to suppress all visible signs c molestation, and affected to sit with calm indifference, waiting till it shoul please him to cease this pastime, and prepare for a run in the garden, by castin his eye on the book and reading or repeating the few words he was require to say. Sometimes he was determined to do his writing badly; and I had to hol his hand to prevent him from purposely blotting or disfiguring the pape Frequently I threatened that, if he did not do better he should have anothe line: then he would stubbornly refuse to write this line; and I, to save my word

id finally to resort to the expedient of holding his fingers upon the pen, and
rcibly drawing his hand up and down, till, in spite of his resistance, the line
.as in some sort completed.

Yet Tom was by no means the most unmanageable of my pupils: sometimes,
my great joy, he would have the sense to see that his wisest policy was to
1ish his tasks, and go out and amuse himself till I and his sisters came to join
.m; which frequently was not at all, for Mary Ann seldom followed his
.ample in this particular: she apparently preferred rolling on the floor to any
:her amusement: down she would drop like a leaden weight; and when I,
ith great difficulty, had succeeded in rooting her thence, I had still to hold
:r up with one arm, while with the other I held the book from which she was
• read or spell her lesson. As the dead weight of the big girl of six became too
:avy for one arm to bear, I transferred it to the other; or, if both were weary
: the burden, I carried her into a corner, and told her she might come out
hen she should find the use of her feet, and stand up: but she generally
referred lying there like a log till dinner or tea time, when, as I could not
:prive her of her meals, she must be liberated, and would come crawling out
ith a grin of triumph on her round, red face. Often she would stubbornly
:fuse to pronounce some particular word in her lesson; and now I regret
1e lost labour I have had in striving to conquer her obstinacy. If I had passed
over as a matter of no consequence, it would have been better for both
arties, than vainly striving to overcome it as I did; but I thought it my
osolute duty to crush this vicious tendency in the bud: and so it was, if I could
ave done it; and, had my powers been less limited, I might have enforced
oedience; but, as it was, it was a trial of strength between her and me, in
hich she generally came off victorious; and every victory served to encourage
1d strengthen her for a future contest. In vain I argued, coaxed, entreated,
ireatened, scolded; in vain I kept her in from play, or if obliged to take her
it, refused to play with her, or to speak kindly, or have anything to do with
:r; in vain I tried to set before her the advantages of doing as she was bid,
1d being loved, and kindly treated in consequence, and the disadvantages of
:rsisting in her absurd perversity. Sometimes, when she would ask me to do
mething for her, I would answer—'Yes, I will, Mary Ann, if you will only
.y that word. Come! you'd better say it at once, and have no more trouble
oout it.'

'No.'

'Then, of course, I can do nothing for you.'

With me, at her age, or under, neglect and disgrace were the most dreadful of
.nishments; but on her they made no impression. Sometimes, exasperated to
ie utmost pitch, I would shake her violently by the shoulder, or pull her long
air, or put her in the corner; for which she punished me with loud, shrill,
iercing screams, that went through my head like a knife. She knew I hated

this, and when she had shrieked her utmost, would look into my face with a air of vindictive satisfaction, exclaiming—'*Now*, then! that's for you!' And the shriek again and again, till I was forced to stop my ears. Often these dreadf cries would bring Mrs. Bloomfield up to inquire what was the matter.

'Mary Ann is a naughty girl, ma'am.'

'But what are these shocking screams?'

'She is screaming in a passion.'

'I never heard such a dreadful noise! You might be killing her. Why is sh not out with her brother?'

'I cannot get her to finish her lessons.'

'But Mary Ann must be a *good* girl, and finish her lessons.' This was bland spoken to the child. 'And I hope I shall *never* hear such terrible cries again

And fixing her cold, stony eyes upon me with a look that could not b mistaken, she would shut the door, and walk away. Sometimes I would try t take the little obstinate creature by surprise, and casually ask her the wor while she was thinking of something else; frequently she would begin to say i and then suddenly check herself, with a provoking look that seemed to sa 'Ah! I'm too sharp for you; you shan't trick it out of me, either.'

On another occasion, I pretended to forget the whole affair; and talked an played with her as usual, till night, when I put her to bed; then bending ove her, while she lay all smiles and good humour, just before departing, I sai as cheerfully and kindly as before—'Now, Mary Ann, just tell me that wor before I kiss you goodnight: you are a good girl now, and, of course, yo will say it.'

'No, I won't.'

'Then I can't kiss you.'

'Well, I don't care.'

In vain I expressed my sorrow; in vain I lingered for some symptom contrition; she really 'didn't care' and I left her alone, and in darknes wondering most of all at this last proof of insensate stubbornness. In *my* child hood I could not imagine a more afflictive punishment, than for my mothe to refuse to kiss me at night: the very idea was terrible. More than the ide I never felt, for, happily, I never committed a fault that was deemed worth of such a penalty; but once I remember, for some transgression of my sister our mother thought proper to inflict it upon her: what *she* felt, I cannot tel but my sympathetic tears and suffering for her sake, I shall not soon forget.

Another troublesome trait in Mary Ann, was her incorrigible propensity t keep running into the nursery, to play with her little sisters and the nurs This was natural enough, but, as it was against her mother's express desir I, of course, forbade her to do so, and did my utmost to keep her with me; bu that only increased her relish for the nursery, and the more I strove to keep he out of it, the oftener she went, and the longer she stayed: to the great di

tisfaction of Mrs. Bloomfield, who, I well knew, would impute all the blame
the matter to me. Another of my trials was the dressing in the morning:
one time she would not be washed; at another she would not be dressed,
iless she might wear some particular frock, that I knew her mother would not
ke her to have; at another she would scream and run away if I attempted to
uch her hair. So that, frequently, when, after much trouble and toil, I had,
length, succeeded in bringing her down, the breakfast was nearly half over;
id black looks from 'mamma,' and testy observations from 'papa,' spoken
me, if not to me, were sure to be my meed: for few things irritated the latter
) much as want of punctuality at meal times. Then, among the minor annoy-
nces, was my inability to satisfy Mrs. Bloomfield with her daughter's dress;
id the child's hair 'was never fit to be seen.' Sometimes, as a powerful
proach to me, she would perform the office of tirewoman herself, and then
omplain bitterly of the trouble it gave her.

When little Fanny came into the schoolroom, I hoped she would be mild
nd inoffensive, at least; but a few days, if not a few hours, sufficed to destroy
ie illusion: I found her a mischievous, intractable little creature, given up to
.lsehood and deception, young as she was, and alarmingly fond of exercising
er two favourite weapons of offence and defence; that of spitting in the faces
f those who incurred her displeasure, and bellowing like a bull when her
nreasonable desires were not gratified. As she, generally, was pretty quiet in
er parents' presence, and they were impressed with the notion of her being
remarkably gentle child, her falsehoods were readily believed, and her loud
proars led them to suspect harsh and injudicious treatment on my part; and
hen, at length, her bad disposition became manifest even to their prejudiced
/es, I felt that the whole was attributed to me.

'What a naughty girl Fanny is getting!' Mrs. Bloomfield would say to her
ouse. 'Don't you observe, my dear, how she is altered since she entered
ie schoolroom? She will soon be as bad as the other two; and, I am sorry to
.y, they have quite deteriorated of late.'

'You may say that,' was the answer. 'I've been thinking that same myself.
thought when we got them a governess they'd improve; but, instead of
iat, they get worse and worse: I don't know how it is with their learning;
ut their habits, I know, make no sort of improvement; they get rougher, and
irtier, and more unseemly, everyday.'

I knew this was all pointed at me; and these, and all similar innuendoes,
ffected me far more deeply than any open accusations would have done; for
gainst the latter I should have been roused to speak in my own defence: now
judged it my wisest plan to subdue every resentful impulse, suppress every
nsitive shrinking, and go on perseveringly, doing my best; for, irksome as my
tuation was, I earnestly wished to retain it. I thought, if I could struggle on
ith unremitting firmness and integrity, the children would in time become

more humanized: every month would contribute to make them some lit
wiser, and, consequently, more manageable; for a child of nine or ten as fran
and ungovernable as these at six and seven would be a maniac.

I flattered myself I was benefiting my parents and sister by my continuan
here; for small as the salary was, I still was earning something, and with stri
economy I could easily manage to have something to spare for them, if th
would favour me by taking it. Then it was by my own will that I had got t
place: I had brought all this tribulation on myself, and I was determined
bear it; nay, more than that, I did not even regret the step I had take
I longed to show my friends that, even now, I was competent to undertake tl
charge, and able to acquit myself honourably to the end; and if ever I felt
degrading to submit so quietly, or intolerable to toil so constantly, I wou
turn towards my home, and say within myself—

> They may crush, but they shall not subdue me!
> 'Tis of thee that I think, not of them.

About Christmas I was allowed to visit home; but my holiday was only
a fortnight's duration: 'For,' said Mrs. Bloomfield, 'I thought, as you had se
your friends so lately, you would not care for a longer stay.' I left her to thi
so still: but she little knew how long, how wearisome those fourteen weeks
absence had been to me; how intensely I had longed for my holidays, ho
greatly I was disappointed at their curtailment. Yet she was not to blame
this; I had never told her my feelings, and she could not be expected to divi
them; I had not been with her a full term, and she was justified in not allowi
me a full vacation.

CHAPTER 4

THE GRANDMAMMA

I spare my readers the account of my delight on coming home, my happine
while there—enjoying a brief space of rest and liberty in that dear, famili
place, among the loving and the loved—and my sorrow on being obliged
bid them, once more, a long adieu.

I returned, however, with unabated vigour to my work—a more arduo
task than anyone can imagine, who has not felt something like the misery
being charged with the care and direction of a set of mischievous turbule
rebels, whom his utmost exertions cannot bind to their duty; while, at the san
time, he is responsible for their conduct to a higher power, who exacts fro
him what cannot be achieved without the aid of the superior's more pote
authority: which, either from indolence, or the fear of becoming unpopul
with the said rebellious gang, the latter refuses to give. I can conceive fe

uations more harassing than that wherein, however you may long for success,
wever you may labour to fulfil your duty, your efforts are baffled and set at
ught by those beneath you, and unjustly censured and misjudged by those
ove.

I have not enumerated half the vexatious propensities of my pupils, or half
e troubles resulting from my heavy responsibilities, for fear of trespassing too
uch upon the reader's patience; as, perhaps, I have already done; but my
sign, in writing the few last pages, was not to amuse, but to benefit those
hom it might concern: he that has no interest in such matters will doubtless
ve skipped them over with a cursory glance, and, perhaps, a malediction
ainst the prolixity of the writer; but if a parent has, therefrom, gathered any
eful hint, or an unfortunate governess received thereby the slightest benefit,
am well rewarded for my pains.

To avoid trouble and confusion, I have taken my pupils one by one, and
scussed their various qualities; but this can give no adequate idea of being
orried by the whole three together; when, as was often the case, all were
termined to 'be naughty, and to tease Miss Grey, and put her in a passion.'
Sometimes, on such occasions, the thought had suddenly occurred to me—
they could see me now!' meaning, of course, my friends at home; and the idea
how they would pity me has made me pity myself—so greatly that I have
d the utmost difficulty to restrain my tears: but I have restrained them, till
y little tormentors were gone to dessert, or cleared off to bed (my only
ospects of deliverance), and then, in all the bliss of solitude, I have given
yself up to the luxury of an unrestricted burst of weeping. But this was
weakness I did not often indulge: my employments were too numerous, my
sure moments too precious, to admit of much time being given to fruitless
mentations.

I particularly remember one wild, snowy afternoon, soon after my return in
nuary; the children had all come up from dinner, loudly declaring that they
ant 'to be naughty'; and they had well kept their resolution, though I had
ked myself hoarse, and wearied every muscle in my throat, in the vain
tempt to reason them out of it. I had got Tom pinned up in a corner, whence,
old him, he should not escape till he had done his appointed task. Mean-
ne, Fanny had possessed herself of my work-bag, and was rifling its contents—
d spitting into it besides. I told her to let it alone, but to no purpose, of
urse. 'Burn it, Fanny!' cried Tom: and *this* command she hastened to obey.
prang to snatch it from the fire, and Tom darted to the door. 'Mary Ann,
ow her desk out of the window!' cried he: and my precious desk, containing
y letters and papers, my small amount of cash, and all my valuables, was
out to be precipitated from the three-story window. I flew to rescue it.
eanwhile Tom had left the room, and was rushing down the stairs, followed
Fanny. Having secured my desk, I ran to catch them, and Mary Ann came

scampering after. All three escaped me, and ran out of the house into the garden, where they plunged about in the snow, shouting and screaming exultant glee.

What must I do? If I followed them, I should probably be unable to capture one, and only drive them farther away, if I did not, how was I to get them in? and what would their parents think of me, if they saw or heard the children rioting, hatless, bonnetless, gloveless, and bootless, in the deep, soft snow. While I stood in this perplexity, just without the door, trying by grim looks and angry words, to awe them into subjection, I heard a voice behind me, harshly piercing tones, exclaiming,—

'Miss Grey! Is it possible! What, in the devil's name, can you be thinking about?'

'I can't get them in, sir,' said I, turning round, and beholding Mr. Bloomfield, with his hair on end, and his pale blue eyes bolting from their sockets.

'But I INSIST upon their being got in!' cried he, approaching nearer, and looking perfectly ferocious.

'Then, sir, you must call them yourself, if you please, for they won't listen to me,' I replied, stepping back.

'Come in with you, you filthy brats; or I'll horsewhip you every one!' roared he; and the children instantly obeyed. 'There, you see! they come at the first word!'

'Yes, when *you* speak.'

'And it's very strange, that when you've the care of 'em, you've no better control over 'em than that!—Now, there they are—gone up stairs with their nasty snowy feet! Do go after 'em and see them made decent, for heaven's sake!'

That gentleman's mother was then staying in the house; and, as I ascended the stairs and passed the drawing-room door, I had the satisfaction of hearing the old lady declaiming aloud to her daughter-in-law to this effect (for I could only distinguish the most emphatic words)—

'Gracious heavens!——never in all my life——!——get their death as sure as——! Do you think, my dear, she's a *proper person?* Take my word for it——'

I heard no more; but that sufficed.

The senior Mrs. Bloomfield had been very attentive and civil to me; and till now, I had thought her a nice kind-hearted, chatty old body. She would often come to me and talk in a confidential strain; nodding and shaking her head, and gesticulating with hands and eyes, as a certain class of old ladies are wont to do: though I never knew one that carried the peculiarity to so great an extent. She would even sympathize with me for the trouble I had with the children, and express at times, by half sentences, interspersed with nods and knowing winks, her sense of the injudicious conduct of their mamma in restricting my power, and neglecting to support me with her authority. Such a mode of testifying disapprobation was not much to my taste; and I generally

fused to take it in, or understand anything more than was openly spoken: at
ast, I never went farther than an implied acknowledgement that, if matters
re otherwise ordered, my task would be a less difficult one, and I should be
tter able to guide and instruct my charge; but now I must be doubly cautious.
therto, though I saw the old lady had her defects (of which one was a prone-
ss to proclaim her perfections), I had always been wishful to excuse them, and
give her credit for all the virtues she professed, and even imagine others yet
told. Kindness, which had been the food of my life through so many years,
d lately been so entirely denied me, that I welcomed with grateful joy the
ghtest semblance of it. No wonder, then, that my heart warmed to the old
ly, and always gladdened at her approach and regretted her departure.

But now, the few words luckily or unluckily heard in passing had wholly
volutionized my ideas respecting her: now I looked upon her as hypocritical
d insincere, a flatterer, and a spy upon my words and deeds. Doubtless it
uld have been my interest still to meet her with the same cheerful smile and
e of respectful cordiality as before; but I could not, if I would: my manner
ered with my feelings, and became so cold and shy that she could not fail to
tice it. She soon did notice it, and *her* manner altered too: the familiar nod
s changed to a stiff bow, the gracious smile gave place to a glare of Gorgon
ocity; her vivacious loquacity was entirely transferred from me to 'the
rling boy and girls,' whom she flattered and indulged more absurdly than
er their mother had done.

I confess I was somewhat troubled at this change: I feared the consequences
her displeasure, and even made some efforts to recover the ground I had
t—and with better apparent success than I could have anticipated. At one
e, I, merely in common civility, asked after her cough; immediately her long
age relaxed into a smile, and she favoured me with a particular history of
t and her other infirmities, followed by an account of her pious resignation,
ivered in the usual emphatic, declamatory style, which no writing could
tray.

But there's one remedy for all, my dear, and that's resignation' (a toss of the
ad), 'resignation to the will of heaven!' (an uplifting of the hands and
es). 'It has always supported me through all my trials, and always will do'
succession of nods). 'But then, it isn't everybody that can say that' (a shake
the head); 'but I'm one of the pious ones, Miss Grey!' (a very significant
d and toss). 'And, thank heaven, I always was' (another nod), 'and I glory
it!' (an emphatic clasping of the hands and shaking of the head). And with
eral texts of scripture, misquoted or misapplied, and religious exclamations
redolent of the ludicrous in the style of delivery and manner of bringing in, if
t in the expressions themselves, that I decline repeating them, she with-
w; tossing her large head in high good humour—with herself at least—and
me hoping that, after all, she was rather weak than wicked.

At her next visit to Wellwood House, I went so far as to say I was glad
see her looking so well. The effect of this was magical: the words, intended
a mark of civility, were received as a flattering compliment; her countenan
brightened up, and from that moment she became as gracious and benign
heart could wish—in outward semblance at least. From what I now saw of h
and what I heard from the children, I knew that, in order to gain her cord
friendship, I had but to utter a word of flattery at each convenient opportuni
but this was against my principles; and for lack of this, the capricious c
dame soon deprived me of her favour again, and I believe did me much sec
injury.

She could not greatly influence her daughter-in-law against me, becau
between that lady and herself there was a mutual dislike—chiefly shown by h
in secret detractions and calumniations; by the other, in an excess of frig
formality in her demeanour; and no fawning flattery of the elder could th
away the wall of ice which the younger interposed between them. But with h
son, the old lady had better success: he would listen to all she had to sa
provided she could soothe his fretful temper, and refrain from irritating h
by her own asperities; and I have reason to believe that she considerab
strengthened his prejudice against me. She would tell him that I shamefu
neglected the children, and even his wife did not attend to them as she oug
and that he must look after them himself, or they would all go to ruin.

Thus urged, he would frequently give himself the trouble of watching the
from the windows during their play; at times, he would follow them throu
the grounds, and too often came suddenly upon them while they were dabbli
in the forbidden well, talking to the coachman in the stables, or revelling in t
filth of the farm-yard—and I, meanwhile wearily standing by, having p
viously exhausted my energy in vain attempts to get them away. Often, t
he would unexpectedly pop his head into the schoolroom while the you
people were at meals, and find them spilling their milk over the table a
themselves, plunging their fingers into their own or each other's mugs,
quarrelling over their victuals like a set of tiger's cubs. If I were quiet at t
moment, I was conniving at their disorderly conduct; if (as was frequently t
case) I happened to be exalting my voice to enforce order, I was using und
violence, and setting the girls a bad example by such ungentleness of tone a
language.

I remember one afternoon in spring when, owing to the rain, they could r
go out; but, by some amazing good fortune, they had all finished their lesso
and yet abstained from running down to tease their parents—a trick th
annoyed me greatly, but which, on rainy days, I seldom could prevent th
doing; because, below, they found novelty and amusement—especially wh
visitors were in the house; and their mother, though she bid me keep th
in the schoolroom, would never chide them for leaving it, or trouble her

send them back. But this day they appeared satisfied with their present
ode, and what is more wonderful still, seemed disposed to play together
thout depending on me for amusement, and without quarrelling with each
her. Their occupation was a somewhat puzzling one: they were all squatted
ether on the floor by the window, over a heap of broken toys and a quantity
birds' eggs—or rather eggshells, for the contents had luckily been abstracted.
ese shells they had broken up and were pounding into small fragments, to
at end I could not imagine; but so long as they were quiet and not in
sitive mischief, I did not care; and, with a feeling of unusual repose, I sat
the fire, putting the finishing stitches to a frock for Mary Ann's doll;
ending, when that was done, to begin a letter to my mother. Suddenly,
door opened, and the dingy head of Mr. Bloomfield looked in.

All very quiet here! What are you doing?' said he. 'No harm *to-day*, at
st,' thought I. But he was of a different opinion. Advancing to the window,
d seeing the children's occupations, he testily exclaimed—'What in the
rld are you about?'

We're grinding eggshells, papa!' cried Tom.

How *dare* you make such a mess, you little devils? Don't you see what con-
nded work you're making of the carpet?' (the carpet was a plain, brown
gget). 'Miss Grey, did you know what they were doing?'

Yes, sir.'

You knew it?'

Yes.'

You *knew* it! and you actually sat there and permitted them to go on,
hout a word of reproof!'

I didn't think they were doing any harm.'

Any harm! Why look there! Just look at that carpet, and see—was there
r anything like it in a Christian house before? No wonder your room is
fit for a pigsty—no wonder your pupils are worse than a litter of pigs!—no
nder—Oh! I declare, it puts me quite past my patience!' and he departed,
tting the door after him with a bang, that made the children laugh.

It puts *me* quite past my patience too!' muttered I, getting up; and, seizing
poker, I dashed it repeatedly into the cinders, and stirred them up with
vonted energy; thus easing my irritation, under pretence of mending the fire.
After this, Mr. Bloomfield was continually looking in to see if the school-
m was in order; and, as the children were continually littering the floor
h fragments of toys, sticks, stones, stubble, leaves, and other rubbish, which
ould not prevent their bringing, or oblige them to gather up, and which
servants refused to 'clean after them,' I had to spend a considerable portion
my valuable leisure moments on my knees upon the floor, in painfully
ucing things to order. Once I told them that they should not taste their
per till they had picked up everything from the carpet; Fanny might have

hers when she had taken up a certain quantity, Mary Ann when she h
gathered twice as many, and Tom was to clear away the rest. Wonderful
state, the girls did their part; but Tom was in such a fury that he flew up
the table, scattered the bread and milk about the floor, struck his siste
kicked the coals out of the coal-pan, attempted to overthrow the table a
chairs, and seemed inclined to make a Douglas-larder of the whole conte
of the room: but I seized upon him, and, sending Mary Ann to call I
mamma, held him, in spite of kicks, blows, yells, and execrations, till M
Bloomfield made her appearance.

'What is the matter with my boy?' said she.

And when the matter was explained to her, all she did was to send for t
nursery-maid to put the room in order, and bring Master Bloomfield
supper.

'There now,' cried Tom, triumphantly, looking up from his viands with
mouth almost too full for speech. 'There now, Miss Grey! you see I have
my supper in spite of you: and I haven't picked up a single thing!'

The only person in the house who had any real sympathy for me was t
nurse; for she had suffered like afflictions, though in a smaller degree; as s
had not the task of teaching, nor was she so responsible for the conduct of I
charge.

'Oh, Miss Grey!' she would say, 'you have some trouble with them childe
'I have indeed, Betty; and I dare say you know what it is.'

'Aye, I do so! But I don't vex myself o'er 'em as you do. And then, you s
I hit 'em a slap sometimes: and them little uns—I gives 'em a good whipp:
now and then: there's nothing else will do for 'em, as what they say. H(
soever, I've lost my place for it.'

'Have you, Betty? I heard you were going to leave.'

'Eh, bless you, yes! Missis gave me warning a three wik sin'. She told
afore Christmas how it mud be, if I hit 'em again; but I couldn't hold
hand off 'em at nothing. I know not how *you* do, for Miss Mary Ann's wo
by the half nor her sisters!'

CHAPTER 5

THE UNCLE

Besides the old lady, there was another relative of the family, whose visits w
a great annoyance to me—this was 'Uncle Robson,' Mrs. Bloomfield's broth
a tall, self-sufficient fellow, with dark hair and sallow complexion like
sister, a nose that seemed to disdain the earth, and little grey eyes, frequer
half-closed, with a mixture of real stupidity and affected contempt of

rrounding objects. He was a thick-set, strongly-built man, but he had found
me means of compressing his waist into a remarkably small compass; and
at, together with the unnatural stiffness of his form, showed that the lofty-
inded, manly Mr. Robson, the scorner of the female sex, was not above the
ppery of stays. He seldom deigned to notice me; and, when he did, it was
th a certain supercilious insolence of tone and manner that convinced me
: was no gentleman: though it was intended to have a contrary effect. But it
as not for that I disliked his coming, so much as for the harm he did the
ildren—encouraging all their evil propensities, and undoing in a few minutes
e little good it had taken me months of labour to achieve.

Fanny and little Harriet he seldom condescended to notice; but Mary Ann
as something of a favourite. He was continually encouraging her tendency to
ffectation (which I had done my utmost to crush), talking about her pretty
ce, and filling her head with all manner of conceited notions concerning her
:rsonal appearance (which I had instructed her to regard as dust in the
ilance compared with the cultivation of her mind and manners); and I never
w a child so susceptible of flattery as she was. Whatever was wrong, in either
:r or her brother, he would encourage by laughing at, if not by actually
aising: people little know the injury they do to children by laughing at their
ults, and making a pleasant jest of what their true friends have endeavoured
teach them to hold in grave abhorrence.

Though not a positive drunkard, Mr. Robson habitually swallowed great
iantities of wine, and took with relish an occasional glass of brandy and
ater. He taught his nephew to imitate him in this to the utmost of his ability,
id to believe that the more wine and spirits he could take, and the better he
:ed them, the more he manifested his bold and manly spirit, and rose superior
his sisters. Mr. Bloomfield had not much to say against it, for his favourite
:verage was gin and water; of which he took a considerable portion every
iy, by dint of constant sipping—and to that, I chiefly attributed his dingy
mplexion and waspish temper.

Mr. Robson likewise encouraged Tom's propensity to persecute the lower
eation, both by precept and example. As he frequently came to course or
oot over his brother-in-law's grounds, he would bring his favourite dogs with
m; and he treated them so brutally that, poor as I was, I would have given
sovereign any day to see one of them bite him, provided the animal could
ive done it with impunity. Sometimes, when in a very complacent mood, he
uld go a-birdnesting with the children: a thing that irritated and annoyed
e exceedingly; as, by frequent and persevering attempts, I flattered myself
iad partly shown them the evil of this pastime, and hoped, in time, to bring
em to some general sense of justice and humanity; but ten minutes' bird-
sting with uncle Robson, or even a laugh from him at some relation of their
·mer barbarities, was sufficient at once to destroy the effect of my whole

elaborate course of reasoning and persuasion. Happily, however, during th
spring, they never, but once, got anything but empty nests, or eggs—bein
too impatient to leave them till the birds were hatched; that once, Tom
who had been with his uncle into the neighbouring plantation, came runnin
in high glee into the garden, with a brood of little callow nestlings in his hand
Mary Ann and Fanny, whom I was just bringing out, ran to admire his spoi
and to beg each a bird for themselves. 'No, not one!' cried Tom. 'They're ;
mine: uncle Robson gave them to me—one, two, three, four, five—you shar
touch one of them! no, not one, for your lives!' continued he, exultingl
laying the nest on the ground, and standing over it with his legs wide apar
his hands thrust into his breeches-pockets, his body bent forward, and his fa
twisted into all manner of contortions in the ecstasy of his delight.

'But you shall see me fettle 'em off. My word, but I *will* wallop 'em! See
I don't now. By gum! but there's rare sport for me in that nest.'

'But, Tom,' said I, 'I shall not allow you to torture those birds. They mu
either be killed at once or carried back to the place you took them from, th
the old birds may continue to feed them.'

'But you don't know where that is, madam: it's only me and uncle Robso
that knows that.'

'But if you don't tell me, I shall kill them myself—much as I hate it.'

'You daren't. You daren't touch them for your life! because you know pa]
and mamma, and uncle Robson, would be angry. Ha, ha! I've caught yo
there, Miss!'

'I shall do what I think right in a case of this sort without consulting an
one. If your papa and mamma don't happen to approve of it, I shall be sorr
to offend them; but your uncle Robson's opinions, of course, are nothir
to me.'

So saying—urged by a sense of duty—at the risk of both making myself si
and incurring the wrath of my employers—I got a large flat stone, that ha
been reared up for a mouse-trap by the gardener, then, having once mo
vainly endeavoured to persuade the little tyrant to let the birds be carri
back, I asked what he intended to do with them. With fiendish glee he con
menced a list of torments; and while he was busied in the relation, I droppe
the stone upon his intended victims and crushed them flat beneath it. Lo
were the outcries, terrible the execrations, consequent upon this darin
outrage; uncle Robson had been coming up the walk with his gun, and w
just then pausing to kick his dog. Tom flew towards him, vowing he wou
make him kick me instead of Juno. Mr. Robson leant upon his gun, an
laughed excessively at the violence of his nephew's passion, and the bitt
maledictions and opprobrious epithets he heaped upon me. 'Well, you
a good un!' exclaimed he, at length, taking up his weapon and proceedin
towards the house. 'Damme, but the lad has some spunk in him, too. Cur

, if ever I saw a nobler little scoundrel than that. He's beyond petticoat
vernment already: by God! he defies mother, granny, governess, and all!
, ha, ha! Never mind, Tom, I'll get you another brood tomorrow.'

'If you do, Mr. Robson, I shall kill them too,' said I.

'Humph!' replied he, and having honoured me with a broad stare—which,
ntrary to his expectations, I sustained without flinching—he turned away
th an air of supreme contempt, and stalked into the house. Tom next went
tell his mamma. It was not her way to say much on any subject; but, when
: next saw me, her aspect and demeanour were doubly dark and chill. After
ne casual remark about the weather, she observed—'I am sorry, Miss Grey,
u should think it necessary to interfere with Master Bloomfield's amuse-
nts; he was *very* much distressed about your destroying the birds.'

When Master Bloomfield's amusements consist in injuring sentient creatures,
nswered, 'I think it my duty to interfere.'

You seemed to have forgotten,' said she, calmly, 'that the creatures were
created for our convenience.'

I thought that doctrine admitted some doubt, but merely replied—'If they
re, we have no right to torment them for our amusement.'

I think,' said she, 'a child's amusement is scarcely to be weighed against the
lfare of a soulless brute.'

But, for the child's own sake, it ought not to be encouraged to have such
usements,' answered I, as meekly as I could, to make up for such unusual
tinacity. ' "Blessed are the merciful, for they shall obtain mercy." '

Oh! of course; but that refers to our conduct towards each other.'

"The merciful man shows mercy to his beast," ' I ventured to add.

I think *you* have not shown much mercy,' replied she with a short, bitter
gh; 'killing the poor birds by wholesale in that shocking manner, and
tting the dear boy to such misery for a mere whim.'

I judged it prudent to say no more. This was the nearest approach to
quarrel I ever had with Mrs. Bloomfield; as well as the greatest number of
rds I ever exchanged with her at one time, since the day of my first arrival.

But Mr. Robson and old Mrs. Bloomfield were not the only guests whose
ning to Wellwood House annoyed me; every visitor disturbed me more or
; not so much because they neglected me (though I did feel their conduct
inge and disagreeable in that respect), as because I found it impossible to
p my pupils away from them, as I was repeatedly desired to do: Tom must
к to them, and Mary Ann must be noticed by them. Neither the one nor the
er knew what is was to feel any degree of shame-facedness, or even common
desty. They would indecently and clamorously interrupt the conversation
heir elders, tease them with the most impertinent questions, roughly collar
gentlemen, climb their knees uninvited, hang about their shoulders or rifle
ir pockets, pull the ladies' gowns, disorder their hair, tumble their collars,

and importunately beg for their trinkets.

Mrs. Bloomfield had the sense to be shocked and annoyed at all this, b
she had not sense to prevent it: she expected me to prevent it. But how cou
I—when the guests, with their fine clothes and new faces, continually flatter
and indulged them, out of complaisance to their parents—how could I, with m
homely garments, everyday face, and honest words, draw them awa
I strained every nerve to do so: by striving to amuse them, I endeavoured
attract them to my side; by the exertion of such authority as I possessed, a
by such severity as I dared to use, I tried to deter them from tormenting t
guests; and by reproaching their unmannerly conduct, to make them asham
to repeat it. But they knew no shame; they scorned authority which had
terrors to back it; and as for kindness and affection, either they had no hear
or such as they had were so strongly guarded, and so well concealed, that
with all my efforts, had not yet discovered how to reach them.

But soon my trials in this quarter came to a close—sooner than I eith
expected or desired; for one sweet evening towards the close of May, as I w
rejoicing in the near approach of the holidays, and congratulating myself up
having made some progress with my pupils (as far as their learning went
least, for I *had* instilled *something* into their heads, and I had, at length, brou
them to be a little—a very little—more rational about getting their lesse
done in time to leave some space for recreation, instead of tormenting the
selves and me all day long to no purpose), Mrs. Bloomfield sent for me, a
calmly told me that after Midsummer my services would be no longer requir
She assured me that my character and general conduct were unexceptionab
but the children had made so little improvement since my arrival, that M
Bloomfield and she felt it their duty to seek some other mode of instructi
Though superior to most children of their years in abilities, they were decide
behind them in attainments: their manners were uncultivated, and th
tempers unruly. And this she attributed to a want of sufficient firmness, a
diligent, persevering care on my part.

Unshaken firmness, devoted diligence, unwearied perseverance, unceas
care, were the very qualifications on which I had secretly prided myself; a
by which I had hoped in time to overcome all difficulties, and obtain succ
at last. I wished to say something in my own justification: but in attempt
to speak, I felt my voice falter; and rather than testify any emotion, or su
the tears to overflow that were already gathering in my eyes, I chose to k
silence, and bear all like a self-convicted culprit.

Thus was I dismissed, and thus I sought my home. Alas! what would t
think of me? unable, after all my boasting, to keep my place, even for a sin
year, as governess to three small children, whose mother was asserted, by
own aunt, to be a 'very nice woman.' Having been thus weighed in the bala
and found wanting, I need not hope they would be willing to try me ag

nd this was an unwelcome thought; for vexed, harassed, disappointed as
had been, and greatly as I had learned to love and value my home, I was
ot yet weary of adventure, nor willing to relax my efforts. I knew that all
arents were not like Mr. and Mrs. Bloomfield, and I was certain all children
ere not like theirs. The next family must be different, and any change must
e for the better. I had been seasoned by adversity, and tutored by experience,
nd I longed to redeem my lost honour in the eyes of those whose opinion was
ore than that of all the world to me.

CHAPTER 6

THE PARSONAGE AGAIN

or a few months I remained peaceably at home, in the quiet enjoyment
f liberty and rest and genuine friendship, from all of which I had fasted so
ng; and in the earnest prosecution of my studies, to recover what I had
st during my stay at Wellwood House, and to lay in new stores for future
se. My father's health was still very infirm, but not materially worse than
hen I last saw him; and I was glad I had it in my power to cheer him by
y return, and to amuse him with singing his favourite songs.

No one triumphed over my failure, or said I had better have taken his or
er advice, and quietly stayed at home. All were glad to have me back again,
nd lavished more kindness than ever upon me, to make up for the sufferings
had undergone; but not one would touch a shilling of what I had so cheerfully
rned and so carefully saved, in the hope of sharing it with them. By dint
f pinching here, and scraping there, our debts were already nearly paid.
Iary had had good success with her drawings; but our father had insisted
pon *her* likewise keeping all the produce of her industry to herself. All we
uld spare from the supply of our humble wardrobe and our little casual
xpenses, he directed us to put into the savings' bank; saying, we knew not
ow soon we might be dependent on that alone for support: for he felt he
ad not long to be with us, and what would become of our mother and us
hen he was gone, God only knew!

Dear papa! if he had troubled himself less about the afflictions that threat-
ned us in case of his death, I am convinced that dreaded event would not
ave taken place so soon. My mother would never suffer him to ponder on the
bject if she could help it.

'Oh, Richard!' exclaimed she, on one occasion, 'if you would but dismiss
ch gloomy subjects from your mind, you would live as long as any of us; at
ast you would live to see the girls married, and yourself a happy grandfather,
ith a canty old dame for your companion.'

My mother laughed, and so did my father: but his laugh soon perished i
a dreary sigh.

'*They* married—poor penniless things!' said he, 'who will take them,
wonder!'

'Why, nobody shall that isn't thankful for them. Wasn't I penniless whe
you took me? and you *pretended*, at least, to be vastly pleased with your acqu
sition. But it's no matter whether they get married or not: we can devis
a thousand honest ways of making a livelihood. And I wonder, Richar¢
you can think of bothering your head about our *poverty* in case of your death
as if *that* would be anything compared with the calamity of losing you—
an affliction that you well know would swallow up all others, and which yo
ought to do your utmost to preserve us from: and there is nothing like a cheerf¢
mind for keeping the body in health.'

'I know, Alice, it is wrong to keep repining as I do, but I cannot help i
you must bear with me.'

'I *won't* bear with you, if I can alter you,' replied my mother: but the harsh
ness of her words was undone by the earnest affection of her tone and pleasar
smile, that made my father smile again, less sadly and less transiently tha
was his wont.

'Mamma,' said I, as soon as I could find an opportunity of speaking wit
her alone, 'my money is but little, and cannot last long; if I could increa¢
it, it would lessen papa's anxiety, on one subject at least. I cannot draw lil
Mary, and so the best thing I could do would be to look out for anothe
situation.'

'And so you would actually try again, Agnes?'

'Decidedly, I would.'

'Why, my dear, I should have thought you had had enough of it.'

'I know,' said I, 'everybody is not like Mr. and Mrs. Bloomfield—'

'Some are worse,' interrupted my mother.

'But not many, I think,' replied I, 'and I'm sure all children are not lil
theirs; for I and Mary were not: we always did as you bid us, didn't we

'Generally: but then, I did not spoil you; and you were not perfect ange
after all: Mary had a fund of quiet obstinacy, and you were somewhat faul¢
in regard to temper; but you were very good children on the whole.'

'I know I was sulky sometimes, and I should have been glad to see the¢
children sulky sometimes too; for then I could have understood them: b¢
they never were, for they *could* not be offended, nor hurt, nor ashamed: the
could not be unhappy in any way, except when they were in a passion

'Well, if they *could* not, it was not their fault: you cannot expect stone to ¦
as clay.'

'No, but still it is very unpleasant to live with such unimpressible, incon
prehensible creatures. You cannot love them; and if you could, your lov

ould be utterly thrown away: they could neither return it, nor value, nor
nderstand it. But, however, even if I should stumble on such a family again,
hich is quite unlikely, I have all this experience to begin with, and I should
anage better another time; and the end and aim of this preamble is, let me
y again.'

'Well, my girl, you are not easily discouraged, I see: I am glad of that.
ut, let me tell you, you are a good deal paler and thinner than when you first
ft home; and we cannot have you undermining your health to hoard up
oney, either for yourself or others.'

'Mary tells me I am changed too; and I don't much wonder at it, for I was
a constant state of agitation and anxiety all day long: but next time I am
etermined to take things coolly.'

After some further discussion, my mother promised once more to assist
e, provided I would wait and be patient; and I left her to broach the matter
• my father, when and how she deemed it most advisable: never doubting
er ability to obtain his consent. Meantime, I searched, with great interest,
e advertising columns of the newspapers, and wrote answers to every
Vanted a Governess' that appeared at all eligible; but all my letters, as well
the replies, when I got any, were dutifully shown to my mother; and she,
• my chagrin, made me reject the situations one after another: these were low
ople, these were too exacting in their demands, and these too niggardly
their remuneration.

'Your talents are not such as every poor clergyman's daughter possesses,
gnes,' she would say, 'and you must not throw them away. Remember,
u promised to be patient: there is no need of hurry: you have plenty of time
fore you, and may have many chances yet.'

At length, she advised me to put an advertisement, myself, in the paper,
ating my qualifications, &c.

'Music, singing, drawing, French, Latin, and German,' said she, 'are no
ean assemblage: many will be glad to have so much in one instructor; and
is time, you shall try your fortune in a somewhat higher family—in that
some genuine, thorough bred gentleman; for such are far more likely to
eat you with proper respect and consideration, than those purseproud
adespeople and arrogant upstarts. I have known several among the higher
nks who treated their governesses quite as one of the family; though some,
allow, are as insolent and exacting as anyone else can be: for there are bad and
od in all classes.'

The advertisement was quickly written and dispatched. Of the two parties
ho answered it, but one would consent to give me fifty pounds, the sum my
other bade me name as the salary I should require; and here, I hesitated
out engaging myself, as I feared the children would be too old, and their
rents would require some one more showy, or more experienced, if not

more accomplished than I. But my mother dissuaded me from declining on that account: I should do vastly well, she said, if I would only throw aside my diffidence, and acquire a little more confidence in myself. I was just to give a plain, true statement of my acquirements and qualifications, and name what stipulations I chose to make, and then await the result. The only stipulation I ventured to propose, was that I might be allowed two months' holidays during the year to visit my friends, at Midsummer and Christmas. The unknown lady, in her reply, made no objection to this, and stated that as to my acquirements, she had no doubt I should be able to give satisfaction; but in the engagement of governesses, she considered those things as but subordinate points; as, being situated in the neighbourhood of O——, she could get masters to supply any deficiencies in that respect: but, in her opinion, next to unimpeachable morality, a mild and cheerful temper and obliging disposition were the most essential requisites.

My mother did not relish this at all, and now made many objections to my accepting the situation; in which my sister warmly supported her: but unwilling to be baulked again, I overruled them all; and, having first obtained the consent of my father (who had, a short time previously, been apprised of these transactions), I wrote a most obliging epistle to my unknown correspondent, and, finally, the bargain was concluded.

It was decreed that on the last day of January I was to enter upon my new office as governess in the family of Mr. Murray, of Horton Lodge, near O——, about seventy miles from our village: a formidable distance to me, as I had never been above twenty miles from home in all the course of my twenty years' sojourn on earth; and as, moreover, every individual in that family and in the neighbourhood was utterly unknown to myself and all my acquaintance. But this rendered it only the more piquant to me. I had now, in some measure, got rid of the *mauvaise honte* that had formerly oppressed me so much; there was a pleasing excitement in the idea of entering these unknown regions, and making my way alone among its strange inhabitants. I now flattered myself I was going to see something of the world: Mr. Murray's residence was near a large town, and not in a manufacturing district, where the people had nothing to do but to make money; his rank, from what I could gather, appeared to be higher than that of Mr. Bloomfield; and, doubtless, he was one of those genuine thoroughbred gentry my mother spoke of, who would treat his governess with due consideration as a respectable well-educated lady, the instructor and guide of his children, and not a mere upper servant. Then, my pupils being older, would be more rational, more teachable, and less troublesome than the last: they would be less confined to the schoolroom, and not require that constant labour and incessant watching; and, finally, bright visions mingled with my hopes, with which the care of children and the mere duties of a governess had little or nothing to do. Thus, the reader will

e that I had no claim to be regarded as a martyr to filial piety, going forth sacrifice peace and liberty for the sole purpose of laying up stores for the mfort and support of my parents: though certainly the comfort of my ther, and the future support of my mother, had a large share in my calcula- ns; and fifty pounds appeared to me no ordinary sum. I must have decent othes becoming my station; I must, it seemed, put out my washing, and so pay for my four annual journeys between Horton Lodge and home; t with strict attention to economy, surely twenty pounds, or little more, would ver those expenses and then there would be thirty for the bank, or little s: what a valuable addition to our stock! Oh, I *must* struggle to keep this uation, whatever it might be! both for my own honour among my friends d for the solid services I might render them by my continuance there.

CHAPTER 7

HORTON LODGE

he 31st of January was a wild, tempestuous day: there was a strong north nd, with a continual storm of snow drifting on the ground and whirling rough the air. My friends would have had me delay my departure, but arful of prejudicing my employers against me by such want of punctuality the commencement of my undertaking, I persisted in keeping the appoint- ent.

I will not inflict upon my readers an account of my leaving home on that rk winter morning: the fond farewells, the long, long journey to O——, e solitary waitings in inns for coaches or trains—for there were some railways en—and, finally, the meeting at O——with Mr. Murray's servant, who had en sent with the phaeton to drive me from thence to Horton Lodge. I will st state that the heavy snow had thrown such impediments in the way of th horses and steam-engines, that it was dark some hours before I reached y journey's end, and that a most bewildering storm came on at last, which ade the few miles space between O——and Horton Lodge a long and formi- ble passage. I sat resigned, with the cold, sharp snow drifting through my il and filling my lap, seeing nothing, and wondering how the unfortunate rse and driver could make their way even as well as they did: and indeed was but a toilsome, creeping style of progression to say the best of it. At length paused; and, at the call of the driver, some one unlatched and rolled back on their creaking hinges what appeared to be the park gates. Then we oceeded along a smoother road, whence, occasionally, I perceived some huge ary mass gleaming through the darkness, which I took to be a portion of snow-clad tree. After a considerable time we paused again, before the

stately portico of a large house with long windows descending to the ground
I rose with some difficulty from under the superincumbent snow-drif
and alighted from the carriage, expecting that a kind and hospitable receptio
would indemnify me for the toils and hardships of the day. A gentleman
person in black opened the door, and admitted me into a spacious hall, lighte
by an amber-coloured lamp suspended from the ceiling; he led me throug
this, along a passage, and, opening the door of a back room, told me that wa
the schoolroom. I entered, and found two young ladies and two young gentl
men—my future pupils, I supposed. After a formal greeting, the elder gir
who was trifling over a piece of canvas and a basket of German wools, aske
if I should like to go upstairs. I replied in the affirmative, of course.

'Matilda, take a candle, and show her her room,' said she.

Miss Matilda, a strapping hoyden of about fourteen, with a short froc
and trousers, shrugged her shoulders and made a slight grimace, but too
a candle and proceeded before me, up the back stairs (a long, steep, doub
flight), and through a long, narrow passage, to a small but tolerably com
fortable room. She then asked me if I would take some tea or coffee. I wa
about to answer No; but remembering that I had taken nothing since seve
o'clock that morning, and feeling faint in consequence, I said I would tak
a cup of tea. Saying she would tell 'Brown,' the young lady departed; and b
the time I had divested myself of my heavy, wet cloak, shawl, bonnet, &c
a mincing damsel came to say the young ladies desired to know wheth
I would take my tea up there or in the schoolroom. Under the plea of fatigu
I chose to take it there. She withdrew; and, after a while, returned again wi
a small tea-tray, and placed it on the chest of drawers which served as a dres
ing-table. Having civilly thanked her, I asked at what time I should b
expected to rise in the morning.

'The young ladies and gentlemen breakfast at half-past eight, ma'am,' sa
she; 'they rise early; but, as they seldom do any lessons before breakfa
I should think it will do if you rise soon after seven.'

I desired her to be so kind as to call me at seven, and, promising to do s
she withdrew. Then, having broken my long fast on a cup of tea and a litt
thin bread and butter, I sat down beside the small, smouldering fire, an
amused myself with a hearty fit of crying; after which, I said my praye
and then, feeling considerably relieved, began to prepare for bed. Findi
that none of my luggage was brought up, I instituted a search for the be
and failing to discover any signs of such a convenience in any corner of t
room, I took my candle and ventured through the long passage, and down t
deep stairs, on a voyage of discovery. Meeting a well-dressed female on t
way, I told her what I wanted; but not without considerable hesitation,
I was not quite sure whether it was one of the upper servants, or Mrs. Murr
herself: it happened, however, to be the lady's-maid. With the air of o

onferring an unusual favour, she vouchsafed to undertake the sending up
f my things; and when I had re-entered my room, and waited and wondered
long time (greatly fearing that she had forgotten or neglected to perform her
romise, and doubting whether to keep waiting or go to bed, or go down again)
y hopes, at length, were revived by the sound of voices and laughter, accom-
anied by the tramp of feet along the passage; and presently the luggage was
rought in by a rough-looking maid and a man, neither of them very respectful
 their demeanour to me. Having shut the door upon their retiring footsteps,
d unpacked a few of my things, I betook myself to rest; gladly enough,
r I was weary in body and mind.

It was with a strange feeling of desolation, mingled with a strong sense of
e novelty of my situation, and a joyless kind of curiosity concerning what was
t unknown, that I awoke the next morning; feeling like one whirled away
y enchantment, and suddenly dropped from the clouds into a remote and
known land, widely and completely isolated from all he had ever seen or
own before; or like a thistle-seed borne on the wind to some strange nook
 uncongenial soil, where it must lie long enough before it can take root
d germinate, extracting nourishment from what appears so alien to its nature:
 indeed, it ever can. But this gives no proper idea of my feelings at all;
d no one that has not lived such a retired, stationary life as mine, can
ssibly imagine what they were: hardly even if he has known what it is to
vake some morning, and find himself in Port Nelson, in New Zealand, with
world of waters between himself and all that knew him.

I shall not soon forget the peculiar feeling with which I raised my blind and
oked out upon the unknown world: a wide, white wilderness was all that
et my gaze; a waste of

> Deserts tossed in snow,
> And heavy-laden groves.

I descended to the schoolroom with no remarkable eagerness to join my
pils, though not without some feeling of curiosity respecting what a further
quaintance would reveal. One thing, among others of more obvious im-
rtance, I determined with myself—I must begin with calling them Miss and
aster. It seemed to me a chilling and unnatural piece of punctilio between
e children of a family and their instructor and daily companion; especially
here the former were in their early childhood, as at Wellwood House; but
en there, my calling the little Bloomfields by their simple names had been
garded as an offensive liberty: as their parents had taken care to show me,
 carefully designating them *Master* and *Miss* Bloomfield, &c., in speaking
 me. I had been very slow to take the hint, because the whole affair struck
e as so very absurd; but now I determined to be wiser, and begin at once
th as much form and ceremony as any member of the family would be

likely to require: and indeed, the children being so much older, there woul
be less difficulty; though the little words Miss and Master seemed to hav
a surprising effect in repressing all familiar, open-hearted kindness, and exti
guishing every gleam of cordiality that might arise between us.

As I cannot, like Dogberry, find it in my heart to bestow *all* my tediousne
upon the reader, I will not go on to bore him with a minute detail of all th
discoveries and proceedings of this and the following day. No doubt he wi
be amply satisfied with a slight sketch of the different members of the famil
and a general view of the first year or two of my sojourn among them.

To begin with the head: Mr. Murray was, by all accounts, a blusterin
roystering, country squire; a devoted fox-hunter, a skilful horse-jockey ar
farrier, an active, practical farmer, and a hearty *bon-vivant*. By all accoun
I say; for, except on Sundays, when he went to church, I never saw hi
from month to month: unless, in crossing the hall or walking in the grounc
the figure of a tall, stout gentleman, with scarlet cheeks and crimson nos
happened to come across me; on which occasions, if he passed near enough
speak, an unceremonious nod, accompanied by a 'Morning, Miss Grey,'
some such brief salutation, was usually vouchsafed. Frequently, indeed, I
loud laugh reached me from afar; and oftener still I heard him swearing ar
blaspheming against the footmen, groom, coachman, or some other haple
dependent.

Mrs. Murray was a handsome, dashing lady of forty, who certainly requir
neither rouge nor padding to add to her charms; and whose chief enjoymer
were, or seemed to be, in giving or frequenting parties, and in dressing at t
very top of the fashion. I did not see her till eleven o'clock on the morni
after my arrival; when she honoured me with a visit, just as my mother mig
step into the kitchen to see a new servant girl: yet not so, either, for my moth
would have seen her immediately after her arrival, and not waited till the ne
day; and, moreover, she would have addressed her in a more kind and frienc
manner, and given her some words of comfort as well as a plain expositi
of her duties; but Mrs. Murray did neither the one nor the other. She j
stepped into the schoolroom on her return from ordering dinner in the hou
keeper's room, bade me good morning, stood for two minutes by the fire, sa
a few words about the weather and the 'rather rough' journey I must have h
yesterday; petted her youngest child—a boy of ten—who had just been wipi
his mouth and hands on her gown, after indulging in some savoury mor
from the housekeeper's stores; told me what a sweet, good boy he was; and th
sailed out, with a self-complacent smile upon her face: thinking, no dou
that she had done quite enough for the present, and had been delightfu
condescending into the bargain. Her children evidently held the same opini
and I alone thought otherwise.

After this she looked in upon me once or twice, during the absence of

upils, to enlighten me concerning my duties towards them. For the girls,
e seemed anxious only to render them as superficially attractive and showily
complished as they could possibly be made, without present trouble or
scomfort to themselves; and I was to act accordingly—to study and strive to
muse and oblige, instruct, refine, and polish, with the least possible exertion
a their part, and no exercise of authority on mine. With regard to the two
ys, it was much the same; only instead of accomplishments, I was to get
e greatest possible quantity of Latin grammar and Valpy's Delectus into
eir heads, in order to fit them for school—the greatest possible quantity at
ast *without* trouble to themselves. John might be a 'little high-spirited,' and
harles might be a little 'nervous and tedious—'

'But at all events, Miss Grey,' said she, 'I hope *you* will keep your temper,
d be mild and patient throughout; especially with the dear little Charles:
is so extremely nervous and susceptible, and so utterly unaccustomed to
ything but the tenderest treatment. You will excuse my naming these
ings to you; for the fact is, I have hitherto found all the governesses, even the
ry best of them, faulty in this particular. They wanted that meek and quiet
irit, which St. Matthew, or some of them, says is better than the putting
of apparel—you will know the passage to which I allude, for you are a cler-
man's daughter. But I have no doubt you will give satisfaction in this respect
well as the rest. And remember, on all occasions, when any of the young
ople do anything improper, if persuasion and gentle remonstrance will
t do, let one of the others come and tell me; for I can speak to them more
ainly than it would be proper for you to do. And make them as happy as you
n, Miss Grey, and I dare say you will do very well.'

I observed that while Mrs. Murray was so extremely solicitous for the comfort
d happiness of her children, and continually talking about it, she never
ce mentioned mine; though they were at home surrounded by friends,
d I an alien among strangers; and I did not yet know enough of the world,
t to be considerably surprised at this anomaly.

Miss Murray, otherwise Rosalie, was about sixteen when I came, and deci-
dly a very pretty girl; and in two years longer, as time more completely
veloped her form and added grace to her carriage and deportment, she
came positively beautiful; and that in no common degree. She was tall and
nder, yet not thin; perfectly formed, exquisitely fair, though not without
brilliant, healthy bloom; her hair, which she wore in a profusion of long
glets, was of a very light brown inclining to yellow; her eyes were pale blue,
t so clear and bright that few would wish them darker; the rest of her
tures were small, not quite regular, and not remarkably otherwise: but
ogether you could not hesitate to pronounce her a lovely girl. I wish I could
as much for mind and disposition as I can for her form and face.
Yet think not I have any dreadful disclosures to make: she was lively, light-

hearted, and could be very agreeable with those who did not cross her wil
Towards me, when I first came, she was cold and haughty, then insolent an
overbearing; but on a further acquaintance, she gradually laid aside he
airs, and in time became as deeply attached to me as it was possible for h
to be to one of my character and position: for she seldom lost sight, for abov
half an hour at a time, of the fact of my being a hireling and a poor curate
daughter. And yet, upon the whole, I believe she respected me more than sh
herself was aware of; because I was the only person in the house who steadi
professed good principles, habitually spoke the truth, and generally endea
oured to make inclination bow to duty: and this I say, not, of course, in con
mendation of myself, but to show the unfortunate state of the family to whic
my services were, for the present, devoted. There was no member of it in who
I regretted this sad want of principle so much as Miss Murray herself; not on
because she had taken a fancy to me, but because there was so much of wh
was pleasant and prepossessing in herself, that, in spite of her failings, I real
liked her—when she did not rouse my indignation, or ruffle my temper by t
great a display of her faults. These, however, I would fain persuade myse
were rather the effect of her education than her disposition: she had never bee
perfectly taught the distinction between right and wrong; she had, like h
brothers and sisters, been suffered, from infancy, to tyrannize over nurse
governesses, and servants; she had not been taught to moderate her desires,
control her temper, or bridle her will, or to sacrifice her own pleasure f
the good of others. Her temper being naturally good, she was never violent
morose, but from constant indulgence and habitual scorn of reason, she w
often testy and capricious; her mind had never been cultivated: her intelle
at best, was somewhat shallow; she possessed considerable vivacity, sor
quickness of perception, and some talent for music and the acquisition
languages, but till fifteen she had troubled herself to acquire nothing;—th
the love of display had roused her faculties, and induced her to apply herse
but only to the more showy accomplishments. And when I came it was t
same: everything was neglected but French, German, music, singing, dancin
fancy-work, and a little drawing—such drawing as might produce the great
show with the smallest labour, and the principal parts of which were genera
done by me. For music and singing, besides my occasional instructions, she h
the attendance of the best master the country afforded; and in these acco
plishments, as well as in dancing, she certainly attained great proficiency.
music, indeed, she devoted too much of her time: as, governess though I w
I frequently told her; but her mother thought that if *she* liked it, she *could*
give too much time to the acquisition of so attractive an art. Of fancy-wo
I knew nothing but what I gathered from my pupil and my own observatio
but no sooner was I initiated, than she made me useful in twenty differe
ways: all the tedious parts of her work were shifted on to my shoulders; su

stretching the frames, stitching in the canvas, sorting the wools and silks, ltting in the grounds, counting the stitches, rectifying mistakes, and finishing e pieces she was tired of.

At sixteen, Miss Murray was something of a romp, yet not more so than is itural and allowable for a girl of that age; but at seventeen, that propensity, :e all other things, began to give way to the ruling passion, and soon was vallowed up in the all-absorbing ambition to attract and dazzle the other sex. ut enough of her: now let us turn to her sister.

Miss Matilda Murray was a veritable hoyden, of whom little need be said. 1e was about two years and a half younger than her sister; her features were rger, her complexion much darker. She might possibly make a handsome 2man; but she was far too big-boned and awkward ever to be called a pretty 'l, and at present she cared little about it. Rosalie knew all her charms, and ought them even greater than they were, and valued them more highly than e ought to have done, had they been three times as great; Matilda thought e was well enough, but cared little about the matter; still less did she care 2out the cultivation of her mind, and the acquisition of ornamental accom- ishments. The manner in which she learnt her lessons and practised her music, 1s calculated to drive any governess to despair. Short and easy as her tasks re, if done at all, they were slurred over, at any time and in any way; but nerally at the least convenient times, and in the way least beneficial to herself, d least satisfactory to me: the short half-hour of practising was horribly ummed through; she, meantime, unsparingly abusing me, either for inter- pting her with corrections, or for not rectifying her mistakes before they were ade, or something equally unreasonable. Once or twice, I ventured to monstrate with her seriously for such irrational conduct; but on each of those casions, I received such reprehensive expostulations from her mother, as nvinced me that, if I wished to keep the situation, I must even let Miss atilda go on in her own way.

When her lessons were over, however, her ill humour was generally over too: 1ile riding her spirited pony, or romping with the dogs or her brothers and ter, but especially with her dear brother John, she was as happy as a lark. an animal, Matilda was all right, full of life, vigour, and activity; as an telligent being, she was barbarously ignorant, indocile, careless and ir- ional; and, consequently, very distressing to one who had the task of ltivating her understanding, reforming her manners, and aiding her to quire those ornamental attainments which, unlike her sister, she despised as 1ch as the rest. Her mother was partly aware of her deficiencies, and gave me 1ny a lecture as to how I should try to form her tastes, and endeavour to 1se and cherish her dormant vanity; and, by insinuating, skilful flattery, to 1 her attention to the desired objects—which I would not do; and how hould prepare and smooth the path of learning till she could glide along it

without the least exertion to herself: which I could not, for nothing can be taught to any purpose without some little exertion on the part of the learner

As a moral agent, Matilda was reckless, headstrong, violent, and unamenable to reason. One proof of the deplorable state of her mind was, that from her father's example she had learned to swear like a trooper. Her mother was greatly shocked at the 'unladylike trick,' and wondered 'how she had picked it up.' 'But you can soon break her of it, Miss Grey,' said she: 'it is only a habit and if you will just gently remind her every time she does so, I am sure she will soon lay it aside.' I not only 'gently reminded' her, I tried to impress upon her how wrong it was, and how distressing to the ears of decent people; but all in vain: I was only answered by a careless laugh, and, 'Oh, Miss Grey, how shocked you are! I'm so glad!' Or, 'Well! I can't help it; papa shouldn't have taught me: I learned it all from him; and may be a bit from the coachman.'

Her brother John, *alias* Master Murray, was about eleven when I came, a fine, stout, healthy boy, frank and good-natured in the main, and might have been a decent lad had he been properly educated; but now he was as rough as a young bear, boisterous, unruly, unprincipled, untaught, unteachable—at least, for a governess under his mother's eye. His masters at school might be able to manage him better—for to school he was sent, greatly to my relief, in the course of a year; in a state, it is true, of scandalous ignorance as to Latin as well as the more useful though more neglected things: and this, doubtless, would all be laid to the account of his education having been entrusted to an ignorant female teacher, who had presumed to take in hand what she was wholly incompetent to perform. I was not delivered from his brother till full twelve months after, when he also was dispatched in the same state of disgraceful ignorance as the former.

Master Charles was his mother's peculiar darling. He was little more than a year younger than John, but much smaller, paler, and less active and robust: a pettish, cowardly, capricious, selfish little fellow, only active in doing mischief, and only clever in inventing falsehoods: not simply to hide his faults, but, in mere malicious wantonness, to bring odium upon others. In fact, Master Charles was a very great nuisance to me: it was a trial of patience to live with him peaceably; to watch over him was worse; and to teach him, or pretend to teach him, was inconceivable. At ten years old, he could not read correctly the easiest line in the simplest book; and as, according to his mother's principles, he was to be told every word, before he had time to hesitate or examine the orthography, and never even to be informed, as a stimulant to exertion, that other boys were more forward than he, it is not surprising that he made but little progress during the two years I had charge of his education. His minute portions of Latin grammar, &c., were to be repeated over to him, till he chose to say he knew them, and then he was to be helped to say them; if he made mistakes in his little easy sums in arithmetic they were to be shown him

ice, and the sum done for him, instead of his being left to exercise his faculties
finding them out himself; so that, of course, he took no pains to avoid
istakes, but frequently set down his figures at random, without any calcula-
on at all.

I did not invariably confine myself to these rules: it was against my con-
ience to do so; but I seldom could venture to deviate from them in the
ightest degree, without incurring the wrath of my little pupil, and sub-
quently of his mamma; to whom he would relate my transgressions, malici-
usly exaggerated, or adorned with embellishments of his own; and often,
a consequence, was I on the point of losing or resigning my situation. But, for
eir sakes at home, I smothered my pride and suppressed my indignation, and
anaged to struggle on till my little tormentor was dispatched to school; his
ther declaring that home education was 'no go for him, it was plain: his
other spoiled him outrageously, and his governess could make no hand of
im at all.'

A few more observations about Horton Lodge and its ongoings, and I have
ne with dry description for the present. The house was a very respectable one;
perior to Mr. Bloomfield's, both in age, size, and magnificence: the garden
as not so tastefully laid out; but instead of the smooth-shaven lawn, the
ung trees guarded by palings, the grove of upstart poplars, and the plantation
firs, there was a wide park, stocked with deer, and beautified by fine old
es. The surrounding country itself was pleasant, as far as fertile fields, flourish-
g trees, quiet green lanes, and smiling hedges with wild flowers scattered
ong their banks, could make it; but it was depressingly flat to one born and
rtured among the rugged hills of —.

We were situated nearly two miles from the village church, and, con-
quently, the family carriage was put in requisition every Sunday morning,
d sometimes oftener. Mr. and Mrs. Murray generally thought it sufficient to
ow themselves at church once in the course of the day; but frequently the
ildren preferred going a second time to wandering about the grounds all the
y with nothing to do. If some of my pupils chose to walk and take me with
em, it was well for me; for otherwise, my position in the carriage was, to be
ushed into the corner farthest from the open window, and with my back to
e horses: a position which invariably made me sick; and, if I were not
tually obliged to leave the church in the middle of the service, my devotions
ere disturbed with a feeling of languor and sickliness, and the tormenting fear
its becoming worse; and a depressing headache was generally my companion
roughout the day, which would otherwise have been of welcome rest, and
ly, calm enjoyment.

'It's very odd, Miss Grey, that the carriage should always make you sick:
never makes *me*,' remarked Miss Matilda.

'Nor me either,' said her sister; 'but I dare say it would, if I sat where she

does—such a nasty, horrid place, Miss Grey; I wonder how you can bear it!

I am obliged to bear it, since no choice is left me—I might have answered; but in tenderness for their feelings I only replied—'Oh! it is but a short way, and if I am not sick in church, I don't mind it.'

If I were called upon to give a description of the usual divisions and arrange-ments of the day, I should find it a very difficult matter. I had all my meals in the schoolroom with my pupils, at such times as suited their fancy: sometimes they would ring for dinner before it was half-cooked; sometimes they would keep it waiting on the table for above an hour, and then be out of humour because the potatoes were cold, and the gravy covered with cakes of solid fat; sometimes they would have tea at four; frequently, they would storm at the servants because it was not in precisely at five; and when these orders were obeyed, by way of encouragement to punctuality, they would keep it on the table till seven or eight.

Their hours of study were managed in much the same way; my judgement or convenience was never once consulted. Sometimes Matilda and John would determine 'to get all the plaguy business over before breakfast,' and send the maid to call me up at half-past five, without any scruple or apology; sometimes I was told to be ready precisely at six, and, having dressed in a hurry, came down to an empty room, and after waiting a long time in suspense, discovered that they had changed their minds, and were still in bed; or perhaps, if it were a fine summer morning, Brown would come to tell me that the young ladies and gentlemen had taken a holiday, and were gone out; and then, I was kept waiting for breakfast till I was almost ready to faint: they having fortified themselves with something before they went.

Often they would do their lessons in the open air; which I had nothing to say against: except that I frequently caught cold by sitting on the damp grass, or from exposure to the evening dew, or some insidious draught, which seemed to have no injurious effect on them. It was quite right that they should be hardy; yet, surely, they might have been taught some consideration for others who were less so. But I must not blame them for what was, perhaps, my own fault; for I never made any particular objections to sitting where they pleased; foolishly choosing to risk the consequences, rather than trouble them for my convenience. Their indecorous manner of doing their lessons was quite as remarkable as the caprice displayed in their choice of time and place. While receiving my instructions, or repeating what they had learned, they would lounge upon the sofa, lie on the rug, stretch, yawn, talk to each other, or look out of the window; whereas, I could not so much as stir the fire, or pick up the handkerchief I had dropped, without being rebuked for inattention by one of my pupils, or told that 'mamma would not like me to be so careless.'

The servants, seeing in what little estimation the governess was held by both parents and children, regulated their behaviour by the same standard. I had

equently stood up for them, at the risk of some injury to myself, against the
rranny and injustice of their young masters and mistresses; and I always
ndeavoured to give them as little trouble as possible: but they entirely
eglected my comfort, despised my requests, and slighted my directions. All
rvants, I am convinced, would not have done so; but domestics in general,
eing ignorant and little accustomed to reason and reflection, are too easily
orrupted by the carelessness and bad example of those above them; and these,
think, were not of the best order to begin with.

I sometimes felt myself degraded by the life I led, and ashamed of submitting
o so many indignities; and sometimes I thought myself a fool for caring so
much about them, and feared I must be sadly wanting in Christian humility, or
that charity which 'suffereth long and is kind, seeketh not her own, is not easily
rovoked, beareth all things, endureth all things.' But, with time and patience,
matters began to be slightly ameliorated: slowly, it is true, and almost imper-
ceptibly; but I got rid of my male pupils (that was no trifling advantage), and
he girls, as I intimated before concerning one of them, became a little less
insolent, and began to show some symptoms of esteem. 'Miss Grey was a queer
eature: she never flattered, and did not praise them half enough; but
whenever she did speak favourably of them, or anything belonging to them,
hey could be quite sure her approbation was sincere. She was very obliging,
uiet, and peaceable in the main, but there were some things that put her out
f temper: they did not much care for that, to be sure, but still it was better
o keep her in tune; as when she was in a good humour she would talk to them,
nd be very agreeable and amusing sometimes, in her way; which was quite
ifferent to mamma's, but still very well for a change. She had her own
opinions on every subject, and kept steadily to them—very tiresome opinions
hey often were; as she was always thinking of what was right and what was
rong, and had a strange reverence for matters connected with religion, and an
naccountable liking to good people.'

CHAPTER 8

THE 'COMING OUT'

t eighteen, Miss Murray was to emerge from the quiet obscurity of the school-
oom into the full blaze of the fashionable world—as much of it, at least, as
uld be had out of London; for her papa could not be persuaded to leave his
ral pleasures and pursuits, even for a few weeks' residence in town. She was to
ake her début on the third of January, at a magnificent ball, which her
amma proposed to give to all nobility and choice gentry of O—— and its
eighbourhood for twenty miles round. Of course, she looked forward to it

with the wildest impatience, and the most extravagant anticipations of deligh

'Miss Grey,' said she, one evening, a month before the all-important day, a
I was perusing a long and extremely interesting letter of my sister's—whic
I had just glanced at in the morning to see that it contained no very bad new
and kept till now, unable before to find a quiet moment for reading it,—'Mi
Grey, do put away that dull, stupid letter, and listen to me! I'm sure my ta
must be far more amusing than that.'

She seated herself on the low stool at my feet; and I, suppressing a sigh
vexation, began to fold up the epistle.

'You should tell the good people at home not to bore you with such lor
letters,' said she; 'and above all, do bid them write on proper notepaper, ar
not on those great vulgar sheets. You should see the charming little ladyli
notes mamma writes to her friends.'

'The good people at home,' replied I, 'know very well that the longer the
letters are, the better I like them. I should be very sorry to receive a charmi
little ladylike note from any of them; and I thought you were too much
a lady yourself, Miss Murray, to talk about the "vulgarity" of writing on a lar
sheet of paper.'

'Well, I only said it to tease you. But now I want to talk about the ball; ar
to tell you that you positively must put off your holidays till it is over.'

'Why so?—I shall not be present at the ball.'

'No, but you will see the rooms decked out before it begins, and hear th
music, and, above all, see me in my splendid new dress. I shall be so charmin
you'll be ready to worship me—you really must stay.'

'I should like to see you very much; but I shall have many opportuniti
of seeing you equally charming, on the occasion of some of the numberless ba
and parties that are to be, and I cannot disappoint my friends by postponi
my return so long.'

'Oh, never mind your friends! Tell them we won't let you go.'

'But, to say the truth, it would be a disappointment to myself: I long to s
them as much as they to see me—perhaps more.'

'Well, but it is such a short time.'

'Nearly a fortnight by my computation; and, besides, I cannot bear th
thoughts of a Christmas spent from home: and, moreover, my sister is goi
to be married.'

'Is she—when?'

'Not till next month; but I want to be there to assist her in making prepar
tions, and to make the best of her company while we have her.'

'Why didn't you tell me before?'

'I've only got the news in this letter, which you stigmatize as dull and stupi
and won't let me read.'

'To whom is she to be married?'

'To Mr. Richardson, the vicar of a neighbouring parish.'

'Is he rich?'

'No; only comfortable.'

'Is he handsome?'

'No, only decent.'

'Young?'

'No; only middling.'

'O mercy! what a wretch! What sort of a house is it?'

'A quiet little vicarage, with an ivy-clad porch, an old-fashioned garden, nd——'

'O stop!—you'll make me sick. How *can* she bear it?'

'I expect she'll not only be able to bear it, but to be very happy. You did ot ask me if Mr. Richardson were a good, wise, or amiable man; I could have nswered Yes, to all these questions—at least so Mary thinks, and I hope she ill not find herself mistaken.'

'But—miserable creature! how can she think of spending her life there, ooped up with that nasty old man; and *no* hope of change?'

'He is not old: he's only six or seven and thirty; and she herself is twenty- ght, and as sober as if she were fifty.'

'Oh! that's better then—they're well matched: but do they call him the worthy vicar"?'

'I don't know; but if they do, I believe he merits the epithet.'

'Mercy, how shocking! and will she wear a white apron, and make pies nd puddings?'

'I don't know about the white apron, but I dare say she will make pies and uddings now and then; but that will be no great hardship, as she has done it efore.'

'And will she go about in a plain shawl, and a large straw bonnet, carrying acts and bone soup to her husband's poor parishioners?'

'I'm not clear about that; but I dare say she will do her best to make them omfortable in body and mind, in accordance with our mother's example.'

CHAPTER 9

THE BALL

Now, Miss Grey,' exclaimed Miss Murray, immediately I entered the school- oom, after having taken off my outdoor garments, upon returning from my ur weeks' recreation, 'Now—shut the door, and sit down, and I'll tell you ll about the ball.'

'No,—damn it, no!' shouted Miss Matilda. 'Hold your tongue, can't ye? and

let me tell her about my new mare—*such* a splendour, Miss Grey! a fine bloo
mare—'

'Do be quiet, Matilda; and let me tell my news first.'

'No, no, Rosalie; you'll be such a damned long time over it—she shall hea
me first—I'll be hanged if she doesn't!'

'I'm sorry to hear, Miss Matilda, that you've not got rid of that shockin
habit yet.'

'Well, I can't help it: but I'll never say a wicked word again, if you'll onl
listen to me, and tell Rosalie to hold her confounded tongue.'

Rosalie remonstrated, and I thought I should have been torn in piece
between them; but Miss Matilda having the loudest voice, her sister at lengt
gave in, and suffered her to tell her story first! so I was doomed to hear a lon
account of her splendid mare, its breeding and pedigree, its paces, its actio
its spirit, &c., and of her own amazing skill and courage in riding it; concludin
with an assertion that she could clear a five-barred gate 'like winking,' tha
papa said she might hunt next time the hounds met, and mamma had ordere
a bright scarlet hunting habit for her.

'Oh, Matilda! what stories you are telling!' exclaimed her sister.

'Well,' answered she, no whit abashed, 'I know I *could* clear a five-barre
gate, if I tried, and papa *will* say I may hunt, and mamma *will* order th
habit when I ask it.'

'Well, now get along,' replied Miss Murray; 'and do, dear Matilda, try t
be a little more ladylike. Miss Grey, I wish you *would* tell her not to use suc
shocking words; she *will* call her horse a mare: it is so *inconceivably* shockin
and then she uses such dreadful expressions in describing it: she *must* hav
learned it from the grooms. It nearly puts me into fits when she begins

'I learned it from papa, you ass! and his jolly friends,' said the young lad
vigorously cracking a hunting-whip, which she habitually carried in he
hand. 'I'm as good a judge of horseflesh as the best of'm.'

'Well, now get along, you shocking girl! I really shall take a fit if you g
on in such a way. And now, Miss Grey, attend to me; I'm going to tell yc
about the ball. You must be dying to hear about it, I know. Oh, *such* a bal
You never saw or heard, or read, or dreamt of anything like it in all you
life! The decorations, the entertainment, the supper, the music were indescr
bable! and then the guests! There were two noblemen, three baronets, an
five titled ladies, and other ladies and gentlemen innumerable. The ladie
of course, were of no consequence to me, except to put me in a good humo
with myself, by showing how ugly and awkward most of them were; an
the best, mamma told me,—the most transcendent beauties among ther
were nothing to me. As for *me*, Miss Grey—I'm so *sorry* you didn't see m
I was *charming*—wasn't I, Matilda?'

'Middling.'

'No, but I really *was*—at least so mamma said—and Brown and Williamson. Brown said she was sure no gentleman could set eyes on me without falling in love that minute; and so I may be allowed to be a little vain. I know you think me a shocking, conceited, frivolous girl; but, then, you know, I don't attribute it *all* to my personal attractions: I give some praise to the hairdresser, and some to my exquisitely lovely dress—you must see it to-morrow—white gauze over pink satin—and so *sweetly* made! and a necklace and bracelet of beautiful, large pearls!'

'I have no doubt you looked very charming: but should that delight you so very much?'

'Oh, no!—not that alone: but, then, I was so much admired; and I made so many conquests in that one night—you'd be astonished to hear—'

'But what good will they do you?'

'What good! Think of any woman asking that!'

'Well, I should think one conquest would be enough; and too much, unless the subjugation were mutual.'

'Oh, but you know I never agree with you on those points. Now, wait a bit, and I'll tell you my principal admirers—those who made themselves very conspicuous that night and after: for I've been to two parties since. Unfortunately the two noblemen, Lord G— and Lord F—, were married, or I might have condescended to be particularly gracious to *them*; as it was, I did not: though Lord F—, who hates his wife, was evidently struck with me. He asked me to dance with him twice—he is a charming dancer, by the by, and so am I: you can't think how well I did—I was astonished at myself. My lord was very complimentary too—rather too much so in fact—and I thought proper to be a little haughty and repellent; but I had the pleasure of seeing his nasty, cross wife ready to perish with spite and vexation—'

'Oh, Miss Murray! you don't mean to say that such a thing could really give you pleasure! However cross or—'

'Well, I know it's very wrong;—but never mind! I mean to be good some time—only don't preach now, there's a good creature. I haven't told you half yet. Let me see. Oh! I was going to tell you how many unmistakable admirers I had:—Sir Thomas Ashby was one,—Sir Hugh Meltham and Sir Broadley Wilson are old codgers, only fit companions for papa and mamma. Sir Thomas is young, rich, and gay; but an ugly beast, nevertheless: however, mamma says I should not mind that after a few months' acquaintance. Then, there was Henry Meltham, Sir Hugh's younger son; rather good-looking, and a pleasant fellow to flirt with: but *being* a younger son, that is all he is good for; then there was young Mr. Green, rich enough, but of no family, and a great stupid fellow, a mere country booby; and then, our good rector, Mr. Hatfield: an *humble* admirer he ought to consider himself; but I fear he has forgotten to number humility among his stock of Christian virtues.'

'Was Mr. Hatfield at the ball?'

'Yes, to be sure. Did you think he was too good to go?'

'I thought he might consider it unclerical.'

'By *no* means. He did not profane his cloth by dancing; but it was with difficulty he could refrain, poor man: he looked as if he were dying to as my hand just for *one* set; and—oh! by the by—he's got a new curate: that seed old fellow Mr. Bligh has got his long-wished-for living at last, and is gone.'

'And what is the new one like?'

'Oh, *such* a beast! Weston his name is. I can give you his description in thre words—an insensate, ugly, stupid blockhead. That's four, but no matter— enough of *him* now.'

Then she returned to the ball, and gave me a further account of her deport ment there, and at the several parties she had since attended; and furthe particulars respecting Sir Thomas Ashby and Messrs. Meltham, Green, an Hatfield, and the ineffaceable impression she had wrought upon each of them

'Well, which of the four do you like best?' said I, suppressing my third c fourth yawn.

'I detest them all!' replied she, shaking her bright ringlets in vivaciou scorn.

'That means, I suppose, "I like them all"—but which most?'

'No, I really detest them all; but Harry Meltham is the handsomest an most amusing, and Mr. Hatfield the cleverest, Sir Thomas the wickedes and Mr. Green the most stupid. But the one I'm to have, I suppose, if I'r doomed to have any of them, is Sir Thomas Ashby.'

'Surely not, if he's so wicked, and if you dislike him?'

'Oh, I don't mind his being wicked: he's all the better for that; and for disliking him—I shouldn't greatly object to being Lady Ashby of Ashb Park, if I must marry. But if I could be always young, I would be alway single. I should like to enjoy myself thoroughly, and coquet with all the worl till I am on the verge of being called an old maid; and then, to escape th infamy of that, after having made ten thousand conquests, to break all the hearts save one, by marrying some high-born, rich, indulgent husban whom, on the other hand, fifty ladies were dying to have.'

'Well, as long as you entertain these views, keep single by all means, an never marry at all: not even to escape the infamy of old-maidenhood.'

CHAPTER 10

THE CHURCH

'Well, Miss Grey, what do you think of the new curate?' asked Miss Murra on our return from church the Sunday after the recommencement of our dutie

'I can scarcely tell,' was my reply: 'I have not even heard him preach.'

'Well, but you saw him, didn't you?'

'Yes, but I cannot pretend to judge of a man's character by a single, cursory ance at his face.'

'But isn't he ugly?'

'He did not strike me as being particularly so; I don't dislike that cast of untenance: but the only thing I particularly noticed about him was his yle of reading; which appeared to me good—infinitely better, at least, than r. Hatfield's. He read the Lessons as if he were bent on giving full effect to ery passage: it seemed as if the most careless person could not have helped tending, nor the most ignorant have failed to understand; and the prayers e read as if he were not reading at all, but praying earnestly and sincerely om his own heart.'

'Oh, yes, that's all he is good for: he can plod through the service well nough; but he has not a single idea beyond it.'

'How do you know?'

'Oh! I know perfectly well; I am an excellent judge in such matters. Did u see how he went out of church? stumping along—as if there were nobody ere but himself—never looking to the right hand or the left, and evidently inking of nothing but just getting out of the church, and, perhaps, home to s dinner: his great stupid head could contain no other idea.'

'I suppose you would have had him cast a glance into the squire's pew,' id I, laughing at the vehemence of her hostility.

'Indeed! I should have been highly indignant if he had dared to do such thing!' replied she, haughtily tossing her head; then, after a moment's flection, she added—'Well, well! I suppose he's good enough for his place: ut I'm glad I'm not dependent on *him* for amusement—that's all. Did you see ow Mr. Hatfield hurried out to get a bow from me, and be in time to put us to the carriage?'

'Yes,' answered I; internally adding, 'and I thought it somewhat derogatory his dignity as a clergyman to come flying from the pulpit in such eager aste to shake hands with the squire, and hand his wife and daughters into eir carriage: and, moreover, I owe him a grudge for nearly shutting me ut of it;' for, in fact, though I was standing before his face, close beside the rriage steps, waiting to get in, he would persist in putting them up and losing the door, till one of the family stopped him by calling out that the overness was not in yet; then, without a word of apology, he departed, ishing them good morning, and leaving the footman to finish the business.

Nota bene.—Mr. Hatfield never spoke to me, neither did Sir Hugh or Lady eltham, nor Mr. Harry or Miss Meltham, nor Mr. Green or his sisters, or any other lady or gentleman who frequented that church: nor, in fact, nyone that visited at Horton Lodge.

Miss Murray ordered the carriage again, in the afternoon, for herse and her sister: she said it was too cold for them to enjoy themselves in the ga den: and besides, she believed Harry Meltham would be at church. 'For said she, smiling slyly at her own fair image in the glass, 'he has been a mo exemplary attendant at church these last few Sundays: you would thin he was quite a good Christian. And you may go with us, Miss Grey: I wa you to see him; he is so greatly improved since he returned from abroad—yo can't think! And besides, then you will have an opportunity of seeing t beautiful Mr. Weston again, and of hearing him preach.'

I did hear him preach, and was decidedly pleased with the evangelical tru of his doctrine, as well as the earnest simplicity of his manner, and the clearne and force of his style. It was truly refreshing to hear such a sermon, aft being so long accustomed to the dry, prosy discourses of the former curat and the still less edifying harangues of the rector. Mr. Hatfield would con sailing up the aisle, or rather sweeping along like a whirlwind, with his ri silk gown flying behind him and rustling against the pew doors, mount the pu pit like a conqueror ascending his triumphal car; then, sinking on the velv cushion in an attitude of studied grace, remain in silent prostration for a ce tain time; then mutter over a Collect, and gabble through the Lord's Praye rise, draw off one bright lavender glove, to give the congregation the benef of his sparkling rings, lightly pass his fingers through his well-curled hai flourish a cambric handkerchief, recite a very short passage, or, perhap a mere phrase of Scripture, as a head-piece to his discourse, and, finall deliver a composition which, as a composition, might be considered goo though far too studied and too artificial to be pleasing to me: the propositio were well laid down, the arguments logically conducted; and yet, it w sometimes hard to listen quietly throughout, without some slight demonstratio of disapproval or impatience.

His favourite subjects were church discipline, rites and ceremonies, apost lical succession, the duty of reverence and obedience to the clergy, the atrocio criminality of dissent, the absolute necessity of observing all the forms godliness, the reprehensible presumption of individuals who attempted think for themselves in matters connected with religion, or to be guided their own interpretations of Scripture, and, occasionally (to please his wealth parishioners) the necessity of deferential obedience from the poor to the rich supporting his maxims and exhortations throughout with quotations fro the Fathers: with whom he appeared to be far better acquainted than with t Apostles and Evangelists, and whose importance he seemed to consider least equal to theirs. But now and then he gave us a sermon of a differe order—what some would call a very good one; but sunless and severe: repr senting the Deity as a terrible task-master, rather than a benevolent fathe Yet, as I listened, I felt inclined to think the man was sincere in all he sai

e must have changed his views, and become decidedly religious; gloomy
nd austere, yet still devout. But such illusions were usually dissipated, on
oming out of church, by hearing his voice in jocund colloquy with some
f the Melthams or Greens, or, perhaps, the Murrays themselves; probably
aughing at his own sermon, and hoping that he had given the rascally people
omething to think about; perchance, exulting in the thought that old Betty
Holmes would now lay aside the sinful indulgence of her pipe, which had
een her daily solace for upwards of thirty years; that George Higgins would
e frightened out of his Sabbath evening walks, and Thomas Jackson would
e sorely troubled in his conscience, and shaken in his sure and certain hope
f a joyful resurrection at the last day.

Thus, I could not but conclude that Mr. Hatfield was one of those who
ind heavy burdens, and grievous to be borne, and lay them upon men's
houlders, while they themselves will not move them with one of their fingers';
nd who 'make the word of God of none effect by their traditions, teaching
or doctrines the commandments of men.' I was well pleased to observe that
e new curate resembled him, as far as I could see, in none of these par-
culars.

'Well, Miss Grey, what do you think of him now?' said Miss Murray, as
e took our places in the carriage after service.

'No harm still,' replied I.

'No harm!' repeated she, in amazement. 'What do you mean?'

'I mean, I think no worse of him than I did before.'

'No worse! I should think not indeed—quite the contrary! Is he not greatly
mproved?'

'Oh, yes; very much indeed,' replied I; for I had now discovered that it
as Harry Meltham she meant, not Mr. Weston. That gentleman had eagerly
ome forward to speak to the young ladies: a thing he would hardly have
entured to do had their mother been present; he had likewise politely handed
em into the carriage. He had not attempted to shut me out, like Mr. Hatfield;
either, of course, had he offered me his assistance (I should not have accepted
, if he had), but as long as the door remained open he had stood smirking
nd chatting with them, and then lifted his hat and departed to his own
bode: but I had scarcely noticed him all the time. My companions, however,
ad been more observant; and, as we rolled along, they discussed between
em not only his looks, words, and actions, but every feature of his face,
nd every article of his apparel.

'You shan't have him all to yourself, Rosalie,' said Miss Matilda at the close
f this discussion; 'I like him: I know he'd make a nice, jolly companion for
e.'

'Well, you're quite welcome to him, Matilda,' replied her sister, in a tone
f affected indifference.

673

'And I'm sure,' continued the other, 'he admires me quite as much as he does you; doesn't he, Miss Grey?'

'I don't know; I'm not acquainted with his sentiments.'

'Well, but he *does* though.'

'My *dear* Matilda! nobody will ever admire you till you get rid of your rough, awkward manners.'

'Oh, stuff! Harry Meltham likes such manners; and so do papa's friends.'

'Well, you *may* captivate old men, and younger sons; but nobody else, I am sure, will ever take a fancy to you.'

'I don't care: I'm not always grubbing after money, like you and mamma. If my husband is able to keep a few good horses and dogs, I shall be quite satisfied; and all the rest may go to the devil!'

'Well, if you use such shocking expressions, I'm sure no real gentleman will ever venture to come near you. Really, Miss Grey, you should not let her do so.'

'I can't possibly prevent it, Miss Murray.'

'And you're quite mistaken, Matilda, in supposing that Harry Meltham admires you: I assure you he does nothing of the kind.'

Matilda was beginning an angry reply; but, happily, our journey was now at an end; and the contention was cut short by the footman opening the carriage door, and letting down the steps for our descent.

CHAPTER 11

THE COTTAGERS

As I had now only one regular pupil—though she contrived to give me as much trouble as three or four ordinary ones, and though her sister still took lessons in German and drawing—I had considerably more time at my own disposal than I had ever been blessed with before, since I had taken upon me the governess's yoke; which time I devoted partly to correspondence with my friends, partly to reading, study, and the practice of music, singing, &c., partly to wandering in the grounds or adjacent fields, with my pupils if they wanted me, alone if they did not.

Often, when they had no more agreeable occupation at hand, the Miss Murray would amuse themselves with visiting the poor cottagers on their father's estate, to receive their flattering homage, or to hear the old stories or gossiping news of the garrulous old women; or, perhaps, to enjoy the pure pleasure of making the poor people happy with their cheering presence and their occasional gifts, so easily bestowed, so thankfully received. Sometimes I was called upon to accompany one or both of the sisters in these visits;

ıd sometimes I was desired to go alone, to fulfil some promise which they
ıd been more ready to make than to perform; to carry some small donation,
' read to one who was sick or seriously disposed: and thus I made a few
:quaintances among the cottagers; and, occasionally, I went to see them on
ıy own account.

I generally had more satisfaction in going alone than with either of the
ıung ladies; for they, chiefly owing to their defective education, comported
emselves towards their inferiors in a manner that was highly disagreeable
r me to witness. They never, in thought, exchanged places with them;
ıd, consequently, had no consideration for their feelings, regarding them as
ı order of beings entirely different from themselves. They would watch the
ıor creatures at their meals, making uncivil remarks about their food, and
eir manner of eating; they would laugh at their simple notions and provincial
:pressions, till some of them scarcely durst venture to speak; they would
ıll the grave elderly men and women old fools and silly old blockheads to
eir faces; and all this without meaning to offend. I could see that the people
ere often hurt and annoyed by such conduct, though their fear of the 'grand
dies' prevented them from testifying any resentment; but *they* never perceived

They thought that, as these cottagers were poor and untaught, they must
: stupid and brutish; and as long as they, their superiors, condescended
talk to them, and to give them shillings and half-crowns, or articles of
»thing, they had a right to amuse themselves, even at their expense; and the
:ople must adore them as angels of light, condescending to minister to their
:cessities, and enlighten their humble dwellings.

I made many and various attempts to deliver my pupils from these delusive
»tions without alarming their pride—which was easily offended, and not
on appeased—but with little apparent result; and I know not which was
e more reprehensible of the two: Matilda was more rude and boisterous;
ıt from Rosalie's womanly age and ladylike exterior better things were
pected: yet she was as provokingly careless and inconsiderate as a giddy
ıild of twelve.

One bright day in the last week of February I was walking in the park,
ıjoying the threefold luxury of solitude, a book, and pleasant weather; for
ıss Matilda had set out on her daily ride, and Miss Murray was gone in
e carriage with her mamma to pay some morning calls. But it struck me
at I ought to leave these selfish pleasures, and the park with its glorious
nopy of bright blue sky, the west wind sounding through its yet leafless
anches, the snow-wreaths still lingering in its hollows, but melting fast
'neath the sun, and the graceful deer browsing on its moist herbage already
suming the freshness and verdure of spring—and go to the cottage of one
ıncy Brown, a widow, whose son was at work all day in the fields, and who
ıs afflicted with an inflammation in the eyes; which had for some time

incapacitated her from reading: to her own great grief, for she was a woma
of a serious, thoughtful turn of mind. I accordingly went, and found h
alone, as usual, in her little, close, dark cottage, redolent of smoke and co
fined air, but as tidy and clean as she could make it. She was seated besi
her little fire (consisting of a few red cinders and a bit of stick), busily knittin
with a small sackcloth cushion at her feet, placed for the accommodatio
of her gentle friend the cat; who was seated thereon with her long tail ha
encircling her velvet paws, and her half-closed eyes dreamily gazing on t
low, crooked fender.

'Well, Nancy, how are you to-day?'

'Why, middling, miss, i' myseln—my eyes is no better, but I'm a deal easi
i' my mind nor I have been,' replied she, rising to welcome me with a co
tented smile: which I was glad to see, for Nancy had been somewhat afflicte
with religious melancholy. I congratulated her upon the change. She agree
that it was a great blessing, and expressed herself 'right down thankful for i
adding, 'If it please God to spare my sight, and make me so as I can read n
Bible again, I think I shall be as happy as a queen.'

'I hope He will, Nancy,' replied I; 'and, meantime, I'll come and read
you now and then, when I have a little time to spare.'

With expressions of grateful pleasure, the poor woman moved to get n
a chair; but, as I saved her the trouble, she busied herself with stirring the fir
and adding a few more sticks to the decaying embers; and then, taking h
well-used Bible from the shelf, dusted it carefully, and gave it me. On m
asking if there was any particular part she should like me to read, she a
swered,—'Well, Miss Grey, if it's all the same to you I should like to hear th
chapter in the First Epistle of St. John, that says, "God is love, and he th
dwelleth in love dwelleth in God, and God in him." '

With a little searching, I found these words in the fourth chapter. Whe
I came to the seventh verse she interrupted me, and with needless apologies f
such a liberty, desired me to read it very slowly, that she might take it all i
and dwell on every word; hoping I would excuse her, as she was but a 'simp
body.'

'The wisest person,' I replied, 'might think over each of these verses for a
hour, and be all the better for it; and I would rather read them slowly tha
not.'

Accordingly, I finished the chapter as slowly as need be, and at the sam
time as impressively as I could; my auditor listened most attentively all th
while, and sincerely thanked me when I had done. I sat still about half a minu
to give her time to reflect upon it; when, somewhat to my surprise, she bro
the pause by asking me how I liked Mr. Weston?

'I don't know,' I replied, a little startled by the suddenness of the questio
'I think he preaches very well.'

'Aye, he does so; and talks well too.'

'Does he?'

'He does. Maybe you haven't seen him—not to talk to him much yet?'

'No, I never see anyone to talk to—except the young ladies of the hall.'

'Ah; they're nice, kind young ladies; but they can't talk as he does.'

'Then he comes to see you, Nancy?'

'He does, Miss; and I'se thankful for it. He comes to see all us poor bodies deal ofter nor Maister Bligh, or th' Rector ever did; an' it's well he does, for 's always welcome: we can't say as much for th' Rector—there is 'at says ey're fair feared on him. When he comes into a house, they say he's sure find summut wrong, and begin a calling 'em as soon as he crosses th' orstuns: but maybe he thinks it his duty-like to tell 'em what's wrong. And ry oft he comes o' purpose to reprove folk for not coming to church, or not eeling an' standing when other folk does, or going to the Methody chapel, summut o' that sort: but I can't say 'at he ever fund much fault wi' me. e came to see me once or twice, afore Maister Weston come, when I was so troubled in my mind; and as I had only very poor health besides, I made ld to send for him—and he came right enough. I was sore distressed, Miss rey—thank God, it's owered now—but when I took my Bible, I could get comfort of it at all. That very chapter 'at you've just been reading troubled e as much as aught— "He that loveth not, knoweth not God." It seemed arsome to me; for I felt that I loved neither God nor man as I should do, d could not, if I tried ever so. And th' chapter afore, where it says—"He at is born of God cannot commit sin." And another place where it says— Love is the fulfilling of the Law." And many, many others, Miss: I should ir weary you out, if I was to tell them all. But all seemed to condemn me, d to show me 'at I was not in the right way; and as I knew not how to get to it, I sent our Bill to beg Maister Hatfield to be as kind as look in on me me day; and when he came, I told him all my troubles.'

'And what did he say, Nancy?'

'Why, Miss, he seemed to scorn me. I might be mista'en—but he like gave sort of a whistle, and I saw a bit of a smile on his face; and he said, "Oh it's stuff! You've been among the Methodists, my good woman." But I told m I'd never been near the Methodies. And then he said—"Well," says he, ou must come to church, where you'll hear the Scriptures properly explained, stead of sitting poring over your Bible at home."

'But I told him I always used coming to church when I had my health; t this very cold winter weather I hardly durst venture so far—and me so bad i' th' rheumatiz and all.

'But he says, "It'll do your rheumatiz good to hobble to church: there's thing like exercise for the rheumatiz. You can walk about the house well ough; why can't you walk to church? The fact is," says he, "you're getting

too fond of your ease. It 's always easy to find excuses for shirking one's duty.

'But then, you know, Miss Grey, it wasn't so. However, I told him I'd tr
"But please, sir," says I, "if I do go to church, what the better shall I be
I want to have my sins blotted out, and to feel that they are remembered r
more against me, and that the love of God is shed abroad in my heart; and
I can get no good by reading my Bible an' saying my prayers at home, wha
good shall I get by going to church?"

' "The church," says he, "is the place appointed by God for His worship
It's your duty to go there as often as you can. If you want comfort, you mu
seek it in the path of duty"—an' a deal more he said, but I cannot rememb
all his fine words. However, it all came to this, that I was to come to churc
as oft as ever I could, and bring my prayer-book with me, an' read up all th
sponsors after the clerk, an' stand, an' kneel, an' sit, an' do all as I should, ar
take the Lord's Supper at every opportunity, an' hearken his sermons, ar
Maister Bligh's, an' it 'ud be all right: if I went on doing my duty, I shoul
get a blessing at last.

' "But if you get no comfort that way," says he, "it's all up."

' "Then sir," says I, "should you think I'm a reprobate?"

' "Why," says he—he says, "if you do your best to get to heaven and can
manage it, you must be one of those that seek to enter in at the strait gate an
shall not be able."

'An' then he asked me if I'd seen any of ladies o' th' Hall about that mornin
so I told him where I had seen the young missis go on th' Moss-lane;
an' he kicked my poor cat right across th' floor, an' went after 'em as gay
a lark: but I was very sad. That last word o' his fair sunk into my heart, a
lay there like a lump o' lead, till I was weary to bear it.

'Howsever, I follered his advice: I thought he meant it all for th' be
though he *had* a queer way with him. But you know, Miss, he 's rich an' youn
and such like cannot right understand the thoughts of a poor old woman su
as me. But, howsever, I did my best to do all as he bade me—but maybe I'
plaguing you, Miss, wi' my chatter.'

'Oh no, Nancy! Go on, and tell me all.'

'Well, my rheumatiz got better—I know not whether wi' going to chur
or not, but one frosty Sunday I got this cold i' my eyes. Th' inflammati
didn't come on all at once like, but bit by bit—but I wasn't going to tell y
about my eyes, I was talking about my trouble o' mind;—and to tell the trut
Miss Grey, I don't think it was anyways eased by coming to church—noug
to speak on, at least: I like got my health better; but that didn't mend my so
I hearkened and hearkened the ministers, and read an' read at my praye
book; but it was all like sounding brass, and a tinkling cymbal: the sermo
I couldn't understand, an' th' prayer-book only served toshow me how wick
I was, that I could read such good words an' never be no better for it, a

tens feel it a sore labour an' a heavy task beside, instead of a blessing and privilege as all good Christians does. It seemed like as all were barren an' ᴵrk to me. And then, them dreadful words, "Many shall seek to enter in, ᴵd shall not be able." They like as they fair dried up my sperrit.

'But one Sunday, when Maister Hatfield gave out about the sacrament, ᴵnoticed where he said, "If there be any of you that cannot quiet his own ᴵnscience, but requireth further comfort or counsel, let him come to me, or ᴵme other discreet and learned minister of God's word, and open his grief!" ᴵ, next Sunday morning, afore service, I just looked into the vestry, an' began talking to th' Rector again. I hardly could fashion to take such a liberty, but ᴵhought when my soul was at stake I shouldn't stick at a trifle. But he said he ᴵdn't time to attend to me then.

' "And, indeed," says he, "I've nothing to say to you but what I've said ᴵfore. Take the sacrament, of course, and go on doing your duty; and if that ᴵon't serve you, nothing will. So don't bother me any more."

'So then, I went away. But I heard Maister Weston—Maister Weston was ᴵere, Miss—this was his first Sunday at Horton, you know, an' he was i' th' ᴵstry in his surplice, helping th' Rector on with gown—'

'Yes, Nancy.'

'And I heard him ask Maister Hatfield who I was; an' he says, "Oh, she's ᴵcanting old fool."

'And I was very ill grieved, Miss Grey; but I went to my seat, and I tried ᴵdo my duty as aforetime: but I like got no peace. An' I even took the sacra-ᴵent; but I felt as though I were eating and drinking to my own damnation ᴵ th' time. So I went home, sorely troubled.

'But next day, afore I'd gotten fettled up—for indeed, Miss, I'd no heart to ᴵeeping an' fettling, an' washing pots; so I sat me down i' th' muck—who ᴵould come in but Maister Weston! I started siding stuff then, an' sweeping ᴵ' doing; and I expected he'd begin a calling me for my idle ways, as Maister ᴵatfield would a' done; but I was mista'en: he only bid me good mornin' like, ᴵ a quiet dacent way. So I dusted him a chair, an' fettled up th' fireplace a bit; ᴵt I hadn't forgotten th' Rector's words, so says I, "I wonder, sir, you should ᴵve yourself that trouble, to come so far to see a 'canting old fool,' such as me."

'He seemed taken aback at that; but he would fain persuade me 'at the ᴵctor was only in jest; and when that wouldn't do, he says, "Well, Nancy, ᴵu shouldn't think so much about it: Mr. Hatfield was a little out of humour ᴵst then: you know we're none of us perfect—even Moses spoke unadvisedly ᴵith his lips. But now sit down a minute, if you can spare the time, and tell me ᴵ your doubts and fears; and I'll try to remove them."

'So I sat me down anent him. He was quite a stranger, you know, Miss Grey, ᴵd even *younger* nor Maister Hatfield, I believe; an' I had thought him not ᴵ pleasant looking as him, and rather a bit crossish, at first to look at; but he

spake so civil like—and when th' cat, poor thing, jumped on to his knee, h
only stroked her, and gave a bit of a smile: so I thought that was a good sig⟩
for once, when she did so to th' Rector, he knocked her off, like as it mig⟩
be in scorn and anger, poor thing. But you can't expect a cat to know manne⟨
like a Christian, you know, Miss Grey.'

'No; of course not, Nancy. But what did Mr. Weston say then?'

'He said naught; but he listened to me as steady an' patient as could b⟨
an' never a bit o' scorn about him; so I went on, an' told him all, just as I'⟨
telled you—an' more too.

' "Well," says he, "Mr. Hatfield was quite right in telling you to persever⟨
in doing your duty; but in advising you to go to church and attend to th⟨
service, and so on, he didn't mean that was the whole of a Christian's dut⟨
he only thought you might there learn what more was to be done, and be le⟨
to take delight in those exercises, instead of finding them a task and a burde⟨
And if you had asked him to explain those words that trouble you so muc⟨
I think he would have told you, that if many shall seek to enter in at the stra⟨
gate and shall not be able, it is their own sins that hinder them; just as a ma⟨
with a large sack on his back might wish to pass through a narrow doorwa⟨
and find it impossible to do so unless he would leave his sack behind hir⟨
But you Nancy, I dare say, have no sins that you would not gladly thro⟨
aside, if you knew how?"

' "Indeed, sir, you speak truth," said I.

' "Well," says he, "you know the first and great commandment—and th⟨
second, which is like unto it—on which two commandments hang all the la⟨
and the prophets? You say you cannot love God; but it strikes me that if y⟨
rightly consider who and what He is, you cannot help it. He is your fath⟨
your best friend: every blessing, everything good, pleasant, or useful, com⟨
from Him; and everything evil, everything you have reason to hate, to shu⟨
or to fear, comes from Satan—*His* enemy as well as ours. And for *this* cau⟨
was God manifest in the flesh, that He might destroy the works of the dev⟨
in one word, God is LOVE; and the more of love we have within us, the near⟨
we are to Him, and the more of His spirit we possess."

' "Well, sir," I said, "if I can always think on these things, I think I mig⟨
well love God: but how can I love my neighbours, when they vex me, and I⟨
so contrairy and sinful as some on 'em is?"

' "It may seem a hard matter," says he, "to love our neighbours, who ha⟨
so much of what is evil about them, and whose faults so often awaken the e⟨
that lingers within ourselves; but remember that *He* made them, and *He* lov⟨
them; and whosoever loveth him that begat, loveth him that is begotten als⟨
And if God so loveth us, that He gave His only begotten Son to die for us, ⟨
ought also to love one another. But if you cannot feel positive affection for tho⟨
who do not care for you, you can at least try to do to them as you would th⟨

ould do unto you: you can endeavour to pity their failings and excuse their fences, and to do all the good you can to those about you. And if you custom yourself to this, Nancy, the very effort itself will make you love them some degree—to say nothing of the goodwill your kindness would beget in em, though they might have little else that is good about them. If we love od and wish to serve Him, let us try to be like Him, to do His work, to labour r His glory—which is the good of man—to hasten the coming of His king- m, which is the peace and happiness of all the world: however powerless we ay seem to be, in doing all the good we can through life, the humblest of us ay do much towards it; and let us dwell in love, that He may dwell in us and e in Him. The more happiness we bestow, the more we shall receive, even re; and the greater will be our reward in heaven when we rest from our bours." I believe, Miss, them is his very words, for I've thought 'em ower any a time. An' then he took that Bible, an' read bits here and there, an' plained 'em as clear as the day: and it seemed like as a new light broke in a my soul; an' I felt fair a glow about my heart, an' only wished poor Bill a' all the world could ha' been there, an' heard it all, and rejoiced wi' me.

'After he was gone, Hannah Rogers, one o' th' neighbours, came in and anted me to help her to wash. I telled her I couldn't just then, for I hadn't t on th' potaties for th' dinner, nor washed up th' breakfast stuff yet. So then e began a-calling me for my nasty idle ways. I was a little bit vexed at first, t I never said nothing wrong to her: I only telled her, like all in a quiet way t I'd had th' new parson to see me; but I'd get done as quick as ever I could, a' then come an' help her. So then she softened down; and my heart like as it armed towards her, an' in a bit we was very good friends. An' so it is, Miss rey, "a soft answer turneth away wrath; but grievous words stir up anger." isn't only in them you speak to, but in yourself.'

'Very true, Nancy, if we could always remember it.'

'Aye, if we could!'

'And did Mr. Weston ever come to see you again?'

'Yes, many a time; and since my eyes has been so bad, he's sat an' read me by the half-hour together: but you know, Miss, he has other folks to see, d other things to do—God bless him! An' that next Sunday he preached *such* sermon! His text was, "Come unto me all ye that labour and are heavy laden, d I will give you rest," and them two blessed verses that follows. You wasn't ere, miss, you was with your friends then—but it made me *so* happy! And am happy now, thank God! an' I take a pleasure, now, in doing little bits jobs for my neighbours—such as a poor old body at's half blind can do; and ey take it kindly of me, just as he said. You see, Miss, I'm knitting a pair stockings now;—they're for Thomas Jackson: he's a queerish old body, an' e've had many about at threaping, one anent t'other; an' at times we've ffered sorely. So I thought I couldn't do better nor knit him a pair o' warm

681

stockings; an' I've felt to like him a deal better, poor old man, sin' I bega: It's turned out just as Maister Weston said.'

'Well, I'm very glad to see you so happy, Nancy, and so wise: but I mu go now; I shall be wanted at the Hall,' said I; and bidding her good-by I departed, promising to come again when I had time, and feeling nearly happy as herself.

At another time I went to read to a poor labourer who was in the last stag of consumption. The young ladies had been to see him, and somehow a promi of reading had been extracted from them; but it was too much trouble, so the begged *me* to do it instead. I went, willingly enough; and there too I w gratified with the praises of Mr. Weston, both from the sick man and his wif The former told me that he derived great comfort and benefit from the visits the new parson, who frequently came to see him, and was 'another guess so of man,' to Mr. Hatfield; who before the other's arrival at Horton had now am then paid him a visit; on which occasions he would always insist upon havin the cottage door kept open, to admit the fresh air for his own convenienc without considering how it might injure the sufferer; and having opened h prayer-book and hastily read over a part of the Service for the sick, wou hurry away again: if he did not stay to administer some harsh rebuke to th afflicted wife, or to make some thoughtless, not to say heartless, observatio rather calculated to increase than diminish the troubles of the suffering pa:

'Whereas,' said the man, 'Maister Weston 'ull pray with me quite in a d ferent fashion, an' talk to me as kind as owt; an' oft read to me too, an' beside me just like a brother.'

'Just for all the world!' exclaimed his wife; 'an' about a three wik si when he seed how poor Jem shivered wi' cold, an' what pitiful fires we ke he axed if wer stock of coals was nearly done. I telled him it was, an' we w ill set to get more: but you know mum I didn't think o' him helping us; b howsever, he sent us a sack o' coals next day; an' we've had good fires ev sin': an' a great blessing it is, this winter time. But that's his way, Miss Gre when he comes into a poor body's house a seein' sick folk, he like notices wh they most stand i' need on; an' if he thinks they can't readily get it thersel he never says nowt about it, but just gets it for 'em. An' it isn't everybody ' 'ud do that, 'at has as little as he has: for you know, mum, he's now't at a to live on but what he gets fra' th' rector, an' that's little enough they sa

I remembered then, with a species of exultation, that he had frequently be styled a vulgar brute by the amiable Miss Murray, because he wore a silv watch, and clothes not quite so bright and fresh as Mr. Hatfield's.

In returning to the Lodge I felt very happy, and thanked God that I h now something to think about; something to dwell on as a relief from t weary monotony, the lonely drudgery, of my present life: for I *was* lone Never, from month to month, from year to year, except during my brief int

ls of rest at home, did I see one creature to whom I could open my heart,
freely speak my thoughts with any hope of sympathy, or even comprehen-
on: never one, unless it were poor Nancy Brown, with whom I could enjoy
single moment of real social intercourse, or whose conversation was calculated
render me better, wiser, or happier than before; or who, as far as I could see,
uld be greatly benefited by mine. My only companions had been unamiable
ildren, and ignorant, wrong-headed girls; from whose fatiguing folly, un-
roken solitude was often a relief most earnestly desired and dearly prized. But
be restricted to such associates was a serious evil, both in its immediate
fects and the consequences that were likely to ensue. Never a new idea or
rring thought came to me from without; and such as rose within me were,
r the most part, miserably crushed at once, or doomed to sicken and fade
vay, because they could not see the light.

Habitual associates are known to exercise a great influence over each other's
inds and manners. Those whose actions are for ever before our eyes, whose
ords are ever in our ears, will naturally lead us, albeit against our will, slowly,
adually, imperceptibly, perhaps, to act and speak as they do. I will not
esume to say how far this irresistible power of assimilation extends; but if one
vilized man were doomed to pass a dozen years amid a race of intractable
vages, unless he had power to improve them, I greatly question whether, at
e close of that period, he would not have become, at least, a barbarian
mself. And I, as I could not make my young companions better, feared
ceedingly that they would make me worse—would gradually bring my
elings, habits, capacities, to the level of their own; without, however, im-
rting to me their light-heartedness and cheerful vivacity.

Already, I seemed to feel my intellect deteriorating, my heart petrifying,
y soul contracting; and I trembled lest my very moral perceptions should
come deadened, my distinctions of right and wrong confounded, and all my
tter faculties be sunk, at last, beneath the baneful influence of such a mode
life. The gross vapours of earth were gathering around me, and closing in
on my inward heaven; and thus it was that Mr. Weston rose at length upon
e, appearing like the morning-star in my horizon, to save me from the fear
utter darkness; and I rejoiced that I had now a subject for contemplation
at was above me, not beneath. I was glad to see that all the world was not
ade up of Bloomfields, Murrays, Hatfields, Ashbys, &c.; and that human
cellence was not a mere dream of the imagination. When we hear a little
od and no harm of a person, it is easy and pleasant to imagine more: in short
is needless to analyse all my thoughts; but Sunday was now become a day of
culiar delight to me (I was now almost broken-in to the back corner in the
rriage), for I liked to hear him—and I liked to see him, too; though I knew
was not handsome, or even what is called agreeable, in outward aspect: but,
rtainly, he was not ugly.

In stature he was a little, a very little, above the middle size; the outlin of his face would be pronounced too square for beauty, but to me it announce decision of character; his dark brown hair was not carefully curled, lik Mr. Hatfield's, but simply brushed aside over a broad white forehead; th eyebrows, I suppose, were too projecting, but from under those dark brow there gleamed an eye of singular power, brown in colour, not large, and som what deep-set, but strikingly brilliant, and full of expression; there was cha acter, too, in the mouth, something that bespoke a man of firm purpose an a habitual thinker; and when he smiled—but I will not speak of that yet, fo at the time I mention, I had never seen him smile: and, indeed, his gener appearance did not impress me with the idea of a man given to such a r laxation, nor of such an individual as the cottagers described him. I had ear formed my opinion of him; and, in spite of Miss Murray's objurgations, w fully convinced that he was a man of strong sense, firm faith, and ardent piet but thoughtful and stern: and when I found that. to his other good qualitie was added that of true benevolence and gentle, considerate kinaness, th discovery, perhaps, delighted me the more, as I had not been prepared expect it.

CHAPTER 12

THE SHOWER

The next visit I paid to Nancy Brown was in the second week in March: fe though I had many spare minutes during the day, I seldom could look upon a hour as entirely my own; since, where everything was left to the caprices Miss Matilda and her sister, there could be no order or regularity. Whatev occupation I chose, when not actually busied about them or their concern I had, as it were, to keep my loins girded, my shoes on my feet, and my staff my hand; for not to be immediately forthcoming when called for, was regard as a grave and inexcusable offence: not only by my pupils and their mothe but by the very servant, who came in breathless haste to call me, exclaimin 'You're to go to the schoolroom *directly*, mum—the young ladies is WAITING Climax of horror! actually waiting for their governess!!!

But this time I was pretty sure of an hour or two to myself; for Matild was preparing for a long ride, and Rosalie was dressing for a dinner party Lady Ashby's: so I took the opportunity of repairing to the widow's cottag where I found her in some anxiety about her cat, which had been absent a day. I comforted her with as many anecdotes of that animal's roving propens ties as I could recollect. 'I'm feared o' th' gamekeepers,' said she, 'that's 'at I think on. If th' young gentlemen had been at home, I should a' thoug

ey'd been setting their dogs at her, an' worried her, poor thing, as they did
any a poor thing's cat; but I haven't that to be feared on now.' Nancy's eyes
ere better, but still far from well: she had been trying to make a Sunday shirt
r her son, but told me she could only bear to do a little bit at it now and
en, so that it progressed but slowly, though the poor lad wanted it sadly. So
proposed to help her a little, after I had read to her, for I had plenty of time
at evening, and need not return till dusk. She thankfully accepted the offer.
n' you'll be a bit o' company for me too, miss,' said she; 'I like as I feel
nesome without my cat.' But when I had finished reading, and done the half
f a seam, with Nancy's capacious brass thimble fitted on to my finger by
eans of a roll of paper, I was disturbed by the entrance of Mr. Weston, with
e identical cat in his arms. I now saw that he could smile, and very
leasantly too.

'I've done you a piece of good service, Nancy,' he began: then seeing me,
e acknowledged my presence by a slight bow. I should have been invisible
Hatfield, or any other gentleman of those parts. 'I've delivered your cat,'
e continued, 'from the hands, or rather the gun, of Mr. Murray's game-
eeper.'

'God bless you, sir!' cried the grateful old woman, ready to weep for joy as
e received her favourite from his arms.

'Take care of it,' said he, 'and don't let it go near the rabbit warren, for the
amekeeper swears he'll shoot it if he sees it there again: he would have
one so to-day, if I had not been in time to stop him. I believe it is raining,
iss Grey,' added he, more quietly, observing that I had put aside my work,
nd was preparing to depart. 'Don't let me disturb you—I shan't stay two
inutes.'

'You'll *both* stay while this shower gets owered,' said Nancy, as she stirred
e fire, and placed another chair beside it; 'what! there's room for all.'

'I can see better here, thank you, Nancy,' replied I, taking my work to the
indow, where she had the goodness to suffer me to remain unmolested, while
e got a brush to remove the cat's hairs from Mr. Weston's coat, carefully
iped the rain from his hat, and gave the cat its supper, busily talking all the
me: now thanking her clerical friend for what he had done; now wondering
ow the cat had found out the warren; and now lamenting the probable
nsequences of such a discovery. He listened with a quiet, good-natured
nile, and at length took a seat in compliance with her pressing invitations,
ut repeated that he did not mean to stay.

'I have another place to go to,' said he, 'and I see' (glancing at the book
n the table) 'some one else has been reading to you.'

'Yes, sir; Miss Grey has been as kind as read me a chapter; an' now she's
elping me with a shirt for our Bill—but I'm feared she'll be cold there. Won't
ou come to th' fire, Miss?'

'No, thank you, Nancy, I'm quite warm. I must go as soon as this shower is over.'

'Oh, Miss! You said you could stop while dusk!' cried the provoking old woman, and Mr. Weston seized his hat.

'Nay, sir,' exclaimed she, 'pray don't go now, while it rains so fast.'

'But it strikes me I'm keeping your visitor away from the fire.'

'No, you're not, Mr. Weston,' replied I, hoping there was no harm in a falsehood of that description.

'No, sure!' cried Nancy. 'What, there's lots o' room!'

'Miss Grey,' said he, half-jestingly, as if he felt it necessary to change the present subject, whether he had anything particular to say or not, 'I wish you would make my peace with the squire, when you see him. He was by when I rescued Nancy's cat, and did not quite approve of the deed. I told him I thought he might better spare all his rabbits than she her cat, for which audacious assertion he treated me to some rather ungentlemanly language; and I fear I retorted a trifle too warmly.'

'Oh, lawful sir! I hope you didn't fall out wi' th' maister for sake o' my cat; he cannot bide answering again—can th' maister.'

'Oh! it's no matter, Nancy: I don't care about it, really; I said nothing very uncivil; and I suppose Mr. Murray is accustomed to use rather strong language when he's heated.'

'Aye, sir: it's a pity!'

'And now, I really must go. I have to visit a place a mile beyond this; and you would not have me to return in the dark: besides, it has nearly done raining now—so good evening, Nancy. Good evening, Miss Grey.'

'Good evening, Mr. Weston; but don't depend upon me for making your peace with Mr. Murray, for I never see him—to speak to.'

'Don't you? it can't be helped then,' replied he in dolorous resignation: then with a peculiar half-smile, he added, 'But never mind; I imagine the squire has more to apologize for than I;' and left the cottage.

I went on with my sewing as long as I could see, and then bade Nancy good evening; checking her too lively gratitude by the undeniable assurance that I had only done for her what she would have done for me, if she had been in my place and I in hers. I hastened back to Horton Lodge, where, having entered the schoolroom, I found the tea-table all in confusion, the tray flooded with slops, and Miss Matilda in a most ferocious humour.

'Miss Grey, whatever have you been about? I've had tea half an hour ago, and had to make it myself, and drink it all alone! I wish you would come in sooner!'

'I've been to see Nancy Brown. I thought you would not be back from your ride.'

'How could I ride in the rain, I should like to know? That damned pelting

ower was vexatious enough—coming on when I was just in full swing: and
en to come and find nobody in to tea!—and you know I can't make the tea
I like it.'

'I didn't think of the shower,' replied I (and, indeed, the thought of its
riving her home had never entered my head).

'No, of course; you were under shelter yourself, and you never thought of
ther people.'

I bore her coarse reproaches with astonishing equanimity, even with cheer-
lness; for I was sensible that I had done more good to Nancy Brown than
arm to her: and perhaps some other thoughts assisted to keep up my spirits,
nd impart a relish to the cup of cold, overdrawn tea, and a charm to the other-
ise unsightly table; and—I had almost said—to Miss Matilda's unamiable
ce. But she soon betook herself to the stables, and left me to the quiet enjoy-
ent of my solitary meal.

CHAPTER 13

THE PRIMROSES

iss Murray now always went twice to church, for she so loved admiration
at she could not bear to lose a single opportunity of obtaining it; and she
as so sure of it wherever she showed herself, that whether Harry Meltham and
r. Green were there or not, there was certain to be somebody present who
ould not be insensible to her charms: besides the Rector, whose official
pacity generally obliged him to attend. Usually, also, if the weather per-
itted, both she and her sister would walk home; Matilda, because she hated
e confinement of the carriage; she, because she disliked the privacy of it, and
joyed the company that generally enlivened the first mile of the journey in
alking from the church to Mr. Green's park-gates: near which commenced
e private road to Horton Lodge, which lay in the opposite direction; while
e highway conducted in a straight-forward course to the still more distant
ansion of Sir Hugh Meltham. Thus there was always a chance of being
companied, so far, either by Harry Meltham, with or without Miss Meltham,
Mr. Green, with perhaps one or both of his sisters, and any gentlemen
sitors they might have.

Whether I walked with the young ladies or rode with their parents depended
pon their own capricious will: if they chose to 'take' me, I went; if, for
asons best known to themselves, they chose to go alone, I took my seat in
e carriage. I liked walking better, but a sense of reluctance to obtrude my
resence on anyone who did not desire it, always kept me passive on these and
milar occasions; and I never inquired into the causes of their varying whims.

Indeed, this was the best policy—for to submit and oblige was the governess[']
part, to consult their own pleasure was that of the pupils. But when I did wal[k]
the first half of the journey was generally a great nuisance to me. As none [of]
the before-mentioned ladies and gentlemen ever noticed me, it was disagre[e-]
able to walk beside them, as if listening to what they said, or wishing to [be]
thought one of them, while they talked over me, or across; and if their eyes, [in]
speaking, chanced to fall on me, it seemed as if they looked on vacancy—as [if]
they either did not see me, or were very desirous to make it appear so. It wa[s]
disagreeable, too, to walk behind, and thus appear to acknowledge my ow[n]
inferiority; for, in truth, I considered myself pretty nearly as good as the best [of]
them, and wished them to know that I did so, and not to imagine that I looke[d]
upon myself as a mere domestic, who knew her own place too well to wa[lk]
beside such fine ladies and gentlemen as they were—though her young ladi[es]
might choose to have her with them, and even condescend to converse with h[er]
when no better company were at hand. Thus—I am almost ashamed to confe[ss]
it—but indeed I gave myself no little trouble in my endeavours (if I did keep u[p]
with them) to appear perfectly unconscious or regardless of their presence, [as]
if I were wholly absorbed in my own reflections, or the contemplation [of]
surrounding objects; or, if I lingered behind, it was some bird or insect, som[e]
tree or flower, that attracted my attention, and having duly examined tha[t]
I would pursue my walk alone, at a leisurely pace, until my pupils had bidd[en]
adieu to their companions, and turned off into the quiet private road.

One such occasion I particularly well remember: it was a lovely afternoo[n]
about the close of March; Mr. Green and his sisters had sent their carriage ba[ck]
empty, in order to enjoy the bright sunshine and balmy air in a sociable wa[lk]
home along with their visitors, Captain Somebody and Lieutenant Somebo[dy]
else (a couple of military fops), and the Misses Murray, who, of course, co[n-]
trived to join them. Such a party was highly agreeable to Rosalie; but n[ot]
finding it equally suitable to my taste, I presently fell back, and began [to]
botanize and entomologize along the green banks and budding hedges, till t[he]
company was considerably in advance of me, and I could hear the sweet so[ng]
of the happy lark; then my spirit of misanthropy began to melt away benea[th]
the soft, pure air and genial sunshine: but sad thoughts of early childhood, a[nd]
yearnings for departed joys, or for a brighter future lot, arose instead. As m[y]
eyes wandered over the steep banks covered with young grass and green-leav[ed]
plants, and surmounted by budding hedges, I longed intensely for some famili[ar]
flower that might recall the woody dales or green hillsides of home: the brow[n]
moorlands, of course, were out of the question. Such a discovery would ma[ke]
my eyes gush out with water, no doubt; but that was one of my greate[st]
enjoyments now. At length I descried, high up between the twisted roots of a[n]
oak, three lovely primroses, peeping so sweetly from their hiding-place that t[he]
tears already started at the sight; but they grew so high above me, that I tri[ed]

vain to gather one or two, to dream over and to carry with me: I could not ach them unless I climbed the bank, which I was deterred from doing by earing a footstep at that moment behind me, and was, therefore, about to urn away, when I was startled by the words, 'Allow me to gather them for ou, Miss Grey,' spoken in the grave, low tones of a well-known voice. Immedi ely the flowers were gathered, and in my hand. It was Mr. Weston, of course who else would trouble himself to do so much for *me*?

I thanked him; whether warmly or coldly, I cannot tell: but certain I am at I did not express half the gratitude I felt. It was foolish, perhaps, to feel any atitude at all; but it seemed to me, at that moment, as if this were a re arkable instance of his good nature: an act of kindness which I could not pay, but never should forget: so utterly unaccustomed was I to receive such vilities, so little prepared to expect them from anyone within fifty miles of orton Lodge. Yet this did not prevent me from feeling a little uncomfortable his presence; and I proceeded to follow my pupils at a much quicker pace an before; though, perhaps, if Mr. Weston had taken the hint and let me ass without another word, I might have repented it an hour after: but he did ot. A somewhat rapid walk for me was but an ordinary pace for him.

'Your young ladies have left you alone,' said he.

'Yes, they are occupied with more agreeable company.'

'Then don't trouble yourself to overtake them.'

I slackened my pace; but next moment regretted having done so: my com anion did not speak; and I had nothing in the world to say, and feared he ight be in the same predicament. At length, however, he broke the pause by king, with a certain quiet abruptness peculiar to himself, if I liked flowers.

'Yes; very much,' I answered: 'wild flowers especially.'

'*I* like wild flowers,' said he; 'others I don't care about, because I have no articular associations connected with them—except one or two. What are your vourite flowers?'

'Primroses, blue-bells, and heath-blossoms.'

'Not violets?'

'No; because, as you say, I have no particular associations connected with em; for there are no sweet violets among the hills and valleys round my home.'

'It must be a great consolation to you to have a home, Miss Grey,' observed y companion after a short pause: 'however remote, or however seldom sited, still it is something to look to.'

'It is so much that I think I could not live without it,' replied I, with an thusiasm of which I immediately repented; for I thought it must have unded essentially silly.

'Oh yes; you could,' said he, with a thoughtful smile. 'The ties that bind us life are tougher than you imagine, or than anyone can who has not felt ow roughly they may be pulled without breaking. You might be miserable

without a home, but even *you* could live; and not *so* miserably as you suppos
The human heart is like india-rubber: a little swells it, but a great deal w
not burst it. If "little more than nothing will disturb it, little less than all thin;
will suffice" to break it. As in the outer members of our frame, there is a vit
power inherent in itself, that strengthens it against external violence. Eve;
blow that shakes it will serve to harden it against a future stroke; as consta;
labour thickens the skin of the hand, and strengthens its muscles instead
wasting them away: so that a day of arduous toil that might excoriate a lady
palm, would make no sensible impression on that of a hardy ploughman.

'I speak from experience—partly my own. There was a time when I thoug;
as you do—at least, I was fully persuaded that home and its affections were t;
only things that made life tolerable: that, if deprived of these, existence wou
become a burden hard to be endured; but now I have no home—unless y
would dignify my two hired rooms at Horton by such a name;—and not twel
months ago, I lost the last and dearest of my early friends; and yet, not on
I live, but I am not wholly destitute of hope and comfort, even for this lif
though I must acknowledge that I can seldom enter even an humble cotta;
at the close of the day, and see its inhabitants peaceably gathered around the
cheerful hearth, without a feeling *almost* of envy at their domestic enjoymen

'You don't know what happiness lies before you yet,' said I: 'you are no
only in the commencement of your journey.'

'The best of happiness,' replied he, 'is mine already—the power and the w
to be useful.'

We now approached a stile communicating with a footpath that conduct;
to a farm-house, where, I suppose, Mr. Weston purposed to make hims;
'useful'; for he presently took leave of me, crossed the stile, and traversed t;
path with his usual firm, elastic tread, leaving me to ponder his words
I continued my course alone. I had heard before that he had lost his moth;
not many months before he came. She then was the last and dearest of his ear
friends; and he had *no home*. I pitied him from my heart: I almost wept f
sympathy. And this, I thought, accounted for the shade of premature thougl
fulness that so frequently clouded his brow, and obtained for him the reputati;
of a morose and sullen disposition with the charitable Miss Murray and ;
her kin. 'But,' thought I, 'he is not so miserable as I should be under su;
a deprivation: he leads an active life; and a wide field for useful exertion li
before him. He can *make* friends; and he can make a home too, if he pleas;
and, doubtless, he will please some time. God grant the partner of that hon
may be worthy of his choice, and make it a happy one—such a home as
deserves to have! And how delightful it would be to——' But no matter wh
I thought.

I began this book with the intention of concealing nothing; that those w;
liked might have the benefit of perusing a fellow creature's heart: but we ha

me thoughts that all the angels in heaven are welcome to behold, but not our rother men—not even the best and kindest among them.

By this time the Greens had taken themselves to their own abode, and the Iurrays had turned down the private road, whither I hastened to follow them. found the two girls warm in an animated discussion on the respective merits f the two young officers; but on seeing me Rosalie broke off in the middle of sentence to exclaim, with malicious glee—

'Oh, ho, Miss Grey! you're come at last, are you? No *wonder* you lingered long behind; and no *wonder* you always stand up so vigorously for Mr. Weston hen I abuse him. Ah, ha! I see it all now!'

'Now, come, Miss Murray, don't be foolish,' said I, attempting a good-atured laugh; 'you know such nonsense can make no impression on me.'

But she still went on talking such intolerable stuff—her sister helping her ith appropriate fiction coined for the occasion—that I thought it necessary say something in my own justification.

'What folly all this is!' I exclaimed. 'If Mr. Weston's road happened to be ae same as mine for a few yards, and if he chose to exchange a word or two passing, what is there so remarkable in that? I assure you, I never spoke to im before; except once.'

'Where? where? and when?' cried they eagerly.

'In Nancy's cottage.'

'Ah, ha! you've met him there, have you?' exclaimed Rosalie, with exultant ughter. 'Ah! now, Matilda, I've found out why she's so fond of going to ancy Brown's! she goes there to flirt with Mr. Weston.'

'Really, that is not worth contradicting!—I only saw him there once, I tell ɔu—and how could I know he was coming?'

Irritated as I was at their foolish mirth and vexatious imputations, the neasiness did not continue long; when they had had their laugh out, they turned again to the captain and lieutenant; and, while they disputed and ɔmmented upon them, my indignation rapidly cooled; the cause of it was uickly forgotten, and I turned my thoughts into a pleasanter channel. Thus e proceeded up the park, and entered the hall; and as I ascended the stairs my own chamber, I had but one thought within me: my heart was filled to ⁄erflowing with one single earnest wish. Having entered the room, and shut ae door, I fell upon my knees and offered up a fervent but not impetuous ayer: 'Thy will be done,' I strove to say throughout; but, 'Father, all things e possible with Thee, and may it be Thy will,' was sure to follow. That ish—that prayer—both men and women would have scorned me for—'But ather, *Thou* wilt *not* despise!' I said, and felt that it was true. It seemed to me ɑt another's welfare was at least as ardently implored for as my own; nay, en *that* was the principal object of my heart's desire. I might have been de-iving myself; but that idea gave me confidence to ask, and power to hope

I did not ask in vain. As for the primroses, I kept two of them in a glass in m room until they were completely withered, and the housemaid threw them ou and the petals of the other I pressed between the leaves of my Bible—I ha them still, and mean to keep them always.

CHAPTER 14

THE RECTOR

The following day was as fine as the preceding one. Soon after breakfa Miss Matilda, having galloped and blundered through a few unprofitab lessons, and vengeably thumped the piano for an hour, in a terrible humo with both me and it, because her mamma would not give her a holida had betaken herself to her favourite places of resort, the yards, the stable and the dog-kennels; and Miss Murray was gone forth to enjoy a quiet ramb with a new fashionable novel for her companion, leaving me in the scho room hard at work upon a water-colour drawing which I had promised to (for her, and which she insisted upon my finishing that day.

At my feet lay a little rough terrier. It was the property of Miss Matild but she hated the animal, and intended to sell it, alleging that it was qui spoiled. It was really an excellent dog of its kind; but she affirmed it was for nothing, and had not even the sense to know its own mistress.

The fact was, she had purchased it when but a small puppy, insisting first that no one should touch it but herself; but, soon becoming tired of helpless and troublesome a nursling, she had gladly yielded to my entreati to be allowed to take charge of it; and I, by carefully nursing the little creatu from infancy to adolescence, of course, had obtained its affections: a rewa I should have greatly valued, and looked upon as far outweighing all th trouble I had had with it, had not poor Snap's grateful feelings expose him to many a harsh word and many a spiteful kick and pinch from its owne and were he not now in danger of being 'put away,' in consequence, transferred to some rough, stony-hearted master. But how could I help i I could not make the dog hate me, by cruel treatment; and she would n propitiate him by kindness.

However, while I thus sat, working away with my pencil, Mrs. Murra came, half-sailing, half-bustling into the room.

'Miss Grey,' she began,—'dear! how can you sit at your drawing su a day as this?' (She thought I was doing it for my own pleasure.) 'I won you don't put on your bonnet and go out with the young ladies.'

'I think, ma'am, Miss Murray is reading; and Miss Matilda is amusi herself with her dogs.'

'If you would try to amuse Miss Matilda yourself a little more, I think she
would not be *driven* to seek amusement in the companionship of dogs and
horses, and grooms, so much as she is; and if you would be a little more cheerful
and conversable with Miss Murray, she would not so often go wandering in
the fields with a book in her hand. However, I don't want to vex you,' added
she, seeing, I suppose, that my cheeks burned and my hand trembled with
some unamiable emotion. 'Do, pray, try not to be so touchy,—there's no
speaking to you else. And tell me if you know where Rosalie is gone: and why
she likes to be so much alone?'

'She says she likes to be alone when she has a new book to read.'

'But why can't she read it in the park or the garden?—why should she go
into the fields and lanes? And how is it that that Mr. Hatfield so often finds
her out? She told me last week he'd walked his horse by her side all up Moss
Lane; and now I'm sure it was he I saw from my dressing-room window,
walking so briskly past the park-gates, and on towards the field where she
so frequently goes. I wish you would go and see if she is there; and just gently
remind her that it is not proper for a young lady of her rank and prospects
to be wandering about by herself in that manner, exposed to the attentions of
anyone that presumes to address her; like some poor neglected girl that has
no park to walk in, and no friends to take care of her: and tell her that her
papa would be extremely angry if he knew of her treating Mr. Hatfield in
the familiar manner that I fear she does; and—oh! if you—if *any* governess
had but half a mother's watchfulness—half a mother's anxious care, I should
be saved this trouble; and you would see at once the necessity of keeping your
eye upon her, and making your company agreeable to —— Well, go—go;
there's no time to be lost,' cried she, seeing that I had put away my drawing-
materials, and was waiting in the doorway for the conclusion of her address.

According to her prognostications, I found Miss Murray in her favourite
field just without the park; and, unfortunately, not alone; for the tall, stately
figure of Mr. Hatfield was slowly sauntering by her side.

Here was a poser for me. It was my duty to interrupt the *tête-à-tête*:
but how was it to be done? Mr. Hatfield could not be driven away by so
insignificant a person as I; and to go and place myself on the other side of
Miss Murray, and intrude my unwelcome presence upon her without noticing
her companion, was a piece of rudeness I could not be guilty of: neither had
I the courage to cry aloud from the top of the field that she was wanted
elsewhere. So I took the intermediate course of walking slowly, but steadily
towards them; resolving, if my approach failed to scare away the beau, to pass
by and tell Miss Murray her mamma wanted her.

She certainly looked very charming as she strolled, lingering along under
the budding horse-chestnut trees that stretched their long arms over the park-
palings, with her closed book in one hand, and in the other a graceful sprig

of myrtle, which served her as a very pretty plaything; her bright ringle[
escaping profusely from her little bonnet, and gently stirred by the breez[
her fair cheek flushed with gratified vanity, her smiling blue eyes, now sly[
glancing towards her admirer, now gazing downwards at her myrtle spri[
But Snap, running before me, interrupted her in the midst of some half-per[
half-playful repartee, by catching hold of her dress and vehemently tuggi[
thereat; till Mr. Hatfield, with his cane, administered a resounding thwa[
upon the animal's skull, and sent it yelping back to me, with a clamoro[
outcry that afforded the reverend gentleman great amusement: but seei[
me so near, he thought, I suppose, he might as well be taking his departur[
and as I stooped to caress the dog, with ostentatious pity to show my disa[
proval of his severity, I heard him say,—'When shall I see you again, M[
Murray?'

'At church, I suppose,' replied she, 'unless your business chances to bri[
you here again, at the precise moment when I happen to be walking by[

'I could always manage to have business here, if I knew precisely when a[
where to find you.'

'But if I would, I could not inform you, for I am so immethodical, I nev[
can tell to-day what I shall do to-morrow.'

'Then give me that, meantime, to comfort me,' said he, half jestingly and h[
in earnest, extending his hand for the sprig of myrtle.

'No, indeed, I shan't.'

'Do! *pray* do! I shall be the most miserable of men if you don't. You cann[
be so cruel as to deny me a favour so easily granted and yet so highly prize[
pleaded he as ardently as if his life depended on it.

By this time I stood within a very few yards of them, impatiently waiting [
departure.

'There then! take it and go,' said Rosalie.

He joyfully received the gift, murmured something that made her blush a[
toss her head, but with a little laugh that showed her displeasure was entir[
affected; and then with a courteous salutation withdrew.

'Did you ever see such a man, Miss Grey?' said she, turning to me; 'I'[
so *glad* you came! I thought I never *should* get rid of him; and I was so terri[
afraid of papa seeing him.'

'Has he been with you long?'

'No, not long, but he's so extremely impertinent: and he's always hangi[
about, pretending his business or his clerical duties require his attendan[
in these parts, and really watching for poor me, and pouncing upon [
wherever he sees me.'

'Well, your mamma thinks you ought not to go beyond the park or gard[
without some discreet, matronly person like me to accompany you, and ke[
off all intruders. She descried Mr. Hatfield hurrying past the park-gates, a[

rthwith dispatched me with instructions to seek you up and to take care
you, and likewise to warn ——'

'Oh, mamma's so tiresome! As if I couldn't take care of myself. She both-
ed me before about Mr. Hatfield; and I told her she might trust me: I never
ould forget my rank and station for the most delightful man that ever
reathed. I wish he would go down on his knees to-morrow, and implore
e to be his wife, that I might just show her how mistaken she is in sup-
osing that I could ever—— Oh, it provokes me so! To think that I could
e such a fool as to fall in *love*! It is quite beneath the dignity of a woman to
o such a thing. Love! I detest the word! as applied to one of our sex, I think
a perfect insult. A preference I *might* acknowledge; but never for one like
or Mr. Hatfield, who has not seven hundred a year to bless himself with.
like to talk to him, because he's so clever and amusing—I wish Sir Thomas
shby were half as nice; besides, I must have *somebody* to flirt with, and no
se has the sense to come here; and when we go out, mamma won't let me
irt with anybody but Sir Thomas—if he's there; and if he's *not* there I'm
ound hand and foot, for fear somebody should go and make up some exagge-
ted story, and put it into his head that I'm engaged, or likely to be engaged,
somebody else; or, what is more probable, for fear his nasty old mother
ould see or hear of my ongoings, and conclude that I'm not a fit wife for
er excellent son: as if the said son were not the greatest scamp in Christen-
om; and as if any woman of common decency were not a world too good
r him.'

'Is it really so, Miss Murray? and does your mamma know it, and yet wish
ou to marry him?'

'To be sure she does! She knows more against him than I do, I believe:
e keeps it from me lest I should be discouraged; not knowing how little
care about such things. For it's no great matter, really: he'll be all right
hen he's married, as mamma says; and reformed rakes make the best
usbands, *everybody* knows. I only wish he were not so ugly—*that's* all *I* think
out: but then there's no choice here in the country; and papa *will not*
t us go to London—'

'But I should think Mr. Hatfield would be far better.'

'And so he would, if he were lord of Ashby Park—there's not a doubt of
but the fact is, I *must* have Ashby Park, whoever shares it with me.'

'But Mr. Hatfield thinks you like him all this time; you don't consider how
tterly he will be disappointed when he finds himself mistaken.'

'*No*, indeed! It will be a proper punishment for his presumption—for ever
ring to think I could like him. I should enjoy nothing so much as lifting the
il from his eyes.'

'The sooner you do it the better then.'

'No; I tell you, I like to amuse myself with him. Besides, he doesn't really

think I like him. I take good care of that: you don't know how cleverly manage. He may presume to think he can *induce* me to like him; for whic I shall punish him as he deserves.'

'Well, mind you don't give too much reason for such presumption—that all,' replied I.

But all my exhortations were in vain: they only made her somewhat mo solicitous to disguise her wishes and her thoughts from me. She talked n more to me about the Rector; but I could see that her mind, if not her hear was fixed upon him still, and that she was intent upon obtaining anothe interview: for though, in compliance with her mother's request, I was no constituted the companion of her rambles for a time, she still persisted wandering in the fields and lanes that lay in the nearest proximity to th road; and, whether she talked to me or read the book she carried in he hand, she kept continually pausing to look round her, or gaze up the road see if anyone was coming; and if a horseman trotted by, I could tell by h unqualified abuse of the poor equestrian, whoever he might be, that she hate him *because* he was not Mr. Hatfield.

'Surely,' thought I, 'she is not so indifferent to him as she believes herse to be, or would have others to believe her; and her mother's anxiety is n so wholly causeless as she affirms.'

Three days passed away, and he did not make his appearance. On th afternoon of the fourth, as we were walking beside the park palings in th memorable field, each furnished with a book (for I always took care to provi myself with something to be doing when she did not require me to talk she suddenly interrupted my studies by exclaiming—

'Oh, Miss Grey! do be so kind as to go and see Mark Wood, and take h wife half a crown from me—I should have given or sent it a week ago, b quite forgot. There!' said she, throwing me her purse, and speaking ve fast—'Never mind getting it out now, but take the purse and give them wh you like; I would go with you, but I want to finish this volume. I'll come an meet you when I've done it. Be quick, will you—and—oh, wait; hadn't yo better read to him a bit? Run to the house and get some sort of a good boo Anything will do.'

I did as I was desired; but, suspecting something from her hurried mann and the suddenness of the request, I just glanced back before I quitted th field, and there was Mr. Hatfield about to enter at the gate below. By sendin me to the house for a book, she had just prevented my meeting him on th road.

'Never mind!' thought I, 'there'll be no great harm done. Poor Mark w be glad of the half-crown, and perhaps of the good book too; and if the Rect does steal Miss Rosalie's heart, it will only humble her pride a little; and they do get married at last, it will only save her from a worse fate; and sh

will be quite a good enough partner for him, and he for her.'

Mark Wood was the consumptive labourer whom I mentioned before. He was now rapidly wearing away. Miss Murray, by her liberality, obtained literally the blessing of him that was ready to perish; for though the half-crown could be of very little service to him, he was glad of it for the sake of his wife and children, so soon to be widowed and fatherless. After I had sat a few minutes, and read a little for the comfort and edification of himself and his afflicted wife, I left them; but I had not proceeded fifty yards before I encountered Mr. Weston, apparently on his way to the same abode. He greeted me in his usual quiet, unaffected way, stopped to inquire about the condition of the sick man and his family, and with a sort of unconscious, brotherly disregard to ceremony, took from my hand the book out of which I had been reading, turned over its pages, made a few brief but very sensible remarks, and restored it; then told me about some poor sufferer he had just been visiting, talked a little about Nancy Brown, made a few observations upon my little rough friend the terrier, that was frisking at his feet, and finally upon the beauty of the weather, and departed.

I have omitted to give a detail of his words, from a notion that they would not interest the reader as they did me, and not because I have forgotten them. No; I remember them well; for I thought them over and over again in the course of that day and many succeeding ones, I know not how often; and recalled every intonation of his deep, clear voice, every flash of his quick, brown eye, and every gleam of his pleasant, but too transient smile. Such confession will look very absurd, I fear; but no matter: I have written it: and they that read it will not know the writer.

While I was walking along, happy within, and pleased with all around, Miss Murray came hastening to meet me; her buoyant step, flushed cheek, and radiant smiles showing that she, too, was happy, in her own way. Running up to me, she put her arm through mine, and without waiting to recover breath, began—'Now, Miss Grey, think yourself highly honoured, for I'm come to tell you my news before I've breathed a word of it to anyone else.'

'Well, what is it?'

'Oh, *such* news! In the first place, you must know that Mr. Hatfield came upon me just after you were gone. I was in *such* a way for fear papa or mamma should see him; but you know I couldn't call you back again, and so I—oh, dear! I can't tell you all about it now, for there's Matilda, I see, in the park, and I must go and open my budget to her. But, however, Hatfield was most uncommonly audacious, unspeakably complimentary, and unprecedently tender—tried to be so, at least—he didn't succeed very well in *that*, because it's not his vein. I'll tell you all he said another time.'

'But what did *you* say—I'm more interested in that?'

'I'll tell you that, too, at some future period. I happened to be in a very good

humour just then; but, though I was complaisant and gracious enough,
I took care not to compromise myself in any possible way. But, however
the conceited wretch chose to interpret my amiability of temper his own
way, and at length presumed upon my indulgence so far—what do you think
—he actually—made me an offer!'

'And you——'

'I proudly drew myself up, and with the greatest coolness expressed my
astonishment at such an occurrence, and hoped he had seen nothing in my
conduct to justify his expectations. You should have *seen* how his countenance
fell! He went perfectly white in the face. I assured him that I esteemed him
and all that, but could not possibly accede to his proposals; and if I did, papa
and mamma could never be brought to give their consent.'

' "But if they could," said he, "would yours be wanting?"

' "Certainly, Mr. Hatfield," I replied, with a cool decision which quelled
all hope at once. Oh, if you had seen how dreadfully mortified he was—how
crushed to the earth by his disappointment! really, I almost pitied him
myself.

'One more desperate attempt, however, he made. After a silence of consider-
able duration, during which he struggled to be calm, and I to be grave—for
I felt a strong propensity to laugh—which would have ruined all—he said
with the ghost of a smile—"But tell me plainly, Miss Murray, if I had the
wealth of Sir Hugh Meltham, or the prospects of his eldest son, would you
still refuse me? answer me truly, upon your honour."

' "Certainly," said I. "That would make no difference whatever."

'It was a great lie, but he looked so confident in his own attractions still
that I determined not to leave him one stone upon another. He looked me
full in the face; but I kept my countenance so well that he could not imagine
I was saying anything more than the actual truth.

' "Then it's all over, I suppose," he said, looking as if he could have died
on the spot with vexation and the intensity of his despair. But he was angry
as well as disappointed. There was he, suffering so unspeakably, and there
was I, the pitiless cause of it all, so utterly impenetrable to all the artillery of
his looks and words, so calmly cold and proud, he could not but feel some
resentment; and with singular bitterness he began—"I certainly did not
expect this, Miss Murray. I might say something about your past conduct
and the hopes you have led me to foster, but I forbear, on condition——"

' "No conditions, Mr. Hatfield!" said I, now truly indignant at his insolence.

' "Then let me beg it as a favour," he replied, lowering his voice at once,
and taking a humbler tone: "let me entreat that you will not mention this
affair to anyone whatever. If you will keep silence about it, there need be no
unpleasantness on either side—nothing, I mean, beyond what is quite un-
avoidable: for my own feelings I will endeavour to keep to myself, if I cannot

nnihilate them—I will try to forgive, if I cannot forget the cause of my suffer-
ngs. I will not suppose, Miss Murray, that you know how deeply you have
njured me. I would not have you aware of it; but if, in addition to the injury
ou have already done me—pardon me, but whether innocently or not,
ou *have* done it—and if you add to it by giving publicity to this unfortunate
ffair, or naming it *at all*, you will find that I too can speak, and though you
corned my love, you will hardly scorn my——"

'He stopped, but he bit his bloodless lip, and looked so terribly fierce that
was quite frightened. However, my pride upheld me still, and I answered
isdainfully—"I do not know what motive you suppose I could have for
aming it to anyone, Mr. Hatfield; but if I were disposed to do so, you would
ot deter me by threats; and it is scarcely the part of a gentleman to attempt it."

' "Pardon me, Miss Murray," said he, "I have loved you so intensely—I
o still adore you so deeply, that I would not willingly offend you; but though
never have loved, and never *can* love any woman as I have loved you, it is
qually certain that I never was so ill-treated by any. On the contrary, I have
lways found your sex the kindest and most tender and obliging of God's
reation, till now." (Think of the conceited fellow saying that!) "And the
ovelty and harshness of the lesson you have taught me to-day, and the bitter-
ess of being disappointed in the only quarter on which the happiness of
y life depended, must excuse any appearance of asperity. If my presence
disagreeable to you, Miss Murray," he said (for I was looking about me to
ow how little I cared for him, so he thought I was tired of him, I suppose),
-'if my presence is disagreeable to you, Miss Murray, you have only to
romise me the favour I named, and I will relieve you at once. There are
any ladies—some even in this parish—who would be delighted to accept
hat you have so scornfully trampled under your feet. They would be naturally
clined to hate one whose surpassing loveliness has so completely estranged my
eart from them and blinded me to their attractions; and a single hint of
e truth from me to one of these, would be sufficient to raise such a talk
gainst you as would seriously injure your prospects, and diminish your
hance of success with any other gentleman you or your mamma might design
 entangle."

' "What do you mean, sir?" said I, ready to stamp with passion.

' "I mean that this affair from beginning to end appears to me like a case
f arrant flirtation, to say the least of it—such a case as you would find it
ather inconvenient to have blazoned through the world: especially with the
dditions and exaggerations of your female rivals, who would be too glad
 publish the matter, if I only gave them a handle to it. But I promise you,
n the faith of a gentleman, that no word or syllable that could tend to your
rejudice shall ever escape my lips, provided you will——"

' "Well, well, I won't mention it," said I. "You may rely upon my silence,

if that can afford you any consolation."

' "You promise it?"

' "Yes," I answered, for I wanted to get rid of him now.

' "Farewell, then!" said he, in a most doleful heartsick tone; and with a look where pride vainly struggled against despair, he turned and went away: longing, no doubt, to get home, that he might shut himself up in his study and cry—if he doesn't burst into tears before he gets there.'

'But you have broken your promise already,' said I, truly horrified at her perfidy.

'Oh! it's only to you; I know you won't repeat it.'

'Certainly, I shall not: but you say you are going to tell your sister; and she will tell your brothers when they come home, and Brown immediately if you do not tell her yourself; and Brown will blazon it, or be the means of blazoning it throughout the country.'

'No, indeed, she won't. We shall not tell her at all, unless it be under the promise of the strictest secrecy.'

'But how can you expect her to keep her promises better than her more enlightened mistress?'

'Well, well, she shan't hear it then,' said Miss Murray, somewhat snappishly.

'But you will tell your mamma, of course,' pursued I; 'and she will tell your papa.'

'Of course, I shall tell mamma, that is the very thing that pleases me so much. I shall now be able to convince her how mistaken she was in her fears about me.'

'Oh, *that's* it, is it? I was wondering what it was that delighted you so much.'

'Yes; and another thing is, that I've humbled Mr. Hatfield so charmingly, and another—why, you must allow me some share of female vanity: I don't pretend to be without that most essential attribute of our sex—and if you had seen poor Hatfield's intense eagerness in making his ardent declaration and his flattering proposal, and his agony of mind, that no effort of pride could conceal, on being refused, you would have allowed I had some cause to be gratified.'

'The greater his agony, I should think, the less your cause for gratification.'

'Oh, nonsense!' cried the young lady, shaking herself with vexation. 'You either can't understand me or you won't. If I had not confidence in your magnanimity, I should think you envied me. But you will, perhaps, comprehend this cause of pleasure—which is as great as any—namely, that I am delighted with myself for my prudence, my self-command, my heartlessness, you please. I was not a bit taken by surprise, not a bit confused, or awkward, or foolish; I just acted and spoke as I ought to have done, and was completely my own mistress throughout. And here was a man, decidedly good-looking—

ne and Susan Green call him bewitchingly handsome—I suppose they're
o of the ladies he pretends would be so glad to have him; but, however, he
as certainly a very clever, witty, agreeable companion—not what *you* call
ever, but just enough to make him entertaining; and a man one needn't be
hamed of anywhere, and would not soon grow tired of; and to confess the
uth, I rather liked him—better even, of late, than Harry Meltham—and he
idently idolized me; and yet, though he came upon me all alone and
prepared, I had the wisdom, and the pride, and the strength to refuse him—
d so scornfully and coolly as I did: I have good reason to be proud of that!'
'And are you equally proud of having told him that his having the wealth
Sir Hugh Meltham would make no difference to you when that was not
e case; and of having promised to tell no one of his misadventure, apparently
thout the slightest intention of keeping your promise?'
'Of course! what else could I do? You would not have had me—but I see,
iss Grey, you're not in a good temper. Here's Matilda; I'll see what she
d mamma have to say about it.'
She left me, offended at my want of sympathy, and thinking, no doubt, that
envied her. I did not—at least, I firmly believed I did not. I was sorry for
r; I was amazed, disgusted at her heartless vanity; I wondered why so much
auty should be given to those who made so bad a use of it, and denied to
me who would make it a benefit to both themselves and others.
But, God knows best, I concluded. There are, I suppose, some men as vain,
selfish, and as heartless as she is, and, perhaps, such women may be useful
punish them.

CHAPTER 15

THE WALK

) dear! I wish Hatfield had not been so precipitate!' said Rosalie next day
four p.m., as, with a portentous yawn, she laid down her worsted-work
d looked listlessly towards the window. 'There's no inducement to go out
w; and nothing to look forward to. The days will be so long and dull when
ere are no parties to enliven them; and there are none this week, or next
her, that I know of.'
'Pity you were so cross to him,' observed Matilda, to whom this lamentation
as addressed. 'He'll never come again: and I suspect you liked him after
. I hoped you would have taken him for your beau, and left dear Harry
me.'
'Humph! my beau must be an Adonis indeed, Matilda, the admired of all
holders, if I am to be contented with him alone. I'm sorry to lose Hatfield,

I confess; but the first decent man, or number of men, that come to supp
his place, will be more than welcome. It's Sunday to-morrow—I do wond
how he'll look, and whether he'll be able to go through the service. Most like
he'll pretend he's got a cold and make Mr. Weston do it all.'

'Not he!' exclaimed Matilda, somewhat contemptuously. 'Fool as he is, h
not so soft as that comes to.'

Her sister was slightly offended; but the event proved Matilda was righ
the disappointed lover performed his pastoral duties as usual. Rosalie, indee
affirmed he looked very pale and dejected: he might be a little paler; but t
difference, if any, was scarcely perceptible. As for his dejection, I certainly d
not hear his laugh ringing from the vestry as usual, nor his voice loud
hilarious discourse; though I did hear it uplifted in rating the sexton
a manner that made the congregation stare; and, in his transits to and fro
the pulpit and the communion table there was more of solemn pomp, and le
of that irreverent, self-confident, or rather self-delighted imperiousness wi
which he usually swept along—that air that seemed to say, 'You all reveren
and adore me, I know; but if anyone does not, I defy him to the teeth!' But t
most remarkable change was, that he never once suffered his eyes to wand
in the direction of Mr. Murray's pew, and did not leave the church till we we
gone.

Mr. Hatfield had doubtless received a very severe blow; but his pri
impelled him to use every effort to conceal the effects of it. He had be
disappointed in his certain hope of obtaining not only a beautiful, and, to hi
highly attractive wife, but one whose rank and fortune might give brillian
to far inferior charms: he was likewise, no doubt, intensely mortified by h
repulse, and deeply offended at the conduct of Miss Murray throughout.
would have given him no little consolation to have known how disappointe
she was to find him apparently so little moved, and to see that he was able
refrain from casting a single glance at her throughout both services; though, s
declared, it showed he was thinking of her all the time, or his eyes would ha
fallen upon her, if it were only by chance: but if they had so chanced
fall, she would have affirmed it was because they could not resist the attractio
It might have pleased him too, in some degree, to have seen how dull a
dissatisfied she was throughout that week (the greater part of it, at least), f
lack of her usual source of excitement; and how often she regretted havi
'used him up so soon,' like a child that, having devoured its plum-cake t
hastily, sits sucking its fingers, and vainly lamenting its greediness.

At length I was called upon, one fine morning, to accompany her in a w
to the village. Ostensibly she went to get some shades of Berlin wool, at a tol
ably respectable shop that was chiefly supported by the ladies of the vicini
really—I trust there is no breach of charity in supposing that she went with t
idea of meeting either with the Rector himself, or some other admirer by t

ay; for as we went along, she kept wondering 'what Hatfield would do or say, we met him,' &c., &c.; as we passed Mr. Green's park-gates, she 'wondered hether he was at home—great stupid blockhead'; as Lady Meltham's carriage assed us, she 'wondered what Mr. Harry was doing this fine day'; and then egan to abuse his elder brother for being 'such a fool as to get married and go nd live in London.'

'Why,' said I, 'I thought you wanted to live in London yourself.'

'Yes, because it's so dull here: but then he makes it still duller by taking imself off; and if he were not married I might have him instead of that dious Sir Thomas.'

Then, observing the prints of a horse's feet on the somewhat miry road, she vondered whether it was a gentleman's horse,' and finally concluded it was, r the impressions were too small to have been made by a 'great, clumsy cart-orse'; and then she 'wondered who the rider could be,' and whether we should eet him coming back, for she was sure he had only passed that morning; nd lastly, when we entered the village and saw only a few of its humble inhabi-nts moving about, she 'wondered why the stupid people couldn't keep in their ouses; she was sure she didn't want to see their ugly faces, and dirty, vulgar lothes—it wasn't for that she came to Horton!'

Amid all this, I confess, I wondered, too, in secret, whether we should meet r catch a glimpse of somebody else; and as we passed his lodgings, I even went far as to wonder whether he was at the window. On entering the shop, liss Murray desired me to stand in the doorway while she transacted her usiness, and tell her if anyone passed. But alas! there was no one visible esides the villagers, except Jane and Susan Green coming down the single reet, apparently returning from a walk.

'Stupid things!' muttered she, as she came out after having concluded her argain. 'Why couldn't they have their dolt of a brother with them? even *he* ould be better than nothing.'

She greeted them, however, with a cheerful smile, and protestations of easure at the happy meeting equal to their own. They placed themselves one 1 each side of her, and all three walked away chatting and laughing as young dies do when they get together, if they be but on tolerably intimate terms. ut I, feeling myself to be one too many, left them to their merriment and gged behind as usual on such occasions: I had no relish for walking beside iss Green or Miss Susan like one deaf and dumb, who could neither speak r be spoken to.

But this time I was not long alone. It struck me, at first, as very odd, that st as I was thinking about Mr. Weston he should come up and accost me; but terwards, on due reflection, I thought there was nothing odd about it, unless were the fact of his speaking to me; for on such a morning and so near s own abode, it was natural enough that he should be about; and as for my

thinking of him, I had been doing that, with little intermission, ever sinc
we set out on our journey; so there was nothing remarkable in that.

'You are alone again, Miss Grey,' said he.

'Yes.'

'What kind of people are those ladies—the Misses Green?'

'I really don't know.'

'That's strange—when you live so near and see them so often!'

'Well, I suppose they are lively, good-tempered girls; but I imagine yo
must know them better than I do, yourself, for I never exchanged a word wit
either of them.'

'Indeed! They don't strike me as being particularly reserved.'

'Very likely they are not so to people of their own class; but they consid
themselves as moving in quite a different sphere from me!'

He made no reply to this; but after a short pause he said—'I suppose it
these things, Miss Grey, that make you think you could not live withou
a home?'

'Not exactly. The fact is I am too socially disposed to be able to live co
tentedly without a friend; and as the only friends I have, or am likely to hav
are at home, if it—or rather, if they were gone—I will not say I could n
live—but I would rather not live in such a desolate world.'

'But why do you say the only friends you are likely to have? Are you s
unsociable that you cannot make friends?'

'No, but I never made one yet; and in my present position there is n
possibility of doing so, or even of forming a common acquaintance. The fau
may be partly in myself, but I hope not altogether.'

'The fault is partly in society, and partly, I should think, in your immedia
neighbours: and partly, too, in yourself; for many ladies, in your positio
would make themselves be noticed and accounted of. But your pupils should l
companions for you in some degree; they cannot be many years younger tha
yourself.'

'Oh, yes, they are good company sometimes; but I cannot call them friend
nor would they think of bestowing such a name on me—they have other co
panions better suited to their tastes.'

'Perhaps you are too wise for them. How do you amuse yourself whe
alone—do you read much?'

'Reading is my favourite occupation, when I have leisure for it and bool
to read.'

From speaking of books in general, he passed to different books in particula
and proceeded by rapid transitions from topic to topic, till several matter
both of taste and opinion, had been discussed considerably within the space
half an hour but without the embellishment of many observations from himsel
he being evidently less bent upon communicating his own thoughts and pr

lilections, than on discovering mine. He had not the tact, or the art, to effect uch a purpose by skilfully drawing out my sentiments or ideas through the real r apparent statement of his own, or leading the conversation by imperceptible radations to such topics as he wished to advert to: but such gentle abruptness, nd such single-minded straightforwardness could not possibly offend me.

'And why should he interest himself at all in my moral and intellectual apacities: what is it to him what I think or feel?' I asked myself. And my eart throbbed in answer to the question.

But Jane and Susan Green soon reached their home. As they stood parleying t the park-gates, attempting to persuade Miss Murray to come in, I wished Ir. Weston would go, that she might not see him with me when she turned ound; but, unfortunately, his business, which was to pay one more visit to poor Iark Wood, led him to pursue the same path as we did, till nearly the close f our journey. When, however, he saw that Rosalie had taken leave of her iends and I was about to join her, he would have left me and passed on at quicker pace; but, as he civilly lifted his hat in passing her, to my surprise, astead of returning the salute with a stiff, ungracious bow, she accosted him vith one of her sweetest smiles, and, walking by his side, began to talk to him vith all imaginable cheerfulness and affability; and so we proceeded all three ogether.

After a short pause in the conversation, Mr. Weston made some remark ddressed particularly to me, as referring to something we had been talking of efore; but, before I could answer, Miss Murray replied to the observation nd enlarged upon it: he rejoined; and, from thence to the close of the inter-iew, she engrossed him entirely to herself. It might be partly owing to my own upidity, my want of tact and assurance: but I felt myself wronged: I trembled ith apprehension; and I listened with envy to her easy, rapid flow of utterance, nd saw with anxiety the bright smile with which she looked into his face om time to time: for she was walking a little in advance, for the purpose (as judged) of being seen as well as heard. If her conversation was light and ivial, it was amusing, and she was never at a loss for something to say, or for uitable words to express it in. There was nothing pert or flippant in her aanner now, as when she walked with Mr. Hatfield; there was only a gentle, layful kind of vivacity, which I thought must be peculiarly pleasing to a man f Mr. Weston's disposition and temperament.

When he was gone she began to laugh, and muttered to herself. 'I thought could do it!'

'Do what?' I asked.

'Fix that man.'

'What in the world do you mean?'

'I mean that he will go home and dream of me. I have shot him through te heart!'

'How do you know?'

'By many infallible proofs: more especially the look he gave me when he went away. It was not an impudent look—I exonerate him from that—it was a look of reverential, tender adoration. Ha, ha! he's not quite such a stupid blockhead as I thought him!'

I made no answer, for my heart was in my throat, or something like it, and I could not trust myself to speak. 'O God, avert it!' I cried, internally—'for his sake, not for mine!'

Miss Murray made several trivial observations as we passed up the park to which (in spite of my reluctance to let one glimpse of my feelings appear) I could only answer by monosyllables. Whether she intended to torment me, or merely to amuse herself, I could not tell—and did not much care; but I thought of the poor man and his one lamb, and the rich man with his thousand flocks; and I dreaded I knew not what for Mr. Weston, independently of my own blighted hopes.

Right glad was I to get into the house, and find myself alone once more in my own room. My first impulse was to sink into the chair beside the bed, and laying my head on the pillow, to seek relief in a passionate burst of tears: there was an imperative craving for such an indulgence; but, alas! I must restrain and swallow back my feelings still: there was the bell—the odious bell for the schoolroom dinner; and I must go down with a calm face, and smile and laugh, and talk nonsense—yes, and eat, too, if possible, as if all was right, and I was just returned from a pleasant walk.

CHAPTER 16

THE SUBSTITUTION

Next Sunday was one of the gloomiest of April days—a day of thick, dark clouds, and heavy showers. None of the Murrays were disposed to attend church in the afternoon, excepting Rosalie: she was bent upon going as usual; so she ordered the carriage, and I went with her: nothing loath, of course, for at church I might look without fear of scorn or censure upon a form and face more pleasing to me than the most beautiful of God's creations; I might listen without disturbance to a voice more charming than the sweetest music to my ears; I might seem to hold communion with that soul in which I felt so deeply interested, and imbibe its purest thoughts and holiest aspirations, with no alloy to such felicity except the secret reproaches of my conscience, which would too often whisper that I was deceiving my own self, and mocking God with the service of a heart more bent upon the creature than the Creator.

Sometimes such thoughts would give me trouble enough; but sometimes

could quiet them with thinking—it is not the man, it is his goodness that
love. 'Whatsoever things are pure, whatsoever things are lovely, whatsoever
things are honest and of good report, think on these things.' We do well to
worship God in His works; and I know none of them in which so many of His
attributes—so much of His own spirit shines, as in this His faithful servant;
whom to know and not to appreciate, were obtuse insensibility in me, who have
o little else to occupy my heart.

Almost immediately after the conclusion of the service, Miss Murray left the
church. We had to stand in the porch, for it was raining, and the carriage
was not yet come. I wondered at her coming forth so hastily, for neither young
Meltham nor Squire Green was there; but I soon found it was to secure
an interview with Mr. Weston as he came out, which he presently did. Having
saluted us both, he would have passed on, but she detained him; first with
observations upon the disagreeable weather, and then with asking if he would
be so kind as to come some time to-morrow to see the granddaughter of the old
woman who kept the porter's lodge, for the girl was ill of a fever, and wished
o see him. He promised to do so.

'And at what time will you be most likely to come, Mr. Weston? The old
woman will like to know when to expect you—you know such people think
more about having their cottages in order when decent people come to see
them than we are apt to suppose.'

Here was a wonderful instance of consideration from the thoughtless Miss
Murray. Mr. Weston named an hour in the morning at which he would
endeavour to be there. By this time the carriage was ready, and the footman
was waiting, with an open umbrella, to escort Miss Murray through the
churchyard. I was about to follow; but Mr. Weston had an umbrella too, and
offered me the benefit of its shelter, for it was raining heavily.

'No,—thank you, I don't mind the rain,' I said. I always lacked common
sense when taken by surprise.

'But you don't *like* it, I suppose?—an umbrella will do you no harm at any
rate,' he replied, with a smile that showed he was not offended; as a man
of worse temper or less penetration would have been at such a refusal of his
aid. I could not deny the truth of this assertion, and so went with him to the
carriage; he even offered me his hand on getting in: an unnecessary piece of
civility, but I accepted that too, for fear of giving offence. One glance he gave,
one little smile at parting—it was but for a moment; but therein I read, or
thought I read, a meaning that kindled in my heart a brighter flame of hope
than had ever yet arisen.

'I would have sent the footman back for you, Miss Grey, if you'd waited
moment—you needn't have taken Mr. Weston's umbrella,' observed Rosalie,
with a very unamiable cloud upon her pretty face.

'I would have come without an umbrella, but Mr. Weston offered me the

benefit of his, and I could not have refused it more than I did without offending him,' replied I, smiling placidly; for my inward happiness made that amusing which would have wounded me at another time.

The carriage was now in motion. Miss Murray bent forwards, and looked out of the window as we were passing Mr. Weston. He was pacing homeward along the causeway, and did not turn his head.

'Stupid ass!' cried she, throwing herself back again in the seat. 'You don't know *what* you've lost by not looking this way!'

'What has he lost?'

'A bow from me, that would have raised him to the seventh heaven!'

I made no answer. I saw she was out of humour, and I derived a secret gratification from the fact, not that she was vexed, but that she thought she had reason to be so. It made me think my hopes were not entirely the offspring of my wishes and imagination.

'I mean to take up Mr. Weston instead of Mr. Hatfield,' said my companion, after a short pause, resuming something of her usual cheerfulness. 'The ball at Ashby Park takes place on Tuesday, you know; and mamma thinks it very likely that Sir Thomas will propose to me then: such things are often done in the privacy of the ballroom, when gentlemen are most easily ensnared, and ladies most enchanting. But if I am to be married so soon, I must make the best of the present time: I am determined Hatfield shall not be the only man who shall lay his heart at my feet, and implore me to accept the worthless gift in vain.'

'If you mean Mr. Weston to be one of your victims,' said I, with affected indifference, 'you will have to make such overtures yourself that you will find it difficult to draw back when he asks you to fulfil the expectations you have raised.'

'I don't suppose he will ask me to *marry* him—nor should I desire it: that would be *rather* too much presumption! but I intend him to feel my power. He has felt it already, indeed: but he shall *acknowledge* it too; and what visionary hopes he may have, he must keep to himself, and only amuse me with the result of them—for a time.'

'Oh! that some kind spirit would whisper those words in his ear!' I inwardly exclaimed. I was far too indignant to hazard a reply to her observation aloud, and nothing more was said about Mr. Weston that day, by me or in my hearing. But next morning, soon after breakfast, Miss Murray came into the schoolroom where her sister was employed at her studies, or rather her lessons, for studies they were not, and said, 'Matilda, I want you to take a walk with me about eleven o'clock.'

'Oh, I can't, Rosalie! I have to give orders about my new bridle and saddle-cloth, and speak to the ratcatcher about his dogs: Miss Grey must go with you.'

'No, I want *you*,' said Rosalie; and calling her sister to the window, she

hispered an explanation in her ear; upon which the latter consented to go. I remembered that eleven was the hour at which Mr. Weston proposed to ome to the porter's lodge; and remembering that I beheld the whole con- ivance. Accordingly, at dinner, I was entertained with a long account of ow Mr. Weston had overtaken them as they were walking along the road; nd how they had had a long walk and talk with him, and really found him uite an agreeable companion; and how he must have been, and evidently as, delighted with them and their amazing condescension, &c. &c.

CHAPTER 17

CONFESSIONS

s I am in the way of confessions, I may as well acknowledge that, about this me, I paid more attention to dress than ever I had done before. This is not ying much; for hitherto I had been a little neglectful in that particular: but ow, also, it was no uncommon thing to spend as much as two minutes in the ontemplation of my own image in the glass; though I never could derive any onsolation from such a study. I could discover no beauty in those 'marked atures, that pale hollow cheek, and ordinary dark brown hair; there might e intellect in the forehead, there might be expression in the dark grey eyes: ut what of that?—a low Grecian brow, and large black eyes devoid of ntiment would be esteemed far preferable. It is foolish to wish for beauty. ensible people never either desire it for themselves, or care about it in others. the mind be but well cultivated, and the heart well disposed, no one ever res for the exterior. So said the teachers of our childhood; and so say we to e children of the present day. All very judicious and proper, no doubt; but e such assertions supported by actual experience?

We are naturally disposed to love what gives us pleasure, and what more easing than a beautiful face—when we know no harm of the possessor at ast? A little girl loves her bird—Why? Because it lives and feels; because it is lpless and harmless? A toad, likewise, lives and feels, and is equally helpless d harmless; but though she would not hurt a toad, she cannot love it like e bird, with its graceful form, soft feathers, and bright, speaking eyes. If woman is fair and amiable, she is praised for both qualities, but especially e former, by the bulk of mankind: if, on the other hand, she is disagreeable person and character, her plainness is commonly inveighed against as her eatest crime, because, to common observers, it gives the greatest offence; hile, if she is plain and good, provided she is a person of retired manners and cluded life, no one ever knows of her goodness, except her immediate con- xions. Others, on the contrary, are disposed to form unfavourable opinions

of her mind and disposition, if it be but to excuse themselves for their instinctive dislike of one so unfavoured by nature; and vice versa with her whose angel form conceals a vicious heart, or sheds a false, deceitful charm over defects and foibles that would not be tolerated in another. They that have beauty, let them be thankful for it, and make a good use of it, like any other talent; they that have it not, let them console themselves, and do the best they can without it certainly, though liable to be over-estimated, it is a gift of God, and not to be despised. Many will feel this who have felt that they could love, and whose hearts tell them that they are worthy to be loved again; while yet they are debarred by the lack of this or some such seeming trifle, from giving and receiving that happiness they seem almost made to feel and to impart. As well might the humble glow-worm despise that power of giving light without which the roving fly might pass her and repass her a thousand times, and never rest beside her: she might hear her winged darling buzzing over and around her he vainly seeking her, she longing to be found, but with no power to make her presence known, no voice to call him, no wings to follow his flight;—the fly must seek another mate, the worm must live and die alone.

Such were some of my reflections about this period. I might go on prosing more and more, I might dive much deeper, and disclose other thoughts propose questions the reader might be puzzled to answer, and deduce arguments that might startle his prejudices, or, perhaps, provoke his ridicule because he could not comprehend them; but I forbear.

Now, therefore, let us return to Miss Murray. She accompanied her mamma to the ball on Tuesday; of course splendidly attired, and delighted with her prospects and her charms. As Ashby Park was nearly ten miles distant from Horton Lodge, they had to set out pretty early, and I intended to have spent the evening with Nancy Brown, whom I had not seen for a long time; but my kind pupil took care I should spend it neither there nor anywhere else beyond the limits of the schoolroom, by giving me a piece of music to copy, which kept me closely occupied till bed-time. About eleven next morning, as soon as she had left her room, she came to tell me her news. Sir Thomas had indeed proposed to her at the ball: an event which reflected great credit on her mamma's sagacity, if not upon her skill in contrivance. I rather incline to the belief that she had first laid her plans, and then predicted their success. The offer had been accepted, of course, and the bridegroom elect was coming that day to settle matters with Mr. Murray.

Rosalie was pleased with the thoughts of becoming mistress of Ashby Park she was elated with the prospect of the bridal ceremony and its attendant splendour and éclat, the honeymoon spent abroad, and the subsequent gaieties she expected to enjoy in London and elsewhere; she appeared pretty well pleased too, for the time being, with Sir Thomas himself, because she had so lately seen him, danced with him, and been flattered by him; but, after all, she

emed to shrink from the idea of being so soon united: she wished the ceremony
be delayed some months, at least; and I wished it too. It seemed a horrible
ning to hurry on the inauspicious match, and not to give the poor creature
me to think and reason on the irrevocable step she was about to take. I made
o pretension to 'a mother's watchful, anxious care,' but I was amazed and
orrified at Mrs. Murray's heartlessness, or want of thought for the real good
f her child; and, by my unheeded warnings and exhortations, I vainly strove
remedy the evil. Miss Murray only laughed at what I said; and I soon
und that her reluctance to an immediate union arose chiefly from a desire
do what execution she could among the young gentlemen of her acquaint-
nce, before she was incapacitated from further mischief of the kind. It was
r this cause that, before confiding to me the secret of her engagement, she had
xtracted a promise that I would not mention a word on the subject to anyone.
nd when I saw this, and when I beheld her plunge more recklessly than ever
to the depths of heartless coquetry, I had no more pity for her. 'Come what
ill,' I thought, 'she deserves it. Sir Thomas cannot be too bad for her; and the
oner she is incapacitated from deceiving and injuring others the better.'

The wedding was fixed for the first of June. Between that and the critical
all was little more than six weeks; but, with Rosalie's accomplished skill and
solute exertion, much might be done, even within that period: especially as
ir Thomas spent most of the interim in London; whither he went up, it was
id, to settle affairs with his lawyer, and make other preparations for the
pproaching nuptials. He endeavoured to supply the want of his presence by
pretty constant fire of *billets-doux*; but these did not attract the neighbours'
ttention, and open their eyes, as personal visits would have done; and old
ady Ashby's haughty, sour spirit of reserve withheld her from spreading the
ws, while her indifferent health prevented her coming to visit her future
aughter-in-law; so that, altogether, this affair was kept far closer than such
ings usually are.

Rosalie would sometimes show her lover's epistles to me, to convince me
hat a kind, devoted husband he would make. She showed me the letters of
other individual, too, the unfortunate Mr. Green, who had not the courage,
, as she expressed it, the 'spunk,' to plead his cause in person, but whom one
nial would not satisfy: he must write again and again. He would not have
ne so if he could have seen the grimaces his fair idol made over his moving
peals to her feelings, and heard her scornful laughter, and the opprobrious
ithets she heaped upon him for his perseverance.

'Why don't you tell him, at once, that you are engaged?' I asked.

'Oh, I don't want him to know that,' replied she. 'If he knew it, his sisters
d everybody would know it, and then there would be an end of my—ahem!
nd, besides, if I told him that, he would think my engagement was the only
stacle, and that I would have him if I were free; which I could not bear that

any man should think, and he, of all others, at least. Besides, I don't care fo
his letters,' she added, contemptuously; 'he may write as often as he please
and look as great a calf as he likes when I meet him; it only amuses me.'

Meantime, young Meltham was pretty frequent in his visits to the house o
transits past it; and, judging by Matilda's execrations and reproaches, her siste
paid more attention to him than civility required: in other words, she carrie
on as animated a flirtation as the presence of her parents would admit. Sh
made some attempts to bring Mr. Hatfield once more to her feet; but findin
them unsuccessful, she repaid his haughty indifference with still loftier scorr
and spoke of him with as much disdain and detestation as she had formerl
done of his curate. But, amid all this, she never for a moment lost sight c
Mr. Weston. She embraced every opportunity of meeting him, tried every ar
to fascinate him, and pursued him with as much perseverance as if she reall
loved him and no other, and the happiness of her life depended upon elicitin
a return of affection. Such conduct was completely beyond my comprehensior
Had I seen it depicted in a novel, I should have thought in unnatural; ha
I heard it described by others, I should have deemed it a mistake or a
exaggeration; but when I saw it with my own eyes, and suffered from it too
I could only conclude that excessive vanity, like drunkeness, hardens the hear
enslaves the faculties, and perverts the feelings; and that dogs are not the onl
creatures which, when gorged to the throat, will yet gloat over what the
cannot devour, and grudge the smallest morsel to a starving brother.

She now became extremely beneficent to the poor cottagers. Her acquaintanc
among them was more widely extended, her visits to their humble dwelling
were more frequent and excursive than they had ever been before. Hereby
she earned among them the reputation of a condescending and very charitabl
young lady; and their encomiums were sure to be repeated to Mr. Westor
whom also she had thus a daily chance of meeting in one or other of thei
abodes, or in her transits to and fro; and often, likewise, she could gathe
through their gossip, to what places he was likely to go at such and suc
a time, whether to baptize a child, or to visit the aged, the sick, the sad, or th
dying; and most skilfully she laid her plans accordingly. In these excursior
she would sometimes go with her sister—whom, by some means, she ha
persuaded or bribed to enter into her schemes—sometimes alone, never, nov
with me; so that I was debarred the pleasure of seeing Mr. Weston, or hearin
his voice even in conversation with another: which would certainly have bee
a very great pleasure, however hurtful or however fraught with pain. I coul
not even see him at church: for Miss Murray, under some trivial pretext, chos
to take possession of that corner in the family pew which had been mine ev
since I came; and, unless I had the presumption to station myself betwee
Mr. and Mrs. Murray, I must sit with my back to the pulpit, which I accor
ingly did.

Now, also, I never walked home with my pupils: they said their mamma thought it did not look well to see three people out of the family walking, and only two going in the carriage; and, as they greatly preferred walking in fine weather, I should be honoured by going with the seniors. 'And, besides,' said they, 'you can't walk as fast as we do; you know you're always lagging behind.' I knew these were false excuses, but I made no objections, and never contradicted such assertions, well knowing the motives which dictated them. And in the afternoons, during those six memorable weeks, I never went to church at all. If I had a cold, or any slight indisposition, they took advantage of that to make me stay at home; and often they would tell me they were not going again that day, themselves, and then pretend to change their minds, and set off without telling me; so managing their departure that I never discovered the change of purpose till too late. Upon their return home, on one of these occasions, they entertained me with an animated account of a conversation they had had with Mr. Weston as they came along. 'And he asked if you were ill, Miss Grey,' said Matilda; 'but we told him you were quite well, only you didn't want to come to church—so he'll think you're turned wicked.'

All chance meetings on week-days were likewise carefully prevented; for, lest I should go to see poor Nancy Brown or any other person, Miss Murray took good care to provide sufficient employment for all my leisure hours. There was always some drawing to finish, some music to copy, or some work to do, sufficient to incapacitate me from indulging in anything beyond a short walk about the grounds, however she or her sister might be occupied.

One morning, having sought and waylaid Mr. Weston, they returned in high glee to give me an account of their interview. 'And he asked after you again,' said Matilda, in spite of her sister's silent but imperative intimation that she should hold her tongue. 'He wondered why you were never with us, and thought you must have delicate health, as you came out so seldom.'

'He didn't, Matilda—what nonsense you're talking!'

'Oh, Rosalie, what a lie! He did, you know; and you said—Don't, Rosalie—hang it!—I won't be pinched so! And, Miss Grey, Rosalie told him you were quite well, but you were always so buried in your books that you had no pleasure in anything else.'

'What an idea he must have of me!' I thought.

'And,' I asked, 'does old Nancy ever inquire about me?'

'Yes; and we tell her you are so fond of reading and drawing that you can do nothing else.'

'That is not the case though; if you had told her I was so busy I *could* not come to see her, it would have been nearer the truth.'

'I don't think it would,' replied Miss Murray, suddenly kindling up; 'I'm sure you have plenty of time to yourself now, when you have so little teaching to do.'

It was no use beginning to dispute with such indulged, unreasoning creatures so I held my peace. I was accustomed, now, to keeping silence when thing distasteful to my ear were uttered; and now, too, I was used to wearing a placid smiling countenance when my heart was bitter within me. Only those who have felt the like can imagine my feelings, as I sat with an assumption of smiling indifference, listening to the accounts of those meetings and interview with Mr. Weston, which they seemed to find such pleasure in describing to me and hearing things asserted of him which, from the character of the man I knew to be exaggerations and perversions of the truth, if not entirely false—things derogatory to him, and flattering to them—especially to Miss Murray—which I burned to contradict, or, at least, to show my doubts about, but dare not; lest, in expressing my disbelief, I should display my interest too. Other things I heard, which I felt or feared were indeed too true: but I must still conceal my anxiety respecting him, my indignation against them, beneath a careless aspect; others, again, mere hints of something said or done, which I longed to hear more of, but could not venture to inquire. So passed the weary time. I could not even comfort myself with saying. 'She will soon be married; and then there may be hope.'

Soon after her marriage the holidays would come; and when I returned from home, most likely, Mr. Weston would be gone, for I was told that he and the Rector could not agree (the Rector's fault, of course), and he was about to remove to another place.

No—besides my hope in God, my only consolation was in thinking that though he knew it not, I was more worthy of his love than Rosalie Murray charming and engaging as she was; for I could appreciate his excellence, which she could not: I would devote my life to the promotion of his happiness; she would destroy his happiness for the momentary gratification of her own vanity 'Oh, if he could but know the difference!' I would earnestly exclaim. 'But no I would not have him see my heart: yet, if he could but know her hollowness her worthless, heartless frivolity, he would then be safe, and I should be *almost* happy, though I might never see him more!'

I fear, by this time, the reader is wellnigh disgusted with the folly and weakness I have so freely laid before him. I never disclosed it then, and would not have done so had my own sister or my mother been with me in the house I was a close and resolute dissembler—in this one case at least. My prayer my tears, my wishes, fears, and lamentations, were witnessed by myself and heaven alone.

When we are harassed by sorrows or anxieties, or long oppressed by any powerful feelings which we must keep to ourselves, for which we can obtain and seek no sympathy from any living creature, and which yet we cannot, or will not wholly crush, we often naturally seek relief in poetry—and often find it, too —whether in the effusions of others, which seem to harmonize with our

existing case, or in our own attempts to give utterance to those thoughts and feelings in strains less musical, perchance, but more appropriate, and therefore more penetrating and sympathetic, and, for the time, more soothing, or more powerful to rouse and to unburden the oppressed and swollen heart. Before this time, at Wellwood House and here, when suffering from home-sick melancholy, I had sought relief twice or thrice at this secret source of consolation; and now I flew to it again, with greater avidity than ever, because I seemed to need it more. I still preserve those relics of past sufferings and experience, like pillars of witness set up in travelling through the vale of life, to mark particular occurrences. The footsteps are obliterated now; the face of the country may be changed; but the pillar is still there, to remind me how all things were when it was reared. Lest the reader should be curious to see any of these effusions, I will favour him with one short specimen: cold and languid as the lines may seem, it was almost a passion of grief to which they owed their being.

> O, they have robbed me of the hope
> My spirit held so dear,
> They will not let me hear that voice
> My soul delights to hear.
>
> They will not let me see that face
> I so delight to see;
> And they have taken all thy smiles,
> And all thy love from me.
>
> Well, let them seize on all they can;—
> One treasure still is mine,—
> A heart that loves to think on thee,
> And feels the worth of thine.

Yes, at least, they could not deprive me of that: I could think of him day and night; and I could feel that he was worthy to be thought of. Nobody knew him as I did; nobody could appreciate him as I did; nobody could love him as I—could, if I might: but there was the evil. What business had I to think so much of one that never thought of me? Was it not foolish? was it not wrong? Yet, if I found such deep delight in thinking of him, and if I kept those thoughts to myself, and troubled no one else with them, where was the harm of it? I would ask myself. And such reasoning prevented me from making any sufficient effort to shake off my fetters.

But, if those thoughts brought delight, it was a painful, troubled pleasure, so near akin to anguish; and one that did me more injury than I was aware of. It was an indulgence that a person of more wisdom or more experience would doubtless have denied herself. And yet, how dreary to turn my eyes from the contemplation of that bright object and force them to dwell on the dull, grey, desolate prospect around: the joyless, hopeless, solitary path that lay

before me. It was wrong to be so joyless, so desponding; I should have made God my friend, and to do His will the pleasure and the business of my life but faith was weak, and passion was too strong.

In this time of trouble I had two other causes of affliction. The first may seem a trifle, but it cost me many a tear: Snap, my little dumb, rough-visaged but bright-eyed, warm-hearted companion, the only thing I had to love me was taken away, and delivered over to the tender mercies of the village rat catcher, a man notorious for his brutal treatment of his canine slaves. The other was serious enough: my letters from home gave intimation that my father's health was worse. No boding fears were expressed, but I was grown timid and despondent, and could not help fearing that some dreadful calamity awaited us there. I seemed to see the black clouds gathering round my native hills, and to hear the angry muttering of a storm that was about to burst, and desolate our hearth.

CHAPTER 18

MIRTH AND MOURNING

The 1st of June arrived at last: and Rosalie Murray was transmuted into Lady Ashby. Most splendidly beautiful she looked in her bridal costume. Upon her return from church, after the ceremony, she came flying into the schoolroom flushed with excitement, and laughing, half in mirth, and half in reckless desperation, as it seemed to me.

'Now, Miss Grey, I'm Lady Ashby!' she exclaimed. 'It's done, my fate is sealed: there's no drawing back now. I'm come to receive your congratulations and bid you good-bye; and then I'm off for Paris, Rome, Naples, Switzerland, London—oh, dear! what a deal I shall see and hear before I come back again. But don't forget me: I shan't forget you, though I've been a naughty girl. Come, why don't you congratulate me?'

'I cannot congratulate you,' I replied, 'till I know whether this change is really for the better; but I sincerely hope it is; and I wish you true happiness and the best of blessings.'

'Well, good-bye, the carriage is waiting, and they're calling me.'

She gave me a hasty kiss, and was hurrying away; but, suddenly returning, embraced me with more affection than I thought her capable of evincing, and departed with tears in her eyes. Poor girl! I really loved her then; and forgave her from my heart all the injury she had done me—and others also: she had not half known it, I was sure; and I prayed God to pardon her too.

During the remainder of that day of festal sadness, I was left to my own devices. Being too much unhinged for any steady occupation, I wandered

bout with a book in my hand for several hours, more thinking than reading,
r I had many things to think about. In the evening, I made use of my
berty to go and see my old friend Nancy once again; to apologize for my
ng absence (which must have seemed so neglectful and unkind) by telling
e how busy I had been; and to talk, or read, or work for her, whichever
ight be most acceptable, and also, of course, to tell her the news of this im-
ortant day: and perhaps to obtain a little information from her in return,
specting Mr. Weston's expected departure. But of this she seemed to know
othing, and I hoped, as she did, that it was all a false report. She was very
ad to see me; but, happily, her eyes were now so nearly well that she was
most independent of my services. She was deeply interested in the wedding;
ut while I amused her with the details of the festive day, the splendours
the bridal party and of the bride herself, she often sighed and shook her head,
nd wished good might come of it; she seemed, like me, to regard it rather
a theme for sorrow than rejoicing. I sat a long time talking to her about
at and other things—but *no one came.*

Shall I confess that I sometimes looked towards the door with a half-expectant
ish to see it open and give entrance to Mr. Weston, as had happened once
fore? and that, returning through the lanes and fields, I often paused to
ok round me, and walked more slowly than was at all necessary—for,
ough a fine evening, it was not a hot one—and, finally, felt a sense of empti-
ss and disappointment at having reached the house without meeting or
en catching a distant glimpse of anyone, except a few labourers returning
om their work?

Sunday, however, was approaching: I should see him then: for now that
iss Murray was gone, I could have my old corner again. I should see him,
d by look, speech, and manner, I might judge whether the circumstance
her marriage had very much afflicted him. Happily, I could perceive no
adow of a difference: he wore the same aspect as he had worn two months
o—voice, look, manner, all alike unchanged: there was the same keen-
hted, unclouded truthfulness in his discourse, the same forcible clearness
his style, the same earnest simplicity in all he said and did, that made itself,
t marked by the eye and ear, but felt upon the hearts of his audience.
I walked home with Miss Matilda; but *he did not join us.* Matilda was now
dly at a loss for amusement, and woefully in want of a companion: her broth-
s at school, her sister married and gone, she too young to be admitted
to society; for which, from Rosalie's example, she was in some degree
ginning to acquire a taste—a taste at least for the company of certain
sses of gentlemen; at this dull time of year—no hunting going on, no shooting
en—for, though she might not join in that, it was *something* to see her father
the gamekeeper go out with the dogs, and to talk with them on their return,
out the different birds they had bagged. Now, also, she was denied the solace

which the companionship of the coachman, grooms, horses, greyhounds and pointers might have afforded; for her mother having, notwithstanding the disadvantages of a country life, so satisfactorily disposed of her elder daughter, the pride of her heart had begun seriously to turn her attention to the younger; and, being truly alarmed at the roughness of her manners, and thinking it high time to work a reform, had been roused at length to exert her authority, and prohibited entirely the yards, stables, kennels, and coach house. Of course, she was not implicitly obeyed; but, indulgent as she had hitherto been, when once her spirit was roused, her temper was not so gentle as she required that of her governesses to be, and her will was not to be thwarted with impunity. After many a scene of contention between mother and daughter, many a violent outbreak which I was ashamed to witness, in which the father's authority was often called in to confirm with oaths and threats the mother's slighted prohibitions—for even *he* could see that 'Tilly, though she would have made a fine lad, was not quite what a young lady ought to be'— Matilda at length found that her easiest plan was to keep clear of the forbidden regions; unless she could now and then steal a visit without her watchful mother's knowledge.

Amid all this, let it not be imagined that I escaped without many a reprimand, and many an implied reproach, that lost none of its sting from not being openly worded; but rather wounded the more deeply, because, from that very reason, it seemed to preclude self-defence. Frequently, I was told to amuse Miss Matilda with other things, and to *remind* her of her mother's precepts and prohibitions. I did so to the best of my power: but she would not be amused against her will, and could not against her taste; and though I went beyond mere reminding, such gentle remonstrances as I could use were utterly ineffectual.

'*Dear* Miss Grey! it is the *strangest* thing. I suppose you can't help it, if it is not in your nature—but I *wonder* you can't win the confidence of that girl, and make your society at *least* as agreeable to her as that of Robert or Joseph.'

'They can talk the best about the things in which she is most interested,' I replied.

'Well! that is a strange confession, *however*, to come from her *governess.* Who is to form a young lady's tastes, I wonder, if the governess doesn't do it? I *have* known governesses who have so completely identified themselves with the reputation of their young ladies for elegance and propriety in mind and manners, that they would *blush* to speak a word against them; and to hear the slightest blame imputed to their pupils was worse than to be censured in their own persons—and I really think it very natural, for my part.'

'Do you, ma'am?'

'Yes, of course: the young lady's proficiency and elegance is of more consequence to the governess than her own, as well as to the world. If she wishes

prosper in her vocation she must devote all her energies to her business: all her ideas and all her ambition will tend to the accomplishment of that one object. When we wish to decide upon the merits of a governess, we naturally look at the young ladies she professes to have educated, and judge accordingly. The *judicious* governess knows this: she knows that, while she lives in obscurity herself, her pupil's virtues and defects will be open to every eye; and that, unless she loses sight of herself in their cultivation, she need not hope for success. You see Miss Grey, it is just the same as any other trade or profession: they that wish to prosper must devote themselves body and soul to their calling; and if they begin to yield to indolence or self-indulgence they are speedily distanced by wiser competitors: there is little to choose between a person that ruins her pupils by neglect, and one that corrupts them by her example. You will excuse my dropping these little hints: you know it is all for your own good. Many ladies would speak to you much more strongly; and many would not trouble themselves to speak at all, but quietly look out for a substitute. That, of course, would be the *easiest* plan: but I know the advantages of a place like this to a person in your situation; and I have no desire to part with you, as I am sure you would do very well if you will only think of these things and try to exert yourself a *little* more: then, I am convinced, you would *soon* acquire that delicate tact which alone is wanting to give you a proper influence over the mind of your pupil.'

I was about to give the lady some idea of the fallacy of her expectations; but she sailed away as soon as she had concluded her speech. Having said what she wished, it was no part of her plan to await my answer: it was my business to hear, and not to speak.

However, as I have said, Matilda at length yielded in some degree to her mother's authority (pity it had not been exerted before); and being thus deprived of almost every source of amusement, there was nothing for it but to take long rides with the groom and long walks with the governess, and to visit the cottages and farm-houses on her father's estate, to kill time in chatting with the old men and women that inhabited them. In one of these walks, it was our chance to meet Mr. Weston. This was what I had long desired; but now, for a moment, I wished either he or I were away: I felt my heart throb so violently that I dreaded lest some outwards signs of emotion should appear; but I think he hardly glanced at me, and I was soon calm enough. After a brief salutation to both, he asked Matilda if she had lately heard from her sister.

'Yes,' replied she. 'She was at Paris when she wrote, and very well, and very happy.'

She spoke the last word emphatically, and with a glance impertinently sly. He did not seem to notice it, but replied, with equal emphasis, and very seriously—

'I hope she will continue to be so.'

'Do you think it likely?' I ventured to inquire: for Matilda had started o‹ in pursuit of her dog, that was chasing a leveret.

'I cannot tell,' replied he. 'Sir Thomas may be a better man than I suppose but, from all I have heard and seen, it seems a pity that one so young and gay and—and *interesting*, to express many things by one word—whose greates‹ if not her only fault, appears to be thoughtlessness—no trifling fault to b‹ sure, since it renders the possessor liable to almost every other, and expose‹ him to so many temptations: but it seems a pity that she should be throw‹ away on such a man. It was her mother's wish, I suppose?'

'Yes; and her own too, I think, for she always laughed at my attempts t‹ dissuade her from the step.'

'You did attempt it? Then, at least, you will have the satisfaction of know‹ ing that it is no fault of yours, if any harm should come of it. As for Mr‹ Murray, I don't know how she can justify her conduct: if I had sufficien‹ acquaintance with her, I'd ask her.'

'It seems unnatural: but some people think rank and wealth the chief good‹ and, if they can secure that for their children, they think they have don‹ their duty.'

'True: but is it not strange that persons of experience, who have been marrie‹ themselves, should judge so falsely?'

Matilda now came panting back, with the lacerated body of the young ha‹ in her hand.

'Was it your intention to kill that hare, or to save it, Miss Murray‹ asked Mr. Weston, apparently puzzled at her gleeful countenance.

'I pretended to want to save it,' she answered, honestly enough, 'as it wa‹ so glaringly out of season; but I was better pleased to see it killed. Howeve‹ you can both witness that I couldn't help it: Prince was determined to hav‹ her; and he clutched her by the back, and killed her in a minute! Wasn‹ it a noble chase?'

'Very! for a young lady after a leveret.'

There was a quiet sarcasm in the tone of his reply which was not lost up‹ her; she shrugged her shoulders, and, turning away with a significant 'Humph‹ asked me how I had enjoyed the fun. I replied that I saw no fun in the matte‹ but admitted that I had not observed the transaction very narrowly.

'Didn't you see how it doubled—just like an old hare? and didn't you he‹ it scream?'

'I'm happy to say I did not.'

'It cried out just like a child.'

'Poor little thing! What will you do with it?'

'Come along—I shall leave it in the first house we come to. I don't want‹ take it home, for fear papa should scold me for letting the dog kill it.'

Mr. Weston was now gone, and we too went on our way; but as we returned, after having deposited the hare in a farm-house, and demolished some spice-cake and currant wine in exchange, we met him returning also from the execution of his mission, whatever it might be. He carried in his hand a cluster of beautiful bluebells which he offered to me; observing, with a smile, that though he had seen so little of me for the last two months, he had not forgotten that bluebells were numbered among my favourite flowers. It was done as a simple act of goodwill, without compliment or remarkable courtesy, or any look that could be construed into 'reverential, tender adoration' (*vide* Rosalie Murray); but still, it was something to find my unimportant saying so well remembered: it was something that he had noticed so accurately the time had ceased to be visible.

'I was told,' said he, 'that you were a perfect bookworm, Miss Grey: so completely absorbed in your studies that you were lost to every other pleasure.'

'Yes, and it's quite true!' cried Matilda.

'No, Mr. Weston; don't believe it: it's a scandalous libel. These young ladies are too fond of making random assertions at the expense of their friends; and you ought to be careful how you listen to them.'

'I hope *this* assertion is groundless, at any rate.'

'Why? Do you particularly object to ladies' studying?'

'No; but I object to anyone so devoting himself or herself to study, as to lose sight of everything else. Except under peculiar circumstances, I consider very close and constant study as a waste of time, and an injury to the mind as well as the body.'

'Well, I have neither the time nor the inclination for such transgressions.'

We parted again.

Well! what is there remarkable in all this? Why have I recorded it? Because, reader, it was important enough to give me a cheerful evening, a night of pleasing dreams, and a morning of felicitous hopes. Shallow-brained cheerfulness, foolish dreams, unfounded hopes, you would say; and I will not venture to deny it: suspicions to that effect arose too frequently in my own mind. But our wishes are like tinder: the flint and steel of circumstances are continually striking out sparks, which vanish immediately, unless they chance to fall upon the tinder of our wishes; then, they instantly ignite, and the flame of hope is kindled in a moment.

But alas! that very morning, my flickering flame of hope was dismally quenched by a letter from my mother, which spoke so seriously of my father's increasing illness, that I feared there was little or no chance of his recovery; and, close at hand as the holidays were, I almost trembled lest they should come too late for me to meet him in this world. Two days after, a letter from Mary told me his life was despaired of, and his end seemed fast approaching. Then, immediately, I sought permission to anticipate the vacation, and

go without delay. Mrs. Murray stared, and wondered at the unwonted energy and boldness with which I urged the request, and thought there was no occasion to hurry; but finally gave me leave: stating, however, that there was 'no need to be in such agitation about the matter—it might prove a false alarm after all; and if not—why, it was only in the common course of nature we must all die some time; and I was not to suppose myself the only afflicted person in the world'; and concluding with saying I might have the phaeton to take me to O——. 'And instead of *repining*, Miss Grey, be thankful for the *privileges* you enjoy. There's many a poor clergyman whose family would be plunged into ruin by the event of his death; but *you*, you see, have influential friends ready to continue their patronage, and to show you every consideration.'

I thanked her for her 'consideration,' and flew to my room to make some hurried preparations for my departure. My bonnet and shawl being on, and a few things hastily crammed into my largest trunk, I descended. But I might have done the work more leisurely, for no one else was in a hurry and I had still a considerable time to wait for the phaeton. At length it came to the door, and I was off: but, oh, what a dreary journey was that! how utterly different from my former passages homewards! Being too late for the last coach to ——, I had to hire a cab for ten miles, and then a car to take me over the rugged hills. It was half-past ten before I reached home. They were not in bed.

My mother and sister both met me in the passage—sad—silent—pale I was so much shocked and terror-stricken that I could not speak, to ask the information I so much longed yet dreaded to obtain.

'Agnes?' said my mother, struggling to repress some strong emotion.

'Oh, Agnes!' cried Mary, and burst into tears.

'How is he?' I asked, gasping for the answer.

'Dead!'

It was the reply I had anticipated: but the shock seemed none the less tremendous.

CHAPTER 19

THE LETTER

My father's mortal remains had been consigned to the tomb; and we, with sad faces and sombre garments, sat lingering over the frugal breakfast-table revolving plans for our future life. My mother's strong mind had not given way beneath even this affliction: her spirit, though crushed, was not broken Mary's wish was that I should go back to Horton Lodge, and that our mother

hould come and live with her and Mr. Richardson at the vicarage: she
ffirmed that he wished it no less than herself, and that such an arrange-
ment could not fail to benefit all parties; for my mother's society and expe-
ience would be of inestimable value to them, and they would do all they
ould to make her happy. But no arguments or entreaties could prevail:
my mother was determined not to go. Not that she questioned, for a moment,
he kind wishes and intentions of her daughter; but she affirmed that so
ong as God spared her health and strength, she would make use of them
o earn her own livelihood, and be chargeable to no one; whether her depen-
ence would be felt as a burden or not. If she could afford to reside as a lodger
n —— vicarage, she would choose that house before all others as the place of
er abode; but not being so circumstanced, she would never come under
ts roof, except as an occasional visitor: unless sickness or calamity should
ender her assistance really needful, or until age or infirmity made her
ncapable of maintaining herself.

'No, Mary,' said she, 'if Richardson and you have anything to spare, you
must lay it aside for your family; and Agnes and I must gather honey for
urselves. Thanks to my having had daughters to educate, I have not for-
otten my accomplishments. God willing, I will check this vain repining,'
-she said, while the tears coursed one another down her cheeks in spite of
er efforts; but she wiped them away, and resolutely shaking back her head,
ontinued, 'I will exert myself, and look out for a small house, commodiously
tuated in some populous but healthy district, where we will take a few young
adies to board and educate—if we can get them—and as many day-pupils
s will come, or as we can manage to instruct. Your father's relations and old
iends will be able to send us some pupils, or to assist us with their recom-
nendations, no doubt: I shall not apply to my own. What say you to it,
gnes? will you be willing to leave your present situation and try?'

'Quite willing, mamma; and the money I have saved will do to furnish
he house. It shall be taken from the bank directly.'

'When it is wanted: we must get the house, and settle all preliminaries first.'
Mary offered to lend the little she possessed; but my mother declined it,
aying, that we must begin on an economical plan; and she hoped that the
hole or part of mine, added to what we could get by the sale of the furniture,
nd what little our dear papa had contrived to lay aside for her since the debts
ere paid, would be sufficient to last us till Christmas; when, it was hoped,
omething would accrue from our united labours. It was finally settled that
is should be our plan; and that inquiries and preparations should immedia-
ly be set on foot; and while my mother busied herself with these, I should
turn to Horton Lodge at the close of my four weeks' vacation, and give
otice for my final departure when things were in train for the speedy com-
encement of our school.

We were discussing these affairs on the morning I have mentioned, abou a fortnight after my father's death, when a letter was brought in for m mother, on beholding which the colour mounted to her face—lately pal enough with anxious watchings and excessive sorrow. 'From my father! murmured she, as she hastily tore off the cover. It was many years since sh had heard from any of her own relations before. Naturally wondering wha the letter might contain, I watched her countenance while she read it, and wa somewhat surprised to see her bite her lip and knit her brows as if in anger When she had done, she somewhat irreverently cast it on the table, sayin with a scornful smile,—'Your grandpapa has been so kind as to write t me. He says he has no doubt I have long repented of my "unfortunate mar riage," and if I will only acknowledge this, and confess I was wrong in neg lecting his advice, and that I have justly suffered for it, he will make a lad of me once again—if that be possible after my long degradation—and remem ber my girls in his will. Get my desk, Agnes, and send these things away I will answer the letter directly. But first, as I may be depriving you bot of a legacy, it is just that I should tell you what I mean to say. I shall sa that he is mistaken in supposing that I can regret the birth of my daughter (who have been the pride of my life, and are likely to be the comfort of m old age), or the thirty years I have passed in the company of my best and deare friend;—that, had our misfortunes been three times as great as they wer (unless they had been of my bringing on), I should still the more rejoice t have shared them with your father, and administered what consolation I wa able; and, had his sufferings in illness been ten times what they were, I coul not regret having watched over and laboured to relieve them;—that, he had married a richer wife, misfortunes and trials would no doubt hav come upon him still; while I am egotist enough to imagine that no othe woman could have cheered him through them so well: not that I am superic to the rest, but I was made for him, and he for me; and I can no more repen the hours, days, years of happiness we have spent together, and which neithe could have had without the other, than I can the privilege of having been h nurse in sickness, and his comfort in affliction.

'Will this do, children?—or shall I say we are all very sorry for what ha happened during the last thirty years, and my daughters wish they ha never been born; but since they have had that misfortune, they will be thankf for any trifle their grandpapa will be kind enough to bestow?'

Of course, we both applauded our mother's resolution; Mary cleared awa the breakfast things; I brought the desk; the letter was quickly written an dispatched; and, from that day, we heard no more of our grandfather, ti we saw his death announced in the newspaper a considerable time after— all his worldly possessions, of course, being left to our wealthy, unknow cousins.

CHAPTER 20

THE FAREWELL

house in A——, the fashionable watering-place, was hired for our seminary;
d a promise of two or three pupils was obtained to commence with. I re-
rned to Horton Lodge about the middle of July, leaving my mother to
nclude the bargain for the house, to obtain more pupils, to sell off the
rniture of our old abode, and to fit out the new one.

We often pity the poor, because they have no leisure to mourn their departed
latives, and necessity obliges them to labour through their severest afflictions:
t is not active employment the best remedy for overwhelming sorrow—the
rest antidote for despair? It may be a rough comforter: it may seem hard to
harassed with the cares of life when we have no relish for its enjoyments; to
goaded to labour when the heart is ready to break, and the vexed spirit
plores for rest only to weep in silence: but is not labour better than the rest
covet? and are not those petty, tormenting cares less hurtful than a con-
ual brooding over the great affliction that oppresses us? Besides, we cannot
ve cares, and anxieties, and toil, without hope—if it be but the hope of
filling our joyless task, accomplishing some needful project, or escaping
me further annoyance. At any rate, I was glad my mother had so much
ployment for every faculty of her action-loving frame. Our kind neighbours
mented that she, once so exalted in wealth and station, should be reduced to
ch extremity in her time of sorrow; but I am persuaded that she would have
ffered thrice as much had she been left in affluence, with liberty to remain in
at house, the scene of her early happiness and late affliction, and no stern
cessity to prevent her from incessantly brooding over and lamenting her
reavement.

I will not dilate upon the feelings with which I left the old house, the well-
own garden, the little village church—then doubly dear to me, because my
ther, who, for thirty years, had taught and prayed within its walls, lay
mbering now beneath its flags—and the old bare hills, delightful in their
ry desolation, with the narrow vales between, smiling in green wood and
arkling water—the house where I was born, the scene of all my early associa-
ns, the place where throughout life my earthly affections had been centred;
and left them to return no more! True, I was going back to Horton Lodge,
ere, amid many evils, one source of pleasure yet remained: but it was
easure mingled with excessive pain; and my stay, alas! was limited to six
eks. And even of that precious time, day after day slipped by and I did not
him: except at church, I never saw him for a fortnight after my return.
seemed a long time to me: and, as I was often out with my rambling pupil,
course hopes would keep rising, and disappointments would ensue; and,

then, I would say to my own heart, 'Here is a convincing proof—if you woul
but have the sense to see it, or the candour to acknowledge it—that he does no
care for you. If he only thought *half* as much about you as you do about him
he would have contrived to meet you many times ere this: you must know tha
by consulting your own feelings. Therefore, have done with this nonsense
you have no ground for hope: dismiss, at once, these hurtful thoughts an
foolish wishes from your mind, and turn to your own duty, and the dull blan
life that lies before you. You might have *known* such happiness was no
for you.'

But I saw him at last. He came suddenly upon me as I was crossing a fiel
in returning from a visit to Nancy Brown, which I had taken the opportunity o
paying while Matilda Murray was riding her matchless mare. He must hav
heard of the heavy loss I had sustained: he expressed no sympathy, offered n
condolence: but almost the first words he uttered were,—'How is your mother
And this was no matter-of-course question, for I never told him that I ha
a mother: he must have learned the fact from others, if he knew it at al
and, besides, there was sincere goodwill, and even deep, touching, unobtrusi
sympathy in the tone and manner of the inquiry. I thanked him with du
civility, and told him she was as well as could be expected. 'What will she do
was the next question. Many would have deemed it an impertinent one, an
given an evasive reply; but such an idea never entered my head, and I ga
a brief but plain statement of mother's plans and prospects.

'Then you will leave this place shortly?' said he.

'Yes, in a month.'

He paused a minute, as if in thought. When he spoke again, I hoped it wou
be to express his concern at my departure; but it was only to say—'I shou
think you will be willing enough to go?'

'Yes—for some things,' I replied.

'For *some* things only—I wonder what should make you regret it!'

I *was* annoyed at this in some degree; because it embarrassed me: I had on
one reason for regretting it; and that was a profound secret, which he had n
business to trouble me about.

'Why,' said I—'why should you suppose that I dislike the place?'

'You told me so yourself,' was the decisive reply. 'You said, at least, that y
could not live contentedly, without a friend; and that you had no friend he
and no possibility of making one—and besides, I know you *must* dislike it.'

'But if you remember rightly, I said, or meant to say, I could not li
contentedly without a friend in the *world*: I was not so unreasonable as
require one always near me. I think I could be happy in a house full of enemi
if——' but no; that sentence must not be continued—I paused, and hast
added—'And besides, we cannot well leave a place where we have lived
two or three years, without some feeling of regret.'

726

'Will you regret to part with Miss Murray, your sole remaining pupil and companion?'

'I dare say I shall in some degree: it was not without sorrow I parted with her sister.'

'I can imagine that.'

'Well, Miss Matilda is quite as good—better, in one respect.'

'What is that?'

'She's honest.'

'And the other is not?'

'I should not call her *dis*honest; but it must be confessed, she's a little artful.'

'*Artful* is she?—I saw she was giddy and vain—and now,' he added, after pause, 'I can well believe she was artful too; but so excessively so as to assume n aspect of extreme simplicity and unguarded openness. Yes,' continued he, ausingly, 'that accounts for some little things that puzzled me a trifle before.'

After that, he turned the conversation to more general subjects. He did not eve me till we had nearly reached the park gates: he had certainly stepped little out of his way to accompany me so far, for he now went back and isappeared down Mosslane, the entrance of which we had passed some time efore. Assuredly I did not regret this circumstance: if sorrow had any place a my heart, it was that he was gone at last—that he was no longer walking by y side, and that that short interval of delightful intercourse was at an end. Ie had not breathed a word of love, or dropped one hint of tenderness or ffection, and yet I had been supremely happy. To be near him, to hear him lk as he did talk; and to feel that he thought me worthy to be so spoken to— apable of understanding and duly appreciating such discourse—was enough.

'Yes, Edward Weston, I could indeed be happy in a house full of enemies, if had but one friend, who truly, deeply, and faithfully loved me; and if that iend were you—though we might be far apart—seldom to hear from each ther, still more seldom to meet—though toil, and trouble, and vexation might rround me, still—it would be too much happiness for me to dream of! Yet ho can tell,' said I within myself, as I proceeded up the park,—'who can tell hat this one month may bring forth? I have lived nearly three-and-twenty ars, and I have suffered much, and tasted little pleasure yet: is it likely my e all through will be so clouded? Is it not possible that God may hear my ayers, disperse these gloomy shadows, and grant me some beams of heaven's nshine yet? Will he entirely deny to me those blessings which are so freely ven to others, who neither ask them nor acknowledge them when received? ay I not still hope and trust?' I did hope and trust for a while: but, alas, alas! e time ebbed away: one week followed another, and, excepting one distant impse and two transient meetings—during which scarcely anything was said while I was walking with Miss Matilda, I saw nothing of him: except, of urse, at church.

And now, the last Sunday was come, and the last service. I was often on the point of melting into tears during the sermon—the last I was to hear from him: the best I should hear from anyone, I was well assured. It was over—the congregation were departing; and I must follow. I had then seen him, and heard his voice, too, probably for the last time. In the churchyard, Matilda was pounced upon by the two Misses Green. They had many inquiries to make about her sister, and I know not what besides. I only wished they would have done, that we might hasten back to Horton Lodge: I longed to seek the retirement of my own room, or some sequestered nook in the grounds, that I might deliver myself up to my feelings—to weep my last farewell, and lament my false hopes and vain delusions. Only this once, and then adieu to fruitless dreaming—thenceforth, only sober, solid, sad reality should occupy my mind. But while I thus resolved, a low voice close beside me said—'I suppose you are going this week, Miss Grey?' 'Yes,' I replied. I was very much startled; and had I been at all hysterically inclined, I certainly should have committed myself in some way then. Thank God, I was not.

'Well,' said Mr. Weston, 'I want to bid you good-bye—it is not likely I shall see you again before you go.'

'Good-bye, Mr. Weston,' I said. Oh, how I struggled to say it calmly! I gave him my hand. He retained it a few seconds in his.

'It is possible we may meet again,' said he; 'will it be of any consequence to you whether we do or not?'

'Yes, I should be very glad to see you again.'

I *could* say no less. He kindly pressed my hand, and went. Now, I was happy again—though more inclined to burst into tears than ever. If I had been forced to speak at that moment, a succession of sobs would have inevitably ensued; and as it was, I could not keep the water out of my eyes. I walked along with Miss Murray, turning aside my face, and neglecting to notice several successive remarks, till she bawled out that I was either deaf or stupid; and then (having recovered my self-possession), as one awakened from a fit of abstraction, I suddenly looked up and asked what she had been saying.

CHAPTER 21

THE SCHOOL

I left Horton Lodge, and went to join my mother in our new abode at A——. I found her well in health, resigned in spirit, and even cheerful, though subdued and sober, in her general demeanour. We had only three boarders and half a dozen day-pupils to commence with; but by due care and diligence we hoped ere long to increase the number of both.

I set myself with befitting energy to discharge the duties of this new mode of
life. I call it *new,* for there was, indeed, a considerable difference between
working with my mother in a school of our own, and working as a hireling
among strangers, despised and trampled upon by old and young; and for the
first few weeks I was by no means unhappy. 'It is possible we may meet again,'
and 'will it be of any consequence to you whether we do or not?'—Those
words still rang in my ear and rested on my heart: they were my secret solace
and support. 'I shall see him again.—He will come; or he will write.' No pro-
mise, in fact, was too bright or too extravagant for Hope to whisper in my ear.
I did not believe half of what she told me: I pretended to laugh at it all; but
I was far more credulous than I myself supposed; otherwise, why did my heart
leap up when a knock was heard at the front door, and the maid, who opened
it, came to tell my mother a gentleman wished to see her? and why was I out
of humour for the rest of the day, because it proved to be a music-master
come to offer his services to our school? and what stopped my breath for
a moment, when the postman having brought a couple of letters, my mother
said, 'Here Agnes, this is for you,' and threw one of them to me? and what
made the hot blood rush into my face when I saw it was directed in a gentle-
man's hand? and why?—oh! why did that cold, sickening sense of disappoint-
ment fall upon me, when I had torn open the cover and found it was *only*
a letter from Mary, which, for some reason or other, her husband had directed
for her?

Was it then come to this—that I should be *disappointed* to receive a letter
from my only sister: and because it was not written by a comparative stranger?
Dear Mary! and she had written it so kindly—and thinking I should be so
pleased to have it!—I was not worthy to read it! And I believe, in my indigna-
tion against myself, I should have put it aside till I had schooled myself into
a better frame of mind, and was become more deserving of the honour and
privilege of its perusal: but there was my mother looking on, and wishful to
know what news it contained; so I read it and delivered it to her, and then went
into the schoolroom to attend to the pupils: but amidst the cares of copies and
sums—in the intervals of correcting errors here, and reproving derelictions of
duty there, I was inwardly taking myself to task with far sterner severity.
'What a fool you must be,' said my head to my heart, or my sterner to my softer
self;—'how could you ever dream that he would write to *you*? What grounds
have you for such a hope—or that he will see you, or give himself any trouble
about you—or even think of you again?' 'What grounds?'—and then Hope
set before me that last, short interview, and repeated the words I had so faith-
fully treasured in my memory. 'Well, and what was there in that?—Who ever
hung his hopes upon so frail a twig? What was there in those words that any
common acquaintance might not say to another? Of course, it was possible you
might meet again: he might have said so if you had been going to New Zea-

land; but that did not imply any *intention* of seeing you—and then, as to th
question that followed, anyone might ask that: and how did you answer?—
Merely with a stupid, commonplace reply, such as you would have given t
Master Murray, or anyone else you had been on tolerably civil terms with
'But, then,' persisted Hope, 'the tone and manner in which he spoke.' 'Oh, tha
is nonsense! he always speaks impressively; and at that moment there were th
Greens and Miss Matilda Murray just before, and other people passing by, an
he was obliged to stand close beside you, and to speak very low, unless h
wished everybody to hear what he said; which—though it was nothing at a
particular—of course, he would rather not.' But then, above all, that emphatic
yet gentle pressure of the hand, which seemed to say, '*Trust me;*' and man
other things besides—too delightful, almost too flattering, to be repeated eve
to oneself. 'Egregious folly—too absurd to require contradiction—mere inven
tions of the imagination, which you ought to be ashamed of. If you would bu
consider your own unattractive exterior, your unamiable reserve, your foolis
diffidence—which must make you appear cold, dull, awkward, and perhap
ill-tempered too;—if you had but rightly considered these from the beginning
you would never have harboured such presumptuous thoughts: and now tha
you have been so foolish, pray repent and amend, and let us have no mor
of it!'

I cannot say that I implicitly obeyed my own injunctions: but such reasonin
as this became more and more effective as time wore on, and nothing wa
seen or heard of Mr. Weston; until at last, I gave up hoping, for even my hear
acknowledged it was all in vain. But still, I would think of him: I would cheris
his image in my mind; and treasure every word, look, and gesture that m
memory could retain; and brood over his excellencies and his peculiarities, and
in fact, all I had seen, heard, or imagined respecting him.

'Agnes, this sea air and change of scene do *you* no good, I think: I never sav
you look so wretched. It must be that you sit too much, and allow the care
of the schoolroom to worry you. You must learn to take things easy, and to b
more active and cheerful; you must take exercise whenever you can get it, an
leave the most tiresome duties to me; they will only serve to exercise m
patience, and, perhaps, try my temper a little.'

So said my mother, as we sat at work one morning during the Easter hol
days. I assured her that my employments were not at all oppressive; that I wa
well; or, if there was anything amiss, it would be gone as soon as the tryin
months of spring were over: when summer came I should be as strong an
hearty as she could wish to see me: but inwardly her observation startled me
I knew my strength was declining, my appetite had failed, and I was grow
listless and desponding;—and if, indeed, he could never care for me, an
I could never see him more—if I was forbidden to minister to his happiness—
forbidden, for ever, to taste the joys of love, to bless and to be blessed—then

730

fe must be a burden, and if my Heavenly Father would call me away, I should e glad to rest. But it would not do to die and leave my mother. Selfish, nworthy daughter, to forget her for a moment! Was not her happiness committed in a great measure to my charge?—and the welfare of our young pupils oo? Should I shrink from the work that God had set before me, because it was ot fitted to my taste? Did not He know best what I should do, and where ought to labour? and should I long to quit His service before I had finished ny task, and expect to enter into His rest without having laboured to earn it? No; by His help I will arise and address myself diligently to my appointed uty. If happiness in this world is not for me, I will endeavour to promote the relfare of those around me, and my reward shall be hereafter.' So said I in ny heart; and from that hour I only permitted my thoughts to wander to dward Weston—or at least to dwell upon him now and then—as a treat for are occasions: and, whether it was really the approach of summer, or the ffect of these good resolutions, or the lapse of time, or all together, tranquillity f mind was soon restored; and bodily health and vigour began likewise, slowly, ut surely, to return.

Early in June, I received a letter from Lady Ashby, late Miss Murray. She ad written to me twice or thrice before, from the different stages of her bridal our, always in good spirits, and professing to be very happy. I wondered every me that she had not forgotten me, in the midst of so much gaiety and variety f scene. At length, however, there was a pause; and it seemed she had forotten me, for upwards of seven months passed away and no letter. Of course, did not break my heart about *that*, though I often wondered how she was etting on; and when this last epistle so unexpectedly arrived, I was glad nough to receive it. It was dated from Ashby Park, where she was come to ttle down at last, having previously divided her time between the continent nd the metropolis. She made many apologies for having neglected me so long, ssured me she had not forgotten me, and had often intended to write, &c., &c., ut had always been prevented by something. She acknowledged that she had een leading a very dissipated life, and I should think her very wicked and ery thoughtless; but, notwithstanding that, she thought a great deal, and, mong other things, that she should vastly like to see me. 'We have been veral days here already,' wrote she. 'We have not a single friend with us, and re likely to be very dull. You know I never had a fancy for living with my usband like two turtles in a nest, were he the most delightful creature that ver wore a coat; so do take pity upon me and come. I suppose your midummer holidays commence in June, the same as other people's, therefore you annot plead want of time; and you must and shall come—in fact, I shall die if ou don't. I want you to visit me as a *friend,* and stay a long time. There is obody with me, as I told you before, but Sir Thomas and old Lady Ashby: ut you needn't mind them—they'll trouble us but little with their company.

And you shall have a room to yourself, whenever you like to retire to it, an
plenty of books to read when my company is not sufficiently amusing. I forge
whether you like babies; if you do, you may have the pleasure of seeing mine—
the most charming child in the world, no doubt; and all the more so, that I am
not troubled with nursing it—I was determined I wouldn't be bothered wit
that. Unfortunately, it is a girl, and Sir Thomas has never forgiven me: bu
however, if you will only come, I promise you shall be its governess as soon a
it can speak; and you shall bring it up in the way it should go, and mak
a better woman of it than its mamma. And you shall see my poodle, too
a splendid little charmer imported from Paris: and two fine Italian painting
of great value—I forget the artist. Doubtless you will be able to discove
prodigious beauties in them, which you must point out to me, as I only admir
by hearsay; and many elegant curiosities besides, which I purchased at Rom
and elsewhere; and, finally, you shall see my new home—the splendid hous
and grounds I used to covet so greatly. Alas! how far the promise of anticipatio
exceeds the pleasure of possession! There's a fine sentiment! I assure you I ar
become quite a grave old matron: pray come, if it be only to witness th
wonderful change. Write by return of post, and tell me when your vacatio
commences, and say that you will come the day after, and stay till the da
before it closes—in mercy to

'Yours affectionately,

'ROSALIE ASHBY.'

I showed this strange epistle to my mother, and consulted her on wha
I ought to do. She advised me to go; and I went—willing enough to see Lad
Ashby, and her baby too, and to do anything I could to benefit her, by cor
solation or advice; for I imagined she must be unhappy, or she would no
have applied to me thus—but feeling, as may readily be conceived, tha
in accepting the invitation, I made a great sacrifice for her, and did violenc
to my feelings in many ways, instead of being delighted with the honourabl
distinction of being entreated by the baronet's lady to visit her as a frien
However, I determined my visit should be only for a few days at most; an
I will not deny that I derived some consolation from the idea that, as Ashb
Park was not very far from Horton, I might possibly see Mr. Weston, or, a
least, hear something about him.

CHAPTER 22

THE VISIT

Ashby Park was certainly a very delightful residence. The mansion was statel
without, commodious and elegant within; the park was spacious and beautifu

732

iefly on account of its magnificent old trees, its stately herds of deer, its broad
eet of water, and the ancient woods that stretched beyond it: for there was
o broken ground to give variety to the landscape, and but very little of that
ndulating swell which adds so greatly to the charm of park scenery. And so,
is was the place Rosalie Murray had so longed to call her own, that she must
ave a share of it, on whatever terms it might be offered—whatever price was
be paid for the title of mistress, and whoever was to be her partner in the
onour and bliss of such a possession! Well! I am not disposed to censure
er now.

She received me very kindly; and, though I was a poor clergyman's daughter,
governess, and a schoolmistress, she welcomed me with unaffected pleasure to
er home; and—what surprised me rather—took some pains to make my visit
greeable. I could see, it is true, that she expected me to be greatly struck
ith the magnificence that surrounded her; and, I confess, I was rather
nnoyed at her evident efforts to reassure me, and prevent me from being over-
helmed by so much grandeur—too much awed at the idea of encountering her
usband and mother-in-law, or too much ashamed of my own humble appear-
nce. I was not ashamed of it at all; for, though plain, I had taken good care
ot to be shabby or mean, and should have been pretty considerably at my
ase, if my condescending hostess had not taken such manifest pains to make
e so; and, as for the magnificence that surrounded her, nothing that met
y eyes struck me or affected me half so much as her own altered appearance.
hether from the influence of fashionable dissipation, or some other evil,
space of little more than twelve months had had the effect that might be
xpected from as many years, in reducing the plumpness of her form, the fresh-
ess of her complexion, the vivacity of her movements, and the exuberance of
er spirits.

I wished to know if she was unhappy; but I felt it was not my province to
quire: I might endeavour to win her confidence; but, if she chose to conceal
er matrimonial cares from me, I would trouble her with no obtrusive
uestions. I, therefore, at first, confined myself to a few general inquiries about
er health and welfare, and a few commendations on the beauty of the park,
nd of the little girl that should have been a boy: a small delicate infant of
ven or eight weeks old, whom its mother seemed to regard with no remarkable
egree of interest or affection, though full as much as I expected her to show.
Shortly after my arrival, she commissioned her maid to conduct me to my
om and see that I had everything I wanted: it was a small, unpretending, but
fficiently comfortable apartment. When I descended thence—having divested
yself of all travelling encumbrances, and arranged my toilet with due con-
deration for the feelings of my lady hostess—she conducted me herself to the
om I was to occupy when I chose to be alone, or when she was engaged with
sitors, or obliged to be with her mother-in-law, or otherwise prevented, as

she said, from enjoying the pleasure of my society. It was a quiet, tidy littl
sitting-room; and I was not sorry to be provided with such a harbour
refuge.

'And some time,' said she, 'I will show you the library: I never examined i
shelves, but, I dare say, it is full of wise books; and you may go and burro
among them whenever you please. And now you shall have some tea—it wi
soon be dinner-time, but, I thought as you were accustomed to dine at on
you would perhaps like better to have a cup of tea about this time, and to din
when we lunch; and then, you know, you can have your tea in this room, an
that will save you from having to dine with Lady Ashby and Sir Thoma
which would be rather awkward—at least, not awkward, but rather—a—yo
know what I mean. I thought you mightn't like it so well—especially as w
may have other ladies and gentlemen to dine with us occasionally.'

'Certainly,' said I, 'I would much rather have it as you say; and, if you hav
no objection, I should prefer having all my meals in this room.'

'Why so?'

'Because, I imagine, it would be more agreeable to Lady Ashby and S
Thomas.'

'Nothing of the kind.'

'At any rate, it would be more agreeable to me.'

She made some faint objections, but soon conceded; and I could see tha
the proposal was a considerable relief to her.

'Now, come into the drawing-room,' said she. 'There's the dressing bell; bi
I won't go yet: it's no use dressing when there's no one to see you; and I wa
to have a little discourse.'

The drawing-room was certainly an imposing apartment, and very elegantl
furnished; but I saw its young mistress glance towards me as we entered, as
to notice how I was impressed by the spectacle, and accordingly I determine
to preserve an aspect of stony indifference, as if I saw nothing at all remarkabl
But this was only for a moment: immediately conscience whispered, 'Wh
should I disappoint her to save my pride? No—rather let me sacrifice my pric
to give her a little innocent gratification.' And I honestly looked round, an
told her it was a noble room, and very tastefully furnished. She said little, b
I saw she was pleased.

She showed me her fat French poodle, that lay curled up on a silk cushio
and the two fine Italian paintings: which, however, she would not give m
time to examine, but, saying I must look at them some other day, insisted upo
my admiring the little jewelled watch she had purchased in Geneva; an
then she took me round the room to point out sundry articles of *vertu* she ha
brought from Italy: an elegant little timepiece, and several busts, small gracef
figures, and vases, all beautifully carved in white marble. She spoke of the
with animation, and heard my admiring comments with a smile of pleasur

at soon, however, vanished, and was followed by a melancholy sigh; as if consideration of the insufficiency of all such baubles to the happiness of the uman heart, and their woeful inability to supply its insatiate demands.

Then, stretching herself upon a couch, she motioned me to a capacious easy hair that stood opposite—not before the fire, but before a wide open window; r it was summer, be it remembered; a sweet, warm evening in the latter half June. I sat for a moment in silence, enjoying the still, pure air, and the elightful prospect of the park that lay before me, rich in verdure and foliage, id basking in yellow sunshine, relieved by the long shadows of declining day. ut I must take advantage of this pause: I had inquiries to make, and, like e substance of a lady's postscript, the most important must come last. So began with asking after Mr. and Mrs. Murray, and Miss Matilda and the ung gentlemen.

I was told that papa had the gout, which made him very ferocious; and that would not give up his choice wines, and his substantial dinners and suppers, d had quarrelled with his physician, because the latter had dared to say that medicine could cure him while he lived so freely; that mamma and the st were well. Matilda was still wild and reckless, but she had got a fashionable overness, and was considerably improved in her manners, and soon to be troduced to the world; and John and Charles (now at home for the holidays) ere, by all accounts, 'fine, bold, unruly, mischievous boys.'

'And how are the other people getting on?' said I—'the Greens, for instance?'

'Ah! Mr. Green is heart-broken, you know,' replied she, with a languid nile: 'he hasn't got over his disappointment yet, and never will, I suppose. e's doomed to be an old bachelor; and his sisters are doing their best to get arried.'

'And the Melthams?'

'Oh, they're jogging on as usual, I suppose: but I know very little about any them—except Harry,' said she, blushing slightly, and smiling again. 'I saw great deal of him while we were in London; for, as soon as he heard we were ere, he came up under pretence of visiting his brother, and either followed e, like a shadow, wherever I went, or met me, like a reflection, at every turn. ou needn't look so shocked, Miss Grey; I was very discreet, I assure you: ut, you know, one can't help being admired. Poor fellow! He was not my only orshipper; though he was certainly the most conspicuous, and, I think, the ost devoted among them all. And that detestable—ahem—and Sir Thomas ose to take offence at him—or my profuse expenditure, or something— don't exactly know what—and hurried me down to the country at a moment's tice; where I'm to play the hermit, I suppose, for life.'

And she bit her lip, and frowned vindictively upon the fair domain she had ce so coveted to call her own.

'And Mr. Hatfield,' said I, 'what is become of him?'

Again she brightened up, and answered gaily—

'Oh! he made up to an elderly spinster, and married her, not long sinc weighing her heavy purse against her faded charms, and expecting to find th solace in gold which was denied him in love, ha, ha!'

'Well, and I think that's all—except Mr. Weston: what is he doing?'

'I don't know, I'm sure. He's gone from Horton.'

'How long since? and where is he gone to?'

'I know nothing about him,' replied she, yawning—'except that he we about a month ago—I never asked where,' (I would have asked whether it w to a living or merely another curacy, but thought it better not) 'and the peop made a great rout about his leaving,' continued she, 'much to Mr. Hatfield displeasure; for Hatfield didn't like him, because he had too much influen with the common people, and because he was not sufficiently tractable an submissive to him—and for some other unpardonable sins, I don't know wha But now I positively must go and dress: the second bell will ring directly, an if I come to dinner in this guise, I shall never hear the end of it from Lac Ashby. It's a strange thing one can't be mistress in one's own house! Just rir the bell, and I'll send for my maid, and tell them to get you some tea. On think of that intolerable woman—'

'Who—your maid?'

'No;—my mother-in-law—and my unfortunate mistake! Instead of lettir her take herself off to some other house, as she offered to do when I marrie I was fool enough to ask her to live here still, and direct the affairs of the hou for me; because, in the first place, I hoped we should spend the greater pa of the year in town, and in the second place, being so young and inexperience I was frightened at the idea of having a houseful of servants to manage, an dinners to order, and parties to entertain, and all the rest of it, and I thoug she might assist me with her experience; never dreaming she would pro a usurper, a tyrant, an incubus, a spy, and everything else that's detestab I wish she was dead!'

She then turned to give her orders to the footman, who had been standi bolt upright within the door for the last half-minute, and had heard the latt part of her animadversions; and, of course, made his own reflections upon ther notwithstanding the inflexible, wooden countenance he thought proper preserve in the drawing-room. On my remarking afterwards that he must ha heard her, she replied—

'Oh, no matter! I never care about the footmen; they're mere automaton it's nothing to them what their superiors say or do; they won't dare to repe it; and as to what they think—if they presume to think at all—of course, nobo cares for that. It would be a pretty thing indeed, if we were to be tongue-ti by our servants!'

So saying, she ran off to make her hasty toilet, leaving me to pilot my wa

ck to my sitting-room, where, in due time, I was served with a cup of tea. After that, I sat musing on Lady Ashby's past and present condition; and on that little information I had obtained respecting Mr. Weston, and the small ance there was of ever seeing or hearing anything more of him throughout y quiet, drab-coloured life: which, henceforth, seemed to offer no alternative tween positive rainy days, and days of dull grey clouds without downfall. t length, however, I began to weary of my thoughts, and to wish I knew where find the library my hostess had spoken of; and to wonder whether I was to main there doing nothing till bedtime.

As I was not rich enough to possess a watch, I could not tell how time was assing, except by observing the slowly lengthening shadows from the window; hich presented a side view, including a corner of the park, a clump of trees, hose topmost branches had been colonized by an innumerable company of isy rooks, and a high wall with a massive wooden gate: no doubt communi- ating with the stable-yard, as a broad carriage-road swept up to it from the irk. The shadow of this wall soon took possession of the whole of the ground far as I could see, forcing the golden sunlight to retreat inch by inch, and at st take refuge in the very tops of the trees. Ere long, even they were left in adow—the shadow of the distant hills, or of the earth itself; and, in sympathy r the busy citizens of the rookery, I regretted to see their habitation, so lately athed in glorious light, reduced to the sombre, work-a-day hue of the lower orld, or of my own world within. For a moment, such birds as soared above e rest might still receive the lustre on their wings, which imparted to their ble plumage the hue and brilliance of deep red gold; at last, that too de- arted. Twilight came stealing on; the rooks became more quiet; I became ore weary, and wished I were going home to-morrow. At length it grew dark; nd I was thinking of ringing for a candle, and betaking myself to bed, when y hostess appeared, with many apologies for having neglected me so long, nd laying all the blame upon that 'nasty old woman,' as she called her mother- -law.

'If I didn't sit with her in the drawing-room while Sir Thomas is taking his ine,' said she, 'she would never forgive me; and, then, if I leave the room the stant he comes—as I have done once or twice—it is an unpardonable offence gainst her dear Thomas. *She* never showed such disrespect to *her* husband; nd as for affection, wives never think of that now-a-days, she supposes: but ings were different in *her* time—as if there was any good to be done by staying the room, when he does nothing but grumble and scold when he's in a bad umour, talk disgusting nonsense when he's in a good one, and go to sleep on e sofa when he's too stupid for either; which is most frequently the case now, hen he has nothing to do but to sot over his wine.'

'But could you not try to occupy his mind with something better; and engage im to give up such habits? I'm sure you have powers of persuasion, and

qualifications for amusing a gentleman, which many ladies would be glad to possess.'

'And so you think I would lay myself out for his amusement! No; that's not *my* idea of a wife. It's the husband's part to please the wife, not hers to please him; and if he isn't satisfied with her as she is—and thankful to possess her too—he isn't worthy of her, that's all. And as for persuasion, I assure you I shan't trouble myself with that: I've enough to do to bear with him as he is, without attempting to work a reform. But I'm sorry I left you so long alone, Miss Grey. How have you passed the time?'

'Chiefly in watching the rooks.'

'Mercy, how dull you must have been! I really must show you the library, and you must ring for everything you want, just as you would in an inn, and make yourself comfortable. I have selfish reasons for wishing to make you happy, because I want you to stay with me, and not fulfil your horrid threat of running away in a day or two.'

'Well, don't let me keep you out of the drawing-room any longer to-night, for at present I am tired, and wish to go to bed.'

CHAPTER 23

THE PARK

I came down a little before eight, next morning, as I knew by the striking of a distant clock. There was no appearance of breakfast. I waited above an hour before it came, still vainly longing for access to the library; and, after that lonely repast was concluded, I waited again about an hour and a half in great suspense and discomfort, uncertain what to do. At length, Lady Ashby came to bid me good morning. She informed me she had only just breakfasted, and now wanted me to take an early walk with her in the park. She asked how long I had been up, and on receiving my answer, expressed the deepest regret, and again promised to show me the library. I suggested she had better do so at once, and then there would be no further trouble either with remembering or forgetting. She complied, on condition that I would not think of reading, or bothering with the books now; for she wanted to show me the gardens, and take a walk in the park with me, before it became too hot for enjoyment: which, indeed, was nearly the case already. Of course, I readily assented; and we took our walk accordingly.

As we were strolling in the park, talking of what my companion had seen and heard during her travelling experience, a gentleman on horseback rode up and passed us. As he turned, in passing, and stared me full in the face, I had a good opportunity of seeing what he was like. He was tall, thin, and wasted,

ith a slight stoop in the shoulders, a pale face, but somewhat blotchy, and
isagreeably red about the eyelids, plain features, and a general expression of
anguor and flatness, relieved by a sinister expression in the mouth and the
ull, soulless eyes.

'I detest that man!' whispered Lady Ashby, with bitter emphasis, as he
owly trotted by.

'Who is it?' I asked, unwilling to suppose that she should so speak of her
usband.

'Sir Thomas Ashby,' she replied, with dreary composure.

'And do you *detest* him, Miss Murray?' said I, for I was too much shocked
to remember her name at the moment.

'Yes, I do, Miss Grey, and despise him too; and if you knew him you would
ot blame me.'

'But you knew what he was before you married him.'

'No; I only thought so: I did not half know him really. I know you warned
me against it, and I wish I had listened to you: but it's too late to regret that
ow. And besides, mamma ought to have known better than either of us, and
he never said anything against it—quite the contrary. And then I thought
e adored me, and would let me have my own way: he did pretend to do so
t first, but now he does not care a bit about me. Yet I should not care for that:
e might do as he pleased, if I might only be free to amuse myself and to stay
a London, or have a few friends down here: but *he will* do as he pleases, and
must be a prisoner and a slave. The moment he saw I could enjoy myself
vithout him, and that others knew my value better than himself, the selfish
vretch began to accuse me of coquetry and extravagance; and to abuse Harry
Ieltham, whose shoes he was not worthy to clean. And then, he must needs
ave me down in the country, to lead the life of a nun, lest I should dishonour
im or bring him to ruin; as if he had not been ten times worse every way, with
is betting book, and his gaming table, and his opera girls, and his Lady This
nd Mrs. That—yes, and his bottles of wine, and glasses of brandy and water
oo! Oh, I would give ten thousand worlds to be Miss Murray again! It is *too*
ad to feel life, health, and beauty wasting away, unfelt and unenjoyed, for
ich a brute as that!' exclaimed she, fairly bursting into tears in the bitterness
f her vexation.

Of course, I pitied her exceedingly; as well for her false idea of happiness and
isregard of duty, as for the wretched partner with whom her fate was linked.
said what I could to comfort her, and offered such counsels as I thought she
ost required: advising her, first, by gentle reasoning, by kindness, example,
nd persuasion, to try to ameliorate her husband; and then, when she had done
ll she could, if she still found him incorrigible, to endeavour to abstract
erself from him—to wrap herself up in her own integrity, and trouble herself
s little about him as possible. I exhorted her to seek consolation in doing her

duty to God and man, to put her trust in Heaven, and solace herself with th
care and nurture of her little daughter; assuring her she would be ampl
rewarded by witnessing its progress in strength and wisdom, and receiving i
genuine affection.

'But I can't devote myself entirely to a child,' said she: 'it may die—whic
is not at all improbable.'

'But, with care, many a delicate infant has become a strong man or woman

'But it may grow so intolerably like its father that I shall hate it.'

'That is not likely; it is a little girl, and strongly resembles its mother.'

'No matter; I should like it better if it were a boy—only that its father wi
leave it no inheritance that he can possibly squander away. What pleasure ca
I have in seeing a girl grow up to eclipse me, and enjoy those pleasures tha
I am for ever debarred from? But supposing I could be so generous as to tak
delight in this, still it is *only* a child; and I can't centre all my hopes in a chil
that is only one degree better than devoting oneself to a dog. And as for all th
wisdom and goodness you have been trying to instil into me—that is all ver
right and proper I dare say, and if I were some twenty years older, I migh
fructify by it: but people must enjoy themselves when they are young; and
others won't let them—why, they must hate them for it!'

'The best way to enjoy yourself is to do what is right and hate nobod
The end of Religion is not to teach us how to die, but how to live; and th
earlier you become wise and good, the more of happiness you secure. An
now, Lady Ashby, I have one more piece of advice to offer you, which i
that you will not make an enemy of your mother-in-law. Don't get into th
the way of holding her at arm's length, and regarding her with jealous di
trust. I never saw her, but I have heard good as well as evil respecting he
and I imagine that, though cold and haughty in her general demeanou
and even exacting in her requirements, she has strong affections for thos
who can reach them; and, though so blindly attached to her son, she is n
without good principles, or incapable of hearing reason. If you would bu
conciliate her a little, and adopt a friendly, open manner—and even confic
your grievances to her—*real* grievances, such as you have a right to complai
of—it is my firm belief that she would, in time, become your faithful frien
and a comfort and support to you, instead of the incubus you describe her

But I fear my advice had little effect upon the unfortunate young lady
and, finding I could render myself so little serviceable, my residence at Ashb
Park became doubly painful. But still, I must stay out that day and the fo
lowing one, as I had promised to do so: though, resisting all entreaties an
inducements to prolong my visit further, I insisted upon departing the nex
morning; affirming that my mother would be lonely without me, and tha
she impatiently expected my return. Nevertheless, it was with a heavy hea
that I bade adieu to poor Lady Ashby, and left her in her princely hom

t was no slight additional proof of her unhappiness, that she should so cling
o the consolation of my presence, and earnestly desire the company of one
vhose general tastes and ideas were so little congenial to her own—whom
he had completely forgotten in her hours of prosperity, and whose presence
vould be rather a nuisance than a pleasure, if she could but have half her
eart's desire.

CHAPTER 24

THE SANDS

Our school was not situated in the heart of the town: on entering A——from
he north-west there is a row of respectable-looking houses, on each side of the
road, white road, with narrow slips of garden-ground before them, venetian
blinds to the windows, and a flight of steps leading to each trim, brass-handled
oor. In one of the largest of these habitations dwelt my mother and I, with
uch young ladies as our friends and the public chose to commit to our charge.
Consequently, we were a considerable distance from the sea, and divided from
t by a labyrinth of streets and houses. But the sea was my delight; and I would
ften gladly pierce the town to obtain the pleasure of a walk beside it, whether
vith the pupils, or alone with my mother during the vacations. It was delightful
o me at all times and seasons, but especially in the wild commotion of a rough
ea-breeze, and in the brilliant freshness of a summer morning.

I awoke early on the third morning after my return from Ashby Park— the
un was shining through the blind, and I thought how pleasant it would be to
ass through the quiet town and take a solitary ramble on the sands while half
he world was in bed. I was not long in forming the resolution, nor slow to act
pon it. Of course I would not disturb my mother, so I stole noiselessly down-
tairs, and quietly unfastened the door. I was dressed and out, when the church
lock struck a quarter to six. There was a feeling of freshness and vigour in the
ery streets; and when I got free of the town, when my foot was on the sands
nd my face towards the broad, bright bay, no language can describe the effect
f the deep, clear azure of the sky and ocean, the bright morning sunshine on
he semicircular barrier of craggy cliffs surmounted by green swelling hills, and
n the smooth, wide sands, and the low rocks out at sea—looking, with their
lothing of weeds and moss, like little grass-grown islands—and above all, on
he brilliant, sparkling waves. And then, the unspeakable purity and fresh-
ess of the air! there was just enough heat to enhance the value of the breeze,
nd just enough wind to keep the whole sea in motion, to make the waves come
ounding to the shore, foaming and sparkling, as if wild with glee. Nothing
lse was stirring—no living creature was visible besides myself. My footsteps

were the first to press the firm, unbroken sands;—nothing before had trampled them since last night's flowing tide had obliterated the deepest marks of yesterday, and left it fair and even, except where the subsiding water had left behind it the traces of dimpled pools and little running streams.

Refreshed, delighted, invigorated, I walked along, forgetting all my cares, feeling as if I had wings to my feet, and could go at least forty miles without fatigue, and experiencing a sense of exhilaration to which I had been an entire stranger since the days of early youth. About half-past six, however, the grooms began to come down to air their master's horses—first one, and then another till there were some dozen horses and five or six riders: but that need not trouble me, for they would not come as far as the low rocks which I was now approaching. When I had reached these, and walked over the moist, slippery seaweed (at the risk of floundering into one of the numerous pools of clear salt water that lay between them), to a little mossy promontory with the sea splashing round it, I looked back again to see who next was stirring. Still there were only the early grooms with their horses, and one gentleman with a little dark speck of a dog running before him, and one water-cart coming out of the town to get water for the baths. In another minute or two, the distant bathing machines would begin to move, and then the elderly gentlemen of regular habits, and sober quaker ladies would be coming to take their salutary morning walks. But however interesting such a scene might be, I could not wait to witness it, for the sun and the sea so dazzled my eyes in that direction, that I could but afford one glance; and then I turned again to delight myself with the sight and the sound of the sea dashing against my promontory—with no prodigious force, for the swell was broken by the tangled seaweed and the unseen rocks beneath; otherwise I should soon have been deluged with spray. But the tide was coming in; the water was rising; the gulfs and lakes were filling; the straits were widening, it was time to seek some safer footing; so I walked, skipped, and stumbled back to the smooth, wide sands, and resolved to proceed to a certain bold projection in the cliffs, and then return.

Presently, I heard a snuffling sound behind me, and then a dog came frisking and wriggling to my feet. It was my own Snap—the little, dark, wire-haired terrier! When I spoke his name, he leapt up in my face and yelled for joy. Almost as much delighted as himself, I caught the little creature in my arms, and kissed him repeatedly. But how came he to be there? He could not have dropped from the sky, or come all that way alone: it must be either his master the rat-catcher, or somebody else that had brought him; so, repressing my extravagant caresses, and endeavouring to repress his likewise, I looked round and beheld—Mr. Weston!

'Your dog remembers you well, Miss Grey,' said he, warmly grasping the hand I offered him without clearly knowing what I was about. 'You rise early.'

'Not often so early as this,' I replied, with amazing composure, considering

l the circumstances of the case.

'How far do you propose to extend your walk?'

'I was thinking of returning—it must be almost time, I think.'

He consulted his watch—a gold one now—and told me it was only five minutes past seven.

'But, doubtless, you have had a long enough walk,' said he, turning towards ae town, to which I now proceeded leisurely to retrace my steps; and he alked beside me.

'In what part of the town do you live?' asked he. 'I never could discover.'

Never could discover? Had he endeavoured to do so then? I told him the lace of our abode. He asked how we prospered in our affairs. I told him we ere doing very well—that we had had a considerable addition to our pupils fter the Christmas vacation, and expected a still further increase at the close f this.

'You must be an accomplished instructor,' he observed.

'No, it is my mother,' I replied; 'she manages things so well, and is so active, nd clever, and kind.'

'I should like to know your mother. Will you introduce me to her some time, ' I call?'

'Yes, willingly.'

'And will you allow me the privilege of an old friend. of looking in upon you ow and then?'

'Yes, if—I suppose so.'

This was a very foolish answer, but the truth was, I considered that I had o right to invite anyone to my mother's house without her knowledge; and if had said, 'yes, if my mother does not object,' it would appear as if by his uestion I understood more than was expected; so, *supposing* she would not, added, 'I suppose so:' but of course I should have said something more nsible and more polite, if I had had my wits about me. We continued our alk for a minute in silence; which, however, was shortly relieved (no small elief to me), by Mr. Weston commenting upon the brightness of the morning nd the beauty of the bay, and then upon the advantages A—— possessed over any other fashionable places of resort.

'You don't ask what brings me to A——,' said he. 'You can't suppose I'm ch enough to come for my own pleasure.'

'I heard you had left Horton.'

'You didn't hear, then, that I had got the living of F——?'

F—— was a village about two miles distant from A——.

'No,' said I; 'we live so completely out of the world, even here, that news ldom reaches me through any quarter; except through the medium of the—— *azette*. But, I hope you like your new parish; and that I may congratulate you n the acquisition?'

'I expect to like my parish better a year or two hence, when I have worke certain reforms I have set my heart upon—or, at least, progressed some ste towards such an achievement. But you may congratulate me now; for I fin it very agreeable to *have* a parish all to myself, with nobody to interfere wi me—to thwart my plans or cripple my exertions: and besides, I have a r spectable house in a rather pleasant neighbourhood, and three hundre pounds a year; and, in fact, I have nothing but solitude to complain of, an nothing but a companion to wish for.'

He looked at me as he concluded; and the flash of his dark eyes seemed set my face on fire: greatly to my own discomfiture, for to evince confusio at such a juncture was intolerable. I made an effort, therefore, to remedy t evil, and disclaim all personal application of the remark by a hasty, ill-expresse reply, to the effect that, if he waited till he was well known in the neighbou hood, he might have numerous opportunities for supplying his want among th residents of F—— and its vicinity, or the visitors of A——, if he required s ample a choice: not considering the compliment implied by such an assertio till his answer made me aware of it.

'I am not so presumptuous as to believe that,' said he, 'though you tell it me but if it were so, I am rather particular in my notions of a companion for lif and perhaps I might not find one to suit me among the ladies you mention

'If you require perfection, you never will.'

'I do not—I have no right to require it, as being so far from perfect mysel

Here the conversation was interrupted by a water-cart lumbering past us, f we were now come to the busy part of the sands; and, for the next eight ten minutes, between carts and horses, and asses, and men, there was littl room for social intercourse, till we had turned our backs upon the sea, an began to ascend the precipitous road leading into the town. Here my com panion offered me his arm, which I accepted, though not with the intentio of using it as a support.

'You don't often come on to the sands, I think,' said he, 'for I have walke there many times, both morning and evening, since I came, and never see you till now; and several times, in passing through the town, too, I hav looked about for your school—but I did not think of the —— Road; and on or twice I made inquiries, but without obtaining the requisite information.'

When we had surmounted the acclivity, I was about to withdraw my ar from his, but by a slight tightening of the elbow was tacitly informed that suc was not his will, and accordingly desisted. Discoursing on different subject we entered the town, and passed through several streets. I saw that he w going out of his way to accompany me, notwithstanding the long walk th was yet before him; and, fearing that he might be inconveniencing himse from motives of politeness, I observed—

'I fear I am taking you out of your way, Mr. Weston—I believe the roa

F——lies quite in another direction.

'I'll leave you at the end of the next street,' said he.

'And when will you come to see mamma?'

'To-morrow—God willing.'

The end of the next street was nearly the conclusion of my journey. He opped there, however, bid me good morning, and called Snap, who seemed little doubtful whether to follow his old mistress or his new master, but otted away upon being summoned by the latter.

'I won't offer to restore him to you, Miss Grey,' said Mr. Weston, smiling, ecause I like him.'

'Oh, I don't want him,' replied I, 'now that he has a good master; I'm quite tisfied.'

'You take it for granted that I *am* a good one, then?'

The man and the dog departed; and I returned home, full of gratitude to eaven for so much bliss, and praying that my hopes might not again be ushed.

CHAPTER 25

CONCLUSION

Vell, Agnes, you must not take such long walks again before breakfast,' said y mother, observing that I drank an extra cup of coffee and ate nothing pleading the heat of the weather, and the fatigue of my long walk as an cuse. I certainly did feel feverish, and tired too.

'You always do things by extremes: now, if you had taken a *short* walk every orning, and would continue to do so, it would do you good.'

'Well, mamma, I will.'

'But this is worse than lying in bed or bending over your books: you have ite put yourself into a fever.'

'I won't do it again,' said I.

I was racking my brains with thinking how to tell her about Mr. Weston, r she must know he was coming to-morrow. However, I waited till the break- st things were removed, and I was more calm and cool; and then, having sat wn to my drawing, I began—

'I met an old friend on the sands to-day, mamma.'

'An old friend! Who could it be?'

'Two old friends, indeed. One was a dog;' and then I reminded her of Snap, hose history I had recounted before, and related the incident of his sudden ppearance and remarkable recognition; 'and the other,' continued I, 'was r. Weston, the curate of Horton.'

'Mr. Weston! I never heard of him before.'

'Yes, you have: I've mentioned him several times, I believe: but you don remember.'

'I've heard you speak of Mr. Hatfield.'

'Mr. Hatfield was the rector, and Mr. Weston the curate: I used to mention him sometimes in contradistinction to Mr. Hatfield, as being a more efficien clergyman. However, he was on the sands this morning with the dog—he ha bought it, I suppose, from the rat-catcher; and he knew me as well as it did probably through its means: and I had a little conversation with him, in th course of which, as he asked about our school, I was led to say somethin about you and your good management; and he said he should like to know yo and asked if I would introduce him to you, if he should take the liberty calling to-morrow; so I said I would. Was I right?'

'Of course. What kind of a man is he?'

'A very *respectable* man, I think: but you will see him to-morrow. He is th new vicar of F——, and as he has only been there a few weeks, I suppose has made no friends yet, and wants a little society.'

The morrow came. What a fever of anxiety and expectation I was in fro breakfast till noon—at which time he made his appearance! Having introduce him to my mother, I took my work to the window, and sat down to await th result of the interview. They got on extremely well together; greatly to n satisfaction, for I had felt very anxious about what my mother would think him. He did not stay long that time: but when he rose to take leave, she sa she should be happy to see him, whenever he might find it convenient to ca again; and when he was gone, I was gratified by hearing her say,—

'Well! I think he's a very sensible man. But why did you sit back ther Agnes,' she added, 'and talk so little?'

'Because you talked so well, mamma, I thought you required no assistan from me: and, besides, he was your visitor, not mine.'

After that, he often called upon us—several times in the course of a wee He generally addressed most of his conversation to my mother: and no wonde for she *could* converse. I almost envied the unfettered, vigorous fluency of h discourse, and the strong sense evinced by everything she said—and yet, I d not; for, though I occasionally regretted my own deficiencies for his sake, gave me very great pleasure to sit and hear the two beings I loved and honour above every one else in the world, discoursing together so amicably, so wise and so well. I was not always silent, however; nor was I at all neglected. I w quite as much noticed as I would wish to be: there was no lack of kind wor and kinder looks, no end of delicate attentions, too fine and subtle to be grasp by words, and therefore indescribable—but deeply felt at heart.

Ceremony was quickly dropped between us: Mr. Weston came as expected guest, welcome at all times, and never deranging the economy of o

ousehold affairs. He even called me 'Agnes': the name had been timidly poken at first, but, finding it gave no offence in any quarter, he seemed reatly to prefer that appellation to 'Miss Grey'; and so did I. How tedious and loomy were those days in which he did not come! And yet not miserable; for had still the remembrance of the last visit and the hope of the next to cheer 1e. But when two or three days passed without my seeing him, I certainly felt ery anxious—absurdly, unreasonably so; for, of course, he had his own usiness and the affairs of his parish to attend to. And I dreaded the close of 1e holidays, when *my* business also would begin, and I should be sometimes nable to see him, and sometimes—when my mother was in the schoolroom— bliged to be with him alone: a position I did not at all desire, in the house; 1ough to meet him out of doors, and walk beside him, had proved by no 1eans disagreeable.

One evening, however, in the last week of the vacation, he arrived—un- xpectedly: for a heavy and protracted thundershower during the afternoon ad almost destroyed my hopes of seeing him that day; but now the storm was ver, and the sun was shining brightly.

'A beautiful evening, Mrs. Grey!' said he, as he entered. 'Agnes, I want you) take a walk with me to——' (he named a certain part of the coast—a bold ill on the land side, and towards the sea a steep precipice, from the summit f which a glorious view is to be had). 'The rain has laid the dust, and cooled nd cleared the air, and the prospect will be magnificent. Will you come?'

'Can I go, mamma?'

'Yes; to be sure.'

I went to get ready, and was down again in a few minutes; though, of ourse, I took a little more pains with my attire than if I had merely been going ut on some shopping expedition alone. The thundershower had certainly had most beneficial effect upon the weather, and the evening was most delightful. 1r. Weston would have me to take his arm: he said little during our passage 1rough the crowded streets, but walked very fast, and appeared grave and bstracted. I wondered what was the matter, and felt an indefinite dread that >mething unpleasant was on his mind; and vague surmises, concerning what might be, troubled me not a little, and made me grave and silent enough. ut these fantasies vanished upon reaching the quiet outskirts of the town; for s soon as we came within sight of the venerable old church, and the —— hill, 'ith the deep blue sea beyond it, I found my companion was cheerful enough.

'I'm afraid I've been walking too fast for you, Agnes,' said he: 'in my im- atience to be rid of the town, I forgot to consult your convenience; but now, 'e'll walk as slowly as you please. I see, by those light clouds in the west, 1ere will be a brilliant sunset, and we shall be in time to witness its effect upon 1e sea, at the most moderate rate of progression.'

When we had got about half-way up the hill, we fell into silence again;

which, as usual, he was the first to break.

'My house is desolate yet, Miss Grey,' he smilingly observed, 'and I a acquainted now with all the ladies in my parish, and several in this town too and many others I know by sight and by report; but not one of them will su me for a companion: in fact, there is only one person in the world that wil and that is yourself; and I want to know your decision?'

'Are you in earnest, Mr. Weston?'

'In earnest! How could you think I should jest on such a subject?'

He laid his hand on mine that rested on his arm: he must have felt tremble—but it was no great matter now.

'I hope I have not been too precipitate,' he said, in a serious tone. 'You mu have known that it was not my way to flatter and talk soft nonsense, or eve to speak the admiration that I felt: and that a single word or glance of min meant more than the honeyed phrases and fervent protestations of most othe men.'

I said something about not liking to leave my mother, and doing nothin without her consent.

'I settled everything with Mrs. Grey, while you were putting on you bonnet,' replied he. 'She said I might have her consent, if I could obtain yours and I asked her, in case I should be so happy, to come and live with us—fo I was sure you would like it better. But she refused, saying she could no afford to employ an assistant, and would continue the school till she coul purchase an annuity sufficient to maintain her in comfortable lodgings; and meantime, she would spend her vacations alternately with us and your siste and should be quite contented if you were happy. And so now I have over ruled your objections on her account. Have you any other?'

'No—none.'

'You love me then?' said he, fervently pressing my hand.

'Yes.'

Here I pause. My Diary, from which I have compiled these pages, goes bu little further. I could go on for years; but I will content myself with adding that I shall never forget that glorious summer evening, and always remembe with delight that steep hill, and the edge of the precipice where we stoo together, watching the splendid sunset mirrored in the restless world of wate at our feet—with hearts filled with gratitude to heaven, and happiness, an love—almost too full for speech.

A few weeks after that, when my mother had supplied herself with a assistant, I became the wife of Edward Weston; and never have found cause t repent it, and am certain that I never shall. We have had trials, and we kno that we must have them again; but we bear them well together, and endeavou to fortify ourselves and each other against the final separation—that greates

all afflictions to the survivor. But, if we keep in mind the glorious heaven beyond, where both may meet again, and sin and sorrow are unknown, surely that too may be borne: and, meantime, we endeavour to live to the glory of Him who has scattered so many blessings in our path.

Edward, by his strenuous exertions, has worked surprising reforms in his parish, and is esteemed and loved by its inhabitants—as he deserves; for whatever his faults may be as a man (and no one is entirely without), I defy anybody to blame him as a pastor, a husband, or a father.

Our children, Edward, Agnes, and little Mary, promise well; their education, for the time being, is chiefly committed to me; and they shall want no good thing that a mother's care can give. Our modest income is amply sufficient for our requirements: and by practising the economy we learnt in harder times, and never attempting to imitate our richer neighbours, we manage not only to enjoy comfort and contentment ourselves, but to have every year something to lay by for our children, and something to give to those who need it.

And now I think I have said sufficient.